THE CLASSIC SCIENCE FICTION COLLECTION

THE CLASSIC SCIENCE FICTION COLLECTION

SIRIUS

SIRIUS

This edition published in 2025 by Sirius Publishing, a division of
Arcturus Publishing Limited,
26/27 Bickels Yard, 151–153 Bermondsey Street,
London SE1 3HA

Cover design: Peter Ridley
Cover illustration: Jarmo Piironen

ISBN: 978-1-3988-6164-0
AD006078NT

Printed in China

CONTENTS

INTRODUCTION

Science fiction today has become almost synonymous with the space opera. The success of the *Star Wars* franchise has inspired hundreds of writers to create their own epic tales of galactic empires, alien races, and space flights. In the early 20th century, as science fiction was first beginning to emerge as a separate genre, the very idea of spaceflight seemed fantastical. Voyages to the moon, experimental rocket ships, and the possibility of life beyond the stars fascinated readers.

There is much more to science fiction though than a fascination with the stars. Since the origins of the genre in the late 19th century, writers have used the possibilities of new inventions, alien encounters, time travel, and alternative forms of society to explore all elements of the human condition. The range of invasion stories, which spawned almost an entire genre of its own in the years leading up to World War I, reflected the increasing tensions in world politics.

Some tales are filled with optimism. Science very well could create new possibilities for the world. No one could deny the wonder of pushing back the frontiers and exploring our own galaxy, finding new worlds to colonize, new species to meet, and the chance radically to change the way we live.

But more writers used the genre as a warning beacon. Scientific innovation could lead to unexpected consequences. Inventors often unleash their new creations on the world with the best of intentions, but either the unpredictability of human nature or the fragile nature of their creations results in disastrous consequences. In the most extreme examples, these result in an apocalypse, wiping the slate clean of the mistakes of the past. Others saw how advances in technology could be exploited by those in power, creating dystopian societies.

Yet even in post-apocalyptic fiction there is often a glimmer of hope. As society disintegrates and the base impulses of human nature reveal themselves, individuals and groups of family and friends perform great acts of heroism and cooperation as they begin to rebuild the world they have lost.

The characters in this volume range from accomplished scientists to boisterous heroes. As they search for new ideas, alien races or pursue justice in an unjust world, they show how there are some things that are universal to all times and to all worlds.

The emergence of pulp magazines like the *Argosy, Amazing Stories* and *Weird Tales* provided writers like Stanley Weinbaum, Austin Hall, and Charles B. Stilson with new outlets for their imagination. The art of the short story thrived.

Jules Verne (1828–1905) and H. G. Wells (1866–1946) are rightfully revered as two of the fathers of the modern science-fiction genre. Verne trained as a lawyer as a young man but found that his passion lay in writing. Working with the publisher Pierre-Jules Hetzel, he published some of the most iconic works of the genre—*Journey to the Centre of the Earth* (1864), *Twenty Thousand Leagues Under the Sea* (1870), and *Around the World in Eighty Days* (1873). One of the most popular writers worldwide, his works took readers on a fascinating adventure to places they would never manage to visit themselves. As we can see in this volume, he also took his imagination to space in "Off on a Comet" and, with the aid of his son Michel, to a world far in the future in "The Day of an American Journalist in 2889."

H. G. Wells was a prolific writer, producing more than fifty novels and countless short stories over the course of his career. Inspired to write after an accident confined him to his bed as a child, he used his scientific training to create astonishingly plausible scenarios of the future. "The Star" is an ominous tale of an extra-planetary body on a collision course with earth, while in "The Crystal Egg" the titular object provides a window into Martian society.

Many writers better known for their non-genre fiction also dabbled in science fiction when it suited them. In this volume, you will find stories by Rudyard Kipling, Jack London, and Nathaniel Hawthorne which demonstrate that they were not above turning to the immense possibilities that science fiction could offer.

Mars was a popular topic for science fiction writers. Following in the footsteps of H. G. Wells' "The War of the Worlds," Miles J. Breuer's "The Raid From Mars" is an classic invasion story about Martians attacking earth in search of radium. Stanley Weinbaum's "A Martian Odyssey" is another classic tale of alien encounters on the red planet that takes a different approach. While earlier writers had tended to focus on the threat that alien beings might pose to humanity, Weinbaum instead focused on the joy of discovery and the possibility, however remote, of cooperation between the species.

A few authors took on the challenge of writing complete space operas, featuring flamboyant heroes, galactic empires, existential threats, and epic adventures in the concise form of the short story. No one did this better than George Griffith. His series featured Rollo Aubrey and Lilla Zaidie gallivanting across space in their spaceship, the Astronef. Immensely popular in their own day, these stories first appeared in *Pearson's Magazine* and display an unbridled exuberance for space travel and the possibilities it presents. Homer Eon Flint's "The Emancipatrix" tells of contact with aliens in a distant solar system. Like many pulp writers, Flint wrote primarily to entertain, but infused his writing with an undercurrent of social and political issues.

A few writers explored how the earth might be different with a few small changes. Rokeya Hossain's feminist utopia "Sultana's Dream" imagines a society in which the roles of men and women are reversed and the problems of the world—crime, poverty and excessive work—no longer exist.

Edward Page Mitchell's stories envisage change on a less radical scale. Featuring earnest scientists, mathematical problems and the creation of machines and robots to assist humanity, they are fascinating studies of an individual's pursuit of their own scientific goals.

At times, scientific discoveries lead to disaster. Grant Allen's "The Thames Valley Catastrophe" imagines the panic unleashed after a volcanic eruption destroys London. "By the Waters of Babylon" by Stephen Vincent Benét is a tale set in a world after the fall of industrialized society, where the great men of the past are viewed as gods to the modern-day inhabitants.

Many more stories in this volume feature robots, dystopias, the adventures of space flight, and the perils of time travel. Between them, there is no area of the imagination left unexplored. At times they reveal new truths about human nature; at others they predict future events and invention. There is something for everyone here and each of these classic stories have been chosen to thrill and entertain you.

THE FLOWERING OF THE STRANGE ORCHID

by H. G. Wells

The buying of orchids always has in it a certain speculative flavour. You have before you the brown shrivelled lump of tissue, and for the rest you must trust your judgment, or the auctioneer, or your good luck, as your taste may incline. The plant may be moribund or dead, or it may be just a respectable purchase, fair value for your money, or perhaps—for the thing has happened again and again—there slowly unfolds before the delighted eyes of the happy purchaser, day after day, some new variety, some novel richness, a strange twist of the labellum, or some subtler colouration or unexpected mimicry. Pride, beauty, and profit blossom together on one delicate green spike, and, it may be, even immortality. For the new miracle of nature may stand in need of a new specific name, and what so convenient as that of its discoverer? "John-smithia"! There have been worse names.

It was perhaps the hope of some such happy discovery that made Winter Wedderburn such a frequent attendant at these sales—that hope, and also, maybe, the fact that he had nothing else of the slightest interest to do in the world. He was a shy, lonely, rather ineffectual man, provided with just enough income to keep off the spur of necessity, and not enough nervous energy to make him seek any exacting employments. He might have collected stamps or coins, or translated Horace, or bound books, or invented new species of diatoms. But, as it happened, he grew orchids, and had one ambitious little hothouse. "I have a fancy," he said over his coffee, "that something is going to happen to me today." He spoke—as he moved and thought—slowly.

"Oh, don't say that!" said his housekeeper—who was also his remote cousin. For "something happening" was a euphemism that meant only one thing to her.

"You misunderstand me. I mean nothing unpleasant… though what I do mean I scarcely know. "Today," he continued, after a pause, "Peters' are going to sell a batch of plants from the Andamans and the Indies. I shall go up and see what they have. It may be I shall buy something good unawares. That may be it."

He passed his cup for his second cupful of coffee.

"Are these the things collected by that poor young fellow you told me of the other day?" asked his cousin, as she filled his cup.

"Yes," he said, and became meditative over a piece of toast. "Nothing ever does happen to me," he remarked presently, beginning to think aloud. "I wonder why? Things enough happen to other people. There is Harvey. Only the other week; on Monday he picked up sixpence, on Wednesday his chicks all had the staggers, on Friday his cousin came home from Australia, and on Saturday he broke his ankle. What a whirl of excitement!—compared to me."

"I think I would rather be without so much excitement," said his housekeeper. "It can't be good for you."

"I suppose it's troublesome. Still… you see, nothing ever happens to me. When I was a little boy I never had accidents. I never fell in love as I grew up. Never married… I wonder how it feels to have something happen to you, something really remarkable.

"That orchid-collector was only thirty-six—twenty years younger than myself—when he died. And he had been married twice and divorced once; he had had malarial fever four times, and once he broke his thigh. He killed a Malay once, and once he was wounded by a poisoned dart. And in the end he was killed by jungle-leeches. It must have all been very troublesome, but then it must have been very interesting, you know—except, perhaps, the leeches."

"I am sure it was not good for him," said the lady with conviction.

"Perhaps not." And then Wedderburn looked at his watch. "Twenty-three minutes past eight. I am going up by the quarter to twelve train, so that there is plenty of time. I think I shall wear my alpaca jacket—it is quite warm enough—and my grey felt hat and brown shoes. I suppose—"

He glanced out of the window at the serene sky and sunlit garden, and then nervously at his cousin's face. "I think you had better take an umbrella if you are going to London," she said in a voice that admitted of no denial. "There's all between here and the station coming back."

When he returned he was in a state of mild excitement. He had made a purchase. It was rare that he could make up his mind quickly enough to buy, but this time he had done so.

"There are Vandas," he said, "and a Dendrobe and some Palaeonophis."

He surveyed his purchases lovingly as he consumed his soup. They were laid out on the spotless tablecloth before him, and he was telling his cousin all about them as he slowly meandered through his dinner. It was his custom to live all his visits to London over again in the evening for her and his own entertainment.

"I knew something would happen today. And I have bought all these. Some of them—some of them—I feel sure, do you know, that some of them will be remarkable. I don't know how it is, but I feel just as sure as if some one had told me that some of these will turn out remarkable.

"That one"—he pointed to a shrivelled rhizome—"was not identified. It may be a Palaeonophis—or it may not. It may be a new species, or even a new genus. And it was the last that poor Batten ever collected."

"I don't like the look of it," said his housekeeper. "It's such an ugly shape."

"To me it scarcely seems to have a shape."

"I don't like those things that stick out," said his housekeeper.

"It shall be put away in a pot tomorrow."

"It looks," said the housekeeper, "like a spider shamming dead."

Wedderburn smiled and surveyed the root with his head on one side. "It is certainly not a pretty lump of stuff. But you can never judge of these things from their dry appearance. It may turn out to be a very beautiful orchid indeed. How busy I shall be tomorrow! I must see to-night just exactly what to do with these things, and tomorrow I shall set to work."

"They found poor Batten lying dead, or dying, in a mangrove swamp—I forget which," he began again presently, "with one of these very orchids crushed up under his body. He had been unwell for some days with some kind of native fever, and I suppose he fainted. These mangrove swamps are very unwholesome. Every drop of blood, they say, was taken out of him by the jungle-leeches. It may be that very plant that cost him his life to obtain."

"I think none the better of it for that."

"Men must work though women may weep," said Wedderburn with profound gravity.

"Fancy dying away from every comfort in a nasty swamp! Fancy being ill of fever with nothing to take but chlorodyne and quinine—if men were left to themselves they would live on chlorodyne and quinine—and no one round you but horrible natives! They say the Andaman islanders are most disgusting wretches—and, anyhow, they can scarcely make good nurses, not having the necessary training. And just for people in England to have orchids!"

"I don't suppose it was comfortable, but some men seem to enjoy that kind of thing," said Wedderburn. "Anyhow, the natives of his party were sufficiently civilised to take care of all his collection until his colleague, who was an ornithologist, came back again from the interior; though they could not tell the species of the orchid, and had let it wither. And it makes these things more interesting."

"It makes them disgusting. I should be afraid of some of the malaria clinging to them. And just think, there has been a dead body lying across that ugly thing! I never thought of that before. There! I declare I cannot eat another mouthful of dinner."

"I will take them off the table if you like, and put them in the window-seat. I can see them just as well there."

The next few days he was indeed singularly busy in his steamy little hothouse, fussing about with charcoal, lumps of teak, moss, and all the other mysteries of the orchid cultivator. He considered he was having a wonderfully eventful time. In the evening he would talk about these new orchids to his friends, and over and over again he reverted to his expectation of something strange. Several of the Vandas and the Dendrobium died under his care, but presently the strange orchid began to show signs of life. He was delighted, and took his housekeeper right away from jam-making to see it at once, directly he made the discovery.

"That is a bud," he said, "and presently there will be a lot of leaves there, and those little things coming out here are aerial rootlets."

"They look to me like little white fingers poking out of the brown," said his housekeeper. "I don't like them."

"Why not?"

"I don't know. They look like fingers trying to get at you. I can't help my likes and dislikes."

"I don't know for certain, but I don't think there are any orchids I know that have aerial rootlets quite like that. It may be my fancy, of course. You see they are a little flattened at the ends."

"I don't like 'em," said his housekeeper, suddenly shivering and turning away. "I know it's very silly of me—and I'm very sorry, particularly as you like the thing so much. But I can't help thinking of that corpse."

"But it may not be that particular plant. That was merely a guess of mine."

His housekeeper shrugged her shoulders. "Anyhow I don't like it," she said.

Wedderburn felt a little hurt at her dislike to the plant. But that did not prevent his talking to her about orchids generally, and this orchid in particular, whenever he felt inclined. "There are such queer things about orchids," he said one day; "such possibilities of surprises. You know, Darwin studied their fertilisation, and showed that the whole structure of an ordinary orchid flower was contrived in order that moths might carry the pollen from plant to plant. Well, it seems that there are lots of orchids known the flower of which cannot possibly be used for fertilisation in that way. Some of the Cypripediums, for instance; there are no insects known that can possibly fertilise them, and some of them have never been found with seed."

"But how do they form new plants?"

"By runners and tubers, and that kind of outgrowth. That is easily explained. The puzzle is, what are the flowers for? Very likely," he added, "my orchid may be something extraordinary in that way. If so I shall study it. I have often thought of making researches as Darwin did. But hitherto I have not found the time, or something else has happened to prevent it. The leaves are beginning to unfold now. I do wish you would come and see them!"

But she said that the orchid-house was so hot it gave her the headache. She had seen the plant once again, and the aerial rootlets, which were now some of them more than a foot long, had unfortunately reminded her of tentacles reaching out after something; and they got into her dreams, growing after her with incredible rapidity. So that she had settled to her entire satisfaction that she would not see that plant again, and Wedderburn had to admire its leaves alone. They were of the ordinary broad form, and a deep glossy green, with splashes and dots of deep red towards the base. He knew of no other leaves quite like them. The plant was placed on a low bench near the thermometer, and close by was a simple arrangement by which a tap dripped on the hot-water pipes and kept the air steamy. And he spent his afternoons now with some regularity meditating on the approaching flowering of this strange plant. And at last the great thing happened. Directly he entered the little glass house he knew that the spike had burst out, although his great Palaeonophis Lowii hid the corner where his new darling stood. There was a new odour in the air, a rich, intensely sweet scent, that overpowered every other in that crowded, steaming little greenhouse.

Directly he noticed this he hurried down to the strange orchid. And, behold! the trailing green spikes bore now three great splashes of blossom, from which this overpowering sweetness proceeded. He stopped before them in an ecstasy of admiration.

The flowers were white, with streaks of golden orange upon the petals; the heavy labellum was coiled into an intricate projection, and a wonderful bluish purple mingled there with the gold. He could see at once that the genus was altogether a new one. And the insufferable scent! How hot the place was! The blossoms swam before his eyes.

He would see if the temperature was right. He made a step towards the thermometer. Suddenly everything appeared unsteady. The bricks on the floor were dancing up and down. Then the white blossoms, the green leaves behind them, the whole greenhouse, seemed to sweep sideways, and then in a curve upward.

* * * * *

At half-past four his cousin made the tea, according to their invariable custom. But Wedderburn did not come in for his tea. “He is worshipping that horrid orchid,” she told herself, and waited ten minutes. “His watch must have stopped. I will go and call him.”

She went straight to the hothouse, and, opening the door, called his name. There was no reply. She noticed that the air was very close, and loaded with an intense perfume. Then she saw something lying on the bricks between the hot-water pipes.

For a minute, perhaps, she stood motionless. He was lying, face upward, at the foot of the strange orchid. The tentacle-like aerial rootlets no longer swayed freely in the air, but were crowded together, a tangle of grey ropes, and stretched tight, with their ends closely applied to his chin and neck and hands. She did not understand. Then she saw from under one of the exultant tentacles upon his cheek there trickled a little thread of blood. With an inarticulate cry she ran towards him, and tried to pull him away from the leech-like suckers. She snapped two of these tentacles, and their sap dripped red.

Then the overpowering scent of the blossom began to make her head reel. How they clung to him! She tore at the tough ropes, and he and the white inflorescence swam about her. She felt she was fainting, knew she must not. She left him and hastily opened the nearest door, and, after she had panted for a moment in the fresh air, she had a brilliant inspiration. She caught up a flower-pot and smashed in the windows at the end of the greenhouse. Then she re-entered. She tugged now with renewed strength at Wedderburn's motionless body, and brought the strange orchid crashing to the floor. It still clung with the grimmest tenacity to its victim. In a frenzy, she lugged it and him into the open air.

Then she thought of tearing through the sucker rootlets one by one, and in another minute she had released him and was dragging him away from the horror.

He was white and bleeding from a dozen circular patches. The odd-job man was coming up the garden, amazed at the smashing of glass, and saw her emerge, hauling the inanimate body with red-stained hands. For a moment he thought impossible things.

"Bring some water!" she cried, and her voice dispelled his fancies. When, with unnatural alacrity, he returned with the water, he found her weeping with excitement, and with Wedderburn's head upon her knee, wiping the blood from his face.

"What's the matter?" said Wedderburn, opening his eyes feebly, and closing them again at once.

"Go and tell Annie to come out here to me, and then go for Dr. Haddon at once," she said to the odd-job man so soon as he brought the water; and added, seeing he hesitated, "I will tell you all about it when you come back."

Presently Wedderburn opened his eyes again, and, seeing that he was troubled by the puzzle of his position, she explained to him, "You fainted in the hothouse."

"And the orchid?"

"I will see to that," she said. Wedderburn had lost a good deal of blood, but beyond that he had suffered no very great injury. They gave him brandy mixed with some pink extract of meat, and carried him upstairs to bed. His housekeeper told her incredible story in fragments to Dr. Haddon. "Come to the orchid-house and see," she said. The cold outer air was blowing in through the open door, and the sickly perfume was almost dispelled. Most of the torn aerial rootlets lay already withered amidst a number of dark stains upon the bricks. The stem of the inflorescence was broken by the fall of the plant, and the flowers were growing limp and brown at the edges of the petals. The doctor stooped towards it, then saw that one of the aerial rootlets still stirred feebly, and hesitated.

The next morning the strange orchid still lay there, black now and putrescent. The door banged intermittently in the morning breeze, and all the array of Wedderburn's orchids was shrivelled and prostrate. But Wedderburn himself was bright and garrulous upstairs in the glory of his strange adventure.

THE STAR

by H. G. Wells

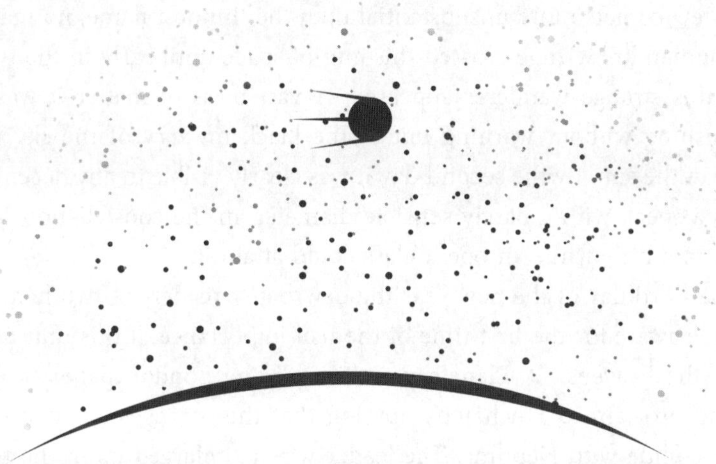

It was on the first day of the new year that the announcement was made, almost simultaneously from three observatories, that the motion of the planet Neptune, the outermost of all the planets that wheel about the sun, had become very erratic. Ogilvy had already called attention to a suspected retardation in its velocity in December. Such a piece of news was scarcely calculated to interest a world the greater portion of whose inhabitants were unaware of the existence of the planet Neptune, nor outside the astronomical profession did the subsequent discovery of a faint remote speck of light in the region of the perturbed planet cause any very great excitement. Scientific people, however, found the intelligence remarkable enough, even before it became known that the new body was rapidly growing larger and brighter, that its motion was quite different from the orderly progress of the planets, and that the deflection of Neptune and its satellite was becoming now of an unprecedented kind.

Few people without a training in science can realise the huge isolation of the solar system. The sun with its specks of planets, its dust of planetoids, and its impalpable comets, swims in a vacant immensity that almost defeats the imagination. Beyond the orbit of Neptune there is space, vacant so far as human observation has penetrated, without warmth or light or sound, blank emptiness, for twenty million times a million miles. That is the smallest estimate of the distance to be traversed before the very nearest of the stars is attained. And, saving a few comets more unsubstantial than the thinnest flame, no matter had ever to human knowledge crossed this gulf of space until early in the twentieth century this strange wanderer appeared. A vast mass of matter it was, bulky, heavy, rushing without warning out of the black mystery of the sky into the radiance of the sun. By the second day it was clearly visible to any decent instrument, as a speck with a barely sensible diameter, in the constellation Leo near Regulus. In a little while an opera glass could attain it.

On the third day of the new year the newspaper readers of two hemispheres were made aware for the first time of the real importance of this unusual apparition in the heavens. "A Planetary Collision," one London paper headed the news, and proclaimed Duchaine's opinion that this strange new planet would probably collide with Neptune. The leader-writers enlarged upon the topic. So that in most of the capitals of the world, on January 3rd, there was an expectation, however vague, of some imminent phenomenon in the sky; and as the night followed the sunset round the globe, thousands of men turned their eyes skyward to see—the old familiar stars just as they had always been.

Until it was dawn in London and Pollux setting and the stars overhead grown pale. The Winter's dawn it was, a sickly filtering accumulation of daylight, and the light of gas and candles shone yellow in the windows to show where people were astir. But the yawning policeman saw the thing, the busy crowds in the markets stopped agape, workmen going to their work betimes, milkmen, the drivers of news-carts, dissipation going home jaded and pale, homeless wanderers, sentinels on their beats, and, in the country, labourers trudging afield, poachers slinking home, all over the dusky quickening country it could be seen—and out at sea by seamen watching for the day—a great white star, come suddenly into the westward sky!

Brighter it was than any star in our skies; brighter than the evening star at its brightest. It still glowed out white and large, no mere twinkling spot of light, but a small, round, clear shining disc, an hour after the day had come. And where science has not reached, men stared and feared, telling one another of the wars and pestilences that are foreshadowed by these fiery signs in the Heavens. Sturdy Boers, dusky Hottentots, Gold Coast negroes, Frenchmen, Spaniards, Portuguese, stood in the warmth of the sunrise watching the setting of this strange new star.

And in a hundred observatories there had been suppressed excitement, rising almost to shouting pitch, as the two remote bodies had rushed together, and a hurrying to and fro, to gather photographic apparatus and spectroscope, and this appliance and that, to record this novel, astonishing sight, the destruction of a world. For it was a world, a sister planet of our earth, far greater than our earth indeed, that had so suddenly flashed into flaming death. Neptune it was had been struck, fairly and squarely, by the strange planet from outer space, and the heat of the concussion had incontinently turned two solid globes into one vast mass of incandescence. Round the world that day, two hours before the dawn, went the pallid great white star, fading only as it sank westward and the sun mounted above it. Everywhere men marvelled at it, but of all those who saw it none could have marvelled more than those sailors, habitual watchers of the stars, who far away at sea had heard nothing of its advent and saw it now rise like a pigmy moon and climb zenithward and hang overhead and sink westward with the passing of the night.

And when next it rose over Europe everywhere were crowds of watchers on hilly slopes, on house-roofs, in open spaces, staring eastward for the rising of the great new star. It rose with a white glow in front of it, like the glare of a white fire, and those who had seen it come into existence the night before cried out at the sight of it. "It is larger," they cried. "It is brighter!" And indeed the moon, a quarter full and sinking in the west, was in its apparent size beyond comparison, but scarcely in all its breadth had it as much brightness now as the little circle of the strange new star.

"It is brighter!" cried the people clustering in the streets. But in the dim observatories the watchers held their breath and peered at one another. "*It is nearer*!" they said. "*Nearer*!"

And voice after voice repeated, "It is nearer," and the clicking telegraph took that up, and it trembled along telephone wires, and in a thousand cities grimy compositors fingered the type. "It is nearer." Men writing in offices, struck with a strange realisation, flung down their pens, men talking in a thousand places suddenly came upon a grotesque possibility in those words, "It is nearer." It hurried along awakening streets, it was shouted down the frost-stilled ways of quiet villages, men who had read these things from the throbbing tape stood in yellow-lit doorways shouting the news to the passers-by. "It is nearer," Pretty women, flushed and glittering, heard the news told jestingly between the dances, and feigned an intelligent interest they did not feel. "Nearer! Indeed. How curious! How very, very clever people must be to find out things like that!"

Lonely tramps faring through the wintry night murmured those words to comfort themselves—looking skyward. "It has need to be nearer, for the night's as cold as charity. Don't seem much warmth from it if it *is* nearer, all the same."

"What is a new star to me?" cried the weeping woman, kneeling beside her dead.

The schoolboy, rising early for his examination work, puzzled it out for himself—with the great white star shining broad and bright through the frost-flowers of his window. "Centrifugal, centripetal," he said, with his chin on his fist. "Stop a planet in its flight, rob it of its centrifugal force, what then? Centripetal has it, and down it falls into the sun! And this—!

"Do *we* come in the way? I wonder—"

The light of that day went the way of its brethren, and with the later watches of the frosty darkness rose the strange star again. And it was now so bright that the waxing moon seemed but a pale yellow ghost of itself, hanging huge in the sunset. In a South African city a great man had married, and the streets were alight to welcome his return with his bride. "Even the skies have illuminated," said the flatterer. Under Capricorn, two negro lovers, daring the wild beasts and evil spirits for love of one another, crouched together in a cane brake where the fire-flies hovered. "That is our star," they whispered, and felt strangely comforted by the sweet brilliance of its light.

The master mathematician sat in his private room and pushed the papers from him. His calculations were already finished. In a small white phial there still remained a little of the drug that had kept him awake and active for four long nights. Each day, serene, explicit, patient as ever, he had given his lecture to his students, and then had come back at once to this momentous calculation. His face was grave, a little drawn and hectic from his drugged activity. For some time he seemed lost in thought. Then he went to the window, and the blind went up with a click. Half-way up the sky, over the clustering roofs, chimneys, and steeples of the city, hung the star.

He looked at it as one might look into the eyes of a brave enemy. "You may kill me," he said after a silence. "But I can hold you—and all the universe for that matter—in the grip of this small brain. I would not change. Even now."

He looked at the little phial. "There will be no need of sleep again," he said. The next day at noon, punctual to the minute, he entered his lecture theatre, put his hat on the end of the table as his habit was, and carefully selected a large piece of chalk. It was a joke among his students that he could not lecture without that piece of chalk to fumble in his fingers, and once he had been stricken to impotence by their hiding his supply. He came and looked under his grey eyebrows at the rising tiers of young fresh faces, and spoke with his accustomed studied commonness of phrasing.

"Circumstances have arisen—circumstances beyond my control," he said, and paused, "which will debar me from completing the course I had designed. It would seem, gentlemen, if I may put the thing clearly and briefly, that—Man has lived in vain."

The students glanced at one another. Had they heard aright? Mad? Raised eyebrows and grinning lips there were, but one or two faces remained intent upon his calm grey-fringed face. "It will be interesting," he was saying, "to devote this morning to an exposition, so far as I can make it clear to you, of the calculations that have led me to this conclusion. Let us assume—"

He turned towards the blackboard, meditating a diagram in the way that was usual to him. "What was that about 'lived in vain'?" whispered one student to another. "Listen," said the other, nodding towards the lecturer.

And presently they began to understand.

* * * * *

That night the star rose later, for its proper eastward motion had carried it some way across Leo towards Virgo, and its brightness was so great that the sky became a luminous blue as it rose, and every star was hidden in its turn, save only Jupiter near the zenith, Capella, Aldebaran, Sirius, and the pointers of the Bear. It was very white and beautiful. In many parts of the world that night a pallid halo encircled it about. It was perceptibly larger; in the clear refractive sky of the tropics it seemed as if it were nearly a quarter the size of the moon. The frost was still on the ground in England, but the world was as brightly lit as if it were midsummer moonlight. One could see to read quite ordinary print by that cold, clear light, and in the cities the lamps burnt yellow and wan.

And everywhere the world was awake that night, and throughout Christendom a sombre murmur hung in the keen air over the country-side like the belling of bees in the heather, and this murmurous tumult grew to a clangour in the cities. It was the tolling of the bells in a million belfry towers and steeples, summoning the people to sleep no more, to sin no more, but to gather in their churches and pray. And overhead, growing larger and brighter, as the earth rolled on its way and the night passed, rose the dazzling star.

And the streets and houses were alight in all the cities, the shipyards glared, and whatever roads led to high country were lit and crowded all night long. And in all the seas about the civilized lands, ships with throbbing engines, and ships with bellying sails, crowded with men and living creatures, were standing out to ocean and the north. For already the warning of the master mathematician had been telegraphed all over the world and translated into a hundred tongues. The new planet and Neptune, locked in a fiery embrace, were whirling headlong, ever faster and faster towards the sun. Already every second this blazing mass flew a hundred miles, and every second its terrific velocity increased. As it flew now, indeed, it must pass a hundred million of miles, wide of the earth and scarcely affect it. But near its destined path, as yet only slightly perturbed, spun the mighty planet Jupiter and his moons sweeping splendid round the sun. Every moment now the attraction between the fiery star and the greatest of the planets grew stronger. And the result of that attraction? Inevitably Jupiter would be deflected from its orbit into an elliptical path, and the burning star, swung by his attraction wide of its sunward rush, would "describe a curved path," and perhaps collide with, and certainly pass very close to, our earth. "Earthquakes, volcanic outbreaks, cyclones, sea waves, floods, and a steady rise in temperature to I know not what limit"—so prophesied the master mathematician.

And overhead, to carry out his words, lonely and cold and livid blazed the star of the coming doom.

To many who stared at it that night until their eyes ached it seemed that it was visibly approaching. And that night, too, the weather changed, and the frost that had gripped all Central Europe and France and England softened towards a thaw.

But you must not imagine, because I have spoken of people praying through the night and people going aboard ships and people fleeing towards mountainous country, that the whole world was already in a terror because of the star. As a matter of fact, use and wont still ruled the world, and save for the talk of idle moments and the splendour of the night, nine human beings out of ten were still busy at their common occupations. In all the cities the shops, save one here and there, opened and closed at their proper hours, the doctor and the undertaker plied their trades, the workers gathered in the factories, soldiers drilled, scholars studied, lovers sought one another, thieves lurked and fled, politicians planned their schemes. The presses of the newspapers roared through the nights, and many a priest of this church and that would not open his holy building to further what he considered a foolish panic. The newspapers insisted on the lesson of the year 1000—for then, too, people had anticipated the end. The star was no star—mere gas—a comet; and were it a star it could not possibly strike the earth. There was no precedent for such a thing. Common-sense was sturdy everywhere, scornful, jesting, a little inclined to persecute the obdurate fearful. That night, at seven-fifteen by Greenwich time, the star would be at its nearest to Jupiter. Then the world would see the turn things would take. The master mathematician's grim warnings were treated by many as so much mere elaborate self-advertisement. Common-sense at last, a little heated by argument, signified its unalterable convictions by going to bed. So, too, barbarism and savagery, already tired of the novelty, went about their nightly business, and, save for a howling dog here and there, the beast world left the star unheeded.

And yet, when at last the watchers in the European States saw the star rise, an hour later, it is true, but no larger than it had been the night before, there were still plenty awake to laugh at the master mathematician—to take the danger as if it had passed.

But hereafter the laughter ceased. The star grew—it grew with a terrible steadiness hour after hour, a little larger each hour, a little nearer the midnight zenith, and brighter and brighter, until it had turned night into a second day. Had it come straight to the earth instead of in a curved path, had it lost no velocity to Jupiter, it must have leapt the intervening gulf in a day; but as it was, it took five days altogether to come by our planet. The next night it had become a third the size of the moon before it set to English eyes, and the thaw was assured. It rose over America near the size of the moon, but blinding white to look at, and *hot*; and a breath of hot wind blew now with its rising and gathering strength, and in Virginia, and Brazil, and down the St. Lawrence valley, it shone intermittently through a driving reek of thunder-clouds, flickering violet lightning, and hail unprecedented. In Manitoba was a thaw and devastating floods. And upon all the mountains of the earth the snow and ice began to melt that night, and all the rivers coming out of high country flowed thick and turbid, and soon—in their upper reaches—with swirling trees and the bodies of beasts and men. They rose steadily, steadily in the ghostly brilliance, and came trickling over their banks at last, behind the flying population of their valleys.

And along the coast of Argentina and up the South Atlantic the tides were higher than had ever been in the memory of man, and the storms drove the waters in many cases scores of miles inland, drowning whole cities. And so great grew the heat during the night that the rising of the sun was like the coming of a shadow. The earthquakes began and grew until all down America from the Arctic Circle to Cape Horn, hillsides were sliding, fissures were opening, and houses and walls crumbling to destruction. The whole side of Cotopaxi slipped out in one vast convulsion, and a tumult of lava poured out so high and broad and swift and liquid that in one day it reached the sea.

So the star, with the wan moon in its wake, marched across the Pacific, trailed the thunder-storms like the hem of a robe, and the growing tidal wave that toiled behind it, frothing and eager, poured over island and island and swept them clear of men: until that wave came at last—in a blinding light and with the breath of a furnace, swift and terrible it came—a wall of water, fifty feet high, roaring hungrily, upon the long coasts of Asia, and swept inland across the plains of China. For a space the star, hotter now and larger and brighter than the sun in its strength, showed with pitiless brilliance the wide and populous country; towns and villages with their pagodas and trees, roads, wide cultivated fields, millions of sleepless people staring in helpless terror at the incandescent sky; and then, low and growing, came the murmur of the flood. And thus it was with millions of men that night—a flight nowhither, with limbs heavy with heat and breath fierce and scant, and the flood like a wall swift and white behind. And then death.

China was lit glowing white, but over Japan and Java and all the islands of Eastern Asia the great star was a ball of dull red fire because of the steam and smoke and ashes the volcanoes were spouting forth to salute its coming. Above was the lava, hot gases and ash, and below the seething floods, and the whole earth swayed and rumbled with the earthquake shocks. Soon the immemorial snows of Thibet and the Himalaya were melting and pouring down by ten million deepening converging channels upon the plains of Burmah and Hindostan. The tangled summits of the Indian jungles were aflame in a thousand places, and below the hurrying waters around the stems were dark objects that still struggled feebly and reflected the blood-red tongues of fire. And in a rudderless confusion a multitude of men and women fled down the broad river-ways to that one last hope of men—the open sea.

Larger grew the star, and larger, hotter, and brighter with a terrible swiftness now. The tropical ocean had lost its phosphorescence, and the whirling steam rose in ghostly wreaths from the black waves that plunged incessantly, speckled with storm-tossed ships.

And then came a wonder. It seemed to those who in Europe watched for the rising of the star that the world must have ceased its rotation. In a thousand open spaces of down and upland the people who had fled thither from the floods and the falling houses and sliding slopes of hill watched for that rising in vain. Hour followed hour through a terrible suspense, and the star rose not. Once again men set their eyes upon the old constellations they had counted lost to them for ever. In England it was hot and clear overhead, though the ground quivered perpetually, but in the tropics, Sirius and Capella and Aldebaran showed through a veil of steam. And when at last the great star rose near ten hours late, the sun rose close upon it, and in the centre of its white heart was a disc of black.

Over Asia it was the star had begun to fall behind the movement of the sky, and then suddenly, as it hung over India, its light had been veiled. All the plain of India from the mouth of the Indus to the mouths of the Ganges was a shallow waste of shining water that night, out of which rose temples and palaces, mounds and hills, black with people. Every minaret was a clustering mass of people, who fell one by one into the turbid waters, as heat and terror overcame them. The whole land seemed a-wailing, and suddenly there swept a shadow across that furnace of despair, and a breath of cold wind, and a gathering of clouds, out of the cooling air. Men looking up, near blinded, at the star, saw that a black disc was creeping across the light. It was the moon, coming between the star and the earth. And even as men cried to God at this respite, out of the East with a strange inexplicable swiftness sprang the sun. And then star, sun, and moon rushed together across the heavens.

So it was that presently to the European watchers star and sun rose close upon each other, drove headlong for a space and then slower, and at last came to rest, star and sun merged into one glare of flame at the zenith of the sky. The moon no longer eclipsed the star but was lost to sight in the brilliance of the sky. And though those who were still alive regarded it for the most part with that dull stupidity that hunger, fatigue, heat and despair engender, there were still men who could perceive the meaning of these signs. Star and earth had been at their nearest, had swung about one another, and the star had passed. Already it was receding, swifter and swifter, in the last stage of its headlong journey downward into the sun.

And then the clouds gathered, blotting out the vision of the sky, the thunder and lightning wove a garment round the world; all over the earth was such a downpour of rain as men had never before seen, and where the volcanoes flared red against the cloud canopy there descended torrents of mud. Everywhere the waters were pouring off the land, leaving mud-silted ruins, and the earth littered like a storm-worn beach with all that had floated, and the dead bodies of the men and brutes, its children. For days the water streamed off the land, sweeping away soil and trees and houses in the way, and piling huge dykes and scooping out Titanic gullies over the country-side. Those were the days of darkness that followed the star and the heat. All through them, and for many weeks and months, the earthquakes continued.

But the star had passed, and men, hunger-driven and gathering courage only slowly, might creep back to their ruined cities, buried granaries, and sodden fields. Such few ships as had escaped the storms of that time came stunned and shattered and sounding their way cautiously through the new marks and shoals of once familiar ports. And as the storms subsided men perceived that everywhere the days were hotter than of yore, and the sun larger, and the moon, shrunk to a third of its former size, took now fourscore days between its new and new.

But of the new brotherhood that grew presently among men, of the saving of laws and books and machines, of the strange change that had come over Iceland and Greenland and the shores of Baffin's Bay, so that the sailors coming there presently found them green and gracious, and could scarce believe their eyes, this story does not tell. Nor of the movement of mankind, now that the earth was hotter, northward and southward towards the poles of the earth. It concerns itself only with the coming and the passing of the star.

The Martian astronomers—for there are astronomers on Mars, although they are very different beings from men—were naturally profoundly interested by these things. They saw them from their own standpoint of course. "Considering the mass and temperature of the missile that was flung through our solar system into the sun," one wrote, "it is astonishing what a little damage the earth, which it missed so narrowly, has sustained. All the familiar continental markings and the masses of the seas remain intact, and indeed the only difference seems to be a shrinkage of the white discolouration (supposed to be frozen water) round either pole." Which only shows how small the vastest of human catastrophes may seem at a distance of a few million miles.

THE CRYSTAL EGG

by H. G. Wells

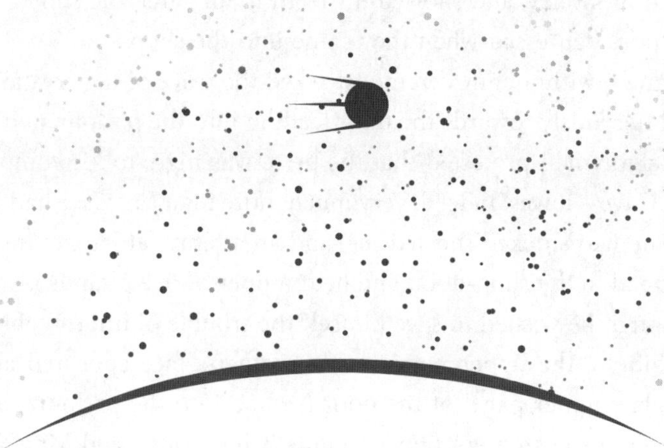

There was, until a year ago, a little and very grimy-looking shop near Seven Dials over which, in weather-worn yellow lettering, the name of "C. Cave, Naturalist and Dealer in Antiquities," was inscribed. The contents of its window were curiously variegated. They comprised some elephant tusks and an imperfect set of chessmen, beads and weapons, a box of eyes, two skulls of tigers and one human, several moth-eaten stuffed monkeys (one holding a lamp), an old-fashioned cabinet, a fly-blown ostrich egg or so, some fishing-tackle, and an extraordinarily dirty, empty glass fish-tank. There was also, at the moment the story begins, a mass of crystal, worked into the shape of an egg and brilliantly polished. And at that two people, who stood outside the window, were looking, one of them a tall, thin clergyman, the other a black-bearded young man of dusky complexion and unobtrusive costume. The dusky young man spoke with eager gesticulation, and seemed anxious for his companion to purchase the article.

While they were there, Mr. Cave came into his shop, his beard still wagging with the bread and butter of his tea. When he saw these men and the object of their regard, his countenance fell. He glanced guiltily over his shoulder, and softly shut the door. He was a little old man, with pale face and peculiar watery blue eyes; his hair was a dirty grey, and he wore a shabby blue frock-coat, an ancient silk hat, and carpet slippers very much down at heel. He remained watching the two men as they talked. The clergyman went deep into his trouser pocket, examined a handful of money, and showed his teeth in an agreeable smile. Mr. Cave seemed still more depressed when they came into the shop.

The clergyman, without any ceremony, asked the price of the crystal egg. Mr. Cave glanced nervously towards the door leading into the parlour, and said five pounds. The clergyman protested that the price was high, to his companion as well as to Mr. Cave—it was, indeed, very much more than Mr. Cave had intended to ask, when he had stocked the article—and an attempt at bargaining ensued. Mr. Cave stepped to the shop-door, and held it open. "Five pounds is my price," he said, as though he wished to save himself the trouble of unprofitable discussion. As he did so, the upper portion of a woman's face appeared above the blind in the glass upper panel of the door leading into the parlour, and stared curiously at the two customers. "Five pounds is my price," said Mr. Cave, with a quiver in his voice.

The swarthy young man had so far remained a spectator, watching Cave keenly. Now he spoke. "Give him five pounds," he said. The clergyman glanced at him to see if he were in earnest, and, when he looked at Mr. Cave again, he saw that the latter's face was white. "It's a lot of money," said the clergyman, and diving into his pocket, began counting his resources. He had little more than thirty shillings, and he appealed to his companion, with whom he seemed to be on terms of considerable intimacy. This gave Mr. Cave an opportunity of collecting his thoughts, and he began to explain in an agitated manner that the crystal was not, as a matter of fact, entirely free for sale. His two customers were naturally surprised at this, and inquired why he had not thought of that before he began to bargain. Mr. Cave became confused, but he stuck to his story, that the crystal was not in the market that afternoon, that a probable purchaser of it had already appeared. The two, treating this as an attempt to raise the price still further, made as if they would leave the shop. But at this point the parlour door opened, and the owner of the dark fringe and the little eyes appeared.

She was a coarse-featured, corpulent woman, younger and very much larger than Mr. Cave; she walked heavily, and her face was flushed. "That crystal is for sale," she said. "And five pounds is a good enough price for it. I can't think what you're about Cave, not to take the gentleman's offer!"

Mr. Cave, greatly perturbed by the irruption, looked angrily at her over the rims of his spectacles, and without excessive assurance, asserted his right to manage his business in his own way. An altercation began. The two customers watched the scene with interest and some amusement, occasionally assisting Mrs. Cave with suggestions. Mr. Cave, hard driven, persisted in a confused and impossible story of an enquiry for the crystal that morning, and his agitation became painful. But he stuck to his point with extraordinary persistence. It was the young Oriental who ended this curious controversy. He proposed that they should call again in the course of two days—so as to give the alleged enquirer a fair chance. "And then we must insist," said the clergyman. "Five pounds." Mrs. Cave took it on herself to apologise for her husband, explaining that he was sometimes "a little odd," and as the two customers left, the couple prepared for a free discussion of the incident in all its bearings.

Mrs. Cave talked to her husband with singular directness. The poor little man, quivering with emotion, muddled himself between his stories, maintaining on the one hand that he had another customer in view, and on the other asserting that the crystal was honestly worth ten guineas. "Why did you ask five pounds?" said his wife. "Do let me manage my business my own way!" said Mr. Cave.

Mr. Cave had living with him a step-daughter and a step-son, and at supper that night the transaction was re-discussed. None of them had a high opinion of Mr. Cave's business methods, and this action seemed a culminating folly.

"It's my opinion he's refused that crystal before," said the step-son, a loose-limbed lout of eighteen.

"But Five Pounds!" said the step-daughter, an argumentative young woman of six-and-twenty.

Mr. Cave's answers were wretched; he could only mumble weak assertions that he knew his own business best. They drove him from his half-eaten supper into the shop, to close it for the night, his ears aflame and tears of vexation behind his spectacles. "Why had he left the crystal in the window so long? The folly of it!" That was the trouble closest in his mind. For a time he could see no way of evading sale.

After supper his step-daughter and step-son smartened themselves up and went out and his wife retired upstairs to reflect upon the business aspects of the crystal, over a little sugar and lemon and so forth in hot water. Mr. Cave went into the shop, and stayed there until late, ostensibly to make ornamental rockeries for gold-fish cases but really for a private purpose that will be better explained later. The next day Mrs. Cave found that the crystal had been removed from the window, and was lying behind some second-hand books on angling. She replaced it in a conspicuous position. But she did not argue further about it, as a nervous headache disinclined her from debate. Mr. Cave was always disinclined. The day passed disagreeably. Mr. Cave was, if anything, more absent-minded than usual, and uncommonly irritable withal. In the afternoon, when his wife was taking her customary sleep, he removed the crystal from the window again.

The next day Mr. Cave had to deliver a consignment of dog-fish at one of the hospital schools, where they were needed for dissection. In his absence Mrs. Cave's mind reverted to the topic of the crystal, and the methods of expenditure suitable to a windfall of five pounds. She had already devised some very agreeable expedients, among others a dress of green silk for herself and a trip to Richmond, when a jangling of the front door bell summoned her into the shop. The customer was an examination coach who came to complain of the non-delivery of certain frogs asked for the previous day. Mrs. Cave did not approve of this particular branch of Mr. Cave's business, and the gentleman, who had called in a somewhat aggressive mood, retired after a brief exchange of words—entirely civil so far as he was concerned. Mrs. Cave's eye then naturally turned to the window; for the sight of the crystal was an assurance of the five pounds and of her dreams. What was her surprise to find it gone!

She went to the place behind the locker on the counter, where she had discovered it the day before. It was not there; and she immediately began an eager search about the shop.

When Mr. Cave returned from his business with the dog-fish, about a quarter to two in the afternoon, he found the shop in some confusion, and his wife, extremely exasperated and on her knees behind the counter, routing among his taxidermic material. Her face came up hot and angry over the counter, as the jangling bell announced his return, and she forthwith accused him of "hiding it."

"Hid what?" asked Mr. Cave.

"The crystal!"

At that Mr. Cave, apparently much surprised, rushed to the window. "Isn't it here?" he said. "Great Heavens! What has become of it?"

Just then, Mr. Cave's step-son re-entered the shop from the inner room—he had come home a minute or so before Mr. Cave—and he was blaspheming freely. He was apprenticed to a second-hand furniture dealer down the road, but he had his meals at home, and he was naturally annoyed to find no dinner ready.

But when he heard of the loss of the crystal, he forgot his meal, and his anger was diverted from his mother to his step-father. Their first idea, of course, was that he had hidden it. But Mr. Cave stoutly denied all knowledge of its fate—freely offering his bedabbled affidavit in the matter—and at last was worked up to the point of accusing, first, his wife and then his step-son of having taken it with a view to a private sale. So began an exceedingly acrimonious and emotional discussion, which ended for Mrs. Cave in a peculiar nervous condition midway between hysterics and amuck, and caused the step-son to be half-an-hour late at the furniture establishment in the afternoon. Mr. Cave took refuge from his wife's emotions in the shop.

In the evening the matter was resumed, with less passion and in a judicial spirit, under the presidency of the step-daughter. The supper passed unhappily and culminated in a painful scene. Mr. Cave gave way at last to extreme exasperation, and went out banging the front door violently. The rest of the family, having discussed him with the freedom his absence warranted, hunted the house from garret to cellar, hoping to light upon the crystal.

The next day the two customers called again. They were received by Mrs. Cave almost in tears. It transpired that no one could imagine all that she had stood from Cave at various times in her married pilgrimage… She also gave a garbled account of the disappearance. The clergyman and the Oriental laughed silently at one another, and said it was very extraordinary. As Mrs. Cave seemed disposed to give them the complete history of her life they made to leave the shop. Thereupon Mrs. Cave, still clinging to hope, asked for the clergyman's address, so that, if she could get anything out of Cave, she might communicate it. The address was duly given, but apparently was afterwards mislaid. Mrs. Cave can remember nothing about it.

In the evening of that day, the Caves seem to have exhausted their emotions, and Mr. Cave, who had been out in the afternoon, supped in a gloomy isolation that contrasted pleasantly with the impassioned controversy of the previous days. For some time matters were very badly strained in the Cave household, but neither crystal nor customer reappeared.

Now without mincing the matter, we must admit that Mr. Cave was a liar. He knew perfectly well where the crystal was. It was in the rooms of Mr. Jacoby Wace, Assistant Demonstrator at St. Catherine's Hospital, Westbourne Street. It stood on the sideboard partially covered by a black velvet cloth, and beside a decanter of American whisky. It is from Mr. Wace, indeed, that the particulars upon which this narrative is based were derived. Cave had taken off the thing to the hospital hidden in the dog-fish sack, and there had pressed the young investigator to keep it for him. Mr. Wace was a little dubious at first. His relationship to Cave was peculiar. He had a taste for singular characters, and he had more than once invited the old man to smoke and drink in his rooms, and to unfold his rather amusing views of life in general and of his wife in particular. Mr. Wace had encountered Mrs. Cave too, on occasions when Mr. Cave was not at home to attend to him. He knew the constant interference to which Cave was subjected, and having weighed the story judicially, he decided to give the crystal a refuge. Mr. Cave promised to explain the reasons for his remarkable affection for the crystal more fully on a later occasion, but he spoke distinctly of seeing visions therein. He called on Mr. Wace the same evening.

He told a complicated story. The crystal he said had come into his possession with other oddments at the forced sale of another curiosity dealer's effects, and not knowing what its value might be, he had ticketed it at ten shillings. It had hung upon his hands at that price for some months, and he was thinking of "reducing the figure," when he made a singular discovery.

At that time his health was very bad—and it must be borne in mind that, throughout all this experience, his physical condition was one of ebb—and he was in considerable distress by reason of the negligence, the positive ill-treatment even, he received from his wife and step-children. His wife was vain, extravagant, unfeeling and had a growing taste for private drinking; his step-daughter was mean and over-reaching; and his step-son had conceived a violent dislike for him, and lost no chance of showing it. The requirements of his business pressed heavily upon him, and Mr. Wace does not think that he was altogether free from occasional intemperance. He had begun life in a comfortable position, he was a man of fair education, and he suffered, for weeks at a stretch, from melancholia and insomnia. Afraid to disturb his family, he would slip quietly from his wife's side, when his thoughts became intolerable, and wander about the house. And about three o'clock one morning, late in August, chance directed him into the shop.

The dirty little place was impenetrably black except in one spot, where he perceived an unusual glow of light. Approaching this, he discovered it to be the crystal egg, which was standing on the corner of the counter towards the window. A thin ray smote through a crack in the shutters, impinged upon the object, and seemed as it were to fill its entire interior.

It occurred to Mr. Cave that this was not in accordance with the laws of optics as he had known them in his younger days. He could understand the rays being refracted by the crystal and coming to a focus in its interior, but this diffusion jarred with his physical conceptions. He approached the crystal nearly, peering into it and round it, with a transient revival of the scientific curiosity that in his youth had determined his choice of a calling. He was surprised to find the light not steady, but writhing within the substance of the egg, as though that object was a hollow sphere of some luminous vapour. In moving about to get different points of view, he suddenly found that he had come between it and the ray, and that the crystal none the less remained luminous. Greatly astonished, he lifted it out of the light ray and carried it to the darkest part of the shop. It remained bright for some four or five minutes, when it slowly faded and went out. He placed it in the thin streak of daylight, and its luminousness was almost immediately restored.

So far, at least, Mr. Wace was able to verify the remarkable story of Mr. Cave. He has himself repeatedly held this crystal in a ray of light (which had to be of a less diameter than one millimetre). And in a perfect darkness, such as could be produced by velvet wrapping, the crystal did undoubtedly appear very faintly phosphorescent. It would seem, however, that the luminousness was of some exceptional sort, and not equally visible to all eyes; for Mr. Harbinger—whose name will be familiar to the scientific reader in connection with the Pasteur Institute—was quite unable to see any light whatever. And Mr. Wace's own capacity for its appreciation was out of comparison inferior to that of Mr. Cave's. Even with Mr. Cave the power varied very considerably: his vision was most vivid during states of extreme weakness and fatigue.

Now, from the outset this light in the crystal exercised a curious fascination upon Mr. Cave. And it says more for his loneliness of soul than a volume of pathetic writing could do, that he told no human being of his curious observations. He seems to have been living in such an atmosphere of petty spite that to admit the existence of a pleasure would have been to risk the loss of it. He found that as the dawn advanced, and the amount of diffused light increased, the crystal became to all appearance non-luminous. And for some time he was unable to see anything in it, except at night-time, in dark corners of the shop.

But the use of an old velvet cloth, which he used as a background for a collection of minerals, occurred to him, and by doubling this, and putting it over his head and hands, he was able to get a sight of the luminous movement within the crystal even in the day-time. He was very cautious lest he should be thus discovered by his wife, and he practised this occupation only in the afternoons, while she was asleep upstairs, and then circumspectly in a hollow under the counter. And one day, turning the crystal about in his hands, he saw something. It came and went like a flash, but it gave him the impression that the object had for a moment opened to him the view of a wide and spacious and strange country; and turning it about, he did, just as the light faded, see the same vision again.

Now, it would be tedious and unnecessary to state all the phases of Mr. Cave's discovery from this point. Suffice that the effect was this: the crystal, being peered into at an angle of about 137 degrees from the direction of the illuminating ray, gave a clear and consistent picture of a wide and peculiar countryside. It was not dream-like at all: it produced a definite impression of reality, and the better the light the more real and solid it seemed. It was a moving picture: that is to say, certain objects moved in it, but slowly in an orderly manner like real things, and according as the direction of the lighting and vision changed, the picture changed also. It must, indeed, have been like looking through an oval glass at a view, and turning the glass about to get at different aspects.

Mr. Cave's statements, Mr. Wace assures me, were extremely circumstantial, and entirely free from any of that emotional quality that taints hallucinatory impressions. But it must be remembered that all the efforts of Mr. Wace to see any similar clarity in the faint opalescence of the crystal were wholly unsuccessful, try as he would. The difference in intensity of the impressions received by the two men was very great, and it is quite conceivable that what was a view to Mr. Cave was a mere blurred nebulosity to Mr. Wace.

The view, as Mr. Cave described it, was invariably of an extensive plain, and he seemed always to be looking at it from a considerable height, as if from a tower or a mast. To the east and to the west the plain was bounded at a remote distance by vast reddish cliffs, which reminded him of those he had seen in some picture; but what the picture was Mr. Wace was unable to ascertain. These cliffs passed north and south—he could tell the points of the compass by the stars that were visible of a night—receding in an almost illimitable perspective and fading into the mists of the distance before they met. He was nearer the eastern set of cliffs, on the occasion of his first vision the sun was rising over them, and black against the sunlight and pale against their shadow appeared a multitude of soaring forms that Mr. Cave regarded as birds. A vast range of buildings spread below him; he seemed to be looking down upon them; and as they approached the blurred and refracted edge of the picture, they became indistinct. There were also trees curious in shape, and in colouring, a deep mossy green and an exquisite grey, beside a wide and shining canal. And something great and brilliantly coloured flew across the picture. But the first time Mr. Cave saw these pictures he saw only in flashes, his hands shook, his head moved, the vision came and went, and grew foggy and indistinct. And at first he had the greatest difficulty in finding the picture again once the direction of it was lost.

His next clear vision, which came about a week after the first, the interval having yielded nothing but tantalising glimpses and some useful experience, showed him the view down the length of the valley. The view was different, but he had a curious persuasion, which his subsequent observations abundantly confirmed, that he was regarding this strange world from exactly the same spot, although he was looking in a different direction. The long facade of the great building, whose roof he had looked down upon before, was now receding in perspective. He recognised the roof. In the front of the facade was a terrace of massive proportions and extraordinary length, and down the middle of the terrace, at certain intervals, stood huge but very graceful masts, bearing small shiny objects which reflected the setting sun. The import of these small objects did not occur to Mr. Cave until some time after, as he was describing the scene to Mr. Wace. The terrace overhung a thicket of the most luxuriant and graceful vegetation, and beyond this was a wide grassy lawn on which certain broad creatures, in form like beetles but enormously larger, reposed. Beyond this again was a richly decorated causeway of pinkish stone; and beyond that, and lined with dense red weeds, and passing up the valley exactly parallel with the distant cliffs, was a broad and mirror-like expanse of water. The air seemed full of squadrons of great birds, manoeuvring in stately curves; and across the river was a multitude of splendid buildings, richly coloured and glittering with metallic tracery and facets, among a forest of moss-like and lichenous trees. And suddenly something flapped repeatedly across the vision, like the fluttering of a jewelled fan or the beating of a wing, and a face, or rather the upper part of a face with very large eyes, came as it were close to his own and as if on the other side of the crystal. Mr. Cave was so startled and so impressed by the absolute reality of these eyes, that he drew his head back from the crystal to look behind it. He had become so absorbed in watching that he was quite surprised to find himself in the cool darkness of his little shop, with its familiar odour of methyl, mustiness, and decay. And as he blinked about him, the glowing crystal faded, and went out.

Such were the first general impressions of Mr. Cave. The story is curiously direct and circumstantial. From the outset, when the valley first flashed momentarily on his senses, his imagination was strangely affected, and as he began to appreciate the details of the scene he saw, his wonder rose to the point of a passion. He went about his business listless and distraught, thinking only of the time when he should be able to return to his watching. And then a few weeks after his first sight of the valley came the two customers, the stress and excitement of their offer, and the narrow escape of the crystal from sale, as I have already told.

Now, while the thing was Mr. Cave's secret, it remained a mere wonder, a thing to creep to covertly and peep at, as a child might peep upon a forbidden garden. But Mr. Wace has, for a young scientific investigator, a particularly lucid and consecutive habit of mind. Directly the crystal and its story came to him, and he had satisfied himself, by seeing the phosphorescence with his own eyes, that there really was a certain evidence for Mr. Cave's statements, he proceeded to develop the matter systematically. Mr. Cave was only too eager to come and feast his eyes on this wonderland he saw, and he came every night from half-past eight until half-past ten, and sometimes, in Mr. Wace's absence, during the day. On Sunday afternoons, also he came. From the outset Mr. Wace made copious notes, and it was due to his scientific method that the relation between the direction from which the initiating ray entered the crystal and the orientation of the picture were proved. And by covering the crystal in a box perforated only with a small aperture to admit the exciting ray, and by substituting black holland for his buff blinds, he greatly improved the conditions of the observations; so that in a little while they were able to survey the valley in any direction they desired.

So having cleared the way, we may give a brief account of this visionary world within the crystal. The things were in all cases seen by Mr. Cave, and the method of working was invariably for him to watch the crystal and report what he saw, while Mr. Wace (who as a science student had learnt the trick of writing in the dark) wrote a brief note of his report. When the crystal faded, it was put into its box in the proper position and the electric light turned on. Mr. Wace asked questions, and suggested observations to clear up difficult points. Nothing, indeed, could have been less visionary and more matter-of-fact.

The attention of Mr. Cave had been speedily directed to the bird-like creatures he had seen so abundantly present in each of his earlier visions. His first impression was soon corrected, and he considered for a time that they might represent a diurnal species of bat. Then he thought, grotesquely enough, that they might be cherubs. Their heads were round, and curiously human, and it was the eyes of one of them that had so startled him on his second observation. They had broad, silvery wings, not feathered, but glistening almost as brilliantly as new-killed fish and with the same subtle play of colour, and these wings were not built on the plan of a bird-wing or bat, Mr. Wace learned, but supported by curved ribs radiating from the body. (A sort of butterfly wing with curved ribs seems best to express their appearance.) The body was small, but fitted with two bunches of prehensile organs, like long tentacles, immediately under the mouth. Incredible as it appeared to Mr. Wace, the persuasion at last became irresistible, that it was these creatures which owned the great quasi-human buildings and the magnificent garden that made the broad valley so splendid. And Mr. Cave perceived that the buildings, with other peculiarities, had no doors, but that the great circular windows, which opened freely, gave the creatures egress and entrance. They would alight upon their tentacles, fold their wings to a smallness almost rod-like, and hop into the interior. But among them was a multitude of smaller-winged creatures, like great dragon-flies and moths and flying beetles, and across the greensward brilliantly-coloured gigantic ground-beetles crawled lazily to and fro. Moreover, on the causeways and terraces, large-headed creatures similar to the greater winged flies, but wingless, were visible, hopping busily upon their hand-like tangle of tentacles.

Allusion has already been made to the glittering objects upon masts that stood upon the terrace of the nearer building. It dawned upon Mr. Cave, after regarding one of these masts very fixedly on one particularly vivid day, that the glittering object there was a crystal exactly like that into which he peered. And a still more careful scrutiny convinced him that each one in a vista of nearly twenty carried a similar object.

Occasionally one of the large flying creatures would flutter up to one, and folding its wings and coiling a number of its tentacles about the mast, would regard the crystal fixedly for a space—, sometimes for as long as fifteen minutes. And a series of observations, made at the suggestion of Mr. Wace, convinced both watchers that, so far as this visionary world was concerned, the crystal into which they peered actually stood at the summit of the end-most mast on the terrace, and that on one occasion at least one of these inhabitants of this other world had looked into Mr. Cave's face while he was making these observations.

So much for the essential facts of this very singular story. Unless we dismiss it all as the ingenious fabrication of Mr. Wace, we have to believe one of two things: either that Mr. Cave's crystal was in two worlds at once, and that, while it was carried about in one, it remained stationary in the other, which seems altogether absurd; or else that it had some peculiar relation of sympathy with another and exactly similar crystal in this other world, so that what was seen in the interior of the one in this world, was under suitable conditions, visible to an observer in the corresponding crystal in the other world; and vice versa. At present indeed, we do not know of any way in which two crystals could so come *en rapport*, but nowadays we know enough to understand that the thing is not altogether impossible. This view of the crystals as *en rapport* was the supposition that occurred to Mr. Wace, and to me at least it seems extremely plausible … .

And where was this other world? On this also, the alert intelligence of Mr. Wace speedily threw light. After sunset, the sky darkened rapidly—there was a very brief twilight interval indeed—and the stars shone out. They were recognisably the same as those we see, arranged in the same constellations. Mr. Cave recognised the Bear, the Pleiades, Aldebaran, and Sirius: so that the other world must be somewhere in the solar system, and at the utmost, only a few hundreds of millions of miles from our own. Following up this clue, Mr. Wace learned that the midnight sky was a darker blue even than our midwinter sky, and that the sun seemed a little smaller. And there were two small moons! "Like our moon but smaller, and quite differently marked" one of which moved so rapidly that its motion was clearly visible as one regarded it. These moons were never high in the sky, but vanished as they rose: that is, every time they revolved they were eclipsed because they were so near their primary planet. And all this answers quite completely although, Mr. Cave did not know it, to what must be the condition of things on Mars.

Indeed, it seems an exceedingly plausible conclusion that peering into this crystal Mr. Cave did actually see the planet Mars and its inhabitants. And if that be the case, then the evening star that shone so brilliantly in the sky of that distant vision, was neither more nor less than our own familiar earth.

For a time the Martians—if they were Martians—do not seem to have known of Mr. Cave's inspection. Once or twice one would come to peer, and go away very shortly to some other mast, as though the vision was unsatisfactory. During this time Mr. Cave was able to watch the proceedings of these winged people without being disturbed by their attentions, and although his report is necessarily vague and fragmentary, it is nevertheless very suggestive. Imagine the impression of humanity a Martian observer would get who, after a difficult process of preparation and with considerable fatigue to the eyes, was able to peer at London from the steeple of St. Martin's Church for stretches, at longest, of four minutes at a time. Mr. Cave was unable to ascertain if the winged Martians were the same as the Martians who hopped about the causeways and terraces, and if the latter could put on wings at will. He several times saw certain clumsy bipeds, dimly suggestive of apes, white and partially translucent, feeding among certain of the lichenous trees, and once some of these fled before one of the hopping, round-headed Martians. The latter caught one in its tentacles, and then the picture faded suddenly and left Mr. Cave most tantalisingly in the dark. On another occasion a vast thing, that Mr. Cave thought at first was some gigantic insect, appeared advancing along the causeway beside the canal with extraordinary rapidity. As this drew nearer Mr. Cave perceived that it was a mechanism of shining metals and of extraordinary complexity. And then, when he looked again, it had passed out of sight.

After a time Mr. Wace aspired to attract the attention of the Martians, and the next time that the strange eyes of one of them appeared close to the crystal Mr. Cave cried out and sprang away, and they immediately turned on the light and began to gesticulate in a manner suggestive of signalling. But when at last Mr. Cave examined the crystal again the Martian had departed.

Thus far these observations had progressed in early November, and then Mr. Cave, feeling that the suspicions of his family about the crystal were allayed, began to take it to and fro with him in order that, as occasion arose in the daytime or night, he might comfort himself with what was fast becoming the most real thing in his existence.

In December Mr. Wace's work in connection with a forthcoming examination became heavy, the sittings were reluctantly suspended for a week, and for ten or eleven days—he is not quite sure which—he saw nothing of Cave. He then grew anxious to resume these investigations, and the stress of his seasonal labours being abated, he went down to Seven Dials. At the corner he noticed a shutter before a bird fancier's window, and then another at a cobbler's. Mr. Cave's shop was closed.

He rapped and the door was opened by the step-son in black. He at once called Mrs. Cave, who was, Mr. Wace could not but observe, in cheap but ample widow's weeds of the most imposing pattern. Without any very great surprise Mr. Wace learnt that Cave was dead and already buried. She was in tears, and her voice was a little thick. She had just returned from Highgate. Her mind seemed occupied with her own prospects and the honourable details of the obsequies, but Mr. Wace was at last able to learn the particulars of Cave's death. He had been found dead in his shop in the early morning, the day after his last visit to Mr. Wace, and the crystal had been clasped in his stone-cold hands. His face was smiling, said Mrs. Cave, and the velvet cloth from the minerals lay on the floor at his feet. He must have been dead five or six hours when he was found.

This came as a great shock to Wace, and he began to reproach himself bitterly for having neglected the plain symptoms of the old man's ill-health. But his chief thought was of the crystal. He approached that topic in a gingerly manner, because he knew Mrs. Cave's peculiarities. He was dumbfounded to learn that it was sold.

Mrs. Cave's first impulse, directly Cave's body had been taken upstairs, had been to write to the mad clergyman who had offered five pounds for the crystal, informing him of its recovery; but after a violent hunt in which her daughter joined her, they were convinced of the loss of his address. As they were without the means required to mourn and bury Cave in the elaborate style the dignity of an old Seven Dials inhabitant demands, they had appealed to a friendly fellow-tradesman in Great Portland Street. He had very kindly taken over a portion of the stock at a valuation. The valuation was his own and the crystal egg was included in one of the lots. Mr. Wace, after a few suitable consolatory observations, a little off-handedly proffered perhaps, hurried at once to Great Portland Street. But there he learned that the crystal egg had already been sold to a tall, dark man in grey. And there the material facts in this curious, and to me at least very suggestive, story come abruptly to an end. The Great Portland Street dealer did not know who the tall dark man in grey was, nor had he observed him with sufficient attention to describe him minutely. He did not even know which way this person had gone after leaving the shop. For a time Mr. Wace remained in the shop, trying the dealer's patience with hopeless questions, venting his own exasperation. And at last, realising abruptly that the whole thing had passed out of his hands, had vanished like a vision of the night, he returned to his own rooms, a little astonished to find the notes he had made still tangible and visible upon his untidy table.

His annoyance and disappointment were naturally very great. He made a second call (equally ineffectual) upon the Great Portland Street dealer, and he resorted to advertisements in such periodicals as were likely to come into the hands of a bric-a-brac collector. He also wrote letters to '*The Daily Chronicle*' and '*Nature*', but both those periodicals, suspecting a hoax, asked him to reconsider his action before they printed, and he was advised that such a strange story, unfortunately so bare of supporting evidence, might imperil his reputation as an investigator. Moreover, the calls of his proper work were urgent. So that after a month or so, save for an occasional reminder to certain dealers, he had reluctantly to abandon the quest for the crystal egg, and from that day to this it remains undiscovered. Occasionally however, he tells me, and I can quite believe him, he has bursts of zeal, in which he abandons his more urgent occupation and resumes the search.

Whether or not it will remain lost for ever, with the material and origin of it, are things equally speculative at the present time. If the present purchaser is a collector, one would have expected the enquiries of Mr. Wace to have readied him through the dealers. He has been able to discover Mr. Cave's clergyman and "Oriental—" no other than the Rev. James Parker and the young Prince of Bosso-Kuni in Java. I am obliged to them for certain particulars. The object of the Prince was simply curiosity—and extravagance. He was so eager to buy, because Cave was so oddly reluctant to sell. It is just as possible that the buyer in the second instance was simply a casual purchaser and not a collector at all, and the crystal egg, for all I know, may at the present moment be within a mile of me, decorating a drawing-room or serving as a paper-weight—its remarkable functions all unknown. Indeed, it is partly with the idea of such a possibility that I have thrown this narrative into a form that will give it a chance of being read by the ordinary consumer of fiction.

My own ideas in the matter are practically identical with those of Mr. Wace. I believe the crystal on the mast in Mars and the crystal egg of Mr. Cave's to be in some physical, but at present quite inexplicable, way *en rapport*, and we both believe further that the terrestrial crystal must have been—possibly at some remote date—sent hither from that planet, in order to give the Martians a near view of our affairs. Possibly the fellows to the crystals in the other masts are also on our globe. No theory of hallucination suffices for the facts.

THE NEW ACCELERATOR

by H. G. Wells

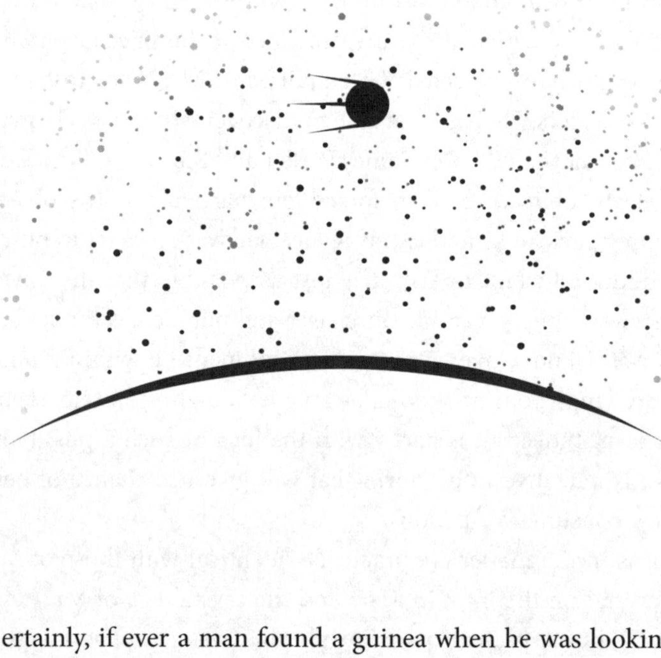

Certainly, if ever a man found a guinea when he was looking for a pin it is my good friend Professor Gibberne. I have heard before of investigators shooting the mark, but never quite to the extent that he has done. He has really, this time at any rate, without any touch of exaggeration in the phrase, found something to revolutionize human life. And that when he was simply seeking an all-round nervous stimulant to bring languid people up to the stresses of these pushful days. I have tasted the stuff now several times, and I cannot do better than describe the effect the thing had on me. That there are astonishing experiences in store for all in search of new sensations will become apparent enough.

Professor Gibberne, as many people know, is my neighbour in Folkestone. Unless my memory plays me a trick, his portrait at various ages has already appeared in various magazines, but I am unable to look it up, because I have lent my volume to someone who has never sent it back. The reader may, perhaps, recall the high forehead and the singularly long black eyebrows that give such a Mephistophelian touch to his face. He occupies one of those pleasant little detached houses in the mixed style that make the western end of the Upper Sandgate Road so interesting. His is the one with the Flemish gables and portico, and it is in the little room with the mullioned bay window that he works when he is down here, and in which of an evening we have so often smoked and talked together. He is a mighty jester, but, besides, he likes to talk to me about his work; he is one of those men who find a help and stimulus in talking, and so I have been able to follow the conception of the New Accelerator right up from a very early stage. Of course, the greater portion of his experimental work is not done in Folkestone, but in Gower Street, in the fine new laboratory next to the hospital that he has been the first to use.

As everyone knows, or at least as all intelligent people know, the special field in which Gibberne has gained so great and deserved a reputation among physiologists includes the action of drugs upon the nervous system. On the subjects of soporifics, sedatives, and anaesthetics he is, I am told, unequalled. He is also a chemist of considerable eminence, and I suppose in the subtle and complex jungle of riddles that shadows the ganglion cell and the axis fibre there are little cleared places of his making, little glades of illumination, which, until he sees fit to publish his results, are still inaccessible to every other living man. And in the last few years he has been particularly assiduous upon the question of nervous stimulants, and already, before the discovery of the New Accelerator, had attained great success with them. Medical science has to thank him for at least three distinct and absolutely safe invigorators of unrivalled value to practising men. In cases of exhaustion the preparation known as Gibberne's B Syrup has, I suppose, saved more lives already than any lifeboat on the coast.

"But none of these little things begin to satisfy me yet," he told me nearly a year ago. "Either they increase the central energy without affecting the nerves or they simply increase the available energy by lowering the nervous conductivity; and all of them are unequal and local in their operation. One wakes up the heart and viscera and leaves the brain stupefied, one gets at the brain, champagne fashion, and does nothing good for the solar plexus, and what I want, and what, if it's an earthly possibility, I mean to have—is a stimulant that stimulates all round, that wakes you up for a time from the crown of your head to the tip of your great toe, and makes you go two—or even three to everybody else's one. Eh? That's the thing I'm after."

"It would tire a man," I said.

"Not a doubt of it. And you'd eat double or treble—and all that. But just think what the thing would mean. Imagine yourself with a little phial like this"—he held up a little bottle of green glass and marked his points with it—"and that in this precious phial is the power to think twice as fast, move twice as quickly, do twice as much work in a given time as you could otherwise do."

"But is such a thing possible?"

"I believe so. If it isn't, I've wasted my time for a year. These various preparations of the hypo-phosphites, for example, seem to show that something of the sort… Even if it was only one and a half times as fast it would do."

"It *would* do," I said.

"If you were a statesman in a corner, for example, time rushing up against you, something urgent to be done, eh?"

"He could dose his private secretary," I said.

"And gain—double time. And think if *you*, for example, wanted to finish a book."

"Usually," I said, "I wish I'd never begun 'em."

"Or a doctor, driven to death, wants to sit down and think out a case. Or a barrister—or a man cramming for an examination."

"Worth a guinea a drop," said I, "and more—to men like that."

"And in a duel, again," said Gibberne, "where it all depends on your quickness in pulling the trigger."

"Or in fencing," I echoed.

"You see," said Gibberne, "if I get it as an all-round thing it will really do you no harm at all—except perhaps to an infinitesimal degree it brings you nearer old age. You will just have lived twice to other peoples once—

"I suppose," I meditated, "in a duel—it would be fair?"

"That's a question for the seconds," said Gibberne.

I harked back further. "And you really think such a thing *is* possible?" I said.

"As possible," said Gibberne, and glanced at something that went throbbing by the window, "as a motorbus. As a matter of fact—"

He paused and smiled at me deeply, and tapped slowly on the edge of his desk with the green phial.

"I think I know the stuff… Already I've got something coming." The nervous smile upon his face betrayed the gravity of his revelation. He rarely talked of his actual experimental work, unless things were very near the end. "And it may be, it may be—I shouldn't be surprised—it may even do the thing at a greater rate than twice."

"It will be rather a big thing," I hazarded.

"It will be, I think, rather a big thing."

But I don't think he quite knew what a big thing it was to be, for all that.

I remember we had several talks about the stuff after that. "The New Accelerator," he called it, and his tone about it grew more confident on each occasion. Sometimes he talked nervously of unexpected physiological results its use might have, and then he would get a little unhappy; at others he was frankly mercenary, and we debated long and anxiously how the preparation might be turned to commercial account. "It's a good thing," said Gibberne, "a tremendous thing. I know I'm giving the world something, and I think it only reasonable we should expect the world to pay. The dignity of science is all very well, but I think somehow I must have the monopoly of the stuff for say, ten years. I don't see why all the fun in life should go to the dealers in ham."

It seemed to me that Gibberne was really preparing no less than the absolute acceleration of life. Suppose a man repeatedly dosed with such a preparation; he would live an active and record life indeed, but he would be an adult at eleven, middle-aged at twenty-five and by thirty well on the road to senile decay. It seemed to me that so far Gibberne was going to do for anyone who took his drug, exactly what Nature has done for the Jews and Orientals, who are men in their teens and aged by fifty, and quicker in thought and act than we are all the time. The marvel of drugs has always been great to my mind; you can madden a man, calm a man, make him incredibly strong and alert or a helpless log, quicken this passion and allay that, all by means of drugs, and here was a new miracle to be added to this strange armoury of phials the doctors use! But Gibberne was far too eager upon his technical points to enter very keenly into my aspect of the question.

It was the 7th or 8th of August when he told me the distillation that would decide his failure or success for a time was going forward as we talked, and it was on the 10th that he told me the thing was done and the New Accelerator a tangible reality in the world. I met him as I was going up the Sandgate Hill toward Folkestone—I think I was going to get my hair cut, and he came hurrying down to meet me—I suppose he was coming to my house to tell me at once of his success. I remember that his eyes were unusually bright and his face flushed, and I noted the swift alacrity of his step.

"It's done," he cried, and gripped my hand, speaking very fast; "it's more than done. Come up to my house and see."

"Really?"

"Really!" he shouted. "Incredibly! Come up and see."

"And it does—twice?"

"It does more, much more. It scares me. Come up and see the stuff. Taste it! Try it! It's the most amazing stuff on earth." He gripped my arm and, walking at such a pace that he forced me into a trot, went shouting with me up the hill. A whole *power-bus* of people turned and stared at us in unison after the manner of people in *power-buses*. It was one of those hot, clear days that Folkestone sees so much of, every colour incredibly bright and every outline hard. There was a breeze, of course, but not so much breeze as sufficed under these conditions to keep me cool and dry. I panted for mercy.

"I'm not walking fast, am I?" cried Gibberne, and slackened his pace to a quick march.

"You've been taking some of this stuff," I puffed.

"No," he said. "At the utmost a drop of water that stood in a beaker from which I had washed out the last traces of the stuff. I took some last night you know. But that is ancient history, now."

"And it goes twice?" I said, nearing his doorway in a grateful perspiration.

"It goes a thousand times, many thousand times," cried Gibberne, with a dramatic gesture, flinging open his Early English carved oak gate.

"Phew," said I, and followed him to the door.

"I don't know how many times it goes," he said, with his latch-key in his hand.

"And you—"

"It throws all sorts of light on nervous physiology, it kicks the theory of vision into a perfectly new shape." … "Heaven knows how many thousand times. We'll try all that after. The thing is to try the stuff now."

"Try the stuff?" I said, as we went along the passage.

"Rather," said Gibberne, turning on me in his study. "There it is in that little green phial there. Unless you happen to be afraid."

I am a careful man by nature, and only theoretically adventurous. I *was* afraid. But on the other hand, there is pride.

"Well," I haggled. "You say you've tried it?"

"I've tried it," he said, "and I don't look hurt by it, do I? I don't even look livery and I *feel*—"

I sat down. "Give me the potion," I said. "If the worst comes to the worst it will save having my hair cut, and that I think is one of the most hateful duties of a civilized man. How do you take the mixture?"

"With water," said Gibberne, whacking down a carafe.

He stood up in front of his desk and regarded me in his easy chair; his manner was suddenly affected by a touch of the Harley Street specialist. "It's rum stuff, you know," he said.

I made a gesture with my hand.

"I must warn you in the first place as soon as you've got it down to shut your eyes, and open them very cautiously in a minute or so's time. One still sees. The sense of vision is a question of length of vibration, consequently of frequency of impacts; but there's a kind of shock to the retina, a nasty giddy confusion just at the time, if the eyes are open. Keep 'em shut."

"Shut," I said. "Good!"

"And the next thing is, keep still. Don't begin to whack about. You may fetch something a nasty rap if you do. Remember you will be going several thousand times faster than you ever did before, heart, lungs, muscles, brain—everything—and you will hit hard without knowing it. You won't know it, you know. You'll feel just as you do now. Only everything in the world will seem to be going ever so many thousand times slower than it ever went before. That's what makes it so deuced queer."

"Lor'," I said. "And you mean—"

"You'll see," said he, and took up a little measure. He glanced at the material on his desk. "Glasses," he said, "water. All here. Mustn't take too much for the first attempt."

The little phial glucked out its precious contents. "Don't forget what I told you," he said, turning the contents of the measure in the manner of an Italian waiter measuring whisky. "Sit with the eyes tightly shut and in absolute stillness for two minutes," he said. "Then you will hear me speak."

He added an inch or so of water to the little dose in each glass.

"By-the-by," he said, "don't put your glass down. Keep it in your hand and rest your hand on your knee. Yes—so, and now—"

He raised his glass.

"The New Accelerator," I said.

"The New Accelerator," he answered, and we touched glasses and drank, and instantly I closed my eyes.

You know that blank non-existence into which one drops when one has taken "gas." For an indefinite interval it was like that. Then I heard Gibberne telling me to wake up, and I stirred and opened my eyes. There he stood as he had been standing, glass still in hand. It was empty, that was all the difference.

"Well?" said I.

"Nothing out of the way?"

"Nothing. A slight feeling of exhilaration, perhaps. Nothing more."

"Sounds?"

"Things are still," I said. "By Jove! Yes! They *are* still. Except the sort of faint pat, patter, like rain falling on different things. What is it?"

"Analyzed sounds," I think he said, but I am not sure. He glanced at the window. "Have you ever seen a curtain before a window fixed in that way before?"

I followed his eyes, and there was the end of the curtain, frozen as it were, corner high, in the act of flapping briskly in the breeze.

"No," said I; "that's odd."

"And here," he said, and opened the hand that held the glass. Naturally I winced, expecting the glass to smash. But so far from smashing it did not even seem to stir; it hung in mid-air—motionless. "Roughly speaking," said Gibberne, "an object in these latitudes falls 16 feet in a second now. Only, you see, it hasn't fallen yet for the hundredth part of a second. That gives you some idea of the pace of my Accelerator." And he waved his hand round and round, over and under the slowly sinking glass. Finally he took it by the bottom, pulled it down, and placed it very carefully on the table. "Eh?" he said to me and laughed.

"That seems all right," I said, and began very gingerly to raise myself from my chair. I felt perfectly well, very light and comfortable, and quite confident in my mind. I was going fast all over. My heart, for example, was beating a thousand times a second, but that caused me no discomfort at all. I looked out of the window. An immovable cyclist, head down and with a frozen puff of dust behind his driving-wheel, scorched to overtake a galloping *char-a-banc* that did not stir. I gaped in amazement at this incredible spectacle. "Gibberne," I cried, "how long will this confounded stuff last?"

"Heaven knows!" he answered. "Last time I took it I went to bed and slept it off. I tell you, I was frightened. It must have lasted some minutes, I think—it seemed like hours. But after a bit it slows down rather suddenly, I believe."

I was proud to observe that I did not feel frightened—I suppose because there were two of us.

"Why shouldn't we go out?" I asked.

"Why not?"

"They'll see us."

"Not they. Goodness no! We shall be going a thousand times faster than the quickest conjuring trick that was ever done. Come along! Which way shall we go? Window, or door?"

And out by the window we went.

Assuredly of all the strange experiences that I have ever had, or imagined, or read of other people having or imagining, that little raid I made with Gibberne on the Folkestone Leas, under the influence of the New Accelerator, was the strangest and maddest of all. We went out by his gate into the road, and there we made a minute examination of the statuesque passing traffic. The tops of the wheels and some of the legs of the horses of this *char-a-banc*, the end of the whip-lash and the lower jaw of the conductor—who was just beginning to yawn—were perceptibly in motion, but all the rest of the lumbering conveyance seemed still. And quite noiseless except for a faint rattling that came from one man's throat! And as parts of this frozen edifice there were a driver, you know, and a conductor, and eleven people! The effect as we walked about the thing began by being madly queer, and ended by being—disagreeable. There they were, people like ourselves and yet not like ourselves, frozen in careless attitudes, caught in mid-gesture. A girl and a man smiled at one another, a leering smile that threatened to last for evermore; a woman in a floppy capelline rested her arm on the rail and stared at Gibberne's house with the unwinking stare of eternity; a man stroked his mustache like a figure of wax, and another stretched a tiresome stiff hand with extended fingers towards his loosened hat. We stared at them, we laughed at them, we made faces at them, and then a sort of disgust of them came upon us, and we turned away and walked around in front of the cyclist towards the Leas.

"Goodness!" cried Gibberne, suddenly; "look there!"

He pointed, and there at the tip of his finger and sliding down the air with wings flapping slowly and at the speed of an exceptionally languid snail— was a bee.

And so we came out upon the Leas. There the thing seemed madder than ever. The band was playing in the upper stand, though all the sound it made for us was a low-pitched, wheezy rattle, a sort of prolonged last sigh that passed at times into a sound like the slow, muffled ticking of some monstrous clock. Frozen people stood erect, strange, silent, self-conscious-looking dummies hung unstably in mid-stride, promenading upon the grass. I passed close to a little poodle dog suspended in the act of leaping, and watched the slow movement of his legs as he sank to earth. "Lord, look *here*!" cried Gibberne, and we halted a moment before a magnificent person in white faint-striped flannels, white shoes, and a Panama hat, who turned back to wink at two gaily dressed ladies he had passed. A wink, studied with such leisurely deliberation as we could afford, is an unattractive thing. It loses any quality of alert gaiety, and one remarks that the winking eye does not completely close, that under its drooping lid appears the lower edge of an eyeball and a little line of white. "Heaven give me memory," said I, "and I will never wink again."

"Or smile," said Gibberne, with his eye on the lady's answering teeth.

"It's infernally hot, somehow," said I. "Let's go slower."

"Oh, come along!" said Gibberne.

We picked our way among the bath-chairs in the path. Many of the people sitting in the chairs seemed almost natural in their passive poses, but the contorted scarlet of the bandsmen was not a restful thing to see. A purple-faced little gentleman was frozen in the midst of a violent struggle to refold his newspaper against the wind; there were many evidences that all these people in their sluggish way were exposed to a considerable breeze, a breeze that had no existence so far as our sensations went. We came out and walked a little way from the crowd, and turned and regarded it. To see all that multitude changed to a picture, smitten rigid, as it were, into the semblance of realistic wax, was impossibly wonderful. It was absurd, of course, but it filled me with an irrational, an exultant sense of superior advantage. Consider the wonder of it! All that I had said and thought, and done since the stuff had begun to work in my veins had happened, so far as those people, so far as the world in general went, in the twinkling of an eye. "The New Accelerator—" I began, but Gibberne interrupted me.

"There's that infernal old woman!" he said.

"What old woman?"

"Lives next door to me," said Gibberne. "Has a lapdog that yaps. Gods! The temptation is strong!"

There is something very boyish and impulsive about Gibberne at times. Before I could expostulate with him he had dashed forward, snatched the unfortunate animal out of visible existence, and was running violently with it towards the cliff of the Leas. It was most extraordinary. The little brute, you know, didn't bark or wriggle or make the slightest sign of vitality. It kept quite stiffly in an attitude of somnolent repose, and Gibberne held it by the neck. It was like running about with a dog of wood. "Gibberne," I cried, "put it down!" Then I said something else. "If you run like that, Gibberne," I cried "you'll set your clothes on fire. Your linen trousers are going brown as it is!"

He clapped his hand on his thigh and stood hesitating on the verge. "Gibberne," I cried, coming up, "put it down. This heat is too much! It's our running so. Two or three miles a second! Friction of the air!"

"What?" he said, glancing at the dog.

"Friction of the air," I shouted. "Friction of the air. Going too fast. Like meteorites and things. Too hot. And, Gibberne! Gibberne! I'm all over pricking and a sort of perspiration. You can see people stirring slightly. I believe the stuff's working off! Put that dog down."

"Eh?" he said.

"It's working off," I repeated. "We're too hot and the stuff's working off! I'm wet through."

He stared at me. Then at the band, the wheezy rattle of whose performance was certainly going faster. Then with a tremendous sweep of his arm he hurled the dog away from him and it went spinning upward, still inanimate, and hung at last over the grouped parasols of a knot of chattering people. Gibberne was gripping my elbow. "By Jove!" he cried. "I believe it is! A sort of hot pricking and—yes. That man's moving his pocket-handkerchief! Perceptibly. We must get out of this sharp."

But we could not get out of it sharply enough. Luckily, perhaps; For we might have run, and if we had run we should, I believe, have burst into flames. Almost certainly we should have burst into flames! You know we had neither of us thought of that… . But before we could even begin to run the action of the drug had ceased. It was the business of a minute fraction of a second. The effect of the New Accelerator passed like the drawing of a curtain, vanished in the movement of a hand. I heard Gibberne's voice in infinite alarm, "Sit down," he said, and flop, down upon the turf at the edge of the Leas I sat—scorching as I sat. There is a patch of burnt grass there still where I sat down. The whole stagnation seemed to wake up as I did so, the disarticulated vibration of the band rushed together into a blast of music, the promenaders put their feet down and walked their ways, the papers and flags began flapping, smiles passed into words, the winker finished his wink and went on his way complacently, and all the seated people moved and spoke.

The whole world had come alive again, was going as fast as we were, or rather we were going no faster than the rest of the world. It was like slowing down as one comes into a railway station. Everything seemed to spin around for a second or two, I had the most transient feeling of nausea, and that was all. And the little dog which had seemed to hang for a moment when the force of Gibberne's arm was expended fell with a swift acceleration clean through a lady's parasol!

That was the saving of us. Unless it was for one corpulent old gentleman in a bath-chair, who certainly did start at the sight of us and afterwards regarded us at intervals with a darkly suspicious eye, and finally, I believe, said something to his nurse about us, I doubt if a solitary person remarked our sudden appearance among them. Plop! We must have appeared abruptly. We ceased to smoulder almost at once, though the turf beneath me was uncomfortably hot. The attention of everyone, including even the Amusements' Association Band, which on this occasion, for the only time in its history, got out of tune, was arrested by the amazing fact, and the still more amazing yapping and uproar caused by the fact that a respectable, overfed lapdog sleeping quietly to the east of the bandstand should suddenly fall through the parasol of a lady on the west—in a slightly singed condition due to the extreme velocity of its movements through the air. In these absurd days, too, when we are all trying to be as psychic, and silly, and superstitious as possible! People got up and trod on other people, chairs were overturned, the Leas policeman ran. How the matter settled itself I do not know—we were much too anxious to disentangle ourselves from the affair and get out of range of the eye of the old gentleman in the bath-chair to make minute inquiries. As soon as we were sufficiently cool and sufficiently recovered from our giddiness and nausea and confusion of mind to do so we stood up and, skirting the crowd, directed our steps back along the road below the Metropole towards Gibberne's house. But amidst the din I heard very distinctly the gentleman who had been sitting beside the lady of the ruptured sunshade using quite unjustifiable threats and language to one of those chair-attendants who have "inspector" written on their caps.

"If you didn't throw the dog," he said, "who *did*?"

The sudden return of movement and familiar noises, and our natural anxiety about ourselves (our clothes were still dreadfully hot, and the fronts of the thighs of Gibberne's white trousers were scorched a drabbish brown), prevented the minute observations I should have liked to make on all these things. Indeed, I really made no observations of any scientific value on that return. The bee, of course, had gone. I looked for that cyclist, but he was already out of sight as we came into the Upper Sandgate Road or hidden from us by traffic; the *char-a-banc*, however, with its people now all alive and stirring, was clattering along at a spanking pace almost abreast of the nearer church.

We noted, however, that the window-sill on which we had stepped in getting out of the house was slightly singed, and that the impressions of our feet on the gravel of the path were unusually deep.

So it was I had my first experience of the New Accelerator. Practically we had been running about and saying and doing all sorts of things in the space of a second or so of time. We had lived half an hour while the hand had played, perhaps two bars. But the effect it had upon us was that the whole world had stopped for our convenient inspection. Considering all things, and particularly considering our rashness in venturing out of the house, the experience might certainly have been much more disagreeable than it was. It showed, no doubt, that Gibberne has still much to learn before his preparation is a manageable convenience, but its practicability is certainly demonstrated beyond all cavil.

Since that adventure he has been steadily bringing its use under control, and I have several times and without the slightest bad result, taken measured doses under his direction; though I must confess I have not yet ventured abroad again while under its influence. I may mention, for example, that this story has been written at one sitting and without interruption, except for the nibbling of some chocolate, by its means. I began at 6:25, and my watch is now very nearly at the minute past the half-hour. The convenience of securing a long, uninterrupted spell of work in the midst of a day full of engagements cannot be exaggerated. Gibberne is now working at the quantitative handling of his preparation, with especial reference to its distinctive effects upon different types of constitution. He then hopes to find a Retarder with which to dilute its present rather excessive potency. The Retarder will, of course, have an effect the reverse of the Accelerator's; used alone it should enable the patient to spread a few seconds over many hours of ordinary time, and so to maintain an apathetic inaction, a glacier-like absence of alacrity, amidst the most animated or irritating surroundings. The two things together must necessarily work an entire revolution in civilized existence. It is the beginning of our escape from that Time Garment of which Carlyle speaks. While this Accelerator will enable us to concentrate ourselves with tremendous impact upon any moment or occasion that demands our utmost sense and vigour, the Retarder will enable us to pass in passive tranquility through infinite hardship and tedium. Perhaps I am a little optimistic about the Retarder, which has indeed still to be discovered, but about the Accelerator there is no possible sort of doubt whatever. Its appearance upon the market in a convenient, controllable, and assimilable form is a matter of the next few months. It will be obtainable of all chemists and druggists, in small green bottles, at a high but, considering its extraordinary qualities, by no means excessive price. Gibberne's Nervous Accelerator it will be called, and he hopes to be able to supply it in three strengths; one in 200, one in 900, and one in 2,000, distinguished by yellow, pink, and white labels respectively.

No doubt its use renders a great number of very extraordinary things possible; for, of course, the most remarkable and, possibly, even criminal proceedings may be effected with impunity by thus dodging, as it were, into the interstices of time. Like all potent preparations it will be liable to abuse. We have, however, discussed this aspect of the question very thoroughly, and we have decided that this is purely a matter of medical jurisprudence and altogether outside our province. We shall manufacture and sell the Accelerator, and, as for the consequences—we shall see.

THE CHRONIC ARGONAUTS

by H. G. Wells

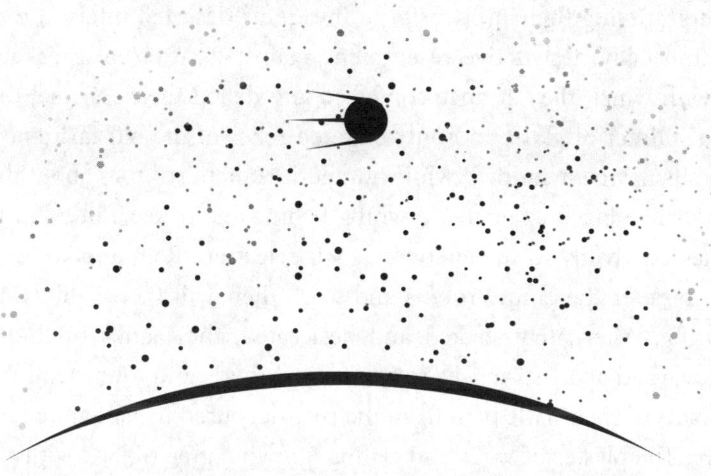

I
BEING THE ACCOUNT OF DR. NEBOGIPFEL'S SOJOURN IN LLYDDWDD

About half-a-mile outside the village of Llyddwdd by the road that goes up over the eastern flank of the mountain called Pen-y-pwll to Rwstog is a large farm-building known as the Manse. It derives this title from the fact that it was at one time the residence of the minister of the Calvinistic Methodists. It is a quaint, low, irregular erection, lying back some hundred yards from the railway, and now fast passing into a ruinous state.

Since its construction in the latter half of the last century this house has undergone many changes of fortune, having been abandoned long since by the farmer of the surrounding acres for less pretentious and more commodious headquarters. Among others Miss Carnot, "the Gallic Sappho" at one time made it her home, and later on an old man named Williams became its occupier. The foul murder of this tenant by his two sons was the cause of its remaining for some considerable period uninhabited; with the inevitable consequence of its undergoing very extensive dilapidation.

The house had got a bad name, and adolescent man and Nature combined to bring swift desolation upon it. The fear of the Williamses which kept the Llyddwdd lads from gratifying their propensity to invade its deserted interior, manifested itself in unusually destructive resentment against its external breakables. The missiles with which they at once confessed and defied their spiritual dread, left scarcely a splinter of glass, and only battered relics of the old-fashioned leaden frames, in its narrow windows, while numberless shattered tiles about the house, and four or five black apertures yawning behind the naked rafters in the roof, also witnessed vividly to the energy of their rejection. Rain and wind thus had free way to enter the empty rooms and work their will there, old Time aiding and abetting. Alternately soaked and desiccated, the planks of flooring and wainscot warped apart strangely, split here and there, and tore themselves away in paroxysms of rheumatic pain from the rust-devoured nails that had once held them firm. The plaster of walls and ceiling, growing green-black with a rain-fed crust of lowly life, parted slowly from the fermenting laths; and large fragments thereof falling down inexplicably in tranquil hours, with loud concussion and clatter, gave strength to the popular superstition that old Williams and his sons were fated to re-enact their fearful tragedy until the final judgment. White roses and daedal creepers, that Miss Carnot had first adorned the walls with, spread now luxuriantly over the lichen-filmed tiles of the roof, and in slender graceful sprays timidly invaded the ghostly cobweb-draped apartments. Fungi, sickly pale, began to displace and uplift the bricks in the cellar floor; while on the rotting wood everywhere they clustered, in all the glory of the purple and mottled crimson, yellow-brown and hepatite. Woodlice and ants, beetles and moths, winged and creeping things innumerable, found each day a more congenial home among the ruins; and after them in ever-increasing multitudes swarmed the blotchy toads. Swallows and martins built every year more thickly in the silent, airy, upper chambers. Bats and owls struggled for the crepuscular corners of the lower rooms. Thus, in the Spring of the year eighteen hundred and eighty-seven, was Nature taking over, gradually but certainly, the tenancy of the old Manse. "The house was falling into decay," as men who do not appreciate the application of human derelicts to other beings' use would say, "surely and swiftly." But it was destined nevertheless to shelter another human tenant before its final dissolution.

There was no intelligence of the advent of a new inhabitant in quiet Llyddwdd. He came without a solitary premonition out of the vast unknown into the sphere of minute village observation and gossip. He fell into the Llyddwdd world, as it were, like a thunderbolt falling in the daytime. Suddenly, out of nothingness, he was. Rumour, indeed, vaguely averred that he was seen to arrive by a certain train from London, and to walk straight without hesitation to the old Manse, giving neither explanatory word nor sign to mortal as to his purpose there: but then the same fertile source of information also hinted that he was first beheld skimming down the slopes of steep Pen-y-pwll with exceeding swiftness, riding, as it appeared to the intelligent observer, upon an instrument not unlike a sieve and that he entered the house by the chimney. Of these conflicting reports, the former was the first to be generally circulated, but the latter, in view of the bizarre presence and eccentric ways of the newest inhabitant, obtained wider credence. By whatever means he arrived, there can be no doubt that he was in, and in possession of the Manse, on the first of May; because on the morning of that day he was inspected by Mrs. Morgan ap Lloyd Jones, and subsequently by the numerous persons her report brought up the mountain slope, engaged in the curious occupation of nailing sheet-tin across the void window sockets of his new domicile—"blinding his house", as Mrs. Morgan ap Lloyd Jones not inaptly termed it.

He was a small-bodied, sallow faced little man, clad in a close-fitting garment of some stiff, dark material, which Mr. Parry Davies the Llyddwdd shoemaker, opined was leather. His aquiline nose, thin lips, high cheek-ridges, and pointed chin, were all small and mutually well proportioned; but the bones and muscles of his face were rendered excessively prominent and distinct by his extreme leanness. The same cause contributed to the sunken appearance of the large eager-looking grey eyes, that gazed forth from under his phenomenally wide and high forehead. It was this latter feature that most powerfully attracted the attention of an observer. It seemed to be great beyond all preconceived ratio to the rest of his countenance. Dimensions, corrugations, wrinkles, venation, were alike abnormally exaggerated. Below it his eyes glowed like lights in some cave at a cliff's foot. It so over-powered and suppressed the rest of his face as to give an unhuman appearance almost, to what would otherwise have been an unquestionably handsome profile. The lank black hair that hung unkempt before his eyes served to increase rather than conceal this effect, by adding to unnatural altitude a suggestion of hydrocephalic projection: and the idea of something ultra human was furthermore accentuated by the temporal arteries that pulsated visibly through his transparent yellow skin. No wonder, in view even of these things, that among the highly and over-poetical Cymric of Llyddwdd the sieve theory of arrival found considerable favour.

It was his bearing and actions, however, much more than his personality, that won over believers to the warlock notion of matters. In almost every circumstance of life the observant villagers soon found his ways were not only not their ways, but altogether inexplicable upon any theory of motives they could conceive. Thus, in a small matter at the beginning, when Arthur Price Williams, eminent and famous in every tavern in Caernarvonshire for his social gifts, endeavoured, in choicest Welsh and even choicer English, to inveigle the stranger into conversation over the sheet-tin performance, he failed utterly. Inquisitional supposition, straightforward enquiry, offer of assistance, suggestion of method, sarcasm, irony, abuse, and at last, gage of battle, though shouted with much effort from the road hedge, went unanswered and apparently unheard. Missile weapons, Arthur Price Williams found, were equally unavailing for the purpose of introduction, and the gathered crowd dispersed with unappeased curiosity and suspicion. Later in the day, the swarth apparition was seen striding down the mountain road towards the village, hatless, and with such swift width of step and set resolution of countenance, that Arthur Price Williams, beholding him from afar from the Pig and Whistle doorway was seized with dire consternation, and hid behind the Dutch oven in the kitchen till he was past. Wild panic also smote the schoolhouse as the children were coming out, and drove them indoors like leaves before a gale. He was merely seeking the provision shop, however, and erupted thencefrom after a prolonged stay, loaded with a various armful of blue parcels, a loaf, herrings, pigs' trotters, salt pork, and a black bottle, with which he returned in the same swift projectile gait to the Manse. His way of shopping was to name, and to name simply, without solitary other word of explanation, civility or request, the article he required.

The shopkeeper's crude meteorological superstitions and inquisitive commonplaces, he seemed not to hear, and he might have been esteemed deaf if he had not evinced the promptest attention to the faintest relevant remark. Consequently it was speedily rumoured that he was determined to avoid all but the most necessary human intercourse. He lived altogether mysteriously, in the decaying manse, without mortal service or companionship, presumably sleeping on planks or litter, and either preparing his own food or eating it raw. This, coupled with the popular conception of the haunting patricides, did much to strengthen the popular supposition of some vast gulf between the newcomer and common humanity. The only thing that was inharmonious with this idea of severance from mankind was a constant flux of crates filled with grotesquely contorted glassware, cases of brazen and steel instruments, huge coils of wire, vast iron and fire-clay implements, of inconceivable purpose, jars and phials labelled in black and scarlet—POISON, huge packages of books, and gargantuan rolls of cartridge paper, which set in towards his Llyddwdd quarters from the outer world. The apparently hieroglyphic inscriptions on these various consignments revealed at the profound scrutiny of Pugh Jones that the style and title of the new inhabitant was Dr. Moses Nebogipfel, Ph.D., F.R.S., N.W.R., PAID: at which discovery much edification was felt, especially among the purely Welsh-speaking community. Further than this, these arrivals, by their evident unfitness for any allowable mortal use, and inferential diabolicalness, filled the neighbourhood with a vague horror and lively curiosity, which were greatly augmented by the extraordinary phenomena, and still more extraordinary accounts thereof, that followed their reception in the Manse.

The first of these was on Wednesday, the fifteenth of May, when the Calvinistic Methodists of Llyddwdd had their annual commemoration festival; on which occasion, in accordance with custom, dwellers in the surrounding parishes of Rwstog, Pen-y-garn, Caergyllwdd, Llanrdd, and even distant Llanrwst flocked into the village. Popular thanks to Providence were materialised in the usual way, by means of plum-bread and butter, mixed tea, terza, consecrated flirtations, kiss-in-the-ring, rough-and-tumble football, and vituperative political speech-making. About half-past eight the fun began to tarnish, and the assembly to break up; and by nine numerous couples and occasional groups were wending their way in the darkling along the hilly Llyddwdd and Rwstog road. It was a calm warm night; one of those nights when lamps, gas and heavy sleep seem stupid ingratitude to the Creator. The zenith sky was an ineffable deep lucent blue, and the evening star hung golden in the liquid darkness of the west. In the north-north-west, a faint phosphorescence marked the sunken day. The moon was just rising, pallid and gibbous over the huge haze-dimmed shoulder of Pen-y-pwll. Against the wan eastern sky, from the vague outline of the mountain slope, the Manse stood out black, clear and solitary. The stillness of the twilight had hushed the myriad murmurs of the day. Only the sounds of footsteps and voices and laughter, that came fitfully rising and falling from the roadway, and an intermittent hammering in the darkened dwelling, broke the silence. Suddenly a strange whizzing, buzzing whirr filled the night air, and a bright flicker glanced across the dim path of the wayfarers. All eyes were turned in astonishment to the old Manse. The house no longer loomed a black featureless block but was filled to overflowing with light. From the gaping holes in the roof, from chinks and fissures amid tiles and brickwork, from every gap which Nature or man had pierced in the crumbling old shell, a blinding blue-white glare was streaming, beside which the rising moon seemed a disc of opaque sulphur. The thin mist of the dewy night had caught the violet glow and hung, unearthly smoke, over the colourless blaze. A strange turmoil and outcrying in the old Manse now began, and grew ever more audible to the clustering spectators, and therewith came clanging loud impacts against the window-guarding tin. Then from the gleaming roof-gaps of the house suddenly vomited forth a wonderous swarm of heteromerous living things—swallows, sparrows, martins, owls, bats, insects in visible multitudes, to hang for many minutes a noisy, gyring, spreading cloud over the black gables and chimneys… and then slowly to thin out and vanish away in the night.

As this tumult died away the throbbing humming that had first arrested attention grew once more in the listener's hearing, until at last it was the only sound in the long stillness. Presently, however, the road gradually awoke again to the beating and shuffling of feet, as the knots of Rwstog people, one by one, turned their blinking eyes from the dazzling whiteness and, pondering deeply, continued their homeward way.

The cultivated reader will have already discerned that this phenomenon, which sowed a whole crop of uncanny thoughts in the minds of these worthy folk, was simply the installation of the electric light in the Manse. Truly, this last vicissitude of the old house was its strangest one. Its revival to mortal life was like the raising of Lazarus. From that hour forth, by night and day, behind the tin-blinded windows, the tamed lightning illuminated every corner of its quickly changing interior. The almost frenzied energy of the lank-haired, leather-clad little doctor swept away into obscure holes and corners and common destruction, creeper sprays, toadstools, rose leaves, birds' nests, birds' eggs, cobwebs, and all the coatings and lovingly fanciful trimmings with which that maternal old dotard, Dame Nature, had tricked out the decaying house for its lying in state. The magneto-electric apparatus whirred incessantly amid the vestiges of the wainscoted dining-room, where once the eighteenth-century tenant had piously read morning prayer and eaten his Sunday dinner; and in the place of his sacred symbolical sideboard was a nasty heap of coke. The oven of the bakehouse supplied substratum and material for a forge, whose snorting, panting bellows, and intermittent, ruddy spark-laden blast made the benighted, but Bible-lit Welsh women murmur in liquid Cymric, as they hurried by: "Whose breath kindleth coals, and out of his mouth is a flame of fire." For the idea these good people formed of it was that a tame, but occasionally restive, leviathan had been added to the terrors of the haunted house. The constantly increasing accumulation of pieces of machinery, big brass castings, block tin, casks, crates, and packages of innumerable articles, by their demands for space, necessitated the sacrifice of most of the slighter partitions of the house, and the beams and flooring of the upper chambers were also mercilessly sawn away by the tireless scientist in such a way as to convert them into mere shelves and corner brackets of the atrial space between cellars and rafters. Some of the sounder planking was utilised in the making of a rude broad table, upon which files and heaps of geometrical diagrams speedily accumulated. The production of these latter seemed to be the object upon which the mind of Dr. Nebogipfel was so inflexibly set. All other circumstances of his life were made entirely subsidiary to this one occupation. Strangely complicated traceries of lines they were—plans, elevations, sections by surfaces and solids, that, with the help of logarithmic mechanical apparatus and involved curvigraphical machines, spread swiftly under his expert hands over yard after yard of paper. Some of these symbolised shapes he despatched to London, and they presently returned, realised, in forms of brass and ivory, and nickel and mahogany. Some of them he himself translated into solid models of metal and wood; occasionally casting the metallic ones in moulds of sand, but often labouriously hewing them out of the block for greater precision of dimension. In this second process, among other appliances, he employed a steel circular saw set with diamond powder and made to rotate with extraordinary swiftness, by means of steam and multiplying gear. It was this latter thing, more than all else, that filled Llyddwdd with a sickly loathing of the Doctor as a man of blood and darkness. Often in the silence of midnight—for the newest inhabitant heeded the sun but little in his incessant research—the awakened dwellers around Pen-y-pwll would hear, what was at first a complaining murmur, like the groaning of a wounded man, "gurr-urrurr-URR", rising by slow gradations in pitch and intensity to the likeness of a voice in despairing passionate protest, and at last ending abruptly in a sharp piercing shriek that rang in the ears for hours afterwards and begot numberless gruesome dreams.

The mystery of all these unearthly noises and inexplicable phenomena, the Doctor's inhumanly brusque bearing and evident uneasiness when away from his absorbing occupation, his entire and jealous seclusion, and his terrifying behaviour to certain officious intruders, roused popular resentment and curiously to the highest, and a plot was already on foot to make some sort of popular inquisition (probably accompanied by an experimental ducking) into his proceedings, when the sudden death of the hunchback Hughes in a fit, brought matters to an unexpected crisis. It happened in broad daylight, in the roadway just opposite the Manse. Half a dozen people witnessed it. The unfortunate creature was seen to fall suddenly and roll about on the pathway, struggling violently, as it appeared to the spectators, with some invisible assailant. When assistance reached him he was purple in the face and his blue lips were covered with a glairy foam. He died almost as soon as they laid hands on him.

Owen Thomas, the general practitioner, vainly assured the excited crowd which speedily gathered outside the Pig and Whistle, whither the body had been carried, that death was unquestionably natural. A horrible zymotic suspicion had gone forth that the deceased was the victim of Dr. Nebogipfel's imputed aerial powers. The contagion was with the news that passed like a flash through the village and set all Llyddwdd seething with a fierce desire for action against the worker of this iniquity. Downright superstition, which had previously walked somewhat modestly about the village, in the fear of ridicule and the Doctor, now appeared boldly before the sight of all men, clad in the terrible majesty of truth. People who had hitherto kept entire silence as to their fears of the imp-like philosopher suddenly discovered a fearsome pleasure in whispering dread possibilities to kindred souls, and from whispers of possibilities their sympathy-fostered utterances soon developed into unhesitating asserverations in loud and even high-pitched tones. The fancy of a captive leviathan, already alluded to, which had up to now been the horrid but secret joy of a certain conclave of ignorant old women, was published to all the world as indisputable fact; it being stated, on her own authority, that the animal had, on one occasion, chased Mrs. Morgan ap Lloyd Jones almost into Rwstog. The story that Nebogipfel had been heard within the Manse chanting, in conjunction with the Williamses, horrible blasphemy, and that a "black flapping thing, of the size of a young calf", had thereupon entered the gap in the roof, was universally believed in. A grisly anecdote, that owed its origination to a stumble in the churchyard, was circulated, to the effect that the Doctor had been caught ghoulishly tearing with his long white fingers at a new-made grave. The numerously attested declaration that Nebogipfel and the murdered Williams had been seen hanging the sons on a ghostly gibbet, at the back of the house, was due to the electric illumination of a fitfully wind-shaken tree. A hundred like stories hurtled thickly about the village and darkened the moral atmosphere. The Reverend Elijah Ulysses Cook, hearing of the tumult, sallied forth to allay it, and narrowly escaped drawing on himself the gathering lightning.

By eight o'clock (it was Monday the twenty-second of July) a grand demonstration had organised itself against the "necromancer". A number of bolder hearts among the men formed the nucleus of the gathering, and at nightfall Arthur Price Williams, John Peters, and others brought torches and raised their spark-raining flames aloft with curt ominous suggestions. The less adventurous village manhood came straggling late to the rendezvous, and with them the married women came in groups of four or five, greatly increasing the excitement of the assembly with their shrill hysterical talk and active imaginations. After these the children and young girls, overcome by undefinable dread, crept quietly out of the too silent and shadowy houses into the yellow glare of the pine knots, and the tumultuary noise of the thickening people. By nine, nearly half the Llyddwdd population was massed before the Pig and Whistle. There was a confused murmur of many tongues, but above all the stir and chatter of the growing crowd could be heard the coarse, cracked voice of the blood-thirsty old fanatic, Pritchard, drawing a congenial lesson from the fate of the four hundred and fifty idolators of Carmel.

Just as the church clock was beating out the hour, an occultly originated movement up hill began, and soon the whole assembly, men, women, and children, was moving in a fear-compacted mass, towards the ill-fated doctor's abode. As they left the brightly-lit public house behind them, a quavering female voice began singing one of those grim-sounding canticles that so satisfy the Calvinistic ear. In a wonderfully short time, the tune had been caught up, first by two or three, and then by the whole procession, and the manifold shuffling of heavy shoon grew swiftly into rhythm with the beats of the hymn. When, however, their goal rose, like a blazing star, over the undulation of the road, the volume of the chanting suddenly died away, leaving only the voices of the ringleaders, shouting indeed now somewhat out of tune, but, if anything, more vigorously than before. Their persistence and example nevertheless failed to prevent a perceptible breaking and slackening of the pace, as the Manse was neared, and when the gate was reached, the whole crowd came to a dead halt. Vague fear for the future had begotten the courage that had brought the villagers thus far: fear for the present now smothered its kindred birth. The intense blaze from the gaps in the death-like silent pile lit up rows of livid, hesitating faces: and a smothered, frightened sobbing broke out among the children. "Well," said Arthur Price Williams, addressing Jack Peters, with an expert assumption of the modest discipleship, "what do we do now, Jack?" But Peters was regarding the Manse with manifest dubiety, and ignored the question. The Llyddwdd witch-find seemed to be suddenly aborting.

At this juncture old Pritchard suddenly pushed his way forward, gesticulating weirdly with his bony hands and long arms. "What!" he shouted, in broken notes, "fear ye to smite when the Lord hateth? Burn the warlock!" And seizing a flambeau from Peters, he flung open the rickety gate and strode on down the drive, his torch leaving a coiling trail of scintillant sparks on the night wind. "Burn the warlock," screamed a shrill voice from the wavering crowd, and in a moment the gregarious human instinct had prevailed. With an outburst of incoherent, threatening voice, the mob poured after the fanatic.

Woe betide the Philosopher now! They expected barricaded doors; but with a groan of a conscious insufficiency, the hinge-rusted portals swung at the push of Pritchard. Blinded by the light, he hesitated for a second on the threshold, while his followers came crowding up behind him.

Those who were there say that they saw Dr. Nebogipfel, standing in the toneless electric glare, on a peculiar erection of brass and ebony and ivory; and that he seemed to be smiling at them, half pityingly and half scornfully, as it is said martyrs are wont to smile. Some assert, moreover, that by his side was sitting a tall man, clad in ravenswing, and some even aver that this second man—whom others deny—bore on his face the likeness of the Reverend Elijah Ulysses Cook, while others declare that he resembled the description of the murdered Williams. Be that as it may, it must now go unproven for ever, for suddenly a wonderous thing smote the crowd as it swarmed in through the entrance. Pritchard pitched headlong on the floor senseless. While shouts and shrieks of anger, changed in mid utterance to yells of agonising fear, or to the mute gasp of heart-stopping horror: and then a frantic rush was made for the doorway.

For the calm, smiling doctor, and his quiet, black-clad companion, and the polished platform which upbore them, had vanished before their eyes!

II
HOW AN ESOTERIC STORY BECAME POSSIBLE

A silvery-foliaged willow by the side of a mere. Out of the cress-spangled waters below, rise clumps of sedge-blades, and among them glows the purple fleur-de-lys, and sapphire vapour of forget-me-nots. Beyond is a sluggish stream of water reflecting the intense blue of the moist Fenland sky; and beyond that a low osier-fringed eyot. This limits all the visible universe, save some scattered pollards and spear-like poplars showing against the violet distance. At the foot of the willow reclines the Author watching a copper butterfly fluttering from iris to iris.

Who can fix the colours of the sunset? Who can take a cast of flame? Let him essay to register the mutations of mortal thought as it wanders from a copper butterfly to the disembodied soul, and thence passes to spiritual motions and the vanishing of Dr. Moses Nebogipfel and the Rev. Elijah Ulysses Cook from the world of sense.

As the author lay basking there and speculating, as another once did under the Budh tree, on mystic transmutations, a presence became apparent. There was a somewhat on the eyot between him and the purple horizon—an opaque reflecting entity, making itself dimly perceptible by reflection in the water to his averted eyes. He raised them in curious surprise.

What was it?

He stared in stupefied astonishment at the apparition, doubted, blinked, rubbed his eyes, stared again, and believed. It was solid, it cast a shadow, and it upbore two men. There was white metal in it that blazed in the noontide sun like incandescent magnesium, ebony bars that drank in the light, and white parts that gleamed like polished ivory. Yet withal it seemed unreal. The thing was not square as a machine ought to be, but all awry: it was twisted and seemed falling over, hanging in two directions, as those queer crystals called triclinic hang; it seemed like a machine that had been crushed or warped; it was suggestive and not confirmatory, like the machine of a disordered dream. The men, too, were dream-like. One was short, intensely sallow, with a strangely-shaped head, and clad in a garment of dark olive green, the other was, grotesquely out of place, evidently a clergyman of the Established Church, a fair-haired, pale-faced respectable-looking man.

Once more doubt came rushing in on the author. He sprawled back and stared at the sky, rubbed his eyes, stared at the willow wands that hung between him and the blue, closely examined his hands to see if his eyes had any new things to relate about them, and then sat up again and stared at the eyot. A gentle breeze stirred the osiers; a white bird was flapping its way through the lower sky. The machine of the vision had vanished! It was an illusion—a projection of the subjective—an assertion of the immateriality of mind. "Yes," interpolated the sceptic faculty, "but how comes it that the clergyman is still there?"

The clergyman had not vanished. In intense perplexity the author examined this black-coated phenomenon as he stood regarding the world with hand-shaded eyes. The author knew the periphery of that eyot by heart, and the question that troubled him was, "Whence?" The clergyman looked as Frenchmen look when they land at Newhaven—intensely travel-worn; his clothes showed rubbed and seamy in the bright day. When he came to the edge of the island and shouted a question to the author, his voice was broken and trembled. "Yes," answered the author, "it is an island. How did you get there?"

But the clergyman, instead of replying to this asked a very strange question.

He said "Are you in the nineteenth century?" The author made him repeat that question before he replied. "Thank heaven," cried the clergyman rapturously. Then he asked very eagerly for the exact date.

"August the ninth, eighteen hundred and eighty-seven," he repeated after the author. "Heaven be praised!" and sinking down on the eyot so that the sedges hid him, he audibly burst into tears.

Now the author was mightily surprised at all this, and going a certain distance along the mere, he obtained a punt, and getting into it he hastily poled to the eyot where he had last seen the clergyman. He found him lying insensible among the reeds, and carried him in his punt to the house where he lived, and the clergyman lay there insensible for ten days.

Meanwhile, it became known that he was the Rev. Elijah Cook, who had disappeared from Llyddwdd with Dr. Moses Nebogipfel three weeks before.

On August 19th, the nurse called the author out of his study to speak to the invalid. He found him perfectly sensible, but his eyes were strangely bright, and his face was deadly pale. "Have you found out who I am?" he asked.

"You are the Rev. Elijah Ulysses Cook, Master of Arts, of Pembroke College, Oxford, and Rector of Llyddwdd, near Rwstog, in Caernarvon."

He bowed his head. "Have you been told anything of how I came here?"

"I found you among the reeds," I said. He was silent and thoughtful for a while. "I have a deposition to make. Will you take it? It concerns the murder of an old man named Williams, which occurred in 1862, this disappearance of Dr. Moses Nebogipfel, the abduction of a ward in the year 4003—"

The author stared.

"The year of our Lord 4003," he corrected. "She would come. Also several assaults on public officials in the years 17,901 and 2."

The author coughed.

"The years 17,901 and 2, and valuable medical, social, and physiographical data for all time."

After a consultation with the doctor, it was decided to have the deposition taken down, and this is which constitutes the remainder of the story of the Chronic Argonauts.

On August 28th, 1887, the Rev Elijah Cook died. His body was conveyed to Llyddwdd, and buried in the churchyard there.

III
THE ESOTERIC STORY BASED ON THE CLERGYMAN'S DEPOSITIONS

THE ANACHRONIC MAN

Incidentally it has been remarked in the first part, how the Reverend Elijah Ulysses Cook attempted and failed to quiet the superstitious excitement of the villagers on the afternoon of the memorable twenty-second of July. His next proceeding was to try and warn the unsocial philosopher of the dangers which impended. With this intent he made his way from the rumour-pelted village, through the silent, slumbrous heat of the July afternoon, up the slopes of Pen-y-pwll, to the old Manse. His loud knocking at the heavy door called forth dull resonance from the interior, and produced a shower of lumps of plaster and fragments of decaying touchwood from the rickety porch, but beyond this the dreamy stillness of the summer mid-day remained unbroken. Everything was so quiet as he stood there expectant, that the occasional speech of the haymakers a mile away in the fields, over towards Rwstog, could be distinctly heard. The reverend gentleman waited, then knocked again, and waited again, and listened, until the echoes and the patter of rubbish had melted away into the deep silence, and the creeping in the blood-vessels of his ears had become oppressively audible, swelling and sinking with sounds like the confused murmuring of a distant crowd, and causing a suggestion of anxious discomfort to spread slowly over his mind.

Again he knocked, this time loud, quick blows with his stick, and almost immediately afterwards, leaning his hand against the door, he kicked the panels vigorously. There was a shouting of echoes, a protesting jarring of hinges, and then the oaken door yawned and displayed, in the blue blaze of the electric light, vestiges of partitions, piles of planking and straw, masses of metal, heaps of papers and overthrown apparatus, to the rector's astonished eyes. "Doctor Nebogipfel, excuse my intruding," he called out, but the only response was a reverberation among the black beams and shadows that hung dimly above. For almost a minute he stood there, leaning forward over the threshold, staring at the glittering mechanisms, diagrams, books, scattered indiscriminately with broken food, packing cases, heaps of coke, hay, and microcosmic lumber, about the undivided house cavity; and then, removing his hat and treading stealthily, as if the silence were a sacred thing, he stepped into the apparently deserted shelter of the Doctor.

His eyes sought everywhere, as he cautiously made his way through the confusion, with a strange anticipation of finding Nebogipfel hidden somewhere in the sharp black shadows among the litter, so strong in him was an indescribable sense of perceiving presence. This feeling was so vivid that, when, after an abortive exploration, he seated himself upon Nebogipfel's diagram-covered bench, it made him explain in a forced hoarse voice to the stillness—"He is not here. I have something to say to him. I must wait for him." It was so vivid, too, that the trickling of some grit down the wall in the vacant corner behind him made him start round in a sudden perspiration. There was nothing visible there, but turning his head back, he was stricken rigid with horror by the swift, noiseless apparition of Nebogipfel, ghastly pale, and with red stained hands, crouching upon a strange-looking metallic platform, and with his deep grey eyes looking intently into the visitor's face.

Cook's first impulse was to yell out his fear, but his throat was paralysed, and he could only stare fascinated at the bizarre countenance that had thus clashed suddenly into visibility. The lips were quivering and the breath came in short convulsive sobs. The un-human forehead was wet with perspiration, while the veins were swollen, knotted and purple. The Doctor's red hands, too, he noticed, were trembling, as the hands of slight people tremble after intense muscular exertion, and his lips closed and opened as if he, too, had a difficulty in speaking as he gasped, "Who—what do you do here?"

Cook answered not a word, but stared with hair erect, open mouth, and dilated eyes, at the dark red unmistakeable smear that streaked the pure ivory and gleaming nickel and shining ebony of the platform.

"What are you doing here?" repeated the doctor, raising himself. "What do you want?"

Cook gave a convulsive effort. "In Heaven's name, what are you?" he gasped; and then black curtains came closing in from every side, sweeping the squatting dwarfish phantasm that reeled before him into rayless, voiceless night.

The Reverend Elijah Ulysses Cook recovered his perceptions to find himself lying on the floor of the old Manse, and Doctor Nebogipfel, no longer blood-stained and with all trace of his agitation gone, kneeling by his side and bending over him with a glass of brandy in his hand. "Do not be alarmed, sir," said the philosopher with a faint smile, as the clergyman opened his eyes. "I have not treated you to a disembodied spirit, or anything nearly so extraordinary… may I offer you this?"

The clergyman submitted quietly to the brandy, and then stared perplexed into Nebogipfel's face, vainly searching his memory for what occurrences had preceded his insensibility. Raising himself at last, into a sitting posture, he saw the oblique mass of metals that had appeared with the doctor, and immediately all that happened flashed back upon his mind. He looked from this structure to the recluse, and from the recluse to the structure.

"There is absolutely no deception, sir," said Nebogipfel with the slightest trace of mockery in his voice. "I lay no claim to work in matters spiritual. It is a bona fide mechanical contrivance, a thing emphatically of this sordid world. Excuse me—just one minute." He rose from his knees, stepped upon the mahogany platform, took a curiously curved lever in his hand and pulled it over. Cook rubbed his eyes. There certainly was no deception. The doctor and the machine had vanished.

The reverend gentleman felt no horror this time, only a slight nervous shock, to see the doctor presently re-appear "in the twinkling of an eye" and get down from the machine. From that he walked in a straight line with his hands behind his back and his face downcast, until his progress was stopped by the intervention of a circular saw; then, turning round sharply on his heel, he said:

"I was thinking while I was… away… Would you like to come? I should greatly value a companion."

The clergyman was still sitting, hatless, on the floor. "I am afraid," he said slowly, "you will think me stupid—"

"Not at all," interrupted the doctor. "The stupidity is mine. You desire to have all this explained… wish to know where I am going first. I have spoken so little with men of this age for the last ten years or more that I have ceased to make due allowances and concessions for other minds. I will do my best, but that I fear will be very unsatisfactory. It is a long story… do you find that floor comfortable to sit on? If not, there is a nice packing case over there, or some straw behind you, or this bench—the diagrams are done with now, but I am afraid of the drawing pins. You may sit on the Chronic Argo!"

"No, thank you," slowly replied the clergyman, eyeing that deformed structure thus indicated, suspiciously; "I am quite comfortable here."

"Then I will begin. Do you read fables? Modern ones?"

"I am afraid I must confess to a good deal of fiction," said the clergyman deprecatingly. "In Wales the ordained ministers of the sacraments of the Church have perhaps too large a share of leisure—"

"Have you read the Ugly Duckling?"

"Hans Christian Andersen's—yes—in my childhood."

"A wonderful story—a story that has ever been full of tears and heart swelling hopes for me, since first it came to me in my lonely boyhood and saved me from unspeakable things. That story, if you understand it well, will tell you almost all that you should know of me to comprehend how that machine came to be thought of in a mortal brain… Even when I read that simple narrative for the first time, a thousand bitter experiences had begun the teaching of my isolation among the people of my birth—I knew the story was for me. The ugly duckling that proved to be a swan, that lived through all contempt and bitterness, to float at last sublime. From that hour forth, I dreamt of meeting with my kind, dreamt of encountering that sympathy I knew was my profoundest need. Twenty years I lived in that hope, lived and worked, lived and wandered, loved even, and at last, despaired. Only once among all those millions of wondering, astonished, indifferent, contemptuous, and insidious faces that I met with in that passionate wandering, looked one upon me as I desired… looked—"

He paused. The Reverend Cook glanced up into his face, expecting some indication of the deep feeling that had sounded in his last words. It was downcast, clouded, and thoughtful, but the mouth was rigidly firm.

"In short, Mr. Cook, I discovered that I was one of those superior Cagots called a genius—a man born out of my time—a man thinking the thoughts of a wiser age, doing things and believing things that men now cannot understand, and that in the years ordained to me there was nothing but silence and suffering for my soul—unbroken solitude, man's bitterest pain. I knew I was an Anachronic Man; my age was still to come. One filmy hope alone held me to life, a hope to which I clung until it had become a certain thing. Thirty years of unremitting toil and deepest thought among the hidden things of matter and form and life, and then that, the Chronic Argo, the ship that sails through time, and now I go to join my generation, to journey through the ages till my time has come."

IV
THE CHRONIC ARGO

Dr. Nebogipfel paused, looked in sudden doubt at the clergyman's perplexed face. "You think that sounds mad," he said, "to travel through time?"

"It certainly jars with accepted opinions," said the clergyman, allowing the faintest suggestion of controversy to appear in his intonation, and speaking apparently to the Chronic Argo. Even a clergyman of the Church of England you see can have a suspicion of illusions at times.

"It certainly does jar with accepted opinions," agreed the philosopher cordially. "It does more than that—it defies accepted opinions to mortal combat. Opinions of all sorts, Mr. Cook—Scientific Theories, Laws, Articles of Belief, or, to come to elements, Logical Premises, Ideas, or whatever you like to call them—all are, from the infinite nature of things, so many diagrammatic caricatures of the ineffable—caricatures altogether to be avoided save where they are necessary in the shaping of results—as chalk outlines are necessary to the painter and plans and sections to the engineer. Men, from the exigencies of their being, find this hard to believe."

The Rev. Elijah Ulysses Cook nodded his head with the quiet smile of one whose opponent has unwittingly given a point.

"It is as easy to come to regard ideas as complete reproductions of entities as it is to roll off a log. Hence it is that almost all civilised men believe in the reality of the Greek geometrical conceptions."

"Oh! pardon me, sir," interrupted Cook. "Most men know that a geometrical point has no existence in matter, and the same with a geometrical line. I think you underrate… "

"Yes, yes, those things are recognised," said Nebogipfel calmly; "but now… a cube. Does that exist in the material universe?"

"Certainly."

"An instantaneous cube?"

"I don't know what you intend by that expression."

"Without any other sort of extension; a body having length, breadth, and thickness, exists?"

"What other sort of extension can there be?" asked Cook, with raised eyebrows.

"Has it never occurred to you that no form can exist in the material universe that has no extension in time?… Has it never glimmered upon your consciousness that nothing stood between men and a geometry of four dimensions—length, breadth, thickness, and duration—but the inertia of opinion, the impulse from the Levantine philosophers of the bronze age?"

"Putting it that way," said the clergyman, "it does look as though there was a flaw somewhere in the notion of tridimensional being; but"… He became silent, leaving that sufficiently eloquent "but" to convey all the prejudice and distrust that filled his mind.

"When we take up this new light of a fourth dimension and reexamine our physical science in its illumination," continued Nebogipfel, after a pause, "we find ourselves no longer limited by hopeless restriction to a certain beat of time—to our own generation. Locomotion along lines of duration—chronic navigation comes within the range, first, of geometrical theory, and then of practical mechanics. There was a time when men could only move horizontally and in their appointed country. The clouds floated above them, unattainable things, mysterious chariots of those fearful gods who dwelt among the mountain summits. Speaking practically, men in those days were restricted to motion in two dimensions; and even there circumambient ocean and hypoborean fear bound him in. But those times were to pass away. First, the keel of Jason cut its way between the Symplegades, and then in the fulness of time, Columbus dropped anchor in a bay of Atlantis. Then man burst his bidimensional limits, and invaded the third dimension, soaring with Montgolfier into the clouds, and sinking with a diving bell into the purple treasure-caves of the waters. And now another step, and the hidden past and unknown future are before us. We stand upon a mountain summit with the plains of the ages spread below."

Nebogipfel paused and looked down at his hearer.

The Reverend Elijah Cook was sitting with an expression of strong distrust on his face. Preaching much had brought home certain truths to him very vividly, and he always suspected rhetoric. "Are those things figures of speech," he asked; "or am I to take them as precise statements? Do you speak of travelling through time in the same way as one might speak of Omnipotence making His pathway on the storm, or do you—a—mean what you say?"

Dr. Nebogipfel smiled quietly. "Come and look at these diagrams," he said, and then with elaborate simplicity he commenced to explain again to the clergyman the new quadridimensional geometry. Insensibly Cook's aversion passed away, and seeming impossibility grew possible, now that such tangible things as diagrams and models could be brought forward in evidence. Presently he found himself asking questions, and his interest grew deeper and deeper as Nebogipfel slowly and with precise clearness unfolded the beautiful order of his strange invention. The moments slipped away unchecked, as the Doctor passed on to the narrative of his research, and it was with a start of surprise that the clergyman noticed the deep blue of the dying twilight through the open doorway.

"The voyage," said Nebogipfel concluding his history, "will be full of undreamt-of dangers—already in one brief essay I have stood in the very jaws of death—but it is also full of the divines' promise of undreamt-of joy. Will you come? Will you walk among the people of the Golden Years?… "

But the mention of death by the philosopher had brought flooding back to the mind of Cook, all the horrible sensations of that first apparition.

"Dr. Nebogipfel… one question?" He hesitated. "On your hands… Was it blood?"

Nebogipfel's countenance fell. He spoke slowly.

"When I had stopped my machine, I found myself in this room as it used to be. Hark!"

"It is the wind in the trees towards Rwstog."

"It sounded like the voices of a multitude of people singing… when I had stopped I found myself in this room as it used to be. An old man, a young man, and a lad were sitting at a table—reading some book together. I stood behind them unsuspected. 'Evil spirits assailed him,' read the old man; 'but it is written, to him that overcometh shall be given life eternal'. They came as entreating friends, but he endured through all their snares. They came as principalities and powers, but he defied them in the name of the King of Kings. Once even it is told that in his study, while he was translating the New Testament into German, the Evil One himself appeared before him…' Just then the lad glanced timorously round, and with a fearful wail fainted away…"

"The others sprang at me… It was a fearful grapple… The old man clung to my throat, screaming 'Man or Devil, I defy thee…'

"I could not help it. We rolled together on the floor… the knife his trembling son had dropped came to my hand… Hark!"

He paused and listened, but Cook remained staring at him in the same horror-stricken attitude he had assumed when the memory of the blood-stained hands had rushed back over his mind.

"Do you hear what they are crying? Hark!"

Burn the warlock! Burn the murderer!

"Do you hear? There is no time to be lost."

Slay the murderer of cripples. Kill the devil's claw!

"Come! Come!"

Cook, with a convulsive effort, made a gesture of repugnance and strode to the doorway. A crowd of black figures roaring towards him in the red torchlight made him recoil. He shut the door and faced Nebogipfel.

The thin lips of the Doctor curled with a contemptuous sneer. "They will kill you if you stay," he said; and seizing his unresisting vistor by the wrist, he forced him towards the glittering machine. Cook sat down and covered his face with his hands.

In another moment the door was flung open, and old Pritchard stood blinking on the threshold.

A pause. A hoarse shout changing suddenly into a sharp shrill shriek.

A thunderous roar like the bursting forth of a great fountain of water.

The voyage of the Chronic Argonauts had begun.

OFF ON A COMET, OR HECTOR SERVADAC

by Jules Verne

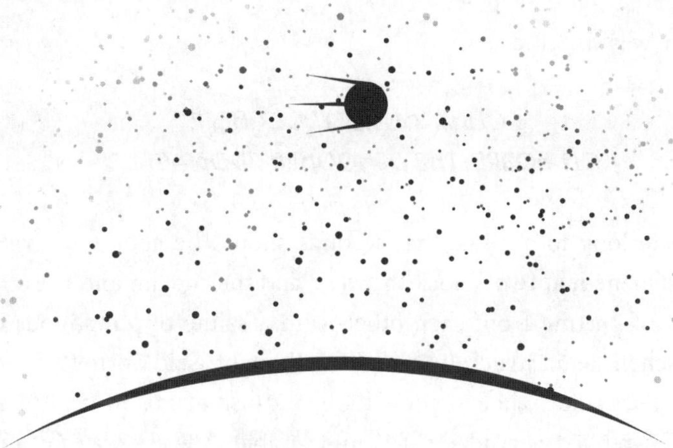

I
A CHALLENGE

"Nothing, sir, can induce me to surrender my claim."

"I am sorry, count, but in such a matter your views cannot modify mine."

"But allow me to point out that my seniority unquestionably gives me a prior right."

"Mere seniority, I assert, in an affair of this kind, cannot possibly entitle you to any prior claim whatever."

"Then, captain, no alternative is left but for me to compel you to yield at the sword's point."

"As you please, count; but neither sword nor pistol can force me to forego my pretensions. Here is my card."

"And mine."

This rapid altercation was thus brought to an end by the formal interchange of the names of the disputants. On one of the cards was inscribed:

CAPTAIN. HECTOR SERVADAC.
STAFF OFFICER. MOSTAGANEM.

On the other was the title:

COUNT WASSILI TIMASCHEFF.
ON BOARD THE SCHOONER "DOBRYNA."

It did not take long to arrange that seconds should be appointed, who would meet in Mostaganem at two o'clock that day; and the captain and the count were on the point of parting from each other, with a salute of punctilious courtesy, when Timascheff, as if struck by a sudden thought, said abruptly: "Perhaps it would be better, captain, not to allow the real cause of this to transpire."

"Far better," replied Servadac; "it is undesirable in every way for any names to be mentioned."

"In that case, however," continued the count, "it will be necessary to assign an ostensible pretext of some kind. Shall we allege a musical dispute—a contention in which I feel bound to defend Wagner, while you are the zealous champion of Rossini?"

"I am quite content," answered Servadac, with a smile; and with another low bow they parted.

The scene as here depicted, took place upon the extremity of a little cape on the Algerian coast, between Mostaganem and Tenes, about two miles from the mouth of the Shelif. The headland rose more than sixty feet above the sea-level, and the azure waters of the Mediterranean, as they softly kissed the strand, were tinged with the reddish hue of the ferriferous rocks that formed its base. It was the 31st of December. The noontide sun, which usually illuminated the various projections of the coast with a dazzling brightness, was hidden by a dense mass of cloud, and the fog, which for some unaccountable cause, had hung for the last two months over nearly every region in the world, causing serious interruption to traffic between continent and continent, spread its dreary veil across land and sea.

After taking leave of the staff-officer, Count Wassili Timascheff wended his way down to a small creek, and took his seat in the stern of a light four-oar that had been awaiting his return; this was immediately pushed off from shore, and was soon alongside a pleasure-yacht, that was lying to, not many cable lengths away.

At a sign from Servadac, an orderly, who had been standing at a respectful distance, led forward a magnificent Arabian horse; the captain vaulted into the saddle, and followed by his attendant, well mounted as himself, started off towards Mostaganem. It was half-past twelve when the two riders crossed the bridge that had been recently erected over the Shelif, and a quarter of an hour later their steeds, flecked with foam, dashed through the Mascara Gate, which was one of five entrances opened in the embattled wall that encircled the town.

At that date, Mostaganem contained about fifteen thousand inhabitants, three thousand of whom were French. Besides being one of the principal district towns of the province of Oran, it was also a military station. Mostaganem rejoiced in a well-sheltered harbour, which enabled it to utilize all the rich products of the Mina and the Lower Shelif. It was the existence of so good a harbour amidst the exposed cliffs of this coast that had induced the owner of the *Dobryna* to winter in these parts, and for two months the Russian standard had been seen floating from her yard, whilst on her mast-head was hoisted the pennant of the French Yacht Club, with the distinctive letters M. C. W. T., the initials of Count Timascheff.

Having entered the town, Captain Servadac made his way towards Matmore, the military quarter, and was not long in finding two friends on whom he might rely—a major of the 2nd Fusileers, and a captain of the 8th Artillery. The two officers listened gravely enough to Servadac's request that they would act as his seconds in an affair of honour, but could not resist a smile on hearing that the dispute between him and the count had originated in a musical discussion. Surely, they suggested, the matter might be easily arranged; a few slight concessions on either side, and all might be amicably adjusted. But no representations on their part were of any avail. Hector Servadac was inflexible.

"No concession is possible," he replied, resolutely. "Rossini has been deeply injured, and I cannot suffer the injury to be unavenged. Wagner is a fool. I shall keep my word. I am quite firm."

"Be it so, then," replied one of the officers; "and after all, you know, a sword-cut need not be a very serious affair."

"Certainly not," rejoined Servadac; "and especially in my case, when I have not the slightest intention of being wounded at all."

Incredulous as they naturally were as to the assigned cause of the quarrel, Servadac's friends had no alternative but to accept his explanation, and without further parley they started for the staff office, where, at two o'clock precisely, they were to meet the seconds of Count Timascheff. Two hours later they had returned. All the preliminaries had been arranged; the count, who like many Russians abroad was an aide-de-camp of the Czar, had of course proposed swords as the most appropriate weapons, and the duel was to take place on the following morning, the first of January, at nine o'clock, upon the cliff at a spot about a mile and a half from the mouth of the Shelif. With the assurance that they would not fail to keep their appointment with military punctuality, the two officers cordially wrung their friend's hand and retired to the Zulma Café for a game at piquet. Captain Servadac at once retraced his steps and left the town.

For the last fortnight Servadac had not been occupying his proper lodgings in the military quarters; having been appointed to make a local levy, he had been living in a gourbi, or native hut, on the Mostaganem coast, between four and five miles from the Shelif. His orderly was his sole companion, and by any other man than the captain the enforced exile would have been esteemed little short of a severe penance.

On his way to the gourbi, his mental occupation was a very labourious effort to put together what he was pleased to call a rondo, upon a model of versification all but obsolete. This rondo, it is unnecessary to coneal, was to be an ode addressed to a young widow by whom he had been captivated, and whom he was anxious to marry, and the tenor of his muse was intended to prove that when once a man has found an object in all respects worthy of his affections he should love her "in all simplicity." Whether the aphorism was universally true was not very material to the gallant captain, whose sole ambition at present was to construct a roundelay of which this should be the prevailing sentiment. He indulged the fancy that he might succeed in producing a composition which would have a fine effect here in Algeria, where poetry in that form was all but unknown.

"I know well enough," he said repeatedly to himself, "what I want to say. I want to tell her that I love her sincerely, and wish to marry her; but, confound it! the words won't rhyme. Plague on it! Does nothing rhyme with 'simplicity'? Ah! I have it now:

'LOVERS SHOULD, WHOE'ER THEY BE,
LOVE IN ALL SIMPLICITY.'

"But what next? how am I to go on? I say, Ben Zoof," he called aloud to his orderly, who was trotting silently close in his rear, "did you ever compose any poetry?"

"No, captain," answered the man promptly: "I have never made any verses, but I have seen them made fast enough at a booth during the fête of Montmartre,"

"Can you remember them?"

"Remember them! to be sure I can. This is the way they began:

'COME IN! COME IN! YOU'LL NOT REPENT
THE ENTRANCE MONEY YOU HAVE SPENT;
THE WONDROUS MIRROR IN THIS PLACE,
REVEALS YOUR FUTURE SWEETHEART'S FACE.'"

"Bosh!" cried Servadac in disgust; "your verses are detestable trash."

"As good as any others, captain, squeaked through a reed pipe."

"Hold your tongue, man," said Servadac peremptorily; "I have made another couplet.

'LOVERS SHOULD, WHOE'ER THEY BE,
LOVE IN ALL SIMPLICITY;
LOVER, LOVING HONESTLY,
OFFER I MYSELF TO THEE."

Beyond this, however, the captain's poetical genius was impotent to carry him; his further efforts were unavailing, and when at six o'clock he reached the gourbi, the four lines still remained the limit of his composition.

II
CAPTAIN SERVADAC AND HIS ORDERLY

At the time of which I write, there might be seen in the registers of the Minister of War the following entry:

SERVADAC (*HECTOR*), BORN AT ST. TRÉLODY IN THE DISTRICT OF LESPARRE, DEPARTMENT OF THE GIRONDE, JULY 19TH, 18—.

PROPERTY: 1200 FRANCS IN RENTES.
LENGTH OF SERVICE: FOURTEEN YEARS, THREE MONTHS, AND FIVE DAYS.
SERVICE: TWO YEARS AT SCHOOL AT ST. CYR; TWO YEARS AT L'ECOLE D'APPLICATION; TWO YEARS IN THE 8TH REGIMENT OF THE LINE; TWO YEARS IN THE 3RD LIGHT CAVALRY; SEVEN YEARS IN ALGERIA.
CAMPAIGNS: SOUDAN AND JAPAN.
RANK: CAPTAIN ON THE STAFF AT MOSTAGANEM.
DECORATIONS: CHEVALIER OF THE LEGION OF HONOUR, MARCH 13TH, 18—.

Hector Servadac was thirty years of age, an orphan without lineage and almost without means. Thirsting for glory rather than for gold, slightly scatter-brained, but warm-hearted, generous, and brave, he was eminently fitted to be the protêgé of the god of battles.

For the first year and a half of his existence he had been the foster-child of the sturdy wife of a vine-dresser of Médoc—a lineal descendant of the heroes of ancient prowess; in a word, he was one of those individuals whom nature seems to have predestined for remarkable things, and around whose cradle have hovered the fairy god-mothers of adventure and good luck.

In appearance Hector Servadac was quite the type of an officer; he was rather more than five feet six inches high, slim and graceful, with dark curling hair and mustaches, well-formed hands and feet, and a clear blue eye. He seemed born to please without being conscious of the power he possessed. It must be owned, and no one was more ready to confess it than himself, that his literary attainments were by no means of a high order. "We don't spin tops" is a favourite saying amongst artillery officers, indicating that they do not shirk their duty for frivolous pursuits; but it must be confessed that Servadac, being naturally idle, was very much given to "spinning tops." His good abilities, however, and his ready intelligence had carried him successfully through the curriculum of his early career. He was a good draughtsman, an excellent rider—having thoroughly mastered the successor to the famous "Uncle Tom" at the riding-school of St. Cyr—and in the records of his military service his name had several times been included in the order of the day.

The following episode may suffice, in a certain degree, to illustrate his character. Once, in action, he was leading a detachment of infantry through an intrenchment. They came to a place where the side-work of the trench had been so riddled by shell that a portion of it had actually fallen in, leaving an aperture quite unsheltered from the grape-shot that was pouring in thick and fast. The men hesitated. In an instant Servadac mounted the sidework, laid himself down in the gap, and thus filling up the breach by his own body, shouted, "March on!"

And through a storm of shot, not one of which touched the prostrate officer, the troop passed in safety.

Since leaving the military college, Servadac, with the exception of his two campaigns in the Soudan and Japan, had been always stationed in Algeria. He had now a staff appointment at Mostaganem, and had lately been entrusted with some topographical work on the coast between Tenes and the Shelif. It was a matter of little consequence to him that the gourbi, in which of necessity he was quartered, was uncomfortable and ill-contrived; he loved the open air, and the independence of his life suited him well. Sometimes he would wander on foot upon the sandy shore, and sometimes he would enjoy a ride along the summit of the cliff; altogether being in no hurry at all to bring his task to an end. His occupation, moreover, was not so engrossing but that he could find leisure for taking a short railway journey once or twice a week; so that he was ever and again putting in an appearance at the general's receptions at Oran, and at the fêtes given by the governor at Algiers.

It was on one of these occasions that he had first met Madame de L—, the lady to whom he was desirous of dedicating the rondo, the first four lines of which had just seen the light. She was a colonel's widow, young and handsome, very reserved, not to say haughty in her manner, and either indifferent or impervious to the admiration which she inspired. Captain Servadac had not yet ventured to declare his attachment; of rivals he was well aware he had not a few, and amongst these not the least formidable was the Russian Count Timasheff. And although the young widow was all unconscious of the share she had in the matter, it was she, and she alone, who was the cause of the challenge just given and accepted by her two ardent admirers.

During his residence in the gourbi, Hector Servadac's sole companion was his orderly, Ben Zoof. Ben Zoof was devoted, body and soul, to his superior officer. His own personal ambition was so entirely absorbed in his master's welfare, that it is certain no offer of promotion—even had it been that of aide-de-camp to the Governor-General of Algiers—would have induced him to quit that master's service. His name might seem to imply that he was a native of Algeria; but such was by no means the case. His true name was Laurent; he was a native of Montmartre in Paris, and how or why he had obtained his patronymic was one of those anomalies which the most sagacious of etymologists would find it hard to explain.

Born on the hill of Montmartre, between the Solferino tower and the mill of La Galette, Ben Zoof had ever possessed the most unreserved admiration for his birthplace; and to his eyes the heights and district of Montmartre represented an epitome of all the wonders of the world. In all his travels, and these had been not a few, he had never beheld scenery which could compete with that of his native home. No cathedral—not even Burgos itself—could vie with the church at Montmartre. Its race-course could well hold its own against that at Pentélique; its reservoir would throw the Mediterranean into the shade; its forests had flourished long before the invasion of the Celts; and its very mill produced no ordinary flour, but provided material for cakes of world-wide renown. To crown all, Montmartre boasted a mountain—a veritable mountain; envious tongues indeed might pronounce it little more than a hill; but Ben Zoof would have allowed himself to be hewn in pieces rather than admit that it was anything less than fifteen thousand feet in height.

Ben Zoof's most ambitious desire was to induce the captain to go with him and end his days in his much-loved home, and so incessantly were Servadac's ears besieged with descriptions of the unparalleled beauties and advantages of this eighteenth arrondissement of Paris, that he could scarcely hear the name of Montmartre without a conscious thrill of aversion. Ben Zoof, however, did not despair of ultimately converting the captain, and meanwhile had resolved never to leave him. When a private in the 8th Cavalry, he had been on the point of quitting the army at twenty-eight years of age, but unexpectedly he had been appointed orderly to Captain Servadac. Side by side they fought in two campaigns. Servadac had saved Ben Zoof's life in Japan; Ben Zoof had rendered his master a like service in the Soudan. The bond of union thus effected could never be severed; and although Ben Zoof's achievements had fairly earned him the right of retirement, he firmly declined all honours or any pension that might part him from his superior officer. Two stout arms, an iron constitution, a powerful frame, and an indomitable courage were all loyally devoted to his master's service, and fairly entitled him to his *soi-disant* designation or "The Rampart of Montmartre." Unlike his master, he made no pretension to any gift of poetic power, but his inexhaustible memory made him a living encyclopaedia; and for his stock of anecdotes and troopers's tales he was matchless.

Thoroughly appreciating his servant's good qualities, Captain Servadac endured with imperturbable good humour those idiosyncrasies, which in a less faithful follower would have been intolerable, and from time to time he would drop a word of sympathy that served to deepen his subordinate's devotion. On one occasion, when Ben Zoof had mounted his hobby-horse, and was indulging in high-flown praises about his beloved eighteenth arrondissement, the captain had remarked gravely, "Do you know, Ben Zoof, that Montmartre only requires a matter of some thirteen thousand feet to make it as high as Mont Blanc?"

Ben Zoof's eyes glistened with delight; and from that moment Hector Servadac and Montmartre held equal places in his affection.

III
INTERRUPTED EFFUSIONS

Composed of mud and loose stones, and covered with a thatch of turf and straw, known to the natives by the name of "driss," the gourbi, though a grade better than the tents of the nomad Arabs, was yet far inferior to any habitation built of brick or stone. It adjoined an old stone hostelry, previously occupied by a detachment of engineers, and which now afforded shelter for Ben Zoof and the two horses. It still contained a considerable number of tools, such as mattocks, shovels, and pick-axes.

Uncomfortable as was their temporary abode Servadac and his attendant made no complaints; neither of them was dainty in the matter either of board or lodging. After dinner, leaving his orderly to stow away the remains of the repast in what he was pleased to term the "cupboard of his stomach," Captain Servadac turned out into the open air to smoke his pipe upon the edge of the cliff. The shades of night were drawing on. An hour previously, veiled in heavy clouds, the sun had sunk below the horizon that bounded the plain beyond the Shelif.

The sky presented a most singular appearance. Towards the north, although the darkness rendered it impossible to see beyond a quarter of a mile, the upper strata of the atmosphere were suffused with a rosy glare. No well-defined fringe of light, nor arch of luminous rays, betokened a display of aurora borealis, even had such a phenomenon been possible in these latitudes; and the most experienced meteorologist would have been puzzled to explain the cause of this striking illumination on this 31st of December, the last evening of the passing year.

But Captain Servadac was no meteorologist, and it is to be doubted whether, since leaving school, he had ever opened his "Course of Cosmography." Besides, he had other thoughts to occupy his mind. The prospects of the morrow offered serious matter for consideration. The captain was actuated by no personal animosity against the count; though rivals, the two men regarded each other with sincere respect; they had simply reached a crisis in which one of them was *de trop*; which of them, fate must decide.

At eight o'clock. Captain Servadac re-entered the gourbi, the single apartment of which contained his bed, a small writing-table, and some trunks that served instead of cupboards. The orderly performed his culinary operations in the adjoining building, which he also used as a bed-room, and where, extended on what he called his "good oak mattress," he would sleep soundly as a doormouse for twelve hours at a stretch. Ben Zoof had not yet received his orders to retire, and ensconcing himself in a corner of the gourbi, he endeavoured to doze—a task which the unusual agitation of his master rendered somewhat difficult. Captain Servadac was evidently in no hurry to betake himself to rest, but seating himself at his table, with a pair of compasses and a sheet of drawing-paper, he began to draw, with red and blue crayons, a variety of coloured lines, which could hardly be supposed to have much connection with a topographical survey. In truth, his character of staff-officer was now entirely absorbed in that of Gascon poet. Whether he imagined that the compasses would bestow upon his verses the measure of a mathematical accuracy, or whether he fancied that the parti-coloured lines would lend variety to his rhythm, it is impossible to determine; be that as it may, he was devoting all his energies to the compilation of his rondo, and supremely difficult he found the task.

"Hang it!" he ejaculated, "whatever induced me to choose this meter? It is as hard to find rhymes as to rally fugitives in a battle. But, by all the powers,' it shan't be said that a French officer cannot cope with a piece of poetry. One battalion has fought—now for the rest!"

Perseverance had its reward. Presently two lines, one red, the other blue, appeared upon the paper, and the captain murmured:

"WORDS. MERE WORDS. CANNOT AVAIL.
TELLING TRUE HEART'S TENDER TALE."

"What on earth ails my master?" muttered Ben Zoof; "for the last hour he has been as fidgety as a bird returning after its winter migration."

Servadac suddenly started from his seat, and as he paced the room with all the frenzy of poetic inspiration, read out:

"EMPTY WORDS CANNOT CONVEY
ALL A LOVER'S HEART WOULD SAY."

"Well, to be sure, he is at his everlasting verses again!" said Ben Zoof to himself, as he roused himself in his corner. "Impossible to sleep in such a noise;" and he gave vent to a loud groan.

"How now, Ben Zoof?" said the captain sharply. "What ails you?"

"Nothing, sir, only the nightmare."

"Curse the fellow, he has quite interrupted me!" ejaculated the captain. "Ben Zoof!" he called aloud.

"Here, sir!" was the prompt reply; and in an instant the orderly was upon his feet, standing in a military attitude, one hand to his forehead, the other closely pressed to his trouser-seam.

"Stay where you are! don't move an inch!" shouted Servadac; "I have just thought of the end of my rondo."

And in a voice of inspiration, accompanying his words with dramatic gestures, Servadac began to declaim:

"LISTEN, LADY, TO MY VOWS—
O, CONSENT TO BE MY SPOUSE;
CONSTANT EVER I WILL BE,
CONSTANT ... ."

No closing lines were uttered. All at once, with unutterable violence, the captain and his orderly were dashed, face downwards, to the ground.

IV
A CONVULSION OF NATURE

Whence came it that at that very moment the horizon underwent so strange and sudden a modification, that the eye of the most praticed mariner could not distinguish between sea and sky?

Whence came it that the billows raged and rose to a height hitherto unregistered in the records of science?

Whence came it that the elements united in one deafening crash; that the earth groaned as though the whole framework of the globe were ruptured; that the waters roared from their innermost depths; that the air shrieked with all the fury of a cyclone?

Whence came it that a radiance, intenser than the effulgence of the Northern

Lights, overspread the firmament, and momentarily dimmed the splendour of the brightest stars?

Whence came it that the Mediterranean, one instant emptied of its waters, was the next flooded with a foaming surge?

Whence came it that in the space of a few seconds the moon's disc reached a magnitude as though it were but a tenth part of its ordinary distance from the earth?

Whence came it that a new blazing spheroid, hitherto unknown to astronomy, now appeared suddenly in the firmament, though it were but to lose itself immediately behind masses of accumulated cloud?

What phenomenon was this that had produced a cataclysm so tremendous in effect upon earth, sky, and sea?

Was it possible that a single human being could have survived the convulsion? and if so, could he explain its mystery?

V
A MYSTERIOUS SEA

Violent as the commotion had been, that portion of the Algerian coast which is bounded on the north by the Mediterranean, and on the west by the right bank of the Shelif, appeared to have suffered little change. It is true that indentations were perceptible in the fertile plain, and the surface of the sea was ruffled with an agitation that was quite unusual; but the rugged outline of the cliff was the same as heretofore, and the aspect of the entire scene appeared unaltered. The stone hostelry, with the exception of some deep clefts in its walls, had sustained little injury; but the gourbi, like a house of cards destroyed by an infant's breath, had completely subsided, and its two inmates lay motionless, buried under the sunken thatch.

It was two hours after the catastrophe that Captain Servadac regained consciousness; he had some trouble to collect his thoughts, and the first sounds that escaped his lips were the concluding words of the rondo which had been so ruthlessly interrupted;

"CONSTANT EVER I WILL BE,
CONSTANT ..."

His next thought was to wonder what had happened; and in order to find an answer, he pushed aside the broken thatch, so that his head appeared above the *débris.* "The gourbi leveled to the ground!" he exclaimed, "surely a waterspout has passed along the coast."

He felt all over his body to perceive what injuries he had sustained, but not a sprain nor a scratch could he discover. "Where are you, Ben Zoof?" he shouted.

"Here, sir!" and with military promptitude a second head protruded from the rubbish.

"Have you any notion what has happened, Ben Zoof?"

"I've a notion, captain, that it's all up with us."

"Nonsense, Ben Zoof; it is nothing but a waterspout!"

"Very good, sir;" was the philosophical reply, immediately followed by the query, "Any bones broken, sir?"

"None whatever," said the captain.

Both men were soon on their feet, and began to make a vigorous clearance of the ruins, beneath which they found that their arms, cooking utensils, and other property, had sustained little injury. "By-the-by, what o'clock is it?" asked the captain.

"It must be eight o'clock, at least," said Ben Zoof, looking at the sun, which was a considerable height above the horizon. "It is almost time for us to start."

"To start! what for?"

"To keep your appointment with Count Timascheff."

"By Jove! I had forgotten all about it!" exclaimed Servadac. Then looking at his watch, he cried, "What are you thinking of, Ben Zoof? It is scarcely two o'clock.

"Two in the morning, or two in the afternoon?" asked Ben Zoof, again regarding the sun.

Servadac raised his watch to his ear. "It is going," said he; "but, by all the wines of Médoc, I am puzzled. Don't you see the sun is in the west? It must be near setting."

"Setting, captain! Why, it is rising finely, like a conscript at the sound of the reveille. It is considerably higher since we have been talking."

Incredible as it might appear, the fact was undeniable that the sun was rising over the Shelif from that quarter of the horizon behind which it usually sank for the latter portion of its daily round. They were utterly bewildered. Some mysterious phenomenon must not only have altered the position of the sun in the sidereal system, but must even have brought about an important modification of the earth's rotation on her axis.

Captain Servadac consoled himself with the prospect of reading an explanation of the mystery in next week's newspapers, and turned his attention to what was to him of more immediate importance. "Come, let us be off," said he to his orderly; "though heaven and earth be topsy-turvy, I must be at my post this morning."

"To do Count Timascheff the honour of running him through the body," added Ben Zoof.

If Servadac and his orderly had been less preoccupied, they would have noticed that a variety of other physical changes besides the apparent alteration in the movement of the sun had been evolved during the atmospheric disturbances of that New Year's night. As they descended the steep footpath leading from the cliff towards the Shelif, they were conscious that their respiration became forced and rapid, like that of a mountaineer when he has reached an altitude where the air has become less charged with oxygen. They were also conscious that their voices were thin and feeble; either they must themselves have become rather deaf or it was evident that the air had become less capable of transmitting sound.

The weather, which on the previous evening had been very foggy, had entirely changed. The sky had assumed a singular tint, and was soon covered with lowering clouds that completely hid the sun. There were, indeed, all the signs of a coming storm, but the vapour, on account of the insufficient condensation, failed to fall.

The sea appeared quite deserted, a most unusual circumstance along this coast, and not a sail nor a trail of smoke broke the gray monotony of water and sky. The limits of the horizon, too, had become much circumscribed. On land, as well as on sea, the remote distance had completely disappeared, and it seemed as though the globe had assumed a more decided convexity.

At the pace at which they were walking, it was very evident that the captain and his attendant would not take long to accomplish the three miles that lay between the gourbi and the place of rendezvous. They did not exchange a word, but each was conscious of an unusual buoyancy, which appeared to lift up their bodies and give as it were, wings to their feet. If Ben Zoof had expressed his sensations in words, he would have said that he felt "up to anything," and he had even forgotten to taste so much as a crust of bread, a lapse of memory of which the worthy soldier was rarely guilty.

As these thoughts were crossing his mind, a harsh bark was heard to the left of the footpath, and a jackal was seen emerging from a large grove of lentisks.

Regarding the two wayfarers with manifest uneasiness, the beast took up its position at the foot of a rock, more than thirty feet in height. It belonged to an African species distinguished by a black spotted skin, and a black line down the front of the legs. At night-time when they scour the country in herds, the creatures are somewhat formidable, but singly they are no more dangerous than a dog. Though by no means afraid of them, Ben Zoof had a particular aversion to jackals, perhaps because they had no place among the fauna of his beloved Montmartre. He accordingly began to make threatening gestures, when, to the unmitigated astonishment of himself and the captain, the animal darted forward, and in one single bound gained the summit of the rock.

"Good Heavens!" cried Ben Zoof, "that leap must have been thirty feet at least."

"True enough," replied the captain; "I never saw such a jump."

Meantime the jackal had seated itself upon its haunches, and was staring at the two men with an air of impudent defiance. This was too much for Ben Zoof's forbearance, and stooping down he caught up a huge stone, when to his surprise, he found that it was no heavier than a piece of petrified sponge. "Confound the brute!" he exclaimed, "I might as well throw a piece of bread at him. What accounts for its being as light as this?"

Nothing daunted, however, he hurled the stone into the air. It missed its aim; but the jackal, deeming it on the whole prudent to decamp, disappeared across the trees and hedges with a series of bounds, which could only be likened to those that might be made by an india-rubber kangaroo. Ben Zoof was sure that his own powers of propelling must equal those of a howitzer, for his stone, after a lengthened flight through the air, fell to the ground full five hundred paces the other side of the rock.

The orderly was now some yards ahead of his master, and had reached a ditch full of water, and about ten feet wide. With the intention of clearing it, he made a spring, when a loud cry burst from Servadac. "Ben Zoof, you idiot! What are you about? You will break your back!"

And well might he be alarmed, for Ben Zoof had sprung to a height of forty feet into the air. Fearful of the consequences that would attend the descent of his servant to *terra firma*, Servadac bounded forwards, to be on the other side of the ditch in time to break his fall. But the muscular effort that he made carried him in his turn to an altitude of thirty feet; in his ascent he passed Ben Zoof, who had already commenced his downward course; and then, obedient to the laws of gravitation, he descended with increasing rapidity, and alighted upon the earth without experiencing a shock greater than if he had merely made a bound of four or five feet high.

Ben Zoof burst into a roar of laughter. "Bravo!" he said, "we should make a good pair of clowns."

But the captain was inclined to take a more serious view of the matter. For a few seconds he stood lost in thought, then said solemnly, "Ben Zoof, I must be dreaming. Pinch me hard; I must be either asleep or mad."

"It is very certain that something has happened to us," said Ben Zoof. "I have occasionally dreamed that I was a swallow flying over the Montmartre, but I never experienced anything of this kind before; it must be peculiar to the coast of Algeria."

Servadac was stupefied; he felt instinctively that he was not dreaming, and yet was powerless to solve the mystery. He was not, however, the man to puzzle himself for long over any insoluble problem. "Come what may," he presently exclaimed, "we will make up our minds for the future to be surprised at nothing."

"Right, captain," replied Ben Zoof; "and, first of all, let us settle our little score with Count Timascheff."

Beyond the ditch lay a small piece of meadow land, about an acre in extent. A soft and delicious herbage carpeted the soil, whilst trees formed a charming framework to the whole. No spot could have been chosen more suitable for the meeting between the two adversaries.

Servadac cast a hasty glance round. No one was in sight. "We are the first on the field," he said.

"Not so sure of that, sir," said Ben Zoof.

"What do you mean?" asked Servadac, looking at his watch, which he had set as nearly as possible by the sun before leaving the gourbi; "it is not nine o'clock yet."

"Look up there, sir. I am much mistaken if that is not the sun;" and as Ben Zoof spoke, he pointed directly overhead to where a faint white disc was dimly visible through the haze of clouds.

"Nonsense!" exclaimed Servadac. "How can the sun be in the zenith, in the month of January, in lat. 39° N.?"

"Can't say, sir. I only know the sun is there; and at the rate he has been traveling, I would lay my cap to a dish of couscous that in less than three hours he will have set."

Hector Servadac mute and motionless, stood with folded arms. Presently he roused himself, and began to look about again. "What means all this?" he murmured. "Laws of gravity disturbed! Points of the compass reversed! The length of day reduced one half! Surely this will indefinitely postpone my meeting with the count. Something has happened; Ben Zoof and I cannot both be mad!"

The orderly, meantime, surveyed his master with the greatest equanimity; no phenomenon, however extraordinary, would have drawn from him a single exclamation of surprise. "Do you see anyone, Ben Zoof?" asked the captain, at last.

"No one, sir; the count has evidently been and gone."

"But supposing that to be the case," persisted the captain, "my seconds would have waited, and not seeing me, would have come on towards the gourbi. I can only conclude that they have been unable to get here; and as for Count Timascheff—"

Without finishing his sentence, Captain Servadac, thinking it just probable that the count, as on the previous evening, might come by water, walked to the ridge of rock that overhung the shore, in order to ascertain if the *Dobryna* were anywhere in sight. But the sea was deserted, and for the first time the captain noticed that, although the wind was calm, the waters were unusually agitated, and seethed and foamed as though they were boiling. It was very certain that the yacht would have found a difficulty in holding her own in such a swell. Another thing that now struck Servadac was the extraordinary contraction of the horizon. Under ordinary circumstances, his elevated position would have allowed him a radius of vision at least five and twenty miles in length; but the terrestrial sphere seemed, in the course of the last few hours, to have become considerably reduced in volume, and he could now see for a distance of only six miles in every direction.

Meantime, with the agility of a monkey, Ben Zoof had clambered to the top of a eucalyptus, and from his lofty perch was surveying the country to the south, as well as towards both Tenes and Mostaganem. On descending, he informed the captain that the plain was deserted.

"We will make our way to the river, and get over into Mostaganem," said the captain.

The Shelif was not more than a mile and a half from the meadow, but no time was to be lost if the two men were to reach the town before nightfall. Though still hidden by heavy clouds, the sun was evidently declining fast; and what was equally inexplicable, it was not following the oblique curve that in these latitudes and at this time of year might be expected, but was sinking perpendicularly down to the horizon.

As he went along, Captain Servadac pondered deeply. Perchance some unheard-of phenomenon had modified the rotary motion of the globe; or perhaps the Algerian coast had been transported beyond the equator into the southern hemisphere. Yet the earth, with the exception of the alteration in its convexity, in this part of Africa at least, seemed to have undergone no change of any very great importance. As far as the eye could reach, the shore was, as it had ever been, a succession of cliffs, beach, and arid rocks, tinged with a red ferruginous hue. To the south—if south, in this inverted order of things, it might still be called—the face of the country also appeared unaltered, and some leagues away, the peaks of the Merdeyah mountains still retained their accustomed outline.

Presently a rift in the clouds gave passage to an oblique ray of light that clearly proved that the sun was setting in the east.

"Well, I am curious to know what they think of all this at Mostaganem," said the captain. "I wonder, too, what the Minister of War will say when he receives a telegram informing him that his African colony has become, not morally, but physically disorganised; that the cardinal points are at variance with ordinary rules, and that the sun in the month of January is shining down vertically upon our heads."

Ben Zoof, whose ideas of discipline were extremely rigid, at once suggested that the colony should be put under the surveillance of the police, that the cardinal points should be placed under restraint, and that the sun should be shot for breach of discipline.

Meantime, they were both advancing with the utmost speed. The decompression of the atmosphere made the specific gravity of their bodies extraordinarily light, and they ran like hares and leaped like chamois. Leaving the devious windings of the footpath, they went as a crow would fly across the country. Hedges, trees, and streams were cleared at a bound, and under these conditions Ben Zoof felt that he could have overstepped Montmartre at a single stride. The earth seemed as elastic as the spring-board of an acrobat; they scarcely touched it with their feet, and their only fear was lest the height to which they were propelled would consume the time which they were saving by their short cut across the fields.

It was not long before their wild career brought them to the right bank of the Shelif. Here they were compelled to stop, for not only had the bridge completely disappeared, but the river itself no longer existed. Of the left bank there was not the slightest trace, and the right bank, which on the previous evening had bounded the yellow stream, as it murmured peacefully along the fertile plain, had now become the shore of a tumultuous ocean, its azure waters extending westwards far as the eye could reach, and annihilating the tract of country which had hitherto formed the district of Mostaganem. The shore coincided exactly with what had been the right bank of the Shelif, and in a slightly curved line ran north and south, whilst the adjacent groves and meadows all retained their previous positions. But the river-bank had become the shore of an unknown sea.

Eager to throw some light upon the mystery, Servadac hurriedly made his way through the oleander bushes that overhung the shore, took up some water in the hollow of his hand, and carried it to his lips. "Salt as brine!" he exclaimed, as soon as he had tasted it. "The sea has undoubtedly swallowed up all the western part of Algeria."

"It will not last long, sir," said Ben Zoof, "It is, probably, only a severe flood."

The captain shook his head. "Worse than that, I fear, Ben Zoof," he replied with emotion. "It is a catastrophe that may have very serious consequences. What can have become of all my friends and fellow-officers?"

Ben Zoof was silent. Rarely had he seen his master so much agitated; and though himself inclined to receive these phenomena with philosophic indifference, his notions of military duty caused his countenance to reflect the captain's expression of amazement.

But there was little time for Servadac to examine the changes which a few hours had wrought. The sun had already reached the eastern horizon, and just as though it were crossing the ecliptic under the tropics, it sank like a cannon ball into the sea. Without any warning, day gave place to night, and earth, sea, and sky were immediately wrapped in profound obscurity.

VI
THE CAPTAIN MAKES AN EXPLORATION

Hector Servadac was not the man to remain long unnerved by any untoward event. It was part of his character to discover the why and the wherefore of everything that came under his observation, and he would have faced a cannon ball the more unflinchingly from understanding the dynamic force by which it was propelled. Such being his temperament, it may well be imagined that he was anxious not to remain long in ignorance of the cause of the phenomena which had been so startling in their consequences.

"We must inquire into this tomorrow," he exclaimed, as darkness fell suddenly upon them. Then, after a pause, he added: "That is to say, if there is to be a tomorrow; for if I were to be put to the torture, I could not tell what has become of the sun."

"May I ask, sir, what we are to do now?" put in Ben Zoof.

"Stay where we are for the present; and when daylight appears—if it ever does appear—we will explore the coast to the west and south, and return to the gourbi. If we can find out nothing else, we must at least discover where we are."

"Meanwhile, sir, may we go to sleep?"

"Certainly, if you like, and if you can."

Nothing loath to avail himself of his master's permission, Ben Zoof crouched down in an angle of the shore, threw his arms over his eyes, and very soon slept the sleep of the ignorant, which is often sounder than the sleep of the just.

Overwhelmed by the questions that crowded upon his brain, Captain Servadac could only wander up and down the shore. Again and again he asked himself what the catastrophe could portend. Had the towns of Algiers, Oran, and Mostaganem escaped the inundation? Could he bring himself to believe that all the inhabitants, his friends, and comrades had perished; or was it not more probable that the Mediterranean had merely invaded the region of the mouth of the Shelif? But this supposition did not in the least explain the other physical disturbances. Another hypothesis that presented itself to his mind was that the African coast might have been suddenly transported to the equatorial zone. But although this might get over the difficulty of the altered altitude of the sun and the absence of twilight, yet it would neither account for the sun setting in the east, nor for the length of the day being reduced to six hours.

"We must wait till tomorrow," he repeated; adding, for he had become distrustful of the future, "that is to say, if tomorrow ever comes."

Although not very learned in astronomy, Servadac was acquainted with the position of the principal constellations. It was therefore a considerable disappointment to him that, in consequence of the heavy clouds, not a star was visible in the firmament. To have ascertained that the pole-star had become displaced would have been an undeniable proof that the earth was revolving on a new axis; but not a rift appeared in the lowering clouds, which seemed to threaten torrents of rain.

It happened that the moon was new on that very day; naturally, therefore, it would have set at the same time as the sun. What, then, was the captain's bewilderment when, after he had been walking for about an hour and a half, he noticed on the western horizon a strong glare that penetrated even the masses of the clouds.

"The moon in the west!" he cried aloud; but suddenly bethinking himself, he added: "But no, that cannot be the moon; unless she has shifted very much nearer the earth, she could never give a light as intense as this."

As he spoke the screen of vapour was illuminated to such a degree that the whole country was, as it were, bathed in twilight. "What can this be?" soliloquized the captain. "It cannot be the sun, for the sun set in the east only an hour and a half ago. Would that those clouds would disclose what enormous luminary lies behind them! What a fool I was not to have learnt more astronomy! Perhaps, after all, I am racking my brain over something that is quite in the ordinary course of nature."

But, reason as he might, the mysteries of the heavens still remained impenetrable. For about an hour some luminous body, the disc evidently of gigantic dimensions, shed its rays upon the upper strata of the clouds; then, marvellous to relate, instead of obeying the ordinary laws of celestial mechanism, and descending upon the opposite horizon, it seemed to retreat farther off, grew dimmer, and vanished.

The darkness that returned to the face of the earth was not more profound than the gloom which fell upon the captain's soul. Everything was incomprehensible. The simplest mechanical rules seemed falsified; the planets had defied the laws of gravitation; the motions of the celestial spheres were erroneous as those of a watch with a defective mainspring, and there was reason to fear that the sun would never again shed his radiance upon the earth.

But these last fears were groundless. In three hours' time, without any intervening twilight, the morning sun made its appearance in the west, and day once more had dawned. On consulting his watch, Servadac found that night had lasted precisely six hours. Ben Zoof, who was unaccustomed to so brief a period of repose, was still slumbering soundly.

"Come, wake up!" said Servadac, shaking him by the shoulder; "it is time to start."

"Time to start?" exclaimed Ben Zoof, rubbing his eyes. "I feel as if I had only just gone to sleep."

"You have slept all night, at any rate," replied the captain; "it has only been for six hours, but you must make it enough."

"Enough it shall be, sir," was the submissive rejoinder.

"And now," continued Servadac, "we will take the shortest way back to the gourbi, and see what our horses think about it all."

"They will think that they ought to be groomed," said the orderly.

"Very good; you may groom them and saddle them as quickly as you like. I want to know what has become of the rest of Algeria: if we cannot get round by the south to Mostaganem, we must go eastwards to Tenes." And forthwith they started. Beginning to feel hungry, they had no hesitation in gathering figs, dates, and oranges from the plantations that formed a continuous rich and luxuriant orchard along their path. The district was quite deserted, and they had no reason to fear any legal penalty.

In an hour and a half they reached the gourbi. Everything was just as they had left it, and it was evident that no one had visited the place during their absence. All was desolate as the shore they had quitted.

The preparations for the expedition were brief, and simple. Ben Zoof saddled the horses and filled his pouch with biscuits and game; water, he felt certain, could be obtained in abundance from the numerous affluents of the Shelif, which, although they had now become tributaries of the Mediterranean, still meandered through the plain. Captain Servadac mounted his horse Zephyr, and Ben Zoof simultaneously got astride his mare Gelette, named after the mill of Montmartre. They galloped off in the direction of the Shelif, and were not long in discovering that the diminution in the pressure of the atmosphere had precisely the same effect upon their horses as it had had upon themselves. Their muscular strength seemed five times as great as hitherto; their hoofs scarcely touched the ground, and they seemed transformed from ordinary quadrupeds into veritable hippogriffs. Happily, Servadac and his orderly were fearless riders; they made no attempt to curb their steeds, but even urged them to still greater exertions. Twenty minutes sufficed to carry them over the four or five miles that intervened between the gourbi and the mouth of the Shelif; then, slackening their speed, they proceeded at a more leisurely pace to the southeast, along what had once been the right bank of the river, but which, although it still retained its former characteristics, was now the boundary of a sea, which extending farther than the limits of the horizon, must have swallowed up at least a large portion of the province of Oran. Captain Servadac knew the country well; he had at one time been engaged upon a trigonometrical survey of the district, and consequently had an accurate knowledge of its topography. His idea now was to draw up a report of his investigations: to whom that report should be delivered was a problem he had yet to solve.

During the four hours of daylight that still remained, the travellers rode about twenty-one miles from the river mouth. To their vast surprise, they did not meet a single human being. At nightfall they again encamped in a slight bend of the shore, at a point which on the previous evening had faced the mouth of the Mina, one of the left-hand affluents of the Shelif, but now absorbed into the newly revealed ocean. Ben Zoof made the sleeping accommodation as comfortable as the circumstances would allow; the horses were hobbled and turned out to feed upon the rich pasture that clothed the shore, and the night passed without special incident.

At sunrise on the following morning, the 2nd of January, or what, according to the ordinary calendar, would have been the night of the 1st, the captain and his orderly remounted their horses, and during the six-hours' day accomplished a distance of forty-two miles. The right bank of the river still continued to be the margin of the land, and only in one spot had its integrity been impaired. This was about twelve milee from the Mina, and on the site of the annex or suburb of Surkelmittoo. Here a large portion of the bank had been swept away, and the hamlet, with its eight hundred inhabitants, had no doubt been swallowed up by the encroaching waters. It seemed, therefore, more than probable that a similar fate had overtaken the larger towns beyond the Shelif.

In the evening the explorers encamped, as previously, in a nook of the shore which here abruptly terminated their new domain, not far from where they might have expected to find the important village of Memounturroy; but of this, too, there was now no trace. "I had quite reckoned upon a supper and a bed at Orleansville to-night," said Servadac, as, full of despondency, he surveyed the waste of water.

"Quite impossible," replied Ben Zoof, "except you had gone by a boat. But cheer up, sir, cheer up; we will soon devise some means for getting across to Mostaganem."

"If, as I hope," rejoined the captain, "we are on a peninsula, we are more likely to get to Tenes; there we shall hear the news."

"Far more likely to carry the news ourselves," answered Ben Zoof, as he threw himself down for his night's rest.

Six hours later, only waiting for sunrise, Captain Servadac set himself in movement again to renew his investigations. At this spot the shore, that hitherto had been running in a southeasterly direction, turned abruptly to the north, being no longer formed by the natural bank of the Shelif, but consisting of an absolutely new coast-line. No land was in sight. Nothing could be seen of Orleansville, which ought to have been about six miles to the southwest; and Ben Zoof, who had mounted the highest point of view attainable, could distinguish sea, and nothing but sea, to the farthest horizon.

Quitting their encampment and riding on, the bewildered explorers kept close to the new shore. This, since it had ceased to be formed by the original river bank, had considerably altered its aspect. Frequent landslips occurred, and in many places deep chasms rifted the ground; great gaps furrowed the fields, and trees, half uprooted, overhung the water, remarkable by the fantastic distortions of their gnarled trunks, looking as though they had been chopped by a hatchet.

The sinuosities of the coast line, alternately gully and headland, had the effect of making a devious progress for the travellers, and at sunset, although they had accomplished more than twenty miles, they had only just arrived at the foot of the Merdeyah Mountains, which, before the cataclysm, had formed the extremity of the chain of the Little Atlas. The ridge, however, had been violently ruptured, and now rose perpendicularly from the water.

On the following morning Servadac and Ben Zoof traversed one of the mountain gorges; and next, in order to make a more thorough acquaintance with the limits and condition of the section of Algerian territory of which they seemed to be left as the sole occupants, they dismounted, and proceeded on foot to the summit of one of the highest peaks. From this elevation they ascertained that from the base of the Merdeyah to the Mediterranean, a distance of about eighteen miles, a new coast line had come into existence; no land was visible in any direction; no isthmus existed to form a connecting link with the territory of Tenes, which had entirely disappeared. The result was that Captain Servadac was driven to the irresistible conclusion that the tract of land which he had been surveying was not, as he had at first imagined, a peninsula; it was actually an island.

Strictly generally speaking, this island was quadrilateral, but the sides were so irregular that it was much more nearly a triangle, the comparison of the sides exhibiting these proportions: The section of the right bank of the Shelif, seventy-two miles; the southern boundary from the Shelif to the chain of the Little Atlas, twenty-one miles; from the Little Atlas to the Mediterranean, eighteen miles; and sixty miles of the shore of the Mediterranean itself, making in all an entire circumference of about 171 miles.

"What does it all mean?" exclaimed the captain, every hour growing more and more bewildered.

"The will of providence, and we must submit," replied Ben Zoof, calm and undisturbed. With this reflection, the two men silently descended the mountain and remounted their horses. Before evening they had reached the Mediterranean. On their road they failed to discern a vestige of the little town of Montenotte; like Tenes, of which not so much as a ruined cottage was visible on the horizon, it seemed to be annihilated.

On the following day, the 6th of January, the two men made a forced march along the coast of the Mediterranean, which they found less altered than the captain had at first supposed; but four villages had entirely disappeared, and the headlands, unable to resist the shock of the convulsion, had been detached from the mainland.

The circuit of the island had been now completed, and the explorers, after a period of sixty hours, found themselves once more beside the ruins of their gourbi. Five days, or what, according to the established order of things, would have been two days and a half, had been occupied in tracing the boundaries of their new domain; and they had ascertained beyond a doubt that they were the sole human inhabitants left upon the island.

"Well, sir, here you are. Governor General of Algeria!" exclaimed Ben Zoof, as they reached the gourbi.

"With not a soul to govern," gloomily rejoined the captain.

"How so? Do you not reckon me?"

"Pshaw! Ben Zoof, what are you?"

"What am I? Why, I am the population."

The captain deigned no reply, but, muttering some expressions of regret for the fruitless trouble he had taken about his rondo, betook himself to rest.

VII
BEN ZOOF WATCHES IN VAIN

In a few minutes the governor general and his population were asleep. The gourbi being in ruins, they were obliged to put up with the best accommodation they could find in the adjacent erection. It must be owned that the captain's slumbers were by no means sound; he was agitated by the consciousness that he had hitherto been unable to account for his strange experiences by any reasonable theory. Though far from being advanced in the knowledge of natural philosophy, he had been instructed, to a certain degree, in its elementary principles; and, by an effort of memory, he managed to recall some general laws which he had almost forgotten. He could understand that an altered inclination of the earth's axis with regard to the ecliptic would introduce a change of position in the cardinal points, and bring about a displacement of the sea; but the hypothesis entirely failed to account, either for the shortening of the days, or for the diminution in the pressure of the atmosphere. He felt that his judgment was utterly baffled; his only remaining hope was that the chain of marvels was not yet complete, and that something farther might throw some light upon the mystery.

Ben Zoof's first care on the following morning was to provide a good breakfast. To use his own phrase, he was as hungry as the whole population of three million Algerians, of whom he was the representative, and he must have enough to eat. The catastrophe which had overwhelmed the country had left a dozen eggs uninjured, and upon these, with a good dish of his famous couscous, he hoped that he and his master might have a sufficiently substantial meal. The stove was ready for use, the copper skillet was as bright as hands could make it, and the beads of condensed steam upon the surface of a large stone alcarraza gave evidence that it was supplied with water. Ben Zoof at once lighted a fire, singing all the time, according to his wont, a snatch of an old military refrain.

Ever on the lookout for fresh phenomena, Captain Servadac watched the preparations with a curious eye. It struck him that perhaps the air, in its strangely modified condition, would fail to supply sufficient oxygen, and that the stove in consequence might not fulfill its function. But no; the fire was lighted just as usual, and fanned into vigour by Ben Zoof applying his mouth in lieu of bellows, and a bright flame started up from the midst of the twigs and coal. The skillet was duly set upon the stove, and Ben Zoof was prepared to wait awhile for the water to boil. Taking up the eggs, he was surprised to notice that they hardly weighed more than they would if they had been mere shells; but he was still more surprised when he saw that before the water had been two minutes over the fire it was at full boil.

"By jingo!" he exclaimed, "a precious hot fire!"

Servadac reflected. "It cannot be that the fire is hotter," he said, "the peculiarity must be in the water." And taking down a centigrade thermometer, which hung upon the wall, he plunged it into the skillet. Instead of 100°, the instrument registered only 66°.

"Take my advice, Ben Zoof," he said, "leave your eggs in the saucepan a good quarter of an hour."

"Boil them hard ! That will never do," objected the orderly.

"You will not find them hard, my good fellow. Trust me, we shall be able to dip our sippets into the yolks easily enough."

The captain was quite right in his conjecture, that this new phenomenon was caused by a diminution in the pressure of the atmosphere. Water boiling at a temperature of 66° was itself an evidence that the ocean of air above the earth's surface had been reduced by one-third of its quantity. The identical phenomenon would have occurred at the summit of a mountain 35,000 feet high; and had Servadac been in possession of a barometer, he would have immediately discovered the fact that only now for the first time, as the result of experiment, revealed itself to him—a fact, moreover, which accounted for the effect upon the blood-vessels which both he and Ben Zoof had experienced, as well as for the attenuation of their voices and their accelerated breathing. "And yet," he agreed with himself, "if our encampment has been projected to so great an elevation, how is it that the sea remains at its proper level?"

Once again Hector Servadac, though capable of tracing consequences, felt himself totally at a loss to comprehend their cause; hence his agitation and bewilderment!

After their prolonged immersion in the boiling water, the eggs were found to be only just sufficiently cooked; the couscous was very much in the same condition; and Ben Zoof came to the conclusion that in future he must be careful to commence his culinary operations an hour earlier. He was rejoiced at last to help his master, who, in spite of his perplexed preoccupation, seemed to have a very fair appetite for breakfast.

"Well, captain?" said Ben Zoof presently, such being his ordinary way of opening conversation.

"Well, Ben Zoof?" was the captain's invariable response to his servant's formula.

"What are we to do now, sir?"

"We can only for the present wait patiently where we are. We are encamped upon an island, and therefore we can only be rescued by sea."

"But do you suppose that any of our friends are still alive?" asked Ben Zoof.

"Oh, I think we must indulge the hope that this catastrophe has not extended far. We must trust that it has limited its mischief to some small portion of the Algerian coast, and that our friends are all alive and well. No doubt the governor general will be anxious to investigate the full extent of the damage, and will send a vessel from Algiers to explore. It is not likely that we shall be forgotten. What you have to do then, Ben Zoof, is to keep a sharp lookout, and to be ready, in case a vessel should appear, to make signals at once."

"But if no vessel should appear!" sighed the orderly.

"Then we must build a boat, and go in search of those who do not come in search of us."

"Very good. But what sort of a sailor are you?"

"Everyone can be a sailor when he must," said Servadac calmly.

Ben Zoof said no more. For several succeeding days he scanned the horizon unintermittently with his telescope. His watching was in vain. No ship appeared upon the desert sea. "By the name of a Kabyle!" he broke out impatiently, "his Excellency is grossly negligent!"

Although the days and nights had become reduced from twenty-four hours to twelve, Captain Servadac would not accept the new condition of things, but resolved to adhere to the computations of the old calendar. Notwithstanding, therefore, that the sun had risen and set twelve times since the commencement of the new year, he persisted in calling the following day the 6th of January. His watch enabled him to keep an accurate account of the passing hours.

In the course of his life, Ben Zoof had read a few books. After pondering one day, he said; "It seems to me, captain, that you have turned into Robinson Crusoe, and that I am your man Friday. I hope I have not become a negro."

"No," replied the captain. "Your complexion isn't the fairest in the world, but you are not black yet."

"Well, I had much sooner be a white Friday than a black one," rejoined Ben Zoof.

Still no ship appeared; and Captain Servadac, after the example of all previous Crusoes, began to consider it advisable to investigate the resources of his domain. The new territory of which he had become the monarch he named Gourbi Island. It had a superficial area of about nine hundred square miles. Bullocks, cows, goats, and sheep existed in considerable numbers; and as there seemed already to be an abundance of game, it was hardly likely that a future supply would fail them. The condition of the cereals was such as to promise a fine ingathering of wheat, maize, and rice; so that for the governor and his population, with their two horses, not only was there ample provision, but even if other human inhabitants besides themselves should yet be discovered, there was not the remotest prospect of any of them perishing by starvation.

From the 6th to the 13th of January the rain came down in torrents; and, what was quite an unusual occurrence at this season of the year, several heavy storms broke over the island. In spite, however, of the continual downfall, the heavens still remained veiled in cloud. Servadac, moreover, did not fail to observe that for the season the temperature was unusually high; and, as a matter still more surprising, that it kept steadily increasing, as though the earth were gradually and continuously approximating to the sun. In proportion to the rise of temperature, the light also assumed greater intensity; and if it had not been for the screen of vapour interposed between the sky and the island, the irradiation which would have illumined all terrestrial objects would have been vivid beyond all precedent.

But neither sun, moon, nor star ever appeared; and Servadac's irritation and annoyance at being unable to identify any one point of the firmament may be more readily imagined than described. On one occasion Ben Zoof endeavoured to mitigate his master's impatience by exhorting him to assume the resignation, even if he did not feel the indifference, which he himself experienced; but his advice was received with so angry a rebuff that he retired in all haste, abashed, to resume his watchman's duty, which he performed with exemplary perseverance. Day and night, with the shortest possible intervals of rest, despite wind, rain, and storm, he mounted guard upon the cliff—but all in vain. Not a speck appeared upon the desolate horizon. To say the truth, no vessel could have stood against the weather. The hurricane raged with tremendous fury, and the waves rose to a height that seemed to defy calculation. Never, even in the second era of creation, when, under the influence of internal heat, the waters rose in vapour to descend in deluge back upon the world, could meteorological phenomena have been developed with more impressive intensity.

But by the night of the 13th the tempest appeared to have spent its fury; the wind dropped; the rain ceased as if by a spell; and Servadac, who for the last six days had confined himself to the shelter of his roof, hastened to join Ben Zoof at his post upon the cliff. Now, he thought, there might be a chance of solving his perplexity; perhaps now the huge disc, of which he had an imperfect glimpse on the night of the 31st of December, might again reveal itself; at any rate, he hoped for an opportunity of observing the constellations in a clear firmament above.

The night was magnificent. Not a cloud dimmed the lustre of the stars, which spangled the heavens in surpassing brilliancy, and several nebulae which hitherto no astronomer had been able to discern without the aid of a telescope were clearly visible to the naked eye.

By a natural impulse, Servadac's first thought was to observe the position of the pole-star. It was in sight, but so near to the horizon as to suggest the utter impossibility of its being any longer the central pivot of the sidereal system; it occupied a position through which it was out of the question that the axis of the earth indefinitely prolonged could ever pass. In his impression he was more thoroughly confirmed when, an hour later, he noticed that the star had approached still nearer the horizon, as though it had belonged to one of the zodiacal constellations.

The pole-star being manifestly thus displaced, it remained to be discovered whether any other of the celestial bodies had become a fixed centre around which the constellations made their apparent daily revolutions. To the solution of this problem Servadac applied himself with the most thoughtful diligence. After patient observation, he satisfied himself that the required conditions were answered by a certain star that was stationary not far from the horizon. This was

Vega, in the constellation Lyra, a star which, according to the precession of the equinoxes, will take the place of our pole-star 12,000 years hence. The most daring imagination could not suppose that a period of 12,000 years had been crowded into the space of a fortnight; and therefore the captain came, as to an easier conclusion, to the opinion that the earth's axis had been suddenly and immensely shifted; and from the fact that the axis, if produced, would pass through a point so litle removed above the horizon, he deduced the inference that the Mediterranean must have been transported to the equator.

Lost in a bewildering maze of thought, he gazed long and intently upon the heavens. His eyes wandered from where the tail of the Great Bear, now a zodiacal constellation, was scarcely visible above the waters, to where the stars of the southern hemisphere were just breaking on his view. A cry from Ben Zoof recalled him to himself.

"The moon!" shouted the orderly, as though overjoyed at once again beholding what the poet has called:

"THE KIND COMPANION OF TERRESTRIAL NIGHT;"

and he pointed to a disc that was rising at a spot precisely opposite the place where they would have expected to see the sun. "The moon!" again he cried.

But Captain Servadac could not altogether enter into his servant's enthusiasm. If this were actually the moon, her distance from the earth must have been increased by some millions of miles. He was rather disposed to suspect that it was not the earth's satellite at all, but some planet with its apparent magnitude greatly enlarged by its approximation to the earth. Taking up the powerful field-glass which he was accustomed to use in his surveying operations, he proceeded to investigate more carefully the luminous orb. But he failed to trace any of the lineaments, supposed to resemble a human face, that mark the lunar surface; he failed to decipher any indications of hill and plain; nor could he make out the aureole of light which emanates from what astronomers have designated Mount Tycho. "It is not the moon," he said slowly.

"Not the moon?" cried Ben Zoof. "Why not?"

"It is not the moon," again affirmed the captain.

"Why not?" repeated Ben Zoof, unwilling to renounce his first impression.

"Because there is a small satellite in attendance." And the captain drew his servant's attention to a bright speck, apparently about the size of one of Jupiter's satellites seen through a moderate telescope, that was clearly visible just within the focus of his glass.

Here, then, was a fresh mystery. The orbit of this planet was assuredly interior to the orbit of the earth, because it accompanied the sun in its apparent motion; yet it was neither Mercury nor Venus, because neither one nor the other of these has any satellite at all.

The captain stamped and stamped again with mingled vexation, agitation, and bewilderment. "Confound it!" he cried, "if this is neither Venus nor Mercury, it must be the moon; but if it is the moon, whence, in the name of all the gods, has she picked up another moon for herself?"

The captain was in dire perplexity.

VIII
VENUS IN PERILOUS PROXIMITY

The light of the returning sun soon extinguished the glory of the stars, and rendered it necessary for the captain to postpone his observations. He had sought in vain for further trace of the huge disc that had so excited his wonder on the first and it seemed most probable that, in its irregular orbit, it had been carried beyond the range of vision.

The weather was still superb. The wind, after veering to the west, had sunk to a perfect calm. Pursuing its inverted course, the sun rose and set with undeviating regularity; and the days and nights were still divided into periods of precisely six hours each—a sure proof that the sun remained close to the new equator which manifestly passed through Gourbi Island.

Meanwhile the temperature was steadily increasing. The captain kept his thermometer close at hand where he could repeatedly consult it, and on the 15th he found that it registered 50° centigrade in the shade.

No attempt had been made to rebuild the gourbi, but the captain and Ben Zoof managed to make up quarters sufficiently comfortable in the principal apartment of the adjoining structure, where the stone walls, that at first afforded a refuge from the torrents of rain, now formed an equally acceptable shelter from the burning sun. The heat was becoming insufferable, surpassing the heat of Senegal and other equatorial regions; not a cloud ever tempered the intensity of the solar rays; and unless some modification ensued, it seemed inevitable that all vegetation should become scorched and burnt off from the face of the island.

In spite, however, of the profuse perspirations from which he suffered, Ben Zoof, constant to his principles, expressed no surprise at the unwonted heat. No remonstrances from his master could induce him to abandon his watch from the cliff. To withstand the vertical beams of that noontide sun would seem to require a skull of brass and a brain of adamant; but yet, hour after hour, he would remain conscientiously scanning the surface of the Mediterranean, which, calm and deserted, lay outstretched before him. On one occasion, Servadac, in reference to his orderly's indomitable perseverance, happened to remark that he thought he must have been born in the heart of equatorial Africa; to which Ben Zoof replied, with the utmost dignity, that he was born at Montmartre, which was all the same. The worthy fellow was unwilling to own that, even in the matter of heat, the tropics could in any way surpass his own much-loved home.

This unprecedented temperature very soon began to take effect upon the products of the soil. The sap rose rapidly in the trees, so that in the course of a few days buds, leaves, flowers, and fruit had come to full maturity. It was the same with the cereals; wheat and maize sprouted and ripened as if by magic, and for a while a rank and luxuriant pasturage clothed the meadows. Summer and autumn seemed blended into one. If Captain Servadac had been more deeply versed in astronomy, he would perhaps have been able to bring to bear his knowledge that if the axis of the earth, as everything seemed to indicate, now formed a right angle with the plane of the ecliptic, her various seasons, like those of the planet Jupiter, would become limited to certain zones, in which they would remain invariable. But even if he had understood the *rationale* of the change, the convulsion that had brought it about would have been as much a mystery as ever.

The precocity of vegetation caused some embarrassment. The time for the corn and fruit harvest had fallen simultaneously with that of the hay making; and as the extreme heat precluded any prolonged exertions, it was evident "the population" of the island would find it difficult to provide the necessary amount of labour. Not that the prospect gave them much concern: the provisions of the gourbi were still far from exhausted, and now that the roughness of the weather had so happily subsided, they had every encouragement to hope that a ship of some sort would soon appear. Not only was that part of the Mediterranean systematically frequented by the government steamers that watched the coast, but vessels of all nations were constantly cruising off the shore.

In spite, however, of all their sanguine speculations, no ship appeared. Ben Zoof admitted the necessity of extemporizing a kind of parasol for himself, otherwise he must literally have been roasted to death upon the exposed summit of the cliff.

Meanwhile, Servadac was doing his utmost—it must be acknowledged, with indifferent success—to recall the lessons of his school-days. He would plunge into the wildest speculations in his endeavours to unravel the difficulties of the new situation, and struggled into a kind of conviction that if there had been a change of manner in the earth's rotation on her axis, there would be a corresponding change in her revolution round the sun, which would involve the consequence of the length of the year being either diminished or increased.

Independently of the increased and increasing heat, there was another very conclusive demonstration that the earth had thus suddenly approached nearer to the sun. The diameter of the solar disc was now exactly twice what it ordinarily looks to the naked eye; in fact, it was precisely such as it would appear to an observer on the surface of the planet Venus. The most obvious inference would therefore be that the earth's distance from the sun had been diminished from 91,000,000 to 66,000,000 miles. If the just equilibrium of the earth had thus been destroyed, and should this diminution of distance still continue, would there not be reason to fear that the terrestrial world would be carried onwards to actual contact with the sun, which must result in its total annihilation?

The continuance of the splendid weather afforded Servadac every facility for observing the heavens. Night after night, constellations in their beauty lay stretched before his eyes—an alphabet which, to his mortification, not to say his rage, he was unable to decipher. In the apparent dimensions of the fixed stars, in their distance, in their relative position with regard to each other, he could observe no change. Although it is established that our sun is approaching the constellation of Hercules at the rate of more than 126,000,000 miles a year, and although Arcturus is travelling through space at the rate of fifty-four miles a second—three times faster than the earth goes round the sun,—yet such is the remoteness of those stars that no appreciable change is evident to the senses. The fixed stars taught him nothing.

Far otherwise was it with the planets. The orbits of Venus and Mercury are within the orbit of the earth, Venus rotating at an average distance of 66,130,000 miles from the sun, and Mercury at that of 35,393,000. After pondering long, and as profoundly as he could, upon these figures, Captain Servadac came to the conclusion that, as the earth was now receiving about double the amount of light and heat that it had been receiving before the catastrophe, it was receiving about the same as the planet Venus; he was driven, therefore, to the estimate of the measure in which the earth must have approximated to the sun, a deduction in which he was confirmed when the opportunity came for him to observe Venus herself in the splendid proportions that she now assumed.

That magnificent planet which—as Phosphorus or Lucifer, Hesperus or Vesper, the evening star, the morning star, or the shepherd's star—has never failed to attract the rapturous admiration of the most indifferent observers, here revealed herself with unprecedented glory, exhibiting all the phases of a lustrous moon in miniature. Various indentations in the outline of its crescent showed that the solar beams were refracted into regions of its surface where the sun had already set, and proved, beyond a doubt, that the planet had an atmosphere of her own; and certain luminous points projecting from the crescent as plainly marked the existence of mountains. As the result of Servadac's computations he formed the opinion that Venus could hardly be at a greater distance than 6,000,000 miles from the earth.

"And a very safe distance, too," said Ben Zoof, when his master told him the conclusion at which he had arrived.

"All very well for two armies, but for a couple of planets not quite so safe, perhaps, as you may imagine. It is my impression that it is more than likely we may run foul of Venus," said the captain.

"Plenty of air and water there, sir?" inquired the orderly.

"Yes; as far as I can tell, plenty," replied Servadac.

"Then why shouldn't we go and visit Venus?"

Servadac did his best to explain that as the two planets were of about equal volume, and were travelling with great velocity in opposite directions, any collision between them must be attended with the most disastrous consequences to one or both of them. But Ben Zoof failed to see that, even at the worst, the catastrophe could be much more serious than the collision of two railway trains.

The captain became exasperated. "You idiot!" he angrily exclaimed; "cannot you understand that the planets are travelling a thousand times faster than the fastest express, and that if they meet, either one or the other must be destroyed? What would become of your darling Montmartre then?"

The captain had touched a tender chord. For a moment Ben Zoof stood with clenched teeth and contracted muscles; then, in a voice of real concern, he inquired whether anything could be done to avert the calamity.

"Nothing whatever; so you may go about your own business," was the captain's brusque rejoinder.

All discomfited and bewildered, Ben Zoof retired without a word.

During the ensuing days the distance between the two planets continued to decrease, and it became more and more obvious that the earth, on her new orbit, was about to cross the orbit of Venus. Throughout this time the earth had been making a perceptible approach towards Mercury, and that planet—which is rarely visible to the naked eye, and then only at what are termed the periods of its greatest eastern and western elongations—now appeared in all its splendour. It amply justified the epithet of "sparkling" which the ancients were accustomed to confer upon it, and could scarcely fail to awaken anew interest. The periodic recurrence of its phases; its reflection of the sun's rays, shedding upon it a light and a heat seven times greater than that received by the earth; its glacial and its torrid zones, which, on account of the great inclination of the axis, are scarcely separable; its equatorial hands; its mountains eleven miles high;—were all subjects of observation worthy of the most studious regard.

But no danger was to be apprehended from Mercury; with Venus only did collision appear imminent. By the 18th of January the distance between that planet and the earth had become reduced to between two and three millions of miles, and the intensity of its light cast heavy shadows from all terrestrial objects. It might be observed to turn upon its own axis in twenty-three hours twenty-one minutes—an evidence, from the unaltered duration of its days, that the planet had not shared in the disturbance. On its disc the clouds formed from its atmospheric vapour were plainly perceptible, as also were the seven spots, which, according to Bianchini, are a chain of seas. It was now visible in broad daylight. Bonaparte, when under the Directory, once had his attention called to Venus at noon, and immediately hailed it joyfully, recognizing it as his own peculiar star in the ascendant. Captain Servadac, it may well be imagined, did not experience the same gratifying emotion.

On the 20th, the distance between the two bodies had again sensibly diminished. The captain had ceased to be surprised that no vessel had been sent to rescue himself and his companion from their strange imprisonment; the governor general and the minister of war were doubtless far differently occupied, and their interests far otherwise engrossed. What sensational articles, he thought, must now be teeming to the newspapers! What crowds must be flocking to the churches! The end of the world approaching! the great climax close at hand! Two days more, and the earth, shivered into a myriad atoms, would be lost in boundless space!

These dire forebodings, however, were not destined to be realized. Gradually the distance between the two planets began to increase; the planes of their orbits did not coincide, and accordingly the dreaded catastrophe did not ensue. By the 25th, Venus was sufficiently remote to preclude any further fear of collision. Ben Zoof gave a sigh of relief when the captain communicated the glad intelligence.

Their proximity to Venus had been close enough to demonstrate that beyond a doubt that planet has no moon or eatellite such as Cassini, Short, Montaigne of Limoges, Montbarron, and some other astronomers have imagined to exist. "Had there been such a satellite," said Servadac, "we might have captured it in passing. But what can be the meaning," he added seriously, "of all this displacement of the heavenly bodies?"

"What is that great building at Paris, captain, with a top like a cap?" asked Ben Zoof.

"Do you mean the Observatory?"

"Yes, the Observatory. Are there not people living in the Observatory who could explain all this?"

"Very likely; but what of that?"

"Let us be philosophers, and wait patiently until we can hear their explanation."

Servadac smiled. "Do you know what it is to be a philosopher, Ben Zoof?" he asked.

"I am a soldier, sir," was the servant's prompt rejoinder, "and I have learnt to know that 'what can't be cured must be endured.'"

The captain made no reply, but for a time, at least, he desisted from puzzling himself over matters which he felt he was utterly incompetent to explain. But an event soon afterwards occurred which awakened his keenest interest.

About nine o'clock on the morning of the 27th, Ben Zoof walked deliberately into his master's apartment, and, in reply to a question as to what he wanted, announced with the utmost composure that a ship was in sight.

"A ship!" exclaimed Servadac, starting to his feet. "A ship! Ben Zoof, you donkey! you speak as unconcernedly as though you were telling me that my dinner was ready."

"Are we not philosophers, captain?" said the orderly.

But the captain was out of hearing.

IX
INQUIRIES UNSATISFIED

Fast as his legs could carry him, Servadac had made his way to the top of the cliff. It was quite true that a vessel was in sight, hardly more than six miles from the shore; but owing to the increase in the earth's convexity, and the consequent limitation of the range of vision, the rigging of the topmasts alone was visible above the water. This was enough, however, to indicate that the ship was a schooner—an impression that was confirmed when, two hours later, she came entirely in sight.

"The *Dobryna!*" exclaimed Servadac, keeping his eye unmoved at his telescope.

"Impossible sir!" rejoined Ben Zoof; "there are no signs of smoke.

"The *Dobryna!*" repeated the captain, positively. "She is under sail; but she is Count Timascheff's yacht."

He was right. If the count were on board, a strange fatality was bringing him to the presence of his rival. But no longer now could Servadac regard him in the light of an adversary; circumstances had changed, and all animosity was absorbed in the eagerness with which he hailed the prospect of obtaining some information about the recent startling and inexplicable events. During the twenty-seven days that she had been absent, the *Dobryna*, he conjectured, would have explored the Mediterranean, would very probably have visited Spain, France, or Italy, and accordingly would convey to Gourbi Island some intelligence from one or other of those countries. He reckoned, therefore, not only upon ascertaining the extent of the late catastrophe, but upon learning its cause. Count Timascheff was, no doubt, magnanimously coming to the rescue of himself and his orderly.

The wind being adverse, the *Dobryna* did not make very rapid progress; but as the weather, in spite of a few clouds, remained calm, and the sea was quite smooth, she was enabled to hold a steady course. It seemed unaccountable that she should not use her engine, as whoever was on board, would be naturally impatient to reconnoitre the new island, which must just have come within their view. The probability that suggested itself was that the schooner's fuel was exhausted.

Servadac took it for granted that the *Dobryna* was endeavouring to put in. It occurred to him, however, that the count, on discovering an island where he had expected to find the mainland of Africa, would not unlikely be at a loss for a place of anchorage. The yacht was evidently making her way in the direction of the former mouth of the Shelif, and the captain was struck with the idea that he would do well to investigate whether there was any suitable harbour towards which he might signal her. Zephyr and Gallette were soon saddled, and in twenty minutes had carried their riders to the western extremity of the island, where they both dismounted and began to explore the coast.

They were not long in ascertaining that on the farther side of the point there was a small well-sheltered creek of sufficient depth to accommodate a vessel of moderate tonnage. A narrow channel formed a passage through the ridge of rocks that protected it from the open sea, and which, even in the roughest weather, would ensure the calmness of its waters.

Whilst examining the rocky shore, the captain observed, to his great surprise, long and well-defined rows of seaweed, which undoubtedly betokened that there had been a very considerable ebb and flow of the waters—a thing unknown in the Mediterranean, where there is scarcely any perceptible tide. What, however, seemed most remarkable, was the manifest evidence that ever since the highest flood (which was caused, in all probability, by the proximity of the body of which the huge disc had been so conspicuous on the night of the 31st of December) the phenomenon had been gradually lessening, and in fact was now reduced to the normal limits which had characterized it before the convulsion.

Without doing more than note the circumstance, Servadac turned his entire attention to the *Dobryna*, which, now little more than a mile from shore, could not fail to see and understand his signals. Slightly changing her course, she first lowered her mainsail, and, in order to facilitate the movements of her helmsman, soon carried nothing but her two topsails, brigantine and jib. After rounding the peak, she steered direct for the channel to which Servadac by his gestures was pointing her, and was not long in entering the creek. As soon as the anchor, imbedded in the sandy bottom, had made good its hold, a boat was lowered. In a few minutes more Count Timascheff had landed on the island. Captain Servadac hastened towards him.

"First of all, count," he exclaimed impetuously, "before we speak one other word, tell me what has happened."

The count, whose imperturbable composure presented a singular contrast to the French officer's enthusiastic vivacity, made a stiff bow, and in his Russian accent replied: "First of all, permit me to express my surprise at seeing you here. I left you on a continent, and here I have the honour of finding you on an island."

"I assure you, count, I have never left the place."

"I am quite aware of it, Captain Servadac, and I now beg to offer you my sincere apologies for failing to keep my appointment with you."

"Never mind, now," interposed the captain; "we will talk of that by-and-by. First, tell me what has happened."

"The very question I was about to put to you, Captain Servadac."

"Do you mean to say you know nothing of the cause, and can tell me nothing of the extent, of the catastrophe which has transformed this part of Africa into an island?"

"Nothing more than you know yourself."

"But surely, Count Timascheff, you can inform me whether upon the northern shore of the Mediterranean—"

"Are you certain that this is the Mediterranean?" asked the count significantly, and added, "I have discovered no sign of land."

The captain stared in silent bewilderment. For some moments he seemed perfectly stupefied; then, recovering himself, he began to overwhelm the count with a torrent of questions. Had he noticed, ever since the 1st of January, that the sun had risen in the west? Had he noticed that the days had been only six hours long, and that the weight of the atmosphere was so much diminished? Had he observed that the moon had quite disappeared, and that the earth had been in imminent hazard of running foul of the planet Venus? Was he aware, in short, that the entire motions of the terrestrial sphere had undergone a complete modification? To all these inquiries, the count responded in the affirmative. He was acquainted with everything that had transpired; but, to Servadac's increasing astonishment, he could throw no light upon the cause of any of the phenomena.

"On the night of the 31st of December," he said, "I was proceeding by sea to our appointed place of meeting, when my yacht was suddenly caught on the crest of an enormous wave, and carried to a height which it is beyond my power to estimate. Some mysterious force seemed to have brought about a convulsion of the elements. Our engine was damaged, nay disabled, and we drifted entirely at the mercy of the terrible hurricane that raged during the succeeding days. That the *Dobryna* escaped at all is little less than a miracle, and I can only attribute her safety to the fact that she occupied the centre of the vast cyclone, and consequently did not experience much change of position."

He paused, and added: "Your island is the first land we have seen."

"Then let us put out to sea at once and ascertain the extent of the disaster," cried the captain eagerly. "You will take me on board, count, will you not?"

"My yacht is at your service, sir, even should you require to make a tour round the world."

"A tour round the Mediterranean will suffice for the present, I think," said the captain, smiling.

The count shook his head.

"I am not sure," said he, "but what the tour of the Mediterranean will prove to be the tour of the world."

Servadac made no reply, but for a time remained silent and absorbed in thought.

After the silence was broken, they consulted as to what course was best to pursue; and the plan they proposed was, in the first place, to discover how much of the African coast still remained, and to carry on the tidings of their own experiences to Algiers; or, in the event of the southern shore having actually disappeared, they would make their way northwards and put themselves in communication with the population on the southern shores of Europe.

Before starting, it was indispensable that the engine of the *Dobryna* should be repaired: to sail under canvas only would in contrary winds and rough seas be both tedious and difficult. The stock of coal on board was adequate for two months' consumption; but as it would at the expiration of that time be exhausted, it was obviously the part of prudence to employ it in reaching a port where fuel could be replenished.

The damage sustained by the engine proved to be not very serious; and in three days after her arrival the *Dobryna* was again ready to put to sea.

Servadac employed the interval in making the count acquainted with all he knew about his small domain. They made an entire circuit of the island, and both agreed that it must be beyond the limits of that circumscribed territory that they must seek an explanation of what had so strangely transpired.

It was on the last day of January that the repairs of the schooner were completed. A slight diminution in the excessively high temperature which had prevailed for the last few weeks, was the only apparent change in the general order of things; but whether this was to be attributed to any alteration in the earth's orbit was a question which would still require several days to decide. The weather remained fine, and although a few clouds had accumulated, and might have caused a trifling fall of the barometer, they were not sufficiently threatening to delay the departure of the *Dobryna*.

Doubts now arose, and some discussion followed, whether or not it was desirable for Ben Zoof to accompany his master. There were various reasons why he should be left behind, not the least important being that the schooner had no accommodation for horses, and the orderly would have found it hard to part with Zephyr, and much more with his own favourite Galette; besides, it was advisable that there should be some one left to receive any strangers that might possibly arrive, as well as to keep an eye upon the herds of cattle which, in the dubious prospect before them, might prove to be the sole resource of the survivors of the catastrophe. Altogether, taking into consideration that the grave fellow would incur no personal risk by remaining upon the island, the captain was induced with much reluctance to forego the attendance of his servant, hoping very shortly to return and to restore him to his country, when he had ascertained the solution of the mysteries in which they were enveloped.

On the 31st, then, Ben Zoof was "invested with governor's powers," and took an affecting leave of his master, begging him, if chance should carry him near Montmartre, to ascertain whether the beloved "mountain" had been left unmoved.

Farewells over, the *Dobryna* was carefully steered through the creek, and was soon upon the open seas.

X
A SEARCH FOR ALGERIA

The *Dobryna*, a strong craft of 200 tons burden, had been built in the famous shipbuilding yards of the Isle of Wight. Her sea-going qualities were excellent, and would have amply sufficed for a circumnavigation of the globe.

Count Timascheff was himself no sailor, but had the greatest confidence in leaving the command of his yacht in the hands of Lieutenant Procope, a man of about thirty years of age, and an excellent seaman. Born on the count's estates, the son of a serf who had been emancipated long before the famous edict of the Emperor Alexander, Procope was sincerely attached, by a tie of gratitude as well as of duty and affection, to his patron's service. After an apprenticeship on a merchant ship he had entered the imperial navy, and had already reached the rank of lieutenant when the count appointed him to the charge of his own private yacht, in which he was accustomed to spend by far the greater part of his time, throughout the winter generally cruising in the Mediterranean, whilst in the summer he visited more northern waters.

The ship could not have been in better hands. The lieutenant was well informed in many matters outside the pale of his profession, and his attainments were alike creditable to himself and to the liberal friend who had given him his education. He had an excellent crew, consisting of Tiglew, the engineer, four sailors named Niegoch, Tolstoy, Etkef, and Ponafka, and Mochel the cook. These men, without exception, were all sons of the count's tenants, and so tenaciously, even out at sea, did they cling to their old traditions, that it mattered little to them what physical disorganization ensued, so long as they felt they were sharing the experiences of their lord and master. The late astounding events, however, had rendered Procope manifestly uneasy, and not the less so from his consciousness that the count secretly partook of his own anxiety.

Steam up and canvas spread, tha schooner started eastward. With a favourable wind she would certainly have made eleven knots an hour had not the high waves somewhat impeded her progress. Although only a moderate breeze was blowing, the sea was rough, a circumstance to be accounted for only by the diminution in the force of the earth's attraction rendering the liquid particles so buoyant, that by the mere effect of oscillation they were carried to a height that was quite unprecedented. M. Arago has fixed twenty-five or twenty-six feet as the maximum elevation ever attained by the highest waves, and his astonishment would have been very great to see them rising fifty or even sixty feet. Nor did these waves in the usual way partially unfurl themselves and rebound against the sides of the vessel; they might rather be described as long undulations carrying the schooner (its weight diminished from the same cause as that of the water) alternately to such heights and depths, that if Captain Servadac had been subject to seasickness he must have found himself in sorry plight. As the pitching, however, was the result of a long uniform swell, the yacht did not labour much harder than she would against the ordinary short strong waves of the Mediterranean; the main inconvenience that was experienced was the diminution in her proper rate of speed.

For a few miles she followed the line hitherto presumably occupied by the coast of Algeria; but no land appeared to the south. The changed positions of the planets rendered them of no avail for purposes of nautical observation, nor could Lieutenant Procope calculate his latitude and longitude by the altitude of the sun, as his reckonings would be useless when applied to charts that had been constructed for the old order of things; but nevertheless, by means of the log, which gave him the rate of progress, and by the compass which indicated the direction in which they were sailing, he was able to form an estimate of his position that was sufficiently free from error for his immediate need.

Happily the recent phenomena had no effect upon the compass; the magnetic needle, which in these regions had pointed about 22° from the north pole, had never deviated in the least—a proof that, although east and west had apparently changed places, north and south continued to retain their normal position as cardinal points. The log and the compass, therefore, were now to be called upon to do the work of the sextant and chronometer, which had become utterly useless.

On the first morning of the cruise Lieutenant Procope, who, like most Russians, spoke French fluently, was explaining these peculiarities to Captain Servadac; the count was present, and the conversation perpetually recurred, as naturally it would, to the phenomena which remained so inexplicable to them all.

"It is very evident," said the lieutenant, "that ever since the 1st of January the earth has been moving in a new orbit, and from some unknown cause has drawn nearer to the sun."

"No doubt about that," said Servadac; "and I suppose that, having crossed the orbit of Venus, we have a good chance of running into the orbit of Mercury."

"And finish up by a collision with the sun!" added the count.

"There is no fear of that, sir. The earth has undoubtedly entered upon a new orbit, but she is not incurring any probable risk of being precipitated into the sun."

"Can you satisfy us of that?" asked the count.

"I can, sir. I can give you a proof which I think you will own is conclusive. If, as you suppose, the earth is being drawn on so as to be precipitated against the sun, the great centre of attraction of our system, it could only be because the centrifugal and centripetal forces that cause the planets to rotate in their several orbits had been entirely suspended: in that case, indeed, the earth would rush onwards towards the sun, and in sixty-four days and a half the catastrophe you dread would inevitably happen."

"And what demonstration do you offer," asked Servadac eagerly, "that it will not happen?"

"Simply this, captain: that since the earth entered her new orbit half the sixty-four days has already elapsed, and yet it is only just recently that she has crossed the orbit of Venus, hardly one-third of the distance to be traversed to reach the sun."

The lieutenant paused to allow time for reflection, and added: "Moreover, I have every reason to believe that we are not so near the sun as we have been. The temperature has been gradually diminishing; the heat upon Gourbi Island is not greater now than we might ordinarily expect to find in Algeria. At the same time, we have the problem still unsolved that the Mediterranean has evidently been transported to the equatorial zone."

Both the count and the captain expressed themselves reassured by his representations, and observed that they must now do all in their power to discover what had become of the vast continent of Africa, of which, they were hitherto failing so completely to find a vestige.

Twenty-four hours after leaving the island, the *Dobryna* had passed over the sites where Tenes, Cherchil, Koleah, and Sidi-Feruch once had been, but of these towns not one appeared within range of the telescope. Ocean reigned supreme. Lieutenant Procope was absolutely certain that he had not mistaken his direction; the compass showed that the wind had never shifted from the west, and this, with the rate of speed as estimated by the log, combined to assure him that at this date, the 2nd of February, the schooner was in lat. 36° 49' N. and long. 3° 25' E., the very spot which ought to have been occupied by the Algerian capital. But Algiers, like all the other coast-towns, had apparently been absorbed into the bowels of the earth.

Captain Servadac, with clenched teeth and knitted brow, stood sternly, almost fiercely, regarding the boundless waste of water. His pulse beat fast as he recalled the friends and comrades with whom he had spent the last few years in that vanished city. All the images of his past life floated upon his memory; his thoughts sped away to his native France, only to return again to wonder whether the depths of ocean would reveal any traces of the Algerian metropolis.

"Is it not impossible," he murmured aloud, "that any city should disappear so completely? Would not the loftiest eminences of the city at least be visible? Surely some portion of the Casbah must still rise above the waves? The imperial fort, too, was built upon an elevation of 750 feet; it is incredible that it should be so totally submerged. Unless some vestiges of these are found, I shall begin to suspect that the whole of Africa has been swallowed in some vast abyss."

Another circumstance was most remarkable. Not a material object of any kind was to be noticed floating on the surface of the water; not one branch of a tree had been seen drifting by, nor one spar belonging to one of the numerous vessels that a month previously had been moored in the magnificent bay which stretched twelve miles across from Cape Matafuz to Point Pexade. Perhaps the depths might disclose what the surface failed to reveal, and Count Timascheff, anxious that Servadac should have every facility afforded him for solving his doubts, called for the sounding-line. Forthwith, the lead was greased and lowered. To the surprise of all, and especially of Lieutenant Procope, the line indicated a bottom at a nearly uniform depth of from four to five fathoms; and although the sounding was persevered with continuously for more than two hours over a considerable area, the differences of level were insignificant, not corresponding in any degree to what would be expected over the site of a city that had been terraced like the seats of an amphitheatre. Astounding as it seemed, what alternative was left but to suppose that the Algerian capital had been completely levelled by the flood?

The sea-bottom was composed of neither rock, mud, sand, nor shells; the sounding-lead brought up nothing but a kind of metallic dust, which glittered with a strange iridescence, and the nature of which it was impossible to determine, as it was totally unlike what had ever been known to be raised from the bed of the Mediterranean.

"You must see, lieutenant, I should think, that we are not so near the coast of Algeria as you imagined."

The lieutenant shook his head. After pondering awhile, he said: "If we were farther away I should expect to find a depth of two or three hundred fathoms instead of five fathoms. Five fathoms! I confess I am puzzled."

For the next thirty-six hours, until the 4th of February, the sea was examined and explored with the most unflagging perseverance. Its depth remained invariable, still four, or at most five, fathoms; and although its bottom was assiduously dredged, it was only to prove it barren of marine production of any type.

The yacht made its way to lat. 36° north, by reference to the charts it was tolerably certain that she was cruising over the site of the Sahel, the ridge that had separated the rich plain of the Mitidja from the sea, and of which the highest peak, Mount Bourjerah, had reached an altitude of 1,200 feet; but even this peak, which might have been expected to emerge like an islet above the surface of the sea, was nowhere to be traced. Nothing was to be done but to put about, and return in disappointment towards the north.

Thus the *Dobryna* regained the waters of the Mediterranean without discovering a trace of the missing province of Algeria.

XI
AN ISLAND TOMB

No longer then, could there be any doubt as to the annihilation of a considerable portion of the colony. Not merely had there been a submersion of the land, but the impression was more and more confirmed that the very bowels of the earth must have yawned and closed again upon a large territory. Of the rocky substratum of the province it became more evident than ever that not a trace remained, and a new soil of unknown formation had certainly taken the place of the old sandy sea-bottom. As it altogether transcended the powers of those on board to elucidate the origin of this catastrophe, it was felt to be incumbent on them at least to ascertain its extent.

After a long and somewhat wavering discussion, it was at length decided that the schooner should take advantage of the favourable wind and weather, and proceed at first towards the east, thus following the outline of what had formerly represented the coast of Africa, until that coast had been lost in boundless sea.

Not a vestige of it all remained; from Cape Matafuz to Tunis it had all gone, as though it had never been. The maritime town of Dellis, built like Algiers, amphitheatre-wise, had totally disappeared; the highest points were quite invisible; not a trace on the horizon was left of the Jurjura chain, the topmost point of which was known to have an altitude of more than 7,000 feet.

Unsparing of her fuel, the *Dobryna* made her way at full steam towards Cape Blanc. Neither Cape Negro nor Cape Serrat was to be seen. The town of Bizerta, once charming in its oriental beauty, had vanished utterly; its maraboute, or temple-tombs, shaded by magnificent palms that fringed the gulf, which by reason of its narrow mouth had the semblance of a lake, all had disappeared, giving place to a vast waste of sea, the transparent waters of which, as still demonstrated by the sounding-line, had ever the same uniform and arid bottom.

In the course of the day the schooner rounded the point where, five weeks previously, Cape Blanc had been so conspicuous an object, and she was now stemming the waters of what once had been the Bay of Tunis. But bay there was none, and the town from which it had derived its name, with the Arsenal, the Goletta, and the two peaks of Bou-Kournein, had all vanished from the view. Cape Bon, too, the most northern promontory of Africa and the point of the continent nearest to the island of Sicily, had been included in the general devastation.

Before the occurrence of the recent prodigy, the bottom of the Mediterranean just at this point had formed a sudden ridge across the Straits of Libya. The sides of the ridge had shelved to so great an extent that, while the depth of water on the summit had been little more than eleven fathoms, that on either hand of the elevation was little short of a hundred fathoms. A formation such as this plainly indicated that at some remote epoch Cape Bon had been connected with Cape Furina, the extremity of Sicily, in the same manner as Cauta has doubtless been connected with Gibraltar.

Lieutenant Procope was too well acquainted with the Mediterranean to be unaware of this peculiarity, and would not lose the opportunity of ascertaining whether the submarine ridge still existed, or whether the sea-bottom between Sicily and Africa had undergone any modification.

Both Timascheff and Servadac were much interested in watching the operations. At a sign from the lieutenant, a sailor who was stationed at the foot of the fore-shrouds dropped the sounding-lead into the water, and in reply to Procope's inquiries, reported—"Five fathoms and a flat bottom."

The next aim was to determine the amount of depression on either side of the ridge, and for this purpose the *Dobryna* was shifted for a distance of half a mile both to the right and left, and the soundings taken at each station. "Five fathoms and a flat bottom," was the unvaried announcement after each operation. Not only, therefore, was it evident that the submerged chain between Cape Bon and Cape Furina no longer existed, but it was equally clear that the convulsion had caused a general levelling of the sea-bottom, and that the soil, degenerated, as it has been said, into a metallic dust of unrecognized composition, bore no trace of the sponges, sea-anemones, star-fish, sea-nettles, hydrophytes, and shells with which the submarine rocks of the Mediterranean had hitherto been prodigally clothed.

The *Dobryna* now put about and resumed her explorations in a southerly direction. It remained, however, as remarkable as ever how completely throughout the voyage the sea continued to be deserted; all expectations of hailing a vessel bearing news from Europe were entirely falsified, so that more and more each member of the crew began to be conscious of his isolation, and to believe that the schooner, like a second Noah's ark, carried the sole survivors of a calamity that had overwhelmed the earth.

On the 9th of February the *Dobryna* passed over the site of the city of Dido, the ancient Byrsa—a Carthage, however, which was now more completely annihilated than ever Punic Carthage had been destroyed by Scipio Africanus or Roman Carthage by Hassan the Saracen.

In the evening, as the sun was sinking below the eastern horizon, Captain Servadac was lounging moodily against the taffrail. From the heaven above, where stars kept peeping fitfully from behind the moving clouds, his eye wandered mechanically to the waters below, where the long waves were rising and falling with the evening breeze.

All at once, his attention was arrested by a luminous speck straight ahead on the southern horizon. At first, imagining that he was the victim of some spectral illusion, he observed it with silent attention; but when, after some minutes, he became convinced that what he saw was actually a distant light, he appealed to one of the sailors, by whom his impression was fully corroborated. The intelligence was immediately imparted to Count Timascheff and the lieutenant.

"Is it land, do you suppose?" inquired Servadac, eagerly.

"I should be more inclined to think it is a light on board some ship," replied the count.

"Whatever it is, in another hour we shall know all about it," said Servadac.

"No, captain," interposed Lieutenant Procope; "we shall know nothing until tomorrow."

"What! not bear down upon it at once?" asked the count in surprise.

"No, sir; I should much rather lie to and wait till daylight. If we are really near land, I should be afraid to approach it in the dark."

The count expressed his approval of the lieutenant's caution, and thereupon all sail was shortened so as to keep the *Dobryna* from making any considerable progress all through the hours of night. Few as those hours were, they seemed to those on board as if their end would never come. Fearful lest the faint glimmer should at any moment cease to be visible, Hector Servadac did not quit his post upon the deck; but the light continued unchanged. It shone with about the same degree of lustre as a star of the second magnitude, and from the fact of its remaining stationary, Procope became more and more convinced that it was on land and did not belong to a passing vessel.

At sunrise every telescope was pointed with keenest interest towards the centre of attraction. The light, of course, had ceased to be visible, but in the direction where it had been seen, and at a distance of about ten miles, there was the distinct outline of a solitary island of very small extent; rather, as the count observed, it had the appearance of being the projecting summit of a mountain all but submerged. Whatever it was, it was agreed that its true character must be ascertained, not only to gratify their own curiosity, but for the benefit of all future navigators. The schooner accordingly was steered directly towards it, and in less than an hour had cast anchor within a few cables' lengths of the shore.

The little island proved to be nothing more than an arid rock rising abruptly about forty feet above the water. It had no outlying reefs, a circumstance that seemed to suggest the probability that in the recent convulsion it had sunk gradually, until it had reached its present position of equilibrium.

Without removing his eye from his telescope, Servadac exclaimed: "There is a habitation on the place; I can see an erection of some kind quite distinctly. Who can tell whether we shall not come across a human being?"

Lieutenant Procope looked doubtful. The island had all the appearance of being deserted, nor did a cannon-shot fired from the schooner have the effect of bringing any resident to the shore. Nevertheless, it was undeniable that there was a stone building situated on the top of the rock, and that this building had much the character of an Arabian mosque.

The boat was lowered and manned by the four sailors; Servadac, Timascheff and Procope were quickly rowed ashore, and lost no time in commencing their ascent of the steep acclivity. Upon reaching the summit, they found their progress arrested by a kind of wall, or rampart of singular construction, its materials consisting mainly of vases, fragments of columns, carved bas-reliefs, statues, and portions of broken stelæ, all piled promiscuously together without any pretence to artistic arrangement. They made their way into the enclosure, and finding an open door, they passed through and soon came to a second door, also open, which admitted them to the interior of the mosque, consisting of a single chamber, the walls of which were ornamented in the Arabian style by sculptures of indifferent execution. In the centre was a tomb of the very simplest kind, and above the tomb was suspended a large silver lamp with a capacious reservoir of oil, in which floated a long lighted wick, the flame of which was evidently the light that had attracted Servadac's attention on the previous night.

"Must there not have been a custodian of the shrine?" they mutually asked; but if such there had ever been, he must, they concluded, either have fled or have perished on that eventful night. Not a soul was there in charge, and the sole living occupants were a flock of wild cormorants which, startled at the entrance of the intruders, rose on wing, and took a rapid flight towards the south.

An old French prayer-book was lying on the corner of the tomb; the volume was open, and the page exposed to view was that which contained the office for the celebration of the 25th of August. A sudden revelation dashed across Servadac's mind. The solemn isolation of the island tomb, the open breviary, the ritual of the ancient anniversary, all combined to apprise him of the sanctity of the spot upon which he stood.

"The tomb of St. Louis!" he exclaimed, and his companions involuntarily followed his example, and made a reverential obeisance to the venerated monument.

It was, in truth, the very spot on which tradition asserts that the canonized monarch came to die, a spot to which for six centuries and more his countrymen had paid the homage of a pious regard. The lamp that had been kindled at the memorial shrine of a saint was now in all probability the only beacon that threw a light across the waters of the Mediterranean, and even this ere long must itself expire.

There was nothing more to explore. The three together quitted the mosque, and descended the rock to the shore, whence their boat re-conveyed them to the schooner, which was soon again on her southward voyage; and it was not long before the tomb of St. Louis, the only spot that had survived the mysterious shock, was lost to view.

XII
AT THE MERCY OF THE WINDS

As the affrighted cormorants had winged their flight towards the south, there sprang up a sanguine hope on board the schooner that land might be discovered in that direction. Thither, accordingly, it was determined to proceed, and in a few hours after quitting the island of the tomb, the *Dobryna* was traversing the shallow waters that now covered the peninsula of Dakhul, which had separated the Bay of Tunis from the Gulf of Hammamet. For two days she continued an undeviating course, and after a futile search for the coast of Tunis, reached the latitude of 34° north.

Here, on the 11th of February, there suddenly arose the cry of "Land!" and in the extreme horizon, right ahead, where land had never been before, it was true enough that a shore was distinctly to be seen. What could it be? It could not be the coast of Tripoli; for not only would that low-lying shore be quite invisible at such a distance, but it was certain, moreover, that it lay two degrees at least still further south. It was soon observed that this newly discovered land was of very irregular elevation, that it extended due east and west across the horizon, thus dividing the gulf into two separate sections and completely concealing the island of Jerba, which must lie behind. Its position was duly traced on the *Dobryna's* chart.

"How strange," exclaimed Hector Servadac, "that after sailing all this time over sea where we expected to find land, we have at last come upon land where we thought to find sea!"

"Strange, indeed," replied Lieutenant Procope; "and what appears to me almost as remarkable is that we have never once caught sight either of one of the Maltese tartans or one of the Levantine xebecs that traffic so regularly on the Mediterranean."

"Eastwards or westwards," asked the count—"which shall be our course? All farther progress to the south is checked."

"Westwards, by all means," replied Servadac quickly. "I am longing to know whether anything of Algeria is left beyond the Shelif; besides, as we pass Gourbi Island we might take Ben Zoof on board, and then make away for Gibraltar, where we should be sure to learn something, at least, of European news."

With his usual air of stately courtesy, Count Timascheff begged the captain to consider the yacht at his own disposal, and desired him to give the lieutenant instructions accordingly.

Lieutenant Procope, however, hesitated, and after revolving matters for a few moments in his mind, pointed out that as the wind was blowing directly from the west, and seemed likely to increase, if they went to the west in the teeth of the weather, the schooner would be reduced to the use of her engine only, and would have much difficulty in making good headway; on the other hand, by taking an eastward course, not only would they have the advantage of the wind, but, under steam and canvas might hope in a few days to be off the coast of Egypt, and from Alexandria or some other port they would have the same opportunity of getting tidings from Europe as they would at Gibraltar.

Intensely anxious as he was to revisit the province of Oran, and eager, too, to satisfy himself of the welfare of his faithful Ben Zoof, Servadac could not but own the reasonableness of the lieutenant's objections, and yielded to the proposal that the eastward course should be adopted. The wind gave signs, only too threatening, of the breeze rising to a gale; but, fortunately, the waves did not culminate in combers, but rather in a long swell which ran in the same direction as the vessel.

During the last fortnight the high temperature had been gradually diminishing, until it now reached an average of 20° Cent. (or 68° Fahr.), and sometimes descended as low as 15°. That this diminution was to be attributed to the change in the earth's orbit was a question that admitted of little doubt. After approaching so near to the sun as to cross the orbit of Venus, the earth must now have receded so far from the sun that its normal distance of ninety-one millions of miles was greatly increased, and the probability was great that it was approximating to the orbit of Mars, that planet which in its physical constitution most nearly resembles our own. Nor was this supposition suggested merely by the lowering of the temperature; it was strongly corroborated by the reduction of the apparent diameter of the sun's disc to the precise dimensions which it would assume to an observer actually stationed on the surface of Mars. The necessary inference that seemed to follow from these phenomena was that the earth had been projected into a new orbit, which had the form of a very elongated ellipse.

Very slight, however, in comparison was the regard which these astronomical wonders attracted on board the *Dobryna*. All interest there was too much absorbed in terrestrial matters, and in ascertaining what changes had taken place in the configuration of the earth itself, to permit much attention to be paid to its erratic movements through space.

The schooner kept bravely on her way, but well out to sea, at a distance of two miles from land. There was good need of this precaution, for so precipitous was the shore that a vessel driven upon it must inevitably have gone to pieces; it did not offer a single harbour of refuge, but, smooth and perpendicular as the walls of a fortress, it rose to a height of two hundred, and occasionally of three hundred feet. The waves dashed violently against its base. Upon the general substratum rested a massive conglomerate, the crystallizations of which rose like a forest of gigantic pyramids and obelisks.

But what struck the explorers more than anything was the appearance of singular newness that pervaded the whole of the region. It all seemed so recent in its formation that the atmosphere had had no opportunity of producing its wonted effect in softening the hardness of its lines, in rounding the sharpness of its angles, or in modifying the colour of its surface; its outline was clearly marked against the sky, and its substance, smooth and polished as though fresh from a founder's mould, glittered with the metallic brilliancy that is characteristic of pyrites. It seemed impossible to come to any other conclusion but that the land before them, continent or island, had been upheaved by subterranean forces above the surface of the sea, and that it was mainly composed of the same metallic element as had characterized the dust so frequently uplifted from the bottom.

The extreme nakedness of the entire tract was likewise very extraordinary. Elsewhere, in various quarters of the globe, there may be sterile rocks, but there are none so adamant as to be altogether unfurrowed by the crevices engendered in the moist residuum of the condensed vapour; elsewhere there may be barren steeps, but none so arid as not to afford some hold to vegetation, however low and elementary may be its type; but here all was bare, and blank, and desolate—not a symptom of vitality was visible.

Such being the condition of the adjacent land, it could hardly be a matter of surprise that all the sea-birds, the albatross, the gull, the sea-mew, sought continual refuge on the schooner; day and night they perched fearlessly upon the yards, the report of a gun failing to dislodge them, and when food of any sort was thrown upon the deck, they would dart down and fight with eager voracity for the prize. Their extreme avidity was recognized as a proof that any land where they could obtain a sustenance must be very remote.

Onwards thus for several days the *Dobryna* followed the contour of the inhospitable coast, of which the features would occasionally change, sometimes for two or three miles assuming the form of a simple arris, sharply defined as though cut by a chisel, when suddenly the prismatic lamellæ soaring in rugged confusion would again recur; but all along there was the same absence of beach or tract of sand to mark its base, neither were there any of those shoals of rock that are ordinarily found in shallow water. At rare intervals there were some narrow fissures, but not a creek available for a ship to enter to replenish its supply of water; and the wide roadsteads were unprotected and exposed to well-nigh every point of the compass.

But after sailing two hundred and forty miles, the progress of the *Dobryna* was suddenly arrested. Lieutenant Procope, who had sedulously inserted the outline of the newly revealed shore upon the maps, announced that it had ceased to run east and west, and had taken a turn due north, thus forming a barrier to their continuing their previous direction. It was, of course, impossible to conjecture how far this barrier extended; it coincided pretty nearly with the fourteenth meridian of east longitude; and if it reached, as probably it did, beyond Sicily to Italy, it was certain that the vast basin of the Mediterranean, which had washed the shores alike of Europe, Asia, and Africa, must have been reduced to about half its original area.

It was resolved to proceed upon the same plan as heretofore, following the boundary of the land at a safe distance. Accordingly, the head of the *Dobryna* was pointed north, making straight, as it was presumed, for the south of Europe. A hundred miles, or somewhat over, in that direction, and it was to be anticipated she would come in sight of Malta, if only that ancient island, the heritage in succession of Phœenicians Carthaginians, Sicilians, Romans, Vandals, Greeks, Arabians, and the knights of Rhodes, should still be undestroyed.

But Malta, too, was gone; and when, upon the 14th, the sounding-line was dropped upon its site, it was only with the same result so oftentimes obtained before.

"The devastation is not limited to Africa," observed the count.

"Assuredly not," assented the lieutenant; adding, "and I confess I am almost in despair whether we shall ever ascertain its limits. To what quarter of Europe, if Europe still exists, do you propose that I should now direct your course?"

"To Sicily, Italy, France!" ejaculated Servadac, eagerly,—"anywhere where we can learn the truth of what has befallen us."

"How if we are the sole survivors?" said the count, gravely.

Hector Servadac was silent; his own secret presentiment so thoroughly coincided with the doubts expressed by the count, that he refrained from saying another word.

The coast, without deviation, still tended towards the north. No alternative, therefore, remained than to take a westerly course and to attempt to reach the northern shores of the Mediterranean. On the 16th day the *Dobryna* essayed to start upon her altered way, but it seemed as if the elements had conspired to obstruct her progress. A furious tempest arose; the wind beat dead in the direction of the coast, and the danger incurred by a vessel of a tonnage so light was necessarily very great.

Lieutenant Procope was extremely uneasy. He took in all sail, struck his topmasts, and resolved to rely entirely on his engine. But the peril seemed only to increase. Enormous waves caught the schooner and carried her up to their crests, whence again she was plunged deep into the abysses that they left. The screw failed to keep its hold upon the water, but continually revolved with useless speed in the vacant air; and thus, although the steam was forced on to the extremest limit consistent with safety, the vessel held her way with the utmost difficulty, and recoiled before the hurricane.

Still, not a single resort for refuge did the inhospitable shore present. Again and again the lieutenant asked himself what would become of him and his comrades, even if they should survive the peril of shipwreck, and gain a footing upon the cliff. What resources could they expect to find upon that scene of desolation? What hope could they entertain that any portion of the old continent still existed beyond that dreary barrier?

It was a trying time, but throughout it all the crew behaved with the greatest courage and composure; confident in the skill of their commander, and in the stability of their ship, they performed their duties with steadiness and unquestioning obedience.

But neither skill, nor courage, nor obedience could avail; all was in vain, Despite the strain put upon her engine, the schooner, bare of canvas (for not even the smallest stay-sail could have withstood the violence of the storm), was drifting with terrific speed towards the menacing precipices, which were only a few short miles to leeward. Fully alive to the hopelessness of their situation, the crew were all on deck.

"All over with us, sir !" said Procope to the count. "I have done everything that man could do; but our case is desperate. Nothing short of a miracle can save us now. Within an hour we must go to pieces upon yonder rocks."

"Let us, then, commend ourselves to the providence of Him to Whom nothing is impossible," replied the count, in a calm, clear voice that could be distinctly heard by all; and as he spoke, he reverently uncovered an example in which he was followed by all the rest.

The destruction of the vessel seeming thus inevitable, Lieutenant Procope took the best measures he could to insure a few days' supply of food for any who might escape ashore. He ordered several cases of provisions and kegs of water to be brought on deck, and saw that they were securely lashed to some empty barrels, to make them float after the ship had gone down.

Less and less grew the distance from the shore, but no creek, no inlet, could be discerned in the towering wall of cliff, which seemed about to topple over and involve them in annihilation. Except a change of wind, or, as Procope observed a supernatural rifting of the rock, nothing could bring deliverance now. But the wind did not veer, and in a few minutes more the schooner was hardly three cables' distance from the fatal land. All were aware that their last moment had arrived. Servadac and the count grasped each others' hands for a long farewell; and, tossed by the tremendous waves, the schooner was on the very point of being hurled upon the cliff, when a ringing shout was heard. "Quick, boys, quick! Hoist the jib, and right the helm!"

Sudden and startling as the unexpected orders were, they were executed as if by magic.

The lieutenant, who had shouted from the bow, rushed astern and took the helm, and before anyone had time to speculate upon the object of his manoeuvres, he shouted again, "Look out! sharp! watch the sheets!"

An involuntary cry broke forth from all on board. But it was no cry of terror. Right ahead was a narrow opening in the solid rock; it was hardly forty feet wide. Whether it was a passage or not, it mattered little; it was at least a refuge; and, driven by wind and wave, the *Dobryna*, under the dexterous guidance of the lieutenant, dashed in between its perpendicular walls.

Had she not immured herself in a perpetual prison?

XIII
A ROYAL SALUTE

"Then I take your bishop, major," said Colonel Murphy, as he made a move that he had taken since the previous evening to consider.

"I was afraid you would," replied Major Oliphsut, looking intently at the chess-board.

Such was the way in which a long silence was broken on the morning of the 17th of February by the old calendar.

Another day elapsed before another move was made. It was a protracted game; it had, in fact, already lasted some months—the players being so deliberate, and so fearful of taking a step without the most mature consideration, that even now they were only making the twentieth move.

Both of them, moreover, were rigid disciples of the renowned Philidor, who pronounces that to play the pawns well is "the soul of chess"; and, accordingly, not one pawn had been sacrificed without a most vigorous defence.

The men who were thus beguiling their leisure were two officers in the British army—Colonel Heneage Finch Murphy and Major Sir John Temple Oliphant. Remarkably similar in personal appearance, they were hardly less so in personal character. Both of them were about forty years of age; both of them were tall and fair, with bushy whiskers and mustaches; both of them were phlegmatic in temperament, and both much addicted to the wearing of their uniforms. They were proud of their nationality, and exhibited a manifest dislike, verging upon contempt, for everything foreign. Probably they would have felt no surprise if they had been told that Anglo-Saxons were fashioned out of some specific clay, the properties of which surpassed the investigation of chemical analysis. Without any intentional disparagement they might, in a certain way, be compared to two scarecrows which, though perfectly harmless in themselves, inspire some measure of respect, and are excellently adapted to protect the territory intrusted to their guardianship.

English-like, the two officers had made themselves thoroughly at home in the station abroad in which it had been their lot to be quartered. The faculty of colonization seems to be indigenous to the native character; once let an Englishman plant his national standard on the surface of the moon, and it would not be long before a colony would be established around it.

The officers had a servant, named Kirke, and a company of ten soldiers of the line. This party of thirteen men were apparently the sole survivors of an overwhelming catastrophe, which on the 1st of January had transformed an enormous rock, garrisoned with well-nigh two thousand troops, into an insignificant island far out to sea. But although the transformation had been so marvellous, it cannot be said that either Colonel Murphy or Major Oliphant had made much demonstration of astonishment.

"This is all very peculiar, Sir John," observed the colonel.

"Yes, colonel; very peculiar," replied the major.

"England will be sure to send for us," said one officer.

"No doubt she will," answered the other.

Accordingly, they came to the mutual resolution that they would "stick to their post."

To say the truth, it would have been a difficult matter for the gallant officers to do otherwise; they had but one small boat; therefore, it was well that they made a virtue of necessity, and resigned themselves to patient expectation of the British ship which, in due time, would bring relief.

They had no fear of starvation. Their island was mined with subterranean stores, more than ample for thirteen men—nay, for thirteen Englishmen—for the next five years at least. Preserved meat, ale, brandy—all were in abundance; consequently, as the men expressed it, they were in this respect "all right."

Of course, the physical changes that had taken place had attracted the notice both of officers and men. But the reversed position of east and west, the diminution of the force of gravity, the altered rotation of the earth, and her projection upon a new orbit, were all things that gave them little concern and no uneasiness; and when the colonel and the major had replaced the pieces on the board which had been disturbed by the convulsion, any surprise they might have felt at the chess-men losing some portion of their weight was quite forgotten in the satisfaction of seeing them retain their equilibrium.

One phenomenon, however, did not fail to make its due impression upon the men; this was the diminution in the length of day and night. Three days after the catastrophe, Corporal Pim, on behalf of himself and his comrades, solicited a formal interview with the officers. The request having been granted, Pim, with the nine soldiers, all punctiliously wearing the regimental tunic of scarlet and trousers of invisible green, presented themselves at the door of the colonel's room, where he and his brother-officer were continuing their game. Raising his hand respectfully to his cap, which he wore poised jauntily over his right ear, and scarcely held on by the strap below his under lip, the corporal waited permission to speak.

After a lingering survey of the chess-board, the colonel slowly lifted his eyes, and said with official dignity, "Well, men, what is it?"

"First of all, sir," replied the corporal, "we want to speak to you about our pay, and then we wish to have a word with the major about our rations."

"Say on, then," said Colonel Murphy. "What is it about your pay?"

"Just this, sir; as the days are only half as long as they were, we should like to know whether our pay is to be diminished in proportion."

The colonel was taken somewhat aback, and did not reply immediately, though by some significant nods towards the major, he indicated that he thought the question very reasonable. After a few moments' reflection, he replied, "It must, I think, be allowed that your pay was calculated from sunrise to sunrise; there was no specification of what the interval should be. Your pay will continue as before. England can afford it.

A buzz of approval burst involuntarily from all the men, but military discipline and the respect due to their officers' kept them in check from any boisterous demonstration of their satisfaction.

"And now, corporal, what is your business with me?" asked Major Oliphant.

"We want to know whether, as the days are only six hours long, we are to have but two meals instead of four?"

The officers looked at each other, and by their glances agreed that the corporal was a man of sound common sense.

"Eccentricities of nature," said the major, "cannot interfere with military regulations. It is true that there will be but an interval of an hour and a half between them, but the rule stands good—four meals a day. England is too rich to grudge her soldiers any of her soldiers' due. Yes; four meals a day."

"Hurrah!" shouted the soldiers, unable this time to keep their delight within the bounds of military decorum; and, turning to the right-about, they marched away, leaving the officers to renew the all absorbing game.

However confident everyone upon the island might profess to be that succour would be sent them from their native land—for Britain never abandons any of her sons—it could not be disguised that that succour was somewhat tardy in making its appearance. Many and various were the conjectures to account for the delay. Perhaps England was engrossed with domestic matters, or perhaps she was absorbed in diplomatic difficulties; or perchance, more likely than all, Northern Europe had received no tidings of the convulsion that had shattered the south. The whole party throve remarkably well upon the liberal provisions of the commissariat department, and if the officers failed to show the same tendency to *embonpoint* which was fast becoming characteristic of the men, it was only because they deemed it due to their rank to curtail any indulgences which might compromise the fit of their uniform.

On the whole, time passed indifferently well. An Englishman rarely suffers from *ennui*, and then only in his own country, when required to conform to what he calls "the humbug of society"; and the two officers, with their similar tastes, ideas, and dispositions, got on together admirably. It is not to be questioned that they were deeply affected by a sense of regret for their lost comrades, and astounded beyond measure at finding themselves the sole survivors of a garrison of 1,895 men, but with true British pluck and self-control, they had done nothing more than draw up a report that 1883 names were missing from the muster-roll.

The island itself, the sole surviving fragment of an enormous pile of rock that had reared itself some 1,600 feet above the sea, was not, strictly speaking, the only land that was visible; for about twelve miles to the south there was another island, apparently the very counterpart of what was now occupied by the Englishmen. It was only natural that this should awaken some interest even in the most imperturbable minds, and there was no doubt that the two officers, during one of the rare intervals when they were not absorbed in their game, had decided that it would be desirable at least to ascertain whether the island was deserted, or whether it might not be occupied by some others, like themselves, survivors from the general catastrophe. Certain it is that one morning, when the weather was bright and calm, they had embarked alone in the little boat, and been absent for seven or eight hours. Not even to Corporal Pim did they communicate the object of their excursion, nor say one syllable as to its result, and it could only be inferred from their manner that they were quite satisfied with what they had seen; and very shortly afterwards Major Oliphant was observed to draw up a lengthy document, which was no sooner finished than it was formally signed and sealed with the seal of the 33rd Regiment. It was directed:

TO THE FIRST LORD OF THE ADMIRALTY.
LONDON.

and kept in readiness for transmission by the first ship that should hail in sight. But time elapsed, and here was the 18th of February without an opportunity having been afforded for any communication with the British Government.

At breakfast that morning, the colonel observed to the major that he was under the most decided impression that the 18th of February was a royal anniversary;

and he went on to say that, although he had received no definite instructions on the subject, he did not think that the peculiar circumstances under which they found themselves should prevent them from giving the day its due military honours.

The major quite concurred; and it was mutually agreed that the occasion must be honoured by a bumper of port, and by a royal salute. Corporal Pim must be sent for. The corporal soon made his appearance, smacking his lips, having, by a ready intuition, found a pretext for a double morning ration of spirits.

"The 18th of February, you know, Pim," said the colonel; "we must have a salute of twenty-one guns."

"Very good," replied Pim, a man of few words.

"And take care that your fellows don't get their arms and legs blown off," added the officer.

"Very good, sir," said the corporal; and he made his salute and withdrew.

Of all the bombs, howitzers, and various species of artillery with which the fortress had been crowded, one solitary piece remained. This was a cumbrous muzzle-loader of 9-inch calibre, and, in default of the smaller ordnance generally employed for the purpose, had to be brought into requisition for the royal salute.

A sufficient number of charges having been provided, the corporal brought his men to the reduct, whence the gun's mouth projected over a sloping embrasure. The two officers, in cocked hats and full staff uniform, attended to take charge of the proceedings. The gun was manoeuvred in strict accordance with the rules of "The Artilleryman's Manual," and the firing commenced.

Not unmindful of the warning he had received, the corporal was most careful between each discharge to see that every vestige of fire was extinguished, so as to prevent an untimely explosion while the men were reloading; and accidents, such as so frequently mar public rejoicings, were all happily avoided.

Much to the chagrin of both Colonel Murphy and Major Oliphant, the effect of the salute fell altogether short of their anticipations. The weight of the atmosphere was so reduced that there was comparatively little resistance to the explosive force of the gases, liberated at the cannon's mouth, and there was consequently none of the reverberation, like rolling thunder, that ordinarily follows the discharge of heavy artillery.

Twenty times had the gun been fired, and it was on the point of being loaded for the last time, when the colonel laid his hand upon the arm of the man who had the ramrod. "Stop!" he said; "we will have a ball this time. Let us put the range of the piece to the test."

"A good idea!" replied the major. "Corporal, you hear the orders."

In quick time an artillery-wagon was on the spot, and the men lifted out a full-sized shot, weighing 200 lbs., which, under ordinary circumstances, the cannon would carry about four miles. It was proposed, by means of telescopes, to note the place where the ball first touched the water, and thus to obtain an approximation sufficiently accurate as to the true range.

Having been duly charged with powder and ball, the gun was raised to an angle of something under 45°, so as to allow proper development to the curve that the projectile would make, and, at a signal from the major, the light was applied to the priming.

"Heavens!" "By all that's good!" exclaimed both officers in one breath, as, standing open-mouthed, they hardly knew whether they were to believe the evidence of their own senses. "Is it possible?"

The diminution of the force of attraction at the earth's surface was so considerable that the ball had sped beyond the horizon.

"Incredible!" ejaculated the colonel.

"Incredible!" echoed the major.

"Six miles at least!" observed the one.

"Ay, more than that!" replied the other.

Awhile, they gazed at the sea and at each other in mute amazement. But in the midst of their perplexity, what sound was that which startled them? Was it mere fancy? Was it the reverberation of the cannon still booming in their ears? Or was it not truly the report of another and a distant gun in answer to their own? Attentively and eagerly they listened. Twice, thrice did the sound repeat itself. It was quite distinct. There could be no mistake.

"I told you so," cried the colonel, triumphantly. "I knew our country would not forsake us; it is an English ship, no doubt."

In half an hour two masts were visible above the horizon. "See! Was I not right? Our country was sure to send to our relief. Here is the ship."

"Yes," replied the major; "she responded to our gun."

"It is to be hoped," muttered the corporal, "that our ball has done her no damage."

Before long the hull was full in sight. A long trail of smoke betokened her to be a steamer; and very soon, by the aid of the glass, it could be ascertained that she was a schooner-yacht, and making straight for the island. A flag at her masthead fluttered in the breeze, and towards this the two officers, with the keenest attention, respectively adjusted their glasses.

Simultaneously the two telescopes were lowered. The colonel and the major stared at each other in blank astonishment. "Russian!" they gasped.

And true it was that the flag that floated at the head of yonder mast was the blue cross of Russia.

XIV
SENSITIVE NATIONALITY

When the schooner had approached the island, the Englishmen were able to make out the name "*Dobryna*" painted on the stern. A sinuous irregularity of the coast had formed a kind of cove, which, though hardly spacious enough for a few fishing-smacks, would afford the yacht a temporary anchorage, so long as the wind did not blow violently from either west or south. Into this cove the *Dobryna* was duly signalled, and as soon as she was safely moored, she lowered her four-oar, and Count Timascheff and Captain Servadac made their way at once to land.

Colonel Heneage Finch Murphy and Major Sir John Temple Oliphant stood, grave and prim, formally awaiting the arrival of their visitors. Captain Servadac, with the uncontrolled vivacity natural to a Frenchman, was the first to speak.

"A joyful sight, gentlemen!" he exclaimed. "It will give us unbounded pleasure to shake hands again with some of our fellow-creatures. You, no doubt have escaped the same disaster as ourselves."

But the English officers, neither by word nor gesture, made the slightest acknowledgment of this familiar greeting.

"What news can you give us of France, England, or Russia?" continued Servadac, perfectly unconscious of the stolid rigidity with which his advances were received. "We are anxious to hear anything you can tell us. Have you had communications with Europe? Have you—"

"To whom have we the honour of speaking?" at last interposed Colonel Murphy, in the coldest and most measured tone, and drawing himself up to his full height.

"Ah! how stupid! I forgot," said Servadac, with the slightest possible shrug of the shoulders; "we have not been introduced."

Then, with a wave of his hand towards his companion, who meanwhile had exhibited a reserve hardly less than that of the British officers, he said:

"Allow me to introduce you to Count Wassili Timascheff."

"Major Sir John Temple Oliphant," replied the colonel.

The Russian and the Englishman mutually exchanged the stiffest of bows.

"I have the pleasure of introducing Captain Servadac," said the count in his turn.

"And this is Colonel Heneage Finch Murphy," was the major's grave rejoinder.

More bows were interchanged and the ceremony brought to its due conclusion. It need hardly be said that the conversation had been carried on in French, a language which is generally known both by Russians and Englishmen—a circumstance that is probably in some measure to be accounted for by the refusal of Frenchmen to learn either Russian or English.

The formal preliminaries of etiquette being thus complete, there was no longer any obstacle to a freer intercourse. The colonel, signing to his guests to follow, led the way to the apartment occupied jointly by himself and the major, which, although only a kind of casemate hollowed in the rock, nevertheless wore a general air of comfort. Major Oliphant accompanied them, and all four having taken their seats, the conversation started.

Irritated and disgusted at all the cold formalities, Hector Servadac resolved to leave all the talking to the count; and he, quite aware that the Englishmen would adhere to the fiction that they could be supposed to know nothing that had transpired previous to the introduction, felt himself obligated to recapitulate matters from the very beginning.

"You must be aware, gentlemen," began the count, "that a most singular catastrophe occurred on the 1st of January last. Its cause, its limits we have utterly failed to discover, but from the appearance of the island on which we find you here, you have evidently experienced its devastating consequences."

The Englishmen, in silence, bowed assent.

"Captain Servadac, who accompanies me," continued the count, "has been most severely tried by the disaster. Engaged as he was in an important mission as a staff-officer in Algeria—"

"A French colony, I believe," interposed Major Oliphant, half shutting his eyes with an expression of supreme indifference.

Servadac was on the point of making some cutting retort, but Count Timascheff, without allowing the interruption to be noticed, calmly continued his narrative:

"It was near the mouth of the Shelif that a portion of Africa, on that eventful night, was transformed into an island which alone survived; the rest of the vast continent disappeared as completely as if it had never been."

The announcement seemed by no means startling to the phlegmatic colonel.

"Indeed!" was all he said.

"And where were you?" asked Major Oliphant.

"I was out at sea, cruising in my yacht hard by; and I look upon it as a miracle, and nothing less, that I and my crew escaped with our lives."

"I congratulate you on your luck," replied the major.

The count resumed: "It was about a month after the great disruption that I was sailing—my engine having sustained some damage in the shock—along the Algerian coast, and had the pleasure of meeting with my previous acquaintance, Captain Servadac, who was resident upon the island with his orderly, Ben Zoof."

"Ben who?" inquired the major.

"Zoof! Ben Zoof!" ejaculated Servadac, who could scarcely shout loud enough to relieve his pent-up feelings.

Ignoring this ebulition of the captain's spleen, the count went on to say: "Captain Servadac was naturally most anxious to get what news he could. Accordingly, he left his servant on the island in charge of his horses, and came on board the *Dobryna* with me. We were quite at a loss to know where we should steer, but decided to direct our course to what previously had been the east, in order that we might, if possible, discover the colony of Algeria; but of Algeria not a trace remained."

The colonel curled his lip, insinuating only too plainly that to him it was by no means surprising that a French colony should be wanting in the element of stability. Servadac observed the supercilious look, and half rose to his feet, but, smothering his resentment, took his seat again without speaking.

"The devastation, gentlemen," said the count, who persistently refused to recognize the Frenchman's irritation, "everywhere was terrible and complete. Not only was Algeria lost, but there was no trace of Tunis, except one solitary rock which was crowned by an ancient tomb of one of the kings of France—"

"Louis the Ninth, I presume," observed the colonel.

"Saint Louis," blurted out Servadac, savagely. Colonel Murphy slightly smiled.

Proof against all interruption, Count Timascheff, as if he had not heard it, went on without pausing. He related how the schooner had pushed her way onwards to the south, and had reached the Gulf of Cabes; and how she had ascertained for certain that the Sahara Sea had no longer an existsnce.

The smile of disdain again crossed the colonel's face; he could not conceal his opinion that such a destiny for the work of a Frenchman could be no matter of surprise.

"Our next discovery," continued the count, "was that a new coast had been upheaved right along in front of the coast of Tripoli, the geological formation of which was altogether strange, and which extended to the north as far as the proper place of Malta."

"And Malta," cried Servadac, unable to control himself any longer; "Malta—town, forts, soldiers, governor, and all—has vanished just like Algeria."

For a moment a cloud rested upon the colonel's brow, only to give place to an expression of decided incredulity.

"The statement seems highly incredible," he said.

"Incredible?" repeated Servadac. "Why is it that you doubt my word?"

The captain's rising wrath did not prevent the colonel from replying coolly, "Because Malta belongs to England."

"I can't help that," answered Servadac, sharply; "it has gone just as utterly as if it had belonged to China."

Colonel Murphy turned deliberately away from Servadac, and appealed to the count: "Do you not think you may have made some error, count, in reckoning the bearings of your yacht?"

"No, colonel, I am quite certain of my reckonings; and not only can I testify that Malta has disappeared, but I can affirm that a large section of the Mediterranean has been closed in by a new continent. After the most anxious investigation, we could discover only one narrow opening in all the coast, and it is by following that little channel that we have made our way hither. England, I fear, has suffered grievously by the late catastrophe. Not only has Malta been entirely lost, but of the Ionian Islands that were under England's protection, there seems to be but little left."

"Ay, you may depend upon it," said Servadac, breaking in upon the conversation petulantly, "your grand resident Lord High Commissioner has not much to congratulate himself about in the condition of Corfu."

The Englishmen were mystified.

"Corfu, did you say?" asked Major Oliphant.

"Yes, Corfu; I said Corfu," replied Servadac, with a sort of malicious triumph.

The officers were speechless with astonishment. The silence of bewilderment was broken at length by Count Timascheff making inquiry whether nothing had been heard from England, either by telegraph or by any passing ship.

"No," said the colonel; "not a ship has passed; and the cable is broken."

"But do not the Italian telegraphs assist you?" continued the count.

"Italian! I do not comprehend you. You must mean the Spanish, surely."

"How?" demanded Timascheff.

"Confound it!" cried the impatient Servadac. "What matters whether it be Spanish or Italian? Tell us, have you had no communication at all from Europe?—no news of any sort from London?"

"Hitherto, none whatever," replied the colonel; adding with a stately emphasis, "but we shall be sure to have tidings from England before long."

"Whether England is still in existence or not, I suppose," said Servadac, in a tone of irony.

The Englishmen started simultaneously to their feet.

"England in existence?" the colonel cried. "England! Ten times more probable that France—"

"France!" shouted Servadac in a passion. "France is not an island that can be submerged; France is an integral portion of a solid continent. France, at least, is safe."

A scene appeared inevitable, and Count Timascheff's efforts to conciliate the excited parties were of small avail.

"You are at home here," said Servadac, with as much calmness as he could command; "it will be advisable, I think, for this discussion to be carried on in the open air." And hurriedly he left the room. Followed immediately by the others, he led the way to a level piece of ground, which he considered he might fairly claim as neutral territory.

"Now, gentlemen," he began haughtily, "permit me to represent that, in spite of any loss France may have sustained in the fate of Algeria, France is ready to answer any provocation that affects her honour. Here I am the representative of my country, and here, on neutral ground—"

"Neutral ground?" objected Colonel Murphy; "I beg your pardon. This, Captain Servadac, is English territory. Do you not see the English flag?" and, as he spoke, he pointed with national pride to the British standard floating over the top of the island.

"Pshaw!" cried Servadac, with a contemptuous sneer; "that flag, you know, has been hoisted but a few short weeks."

"That flag has floated where it is for ages," asserted the colonel.

"An imposture!" shouted Servadac, as he stamped with rage.

Recovering his composure in a degree, he continued:

"Can you suppose that I am not aware that this island on which we find you is what remains of the Ionian representative republic, over which you English exercise the right of protection, but have no claim of government?"

The colonel and the major looked at each other in amazement.

Although Count Timascheff secretly sympathized with Servadac he had carefully refrained from taking part in the dispute; but he was on the point of interfering, when the colonel, in a greatly subdued tone, begged to be allowed to speak.

"I begin to apprehend," he said, "that you must be labouring under some strange mistake. There is no room for questioning that the territory here is England's—England's by right of conquest; ceded to England by the Treaty of Utrecht. Three times, indeed—in 1727, 1779, and 1792—France and Spain have disputed our title, but always to no purpose. You are, I assure you, at the present moment, as much on English soil as if you were in London, in the middle of Trafalgar Square."

It was now the turn of the captain and the count to look surprised. "Are we not, then, in Corfu?" they asked.

"You are at Gibraltar," replied the colonel.

Gibraltar! The word fell like a thunderclap upon their ears. Gibraltar! the western extremity of the Mediterranean! Why, had they not been sailing persistently to the east? Could they be wrong in imagining that they had reached the Ionian Islands? What new mystery was this?

Count Timascheff was about to proceed with a more rigorous investigation, when the attention of all was arrested by a loud outcry. Turning round, they saw that the crew of the *Dobryna* was in hot dispute with the English soldiers. A general altercation had arisen from a disagreement between the sailor Panofka and Corporal Pim. It had transpired that the cannon-ball fired in experiment from the island had not only damaged one of the spars of the schooner, but had broken Panofka's pipe, and, moreover, had just grazed his nose, which, for a Russian's, was unusually long. The discussion over this mishap led to mutual recriminations, till the sailors had almost come to blows with the garrison.

Servadac was just in the mood to take Panofka's part, which drew fom Major Oliphant the remark that England could not be held responsible for any accidental injury done by her cannon, and if the Russian's long nose came in the way of the ball, the Russian must submit to the mischance.

This was too much for Count Timascheff, and having poured out a torrent of angry invective against the English officers, he ordered his crew to embark immediately.

"We shall meet again," said Servadac, as they pushed off from shore.

"Whenever you please," was the cool reply.

The geographical mystery haunted the minds of both the count and the captain, and they felt they could never rest till they had ascertained what had become of their respective countries. They were glad to be on board again, that they might resume their voyage of investigation, and in two hours were out of sight of the sole remaining fragment of Gibraltar.

XV
AN ENIGMA FROM THE SEA

Lieutenant Procope had been left on board in charge of the *Dobryna*, and on resuming the voyage it was a task of some difficulty to make him understand the fact that had just come to light. Some hours were spent in discussion and in attempting to penetrate the mysteries of the situation.

There were certain things of which they were perfectly certain. They could be under no misapprehension as to the distance they had positively sailed from Gourbi Island towards the east before their further progress was arrested by the unknown shore; as nearly as possible that was fifteen degrees; the length of the narrow strait by which they had made their way across that land to regain the open sea was about three miles and a half; thence onward to the island, which they had been assured, on evidence that they could not disbelieve, to be upon the site of Gibraltar, was four degrees; while from Gibraltar to Gourbi Island was seven degrees or but little more. What was it altogether? Was it not less than thirty degrees? In that latitude, the degree of longitude represents eight and forty miles. What, then, did it all amount to? Indubitably, to less than 1,400 miles. So brief a voyage would bring the *Dobryna* once again to her starting point, or, in other words, would enable her to complete the circumnavigation of the globe. How changed the condition of things! Previously, to sail from Malta to Gibraltar by an eastward course would have involved the passage of the Suez Canal, the Red Sea, the Indian Ocean, the Pacific, the Atlantic; but what had happened now? Why, Gibraltar had been reached as if it had been just at Corfu, and some three hundred and thirty degrees of the earth's circuit had vanished utterly.

After allowing for a certain margin of miscalculation, the main fact remained undeniable; and the necessary inference that Lieutenant Procope drew from the round of the earth being completed in 1,400 miles, was that the earth's diameter had been reduced by about fifteen sixteenths of its length.

"If that be so," observed the count, "it accounts for some of the strange phenomena we witness. If our world has become so insignificant a spheroid, not only has its gravity diminished, but its rotary speed has been accelerated; and this affords an adequate explanation of our days and nights being thus curtailed. But how about the new orbit in which we are moving?"

He paused and pondered, and then looked at Procope as though awaiting from him some further elucidation of the difficulty. The lieutenant hesitated. When, in a few moments, he began to speak. Servadac smiled intelligently, anticipating the answer he was about to hear.

"My conjecture is," said Procope, "that a fragment of considerable magnitude has been detached from the earth; that it has carried with it an envelope of the earth's atmosphere, and that it is now travelling through the solar system in an orbit that does not correspond at all with the proper orbit of the earth."

The hypothesis was plausible; but what a multitude of bewildering speculations it entailed! If, in truth, a certain mass had been broken off from the terrestrial sphere, whither would it wend its way? What would be the measure of the eccentricity of its path? What would be its period round the sun? Might it not, like a comet, be carried away into the vast infinity of space? or, on the other hand, might it not be attracted to the great central source of light and heat, and be absorbed in it? Did its orbit correspond with the plane of the ecliptic? and was there no chance of its ever uniting again with the globe, from which it had been torn off by so sudden and violent a disruption.

A thoughtful silence fell upon them all, which Servadac was the first to break. "Lieutenant," he said, "your explanation is ingenious, and accounts for many appearances; but it seems to me that in one point it fails."

"How so?" replied Procope. "To my mind the theory meets all objections."

"I think not," Servadac answered. "In one point, at least, it appears to me to break down completely."

"What is that?" asked the lieutenant.

"Stop a moment," said the captain. "Let us see that we understand each other right. Unless I mistake you, your hypothesis is that a fragment of the earth, comprising the Mediterranean and its shores from Gibraltar to Malta, has been developed into a new asteroid, which is started on an independent orbit in the solar regions. Is not that your meaning?"

"Precisely so," the lieutenant acquiesced.

"Well, then," continued Servadac, "it seems to me to be at fault in this respect: it fails, and fails completely, to account for the geological character of the land that we have found now encompassing this sea. Why, if the new land is a fragment of the old—why does it not retain its old formation? What has become of the granite and the calcareous deposits? How is it that these should all be changed into a mineral concrete with which we have no acquaintance?"

No doubt, it was a serious objection; for, however likely it might be that a mass of the earth on being detached would be eccentric in its movements, there was no probable reason to be alleged why the material of its substance should undergo so complete a change. There was nothing to account for the fertile shores, rich in vegetation, being transformed into rocks arid and barren beyond precedent.

The lieutenant felt the difficulty, and owned himself unprepared to give at once an adequate solution; nevertheless, he declined to renounce his theory. He asserted that the arguments in favour of it carried conviction to his mind, and that he entertained no doubt but that, in the course of time, all apparently antagonistic circumstances would be explained so as to become consistent with the view he took. He was careful, however, to make it understood that with respect to the original cause of the disruption he had no theory to offer; and although he knew what expansion might be the result of subterranean forces, he did not venture to say that he considered it sufficient to produce so tremendous an effect. The origin of the catastrophe was a problem still to be solved.

"Ah! well," said Servadac, "I don't know that it matters much where our new little planet comes from, or what it is made of, if only it carries France along with it."

"And Russia," added the count.

"And Russia, of course," said Servadac, with a polite bow.

There was, however, not much room for this sanguine expectation, for if a new asteroid had thus been brought into existence, it must be a sphere of extremely limited dimensions, and there could be little chance that it embraced more than the merest fraction of either France or Russia. As to England, the total cessation of all telegraphic communication between her shores and Gibraltar was a virtual proof that England was beyond its compass.

And what was the true measurement of the new little world? At Gourbi Island the days and nights were of equal length, and this seemed to indicate that it was situated on the equator; hence the distance by which the two poles stood apart would be half what had been reckoned would be the distance completed by the *Dobryna* in her circuit. That distance had been already estimated to be something under 1,400 miles, so that the Arctic Pole of their recently fashioned world must be about 350 miles to the north, and the Antarctic about 350 miles to the south of the island. Compare these calculations with the map, and it is at once apparent that the northernmost limit barely touched the coast of Provence, while the southernmost reached to about lat. 29° N., and fell in the heart of the desert. The practical test of these conclusions would be made by future investigation, but meanwhile the fact appeared very much to strengthen the presumption that, if Lieutenant Procope had not arrived at the whole truth, he had made a considerable advance towards it.

The weather, ever since the storm that had driven the *Dobryna* into the creek, had been magnificent. The wind continued favourable, and now under both steam and canvas, she made a rapid progress towards the north, a direction in which she was free to go in consequence of the total disappearance of the Spanish coast, from Gibraltar right away to Alicante. Malaga, Aboeris, Cape Gata, Cartagena. Cape Palos—all were gone. The sea was rolling over the southern extent of the peninsula, so that the yacht advanced to the latitude of Seville before it sighted any land at all, and then, not shores such as the shores of Andalusia, but a bluff and precipitous cliff, in its geological features resembling exactly the stern and barren rock that she had coasted beyond the site of Malta. Here the sea made a decided indentation on the coast; it ran up in an acute-angled triangle till its apex coincided, with the very spot upon which Madrid had stood. But as hitherto the sea had encroached upon the land, the land in its turn now encroached upon the sea; for a frowning headland stood out far into the basin of the Mediterranean, and formed a promontory stretching out beyond the proper places of the Balearic Isles. Curiosity was all alive. There was the intensest interest awakened to determine whether any vestige could be traced of Majorca, Minorca, or any of the group, and it was during a deviation from the direct course for the purpose of a more thorough scrutiny, that one of the sailors raised a thrill of general excitement by shouting, "A bottle in the sea!"

Here, then, at length was a communication from the outer world. Surely now they would find a document which would throw some light upon all the mysteries that had happened? Had not the day now dawned that should set their speculations all at rest?

It was the morning of the 21st of February. The count, the captain, the lieutenant, everybody hurried to the forecastle; the schooner was dexterously put about, and all was eager impatience until the supposed bottle was hauled on deck.

It was not, however, a bottle; it proved to be a round leather telescope-case, about a foot long, and the first thing to do before investigating its contents was to make a careful examination of its exterior. The lid was fastened on by wax, and so securely that it would take a long immersion before any water could penetrate; there was no maker's name to be deciphered; but impressed very plainly with a seal on the wax were the two initials "P. R."

When the scrutiny of the outside was finished, the wax was removed and the cover opened, and the lieutenant drew out a slip of ruled paper, evidently torn from a common note-book. The paper had an inscription written in four lines, which were remarkable for the profusion of notes of admiration and interrogation with which they were interspersed:

"GALLIA???
AB SOLE, AU 15 *FÉV.* 59.000.000 L.!
CHEMIN PARCOURU DE *JANV. À FÉV.* 82.000.000 L.!!
VA BENE! ALL RIGHT!! PARFAIT!!!

There was a general sigh of disappointment. They turned the paper over and over, and handed it from one to another. "What does it all mean?" exclaimed the count.

"Something mysterious here!" said Servadac. "But yet," he continued, after a pause, "one thing is tolerably certain: on the 15th, six days ago, someone was alive to write it."

"Yes; I presume there is no reason to doubt the accuracy of the date," assented the count.

To this strange conglomeration of French, English, Italian, and Latin, there was no signature attached; nor was there anything to give a clue as to the locality in which it had been committed to the waves. A telescope-case would probably be the property of some one on board a ship; and the figures obviously referred to the astronomical wonders that had been experienced.

To these general observations Captain Servadac objected that he thought it unlikely that any one on board a ship would use a telescope-case for this purpose, but would be sure to use a bottle as being more secure; and, accordingly, he should rather be inclined to believe that the message had been set afloat by some *savant* left alone, perchance, upon some isolated coast.

"But, however interesting it might be," observed the count, "to know the author of the lines, to us it is of far greater moment to ascertain their meaning."

And taking up the paper again, he said, "Perhaps we might analyze it word by word, and from its detached parts gather some clue to its sense as a whole."

"What can be the meaning of all that cluster of interrogations after Gallia?" asked Servadac.

Lieutenant Procope, who had hitherto not spoken, now broke his silence by saying, "I beg, gentlemen, to submit my opinion that this document goes very far to confirm my hypothesis that a fragment of the earth has been precipitated into space."

Captain Servadac hesitated, and then replied, "Even if it does, I do not see how it accounts in the least for the geological character of the new asteroid."

"But will you allow me for one minute to take my supposition for granted?" said Procope. "If a new little planet has been formed, as I imagine, by disintegration from the old, I should conjecture that Gallia is the name assigned to it by the writer of this paper. The very notes of interrogation are significant that he was in doubt what he should write."

"You would presume that he was a Frenchman?" asked the count.

"I should think so," replied the lieutenant.

"Not much doubt about that," said Servadac; "it is all in French, except a few scattered words of English, Latin, and Italian, inserted to attract attention. He could not tell into whose hands the message would fall first."

"Well, then," said Count Timascheff, "we seem to have found a name for the new world we occupy."

"But what I was going especially to observe," continued the lieutenant, "is that the distance, 59,000,000 leagues, represents precisely the distance we ourselves were from the sun on the 15th. It was on that day we crossed the orbit of Mars."

"Yes, true," assented the others.

"And the next line," said the lieutenant, after reading it aloud, "apparently registers the distance traversed by Gallia, the new little planet, in her own orbit. Her speed, of course, we know by Kepler's laws, would vary according to her distance from the sun, and if she were—as I conjecture from the temperature at that date—on the 15th of January, at her perihelion, she would be traveling twice as fast as the earth, which moves at the rate of between 50,000 and 60,000 miles an hour."

"You think, then," said Servadac, with a smile, "you have determined the perihelion of our orbit; but how about the aphelion? Can you form a judgment as to what distance we are likely to be carried?"

"You are asking too much," remonstrated the count.

"I confess," said the lieutenant, "that just at present I am not able to clear away the uncertainty of the future; but I feel confident that by careful observation at various points we shall arrive at conclusions which not only will determine our path, but perhaps may clear up the mystery about our geological structure."

"Allow me to ask," said Count Timascheff, "whether such a new asteriod would not be subject to ordinary mechanical laws, and whether, once started, it would not have an orbit that must be immutable?"

"Decidedly it would, so long as it was undisturbed by the attraction of some considerable body; but we must recollect that, compared to the great planets, Gallia must be almost infinitesimally small, and so might be attracted by a force that is irresistible."

"Altogether, then," said Servadac, "we seem to have settled it to our entire satisfaction that we must be the population of a young little world called Gallia. Perhaps some day we may have the honour of being registered among the minor planets."

"No chance of that," quickly rejoined Lieutenant Procope. "Those minor planets all are known to rotate in a narrow zone between the orbits of Mars and Jupiter; in their perihelia they cannot approximate the sun as we have done; we shall not be classed with them."

"Our lack of instruments," said the count, "is much to be deplored; it baffles our investigations in every way."

"Ah, never mind! Keep up your courage, count!" said Servadac, cheerily.

And Lieutenant Procope renewed his assurances that he entertained good hopes that every perplexity would soon be solved.

"I suppose," remarked the count, "that we cannot attribute much importance to the last line:

Va bene! All right!! Parfait!!!

The captain answered, "At least, it shows that whoever wrote it had no murmuring or complaint to make, but was quite content with the new order of things."

XVI
THE RESIDUUM OF A CONTINENT

Almost unconsciously, the voyagers in the *Dobryna* fell into the habit of using Gallia as the name of the new world in which they became aware they must be making an extraordinary excursion through the realms of space. Nothing, however, was allowed to divert them from their ostensible object of making a survey of the coast of the Mediterranean, and accordingly they persevered in following that singular boundary which had revealed itself to their extreme astonishment.

Having rounded the great promontory that had barred her farther progress to the north, the schooner skirted its upper edge. A few more leagues and they ought to be abreast of the shores of France. Yes, of France.

But who shall describe the feelings of Hector Servadac when, instead of the charming outline of his native land, he beheld nothing but a solid boundary of savage rock? Who shall paint the look of consternation with which he gazed upon the stony rampart—rising perpendicularly for a thousand feet—that had replaced the shores of the smiling south? Who shall reveal the burning anxiety with which he throbbed to see beyond that cruel wall?

But there seemed no hope. Onwards and onwards the yacht made her way, and still no sign of France. It might have been supposed that Servadac's previous experiences would have prepared him for the discovery that the catastrophe which had overwhelmed other sites had brought destruction to his own country as well. But he had failed to realize how it might extend to France; and when now he was obliged with his own eye to witness the waves of ocean rolling over what once had been the lovely shores of Provence, he was well-nigh frantic with desperation.

"Am I to believe that Gourbi Island, that little shred of Algeria, constitutes all that is left of our glorious France? No, no! it cannot be. Not yet have we reached the pole of our new world. There is—there must be—something more behind that frowning rock. Oh, that for a moment we could scale its towering height and look beyond! By Heaven, I adjure you, let us disembark, and mount the summit and explore! France lies beyond."

Disembarkation, however, was an utter impossibility. There was no semblance of a creek in which the *Dobryna* could find an anchorage. There was no outlying ridge on which a footing could be gained. The precipice was perpendicular as a wall, its topmost height crowned with the same conglomerate of crystallized lamellæ that had all along been so pronounced a feature.

With her steam at high presure, the yacht made rapid progress towards the east. The weather remained perfectly fine, the temperature became gradually cooler, so that there was little prospect of vapours accumulating in the atmosphere: and nothing more than a few cirri, almost transparent veiled here and there the clear azure of the sky. Throughout the day the pale rays of the sun, apparently lessened in its magnitude, cast only faint and somewhat uncertain shadows; but at night the stars shone with surpassing brilliancy. Of the planets, some, it was observed, seemed to be fading away in remote distance. This was the case with Mars, Venus, and that unknown orb which was moving in the orbit of the minor planets; but Jupiter, on the other hand, had assumed splendid proportions; Saturn was superb in its lustre, and Uranus, which hitherto had been imperceptible without a telescope was pointed out by Lieutenant Procope, plainly visible to the naked eye. The inference was irresistible that Gallia was receding from the sun, and travelling far away across the planetary regions.

On the 24th of February, after following the sinuous course of what before the date of the convulsion had been the coast line of the department of Var, and after a fruitless search for Hyères, the peninsula of St. Tropez, the Lérius Islands, and the gulfs of Cannes and Jouar, the *Dobryna* arrived upon the site of the Cape of Antibes.

Here, quite unexpectedly, the explorers made the discovery that the massive wall of cliff had been rent from the top to the bottom by a narrow rift, like the dry bed of a mountain torrent, and at the base of the opening, level with the sea, was a little strand upon which there was just space enough for their boat to be hauled up.

"Joy! joy!" shouted Servadac, half beside himself with ecstasy; "we can land at last!"

Count Timascheff and the lieutenant were scarcely less impatient than the captain, and little needed his urgent and repeated solicitations: "Come on! Quick! Come on! no time to lose!"

It was half-past seven in the morning, when they set their foot upon this untried land. The bit of strand was only a few square yards in area, quite a narrow strip. Upon it might have been recognized some fragments of that agglutination of yellow limestone which is characteristic of the coast of Provence. But the whole party was far too eager to wait and examine these remnants of the ancient shore; they hurried on to scale the heights.

The narrow ravine was not only perfectly dry, but manifestly had never been the bed of any mountain torrent. The rocks that rested at the bottom—just as those which formed its sides—were of the same lamellous formation as the entire coast, and had not hitherto been subject to the disaggregation which the lapse of time never fails to work. A skilled geologist would probably have been able to assign them their proper scientific classification, but neither Servadac, Timascheff, nor the lieutenant could pretend to any acquaintance with their specific character.

Although, however, the bottom of the chasm had never as yet been the channel of a stream, indications were not wanting that at some future time it would be the natural outlet of accumulated waters; for already, in many places, thin layers of snow were glittering upon the surface of the fractured rocks, and the higher the elevation that was gained, the more these layers were found to increase in area and in depth.

"Here is a trace of fresh water, the first that Gallia has exhibited," said the count to his companions, as they toiled up the precipitous path.

"And probably," replied the lieutenant, "as we ascend we shall find not only snow but ice. We must suppose this Gallia of ours to be a sphere, and if it is so, we must now be very close to her Arctic regions; it is true that her axis is not so much inclined as to prolong day and night as at the poles of the earth, but the rays of the sun must reach us here only very obliquely, and the cold, in all likelihood, will be intense."

"So cold, do you think," asked Servadac, "that animal life must be extinct?"

"I do not say that, captain," answered the lieutenant; "for, however far our little world may be removed from the sun, I do not see why its temperature should fall below what prevails in those outlying regions beyond our system where sky and air are not."

"And what temperature may that be?" inquired the captain with a shudder.

"Fourier estimates that even in those vast unfathomable tracts the temperature never descends lower than 60° below zero," said Procope.

"Sixty! Sixty degrees below zero!" cried the count. "Why, there's not a Russian could endure it!"

"I beg your pardon, count. It is placed on record that the English *have* survived it, or something quite approximate, upon their Arctic expeditions. When Captain Parry was on Melville Island, he knew the thermometer to fall to –56°," said Procope.

As the explorers advanced, they seemed glad to pause from time to time, that they might recover their breath; for the air, becoming more and more rarefied, made respiration somewhat difficult and the ascent fatiguing. Before they had reached an altitude of 600 feet they noticed a sensible diminution of the temperature; but neither cold nor fatigue deterred them, and they were resolved to persevere. Fortunately, the deep striæ or furrows in the surface of the rocks that made the bottom of the ravine in some degree facilitated their progress, but it was not until they had been toiling up for two hours more that they succeeded in reaching the summit of the cliff.

Eagerly and anxiously did they look around. To the south there was nothing but the sea they had traversed; to the north, nothing but one drear, inhospitable stretch.

Servadac could not suppress a cry of dismay. Where was his beloved France? Had he gained this arduous height only to behold the rocks carpeted with ice and snow, and reaching interminably to the far-off horizon? His heart sank within him.

The whole region appeared to consist of nothing but the same strange, uniform mineral conglomerate crystallized into regular hexagonal prisms. But whatever was its geological character it was only too evident that it had entirely replaced the former soil, so that not a vestige of the old continent of Europe could be discerned. The lovely scenery of Provence, with the grace of its rich and undulating landscape; its gardens of citrons and oranges rising tier upon tier from the deep red soil—all, all had vanished. Of the vegetable kingdom, there was not a single representative; the most meagre of Arctic plants, the most insignificant of lichens, could obtain no hold upon that stony waste. Nor did the animal world assert the feeblest sway. The mineral kingdom reigned supreme.

Captain Servadac's deep dejection was in strange contrast to his general hilarity. Silent and tearful, he stood upon an ice-bound rock, straining his eyes across the boundless vista of the mysterious territory. "It cannot be!" he exclaimed. "We must somehow have mistaken our bearings. True, we have encountered this barrier; but France is there beyond! Yes, France is *there!* Come, count, come! By all that's pitiful, I entreat you, come and explore the farthest verge of the ice-bound track!"

He pushed onwards along the rugged surface of the rock, but had not proceeded far before he came to a sudden pause. His foot had come in contact with something hard beneath the snow, and, stooping down, he picked up a little block of stony substance, which the first glance revealed to be of a geological character altogether alien to the universal rocks around. It proved to be a fragment of discoloured marble, on which several letters were inscribed, of which the only part at all decipherable was the syllable "Vil."

"Vil—Villa!" he cried out, in his excitement dropping the marble, which was broken into atoms by the fall.

What else could this fragment be but the sole surviving remnant of some sumptuous mansion that once had stood on this unrivalled site? Was it not the residue of some edifice that had crowned the luxuriant headlands of Antibes, overlooking Nice, and commanding the gorgeous panorama that embraced the Maritime Alps and reached beyond Monaco and Mentone to the Italian height of Bordighera? And did it not give in its sad and too convincing testimony that Antibes itself had been involved in the great destruction? Servadac gazed upon the shattered marble, pensive and disheartened.

Count Timascheff laid his hand kindly on the captain's shoulder, and said, "My friend, do you not remember the motto of the old Hope family?"

He shook his head mournfully.

"*Orbe fracto, spes illœsa*," continued the count—"Though the world be shattered, hope is unimpaired."

Servadac smiled faintly, and replied that he felt rather compelled to take up the despairing cry of Dante, "All hope abandon, ye who enter here."

"Nay, not so," answered the count; "for the present at least, let our maxim be *Nil desperandum!*"

XVII
A SECOND ENIGMA

Upon re-embarking, the bewildered explorers began to discuss the question whether it would not now be desirable to make their way back to Gourbi Island, which was apparently the only spot in their new world from which they could hope to derive their future sustenance. Captain Servadac tried to console himself with the reflection that Gourbi Island was, after all, a fragment of a French colony, and as such almost like a bit of his dear France; and the plan of returning thither was on the point of being adopted, when Lieutenant Procope remarked that they ought to remember that they had not hitherto made an entire circuit of the new shores of the sea on which they were sailing.

"We have," he said, "neither investigated the northern shore from the site of

Cape Antibes to the strait that brought us to Gibraltar, nor have we followed the southern shore that stretches from the strait to the Gulf of Cabes. It is the old coast, and not the new, that we have been tracing; as yet, we cannot say positively that there is no outlet to the south; as yet, we cannot assert that no oasis of the African desert has escaped the catastrophe. Perhaps, even here in the north, we may find that Italy and Sicily and the larger islands of the Mediterranean may still maintain their existence."

"I entirely concur with you," said Count Timascheff, "I quite think we ought to make our survey of the confines of this new basin as complete as possible before we withdraw."

Servadac, although he acknowledged the justness of these observations, could not help pleading that the explorations might be deferred until after a visit had been paid to Gourbi Island.

"Depend upon it, captain, you are mistaken," replied the lieutenant; "the right thing to do is to use the *Dobryna* while she is available."

"Available! What do you mean?" asked the count, somewhat taken by surprise.

"I mean," said Procope, "that the farther this Gallia of ours recedes from the sun, the lower the temperature will fall. It is likely enough, I think, that before long the sea will be frozen over, and navigation will be impossible. Already you have learned something of the difficulties of traversing a field of ice, and I am sure, therefore, you will acquiesce in my wish to continue our explorations while the water is still open."

"No doubt you are right, lieutenant," said the count. "We will continue our search while we can for some remaining fragment of Europe. Who shall tell whether we may not meet with some more survivors from the catastrophe, to whom it might be in our power to afford assistance, before we go into our winter quarters?"

Generous and altogether unselfish as this sentiment really was, it was obviously to the general interest that they should become acquainted, and if possible establish friendly relations, with any human inhabitant who might be sharing their own strange destiny in being rolled away upon a new planet into the infinitude of space. All difference of race, all distinction of nationality, must be merged into the one thought that, few as they were, they were the sole surviving representatives of a world which it seemed exceedingly improbable that they would ever see again; and common sense dictated that they were bound to direct all their energies to insure that their asteroid should at least have a united and sympathizing population.

It was on the 25th of February that the yacht left the little creek in which she had taken refuge, and setting off at full steam eastwards, she continued her way along the northern shore. A brisk breeze tended to increase the keenness of the temperature, the thermometer being, on an average, about two degrees below zero. Salt water freezes only at a lower temperature than fresh; the course of the *Dobryna* was therefore unimpeded by ice, but it could not be concealed that there was the greatest necessity to maintain the utmost possible speed.

The nights continued lovely; the chilled condition of the atmosphere prevented the formation of clouds; the constellations gleamed forth with unsullied lustre; and, much as Lieutenant Procope, from nautical considerations, might regret the absence of the moon, he could not do otherwise than own that the magnificent nights of Gallia were such as must awaken the enthusiasm of an astronomer. And, as if to compensate for the loss of the moonlight, the heavens were illuminated by a superb shower of falling stars, far exceeding, both in number and in brilliancy, the phenomena which are commonly distinguished as the August and November meteors; in fact, Gallia was passing through that meteoric ring which is known to lie exterior to the earth's orbit, but almost concentric with it. The rocky coast, its metallic surface reflecting the glow of the dazzling luminaries, appeared literally stippled with light, whilst the sea, as though spattered with burning hailstones, shone with a phosphorescence that was perfectly splendid. So great, however, was the speed at which Gallia was receding from the sun, that this meteoric storm lasted scarcely more than four and twenty hours.

Next day the direct progress of the *Dobryna* was arrested by a long projection of land, which obliged her to turn southwards, until she reached what formerly would have been the southern extremity of Corsica. Of this, however, there was now no trace; the Strait of Bonfacio had been replaced by a vast expanse of water, which had at first all the appearance of being utterly desert; but on the following morning the explorers unexpectedly sighted a little island, which, unless it should prove, as was only too likely, to be of recent origin they concluded, from its situation, must be a portion of the northernmost territory of Sardinia.

The *Dobryna* approached the land as nearly as was prudent, the boat was lowered, and in a few minutes the count and Servadac had landed upon the islet, which was a mere plot of meadow land, not much more than two acres in extent, dotted here and there with a few myrtle-bushes and lentisks, interspersed with some ancient olives. Having ascertained, as they imagined, that the spot was devoid of living creature, they were on the point of returning to their boat, when their attention was arrested by a faint bleating, and immediately afterwards a solitary she-goat came bounding towards the shore. The creature had dark, almost black hair, and small curved horns, and was a specimen of that domestic breed which, with considerable justice, has gained for itself the title of "the poor man's cow." So far from being alarmed at the presence of strangers, the goat ran nimbly towards them, and then, by its movements and plaintive cries, seemed to be enticing them to follow it.

"Come," said Servadac; "let us see where it will lead us; it is more than probable it is not alone."

The count agreed; and the animal, as if comprehending what was said, trotted on gently for about a hundred paces, and stopped in front of a kind of cave or burrow that was half concealed by a grove of lentisks. Here a little girl, seven or eight years of age, with rich brown hair and lustrous dark eyes, beautiful as one of Murillo's angels, was peeping shyly through the branches. Apparently discovering nothing in the aspect of the strangers to excite her apprehensions, the child suddenly gained confidence, darted forwards with outstretched hands, and in a voice, soft and melodious as the language which she spoke, said in Italian:

"I like you; you will not hurt me, will you?"

"Hurt you, my child?" answered Servadac. "No, indeed; we will be your friends; we will take care of you."

And after a few moments' scrutiny of the pretty maiden, he added:

"Tell us your name, little one."

"Nina!" was the child's reply.

"Well, then, Nina, can you tell us where we are?"

"At Madalena, I think," said the little girl; "at least, I know I was there when that dreadful shock came and altered everything."

The count knew that Madalena was close to Caprera, to the north of Sardinia, which had entirely disappeared in the disaster. By dint of a series of questions, he gained from the child a very intelligent account of her experiences. She told him that she had no parents, and had been employed in taking care of a flock of goats belonging to one of the landowners, when one day, all of a sudden, everything around her, except this little piece of land, had been swallowed up, and that she and Marzy, her pet goat, had been left quite alone. She went on to say that at first she had been very frightened; but when she found that the earth did not shake any more, she had thanked the great God, and had soon made herself very happy living with Marzy. She had enough food, she said, and had been waiting for a boat to fetch her, and now a boat had come and she was quite ready to go away; only they must let her goat go with her: they would both like so much to get back to the old farm.

"Here, at least, is one nice little inhabitant of Gallia," said Captain Servadac, as he caressed the child and conducted her to the boat.

Half an hour later, both Nina and Marzy were safely quartered on board the yacht. It is needless to say that they received the heartiest of welcomes. The Russian sailors, ever superstitious, seemed almost to regard the coming of the child as the appearance of an angel; and, incredible as it may seem, more than one of them wondered whether she had wings, and amongst themselves they commonly referred to her as "the little Madonna."

Soon out of sight of Madalena, the *Dobryna* for some hours held a south-easterly course along the shore, which here was fifty leagues in advance of the former coast-line of Italy, demonstrating that a new continent must have been formed, substituted as it were for the old peninsula, of which not a vestige could be identified. At a latitude corresponding with the latitude of Rome, the sea took the form of a deep gulf, extending back far beyond the site of the Eternal City; the coast making a wide sweep round to the former position of Calabria, and jutting far beyond the outline of "the boot," which Italy resembles. But the beacon of Messina was not to be discerned; no trace, indeed, survived of any portion of Sicily; the very peak of Etna, 11,000 feet as it had reared itself above the level of the sea, had vanished utterly.

Another sixty leagues to the south, and the *Dobryna* sighted the entrance of the strait which had afforded her so providential a refuge from the tempest, and had conducted her to the fragmentary relic of Gibraltar. Hence to the Gulf of Cabes had been already explored, and as it was universally allowed that it was unnecessary to renew the search in that direction, the lieutenant started off in a transverse course, towards a point hitherto uninvestigated. That point was reached on the 3rd of March, and thence the coast was continuously followed, as it led through what had been Tunis, across the province of Constantine, away to the oasis of Ziban; where, taking a sharp turn, it first reached a latitude of 32° N. and then returned again, thus forming a sort of irregular gulf, enclosed by the same unvarying border of mineral concrete. This colossal boundary then stretched away for nearly 150 leagues over the Sahara desert, and, extending to the south of Gourbi Island, occupied what, if Morocco had still existed, would have been its natural frontier.

Adapting her course to these deviations of the coastline, the *Dobryna* was steering northwards, and had barely reached the limit of the bay, when the attention of all on board was arrested by the phenomenon of a volcano, at least 3,000 feet high, its crater crowned with smoke, which occasionally was streaked by tongues of flame.

"A burning mountain!" they exclaimed.

"Gallia, then, has some internal heat," said Servadac.

"And why not, captain?" rejoined the lieutenant. "If our asteroid has carried with it a portion of the old earth's atmosphere, why should it not likewise retain something of its central fire?"

"Ah, well!" said the captain, shrugging his shoulders, "I dare say there is caloric enough in our little world to supply the wants of its population."

Count Timascheff interrupted the silence that followed this conversation by saying, "And now, gentlemen, as our course has brought us on our way once more towards Gibraltar, what do you say to our renewing our acquaintance with the Englishmen? They will be interested in the result of our voyage."

"For my part," said Servadac, "I have no desire that way. They know where to find Gourbi Island; they can betake themselves thither just when they please. They have plenty of provisions. If the water freezes, 120 leagues is no very great distance. The reception they gave us was not so cordial that we need put ourselves out of the way to repeat our visit."

"What you say is too true," replied the count. "I hope we shall show them better manners when they condescend to visit us."

"Ay," said Servadac, "we must remember that we are all one people now; no longer Russian, French, or English. Nationality is extinct."

"I am sadly afraid, however," continued the count, "that an Englishman will be an Englishman ever."

"Yes," said the captain, "that is always their failing."

And thus all further thought of making their way again to the little garrison of Gibraltar was abandoned.

But even if their spirit of courtesy had disposed them to renew their acquaintance with the British officers, there were two circumstances that just then would have rendered such a proposal very inadvisable. In the first place, Lieutenant Procope was convinced that it could not be much longer now before the sea would be entirely frozen; and, besides this, the consumption of their coal, through the speed they had maintained, had been so great that there was only too much reason to fear that fuel would fail them. Anyhow, the strictest economy was necessary, and it was accordingly resolved that the voyage should not be much prolonged. Beyond the volcanic peak, moreover, the waters seemed to expand into a boundless ocean, and it might be a thing full of risk to be frozen up while the yacht was so inadequately provisioned. Taking all these things into account, it was agreed that further investigations should be deferred to a more favourable season, and that, without delay, the *Dobryna* should return to Gourbi Island.

This decision was especially welcome to Hector Servadac, who, throughout the whole of the last five weeks, had been agitated by much anxious thought on account of the faithful servant he had left behind.

The transit from the volcano to the island was not long, and was marked by only one noticeable incident. This was the finding of a second mysterious document, in character precisely similar to what they had found before. The writer of it was evidently engaged upon a calculation, probably continued from day to day, as to the motions of the planet Gallia upon its orbit, and committing the results of his reckonings to the waves as the channel of communication.

Instead of being enclosed in a telescope-case, it was this time secured in a preserved-meat tin, hermetically sealed, and stamped with the same initials on the wax that fastened it. The greatest care was used in opening it, and it was found to contain the following message:

"GALLIA (?)
AB SOLE, AU 1 *MARS*, DIST. 78.000.000 1.!
CHEMIN PARCOURU DE *FÉV.* À *MARS*: 59.000.000 1!
VA BENE! ALL RIGHT! NIL DESPERANDUM!

ENCHANTÉ!"

"Another enigma!" exclaimed Servadac; "and still no intelligible signature, and no address. No clearing up of the mystery!"

"I have no doubt, in my own mind," said the count, "that it is one of a series. It seems to me probable that they are being sent broadcast upon the sea."

"I wonder where the hare-brained *savant* that writes them can be living?" observed Servadac.

"Very likely he may have met with the fate of Æsop's abstracted astronomer, who found himself at the bottom of a well."

"Aye; but where *is* that well?" demanded the captain.

This was a question which the count was incapable of settling; and they could only speculate afresh as to whether the author of the riddles was dwelling upon some solitary island, or, like themselves, was navigating the waters of the new Mediterranean. But they could detect nothing to guide them to a definite decision.

After thoughtfully regarding the document for some time, Lieutenant Procope proceeded to observe that he believed the paper might be considered as genuine, and accordingly, taking its ststements as reliable, he deduced two important conclusions: first, that whereas, in the month of January, the distance traveled by the planet (hypothetically called Gallia) had been recorded as 82,000,000 leagues, the distance travelled in February was only 59,000,000 leagues—a difference of 23,000,000 leagues in one month; secondly, that the distance of the planet from the sun, which on the 15th of February had been 59,000,000 leagues, was on the 1st of March 78,000,000 leagues—an increase of 19,000,000 leagues in a fortnight. Thus, in proportion as Gallia receded from the sun, so did the rate of speed diminish by which she traveled along her orbit; facts to be observed in perfect conformity with the known laws of celestial mechanism.

"And your inference?" asked the count.

"My inference," replied the lieutenant, "is a confirmation of my surmise that we are following an orbit decidedly elliptical, although we have not yet the material to determine its eccentricity,"

"As the writer adheres to the appellation of Gallia, do you not think," asked the count, "that we might call these new waters the Gallian Sea?"

"There can be no reason to the contrary, count," replied the lieutenant; "and as such I will insert it upon my new chart."

"Our friend," said Servadac, "seems to be more and more gratified with the condition of things; not only has he adopted our motto, '*Nil desperandum!*' but see how enthusiastically he has wound up with his '*Enchanté!*'"

The conversation dropped.

A few hours later the man on watch announced that Gourbi Island was in sight.

XVIII
AN UNEXPECTED POPULATION

The *Dobryna* was now back again at the island. Her cruise had lasted from the 31st of January to the 5th of March, a period of thirty-five days (for it was leap year), corresponding to seventy days as accomplished by the new little world.

Many a time during his absence Hector Servadac had wondered how his present vicissitudes would end, and he had felt some misgivings as to whether he should ever again set foot upon the island, and see his faithful orderly, so that it was not without emotion that he had approached the coast of the sole remaining fragment of Algerian soil. But his apprehensions were groundless; Gourbi Island was just as he had left it, with nothing unusual in its aspect, except that a very peculiar cloud was hovering over it, at an altitude of little more than a hundred feet. As the yacht approached the shore, this cloud appeared to rise and fall as if acted upon by some invisible agency, and the captain, after watching it carefully, perceived that it was not an accumulation of vapours at all, but a dense mass of birds packed as closely together as a swarm of herrings, and uttering deafening and discordant cries, amidst which from time to time the noise of the report of a gun could be plainly distinguished.

The *Dobryna* signalized her arrival by firing her cannon, and dropped anchor in the little port of the Shelif. Almost within a minute Ben Zoof was seen running, gun in hand, towards the shore; he cleared the last ridge of rocks at a single bound, and then suddenly halted. For a few seconds he stood motionless, his eyes fixed, as if obeying the instructions of a drill sergeant, on a point some fifteen yards distant, his whole attitude indicating submission and respect; but the sight of the captain, who was landing, was too much for his equanimity, and darting forward, he seized his master's hand and covered it with kisses. Instead, however, of uttering any expressions of welcome or rejoicing at the captain's return, Ben Zoof broke out into the most vehement ejaculations.

"Thieves, captain! beastly thieves! Bedouins! pirates! devils!"

"Why, Ben Zoof, what's the matter?" said Servadac soothingly.

"They are thieves! downright, desperate thieves! those infernal birds! That's what's the matter. It is a good thing you have come. Here have I for a whole month been spending my powder and shot upon them, and the more I kill them, the worse they get; and yet, if I were to leave them alone, we should not have a grain of corn upon the island."

It was soon evident that the orderly had only too much cause for alarm. The crops had ripened rapidly during the excessive heat of January, when the orbit of Gallia was being traversed at its perihelion, and were now exposed to the depredations of many thousands of birds; and although a goodly number of stacks attested the industry of Ben Zoof during the time of the *Dobryna*'s voyage, it was only too apparent that the portion of the harvest that remained ungathered was liable to the most imminent risk of being utterly devoured. It was, perhaps, only natural that this clustered mass of birds, as representing the whole of the feathered tribe upon the surface of Gallia, should resort to Gourbi Island, of which the meadows seemed to be the only spot from which they could get sustenance at all; but as this sustenance would be obtained at the expense, and probably to the serious detriment, of the human population, it was absolutely necessary that every possible resistance should be made to the devastation that was threatened.

Once satisfied that Servadac and his friends would co-operate with him in the raid upon "the thieves," Ben Zoof became calm and content, and began to make various inquiries. "And what has become," he said, "of all our old comrades in Africa?"

"As far as I can tell you," answered the captain, "they are all in Africa still; only Africa isn't by any means where we expected to find it."

"And France? Montmartre?" continued Ben Zoof eagerly. Here was the cry of the poor fellow's heart.

As briefly as he could, Servadac endeavoured to explain the true condition of things; he tried to communicate the fact that Paris, France, Europe, nay, the whole world was more than eighty millions of leagues away from Gourbi Island; as gently and cautiously as he could he expressed his fear that they might never see Europe, France, Paris, Montmartre again.

"No, no, sir!" protested Ben Zoof emphatically; "that is all nonsense. It is altogether out of the question to suppose that we are not to see Montmartre again." And the orderly shook his head resolutely, with the air of a man determined, in spite of argument, to adhere to his own opinion.

"Very good, my brave fellow," replied Servadac, "hope on, hope while you may. The message has come to us over the sea, 'Never despair'; but one thing, nevertheless, is certain; we must forthwith commence arrangements for making this island our permanent home."

Captain Servadac now led the way to the gourbi, which, by his servant's exertions, had been entirely rebuilt; and here he did the honours of his modest establishment to his two guests, the count and the lieutenant, and gave a welcome, too, to little Nina, who had accompanied them on shore, and between whom and Ben Zoof the most friendly relations had already been established.

The adjacent building continued in good preservation, and Captain Servadac's satisfaction was very great in finding the two horses, Zephyr and Galette, comfortably housed in there and in good condition.

After the enjoyment of some refreshment, the party proceeded to a general consultation as to what steps must be taken for their future welfare. The most pressing matter that came before them was the consideration of the means to be adopted to enable the inhabitants of Gallia to survive the terrible cold, which, in their ignorance of the true eccentricity of their orbit, might, for aught they knew, last for an almost indefinite period. Fuel was far from abundant; of coal there was none; trees and shrubs were few in number, and to cut them down in prospect of the cold seemed a very questionable policy; but there was no doubt that some expedient must be devised to prevent disaster, and that without delay.

The victualling of the little colony offered no immediate difficulty. Water was abundant, and the cisterns could hardly fail to be replenished by the numerous streams that meandered along the plains; moreover, the Gallian Sea would ere long be frozen over, and the melted ice, (water in its congealed state being divested of every particle of salt) would afford a supply of drink that could not be exhausted. The crops that were now ready for the harvest, and the flocks and herds scattered over the island, would form an ample reserve. There was little doubt that throughout the winter the soil would remain unproductive, and no fresh fodder for domestic animals could then be obtained; it would therefore be necessary, if the exact duration of Gallia's year should ever be calculated, to proportion the number of animals to be reserved to the real length of the winter.

The next thing requisite was to arrive at a true estimate of the number of the population. Without including the thirteen Englishmen at Gibraltar, about whom he was not particularly disposed to give himself much concern at present, Servadac put down the names of the eight Russians, the two Frenchmen, and the little Italian girl, eleven in all, as the entire list of the inhabitants of Gourbi Island.

"Oh, pardon me," interposed Ben Zoof, "you are mistaking the state of the case altogether. You will be surprised to learn that the total of people on the island is double that. It is twenty-two."

"Twenty-two!" exclaimed the captain; "twenty-two people on this island? What do you mean?"

"The opportunity has not occurred," answered Ben Zoof, "for me to tell you before, but I have had company."

"Explain yourself, Ben Zoof," said Servadac. "What company have you had?"

"You could not suppose," replied the orderly, "that my own unassisted hands could have accomplished all that harvest work that you see has been done."

"I confess," said Lieutenant Procope, "we do not seem to have noticed that."

"Well, then," said Ben Zoof, "if you will be good enough to come with me for about a mile, I shall be able to show you my companions. But we must take our guns."

"Why take our guns?" asked Servadac. "I hope we are not going to fight."

"No, not with men," said Ben Zoof; "but it does not answer to throw a chance away for giving battle to those thieves of birds."

Leaving little Nina and her goat in the gourbi, Servadac, Count Timascheff, and the lieutenant, greatly mystified, took up their guns and followed the orderly. All along their way they made unsparing slaughter of the birds that hovered over and around them. Nearly every species of the feathered tribe seemed to have its representative in that living cloud. There were wild ducks in thousands; snipe, larks, rooks, and swallows; a countless variety of sea-birds—widgeons, gulls, and seamews; beside a quantity of game—quails, partridges, and woodcocks. The sportsmen did their best; every shot told; and the depredators fell by dozens on either hand.

Instead of following the northern shore of the island, Ben Zoof cut obliquely across the plain. Making their progress with the unwonted rapidity which was attributable to their specific lightness, Servadac and his companions soon found themselves near a grove of sycamores and eucalyptus massed in picturesque confusion at the base of a little hill. Here they halted.

"Ah! the vagabonds! the rascals! the thieves!" suddenly exelaimed Ben Zoof, stamping his foot with rage.

"How now? Are your friends the birds at their pranks again?" asked the captain.

"No, I don't mean the birds: I mean those lazy beggars that are shirking their work. Look here; look there!" And as Ben Zoof spoke, he pointed to some scythes, and sickles, and other implements of husbandry that had been left upon the ground.

"What is it you mean?" asked Servadac, getting somewhat impatient.

"Hush, hush! listen!" was all Ben Zoof's reply; and he raised his finger as if in warning.

Listening attentively, Servadac and his associates could distinctly recognize a human voice, accompanied by the notes of a guitar and by the measured click of castanets.

"Spaniards!" said Servadac.

"No mistake about that, sir," replied Ben Zoof; "a Spaniard would rattle his castanets at the cannon's mouth.

"But what is the meaning of it all?" asked the captain, more puzzled than before.

"Hark!" said Ben Zoof; "it is the old man's turn."

And then a voice, at once gruff and harsh, was heard vociferating, "My money! my money! when will you pay me my money? Pay me what you owe me, you miserable majos."

Meanwhile the song continued:

> *"TU SANDUNGA Y CIGARRO.*
> *Y UNA CANA DE JEREZ.*
> *MI JAMELGO Y UN TRABUCO.*
> *QUE MAS GLORIA PUEDE HAVER?"*

Servadac's knowledge of Gascon enabled him partially to comprehend the rollicking tenor of the Spanish patriotic air, but his attention was again arrested by the voice of the old man growling savagely, "Pay me you shall; yes, by the God of Abraham, you shall pay me."

"A Jew!" exclaimed Servadac.

"Ay, sir, a German Jew," said Ben Zoof.

The party was on the point of entering the thicket, when a singular spectacle made them pause. A group of Spaniards had just begun dancing their national fandango, and the extraordinary lightness which had become the physical property of every object in the new planet made the dancers bound to a height of thirty feet or more into the air, considerably above the tops of the trees. What followed was irresistibly comic. Four sturdy majos had dragged along with them an old man incapable of resistance, and compelled him, *nolens volens*, to join in the dance; and as they all kept appearing and disappearing above the bank of foliage, their grotesque attitudes, combined with the pitiable countenance of their helpless victim, could not do otherwise than recall most forcibly the story of Sancho Panza tossed in a blanket by the merry drapers of Segovia.

Servadac, the count, Procope, and Ben Zoof now proceeded to make their way through the thicket until they came to a little glade, where two men were stretched idly on the grass, one of them playing the guitar, and the other a pair of castanets; both were exploding with laughter, as they urged the performers to greater and yet greater exertions in the dance. At the sight of strangers they paused in their music, and simultaneously the dancers, with their victim, alighted gently on the sward.

Breathless and half exhausted as was the Jew, he rushed with an effort towards Servadac, and exclaimed in French, marked by a strong Teutonic accent, "Oh, my Lord Governor, help me, help! These rascals defraud me of my rights; they rob me; but, in the name of the God of Israel, I ask you to see justice done!"

The captain glanced inquiringly towards Ben Zoof, and the orderly, by a significant nod, made his master understand that he was to play the part that was implied by the title. He took the cue, and promptly ordered the Jew to hold his tongue at once. The man bowed his head in servile submission, and folded his hands upon his breast.

Servadac surveyed him leisurely. He was a man of about fifty, but from his appearance might well have been taken for at least ten years older. Small and skinny, with eyes bright and cunning, a hooked nose, a short yellow beard, unkempt hair, huge feet, and long bony hands, he presented all the typical characteristics of the German Jew, the heartless, wily usurer, the hardened miser and skinflint. As iron is attracted by the magnet, so was this Shylock attracted by the sight of gold, nor would he have hesitated to draw the life-blood of his creditors, if by such means he could secure his claims.

His name was Isaac Hakkabut, and he was a native of Cologne. Nearly the whole of his time, however, he informed Captain Servadac, had been spent upon the sea, his real business being that of a merchant trading at all the ports of the Mediterranean. A tartan, a small vessel of two hundred tons burden, conveyed his entire stock of merchandise, and, to say the truth, was a sort of floating emporium, conveying nearly every possible article of commerce, from a lucifer match to the radiant fabrics of Frankfort and Epinal. Without wife or children, and having no settled home, Isaac Hakkabut lived almost entirely on board the *Hansa*, as he had named his tartan; and engaging a mate, with a crew of three men, as being adequate to work so light a craft, he cruised along the coasts of Algeria, Tunis, Egypt, Turkey, and Greece, visiting moreover, most of the harbours of the Levant. Careful to be always well supplied with the products in most general demand—coffee, sugar, rice, tobacco, cotton stuffs, and gunpowder—and being at all times ready to barter, and prepared to deal in secondhand wares, he had contrived to amass considerable wealth.

On the eventful night of the 1st of January the *Hansa* had been at Cente, the point on the coast of Morocco exactly opposite Gibraltar. The mate and three sailors had all gone on shore, and, in common with many of their fellow-creatures, had entirely disappeared; but the most projecting rock of Ceuta had been undisturbed by the general catastrophe, and half a score of Spaniards, who had happened to be upon it, had escaped with their lives. They were all Andalusian majos, agricultural labourers, and naturally as careless and apathetic as men of their class usually are, but they could not help being very considerably embarrassed when they discovered that they were left in solitude upon a detached and isolated rock. They took what mutual counsel they could, but became only more and more perplexed. One of them was named Negrete, and he, as having travelled somewhat more than the rest, was tacitly recognized as a sort of leader; but although he was by far the most enlightened of them all, he was quite incapable of forming the least conception of the nature of what had occurred. The one thing upon which they could not fail to be conscious was that they had no prospect of obtaining provisions, and consequently their first business was to devise a scheme for getting away from their present abode. The *Hansa* was lying off shore. The Spaniards would not have had the slightest hesitation in summarily taking possession of her, but their utter ignorance of seamanship made them reluctantly come to the conclusion that the more prudent policy was to make terms with the owner.

And now came a singular part of the story. Negrete and his companions had meanwhile received a visit from two English officers from Gibraltar. What passed between them the Jew did not know; he only knew that, immediately after the conclusion of the interview, Negrete came to him and ordered him to set sail at once for the nearest point of Morocco. The Jew, afraid to disobey, but with his eye ever upon the main chance, stipulated that at the end of their voyage the Spaniards should pay for their passage—terms to which, as they would to any other, they did not demur, knowing that they had not the slightest intention of giving him a single real.

The *Hansa* had weighed anchor on the 3rd of February. The wind blew from the west, and consequently the working of the tartan was easy enough, The unpracticed sailors had only to hoist their sails and, though they were quite unconscious of the fact, the breeze carried them to the only spot upon the little world they occupied which could afford them a refuge.

Thus it fell out that one morning Ben Zoof, from his lookout on Gourbi Island, saw a ship, not the *Dobryna*, appear upon the horizon, and make quietly down towards what had formerly been the right bank of the Shelif.

Such was Ben Zoofs version of what had occurred, as he had gathered it from the new-comers. He wound up his recital by remarking that the cargo of the

Hansa would be of immense service to them; he expected, indeed, that Isaac Hakkabut would be difficult to manage, but considered there could be no harm in appropriating the goods for the common welfare, since there could be no opportunity now for selling them.

Ben Zoof added, "And as to the difficulties between the Jew and his passengers, I told him that the governor general was absent on a tour of inspection, and that he would see everything equitably settled."

Smiling at his orderly's tactics, Servadac turned to Hakkabut, and told him that he would take care that his claims should be duly investigated and all proper demands should be paid. The man appeared satisfied, and, for the time at least, desisted from his complaints and importunities.

When the Jew had retired, Count Timascheff asked "But how in the world can you ever make those fellows pay anything?"

"They have lots of money," said Ben Zoof.

"Not likely," replied the count; "when did you ever know Spaniards like them to have lots of money?"

"But I have seen it myself," said Ben Zoof; "and it is English money."

"English money!" echoed Servadac; and his mind again reverted to the excursion made by the colonel and the major from Gibraltar, about which they had been so reticent.

"We must inquire more about this," he said.

Then, addressing Count Timascheff, he added, "Altogether I think the countries of Europe are fairly represented by the population of Gallia."

"True, captain," answered the count; "we have only a fragment of a world, but it contains natives of France, Russia, Italy, Spain, and England. Even Germany may be said to have a representative in the person of this miserable Jew."

"And even in him," said Servadac, "perhaps we shall not find so indifferent a representative as we at present imagine."

XIX
GALLIA'S GOVERNOR GENERAL

The Spaniards who had arrived on board the *Hansa* consisted of nine men and a lad of twelve years of age, named Pablo. They all received Captain Servadac, whom Ben Zoof introduced as the governor general, with due respect, and returned quickly to their separate tasks. The captain and his friends, followed at some distance by the eager Jew, soon left the glade and directed their steps towards the coast where the *Hansa* was moored.

As they went they discussed their situation. As far as they had ascertained, except Gourbi Island, the sole surviving fragments of the Old World were four small islands: the bit of Gibraltar occupied by the Englishmen; Ceuta, which had just been left by the Spaniards; Madalena, where they had picked up the little Italian girl; and the site of the tomb of Saint Louis on the coast of Tunis. Around these there was stretched out the full extent of the Gallian Sea, which apparently comprised about one-half of the Mediterranean, the whole being encompassed by a barrier like a framework of precipitous cliffs, of an origin and a substance alike unknown.

Of all these spots only two were known to be inhabited: Gibraltar, where the thirteen Englishmen were amply provisioned for some years to come, and their own Gourbi Island. Here there was a population of twenty-two, who would all have to subsist upon the natural products of the soil. It was indeed not to be forgotten that, perchance, upon some remote and undiscovered isle there might be the solitary writer of the mysterious papers which they had found, and if so, that would raise the census of their new asteroid to an aggregate of thirty-six.

Even upon the supposition that at some future date the whole population should be compelled to unite and find a residence upon Gourbi Island, there did not appear any reason to question but that eight hundred acres of rich soil, under good management, would yield them all an ample sustenance. The only critical matter was how long the cold season would last; every hope depended upon the land again becoming productive; at present, it seemed impossible to determine, even if Gallia's orbit were really elliptical, when she would reach her aphelion, and it was consequently necessary that the Gallians for the time being should reckon on nothing beyond their actual and present resources.

These resources were, first, the provisions of the *Dobryna*, consisting of preserved meat, sugar, wine, brandy, and other stores sufficient for about two months; secondly, the valuable cargo of the *Hansa*, which, sooner or later, the owner, whether he would or not, must be compelled to surrender for the common benefit; and lastly, the produce of the island, animal and vegetable, which with proper economy might be made to last for a considerable period.

In the course of the conversation, Count Timascheff took an opportunity of saying that, as Captain Servadac had already been presented to the Spaniards as governor of the island, he thought it advisable that he should really assume that position.

"Every body of men," he observed, "must have a head, and you, as a Frenchman, should, I think, take the command of this fragment of a French colony. My men, I can answer for it, are quite prepared to recognize you as their superior officer."

"Most unhesitatingly," replied Servadac, "I accept the post with all its responsibilities. We understand each other so well that I feel sure we shall try and work together for the common good; and even if it be our fate never again to behold our fellow creatures, I have no misgivings but that we shall be able to cope with whatever difficulties may be before us."

As he spoke, he held out his hand. The count took it, at the same time making a slight bow. It was the first time since their meeting that the two men had shaken hands; on the other hand, not a single word about their former rivalry had ever escaped their lips; perhaps that was all forgotten. The silence of a few moments was broken by Servadac saying, "Do you not think we ought to explain our situation to the Spaniards?"

"No, no, your Excellency," burst in Ben Zoof, emphatically; "the fellows are chicken-hearted enough already; only tell them what has happened, and in sheer despondency they will not do another stroke of work."

"Besides," said Lieutenant Procope, who took very much the same view as the orderly, "they are so miserably ignorant they would be sure to misunderstand you."

"Understand or misunderstand," replied Servadac, "I do not think it matters. They would not care. They are all fatalists. Only give them a guitar and their castanets, and they will soon forget all care and anxiety. For my own part, I must adhere to my belief that it will be advisable to tell them everything. Have you any opinion to offer, count?"

"My own opinion, captain, coincides entirely with yours. I have followed the plan of explaining all I could to my men on board the *Dobryna*, and no inconvenience has arisen."

"Well, then, so let it be," said the captain; adding, "It is not likely that these Spaniards are so ignorant as not to have noticed the change in length of the days; neither can they be unaware of the physical changes that have transpired. They shall certainly be told that we are being carried away into unknown regions of space, and that this island is nearly all that remains of the Old World."

"Ha! ha!" laughed Ben Zoof, aloud; "it will be fine sport to watch the old Jew's face, when he is made to comprehend that he is flying away millions and millions of leagues from all his debtors."

Isaac Hakkabut was about fifty yards behind, and was consequently unable to overhear the conversation. He went shambling along, half whimpering and not infrequently invoking the God of Israel; but every now and then a cunning light gleamed from his eyes, and his lips became compressed with a grim significance.

None of the recent phenomena had escaped his notice, and more than once he had attempted to entice Ben Zoof into conversation upon the subject; but the orderly made no secret of his antipathy to him, and generally replied to his advances either by satire or by banter. He told him that he had everything to gain under the new system of nights and days, for, instead of living the Jew's ordinary life of a century, he would reach to the age of two centuries; and he congratulated him upon the circumstance of things having become so light, because it would prevent him feeling the burden of his years. At another time he would declare that, to an old usurer like him, it could not matter in the least what had become of the moon, as he could not possibly have advanced any money upon her. And when Isaac, undaunted by his jeers, persevered in besetting him with questions, he tried to silence him by saying, "Only wait till the governor general comes; he is a shrewd fellow, and will tell you all about it."

"But will he protect my property?" poor Isaac would ask tremulously.

"To be sure he will! He would confiscate it all rather than that you should be robbed of it."

With this Job's comfort the Jew had been obliged to content himself as best he could, and to await the promised arrival of the governor.

When Servadac and his companions reached the shore, they found that the *Hansa* had anchored in an exposed bay, protected but barely by a few projecting rocks, and in such a position that a gale rising from the west would inevitably drive her on to the land, where she must be dashed in pieces. It would be the height of folly to leave her in her present moorings; without loss of time she must be brought round to the mouth of the Shelif, in immediate proximity to the Russian yacht.

The consciousness that his tartan was the subject of discussion made the Jew give way to such vehement ejaculations of anxiety, that Servadac turned round and peremptorily ordered him to desist from his clamour. Leaving the old man under the surveillance of the count and Ben Zoof, the captain and the lieutenant stepped into a small boat and were soon alongside the floating emporium.

A very short inspection sufficed to make them aware that both the tartan and her cargo were in a perfect state of preservation. In the hold were sugar-loaves by hundreds, chests of tea, bags of coffee, hogsheads of tobacco, pipes of wine, casks of brandy, barrels of dried herrings, bales of cotton, clothing of every kind, shoes of all sizes, caps of various shape, tools, household utensils, china and earthenware, reams of paper, bottles of ink, boxes of lucifer matches, blocks of salt, bags of pepper and spices, a stock of huge Dutch cheeses, and a collection of almanacs and miscellaneous literature. At a rough guess the value could not be much under £5,000 sterling. A new cargo had been taken in only a few days before the catastrophe, and it had been Isaac Hakkabut's intention to cruise from Ceuts to Tripoli, calling wherever he had reason to believe there was likely to be a market for any of his commodities.

"A fine haul, lieutenant," said the captain.

"Yes, indeed," said the lieutenant; "but what if the owner refuses to part with it?"

"No fear; no fear," replied the captain. "As soon as ever the old rascal finds that there are no more Arabs or Algerians for him to fleece, he will be ready enough to transact a little business with us. We will pay him by bills of acceptance on some of his old friends in the Old World."

"But why should he want any payment?" inquired the lieutenant. "Under the circumstances, he must know that you have a right to make a requisition of his goods."

"No, no," quickly rejoined Servadac; "we will not do that. Just because the fellow is a German we shall not be justified in treating him in German fashion. We will transact our business in a business like way. Only let him once realize that he is on a new globe, with no prospect of getting back to the old one, and he will be ready enough to come to terms with us."

"Perhaps you are right," replied the lieutenant; "I hope you are. But anyhow, it will not do to leave the tartan here; not only would she be in danger in the event of a storm, but it is very questionable whether she could resist the pressure of the ice, if the water were to freeze."

"Quite true, Procope; and accordingly I give you the commission to see that your crew bring her round to the Shelif as soon as may be."

"Tomorrow morning it shall be done," answered the lieutenant, promptly.

Upon returning to the shore, it was arranged that the whole of the little colony should forthwith assemble at the gourbi. The Spaniards were summoned and

Isaac, although he could only with reluctance take his wistful gaze from his tartan, obeyed the governor's orders to follow.

An hour later and the entire population of twenty-two had met in the chamber adjoining the gourbi. Young Pablo made his first acquaintance with little Nina, and the child seemed highly delighted to find a companion so nearly of her own age. Leaving the children to entertain each other, Captain Servadac began his address.

Before entering upon further explanation, he said that he counted upon the cordial co-operation of them all for the common welfare.

Negrete interrupted him by declaring that no promises or pledges could be given until he and his countrymen knew how soon they could be sent back to Spain.

"To Spain, do you say?" asked Servadac.

"To Spain!" echoed Isaac Hakkabut, with a hideous yell. "Do they expect to go back to Spain till they have paid their debts? Your Excellency, they owe me twenty reals apiece for their passage here; they owe me two hundred reals. Are they to be allowed… ?"

"Silence Mordecai, you fool!" shouted Ben Zoof, who was accustomed to call the Jew by any Hebrew name that came uppermost to his memory. "Silence!"

Servadac was disposed to appease the old man's anxiety by promising to see that justice was ultimately done; but, in a fever of frantic excitement, he went on to implore that he might have the loan of a few sailors to carry his ship to Algiers.

"I will pay you honestly; I will pay you *well*," he cried; but his ingrained propensity for making a good bargain prompted him to add, "provided you do not overcharge me."

Ben Zoof was about again to interpose some angry exclamation; but Servadac checked him, and continued in Spanish: "Listen to me, my friends. Something very strange has happened. A most wonderful event has cut us off from Spain, from France, from Italy, from every country of Europe. In fact, we have left the Old World entirely. Of the whole earth, nothing remains except this island on which you are now taking refuge. The old globe is far, far away. Our present abode is but an insignificant fragment that is left. I dare not tell you that there is any chance of your ever again seeing your country or your homes."

He paused. The Spaniards evidently had no conception of his meaning.

Negrete begged him to tell them all again. He repeated all that he had said, and by introducing some illustrations from familiar things, he succeeded to a certain extent in conveying some faint idea of the convulsion that had happened. The event was precisely what he had foretold. The communication was received by all alike with the most supreme indifference.

Hakkabut did not say a word. He had listened with manifest attention, his lips twitching now and then as if suppressing a smile. Servadac turned to him, and asked whether he was still disposed to put out to sea and make for Algiers.

The Jew gave a broad grin, which, however, he was careful to conceal from the Spaniards. "Your Excellency jests," he said in French; and turning to Count Timascheff, he added in Russian: "The governor has made up a wonderful tale."

The count turned his back in disgust, while the Jew sidled up to little Nina and muttered in Italian. "A lot of lies, pretty one; a lot of lies!"

"Confound the knave!" exclaimed Ben Zoof; "he gabbles every tongue under the sun!"

"Yes," said Servadac; "but whether he speaks French, Russian, Spanish, German, or Italian, he is neither more nor less than a Jew."

XX
A LIGHT ON THE HORIZON

On the following day, without giving himself any further concern about the Jew's incredulity, the captain gave orders for the *Hansa* to be shifted round to the harbour of the Shelif. Hakkabut raised no objection, not only because he was aware that the move insured the immediate safety of his tartan, but because he was secretly entertaining the hope that he might entice away two or three of the *Dobryna*'s crew and make his escape to Algiers or some other port.

Operations now commenced for preparing proper winter quarters. Spaniards and Russians alike joined heartily in the work, the diminution of atmospheric pressure and of the force of attraction contributing such an increase to their muscular force as materially facilitated all their labours. The first business was to accommodate the building adjacent to the gourbi to the wants of the little colony. Here for the present the Spaniards were lodged, the Russians retaining their berths upon the yacht, while the Jew was permitted to pass his nights upon the *Hansa*. This arrangement, however, could be only temporary. The time could not be far distant when ships' sides and ordinary walls would fail to give an adequate protection from the severity of the cold that must be expected; the stock of fuel was too limited to keep up a permanent supply of heat in their present quarters, and consequently they must be driven to seek some other refuge, the internal temperature of which would at least be bearable.

The plan that seemed to commend itself most to their consideration, was, that they should dig out for themselves some subterraneous pits similar to "silos," such as are used as receptacles for grain. They presumed that when the surface of Gallia should be covered by a thick layer of ice, which is a bad conductor of heat, a sufficient amount of warmth for animal vitality might still be retained in excavations of this kind. After a long consultation they failed to devise any better expedient, and were forced to resign themselves to this species of troglodyte existence.

In one respect they congratulated themselves that they should be better off than many of the whalers in the polar seas, for as it is impossible to get below the surface of a frozen ocean, these adventurers have to seek refuge in huts of wood and snow erected on their ships, which at best can give but slight protection from extreme cold; but here, with a solid subsoil, the Gallians might hope to dig down a hundred feet or so and secure for themselves a shelter that would enable them to brave the hardest severity of climate.

The order, then, was at once given. The work was commenced. A stock of shovels, mattocks, and pickaxes was brought from the gourbi, and with Ben Zoof as overseer, both Spanish majos and Russian sailors set to work with a will.

It was not long, however, before a discovery, more unexpected than agreeable, suddenly arrested their labours. The spot chosen for the excavation was a little to the right of the gourbi, on a slight elevation of the soil. For the first day everything went on prosperously enough; but at a depth of eight feet below the surface, the navvies came in contact with a hard surface, upon which all their tools failed to make the slightest impression. Servadac and the count were at once apprised of the fact, and had little difficulty in recognizing the substance that had revealed itself as the very same which composed the shores as well as the subsoil of the Gallian sea. It evidently formed the universal substructure of the new asteroid. Means for hollowing it failed them utterly. Harder and more resisting than granite, it could not be blasted by ordinary powder; dynamite alone could suffice to rend it.

The disappointment was very great Unless some means of protection were speedily devised, death seemed to be staring them in the face. Were the figures in the mysterious documents correct? If so, Gallia must now be a hundred millions of leagues from the sun, nearly three times the distance of the earth at the remotest section of her orbit. The intensity of the solar light and heat, too, was very seriously diminishing, although Gourbi Island (being on the equator of an orb which had its axis always perpendicular to the plane in which it revolved) enjoyed a position that gave it a permanent summer. But no advantage of this kind could compensate for the remoteness of the sun. The temperature fell steadily; already, to the discomfiture of the little Italian girl, nurtured in sunshine, ice was beginning to form in the crevices of the rocks, and manifestly the time was impending when the sea itself would freeze.

Some shelter must be found before the temperature should fall to 60° below zero. Otherwise death was inevitable. Hitherto, for the last few days, the thermometer had been registering an average of about 6° below zero, and it had become matter of experience that the stove, although replenished with all the wood that was available, was altogether inadequate to effect any sensible mitigation of the severity of the cold. Nor could any amount of fuel be enough. It was certain that ere long the very mercury and spirit in the thermometers would be congealed. Some other resort must assuredly be soon found, or they must perish. That was clear.

The idea of betaking themselves to the *Dobryna* and *Hansa* could not for a moment be seriously entertained; not only did the structure of the vessels make them utterly insufficient to give substantial shelter, but they were totally unfitted to be trusted as to their stability when exposed to the enormous pressure of the accummulated ice.

Neither Servadac, nor the count, nor Lieutenant Procope were men to be easily disheartened, but it could not be concealed that they felt themselves in circumstances by which they were equally harassed and perplexed. The sole expedient that their united counsel could suggest was to obtain a refuge below ground, and *that* was denied them by the strange and impenetrable substratum of the soil; yet hour by hour the sun's disc was lessening in its dimensions, and although at midday some faint radiance and glow were to be distinguished, during the night the painfulness of the cold was becoming almost intolerable.

Mounted upon Zephyr and Galette, the captain and the count scoured the island in search of some available retreat. Scarcely a yard of ground was left unexplored, the horses clearing every obstacle as if they were, like Pegasus, furnished with wings. But all in vain. Soundings were made again and again, but invariably with the same result; the rock, hard as adamant, never failed to reveal itself within a few feet of the surface of the ground.

The excavation of any silo being thus manifestly hopeless, there seemed nothing to be done except to try and render the buildings alongside the gourbi impervious to frost. To contribute to the supply of fuel, orders were given to collect every scrap of wood, dry or green, that the island produced; and this involved the necessity of felling the numerous trees that were scattered over the plain. But toil as they might at the accumulation of firewood, Captain Servadac and his companions could not resist the conviction that the consumption of a very short period would exhaust the total stock. And what would happen then?

Studious if possible to conceal his real misgivings, and anxious that the rest of the party should be affected as little as might be by his own uneasiness, Servadac would wander alone about the island, racking his brain for an idea that would point the way out of the serious difficulty. But still all in vain.

One day he suddenly came upon Ben Zoof, and asked him whether he had no plan to propose. The orderly shook his head, but after a few moments' pondering, said: "Ah! master, if only we were at Montmartre, we would get shelter in the charming stone-quarries."

"Idiot!" replied the captain, angrily, "if we were at Montmartre, you don't suppose that we should need to live in stone-quarries?"

But the means of preservation which human ingenuity had failed to secure were at hand from the felicitous provision of Nature herself. It was on the 10th of March that the captain and Lieutenant Procope started off once more to investigate the northwest corner of the island; on their way their conversation naturally was engrossed by the subject of the dire necessities which only too manifestly were awaiting them. A discussion more than usually animated arose between them, for the two men were not altogether of the same mind as to the measures that ought to be adopted in order to open the fairest chance of avoiding a fatal climax to their exposure; the captain persisted that an entirely new abode must be sought, while the lieutenant was equally bent upon devising a method of some sort by which their present quarters might be rendered sufficiently warm. All at once, in the very heat of his argument, Procope paused; he passed his hand across his eyes, as if to dispel a mist, and stood, with a fixed gaze centred on a point towards the south. "What is that?" he said, with a kind of hesitation. "No, I am not mistaken," he added; "it is a light on the horizon."

"A light!" exclaimed Servadac; "show me where."

"Look there!" answered the lieutenant, and he kept pointing steadily in its direction, until Servadac also distinctly saw the bright speck in the distance.

It increased in clearness in the gathering shades of evening. "Can it be a ship?" asked the captain. "If so, it must be in flames; otherwise we should not be able to see it so far off," replied Procope.

"It does not move," said Servadac;" and unless I am greatly deceived, I can hear a kind of reverberation in the air."

For some seconds the two men stood straining eyes and ears in rapt attention. Suddenly an idea struck Servadac's mind. "The volcano!" he cried; "may it not be the volcano that we saw, whilst we were on board the *Dobryna*?"

The lieutenant agreed that it was very probable.

"Heaven be praised!" ejaculated the captain, and he went on in the tones of a keen excitement: "Nature has provided us with our winter quarters; the stream of burning lava that is flowing there is the gift of a bounteous Providence; it will provide us all the warmth we need. No time to lose! Tomorrow, my dear Procope, tomorrow we will explore it all; no doubt the life, the heat we want is reserved for us in the heart and bowels of our own Gallia!"

Whilst the captain was indulging in his expressions of enthusiasm, Procope was endeavouring to collect his thoughts. Distinctly he remembered the long promontory which had barred the *Dobryna*'s progress while coasting the southern confines of the sea, and which had obliged her to ascend northwards as far as the former latitude of Oran; he remembered also that at the extremity of the promontory there was a rocky headland crowned with smoke; and now he was convinced that he was right in identifying the position, and in believing that the smoke had given place to an eruption of flame.

When Servadac gave him a chance of speaking, he said, "The more I consider it, captain, the more I am satisfied that your conjecture is correct. Beyond a doubt, what we see is the volcano, and tomorrow we will not fail to visit it."

On returning to the gourbi, they communicated their discovery to Count Timascheff only, deeming any further publication of it to be premature. The count at once placed his yacht at their disposal, and expressed his intention of accompanying them. "The yacht, I think," said Procope, "had better remain where she is; the weather is beautifully calm, and the steam-launch will answer our purpose better; at any rate, it will convey us much closer to shore than the schooner."

The count replied that the lieutenant was by all means to use his own discretion, and they all retired for the night.

Like many other modern pleasure-yacht, the *Dobryna*, in addition to her four-oar, was fitted with a fast-going little steam-launch, its screw being propelled, on the Oriolle system, by mean of a boiler, small but very effective. Early next morning, this handy little craft was sufficiently freighted with coal (of which there was still about ten tons on board the *Dobryna*), and manned by nobody except the captain, the count, and the lieutenant, left the harbour of the Shelif, much to the bewilderment of Ben Zoof, who had not yet been admitted into the secret. The orderly, however, consoled himself with the reflection that he had been temporarily invested with the full powers of governor general, an office of which he was not a little proud.

The eighteen miles between the island and the headland were made in something less than three hours. The volcanic eruption was manifestly very considerable, the entire summit of the promontory being enveloped in flames. To produce so large a combustion either the oxygen of Gallia's atmosphere had been brought into contact with the explosive gases contained beneath her soil, or perhaps, still more probable, the volcano, like those in the moon, was fed by an internal supply of oxygen of her own.

It took more than half an hour to settle on a suitable landing-place. At length, a small semi-circular creek was discovered among the rocks, which appeared advantageous, because, if circumstances should so require, it would form a safe anchorage for both the *Dobryna* and the *Hansa*.

The launch securely moored, the passengers landed on the side of the promontory opposite to that on which a torrent of flaming lava was descending to the sea. With much satisfaction they experienced, as they approached the mountain, a sensible difference in the temperature, and their spirits could not do otherwise than rise at the prospect of having their hopes confirmed, that a deliverance from the threatened calamity had so opportunely been found. On they went, up the steep acclivity, scrambling over its rugged projections, scaling the irregularities of its gigantic strata, bounding from point to point with the agility of chamois, but never alighting on anything except the accumulation of the same hexagonal prisms with which they had now become so familiar.

Their exertions were happily rewarded. Behind a huge pyramid rock they found a hole in the mountain-side, like the mouth of a great tunnel. Climbing up to this orifice, which was more than sixty feet above the level of the sea, they ascertained that it opened into a long dark gallery. They entered and groped their way cautiously along the sides. A continuous rumbling, that increased as they advanced, made them aware that they must be approaching the central funnel of the volcano; their only fear was lest some insuperable wall of rock should suddenly bar their further progress.

Servadac was some distance ahead.

"Come on!" he cried cheerily, his voice ringing through the darkness, "come on! Our fire is lighted! no stint of fuel! Nature provides thet! Let us make haste and warm ourselves!"

Inspired by his confidence, the count and the lieutenant advanced bravely along the unseen and winding path. The temperature was now at least fifteen degrees above zero, and the walls of the gallery were beginning to feel quite warm to the touch, an indication, not to be overlooked, that the substance of which the rock was composed was metallic in its nature, and capable of conducting heat.

"Follow me!" shouted Servadac again; "we shall soon find a regular stove!"

Onwards they made their way, until at last a sharp turn brought them into a sudden flood of light. The tunnel had opened into a vast cavern, and the gloom was exchanged for an illumination that was perfectly dazzling. Although the temperature was high, it was not in any way intolerable.

One glance was sufficient to satisfy the explorers that the grateful light and heat of this huge excavation were to be attributed to a torrent of lava that was rolling downwards to the sea, completely subtending the aperture of the cave. Not inaptly might the scene be compared to the celebrated Grotto of the Winds at the rear of the central fall of Niagara, only with the exception that here, instead of a curtain of rushing water, it was a curtain of roaring flame that hung before the cavern's mouth.

"Heaven be praised!" cried Servadac, with glad emotion; "here is all that we hoped for, and more besides!"

XXI
WINTER QUARTERS

The habitation that had now revealed itself, well lighted and thoroughly warm, was indeed marvellous. Not only would it afford ample accommodation for Hector Servadac and "his subjects," as Ben Zoof delighted to call them, but it would provide shelter for the two horses, and for a considerable number of domestic animals.

This enormous cavern was neither more or less than the common junction of nearly twenty tunnels (similar to that which had been traversed by the explorers), forming ramifications in the solid rock, and the pores, as it were, by which the internal heat exuded from the heart of the mountain. Here, as long as the volcano retained its activity, every living creature on the new asteroid might brave the most rigorous of climates; and as Count Timascheff justly remarked, since it was the only burning mountain they had sighted, it was most probably the sole outlet for Gallia's subterranean fires, and consequently the eruption might continue unchanged for ages to come.

But not a day, not an hour, was to be lost now. The steam-launch returned to Gourbi Island, and preparations were forthwith taken in hand for conveying man and beast, corn and fodder, across to the volcanic headland. Loud and hearty were the acclamations of the little colony, especially of the Spaniards, and great was the relief of Nina, when Servadac announced to them the discovery of their future domicile; and with requickened energies they laboured hard at packing, anxious to reach their genial winter quarters without delay.

For three successive days the *Dobryna*, laden to her very gunwale, made a transit to and fro. Ben Zoof was left upon the island to superintend the stowage of the freight, whilst Servadac found abundant occupation in overlooking its disposal within the recesses of the mountain. First of all, the large store of corn and fodder, the produce of the recent harvest, was landed and deposited in one of the vaults, then, on the 15th, about fifty head of live cattle—bullocks, cows, sheep, and pigs—were conveyed to their rocky stalls. These were saved for the sake of preserving the several breeds, the bulk of the island cattle being slaughtered, as the extreme severity of the climate insured all meat remaining fresh for almost an indefinite period. The winter which they were expecting would probably be of unprecedented length; it was quite likely that it would exceed the six months' duration by which many arctic explorers have been tried; but the population of Gallia had no anxiety in the matter of provisions—their stock was far more than adequate; while as for drink, as long as they were satisfied with pure water, a frozen sea would afford them an inexhaustible reservoir.

The need for haste in forwarding their preparations became more and more manifest; the sea threatened to be unnavigable very soon, as ice was already forming which the noonday sun was unable to melt. And if haste were necessary, so also were care, ingenuity, and forethought. It was indispensable that the space at their command should be properly utilized, and yet that the several portions of the store should all be readily accessible.

On further investigation an unexpected number of galleries was discovered, so that, in fact, the interior of the mountain was like a vast bee-hive perforated with innumerable cells; and in compliment to the little Italian it was unanimously voted by the colony that their new home should be called "Nina's Hive."

The first care of Captain Servadac was to ascertain how he could make the best possible use of the heat which nature had provided for them so opportunely and with so lavish a hand. By opening fresh vents in the solid rock (which by the action of the heat was here capable of fissure) the stream of burning lava was diverted into several new channels, where it could be available for daily use; and thus Mocbal, the *Dobryna*'s cook, was furnished with an admirable kitchen, provided with a permanent stove, where he was duly installed with all his culinary apparatus.

"What a saving of expense it would be," exclaimed Ben Zoof, "if every household could be furnished with its own private volcano!"

The large cavern at the general junction of the galleries was fitted up as a drawing-room, and arranged with all the best furniture both of the gourbi and of the cabin of the *Dobryna*. Hither was also brought the schooner's library, containing a good variety of French and Russian books; lamps were suspended over the different tables; and the walls of the apartment were tapestried with the sails and adorned with the flags belonging to the yacht. The curtain of fire extending over the opening of the cavern provided it, as already stated, with light and heat.

The torrent of lava fell into a small rock-bound basin that had no apparent communication with the sea, and was evidently the aperture of a deep abyss, of which the waters, heated by the descent of the eruptive matter, would no doubt retain their liquid condition long after the Gallian Sea had become a sheet of ice.

A small excavation to the left of the common hall was allotted for the special use of Servadac and the count; another on the right was appropriated to the lieutenant and Ben Zoof; whilst a third recess, immediately at the back, made a convenient little chamber for Nina. The Spaniards and the Russian sailors took up their sleeping-quarters in the adjacent galleries, and found the temperature quite comfortable.

Such were the internal arrangements of Nina's Hive, the refuge where the little colony were full of hope that they would be able to brave the rigours of the stern winter-time that lay before them—a winter-time during which Gallia might possibly be projected even to the orbit of Jupiter, where the temperature would not exceed one twenty-fifth of the normal winter temperature of the earth.

The only discontented spirit was Isaac Hakkabut. Throughout all the preparations which roused even the Spaniards to activity, the Jew, still incredulous and deaf to every representation of the true state of things, insisted upon remaining in the creek at Gourbi Island; nothing could induce him to leave his tartan, where, like a miser, he would keep guard over his precious cargo, ever grumbling and growling, but with his weather-eye open in the hope of catching sight of some passing sail. It must be owned that the whole party were far from sorry to be relieved of his presence; his uncomely figure and repulsive countenance was a perpetual bugbear. He had given out in plain terms that he did not intend to part with any of his property, except for current money; and Servadac, equally resolute, had strictly forbidden any purchases to be made, hoping to wear out the rascal's obstinacy.

Hakkabut persistently refused to credit the real situation; he could not absolutely deny that some portions of the terrestrial globe had undergone a certain degree of modification, but nothing could bring him to believe that he was not, sooner or later, to resume his old line of business in the Mediterranean. With his wonted distrust of all with whom he came in contact, he regarded every argument that was urged upon him only as evidence of a plot that had been devised to deprive him of his goods. Repudiating, as he did utterly, the hypothesis that a fragment had beome detached from the earth, he scanned the horizon for hours together with an old telescope, the case of which had been patched up till it looked like a rusty stove-pipe, hoping to descry the passing trader with which he might effect some bartering upon advantageous terms.

At first he professed to regard the proposed removal into winter-quarters as an attempt to impose upon his credulity; but the frequent voyages made by the *Dobryna* to the south, and the repeated consignments of corn and cattle, soon served to make him aware that Captain Servadac and his companions were really contemplating a departure from Gourbi Island.

The movement set him thinking. What, he began to ask himself—what if all that was told him was true? What if this sea was no longer the Mediterranean? What if he should never again behold his German fatherland? What if his marts for business were gone for ever? A vague idea of ruin began to take possession of his mind: he must yield to necessity; he must do the best he could. As the result of his cogitations, he occasionally left his tartan and made a visit to the shore. At length he endeavoured to mingle with the busy group, who were hurrying on their preparations; but his advances were only met by jeers and scorn, and, ridiculed by all the rest, he was fain to turn his attention to Ben Zoof, to whom he offered a few pinches of tobacco.

"No, old Zebulon," said Ben Zoof, steadily refusing the gift, "it is against orders to take anything from you. Keep your cargo to yourself; eat and drink it all if you can; we are not to touch it."

Finding the subordinates incorruptible, Isaac determined to go to the fountain-head. He addressed himself to Servadac, and begged him to tell him the whole truth, piteously adding that surely it was unworthy of a French officer to deceive a poor old man like himself.

"Tell you the truth, man!" cried Servadac. "Confound it, I have told you the truth twenty times. Once for all, I tell you now, you have left yourself barely time enough to make your escape to yonder mountain."

"God and Mahomet have mercy on me!" muttered the Jew, whose creed frequently assumed a very ambiguous character.

"I will tell you what," continued the captain—"you shall have a few men to work the *Hansa* across, if you like."

"But I want to go to Algiers," whispered Hakkabut.

"How often am I to tell you that Algiers is no longer in existence? Only say yes or no—are you coming with us into winter-quarters?"

"God of Israel! what is to become of all my proparty?"

"But, mind you," continued the captain, not heeding the interruption, "if you do not choose voluntarily to come with us, I shall have the *Hansa*, by my orders, removed to a place of safety. I am not going to let your cursed obstinancy incur the risk of losing your cargo altogether."

"Merciful Heaven! I shall be ruined!" moaned Isaac, in despair.

"You are going the right way to ruin yourself and it would serve you right to leave you to your own devices. But be off! I have no more to say."

And, turning contemptuously on his heel, Servadac left the old man vociferating bitterly, and with uplifted hands protesting vehemently against the rapacity of the Gentiles.

By the 20th all preliminary arrangements were complete, and everything ready for a final departure from the island. The thermometer stood on an average at 8° below zero, and the water in the cistern was completely frozen. It was determined, therefore, for the colony to embark on the following day, and take up their residence in Nina's Hive.

A final consultation was held about the *Hansa*. Lieutenant Procope pronounced his decided conviction that it would be impossible for the tartan to resist the pressure of the ice in the harbour of the Shelif, and that there would be far more safety in the proximity of the volcano. It was agreed on all hands that the vessel must be shifted; and accordingly orders were given, four Russian sailors were sent on board, and only a few minutes elapsed after the *Dobryna* had weighed anchor, before the great lateen sail "of the tartan" was unfurled, and the "shop-ship," as Ben Zoof delighted to call it, was also on her way to the southward.

Long and loud were the lamentations of the Jew. He kept exclaiming that he had given no orders, that he was being moved against his will, that he had asked for no assistance, and needed none; but it required no very keen discrimination to observe that all along there was a lurking gleam of satisfaction in his little gray eyes, and when, a few hours later, he found himself securely anchored, and his property in a place of safety, he quite chuckled with glee.

"God of Israel!" he said in an undertone, "they have made no charge; the idiots have piloted me here for nothing."

For nothing! His whole nature exulted in the consciousness that he was enjoying a service that had been rendered gratuitously.

Destitute of human inhabitants, Gourbi Island was now left to the tenancy of such birds and beasts as had escaped the recent promiscuous slaughter. Birds, indeed, that had migrated in search of warmer shores, had returned, proving that this fragment of the French colony was the only shred of land that could yield them any sustenance; but their life must necessarily be short. It was utterly impossible that they could survive the cold that would soon ensue.

The colony took possession of their new abode with but few formalities. Everyone, however, approved of all the internal arrangements of Nina's Hive, and were profuse in their expressions of satisfaction at finding themselves located in such comfortable quarters. The only malcontent was Hakkabut; he had no share in the general enthusiasm, refused even to enter or inspect any of the galleries, and insisted on remaining on board his tartan.

"He is afraid," said Ben Zoof, "that he will have to pay for his lodgings. But wait a bit; we shall see how he stands the cold out there; the frost, no doubt, will drive the old fox out of his hole."

Towards evening the pots were set boiling, and a bountiful supper, to which all were invited, was spread in the central hall. The stores of the

Dobryna contained some excellent wine, some of which was broached to do honour to the occasion. The health of the governor general was drunk, as well as the toast "Success to his council," to which Ben Zoof was called upon to return thanks. The entertainment passed off merrily. The Spaniards were in the best of spirits; one of them played the guitar, another the castanets, and the rest joined in a ringing chorus. Ben Zoof contributed the famous Zouave refrain, well known throughout the French army, but rarely performed in finer style than by this *virtuoso*:

"MISTI GOTH DAR DAR TIRE LYRE!
FLIC! FLOC! FLAC! LIRETTE, LIRA!
FAR LA RIRA,
TOUR TALA RIRE,
TOUR LA RIBAUD,
RICANDEAU,
SANS REPOS, RÉPIT, RÉPIT, REPOS, RIS POT, RIPETTE!
SI VOUS ATTRAPEZ MON REFRAIN,

FAMEUX VOUS ÊTES."

The concert was succeeded by a ball, unquestionably the first that had ever taken place in Gallia. The Russian sailors exhibited some of their national dances, which gained considerable applause, even though they followed upon the marvelous fandangos of the Spaniards. Ben Zoof, in his turn, danced a *pas seul* (often performed in the Elysée Montmartre) with an elegance and vigour that earned many compliments from Negrete.

It was nine o'clock before the festivities came to an end, and by that time the company, heated by the high temperature of the hall, and by their own exertions, felt the want of a little fresh air. Accordingly the greater portion of the party, escorted by Ben Zoof, made their way into one of the adjacent galleries that led to the shore. Bervadac, with the count and lieutenant, did not follow immediately; but shortly afterwards they proceeded to join them, when on their way they were startled by loud cries from those in advance.

Their first impression was that they were cries of distress, and they were greatly relieved to find that they were shouts of delight, which the dryness and purity of the atmosphere caused to re-echo like a volley of musketry.

Reaching the mouth of the gallery, they found the entire group pointing with eager interest to the sky.

"Well, Ben Zoof," asked the captain, "what's the matter now?"

"Oh, your Excellency," ejaculated the orderly, "look there! look there! The moon! the moon's come back!"

And, sure enough, what was apparently the moon was rising above the mists of evening.

XXII
A FROZEN OCEAN

The moon! She had disappeared for weeks; was she now returning? Had she been faithless to the earth? and had she now approached to be a satellite of the new-born world?

"Impossible!" said Lieutenant Procope; "the earth is millions and millions of leagues away, and it is not probable that the moon has ceased to revolve about her."

"Why not?" remonstrated Servadac. "It would not be more strange than the other phenomena which we have lately witnessed. Why should not the moon have fallen within the limits of Gallia's attraction, and become her satellite?"

"Upon that supposition," put in the count, "I should think that it would be altogether unlikely that three months would elapse without our seeing her."

"Quite incredible!" continued Procope. "And there is another thing which totally disproves the captain's hypothesis; the magnitude of Gallia is far too insignificant for her power of attraction to carry off the moon."

"But," persisted Servadac, "why should not the same convulsion that tore us away from the earth have torn away the moon as well? After wandering about as she would for a while in the solar regions, I do not see why she should not have attached herself to us."

The lieutenant repeated his conviction that it was not likely.

"But why not?" again asked Servadac impetuously.

"Because, I tell you, the mass of Gallia is so inferior to that of the moon, that Gallia would become the moon's satellite; the moon could not possibly become hers."

"Assuming, however," continued Servadac, "such to be the case—"

"I am afraid," said the lieutenant, interrupting him, "that I cannot assume anything of the sort even for a moment."

Servadac smiled good-humoredly.

"I confess you seem to have the best of the argument, and if Gallia had become a satellite of the moon, it would not have taken three months to catch sight of her. I suppose you are right."

While this discussion had been going on, the satellite, or whatever it might be, had been rising steadily above the horizon, and had reached a position favourable for observation. Telescopes were brought, and it was very soon ascertained, beyond a question, that the new luminary was not the well-known Phœbe of terrestrial nights; it had no feature in common with the moon. Although it was apparently much nearer to Gallia than the moon to the earth, its superficies was hardly one-tenth as large, and so feebly did it reflect the light of the remote sun, that it scarcely emitted radiance enough to extinguish the dim lustre of stars of the eighth magnitude. Like the sun, it had risen in the west, and was now at its full. To confuse its identity with the moon was absolutely impossible; not even Servadac could discover a trace of the seas, chasms, craters, and mountains which have been so minutely delineated in lunar charts; and it could not be denied that any transient hope that had been excited as to their once again being about to enjoy the peaceful smiles of "the queen of night" must all be given up.

Count Timascheff finally suggested, though somewhat doubtfully, the question of the probability that Gallic, in her course across the zone of the minor planets, had carried off one of them; but whether it was one of the 169 asteroids already included in the astronomical catalogues, or one previously unknown, he did not presume to determine. The idea to a certain extent was plausible, inasmuch as it has been ascertained that several of the telescopic planets are of such small dimensions that a good walker might make a circuit of them in four and twenty hours; consequently Gallia, being of superior volume, might be supposed capable of exercising a power of attraction upon any of these miniature microcosms.

The first night in Nina's Hive passed without special incident; and next morning a regular scheme of life was definitely laid down. "My lord governor," as Ben Zoof, until he was peremptorily forbidden, delighted to call Servadac, had a wholesome dread of idleness and its consequences, and insisted upon each member of the party undertaking some special duty to fulfill. There was plenty to do. The domestic animals required a great deal of attention; a supply of food had to be secured and preserved; fishing had to be carried on while the condition of the sea would allow it; and in several places the galleries had to be further excavated to render them more available for use. Occupation, then, need never be wanting, and the daily round of labour could go on in orderly routine.

A perfect concord ruled the little colony. The Russians and Spaniards amalgamated well, and both did their best to pick up various scraps of French, which was considered the official language of the place. Servadac himself undertook the tuition of Pablo and Nina, Ben Zoof being their companion in play-hours, when he entertained them with enchanting stories in the best Parisian French, about "a lovely city at the foot of a mountain," where he always promised one day to take them.

The end of March came, but the cold was not intense to such a degree as to confine any of the party to the interior of their ;esort; several excursions were made along the shore, and for a radius of three or four miles the adjacent district was carefully explored. Investigation, however, always ended in the same result; turn their course in whatever direction they would, they found that the country retained everywhere its desert character, rocky, barren, and without a trace of vegetation. Here and there a slight layer of snow or a thin coating of ice arising from atmospheric condensation indicated the existence of superficial moisture, but it would require a period indefinitely long, exceeding human reckoning, before that moisture could collect into a stream and roll downwards over the stony strata to the sea. It seemed at present out of their power to determine whether the land upon which they were so happily settled was an island or a continent, and till the cold was abated they feared to undertake any lengthened expedition to ascertain the actual extent of the strange concrete of metallic crystallization.

By ascending one day to the summit of the volcano. Captain Servadac and the count succeeded in getting a general idea of the aspect of the country. The mountain itself was an enormous block rising symmetrically to a height of nearly 3,000 feet above the level of the sea, in the form of a truncated cone, of which the topmost section was crowned by a wreath of smoke issuing continuously from the mouth of a narrow crater.

Under the old condition of terrestrial things, the ascent of this steep acclivity would have been attended with much fatigue, but as the effect of the altered condition of the law of gravity, the travellers performed perpetual prodigies in the way of agility, and in little over an hour reached the edge of the crater, without more sense of exertion than if they had traversed a couple of miles on level ground. Gallia had its drawbacks, but it had some compensating advantages.

Telescopes in hand, the explorers from the summit scanned the surrounding view. Their anticipations had already realized what they saw. Just as they expected, on the north, east, and west lay the Gallian Sea, smoothed and motionless as a sheet of glass, the cold having, as it were, congealed the atmosphere so that there was not a breath of wind. Towards the south there seemed no limit to the land, and the volcano formed the apex of a triangle, of which the base was beyond the reach of vision. Viewed even from this height, whence distance would do much to soften the general asperity, the surface nevertheless seemed to be bristling with its myriads of hexagonal lamellæ, and to present difficulties which, to an ordinary pedestrian, would be insurmountable.

"Oh for some wings, or else a balloon!" cried Servadac, as he gazed around him; and then, looking down to the rock upon which they were standing, he added, "We seem to have been transplanted to a soil strange enough in its chemical character to bewilder the *savants* of a museum."

"And do you observe, captain," asked the count, "how the convexity of our little world curtails our view? See, how circumscribed is the horizon!"

Servadac replied that he had noticed the same circumstance from the top of the cliffs of Gourbi Island.

"Yes," said the count; "it becomes more and more obvious that ours is a very tiny world, and that Gourbi Island is the sole productive spot upon its surface. We have had a short summer, and who knows whether we are not entering upon a winter that may last for years, perhaps for centuries?"

"But we must not mind, count," said Servadac, smiling. "We have agreed, you know, that, come what may, we are to be philosophers."

"Ay, true, my friend," rejoined the count; "we must be philosophers and something more; we must be grateful to the good Protector who has hitherto befriended us, and we must trust His mercy to the end."

For a few moments they both stood in silence, and contemplated land and sea; then, having given a last glance over the dreary panorama, they prepared to wend their way down the mountain. Before they commenced their descent, however, they resolved to make a closer examination of the crater. They were particularly struck by what seemed to them almost the mysterious calmness with which the eruption was effected. There was none of the wild disorder and deafening tumult that usually accompany the discharge of volcanic matter, but the heated lava, rising with a uniform gentleness, quietly overran the limits of the crater, like the flow of water from the bosom of a peaceful lake. Instead of a boiler exposed to the action of an angry fire, the crater rather resembled a brimming basin, of which the contents were noiselessly escaping. Nor were there any igneous stones or red-hot cinders mingled with the smoke that crowned the summit; a circumstance that quite accorded with the absence of the pumice-stones, obsidians, and other minerals of volcanic origin with which the base of a burning mountain is generally strewn.

Captain Servadac was of opinion that this peculiarity augured favourably for the continuance of the eruption. Extreme violence in physical, as well as in moral nature, is never of long duration. The most terrible storms, like the most violent fits of passion, are not lasting; but here the calm flow of the liquid fire appeared to be supplied from a source that was inexhaustible, in the same way as the waters of Niagara, gliding on steadily to their final plunge, would defy all effort to arrest their course.

Before the evening of this day closed in, a most important change was effected in the condition of the Gallian Sea by the intervention of human agency. Notwithstanding the increasing cold, the sea, unruffled as it was by a breath of wind, still retained its liquid state. It is an established fact that water, under this condition of absolute stillness, will remain uncongealed at a temperature several degrees below zero, whilst experiment, at the same time, shows that a very slight shock will often be sufficient to convert it into solid ice.

It had occurred to Servadac that if some communication could be opened with Gourbi Island, there would be a fine scope for hunting expeditions. Having this ultimate object in view, he assembled his little colony upon a projecting rock at the extremity of the promontory, and having called Nina and Pablo out to him in front, he said: "Now, Nina, do you think you could throw something into the sea?"

"I think I could," replied the child, "but I am sure that Pablo would throw it a great deal further than I can."

"Never mind, you shall try first."

Putting a fragment of ice into Nina's hand, he addressed himself to Pablo:

"Look out, Pablo ; you shall see what a nice little fairy Nina is! Throw, Nina, throw, as hard as you can."

Nina balanced the piece of ice two or three times in her hand, and threw it forward with all her strength.

A sudden thrill seemed to vibrate across the motionless waters to the distant horizon, and the Gallian Sea had become a solid sheet of ice!

XXIII
A CARRIER-PIGEON

When, three hours after sunset, on the 23rd of March, the Gallian moon rose upon the western horizon, it was observed that she had entered upon her last quarter. She had taken only four days to pass from syzygy to quadrature, and it was consequently evident that she would be visible for little more than a week at a time, and that her lunation would be accomplished within sixteen days. The lunar months, like the solar days, had been diminished by one-half. Three days later the moon was in conjunction with the sun, and was consequently lost to view; Ben Zoof, as the first observer of the satellite, was extremely interested in its movements, and wondered whether it would ever reappear.

On the 26th, under an atmosphere perfectly clear and dry, the thermometer fell to 12° C. below zero. Of the present distance of Gallia from the sun, and the number of leagues she had traversed since the receipt of the last mysterious document, there were no means of judging; the extent of diminution in the apparent disc of the sun did not afford sufficient basis even for an approximate calculation; and Captain Servadac was perpetually regretting that they could receive no further tidings from the anonymous correspondent, whom he persisted in regarding as a fellow-countryman.

The solidity of the ice was perfect; the utter stillness of the air at the time when the final congelation of the waters had taken place had resulted in the formation of a surface that for smoothness would rival a skating-rink; without a crack or flaw it extended far beyond the range of vision.

The contrast to the ordinary aspect of polar seas was very remarkable. There, the ice-fields are an agglomeration of hummocks and icebergs, massed in wild confusion, often towering higher than the masts of the largest whalers, and from the instability of their foundations liable to an instantaneous loss of equilibrium; a breath of wind, a slight modification of the temperature, not infrequently serving to bring about a series of changes outrivalling the most elaborate transformation scenes of a pantomime. Here, on the contrary, the vast white plain was level as the desert of Sahara or the Russian steppes; the waters of the Gallian Sea were imprisoned beneath the solid sheet, which became continually thicker in the increasing cold.

Accustomed to the uneven crystallizations of their own frozen seas, the

Russians could not be otherwise than delighted with the polished surface that afforded them such excellent opportunity for enjoying their favourite pastime of skating. A supply of skates, found hidden away amongst the *Dobryna's* stores, was speedily brought into use. The Russians undertook the instruction of the Spaniards, and at the end of a few days, during which the temperature was only endurable through the absence of wind, there was not a Gallian who could not skate tolerably well, while many of them could describe figures involving the most complicated curves. Nina and Pablo earned loud applause by their rapid proficiency; Captain Servadac, an adept in athletics, almost outvied his instructor, the count; and Ben Zoof, who had upon some rare occasions skated upon the Lake of Montmartre (in his eyes, of course, a sea), performed prodigies in the art.

This exercise was not only healthful in itself, but it was acknowledged that, in ease of necessity, it might become a very useful means of locomotion. As Captain Servadac remarked, it was almost a substitute for railways, and as if to illustrate this proposition, Lieutenant Procope, perhaps the greatest expert in the party, accomplished the twenty miles to Gourbi Island and back in considerably less than four hours.

The temperature, meanwhile, continued to decrease, and the average reading of the thermometer was about 16° C. below zero; the light also diminished in proportion, and all objects appeared to be enveloped in a half-defined shadow, as though the sun were undergoing a perpetual eclipse. It was not surprising that the effect of this continuously overhanging gloom should be to induce a frequent depression of spirits amongst the majority of the little population, exiles as they were from their mother earth, and not unlikely, as it seemed, to be swept far away into the regions of another planetary sphere. Probably Count Timascheff, Captain Servadac, and Lieutenant Procope were the only members of the community who could bring any scientific judgment to bear upon the uncertainty that was before them, but a general sense of the strangeness of their situation could not fail at times to weigh heavily upon the minds of all. Under these circumstances it was very necessary to counteract the tendency to despond by continual diversion; and the recreation of skating thus opportunely provided, seemed just the thing to arouse the flagging spirits, and to restore a wholesome excitement.

With dogged obstinacy, Isaac Hakkabut refused to take any share either in the labours or the amusements of the colony. In spite of the cold, he had not been seen since the day of his arrival from Gourbi Island. Captain Servadac had strictly forbidden any communication with him; and the smoke that rose from the cabin chimney of the *Hansa* was the sole indication of the proprietor being still on board. There was nothing to prevent him, if he chose, from partaking gratuitously of the volcanic light and heat which were being enjoyed by all besides; but rather than abandon his close and personal oversight of his precious cargo, he preferred to sacrifice his own slender stock of fuel.

Both the schooner and the tartan had been carefully moored in the way that seemed to promise best for withstanding the rigour of the winter. After seeing the vessels made secure in the frozen creek, Lieutenant Procope, following the example of many Arctic explorers, had the precaution to have the ice bevelled away from the keels, so that there should be no risk of the ships' sides being crushed by the increasing pressure; he hoped that they would follow any rise in the level of the ice-field, and when the thaw should come, that they would easily regain their proper water-line.

On his last visit to Gourbi Island, the lieutenant had ascertained that north, east, and west, far as the eye could reach, the Gallian Sea had become one uniform sheet of ice. One spot alone refused to freeze; this was the pool immediately below the central cavern, the receptacle for the stream of burning lava. It was entirely enclosed by rocks, and if ever a few icicles were formed there by the action of the cold, they were very soon melted by the fiery shower. Hissing and spluttering as the hot lava came in contact with it, the water was in a continual state of ebullition, and the fish that abounded in its depths defied the angler's craft; they were, as Ben Zoof remarked, "too much boiled to bite."

At the beginning of April the weather changed. The sky became overcast, but there was no rise in the temperature. Unlike the polar winters of the earth, which ordinarily are affected by atmospheric influence, and liable to slight intermissions of their severity at various shiftings of the wind, Gallia's winter was caused by her immense distance from the source of all light and heat, and the cold was consequently destined to go on steadily increasing until it reached the limit ascertained by Fourier to be the normal temperature of the realms of space. With the over-clouding of the heavens there arose a violent tempest; but although the wind raged with an almost inconceivable fury, it was unaccompanied by either snow or rain. Its effect upon the burning curtain that covered the aperture of the central hall was very remarkable. So far from there being any likelihood of the fire being extinguished by the vehemence of the current of air, the hurricane seemed rather to act as a ventilator, which fanned the flame into greater activity, and the utmost care was necessary to avoid being burnt by the fragments of lava that were drifted into the interior of the grotto. More than once the curtain itself was rifted entirely asunder, but only to close up again immediately after allowing a momentary draught of cold air to penetrate the hall in a way that was refreshing and rather advantageous than otherwise.

On the 4th of April, after an absence of about four days, the new satellite, to Ben Zoof's great satisfaction, made its reappearance in a crescent form, a circumstance that seemed to justify the anticipation that henceforward it would continue to make a periodic revolution every fortnight.

The crust of ice and snow was far too stout for the beaks of the strongest birds to penetrate, and accordingly large swarms had left the island, and, following the human population, had taken refuge on the volcanic promontory; not that there the barren shore had anything in the way of nourishment to offer them, but their instinct impelled them to haunt now the very habitations which formerly they would have shunned. Scraps of food were thrown to them from the galleries; these were speedily devoured, but were altogether inadequate in quantity to meet the demand. At length, emboldened by hunger, several hundred birds ventured through the tunnel, and took up their quarters actually in Nina's Hive. Congregating in the large hall, the half-famished creatures did not hesitate to snatch bread, meat, or food of any description from the hands of the residents as they sat at table, and soon became such an intolerable nuisance that it formed one of the daily diversions to hunt them down; but although they were vigorously attacked by stones and sticks, and even occasionally by shot, it was with some difficulty that their number could be sensibly reduced.

By a systematic course of warfare the bulk of the birds were all expelled, with the exception of about a hundred, which began to build in the crevices of the rocks. These were left in quiet possession of their quarters, as not only was it deemed advisable to perpetuate the various breeds, but it was found that these birds acted as a kind of police, never failing either to chase away or to kill any others of their species who infringed upon what they appeared to regard as their own special privilege in intruding within the limits of their domain.

On the 15th loud cries were suddenly heard issuing from the mouth of the principal gallery.

"Help, help! I shall be killed!"

Pablo in a moment recognized the voice as Nina's. Outrunning even Ben Zoof he hurried to the assistance of his little playmate, and discovered that she was being attacked by half a dozen great sea-gulls, and only after receiving some severe blows from their beaks could he succeed by means of a stout cudgel in driving them away.

"Tell me, Nina, what is this?" he asked as soon as the tumult had subsided.

The child pointed to a bird which she was caressing tenderly in her bosom.

"A pigeon!" exclaimed Ben Zoof, who had reached the scene of the commotion. "A carrier-pigeon! And by all the saints of Montmartre, there is a little bag attached to its neck!"

He took the bird, and rushing into the hall placed it in Servadac's hands.

"Another message, no doubt," cried the captain, "from our unknown friend. Let us hope that this time he has given us his name and address."

All crowded round, eager to hear the news. In the struggle with the gulls the bag had been partially torn open, but still contained the following dispatch:

"GALLIA!"

CHEMIN PARCOURU DU JE1 MARS AU 1ER AVRIL: 39.000.000 L.!
DISTANCE DU SOLEIL: 110.000.000 1.!
CAPTÉ NÉRINA EN PASSANT.
VIVRES VONT MANQUER ET.... "

The rest of the document had been so damaged by the beaks of the gulls that it was illegible. Servadac was wild with vexation. He felt more and more convinced that the writer was a Frenchman, and that the last line indicated that he was in distress from scarcity of food. The very thought of a fellow-countryman in peril of starvation drove him well-nigh to distraction, and it was in vain that search was made everywhere near the scene of conflict in hopes of finding the missing scrap that might bear a signature or address.

Suddenly little Nina, who had again taken possession of the pigeon, and was hugging it to her breast, said:

"Look here, Ben Zoof!"

And as she spoke she pointed to the left wing of the bird.

The wing bore the faint impress of a postage stamp, and the one word:

"FORMENTERA."

XXIV
A SLEDGE-RIDE

Formentera was at once recognized by Servadac and the count as the name of one of the smallest of the Balearic Islands. It was more than probable that the unknown writer had thence sent out the mysterious documents, and from the message just come to hand by the carrier-pigeon, it appeared all but certain that at the beginning of April, a fortnight back, he had still been there. In one important particular the present communication differed from those that had preceded it: it was written entirely in French, and exhibited none of the ecstatic exclamations in other languages that had been remarkable in the two former papers. The concluding line, with its intimation of failing provisions, amounted almost to an appeal for help. Captain Servadac briefly drew attention to these points, and concluded by saying, "My friends, we must, without delay, hasten to the assistance of this unfortunate man."

"For my part," said the count, "I am quite ready to accompany you; it is not unlikely that he is not alone in his distress."

Lieutenant Procope expressed much surprise.

"We must have passed close to Formentera," he said, "when we explored the site of the Balearic Isles; this fragment must be very small; it must be smaller than the remaining splinter of Gibraltar or Ceuta; otherwise, surely it would never have escaped our observation."

"However small it may be," replied Servadac, "we must find it. How far off do you suppose it is?"

"It must be a hundred and twenty leagues away," said the lieutenant, thoughtfully; "and I do not quite understand how you would propose to get there."

"Why, on skates of course; no difficulty in that, I should imagine," answered Servadac, and he appealed to the count for confirmation of his opinion.

The count assented, but Procope looked doubtful.

"Your enterprise is generous," he said, "and I should be most unwilling to throw any unnecessary obstacle in the way of its execution; but, pardon me, if I submit to you a few considerations which to my mind are very important. First of all, the thermometer is already down to 22° below zero, and the keen wind from the south is making the temperature absolutely unendurable; in the second place, supposing you travel at the rate of twenty leagues a day, you would be exposed for at least six consecutive days; and thirdly, your expedition will be of small avail unless you convey provisions not only for yourselves, but for those whom you hope to relieve."

"We can carry our own provisions on our backs in knapsacks," interposed Servadac, quickly, unwilling to recognize any difficulty in the way.

"Granted that you can," answered the lieutenant, quietly; "but where, on this level ice-field, will you find shelter in your periods of rest? You must perish with cold; you will not have the chance of digging out ice-huts like the Esquimaux."

"As to rest," said Servadac, "we shall take none; we shall keep on our way continuously; by travelling day and night without intermission, we shall not be more than three days in reaching Formentera."

"Believe me," persisted the lieutenant, calmly, "your enthusiasm is carrying you too far; the feat you propose is impossible; but even conceding the possibility of your success in reaching your destination, what service do you imagine that you, half-starved and half-frozen yourself, could render to those who are already perishing by want and exposure? You would only bring them away to die."

The obvious and dispassionate reasoning of the lieutenant could not fail to impress the minds of those who listened to him; the impracticability of the journey became more and more apparent; unprotected on that drear expanse, any traveller must assuredly succumb to the snow-drifts that were continually being whirled across it. But Hector Servadac, animated by the generous desire of rescuing a suffering fellow-creature, could scarcely be brought within the bounds of common sense. Against his better judgment he was still bent upon the expedition, and Ben Zoof declared himself ready to accompany his master in the event of Count Timascheff hesitating to encounter the peril which the undertaking involved. But the count entirely repudiated all idea of shrinking from what, quite as much as the captain, he regarded as a sacred duty, and turning to Lieutenant Procope, told him that unless some better plan could be devised, he was prepared to start off at once and make the attempt to skate across to Formentera. The lieutenant, who was lost in thought, made no immediate reply.

"I wish we had a sledge," said Ben Zoof.

"I dare say that a sledge of some sort could be contrived," said the count; "but then we should have no dogs or reindeers to draw it."

"Why not rough-shoe the two horses?"

"They would never be able to endure the cold," objected the count.

"Never mind," said Servadac, "let us get our sledge and put them to the test. Something must be done!"

"I think," said Lieutenant Procope, breaking his thoughtful silence, "that I can tell you of a sledge already provided for your hand, and I can suggest a motive power surer and swifter than horses."

"What do you mean?" was the eager inquiry.

"I mean the *Dobryna*'s yawl," answered the lieutenant; "and I have no doubt that the wind would carry her rapidly along the ice."

The idea seemed admirable. Lieutenant Procope was well aware to what marvellous perfection the Americans had brought their sail-sledges, and had heard how in the vast prairies of the United States they had been known to outvie the speed of an express train, occasionally attaining a rate of more than a hundred miles an hour. The wind was still blowing hard from the south, and assuming that the yawl could be propelled with a velocity of about fifteen or at least twelve leagues an hour, he reckoned that it was quite possible to reach Formentera within twelve hours, that is to say, in a single day between the intervals of sunrise and sunrise.

The yawl was about twelve feet long, and capable of holding five or six people. The addition of a couple of iron runners would be all that was requisite to convert it into an excellent sledge, which, if a sail were hoisted, might be deemed certain to make a rapid progress over the smooth surface of the ice. For the protection of the passengers it was proposed to erect a kind of wooden roof lined with strong cloth; beneath this could be packed a supply of provisions, some warm furs, some cordials, and a portable stove to be heated by spirits of wine.

For the outward journey the wind was as favourable as could be desired; but it was to be apprehended that, unless the direction of the wind should change, the return would be a matter of some difficulty; a system of tacking might be carried out to a certain degree, but it was not likely that the yawl would answer her helm in any way corresponding to what would occur in the open sea. Captain Servadac, however, would not listen to any representation of probable difficulties; the future, he said, must provide for itself.

The engineer and several of the sailors set vigorously to work, and before the close of the day the yawl was furnished with a pair of stout iron runners, curved upwards in front, and fitted with a metal fin designed to assist in maintaining the directness of her course; the roof was put on, and beneath it were stored the provisions, the wraps, and the cooking utensils.

A strong desire was expressed by Lieutenant Procope that he should be allowed to accompany Captain Servadac instead of Count Timascheff. It was inadvisable for all three of them to go, as, in case of there being several persons to be rescued, the space at their command would be quite inadequate. The lieutenant urged that he was the most experienced seaman, and as such was best qualified to take command of the sledge and the management of the sails; and as it was not to be expected that Servadac would resign his intention of going in person to relieve his fellow-countryman, Procope submitted his own wishes to the count. The count was himself very anxious to have his share in the philanthropic enterprise, and demurred considerably to the proposals; he yielded, however, after a time, to Servadac's representations that in the event of the expedition proving disastrous, the little colony would need his services alike as governor and protector, and overcoming his reluctance to be left out of the perilous adventure, was prevailed upon to remain behind for the general good of the community at Nina's Hive.

At sunrise on the following morning, the 16th of April, Captain Servadac and the lieutenant took their places in the yawl. The thermometer was more than 20° below zero, and it was with deep emotion that their companions beheld them thus embarking upon the vast white plain. Ben Zoof's heart was too full for words; Count Timascheff could not forbear pressing his two brave friends to his bosom; the Spaniards and the Russian sailors crowded round for a farewell shake of the hand, and little Nina, her great eyes flooded with tears, held up her face for a parting kiss. The sad scene was not permitted to last long. The sail was quickly hoisted, and the sledge, just as if it had expanded a huge white wing, was in a little while carried far away beyond the horizon.

Light and unimpeded, the yawl scudded on with incredible speed. Two sails, a mainsail and a jib, were arranged to catch the wind to the greatest advantage, and the travellers estimated that their progress would be little under the rate of twelve leagues an hour. The motion of their novel vehicle was singularly gentle, the oscillation being less than that of an ordinary railway-carriage, while the diminished force of gravity contributed to the swiftness. Except that the clouds of ice-dust raised by the metal runners were an evidence that they had not actually left the level surface of the ice, the captain and lieutenant might again and again have imagined that they were being conveyed through the air in a balloon.

Lieutenant Procope, with his head all muffled up for fear of frost-bite, took an occasional peep through an aperture that, had been intentionally left in the roof, and by the help of a compass, maintained a proper and straight course for Formentera. Nothing could be more dejected than the aspect of that frozen sea;

not a single living creature relieved the solitude; both the travellers, Procope from a scientific point of view, Servadac from an aesthetic, were alike impressed by the solemnity of the scene, and when the lengthened shadow of the sail cast upon the ice by the oblique rays of the setting sun had disappeared, and day had given place to night, the two men, drawn together as by an involuntary impulse, mutually held each other's hands in silence.

There had been a new moon on the previous evening; but, in the absence of moonlight, the constellations shone with remarkable brilliancy. The new pole-star close upon the horizon was resplendent, and even had Lieutenant Procope been destitute of a compass, he would have had no difficulty in holding his course by the guidance of that alone. However great was the distance that separated Gallia from the sun, it was after all manifestly insignificant in comparison with the remoteness of the nearest of the fixed stars.

Observing that Servadac was completely absorbed in his own thoughts, Lieutenant Procope had leisure to contemplate some of the present perplexing problems, and to ponder over the true astronomical position. The last of the three mysterious documents had represented that Gallia, in conformity with Kepler's second law, had travelled along her orbit during the month of March twenty millions of leagues less than she had done in the previous month; yet, in the same time, her distance from the sun had nevertheless been increased by thirty-two millions of leagues. She was now, therefore, in the centre of the zone of telescopic planets that revolve between the orbits of Mars and Jupiter, and had captured for herself a satellite which, according to the document, was Nerina, one of the asteroids most recently identified. If thus, then, it was within the power of the unknown writer to estimate with such apparent certainty Gallia's exact position, was it not likely that his mathematical calculations would enable him to arrive at some definite conclusion as to the date at which she would begin again to approach the sun? Nay, was it not to be expected that he had already estimated, with sufficient approximation to truth, what was to be the true length of the Gallian year?

So intently had they each separately been following their own train of thought, that daylight reappeared almost before the travellers were aware of it. On consulting their instruments, they found that they must have travelled close upon a hundred leagues since they started, and they resolved to slacken their speed. The sails were accordingly taken in a little, and in spite of the intensity of the cold, the explorers ventured out of their shelter, in order that they might reconnoiter the plain, which was apparently as boundless as ever. It was completely desert; not so much as a single point of rock relieved the bare uniformity of its surface.

"Are we not considerably to the west of Formentera?" asked Servadac, after examining the chart.

"Most likely," replied Procope. "I have taken the same course as I should have done at sea, and I have kept some distance to windward of the island; we can bear straight down upon it whenever we like."

"Bear down then, now; and as quickly as you can. The yawl was at once put with her head to the northeast, and Captain Servadac, in defiance of the icy blast, remained standing at the bow, his gaze fixed on the horizon.

All at once his eye brightened.

"Look! look!" he exclaimed, pointing to a faint outline that broke the monotony of the circle that divided the plain from the sky.

In an instant the lieutenant had seized his telescope.

"I see what you mean," said he; "it is a pylon that has been used for some geodesic survey."

The next moment the sail was filled, and the yawl was bearing down upon the object with inconceivable swiftness, both Captain Servadac and the lieutenant too excited to utter a word. Mile after mile the distance rapidly grew less, and as they drew nearer the pylon they could see that it was erected on a low mass of rocks that was the sole interruption to the dull level of the field of ice. No wreath of smoke rose above the little island; it was manifestly impossible, they conceived, that any human being could there have survived the cold; the sad presentiment forced itself upon their minds that it was a mere cairn to which they had been hurrying.

Ten minutes later, and they were so near the rock that the lieutenant took in his sail, convinced that the impetus already attained would be sufficient to carry him to the land. Servadac's heart bounded as he caught sight of a fragment of blue canvas fluttering in the wind from the top of the pylon: it was all that now remained of the French national standard. At the foot of the pylon stood a miserable shed, its shutters tightly closed. No other habitation was to be seen; the entire island was less than a quarter of a mile in circumference; and the conclusion was irresistible that it was the sole surviving remnant of Formentera, once a member of the Balearic Archipelago.

To leap on shore, to clamber over the slippery stones, and to reach the cabin was but the work of a few moments. The worm-eaten door was bolted on the inside. Servadac began to knock with all his might. No answer. Neither shouting nor knocking could draw forth a reply.

"Let us force it open, Procope!" he said.

The two men put their shoulders to the door, which soon yielded to their vigorous efforts, and they found themselves inside the shed, and in almost total darkness. By opening a shutter they admitted what daylight they could, At first sight the wretched place seemed to be deserted; the little grate contained the ashes of a fire long since extinguished; all looked black and desolate. Another instant's investigation, however, revealed a bed in the extreme corner, and extended on the bed a human form.

"Dead!" sighed Servadac; "dead of cold and hunger!"

Lieutenant Procope bent down and anxiously contemplated the body.

"No; he is alive!" he said, and drawing a small flask from his pocket he poured a few drops of brandy between the lips of the senseless man.

There was a faint sigh, followed by a feeble voice, which uttered the one word, "Gallia?"

"Yes, yes! Gallia!" echoed Servadac, eagerly.

"My comet, my comet!" said the voice, so low as to be almost inaudible, and the unfortunate man relapsed again into unconsciousness.

"Where have I seen this man?" thought Servadac to himself; "his face is strangely familiar to me."

But it was no time for deliberation. Not a moment was to be lost in getting the unconscious astronomer away from his desolate quarters. He was soon conveyed to the yawl; his books, his scanty wardrobe, his papers, his instruments, and the blackboard which had served for his calculations, were quickly collected; the wind, by a fortuitous providence, had shifted into a favourable quarter; they set their sail with all speed, and ere long were on their journey back from Formentera.

Thirty-six hours later, the brave travellers were greeted by the acclamations of their fellow-colonists, who had been most anxiously awaiting their reappearance, and the still senseless savant, who had neither opened his eyes nor spoken a word throughout the journey, was safely deposited in the warmth and security of the great hall of Nina's Hive.

The Day of an American Journalist in 2889

by Jules Verne (with Michel Verne)

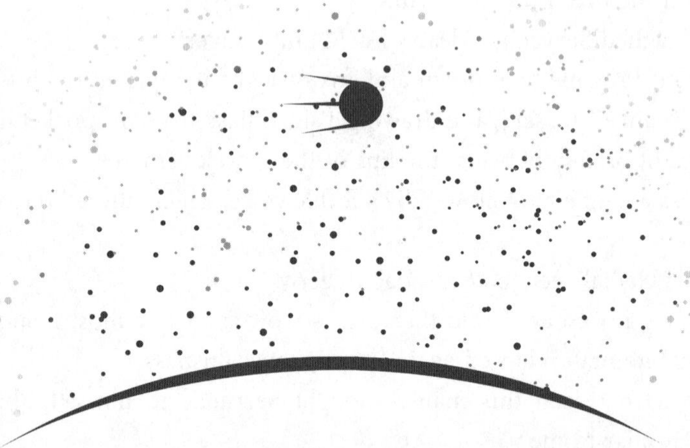

Little though they seem to think of it, the people of this twenty-ninth century live continually in fairyland. Surfeited as they are with marvels, they are indifferent in presence of each new marvel. To them all seems natural. Could they but duly appreciate the refinements of civilization in our day; could they but compare the present with the past, and so better comprehend the advance we have made! How much fairer they would find our modern towns, with populations amounting sometimes to 10,000,000 souls; their streets 300 feet wide, their houses 1000 feet in height; with a temperature the same in all seasons; with their lines of aerial locomotion crossing the sky in every direction! If they would but picture to themselves the state of things that once existed, when through muddy streets rumbling boxes on wheels, drawn by horses—yes, by horses!—were the only means of conveyance. Think of the railroads of the olden time, and you will be able to appreciate the pneumatic tubes through which today one travels at the rate of 1000 miles an hour. Would not our contemporaries prize the telephone and the telephote more highly if they had not forgotten the telegraph?

Singularly enough, all these transformations rest upon principles which were perfectly familiar to our remote ancestors, but which they disregarded. Heat, for instance, is as ancient as man himself; electricity was known 3000 years ago, and steam 1100 years ago. Nay, so early as ten centuries ago it was known that the differences between the several chemical and physical forces depend on the mode of vibration of the etheric particles, which is for each specifically different. When at last the kinship of all these forces was discovered, it is simply astounding that 500 years should still have to elapse before men could analyze and describe the several modes of vibration that constitute these differences. Above all, it is singular that the mode of reproducing these forces directly from one another, and of reproducing one without the others, should have remained undiscovered till less than a hundred years ago. Nevertheless, such was the course of events, for it was not till the year 2792 that the famous Oswald Nier made this great discovery.

Truly was he a great benefactor of the human race. His admirable discovery led to many another. Hence is sprung a pleiad of inventors, its brightest star being our great Joseph Jackson. To Jackson we are indebted for those wonderful instruments the new accumulators. Some of these absorb and condense the living force contained in the sun's rays; others, the electricity stored in our globe; others again, the energy coming from whatever source, as a waterfall, a stream, the winds, etc. He, too, it was that invented the transformer, a more wonderful contrivance still, which takes the living force from the accumulator, and, on the simple pressure of a button, gives it back to space in whatever form may be desired, whether as heat, light, electricity, or mechanical force, after having first obtained from it the work required. From the day when these two instruments were contrived is to be dated the era of true progress. They have put into the hands of man a power that is almost infinite. As for their applications, they are numberless. Mitigating the rigours of winter, by giving back to the atmosphere the surplus heat stored up during the summer, they have revolutionized agriculture. By supplying motive power for aerial navigation, they have given to commerce a mighty impetus. To them we are indebted for the continuous production of electricity without batteries or dynamos, of light without combustion or incandescence, and for an unfailing supply of mechanical energy for all the needs of industry.

Yes, all these wonders have been wrought by the accumulator and the transformer. And can we not to them also trace, indirectly, this latest wonder of all, the great "Earth Chronicle" building in 253rd Avenue, which was dedicated the other day? If George Washington Smith, the founder of the Manhattan "Chronicle", should come back to life today, what would he think were he to be told that this palace of marble and gold belongs to his remote descendant, Fritz Napoleon Smith, who, after thirty generations have come and gone, is owner of the same newspaper which his ancestor established!

For George Washington Smith's newspaper has lived generation after generation, now passing out of the family, now coming back to it. When, 200 years ago, the political centre of the United States was transferred from Washington to Centropolis, the newspaper followed the government and assumed the name of Earth Chronicle. Unfortunately, it was unable to maintain itself at the high level of its name. Pressed on all sides by rival journals of a more modern type, it was continually in danger of collapse. Twenty years ago its subscription list contained but a few hundred thousand names, and then Mr. Fritz Napoleon Smith bought it for a mere trifle, and originated telephonic journalism.

Every one is familiar with Fritz Napoleon Smith's system—a system made possible by the enormous development of telephony during the last hundred years. Instead of being printed, the Earth Chronicle is every morning spoken to subscribers, who, in interesting conversations with reporters, statesmen, and scientists, learn the news of the day. Furthermore, each subscriber owns a phonograph, and to this instrument he leaves the task of gathering the news whenever he happens not to be in a mood to listen directly himself. As for purchasers of single copies, they can at a very trifling cost learn all that is in the paper of the day at any of the innumerable phonographs set up nearly everywhere.

Fritz Napoleon Smith's innovation galvanized the old newspaper. In the course of a few years the number of subscribers grew to be 80,000,000, and Smith's wealth went on growing, till now it reaches the almost unimaginable figure of $10,000,000,000. This lucky hit has enabled him to erect his new building, a vast edifice with four façades each 3,250 feet in length, over which proudly floats the hundred-starred flag of the Union. Thanks to the same lucky hit, he is today king of newspaperdom; indeed, he would be king of all the Americans, too, if Americans could ever accept a king. You do not believe it? Well, then, look at the plenipotentiaries of all nations and our own ministers themselves crowding about his door, entreating his counsels, begging for his approbation, imploring the aid of his all-powerful organ. Reckon up the number of scientists and artists that he supports, of inventors that he has under his pay.

Yes, a king is he. And in truth his is a royalty full of burdens. His labours are incessant, and there is no doubt at all that in earlier times any man would have succumbed under the overpowering stress of the toil which Mr. Smith has to perform. Very fortunately for him, thanks to the progress of hygiene, which, abating all the old sources of unhealthfulness, has lifted the mean of human life from 37 up to 52 years, men have stronger constitutions now than heretofore. The discovery of nutritive air is still in the future, but in the meantime men today consume food that is compounded and prepared according to scientific principles, and they breathe an atmosphere freed from the micro-organisms that formerly used to swarm in it; hence they live longer than their forefathers and know nothing of the innumerable diseases of olden times.

Nevertheless, and notwithstanding these considerations, Fritz Napoleon Smith's mode of life may well astonish one. His iron constitution is taxed to the utmost by the heavy strain that is put upon it. Vain the attempt to estimate the amount of labour he undergoes; an example alone can give an idea of it. Let us then go about with him for one day as he attends to his multifarious concernments. What day? That matters little; it is the same every day. Let us then take at random September 25th of this present year 2889.

This morning Mr. Fritz Napoleon Smith awoke in very bad humor. His wife having left for France eight days ago, he was feeling disconsolate. Incredible though it seems, in all the ten years since their marriage, this is the first time that Mrs. Edith Smith, the professional beauty, has been so long absent from home; two or three days usually suffice for her frequent trips to Europe. The first thing that Mr. Smith does is to connect his phonotelephote, the wires of which communicate with his Paris mansion. The telephote! Here is another of the great triumphs of science in our time. The transmission of speech is an old story; the transmission of images by means of sensitive mirrors connected by wires is a thing but of yesterday. A valuable invention indeed, and Mr. Smith this morning was not niggard of blessings for the inventor, when by its aid he was able distinctly to see his wife notwithstanding the distance that separated him from her. Mrs. Smith, weary after the ball or the visit to the theatre the preceding night, is still abed, though it is near noontide at Paris. She is asleep, her head sunk in the lace-covered pillows. What? She stirs? Her lips move. She is dreaming perhaps? Yes, dreaming. She is talking, pronouncing a name, his name—Fritz! The delightful vision gave a happier turn to Mr. Smith's thoughts. And now, at the call of imperative duty, light-hearted he springs from his bed and enters his mechanical dresser.

Two minutes later the machine deposited him all dressed at the threshold of his office. The round of journalistic work was now begun. First he enters the hall of the novel-writers, a vast apartment crowned with an enormous transparent cupola. In one corner is a telephone, through which a hundred Earth Chronicle littérateurs in turn recount to the public in daily instalments a hundred novels. Addressing one of these authors who was waiting his turn, "Capital! Capital! my dear fellow," said he, "your last story. The scene where the village maid discusses interesting philosophical problems with her lover shows your very acute power of observation. Never have the ways of country folk been better portrayed. Keep on, my dear Archibald, keep on! Since yesterday, thanks to you, there is a gain of 5000 subscribers."

"Mr. John Last," he began again, turning to a new arrival, "I am not so well pleased with your work. Your story is not a picture of life; it lacks the elements of truth. And why? Simply because you run straight on to the end; because you do not analyze. Your heroes do this thing or that from this or that motive, which you assign without ever a thought of dissecting their mental and moral natures. Our feelings, you must remember, are far more complex than all that. In real life every act is the resultant of a hundred thoughts that come and go, and these you must study, each by itself, if you would create a living character. 'But,' you will say, 'in order to note these fleeting thoughts one must know them, must be able to follow them in their capricious meanderings.' Why, any child can do that, as you know. You have simply to make use of hypnotism, electrical or human, which gives one a two-fold being, setting free the witness-personality so that it may see, understand, and remember the reasons which determine the personality that acts. Just study yourself as you live from day to day, my dear Last. Imitate your associate whom I was complimenting a moment ago. Let yourself be hypnotized. What's that? You have tried it already? Not sufficiently, then, not sufficiently!"

Mr. Smith continues his round and enters the reporters' hall. Here 1500 reporters, in their respective places, facing an equal number of telephones, are communicating to the subscribers the news of the world as gathered during the night. The organization of this matchless service has often been described. Besides his telephone, each reporter, as the reader is aware, has in front of him a set of commutators, which enable him to communicate with any desired telephotic line. Thus the subscribers not only hear the news but see the occurrences. When an incident is described that is already past, photographs of its main features are transmitted with the narrative. And there is no confusion withal. The reporters' items, just like the different stories and all the other component parts of the journal, are classified automatically according to an ingenious system, and reach the hearer in due succession. Furthermore, the hearers are free to listen only to what specially concerns them. They may at pleasure give attention to one editor and refuse it to another.

Mr. Smith next addresses one of the ten reporters in the astronomical department—a department still in the embryonic stage, but which will yet play an important part in journalism.

"Well, Cash, what's the news?"

"We have phototelegrams from Mercury, Venus, and Mars."

"Are those from Mars of any interest?"

"Yes, indeed. There is a revolution in the Central Empire."

"And what of Jupiter?" asked Mr. Smith.

"Nothing as yet. We cannot quite understand their signals. Perhaps ours do not reach them."

"That's bad," exclaimed Mr. Smith, as he hurried away, not in the best of humour, toward the hall of the scientific editors.

With their heads bent down over their electric computers, thirty scientific men were absorbed in transcendental calculations. The coming of Mr. Smith was like the falling of a bomb among them.

"Well, gentlemen, what is this I hear? No answer from Jupiter? Is it always to be thus? Come, Cooley, you have been at work now twenty years on this problem, and yet—"

"True enough," replied the man addressed. "Our science of optics is still very defective, and through our mile-and-three-quarter telescopes."

"Listen to that, Peer," broke in Mr. Smith, turning to a second scientist. "Optical science defective! Optical science is your specialty. But," he continued, again addressing William Cooley, "failing with Jupiter, are we getting any results from the moon?"

"The case is no better there."

"This time you do not lay the blame on the science of optics. The moon is immeasurably less distant than Mars, yet with Mars our communication is fully established. I presume you will not say that you lack telescopes?"

"Telescopes? O no, the trouble here is about inhabitants!"

"That's it," added Peer.

"So, then, the moon is positively uninhabited?" asked Mr. Smith.

"At least," answered Cooley, "on the face which she presents to us. As for the opposite side, who knows?"

"Ah, the opposite side! You think, then," remarked Mr. Smith, musingly, "that if one could but—"

"Could what?"

"Why, turn the moon about-face."

"Ah, there's something in that," cried the two men at once. And indeed, so confident was their air, they seemed to have no doubt as to the possibility of success in such an undertaking.

"Meanwhile," asked Mr. Smith, after a moment's silence, "have you no news of interest today?"

"Indeed we have," answered Cooley. "The elements of Olympus are definitively settled. That great planet gravitates beyond Neptune at the mean distance of 11,400,799,642 miles from the sun, and to traverse its vast orbit takes 1311 years, 294 days, 12 hours, 43 minutes, 9 seconds."

"Why didn't you tell me that sooner?" cried Mr. Smith. "Now inform the reporters of this straightaway. You know how eager is the curiosity of the public with regard to these astronomical questions. That news must go into today's issue."

Then, the two men bowing to him, Mr. Smith passed into the next hall, an enormous gallery upward of 3200 feet in length, devoted to atmospheric advertising. Every one has noticed those enormous advertisements reflected from the clouds, so large that they may be seen by the populations of whole cities or even of entire countries. This, too, is one of Mr. Fritz Napoleon Smith's ideas, and in the Earth Chronicle building a thousand projectors are constantly engaged in displaying upon the clouds these mammoth advertisements.

When Mr. Smith today entered the sky-advertising department, he found the operators sitting with folded arms at their motionless projectors, and inquired as to the cause of their inaction. In response, the man addressed simply pointed to the sky, which was of a pure blue. "Yes," muttered Mr. Smith, "a cloudless sky! That's too bad, but what's to be done? Shall we produce rain? That we might do, but is it of any use? What we need is clouds, not rain. Go," said he, addressing the head engineer, "go see Mr. Samuel Mark, of the meteorological division of the scientific department, and tell him for me to go to work in earnest on the question of artificial clouds. It will never do for us to be always thus at the mercy of cloudless skies!"

Mr. Smith's daily tour through the several departments of his newspaper is now finished. Next, from the advertisement hall he passes to the reception chamber, where the ambassadors accredited to the American government are awaiting him, desirous of having a word of counsel or advice from the all-powerful editor. A discussion was going on when he entered. "Your Excellency will pardon me," the French Ambassador was saying to the Russian, "but I see nothing in the map of Europe that requires change. 'The North for the Slavs?' Why, yes, of course; but the South for the Matins. Our common frontier, the Rhine, it seems to me, serves very well. Besides, my government, as you must know, will firmly oppose every movement, not only against Paris, our capital, or our two great prefectures, Rome and Madrid, but also against the kingdom of Jerusalem, the dominion of Saint Peter, of which France means to be the trusty defender."

"Well said!" exclaimed Mr. Smith. "How is it," he asked, turning to the Russian ambassador, "that you Russians are not content with your vast empire, the most extensive in the world, stretching from the banks of the Rhine to the Celestial Mountains and the Kara-Korum, whose shores are washed by the Frozen Ocean, the Atlantic, the Mediterranean, and the Indian Ocean? Then, what is the use of threats? Is war possible in view of modern inventions-asphyxiating shells capable of being projected a distance of 60 miles, an electric spark of 90 miles, that can at one stroke annihilate a battalion; to say nothing of the plague, the cholera, the yellow fever, that the belligerents might spread among their antagonists mutually, and which would in a few days destroy the greatest armies?"

"True," answered the Russian; "but can we do all that we wish? As for us Russians, pressed on our eastern frontier by the Chinese, we must at any cost put forth our strength for an effort toward the west."

"O, is that all? In that case," said Mr. Smith, "the thing can be arranged. I will speak to the Secretary of State about it. The attention of the Chinese government shall be called to the matter. This is not the first time that the Chinese have bothered us."

"Under these conditions, of course—" And the Russian ambassador declared himself satisfied.

"Ah, Sir John, what can I do for you?" asked Mr. Smith as he turned to the representative of the people of Great Britain, who till now had remained silent.

"A great deal," was the reply. "If the Earth Chronicle would but open a campaign on our behalf—"

"And for what object?"

"Simply for the annulment of the Act of Congress annexing to the United States the British islands."

Though, by a just turn-about of things here below, Great Britain has become a colony of the United States, the English are not yet reconciled to the situation. At regular intervals they are ever addressing to the American government vain complaints.

"A campaign against the annexation that has been an accomplished fact for 150 years!" exclaimed Mr. Smith. "How can your people suppose that I would do anything so unpatriotic?"

"We at home think that your people must now be sated. The Monroe doctrine is fully applied; the whole of America belongs to the Americans. What more do you want? Besides, we will pay for what we ask."

"Indeed!" answered Mr. Smith, without manifesting the slightest irritation. "Well, you English will ever be the same. No, no, Sir John, do not count on me for help. Give up our fairest province, Britain? Why not ask France generously to renounce possession of Africa, that magnificent colony the complete conquest of which cost her the labour of 800 years? You will be well received!"

"You decline! All is over then!" murmured the British agent sadly. "The United Kingdom falls to the share of the Americans; the Indies to that of—"

"The Russians," said Mr. Smith, completing the sentence.

"Australia—"

"Has an independent government."

"Then nothing at all remains for us!" sighed Sir John, downcast.

"Nothing?" asked Mr. Smith, laughing. "Well, now, there's Gibraltar!"

With this sally, the audience ended. The clock was striking twelve, the hour of breakfast. Mr. Smith returns to his chamber. Where the bed stood in the morning a table all spread comes up through the floor. For Mr. Smith, being above all a practical man, has reduced the problem of existence to its simplest terms. For him, instead of the endless suites of apartments of the olden time, one room fitted with ingenious mechanical contrivances is enough. Here he sleeps, takes his meals, in short, lives.

He seats himself. In the mirror of the phonotelephote is seen the same chamber at Paris which appeared in it this morning. A table furnished forth is likewise in readiness here, for notwithstanding the difference of hours, Mr. Smith and his wife have arranged to take their meals simultaneously. It is delightful thus to take breakfast tête-a-tête with one who is 3000 miles or so away. Just now, Mrs. Smith's chamber has no occupant.

"She is late! Woman's punctuality! Progress everywhere except there!" muttered Mr. Smith as he turned the tap for the first dish. For like all wealthy folk in our day, Mr. Smith has done away with the domestic kitchen and is a subscriber to the Grand Alimentation Company, which sends through a great network of tubes to subscribers' residences all sorts of dishes, as a varied assortment is always in readiness. A subscription costs money, to be sure, but the cuisine is of the best, and the system has this advantage, that it does away with the pestering race of the cordons-bleus. Mr. Smith received and ate, all alone, the hors-d'oeuvre, entrées, rôti and legumes that constituted the repast. He was just finishing the dessert when Mrs. Smith appeared in the mirror of the telephote.

"Why, where have you been?" asked Mr. Smith through the telephone.

"What! You are already at the dessert? Then I am late," she exclaimed, with a winsome naïveté. "Where have I been, you ask? Why, at my dress-maker's. The hats are just lovely this season! I suppose I forgot to note the time, and so am a little late."

"Yes, a little," growled Mr. Smith; "so little that I have already quite finished breakfast. Excuse me if I leave you now, but I must be going."

"O certainly, my dear; good-by till evening."

Smith stepped into his air-coach, which was in waiting for him at a window. "Where do you wish to go, sir?" inquired the coachman.

"Let me see; I have three hours," Mr. Smith mused. "Jack, take me to my accumulator works at Niagara."

For Mr. Smith has obtained a lease of the great falls of Niagara. For ages the energy developed by the falls went unutilized. Smith, applying Jackson's invention, now collects this energy, and lets or sells it. His visit to the works took more time than he had anticipated. It was four o'clock when he returned home, just in time for the daily audience which he grants to callers.

One readily understands how a man situated as Smith is must be beset with requests of all kinds. Now it is an inventor needing capital; again it is some visionary who comes to advocate a brilliant scheme which must surely yield millions of profit. A choice has to be made between these projects, rejecting the worthless, examining the questionable ones, accepting the meritorious. To this work Mr. Smith devotes every day two full hours.

The callers were fewer today than usual—only twelve of them. Of these, eight had only impracticable schemes to propose. In fact, one of them wanted to revive painting, an art fallen into desuetude owing to the progress made in colour-photography. Another, a physician, boasted that he had discovered a cure for nasal catarrh! These impracticables were dismissed in short order. Of the four projects favourably received, the first was that of a young man whose broad forehead betokened his intellectual power.

"Sir, I am a chemist," he began, "and as such I come to you."

"Well!"

"Once the elementary bodies," said the young chemist, "were held to be sixty-two in number; a hundred years ago they were reduced to ten; now only three remain irresolvable, as you are aware."

"Yes, yes."

"Well, sir, these also I will show to be composite. In a few months, a few weeks, I shall have succeeded in solving the problem. Indeed, it may take only a few days."

"And then?"

"Then, sir, I shall simply have determined the absolute. All I want is money enough to carry my research to a successful issue."

"Very well," said Mr. Smith. "And what will be the practical outcome of your discovery?"

"The practical outcome? Why, that we shall be able to produce easily all bodies whatever—stone, wood, metal, fibres—"

"And flesh and blood?" queried Mr. Smith, interrupting him. "Do you pretend that you expect to manufacture a human being out and out?"

"Why not?"

Mr. Smith advanced $100,000 to the young chemist, and engaged his services for the Earth Chronicle laboratory.

The second of the four successful applicants, starting from experiments made so long ago as the nineteenth century and again and again repeated, had conceived the idea of removing an entire city all at once from one place to another. His special project had to do with the city of Granton, situated, as everybody knows, some fifteen miles inland. He proposes to transport the city on rails and to change it into a watering-place. The profit, of course, would be enormous. Mr. Smith, captivated by the scheme, bought a half-interest in it.

"As you are aware, sir," began applicant No. 3, "by the aid of our solar and terrestrial accumulators and transformers, we are able to make all the seasons the same. I propose to do something better still. Transform into heat a portion of the surplus energy at our disposal; send this heat to the poles; then the polar regions, relieved of their snow-cap, will become a vast territory available for man's use. What think you of the scheme?"

"Leave your plans with me, and come back in a week. I will have them examined in the meantime."

Finally, the fourth announced the early solution of a weighty scientific problem. Every one will remember the bold experiment made a hundred years ago by Dr. Nathaniel Faithburn. The doctor, being a firm believer in human hibernation—in other words, in the possibility of our suspending our vital functions and of calling them into action again after a time—resolved to subject the theory to a practical test. To this end, having first made his last will and pointed out the proper method of awakening him; having also directed that his sleep was to continue a hundred years to a day from the date of his apparent death, he unhesitatingly put the theory to the proof in his own person.

Reduced to the condition of a mummy, Dr. Faithburn was coffined and laid in a tomb. Time went on. September 25th, 2889, being the day set for his resurrection, it was proposed to Mr. Smith that he should permit the second part of the experiment to be performed at his residence this evening.

"Agreed. Be here at ten o'clock," answered Mr. Smith; and with that the day's audience was closed.

Left to himself, feeling tired, he lay down on an extension chair. Then, touching a knob, he established communication with the Central Concert Hall, whence our greatest maestros send out to subscribers their delightful successions of accords determined by recondite algebraic formulas. Night was approaching. Entranced by the harmony, forgetful of the hour, Smith did not notice that it was growing dark. It was quite dark when he was aroused by the sound of a door opening. "Who is there?" he asked, touching a commutator.

Suddenly, in consequence of the vibrations produced, the air became luminous.

"Ah! you, Doctor?"

"Yes," was the reply. "How are you?"

"I am feeling well."

"Good! Let me see your tongue. All right! Your pulse. Regular! And your appetite?"

"Only passably good."

"Yes, the stomach. There's the rub. You are over-worked. If your stomach is out of repair, it must be mended. That requires study. We must think about it."

"In the meantime," said Mr. Smith, "you will dine with me."

As in the morning, the table rose out of the floor. Again, as in the morning, the potage, rôti, ragoûts, and legumes were supplied through the food-pipes. Toward the close of the meal, phonotelephotic communication was made with Paris. Smith saw his wife, seated alone at the dinner-table, looking anything but pleased at her loneliness.

"Pardon me, my dear, for having left you alone," he said through the telephone. "I was with Dr. Wilkins."

"Ah, the good doctor!" remarked Mrs. Smith, her countenance lighting up.

"Yes. But, pray, when are you coming home?"

"This evening."

"Very well. Do you come by tube or by air-train?"

"Oh, by tube."

"Yes; and at what hour will you arrive?"

"About eleven, I suppose."

"Eleven by Centropolis time, you mean?"

"Yes."

"Good-by, then, for a little while," said Mr. Smith as he severed communication with Paris.

Dinner over, Dr. Wilkins wished to depart. "I shall expect you at ten," said Mr Smith. "Today, it seems, is the day for the return to life of the famous Dr. Faithburn. You did not think of it, I suppose. The awakening is to take place here in my house. You must come and see. I shall depend on your being here."

"I will come back," answered Dr. Wilkins.

Left alone, Mr. Smith busied himself with examining his accounts—a task of vast magnitude, having to do with transactions which involve a daily expenditure of upward of $800,000. Fortunately, indeed, the stupendous progress of mechanic art in modern times makes it comparatively easy. Thanks to the Piano Electro-Reckoner, the most complex calculations can be made in a few seconds. In two hours Mr. Smith completed his task. Just in time. Scarcely had he turned over the last page when Dr. Wilkins arrived. After him came the body of Dr. Faithburn, escorted by a numerous company of men of science. They commenced work at once. The casket being laid down in the middle of the room, the telephote was got in readiness. The outer world, already notified, was anxiously expectant, for the whole world could be eye-witnesses of the performance, a reporter meanwhile, like the chorus in the ancient drama, explaining it all viva voce through the telephone.

"They are opening the casket," he explained. "Now they are taking Faithburn out of it—a veritable mummy, yellow, hard, and dry. Strike the body and it resounds like a block of wood. They are now applying heat; now electricity. No result. These experiments are suspended for a moment while Dr. Wilkins makes an examination of the body. Dr. Wilkins, rising, declares the man to be dead. 'Dead!' exclaims every one present. 'Yes,' answers Dr. Wilkins, 'dead!' 'And how long has he been dead?' Dr. Wilkins makes another examination. 'A hundred years,' he replies."

The case stood just as the reporter said. Faithburn was dead, quite certainly dead! "Here is a method that needs improvement," remarked Mr. Smith to Dr. Wilkins, as the scientific committee on hibernation bore the casket out. "So much for that experiment. But if poor Faithburn is dead, at least he is sleeping," he continued. "I wish I could get some sleep. I am tired out, Doctor, quite tired out! Do you not think that a bath would refresh me?"

"Certainly. But you must wrap yourself up well before you go out into the hall-way. You must not expose yourself to cold."

"Hall-way? Why, Doctor, as you well know, everything is done by machinery here. It is not for me to go to the bath; the bath will come to me. Just look!" and he pressed a button. After a few seconds a faint rumbling was heard, which grew louder and louder. Suddenly the door opened, and the tub appeared.

Such, for this year of grace 2889, is the history of one day in the life of the editor of the Earth Chronicle. And the history of that one day is the history of 365 days every year, except leap-years, and then of 366 days—for as yet no means has been found of increasing the length of the terrestrial year.

A MARTIAN ODYSSEY

by Stanley G. Weinbaum

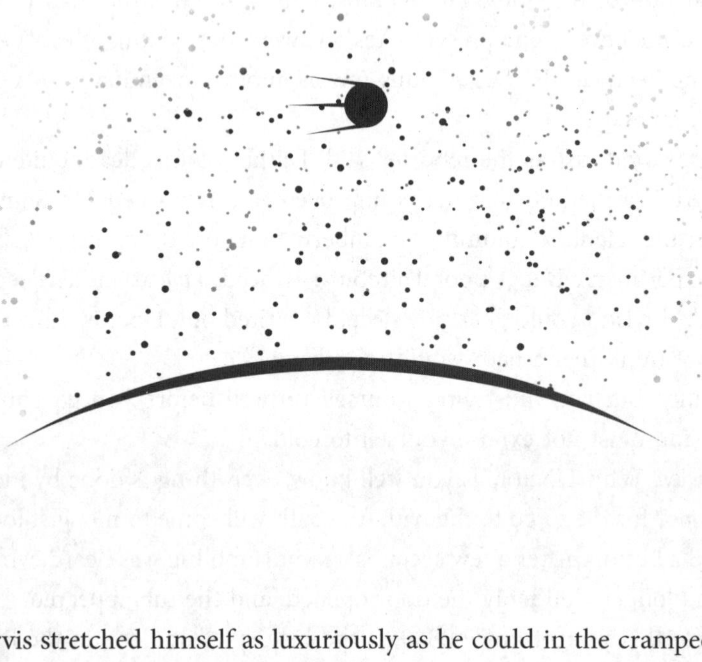

Jarvis stretched himself as luxuriously as he could in the cramped general quarters of the *Ares*.

"Air you can breathe!" he exulted. "It feels as thick as soup after the thin stuff out there!" He nodded at the Martian landscape stretching flat and desolate in the light of the nearer moon, beyond the glass of the port.

The other three stared at him sympathetically—Putz, the engineer, Leroy, the biologist, and Harrison, the astronomer and captain of the expedition. Dick Jarvis was chemist of the famous crew, the *Ares* expedition, first human beings to set foot on the mysterious neighbour of the earth, the planet Mars. This, of course, was in the old days, less than twenty years after the mad American Doheny perfected the atomic blast at the cost of his life, and only a decade after the equally mad Cardoza rode on it to the moon. They were true pioneers, these four of the *Ares*. Except for a half-dozen moon expeditions and the ill-fated de Lancey flight aimed at the seductive orb of Venus, they were the first men to feel other gravity than earth's, and certainly the first successful crew to leave the earth-moon system. And they deserved that success when one considers the difficulties and discomforts—the months spent in acclimatization chambers back on earth, learning to breathe the air as tenuous as that of Mars, the challenging of the void in the tiny rocket driven by the cranky reaction motors of the twenty-first century, and mostly the facing of an absolutely unknown world.

Jarvis stretched and fingered the raw and peeling tip of his frost-bitten nose. He sighed again contentedly.

"Well," exploded Harrison abruptly, "are we going to hear what happened? You set out all shipshape in an auxiliary rocket, we don't get a peep for ten days, and finally Putz here picks you out of a lunatic ant-heap with a freak ostrich as your pal! Spill it, man!"

"Speel?" queried Leroy perplexedly. "Speel what?"

"He means '*spiel*,'" explained Putz soberly. "It iss to tell."

Jarvis met Harrison's amused glance without the shadow of a smile. "That's right, Karl," he said in grave agreement with Putz. "*Ich spiel es!*" He grunted comfortably and began.

"According to orders," he said, "I watched Karl here take off toward the North, and then I got into my flying sweat-box and headed South. You'll remember, Cap—we had orders not to land, but just scout about for points of interest. I set the two cameras clicking and buzzed along, riding pretty high—about two thousand feet—for a couple of reasons. First, it gave the cameras a greater field, and second, the under-jets travel so far in this half-vacuum they call air here that they stir up dust if you move low."

"We know all that from Putz," grunted Harrison. "I wish you'd saved the films, though. They'd have paid the cost of this junket; remember how the public mobbed the first moon pictures?"

"The films are safe," retorted Jarvis. "Well," he resumed, "as I said, I buzzed along at a pretty good clip; just as we figured, the wings haven't much lift in this air at less than a hundred miles per hour, and even then I had to use the under-jets.

"So, with the speed and the altitude and the blurring caused by the under-jets, the seeing wasn't any too good. I could see enough, though, to distinguish that what I sailed over was just more of this grey plain that we'd been examining the whole week since our landing—same blobby growths and the same eternal carpet of crawling little plant-animals, or biopods, as Leroy calls them. So I sailed along, calling back my position every hour as instructed, and not knowing whether you heard me."

"I did!" snapped Harrison.

"A hundred and fifty miles south," continued Jarvis imperturbably, "the surface changed to a sort of low plateau, nothing but desert and orange-tinted sand. I figured that we were right in our guess, then, and this grey plain we dropped on was really the Mare Cimmerium which would make my orange desert the region called Xanthus. If I were right, I ought to hit another grey plain, the Mare Chronium in another couple of hundred miles, and then another orange desert, Thyle I or II. And so I did."

"Putz verified our position a week and a half ago!" grumbled the captain. "Let's get to the point."

"Coming!" remarked Jarvis. "Twenty miles into Thyle—believe it or not—I crossed a canal!"

"Putz photographed a hundred! Let's hear something new!"

"And did he also see a city?"

"Twenty of 'em, if you call those heaps of mud cities!"

"Well," observed Jarvis, "from here on I'll be telling a few things Putz didn't see!" He rubbed his tingling nose, and continued. "I knew that I had sixteen hours of daylight at this season, so eight hours—eight hundred miles—from here, I decided to turn back. I was still over Thyle, whether I or II I'm not sure, not more than twenty-five miles into it. And right there, Putz's pet motor quit!"

"Quit? How?" Putz was solicitous.

"The atomic blast got weak. I started losing altitude right away, and suddenly there I was with a thump right in the middle of Thyle! Smashed my nose on the window, too!" He rubbed the injured member ruefully.

"Did you maybe try vashing der combustion chamber mit acid sulphuric?" inquired Putz. "Sometimes der lead giffs a secondary radiation—"

"Naw!" said Jarvis disgustedly. "I wouldn't try that, of course—not more than ten times! Besides, the bump flattened the landing gear and busted off the under-jets. Suppose I got the thing working—what then? Ten miles with the blast coming right out of the bottom and I'd have melted the floor from under me!"

He rubbed his nose again. "Lucky for me a pound only weighs seven ounces here, or I'd have been mashed flat!"

"I could have fixed!" ejaculated the engineer. "I bet it vas not serious."

"Probably not," agreed Jarvis sarcastically. "Only it wouldn't fly. Nothing serious, but I had my choice of waiting to be picked up or trying to walk back—eight hundred miles, and perhaps twenty days before we had to leave! Forty miles a day! Well," he concluded, "I chose to walk. Just as much chance of being picked up, and it kept me busy."

"We'd have found you," said Harrison.

"No doubt. Anyway, I rigged up a harness from some seat straps, and put the water tank on my back, took a cartridge belt and revolver, and some iron rations, and started out."

"Water tank!" exclaimed the little biologist, Leroy. "She weigh one-quarter ton!"

"Wasn't full. Weighed about two hundred and fifty pounds earth-weight, which is eighty-five here. Then, besides, my own personal two hundred and ten pounds is only seventy on Mars, so, tank and all, I grossed a hundred and fifty-five, or fifty-five pounds less than my everyday earth-weight. I figured on that when I undertook the forty-mile daily stroll. Oh—of course I took a thermo-skin sleeping bag for these wintry Martian nights.

"Off I went, bouncing along pretty quickly. Eight hours of daylight meant twenty miles or more. It got tiresome, of course—plugging along over a soft sand desert with nothing to see, not even Leroy's crawling biopods. But an hour or so brought me to the canal—just a dry ditch about four hundred feet wide, and straight as a railroad on its own company map.

"There'd been water in it sometime, though. The ditch was covered with what looked like a nice green lawn. Only, as I approached, the lawn moved out of my way!"

"Eh?" said Leroy.

"Yeah, it was a relative of your biopods. I caught one—a little grass-like blade about as long as my finger, with two thin, stemmy legs."

"He is where?" Leroy was eager.

"He is let go! I had to move, so I plowed along with the walking grass opening in front and closing behind. And then I was out on the orange desert of Thyle again.

"I plugged steadily along, cussing the sand that made going so tiresome, and, incidentally, cussing that cranky motor of yours, Karl. It was just before twilight that I reached the edge of Thyle, and looked down over the gray Mare Chronium. And I knew there was seventy-five miles of *that* to be walked over, and then a couple of hundred miles of that Xanthus desert, and about as much more Mare Cimmerium. Was I pleased? I started cussing you fellows for not picking me up!"

"We were trying, you sap!" said Harrison.

"That didn't help. Well, I figured I might as well use what was left of daylight in getting down the cliff that bounded Thyle. I found an easy place, and down I went. Mare Chronium was just the same sort of place as this—crazy leafless plants and a bunch of crawlers; I gave it a glance and hauled out my sleeping bag. Up to that time, you know, I hadn't seen anything worth worrying about on this half-dead world—nothing dangerous, that is."

"Did you?" queried Harrison.

"*Did I!* You'll hear about it when I come to it. Well, I was just about to turn in when suddenly I heard the wildest sort of shenanigans!"

"Vot iss shenanigans?" inquired Putz.

"He says, 'Je ne sais quoi,'" explained Leroy. "It is to say, 'I don't know what.'"

"That's right," agreed Jarvis. "I didn't know what, so I sneaked over to find out. There was a racket like a flock of crows eating a bunch of canaries—whistles, cackles, caws, trills, and what have you. I rounded a clump of stumps, and there was Tweel!"

"Tweel?" said Harrison, and "Tveel?" said Leroy and Putz.

"That freak ostrich," explained the narrator. "At least, Tweel is as near as I can pronounce it without sputtering. He called it something like 'Trrrweerrlll.'"

"What was he doing?" asked the Captain.

"He was being eaten! And squealing, of course, as any one would."

"Eaten! By what?"

"I found out later. All I could see then was a bunch of black ropy arms tangled around what looked like, as Putz described it to you, an ostrich. I wasn't going to interfere, naturally; if both creatures were dangerous, I'd have one less to worry about.

"But the bird-like thing was putting up a good battle, dealing vicious blows with an eighteen-inch beak, between screeches. And besides, I caught a glimpse or two of what was on the end of those arms!" Jarvis shuddered. "But the clincher was when I noticed a little black bag or case hung about the neck of the bird-thing! It was intelligent! That or tame, I assumed. Anyway, it clinched my decision. I pulled out my automatic and fired into what I could see of its antagonist.

"There was a flurry of tentacles and a spurt of black corruption, and then the thing, with a disgusting sucking noise, pulled itself and its arms into a hole in the ground. The other let out a series of clacks, staggered around on legs about as thick as golf sticks, and turned suddenly to face me. I held my weapon ready, and the two of us stared at each other.

"The Martian wasn't a bird, really. It wasn't even bird-like, except just at first glance. It had a beak all right, and a few feathery appendages, but the beak wasn't really a beak. It was somewhat flexible; I could see the tip bend slowly from side to side; it was almost like a cross between a beak and a trunk. It had four-toed feet, and four-fingered things—hands, you'd have to call them, and a little roundish body, and a long neck ending in a tiny head—and that beak. It stood an inch or so taller than I, and—well, Putz saw it!"

The engineer nodded. "*Ja!* I saw!"

Jarvis continued. "So—we stared at each other. Finally the creature went into a series of clackings and twitterings and held out its hands toward me, empty. I took that as a gesture of friendship."

"Perhaps," suggested Harrison, "it looked at that nose of yours and thought you were its brother!"

"Huh! You can be funny without talking! Anyway, I put up my gun and said 'Aw, don't mention it,' or something of the sort, and the thing came over and we were pals.

"By that time, the sun was pretty low and I knew that I'd better build a fire or get into my thermo-skin. I decided on the fire. I picked a spot at the base of the Thyle cliff, where the rock could reflect a little heat on my back. I started breaking off chunks of this desiccated Martian vegetation, and my companion caught the idea and brought in an armful. I reached for a match, but the Martian fished into his pouch and brought out something that looked like a glowing coal; one touch of it, and the fire was blazing—and you all know what a job we have starting a fire in this atmosphere!

"And that bag of his!" continued the narrator. "That was a manufactured article, my friends; press an end and she popped open—press the middle and she sealed so perfectly you couldn't see the line. Better than zippers.

"Well, we stared at the fire a while and I decided to attempt some sort of communication with the Martian. I pointed at myself and said 'Dick'; he caught the drift immediately, stretched a bony claw at me and repeated 'Tick.' Then I pointed at him, and he gave that whistle I called Tweel; I can't imitate his accent.

Things were going smoothly; to emphasize the names, I repeated 'Dick,' and then, pointing at him, 'Tweel.'

"There we stuck! He gave some clacks that sounded negative, and said something like 'P-p-p-proot.' And that was just the beginning; I was always 'Tick,' but as for him—part of the time he was 'Tweel,' and part of the time he was 'P-p-p-proot,' and part of the time he was sixteen other noises!

"We just couldn't connect. I tried 'rock,' and I tried 'star,' and 'tree,' and 'fire,' and Lord knows what else, and try as I would, I couldn't get a single word! Nothing was the same for two successive minutes, and if that's a language, I'm an alchemist! Finally I gave it up and called him Tweel, and that seemed to do.

"But Tweel hung on to some of my words. He remembered a couple of them, which I suppose is a great achievement if you're used to a language you have to make up as you go along. But I couldn't get the hang of his talk; either I missed some subtle point or we just didn't *think* alike—and I rather believe the latter view.

"I've other reasons for believing that. After a while I gave up the language business, and tried mathematics. I scratched two plus two equals four on the ground, and demonstrated it with pebbles. Again Tweel caught the idea, and informed me that three plus three equals six. Once more we seemed to be getting somewhere.

"So, knowing that Tweel had at least a grammar school education, I drew a circle for the sun, pointing first at it, and then at the last glow of the sun. Then I sketched in Mercury, and Venus, and Mother Earth, and Mars, and finally, pointing to Mars, I swept my hand around in a sort of inclusive gesture to indicate that Mars was our current environment. I was working up to putting over the idea that my home was on the earth.

"Tweel understood my diagram all right. He poked his beak at it, and with a great deal of trilling and clucking, he added Deimos and Phobos to Mars, and then sketched in the earth's moon!

"Do you see what that proves? It proves that Tweel's race uses telescopes—that they're civilized!"

"Does not!" snapped Harrison. "The moon is visible from here as a fifth magnitude star. They could see its revolution with the naked eye."

"The moon, yes!" said Jarvis. "You've missed my point. Mercury isn't visible! And Tweel knew of Mercury because he placed the Moon at the *third* planet, not the second. If he didn't know Mercury, he'd put the earth second, and Mars third, instead of fourth! See?"

"Humph!" said Harrison.

"Anyway," proceeded Jarvis, "I went on with my lesson. Things were going smoothly, and it looked as if I could put the idea over. I pointed at the earth on my diagram, and then at myself, and then, to clinch it, I pointed to myself and then to the earth itself shining bright green almost at the zenith.

"Tweel set up such an excited clacking that I was certain he understood. He jumped up and down, and suddenly he pointed at himself and then at the sky, and then at himself and at the sky again. He pointed at his middle and then at Arcturus, at his head and then at Spica, at his feet and then at half a dozen stars, while I just gaped at him. Then, all of a sudden, he gave a tremendous leap. Man, what a hop! He shot straight up into the starlight, seventy-five feet if an inch! I saw him silhouetted against the sky, saw him turn and come down at me head first, and land smack on his beak like a javelin! There he stuck square in the centre of my sun-circle in the sand—a bull's eye!"

"Nuts!" observed the captain. "Plain nuts!"

"That's what I thought, too! I just stared at him open-mouthed while he pulled his head out of the sand and stood up. Then I figured he'd missed my point, and I went through the whole blamed rigamarole again, and it ended the same way, with Tweel on his nose in the middle of my picture!"

"Maybe it's a religious rite," suggested Harrison.

"Maybe," said Jarvis dubiously. "Well, there we were. We could exchange ideas up to a certain point, and then—blooey! Something in us was different, unrelated; I don't doubt that Tweel thought me just as screwy as I thought him. Our minds simply looked at the world from different viewpoints, and perhaps his viewpoint is as true as ours. But—we couldn't get together, that's all. Yet, in spite of all difficulties, I *liked* Tweel, and I have a queer certainty that he liked me."

"Nuts!" repeated the captain. "Just daffy!"

"Yeah? Wait and see. A couple of times I've thought that perhaps we—" He paused, and then resumed his narrative. "Anyway, I finally gave it up, and got into my thermo-skin to sleep. The fire hadn't kept me any too warm, but that damned sleeping bag did. Got stuffy five minutes after I closed myself in. I opened it a little and bingo! Some eighty-below-zero air hit my nose, and that's when I got this pleasant little frostbite to add to the bump I acquired during the crash of my rocket.

"I don't know what Tweel made of my sleeping. He sat around, but when I woke up, he was gone. I'd just crawled out of my bag, though, when I heard some twittering, and there he came, sailing down from that three-story Thyle cliff to alight on his beak beside me. I pointed to myself and toward the north, and he pointed at himself and toward the south, but when I loaded up and started away, he came along.

"Man, how he travelled! A hundred and fifty feet at a jump, sailing through the air stretched out like a spear, and landing on his beak. He seemed surprised at my plodding, but after a few moments he fell in beside me, only every few minutes he'd go into one of his leaps, and stick his nose into the sand a block ahead of me. Then he'd come shooting back at me; it made me nervous at first to see that beak of his coming at me like a spear, but he always ended in the sand at my side.

"So the two of us plugged along across the Mare Chronium. Same sort of place as this—same crazy plants and same little green biopods growing in the sand, or crawling out of your way. We talked—not that we understood each other, you know, but just for company. I sang songs, and I suspect Tweel did too; at least, some of his trillings and twitterings had a subtle sort of rhythm.

"Then, for variety, Tweel would display his smattering of English words. He'd point to an outcropping and say 'rock,' and point to a pebble and say it again; or he'd touch my arm and say 'Tick,' and then repeat it. He seemed terrifically amused that the same word meant the same thing twice in succession, or that the same word could apply to two different objects. It set me wondering if perhaps his language wasn't like the primitive speech of some earth people—you know, Captain, like the Negritoes, for instance, who haven't any generic words. No word for food or water or man—words for good food and bad food, or rain water and sea water, or strong man and weak man—but no names for general classes. They're too primitive to understand that rain water and sea water are just different aspects of the same thing. But that wasn't the case with Tweel; it was just that we were somehow mysteriously different—our minds were alien to each other. And yet—we *liked* each other!"

"Looney, that's all," remarked Harrison. "That's why you two were so fond of each other."

"Well, I like *you*!" countered Jarvis wickedly. "Anyway," he resumed, "don't get the idea that there was anything screwy about Tweel. In fact, I'm not so sure but that he couldn't teach our highly praised human intelligence a trick or two. Oh, he wasn't an intellectual superman, I guess; but don't overlook the point that he managed to understand a little of my mental workings, and I never even got a glimmering of his."

"Because he didn't have any!" suggested the captain, while Putz and Leroy blinked attentively.

"You can judge of that when I'm through," said Jarvis. "Well, we plugged along across the Mare Chronium all that day, and all the next. Mare Chronium—Sea of Time! Say, I was willing to agree with Schiaparelli's name by the end of that march! Just that grey, endless plain of weird plants, and never a sign of any other life. It was so monotonous that I was even glad to see the desert of Xanthus toward the evening of the second day.

"I was fair worn out, but Tweel seemed as fresh as ever, for all I never saw him drink or eat. I think he could have crossed the Mare Chronium in a couple of hours with those block-long nose dives of his, but he stuck along with me. I offered him some water once or twice; he took the cup from me and sucked the liquid into his beak, and then carefully squirted it all back into the cup and gravely returned it.

"Just as we sighted Xanthus, or the cliffs that bounded it, one of those nasty sand clouds blew along, not as bad as the one we had here, but mean to travel against. I pulled the transparent flap of my thermo-skin bag across my face and managed pretty well, and I noticed that Tweel used some feathery appendages growing like a mustache at the base of his beak to cover his nostrils, and some similar fuzz to shield his eyes."

"He is a desert creature!" ejaculated the little biologist, Leroy.

"Huh? Why?"

"He drink no water—he is adapt' for sand storm—"

"Proves nothing! There's not enough water to waste any where on this desiccated pill called Mars. We'd call all of it desert on earth, you know." He paused. "Anyway, after the sand storm blew over, a little wind kept blowing in our faces, not strong enough to stir the sand. But suddenly things came drifting along from the Xanthus cliffs—small, transparent spheres, for all the world like glass tennis balls! But light—they were almost light enough to float even in this thin air—empty, too; at least, I cracked open a couple and nothing came out but a bad smell. I asked Tweel about them, but all he said was 'No, no, no,' which I took to mean that he knew nothing about them. So they went bouncing by like tumbleweeds, or like soap bubbles, and we plugged on toward Xanthus. Tweel pointed at one of the crystal balls once and said 'rock,' but I was too tired to argue with him. Later I discovered what he meant.

"We came to the bottom of the Xanthus cliffs finally, when there wasn't much daylight left. I decided to sleep on the plateau if possible; anything dangerous, I reasoned, would be more likely to prowl through the vegetation of the Mare Chronium than the sand of Xanthus. Not that I'd seen a single sign of menace, except the rope-armed black thing that had trapped Tweel, and apparently that didn't prowl at all, but lured its victims within reach. It couldn't lure me while I slept, especially as Tweel didn't seem to sleep at all, but simply sat patiently around all night. I wondered how the creature had managed to trap Tweel, but there wasn't any way of asking him. I found that out too, later; it's devilish!

"However, we were ambling around the base of the Xanthus barrier looking for an easy spot to climb. At least, I was. Tweel could have leaped it easily, for the cliffs were lower than Thyle—perhaps sixty feet. I found a place and started up, swearing at the water tank strapped to my back—it didn't bother me except when climbing—and suddenly I heard a sound that I thought I recognized!

"You know how deceptive sounds are in this thin air. A shot sounds like the pop of a cork. But this sound was the drone of a rocket, and sure enough, there went our second auxiliary about ten miles to westward, between me and the sunset!"

"Vas me!" said Putz. "I hunt for you."

"Yeah; I knew that, but what good did it do me? I hung on to the cliff and yelled and waved with one hand. Tweel saw it too, and set up a trilling and twittering, leaping to the top of the barrier and then high into the air. And while I watched, the machine droned on into the shadows to the south.

"I scrambled to the top of the cliff. Tweel was still pointing and trilling excitedly, shooting up toward the sky and coming down head-on to stick upside down on his beak in the sand. I pointed toward the south and at myself, and he said, 'Yes—Yes—Yes'; but somehow I gathered that he thought the flying thing was a relative of mine, probably a parent. Perhaps I did his intellect an injustice; I think now that I did.

"I was bitterly disappointed by the failure to attract attention. I pulled out my thermo-skin bag and crawled into it, as the night chill was already apparent. Tweel stuck his beak into the sand and drew up his legs and arms and looked for all the world like one of those leafless shrubs out there. I think he stayed that way all night."

"Protective mimicry!" ejaculated Leroy. "See? He is desert creature!"

"In the morning," resumed Jarvis, "we started off again. We hadn't gone a hundred yards into Xanthus when I saw something queer! This is one thing Putz didn't photograph, I'll wager!

"There was a line of little pyramids—tiny ones, not more than six inches high, stretching across Xanthus as far as I could see! Little buildings made of pygmy bricks, they were, hollow inside and truncated, or at least broken at the top and empty. I pointed at them and said 'What?' to Tweel, but he gave some negative twitters to indicate, I suppose, that he didn't know. So off we went, following the row of pyramids because they ran north, and I was going north.

"Man, we trailed that line for hours! After a while, I noticed another queer thing: they were getting larger. Same number of bricks in each one, but the bricks were larger.

"By noon they were shoulder high. I looked into a couple—all just the same, broken at the top and empty. I examined a brick or two as well; they were silica, and old as creation itself!"

"How you know?" asked Leroy.

"They were weathered—edges rounded. Silica doesn't weather easily even on earth, and in this climate—!"

"How old you think?"

"Fifty thousand—a hundred thousand years. How can I tell? The little ones we saw in the morning were older—perhaps ten times as old. Crumbling. How old would that make *them*? Half a million years? Who knows?" Jarvis paused a moment. "Well," he resumed, "we followed the line. Tweel pointed at them and said 'rock' once or twice, but he'd done that many times before. Besides, he was more or less right about these.

"I tried questioning him. I pointed at a pyramid and asked 'People?' and indicated the two of us. He set up a negative sort of clucking and said, 'No, no, no. No one-one-two. No two-two-four,' meanwhile rubbing his stomach. I just stared at him and he went through the business again. 'No one-one-two. No two-two-four.' I just gaped at him."

"That proves it!" exclaimed Harrison. "Nuts!"

"You think so?" queried Jarvis sardonically. "Well, I figured it out different! 'No one-one-two!' You don't get it, of course, do you?"

"Nope—nor do you!"

"I think I do! Tweel was using the few English words he knew to put over a very complex idea. What, let me ask, does mathematics make you think of?"

"Why—of astronomy. Or—or logic!"

"That's it! 'No one-one-two!' Tweel was telling me that the builders of the pyramids weren't people—or that they weren't intelligent, that they weren't reasoning creatures! Get it?"

"Huh! I'll be damned!"

"You probably will."

"Why," put in Leroy, "he rub his belly?"

"Why? Because, my dear biologist, that's where his brains are! Not in his tiny head—in his middle!"

"*C'est* impossible!"

"Not on Mars, it isn't! This flora and fauna aren't earthly; your biopods prove that!" Jarvis grinned and took up his narrative. "Anyway, we plugged along across Xanthus and in about the middle of the afternoon, something else queer happened. The pyramids ended."

"Ended!"

"Yeah; the queer part was that the last one—and now they were ten-footers—was capped! See? Whatever built it was still inside; we'd trailed 'em from their half-million-year-old origin to the present.

"Tweel and I noticed it about the same time. I yanked out my automatic (I had a clip of Boland explosive bullets in it) and Tweel, quick as a sleight-of-hand trick, snapped a queer little glass revolver out of his bag. It was much like our weapons, except that the grip was larger to accommodate his four-taloned hand. And we held our weapons ready while we sneaked up along the lines of empty pyramids.

"Tweel saw the movement first. The top tiers of bricks were heaving, shaking, and suddenly slid down the sides with a thin crash. And then—something—something was coming out!

"A long, silvery-grey arm appeared, dragging after it an armoured body. Armoured, I mean, with scales, silver-grey and dull-shining. The arm heaved the body out of the hole; the beast crashed to the sand.

"It was a nondescript creature—body like a big grey cask, arm and a sort of mouth-hole at one end; stiff, pointed tail at the other—and that's all. No other limbs, no eyes, ears, nose—nothing! The thing dragged itself a few yards, inserted its pointed tail in the sand, pushed itself upright, and just sat.

"Tweel and I watched it for ten minutes before it moved. Then, with a creaking and rustling like—oh, like crumpling stiff paper—its arm moved to the mouth-hole and out came a brick! The arm placed the brick carefully on the ground, and the thing was still again.

"Another ten minutes—another brick. Just one of Nature's bricklayers. I was about to slip away and move on when Tweel pointed at the thing and said 'rock'!

I went 'huh?' and he said it again. Then, to the accompaniment of some of his trilling, he said, 'No—no—,' and gave two or three whistling breaths.

"Well, I got his meaning, for a wonder! I said, 'No breath?' and demonstrated the word. Tweel was ecstatic; he said, 'Yes, yes, yes! No, no, no breet!' Then he gave a leap and sailed out to land on his nose about one pace from the monster!

"I was startled, you can imagine! The arm was going up for a brick, and I expected to see Tweel caught and mangled, but—nothing happened! Tweel pounded on the creature, and the arm took the brick and placed it neatly beside the first. Tweel rapped on its body again, and said 'rock,' and I got up nerve enough to take a look myself.

"Tweel was right again. The creature was rock, and it didn't breathe!"

"How you know?" snapped Leroy, his black eyes blazing interest.

"Because I'm a chemist. The beast was made of silica! There must have been pure silicon in the sand, and it lived on that. Get it? We, and Tweel, and those plants out there, and even the biopods are *carbon* life; this thing lived by a different set of chemical reactions. It was silicon life!"

"*La vie silicieuse!*" shouted Leroy. "I have suspect, and now it is proof! I must go see! *Il faut que je—*"

"All right! All right!" said Jarvis. "You can go see. Anyhow, there the thing was, alive and yet not alive, moving every ten minutes, and then only to remove a brick. Those bricks were its waste matter. See, Frenchy? We're carbon, and our waste is carbon dioxide, and this thing is silicon, and *its* waste is silicon dioxide—silica. But silica is a solid, hence the bricks. And it builds itself in, and when it is covered, it moves over to a fresh place to start over. No wonder it creaked! A living creature half a million years old!"

"How you know how old?" Leroy was frantic.

"We trailed its pyramids from the beginning, didn't we? If this weren't the original pyramid builder, the series would have ended somewhere before we found him, wouldn't it?—ended and started over with the small ones. That's simple enough, isn't it?

"But he reproduces, or tries to. Before the third brick came out, there was a little rustle and out popped a whole stream of those little crystal balls. They're his spores, or eggs, or seeds—call 'em what you want. They went bouncing by across Xanthus just as they'd bounced by us back in the Mare Chronium. I've a hunch how they work, too—this is for your information, Leroy. I think the crystal shell of silica is no more than a protective covering, like an eggshell, and that the active principle is the smell inside. It's some sort of gas that attacks silicon, and if the shell is broken near a supply of that element, some reaction starts that ultimately develops into a beast like that one."

"You should try!" exclaimed the little Frenchman. "We must break one to see!"

"Yeah? Well, I did. I smashed a couple against the sand. Would you like to come back in about ten thousand years to see if I planted some pyramid monsters? You'd most likely be able to tell by that time!" Jarvis paused and drew a deep breath. "Lord! That queer creature! Do you picture it? Blind, deaf, nerveless, brainless—just a mechanism, and yet—immortal! Bound to go on making bricks, building pyramids, as long as silicon and oxygen exist, and even afterwards it'll just stop. It won't be dead. If the accidents of a million years bring it its food again, there it'll be, ready to run again, while brains and civilizations are part of the past. A queer beast—yet I met a stranger one!"

"If you did, it must have been in your dreams!" growled Harrison.

"You're right!" said Jarvis soberly. "In a way, you're right. The dream-beast! That's the best name for it—and it's the most fiendish, terrifying creation one could imagine! More dangerous than a lion, more insidious than a snake!"

"Tell me!" begged Leroy. "I must go see!"

"Not *this* devil!" He paused again. "Well," he resumed, "Tweel and I left the pyramid creature and plowed along through Xanthus. I was tired and a little disheartened by Putz's failure to pick me up, and Tweel's trilling got on my nerves, as did his flying nosedives. So I just strode along without a word, hour after hour across that monotonous desert.

"Toward mid-afternoon we came in sight of a low dark line on the horizon. I knew what it was. It was a canal; I'd crossed it in the rocket and it meant that we were just one-third of the way across Xanthus. Pleasant thought, wasn't it? And still, I was keeping up to schedule.

"We approached the canal slowly; I remembered that this one was bordered by a wide fringe of vegetation and that Mud-heap City was on it.

"I was tired, as I said. I kept thinking of a good hot meal, and then from that I jumped to reflections of how nice and home-like even Borneo would seem after this crazy planet, and from that, to thoughts of little old New York, and then to thinking about a girl I know there—Fancy Long. Know her?"

"Vision entertainer," said Harrison. "I've tuned her in. Nice blonde—dances and sings on the *Yerba Mate* hour."

"That's her," said Jarvis ungrammatically. "I know her pretty well—just friends, get me?—though she came down to see us off in the *Ares*. Well, I was thinking about her, feeling pretty lonesome, and all the time we were approaching that line of rubbery plants.

"And then—I said, 'What 'n Hell!' and stared. And there she was—Fancy Long, standing plain as day under one of those crack-brained trees, and smiling and waving just the way I remembered her when we left!"

"Now you're nuts, too!" observed the captain.

"Boy, I almost agreed with you! I stared and pinched myself and closed my eyes and then stared again—and every time, there was Fancy Long smiling and waving! Tweel saw something, too; he was trilling and clucking away, but I scarcely heard him. I was bounding toward her over the sand, too amazed even to ask myself questions.

"I wasn't twenty feet from her when Tweel caught me with one of his flying leaps. He grabbed my arm, yelling, 'No—no—no!' in his squeaky voice. I tried to shake him off—he was as light as if he were built of bamboo—but he dug his claws in and yelled. And finally some sort of sanity returned to me and I stopped less than ten feet from her. There she stood, looking as solid as Putz's head!"

"Vot?" said the engineer.

"She smiled and waved, and waved and smiled, and I stood there dumb as Leroy, while Tweel squeaked and chattered. I *knew* it couldn't be real, yet—there she was!

"Finally I said, 'Fancy! Fancy Long!' She just kept on smiling and waving, but looking as real as if I hadn't left her thirty-seven million miles away.

"Tweel had his glass pistol out, pointing it at her. I grabbed his arm, but he tried to push me away. He pointed at her and said, 'No breet! No breet!' and I understood that he meant that the Fancy Long thing wasn't alive. Man, my head was whirling!

"Still, it gave me the jitters to see him pointing his weapon at her. I don't know why I stood there watching him take careful aim, but I did. Then he squeezed the handle of his weapon; there was a little puff of steam, and Fancy Long was gone! And in her place was one of those writhing, black, rope-armed horrors like the one I'd saved Tweel from!

"The dream-beast! I stood there dizzy, watching it die while Tweel trilled and whistled. Finally he touched my arm, pointed at the twisting thing, and said, 'You one-one-two, he one-one-two.' After he'd repeated it eight or ten times, I got it. Do any of you?"

"*Oui!*" shrilled Leroy. "*Moi—je le comprends!* He mean you think of something, the beast he know, and you see it! *Un chien*—a hungry dog, he would see the big bone with meat! Or smell it—not?"

"Right!" said Jarvis. "The dream-beast uses its victim's longings and desires to trap its prey. The bird at nesting season would see its mate, the fox, prowling for its own prey, would see a helpless rabbit!"

"How he do?" queried Leroy.

"How do I know? How does a snake back on earth charm a bird into its very jaws? And aren't there deep-sea fish that lure their victims into their mouths? Lord!" Jarvis shuddered. "Do you see how insidious the monster is? We're warned now—but henceforth we can't trust even our eyes. You might see me—I might see one of you—and back of it may be nothing but another of those black horrors!"

"How'd your friend know?" asked the captain abruptly.

"Tweel? I wonder! Perhaps he was thinking of something that couldn't possibly have interested me, and when I started to run, he realized that I saw something different and was warned. Or perhaps the dream-beast can only project a single vision, and Tweel saw what I saw—or nothing. I couldn't ask him. But it's just another proof that his intelligence is equal to ours or greater."

"He's daffy, I tell you!" said Harrison. "What makes you think his intellect ranks with the human?"

"Plenty of things! First, the pyramid-beast. He hadn't seen one before; he said as much. Yet he recognized it as a dead-alive automaton of silicon."

"He could have heard of it," objected Harrison. "He lives around here, you know."

"Well how about the language? I couldn't pick up a single idea of his and he learned six or seven words of mine. And do you realize what complex ideas he put over with no more than those six or seven words? The pyramid-monster—the dream-beast! In a single phrase he told me that one was a harmless automaton and the other a deadly hypnotist. What about that?"

"Huh!" said the captain.

"*Huh* if you wish! Could you have done it knowing only six words of English? Could you go even further, as Tweel did, and tell me that another creature was of a sort of intelligence so different from ours that understanding was impossible—even more impossible than that between Tweel and me?"

"Eh? What was that?"

"Later. The point I'm making is that Tweel and his race are worthy of our friendship. Somewhere on Mars—and you'll find I'm right—is a civilization and culture equal to ours, and maybe more than equal. And communication is possible between them and us; Tweel proves that. It may take years of patient trial, for their minds are alien, but less alien than the next minds we encountered—if they *are* minds."

"The next ones? What next ones?"

"The people of the mud cities along the canals." Jarvis frowned, then resumed his narrative. "I thought the dream-beast and the silicon-monster were the strangest beings conceivable, but I was wrong. These creatures are still more alien, less understandable than either and far less comprehensible than Tweel, with whom friendship is possible, and even, by patience and concentration, the exchange of ideas.

"Well," he continued, "we left the dream-beast dying, dragging itself back into its hole, and we moved toward the canal. There was a carpet of that queer walking-grass scampering out of our way, and when we reached the bank, there was a yellow trickle of water flowing. The mound city I'd noticed from the rocket was a mile or so to the right and I was curious enough to want to take a look at it.

"It had seemed deserted from my previous glimpse of it, and if any creatures were lurking in it—well, Tweel and I were both armed. And by the way, that crystal weapon of Tweel's was an interesting device; I took a look at it after the dream-beast episode. It fired a little glass splinter, poisoned, I suppose, and I guess it held at least a hundred of 'em to a load. The propellent was steam—just plain steam!"

"Shteam!" echoed Putz. "From vot come, shteam?"

"From water, of course! You could see the water through the transparent handle and about a gill of another liquid, thick and yellowish. When Tweel squeezed the handle—there was no trigger—a drop of water and a drop of the yellow stuff squirted into the firing chamber, and the water vaporized—pop!—like that. It's not so difficult; I think we could develop the same principle. Concentrated sulphuric acid will heat water almost to boiling, and so will quicklime, and there's potassium and sodium—

"Of course, his weapon hadn't the range of mine, but it wasn't so bad in this thin air, and it *did* hold as many shots as a cowboy's gun in a Western movie. It was effective, too, at least against Martian life; I tried it out, aiming at one of the crazy plants, and darned if the plant didn't wither up and fall apart! That's why I think the glass splinters were poisoned.

"Anyway, we trudged along toward the mud-heap city and I began to wonder whether the city builders dug the canals. I pointed to the city and then at the canal, and Tweel said 'No—no—no!' and gestured toward the south. I took it to mean that some other race had created the canal system, perhaps Tweel's people. I don't know; maybe there's still another intelligent race on the planet, or a dozen others. Mars is a queer little world.

"A hundred yards from the city we crossed a sort of road—just a hard-packed mud trail, and then, all of a sudden, along came one of the mound builders!

"Man, talk about fantastic beings! It looked rather like a barrel trotting along on four legs with four other arms or tentacles. It had no head, just body and members and a row of eyes completely around it. The top end of the barrel-body was a diaphragm stretched as tight as a drum head, and that was all. It was pushing a little coppery cart and tore right past us like the proverbial bat out of Hell. It didn't even notice us, although I thought the eyes on my side shifted a little as it passed.

"A moment later another came along, pushing another empty cart. Same thing—it just scooted past us. Well, I wasn't going to be ignored by a bunch of barrels playing train, so when the third one approached, I planted myself in the way—ready to jump, of course, if the thing didn't stop.

"But it did. It stopped and set up a sort of drumming from the diaphragm on top. And I held out both hands and said, 'We are friends!' And what do you suppose the thing did?"

"Said, 'Pleased to meet you,' I'll bet!" suggested Harrison.

"I couldn't have been more surprised if it had! It drummed on its diaphragm, and then suddenly boomed out, 'We are v-r-r-riends!' and gave its pushcart a vicious poke at me! I jumped aside, and away it went while I stared dumbly after it.

"A minute later another one came hurrying along. This one didn't pause, but simply drummed out, 'We are v-r-r-riends!' and scurried by. How did it learn the phrase? Were all of the creatures in some sort of communication with each other? Were they all parts of some central organism? I don't know, though I think Tweel does.

"Anyway, the creatures went sailing past us, every one greeting us with the same statement. It got to be funny; I never thought to find so many friends on this God-forsaken ball! Finally I made a puzzled gesture to Tweel; I guess he understood, for he said, 'One-one-two—yes!—two-two-four—no!' Get it?"

"Sure," said Harrison, "It's a Martian nursery rhyme."

"Yeah! Well, I was getting used to Tweel's symbolism, and I figured it out this way. 'One-one-two—yes!' The creatures were intelligent. 'Two-two-four—no!' Their intelligence was not of our order, but something different and beyond the logic of two and two is four. Maybe I missed his meaning. Perhaps he meant that their minds were of low degree, able to figure out the simple things—'One-one-two—yes!'—but not more difficult things—'Two-two-four—no!' But I think from what we saw later that he meant the other.

"After a few moments, the creatures came rushing back—first one, then another. Their pushcarts were full of stones, sand, chunks of rubbery plants, and such rubbish as that. They droned out their friendly greeting, which didn't really sound so friendly, and dashed on. The third one I assumed to be my first acquaintance and I decided to have another chat with him. I stepped into his path again and waited.

"Up he came, booming out his 'We are v-r-r-riends' and stopped. I looked at him; four or five of his eyes looked at me. He tried his password again and gave a shove on his cart, but I stood firm. And then the—the dashed creature reached out one of his arms, and two finger-like nippers tweaked my nose!"

"Haw!" roared Harrison. "Maybe the things have a sense of beauty!"

"Laugh!" grumbled Jarvis. "I'd already had a nasty bump and a mean frostbite on that nose. Anyway, I yelled 'Ouch!' and jumped aside and the creature dashed away; but from then on, their greeting was 'We are v-r-r-riends! Ouch!' Queer beasts!

"Tweel and I followed the road squarely up to the nearest mound. The creatures were coming and going, paying us not the slightest attention, fetching their loads of rubbish. The road simply dived into an opening, and slanted down like an old mine, and in and out darted the barrel-people, greeting us with their eternal phrase.

"I looked in; there was a light somewhere below, and I was curious to see it. It didn't look like a flame or torch, you understand, but more like a civilized light, and I thought that I might get some clue as to the creatures' development. So in I went and Tweel tagged along, not without a few trills and twitters, however.

"The light was curious; it sputtered and flared like an old arc light, but came from a single black rod set in the wall of the corridor. It was electric, beyond doubt. The creatures were fairly civilized, apparently.

"Then I saw another light shining on something that glittered and I went on to look at that, but it was only a heap of shiny sand. I turned toward the entrance to leave, and the Devil take me if it wasn't gone!

"I suppose the corridor had curved, or I'd stepped into a side passage. Anyway, I walked back in that direction I thought we'd come, and all I saw was more dimlit corridor. The place was a labyrinth! There was nothing but twisting passages running every way, lit by occasional lights, and now and then a creature running by, sometimes with a pushcart, sometimes without.

"Well, I wasn't much worried at first. Tweel and I had only come a few steps from the entrance. But every move we made after that seemed to get us in deeper. Finally I tried following one of the creatures with an empty cart, thinking that he'd be going out for his rubbish, but he ran around aimlessly, into one passage and out another. When he started dashing around a pillar like one of these Japanese waltzing mice, I gave up, dumped my water tank on the floor, and sat down.

"Tweel was as lost as I. I pointed up and he said 'No—no—no!' in a sort of helpless trill. And we couldn't get any help from the natives. They paid no attention at all, except to assure us they were friends—ouch!

"Lord! I don't know how many hours or days we wandered around there! I slept twice from sheer exhaustion; Tweel never seemed to need sleep. We tried following only the upward corridors, but they'd run uphill a ways and then curve downwards. The temperature in that damned ant hill was constant; you couldn't tell night from day and after my first sleep I didn't know whether I'd slept one hour or thirteen, so I couldn't tell from my watch whether it was midnight or noon.

"We saw plenty of strange things. There were machines running in some of the corridors, but they didn't seem to be doing anything—just wheels turning. And several times I saw two barrel-beasts with a little one growing between them, joined to both."

"Parthenogenesis!" exulted Leroy. "Parthenogenesis by budding like *les tulipes*!"

"If you say so, Frenchy," agreed Jarvis. "The things never noticed us at all, except, as I say, to greet us with 'We are v-r-r-riends! Ouch!' They seemed to have no home-life of any sort, but just scurried around with their pushcarts, bringing in rubbish. And finally I discovered what they did with it.

"We'd had a little luck with a corridor, one that slanted upwards for a great distance. I was feeling that we ought to be close to the surface when suddenly the passage debouched into a domed chamber, the only one we'd seen. And man!—I felt like dancing when I saw what looked like daylight through a crevice in the roof.

"There was a—a sort of machine in the chamber, just an enormous wheel that turned slowly, and one of the creatures was in the act of dumping his rubbish below it. The wheel ground it with a crunch—sand, stones, plants, all into powder that sifted away somewhere. While we watched, others filed in, repeating the process, and that seemed to be all. No rhyme nor reason to the whole thing—but that's characteristic of this crazy planet. And there was another fact that's almost too bizarre to believe.

"One of the creatures, having dumped his load, pushed his cart aside with a crash and calmly shoved himself under the wheel! I watched him being crushed, too stupefied to make a sound, and a moment later, another followed him! They were perfectly methodical about it, too; one of the cartless creatures took the abandoned pushcart.

"Tweel didn't seem surprised; I pointed out the next suicide to him, and he just gave the most human-like shrug imaginable, as much as to say, 'What can I do about it?' He must have known more or less about these creatures.

"Then I saw something else. There was something beyond the wheel, something shining on a sort of low pedestal. I walked over; there was a little crystal about the size of an egg, fluorescing to beat Tophet. The light from it stung my hands and face, almost like a static discharge, and then I noticed another funny thing. Remember that wart I had on my left thumb? Look!" Jarvis extended his hand. "It dried up and fell off—just like that! And my abused nose—say, the pain went out of it like magic! The thing had the property of hard x-rays or gamma radiations, only more so; it destroyed diseased tissue and left healthy tissue unharmed!

"I was thinking what a present *that'd* be to take back to Mother Earth when a lot of racket interrupted. We dashed back to the other side of the wheel in time to see one of the pushcarts ground up. Some suicide had been careless, it seems.

"Then suddenly the creatures were booming and drumming all around us and their noise was decidedly menacing. A crowd of them advanced toward us; we backed out of what I thought was the passage we'd entered by, and they came rumbling after us, some pushing carts and some not. Crazy brutes! There was a whole chorus of 'We are v-r-r-riends! Ouch!' I didn't like the 'ouch'; it was rather suggestive.

"Tweel had his glass gun out and I dumped my water tank for greater freedom and got mine. We backed up the corridor with the barrel-beasts following—about twenty of them. Queer thing—the ones coming in with loaded carts moved past us inches away without a sign.

"Tweel must have noticed that. Suddenly, he snatched out that glowing coal cigar-lighter of his and touched a cart-load of plant limbs. Puff! The whole load was burning—and the crazy beast pushing it went right along without a change of pace! It created some disturbance among our 'V-r-r-riends,' however—and then I noticed the smoke eddying and swirling past us, and sure enough, there was the entrance!

"I grabbed Tweel and out we dashed and after us our twenty pursuers. The daylight felt like Heaven, though I saw at first glance that the sun was all but set, and that was bad, since I couldn't live outside my thermo-skin bag in a Martian night—at least, without a fire.

"And things got worse in a hurry. They cornered us in an angle between two mounds, and there we stood. I hadn't fired nor had Tweel; there wasn't any use in irritating the brutes. They stopped a little distance away and began their booming about friendship and ouches.

"Then things got still worse! A barrel-brute came out with a pushcart and they all grabbed into it and came out with handfuls of foot-long copper darts—sharp-looking ones—and all of a sudden one sailed past my ear—zing! And it was shoot or die then.

"We were doing pretty well for a while. We picked off the ones next to the pushcart and managed to keep the darts at a minimum, but suddenly there was a thunderous booming of 'v-r-r-riends' and 'ouches,' and a whole army of 'em came out of their hole.

"Man! We were through and I knew it! Then I realized that Tweel wasn't. He could have leaped the mound behind us as easily as not. He was staying for me!

"Say, I could have cried if there'd been time! I'd liked Tweel from the first, but whether I'd have had gratitude to do what he was doing—suppose I *had* saved him from the first dream-beast—he'd done as much for me, hadn't he? I grabbed his arm, and said 'Tweel,' and pointed up, and he understood. He said, 'No—no—no, Tick!' and popped away with his glass pistol.

"What could I do? I'd be a goner anyway when the sun set, but I couldn't explain that to him. I said, 'Thanks, Tweel. You're a man!' and felt that I wasn't paying him any compliment at all. A man! There are mighty few men who'd do that.

"So I went 'bang' with my gun and Tweel went 'puff' with his, and the barrels were throwing darts and getting ready to rush us, and booming about being friends. I had given up hope. Then suddenly an angel dropped right down from Heaven in the shape of Putz, with his under-jets blasting the barrels into very small pieces!

"Wow! I let out a yell and dashed for the rocket; Putz opened the door and in I went, laughing and crying and shouting! It was a moment or so before I remembered Tweel; I looked around in time to see him rising in one of his nosedives over the mound and away.

"I had a devil of a job arguing Putz into following! By the time we got the rocket aloft, darkness was down; you know how it comes here—like turning off a light. We sailed out over the desert and put down once or twice. I yelled 'Tweel!' and yelled it a hundred times, I guess. We couldn't find him; he could travel like the wind and all I got—or else I imagined it—was a faint trilling and twittering drifting out of the south. He'd gone, and damn it! I wish—I wish he hadn't!"

The four men of the *Ares* were silent—even the sardonic Harrison. At last little Leroy broke the stillness.

"I should like to see," he murmured.

"Yeah," said Harrison. "And the wart-cure. Too bad you missed that; it might be the cancer cure they've been hunting for a century and a half."

"Oh, that!" muttered Jarvis gloomily. "That's what started the fight!" He drew a glistening object from his pocket.

"Here it is."

A Valley of Dreams

by Stanley G. Weinbaum

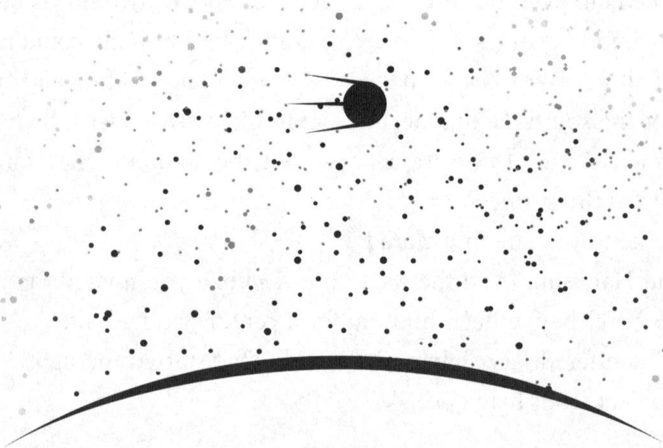

Captain Harrison of the *Ares* expedition turned away from the little telescope in the bow of the rocket. "Two weeks more, at the most," he remarked. "Mars only retrogrades for seventy days in all, relative to the earth, and we've got to be homeward bound during that period, or wait a year and a half for old Mother Earth to go around the sun and catch up with us again. How'd you like to spend a winter here?"

Dick Jarvis, chemist of the party, shivered as he looked up from his notebook. "I'd just as soon spend it in a liquid air tank!" he averred. "These eighty-below zero summer nights are plenty for me."

"Well," mused the captain, "the first successful Martian expedition ought to be home long before then."

"Successful if we get home," corrected Jarvis. "I don't trust these cranky rockets—not since the auxiliary dumped me in the middle of Thyle last week. Walking back from a rocket ride is a new sensation to me."

"Which reminds me," returned Harrison, "that we've got to recover your films. They're important if we're to pull this trip out of the red. Remember how the public mobbed the first moon pictures? Our shots ought to pack 'em to the doors. And the broadcast rights, too; we might show a profit for the Academy."

"What interests me," countered Jarvis, "is a personal profit. A book, for instance; exploration books are always popular. *Martian Deserts*—how's that for a title?"

"Lousy!" grunted the captain. "Sounds like a cook-book for desserts. You'd have to call it 'Love Life of a Martian,' or something like that."

Jarvis chuckled. "Anyway," he said, "if we once get back home, I'm going to grab what profit there is, and never, never, get any farther from the earth than a good stratosphere plane'll take me. I've learned to appreciate the planet after plowing over this dried-up pill we're on now."

"I'll lay you odds you'll be back here year after next," grinned the Captain. "You'll want to visit your pal—that trick ostrich."

"Tweel?" The other's tone sobered. "I wish I hadn't lost him, at that. He was a good scout. I'd never have survived the dream-beast but for him. And that battle with the push-cart things—I never even had a chance to thank him."

"A pair of lunatics, you two," observed Harrison. He squinted through the port at the gray gloom of the Mare Cimmerium. "There comes the sun." He paused. "Listen, Dick—you and Leroy take the other auxiliary rocket and go out and salvage those films."

Jarvis stared. "Me and Leroy?" he echoed ungrammatically. "Why not me and Putz? An engineer would have some chance of getting us there and back if the rocket goes bad on us."

The captain nodded toward the stern, whence issued at that moment a medley of blows and guttural expletives. "Putz is going over the insides of the *Ares*," he announced. "He'll have his hands full until we leave, because I want every bolt inspected. It's too late for repairs once we cast off."

"And if Leroy and I crack up? That's our last auxiliary."

"Pick up another ostrich and walk back," suggested Harrison gruffly. Then he smiled. "If you have trouble, we'll hunt you out in the *Ares*," he finished. "Those films are important." He turned. "Leroy!"

The dapper little biologist appeared, his face questioning.

"You and Jarvis are off to salvage the auxiliary," the Captain said. "Everything's ready and you'd better start now. Call back at half-hour intervals; I'll be listening."

Leroy's eyes glistened. "Perhaps we land for specimens—no?" he queried.

"Land if you want to. This golf ball seems safe enough."

"Except for the dream-beast," muttered Jarvis with a faint shudder. He frowned suddenly. "Say, as long as we're going that way, suppose I have a look for Tweel's home! He must live off there somewhere, and he's the most important thing we've seen on Mars."

Harrison hesitated. "If I thought you could keep out of trouble," he muttered. "All right," he decided. "Have a look. There's food and water aboard the auxiliary; you can take a couple of days. But keep in touch with me, you saps!"

Jarvis and Leroy went through the airlock out to the grey plain. The thin air, still scarcely warmed by the rising sun, bit flesh and lung like needles, and they gasped with a sense of suffocation. They dropped to a sitting posture, waiting for their bodies, trained by months in acclimatization chambers back on earth, to accommodate themselves to the tenuous air. Leroy's face, as always, turned a smothered blue, and Jarvis heard his own breath rasping and rattling in his throat. But in five minutes, the discomfort passed; they rose and entered the little auxiliary rocket that rested beside the black hull of the *Ares*.

The under-jets roared out their fiery atomic blast; dirt and bits of shattered biopods spun away in a cloud as the rocket rose. Harrison watched the projectile trail its flaming way into the south, then turned back to his work.

It was four days before he saw the rocket again. Just at evening, as the sun dropped behind the horizon with the suddenness of a candle falling into the sea, the auxiliary flashed out of the southern heavens, easing gently down on the flaming wings of the under-jets. Jarvis and Leroy emerged, passed through the swiftly gathering dusk, and faced him in the light of the *Ares*. He surveyed the two; Jarvis was tattered and scratched, but apparently in better condition than Leroy, whose dapperness was completely lost. The little biologist was pale as the nearer moon that glowed outside; one arm was bandaged in thermo-skin and his clothes hung in veritable rags. But it was his eyes that struck Harrison most strangely; to one who lived these many weary days with the diminutive Frenchman, there was something queer about them. They were frightened, plainly enough, and that was odd, since Leroy was no coward or he'd never have been one of the four chosen by the Academy for the first Martian expedition. But the fear in his eyes was more understandable than that other expression, that queer fixity of gaze like one in a trance, or like a person in an ecstasy. "Like a chap who's seen Heaven and Hell together," Harrison expressed it to himself. He was yet to discover how right he was.

He assumed a gruffness as the weary pair sat down. "You're a fine looking couple!" he growled. "I should've known better than to let you wander off alone." He paused. "Is your arm all right, Leroy? Need any treatment?"

Jarvis answered. "It's all right—just gashed. No danger of infection here, I guess; Leroy says there aren't any microbes on Mars."

"Well," exploded the Captain, "Let's hear it, then! Your radio reports sounded screwy. 'Escaped from Paradise!' Huh!"

"I didn't want to give details on the radio," said Jarvis soberly. "You'd have thought we'd gone loony."

"I think so, anyway."

"*Moi aussi!*" muttered Leroy. "I too!"

"Shall I begin at the beginning?" queried the chemist. "Our early reports were pretty nearly complete." He stared at Putz, who had come in silently, his face and hands blackened with carbon, and seated himself beside Harrison.

"At the beginning," the Captain decided.

"Well," began Jarvis, "we got started all right, and flew due south along the meridian of the *Ares*, same course I'd followed last week. I was getting used to this narrow horizon, so I didn't feel so much like being cooped under a big bowl, but one does keep overestimating distances. Something four miles away looks eight when you're used to terrestrial curvature, and that makes you guess its size just four times too large. A little hill looks like a mountain until you're almost over it."

"I know that," grunted Harrison.

"Yes, but Leroy didn't, and I spent our first couple of hours trying to explain it to him. By the time he understood (if he does yet) we were past Cimmerium and over that Xanthus desert, and then we crossed the canal with the mud city and the barrel-shaped citizens and the place where Tweel had shot the dream-beast. And nothing would do for Pierre here but that we put down so he could practice his biology on the remains. So we did.

"The thing was still there. No sign of decay; couldn't be, of course, without bacterial forms of life, and Leroy says that Mars is as sterile as an operating table."

"*Comme le coeur d'une fileuse,*" corrected the little biologist, who was beginning to regain a trace of his usual energy. "Like an old maid's heart!"

"However," resumed Jarvis, "about a hundred of the little grey-green biopods had fastened onto the thing and were growing and branching. Leroy found a stick and knocked 'em off, and each branch broke away and became a biopod crawling around with the others. So he poked around at the creature, while I looked away from it; even dead, that rope-armed devil gave me the creeps. And then came the surprise; the thing was part plant!"

"*C'est vrai!*" confirmed the biologist. "It's true!"

"It was a big cousin of the biopods," continued Jarvis. "Leroy was quite excited; he figures that all Martian life is of that sort—neither plant nor animal. Life here never differentiated, he says; everything has both natures in it, even the barrel-creatures—even Tweel! I think he's right, especially when I recall how Tweel rested, sticking his beak in the ground and staying that way all night. I never saw him eat or drink, either; perhaps his beak was more in the nature of a root, and he got his nourishment that way."

"Sounds nutty to me," observed Harrison.

"Well," continued Jarvis, "we broke up a few of the other growths and they acted the same way—the pieces crawled around, only much slower than the biopods, and then stuck themselves in the ground. Then Leroy had to catch a sample of the walking grass, and we were ready to leave when a parade of the barrel-creatures rushed by with their push-carts. They hadn't forgotten me, either; they all drummed out, 'We are v-r-r-iends—ouch!' just as they had before. Leroy wanted to shoot one and cut it up, but I remembered the battle Tweel and I had had with them, and vetoed the idea. But he did hit on a possible explanation as to what they did with all the rubbish they gathered."

"Made mud-pies, I guess," grunted the captain.

"More or less," agreed Jarvis. "They use it for food, Leroy thinks. If they're part vegetable, you see, that's what they'd want—soil with organic remains in it to make it fertile. That's why they ground up sand and biopods and other growths all together. See?"

"Dimly," countered Harrison. "How about the suicides?"

"Leroy had a hunch there, too. The suicides jump into the grinder when the mixture has too much sand and gravel; they throw themselves in to adjust the proportions."

"Rats!" said Harrison disgustedly. "Why couldn't they bring in some extra branches from outside?"

"Because suicide is easier. You've got to remember that these creatures can't be judged by earthly standards; they probably don't feel pain, and they haven't got what we'd call individuality. Any intelligence they have is the property of the whole community—like an ant-heap. That's it! Ants are willing to die for their ant-hill; so are these creatures."

"So are men," observed the captain, "if it comes to that."

"Yes, but men aren't exactly eager. It takes some emotion like patriotism to work 'em to the point of dying for their country; these things do it all in the day's work." He paused.

"Well, we took some pictures of the dream-beast and the barrel-creatures, and then we started along. We sailed over Xanthus, keeping as close to the meridian of the *Ares* as we could, and pretty soon we crossed the trail of the pyramid-builder. So we circled back to let Leroy take a look at it, and when we found it, we landed. The thing had completed just two rows of bricks since Tweel and I left it, and there it was, breathing in silicon and breathing out bricks as if it had eternity to do it in—which it has. Leroy wanted to dissect it with a Boland explosive bullet, but I thought that anything that had lived for ten million years was entitled to the respect due old age, so I talked him out of it. He peeped into the hole on top of it and nearly got beaned by the arm coming up with a brick, and then he chipped off a few pieces of it, which didn't disturb the creature a bit. He found the place I'd chipped, tried to see if there was any sign of healing, and decided he could tell better in two or three thousand years. So we took a few shots of it and sailed on.

"Mid afternoon we located the wreck of my rocket. Not a thing disturbed; we picked up my films and tried to decide what next. I wanted to find Tweel if possible; I figured from the fact of his pointing south that he lived somewhere near Thyle. We plotted our route and judged that the desert we were in now was Thyle II; Thyle I should be east of us. So, on a hunch, we decided to have a look at Thyle I, and away we buzzed."

"*Der* motors?" queried Putz, breaking his long silence.

"For a wonder, we had no trouble, Karl. Your blast worked perfectly. So we hummed along, pretty high to get a wider view, I'd say about fifty thousand feet. Thyle II spread out like an orange carpet, and after a while we came to the grey branch of the Mare Chronium that bounded it. That was narrow; we crossed it in half an hour, and there was Thyle I—same orange-hued desert as its mate. We veered south, toward the Mare Australe, and followed the edge of the desert. And toward sunset we spotted it."

"Shpotted?" echoed Putz. "Vot vas shpotted?"

"The desert was spotted—with buildings! Not one of the mud cities of the canals, although a canal went through it. From the map we figured the canal was a continuation of the one Schiaparelli called Ascanius.

"We were probably too high to be visible to any inhabitants of the city, but also too high for a good look at it, even with the glasses. However, it was nearly sunset, anyway, so we didn't plan on dropping in. We circled the place; the canal went out into the Mare Australe, and there, glittering in the south, was the melting polar ice-cap! The canal drained it; we could distinguish the sparkle of water in it. Off to the southeast, just at the edge of the Mare Australe, was a valley—the first irregularity I'd seen on Mars except the cliffs that bounded Xanthus and Thyle II. We flew over the valley—" Jarvis paused suddenly and shuddered; Leroy, whose colour had begun to return, seemed to pale. The chemist resumed, "Well, the valley looked all right—then! Just a gray waste, probably full of crawlers like the others.

"We circled back over the city; say, I want to tell you that place was—well, gigantic! It was colossal; at first I thought the size was due to that illusion I spoke of—you know, the nearness of the horizon—but it wasn't that. We sailed right over it, and you've never seen anything like it!

"But the sun dropped out of sight right then. I knew we were pretty far south—latitude 60—but I didn't know just how much night we'd have."

Harrison glanced at a Schiaparelli chart. "About 60—eh?" he said. "Close to what corresponds to the Antarctic circle. You'd have about four hours of night at this season. Three months from now you'd have none at all."

"Three months!" echoed Jarvis, surprised. Then he grinned. "Right! I forget the seasons here are twice as long as ours. Well, we sailed out into the desert about twenty miles, which put the city below the horizon in case we overslept, and there we spent the night.

"You're right about the length of it. We had about four hours of darkness which left us fairly rested. We ate breakfast, called our location to you, and started over to have a look at the city.

"We sailed toward it from the east and it loomed up ahead of us like a range of mountains. Lord, what a city! Not that New York mightn't have higher buildings, or Chicago cover more ground, but for sheer mass, those structures were in a class by themselves. Gargantuan!

"There was a queer look about the place, though. You know how a terrestrial city sprawls out, a nimbus of suburbs, a ring of residential sections, factory districts, parks, highways. There was none of that here; the city rose out of the desert as abruptly as a cliff. Only a few little sand mounds marked the division, and then the walls of those gigantic structures.

"The architecture was strange, too. There were lots of devices that are impossible back home, such as set-backs in reverse, so that a building with a small base could spread out as it rose. That would be a valuable trick in New York, where land is almost priceless, but to do it, you'd have to transfer Martian gravitation there!

"Well, since you can't very well land a rocket in a city street, we put down right next to the canal side of the city, took our small cameras and revolvers, and started for a gap in the wall of masonry. We weren't ten feet from the rocket when we both saw the explanation for a lot of the queerness.

"The city was in ruin! Abandoned, deserted, dead as Babylon! Or at least, so it looked to us then, with its empty streets which, if they had been paved, were now deep under sand."

"A ruin, eh?" commented Harrison. "How old?"

"How could we tell?" countered Jarvis. "The next expedition to this golf ball ought to carry an archaeologist—and a philologist, too, as we found out later. But it's a devil of a job to estimate the age of anything here; things weather so slowly that most of the buildings might have been put up yesterday. No rainfall, no earthquakes, no vegetation is here to spread cracks with its roots—nothing. The only ageing factors here are the erosion of the wind—and that's negligible in this atmosphere—and the cracks caused by changing temperature. And one other agent—meteorites. They must crash down occasionally on the city, judging from the thinness of the air, and the fact that we've seen four strike ground right here near the *Ares*."

"Seven," corrected the captain. "Three dropped while you were gone."

"Well, damage by meteorites must be slow, anyway. Big ones would be as rare here as on earth, because big ones get through in spite of the atmosphere, and those buildings could sustain a lot of little ones. My guess at the city's age—and it may be wrong by a big percentage—would be fifteen thousand years. Even that's thousands of years older than any human civilization; fifteen thousand years ago was the Late Stone Age in the history of mankind.

"So Leroy and I crept up to those tremendous buildings feeling like pygmies, sort of awe-struck, and talking in whispers. I tell you, it was ghostly walking down that dead and deserted street, and every time we passed through a shadow, we shivered, and not just because shadows are cold on Mars. We felt like intruders, as if the great race that had built the place might resent our presence even across a hundred and fifty centuries. The place was as quiet as a grave, but we kept imagining things and peeping down the dark lanes between buildings and looking over our shoulders. Most of the structures were windowless, but when we did see an opening in those vast walls, we couldn't look away, expecting to see some horror peering out of it.

"Then we passed an edifice with an open arch; the doors were there, but blocked open by sand. I got up nerve enough to take a look inside, and then, of course, we discovered we'd forgotten to take our flashes. But we eased a few feet into the darkness and the passage debouched into a colossal hall. Far above us a little crack let in a pallid ray of daylight, not nearly enough to light the place; I couldn't even see if the hall rose clear to the distant roof. But I know the place was enormous; I said something to Leroy and a million thin echoes came slipping back to us out of the darkness. And after that, we began to hear other sounds—slithering rustling noises, and whispers, and sounds like suppressed breathing—and something black and silent passed between us and that far-away crevice of light.

"Then we saw three little greenish spots of luminosity in the dusk to our left. We stood staring at them, and suddenly they all shifted at once. Leroy yelled '*Ce sont des yeux!*' and they were! They were eyes!

"Well, we stood frozen for a moment, while Leroy's yell reverberated back and forth between the distant walls, and the echoes repeated the words in queer, thin voices. There were mumblings and mutterings and whisperings and sounds like strange soft laughter, and then the three-eyed thing moved again. Then we broke for the door!

"We felt better out in the sunlight; we looked at each other sheepishly, but neither of us suggested another look at the buildings inside—though we *did* see the place later, and that was queer, too—but you'll hear about it when I come to it. We just loosened our revolvers and crept on along that ghostly street.

"The street curved and twisted and subdivided. I kept careful note of our directions, since we couldn't risk getting lost in that gigantic maze. Without our thermo-skin bags, night would finish us, even if what lurked in the ruins didn't. By and by, I noticed that we were veering back toward the canal, the buildings ended and there were only a few dozen ragged stone huts which looked as though they might have been built of debris from the city. I was just beginning to feel a bit disappointed at finding no trace of Tweel's people here when we rounded a corner and there he was!

"I yelled 'Tweel!' but he just stared, and then I realized that he wasn't Tweel, but another Martian of his sort. Tweel's feathery appendages were more orange hued and he stood several inches taller than this one. Leroy was sputtering in excitement, and the Martian kept his vicious beak directed at us, so I stepped forward as peace-maker. I said 'Tweel?' very questioningly, but there was no result. I tried it a dozen times, and we finally had to give it up; we couldn't connect.

"Leroy and I walked toward the huts, and the Martian followed us. Twice he was joined by others, and each time I tried yelling 'Tweel' at them but they just stared at us. So we ambled on with the three trailing us, and then it suddenly occurred to me that my Martian accent might be at fault. I faced the group and tried trilling it out the way Tweel himself did: 'T-r-r-rwee-r-rl!' Like that.

"And that worked! One of them spun his head around a full ninety degrees, and screeched 'T-r-r-rweee-r-rl!' and a moment later, like an arrow from a bow, Tweel came sailing over the nearer huts to land on his beak in front of me!

"Man, we were glad to see each other! Tweel set up a twittering and chirping like a farm in summer and went sailing up and coming down on his beak, and I would have grabbed his hands, only he wouldn't keep still long enough.

"The other Martians and Leroy just stared, and after a while, Tweel stopped bouncing, and there we were. We couldn't talk to each other any more than we could before, so after I'd said 'Tweel' a couple of times and he'd said 'Tick,' we were more or less helpless. However, it was only mid-morning, and it seemed important to learn all we could about Tweel and the city, so I suggested that he guide us around the place if he weren't busy. I put over the idea by pointing back at the buildings and then at him and us.

"Well, apparently he wasn't too busy, for he set off with us, leading the way with one of his hundred and fifty-foot nosedives that set Leroy gasping. When we caught up, he said something like 'one, one, two—two, two, four—no, no—yes, yes—rock—no breet!' That didn't seem to mean anything; perhaps he was just letting Leroy know that he could speak English, or perhaps he was merely running over his vocabulary to refresh his memory.

"Anyway, he showed us around. He had a light of sorts in his black pouch, good enough for small rooms, but simply lost in some of the colossal caverns we went through. Nine out of ten buildings meant absolutely nothing to us—just vast empty chambers, full of shadows and rustlings and echoes. I couldn't imagine their use; they didn't seem suitable for living quarters, or even for commercial purposes—trade and so forth; they might have been all right as power-houses, but what could have been the purpose of a whole city full? And where were the remains of the machinery?

"The place was a mystery. Sometimes Tweel would show us through a hall that would have housed an ocean-liner, and he'd seem to swell with pride—and we couldn't make a damn thing of it! As a display of architectural power, the city was colossal; as anything else it was just nutty!

"But we did see one thing that registered. We came to that same building Leroy and I had entered earlier—the one with the three eyes in it. Well, we were a little shaky about going in there, but Tweel twittered and trilled and kept saying, 'Yes, yes, yes!' so we followed him, staring nervously about for the thing that had watched us. However, that hall was just like the others, full of murmurs and slithering noises and shadowy things slipping away into corners. If the three-eyed creature were still there, it must have slunk away with the others.

"Tweel led us along the wall; his light showed a series of little alcoves, and in the first of these we ran into a puzzling thing—a very weird thing. As the light flashed into the alcove, I saw first just an empty space, and then, squatting on the floor, I saw—it! A little creature about as big as a large rat, it was, gray and huddled and evidently startled by our appearance. It had the queerest, most devilish little face!—pointed ears or horns and satanic eyes that seemed to sparkle with a sort of fiendish intelligence.

"Tweel saw it, too, and let out a screech of anger, and the creature rose on two pencil-thin legs and scuttled off with a half-terrified, half-defiant squeak. It darted past us into the darkness too quickly even for Tweel, and as it ran, something waved on its body like the fluttering of a cape. Tweel screeched angrily at it and set up a shrill hullabaloo that sounded like genuine rage.

"But the thing was gone, and then I noticed the weirdest of imaginable details. Where it had squatted on the floor was—a book! It had been hunched over a book!

"I took a step forward; sure enough, there was some sort of inscription on the pages—wavy white lines like a seismograph record on black sheets like the material of Tweel's pouch. Tweel fumed and whistled in wrath, picked up the volume and slammed it into place on a shelf full of others. Leroy and I stared dumbfounded at each other.

"Had the little thing with the fiendish face been reading? Or was it simply eating the pages, getting physical nourishment rather than mental? Or had the whole thing been accidental?

"If the creature were some rat-like pest that destroyed books, Tweel's rage was understandable, but why should he try to prevent an intelligent being, even though of an alien race, from *reading*—if it *was* reading? I don't know; I did notice that the book was entirely undamaged, nor did I see a damaged book among any that we handled. But I have an odd hunch that if we knew the secret of the little cape-clothed imp, we'd know the mystery of the vast abandoned city and of the decay of Martian culture.

"Well, Tweel quieted down after a while and led us completely around that tremendous hall. It had been a library, I think; at least, there were thousands upon thousands of those queer black-paged volumes printed in wavy lines of white. There were pictures, too, in some; and some of these showed Tweel's people. That's a point, of course; it indicated that his race built the city and printed the books. I don't think the greatest philologist on earth will ever translate one line of those records; they were made by minds too different from ours.

"Tweel could read them, naturally. He twittered off a few lines, and then I took a few of the books, with his permission; he said 'no, no!' to some and 'yes, yes!' to others. Perhaps he kept back the ones his people needed, or perhaps he let me take the ones he thought we'd understand most easily. I don't know; the books are outside there in the rocket.

"Then he held that dim torch of his toward the walls, and they were pictured. Lord, what pictures! They stretched up and up into the blackness of the roof, mysterious and gigantic. I couldn't make much of the first wall; it seemed to be a portrayal of a great assembly of Tweel's people. Perhaps it was meant to symbolize Society or Government. But the next wall was more obvious; it showed creatures at work on a colossal machine of some sort, and that would be Industry or Science. The back wall had corroded away in part, from what we could see, I suspected the scene was meant to portray Art, but it was on the fourth wall that we got a shock that nearly dazed us.

"I think the symbol was Exploration or Discovery. This wall was a little plainer, because the moving beam of daylight from that crack lit up the higher surface and Tweel's torch illuminated the lower. We made out a giant seated figure, one of the beaked Martians like Tweel, but with every limb suggesting heaviness, weariness. The arms dropped inertly on the chair, the thin neck bent and the beak rested on the body, as if the creature could scarcely bear its own weight. And before it was a queer kneeling figure, and at sight of it, Leroy and I almost reeled against each other. It was, apparently, a man!"

"A man!" bellowed Harrison. "A man you say?"

"I said apparently," retorted Jarvis. "The artist had exaggerated the nose almost to the length of Tweel's beak, but the figure had black shoulder-length hair, and instead of the Martian four, there were *five* fingers on its outstretched hand! It was kneeling as if in worship of the Martian, and on the ground was what looked like a pottery bowl full of some food as an offering. Well! Leroy and I thought we'd gone screwy!"

"And Putz and I think so, too!" roared the captain.

"Maybe we all have," replied Jarvis, with a faint grin at the pale face of the little Frenchman, who returned it in silence. "Anyway," he continued, "Tweel was squeaking and pointing at the figure, and saying 'Tick! Tick!' so he recognized the resemblance—and never mind any cracks about my nose!" he warned the captain. "It was Leroy who made the important comment; he looked at the Martian and said 'Thoth! The god Thoth!'"

"*Oui!*" confirmed the biologist. "*Comme l'Egypte!*"

"Yeah," said Jarvis. "Like the Egyptian ibis-headed god—the one with the beak. Well, no sooner did Tweel hear the name Thoth than he set up a clamour of twittering and squeaking. He pointed at himself and said 'Thoth! Thoth!' and then waved his arm all around and repeated it. Of course he often did queer things, but we both thought we understood what he meant. He was trying to tell us that his race called themselves Thoth. Do you see what I'm getting at?"

"I see, all right," said Harrison. "You think the Martians paid a visit to the earth, and the Egyptians remembered it in their mythology. Well, you're off, then; there wasn't any Egyptian civilization fifteen thousand years ago."

"Wrong!" grinned Jarvis. "It's too bad we *haven't* an archaeologist with us, but Leroy tells me that there was a stone-age culture in Egypt then, the pre-dynastic civilization."

"Well, even so, what of it?"

"Plenty! Everything in that picture proves my point. The attitude of the Martian, heavy and weary—that's the unnatural strain of terrestrial gravitation. The name Thoth; Leroy tells me Thoth was the Egyptian god of philosophy and the inventor of *writing*! Get that? They must have picked up the idea from watching the

Martian take notes. It's too much for coincidence that Thoth should be beaked and ibis-headed, and that the beaked Martians call themselves Thoth."

"Well, I'll be hanged! But what about the nose on the Egyptian? Do you mean to tell me that stone-age Egyptians had longer noses than ordinary men?"

"Of course not! It's just that the Martians very naturally cast their paintings in Martianized form. Don't human beings tend to relate everything to themselves? That's why dugongs and manatees started the mermaid myths—sailors thought they saw human features on the beasts. So the Martian artist, drawing either from descriptions or imperfect photographs, naturally exaggerated the size of the human nose to a degree that looked normal to him. Or anyway, that's my theory."

"Well, it'll do as a theory," grunted Harrison. "What I want to hear is why you two got back here looking like a couple of year-before-last bird's nests."

Jarvis shuddered again, and cast another glance at Leroy. The little biologist was recovering some of his accustomed poise, but he returned the glance with an echo of the chemist's shudder.

"We'll get to that," resumed the latter. "Meanwhile I'll stick to Tweel and his people. We spent the better part of three days with them, as you know. I can't give every detail, but I'll summarize the important facts and give our conclusions, which may not be worth an inflated franc. It's hard to judge this dried-up world by earthly standards.

"We took pictures of everything possible; I even tried to photograph that gigantic mural in the library, but unless Tweel's lamp was unusually rich in actinic rays, I don't suppose it'll show. And that's a pity, since it's undoubtedly the most interesting object we've found on Mars, at least from a human viewpoint.

"Tweel was a very courteous host. He took us to all the points of interest—even the new water-works."

Putz's eyes brightened at the word. "Vater-vorks?" he echoed. "For vot?"

"For the canal, naturally. They have to build up a head of water to drive it through; that's obvious." He looked at the captain. "You told me yourself that to drive water from the polar caps of Mars to the equator was equivalent to forcing it up a twenty-mile hill, because Mars is flattened at the poles and bulges at the equator just like the earth."

"That's true," agreed Harrison.

"Well," resumed Jarvis, "this city was one of the relay stations to boost the flow. Their power plant was the only one of the giant buildings that seemed to serve any useful purpose, and that was worth seeing. I wish you'd seen it, Karl; you'll have to make what you can from our pictures. It's a sun-power plant!"

Harrison and Putz stared. "Sun-power!" grunted the captain. "That's primitive!" And the engineer added an emphatic "*Ja!*" of agreement.

"Not as primitive as all that," corrected Jarvis. "The sunlight focused on a queer cylinder in the centre of a big concave mirror, and they drew an electric current from it. The juice worked the pumps."

"A t'ermocouple!" ejaculated Putz.

"That sounds reasonable; you can judge by the pictures. But the power-plant had some queer things about it. The queerest was that the machinery was tended, not by Tweel's people, but by some of the barrel-shaped creatures like the ones in Xanthus!" He gazed around at the faces of his auditors; there was no comment.

"Get it?" he resumed. At their silence, he proceeded, "I see you don't. Leroy figured it out, but whether rightly or wrongly, I don't know. He thinks that the barrels and Tweel's race have a reciprocal arrangement like—well, like bees and flowers on earth. The flowers give honey for the bees; the bees carry the pollen for the flowers. See? The barrels tend the works and Tweel's people build the canal system. The Xanthus city must have been a boosting station; that explains the mysterious machines I saw. And Leroy believes further that it isn't an intelligent arrangement—not on the part of the barrels, at least—but that it's been done for so many thousands of generations that it's become instinctive—a tropism—just like the actions of ants and bees. The creatures have been bred to it!"

"Nuts!" observed Harrison. "Let's hear you explain the reason for that big empty city, then."

"Sure. Tweel's civilization is decadent, that's the reason. It's a dying race, and out of all the millions that must once have lived there, Tweel's couple of hundred companions are the remnant. They're an outpost, left to tend the source of the water at the polar cap; probably there are still a few respectable cities left somewhere on the canal system, most likely near the tropics. It's the last gasp of a race—and a race that reached a higher peak of culture than Man!"

"Huh?" said Harrison. "Then why are they dying? Lack of water?"

"I don't think so," responded the chemist. "If my guess at the city's age is right, fifteen thousand years wouldn't make enough difference in the water supply—nor a hundred thousand, for that matter. It's something else, though the water's doubtless a factor."

"*Das wasser*," cut in Putz. "Vere goes dot?"

"Even a chemist knows that!" scoffed Jarvis. "At least on earth. Here I'm not so sure, but on earth, every time there's a lightning flash, it electrolyzes some water vapour into hydrogen and oxygen, and then the hydrogen escapes into space, because terrestrial gravitation won't hold it permanently. And every time there's an earthquake, some water is lost to the interior. Slow—but damned certain." He turned to Harrison. "Right, Cap?"

"Right," conceded the captain. "But here, of course—no earthquakes, no thunderstorms—the loss must be very slow. Then why is the race dying?"

"The sun-power plant answers that," countered Jarvis. "Lack of fuel! Lack of power! No oil left, no coal left—if Mars ever had a Carboniferous Age—and no water-power—just the driblets of energy they can get from the sun. That's why they're dying."

"With the limitless energy of the atom?" exploded Harrison.

"They don't know about atomic energy. Probably never did. Must have used some other principle in their space-ship."

"Then," snapped the captain, "what makes you rate their intelligence above the human? We've finally cracked open the atom!"

"Sure we have. We had a clue, didn't we? Radium and uranium. Do you think we'd ever have learned how without those elements? We'd never even have suspected that atomic energy existed!"

"Well? Haven't they—?"

"No, they haven't. You've told me yourself that Mars has only 73 percent of the earth's density. Even a chemist can see that that means a lack of heavy metals—no osmium, no uranium, no radium. They didn't have the clue."

"Even so, that doesn't prove they're more advanced than we are. If they were *more* advanced, they'd have discovered it anyway."

"Maybe," conceded Jarvis. "I'm not claiming that we don't surpass them in some ways. But in others, they're far ahead of us."

"In what, for instance?"

"Well—socially, for one thing."

"Huh? How do you mean?"

Jarvis glanced in turn at each of the three that faced him. He hesitated. "I wonder how you chaps will take this," he muttered. "Naturally, everybody likes his own system best." He frowned. "Look here—on the earth we have three types of society, haven't we? And there's a member of each type right here. Putz lives under a dictatorship—an autocracy. Leroy's a citizen of the Sixth Commune in France. Harrison and I are Americans, members of a democracy. There you are—autocracy, democracy, communism—the three types of terrestrial societies. Tweel's people have a different system from any of us."

"Different? What is it?"

"The one no earthly nation has tried. Anarchy!"

"Anarchy!" the captain and Putz burst out together.

"That's right."

"But—" Harrison was sputtering. "What do you mean—they're ahead of us? Anarchy! Bah!"

"All right—bah!" retorted Jarvis. "I'm not saying it would work for us, or for any race of men. But it works for them."

"But—anarchy!" The captain was indignant.

"Well, when you come right down to it," argued Jarvis defensively, "anarchy is the ideal form of government, if it works. Emerson said that the best government was that which governs least, and so did Wendell Phillips, and I think George Washington. And you can't have any form of government which governs less than anarchy, which is no government at all!"

The captain was sputtering. "But—it's unnatural! Even savage tribes have their chiefs! Even a pack of wolves has its leader!"

"Well," retorted Jarvis defiantly, "that only proves that government is a primitive device, doesn't it? With a perfect race you wouldn't need it at all; government is a confession of weakness, isn't it? It's a confession that part of the people won't cooperate with the rest and that you need laws to restrain those individuals which a psychologist calls anti-social. If there were no anti-social persons—criminals and such—you wouldn't need laws or police, would you?"

"But government! You'd need government! How about public works—wars—taxes?"

"No wars on Mars, in spite of being named after the War God. No point in wars here; the population is too thin and too scattered, and besides, it takes the help of every single community to keep the canal system functioning. No taxes because, apparently, all individuals cooperate in building public works. No competition to cause trouble, because anybody can help himself to anything. As I said, with a perfect race government is entirely unnecessary."

"And do you consider the Martians a perfect race?" asked the captain grimly.

"Not at all! But they've existed so much longer than man that they're evolved, socially at least, to the point where they don't need government. They work together, that's all." Jarvis paused. "Queer, isn't it—as if Mother Nature were carrying on two experiments, one at home and one on Mars. On earth it's trial of an emotional, highly competitive race in a world of plenty; here it's the trial of a quiet, friendly race on a desert, unproductive, and inhospitable world. Everything here makes for cooperation. Why, there isn't even the factor that causes so much trouble at home—sex!"

"Huh?"

"Yeah: Tweel's people reproduce just like the barrels in the mud cities; two individuals grow a third one between them. Another proof of Leroy's theory that Martian life is neither animal nor vegetable. Besides, Tweel was a good enough host to let him poke down his beak and twiddle his feathers, and the examination convinced Leroy."

"*Oui*," confirmed the biologist. "It is true."

"But anarchy!" grumbled Harrison disgustedly. "It would show up on a dizzy, half-dead pill like Mars!"

"It'll be a good many centuries before you'll have to worry about it on earth," grinned Jarvis. He resumed his narrative.

"Well, we wandered through that sepulchral city, taking pictures of everything. And then—" Jarvis paused and shuddered—"then I took a notion to have a look at that valley we'd spotted from the rocket. I don't know why. But when we tried to steer Tweel in that direction, he set up such a squawking and screeching that I thought he'd gone batty."

"If possible!" jeered Harrison.

"So we started over there without him; he kept wailing and screaming, 'No—no—no! Tick!' but that made us the more curious. He sailed over our heads and stuck on his beak, and went through a dozen other antics, but we ploughed on, and finally he gave up and trudged disconsolately along with us.

"The valley wasn't more than a mile southeast of the city. Tweel could have covered the distance in twenty jumps, but he lagged and loitered and kept pointing back at the city and wailing 'No—no—no!' Then he'd sail up into the air and zip down on his beak directly in front of us, and we'd have to walk around him. I'd seen him do lots of crazy things before, of course; I was used to them, but it was as plain as print that he didn't want us to see that valley."

"Why?" queried Harrison.

"You asked why we came back like tramps," said Jarvis with a faint shudder.

"You'll learn. We plugged along up a low rocky hill that bounded it, and as we neared the top, Tweel said, 'No breet', Tick! No breet'!' Well, those were the words he used to describe the silicon monster; they were also the words he had used to tell me that the image of Fancy Long, the one that had almost lured me to the dream-beast, wasn't real. I remembered that, but it meant nothing to me—then!

"Right after that, Tweel said, 'You one-one-two, he one-one-two,' and then I began to see. That was the phrase he had used to explain the dream-beast to tell me that what I thought, the creature thought—to tell me how the thing lured its victims by their own desires. So I warned Leroy; it seemed to me that even the dream-beast couldn't be dangerous if we were warned and expecting it. Well, I was wrong!

"As we reached the crest, Tweel spun his head completely around, so his feet were forward but his eyes looked backward, as if he feared to gaze into the valley. Leroy and I stared out over it, just a gray waste like this around us, with the gleam of the south polar cap far beyond its southern rim. That's what it was one second; the next it was—Paradise!"

"What?" exclaimed the captain.

Jarvis turned to Leroy. "Can you describe it?" he asked.

The biologist waved helpless hands, "*C'est impossible!*" he whispered. "*Il me rend muet!*"

"It strikes me dumb, too," muttered Jarvis. "I don't know how to tell it; I'm a chemist, not a poet. Paradise is as good a word as I can think of, and that's not at all right. It was Paradise and Hell in one!"

"Will you talk sense?" growled Harrison.

"As much of it as makes sense. I tell you, one moment we were looking at a grey valley covered with blobby plants, and the next—Lord! You can't imagine that next moment! How would you like to see all your dreams made real? Every desire you'd ever had gratified? Everything you'd ever wanted there for the taking?"

"I'd like it fine!" said the captain.

"You're welcome, then!—not only your noble desires, remember! Every good impulse, yes—but also every nasty little wish, every vicious thought, everything you'd ever desired, good or bad! The dream-beasts are marvellous salesmen, but they lack the moral sense!"

"The dream-beasts?"

"Yes. It was a valley of them. Hundreds, I suppose, maybe thousands. Enough, at any rate, to spread out a complete picture of your desires, even all the forgotten ones that must have been drawn out of the subconscious. A Paradise—of sorts! I saw a dozen Fancy Longs, in every costume I'd ever admired on her, and some I must have imagined. I saw every beautiful woman I've ever known, and all of them pleading for my attention. I saw every lovely place I'd ever wanted to be, all packed queerly into that little valley. And I saw—other things." He shook his head soberly. "It wasn't all exactly pretty. Lord! How much of the beast is left in us! I suppose if every man alive could have one look at that weird valley, and could see just once what nastiness is hidden in him—well, the world might gain by it. I thanked heaven afterwards that Leroy—and even Tweel—saw their own pictures and not mine!"

Jarvis paused again, then resumed, "I turned dizzy with a sort of ecstasy. I closed my eyes—and with eyes closed, I still saw the whole thing! That beautiful, evil, devilish panorama was in my mind, not my eyes. That's how those fiends work—through the mind. I knew it was the dream-beasts; I didn't need Tweel's wail of 'No breet'! No breet'!' But—*I couldn't keep away!* I knew it was death beckoning, but it was worth it for one moment with the vision."

"Which particular vision?" asked Harrison dryly.

Jarvis flushed. "No matter," he said. "But beside me I heard Leroy's cry of 'Yvonne! Yvonne!' and I knew he was trapped like myself. I fought for sanity; I kept telling myself to stop, and all the time I was rushing headlong into the snare!

"Then something tripped me. Tweel! He had come leaping from behind; as I crashed down I saw him flash over me straight toward—toward what I'd been running to, with his vicious beak pointed right at her heart!"

"Oh!" nodded the captain. "*Her* heart!"

"Never mind that. When I scrambled up, that particular image was gone, and Tweel was in a twist of black ropey arms, just as when I first saw him. He'd missed a vital point in the beast's anatomy, but was jabbing away desperately with his beak.

"Somehow, the spell had lifted, or partially lifted. I wasn't five feet from Tweel, and it took a terrific struggle, but I managed to raise my revolver and put a Boland shell into the beast. Out came a spurt of horrible black corruption, drenching Tweel and me—and I guess the sickening smell of it helped to destroy the illusion of that valley of beauty. Anyway, we managed to get Leroy away from the devil that had him, and the three of us staggered to the ridge and over. I had presence of mind enough to raise my camera over the crest and take a shot of the valley, but I'll bet it shows nothing but gray waste and writhing horrors. What we saw was with our minds, not our eyes."

Jarvis paused and shuddered. "The brute half poisoned Leroy," he continued. "We dragged ourselves back to the auxiliary, called you, and did what we could to treat ourselves. Leroy took a long dose of the cognac that we had with us; we didn't dare try anything of Tweel's because his metabolism is so different from ours that what cured him might kill us. But the cognac seemed to work, and so, after I'd done one other thing I wanted to do, we came back here—and that's all."

"All, is it?" queried Harrison. "So you've solved all the mysteries of Mars, eh?"

"Not by a damned sight!" retorted Jarvis. "Plenty of unanswered questions are left."

"*Ja!*" snapped Putz. "Der evaporation—dot iss shtopped how?"

"In the canals? I wondered about that, too; in those thousands of miles, and against this low air-pressure, you'd think they'd lose a lot. But the answer's simple; they float a skin of oil on the water."

Putz nodded, but Harrison cut in. "Here's a puzzler. With only coal and oil—just combustion or electric power—where'd they get the energy to build a planet-wide canal system, thousands and thousands of miles of 'em? Think of the job we had cutting the Panama Canal to sea level, and then answer that!"

"Easy!" grinned Jarvis. "Martian gravity and Martian air—that's the answer. Figure it out: First, the dirt they dug only weighed a third its earth-weight. Second, a steam engine here expands against ten pounds per square inch less air pressure than on earth. Third, they could build the engine three times as large here with no greater internal weight. And fourth, the whole planet's nearly level. Right, Putz?"

The engineer nodded. "*Ja!* Der shteam—engine—it iss *sieben-und zwanzig*—twenty-seven times so effective here."

"Well, there *does* go the last mystery then," mused Harrison.

"Yeah?" queried Jarvis sardonically. "You answer these, then. What was the nature of that vast empty city? Why do the Martians *need* canals, since we never saw them eat or drink? Did they really visit the earth before the dawn of history, and, if not atomic energy, what powered their ship? Since Tweel's race seems to need little or no water, are they merely operating the canals for some higher creature that does? *Are* there other intelligences on Mars? If not, what was the demon-faced imp we saw with the book? There are a few mysteries for you!"

"I know one or two more!" growled Harrison, glaring suddenly at little Leroy. "You and your visions! 'Yvonne!' eh? Your wife's name is Marie, isn't it?"

The little biologist turned crimson. "*Oui*," he admitted unhappily. He turned pleading eyes on the captain. "Please," he said. "In Paris *tout le monde*—everybody he think differently of those things—no?" He twisted uncomfortably. "Please, you will not tell Marie, *n'est-ce pas*?"

Harrison chuckled. "None of my business," he said. "One more question, Jarvis. What was the one other thing you did before returning here?"

Jarvis looked diffident. "Oh—that." He hesitated. "Well I sort of felt we owed Tweel a lot, so after some trouble, we coaxed him into the rocket and sailed him out to the wreck of the first one, over on Thyle II. Then," he finished apologetically, "I showed him the atomic blast, got it working—and gave it to him!"

"You *what*?" roared the Captain. "You turned something as powerful as that over to an alien race—maybe some day as an enemy race?"

"Yes, I did," said Jarvis. "Look here," he argued defensively. "This lousy, dried-up pill of a desert called Mars'll never support much human population. The Sahara desert is just as good a field for imperialism, and a lot closer to home. So we'll never find Tweel's race enemies. The only value we'll find here is commercial trade with the Martians. Then why shouldn't I give Tweel a chance for survival? With atomic energy, they can run their canal system a hundred per cent instead of only one out of five, as Putz's observations showed. They can repopulate those ghostly cities; they can resume their arts and industries; they can trade with the nations of the earth—and I'll bet they can teach us a few things," he paused, "if they can figure out the atomic blast, and I'll lay odds they can. They're no fools, Tweel and his ostrich-faced Martians!"

THE WORLDS OF IF

by Stanley G. Weinbaum

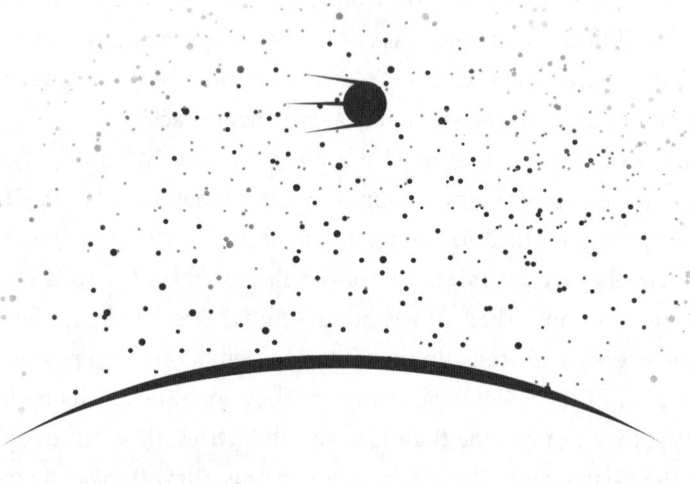

I stopped on the way to the Staten Island Airport to call up, and that was a mistake, doubtless, since I had a chance of making it otherwise. But the office was affable. "We'll hold the ship five minutes for you," the clerk said. "That's the best we can do."

So I rushed back to my taxi and we spun off to the third level and sped across the Staten bridge like a comet treading a steel rainbow. I had to be in Moscow by evening, by eight o'clock, in fact, for the opening of bids on the Ural Tunnel. The Government required the personal presence of an agent of each bidder, but the firm should have known better than to send me, Dixon Wells, even though the N. J. Wells Corporation is, so to speak, my father. I have a—well, an undeserved reputation for being late to everything; something always comes up to prevent me from getting anywhere on time. It's never my fault; this time it was a chance encounter with my old physics professor, old Haskel van Manderpootz. I couldn't very well just say hello and good-bye to him; I'd been a favourite of his back in the college days of 2014.

I missed the airliner, of course. I was still on the Staten Bridge when I heard the roar of the catapult and the Soviet rocket *Baikal* hummed over us like a tracer bullet with a long tail of flame.

We got the contract anyway; the firm wired our man in Beirut and he flew up to Moscow, but it didn't help my reputation. However, I felt a great deal better when I saw the evening papers; the *Baikal*, flying at the north edge of the east-bound lane to avoid a storm, had locked wings with a British fruitship and all but a hundred of her five hundred passengers were lost. I had almost become "the late Mr. Wells" in a grimmer sense.

I'd made an engagement for the following week with old van Manderpootz. It seems he'd transferred to N.Y.U. as head of the department of Newer Physics—that is, of Relativity. He deserved it; the old chap was a genius if ever there was one, and even now, eight years out of college, I remember more from his course than from half a dozen calculus, steam and gas, mechanics, and other hazards on the path to an engineer's education. So on Tuesday night I dropped in an hour or so late, to tell the truth, since I'd forgotten about the engagement until mid-evening.

He was reading in a room as disorderly as ever. "Humph!" he grunted. "Time changes everything but habit, I see. You were a good student, Dick, but I seem to recall that you always arrived in class toward the middle of the lecture."

"I had a course in East Hall just before," I explained. "I couldn't seem to make it in time."

"Well, it's time you learned to be on time," he growled. Then his eyes twinkled. "Time!" he ejaculated. "The most fascinating word in the language. Here we've used it five times (there goes the sixth time—and the seventh!) in the first minute of conversation; each of us understands the other, yet science is just beginning to learn its meaning. Science? I mean that *I* am beginning to learn."

I sat down. "You and science are synonymous," I grinned. "Aren't you one of the world's outstanding physicists?"

"One of them!" he snorted. "One of them, eh! And who are the others?"

"Oh, Corveille and Hastings and Shrimski—"

"Bah! Would you mention them in the same breath with the name of van

Manderpootz? A pack of jackals, eating the crumbs of ideas that drop from my feast of thoughts! Had you gone back into the last century, now—had you mentioned Einstein and de Sitter—there, perhaps, are names worthy to rank with (or just below) van Manderpootz!"

I grinned again in amusement. "Einstein was considered pretty good, wasn't he?" I remarked. "After all, he was the first to tie time and space to the laboratory. Before him they were just philosophical concepts."

"He didn't!" rasped the professor. "Perhaps, in a dim, primitive fashion, he showed the way, but I—*I*, van Manderpootz—am the first to seize time, drag it into my laboratory, and perform an experiment on it."

"Indeed? And what sort of experiment?"

"What experiment, other than simple measurement, is it possible to perform?" he snapped.

"Why—I don't know. To travel in it?"

"Exactly."

"Like these time-machines that are so popular in the current magazines? To go into the future or the past?"

"Bah! Many bahs! The future or the past—pfui! It needs no van Manderpootz to see the fallacy in that. Einstein showed us that much."

"How? It's conceivable, isn't it?"

"Conceivable? And you, Dixon Wells, studied under van Manderpootz!" He grew red with emotion, then grimly calm. "Listen to me. You know how time varies with the speed of a system—Einstein's relativity."

"Yes."

"Very well. Now suppose then that the great engineer Dixon Wells invents a machine capable of travelling very fast, enormously fast, nine-tenths as fast as light. Do you follow? Good. You then fuel this miracle ship for a little jaunt of a half million miles, which, since mass (and with it inertia) increases according to the Einstein formula with increasing speed, takes all the fuel in the world. But you solve that. You use atomic energy. Then, since at nine-tenths light-speed, your ship weighs about as much as the sun, you disintegrate North America to give you sufficient motive power. You start off at that speed, a hundred and sixty-eight thousand miles per second, and you travel for two hundred and four thousand miles. The acceleration has now crushed you to death, but you have penetrated the future." He paused, grinning sardonically. "Haven't you?"

"Yes."

"And how far?"

I hesitated.

"Use your Einstein formula!" he screeched. "How far? I'll tell you. *One second!*" He grinned triumphantly. "That's how possible it is to travel into the future. And as for the past—in the first place, you'd have to exceed light-speed, which immediately entails the use of more than an infinite number of horsepowers. We'll assume that the great engineer Dixon Wells solves that little problem too, even though the energy out-put of the whole universe is not an infinite number of horsepowers. Then he applies this more than infinite power to travel at two hundred and four thousand miles per second for *ten* seconds. He has then penetrated the past. How far?"

Again I hesitated.

"I'll tell you. *One second!*" He glared at me. "Now all you have to do is to design such a machine, and then van Manderpootz will admit the possibility of travelling into the future—for a limited number of seconds. As for the past, I have just explained that all the energy in the universe is insufficient for that."

"But," I stammered, "you just said that you—"

"I did *not* say anything about travelling into either future or past, which I have just demonstrated to you to be impossible—a practical impossibility in the one case and an absolute one in the other."

"Then how *do* you travel in time?"

"Not even van Manderpootz can perform the impossible," said the professor, now faintly jovial. He tapped a thick pad of typewriter paper on the table beside him. "See, Dick, this is the world, the universe." He swept a finger down it. "It is long in time, and"—sweeping his hand across it—"it is broad in space, but"—now jabbing his finger against its centre—"it is very thin in the fourth dimension. Van Manderpootz takes always the shortest, the most logical course. I do not travel along time, into past or future. No. Me, I travel across time, sideways!"

I gulped. "Sideways into time! What's there?"

"What would naturally be there?" he snorted. "Ahead is the future; behind is the past. Those are real, the worlds of past and future. What worlds are neither past nor future, but contemporary and yet—extemporal—existing, as it were, in time parallel to our time?"

I shook my head.

"Idiot!" he snapped. "The conditional worlds, of course! The worlds of 'if.' Ahead are the worlds to be; behind are the worlds that were; to either side are the worlds that might have been—the worlds of 'if!'"

"Eh?" I was puzzled. "Do you mean that you can see what will happen if I do such and such?"

"No!" he snorted. "My machine does not reveal the past nor predict the future. It will show, as I told you, the conditional worlds. You might express it, by 'if I had done such and such, so and so would have happened.' The worlds of the subjunctive mode."

"Now how the devil does it do that?"

"Simple, for van Manderpootz! I use polarized light, polarized not in the horizontal or vertical planes, but in the direction of the fourth dimension—an easy matter. One uses Iceland spar under colossal pressures, that is all. And since the worlds are very thin in the direction of the fourth dimension, the thickness of a single light wave, though it be but millionths of an inch, is sufficient. A considerable improvement over time-travelling in past or future, with its impossible velocities and ridiculous distances!"

"But—are those—worlds of 'if'—real?"

"Real? What is real? They are real, perhaps, in the sense that two is a real number as opposed to √-2, which is imaginary. They are the worlds that would have been *if*— Do you see?"

I nodded. "Dimly. You could see, for instance, what New York would have been like if England had won the Revolution instead of the Colonies."

"That's the principle, true enough, but you couldn't see that on the machine. Part of it, you see, is a Horsten psychomat (stolen from one of my ideas, by the way) and you, the user, become part of the device. Your own mind is necessary to furnish the background. For instance, if George Washington could have used the mechanism after the signing of peace, he could have seen what you suggest. We can't. You can't even see what would have happened if I hadn't invented the thing, but *I* can. Do you understand?"

"Of course. You mean the background has to rest in the past experiences of the user."

"You're growing brilliant," he scoffed. "Yes. The device will show ten hours of what would have happened *if*—condensed, of course, as in a movie, to half an hour's actual time."

"Say, that sounds interesting!"

"You'd like to see it? Is there anything you'd like to find out? Any choice you'd alter?"

"I'll say—a thousand of 'em. I'd like to know what would have happened if I'd sold out my stocks in 2009 instead of '10. I was a millionaire in my own right then, but I was a little—well, a little late in liquidating."

"As usual," remarked van Manderpootz. "Let's go over to the laboratory then."

The professor's quarters were but a block from the campus. He ushered me into the Physics Building, and thence into his own research laboratory, much like the one I had visited during my courses under him. The device—he called it his "subjunctivisor," since it operated in hypothetical worlds—occupied the entire centre table. Most of it was merely a Horsten psychomat, but glittering crystalline and glassy was the prism of Iceland spar, the polarizing agent that was the heart of the instrument.

Van Manderpootz pointed to the headpiece. "Put it on," he said, and I sat staring at the screen of the psychomat. I suppose everyone is familiar with the Horsten psychomat; it was as much a fad a few years ago as the ouija board a century back. Yet it isn't just a toy; sometimes, much as the ouija board, it's a real aid to memory. A maze of vague and coloured shadows is caused to drift slowly across the screen, and one watches them, meanwhile visualizing whatever scene or circumstances he is trying to remember. He turns a knob that alters the arrangement of lights and shadows, and when, by chance, the design corresponds to his mental picture—presto! There is his scene re-created under his eyes. Of course his own mind adds the details. All the screen actually shows are these tinted blobs of light and shadow, but the thing can be amazingly real. I've seen occasions when I could have sworn the psychomat showed pictures almost as sharp and detailed as reality itself; the illusion is sometimes as startling as that.

Van Manderpootz switched on the light, and the play of shadows began. "Now recall the circumstances of, say, a half-year after the market crash. Turn the knob until the picture clears, then stop. At that point I direct the light of the subjunctivisor upon the screen, and you have nothing to do but watch."

I did as directed. Momentary pictures formed and vanished. The inchoate sounds of the device hummed like distant voices, but without the added suggestion of the picture, they meant nothing. My own face flashed and dissolved and then, finally, I had it. There was a picture of myself sitting in an ill-defined room; that was all. I released the knob and gestured.

A click followed. The light dimmed, then brightened. The picture cleared, and amazingly, another figure emerged, a woman. I recognized her; it was Whimsy White, erstwhile star of television and premiere of the "Vision Varieties of '09." She was changed on that picture, but I recognized her.

I'll say I did! I'd been trailing her all through the boom years of '07 to '10, trying to marry her, while old N. J. raved and ranted and threatened to leave everything to the Society for Rehabilitation of the Gobi Desert. I think those threats were what kept her from accepting me, but after I took my own money and ran it up to a couple of million in that crazy market of '08 and '09, she softened.

Temporarily, that is. When the crash of the spring of '10 came and bounced me back on my father and into the firm of N. J. Wells, her favour dropped a dozen points to the market's one. In February we were engaged, in April we were hardly speaking. In May they sold me out. I'd been late again.

And now, there she was on the psychomat screen, obviously plumping out, and not nearly so pretty as memory had pictured her. She was staring at me with an expression of enmity, and I was glaring back. The buzzes became voices.

"You nit-wit!" she snapped. "You can't bury me out here. I want to go back to New York, where there's a little life. I'm bored with you and your golf."

"And I'm bored with you and your whole dizzy crowd."

"At least they're *alive*. You're a walking corpse. Just because you were lucky enough to gamble yourself into the money, you think you're a tin god."

"Well, I *don't* think *you're* Cleopatra! Those friends of yours—they trail after you because you give parties and spend money—*my* money."

"Better than spending it to knock a white walnut along a mountainside!"

"Indeed? You ought to try it, Marie." (That was her real name.) "It might help your figure—though I doubt if anything could!"

She glared in rage and—well, that was a painful half hour. I won't give all the details, but I was glad when the screen dissolved into meaningless coloured clouds.

"Whew!" I said, staring at Van Manderpootz, who had been reading.

"You liked it?"

"Liked it! Say, I guess I was lucky to be cleaned out. I won't regret it from now on."

"That," said the professor grandly, "is van Manderpootz's great contribution to human happiness. 'Of all sad words of tongue or pen, the saddest are these: It might have been!' True no longer, my friend Dick. Van Manderpootz has shown that the proper reading is, 'It might have been—worse!'"

* * * * *

It was very late when I returned home, and as a result, very late when I rose, and equally late when I got to the office. My father was unnecessarily worked up about it, but he exaggerated when he said I'd never been on time. He forgets the occasions when he's awakened me and dragged me down with him. Nor was it necessary to refer so sarcastically to my missing the *Baikal*; I reminded him of the wrecking of the liner, and he responded very heartlessly that if I'd been aboard, the rocket would have been late, and so would have missed colliding with the British fruitship. It was likewise superfluous for him to mention that when he and I had tried to snatch a few weeks of golfing in the mountains, even the spring had been late. I had nothing to do with that.

"Dixon," he concluded, "you have no conception whatever of time. None whatever."

The conversation with van Manderpootz recurred to me. I was impelled to ask, "And have you, sir?"

"I have," he said grimly. "I most assuredly have. Time," he said oracularly, "is money."

You can't argue with a viewpoint like that.

But those aspersions of his rankled, especially that about the *Baikal*. Tardy I might be, but it was hardly conceivable that my presence aboard the rocket could have averted the catastrophe. It irritated me; in a way, it made me responsible for the deaths of those unrescued hundreds among the passengers and crew, and I didn't like the thought.

Of course, if they'd waited an extra five minutes for me, or if I'd been on time and they'd left on schedule instead of five minutes late, or if—*if*!

If! The word called up van Manderpootz and his subjunctivisor—the worlds of "if," the weird, unreal worlds that existed beside reality, neither past nor future, but contemporary, yet extemporal. Somewhere among their ghostly infinities existed one that represented the world that would have been had I made the liner. I had only to call up Haskel van Manderpootz, make an appointment, and then—find out.

Yet it wasn't an easy decision. Suppose—just suppose that I found myself responsible—not legally responsible, certainly; there'd be no question of criminal negligence, or anything of that sort—not even morally responsible, because I couldn't possibly have anticipated that my presence or absence could weigh so heavily in the scales of life and death, nor could I have known in which direction the scales would tip. Just—responsible; that was all. Yet I hated to find out.

I hated equally not finding out. Uncertainty has its pangs too, quite as painful as those of remorse. It might be less nerve-racking to know myself responsible than to wonder, to waste thoughts in vain doubts and futile reproaches. So I seized the visiphone, dialled the number of the University, and at length gazed on the broad, humorous, intelligent features of van Manderpootz, dragged from a morning lecture by my call.

* * * * *

I was all but prompt for the appointment the following evening, and might actually have been on time but for an unreasonable traffic officer who insisted on booking me for speeding. At any rate, van Manderpootz was impressed.

"Well!" he rumbled. "I almost missed you, Dixon. I was just going over to the club, since I didn't expect you for an hour. You're only ten minutes late."

I ignored this. "Professor, I want to use your—uh—your subjunctivisor."

"Eh? Oh, yes. You're lucky, then. I was just about to dismantle it."

"Dismantle it! Why?"

"It has served its purpose. It has given birth to an idea far more important than itself. I shall need the space it occupies."

"But what *is* the idea, if it's not too presumptuous of me to ask?"

"It is not too presumptuous. You and the world which awaits it so eagerly may both know, but you hear it from the lips of the author. It is nothing less than the autobiography of van Manderpootz!" He paused impressively.

I gaped. "Your autobiography?"

"Yes. The world, though perhaps unaware, is crying for it. I shall detail my life, my work. I shall reveal myself as the man responsible for the three years' duration of the Pacific War of 2004."

"You?"

"None other. Had I not been a loyal Netherlands subject at that time, and therefore neutral, the forces of Asia would have been crushed in three months instead of three years. The subjunctivisor tells me so; I would have invented a calculator to forecast the chances of every engagement; van Manderpootz would have removed the hit or miss element in the conduct of war." He frowned solemnly. "There is my idea. The autobiography of van Manderpootz. What do you think of it?"

I recovered my thoughts. "It's—uh—it's colossal!" I said vehemently. "I'll buy a copy myself. Several copies. I'll send 'em to my friends."

"I," said van Manderpootz expansively, "shall autograph your copy for you. It will be priceless. I shall write in some fitting phrase, perhaps something like *Magnificus sed non superbus*. 'Great but not proud!' That well described van

Manderpootz, who despite his greatness is simple, modest, and unassuming. Don't you agree?"

"Perfectly! A very apt description of you. But—couldn't I see your subjunctivisor before it's dismantled to make way for the greater work?"

"Ah! You wish to find out something?"

"Yes, professor. Do you remember the *Baikal* disaster of a week or two ago? I was to have taken that liner to Moscow. I just missed it." I related the circumstances.

"Humph!" he grunted. "You wish to discover what would have happened had you caught it, eh? Well, I see several possibilities. Among the world of 'if' is the one that would have been real if you had been on time, the one that depended on the vessel waiting for your actual arrival, and the one that hung on your arriving within the five minutes they actually waited. In which are you interested?"

"Oh—the last one." That seemed the likeliest. After all, it was too much to expect that Dixon Wells could ever be on time, and as to the second possibility—well, they *hadn't* waited for me, and that in a way removed the weight of responsibility.

"Come on," rumbled van Manderpootz. I followed him across to the Physics Building and into his littered laboratory. The device still stood on the table and I took my place before it, staring at the screen of the Horsten psychomat. The clouds wavered and shifted as I sought to impress my memories on their suggestive shapes, to read into them some picture of that vanished morning.

Then I had it. I made out the vista from the Staten Bridge, and was speeding across the giant span toward the airport. I waved a signal to van Manderpootz, the thing clicked, and the subjunctivisor was on.

The grassless clay of the field appeared. It is a curious thing about the psychomat that you see only through the eyes of your image on the screen. It lends a strange reality to the working of the toy; I suppose a sort of self-hypnosis is partly responsible.

I was rushing over the ground toward the glittering, silver-winged projectile that was the *Baikal*. A glowering officer waved me on, and I dashed up the slant of the gangplank and into the ship; the port dropped and I heard a long "Whew!" of relief.

"Sit down!" barked the officer, gesturing toward an unoccupied seat. I fell into it; the ship quivered under the thrust of the catapult, grated harshly into motion, and then was flung bodily into the air. The blasts roared instantly, then settled to a more muffled throbbing, and I watched Staten Island drop down and slide back beneath me. The giant rocket was under way.

"Whew!" I breathed again. "Made it!" I caught an amused glance from my right. I was in an aisle seat; there was no one to my left, so I turned to the eyes that had flashed, glanced, and froze staring.

It was a girl. Perhaps she wasn't actually as lovely as she looked to me; after all, I was seeing her through the half-visionary screen of a psychomat. I've told myself since that she *couldn't* have been as pretty as she seemed, that it was due to my own imagination filling in the details. I don't know; I remember only that I stared at curiously lovely silver-blue eyes and velvety brown hair, and a small amused mouth, and an impudent nose. I kept staring until she flushed.

"I'm sorry," I said quickly. "I—was startled."

There's a friendly atmosphere aboard a trans-oceanic rocket. The passengers are forced into a crowded intimacy for anywhere from seven to twelve hours, and there isn't much room for moving about. Generally, one strikes up an acquaintance with his neighbours; introductions aren't at all necessary, and the custom is simply to speak to anybody you choose—something like an all-day trip on the railroad trains of the last century, I suppose. You make friends for the duration of the journey, and then, nine times out of ten, you never hear of your travelling companions again.

The girl smiled. "Are you the individual responsible for the delay in starting?"

I admitted it. "I seem to be chronically late. Even watches lose time as soon as I wear them."

She laughed. "Your responsibilities can't be very heavy."

Well, they weren't of course, though it's surprising how many clubs, caddies, and chorus girls have depended on me at various times for appreciable portions of their incomes. But somehow I didn't feel like mentioning those things to the silvery-eyed girl.

We talked. Her name, it developed, was Joanna Caldwell, and she was going as far as Paris. She was an artist, or hoped to be one day, and of course there is no place in the world that can supply both training and inspiration like Paris. So it was there she was bound for a year of study, and despite her demurely humorous lips and laughing eyes, I could see that the business was of vast importance to her. I gathered that she had worked hard for the year in Paris, had scraped and saved for three years as fashion illustrator for some woman's magazine, though she couldn't have been many months over twenty-one. Her painting meant a great deal to her, and I could understand it. I'd felt that way about polo once.

So you see, we were sympathetic spirits from the beginning. I knew that she liked me, and it was obvious that she didn't connect Dixon Wells with the N. J. Wells Corporation. And as for me—well, after that first glance into her cool silver eyes, I simply didn't care to look anywhere else. The hours seemed to drip away like minutes while I watched her.

You know how those things go. Suddenly I was calling her Joanna and she was calling me Dick, and it seemed as if we'd been doing just that all our lives. I'd decided to stop over in Paris on my way back from Moscow, and I'd secured her promise to let me see her. She was different, I tell you; she was nothing like the calculating Whimsy White, and still less like the dancing, simpering, giddy youngsters one meets around at social affairs. She was just Joanna, cool and humorous, yet sympathetic and serious, and as pretty as a Majolica figurine.

We could scarcely realize it when the steward passed along to take orders for luncheon. Four hours out? It seemed like forty minutes. And we had a pleasant feeling of intimacy in the discovery that both of us liked lobster salad and detested oysters. It was another bond; I told her whimsically that it was an omen, nor did she object to considering it so.

Afterwards we walked along the narrow aisle to the glassed-in observation room up forward. It was almost too crowded for entry, but we didn't mind that at all, as it forced us to sit very close together. We stayed long after both of us had begun to notice the stuffiness of the air.

It was just after we had returned to our seats that the catastrophe occurred. There was no warning save a sudden lurch, the result, I suppose, of the pilot's futile last-minute attempt to swerve—just that and then a grinding crash and a terrible sensation of spinning, and after that a chorus of shrieks that were like the sounds of battle.

It *was* battle. Five hundred people were picking themselves up from the floor, were trampling each other, milling around, being cast helplessly down as the great rocket-plane, its left wing but a broken stub, circled downward toward the Atlantic.

The shouts of officers sounded and a loudspeaker blared. "Be calm," it kept repeating, and then, "There has been a collision. We have contacted a surface ship. There is no danger— There is no danger—"

I struggled up from the debris of shattered seats. Joanna was gone; just as I found her crumpled between the rows, the ship struck the water with a jar that set everything crashing again. The speaker blared, "Put on the cork belts under the seats. The life-belts are under the seats."

I dragged a belt loose and snapped it around Joanna, then donned one myself. The crowd was surging forward now, and the tail end of the ship began to drop. There was water behind us, sloshing in the darkness as the lights went out. An officer came sliding by, stooped, and fastened a belt about an unconscious woman ahead of us. "You all right?" he yelled, and passed on without waiting for an answer.

The speaker must have been cut on to a battery circuit. "And get as far away as possible," it ordered suddenly. "Jump from the forward port and get as far away as possible. A ship is standing by. You will be picked up. Jump from the—". It went dead again.

I got Joanna untangled from the wreckage. She was pale; her silvery eyes were closed. I started dragging her slowly and painfully toward the forward port, and the slant of the floor increased until it was like the slide of a ski-jump. The officer passed again. "Can you handle her?" he asked, and again dashed away.

I was getting there. The crowd around the port looked smaller, or was it simply huddling closer? Then suddenly, a wail of fear and despair went up, and there was a roar of water. The observation room walls had given. I saw the green surge of waves, and a billowing deluge rushed down upon us. I had been late again.

That was all. I raised shocked and frightened eyes from the subjunctivisor to face van Manderpootz, who was scribbling on the edge of the table.

"Well?" he asked.

I shuddered. "Horrible!" I murmured. "We—I guess we wouldn't have been among the survivors."

"We, eh? *We?*" His eyes twinkled.

I did not enlighten him. I thanked him, bade him good-night, and went dolorously home.

* * * * *

Even my father noticed something queer about me. The day I got to the office only five minutes late, he called me in for some anxious questioning as to my health. I couldn't tell him anything, of course. How could I explain that I'd been late once too often, and had fallen in love with a girl two weeks after she was dead?

The thought drove me nearly crazy. Joanna! Joanna with her silvery eyes now lay somewhere at the bottom of the Atlantic. I went around half dazed, scarcely speaking. One night I actually lacked the energy to go home and sat smoking in my father's big overstuffed chair in his private office until I finally dozed off. The next morning, when old N. J. entered and found me there before him, he turned pale as paper, staggered, and gasped, "My heart!" It took a lot of explaining to convince him that I wasn't early at the office but just very late going home.

At last I felt that I couldn't stand it. I had to do something—anything at all. I thought finally of the subjunctivisor. I could see—yes, I could see what would have transpired if the ship hadn't been wrecked! I could trace out that weird, unreal romance hidden somewhere in the worlds of "if". I could, perhaps, wring a sombre, vicarious joy from the things that might have been. I could see Joanna once more!

It was late afternoon when I rushed over to van Manderpootz's quarters. He wasn't there; I encountered him finally in the hall of the Physics Building.

"Dick!" he exclaimed. "Are you sick?"

"Sick? No. Not physically. Professor. I've got to use your subjunctivisor again. I've *got* to!"

"Eh? Oh—that toy. You're too late, Dick. I've dismantled it. I have a better use for the space."

I gave a miserable groan and was tempted to damn the autobiography of the great van Manderpootz. A gleam of sympathy showed in his eyes, and he took my arm, dragging me into the little office adjoining his laboratory.

"Tell me," he commanded.

I did. I guess I made the tragedy plain enough, for his heavy brows knit in a frown of pity. "Not even van Manderpootz can bring back the dead," he murmured. "I'm sorry, Dick. Take your mind from the affair. Even were my subjunctivisor available, I wouldn't permit you to use it. That would be but to turn the knife in the wound." He paused. "Find something else to occupy your mind. Do as van Manderpootz does. Find forgetfulness in work."

"Yes," I responded dully. "But who'd want to read my autobiography? That's all right for you."

"Autobiography? Oh! I remember. No, I have abandoned that. History itself will record the life and works of van Manderpootz. Now I am engaged in a far grander project."

"Indeed?" I was utterly, gloomily disinterested.

"Yes. Gogli has been here, Gogli the sculptor. He is to make a bust of me. What better legacy can I leave to the world than a bust of van Manderpootz, sculptured from life? Perhaps I shall present it to the city, perhaps to the university. I would have given it to the Royal Society if they had been a little more receptive, if they—if—*if!*" The last in a shout.

"Huh?"

"*If!*" cried van Manderpootz. "What you saw in the subjunctivisor was what would have happened *if* you had caught the ship!"

"I know that."

"But something quite different might really have happened! Don't you see? She—she— Where are those old newspapers?"

He was pawing through a pile of them. He flourished one finally. "Here! Here are the survivors!"

Like letters of flame, Joanna Caldwell's name leaped out at me. There was even a little paragraph about it, as I saw once my reeling brain permitted me to read:

"At least a score of survivors owe their lives to the bravery of twenty-eight-year-old Navigator Orris Hope, who patrolled both aisles during the panic, lacing life-belts on the injured and helpless, and carrying many to the port. He remained on the sinking liner until the last, finally fighting his way to the surface through the broken walls of the observation room. Among those who owe their lives to the young officer are: Patrick Owensby, New York City; Mrs. Campbell Warren, Boston; Miss Joanna Caldwell, New York City—"

I suppose my shout of joy was heard over in the Administration Building, blocks away. I didn't care; if van Manderpootz hadn't been armoured in stubby whiskers, I'd have kissed him. Perhaps I did anyway; I can't be sure of my actions during those chaotic minutes in the professor's tiny office.

At last I calmed. "I can look her up!" I gloated. "She must have landed with the other survivors, and they were all on that British tramp freighter the *Osgood*, that docked here last week. She must be in New York—and if she's gone over to Paris, I'll find out and follow her!"

Well, it's a queer ending. She was in New York, but—you see, Dixon Wells had, so to speak, known Joanna Caldwell by means of the professor's subjunctivisor, but Joanna had never known Dixon Wells. What the ending might have been if—*if*— But it wasn't; she had married Orris Hope, the young officer who had rescued her. I was late again.

With the Night Mail: A Story of 2000 AD

by Rudyard Kipling

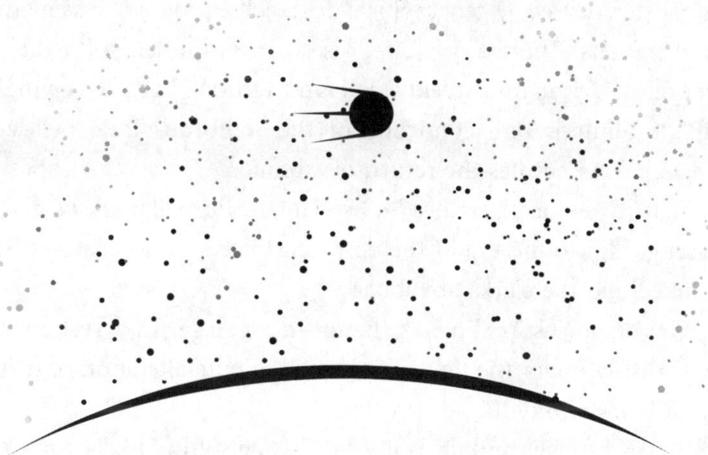

At 21 o'clock of a gusty winter night I stood on the lower stages of one of the G. P. O. outward mail tower. My purpose was a run to Quebec in "postal packet 162 or such other as may be appointed": and the Postmaster General himself countersigned the order. This talisman opened all doors, even those in the despatching-caisson at the foot of the tower, where they were delivering the sorted Continental mail. The bags lay packed close as herrings in the long gray underbodies which our G. P. O. still calls "coaches." Five such coaches were filled as I watched, and were shot up the guides to be locked on to their waiting packets three hundred feet nearer the stars.

From the despatching-caisson I was conducted by a courteous and wonderfully learned official—Mr. L. L. Geary, Second Despatcher of the Western Route—to the Captains' Room (this wakes an echo of old romance), where the mail captains come on for their turn of duty. He introduces me to the captain of "162"—Captain Purnall, and his relief, Captain Hodgson. The one is small and dark: the other large and red; but each has the brooding sheathed glance characteristic of eagles and aeronauts. You can see it in the pictures of our racing professionals, from L. V. Rautsch to little Ada Warrleigh—that fathomless abstraction of eyes habitually turned through naked space.

On the notice-board in the Captains' Room, the pulsing arrows of some twenty indicators register, degree by geographical degree, the progress of as many homeward-bound packets. The word "Cape" rises across the face of a dial; a gong strikes: the South African mid-weekly mail is in at the Highgate Receiving Towers. That is all. It reminds one comically of the traitorous little bell which in pigeon-fanciers' lofts notifies the return of a homer.

"Time for us to be on the move," says Captain Purnall, and we are shot up by the passenger-lift to the top of the despatch-towers. "Our coach will lock on when it is filled and the clerks are aboard."

"No. 162" waits for us in Slip E of the top-most stage. The great curve of her back shines frostily under the lights, and some minute alteration of trim makes her rock a little in her holding-down slips.

Captain Purnall frowns and dives inside. Hissing softly, "162" comes to rest as level as a rule. From her North Atlantic Winter nose-cap (worn bright as diamond with boring through uncounted leagues of hail, snow, and ice) to the inset of her three built-out propeller-shafts is some two hundred and forty feet. Her extreme diameter, carried well forward, is thirty-seven. Contrast this with the nine hundred by ninety-four of any crack liner, and you will realize the power that must drive a hull through all weathers at more than twice the emergency-speed of the "Cyclonic"!

The eye detects no joint in her skin plating save the sweeping hair-crack of the bow-rudder—Magniac's rudder that assured us the dominion of the unstable air and left its inventor penniless and half-blind. It is calculated to Castelli's "gull-wing" curve. Raise a few feet of that all but invisible plate three-eighths of an inch and she will yaw five miles to port or starboard ere she is under control again. Give her full helm and she returns on her track like a whip-lash. Cant the whole forward—a touch on the wheel will suffice—and she sweeps at your good direction up or down. Open the full circle and she presents to the air a mushroom head that will bring her up all standing within a half mile.

* * * * *

"Yes," says Captain Hodgson, answering my thought, "Castelli thought he'd discovered the secret of controlling aeroplanes when he'd only found out how to steer dirigible balloons. Magniac invented his rudder to help war-boats ram each other; and war went out of fashion and Magniac he went out of his mind because he said he couldn't serve his country any more. I wonder if any of us ever know what we're really doing."

"If you want to see the coach locked you'd better go aboard. It's due now," says Mr. Geary. I enter through the door amidships. There is nothing here for display. The inner skin of the gas-tanks comes down to within a foot or two of my head and turns over just short of the turn of the bilges. Liners and yachts disguise their tanks with decoration, but the G. P. O. serves them raw under a lick of gray official paint. The inner skin shuts off fifty feet of the bow and as much of the stern, but the bow-bulkhead is recessed for the lift-shunting apparatus as the stern is pierced for the shaft-tunnels. The engine-room lies almost amidships. Forward of it, extending to the turn of the bow tanks is an aperture—a bottomless hatch at present—into which the coach will be locked. One looks down over the coamings three hundred feet to the despatching-caisson whence voices boom upward. The light below is obscured to a sound of thunder, as the coach rises on its guides. It enlarges rapidly from a postage-stamp to a playing-card; to a punt and last a pontoon. The two clerks, its crew, do not even look up as it comes into place. The Quebec letters fly under their fingers and leap into the docketed racks, while both captains and Mr. Geary satisfy themselves that the coach is locked home. A clerk passes the way-bill over the hatch-coaming. Captain Purnall thumb-marks and passes it to Mr. Geary. Receipt has been given and taken. "Pleasant run," says Mr. Geary, and disappears through the door which a foot high pneumatic compressor locks after him.

"A-ah!" sighs the compressor released. Our holding-down clips part with a tang. We are clear.

Captain Hodgson opens the great colloid underbody-porthole through which I watch million-lighted London slide eastward as the gale gets hold of us. The first of the low winter clouds cuts off the well-known view and darkens Middlesex.

On the south edge of it I can see a packet's postal light ploughing through the white fleece. For an instant she gleams like a star ere she drops toward the Highgate Receiving Towers. "The Bombay Mail," says Captain Hodgson, and looks at his watch. "She's forty minutes late."

"What's our level?" I ask.

"Four thousand. Aren't you coming up on the bridge?"

The bridge (let us ever praise the G. P. O. as a repository of ancientest tradition!) is represented by a view of Captain Hodgson's legs where he stands on the control platform that runs thwartships overhead. The bow colloid is unshuttered and Captain Purnall, one hand on the wheel, is feeling for a fair slant. The dial shows 4,300 feet.

"It's steep to-night," he mutters, as tier on tier of cloud drops under. "We generally pick up an easterly draught below three thousand at this time o' the year. I hate slathering through fluff."

"So does Van Cutsem. Look at him huntin' for a slant," says Captain Hodgson. A fog-light breaks cloud a hundred fathoms below. The Antwerp Night Mail makes her signal and rises between two racing clouds far to port, her flanks blood-red in the glare of Sheerness Double Light. The gale will have us over the North Sea in half an hour, but Captain Purnall lets her go composedly—nosing to every point of the compass as she rises.

"Five thousand—six, six thousand eight hundred"—the dip-dial reads ere we find the easterly drift, heralded by a flurry of snow at the thousand fathom level. Captain Purnall rings up the engines and keys down the governor on the switch before him. There is no sense in urging machinery when Æolus himself gives you good knots for nothing. We are away in earnest now—our nose notched home on our chosen star. At this level the lower clouds are laid out, all neatly combed by the dry fingers of the East. Below that again is the strong westerly blow through which we rose. Overhead, a film of southerly drifting mist draws a theatrical gauze across the firmament. The moonlight turns the lower strata to silver without a stain except where our shadow underruns us. Bristol and Cardiff Double Lights (those statelily inclined beams over Severnmouth) are dead ahead of us; for we keep the Southern Winter Route. Coventry Central, the pivot of the English system, stabs upward once in ten seconds its spear of diamond light to the north; and a point or two off our starboard bow The Leek, the great cloud-breaker of Saint David's Head, swings its unmistakable green beam twenty-five degrees each way. There must be half a mile of fluff over it in this weather, but it does not affect The Leek.

"Our planet's overlighted if anything," says Captain Purnall at the wheel, as Cardiff-Bristol slides under. "I remember the old days of common white verticals that 'ud show two or three thousand feet up in a mist, if you knew where to look for 'em. In really fluffy weather they might as well have been under your hat. One could get lost coming home then, an' have some fun. Now, it's like driving down Piccadilly."

He points to the pillars of light where the cloud-breakers bore through the cloud-floor. We see nothing of England's outlines: only a white pavement pierced in all directions by these manholes of variously coloured fire—Holy Island's white and red—St. Bee's interrupted white, and so on as far as the eye can reach. Blessed be Sargent, Ahrens, and the Dubois brothers, who invented the cloud-breakers of the world whereby we travel in security!

"Are you going to lift for The Shamrock?" asks Captain Hodgson. Cork Light (green, fixed) enlarges as we rush to it. Captain Purnall nods. There is heavy traffic hereabouts—the bank beneath us is streaked with running fissures of flame where the Atlantic boats are hurrying Londonwards just clear of the fluff. Mail-packets are supposed, under the Conference rules, to have the five-thousand-foot lanes to themselves, but the foreigner in a hurry is apt to take liberties with English air. "No. 162" lifts to a long-drawn wail of the breeze in the fore-flange of the rudder and we make Valencia (white, green, white) at a safe 7000 feet, dipping our beam to an incoming Washington packet.

There is no cloud on the Atlantic, and faint streaks of cream round Dingle Bay show where the driven seas hammer the coast. A big S. A. T. A. liner (*Société Anonyme des Transports Aeriens*) is diving and lifting half a mile below us in search of some break in the solid west wind. Lower still lies a disabled Dane: she is telling the liner all about it in International. Our General Communication dial has caught her talk and begins to eavesdrop. Captain Hodgson makes a motion to shut it off but checks himself. "Perhaps you'd like to listen," he says.

"'Argol' of St. Thomas," the G. C. whispers. "Report owners three starboard shaft collar-bearings fused. Can make Flores as we are, but impossible further. Shall we buy spares at Fayal?"

The liner acknowledges and recommends inverting the bearings. The "Argol" answers that she has already done so without effect, and begins to relieve her mind about cheap German enamels for collar-bearings. The Frenchman assents cordially, cries "*Courage, mon ami*," and switches off.

Their lights sink under the curve of the ocean.

"That's one of Lundt & Bleamer's boats," says Captain Hodgson. "Serves 'em right for putting German compos in their thrust-blocks. *She* won't be in Fayal to-night! By the way, wouldn't you like to look round the engine-room?"

I have been waiting eagerly for this invitation and I follow Captain Hodgson from the control-platform, stooping low to avoid the bulge of the tanks. We know that Fleury's gas can lift anything, as the world-famous trials of '17 showed, but its almost indefinite powers of expansion necessitate vast tank room. Even in this thin air the lift-shunts are busy taking out one-third of its normal lift, and still "162" must be checked by an occasional downdraw of the rudder or our flight would become a climb to the stars. Captain Purnall prefers an overlifted to an underlifted ship; but no two captains trim ship alike. "When *I* take the bridge," says Captain Hodgson, "you'll see me shunt forty per cent of the lift out of the gas and run her on the upper rudder. With a swoop upwards instead of a swoop downwards, *as* you say. Either way will do. It's only habit. Watch our dip-dial! Tim fetches her down once every thirty knots as regularly as breathing."

So is it shown on the dip-dial. For five or six minutes the arrow creeps from 6,700 to 7,300. There is the faint "szgee" of the rudder, and back slides the arrow to 6,500 on a falling slant of ten or fifteen knots.

"In heavy weather you jockey her with the screws as well," says Captain Hodgson, and, unclipping the jointed bar which divides the engine-room from the bare deck, he leads me on to the floor. Here we find Fleury's Paradox of the Bulkheaded Vacuum—which we accept now without thought—literally in full blast. The three engines are H. T. & T. assisted-vacuo Fleury turbines running from 3,000 to the Limit—that is to say, up to the point when the blades make the air "bell"—cut out a vacuum for themselves precisely as do over-driven marine propellers. "162's" Limit is low on account of the small size of her nine screws, which, though handier than the old colloid Thelussons, bell sooner. The midships engine, generally used as a reinforce, is not running; so the port and starboard turbine vacuum-chambers draw direct into the return-mains.

The turbines whistle reflectively. From the low-arched expansion-tanks on either side the valves descend pillarwise to the turbine-chests, and thence the obedient gas whirls through the spirals of blades with a force that would whip the teeth out of a power-saw. Behind, is its own pressure held in leash or spurred on by the lift-shunts; before it, the vacuum where Fleury's Ray dances in violet-green bands and whirled tourbillons of flame. The jointed U-tubes of the vacuum-chamber are pressure-tempered colloid (no glass would endure the strain for an instant) and a junior engineer with tinted spectacles watches the Ray intently. It is the very heart of the machine—a mystery to this day. Even Fleury who begat it and, unlike Magniac, died a multi-millionaire, could not explain how the restless little imp shuddering in the U-tube can, in the fractional fraction of a second, strike the furious blast of gas into a chill grayish-green liquid that drains (you can hear it trickle) from the far end of the vacuum through the eduction-pipes and the mains back to the bilges. Here it returns to its gaseous, one had almost written sagacious, state and climbs to work afresh. Bilge-tank, upper tank, dorsal-tank, expansion-chamber, vacuum, main-return (as a liquid), and bilge-tank once more is the ordained cycle. Fleury's Ray sees to that; and the engineer with the tinted spectacles sees to Fleury's Ray. If a speck of oil; if even the natural grease of the human finger touch the hooded terminals, Fleury's Ray will wink and disappear and must be labouriously built up again. This means half a day's work for all hands and an expense of one hundred and seventy-odd pounds to the G. P. O. for radium-salts and such trifles.

"Now look at our thrust-collars. You won't find much German compo there. Full-jewelled, you see," says Captain Hodgson as the engineer shunts open the top of a cap. Our shaft-bearings are C. D. C. (Commercial Diamond Company) stones, ground with as much care as the lens of a telescope. They cost £37 apiece. So far we have not arrived at their term of life. These bearings came from "No. 97," which took them over from the old "Dominion of Light" which had them out of the wreck of the "Perseus" aeroplane in the years when men still flew kites over thorium engines.

They are a shining reproof to all low-grade German "ruby" enamels, so-called "boort" facings, and the dangerous and unsatisfactory alumina compounds which please dividend-hunting owners and turn skippers crazy.

The rudder-gear and the gas lift-shunt, seated side by side under the engine-room dials, are the only machines in visible motion. The former sighs from time to time as the oil plunger rises and falls half an inch. The latter, cased and guarded like the U-tube aft, exhibits another Fleury Ray, but inverted and more green than violet. Its function is to shunt the lift out of the gas, and this it will do without watching. That is all! A tiny pump-rod wheezing and whining to itself beside a sputtering green lamp. A hundred and fifty feet aft down the flat-topped tunnel of the tanks a violet light, restless and irresolute. Between the two, three white-painted turbine-trunks, like eel-baskets laid on their side, accentuate the empty perspectives. You can hear the trickle of the liquefied gas flowing from the vacuum into the bilge-tanks and the soft *gluck-glock* of gas-locks closing as Captain Purnall brings "162" down by the head. The hum of the turbines and the boom of the air on our skin is no more than a cotton-wool wrapping to the universal stillness. And we are running an eighteen-second mile.

I peer from the fore end of the engine-room over the hatch-coamings into the coach. The mail-clerks are sorting the Winnipeg, Calgary, and Medicine Hat bags; but there is a pack of cards ready on the table.

Suddenly a bell thrills; the engineers run to the turbine-valves and stand by; but the spectacled slave of the Ray in the U-tube never lifts his head. He must watch where he is. We are hard-braked and going astern; and there is language from the Control Platform.

"Tim's sparking badly about something," says the unruffled Captain Hodgson. "Let's look."

Captain Purnall is not the man we left half an hour ago, but the embodied authority of the G. P. O. Ahead of us floats an ancient, aluminium-patched, twin-screw tramp of the dingiest, with no more right to the 5,000-foot lanes than has a horse-cart to a town. She carries an obsolete "barbette" conning-tower—a six-foot affair with railed platform forward—and our warning beam plays on the top of it as a policeman's lantern flashes on the area sneak. Like a sneak-thief, too, emerges a shock-headed navigator in his shirt-sleeves. Captain Purnall wrenches open the colloid to talk with him man to man. There are times when Science does not satisfy.

"What under the stars are you doing here, you sky-scraping chimney-sweep?" he shouts as we two drift side by side. "Do you know this is a Mail-lane? You call yourself a skipper, sir? You ain't fit to peddle toy balloons to an Esquimaux. Your name and number! Report and get down!"

"I've been blown up once," the shock-headed man cries, hoarsely, as a dog barking. "I don't care two flips of a contact for anything *you* can do, Postey."

"Don't you, sir? But I'll make you care. I'll have you towed stern first to Disko and broke up. You can't recover insurance if you're broke for obstruction. Do you understand *that?*"

Then the stranger bellows: "Look at my propellers! There's been a wullie-wa down under that has knocked me into umbrella-frames! We've been blown up about forty thousand feet! We're all one conjuror's watch inside! My mate's arm's broke; my engineer's head's cut open; my Ray went out when the engines smashed; and … and … for pity's sake give me my height, Captain! We doubt we're dropping."

"Six thousand eight hundred. Can you hold it?" Captain Purnall overlooks all insults, and leans half out of the colloid, staring and snuffing. The stranger leaks pungently.

"We ought to blow back to St. John's with luck. We're trying to plug the fore-tank now, but she's simply whistling it away," her captain wails.

"She's sinkin' like a log," says Captain Purnall in an undertone. "Call up the Mark Boat, George." Our dip-dial shows that we abreast the tramp have dropped five hundred feet the last few minutes.

Captain Purnall presses a switch and our signal beam begins to swing through the night, twizzling spokes of light across infinity.

"That'll fetch something," he says, while Captain Hodgson watches the General Communicator. He has called up the Banks Mark Boat, a couple of hundred miles west, and is reporting the case.

"I'll stand by you," Captain Purnall roars to the lone figure on the conning-tower.

"Is it as bad as that?" comes the answer. "She isn't insured."

"Might have guessed as much," mutters Hodgson. "Owner's risk is the worst risk of all!"

"Can't I fetch St. John's—not even with this breeze?" the voice quavers.

"Stand by to abandon ship. Haven't you *any* lift in you, fore or aft?"

"Nothing but the midship tanks, and they're none too tight. You see, my Ray gave out and—" he coughs in the reek of the escaping gas.

"You poor devil!" This does not reach our friend. "What does the Mark Boat say, George?"

"Wants to know if there's any danger to traffic. Says she's in a bit of weather herself, and can't quit station. I've turned in a General Call, so even if they don't see our beam some one's bound to—or else we must. Shall I clear our slings? Hold on! Here we are! A Planet liner, too! She'll be up in a tick!"

"Tell her to have her slings ready," cries his brother captain. "There won't be much time to spare ... Tie up your mate," he roars to the tramp.

"My mate's all right. It's my engineer. He's gone crazy."

"Shunt the lift out of him with a spanner. Hurry!"

"But I can make land if I've half a chance."

"You'll make the Atlantic in twenty minutes. You're less than fifty-eight hundred now. Get your log and papers."

A Planet liner—east bound, heaves up in a superb spiral and takes the air of us humming. Her underbody colloid is open and her transporter-slings hang down like tentacles. We shut off our beam as she adjusts herself—steering to a hair—over the tramp's conning-tower. The mate comes up, his arm strapped to his side, and stumbles into the cradle. A man with a ghastly scarlet head follows, shouting that he must go back and build up his Ray. The mate assures him that he will find a nice new Ray all ready in the liner's engine-room. The bandaged head goes up wagging excitedly. A youth and a woman follow. The liner cheers hollowly above us, and we see the passengers' faces at the saloon colloid.

"That's a good girl. What's the fool waiting for now?" says Captain Purnall.

The skipper comes up, still appealing to us to stand by and see him fetch St. John's. He dives below and returns—at which we little human beings in the void cheer louder than ever—with the ship's kitten. Up fly the liner's hissing slings; her underbody crashes home and she hurtles away again. The dial shows less than 3,000 feet.

The Mark Boat signals we must attend to the derelict, now whistling her death song, as she falls beneath us in long sick zigzags.

"Keep our beam on her and send out a General Warning," says Captain Purnall, following her down. There is no need. Not a liner in air but knows the meaning of that vertical beam and gives us and our quarry a wide berth.

"But she'll drown in the water, won't she?" I ask.

"I've known a derelict up-end and sift her engines out of herself and flicker round the Lower Lanes for three weeks on her forward tanks only. We'll run no risks. Pith her, George, and look sharp. There's weather ahead."

Captain Hodgson opens the underbody colloid, swings the heavy pithing-iron out of its rack, which in liners is generally cased as a settee, and at two hundred feet releases the catch. We hear the whir of the crescent-shaped arms opening as they descend. The derelict's forehead is punched in, starred across, and rent diagonally. She falls stern first; our beam upon her; slides like a lost soul down that pitiless ladder of light, and the Atlantic takes her.

"A filthy business," says Hodgson. "I wonder what it must have been like in the old days?"

The thought had crossed my mind, too. What if that wavering carcass had been filled with International-speaking men of all the Internationalities, each one of them taught (*that* is the horror of it!) that after death he would very possibly go for ever to unspeakable torment?

And not half a century since, we (one knows now that we are only our fathers re-enlarged upon the earth), *we*, I say, ripped and rammed and pithed to admiration.

Here Tim, from the control-platform, shouts that we are to get into our inflators and to bring him his at once.

We hurry into the heavy rubber suits—the engineers are already dressed—and inflate at the air-pump taps. G. P. O. inflators are thrice as thick as a racing man's "heavies," and chafe abominably under the armpits. George takes the wheel until Tim has blown himself up to the extreme of rotundity. If you kicked him off the c. p. to the deck he would bounce back. But it is "162" that will do the kicking.

"The Mark Boat's mad—stark ravin' crazy," he snorts, returning to command. "She says there's a bad blow-out ahead and wants me to pull over to Greenland. I'll see her pithed first! We wasted an hour and a quarter over that dead duck down under, and now I'm expected to go rubbin' my back all over the Pole. What does she think a postal packet's made of? Gummed silk? Tell her we're coming on straight."

George buckles him into the Frame and switches on the Direct Control. Now under Tim's left toe lies the port engine Accelerator; under his left heel the Reverse, and so with the other foot. The lift-shunt stops stand out on the rim of the steering-wheel where the fingers of his left hand can play on them. At his right hand is the midships engine lever ready to be thrown into gear at a moment's notice. He leans forward in his belt, eyes glued to the colloid, and one ear cocked toward the General Communicator. Henceforth he is the strength and direction of "162," through whatever may befall.

The Banks Mark Boat is reeling out pages of Aerial Route Directions to the traffic at large. We are to secure all "loose objects"; hood up our Fleury Rays; and "on no account to attempt to clear snow from our conning-towers till the weather abates." Under-powered craft, we are told, can ascend to the limit of their lift, mail-packets to look out for them accordingly; the lanes westward are pitting very badly, with frequent blow-outs, vortices, and laterals."

Still the clear dark holds up unblemished. The only warning is the electric skin-tension (I feel as though I were a lace-maker's pillow) and an irritability which the gibbering of the General Communicator increases almost to hysteria.

We have made eight thousand feet since we pithed the tramp and our turbines are giving us an honest two hundred and ten an hour.

Very far to the west an elongated blur of red, low down, shows us the Banks Mark Boat. There are specks of fire round her rising and falling—bewildered planets about an unstable sun—helpless shipping hanging on to her light for company's sake. No wonder she could not quit station.

She warns us to look out for the back-wash of the bad vortex in which (her beam shows it) she is even now reeling.

The pits of gloom about us begin to fill with very faintly luminous films—wreathing and uneasy shapes. One forms itself into a globe of pale flame that waits shivering with eagerness till we sweep by. It leaps monstrously across the blackness, alights on the precise tip of our nose, pirouettes there an instant, and swings off. Our roaring bow sinks as though that light were lead—sinks and recovers to lurch and stumble again beneath the next blow-out. Tim's fingers on the lift-shunt strike chords of numbers—1:4:7:—2:4:6:—7:5:3; and so on; for he is running by his tanks only, lifting or lowering her against the uneasy air. All three engines are at work; the sooner we have skated over this thin ice the better. Higher we dare not go. The whole upper vault is charged with pale krypton vapours, which our skin friction may excite to unholy manifestations. Between the upper and the lower levels—5,000 and 7,000, hints the Mark Boat—we may perhaps bolt through if … Our bow clothes itself in blue flame and falls like a sword. No human skill can keep pace with the changing tensions. A vortex has us by the beak and we dive down a two-thousand foot slant at an angle (the dip-dial and my bouncing body record it) of thirty-five. Our turbines scream shrilly; the propellers cannot bite on the thin air; Tim shunts the lift out of five tanks at once and by sheer weight drives her bullet wise through the maelstrom till she cushions with a jar on an up-gust, three thousand feet below.

"*Now* we've done it," says George in my ear. "Our skin-friction, that last slide, has played Old Harry with the tensions! Look out for laterals, Tim, she'll want some lifting."

"I've got her," is the answer. "Come *up*, old woman."

She comes up nobly, but the laterals buffet her left and right like the pinions of angry angels. She is jolted off her chosen star twenty degrees to port or starboard, and cuffed into place again, only to be swung away and dropped into a new blow-out. We are never without a corposant grinning on our bows or rolling head over heels from nose to midships, and to the crackle of electricity round and within us is added once or twice the rattle of hail—hail that will never fall on any sea. Slow we must or we may break our back, pitch-poling.

"Air's a perfectly elastic fluid," roars George above the tumult. "About as elastic as a head sea off the Fastnet."

He is less than just to the good element. If one intrudes on the heavens when they are balancing their volt-accounts; if one disturbs the High Gods' market-rates by hurling steel hulls at ninety knots across tremblingly adjusted tensions, one must not complain of any rudeness in the reception. Tim met it with an unmoved countenance, one corner of his under lip caught up on a tooth, his eyes fleeting into the blackness twenty miles ahead, and the fierce sparks flying from his knuckles at every turn of the hand. Now and again he shook his head to clear the sweat trickling from his eyebrows, and it was then that George, watching his chance, would slide down the life-rail and swab his face quickly with a big red handkerchief. I never imagined that a human being could so continuously labour and so collectedly think as did Tim through that Hell's half hour when the flurry was at its worst. We were dragged hither and yon by warm or frozen suctions, belched up on the tops of wulli-was, spun down by vortices and clubbed aside by laterals under a dizzying rush of stars, in the company of a drunken moon. I heard the rushing click of the midship engine lever sliding in and out, the low growl of the lift-shunts and, louder than the yelling winds without, the scream of the bow-rudder gouging into any lull that promised hold for an instant. At last we began to claw up on a cant, bow-rudder and port-propeller together; only the nicest balancing of tanks saved us from spinning like the rifle-bullet of the old days.

"We've got to hitch to windward of that Mark Boat somehow," George cried.

"There's no windward," I protested feebly, where I swung shackled to a stanchion. "How can there be?"

He laughed—as we pitched into a thousand foot blow-out—that red man laughed under his inflated hood.

"Look!" he said. "We must clear those refugees with a high lift."

The Mark Boat was below and a little to the sou'west of us, fluctuating in the centre of her distraught galaxy. The air was thick with moving lights at every level. I take it most of them were lying head to wind but, not being hydras, they failed. An under-tanked Moghrabi boat had risen to the limit of her lift and, finding no improvement, had dropped a couple of thousand. There she met a superb wulli-wa, and was blown up spinning like a dead leaf. Instead of shutting off she braked hard and, naturally, rebounded as from a wall almost into the Mark Boat, whose language (our G. C. took it in) was humanly simple.

"If they'd only ride it out quietly it 'ud be better," said George in a calm, as we climbed like a bat above them all. "But some skippers *will* navigate without lift. What does that Tad-boat think she is doing, Tim?"

"Playin' kiss in the ring," was Tim's unmoved reply. A Trans-Asiatic Direct liner had found a smooth and butted into it full power. But there was a vortex at the tail of that smooth, so the T. A. D. was flipped out like a pea from off a fingernail, braking madly as she fled down and all but over-ending.

"Now I hope she's satisfied," said Tim. "I'm glad I'm not a Mark Boat ... Do I want help?" The G. C. dial had caught his ear. "George, you may tell that gentleman with my love—love, remember, George—that I do not want help. Who *is* the officious sardine-tin?"

"Rimouski drogher on the lookout for a tow."

"Very kind of the Rimouski drogher. This postal packet isn't being towed at present."

"These droghers will go anywhere on a chance of salvage," George explained. "We call 'em kittiwakes."

A long-beaked, bright steel ninety-footer floated at ease for one instant within hail of us, her slings coiled ready for rescues, and a single hand in her open tower. He was smoking. Surrendered to the insurrection of the airs through which we tore our way, he lay in absolute peace. I saw the smoke of his pipe ascend untroubled ere his boat dropped like a stone in a well.

We had just cleared the Mark Boat and her disorderly refugees when the storm ended as suddenly as it had begun. A shooting-star to northward filled the sky with the green blink of a meteorite dissipating itself in our atmosphere.

Said George: "That may iron out all the tensions." Even as he spoke, the conflicting winds came to rest; the levels filled; the laterals died out in long easy swells; the air-ways were smoothed before us. In less than three minutes the covey round the Mark Boat had shipped their power-lights and whirred away upon their businesses.

"What's happened?" I gasped. The nerve-storm within and the volt-tingle without had passed—my inflaters weighed like lead.

"God he knows!" said Captain George soberly "That old shooting-star's skin-friction has discharged the different levels. I've seen it happen before. Phew! What a relief!"

We dropped from twelve to six thousand and got rid of our clammy suits. Tim shut off and stepped out of the Frame. The Mark Boat was coming up behind us. He opened the colloid in that heavenly stillness and mopped his face.

"Hello, Williams!" he cried. "A degree or two out o' station, ain't you?"

"May be," was the answer. "I've had some company this evening."

"So I noticed. Wasn't that quite a little flurry?"

"I warned you. Why didn't you pull out round by Disko? The east-bound packets have."

"Me? Not till I'm running a Polar consumptives sanatorium boat! I was squinting through a colloid before you were out of your cradle, my son."

"I'd be the last man to deny it," the captain of the Mark Boat replies softly. "The way you handled her just now—I'm a pretty fair judge of traffic in a volt-flurry—it was a thousand revolutions beyond anything even I've ever seen."

Tim's back supples visibly to this oiling. Captain George on the c. p. winks and points to the portrait of a singularly attractive maiden pinned up on the telescope-bracket above the steering-wheel.

I see. Wholly and entirely do I see!

There is some talk overhead of "coming round to tea on Friday," a brief report of the derelict's fate, and Tim volunteers as he descends: "For an A. B. C. man young Williams is less of a high-tension fool than some… . Were you thinking of taking her on, George? Then I'll just have a look round that port-thrust—seems to me it's a trifle warm—and we'll fan along."

The Mark Boat hums off joyously and hangs herself up in her appointed eyrie. Here she will stay, a shutterless observatory; a life-boat station; a salvage tug; a court of ultimate appeal-cum-meteorological bureau for three hundred miles in all directions, till Wednesday next when her relief slides across the stars to take her buffeted place. Her black hull, double conning-tower, and ever-ready slings represent all that remains to the planet of that odd old word authority. She is responsible only to the Aerial Board of Control—the A. B. C. of which Tim speaks so flippantly. But that semi-elected, semi-nominated body of a few score of persons of both sexes, controls this planet. "Transportation is Civilization," our motto runs. Theoretically, we do what we please so long as we do not interfere with the traffic *and all it implies.* Practically, the A. B. C. confirms or annuls all international arrangements and, to judge from its last report, finds our tolerant, humorous, lazy little planet only too ready to lay the whole burden of public administration on its shoulders.

I discuss this with Tim, sipping maté on the c. p. while George fans her along over the white blur of the Banks in beautiful upward curves of fifty miles each. The dip-dial translates them on the tape in flowing freehand.

Tim gathers up a skein of it and surveys the last few feet, which record "162's" path through the volt-flurry.

"I haven't had a fever-chart like this to show up in five years," he says ruefully.

A postal packet's dip-dial records every yard of every run. The tapes then go to the A. B. C., which collates and makes composite photographs of them for the instruction of captains. Tim studies his irrevocable past, shaking his head.

"Hello! Here's a fifteen-hundred-foot drop at eighty-five degrees! We must have been standing on our heads then, George."

"You don't say so," George answers. "I fancied I noticed it at the time."

George may not have Captain Purnall's catlike swiftness, but he is all an artist to the tips of the broad fingers that play on the shunt-stops. The delicious flight-curves come away on the tape with never a waver. The Mark Boat's vertical spindle of light lies down to eastward, setting in the face of the following stars. Westward, where no planet should rise, the triple verticals of Trinity Bay (we keep still to the Southern route) make a low-lifting haze. We seem the only thing at rest under all the heavens; floating at ease till the earth's revolution shall turn up our landing-towers.

And minute by minute our silent clock gives us a sixteen-second mile.

"Some fine night," says Tim, "we'll be even with that clock's Master."

"He's coming now," says George, over his shoulder. "I'm chasing the night already."

The stars ahead dim no more than if a film of mist had been drawn under unobserved, but the deep air-boom on our skin changes to a joyful shout.

"The dawn-gust," says Tim. "It'll go on to meet the Sun. Look! Look! There's the dark being crammed back over our bow! Come to the aft colloid. I'll show you something."

The engine-room is hot and stuffy; the clerks in the coach are asleep, and the Slave of the Ray is ready to follow them. Tim slides open the aft colloid and reveals the curve of the world—the ocean's deepest purple—edged with fuming and intolerable gold. Then the Sun rises and through the colloid strikes out our lamps. Tim scowls in his face.

"Squirrels in a cage," he mutters. "That's all we are. Squirrels in a cage! He's going twice as fast as us. Just you wait a few years, my shining friend, and we'll take steps that will amaze you. *We'll* Joshua you!"

Yes, that is our dream: to turn all earth into the Vale of Ajalon at our pleasure. So far, we can drag out the dawn to twice its normal length in these latitudes. But some day—even on the Equator—we shall hold the Sun level in his full stride.

Now we look down on a sea thronged with heavy traffic. A big submersible breaks water suddenly. Another and another follows with a swash and a suck and a savage bubbling of relieved pressures. The deep-sea freighters are rising to lung up after the long night, and the leisurely ocean is all patterned with peacock's eyes of foam.

"We'll lung up, too," says Tim, and when we return to the c. p. George shunts off, the colloids are opened, and the fresh air sweeps her out. There is no hurry. The old contracts (they will be revised at the end of the year) allow twelve hours for a run which any packet can put behind her in ten. So we breakfast in the arms of an easterly slant which pushes us along at a languid twenty.

To enjoy life, and tobacco, begin both on a sunny morning half a mile or so above the dappled Atlantic cloud-belts and after a volt-flurry which has cleared and tempered your nerves. While we discussed the thickening traffic with the superiority that comes of having a high level reserved to ourselves, we heard (and I for the first time) the morning hymn on a Hospital boat.

She was cloaked by a skein of ravelled fluff beneath us and we caught the chant before she rose into the sunlight. "*Oh, ye Winds of God,*" sang the unseen voices: "*bless ye the Lord! Praise Him and magnify Him for ever!*"

We slid off our caps and joined in. When our shadow fell across her great open platforms they looked up and stretched out their hands neighbourly while they sang. We could see the doctors and the nurses and the white-button-like faces of the cot-patients. She passed slowly beneath us, heading northward, her hull, wet with the dews of the night, all ablaze in the sunshine. So took she the shadow of a cloud and vanished, her song continuing. *Oh, ye holy and humble men of heart, bless ye the Lord! Praise Him and magnify Him for ever.*

"She's a public lunger or she wouldn't have been singing the *Benedicite*, and she's a Greenlander or she wouldn't have snow-blinds over her colloids," said George at last. "She'll be bound for Frederikshavn or one of the Glacier sanatoriums for a month. If she was an accident ward she'd be hung up at the eight-thousand-foot level. Yes—consumptives."

"Funny how the new things are the old things. I've read in books," Tim answered, "that savages used to haul their sick and wounded up to the tops of hills because microbes were fewer there. We hoist 'em in sterilized air for a while. Same idea."

"How much do the doctors say we've added to the average life of man?"

"Thirty years," says George with a twinkle in his eye. "Are we going to spend 'em all up here?"

"Flap along, then. Flap along. Who's hindering?" the senior captain laughed, as we went in.

We held a good lift to clear the coastwise and Continental shipping and we had need of it. Though our route is in no sense a populated one, there is a steady trickle of traffic this way along. We met Hudson Bay furriers out of the Great Preserve, hurrying to make their departure from Bonavista with sable and black fox for the insatiable markets. We over-crossed Keewatin liners, small and cramped, but their captains, who see no land between Trepassy and Blanco, know what gold they bring back from West Africa. Trans-Asiatic Directs we met, soberly ringing the world round the Fiftieth Meridian at an honest seventy knots; and white-painted Ackroyd & Hunt fruiters out of the south fled beneath us, their ventilated hulls whistling like Chinese kites. Their market is in the North among the northern sanatoria where you can smell their grapefruit and bananas across the cold snows. Argentine beef boats we sighted too, of enormous capacity and unlovely outline. They, too, feed the northern health stations in icebound ports where submersibles dare not rise.

Yellow-bellied ore-flats and Ungava petrol-tanks punted down leisurely out of the north, like strings of unfrightened wild duck. It does not pay to "fly" minerals and oil a mile farther than is necessary; but the risks of transhipping to submersibles in the ice-pack off Nain or Hebron are so great that these heavy freighters fly down to Halifax direct, and scent the air as they go. They are the biggest tramps aloft except the Athabasca grain tubs. But these last, now that the wheat is moved, are busy, over the world's shoulder, timber-lifting in Siberia.

We held to the St. Lawrence (it is astonishing how the old water-ways still pull us children of the air), and followed his broad line of black between its drifting ice blocks, all down the Park that the wisdom of our fathers—but every one knows the Quebec run.

We dropped to the Heights Receiving Towers twenty minutes ahead of time, and there hung at ease till the Yokohama Intermediate Packet could pull out and give us our proper slip. It was curious to watch the action of the holding-down clips all along the frosty river front as the boats cleared or came to rest. A big Hamburger was leaving Pont Levis and her crew, unshipping the platform railings, began to sing "Elsinore"—the oldest of our chanteys. You know it of course:

MOTHER RUGEN'S TEA-HOUSE ON THE BALTIC—
FORTY COUPLE WALTZING ON THE FLOOR!
AND YOU CAN WATCH MY RAY,
FOR I MUST GO AWAY
AND DANCE WITH ELLA SWEYN AT ELSINORE!

Then, while they sweated home the covering-plates:

NOR-NOR-NOR-NOR-
WEST FROM SOURABAYA TO THE BALTIC!
NINETY KNOT AN HOUR TO THE SKAW!
MOTHER RUGEN'S TEA-HOUSE ON THE BALTIC
AND A DANCE WITH ELLA SWEYN AT ELSINORE!

The clips parted with a gesture of indignant dismissal, as though Quebec, glittering under her snows, were casting out these light and unworthy lovers. Our signal came from the Heights. Tim turned and floated up, but surely then it was with passionate appeal that the great arms flung open from our tower—or did I think so because on the upper staging a little hooded figure also stretched arms wide towards her father?

* * * * *

In ten seconds the coach with its clerks clashed down to the receiving-caisson; the hostlers displaced the engineers at the idle turbines, and Tim, prouder of this than all, introduced me to the maiden of the photograph on the shelf. "And by the way," said he to her, stepping forth in sunshine under the hat of civil life, "I saw young Williams in the Mark Boat. I've asked him to tea on Friday."

WIRELESS

by Rudyard Kipling

"It's a funny thing, this Marconi business, isn't it?" said Mr. Shaynor, coughing heavily. "Nothing seems to make any difference, by what they tell me—storms, hills, or anything; but if that's true we shall know before morning."

"Of course it's true," I answered, stepping behind the counter. "Where's old Mr. Cashell?"

"He's had to go to bed on account of his influenza. He said you'd very likely drop in."

"Where's his nephew?"

"Inside, getting the things ready. He told me that the last time they experimented they put the pole on the roof of one of the big hotels here, and the batteries electrified all the water-supply, and"—he giggled—"the ladies got shocks when they took their baths."

"I never heard of that."

"The hotel wouldn't exactly advertise it, would it? Just now, by what Mr. Cashell tells me, they're trying to signal from here to Poole, and they're using stronger batteries than ever. But, you see, he being the guvnor's nephew and all that (and it will be in the papers too), it doesn't matter how they electrify things in this house. Are you going to watch?"

"Very much. I've never seen this game. Aren't you going to bed?"

"We don't close till ten on Saturdays. There's a good deal of influenza in town, too, and there'll be a dozen prescriptions coming in before morning. I generally sleep in the chair here. It's warmer than jumping out of bed every time. Bitter cold, isn't it?"

"Freezing hard. I'm sorry your cough's worse."

"Thank you. I don't mind cold so much. It's this wind that fair cuts me to pieces." He coughed again hard and hackingly, as an old lady came in for ammoniated quinine. "We've just run out of it in bottles, madam," said Mr. Shaynor, returning to the professional tone, "but if you will wait two minutes, I'll make it up for you, madam."

I had used the shop for some time, and my acquaintance with the proprietor had ripened into friendship. It was Mr. Cashell who revealed to me the purpose and power of Apothecaries' Hall that time a fellow chemist had made an error in a prescription of mine, had lied to cover his sloth, and when error and lie were brought home to him had written vain letters.

"A disgrace to our profession," said the thin, mild-eyed man, hotly, after studying the evidence. "You couldn't do a better service to the profession than report him to Apothecaries' Hall."

I did so, not knowing what djinns I should evoke; and the result was such an apology as one might make who had spent a night on the rack. I conceived great respect for Apothecaries' Hall, and esteem for Mr. Cashell, a zealous craftsman who magnified his calling. Until Mr. Shaynor came down from the North his assistants had by no means agreed with Mr. Cashell. "They forget," said he, "that, first and foremost, the compounder is a medicine-man. On him depends the physician's reputation. He holds it literally in the hollow of his hand, Sir."

Mr. Shaynor's manners had not, perhaps, the polish of the grocery and Italian warehouse next door, but he knew and loved his dispensary work in every detail.

For relaxation he seemed to go no farther afield than the romance of drugs—their discovery, preparation, packing, and export—but it led him to the ends of the earth, and on this subject, and the Pharmaceutical Formulary, and Nicholas Culpepper, most confident of physicians, we met.

Little by little I grew to know something of his beginnings and his hopes - -of his mother, who had been a school-teacher in one of the northern counties, and of his red-headed father, a small job-master at Kirby Moors, who died when he was a child; of the examinations he had passed and of their exceeding and increasing difficulty; of his dreams of a shop in London; of his hate for the price-cutting Co-operative stores; and, most interesting, of his mental attitude towards customers.

"There's a way you get into," he told me, "of serving them carefully, and I hope, politely, without stopping your own thinking. I've been reading Christie's *New Commercial Plants* all this autumn, and that needs keeping your mind on it, I can tell you. So long as it isn't a prescription, of course, I can carry as much as half a page of Christie in my head, and at the same time I could sell out all that window twice over, and not a penny wrong at the end. As to prescriptions, I think I could make up the general run of 'em in my sleep, almost."

For reasons of my own, I was deeply interested in Marconi experiments at their outset in England; and it was of a piece with Mr. Cashell's unvarying thoughtfulness that, when his nephew the electrician appropriated the house for a long-range installation, he should, as I have said, invite me to see the result.

The old lady went away with her medicine, and Mr. Shaynor and I stamped on the tiled floor behind the counter to keep ourselves warm. The shop, by the light of the many electrics, looked like a Paris-diamond mine, for Mr. Cashell believed in all the ritual of his craft. Three superb glass jars— red, green, and blue—of the sort that led Rosamund to parting with her shoes—blazed in the broad plate-glass windows, and there was a confused smell of orris, Kodak films, vulcanite, tooth-powder, sachets, and almond-cream in the air. Mr. Shaynor fed the dispensary stove, and we sucked cayenne-pepper jujubes and menthol lozenges. The brutal east wind had cleared the streets, and the few passers-by were muffled to their puckered eyes. In the Italian warehouse next door some gay feathered birds and game, hung upon hooks, sagged to the wind across the left edge of our window-frame.

"They ought to take these poultry in—all knocked about like that," said Mr. Shaynor. "Doesn't it make you feel fair perishing? See that old hare! The wind's nearly blowing the fur off him."

I saw the belly-fur of the dead beast blown apart in ridges and streaks as the wind caught it, showing bluish skin underneath. "Bitter cold," said Mr. Shaynor, shuddering. "Fancy going out on a night like this! Oh, here's young Mr. Cashell."

The door of the inner office behind the dispensary opened, and an energetic, spade-bearded man stepped forth, rubbing his hands.

"I want a bit of tin-foil, Shaynor," he said. "Good-evening. My uncle told me you might be coming." This to me, as I began the first of a hundred questions.

"I've everything in order," he replied. "We're only waiting until Poole calls us up. Excuse me a minute. You can come in whenever you like—but I'd better be with the instruments. Give me that tin-foil. Thanks."

While we were talking, a girl—evidently no customer—had come into the shop, and the face and bearing of Mr. Shaynor changed. She leaned confidently across the counter.

"But I can't," I heard him whisper uneasily—the flush on his cheek was dull red, and his eyes shone like a drugged moth's. "I can't. I tell you I'm alone in the place."

"No, you aren't. Who's *that*? Let him look after it for half an hour. A brisk walk will do you good. Ah, come now, John."

"But he isn't— "

"I don't care. I want you to; we'll only go round by St. Agnes. If you don't—"

He crossed to where I stood in the shadow of the dispensary counter, and began some sort of broken apology about a lady-friend.

"Yes," she interrupted. "You take the shop for half an hour—to oblige *me*, won't you?"

She had a singularly rich and promising voice that well matched her outline.

"All right," I said. "I'll do it—but you'd better wrap yourself up, Mr. Shaynor."

"Oh, a brisk walk ought to help me. We're only going round by the church." I heard him cough grievously as they went out together.

I refilled the stove, and, after reckless expenditure of Mr. Cashell's coal, drove some warmth into the shop. I explored many of the glass-knobbed drawers that lined the walls, tasted some disconcerting drugs, and, by the aid of a few cardamoms, ground ginger, chloric-ether, and dilute alcohol, manufactured a new and wildish drink, of which I bore a glassful to young Mr. Cashell, busy in the back office. He laughed shortly when I told him that Mr. Shaynor had stepped out—but a frail coil of wire held all his attention, and he had no word for me bewildered among the batteries and rods. The noise of the sea on the beach began to make itself heard as the traffic in the street ceased. Then briefly, but very lucidly, he gave me the names and uses of the mechanism that crowded the tables and the floor.

"When do you expect to get the message from Poole?" I demanded, sipping my liquor out of a graduated glass.

"About midnight, if everything is in order. We've got our installation-pole fixed to the roof of the house. I shouldn't advise you to turn on a tap or anything tonight. We've connected up with the plumbing, and all the water will be electrified." He repeated to me the history of the agitated ladies at the hotel at the time of the first installation.

"But what *is* it?" I asked. "Electricity is out of my beat altogether."

"Ah, if you knew *that* you'd know something nobody knows. It's just it—what we call Electricity, but the magic—the manifestations—the Hertzian waves—are all revealed by *this*. The coherer, we call it."

He picked up a glass tube not much thicker than a thermometer, in which, almost touching, were two tiny silver plugs, and between them an infinitesimal pinch of metallic dust. "That's all," he said, proudly, as though himself responsible for the wonder. "That is the thing that will reveal to us the Powers—whatever the Powers may be—at work—through space—a long distance away."

Just then Mr. Shaynor returned alone and stood coughing his heart out on the mat.

"Serves you right for being such a fool," said young Mr. Cashell, as annoyed as myself at the interruption. "Never mind—we've all the night before us to see wonders."

Shaynor clutched the counter, his handkerchief to his lips. When he brought it away I saw two bright red stains.

"I—I've got a bit of a rasped throat from smoking cigarettes," he panted. "I think I'll try a cubeb."

"Better take some of this. I've been compounding while you've been away." I handed him the brew.

"'Twon't make me drunk, will it? I'm almost a teetotaller. My word! That's grateful and comforting."

He sat down the empty glass to cough afresh.

"Brr! But it was cold out there! I shouldn't care to be lying in my grave a night like this. Don't *you* ever have a sore throat from smoking?" He pocketed the handkerchief after a furtive peep.

"Oh, yes, sometimes," I replied, wondering, while I spoke, into what agonies of terror I should fall if ever I saw those bright-red danger-signals under my nose. Young Mr. Cashell among the batteries coughed slightly to show that he was quite ready to continue his scientific explanations, but I was thinking still of the girl with the rich voice and the significantly cut mouth, at whose command I had taken charge of the shop. It flashed across me that she distantly resembled the seductive shape on a gold-framed toilet-water advertisement whose charms were unholily heightened by the glare from the red bottle in the window. Turning to make sure, I saw Mr. Shaynor's eyes bent in the same direction, and by instinct recognised that the flamboyant thing was to him a shrine. "What do you take for your—cough?" I asked.

"Well, I'm the wrong side of the counter to believe much in patent medicines. But there are asthma cigarettes and there are pastilles. To tell you the truth, if you don't object to the smell, which is very like incense, I believe, though I'm not a Roman Catholic, Blaudett's Cathedral Pastilles relieve me as much as anything."

"Let's try." I had never raided a chemist's shop before, so I was thorough. We unearthed the pastilles—brown, gummy cones of benzoin—and set them alight under the toilet-water advertisement, where they fumed in thin blue spirals.

"Of course," said Mr. Shaynor, to my question, "what one uses in the shop for one's self comes out of one's pocket. Why, stock-taking in our business is nearly the same as with jewellers—and I can't say more than that. But one gets them"—he pointed to the pastille-box—"at trade prices." Evidently the censing of the gay, seven-tinted wench with the teeth was an established ritual which cost something.

"And when do we shut up shop?"

"We stay like this all night. The gov—old Mr. Cashell—doesn't believe in locks and shutters as compared with electric light. Besides it brings trade. I'll just sit here in the chair by the stove and write a letter, if you don't mind. Electricity isn't my prescription."

The energetic young Mr. Cashell snorted within, and Shaynor settled himself up in his chair over which he had thrown a staring red, black, and yellow Austrian jute blanket, rather like a table-cover. I cast about, amid patent medicine pamphlets, for something to read, but finding little, returned to the manufacture of the new drink. The Italian warehouse took down its game and went to bed. Across the street blank shutters flung back the gaslight in cold smears; the dried pavement seemed to rough up in goose-flesh under the scouring of the savage wind, and we could hear, long ere he passed, the policeman flapping his arms to keep himself warm. Within, the flavours of cardamoms and chloric-ether disputed those of the pastilles and a score of drugs and perfume and soap scents. Our electric lights, set low down in the windows before the tunbellied Rosamund jars, flung inward three monstrous daubs of red, blue, and green, that broke into kaleidoscopic lights on the facetted knobs of the drug-drawers, the cut-glass scent flagons, and the bulbs of the sparklet bottles. They flushed the white-tiled floor in gorgeous patches; splashed along the nickel-silver counter-rails, and turned the polished mahogany counter-panels to the likeness of intricate grained marbles—slabs of porphyry and malachite. Mr. Shaynor unlocked a drawer, and ere he began to write, took out a meagre bundle of letters. From my place by the stove, I could see the scalloped edges of the paper with a flaring monogram in the corner and could even smell the reek of chypre. At each page he turned toward the toilet-water lady of the advertisement and devoured her with over-luminous eyes. He had drawn the Austrian blanket over his shoulders, and among those warring lights he looked more than ever the incarnation of a drugged moth—a tiger-moth as I thought.

He put his letter into an envelope, stamped it with stiff mechanical movements, and dropped it in the drawer. Then I became aware of the silence of a great city asleep—the silence that underlaid the even voice of the breakers along the sea-front—a thick, tingling quiet of warm life stilled down for its appointed time, and unconsciously I moved about the glittering shop as one moves in a sick-room. Young Mr. Cashell was adjusting some wire that crackled from time to time with the tense, knuckle-stretching sound of the electric spark. Upstairs, where a door shut and opened swiftly, I could hear his uncle coughing abed.

"Here," I said, when the drink was properly warmed, "take some of this, Mr. Shaynor."

He jerked in his chair with a start and a wrench, and held out his hand for the glass. The mixture, of a rich port-wine colour, frothed at the top.

"It looks," he said, suddenly, "it looks—those bubbles—like a string of pearls winking at you—rather like the pearls round that young lady's neck." He turned again to the advertisement where the female in the dove-coloured corset had seen fit to put on all her pearls before she cleaned her teeth.

"Not bad, is it?" I said.

"Eh?"

He rolled his eyes heavily full on me, and, as I stared, I beheld all meaning and consciousness die out of the swiftly dilating pupils. His figure lost its stark rigidity, softened into the chair, and, chin on chest, hands dropped before him, he rested open-eyed, absolutely still.

"I'm afraid I've rather cooked Shaynor's goose," I said, bearing the fresh drink to young Mr. Cashell. "Perhaps it was the chloric-ether."

"Oh, he's all right." The spade-bearded man glanced at him pityingly. "Consumptives go off in those sort of doses very often. It's exhaustion… I don't wonder. I dare say the liquor will do him good. It's grand stuff," he finished his share appreciatively. "Well, as I was saying—before he interrupted—about this little coherer. The pinch of dust, you see, is nickel filings. The Hertzian waves, you see, come out of space from the station that despatches 'em, and all these little particles are attracted together—cohere, we call it—for just so long as the current passes through them. Now, it's important to remember that the current is an induced current. There are a good many kinds of induction—"

"Yes, but what *is* induction?"

"That's rather hard to explain untechnically. But the long and the short of it is that when a current of electricity passes through a wire there's a lot of magnetism present round that wire; and if you put another wire parallel to, and within what we call its magnetic field—why then, the second wire will also become charged with electricity."

"On its own account?"

"On its own account."

"Then let's see if I've got it correctly. Miles off, at Poole, or wherever it is—"

"It will be anywhere in ten years."

"You've got a charged wire—"

"Charged with Hertzian waves which vibrate, say, two hundred and thirty million times a second." Mr. Cashell snaked his forefinger rapidly through the air.

"All right—a charged wire at Poole, giving out these waves into space. Then this wire of yours sticking out into space—on the roof of the house—in some mysterious way gets charged with those waves from Poole—"

"Or anywhere—it only happens to be Poole tonight."

"And those waves set the coherer at work, just like an ordinary telegraph office ticker?"

"No! That's where so many people make the mistake. The Hertzian waves wouldn't be strong enough to work a great heavy Morse instrument like ours.

They can only just make that dust cohere, and while it coheres (a little while for a dot and a longer while for a dash) the current from this battery—the home battery"—he laid his hand on the thing—"can get through to the Morse printing-machine to record the dot or dash. Let me make it clearer. Do you know anything about steam?"

"Very little. But go on."

"Well, the coherer is like a steam-valve. Any child can open a valve and start a steamer's engines, because a turn of the hand lets in the main steam, doesn't it? Now, this home battery here ready to print is the main steam. The coherer is the valve, always ready to be turned on. The Hertzian wave is the child's hand that turns it."

"I see. That's marvellous."

"Marvellous, isn't it? And, remember, we're only at the beginning. There's nothing we sha'n't be able to do in ten years. I want to live—my God, how I want to live, and see it develop!" He looked through the door at Shaynor breathing lightly in his chair. "Poor beast! And he wants to keep company with Fanny Brand."

"Fanny *who*?" I said, for the name struck an obscurely familiar chord in my brain—something connected with a stained handkerchief, and the word "arterial."

"Fanny Brand—the girl you kept shop for." He laughed, "That's all I know about her, and for the life of me I can't see what Shaynor sees in her, or she in him."

"*Can't* you see what he sees in her?" I insisted. "Oh, yes, if *that's* what you mean. She's a great, big, fat lump of a girl, and so on. I suppose that's why he's so crazy after her. She isn't his sort. Well, it doesn't matter. My uncle says he's bound to die before the year's out. Your drink's given him a good sleep, at any rate." Young Mr. Cashell could not catch Mr. Shaynor's face, which was half turned to the advertisement.

I stoked the stove anew, for the room was growing cold, and lighted another pastille. Mr. Shaynor in his chair, never moving, looked through and over me with eyes as wide and lustreless as those of a dead hare.

"Poole's late," said young Mr. Cashell, when I stepped back. "I'll just send them a call."

He pressed a key in the semi-darkness, and with a rending crackle there leaped between two brass knobs a spark, streams of sparks, and sparks again.

"Grand, isn't it? *That's* the Power—our unknown Power—kicking and fighting to be let loose," said young Mr. Cashell. "There she goes—kick—kick—kick into space. I never get over the strangeness of it when I work a sending-machine—waves going into space, you know. T.R. is our call. Poole ought to answer with L.L.L."

We waited two, three, five minutes. In that silence, of which the boom of the tide was an orderly part, I caught the clear "*kiss—kiss—kiss*" of the halliards on the roof, as they were blown against the installation-pole.

"Poole is not ready. I'll stay here and call you when he is."

I returned to the shop, and set down my glass on a marble slab with a careless clink. As I did so, Shaynor rose to his feet, his eyes fixed once more on the advertisement, where the young woman bathed in the light from the red jar simpered pinkly over her pearls. His lips moved without cessation. I stepped nearer to listen. "And threw—and threw—and threw," he repeated, his face all sharp with some inexplicable agony.

I moved forward astonished. But it was then he found words—delivered roundly and clearly. These:—

And threw warm gules on Madeleine's young breast. The trouble passed off his countenance, and he returned lightly to his place, rubbing his hands.

It had never occurred to me, though we had many times discussed reading and prize-competitions as a diversion, that Mr. Shaynor ever read Keats, or could quote him at all appositely. There was, after all, a certain stained-glass effect of light on the high bosom of the highly-polished picture which might, by stretch of fancy, suggest, as a vile chromo recalls some incomparable canvas, the line he had spoken. Night, my drink, and solitude were evidently turning Mr. Shaynor into a poet. He sat down again and wrote swiftly on his villainous note-paper, his lips quivering.

I shut the door into the inner office and moved up behind him. He made no sign that he saw or heard. I looked over his shoulder, and read, amid half-formed words, sentences, and wild scratches:—

—VERY COLD IT *WAS*. VERY COLD
THE HARE—THE HARE—THE HARE—
THE BIRDS—

He raised his head sharply, and frowned toward the blank shutters of the poulterer's shop where they jutted out against our window. Then one clear line came:—

THE HARE, IN SPITE OF FUR, WAS VERY COLD.

The head, moving machine-like, turned right to the advertisement where the Blaudett's Cathedral pastille reeked abominably. He grunted, and went on:—

INCENSE IN A CENSER— BEFORE HER DARLING PICTURE FRAMED IN GOLD— MAIDEN'S PICTURE—ANGEL'S PORTRAIT—

"Hsh!" said Mr. Cashell guardedly from the inner office, as though in the presence of spirits. "There's something coming through from somewhere; but it isn't Poole." I heard the crackle of sparks as he depressed the keys of the transmitter. In my own brain, too, something crackled, or it might have been the hair on my head. Then I heard my own voice, in a harsh whisper: "Mr. Cashell, there is something coming through here, too. Leave me alone till I tell you."

"But I thought you'd come to see this wonderful thing—Sir," indignantly at the end.

"Leave me alone till I tell you. Be quiet."

I watched—I waited. Under the blue-veined hand—the dry hand of the consumptive—came away clear, without erasure:

And my weak spirit fails To think how the dead must freeze—he shivered as he wrote—

BENEATH THE CHURCHYARD MOULD.

Then he stopped, laid the pen down, and leaned back.

For an instant, that was half an eternity, the shop spun before me in a rainbow-tinted whirl, in and through which my own soul most dispassionately considered my own soul as that fought with an overmastering fear. Then I smelt the strong smell of cigarettes from Mr. Shaynor's clothing, and heard, as though it had been the rending of trumpets, the rattle of his breathing. I was still in my place of observation, much as one would watch a rifle-shot at the butts, half-bent, hands on my knees, and head within a few inches of the black, red, and yellow blanket of his shoulder. I was whispering encouragement, evidently to my other self, sounding sentences, such as men pronounce in dreams.

"If he has read Keats, it proves nothing. If he hasn't—like causes *must* beget like effects. There is no escape from this law. *You* ought to be grateful that you know 'St. Agnes Eve' without the book; because, given the circumstances, such as Fanny Brand, who is the key of the enigma, and approximately represents the latitude and longitude of Fanny Brawne; allowing also for the bright red colour of the arterial blood upon the handkerchief, which was just what you were puzzling over in the shop just now; and counting the effect of the professional environment, here almost perfectly duplicated—the result is logical and inevitable. As inevitable as induction."

Still, the other half of my soul refused to be comforted. It was cowering in some minute and inadequate corner—at an immense distance.

Hereafter, I found myself one person again, my hands still gripping my knees, and my eyes glued on the page before Mr. Shaynor. As dreamers accept and explain the upheaval of landscapes and the resurrection of the dead, with excerpts from the evening hymn or the multiplication-table, so I had accepted the facts, whatever they might be, that I should witness, and had devised a theory, sane and plausible to my mind, that explained them all. Nay, I was even in advance of my facts, walking hurriedly before them, assured that they would fit my theory. And all that I now recall of that epoch-making theory are the lofty words: "If he has read Keats it's the chloric-ether. If he hasn't, it's the identical bacillus, or Hertzian wave of tuberculosis, *plus* Fanny Brand and the professional status which, in conjunction with the main-stream of subconscious thought common to all mankind, has thrown up temporarily an induced Keats."

Mr. Shaynor returned to his work, erasing and rewriting as before with swiftness. Two or three blank pages he tossed aside. Then he wrote, muttering:

THE LITTLE SMOKE OF A CANDLE THAT GOES OUT.

"No," he muttered. "Little smoke—little smoke—little smoke. What else?" He thrust his chin forward toward the advertisement, whereunder the last of the Blaudett's Cathedral pastilles fumed in its holder. "Ah!" Then with relief:—

THE LITTLE SMOKE THAT DIES IN MOONLIGHT COLD.

Evidently he was snared by the rhymes of his first verse, for he wrote and rewrote "gold—cold—mould" many times. Again he sought inspiration from the advertisement, and set down, without erasure, the line I had overheard:

AND THREW WARM GULES ON MADELEINE'S YOUNG BREAST.

As I remembered the original it is "fair"—a trite word—instead of "young," and I found myself nodding approval, though I admitted that the attempt to reproduce "its little smoke in pallid moonlight died" was a failure.

Followed without a break ten or fifteen lines of bald prose—the naked soul's confession of its physical yearning for its beloved—unclean as we count uncleanliness; unwholesome, but human exceedingly; the raw material, so it seemed to me in that hour and in that place, whence Keats wove the twenty-sixth, seventh, and eighth stanzas of his poem. Shame I had none in overseeing this revelation; and my fear had gone with the smoke of the pastille.

"That's it," I murmured. "That's how it's blocked out. Go on! Ink it in, man. Ink it in!"

Mr. Shaynor returned to broken verse wherein "loveliness" was made to rhyme with a desire to look upon "her empty dress." He picked up a fold of the gay, soft blanket, spread it over one hand, caressed it with infinite tenderness, thought, muttered, traced some snatches which I could not decipher, shut his eyes drowsily, shook his head, and dropped the stuff. Here I found myself at fault, for I could not then see (as I do now) in what manner a red, black, and yellow Austrian blanket coloured his dreams.

In a few minutes he laid aside his pen, and, chin on hand, considered the shop with thoughtful and intelligent eyes. He threw down the blanket, rose, passed along a line of drug-drawers, and read the names on the labels aloud. Returning, he took from his desk Christie's *New Commercial Plants* and the old Culpepper that I had given him, opened and laid them side by side with a clerky air, all trace of passion gone from his face, read first in one and then in the other, and paused with pen behind his ear.

"What wonder of Heaven's coming now?" I thought.

"Manna—manna—manna," he said at last, under wrinkled brows. "That's what I wanted. Good! Now then! Now then! Good! Good! Oh, by God, that's good!" His voice rose and he spoke rightly and fully without a falter:—

CANDIED APPLE, QUINCE AND PLUM AND GOURD,
AND JELLIES SMOOTHER THAN THE CREAMY CURD,
AND LUCENT SYRUPS TINCT WITH CINNAMON,
MANNA AND DATES IN ARGOSY TRANSFERRED

FROM FEZ: AND SPICED DAINTIES, EVERY ONE
FROM SILKEN SAMARCAND TO CEDARED LEBANON.

He repeated it once more, using "blander" for "smoother" in the second line; then wrote it down without erasure, but this time (my set eyes missed no stroke of any word) he substituted "soother" for his atrocious second thought, so that it came away under his hand as it is written in the book—as it is written in the book.

A wind went shouting down the street, and on the heels of the wind followed a spurt and rattle of rain.

After a smiling pause—and good right had he to smile—he began anew, always tossing the last sheet over his shoulder:—

"THE SHARP RAIN FALLING ON THE WINDOW-PANE,
RATTLING SLEET—THE WIND-BLOWN SLEET."

Then prose: "It is very cold of mornings when the wind brings rain and sleet with it. I heard the sleet on the window-pane outside, and thought of you, my darling. I am always thinking of you. I wish we could both run away like two lovers into the storm and get that little cottage by the sea which we are always thinking about, my own dear darling. We could sit and watch the sea beneath our windows. It would be a fairyland all of our own—a fairy sea—a fairy sea..."

He stopped, raised his head, and listened. The steady drone of the Channel along the sea-front that had borne us company so long leaped up a note to the sudden fuller surge that signals the change from ebb to flood. It beat in like the change of step throughout an army—this renewed pulse of the sea—and filled our ears till they, accepting it, marked it no longer.

"A FAIRYLAND FOR YOU AND ME
ACROSS THE FOAM—BEYOND ...
A MAGIC FOAM, A PERILOUS SEA."

He grunted again with effort and bit his underlip. My throat dried, but I dared not gulp to moisten it lest I should break the spell that was drawing him nearer and nearer to the high-water mark but two of the sons of Adam have reached. Remember that in all the millions permitted there are no more than five—five little lines—of which one can say: "These are the pure Magic. These are the clear Vision. The rest is only poetry." And Mr. Shaynor was playing hot and cold with two of them!

I vowed no unconscious thought of mine should influence the blindfold soul, and pinned myself desperately to the other three, repeating and rerepeating:

A SAVAGE SPOT AS HOLY AND ENCHANTED
AS E'ER BENEATH A WANING MOON WAS HAUNTED
BY WOMAN WAILING FOR HER DEMON LOVER.

But though I believed my brain thus occupied, my every sense hung upon the writing under the dry, bony hand, all brown-fingered with chemicals and cigarette-smoke.

OUR WINDOWS FRONTING ON THE DANGEROUS FOAM.

(he wrote, after long, irresolute snatches), and then—

"OUR OPEN CASEMENTS FACING DESOLATE SEAS
FORLORN—FORLORN—"

Here again his face grew peaked and anxious with that sense of loss I had first seen when the Power snatched him. But this time the agony was tenfold keener. As I watched it mounted like mercury in the tube. It lighted his face from within till I thought the visibly scourged soul must leap forth naked between his jaws, unable to endure. A drop of sweat trickled from my forehead down my nose and splashed on the back of my hand.

"OUR WINDOWS FACING ON THE DESOLATE SEAS
AND PEARLY FOAM OF MAGIC FAIRYLAND—"

"Not yet—not yet," he muttered, "wait a minute. *Please* wait a minute. I shall get it then—"

OUR MAGIC WINDOWS FRONTING ON THE SEA.
THE DANGEROUS FOAM OF DESOLATE SEAS ..
FOR AYE.

"*Ouh*, my God!"

From head to heel he shook—shook from the marrow of his bones outwards—then leaped to his feet with raised arms, and slid the chair screeching across the tiled floor where it struck the drawers behind and fell with a jar. Mechanically, I stooped to recover it.

As I rose, Mr. Shaynor was stretching and yawning at leisure. "I've had a bit of a doze," he said. "How did I come to knock the chair over? You look rather—"

"The chair startled me," I answered. "It was so sudden in this quiet."

Young Mr. Cashell behind his shut door was offendedly silent. "I suppose I must have been dreaming," said Mr. Shaynor.

"I suppose you must," I said. "Talking of dreams—I—I noticed you writing—before—"

He flushed consciously. "I meant to ask you if you've ever read anything written by a man called Keats."

"Oh! I haven't much time to read poetry, and I can't say that I remember the name exactly. Is he a popular writer?"

"Middling. I thought you might know him because he's the only poet who was ever a druggist. And he's rather what's called the lover's poet."

"Indeed. I must dip into him. What did he write about?"

"A lot of things. Here's a sample that may interest you." Then and there, carefully, I repeated the verse he had twice spoken and once written not ten minutes ago.

"Ah. Anybody could see he was a druggist from that line about the tinctures and syrups. It's a fine tribute to our profession."

"I don't know," said young Mr. Cashell, with icy politeness, opening the door one half-inch, "if you still happen to be interested in our trifling experiments. But, should such be the case—"

I drew him aside, whispering, "Shaynor seemed going off into some sort of fit when I spoke to you just now. I thought, even at the risk of being rude, it wouldn't do to take you off your instruments just as the call was coming through. Don't you see?"

"Granted—granted as soon as asked," he said unbending. "I *did* think it a shade odd at the time. So that was why he knocked the chair down?"

"I hope I haven't missed anything," I said. "I'm afraid I can't say that, but you're just in time for the end of a rather curious performance. You can come in, too, Mr. Shaynor. Listen, while I read it off."

The Morse instrument was ticking furiously. Mr. Cashell interpreted: "'*K.K.V. Can make nothing of your signals.*'" A pause. "'*M.M.V. M.M.V. Signals unintelligible. Purpose anchor Sandown Bay. Examine instruments tomorrow.*' Do you know what that means? It's a couple of men-o'-war working Marconi signals off the Isle of Wight. They are trying to talk to each other. Neither can read the other's messages, but all their messages are being taken in by our receiver here. They've been going on for ever so long. I wish you could have heard it."

"How wonderful!" I said. "Do you mean we're overhearing Portsmouth ships trying to talk to each other—that we're eavesdropping across half South England?"

"Just that. Their transmitters are all right, but their receivers are out of order, so they only get a dot here and a dash there. Nothing clear."

"Why is that?"

"God knows—and Science will know tomorrow. Perhaps the induction is faulty; perhaps the receivers aren't tuned to receive just the number of vibrations per second that the transmitter sends. Only a word here and there. Just enough to tantalise."

Again the Morse sprang to life.

"That's one of 'em complaining now. Listen: '*Disheartening—most disheartening.*' It's quite pathetic. Have you ever seen a spiritualistic seance? It reminds me of that sometimes—odds and ends of messages coming out of nowhere—a word here and there—no good at all."

"But mediums are all impostors," said Mr. Shaynor, in the doorway, lighting an asthma-cigarette. "They only do it for the money they can make. I've seen 'em."

"Here's Poole, at last—clear as a bell. L.L.L. *Now* we sha'n't be long." Mr. Cashell rattled the keys merrily. "Anything you'd like to tell 'em?"

"No, I don't think so," I said. "I'll go home and get to bed. I'm feeling a little tired."

SULTANA'S DREAM

by Rokeya Sakhawat Hossain

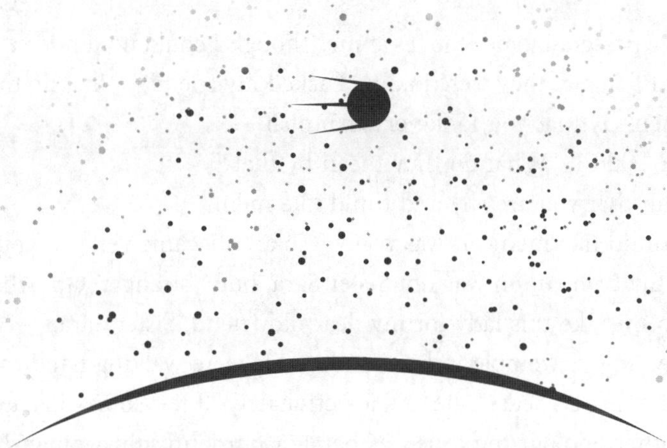

One evening I was lounging in an easy chair in my bedroom and thinking lazily of the condition of Indian womanhood. I am not sure whether I dozed off or not. But, as far as I remember, I was wide awake. I saw the moonlit sky sparkling with thousands of diamond-like stars, very distinctly.

All on a sudden a lady stood before me; how she came in, I do not know. I took her for my friend, Sister Sara.

"Good morning," said Sister Sara. I smiled inwardly as I knew it was not morning, but starry night. However, I replied to her, saying, "How do you do?"

"I am all right, thank you. Will you please come out and have a look at our garden?"

I looked again at the moon through the open window, and thought there was no harm in going out at that time. The men-servants outside were fast asleep just then, and I could have a pleasant walk with Sister Sara.

I used to have my walks with Sister Sara, when we were at Darjeeling. Many a time did we walk hand in hand and talk light-heartedly in the botanical gardens there. I fancied, Sister Sara had probably come to take me to some such garden and I readily accepted her offer and went out with her.

When walking I found to my surprise that it was a fine morning. The town was fully awake and the streets alive with bustling crowds. I was feeling very shy, thinking I was walking in the street in broad daylight, but there was not a single man visible.

Some of the passers-by made jokes at me. Though I could not understand their language, yet I felt sure they were joking. I asked my friend, "What do they say?"

"The women say that you look very mannish."

"Mannish?" said I, "What do they mean by that?"

"They mean that you are shy and timid like men."

"Shy and timid like men?" It was really a joke. I became very nervous, when I found that my companion was not Sister Sara, but a stranger. Oh, what a fool had I been to mistake this lady for my dear old friend, Sister Sara.

She felt my fingers tremble in her hand, as we were walking hand in hand.

"What is the matter, dear?" she said affectionately. "I feel somewhat awkward," I said in a rather apologizing tone, "as being a purdahnishin woman I am not accustomed to walking about unveiled."

"You need not be afraid of coming across a man here. This is Ladyland, free from sin and harm. Virtue herself reigns here."

By and by I was enjoying the scenery. Really it was very grand. I mistook a patch of green grass for a velvet cushion. Feeling as if I were walking on a soft carpet, I looked down and found the path covered with moss and flowers.

"How nice it is," said I.

"Do you like it?" asked Sister Sara. (I continued calling her "Sister Sara," and she kept calling me by my name).

"Yes, very much; but I do not like to tread on the tender and sweet flowers."

"Never mind, dear Sultana; your treading will not harm them; they are street flowers."

"The whole place looks like a garden," said I admiringly. "You have arranged every plant so skillfully."

"Your Calcutta could become a nicer garden than this if only your countrymen wanted to make it so."

"They would think it useless to give so much attention to horticulture, while they have so many other things to do."

"They could not find a better excuse," said she with a smile.

I became very curious to know where the men were. I met more than a hundred women while walking there, but not a single man.

"Where are the men?" I asked her.

"In their proper places, where they ought to be."

"Pray let me know what you mean by 'their proper places'."

"O, I see my mistake, you cannot know our customs, as you were never here before. We shut our men indoors."

"Just as we are kept in the zenana?"

"Exactly so."

"How funny," I burst into a laugh. Sister Sara laughed too.

"But dear Sultana, how unfair it is to shut in the harmless women and let loose the men."

"Why? It is not safe for us to come out of the zenana, as we are naturally weak."

"Yes, it is not safe so long as there are men about the streets, nor is it so when a wild animal enters a marketplace."

"Of course not."

"Suppose, some lunatics escape from the asylum and begin to do all sorts of mischief to men, horses and other creatures; in that case what will your countrymen do?"

"They will try to capture them and put them back into their asylum."

"Thank you! And you do not think it wise to keep sane people inside an asylum and let loose the insane?"

"Of course not!" said I laughing lightly.

"As a matter of fact, in your country this very thing is done! Men, who do or at least are capable of doing no end of mischief, are let loose and the innocent women, shut up in the zenana! How can you trust those untrained men out of doors?"

"We have no hand or voice in the management of our social affairs. In India man is lord and master, he has taken to himself all powers and privileges and shut up the women in the zenana."

"Why do you allow yourselves to be shut up?"

"Because it cannot be helped as they are stronger than women."

"A lion is stronger than a man, but it does not enable him to dominate the human race. You have neglected the duty you owe to yourselves and you have lost your natural rights by shutting your eyes to your own interests."

"But my dear Sister Sara, if we do everything by ourselves, what will the men do then?"

"They should not do anything, excuse me; they are fit for nothing. Only catch them and put them into the zenana."

"But would it be very easy to catch and put them inside the four walls?" said I. "And even if this were done, would all their business—political and commercial—also go with them into the zenana?"

Sister Sara made no reply. She only smiled sweetly. Perhaps she thought it useless to argue with one who was no better than a frog in a well.

By this time we reached Sister Sara's house. It was situated in a beautiful heart-shaped garden. It was a bungalow with a corrugated iron roof. It was cooler and nicer than any of our rich buildings. I cannot describe how neat and how nicely furnished and how tastefully decorated it was.

We sat side by side. She brought out of the parlour a piece of embroidery work and began putting on a fresh design.

"Do you know knitting and needle work?"

"Yes; we have nothing else to do in our zenana."

"But we do not trust our zenana members with embroidery!" she said laughing, "as a man has not patience enough to pass thread through a needlehole even!"

"Have you done all this work yourself?" I asked her pointing to the various pieces of embroidered teapoy cloths.

"Yes."

"How can you find time to do all these? You have to do the office work as well? Have you not?"

"Yes. I do not stick to the laboratory all day long. I finish my work in two hours."

"In two hours! How do you manage? In our land the officers – magistrates, for instance – work seven hours daily."

"I have seen some of them doing their work. Do you think they work all the seven hours?"

"Certainly they do!"

"No, dear Sultana, they do not. They dawdle away their time in smoking.

Some smoke two or three choroots during the office time. They talk much about their work, but do little. Suppose one choroot takes half an hour to burn off, and a man smokes twelve choroots daily; then you see, he wastes six hours every day in sheer smoking."

We talked on various subjects, and I learned that they were not subject to any kind of epidemic disease, nor did they suffer from mosquito bites as we do. I was very much astonished to hear that in Ladyland no one died in youth except by rare accident.

"Will you care to see our kitchen?" she asked me.

"With pleasure," said I, and we went to see it. Of course the men had been asked to clear off when I was going there. The kitchen was situated in a beautiful vegetable garden. Every creeper, every tomato plant was itself an ornament. I found no smoke, nor any chimney either in the kitchen – it was clean and bright; the windows were decorated with flower gardens. There was no sign of coal or fire.

"How do you cook?" I asked.

"With solar heat," she said, at the same time showing me the pipe, through which passed the concentrated sunlight and heat. And she cooked something then and there to show me the process.

"How did you manage to gather and store up the sun-heat?" I asked her in amazement.

"Let me tell you a little of our past history then. Thirty years ago, when our present Queen was thirteen years old, she inherited the throne. She was Queen in name only, the Prime Minister really ruling the country.

"Our good Queen liked science very much. She circulated an order that all the women in her country should be educated. Accordingly a number of girls' schools were founded and supported by the government. Education was spread far and wide among women. And early marriage also was stopped. No woman was to be allowed to marry before she was twenty-one. I must tell you that, before this change we had been kept in strict purdah."

"How the tables are turned," I interposed with a laugh.

"But the seclusion is the same," she said. "In a few years we had separate universities, where no men were admitted."

"In the capital, where our Queen lives, there are two universities. One of these invented a wonderful balloon, to which they attached a number of pipes. By means of this captive balloon which they managed to keep afloat above the cloud-land, they could draw as much water from the atmosphere as they pleased. As the water was incessantly being drawn by the university people no cloud gathered and the ingenious Lady Principal stopped rain and storms thereby."

"Really! Now I understand why there is no mud here!" said I. But I could not understand how it was possible to accumulate water in the pipes. She explained to me how it was done, but I was unable to understand her, as my scientific knowledge was very limited. However, she went on, "When the other university came to know of this, they became exceedingly jealous and tried to do something more extraordinary still. They invented an instrument by which they could collect as much sun-heat as they wanted. And they kept the heat stored up to be distributed among others as required.

"While the women were engaged in scientific research, the men of this country were busy increasing their military power. When they came to know that the female universities were able to draw water from the atmosphere and collect heat from the sun, they only laughed at the members of the universities and called the whole thing 'a sentimental nightmare!'"

"Your achievements are very wonderful indeed! But tell me, how you managed to put the men of your country into the zenana. Did you entrap them first?"

"No."

"It is not likely that they would surrender their free and open air life of their own accord and confine themselves within the four walls of the zenana! They must have been overpowered."

"Yes, they have been!"

"By whom? By some lady-warriors, I suppose?"

"No, not by arms."

"Yes, it cannot be so. Men's arms are stronger than women's. Then?"

"By brain."

"Even their brains are bigger and heavier than women's. Are they not?"

"Yes, but what of that? An elephant also has got a bigger and heavier brain than a man has. Yet man can enchain elephants and employ them, according to their own wishes."

"Well said, but tell me please, how it all actually happened. I am dying to know it!"

"Women's brains are somewhat quicker than men's. Ten years ago, when the military officers called our scientific discoveries 'a sentimental nightmare,' some of the young ladies wanted to say something in reply to those remarks. But both the Lady Principals restrained them and said, they should reply not by word, but by deed, if ever they got the opportunity. And they had not long to wait for that opportunity."

"How marvellous!" I heartily clapped my hands. "And now the proud gentlemen are dreaming sentimental dreams themselves."

"Soon afterwards certain persons came from a neighbouring country and took shelter in ours. They were in trouble having committed some political offence. The king who cared more for power than for good government asked our kind-hearted Queen to hand them over to his officers. She refused, as it was against her principle to turn out refugees. For this refusal the king declared war against our country.

"Our military officers sprang to their feet at once and marched out to meet the enemy. The enemy however, was too strong for them. Our soldiers fought bravely, no doubt. But in spite of all their bravery the foreign army advanced step by step to invade our country.

"Nearly all the men had gone out to fight; even a boy of sixteen was not left home. Most of our warriors were killed, the rest driven back and the enemy came within twenty-five miles of the capital.

"A meeting of a number of wise ladies was held at the Queen's palace to advise as to what should be done to save the land. Some proposed to fight like soldiers; others objected and said that women were not trained to fight with swords and guns, nor were they accustomed to fighting with any weapons. A third party regretfully remarked that they were hopelessly weak of body.

"'If you cannot save your country for lack of physical strength,' said the Queen, 'try to do so by brain power.'

"There was a dead silence for a few minutes. Her Royal Highness said again, 'I must commit suicide if the land and my honour are lost.'

"Then the Lady Principal of the second university (who had collected sun-heat), who had been silently thinking during the consultation, remarked that they were all but lost, and there was little hope left for them. There was, however, one plan which she would like to try, and this would be her first and last efforts; if she failed in this, there would be nothing left but to commit suicide. All present solemnly vowed that they would never allow themselves to be enslaved, no matter what happened.

"The Queen thanked them heartily, and asked the Lady Principal to try her plan. The Lady Principal rose again and said, 'before we go out the men must enter the zenanas. I make this prayer for the sake of purdah.' 'Yes, of course,' replied Her Royal Highness.

"On the following day the Queen called upon all men to retire into zenanas for the sake of honour and liberty. Wounded and tired as they were, they took that order rather for a boon! They bowed low and entered the zenanas without uttering a single word of protest. They were sure that there was no hope for this country at all.

"Then the Lady Principal with her two thousand students marched to the battle field, and arriving there directed all the rays of the concentrated sunlight and heat towards the enemy.

"The heat and light were too much for them to bear. They all ran away panic-stricken, not knowing in their bewilderment how to counteract that scorching heat. When they fled away leaving their guns and other ammunitions of war, they were burnt down by means of the same sun-heat. Since then no one has tried to invade our country any more."

"And since then your countrymen never tried to come out of the zenana?"

"Yes, they wanted to be free. Some of the police commissioners and district magistrates sent word to the Queen to the effect that the military officers certainly deserved to be imprisoned for their failure; but they never neglected their duty and therefore they should not be punished and they prayed to be restored to their respective offices.

"Her Royal Highness sent them a circular letter intimating to them that if their services should ever be needed they would be sent for, and that in the meanwhile they should remain where they were. Now that they are accustomed to the purdah system and have ceased to grumble at their seclusion, we call the system 'Mardana' instead of 'zenana.'"

"But how do you manage," I asked Sister Sara, "to do without the police or magistrates in case of theft or murder?"

"Since the 'Mardana' system has been established, there has been no more crime or sin; therefore we do not require a policeman to find out a culprit, nor do we want a magistrate to try a criminal case."

"That is very good, indeed. I suppose if there was any dishonest person, you could very easily chastise her. As you gained a decisive victory without shedding a single drop of blood, you could drive off crime and criminals too without much difficulty!"

"Now, dear Sultana, will you sit here or come to my parlour?" she asked me.

"Your kitchen is not inferior to a queen's boudoir!" I replied with a pleasant smile, "but we must leave it now; for the gentlemen may be cursing me for keeping them away from their duties in the kitchen so long." We both laughed heartily.

"How my friends at home will be amused and amazed, when I go back and tell them that in the far-off Ladyland, ladies rule over the country and control all social matters, while gentlemen are kept in the Mardanas to mind babies, to cook and to do all sorts of domestic work; and that cooking is so easy a thing that it is simply a pleasure to cook!"

"Yes, tell them about all that you see here."

"Please let me know, how you carry on land cultivation and how you plough the land and do other hard manual work."

"Our fields are tilled by means of electricity, which supplies motive power for other hard work as well, and we employ it for our aerial conveyances too. We have no rail road nor any paved streets here."

"Therefore neither street nor railway accidents occur here," said I. "Do not you ever suffer from want of rainwater?" I asked.

"Never since the 'water balloon' has been set up. You see the big balloon and pipes attached thereto. By their aid we can draw as much rainwater as we require. Nor do we ever suffer from flood or thunderstorms. We are all very busy making nature yield as much as she can. We do not find time to quarrel with one another as we never sit idle. Our noble Queen is exceedingly fond of botany; it is her ambition to convert the whole country into one grand garden."

"The idea is excellent. What is your chief food?"

"Fruits."

"How do you keep your country cool in hot weather? We regard the rainfall in summer as a blessing from heaven."

"When the heat becomes unbearable, we sprinkle the ground with plentiful showers drawn from the artificial fountains. And in cold weather we keep our room warm with sun-heat."

She showed me her bathroom, the roof of which was removable. She could enjoy a shower bath whenever she liked, by simply removing the roof (which was like the lid of a box) and turning on the tap of the shower pipe.

"You are a lucky people!" ejaculated I. "You know no want. What is your religion, may I ask?"

"Our religion is based on Love and Truth. It is our religious duty to love one another and to be absolutely truthful. If any person lies, she or he is...."

"Punished with death?"

"No, not with death. We do not take pleasure in killing a creature of God, especially a human being. The liar is asked to leave this land for good and never to come to it again."

"Is an offender never forgiven?"

"Yes, if that person repents sincerely."

"Are you not allowed to see any man, except your own relations?"

"No one except sacred relations."

"Our circle of sacred relations is very limited; even first cousins are not sacred."

"But ours is very large; a distant cousin is as sacred as a brother."

"That is very good. I see purity itself reigns over your land. I should like to see the good Queen, who is so sagacious and far-sighted and who has made all these rules."

"All right," said Sister Sara.

Then she screwed a couple of seats onto a square piece of plank. To this plank she attached two smooth and well-polished balls. When I asked her what the balls were for, she said they were hydrogen balls and they were used to overcome the force of gravity. The balls were of different capacities to be used according to the different weights desired to be overcome. She then fastened to the air-car two wing-like blades, which, she said, were worked by electricity. After we were comfortably seated she touched a knob and the blades began to whirl, moving faster and faster every moment. At first we were raised to the height of about six or seven feet and then off we flew. And before I could realize that we had commenced moving, we reached the garden of the Queen.

My friend lowered the air-car by reversing the action of the machine, and when the car touched the ground the machine was stopped and we got out.

I had seen from the air-car the Queen walking on a garden path with her little daughter (who was four years old) and her maids of honour.

"Halloo! You here!" cried the Queen addressing Sister Sara. I was introduced to Her Royal Highness and was received by her cordially without any ceremony.

I was very much delighted to make her acquaintance. In the course of the conversation I had with her, the Queen told me that she had no objection to permitting her subjects to trade with other countries. "But," she continued, "no trade was possible with countries where the women were kept in the zenanas and so unable to come and trade with us. Men, we find, are rather of lower morals and so we do not like dealing with them. We do not covet other people's land, we do not fight for a piece of diamond though it may be a thousand-fold brighter than the Koh-i-Noor, nor do we grudge a ruler his Peacock Throne. We dive deep into the ocean of knowledge and try to find out the precious gems, which nature has kept in store for us. We enjoy nature's gifts as much as we can."

After taking leave of the Queen, I visited the famous universities, and was shown some of their manufactories, laboratories and observatories.

After visiting the above places of interest we got again into the air-car, but as soon as it began moving, I somehow slipped down and the fall startled me out of my dream. And on opening my eyes, I found myself in my own bedroom still lounging in the easy-chair!

THE TACHYPOMP

by Edward Page Mitchell

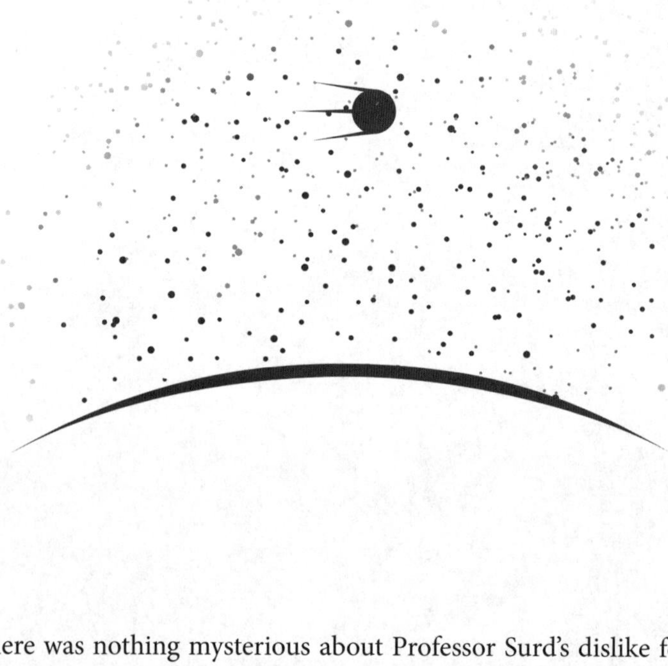

There was nothing mysterious about Professor Surd's dislike for me. I was the only poor mathematician in an exceptionally mathematical class. The old gentleman sought the lecture-room every morning with eagerness, and left it reluctantly. For was it not a thing of joy to find seventy young men who, individually and collectively, preferred *x* to XX; who had rather differentiate than dissipate; and for whom the limbs of the heavenly bodies had more attractions than those of earthly stars upon the spectacular stage?

So affairs went on swimmingly between the Professor of Mathematics and the junior Class at Polyp University. In every man of the seventy the sage saw the logarithm of a possible La Place, of a Sturm, or of a Newton. It was a delightful task for him to lead them through the pleasant valleys of conic sections, and beside the still waters of the integral calculus. Figuratively speaking, his problem was not a hard one. He had only to manipulate, and eliminate, and to raise to a higher power, and the triumphant result of examination day was assured.

But I was a disturbing element, a perplexing unknown quantity, which had somehow crept into the work, and which seriously threatened to impair the accuracy of his calculations. It was a touching sight to behold the venerable mathematician as he pleaded with me not so utterly to disregard precedent in the use of cotangents; or as he urged, with eyes almost tearful, that ordinates were dangerous things to trifle with. All in vain. More theorems went on to my cuff than into my head. Never did chalk do so much work to so little purpose. And, therefore, it came that Furnace Second was reduced to zero in Professor Surd's estimation. He looked upon me with all the horror which an unalgebraic nature could inspire. I have seen the professor walk around an entire square rather than meet the man who had no mathematics in his soul.

For Furnace Second were no invitations to Professor Surd's house. Seventy of the class supped in delegations around the periphery of the professor's tea-table. The seventy-first knew nothing of the charms of that perfect ellipse, with its twin bunches of fuchsias and geraniums in gorgeous precision at the two foci.

This, unfortunately enough, was no trifling deprivation. Not that I longed especially for segments of Mrs. Surd's justly celebrated lemon pies; not that the spheroidal damsons of her excellent preserving had any marked allurements; not even that I yearned to hear the professor's jocose tabletalk about binomials, and chatty illustrations of abstruse paradoxes. The explanation is far different. Professor Surd had a daughter. Twenty years before, he made a proposition of marriage to the present Mrs. S. He added a little corollary to his proposition not long after. The corollary was a girl.

Abscissa Surd was as perfectly symmetrical as Giotto's circle, and as pure, withal, as the mathematics her father taught. It was just when spring was coming to extract the roots of frozen-up vegetation that I fell in love with the corollary. That she herself was not indifferent I soon had reason to regard as a self-evident truth.

The sagacious reader will already recognize nearly all the elements necessary to a well-ordered plot. We have introduced a heroine, inferred a hero, and constructed a hostile parent after the most approved model. A movement for the story, a *Deus ex machina*, is alone lacking. With considerable satisfaction I can promise a perfect novelty in this line, a *Deus ex machina* never before offered to the public.

It would be discounting ordinary intelligence to say that I sought with unwearying assiduity to figure my way into the stern father's good-will; that never did dullard apply himself to mathematics more patiently than I; that never did faithfulness achieve such meagre reward. Then I engaged a private tutor. His instructions met with no better success.

My tutor's name was Jean Marie Rivarol. He was a unique Alsatian; though Gallic in name, thoroughly Teuton in nature; by birth a Frenchman, by education a German. His age was thirty; his profession, omniscience; the wolf at his door, poverty; the skeleton in his closet, a consuming but unrequited passion. The most recondite principles of practical science were his toys; the deepest intricacies of abstract science his diversions. Problems which were foreordained mysteries to me were to him as clear as Tahoe water. Perhaps this very fact will explain our lack of success in the relation of tutor and pupil; perhaps the failure is alone due to my own unmitigated stupidity. Rivarol had hung about the skirts of the University for several years; supplying his few wants by writing for scientific journals, or by giving assistance to students who, like myself, were characterized by a plethora of purse and a paucity of ideas; cooking, studying and sleeping in his attic lodgings; and prosecuting queer experiments all by himself.

We were not long discovering that even this eccentric genius could not transplant brains into my deficient skull. I gave over the struggle in despair. An unhappy year dragged its slow length around. A gloomy year it was, brightened only by occasional interviews with Abscissa, the Abbie of my thoughts and dreams.

Commencement day was coming on apace. I was soon to go forth, with the rest of my class, to astonish and delight a waiting world. The professor seemed to avoid me more than ever. Nothing but the conventionalities, I think kept him from shaping his treatment of me on the basis of unconcealed disgust.

At last, in the very recklessness of despair, I resolved to see him, plead with him, threaten him if need be, and risk all my fortunes on one desperate chance. I wrote him a somewhat defiant letter, stating my aspirations, and, as I flattered myself, shrewdly giving him a week to get over the first shock of horrified surprise. Then I was to call and learn my fate.

During the week of suspense I nearly worried myself into a fever. It was first crazy hope, and then saner despair. On Friday evening, when I presented myself at the professor's door, I was such a haggard, sleepy, dragged-out spectre, that even Miss Jocasta, the harsh-favoured maiden sister of the Surd's, admitted me with commiserate regard, and suggested pennyroyal tea.

Professor Surd was at a faculty meeting. Would I wait?

Yes, till all was blue, if need be. Miss Abbie?

Abscissa had gone to Wheelborough to visit a school friend. The aged maiden hoped I would make myself comfortable, and departed to the unknown haunts which knew Jocasta's daily walk.

Comfortable! But I settled myself in a great uneasy chair and waited, with the contradictory spirit common to such junctures, dreading every step lest it should herald the man whom, of all men, I wished to see.

I had been there at least an hour, and was growing right drowsy.

At length Professor Surd came in. He sat down in the dusk opposite me, and I thought his eyes glinted with malignant pleasure as he said, abruptly:

"So, young man, you think you are a fit husband for my girl?"

I stammered some inanity about making up in affection what I lacked in merit; about my expectations, family and the like. He quickly interrupted me.

"You misapprehend me, sir. Your nature is destitute of those mathematical perceptions and acquirements which are the only sure foundations of character. You have no mathematics in you.

You are fit for treason, stratagems, and spoils—Shakespeare. Your narrow intellect cannot understand and appreciate a generous mind. There is all the difference between you and a Surd, if I may say it, which intervenes between an infinitesimal and an infinite. Why, I will even venture to say that you do not comprehend the Problem of the Couriers!"

I admitted that the Problem of the Couriers should be classed rather without my list of accomplishments than within it. I regretted this fault very deeply, and suggested amendment. I faintly hoped that my fortune would be such—

"Money!" he impatiently exclaimed. "Do you seek to bribe a Roman senator with a penny whistle? Why, boy, do you parade your paltry wealth, which, expressed in mills, will not cover ten decimal places, before the eyes of a man who measures the planets in their orbits, and close crowds infinity itself?"

I hastily disclaimed any intention of obtruding my foolish dollars, and he went on:

"Your letter surprised me not a little. I thought you would be the last person in the world to presume to an alliance here. But having a regard for you personally"—and again I saw malice twinkle in his small eyes—"and still more regard for Abscissa's happiness, I have decided that you shall have her—upon conditions. Upon conditions," he repeated, with a half-smothered sneer.

"What are they?" cried I, eagerly enough. "Only name them."

"Well, sir," he continued, and the deliberation of his speech seemed the very refinement of cruelty, "you have only to prove yourself worthy an alliance with a mathematical family. You have only to accomplish a task which I shall presently give you. Your eyes ask me what it is. I will tell you. Distinguish yourself in that noble branch of abstract science in which, you cannot but acknowledge, you are at present sadly deficient. I will place Abscissa's hand in yours whenever you shall come before me and square the circle to my satisfaction. No! That is too easy a condition. I should cheat myself. Say perpetual motion. How do you like that? Do you think it lies within the range of your mental capabilities? You don't smile. Perhaps your talents don't run in the way of perpetual motion. Several people have found that theirs didn't. I'll give you another chance. We were speaking of the Problem of the Couriers, and I think you expressed a desire to know more of that ingenious question. You shall have the opportunity. Sit down some day, when you have nothing else to do, and discover the principle of infinite speed. I mean the law of motion which shall accomplish an infinitely great distance in an infinitely short time. You may mix in a little practical mechanics, if you choose. Invent some method of taking the tardy Courier over his road at the rate of sixty miles a minute. Demonstrate me this discovery (when you have made it!) mathematically, and approximate it practically, and Abscissa is yours. Until you can, I will thank you to trouble neither myself nor her."

I could stand his mocking no longer. I stumbled mechanically out of the room, and out of the house. I even forgot my hat and gloves. For an hour I walked in the moonlight. Gradually I succeeded to a more hopeful frame of mind. This was due to my ignorance of mathematics. Had I understood the real meaning of what he asked, I should have been utterly despondent.

Perhaps this problem of sixty miles a minute was not so impossible after all. At any rate I could attempt, though I might not succeed. And Rivarol came to my mind. I would ask him. I would enlist his knowledge to accompany my own devoted perseverance. I sought his lodgings at once.

The man of science lived in the fourth story, back. I had never been in his room before. When I entered, he was in the act of filling a beer mug from a carboy labelled *aqua fortis*.

"Seat you," he said. "No, not in that chair. That is my Petty Cash Adjuster."

But he was a second too late. I had carelessly thrown myself into a chair of seductive appearance. To my utter amazement it reached out two skeleton arms and clutched me with a grasp against which I struggled in vain. Then a skull stretched itself over my shoulder and grinned with ghastly familiarity close to my face.

Rivarol came to my aid with many apologies. He touched a spring somewhere and the Petty Cash Adjuster relaxed its horrid hold. I placed myself gingerly in a plain cane-bottomed rocking-chair, which Rivarol assured me was a safe location.

"That seat," he said, "is an arrangement upon which I much felicitate myself. I made it at Heidelberg. It has saved me a vast deal of small annoyance. I consign to its embraces the friends who bore, and the visitors who exasperate, me. But it is never so useful as when terrifying some tradesman with an insignificant account. Hence the pet name which I have facetiously given it. They are invariably too glad to purchase release at the price of a bill receipted. Do you well apprehend the idea?"

While the Alsatian diluted his glass of *aqua fortis*, shook into it an infusion of bitters, and tossed off the bumper with apparent relish, I had time to look around the strange apartment.

The four corners of the room were occupied respectively by a turning lathe, a Rhumkorff Coil, a small steam engine and an orrery in stately motion. Tables, shelves, chairs and floor supported an odd aggregation of tools, retorts, chemicals, gas receivers, philosophical instruments, boots, flasks, paper-collar boxes, books diminutive and books of preposterous size. There were plaster busts of Aristotle, Archimedes, and Comte, while a great drowsy owl was blinking away, perched on the benign brow of Martin Farquhar Tupper. "He always roosts there when he proposes to slumber," explained my tutor. "You are a bird of no ordinary mind. *Schlafen Sie wohl.*"

Through a closet door, half open, I could see a humanlike form covered with a sheet. Rivarol caught my glance.

"That," said he, "will be my masterpiece. It is a Microcosm, an Android, as yet only partially complete. And why not? Albertus Magnus constructed an image perfect to talk metaphysics and confute the schools. So did Sylvester II; so did Robertus Greathead. Roger Bacon made a brazen head that held discourses. But the first named of these came to destruction. Thomas Aquinas got wrathful at some of its syllogisms and smashed its head. The idea is reasonable enough. Mental action will yet be reduced to laws as definite as those which govern the physical. Why should not I accomplish a manikin which shall preach as original discourses as the Reverend Dr. Allchin, or talk poetry as mechanically as Paul Anapest? My android can already work problems in vulgar fractions and compose sonnets. I hope to teach it the Positive Philosophy."

Out of the bewildering confusion of his effects Rivarol produced two pipes and filled them. He handed one to me.

"And here," he said, "I live and am tolerably comfortable. When my coat wears out at the elbows I seek the tailor and am measured for another. When I am hungry I promenade myself to the butcher's and bring home a pound or so of steak, which I cook very nicely in three seconds by this oxy-hydrogen flame. Thirsty, perhaps, I send for a carboy of *aqua fortis*. But I have it charged, all charged. My spirit is above any small pecuniary transaction. I loathe your dirty greenbacks, and never handle what they call scrip."

"But are you never pestered with bills?" I asked. "Don't the creditors worry your life out?"

"Creditors!" gasped Rivarol. "I have learned no such word in your very admirable language. He who will allow his soul to be vexed by creditors is a relic of an imperfect civilization. Of what use is science if it cannot avail a man who has accounts current? Listen. The moment you or any one else enters the outside door this little electric bell sounds me warning. Every successive step on Mrs. Grimler's staircase is a spy and informer vigilant for my benefit. The first step is trod upon. That trusty first step immediately telegraphs your weight. Nothing could be simpler. It is exactly like any platform scale. The weight is registered up here upon this dial. The second step records the size of my visitor's feet. The third his height, the fourth his complexion, and so on. By the time he reaches the top of the first flight I have a pretty accurate description of him right here at my elbow, and quite a margin of time for deliberation and action. Do you follow me? It is plain enough. Only the A B C of my science."

"I see all that," I said, "but I don't see how it helps you any. The knowledge that a creditor is coming won't pay his bill. You can't escape unless you jump out of the window."

Rivarol laughed softly. "I will tell you. You shall see what becomes of any poor devil who goes to demand money of me—of a man of science. Ha! ha! It pleases me. I was seven weeks perfecting my Dun Suppressor. Did you know"—he whispered exultingly—"did you know that there is a hole through the earth's centre? Physicists have long suspected it; I was the first to find it. You have read how Rhuyghens, the Dutch navigator, discovered in Kerguellen's Land an abysmal pit which fourteen hundred fathoms of plumb-line failed to sound. Herr Tom, that hole has no bottom! It runs from one surface of the earth to the antipodal surface. It is diametric. But where is the antipodal spot? You stand upon it. I learned this by the merest chance. I was deep-digging in Mrs. Grimler's cellar, to bury a poor cat I had sacrificed in a galvanic experiment, when the earth under my spade crumbled, caved in, and wonder-stricken I stood upon the brink of a yawning shaft. I dropped a coal-hod in. It went down, down, down, bounding and rebounding. In two hours and a quarter that coal-hod came up again. I caught it and restored it to the angry Grimler. Just think a minute. The coal-hod went down, faster and faster, till it reached the centre of the earth. There it would stop, were it not for acquired momentum. Beyond the centre its journey was relatively upward, toward the opposite surface of the globe. So, losing velocity, it went slower and slower till it reached that surface. Here it came to rest for a second and then fell back again, eight thousand odd miles, into my hands. Had I not interfered with it, it would have repeated its journey, time after time, each trip of shorter extent, like the diminishing oscillations of a pendulum, till it finally came to eternal rest at the centre of the sphere. I am not slow to give a practical application to any such grand discovery. My Dun Suppressor was born of it. A trap, just outside my chamber door: a spring in here: a creditor on the trap: need I say more?"

"But isn't it a trifle inhuman?" I mildly suggested. "Plunging an unhappy being into a perpetual journey to and from Kerguellen's Land, without a moment's warning."

"I give them a chance. When they come up the first time I wait at the mouth of the shaft with a rope in hand. If they are reasonable and will come to terms, I fling them the line. If they perish, 'tis their own fault. Only," he added, with a melancholy smile, "the centre is getting so plugged up with creditors that I am afraid there soon will be no choice whatever for 'em."

By this time I had conceived a high opinion of my tutor's ability. If anybody could send me waltzing through space at an infinite speed, Rivarol could do it. I filled my pipe and told him the story. He heard with grave and patient attention. Then, for full half an hour, he whiffed away in silence. Finally he spoke.

"The ancient cipher has overreached himself. He has given you a choice of two problems, both of which he deems insoluble. Neither of them is insoluble. The only gleam of intelligence Old Cotangent showed was when he said that squaring the circle was too easy. He was right. It would have given you your Liebchen in five minutes. I squared the circle before I discarded pantalets. I will show you the work—but it would be a digression, and you are in no mood for digressions. Our first chance, therefore, lies in perpetual motion. Now, my good friend, I will frankly tell you that, although I have compassed this interesting problem, I do not choose to use it in your behalf. I too, Herr Tom, have a heart. The loveliest of her sex frowns upon me. Her somewhat mature charms are not for Jean Marie Rivarol. She has cruelly said that her years demand of me filial rather than connubial regard. Is love a matter of years or of eternity? This question did I put to the cold, yet lovely Jocasta."

"Jocasta Surd!" I remarked in surprise, "Abscissa's aunt!"

"The same," he said, sadly. "I will not attempt to conceal that upon the maiden Jocasta my maiden heart has been bestowed. Give me your hand, my nephew in affliction as in affection!"

Rivarol dashed away a not discreditable tear, and resumed:

"My only hope lies in this discovery of perpetual motion. It will give me the fame, the wealth. Can Jocasta refuse these? If she can, there is only the trap-door and—Kerguellen's Land!"

I bashfully asked to see the perpetual-motion machine. My uncle in affliction shook his head.

"At another time," he said. "Suffice it at present to say, that it is something upon the principle of a woman's tongue. But you see now why we must turn in your case to the alternative condition—infinite speed. There are several ways in which this may be accomplished, theoretically. By the lever, for instance. Imagine a lever with a very long and a very short arm. Apply power to the shorter arm which will move it with great velocity. The end of the long arm will move much faster. Now keep shortening the short arm and lengthening the long one, and as you approach infinity in their difference of length, you approach infinity in the speed of the long arm. It would be difficult to demonstrate this practically to the professor. We must seek another solution. Jean Marie will meditate. Come to me in a fortnight. Good-night. But stop! Have you the money—*das Geld?*"

"Much more than I need."

"Good! Let us strike hands. Gold and Knowledge; Science and Love. What may not such a partnership achieve? We go to conquer thee, Abscissa. *Vorwärts!*"

When, at the end of a fortnight; I sought Rivarol's chamber, I passed with some little trepidation over the terminus of the Air Line to Kerguellen's Land,

and evaded the extended arms of the Petty Cash Adjuster. Rivarol drew a mug of ale for me, and filled himself a retort of his own peculiar beverage.

"Come," he said at length. "Let us drink success to the TACHYPOMP."

"The TACHYPOMP?"

"Yes. Why not? *Tachu*, quickly, and *pempo, pepompa*, to send. May it send you quickly to your wedding-day. Abscissa is yours. It is done. When shall we start for the prairies?"

"Where is it?" I asked, looking in vain around the room for any contrivance which might seem calculated to advance matrimonial prospects.

"It is here," and he gave his forehead a significant tap. Then he held forth didactically.

"There is force enough in existence to yield us a speed of sixty miles a minute, or even more. All we need is the knowledge how to combine and apply it. The wise man will not attempt to make some great force yield some great speed. He will keep adding the little force to the little force, making each little force yield its little speed, until an aggregate of little forces shall be a great force, yielding an aggregate of little speeds, a great speed. The difficulty is not in aggregating the forces; it lies in the corresponding aggregation of the speeds. One musket ball will go, say a mile. It is not hard to increase the force of muskets to a thousand, yet the thousand musket balls will go no farther, and no faster, than the one. You see, then, where our trouble lies. We cannot readily add speed to speed, as we add force to force. My discovery is simply the utilization of a principle which extorts an increment of speed from each increment of power. But this is the metaphysics of physics. Let us be practical or nothing.

"When you have walked forward, on a moving train, from the rear car, toward the engine, did you ever think what you were really doing?"

"Why, yes, I have generally been going to the smoking car to have a cigar."

"Tut, tut—not that! I mean, did it ever occur to you on such an occasion, that absolutely you were moving faster than the train? The train passes the telegraph poles at the rate of thirty miles an hour, say. You walk toward the smoking car at the rate of four miles an hour. Then you pass the telegraph poles at the rate of thirty-four miles. Your absolute speed is the speed of the engine, plus the speed of your own locomotion. Do you follow me?"

I began to get an inkling of his meaning, and told him so.

"Very well. Let us advance a step. Your addition to the speed of the engine is trivial, and the space in which you can exercise it, limited. Now suppose two stations, A and B, two miles distant by the track. Imagine a train of platform cars, the last car resting at station A. The train is a mile long, say. The engine is therefore within a mile of station B. Say the train can move a mile in ten minutes. The last car, having two miles to go, would reach B in twenty minutes, but the engine, a mile ahead, would get there in ten. You jump on the last car, at A, in a prodigious hurry to reach Abscissa, who is at B. If you stay on the last car it will be twenty long minutes before you see her. But the engine reaches B and the fair lady in ten. You will be a stupid reasoner, and an indifferent lover, if you don't put for the engine over those platform cars, as fast as your legs will carry you. You can run a mile, the length of the train, in ten minutes. Therefore, you reach Abscissa when the engine does, or in ten minutes—ten minutes sooner than if you had lazily sat down upon the rear car and talked politics with the brakeman. You have diminished the time by one half. You have added your speed to that of the locomotive to some purpose. *Nicht wahr?*"

I saw it perfectly; much plainer, perhaps, for his putting in the clause about Abscissa.

He continued, "This illustration, though a slow one, leads up to a principle which may be carried to any extent. Our first anxiety will be to spare your legs and wind. Let us suppose that the two miles of track are perfectly straight, and make our train one platform car, a mile long, with parallel rails laid upon its top. Put a little dummy engine on these rails, and let it run to and fro along the platform car, while the platform car is pulled along the ground track. Catch the idea? The dummy takes your place. But it can run its mile much faster. Fancy that our locomotive is strong enough to pull the platform car over the two miles in two minutes. The dummy can attain the same speed. When the engine reaches B in one minute, the dummy, having gone a mile a-top the platform car, reaches B also. We have so combined the speeds of those two engines as to accomplish two miles in one minute. Is this all we can do? Prepare to exercise your imagination."

I lit my pipe.

"Still two miles of straight track, between A and B. On the track a long platform car, reaching from A to within a quarter of a mile of B. We will now discard ordinary locomotives and adopt as our motive power a series of compact magnetic engines, distributed underneath the platform car, all along its length."

"I don't understand those magnetic engines."

"Well, each of them consists of a great iron horseshoe, rendered alternately a magnet and not a magnet by an intermittent current of electricity from a battery, this current in its turn regulated by clock-work. When the horseshoe is in the circuit, it is a magnet, and it pulls its clapper toward it with enormous power. When it is out of the circuit, the next second, it is not a magnet, and it lets the clapper go. The clapper, oscillating to and fro, imparts a rotatory motion to a fly wheel, which transmits it to the drivers on the rails. Such are our motors. They are no novelty, for trial has proved them practicable.

"With a magnetic engine for every truck of wheels, we can reasonably expect to move our immense car, and to drive it along at a speed, say, of a mile a minute.

"The forward end, having but a quarter of a mile to go, will reach B in fifteen seconds. We will call this platform car number 1. On top of number 1 are laid rails on which another platform car, number 2, a quarter of a mile shorter than number 1, is moved in precisely the same way. Number 2, in its turn, is surmounted by number 3, moving independently of the tiers beneath, and a quarter of a mile shorter than number 2. Number 2 is a mile and a half long; number 3 a mile and a quarter. Above, on successive levels, are number 4, a mile long; number 5, three quarters of a mile; number 6, half a mile; number 7, a quarter of a mile, and number 8, a short passenger car, on top of all.

"Each car moves upon the car beneath it, independently of all the others, at the rate of a mile a minute. Each car has its own magnetic engines. Well, the train being drawn up with the latter end of each car resting against a lofty bumping-post at A, Tom Furnace, the gentlemanly conductor, and Jean Marie Rivarol, engineer, mount by a long ladder to the exalted number 8. The complicated mechanism is set in motion. What happens?

"Number 8 runs a quarter of a mile in fifteen seconds and reaches the end of number 7. Meanwhile number 7 has run a quarter of a mile in the same time and reached the end of number 6; number 6, a quarter of a mile in fifteen seconds, and reached the end of number 5; number 5, the end of number 4; number 4, of number 3; number 3, of number 2; number 2, of number 1. And number 1, in fifteen seconds, has gone its quarter of a mile along the ground track, and has reached station B. All this has been done in fifteen seconds. Wherefore, numbers 1, 2, 3, 4, 5, 6, 7, and 8 come to rest against the bumping-post at B, at precisely the same second. We, in number 8, reach B just when number 1 reaches it. In other words, we accomplish two miles in fifteen seconds. Each of the eight cars, moving at the rate of a mile a minute, has contributed a quarter of a mile to our journey, and has done its work in fifteen seconds. All the eight did their work at once, during the same fifteen seconds. Consequently we have been whizzed through the air at the somewhat startling speed of seven and a half seconds to the mile. This is the Tachypomp. Does it justify the name?"

Although a little bewildered by the complexity of cars, I apprehended the general principle of the machine. I made a diagram, and understood it much better. "You have merely improved on the idea of my moving faster than the train when I was going to the smoking car?"

"Precisely. So far we have kept within the bounds of the practicable. To satisfy the professor, you can theorize in something after this fashion: If we double the number of cars, thus decreasing by one half the distance which each has to go, we shall attain twice the speed. Each of the sixteen cars will have but one eighth of a mile to go. At the uniform rate we have adopted, the two miles can be done in seven and a half instead of fifteen seconds. With thirty-two cars, and a sixteenth of a mile, or twenty rods difference in their length, we arrive at the speed of a mile in less than two seconds; with sixty-four cars, each travelling but ten rods, a mile under the second. More than sixty miles a minute! If this isn't rapid enough for the professor, tell him to go on, increasing the number of his cars and diminishing the distance each one has to run. If sixty-four cars yield a speed of a mile inside the second, let him fancy a Tachypomp of six hundred and forty cars, and amuse himself calculating the rate of car number 640. Just whisper to him that when he has an infinite number of cars with an infinitesimal difference in their lengths, he will have obtained that infinite speed for which he seems to yearn. Then demand Abscissa."

I wrung my friend's hand in silent and grateful admiration. I could say nothing.

"You have listened to the man of theory," he said proudly. "You shall now behold the practical engineer. We will go to the west of the Mississippi and find some suitably level locality. We will erect thereon a model Tachypomp. We will summon thereunto the professor, his daughter, and why not his fair sister Jocasta, as well? We will take them a journey which shall much astonish the venerable Surd. He shall place Abscissa's digits in yours and bless you both with an algebraic formula. Jocasta shall contemplate with wonder the genius of Rivarol. But we have much to do. We must ship to St. Joseph the vast amount of material to be employed in the construction of the Tachypomp. We must engage a small army of workmen to effect that construction, for we are to annihilate time and space. Perhaps you had better see your bankers."

I rushed impetuously to the door. There should be no delay. "Stop! stop! *Um*

Gottes Willen, stop!" shrieked Rivarol. "I launched my butcher this morning and I haven't bolted the-"

But it was too late. I was upon the trap. It swung open with a crash, and I was plunged down, down, down! I felt as if I were falling through illimitable space. I remember wondering, as I rushed through the darkness, whether I should reach Kerguellen's Land or stop at the centre. It seemed an eternity. Then my course was suddenly and painfully arrested.

I opened my eyes. Around me were the walls of Professor Surd's study. Under me was a hard, unyielding plane which I knew too well was Professor Surd's study floor. Behind me was the black, slippery, haircloth chair which had belched me forth, much as the whale served Jonah. In front of me stood Professor Surd himself, looking down with a not unpleasant smile.

"Good evening, Mr. Furnace. Let me help you up. You look tired, sir. No wonder you fell asleep when I kept you so long waiting. Shall I get you a glass of wine? No? By the way, since receiving your letter I find that you are a son of my old friend, Judge Furnace. I have made inquiries, and see no reason why you should not make Abscissa a good husband."

Still I can see no reason why the Tachypomp should not have succeeded. Can you?

THE MAN WITHOUT A BODY

by Edward Page Mitchell

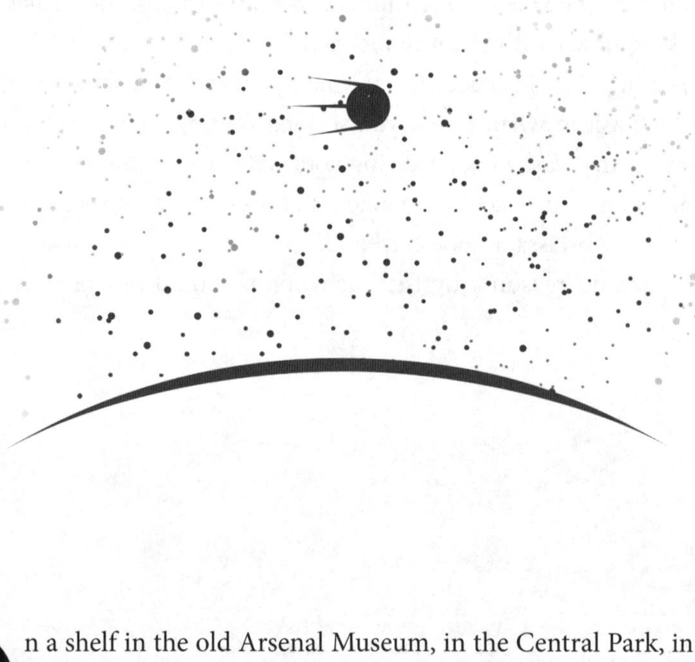

On a shelf in the old Arsenal Museum, in the Central Park, in the midst of stuffed hummingbirds, ermines, silver foxes, and bright-coloured parakeets, there is a ghastly row of human heads. I pass by the mummied Peruvian, the Maori chief, and the Flathead Indian to speak of a Caucasian head which has had a fascinating interest to me ever since it was added to the grim collection a little more than a year ago.

I was struck with the Head when I first saw it. The pensive intelligence of the features won me. The face is remarkable, although the nose is gone, and the nasal fossae are somewhat the worse for wear. The eyes are likewise wanting, but the empty orbs have an expression of their own. The parchmenty skin is so shriveled that the teeth show to their roots in the jaws. The mouth has been much affected by the ravages of decay, but what mouth there is displays character. It seems to say: "Barring certain deficiencies in my anatomy, you behold a man of parts!" The features of the Head are of the Teutonic cast, and the skull is the skull of a philosopher. What particularly attracted my attention, however, was the vague resemblance which this dilapidated countenance bore to some face which had at some time been familiar to me—some face which lingered in my memory, but which I could not place.

After all, I was not greatly surprised, when I had known the Head for nearly a year, to see it acknowledge our acquaintance and express its appreciation of friendly interest on my part by deliberately winking at me as I stood before its glass case.

This was on a Trustees' Day, and I was the only visitor in the hall. The faithful attendant had gone to enjoy a can of beer with his friend, the superintendent of the monkeys.

The Head winked a second time, and even more cordially than before. I gazed upon its efforts with the critical delight of an anatomist. I saw the masseter muscle flex beneath the leathery skin. I saw the play of the glutinators, and the beautiful lateral movement of the internal playtsyma. I knew the Head was trying to speak to me. I noted the convulsive twitchings of the risorius and the zygomatie major, and knew that it was endeavouring to smile.

"Here," I thought, "is either a case of vitality long after decapitation, or, an instance of reflex action where there is no diastaltic or excitor-motory system. In either case the phenomenon is unprecedented, and should be carefully observed. Besides, the Head is evidently well disposed toward me." I found a key on my bunch which opened the glass door.

"Thanks," said the Head. "A breath of fresh air is quite a treat."

"How do you feel?" I asked politely. "How does it seem without a body?"

The Head shook itself sadly and sighed. "I would give," it said, speaking through its ruined nose, and for obvious reasons using chest tones sparingly, "I would give both ears for a single leg. My ambition is principally ambulatory, and yet I cannot walk. I cannot even hop or waddle. I would fain travel, roam, promenade, circulate in the busy paths of men, but I am chained to this accursed shelf. I am no better off than these barbarian heads—I, a man of science! I am compelled to sit here on my neck and see sandpipers and storks all around me, with legs and to spare. Look at that infernal little Oedieneninus longpipes over there. Look at that miserable gray-headed porphyric. They have no brains, no ambition, no yearnings. Yet they have legs, legs, legs, in profusion." He cast an envious glance across the alcove at the tantalizing limbs of the birds in question and added gloomily, "There isn't even enough of me to make a hero for one of Wilkie Collins's novels."

I did not exactly know how to console him in so delicate a manner, but ventured to hint that perhaps his condition had its compensations in immunity from corns and the gout.

"And as to arms," he went on, "there's another misfortune for you! I am unable to brush away the flies that get in here—Lord knows how—in the summertime. I cannot reach over and cuff that confounded Chinook mummy that sits there grinning at me like a jack-in-the-box. I cannot scratch my head or even blow my nose (his nose!) decently when I get cold in this thundering draft. As to eating and drinking, I don't care. My soul is wrapped up in science. Science is my bride, my divinity. I worship her footsteps in the past and hail the prophecy of her future progress. I—"

I had heard these sentiments before. In a flash I had accounted for the familiar look which had haunted me ever since I first saw the Head. "Pardon me," I said, "you are the celebrated Professor Dummkopf?"

"That is, or was, my name," he replied, with dignity.

"And you formerly lived in Boston, where you carried on scientific experiments of startling originality. It was you who first discovered how to photograph smell, how to bottle music, how to freeze the aurora borealis. It was you who first applied spectrW analysis to Mind."

"Those were some of my minor achievements," said the Head, sadly nodding itself—"small when compared with my final invention, the grand discovery which was at the same time my greatest triumph and my ruin. I lost my Body in an experiment."

"How was that?" I asked. "I had not heard."

"No," said the Head. "I being alone and friendless, my disappearance was hardly noticed. I will tell you."

There was a sound upon the stairway. "Hush!" cried the Head. "Here comes somebody. We must not be discovered. You must dissemble."

I hastily closed the door of the glass case, locking it just in time to evade the vigilance of the returning keeper, and dissembled by pretending to examine, with great interest, a nearby exhibit.

On the next Trustees' Day I revisited the museum and gave the keeper of the

Head a dollar on the pretence of purchasing information in regard to the curiosities in his charge. He made the circuit of the hall with me, talking volubly all the while.

"That there," he said, as we stood before the Head, "is a relic of morality presented to the museum fifteen months ago. The head of a notorious murderer guillotined at Paris in the last century, sir."

I fancied that I saw a slight twitching about the corners of Professor Dummkopf's mouth and an almost imperceptible depression of what was once his left eyelid, but he kept his face remarkably well under the circumstances. I dismissed my guide with many thanks for his intelligent services, and, as I had anticipated, he departed forthwith to invest his easily earned dollar in beer, leaving me to pursue my conversation with the Head.

"Think of putting a wooden-headed idiot like that," said the professor, after I had opened his glass prison, "in charge of a portion, however small, of a man of science—of the inventor of the Telepomp! Paris! Murderer! Last century, indeed!" and the Head shook with laughter until I feared that it would tumble off the shelf.

"You spoke of your invention, the Telepomp," I suggested.

"Ah, yes," said the Head, simultaneously recovering its gravity and its centre of gravity; "I promised to tell you how I happen to be a Man without a Body. You see that some three or four years ago I discovered the principle of the transmission of sound by electricity. My telephone, as I called it, would have been an invention of great practical utility if I had been spared to introduce it to the public. But, alas—"

"Excuse the interruption," I said, "but I must inform you that somebody else has recently accomplished the same thing. The telephone is a realized fact."

"Have they gone any further?" he eagerly asked. "Have they discovered the great secret of the transmission of atoms? In other words, have they accomplished the Telepomp?"

"I have heard nothing of the kind," I hastened to assure him, "but what do you mean?"

"Listen," he said. "In the course of my experiments with the telephone I became convinced that the same principle was capable of indefinite expansion. Matter is made up of molecules, and molecules, in their turn, are made up of atoms. The atom, you know, is the unit of being. The molecules differ according to the number and the arrangement of their constituent atoms. Chemical changes are effected by the dissolution of the atoms in the molecules and their rearrangements into molecules of another kind. This dissolution may be accomplished by chemical affinity or by a sufficiently strong electric current. Do you follow me?"

"Perfectly."

"Well, then, following out this line of thought, I conceived a great idea. There was no reason why matter could not be telegraphed, or, to be etymologically accurate, 'telepomped.' It was only necessary to effect at one end of the line the disintegration of the molecules into atoms and to convey the vibrations of the chemical dissolution by electricity to the other pole, where a corresponding reconstruction could be effected from other atoms. As all atoms are alike, their arrangement into molecules of the same order, and the arrangement of those molecules into an organization similar to the original organization, would be practically a reproduction of the original. It would be a materialization—not in the sense of the spiritualists' cant, but in all the truth and logic of stern science. Do you still follow me?"

"It is a little misty," I said, "but I think I get the point. You would telegraph the Idea of the matter, to use the word Idea in Plato's sense."

"Precisely. A candle flame is the same candle flame although the burning gas is continually changing. A wave on the surface of water is the same wave, although the water composing it is shifting as it moves. A man is the same man although there is not an atom in his body which was there five years before. It is the form, the shape, the Idea, that is essential. The vibrations that give individuality to matter may be transmitted to a distance by wire just as readily as the vibrations that give individuality to sound. So I constructed an instrument by which I could pull down matter, so to speak, at the anode and build it up again on the same plan at the cathode. This was my Telepomp."

"But in practice—how did the Telepomp work?"

"To perfection! In my rooms on Joy Street, in Boston, I had about five miles of wire. I had no difficulty in sending simple compounds, such as quartz, starch, and water, from one room to another over this five-mile coil. I shall never forget the joy with which I disintegrated a three-cent postage stamp in one room and found it immediately reproduced at the receiving instrument in another. This success with inorganic matter emboldened me to attempt the same thing with a living organism. I caught a cat—a black and yellow cat—and I submitted him to a terrible current from my two-hundred-cup battery. The cat disappeared in a twinkling. I hastened to the next room and, to my immense satisfaction, found Thomas there, alive and purring, although somewhat astonished. It worked like a charm."

"This is certainly very remarkable."

"Isn't it? After my experiment with the cat, a gigantic idea took possession of me. If I could send a feline being, why not send a human being? If I could transmit a cat five miles by wire in an instant by electricity, why not transmit a man to London by Atlantic cable and with equal dispatch? I resolved to strengthen my already powerful battery and try the experiment. Like a thorough votary of science, I resolved to try the experiment on myself.

"I do not like to dwell upon this chapter of my experience," continued the Head, winking at a tear which had trickled down on to his cheek and which I gently wiped away for him with my own pocket handkerchief. "Suffice it that I trebled the cups in my battery, stretched my wire over housetops to my lodgings in Phillips Street, made everything ready, and with a solemn calmness born of my confidence in the theory, placed myself in the receiving instrument of the Telepomp at my Joy Street office. I was as sure that when I made the connection with the battery I would find myself in my rooms in Phillips Street as I was sure of my existence. Then I touched the key that let on the electricity. Alas!"

For some moments my friend was unable to speak. At last, with an effort, he resumed his narrative.

"I began to disintegrate at my feet and slowly disappeared under my own eyes. My legs melted away, and then my trunk and arms. That something was wrong, I knew from the exceeding slowness of my dissolution, but I was helpless. Then my head went and I lost all consciousness. According to my theory, my head, having been the last to disappear, should have been the first to materialize at the other end of the wire. The theory was confirmed in fact. I recovered consciousness. I opened my eyes in my Phillips Street apartments. My chin was materializing, and with great satisfaction I saw my neck slowly taking shape. Suddenly, and about at the third cervical vertebra, the process stopped. In a flash I knew the reason. I had forgotten to replenish the cups of my battery with fresh sulphuric acid, and there was not electricity enough to materialize the rest of me. I was a Head, but my body was Lord knows where."

I did not attempt to offer consolation. Words would have been mockery in the presence of Professor Dummkopf's grief.

"What matters it about the rest?" he sadly continued. "The house in Phillips Street was full of medical students. I suppose that some of them found my head, and knowing nothing of me or of the Telepomp, appropriated it for purposes of anatomical study. I suppose that they attempted to preserve it by means of some arsenical preparation. How badly the work was done is shown by my defective nose. I suppose that I drifted from medical student to medical student and from anatomical cabinet to anatomical cabinet until some would-be humourist presented me to this collection as a French murderer of the last century. For some months I knew nothing, and when I recovered consciousness I found myself here.

"Such," added the Head, with a dry, harsh laugh, "is the irony of fate!"

"Is there nothing I can do for you?" I asked, after a pause.

"Thank you," the Head replied; "I am tolerably cheerful and resigned. I have lost pretty much all interest in experimental science. I sit here day after day and watch the objects of zoological, ichthyological, ethnological, and conchological interest with which this admirable museum abounds. I don't know of anything you can do for me.

"Stay," he added, as his gaze fell once more upon the exasperating legs of the Oedieneninus longpipes opposite him. "If there is anything I do feel the need of, it is outdoor exercise. Couldn't you manage in some way to take me out for a walk?"

I confess that I was somewhat staggered by this request, but promised to do what I could. After some deliberation, I formed a plan, which was carried out in the following manner:

I returned to the museum that afternoon just before the closing hour, and hid myself behind the mammoth sea cow, or Manatus Americanus. The attendant, after a cursory glance through the hall, locked up the building and departed. Then I came boldly forth and removed my friend from his shelf. With a piece of stout twine, I lashed his one or two vertebrae to the headless vertebrae of a skeleton moa. This gigantic and extinct bird of New Zealand is heavy-legged, full-breasted, tall as a man, and has huge, sprawling feet. My friend, thus provided with legs and arms, manifested extraordinary glee. He walked about, stamped his big feet, swung his wings, and occasionally broke forth into a hilarious shuffle. I was obliged to remind him that he must support the dignity of the venerable bird whose skeleton he had borrowed. I despoiled the African lion of his glass eyes, and inserted them in the empty orbits of the Head. I gave Professor Dummkopf a Fiji war lance for a walking stick, covered him with a Sioux blanket, and then we issued forth from the old arsenal into the fresh night air and the moonlight, and wandered arm in arm along the shores of the quiet lake and through the mazy paths of the Ramble.

THE ABLEST MAN IN THE WORLD

by Edward Page Mitchell

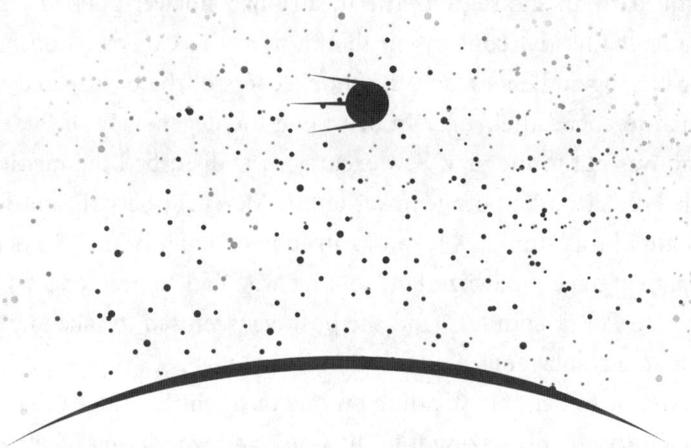

I

It may or may not be remembered that in 1878 General Ignatieff spent several weeks of July at the Badischer Hof in Baden. The public journals gave out that he visited the watering-place for the benefit of his health, said to be much broken by protracted anxiety and responsibility in the service of the Czar. But everybody knew that Ignatieff was just then out of favour at St. Petersburg, and that his absence from the centres of active statecraft at a time when the peace of Europe fluttered like a shuttlecock in the air, between Salisbury and Shouvaloff, was nothing more or less than politely disguised exile.

I am indebted for the following facts to my friend Fisher, of New York, who arrived at Baden on the day after Ignatieff, and was duly announced in the official list of strangers as "Herr Doctor Professor Fischer, mit Frau Gattin and Bed. Nordamerika."

The scarcity of titles among the travelling aristocracy of North America is a standing grievance with the ingenious person who compiles the official list. Professional pride and the instincts of hospitality alike impel him to supply the lack whenever he can. He distributes governor, major-general, and doctor professor with tolerable impartiality, according as the arriving Americans wear a distinguished, a martial, or a studious air. Fisher owed his title to his spectacles.

It was still early in the season. The theatre had not yet opened. The hotels were hardly half full, the concerts in the kiosk at the Conversationshaus were heard by scattering audiences, and the shopkeepers of the bazaar had no better business than to spend their time in bewailing the degeneracy of Baden Baden since an end was put to the play. Few excursionists disturbed the meditations of the shrivelled old custodian of the tower on the Mercuriusberg. Fisher found the place very stupid—as stupid as Saratoga in June or Long Branch in September. He was impatient to get to Switzerland, but his wife had contracted a table d'hôte intimacy with a Polish countess, and she positively refused to take any step that would sever so advantageous a connection.

One afternoon Fisher was standing on one of the little bridges that span the gutter-wide Oosbach, idly gazing into the water and wondering whether a good sized Rangely trout could swim the stream without personal inconvenience, when the porter of the Badischer Hof came to him on the run.

"Herr Doctor Professor!" cried the porter, touching his cap. "I pray you pardon, but the highborn the Baron Savitch out of Moscow, of the General Ignatieff's suite, suffers himself in a terrible fit, and appears to die."

In vain Fisher assured the porter that it was a mistake to consider him a medical expert; that he professed no science save that of draw poker; that if a false impression prevailed in the hotel it was through a blunder for which he was in no way responsible; and that, much as he regretted the unfortunate condition of the highborn the baron out of Moscow, he did not feel that his presence in the chamber of sickness would be of the slightest benefit. It was impossible to eradicate the idea that possessed the porter's mind. Finding himself fairly dragged toward the hotel, Fisher at length concluded to make a virtue of necessity and to render his explanations to the baron's friends.

The Russian's apartments were upon the second floor, not far from those occupied by Fisher. A French valet, almost beside himself with terror, came hurrying out of the room to meet the porter and the doctor professor. Fisher again attempted to explain, but to no purpose. The valet also had explanations to make, and the superior fluency of his French enabled him to monopolize the conversation. No, there was nobody there—nobody but himself, the faithful Auguste of the baron. His Excellency, the General Ignatieff, His Highness, the Prince Koloff, Dr. Rapperschwyll, all the suite, all the world, had driven out that morning to Gernsbach. The baron, meanwhile, had been seized by an effraying malady, and he, Auguste, was desolate with apprehension. He entreated Monsieur to lose no time in parley, but to hasten to the bedside of the baron, who was already in the agonies of dissolution.

Fisher followed Auguste into the inner room. The baron, in his boots, lay upon the bed, his body bent almost double by the unrelenting gripe of a distressful pain. His teeth were tightly clenched, and the rigid muscles around the mouth distorted the natural expression of his face. Every few seconds a prolonged groan escaped him. His fine eyes rolled piteously. Anon, he would press both hands upon his abdomen and shiver in every limb in the intensity of his suffering.

Fisher forgot his explanations. Had he been a doctor professor in fact, he could not have watched the symptoms of the baron's malady with greater interest.

"Can Monsieur preserve him?" whispered the terrified Auguste.

"Perhaps," said Monsieur, dryly.

Fisher scribbled a note to his wife on the back of a card and dispatched it in the care of the hotel porter. That functionary returned with great promptness, bringing a black bottle and a glass. The bottle had come in Fisher's trunk to Baden all the way from Liverpool, had crossed the sea to Liverpool from New York, and had journeyed to New York direct from Bourbon County, Kentucky. Fisher seized it eagerly but reverently, and held it up against the light. There were still three inches or three inches and a half in the bottom. He uttered a grunt of pleasure.

"There is some hope of saving the baron," he remarked to Auguste.

Fully one half of the precious liquid was poured into the glass and administered without delay to the groaning, writhing patient. In a few minutes Fisher had the satisfaction of seeing the baron sit up in bed. The muscles around his mouth relaxed, and the agonized expression was superseded by a look of placid contentment.

Fisher now had an opportunity to observe the personal characteristics of the Russian baron. He was a young man of about thirty-five, with exceedingly handsome and clear-cut features, but a peculiar head. The peculiarity of his head was that it seemed to be perfectly round on top—that is, its diameter from ear to ear appeared quite equal to its anterior and posterior diameter. The curious effect of this unusual conformation was rendered more striking by the absence of all hair. There was nothing on the baron's head but a tightly fitting skullcap of black silk. A very deceptive wig hung upon one of the bed posts.

Being sufficiently recovered to recognize the presence of a stranger, Savitch made a courteous bow.

"How do you find yourself now?" inquired Fisher, in bad French.

"Very much better, thanks to Monsieur," replied the baron, in excellent English, spoken in a charming voice. "Very much better, though I feel a certain dizziness here." And he pressed his hand to his forehead.

The valet withdrew at a sign from his master, and was followed by the porter. Fisher advanced to the bedside and took the baron's wrist. Even his unpractised touch told him that the pulse was alarmingly high. He was much puzzled, and not a little uneasy at the turn which the affair had taken. "Have I got myself and the Russian into an infernal scrape?" he thought. "But no—he's well out of his teens, and half a tumbler of such whiskey as that ought not to go to a baby's head."

Nevertheless, the new symptoms developed themselves with a rapidity and poignancy that made Fisher feel uncommonly anxious. Savitch's face became as white as marble—its paleness rendered startling by the sharp contrast of the black skull cap. His form reeled as he sat on the bed, and he clasped his head convulsively with both hands, as if in terror lest it burst.

"I had better call your valet," said Fisher, nervously.

"No, no!" gasped the baron. "You are a medical man, and I shall have to trust you. There is something-wrong-here." With a spasmodic gesture he vaguely indicated the top of his head.

"But I am not—" stammered Fisher.

"No words!" exclaimed the Russian, imperiously. "Act at once—there must be no delay. Unscrew the top of my head!"

Savitch tore off his skullcap and flung it aside. Fisher has no words to describe the bewilderment with which he beheld the actual fabric of the baron's cranium. The skullcap had concealed the fact that the entire top of Savitch's head was a dome of polished silver.

"Unscrew it!" said Savitch again.

Fisher reluctantly placed both hands upon the silver skull and exerted a gentle pressure toward the left. The top yielded, turning easily and truly in its threads.

"Faster!" said the baron, faintly. "I tell you no time must be lost." Then he swooned.

At this instant there was a sound of voices in the outer room, and the door leading into the baron's bed-chamber was violently flung open and as violently closed. The newcomer was a short, spare man, of middle age, with a keen visage and piercing, deepset little gray eyes. He stood for a few seconds scrutinizing Fisher with a sharp, almost fiercely jealous regard.

The baron recovered his consciousness and opened his eyes.

"Dr. Rapperschwyll!" he exclaimed.

Dr. Rapperschwyll, with a few rapid strides, approached the bed and confronted Fisher and Fisher's patient. "What is all this?" he angrily demanded.

Without waiting for a reply he laid his hand rudely upon Fisher's arm and pulled him away from the baron. Fisher, more and more astonished, made no resistance, but suffered himself to be led, or pushed, toward the door. Dr. Rapperschwyll opened the door wide enough to give the American exit, and then closed it with a vicious slam. A quick click informed Fisher that the key had been turned in the lock.

II

The next morning Fisher met Savitch coming from the Trinkhalle. The baron bowed with cold politeness and passed on. Later in the day a valet de place handed to Fisher a small parcel, with the message: "Dr. Rapperschwyll supposes that this will be sufficient." The parcel contained two gold pieces of twenty marks.

Fisher gritted his teeth. "He shall have back his forty marks," he muttered to himself, "but I will have his confounded secret in return."

Then Fisher discovered that even a Polish countess has her uses in the social economy.

Mrs. Fisher's table d'hôte friend was amiability itself, when approached by Fisher (through Fisher's wife) on the subject of the Baron Savitch of Moscow. Know anything about the Baron Savitch? Of course she did, and about everybody else worth knowing in Europe. Would she kindly communicate her knowledge? Of course she would, and be enchanted to gratify in the slightest degree the charming curiosity of her Americaine. It was quite refreshing for a *blasée* old woman, who had long since ceased to feel much interest in contemporary men, women, things and events, to encounter one so recently from the boundless prairies of the new world as to cherish a piquant inquisitiveness about the affairs of the grand monde. Ah! yes, she would very willingly communicate the history of the Baron Savitch of Moscow, if that would amuse her dear Americaine.

The Polish countess abundantly redeemed her promise, throwing in for good measure many choice bits of gossip and scandalous anecdotes about the Russian nobility, which are not relevant to the present narrative. Her story, as summarized by Fisher, was this:

The Baron Savitch was not of an old creation. There was a mystery about his origin that had never been satisfactorily solved in St. Petersburg or in Moscow. It was said by some that he was a foundling from the Vospitatelnoi Dom. Others believed him to be the unacknowledged son of a certain illustrious personage nearly related to the House of Romanoff. The latter theory was the more probable, since it accounted in a measure for the unexampled success of his career from the day that he was graduated at the University of Dorpat.

Rapid and brilliant beyond precedent this career had been. He entered the diplomatic service of the Czar, and for several years was attached to the legations at Vienna, London, and Paris. Created a baron before his twenty-fifth birthday for the wonderful ability displayed in the conduct of negotiations of supreme importance and delicacy with the House of Hapsburg, he became a pet of Gortchakoff's, and was given every opportunity for the exercise of his genius in diplomacy. It was even said in well informed circles at St. Petersburg that the guiding mind which directed Russia's course throughout the entire Eastern complication, which planned the campaign on the Danube, effected the combinations that gave victory to the Czar's soldiers, and which meanwhile held Austria aloof, neutralized the immense power of Germany, and exasperated England only to the point where wrath expends itself in harmless threats, was the brain of the young Baron Savitch. It was certain that he had been with Ignatieff at Constantinople when the trouble was first fomented, with Shouvaloff in England at the time of the secret conference agreement, with the Grand Duke Nicholas at Adrianople when the protocol of an armistice was signed, and would soon be in Berlin behind the scenes of the Congress, where it was expected that he would outwit the statesmen of all Europe, and play with Bismarck and Disraeli as a strong man plays with two kicking babies.

But the countess had concerned herself very little with this handsome young man's achievements in politics. She had been more particularly interested in his social career. His success in that field had been not less remarkable. Although no one knew with positive certainty his father's name, he had conquered an absolute supremacy in the most exclusive circles surrounding the imperial court. His influence with the Czar himself was supposed to be unbounded. Birth apart, he was considered the best *parti* in Russia. From poverty and by the sheer force of intellect he had won for himself a colossal fortune. Report gave him forty million roubles, and doubtless report did not exceed the fact. Every speculative enterprise which he undertook, and they were many and various, was carried to sure success by the same qualities of cool, unerring judgment, far-reaching sagacity, and apparently superhuman power of organizing, combining, and controlling, which had made him in politics the phenomenon of the age.

About Dr. Rapperschwyll? Yes, the countess knew him by reputation and by sight. He was the medical man in constant attendance upon the Baron Savitch, whose high-strung mental organization rendered him susceptible to sudden and alarming attacks of illness. Dr. Rapperschwyll was a Swiss—had originally been a watchmaker or artisan of some kind, she had heard. For the rest, he was a commonplace little old man, devoted to his profession and to the baron, and evidently devoid of ambition, since he wholly neglected to turn the opportunities of his position and connections to the advancement of his personal fortunes.

Fortified with this information, Fisher felt better prepared to grapple with Rapperschwyll for the possession of the secret. For five days he lay in wait for the Swiss physician. On the sixth day the desired opportunity unexpectedly presented itself.

Half way up the Mercuriusberg, late in the afternoon, he encountered the custodian of the ruined tower, coming down. "No, the tower was not closed. A gentleman was up there, making observations of the country, and he, the custodian, would be back in an hour or two." So Fisher kept on his way.

The upper part of this tower is in a dilapidated condition. The lack of a stairway to the summit is supplied by a temporary wooden ladder. Fisher's head and shoulders were hardly through the trap that opens to the platform, before he discovered that the man already there was the man whom he sought. Dr. Rapperschwyll was studying the topography of the Black Forest through a pair of field glasses.

Fisher announced his arrival by an opportune stumble and a noisy effort to recover himself, at the same instant aiming a stealthy kick at the topmost round of the ladder, and scrambling ostentatiously over the edge of the trap. The ladder went down thirty or forty feet with a racket, clattering and banging against the walls of the tower.

Dr. Rapperschwyll at once appreciated the situation. He turned sharply around, and remarked with a sneer, "Monsieur is unaccountably awkward." Then he scowled and showed his teeth, for he recognized Fisher.

"It is rather unfortunate," said the New Yorker, with imperturbable coolness. "We shall be imprisoned here a couple of hours at the shortest. Let us congratulate ourselves that we each have intelligent company, besides a charming landscape to contemplate."

The Swiss coldly bowed, and resumed his topographical studies. Fisher lighted a cigar.

"I also desire," continued Fisher, puffing clouds of smoke in the direction of the Teufelmfihle, "to avail myself of this opportunity to return forty marks of yours, which reached me, I presume, by a mistake."

"If Monsieur the American physician was not satisfied with his fee," rejoined Rapperschwyll, venomously, "he can without doubt have the affair adjusted by applying to the baron's valet."

Fisher paid no attention to this thrust, but calmly laid the gold pieces upon the parapet, directly under the nose of the Swiss.

"I could not think of accepting any fee," he said, with deliberate emphasis. "I was abundantly rewarded for my trifling services by the novelty and interest of the case."

The Swiss scanned the American's countenance long and steadily with his sharp little gray eyes. At length he said, carelessly:

"Monsieur is a man of science?"

"Yes," replied Fisher, with a mental reservation in favour of all sciences save that which illuminates and dignifies our national game.

"Then," continued Dr. Rapperschwyll, "Monsieur will perhaps acknowledge that a more beautiful or more extensive case of trephining has rarely come under his observation."

Fisher slightly raised his eyebrows.

"And Monsieur will also understand, being a physician," continued Dr. Rapperschwyll, "the sensitiveness of the baron himself, and of his friends upon the subject. He will therefore pardon my seeming rudeness at the time of his discovery."

"He is smarter than I supposed," thought Fisher. "He holds all the cards, while

I have nothing—nothing, except a tolerably strong nerve when it comes to a game of bluff."

"I deeply regret that sensitiveness," he continued, aloud, "for it had occurred to me that an accurate account of what I saw, published in one of the scientific journals of England or America, would excite wide attention, and no doubt be received with interest on the Continent."

"What you saw?" cried the Swiss, sharply. "It is false. You saw nothing—when I entered you had not even removed the—"

Here he stopped short and muttered to himself, as if cursing his own impetuosity. Fisher celebrated his advantage by tossing away his half-burned cigar and lighting a fresh one.

"Since you compel me to be frank," Dr. Rapperschwyll went on, with visibly increasing nervousness, "I will inform you that the baron has assured me that you saw nothing. I interrupted you in the act of removing the silver cap."

"I will be equally frank," replied Fisher, stiffening his face for a final effort. "On that point, the baron is not a competent witness. He was in a state of unconsciousness for some time before you entered. Perhaps I was removing the silver cap when you interrupted me—"

Dr. Rapperschwyll turned pale.

"And, perhaps," said Fisher, coolly, "I was replacing it."

The suggestion of this possibility seemed to strike Rapperschwyll like a sudden thunderbolt from the clouds. His knees parted, and he almost sank to the floor. He put his hands before his eyes, and wept like a child, or, rather, like a broken old man.

"He will publish it! He will publish it to the court and to the world!" he cried, hysterically. "And at this crisis—"

Then, by a desperate effort, the Swiss appeared to recover to some extent his self-control. He paced the diameter of the platform for several minutes, with his head bent and his arms folded across the breast. Turning again to his companion, he said:

"If any sum you may name will—"

Fisher cut the proposition short with a laugh.

"Then," said Rapperschwyll, "if-if I throw myself on your generosity—"

"Well?" demanded Fisher.

"And ask a promise, on your honour, of absolute silence concerning what you have seen?"

"Silence until such time as the Baron Savitch shall have ceased to exist?"

"That will suffice," said Rapperschwyll. "For when he ceases to exist I die. And your conditions?"

"The whole story, here and now, and without reservation."

"It is a terrible price to ask me," said Rapperschwyll, "but larger interests than my pride are at stake. You shall hear the story.

"I was bred a watchmaker," he continued, after a long pause, "in the Canton of Zurich. It is not a matter of vanity when I say that I achieved a marvellous degree of skill in the craft. I developed a faculty of invention that led me into a series of experiments regarding the capabilities of purely mechanical combinations. I studied and improved upon the best automata ever constructed by human ingenuity. Babbage's calculating machine especially interested me. I saw in Babbage's idea the germ of something infinitely more important to the world.

"Then I threw up my business and went to Paris to study physiology. I spent three years at the Sorbonne and perfected myself in that branch of knowledge. Meanwhile, my pursuits had extended far beyond the purely physical sciences. Psychology engaged me for a time; and then I ascended into the domain of sociology, which, when adequately understood, is the summary and final application of all knowledge.

"It was after years of preparation, and as the outcome of all my studies, that the great idea of my life, which had vaguely haunted me ever since the Zurich days, assumed at last a well-defined and perfect form."

The manner of Dr. Rapperschwyll had changed from distrustful reluctance to frank enthusiasm. The man himself seemed transformed. Fisher listened attentively and without interrupting the relation. He could not help fancying that the necessity of yielding the secret, so long and so jealously guarded by the physician, was not entirely distasteful to the enthusiast.

"Now, attend, Monsieur," continued Dr. Rapperschwyll, "to several separate propositions which may seem at first to have no direct bearing on each other.

"My endeavours in mechanism had resulted in a machine which went far beyond Babbage's in its powers of calculation. Given the data, there was no limit to the possibilities in this direction. Babbage's cogwheels and pinions calculated logarithms, calculated an eclipse. It was fed with figures, and produced results in figures. Now, the relations of cause and effect are as fixed and unalterable as the laws of arithmetic. Logic is, or should be, as exact a science as mathematics. My new machine was fed with facts, and produced conclusions. In short, it reasoned; and the results of its reasoning were always true, while the results of human reasoning are often, if not always, false. The source of error in human logic is what the philosophers call the 'personal equation.' My machine eliminated the personal equation; it proceeded from cause to effect, from premise to conclusion, with steady precision. The human intellect is fallible; my machine was, and is, infallible in its processes.

"Again, physiology and anatomy had taught me the fallacy of the medical superstition which holds the gray matter of the brain and the vital principle to be inseparable. I had seen men living with pistol balls imbedded in the medulla oblongata. I had seen the hemispheres and the cerebellum removed from the crania of birds and small animals, and yet they did not die. I believed that, though the brain were to be removed from a human skull, the subject would not die, although he would certainly be divested of the intelligence which governed all save the purely involuntary actions of his body.

"Once more: a profound study of history from the sociological point of view, and a not inconsiderable practical experience of human nature, had convinced me that the greatest geniuses that ever existed were on a plane not so very far removed above the level of average intellect. The grandest peaks in my native country, those which all the world knows by name, tower only a few hundred feet above the countless unnamed peaks that surround them. Napoleon Bonaparte towered only a little over the ablest men around him. Yet that little was everything, and he overran Europe. A man who surpassed Napoleon, as Napoleon surpassed Murat, in the mental qualities which transmute thought into fact, would have made himself master of the whole world.

"Now, to fuse these three propositions into one: suppose that I take a man, and, by removing the brain that enshrines all the errors and failures of his ancestors away back to the origin of the race, remove all sources of weakness in his future career. Suppose, that in place of the fallible intellect which I have removed, I endow him with an artificial intellect that operates with the certainty of universal laws. Suppose that I launch this superior being, who reasons truly, into the burly burly of his inferiors, who reason falsely, and await the inevitable result with the tranquillity of a philosopher.

"Monsieur, you have my secret. That is precisely what I have done. In Moscow, where my friend Dr. Duchat had charge of the new institution of St. Vasili for hopeless idiots, I found a boy of eleven whom they called Stépan Borovitch. Since he was born, he had not seen, heard, spoken or thought. Nature had granted him, it was believed, a fraction of the sense of smell, and perhaps a fraction of the sense of taste, but of even this there was no positive ascertainment. Nature had walled in his soul most effectually. Occasional inarticulate murmurings, and an incessant knitting and kneading of the fingers were his only manifestations of energy. On bright days they would place him in a little rocking-chair, in some spot where the sun fell warm, and he would rock to and fro for hours, working his slender fingers and mumbling forth his satisfaction at the warmth in the plaintive and unvarying refrain of idiocy. The boy was thus situated when I first saw him.

"I begged Stépan Borovitch of my good friend Dr. Duchat. If that excellent man had not long since died he should have shared in my triumph. I took Stépan to my home and plied the saw and the knife. I could operate on that poor, worthless, useless, hopeless travesty of humanity as fearlessly and as recklessly as upon a dog bought or caught for vivisection. That was a little more than twenty years ago. Today Stépan Borovitch wields more power than any other man on the face of the earth. In ten years he will be the autocrat of Europe, the master of the world. He never errs; for the machine that reasons beneath his silver skull never makes a mistake."

Fisher pointed downward at the old custodian of the tower, who was seen toiling up the hill.

"Dreamers," continued Dr. Rapperschwyll, "have speculated on the possibility of finding among the ruins of the older civilizations some brief inscription which shall change the foundations of human knowledge. Wiser men deride the dream, and laugh at the idea of scientific kabbala. The wiser men are fools. Suppose that Aristotle had discovered on a cuneiform-covered tablet at Nineveh the few words, 'Survival of the Fittest.' Philosophy would have gained twenty-two hundred years. I will give you, in almost as few words, a truth equally pregnant. The ultimate evolution of the creature is into the creator. Perhaps it will be twenty-two hundred years before the truth finds general acceptance, yet it is not the less a truth. The Baron Savitch is my creature, and I am his creator—creator of the ablest man in Europe, the ablest man in the world.

"Here is our ladder, Monsieur. I have fulfilled my part of the agreement. Remember yours."

III

After a two months' tour of Switzerland and the Italian lakes, the Fishers found themselves at the Hotel Splendide in Paris, surrounded by people from the States. It was a relief to Fisher, after his somewhat bewildering experience at Baden, followed by a surfeit of stupendous and ghostly snow peaks, to be once more among those who discriminated between a straight flush and a crooked straight, and whose bosoms thrilled responsive to his own at the sight of the star-spangled banner. It was particularly agreeable for him to find at the Hotel Splendide, in a party of Easterners who had come over to see the Exposition, Miss Bella Ward, of Portland, a pretty and bright girl, affianced to his best friend in New York.

With much less pleasure, Fisher learned that the Baron Savitch was in Paris, fresh from the Berlin Congress, and that he was the lion of the hour with the select few who read between the written lines of politics and knew the dummies of diplomacy from the real players in the tremendous game. Dr. Rapperschwyll was not with the baron. He was detained in Switzerland, at the death-bed of his aged mother.

This last piece of information was welcome to Fisher. The more he reflected upon the interview on the Mercuriusberg, the more strongly he felt it to be his intellectual duty to persuade himself that the whole affair was an illusion, not a reality. He would have been glad, even at the sacrifice of his confidence in his own astuteness, to believe that the Swiss doctor had been amusing himself at the expense of his credulity. But the remembrance of the scene in the baron's bedroom at the Badischer Hof was too vivid to leave the slightest ground for this theory. He was obliged to be content with the thought that he should soon place the broad Atlantic between himself and a creature so unnatural, so dangerous, so monstrously impossible as the Baron Savitch.

Hardly a week had passed before he was thrown again into the society of that impossible person.

The ladies of the American party met the Russian baron at a ball in the New Continental Hotel. They were charmed with his handsome face, his refinement of manner, his intelligence and wit. They met him again at the American Minister's, and, to Fisher's unspeakable consternation, the acquaintance thus established began to make rapid progress in the direction of intimacy. Baron Savitch became a frequent visitor at the Hotel Splendide.

Fisher does not like to dwell upon this period. For a month his peace of mind was rent alternately by apprehension and disgust. He is compelled to admit that the baron's demeanor toward himself was most friendly, although no allusion was made on either side to the incident at Baden. But the knowledge that no good could come to his friends from this association with a being in whom the moral principle had no doubt been supplanted by a system of cog-gear, kept him continually in a state of distraction. He would gladly have explained to his American friends the true character of the Russian, that he was not a man of healthy mental organization, but merely a marvel of mechanical ingenuity, constructed upon a principle subversive of all society as at present constituted—in short, a monster whose very existence must ever be revolting to right-minded persons with brains of honest gray and white. But the solemn promise to Dr. Rapperschwyll sealed his lips.

A trifling incident suddenly opened his eyes to the alarming character of the situation, and filled his heart with a new horror.

One evening, a few days before the date designated for the departure of the American party from Havre for home, Fisher happened to enter the private parlour which was, by common consent, the headquarters of his set. At first he thought that the room was unoccupied. Soon he perceived, in the recess of a window, and partly obscured by the drapery of the curtain, the forms of the Baron Savitch and Miss Ward of Portland. They did not observe his entrance. Miss Ward's hand was in the baron's hand, and she was looking up into his handsome face with an expression which Fisher could not misinterpret.

Fisher coughed, and going to another window, pretended to be interested in affairs on the Boulevard. The couple emerged from the recess. Miss Ward's face was ruddy with confusion, and she immediately withdrew. Not a sign of embarrassment was visible on the baron's countenance. He greeted Fisher with perfect self-possession, and began to talk of the great balloon in the Place du Carrousel.

Fisher pitied but could not blame the young lady. He believed her still loyal at heart to her New York engagement. He knew that her loyalty could not be shaken by the blandishments of any man on earth. He recognized the fact that she was under the spell of a power more than human. Yet what would be the outcome? He could not tell her all; his promise bound him. It would be useless to appeal to the generosity of the baron; no human sentiments governed his exorable purposes. Must the affair drift on while he stood tied and helpless? Must this charming and innocent girl be sacrificed to the transient whim of an automaton? Allowing that the baron's intentions were of the most honourable character, was the situation any less horrible? Marry a Machine! His own loyalty to his friend in New York, his regard for Miss Ward, alike loudly called on him to act with promptness.

And, apart from all private interest, did he not owe a plain duty to society, to the liberties of the world? Was Savitch to be permitted to proceed in the career laid out for him by his creator, Dr. Rapperschwyll? He (Fisher) was the only man in the world in a position to thwart the ambitious programme. Was there ever greater need of a Brutus?

Between doubts and fears, the last days of Fisher's stay in Paris were wretched beyond description. On the morning of the steamer day he had almost made up his mind to act.

The train for Havre departed at noon, and at eleven o'clock the Baron Savitch made his appearance at the Hotel Splendide to bid farewell to his American friends. Fisher watched Miss Ward closely. There was a constraint in her manner which fortified his resolution. The baron incidentally remarked that he should make it his duty and pleasure to visit America within a very few months, and that he hoped then to renew the acquaintances now interrupted. As Savitch spoke, Fisher observed that his eyes met Miss Ward's, while the slightest possible blush coloured her cheeks. Fisher knew that the case was desperate, and demanded a desperate remedy.

He now joined the ladies of the party in urging the baron to join them in the hasty lunch that was to precede the drive to the station. Savitch gladly accepted the cordial invitation. Wine he politely but firmly declined, pleading the absolute prohibition of his physician. Fisher left the room for an instant, and returned with the black bottle which had figured in the Baden episode.

"The Baron," he said, "has already expressed his approval of the noblest of our American products, and he knows that this beverage has good medical endorsement." So saying, he poured the remaining contents of the Kentucky bottle into a glass, and presented it to the Russian.

Savitch hesitated. His previous experience with the nectar was at the same time a temptation and a warning, yet he did not wish to seem discourteous. A chance remark from Miss Ward decided him.

"The baron," she said, with a smile, "will certainly not refuse to wish us *bon voyage* in the American fashion."

Savitch drained the glass and the conversation turned to other matters. The carriages were already below. The parting compliments were being made, when Savitch suddenly pressed his hands to his forehead and clutched at the back of a chair. The ladies gathered around him in alarm.

"It is nothing," he said faintly; "a temporary dizziness."

"There is no time to be lost," said Fisher, pressing forward. "The train leaves in twenty minutes. Get ready at once, and I will meanwhile attend to our friend."

Fisher hurriedly led the baron to his own bedroom. Savitch fell back upon the bed. The Baden symptoms repeated themselves. In two minutes the Russian was unconscious.

Fisher looked at his watch. He had three minutes to spare. He turned the key in the lock of the door and touched the knob of the electric annunciator.

Then, gaining the mastery of his nerves by one supreme effort for self-control, Fisher pulled the deceptive wig and the black skullcap from the baron's head. "Heaven forgive me if I am making a fearful mistake!" he thought. But I believe it to be best for ourselves and for the world." Rapidly, but with a steady hand, he unscrewed the silver dome. The Mechanism lay exposed before his eyes. The baron groaned. Ruthlessly Fisher tore out the wondrous machine. He had no time and no inclination to examine it. He caught up a newspaper and hastily enfolded it. He thrust the bundle into his open travelling bag. Then he screwed the silver top firmly upon the baron's head, and replaced the skullcap and the wig.

All this was done before the servant answered the bell. "The Baron Savitch is ill," said Fisher to the attendant, when he came. "There is no cause for alarm. Send at once to the Hotel de l'Athénée for his valet, Auguste." In twenty seconds Fisher was in a cab, whirling toward the Station St. Lazare.

When the steamship Pereire was well out at sea, with Ushant five hundred miles in her wake, and countless fathoms of water beneath her keel, Fisher took a newspaper parcel from his traveling bag. His teeth were firm set and his lips rigid. He carried the heavy parcel to the side of the ship and dropped it into the Atlantic. It made a little eddy in the smooth water, and sank out of sight. Fisher fancied that he heard a wild, despairing cry, and put his hands to his ears to shut out the sound. A gull came circling over the steamer—the cry may have been the gull's.

Fisher felt a light touch upon his arm. He turned quickly around. Miss Ward was standing at his side, close to the rail.

"Bless me, how white you are!" she said. "What in the world have you been doing?"

"I have been preserving the liberties of two continents," slowly replied Fisher, "and perhaps saving your own peace of mind."

"Indeed!" said she; "and how have you done that?"

"I have done it," was Fisher's grave answer, "by throwing overboard the Baron Savitch."

Miss Ward burst into a ringing laugh. "You are sometimes too droll, Mr. Fisher," she said.

THE CRYSTAL MAN

by Edward Page Mitchell

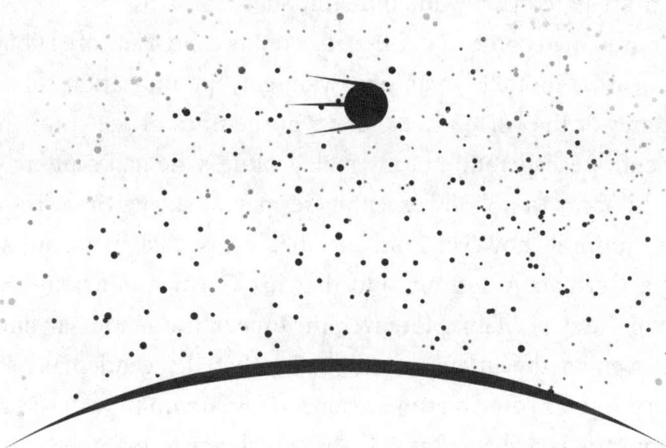

I

Rapidly turning into the Fifth Avenue from one of the cross streets above the old reservoir, at quarter past eleven o'clock on the night of November 6, 1879, I ran plump into an individual coming the other way.

It was very dark on this corner. I could see nothing of the person with whom I had the honour to be in collision. Nevertheless, the quick habit of a mind accustomed to induction had furnished me with several well-defined facts regarding him before I fairly recovered from the shock of the encounter.

These were some of the facts: He was a heavier man than myself, and stiffer in the legs; but he lacked precisely three inches and a half of my stature. He wore a silk hat, a cape or cloak of heavy woollen material, and rubber overshoes or arctics. He was about thirty-five years old, born in America, educated at a German university, either Heidelberg or Freiburg, naturally of hasty temper, but considerate and courteous, in his demeanour to others. He was not entirely at peace with society: there was something in his life or in his present errand which he desired to conceal.

How did I know all this when I had not seen the stranger, and when only a single monosyllable had escaped his lips? Well, I knew that he was stouter than myself, and firmer on his foot, because it was I, not he, who recoiled. I knew that I was just three inches and a half taller than he, for the tip of my nose was still tingling from its contact with the stiff, sharp brim of his hat. My hand, involuntarily raised, had come under the edge of his cape. He wore rubber shoes, for I had not heard a footfall. To an observant ear; the indications of age are as plain in the tones of the voice as to the eye in the lines of the countenance. In the first moment of exasperation of my maladroitness, he had muttered "Ox!" a term that would occur to nobody except a German at such a time. The pronunciation of the guttural, however, told me that the speaker was an American German, not a German American, and that his German education had been derived south of the river Main. Moreover, the tone of the gentleman and scholar was manifest even in the utterance of wrath. That the gentleman was in no particular hurry, but for some reason anxious to remain unknown; was a conclusion drawn from the fact that, after listening in silence to my polite apology, he stooped to recover and restore to me my umbrella, and then passed on as noiselessly as he had approached.

I make it a point to verify my conclusions when possible. So I turned back into the cross street and followed the stranger toward a lamp part way down the block. Certainly, I was not more than five seconds behind him. There was no other road that he could have taken. No house door had opened and closed along the way. And yet, when we came into the light, the form that ought to have been directly in front of me did not appear. Neither man nor man's shadow was visible.

Hurrying on as fast as I could walk to the next gaslight, I paused under the lamp and listened. The street was apparently deserted. The rays from the yellow flame reached only a little way into the darkness. The steps and doorway, however, of the brownstone house facing the street lamp were sufficiently illuminated. The gilt figures above the door were distinct. I recognized the house: the number was a familiar one. While I stood under the gaslight, waiting, I heard a slight noise on these steps, and the click of a key in a lock. The vestibule door of the house was slowly opened, and then closed with a slam that echoed across the street. Almost immediately followed the sound of the opening and shutting of the inner door. Nobody had come out. As far as my eyes could be trusted to report an event hardly ten feet away and in broad light, nobody had gone in.

With a notion that here was scanty material for an exact application of the inductive process, I stood a long time wildly guessing at the philosophy of the strange occurrence. I felt that vague sense of the unexplainable which amounts almost to dread. It was a relief to hear steps on the sidewalk opposite, and turning, to see a policeman swinging his long black club and watching me.

II

This house of chocolate brown, whose front door opened and shut at midnight without indications of human agency, was, as I have said, well known to me. I had left it not more than ten minutes earlier, after spending the evening with my friend Bliss and his daughter Pandora. The house was of the sort in which each storey constitutes a domicile complete in itself. The second floor, or flat, had been inhabited by Bliss since his return from abroad; that is to say, for a twelvemonth. I held Bliss in esteem for his excellent qualities of heart, while his deplorably illogical and unscientific mind commanded my profound pity. I adored Pandora.

Be good enough to understand that my admiration for Pandora Bliss was hopeless, and not only hopeless, but resigned to its hopelessness. In our circle of acquaintance there was a tacit covenant that the young lady's peculiar position as a flirt wedded to a memory should be at all times respected. We adored Pandora mildly, not passionately—just enough to feed her coquetry without excoriating the seared surface of her widowed heart. On her part, Pandora conducted herself with signal propriety. She did not sigh too obtrusively when she flirted: and she always kept her flirtations so well in hand that she could cut them short whenever the fond, sad recollections came.

It was considered proper for us to tell Pandora that she owed it to her youth and beauty to put aside the dead past like a closed book, and to urge her respectfully to come forth into the living present. It was not considered proper to press the subject after she had once replied that this was forever impossible.

The particulars of the tragic episode in Miss Pandora's European experience were not accurately known to us. It was understood, in a vague way, that she had loved while abroad, and trifled with her lover: that he had disappeared, leaving her in ignorance of his fate and in perpetual remorse for her capricious behaviour. From Bliss I had gathered a few, sporadic facts, not coherent enough to form a history of the case. There was no reason to believe that Pandora's lover had committed suicide. His name was Flack. He was a scientific man. In Bliss's opinion he was a fool. In Bliss's opinion Pandora was a fool to pine on his account. In Bliss's opinion all scientific men were more or less fools.

III

That year I ate Thanksgiving dinner with the Blisses. In the evening I sought to astonish the company by reciting the mysterious events on the night of my collision with the stranger. The story failed to produce the expected sensation. Two or three odious people exchanged glances. Pandora, who was unusually pensive, listened with seeming indifference. Her father, in his stupid inability to grasp anything outside the commonplace, laughed outright, and even went so far as to question my trustworthiness as an observer of phenomena.

Somewhat nettled, and perhaps a little shaken in my own faith in the marvel, I made an excuse to withdraw early. Pandora accompanied me to the threshold. "Your story," said she, "interested me strangely. I, too, could report occurrences in and about this house which would surprise you. I believe I am not wholly in the dark. The sorrowful past casts a glimmer of light—but let us not be hasty. For my sake probe the matter to the bottom."

The young woman sighed as she bade me good night. I thought I heard a second sigh, in a deeper tone than hers, and too distinct to be a reverberation.

I began to go downstairs. Before I had descended half a dozen steps I felt a man's hand laid rather heavily upon my shoulder from behind. My first idea was that Bliss had followed me into the hall to apologize for his rudeness. I turned around to meet his friendly overture. Nobody was in sight.

Again the hand touched my arm. I shuddered in spite of my philosophy.

This time the hand gently pulled at my coat sleeve, as if to invite me upstairs. I ascended a step or two, and the pressure on my arm was relaxed. I paused, and the silent invitation was repeated with an urgency that left no doubt as to what was wanted.

We mounted the stairs together, the presence leading the way, I following. What an extraordinary journey it was! The halls were bright with gaslight. By the testimony of my eyes there was no one but myself upon the stairway. Closing my eyes, the illusion, if illusion it could be called, was perfect. I could hear the creaking of the stairs ahead of me, the soft but distinctly audible footfalls synchronous with my own, even the regular breathing of my companion and guide. Extending my arm, I could touch and finger the skirt of his garment—a heavy woollen cloak lined with silk.

Suddenly I opened my eyes. They told me again that I was absolutely alone.

This problem then presented itself to mind: How to determine whether vision was playing me false, while the senses of hearing and feeling correctly informed me, or whether my ears and touch lied, while my eyes reported the truth. Who shall be arbiter when the senses contradict each other? The reasoning faculty? Reason was inclined to recognize the presence of an intelligent being, whose existence was flatly denied by the most trusted of the senses.

We reached the topmost floor of the house. The door leading out of the public hall opened for me, apparently of its own accord. A curtain within seemed to draw itself aside, and hold itself aside long enough to give me ingress to an apartment wherein every appointment spoke of good taste and scholarly habits. A wood fire was burning in the chimney place. The walls were covered with books and pictures. The lounging chairs were capacious and inviting. There was nothing in the room uncanny, nothing weird, nothing different from the furniture of everyday flesh and blood existence.

By this time I had cleared my mind of the last lingering suspicion of the supernatural. These phenomena were perhaps not inexplicable; all that I lacked was the key. The behaviour of my unseen host argued his amicable disposition. I was able to watch with perfect calmness a series of manifestations of independent energy on the part of inanimate objects.

In the first place, a great Turkish easy chair wheeled itself out of a corner of the room and approached the hearth. Then a square-backed Queen Anne chair started from another corner, advancing until it was planted directly opposite the first. A little tripod table lifted itself a few inches above the floor and took a position between the two chairs. A thick octavo volume backed out of its place on the shelf and sailed tranquilly through the air at the height of three or four feet, landing neatly on top of the table. A finely painted porcelain pipe left a hook on the wall and joined the volume. A tobacco box jumped from the mantlepiece. The door of a cabinet swung open, and a decanter and wineglass made the journey in company, arriving simultaneously at the same destination. Everything in the room seemed instinct with the spirit of hospitality.

I seated myself in the easy chair, filled the wineglass, lighted the pipe, and examined the volume. It was the Handbuch der Gewebelehre of Bussius of Vienna. When I had replaced the book upon the table, it deliberately opened itself at the four hundred and forty-third page.

"You are not nervous?" demanded a voice, not four feet from my tympanum.

IV

This voice had a familiar sound. I recognized it as the voice that I heard in the street on the night of November 6, when it called me an ox.

"No," I said. "I am not nervous. I am a man of science, accustomed to regard all phenomena as explainable by natural laws, provided we can discover the laws. No, I am not frightened."

"So much the better. You are a man of science, like myself"—here the voice groaned—"a man of nerve, and a friend of Pandora's."

"Pardon me," I interposed. "Since a lady's name is introduced it would be well to know with whom or with what I am speaking."

"That is precisely what I desire to communicate," replied the voice, "before I ask you to render me a great service. My name is or was Stephen Flack. I am or have been a citizen of the United States. My exact status at present is as great a mystery to myself as it can possibly be to you. But I am, or was, an honest man and a gentleman, and I offer you my hand."

I saw no hand. I reached forth my own, however, and it met the pressure of warm, living fingers.

"Now," resumed the voice, after this silent pact of friendship, "be good enough to read the passage at which I have opened the book upon the table."

Here is a rough translation of what I read in German:

As the colour of the organic tissues constituting the body depends upon the presence of certain proximate principles of the third class, all containing iron as one of the ultimate elements, it follows that the hue may vary according to well-defined chemico-physiological changes. An excess of hematin in the blood globules gives a ruddier tinge to every tissue. The melanin that colours the choroid of the eye, the iris, the hair, may be increased or diminished according to laws recently formulated by Schardt of Basel. In the epidermis the excess of melanin makes the Negro, the deficient supply the albino. The hematin and the melanin, together with the greenish-yellow biliverdine and the reddish-yellow urokacine, are the pigments which impart colour character to tissues otherwise transparent, or nearly so. I deplore my inability to record the result of some highly interesting histological experiments conducted by that indefatigable investigator Fröliker in achieving success in the way of separating pink discolouration of the human body by chemical means.

"For five years," continued my unseen companion when I had finished reading, "I was Fröliker's student and laboratory assistant at Freiburg. Bussius only half guessed at the importance of our experiments. We reached results which were so astounding that public policy required they should not be published, even to the scientific world. Fröliker died a year ago last August.

"I had faith in the genius of this great thinker and admirable man. If he had rewarded my unquestioning loyalty with full confidence, I should not now be a miserable wretch. But his natural reserve, and the jealousy with which all savants guard their unverified results, kept me ignorant of the essential formulas governing our experiments. As his disciple I was familiar with the laboratory details of the work; the master alone possessed the radical secret. The consequence is that I have been led into a misfortune more appalling than has been the lot of any human being since the primal curse fell upon Cain.

"Our efforts were at first directed to the enlargement and variation of the quantity of pigmentary matter in the system. By increasing the proportion of melanin, for instance, conveyed in food to the blood, we were able to make a fair man dark, a dark man black as an African. There was scarcely a hue we could not impart to the skin by modifying and varying our combinations. The experiments were usually tried on me. At different times I have been copper-coloured, violet blue, crimson, and chrome yellow. For one triumphant week I exhibited in my person all the colours of the rainbow. There still remains a witness to the interesting character of our work during this period."

The voice paused, and in a few seconds a hand bell upon the mantel was sounded. Presently an old man with a close-fitting skullcap shuffled into the room.

"Käspar," said the voice, in German, "show the gentleman your hair."

Without manifesting any surprise, and as if perfectly accustomed to receive commands addressed to him out of vacancy, the old domestic bowed and removed his cap. The scanty locks thus discovered were of a lustrous emerald green. I expressed my astonishment.

"The gentleman finds your hair very beautiful," said the voice, again in German. "That is all, Käspar."

Replacing his cap, the domestic withdrew, with a look of gratified vanity on his face.

"Old Käspar was Fröliker's servant, and is now mine. He was the subject of one of our first applications of the process. The worthy man was so pleased with the result that he would never permit us to restore his hair to its original red. He is a faithful soul, and my only intermediary and representative in the visible world.

"Now," continued Flack, "to the story of my undoing. The great histologist with whom it was my privilege to be associated, next turned his attention to another and still more interesting branch of the investigation. Hitherto he had sought merely to increase or to modify the pigments in the tissues. He now began a series of experiments as to the possibility of eliminating those pigments altogether from the system by absorption, exudation, and the use of the chlorides and other chemical agents acting on organic matter. He was only too successful!

"Again I was the subject of experiments which Fröliker supervised, imparting to me only so much of the secret of this process as was unavoidable. For weeks at a time I remained in his private laboratory, seeing no one and seen by no one excepting the professor and the trustworthy Käspar. Herr Fröliker proceeded with caution, closely watching the effect of each new test, and advancing by degrees. He never went so far in one experiment that he was unable to withdraw at discretion. He always kept open an easy road for retreat. For that reason I felt myself perfectly safe in his hands and submitted to whatever he required.

"Under the action of the etiolating drugs which the professor administered in connection with powerful detergents, I became at first pale, white, colourless as an albino, but without suffering in general health. My hair and beard looked like spun glass and my skin like marble. The professor was satisfied with his results, and went no further at this time. He restored to me my normal colour.

"In the next experiment, and in those succeeding, he allowed his chemical agents to take firmer hold upon the tissues of my body. I became not only white, like a bleached man, but slightly translucent, like a porcelain figure. Then again he paused for a while, giving me back my colour and allowing me to go forth into the world. Two months later I was more than translucent. You have seen floating those sea radiates, the medusa or jellyfish, their outlines almost invisible to the eye. Well, I became in the air like a jellyfish in the water. Almost perfectly transparent, it was only by close inspection that old Käspar could discover my whereabouts in the room when he came to bring me food. It was Käspar who ministered to my wants at times when I was cloistered."

"But your clothing?" I inquired, interrupting Flack's narrative. "That must have stood out in strong contrast with the dim aspect of your body."

"Ah, no," said Flack. "The spectacle of an apparently empty suit of clothes moving about the laboratory was too grotesque even for the grave professor. For the protection of his gravity he was obliged to devise a way to apply his process to dead organic matter, such as the wool of my cloak, the cotton of my shirts, and the leather of my shoes. Thus I came to be equipped with the outfit which still serves me.

"It was at this stage of our progress, when we had almost attained perfect transparency, and therefore complete invisibility, that I met Pandora Bliss.

"A year ago last July, in one of the intervals of our experimenting, and at a time when I presented my natural appearance, I went into the Schwarzwald to recuperate. I first saw and admired Pandora at the little village of St. Blasien. They had come from the Falls of the Rhine, and were travelling north; I turned around and travelled north. At the Stern Inn I loved Pandora; at the summit of the Feldberg I madly worshipped her. In the Höllenpass I was ready to sacrifice my life for a gracious word from her lips. On Hornisgrinde I besought her permission to throw myself from the top of the mountain into the gloomy waters of the Mummelsee in order to prove my devotion. You know Pandora. Since you know her, there is no need to apologize for the rapid growth of my infatuation. She flirted with me, laughed with me, laughed at me, drove with me, walked with me through byways in the green woods, climbed with me up aeclivities so steep that climbing together was one delicious, prolonged embrace; talked science with me, and sentiment; listened to my hopes and enthusiasm, snubbed me, froze me, maddened me—all at her sweet will, and all while her matter-of-fact papa dozed in the coffee rooms of the inns over the financial columns of the latest New York newspapers. But whether she loved me I know not to this day.

"When Pandora's father learned what my pursuits were, and what my prospects, he brought our little idyll to an abrupt termination. I think he classed me somewhere between the professional jugglers and the quack doctors. In vain I explained to him that I should be famous and probably rich. 'When you are famous and rich,' he remarked with a grin, 'I shall be pleased to see you at my office in Broad Street.' He carried Pandora off to Paris, and I returned to Freiburg.

"A few weeks later, one bright afternoon in August, I stood in Fröliker's laboratory unseen by four persons who were almost within the radius of my arm's length. Käspar was behind me, washing some test tubes. Fröliker, with a proud smile upon his face, was gazing intently at the place where he knew I ought to be. Two brother professors, summoned on some pretext, were unconsciously almost jostling me with their elbows as they discussed I know not what trivial question. They could have heard my heart beat. 'By the way, Herr Professor,' one asked as he was about to depart, 'has your assistant, Herr Flack, returned from his vacation?' This test was perfect.

"As soon as we were alone, Professor Fröliker grasped my invisible hand, as you have grasped it tonight. He was in high spirits.

"'My dear fellow,' he said, 'tomorrow crowns our work. You shall appear—or rather not appear—before the assembled faculty of the university. I have telegraphed invitations to Heidelberg, to Bonn, to Berlin. Schrotter, Haeckel, Steinmetz, Lavallo, will be here. Our triumph will be in presence of the most eminent physicists of the age. I shall then disclose those secrets of our process which I have hitherto withheld even from you, my co-labourer and trusted friend. But you shall share the glory. What is this I hear about the forest bird that has flown? My boy, you shall be restocked with pigment and go to Paris to seek her with fame in your hands and the blessings of science on your head.'

"The next morning, the nineteenth of August, before I had arisen from my cot bed, Käspar hastily entered the laboratory.

"'Herr Flack! Herr Flack!' he gasped, 'the Herr Doctor Professor is dead of apoplexy.'"

V

The narrative had come to an end. I sat a long time thinking. What could I do? What could I say? In what shape could I offer consolation to this unhappy man?

Flack, the invisible, was sobbing bitterly.

He was the first to speak. "It is hard, hard, hard! For no crime in the eyes of man, for no sin in the sight of God, I have been condemned to a fate ten thousand times worse than hell. I must walk the earth, a man, living, seeing, loving, like other men, while between me and all that makes life worth having there is a barrier fixed forever. Even ghosts have shapes. My life is living death; my existence oblivion. No friend can look me in the face. Were I to clasp to my breast the woman I love, it would only be to inspire terror inexpressible. I see her almost every day. I brush against her skirts as I pass her on the stairs. Did she love me? Does she love me? Would not that knowledge make the curse still more cruel? Yet it was to learn the truth that I brought you here."

Then I made the greatest mistake of my life.

"Cheer up!" I said. "Pandora has always loved you."

By the sudden overturning of the table I knew with what vehemence Flack sprang to his feet. His two hands had my shoulders in a fierce grip.

"Yes," I continued; "Pandora has been faithful to your memory. There is no reason to despair. The secret of Fröliker's process died with him, but why should it not be rediscovered by experiment and induction *ab initio*, with the aid which you can render? Have courage and hope. She loves you. In five minutes you shall hear it from her own lips."

No wail of pain that I ever heard was half so pathetic as his wild cry of joy.

I hurried downstairs and summoned Miss Bliss into the hall. In a few words I explained the situation. To my surprise, she neither fainted nor went into hysterics. "Certainly, I will accompany you," she said, with a smile which I could not then interpret.

She followed me into Flack's room, calmly scrutinizing every corner of the apartment, with the set smile still upon her face. Had she been entering a ball-room she could not have shown greater self-possession. She manifested no astonishment, no terror, when her hand was seized by invisible hands and covered with kisses from invisible lips. She listened with composure to the torrent of loving and caressing words which my unfortunate friend poured into her ears.

Perplexed and uneasy, I watched the strange scene.

Presently Miss Bliss withdrew her hand.

"Really, Mr. Flack," she said with a light laugh, "you are sufficiently demonstrative. Did you acquire the habit on the Continent?"

"Pandora!" I heard him say, "I do not understand."

"Perhaps," she calmly went on, "you regard it as one of the privileges of your invisibility. Let me congratulate you on the success of your experiment. What a clever man your professor—what is his name?—must be. You can make a fortune by exhibiting yourself."

Was this the woman who for months had paraded her inconsolable sorrow for the loss of this very man? I was stupefied. Who shall undertake to analyze the motives of a coquette? What science is profound enough to unravel her unconscionable whims?

"Pandora!" he exclaimed again, in a bewildered voice. "What does it mean? Why do you receive me in this manner? Is that all you have to say to me?"

"I believe that is all," she coolly replied, moving toward the door. "You are a gentleman, and I need not ask you to spare me any further annoyance."

"Your heart is quartz," I whispered, as she passed me in going out. "You are unworthy of him."

Flack's despairing cry brought Käspar into the room. With the instinct acquired by long and faithful service, the old man went straight to the place where his master was. I saw him clutch at the air, as if struggling with and seeking to detain the invisible man. He was flung violently aside. He recovered himself and stood an instant listening, his neck distended, his face pale. Then he rushed out of the door and down the stairs. I followed him.

The street door of the house was open. On the sidewalk Käspar hesitated a few seconds. It was toward the west that he finally turned, running down the street with such speed that I had the utmost difficulty to keep at his side.

It was near midnight. We crossed avenue after avenue. An inarticulate murmur of satisfaction escaped old Käspar's lips. A little way ahead of us we saw a man, standing at one of the avenue corners, suddenly thrown to the ground. We sped on, never relaxing our pace. I now heard rapid footfalls a short distance in advance of us. I clutched Käspar's arm. He nodded.

Almost breathless, I was conscious that we were no longer treading upon pavement, but on boards and amid a confusion of lumber. In front of us were no more lights; only blank vacancy. Käspar gave one mighty spring. He clutched, missed, and fell back with a cry of horror.

There was a dull splash in the black waters of the river at our feet.

A THOUSAND DEATHS

by Jack London

I had been in the water about an hour, and cold, exhausted, with a terrible cramp in my right calf, it seemed as though my hour had come. Fruitlessly struggling against the strong ebb tide, I had beheld the maddening procession of the water-front lights slip by, but now I gave up attempting to breast the stream and contended myself with the bitter thoughts of a wasted career, now drawing to a close.

It had been my luck to come of good, English stock, but of parents whose account with the bankers far exceeded their knowledge of child-nature and the rearing of children. While born with a silver spoon in my mouth, the blessed atmosphere of the home circle was to me unknown. My father, a very learned man and a celebrated antiquarian, gave no thought to his family, being constantly lost in the abstractions of his study; while my mother, noted far more for her good looks than her good sense, sated herself with the adulation of the society in which she was perpetually plunged. I went through the regular school and college routine of a boy of the English bourgeoisie, and as the years brought me increasing strength and passions, my parents suddenly became aware that I was possessed of an immortal soul, and endeavoured to draw the curb. But it was too late; I perpetrated the wildest and most audacious folly, and was disowned by my people, ostracised by the society I had so long outraged, and with the thousand pounds my father gave me, with the declaration that he would neither see me again nor give me more, I took a first-class passage to Australia.

Since then my life had been one long peregrination—from the Orient to the Occident, from the Arctic to the Antarctic—to find myself at last, an able seaman at thirty, in the full vigour of my manhood, drowning in San Francisco bay because of a disastrously successful attempt to desert my ship.

My right leg was drawn up by the cramp, and I was suffering the keenest agony. A slight breeze stirred up a choppy sea, which washed into my mouth and down my throat, nor could I prevent it. Though I still contrived to keep afloat, it was merely mechanical, for I was rapidly becoming unconscious. I have a dim recollection of drifting past the sea-wall, and of catching a glimpse of an upriver steamer's starboard light; then everything became a blank.

* * * * *

I heard the low hum of insect life, and felt the balmy air of a spring morning fanning my cheek. Gradually it assumed a rhythmic flow, to whose soft pulsations my body seemed to respond. I floated on the gentle bosom of a summer's sea, rising and falling with dreamy pleasure on each crooning wave. But the pulsations grew stronger; the humming, louder; the waves, larger, fiercer—I was dashed about on a stormy sea. A great agony fastened upon me. Brilliant, intermittent sparks of light flashed athwart my inner consciousness; in my ears there was the sound of many waters; then a sudden snapping of an intangible something, and I awoke.

The scene, of which I was protagonist, was a curious one. A glance sufficed to inform me that I lay on the cabin floor of some gentleman's yacht, in a most uncomfortable posture. On either side, grasping my arms and working them up and down like pump handles, were two peculiarly clad, dark-skinned creatures. Though conversant with most aboriginal types, I could not conjecture their nationality. Some attachment had been fastened about my head, which connected my respiratory organs with the machine I shall next describe. My nostrils, however, had been closed, forcing me to breathe through my mouth. Foreshortened by the obliquity of my line of vision, I beheld two tubes, similar to small hosing but of different composition, which emerged from my mouth and went off at an acute angle from each other. The first came to an abrupt termination and lay on the floor beside me; the second traversed the floor in numerous coils, connecting with the apparatus I have promised to describe.

In the days before my life had become tangential, I had dabbled not a little in science, and, conversant with the appurtenances and general paraphernalia of the laboratory, I appreciated the machine I now beheld. It was composed chiefly of glass, the construction being of that crude sort which is employed for experimentative purposes. A vessel of water was surrounded by an air chamber, to which was fixed a vertical tube, surmounted by a globe. In the centre of this was a vacuum gauge. The water in the tube moved upwards and downwards, creating alternate inhalations and exhalations, which were in turn communicated to me through the hose. With this, and the aid of the men who pumped my arms, so vigorously, had the process of breathing been artificially carried on, my chest rising and falling and my lungs expanding and contracting, till nature could be persuaded to again take up her wonted labour.

As I opened my eyes the appliance about my head, nostrils and mouth was removed. Draining a stiff three fingers of brandy, I staggered to my feet to thank my preserver, and confronted—my father. But long years of fellowship with danger had taught me self-control, and I waited to see if he would recognise me. Not so; he saw in me no more than a runaway sailor and treated me accordingly.

Leaving me to the care of the blackies, he fell to revising the notes he had made on my resuscitation. As I ate of the handsome fare served up to me, confusion began on deck, and from the chanteys of the sailors and the rattling of blocks and tackles I surmised that we were getting under way. What a lark! Off on a cruise with my recluse father into the wide Pacific! Little did I realise, as I laughed to myself, which side the joke was to be on. Aye, had I known, I would have plunged overboard and welcomed the dirty fo'c'sle from which I had just escaped.

I was not allowed on deck till we had sunk the Farallones and the last pilot boat. I appreciated this forethought on the part of my father and made it a point to thank him heartily, in my bluff seaman's manner. I could not suspect that he had his own ends in view, in thus keeping my presence secret to all save the crew. He told me briefly of my rescue by his sailors, assuring me that the obligation was on his side, as my appearance had been most opportune. He had constructed the apparatus for the vindication of a theory concerning certain biological phenomena, and had been waiting for an opportunity to use it.

"You have proved it beyond all doubt," he said; then added with a sigh, "But only in the small matter of drowning."

But, to take a reef in my yarn—he offered me an advance of two pounds on my previous wages to sail with him, and this I considered handsome, for he really did not need me. Contrary to my expectations, I did not join the sailors' mess, for'ard, being assigned to a comfortable stateroom and eating at the captain's table. He had perceived that I was no common sailor, and I resolved to take this chance for reinstating myself in his good graces. I wove a fictitious past to account for my education and present position, and did my best to come in touch with him. I was not long in disclosing a predilection for scientific pursuits, nor he in appreciating my aptitude. I became his assistant, with a corresponding increase in wages, and before long, as he grew confidential and expounded his theories, I was as enthusiastic as himself.

The days flew quickly by, for I was deeply interested in my new studies, passing my waking hours in his well-stocked library, or listening to his plans and aiding him in his laboratory work. But we were forced to forego many enticing experiments, a rolling ship not being exactly the proper place for delicate or intricate work. He promised me, however, many delightful hours in the magnificent laboratory for which we were bound. He had taken possession of an uncharted South Sea island, as he said, and turned it into a scientific paradise.

We had not been on the island long, before I discovered the horrible mare's nest I had fallen into. But before I describe the strange things which came to pass, I must briefly outline the causes which culminated in as startling an experience as ever fell to the lot of man.

Late in life, my father had abandoned the musty charms of antiquity and succumbed to the more fascinating ones embraced under the general head of biology. Having been thoroughly grounded during his youth in the fundamentals, he rapidly explored all the higher branches as far as the scientific world had gone, and found himself on the no man's land of the unknowable. It was his intention to pre-empt some of this unclaimed territory, and it was at this stage of his investigations that we had been thrown together. Having a good brain, though I say it myself, I had mastered his speculations and methods of reasoning, becoming almost as mad as himself. But I should not say this. The marvellous results we afterwards obtained can only go to prove his sanity. I can but say that he was the most abnormal specimen of cold-blooded cruelty I have ever seen.

After having penetrated the dual mysteries of physiology and psychology, his thought had led him to the verge of a great field, for which, the better to explore, he began studies in higher organic chemistry, pathology, toxicology and other sciences and sub-sciences rendered kindred as accessories to his speculative hypotheses. Starting from the proposition that the direct cause of the temporary and permanent arrest of vitality was due to the coagulation of certain elements and compounds in the protoplasm, he had isolated and subjected these various substances to innumerable experiments. Since the temporary arrest of vitality in an organism brought coma, and a permanent arrest death, he held that by artificial means this coagulation of the protoplasm could be retarded, prevented, and even overcome in the extreme states of solidification. Or, to do away with the technical nomenclature, he argued that death, when not violent and in which none of the organs had suffered injury, was merely suspended vitality; and that, in such instances, life could be induced to resume its functions by the use of proper methods. This, then, was his idea: To discover the method—and by practical experimentation prove the possibility—of renewing vitality in a structure from which life had seemingly fled. Of course, he recognised the futility of such endeavour after decomposition had set in; he must have organisms which but the moment, the hour, or the day before, had been quick with life. With me, in a crude way, he had proved this theory. I was really drowned, really dead, when picked from the water of San Francisco bay—but the vital spark had been renewed by means of his aerotherapeutical apparatus, as he called it.

Now to his dark purpose concerning me. He first showed me how completely I was in his power. He had sent the yacht away for a year, retaining only his two blackies, who were utterly devoted to him. He then made an exhaustive review of his theory and outlined the method of proof he had adopted, concluding with the startling announcement that I was to be his subject.

I had faced death and weighed my chances in many a desperate venture, but never in one of this nature. I can swear I am no coward, yet this proposition of journeying back and forth across the borderland of death put the yellow fear upon me. I asked for time, which he granted, at the same time assuring me that but the one course was open—I must submit. Escape from the Island was out of the question; escape by suicide was not to be entertained, though really preferable to what it seemed I must undergo; my only hope was to destroy my captors. But this latter was frustrated through the precautions taken by my father. I was subjected to a constant surveillance, even in my sleep being guarded by one or the other of the blacks.

Having pleaded in vain, I announced and proved that I was his son. It was my last card, and I had played all my hopes upon it. But he was inexorable; he was not a father but a scientific machine. I wonder yet how it ever came to pass that he married my mother or begat me, for there was not the slightest grain of emotion in his make-up. Reason was all in all to him, nor could he understand such things as love or sympathy in others, except as petty weaknesses which should be overcome. So he informed me that in the beginning he had given me life, and who had better right to take it away than he? Such, he said, was not his desire, however; he merely wished to borrow it occasionally, promising to return it punctually at the appointed time. Of course, there was a liability of mishaps, but I could do no more than take the chances, since the affairs of men were full of such.

The better to insure success, he wished me to be in the best possible condition, so I was dieted and trained like a great athlete before a decisive contest. What could I do? If I had to undergo the peril, it were best to be in good shape. In my intervals of relaxation he allowed me to assist in the arranging of the apparatus and in the various subsidiary experiments. The interest I took in all such operations can be imagined. I mastered the work as thoroughly as he, and often had the pleasure of seeing some of my suggestions or alterations put into effect. After such events I would smile grimly, conscious of officiating at my own funeral.

He began by inaugurating a series of experiments in toxicology. When all was ready, I was killed by a stiff dose of strychnine and allowed to lie dead for some twenty hours. During that period my body was dead, absolutely dead. All respiration and circulation ceased; but the frightful part of it was, that while the protoplasmic coagulation proceeded, I retained consciousness and was enabled to study it in all its ghastly details.

The apparatus to bring me back to life was an air-tight chamber, fitted to receive my body. The mechanism was simple—a few valves, a rotary shaft and crank, and an electric motor. When in operation, the interior atmosphere was alternately condenses and rarefied, thus communicating to my lungs an artificial respiration without the agency of the hosing previously used. Though my body was inert, and, for all I knew, in the first stages of decomposition, I was cognisant of everything that transpired. I knew when they placed me in the chamber, and though all my senses were quiescent, I was aware of hypodermic injections of a compound to react upon the coagulatory process. Then the chamber was closed and the machinery started. My anxiety was terrible; but the circulation became gradually restored, the different organs began to carry on their respective functions, and in an hour's time I was eating a hearty dinner.

It cannot be said that I participated in this series, nor in the subsequent ones, with much verve; but after two ineffectual attempts of escape, I began to take quite an interest. Besides, I was becoming accustomed. My father was beside himself at his success, and as the months rolled by his speculations took wilder and yet wilder flights. We ranged through the three great classes of poisons, the neurotics, the gaseous and the irritants, but carefully avoided some of the mineral irritants and passed the whole group of corrosives. During the poison regime I became quite accustomed to dying, and had but one mishap to shake my growing confidence. Scarifying a number of lesser blood vessels in my arm, he introduced a minute quantity of that most frightful of poisons, the arrow poison, or curare. I lost consciousness at the start, quickly followed by the cessation of respiration and circulation, and so far had the solidification of the protoplasm advanced, that he gave up all hope. But at the last moment he applied a discovery he had been working upon, receiving such encouragement as to redouble his efforts.

In a glass vacuum, similar but not exactly like a Crookes' tube, was placed a magnetic field. When penetrated by polarised light, it gave no phenomena of phosphorescence nor the rectilinear projection of atoms, but emitted non-luminous rays, similar to the X ray. While the X ray could reveal opaque objects hidden in dense mediums, this was possessed of far subtler penetration. By this he photographed my body, and found on the negative an infinite number of blurred shadows, due to the chemical and electric motions still going on. This was an infallible proof that the rigor mortis in which I lay was not genuine; that is, those mysterious forces, those delicate bonds which held my soul to my body, were still in action. The resultants of all other poisons were unapparent, save those of mercurial compounds, which usually left me languid for several days.

Another series of delightful experiments was with electricity. We verified Tesla's assertion that high currents were utterly harmless by passing 100,000 volts through my body. As this did not affect me, the current was reduced to 2,500, and I was quickly electrocuted. This time he ventured so far as to allow me to remain dead, or in a state of suspended vitality, for three days. It took four hours to bring me back.

Once, he superinduced lockjaw; but the agony of dying was so great that I positively refused to undergo similar experiments. The easiest deaths were by asphyxiation, such as drowning, strangling, and suffocation by gas; while those by morphine, opium, cocaine and chloroform, were not at all hard.

Another time, after being suffocated, he kept me in cold storage for three months, not permitting me to freeze or decay. This was without my knowledge, and I was in a great fright on discovering the lapse of time. I became afraid of what he might do with me when I lay dead, my alarm being increased by the predilection he was beginning to betray towards vivisection. The last time I was resurrected, I discovered that he had been tampering with my breast. Though he had carefully dressed and sewed the incisions up, they were so severe that I had to take to my bed for some time. It was during this convalescence that I evolved the plan by which I ultimately escaped.

While feigning unbounded enthusiasm in the work, I asked and received a vacation from my moribund occupation. During this period I devoted myself to laboratory work, while he was too deep in the vivisection of the many animals captured by the blacks to take notice of my work.

It was on these two propositions that I constructed my theory: First, electrolysis, or the decomposition of water into its constituent gases by means of electricity; and, second, by the hypothetical existence of a force, the converse of gravitation, which Astor has named "apergy". Terrestrial attraction, for instance, merely draws objects together but does not combine them; hence, apergy is merely repulsion. Now, atomic or molecular attraction not only draws objects together but integrates them; and it was the converse of this, or a disintegrative force, which I wished to not only discover and produce, but to direct at will. Thus, the molecules of hydrogen and oxygen reacting on each other, separate and create new molecules, containing both elements and forming water. Electrolysis causes these molecules to split up and resume their original condition, producing the two gases separately. The force I wished to find must not only do this with two, but with all elements, no matter in what compounds they exist. If I could then entice my father within its radius, he would be instantly disintegrated and sent flying to the four quarters, a mass of isolated elements.

It must not be understood that this force, which I finally came to control, annihilated matter; it merely annihilated form. Nor, as I soon discovered, had it any effect on inorganic structure; but to all organic form it was absolutely fatal. This partiality puzzled me at first, though had I stopped to think deeper I would have seen through it. Since the number of atoms in organic molecules is far greater than in the most complex mineral molecules, organic compounds are characterised by their instability and the ease with which they are split up by physical forces and chemical reagents.

By two powerful batteries, connected with magnets constructed specially for this purpose, two tremendous forces were projected. Considered apart from each other, they were perfectly harmless; but they accomplished their purpose by focusing at an invisible point in mid-air. After practically demonstrating its success, besides narrowly escaping being blown into nothingness, I laid my trap. Concealing the magnets, so that their force made the whole space of my chamber doorway a field of death, and placing by my couch a button by which I could throw on the current from the storage batteries, I climbed into bed.

The blackies still guarded my sleeping quarters, one relieving the other at midnight. I turned on the current as soon as the first man arrived. Hardly had I begun to doze, when I was aroused by a sharp, metallic tinkle. There, on the mid-threshold, lay the collar of Dan, my father's St. Bernard. My keeper ran to pick it up. He disappeared like a gust of wind, his clothes falling to the floor in a heap. There was a slight wiff of ozone in the air, but since the principal gaseous components of his body were hydrogen, oxygen and nitrogen, which are equally colourless and odourless, there was no other manifestation of his departure. Yet when I shut off the current and removed the garments, I found a deposit of carbon in the form of animal charcoal; also other powders, the isolated, solid elements of his organism, such as sulphur, potassium and iron. Resetting the trap, I crawled back to bed. At midnight I got up and removed the remains of the second black, and then slept peacefully till morning.

I was awakened by the strident voice of my father, who was calling to me from across the laboratory. I laughed to myself. There had been no one to call him and he had overslept. I could hear him as he approached my room with the intention of rousing me, and so I sat up in bed, the better to observe his translation—perhaps apotheosis were a better term. He paused a moment at the threshold, then took the fatal step. Puff! It was like the wind sighing among the pines. He was gone. His clothes fell in a fantastic heap on the floor. Besides ozone, I noticed the faint, garlic-like odour of phosphorus. A little pile of elementary solids lay among his garments. That was all. The wide world lay before me. My captors were no more.

THE SHADOW AND THE FLASH

by Jack London

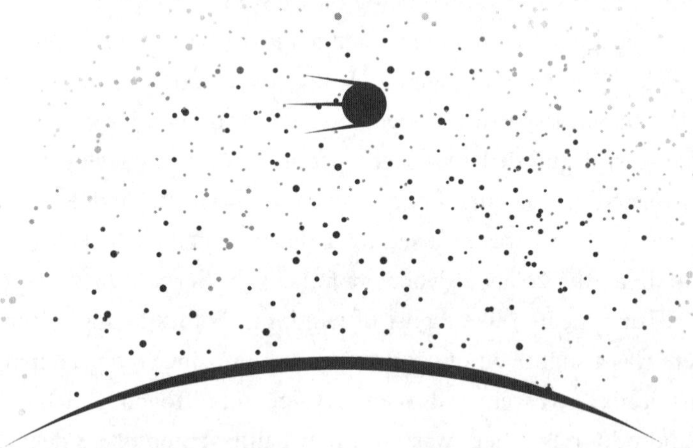

When I look back, I realize what a peculiar friendship it was. First, there was Lloyd Inwood, tall, slender, and finely knit, nervous and dark. And then Paul Tichlorne, tall, slender, and finely knit, nervous and blond. Each was the replica of the other in everything except colour. Lloyd's eyes were black; Paul's were blue. Under stress of excitement, the blood coursed olive in the face of Lloyd, crimson in the face of Paul. But outside this matter of colouring they were as like as two peas. Both were high-strung, prone to excessive tension and endurance, and they lived at concert pitch.

But there was a trio involved in this remarkable friendship, and the third was short, and fat, and chunky, and lazy, and, loath to say, it was I. Paul and Lloyd seemed born to rivalry with each other, and I to be peacemaker between them. We grew up together, the three of us, and full often have I received the angry blows each intended for the other. They were always competing, striving to outdo each other, and when entered upon some such struggle there was no limit either to their endeavours or passions.

This intense spirit of rivalry obtained in their studies and their games. If Paul memorized one canto of "Marmion," Lloyd memorized two cantos, Paul came back with three, and Lloyd again with four, till each knew the whole poem by heart. I remember an incident that occurred at the swimming hole—an incident tragically significant of the life-struggle between them. The boys had a game of diving to the bottom of a ten-foot pool and holding on by submerged roots to see who could stay under the longest. Paul and Lloyd allowed themselves to be bantered into making the descent together. When I saw their faces, set and determined, disappear in the water as they sank swiftly down, I felt a foreboding of something dreadful. The moments sped, the ripples died away, the face of the pool grew placid and untroubled, and neither black nor golden head broke surface in quest of air. We above grew anxious. The longest record of the longest-winded boy had been exceeded, and still there was no sign. Air bubbles trickled slowly upward, showing that the breath had been expelled from their lungs, and after that the bubbles ceased to trickle upward. Each second became interminable, and, unable longer to endure the suspense, I plunged into the water.

I found them down at the bottom, clutching tight to the roots, their heads not a foot apart, their eyes wide open, each glaring fixedly at the other. They were suffering frightful torment, writhing and twisting in the pangs of voluntary suffocation; for neither would let go and acknowledge himself beaten. I tried to break Paul's hold on the root, but he resisted me fiercely. Then I lost my breath and came to the surface, badly scared. I quickly explained the situation, and half a dozen of us went down and by main strength tore them loose. By the time we got them out, both were unconscious, and it was only after much barrel-rolling and rubbing and pounding that they finally came to their senses. They would have drowned there, had no one rescued them.

When Paul Tichlorne entered college, he let it be generally understood that he was going in for the social sciences. Lloyd Inwood, entering at the same time, elected to take the same course. But Paul had had it secretly in mind all the time to study the natural sciences, specializing on chemistry, and at the last moment he switched over. Though Lloyd had already arranged his year's work and attended the first lectures, he at once followed Paul's lead and went in for the natural sciences and especially for chemistry. Their rivalry soon became a noted thing throughout the university. Each was a spur to the other, and they went into chemistry deeper than did ever students before—so deep, in fact, that ere they took their sheepskins they could have stumped any chemistry or "cow college" professor in the institution, save "old" Moss, head of the department, and even him they puzzled and edified more than once. Lloyd's discovery of the "death bacillus" of the sea toad, and his experiments on it with potassium cyanide, sent his name and that of his university ringing round the world; nor was Paul a whit behind when he succeeded in producing laboratory colloids exhibiting amoeba-like activities, and when he cast new light upon the processes of fertilization through his startling experiments with simple sodium chlorides and magnesium solutions on low forms of marine life.

It was in their undergraduate days, however, in the midst of their profoundest plunges into the mysteries of organic chemistry, that Doris Van Benschoten entered into their lives. Lloyd met her first, but within twenty-four hours Paul saw to it that he also made her acquaintance. Of course, they fell in love with her, and she became the only thing in life worth living for. They wooed her with equal ardour and fire, and so intense became their struggle for her that half the student-body took to wagering wildly on the result. Even "old" Moss, one day, after an astounding demonstration in his private laboratory by Paul, was guilty to the extent of a month's salary of backing him to become the bridegroom of Doris Van Benschoten.

In the end she solved the problem in her own way, to everybody's satisfaction except Paul's and Lloyd's. Getting them together, she said that she really could not choose between them because she loved them both equally well; and that, unfortunately, since polyandry was not permitted in the United States she would be compelled to forego the honour and happiness of marrying either of them. Each blamed the other for this lamentable outcome, and the bitterness between them grew more bitter.

But things came to a head enough. It was at my home, after they had taken their degrees and dropped out of the world's sight, that the beginning of the end came to pass. Both were men of means, with little inclination and no necessity for professional life. My friendship and their mutual animosity were the two things that linked them in any way together. While they were very often at my place, they made it a fastidious point to avoid each other on such visits, though it was inevitable, under the circumstances, that they should come upon each other occasionally.

On the day I have in recollection, Paul Tichlorne had been mooning all morning in my study over a current scientific review. This left me free to my own affairs, and I was out among my roses when Lloyd Inwood arrived. Clipping and pruning and tacking the climbers on the porch, with my mouth full of nails, and Lloyd following me about and lending a hand now and again, we fell to discussing the mythical race of invisible people, that strange and vagrant people the traditions of which have come down to us. Lloyd warmed to the talk in his nervous, jerky fashion, and was soon interrogating the physical properties and possibilities of invisibility. A perfectly black object, he contended, would elude and defy the acutest vision.

"Colour is a sensation," he was saying. "It has no objective reality. Without light, we can see neither colours nor objects themselves. All objects are black in the dark, and in the dark it is impossible to see them. If no light strikes upon them, then no light is flung back from them to the eye, and so we have no vision-evidence of their being."

"But we see black objects in daylight," I objected.

"Very true," he went on warmly. "And that is because they are not perfectly black. Were they perfectly black, absolutely black, as it were, we could not see them—ay, not in the blaze of a thousand suns could we see them! And so I say, with the right pigments, properly compounded, an absolutely black paint could be produced which would render invisible whatever it was applied to."

"It would be a remarkable discovery," I said non-committally, for the whole thing seemed too fantastic for aught but speculative purposes.

"Remarkable!" Lloyd slapped me on the shoulder. "I should say so. Why, old chap, to coat myself with such a paint would be to put the world at my feet. The secrets of kings and courts would be mine, the machinations of diplomats and politicians, the play of stock-gamblers, the plans of trusts and corporations. I could keep my hand on the inner pulse of things and become the greatest power in the world. And I—" He broke off shortly, then added, "Well, I have begun my experiments, and I don't mind telling you that I'm right in line for it."

A laugh from the doorway startled us. Paul Tichlorne was standing there, a smile of mockery on his lips.

"You forget, my dear Lloyd," he said.

"Forget what?"

"You forget," Paul went on—"ah, you forget the shadow."

I saw Lloyd's face drop, but he answered sneeringly, "I can carry a sunshade, you know." Then he turned suddenly and fiercely upon him. "Look here, Paul, you'll keep out of this if you know what's good for you."

A rupture seemed imminent, but Paul laughed good-naturedly. "I wouldn't lay fingers on your dirty pigments. Succeed beyond your most sanguine expectations, yet you will always fetch up against the shadow. You can't get away from it. Now I shall go on the very opposite tack. In the very nature of my proposition the shadow will be eliminated—"

"Transparency!" ejaculated Lloyd, instantly. "But it can't be achieved."

"Oh, no; of course not." And Paul shrugged his shoulders and strolled off down the briar-rose path.

This was the beginning of it. Both men attacked the problem with all the tremendous energy for which they were noted, and with a rancour and bitterness that made me tremble for the success of either. Each trusted me to the utmost, and in the long weeks of experimentation that followed I was made a party to both sides, listening to their theorizings and witnessing their demonstrations. Never, by word or sign, did I convey to either the slightest hint of the other's progress, and they respected me for the seal I put upon my lips.

Lloyd Inwood, after prolonged and unintermittent application, when the tension upon his mind and body became too great to bear, had a strange way of obtaining relief. He attended prize fights. It was at one of these brutal exhibitions, whither he had dragged me in order to tell his latest results, that his theory received striking confirmation.

"Do you see that red-whiskered man?" he asked, pointing across the ring to the fifth tier of seats on the opposite side. "And do you see the next man to him, the one in the white hat? Well, there is quite a gap between them, is there not?"

"Certainly," I answered. "They are a seat apart. The gap is the unoccupied seat."

He leaned over to me and spoke seriously. "Between the red-whiskered man and the white-hatted man sits Ben Wasson. You have heard me speak of him. He is the cleverest pugilist of his weight in the country. He is also a Caribbean negro, full-blooded, and the blackest in the United States. He has on a black overcoat buttoned up. I saw him when he came in and took that seat. As soon as he sat down he disappeared. Watch closely; he may smile."

I was for crossing over to verify Lloyd's statement, but he restrained me. "Wait," he said.

I waited and watched, till the red-whiskered man turned his head as though addressing the unoccupied seat; and then, in that empty space, I saw the rolling whites of a pair of eyes and the white double-crescent of two rows of teeth, and for the instant I could make out a negro's face. But with the passing of the smile his visibility passed, and the chair seemed vacant as before.

"Were he perfectly black, you could sit alongside him and not see him," Lloyd said; and I confess the illustration was apt enough to make me well-nigh convinced.

I visited Lloyd's laboratory a number of times after that, and found him always deep in his search after the absolute black. His experiments covered all sorts of pigments, such as lamp-blacks, tars, carbonized vegetable matters, soots of oils and fats, and the various carbonized animal substances.

"White light is composed of the seven primary colours," he argued to me. "But it is itself, of itself, invisible. Only by being reflected from objects do it and the objects become visible. But only that portion of it that is reflected becomes visible. For instance, here is a blue tobacco-box. The white light strikes against it, and, with one exception, all its component colours—violet, indigo, green, yellow, orange, and red—are absorbed. The one exception is *blue*. It is not absorbed, but reflected. Wherefore the tobacco-box gives us a sensation of blueness. We do not see the other colours because they are absorbed. We see only the blue. For the same reason grass is *green*. The green waves of white light are thrown upon our eyes."

"When we paint our houses, we do not apply colour to them," he said at another time. "What we do is to apply certain substances that have the property of absorbing from white light all the colours except those that we would have our houses appear. When a substance reflects all the colours to the eye, it seems to us white. When it absorbs all the colours, it is black. But, as I said before, we have as yet no perfect black. All the colours are not absorbed. The perfect black, guarding against high lights, will be utterly and absolutely invisible. Look at that, for example."

He pointed to the palette lying on his work-table. Different shades of black pigments were brushed on it. One, in particular, I could hardly see. It gave my eyes a blurring sensation, and I rubbed them and looked again.

"That," he said impressively, "is the blackest black you or any mortal man ever looked upon. But just you wait, and I'll have a black so black that no mortal man will be able to look upon it—and see it!"

On the other hand, I used to find Paul Tichlorne plunged as deeply into the study of light polarization, diffraction, and interference, single and double refraction, and all manner of strange organic compounds.

"Transparency: a state or quality of body which permits all rays of light to pass through," he defined for me. "That is what I am seeking. Lloyd blunders up against the shadow with his perfect opaqueness. But I escape it. A transparent body casts no shadow; neither does it reflect light-waves—that is, the perfectly transparent does not. So, avoiding high lights, not only will such a body cast no shadow, but, since it reflects no light, it will also be invisible."

We were standing by the window at another time. Paul was engaged in polishing a number of lenses, which were ranged along the sill. Suddenly, after a pause in the conversation, he said, "Oh! I've dropped a lens. Stick your head out, old man, and see where it went to."

Out I started to thrust my head, but a sharp blow on the forehead caused me to recoil. I rubbed my bruised brow and gazed with reproachful inquiry at Paul, who was laughing in gleeful, boyish fashion.

"Well?" he said.

"Well?" I echoed.

"Why don't you investigate?" he demanded. And investigate I did. Before thrusting out my head, my senses, automatically active, had told me there was nothing there, that nothing intervened between me and out-of-doors, that the aperture of the window opening was utterly empty. I stretched forth my hand and felt a hard object, smooth and cool and flat, which my touch, out of its experience, told me to be glass. I looked again, but could see positively nothing.

"White quartzose sand," Paul rattled off, "sodic carbonate, slaked lime, cutlet, manganese peroxide—there you have it, the finest French plate glass, made by the great St. Gobain Company, who made the finest plate glass in the world, and this is the finest piece they ever made. It cost a king's ransom. But look at it! You can't see it. You don't know it's there till you run your head against it.

"Eh, old boy! That's merely an object-lesson—certain elements, in themselves opaque, yet so compounded as to give a resultant body which is transparent. But that is a matter of inorganic chemistry, you say. Very true. But I dare to assert, standing here on my two feet, that in the organic I can duplicate whatever occurs in the inorganic.

"Here!" He held a test-tube between me and the light, and I noted the cloudy or muddy liquid it contained. He emptied the contents of another test-tube into it, and almost instantly it became clear and sparkling.

"Or here!" With quick, nervous movements among his array of test-tubes, he turned a white solution to a wine colour, and a light yellow solution to a dark brown. He dropped a piece of litmus paper into an acid, when it changed instantly to red, and on floating it in an alkali it turned as quickly to blue.

"The litmus paper is still the litmus paper," he enunciated in the formal manner of the lecturer. "I have not changed it into something else. Then what did I do? I merely changed the arrangement of its molecules. Where, at first, it absorbed all colours from the light but red, its molecular structure was so changed that it absorbed red and all colours except blue. And so it goes, ad infinitum. Now, what I purpose to do is this." He paused for a space. "I purpose to seek—ay, and to find—the proper reagents, which, acting upon the living organism, will bring about molecular changes analogous to those you have just witnessed. But these reagents, which I shall find, and for that matter, upon which I already have my hands, will not turn the living body to blue or red or black, but they will turn it to transparency. All light will pass through it. It will be invisible. It will cast no shadow."

A few weeks later I went hunting with Paul. He had been promising me for some time that I should have the pleasure of shooting over a wonderful dog—the most wonderful dog, in fact, that ever man shot over, so he averred, and continued to aver till my curiosity was aroused. But on the morning in question I was disappointed, for there was no dog in evidence.

"Don't see him about," Paul remarked unconcernedly, and we set off across the fields.

I could not imagine, at the time, what was ailing me, but I had a feeling of some impending and deadly illness. My nerves were all awry, and, from the astounding tricks they played me, my senses seemed to have run riot. Strange sounds disturbed me. At times I heard the swish-swish of grass being shoved aside, and once the patter of feet across a patch of stony ground.

"Did you hear anything, Paul?" I asked once.

But he shook his head, and thrust his feet steadily forward.

While climbing a fence, I heard the low, eager whine of a dog, apparently from within a couple of feet of me; but on looking about me I saw nothing.

I dropped to the ground, limp and trembling.

"Paul," I said, "we had better return to the house. I am afraid I am going to be sick."

"Nonsense, old man," he answered. "The sunshine has gone to your head like wine. You'll be all right. It's famous weather."

But, passing along a narrow path through a clump of cottonwoods, some object brushed against my legs and I stumbled and nearly fell. I looked with sudden anxiety at Paul.

"What's the matter?" he asked. "Tripping over your own feet?"

I kept my tongue between my teeth and plodded on, though sore perplexed and thoroughly satisfied that some acute and mysterious malady had attacked my nerves. So far my eyes had escaped; but, when we got to the open fields again, even my vision went back on me. Strange flashes of vari-coloured, rainbow light began to appear and disappear on the path before me. Still, I managed to keep myself in hand, till the vari-coloured lights persisted for a space of fully twenty seconds, dancing and flashing in continuous play. Then I sat down, weak and shaky.

"It's all up with me," I gasped, covering my eyes with my hands. "It has attacked my eyes. Paul, take me home."

But Paul laughed long and loud. "What did I tell you?—the most wonderful dog, eh? Well, what do you think?"

He turned partly from me and began to whistle. I heard the patter of feet, the panting of a heated animal, and the unmistakable yelp of a dog. Then Paul stooped down and apparently fondled the empty air.

"Here! Give me your fist."

And he rubbed my hand over the cold nose and jowls of a dog. A dog it certainly was, with the shape and the smooth, short coat of a pointer.

Suffice to say, I speedily recovered my spirits and control. Paul put a collar about the animal's neck and tied his handkerchief to its tail. And then was vouchsafed us the remarkable sight of an empty collar and a waving handkerchief cavorting over the fields. It was something to see that collar and handkerchief pin a bevy of quail in a clump of locusts and remain rigid and immovable till we had flushed the birds.

Now and again the dog emitted the vari-coloured light-flashes I have mentioned. The one thing, Paul explained, which he had not anticipated and which he doubted could be overcome.

"They're a large family," he said, "these sun dogs, wind dogs, rainbows, halos, and parhelia. They are produced by refraction of light from mineral and ice crystals, from mist, rain, spray, and no end of things; and I am afraid they are the penalty I must pay for transparency. I escaped Lloyd's shadow only to fetch up against the rainbow flash."

A couple of days later, before the entrance to Paul's laboratory, I encountered a terrible stench. So overpowering was it that it was easy to discover the source—a mass of putrescent matter on the doorstep which in general outlines resembled a dog.

Paul was startled when he investigated my find. It was his invisible dog, or rather, what had been his invisible dog, for it was now plainly visible. It had been playing about but a few minutes before in all health and strength. Closer examination revealed that the skull had been crushed by some heavy blow. While it was strange that the animal should have been killed, the inexplicable thing was that it should so quickly decay.

"The reagents I injected into its system were harmless," Paul explained. "Yet they were powerful, and it appears that when death comes they force practically instantaneous disintegration. Remarkable! Most remarkable! Well, the only thing is not to die. They do not harm so long as one lives. But I do wonder who smashed in that dog's head."

Light, however, was thrown upon this when a frightened housemaid brought the news that Gaffer Bedshaw had that very morning, not more than an hour back, gone violently insane, and was strapped down at home, in the huntsman's lodge, where he raved of a battle with a ferocious and gigantic beast that he had encountered in the Tichlorne pasture. He claimed that the thing, whatever it was, was invisible, that with his own eyes he had seen that it was invisible; wherefore his tearful wife and daughters shook their heads, and wherefore he but waxed the more violent, and the gardener and the coachman tightened the straps by another hole.

Nor, while Paul Tichlorne was thus successfully mastering the problem of invisibility, was Lloyd Inwood a whit behind. I went over in answer to a message of his to come and see how he was getting on. Now his laboratory occupied an isolated situation in the midst of his vast grounds. It was built in a pleasant little glade, surrounded on all sides by a dense forest growth, and was to be gained by way of a winding and erratic path. But I have travelled that path so often as to know every foot of it, and conceive my surprise when I came upon the glade and found no laboratory. The quaint shed structure with its red sandstone chimney was not. Nor did it look as if it ever had been. There were no signs of ruin, no debris, nothing.

I started to walk across what had once been its site. "This," I said to myself, "should be where the step went up to the door." Barely were the words out of my mouth when I stubbed my toe on some obstacle, pitched forward, and butted my head into something that FELT very much like a door. I reached out my hand. It WAS a door. I found the knob and turned it. And at once, as the door swung inward on its hinges, the whole interior of the laboratory impinged upon my vision. Greeting Lloyd, I closed the door and backed up the path a few paces. I could see nothing of the building. Returning and opening the door, at once all the furniture and every detail of the interior were visible. It was indeed startling, the sudden transition from void to light and form and colour.

"What do you think of it, eh?" Lloyd asked, wringing my hand. "I slapped a couple of coats of absolute black on the outside yesterday afternoon to see how it worked. How's your head? you bumped it pretty solidly, I imagine."

"Never mind that," he interrupted my congratulations. "I've something better for you to do."

While he talked he began to strip, and when he stood naked before me he thrust a pot and brush into my hand and said, "Here, give me a coat of this."

It was an oily, shellac-like stuff, which spread quickly and easily over the skin and dried immediately.

"Merely preliminary and precautionary," he explained when I had finished; "but now for the real stuff."

I picked up another pot he indicated, and glanced inside, but could see nothing.

"It's empty," I said.

"Stick your finger in it."

I obeyed, and was aware of a sensation of cool moistness. On withdrawing my hand I glanced at the forefinger, the one I had immersed, but it had disappeared. I moved and knew from the alternate tension and relaxation of the muscles that I moved it, but it defied my sense of sight. To all appearances I had been shorn of a finger; nor could I get any visual impression of it till I extended it under the skylight and saw its shadow plainly blotted on the floor.

Lloyd chuckled. "Now spread it on, and keep your eyes open."

I dipped the brush into the seemingly empty pot, and gave him a long stroke across his chest. With the passage of the brush the living flesh disappeared from beneath. I covered his right leg, and he was a one-legged man defying all laws of gravitation. And so, stroke by stroke, member by member, I painted Lloyd Inwood into nothingness. It was a creepy experience, and I was glad when naught remained in sight but his burning black eyes, poised apparently unsupported in mid-air.

"I have a refined and harmless solution for them," he said. "A fine spray with an air-brush, and presto! I am not."

This deftly accomplished, he said, "Now I shall move about, and do you tell me what sensations you experience."

"In the first place, I cannot see you," I said, and I could hear his gleeful laugh from the midst of the emptiness. "Of course," I continued, "you cannot escape your shadow, but that was to be expected. When you pass between my eye and an object, the object disappears, but so unusual and incomprehensible is its disappearance that it seems to me as though my eyes had blurred. When you move rapidly, I experience a bewildering succession of blurs. The blurring sensation makes my eyes ache and my brain tired."

"Have you any other warnings of my presence?" he asked.

"No, and yes," I answered. "When you are near me I have feelings similar to those produced by dank warehouses, gloomy crypts, and deep mines. And as sailors feel the loom of the land on dark nights, so I think I feel the loom of your body. But it is all very vague and intangible."

Long we talked that last morning in his laboratory; and when I turned to go, he put his unseen hand in mine with nervous grip, and said, "Now I shall conquer the world!" And I could not dare to tell him of Paul Tichlorne's equal success.

At home I found a note from Paul, asking me to come up immediately, and it was high noon when I came spinning up the driveway on my wheel. Paul called me from the tennis court, and I dismounted and went over. But the court was empty. As I stood there, gaping open-mouthed, a tennis ball struck me on the arm, and as I turned about, another whizzed past my ear. For aught I could see of my assailant, they came whirling at me from out of space, and right well was I peppered with them. But when the balls already flung at me began to come back for a second whack, I realized the situation. Seizing a racquet and keeping my eyes open, I quickly saw a rainbow flash appearing and disappearing and darting over the ground. I took out after it, and when I laid the racquet upon it for a half-dozen stout blows, Paul's voice rang out:

"Enough! Enough! Oh! Ouch! Stop! You're landing on my naked skin, you know! Ow! O-w-w! I'll be good! I'll be good! I only wanted you to see my metamorphosis," he said ruefully, and I imagined he was rubbing his hurts.

A few minutes later we were playing tennis—a handicap on my part, for I could have no knowledge of his position save when all the angles between himself, the sun, and me, were in proper conjunction. Then he flashed, and only then.

But the flashes were more brilliant than the rainbow—purest blue, most delicate violet, brightest yellow, and all the intermediary shades, with the scintillant brilliancy of the diamond, dazzling, blinding, iridescent.

But in the midst of our play I felt a sudden cold chill, reminding me of deep mines and gloomy crypts, such a chill as I had experienced that very morning. The next moment, close to the net, I saw a ball rebound in mid-air and empty space, and at the same instant, a score of feet away, Paul Tichlorne emitted a rainbow flash. It could not be he from whom the ball had rebounded, and with sickening dread I realized that Lloyd Inwood had come upon the scene. To make sure, I looked for his shadow, and there it was, a shapeless blotch the girth of his body, (the sun was overhead), moving along the ground. I remembered his threat, and felt sure that all the long years of rivalry were about to culminate in uncanny battle.

I cried a warning to Paul, and heard a snarl as of a wild beast, and an answering snarl. I saw the dark blotch move swiftly across the court, and a brilliant burst of vari-coloured light moving with equal swiftness to meet it; and then shadow and flash came together and there was the sound of unseen blows. The net went down before my frightened eyes. I sprang toward the fighters, crying:

"For God's sake!"

But their locked bodies smote against my knees, and I was overthrown.

"You keep out of this, old man!" I heard the voice of Lloyd Inwood from out of the emptiness. And then Paul's voice crying, "Yes, we've had enough of peace-making!"

From the sound of their voices I knew they had separated. I could not locate Paul, and so approached the shadow that represented Lloyd. But from the other side came a stunning blow on the point of my jaw, and I heard Paul scream angrily, "Now will you keep away?"

Then they came together again, the impact of their blows, their groans and gasps, and the swift flashings and shadow-movings telling plainly of the deadliness of the struggle.

I shouted for help, and Gaffer Bedshaw came running into the court. I could see, as he approached, that he was looking at me strangely, but he collided with the combatants and was hurled headlong to the ground. With despairing shriek and a cry of "O Lord, I've got 'em!" he sprang to his feet and tore madly out of the court.

I could do nothing, so I sat up, fascinated and powerless, and watched the struggle. The noonday sun beat down with dazzling brightness on the naked tennis court. And it was naked. All I could see was the blotch of shadow and the rainbow flashes, the dust rising from the invisible feet, the earth tearing up from beneath the straining foot-grips, and the wire screen bulge once or twice as their bodies hurled against it. That was all, and after a time even that ceased. There were no more flashes, and the shadow had become long and stationary; and I remembered their set boyish faces when they clung to the roots in the deep coolness of the pool.

They found me an hour afterward. Some inkling of what had happened got to the servants and they quitted the Tichlorne service in a body. Gaffer Bedshaw never recovered from the second shock he received, and is confined in a madhouse, hopelessly incurable. The secrets of their marvellous discoveries died with Paul and Lloyd, both laboratories being destroyed by grief-stricken relatives. As for myself, I no longer care for chemical research, and science is a tabooed topic in my household. I have returned to my roses. Nature's colours are good enough for me.

THE ENEMY OF ALL THE WORLD

by Jack London

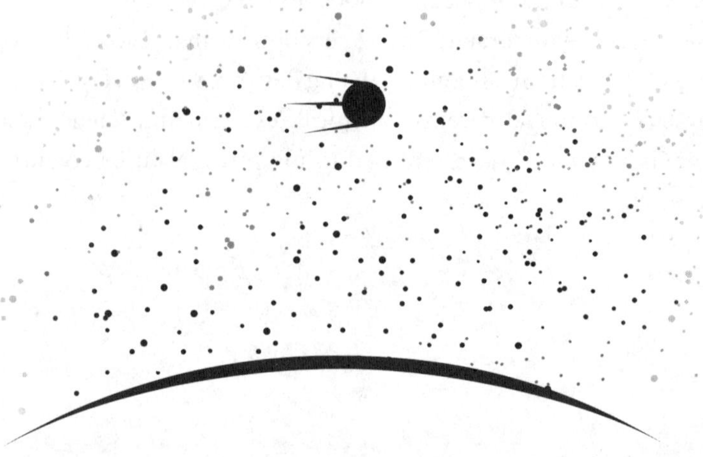

It was Silas Bannerman who finally ran down that scientific wizard and arch-enemy of mankind, Emil Gluck. Gluck's confession, before he went to the electric chair, threw much light upon the series of mysterious events, many apparently unrelated, that so perturbed the world between the years 1933 and 1941. It was not until that remarkable document was made public that the world dreamed of there being any connection between the assassination of the King and Queen of Portugal and the murders of the New York City police officers. While the deeds of Emil Gluck were all that was abominable, we cannot but feel, to a certain extent, pity for the unfortunate, malformed, and maltreated genius. This side of his story has never been told before, and from his confession and from the great mass of evidence and the documents and records of the time we are able to construct a fairly accurate portrait of him, and to discern the factors and pressures that moulded him into the human monster he became and that drove him onward and downward along the fearful path he trod.

Emil Gluck was born in Syracuse, New York, in 1895. His father, Josephus Gluck, was a special policeman and night watchman, who, in the year 1900, died suddenly of pneumonia. The mother, a pretty, fragile creature, who, before her marriage, had been a milliner, grieved herself to death over the loss of her husband. This sensitiveness of the mother was the heritage that in the boy became morbid and horrible.

In 1901, the boy, Emil, then six years of age, went to live with his aunt, Mrs. Ann Bartell. She was his mother's sister, but in her breast was no kindly feeling for the sensitive, shrinking boy. Ann Bartell was a vain, shallow, and heartless woman. Also, she was cursed with poverty and burdened with a husband who was a lazy, erratic ne'er-do-well. Young Emil Gluck was not wanted, and Ann Bartell could be trusted to impress this fact sufficiently upon him. As an illustration of the treatment he received in that early, formative period, the following instance is given.

When he had been living in the Bartell home a little more than a year, he broke his leg. He sustained the injury through playing on the forbidden roof—as all boys have done and will continue to do to the end of time. The leg was broken in two places between the knee and thigh. Emil, helped by his frightened playmates, managed to drag himself to the front sidewalk, where he fainted. The children of the neighbourhood were afraid of the hard-featured shrew who presided over the Bartell house; but, summoning their resolution, they rang the bell and told Ann Bartell of the accident. She did not even look at the little lad who lay stricken on the sidewalk, but slammed the door and went back to her wash-tub. The time passed. A drizzle came on, and Emil Gluck, out of his faint, lay sobbing in the rain. The leg should have been set immediately. As it was, the inflammation rose rapidly and made a nasty case of it. At the end of two hours, the indignant women of the neighbourhood protested to Ann Bartell. This time she came out and looked at the lad. Also she kicked him in the side as he lay helpless at her feet, and she hysterically disowned him. He was not her child, she said, and recommended that the ambulance be called to take him to the city receiving hospital. Then she went back into the house.

It was a woman, Elizabeth Shepstone, who came along, learned the situation, and had the boy placed on a shutter. It was she who called the doctor, and who, brushing aside Ann Bartell, had the boy carried into the house. When the doctor arrived, Ann Bartell promptly warned him that she would not pay him for his services. For two months the little Emil lay in bed, the first month on his back without once being turned over; and he lay neglected and alone, save for the occasional visits of the unremunerated and over-worked physician. He had no toys, nothing with which to beguile the long and tedious hours. No kind word was spoken to him, no soothing hand laid upon his brow, no single touch or act of loving tenderness—naught but the reproaches and harshness of Ann Bartell, and the continually reiterated information that he was not wanted. And it can well be understood, in such environment, how there was generated in the lonely, neglected boy much of the bitterness and hostility for his kind that later was to express itself in deeds so frightful as to terrify the world.

It would seem strange that, from the hands of Ann Bartell, Emil Gluck should have received a college education; but the explanation is simple. Her ne'er-do-well husband, deserting her, made a strike in the Nevada goldfields, and returned to her a many-times millionaire. Ann Bartell hated the boy, and immediately she sent him to the Farristown Academy, a hundred miles away. Shy and sensitive, a lonely and misunderstood little soul, he was more lonely than ever at Farristown. He never came home, at vacation, and holidays, as the other boys did. Instead, he wandered about the deserted buildings and grounds, befriended and misunderstood by the servants and gardeners, reading much, it is remembered, spending his days in the fields or before the fire-place with his nose poked always in the pages of some book. It was at this time that he over-used his eyes and was compelled to take up the wearing of glasses, which same were so prominent in the photographs of him published in the newspapers in 1941.

He was a remarkable student. Application such as his would have taken him far; but he did not need application. A glance at a text meant mastery for him. The result was that he did an immense amount of collateral reading and acquired more in half a year than did the average student in half-a-dozen years. In 1909, barely fourteen years of age, he was ready—"more than ready" the headmaster of the academy said—to enter Yale or Harvard. His juvenility prevented him from entering those universities, and so, in 1909, we find him a freshman at historic Bowdoin College. In 1913 he graduated with highest honours, and immediately afterward followed Professor Bradlough to Berkeley, California. The one friend that Emil Gluck discovered in all his life was Professor Bradlough.

The latter's weak lungs had led him to exchange Maine for California, the removal being facilitated by the offer of a professorship in the State University. Throughout the year 1914, Emil Gluck resided in Berkeley and took special scientific courses. Toward the end of that year two deaths changed his prospects and his relations with life. The death of Professor Bradlough took from him the one friend he was ever to know, and the death of Ann Bartell left him penniless. Hating the unfortunate lad to the last, she cut him off with one hundred dollars.

The following year, at twenty years of age, Emil Gluck was enrolled as an instructor of chemistry in the University of California. Here the years passed quietly; he faithfully performed the drudgery that brought him his salary, and, a student always, he took half-a-dozen degrees. He was, among other things, a Doctor of Sociology, of Philosophy, and of Science, though he was known to the world, in later days, only as Professor Gluck.

He was twenty-seven years old when he first sprang into prominence in the newspapers through the publication of his book, Sex and Progress. The book remains today a milestone in the history and philosophy of marriage. It is a heavy tome of over seven hundred pages, painfully careful and accurate, and startlingly original. It was a book for scientists, and not one calculated to make a stir. But Gluck, in the last chapter, using barely three lines for it, mentioned the hypothetical desirability of trial marriages. At once the newspapers seized these three lines, "played them up yellow," as the slang was in those days, and set the whole world laughing at Emil Gluck, the bespectacled young professor of twenty-seven. Photographers snapped him, he was besieged by reporters, women's clubs throughout the land passed resolutions condemning him and his immoral theories; and on the floor of the California Assembly, while discussing the state appropriation to the University, a motion demanding the expulsion of Gluck was made under threat of withholding the appropriation—of course, none of his persecutors had read the book; the twisted newspaper version of only three lines of it was enough for them. Here began Emil Gluck's hatred for newspaper men. By them his serious and intrinsically valuable work of six years had been made a laughing-stock and a notoriety. To his dying day, and to their everlasting regret, he never forgave them.

It was the newspapers that were responsible for the next disaster that befell him. For the five years following the publication of his book he had remained silent, and silence for a lonely man is not good. One can conjecture sympathetically the awful solitude of Emil Gluck in that populous University; for he was without friends and without sympathy. His only recourse was books, and he went on reading and studying enormously. But in 1927 he accepted an invitation to appear before the Human Interest Society of Emeryville. He did not trust himself to speak, and as we write we have before us a copy of his learned paper. It is sober, scholarly, and scientific, and, it must also be added, conservative. But in one place he dealt with, and I quote his words, "the industrial and social revolution that is taking place in society." A reporter present seized upon the word "revolution," divorced it from the text, and wrote a garbled account that made Emil Gluck appear an anarchist. At once, "Professor Gluck, anarchist," flamed over the wires and was appropriately "featured" in all the newspapers in the land.

He had attempted to reply to the previous newspaper attack, but now he remained silent. Bitterness had already corroded his soul. The University faculty appealed to him to defend himself, but he sullenly declined, even refusing to enter in defence a copy of his paper to save himself from expulsion. He refused to resign, and was discharged from the University faculty. It must be added that political pressure had been put upon the University Regents and the President.

Persecuted, maligned, and misunderstood, the forlorn and lonely man made no attempt at retaliation. All his life he had been sinned against, and all his life he had sinned against no one. But his cup of bitterness was not yet full to overflowing. Having lost his position, and being without any income, he had to find work. His first place was at the Union Iron Works, in San Francisco, where he proved a most able draughtsman. It was here that he obtained his firsthand knowledge of battleships and their construction. But the reporters discovered him and featured him in his new vocation. He immediately resigned and found another place; but after the reporters had driven him away from half-a-dozen positions, he steeled himself to brazen out the newspaper persecution. This occurred when he started his electroplating establishment—in Oakland, on Telegraph Avenue. It was a small shop, employing three men and two boys. Gluck himself worked long hours. Night after night, as Policeman Carew testified on the stand, he did not leave the shop till one and two in the morning. It was during this period that he perfected the improved ignition device for gas-engines, the royalties from which ultimately made him wealthy.

He started his electroplating establishment early in the spring of 1928, and it was in the same year that he formed the disastrous love attachment for Irene Tackley. Now it is not to be imagined that an extraordinary creature such as Emil Gluck could be any other than an extraordinary lover. In addition to his genius, his loneliness, and his morbidness, it must be taken into consideration that he knew nothing about women. Whatever tides of desire flooded his being, he was unschooled in the conventional expression of them; while his excessive timidity was bound to make his love-making unusual. Irene Tackley was a rather pretty young woman, but shallow and light-headed. At the time she worked in a small candy store across the street from Gluck's shop. He used to come in and drink ice-cream sodas and lemon-squashes, and stare at her. It seems the girl did not care for him, and merely played with him. He was "queer," she said; and at another time she called him a crank when describing how he sat at the counter and peered at her through his spectacles, blushing and stammering when she took notice of him, and often leaving the shop in precipitate confusion.

Gluck made her the most amazing presents—a silver tea-service, a diamond ring, a set of furs, opera-glasses, a ponderous History of the World in many volumes, and a motor-cycle all silver-plated in his own shop. Enters now the girl's lover, putting his foot down, showing great anger, compelling her to return Gluck's strange assortment of presents. This man, William Sherbourne, was a gross and stolid creature, a heavy-jawed man of the working class who had become a successful building-contractor in a small way. Gluck did not understand. He tried to get an explanation, attempting to speak with the girl when she went home from work in the evening. She complained to Sherbourne, and one night he gave Gluck a beating. It was a very severe beating, for it is on the records of the Red Cross Emergency Hospital that Gluck was treated there that night and was unable to leave the hospital for a week.

Still Gluck did not understand. He continued to seek an explanation from the girl. In fear of Sherbourne, he applied to the Chief of Police for permission to carry a revolver, which permission was refused, the newspapers as usual playing it up sensationally. Then came the murder of Irene Tackley, six days before her contemplated marriage with Sherbourne. It was on a Saturday night. She had worked late in the candy store, departing after eleven o'clock with her week's wages in her purse. She rode on a San Pablo Avenue surface car to Thirty-fourth Street, where she alighted and started to walk the three blocks to her home. That was the last seen of her alive. Next morning she was found, strangled, in a vacant lot.

Emil Gluck was immediately arrested. Nothing that he could do could save him. He was convicted, not merely on circumstantial evidence, but on evidence "cooked up" by the Oakland police. There is no discussion but that a large portion of the evidence was manufactured. The testimony of Captain Shehan was the sheerest perjury, it being proved long afterward that on the night in question he had not only not been in the vicinity of the murder, but that he had been out of the city in a resort on the San Leandro Road. The unfortunate Gluck received life imprisonment in San Quentin, while the newspapers and the public held that it was a miscarriage of justice—that the death penalty should have been visited upon him.

Gluck entered San Quentin prison on April 17, 1929. He was then thirty-four years of age. And for three years and a half, much of the time in solitary confinement, he was left to meditate upon the injustice of man. It was during that period that his bitterness corroded home and he became a hater of all his kind. Three other things he did during the same period: he wrote his famous treatise, Human Morals, his remarkable brochure, The Criminal Sane, and he worked out his awful and monstrous scheme of revenge. It was an episode that had occurred in his electroplating establishment that suggested to him his unique weapon of revenge. As stated in his confession, he worked every detail out theoretically during his imprisonment, and was able, on his release, immediately to embark on his career of vengeance.

His release was sensational. Also it was miserably and criminally delayed by the soulless legal red tape then in vogue. On the night of February 1, 1932, Tim Haswell, a hold-up man, was shot during an attempted robbery by a citizen of Piedmont Heights. Tim Haswell lingered three days, during which time he not only confessed to the murder of Irene Tackley, but furnished conclusive proofs of the same. Bert Danniker, a convict dying of consumption in Folsom Prison, was implicated as accessory, and his confession followed. It is inconceivable to us of today—the bungling, dilatory processes of justice a generation ago. Emil Gluck was proved in February to be an innocent man, yet he was not released until the following October. For eight months, a greatly wronged man, he was compelled to undergo his unmerited punishment. This was not conducive to sweetness and light, and we can well imagine how he ate his soul with bitterness during those dreary eight months.

He came back to the world in the fall of 1932, as usual a "feature" topic in all the newspapers. The papers, instead of expressing heartfelt regret, continued their old sensational persecution. One paper did more—the San Francisco Intelligencer. John Hartwell, its editor, elaborated an ingenious theory that got around the confessions of the two criminals and went to show that Gluck was responsible, after all, for the murder of Irene Tackley. Hartwell died. And Sherbourne died too, while Policeman Phillipps was shot in the leg and discharged from the Oakland police force.

The murder of Hartwell was long a mystery. He was alone in his editorial office at the time. The reports of the revolver were heard by the office boy, who rushed in to find Hartwell expiring in his chair. What puzzled the police was the fact, not merely that he had been shot with his own revolver, but that the revolver had been exploded in the drawer of his desk. The bullets had torn through the front of the drawer and entered his body. The police scouted the theory of suicide, murder was dismissed as absurd, and the blame was thrown upon the Eureka Smokeless Cartridge Company. Spontaneous explosion was the police explanation, and the chemists of the cartridge company were well bullied at the inquest. But what the police did not know was that across the street, in the Mercer Building, Room 633, rented by Emil Gluck, had been occupied by Emil Gluck at the very moment Hartwell's revolver so mysteriously exploded.

At the time, no connection was made between Hartwell's death and the death of William Sherbourne. Sherbourne had continued to live in the home he had built for Irene Tackley, and one morning in January, 1933, he was found dead. Suicide was the verdict of the coroner's inquest, for he had been shot by his own revolver. The curious thing that happened that night was the shooting of Policeman Phillipps on the sidewalk in front of Sherbourne's house. The policeman crawled to a police telephone on the corner and rang up for an ambulance. He claimed that some one had shot him from behind in the leg. The leg in question was so badly shattered by three .38 calibre bullets that amputation was necessary. But when the police discovered that the damage had been done by his own revolver, a great laugh went up, and he was charged with having been drunk. In spite of his denial of having touched a drop, and of his persistent assertion that the revolver had been in his hip pocket and that he had not laid a finger to it, he was discharged from the force. Emil Gluck's confession, six years later, cleared the unfortunate policeman of disgrace, and he is alive today and in good health, the recipient of a handsome pension from the city.

Emil Gluck, having disposed of his immediate enemies, now sought a wider field, though his enmity for newspaper men and for the police remained always active. The royalties on his ignition device for gasolene-engines had mounted up while he lay in prison, and year by year the earning power of his invention increased. He was independent, able to travel wherever he willed over the earth and to glut his monstrous appetite for revenge. He had become a monomaniac and an anarchist—not a philosophic anarchist, merely, but a violent anarchist. Perhaps the word is misused, and he is better described as a nihilist, or an annihilist. It is known that he affiliated with none of the groups of terrorists. He operated wholly alone, but he created a thousandfold more terror and achieved a thousandfold more destruction than all the terrorist groups added together.

He signalized his departure from California by blowing up Fort Mason. In his confession he spoke of it as a little experiment—he was merely trying his hand. For eight years he wandered over the earth, a mysterious terror, destroying property to the tune of hundreds of millions of dollars, and destroying countless lives. One good result of his awful deeds was the destruction he wrought among the terrorists themselves. Every time he did anything the terrorists in the vicinity were gathered in by the police dragnet, and many of them were executed. Seventeen were executed at Rome alone, following the assassination of the Italian King.

Perhaps the most world-amazing achievement of his was the assassination of the King and Queen of Portugal. It was their wedding day. All possible precautions had been taken against the terrorists, and the way from the cathedral, through Lisbon's streets, was double-banked with troops, while a squad of two hundred mounted troopers surrounded the carriage. Suddenly the amazing thing happened. The automatic rifles of the troopers began to go off, as well as the rifles, in the immediate vicinity, of the double-banked infantry. In the excitement the muzzles of the exploding rifles were turned in all directions. The slaughter was terrible—horses, troops, spectators, and the King and Queen, were riddled with bullets. To complicate the affair, in different parts of the crowd behind the foot-soldiers, two terrorists had bombs explode on their persons. These bombs they had intended to throw if they got the opportunity. But who was to know this? The frightful havoc wrought by the bursting bombs but added to the confusion; it was considered part of the general attack.

One puzzling thing that could not be explained away was the conduct of the troopers with their exploding rifles. It seemed impossible that they should be in the plot, yet there were the hundreds their flying bullets had slain, including the King and Queen. On the other hand, more baffling than ever was the fact that seventy per cent. of the troopers themselves had been killed or wounded. Some explained this on the ground that the loyal foot-soldiers, witnessing the attack on the royal carriage, had opened fire on the traitors. Yet not one bit of evidence to verify this could be drawn from the survivors, though many were put to the torture. They contended stubbornly that they had not discharged their rifles at all, but that their rifles had discharged themselves. They were laughed at by the chemists, who held that, while it was just barely probable that a single cartridge, charged with the new smokeless powder, might spontaneously explode, it was beyond all probability and possibility for all the cartridges in a given area, so charged, spontaneously to explode. And so, in the end, no explanation of the amazing occurrence was reached. The general opinion of the rest of the world was that the whole affair was a blind panic of the feverish Latins, precipitated, it was true, by the bursting of two terrorist bombs; and in this connection was recalled the laughable encounter of long years before between the Russian fleet and the English fishing boats.

And Emil Gluck chuckled and went his way. He knew. But how was the world to know? He had stumbled upon the secret in his old electroplating shop on Telegraph Avenue in the city of Oakland. It happened, at that time, that a wireless telegraph station was established by the Thurston Power Company close to his shop. In a short time his electroplating vat was put out of order. The vat-wiring had many bad joints, and, on investigation, Gluck discovered minute welds at the joints in the wiring. These, by lowering the resistance, had caused an excessive current to pass through the solution, "boiling" it and spoiling the work. But what had caused the welds? was the question in Gluck's mind. His reasoning was simple. Before the establishment of the wireless station, the vat had worked well. Not until after the establishment of the wireless station had the vat been ruined. Therefore the wireless station had been the cause. But how? He quickly answered the question. If an electric discharge was capable of operating a coherer across three thousand miles of ocean, then, certainly, the electric discharges from the wireless station four hundred feet away could produce coherer effects on the bad joints in the vat-wiring.

Gluck thought no more about it at the time. He merely re-wired his vat and went on electroplating. But afterwards, in prison, he remembered the incident, and like a flash there came into his mind the full significance of it. He saw in it the silent, secret weapon with which to revenge himself on the world. His great discovery, which died with him, was control over the direction and scope of the electric discharge. At the time, this was the unsolved problem of wireless telegraphy—as it still is today—but Emil Gluck, in his prison cell, mastered it. And, when he was released, he applied it. It was fairly simple, given the directing power that was his, to introduce a spark into the powder-magazines of a fort, a battleship, or a revolver. And not alone could he thus explode powder at a distance, but he could ignite conflagrations. The great Boston fire was started by him—quite by accident, however, as he stated in his confession, adding that it was a pleasing accident and that he had never had any reason to regret it.

It was Emil Gluck that caused the terrible German-American War, with the loss of 800,000 lives and the consumption of almost incalculable treasure. It will be remembered that in 1939, because of the Pickard incident, strained relations existed between the two countries. Germany, though aggrieved, was not anxious for war, and, as a peace token, sent the Crown Prince and seven battleships on a friendly visit to the United States. On the night of February 15, the seven warships lay at anchor in the Hudson opposite New York City. And on that night Emil Gluck, alone, with all his apparatus on board, was out in a launch. This launch, it was afterwards proved, was bought by him from the Ross Turner Company, while much of the apparatus he used that night had been purchased from the Columbia Electric Works. But this was not known at the time. All that was known was that the seven battleships blew up, one after another, at regular four-minute intervals. Ninety per cent of the crews and officers, along with the Crown Prince, perished. Many years before, the American battleship Maine had been blown up in the harbour of Havana, and war with Spain had immediately followed—though there has always existed a reasonable doubt as to whether the explosion was due to conspiracy or accident. But accident could not explain the blowing up of the seven battleships on the Hudson at four-minute intervals. Germany believed that it had been done by a submarine, and immediately declared war. It was six months after Gluck's confession that she returned the Philippines and Hawaii to the United States.

In the meanwhile Emil Gluck, the malevolent wizard and arch-hater, travelled his whirlwind path of destruction. He left no traces. Scientifically thorough, he always cleaned up after himself. His method was to rent a room or a house, and secretly to install his apparatus—which apparatus, by the way, he so perfected and simplified that it occupied little space. After he had accomplished his purpose he carefully removed the apparatus. He bade fair to live out a long life of horrible crime.

The epidemic of shooting of New York City policemen was a remarkable affair. It became one of the horror mysteries of the time. In two short weeks over a hundred policemen were shot in the legs by their own revolvers. Inspector Jones did not solve the mystery, but it was his idea that finally outwitted Gluck. On his recommendation the policemen ceased carrying revolvers, and no more accidental shootings occurred.

It was in the early spring of 1940 that Gluck destroyed the Mare Island navy-yard. From a room in Vallejo he sent his electric discharges across the Vallejo Straits to Mare Island. He first played his flashes on the battleship Maryland. She lay at the dock of one of the mine-magazines. On her forward deck, on a huge temporary platform of timbers, were disposed over a hundred mines. These mines were for the defence of the Golden Gate. Any one of these mines was capable of destroying a dozen battleships, and there were over a hundred mines. The destruction was terrific, but it was only Gluck's overture. He played his flashes down the Mare Island shore, blowing up five torpedo boats, the torpedo station, and the great magazine at the eastern end of the island. Returning westward again, and scooping in occasional isolated magazines on the high ground back from the shore, he blew up three cruisers and the battleships Oregon, Delaware, New Hampshire, and Florida—the latter had just gone into dry-dock, and the magnificent dry-dock was destroyed along with her.

It was a frightful catastrophe, and a shiver of horror passed through the land. But it was nothing to what was to follow. In the late fall of that year Emil Gluck made a clean sweep of the Atlantic seaboard from Maine to Florida. Nothing escaped. Forts, mines, coast defences of all sorts, torpedo stations, magazines—everything went up. Three months afterward, in midwinter, he smote the north shore of the Mediterranean from Gibraltar to Greece in the same stupefying manner. A wail went up from the nations. It was clear that human agency was behind all this destruction, and it was equally clear, through Emil Gluck's impartiality, that the destruction was not the work of any particular nation. One thing was patent, namely, that whoever was the human behind it all, that human was a menace to the world. No nation was safe. There was no defence against this unknown and all-powerful foe. Warfare was futile—nay, not merely futile but itself the very essence of the peril. For a twelve-month the manufacture of powder ceased, and all soldiers and sailors were withdrawn from all fortifications and war vessels. And even a world-disarmament was seriously considered at the Convention of the Powers, held at The Hague at that time.

And then Silas Bannerman, a secret service agent of the United States, leaped into world-fame by arresting Emil Gluck. At first Bannerman was laughed at, but he had prepared his case well, and in a few weeks the most sceptical were convinced of Emil Gluck's guilt. The one thing, however, that Silas Bannerman never succeeded in explaining, even to his own satisfaction, was how first he came to connect Gluck with the atrocious crimes. It is true, Bannerman was in Vallejo, on secret government business, at the time of the destruction of Mare Island; and it is true that on the streets of Vallejo Emil Gluck was pointed out to him as a queer crank; but no impression was made at the time. It was not until afterward, when on a vacation in the Rocky Mountains and when reading the first published reports of the destruction along the Atlantic Coast, that suddenly Bannerman thought of Emil Gluck. And on the instant there flashed into his mind the connection between Gluck and the destruction. It was only an hypothesis, but it was sufficient. The great thing was the conception of the hypothesis, in itself an act of unconscious cerebration—a thing as unaccountable as the flashing, for instance, into Newton's mind of the principle of gravitation.

The rest was easy. Where was Gluck at the time of the destruction along the Atlantic sea-board? was the question that formed in Bannerman's mind. By his own request he was put upon the case. In no time he ascertained that Gluck had himself been up and down the Atlantic Coast in the late fall of 1940. Also he ascertained that Gluck had been in New York City during the epidemic of the shooting of police officers. Where was Gluck now? was Bannerman's next query. And, as if in answer, came the wholesale destruction along the Mediterranean. Gluck had sailed for Europe a month before— Bannerman knew that. It was not necessary for Bannerman to go to Europe. By means of cable messages and the co-operation of the European secret services, he traced Gluck's course along the Mediterranean and found that in every instance it coincided with the blowing up of coast defences and ships. Also, he learned that Gluck had just sailed on the Green Star liner Plutonic for the United States.

The case was complete in Bannerman's mind, though in the interval of waiting he worked up the details. In this he was ably assisted by George Brown, an operator employed by the Wood's System of Wireless Telegraphy. When the Plutonic arrived off Sandy Hook she was boarded by Bannerman from a Government tug, and Emil Gluck was made a prisoner. The trial and the confession followed. In the confession Gluck professed regret only for one thing, namely, that he had taken his time. As he said, had he dreamed that he was ever to be discovered he would have worked more rapidly and accomplished a thousand times the destruction he did. His secret died with him, though it is now known that the French Government managed to get access to him and offered him a billion francs for his invention wherewith he was able to direct and closely to confine electric discharges. "What!" was Gluck's reply—"to sell to you that which would enable you to enslave and maltreat suffering Humanity?" And though the war departments of the nations have continued to experiment in their secret laboratories, they have so far failed to light upon the slightest trace of the secret. Emil Gluck was executed on December 4, 1941, and so died, at the age of forty-six, one of the world's most unfortunate geniuses, a man of tremendous intellect, but whose mighty powers, instead of making toward good, were so twisted and warped that he became the most amazing of criminals.

* * * * *

—Culled from Mr. A. G. Burnside's "Eccentricitics of Crime," by kind permission of the publishers, Messrs. Holiday and Whitsund.

A CURIOUS FRAGMENT

by Jack London

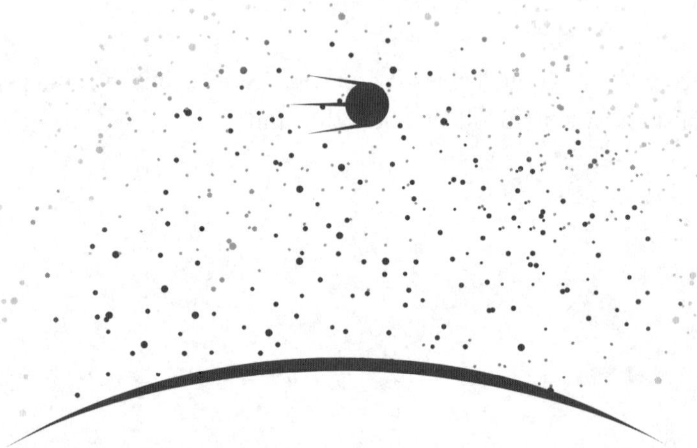

[The capitalist, or industrial oligarch, Roger Vanderwater, mentioned in the narrative, has been identified as the ninth in the line of the Vanderwaters that controlled for hundreds of years the cotton factories of the South. This Roger Vanderwater flourished in the last decades of the twenty-sixth century after Christ, which was the fifth century of the terrible industrial oligarchy that was reared upon the ruins of the early Republic.

From internal evidences we are convinced that the narrative which follows was not reduced to writing till the twenty-ninth century. Not only was it unlawful to write or print such matter during that period, but the working-class was so illiterate that only in rare instances were its members able to read and write. This was the dark reign of the overman, in whose speech the great mass of the people were characterized as the "herd animals." All literacy was frowned upon and stamped out. From the statute-books of the times may be instanced that black law that made it a capital offence for any man, no matter of what class, to teach even the alphabet to a member of the working-class. Such stringent limitation of education to the ruling class was necessary if that class was to continue to rule.

One result of the foregoing was the development of the professional story-tellers. These story-tellers were paid by the oligarchy, and the tales they told were legendary, mythical, romantic, and harmless. But the spirit of freedom never quite died out, and agitators, under the guise of story-tellers, preached revolt to the slave class. That the following tale was banned by the oligarchs we have proof from the records of the criminal police court of Ashbury, wherein, on January 27, 2734, one John Tourney, found guilty of telling the tale in a boozing-ken of labourers, was sentenced to five years' penal servitude in the borax mines of the Arizona Desert.—EDITOR'S NOTE.]

* * * * *

Listen, my brothers, and I will tell you a tale of an arm. It was the arm of Tom Dixon, and Tom Dixon was a weaver of the first class in a factory of that hell-hound and master, Roger Vanderwater. This factory was called "Hell's Bottom" … by the slaves who toiled in it, and I guess they ought to know; and it was situated in Kingsbury, at the other end of the town from Vanderwater's summer palace. You do not know where Kingsbury is? There are many things, my brothers, that you do not know, and it is sad. It is because you do not know that you are slaves. When I have told you this tale, I should like to form a class among you for the learning of written and printed speech. Our masters read and write and possess many books, and it is because of that that they are our masters, and live in palaces, and do not work. When the toilers learn to read and write—all of them—they will grow strong; then they will use their strength to break their bonds, and there will be no more masters and no more slaves.

Kingsbury, my brothers, is in the old State of Alabama. For three hundred years the Vanderwaters have owned Kingsbury and its slave pens and factories, and slave pens and factories in many other places and States. You have heard of the Vanderwaters—who has not?—but let me tell you things you do not know about them. The first Vanderwater was a slave, even as you and I. Have you got that?

He was a slave, and that was over three hundred years ago. His father was a machinist in the slave pen of Alexander Burrell, and his mother was a washerwoman in the same slave pen. There is no doubt about this. I am telling you truth. It is history. It is printed, every word of it, in the history books of our masters, which you cannot read because your masters will not permit you to learn to read. You can understand why they will not permit you to learn to read, when there are such things in the books. They know, and they are very wise. If you did read such things, you might be wanting in respect to your masters, which would be a dangerous thing … to your masters. But I know, for I can read, and I am telling you what I have read with my own eyes in the history books of our masters.

The first Vanderwater's name was not Vanderwater; it was Vange—Bill Vange, the son of Yergis Vange, the machinist, and Laura Carnly, the washerwoman. Young Bill Vange was strong. He might have remained with the slaves and led them to freedom; instead, however, he served the masters and was well rewarded. He began his service, when yet a small child, as a spy in his home slave pen. He is known to have informed on his own father for seditious utterance. This is fact. I have read it with my own eyes in the records. He was too good a slave for the slave pen. Alexander Burrell took him out, while yet a child, and he was taught to read and write. He was taught many things, and he was entered in the secret service of the Government. Of course, he no longer wore the slave dress, except for disguise at such times when he sought to penetrate the secrets and plots of the slaves. It was he, when but eighteen years of age, who brought that great hero and comrade, Ralph Jacobus, to trial and execution in the electric chair. Of course, you have all heard the sacred name of Ralph Jacobus, but it is news to you that he was brought to his death by the first Vanderwater, whose name was Vange. I know. I have read it in the books. There are many interesting things like that in the books.

And after Ralph Jacobus died his shameful death, Bill Vange's name began the many changes it was to undergo. He was known as "Sly Vange" far and wide. He rose high in the secret service, and he was rewarded in grand ways, but still he was not a member of the master class. The men were willing that he should become so; it was the women of the master class who refused to have Sly Vange one of them. Sly Vange gave good service to the masters. He had been a slave himself, and he knew the ways of the slaves. There was no fooling him. In those days the slaves were braver than now, and they were always trying for their freedom. And Sly Vange was everywhere, in all their schemes and plans, bringing their schemes and plans to naught and their leaders to the electric chair. It was in 2255 that his name was next changed for him. It was in that year that the Great Mutiny took place. In that region west of the Rocky Mountains, seventeen millions of slaves strove bravely to overthrow their masters. Who knows, if Sly Vange had not lived, but that they would have succeeded? But Sly Vange was very much alive. The masters gave him supreme command of the situation. In eight months of fighting, one million and three hundred and fifty thousand slaves were killed. Vange, Bill Vange, Sly Vange, killed them, and he broke the Great Mutiny. And he was greatly rewarded, and so red were his hands with the blood of the slaves that thereafter he was called "Bloody Vange." You see, my brothers, what interesting things are to be found in the books when one can read them. And, take my word for it, there are many other things, even more interesting, in the books. And if you will but study with me, in a year's time you can read those books for yourselves—ay, in six months some of you will be able to read those books for yourselves.

Bloody Vange lived to a ripe old age, and always, to the last, was he received in the councils of the masters; but never was he made a master himself. He had first opened his eyes, you see, in a slave pen. But oh, he was well rewarded! He had a dozen palaces in which to live. He, who was no master, owned thousands of slaves. He had a great pleasure yacht upon the sea that was a floating palace, and he owned a whole island in the sea where toiled ten thousand slaves on his coffee plantations. But in his old age he was lonely, for he lived apart, hated by his brothers, the slaves, and looked down upon by those he had served and who refused to be his brothers. The masters looked down upon him because he had been born a slave. Enormously wealthy he died; but he died horribly, tormented by his conscience, regretting all he had done and the red stain on his name.

But with his children it was different. They had not been born in the slave pen, and by the special ruling of the Chief Oligarch of that time, John Morrison, they were elevated to the master class. And it was then that the name of Vange disappears from the page of history. It becomes Vanderwater, and Jason Vange, the son of Bloody Vange, becomes Jason Vanderwater, the founder of the Vanderwater line. But that was three hundred years ago, and the Vanderwaters of today forget their beginnings and imagine that somehow the clay of their bodies is different stuff from the clay in your body and mine and in the bodies of all slaves. And I ask you, Why should a slave become the master of another slave? And why should the son of a slave become the master of many slaves? I leave these questions for you to answer for yourselves, but do not forget that in the beginning the Vanderwaters were slaves.

And now, my brothers, I come back to the beginning of my tale to tell you of Tom Dixon's arm. Roger Vanderwater's factory in Kingsbury was rightly named "Hell's Bottom," but the men who toiled in it were men, as you shall see. Women toiled there, too, and children, little children. All that toiled there had the regular slave rights under the law, but only under the law, for they were deprived of many of their rights by the two overseers of Hell's Bottom, Joseph Clancy and Adolph Munster.

It is a long story, but I shall not tell all of it to you. I shall tell only about the arm. It happened that, according to the law, a portion of the starvation wage of the slaves was held back each month and put into a fund. This fund was for the purpose of helping such unfortunate fellow-workmen as happened to be injured by accidents or to be overtaken by sickness. As you know with yourselves, these funds are controlled by the overseers. It is the law, and so it was that the fund at Hell's Bottom was controlled by the two overseers of accursed memory.

Now, Clancy and Munster took this fund for their own use. When accidents happened to the workmen, their fellows, as was the custom, made grants from the fund; but the overseers refused to pay over the grants. What could the slaves do? They had their rights under the law, but they had no access to the law. Those that complained to the overseers were punished. You know yourselves what form such punishment takes—the fines for faulty work that is not faulty; the overcharging of accounts in the Company's store; the vile treatment of one's women and children; and the allotment to bad machines whereon, work as one will, he starves.

Once, the slaves of Hell's Bottom protested to Vanderwater. It was the time of the year when he spent several months in Kingsbury. One of the slaves could write; it chanced that his mother could write, and she had secretly taught him as her mother had secretly taught her. So this slave wrote a round robin, wherein was contained their grievances, and all the slaves signed by mark. And, with proper stamps upon the envelope, the round robin was mailed to Roger Vanderwater. And Roger Vanderwater did nothing, save to turn the round robin over to the two overseers. Clancy and Munster were angered. They turned the guards loose at night on the slave pen. The guards were armed with pick handles. It is said that next day only half of the slaves were able to work in Hell's Bottom. They were well beaten. The slave who could write was so badly beaten that he lived only three months. But before he died, he wrote once more, to what purpose you shall hear.

Four or five weeks afterward, Tom Dixon, a slave, had his arm torn off by a belt in Hell's Bottom. His fellow-workmen, as usual, made a grant to him from the fund, and Clancy and Munster, as usual, refused to pay it over from the fund. The slave who could write, and who even then was dying, wrote anew a recital of their grievances. And this document was thrust into the hand of the arm that had been torn from Tom Dixon's body.

Now it chanced that Roger Vanderwater was lying ill in his palace at the other end of Kingsbury—not the dire illness that strikes down you and me, brothers; just a bit of biliousness, mayhap, or no more than a bad headache because he had eaten too heartily or drunk too deeply. But it was enough for him, being tender and soft from careful rearing. Such men, packed in cotton wool all their lives, are exceeding tender and soft. Believe me, brothers, Roger Vanderwater felt as badly with his aching head, or *thought* he felt as badly, as Tom Dixon really felt with his arm torn out by the roots.

It happened that Roger Vanderwater was fond of scientific farming, and that on his farm, three miles outside of Kingsbury, he had managed to grow a new kind of strawberry. He was very proud of that new strawberry of his, and he would have been out to see and pick the first ripe ones, had it not been for his illness. Because of his illness he had ordered the old farm slave to bring in personally the first box of the berries. All this was learned from the gossip of a palace scullion, who slept each night in the slave pen. The overseer of the plantation should have brought in the berries, but he was on his back with a broken leg from trying to break a colt. The scullion brought the word in the night, and it was known that next day the berries would come in. And the men in the slave pen of Hell's Bottom, being men and not cowards, held a council.

The slave who could write, and who was sick and dying from the pick-handle beating, said he would carry Tom Dixon's arm; also, he said he must die anyway, and that it mattered nothing if he died a little sooner. So five slaves stole from the slave pen that night after the guards had made their last rounds. One of the slaves was the man who could write. They lay in the brush by the roadside until late in the morning, when the old farm slave came driving to town with the precious fruit for the master. What of the farm slave being old and rheumatic, and of the slave who could write being stiff and injured from his beating, they moved their bodies about when they walked, very much in the same fashion. The slave who could write put on the other's clothes, pulled the broad-brimmed hat over his eyes, climbed upon the seat of the wagon, and drove on to town. The old farm slave was kept tied all day in the bushes until evening, when the others loosed him and went back to the slave pen to take their punishment for having broken bounds.

In the meantime, Roger Vanderwater lay waiting for the berries in his wonderful bedroom—such wonders and such comforts were there that they would have blinded the eyes of you and me who have never seen such things. The slave who could write said afterward that it was like a glimpse of Paradise! And why not? The labour and the lives of ten thousand slaves had gone to the making of that bedchamber, while they themselves slept in vile lairs like wild beasts. The slave who could write brought in the berries on a silver tray or platter—you see, Roger Vanderwater wanted to speak with him in person about the berries.

The slave who could write tottered his dying body across the wonderful room and knelt by the couch of Vanderwater, holding out before him the tray. Large green leaves covered the top of the tray, and these the body-servant alongside whisked away so that Vanderwater could see. And Roger Vanderwater, propped upon his elbow, saw. He saw the fresh, wonderful fruit lying there like precious jewels, and in the midst of it the arm of Tom Dixon as it had been torn from his body, well washed, of course, my brothers, and very white against the blood-red fruit. And also he saw, clutched in the stiff, dead fingers, the petition of his slaves who toiled in Hell's Bottom.

"Take and read," said the slave who could write. And even as the master took the petition, the body-servant, who till then had been motionless with surprise, struck with his fist the kneeling slave upon the mouth. The slave was dying anyway, and was very weak, and did not mind. He made no sound, and, having fallen over on his side, he lay there quietly, bleeding from the blow on the mouth. The physician, who had run for the palace guards, came back with them, and the slave was dragged upright upon his feet. But as they dragged him up, his hand clutched Tom Dixon's arm from where it had fallen on the floor.

"He shall be flung alive to the hounds!" the body-servant was crying in great wrath. "He shall be flung alive to the hounds!"

But Roger Vanderwater, forgetting his headache, still leaning on his elbow, commanded silence, and went on reading the petition. And while he read, there was silence, all standing upright, the wrathful body-servant, the physician, the palace guards, and in their midst the slave, bleeding at the mouth and still holding Tom Dixon's arm. And when Roger Vanderwater had done, he turned upon the slave, saying—

"If in this paper there be one lie, you shall be sorry that you were ever born."

And the slave said, "I have been sorry all my life that I was born."

Roger Vanderwater looked at him closely, and the slave said—

"You have done your worst to me. I am dying now. In a week I shall be dead, so it does not matter if you kill me now."

"What do you with that?" the master asked, pointing to the arm; and the slave made answer—

"I take it back to the pen to give it burial. Tom Dixon was my friend. We worked beside each other at our looms."

There is little more to my tale, brothers. The slave and the arm were sent back in a cart to the pen. Nor were any of the slaves punished for what they had done. Indeed, Roger Vanderwater made investigation and punished the two overseers, Joseph Clancy and Adolph Munster. Their freeholds were taken from them. They were branded, each upon the forehead, their right hands were cut off, and they were turned loose upon the highway to wander and beg until they died. And the fund was managed rightfully thereafter for a time—for a time only, my brothers; for after Roger Vanderwater came his son, Albert, who was a cruel master and half mad.

Brothers, that slave who carried the arm into the presence of the master was my father. He was a brave man. And even as his mother secretly taught him to read, so did he teach me. Because he died shortly after from the pick-handle beating, Roger Vanderwater took me out of the slave pen and tried to make various better things out of me. I might have become an overseer in Hell's Bottom, but I chose to become a story-teller, wandering over the land and getting close to my brothers, the slaves, everywhere. And I tell you stories like this, secretly, knowing that you will not betray me; for if you did, you know as well as I that my tongue will be torn out and that I shall tell stories no more. And my message is, brothers, that there is a good time coming, when all will be well in the world and there will be neither masters nor slaves. But first you must prepare for that good time by learning to read. There is power in the printed word. And here am I to teach you to read, and as well there are others to see that you get the books when I am gone along upon my way—the history books wherein you will learn about your masters, and learn to become strong even as they.

* * * * *

[EDITOR'S NOTE.—From "Historical Fragments and Sketches," first published in fifty volumes in 4427, and now, after two hundred years, because of its accuracy and value, edited and republished by the National Committee on Historical Research.]

THE MAN WHO SAVED THE EARTH

by Austin Hall

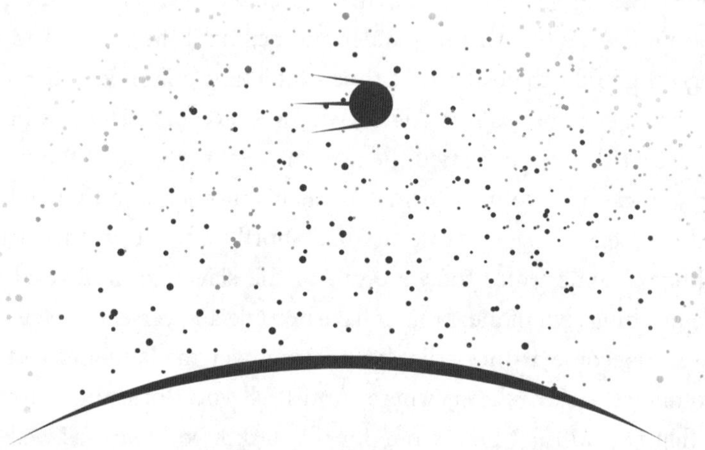

I
THE BEGINNING

Even the beginning. From the start the whole thing has the precision of machine work. Fate and its working—and the wonderful Providence which watches over Man and his future. The whole thing unerring: the incident, the work, the calamity, and the martyr. In the retrospect of disaster we may all of us grow strong in wisdom. Let us go into history.

A hot July day. A sun of scant pity, and a staggering street; panting thousands dragging along, hatless; fans and parasols; the sultry vengeance of a real day of summer. A day of bursting tires; hot pavements, and wrecked endeavour, heart-aches for the seashore, for leafy bowers beside rippling water, a day of broken hopes and listless ambition.

Perhaps Fate chose the day because of its heat and because of its natural benefit on fecundity. We have no way of knowing. But we do know this: the date, the time, the meeting; the boy with the burning glass and the old doctor. So common-place, so trivial and hidden in obscurity! Who would have guessed it? Yet it is—after the creation—one of the most important dates in the world's history.

This is saying a whole lot. Let us go into it and see what it amounts to. Let us trace the thing out in history, weigh it up and balance it with sequence.

Of Charley Huyck we know nothing up to this day. It is a thing which, for some reason, he has always kept hidden. Recent investigation as to his previous life and antecedents have availed us nothing. Perhaps he could have told us; but as he has gone down as the world's great martyr, there is no hope of gaining from his lips what we would so like to know.

After all, it does not matter. We have the day—the incident, and its purport, and its climax of sequence to the day of the great disaster. Also we have the blasted mountains and the lake of blue water which will ever live with his memory. His greatness is not of warfare, nor personal ambition; but of all mankind. The wreaths that we bestow upon him have no doubtful colour. The man who saved the earth!

From such a beginning, Charley Huyck, lean and frail of body, with, even then, the wistfulness of the idealist, and the eyes of a poet. Charley Huyck, the boy, crossing the hot pavement with his pack of papers; the much treasured piece of glass in his pocket, and the sun which only he should master burning down upon him. A moment out of the ages; the turning of a straw destined to out-balance all the previous accumulation of man's history.

The sun was hot and burning, and the child—he could not have been more than ten—cast a glance over his shoulder. It was in the way of calculation. In the heyday of childhood he was not dragged down by the heat and weather: he had the enthusiasm of his half-score of years and the joy of the plaything. We will not presume to call it the spirit of the scientist, though it was, perhaps, the spark of latent investigation that was destined to lead so far.

A moment picked out of destiny! A boy and a plaything. Uncounted millions of boys have played with glass and the sun rays. Who cannot remember the little, round-burning dot in the palm of the hand and the subsequent exclamation?

Charley Huyck had found a new toy, it was a simple thing and as old as glass. Fate will ever be so in her working.

And the doctor? Why should he have been waiting? If it was not destiny, it was at least an accumulation of moment. In the heavy eye-glasses, the square, close-cut beard; and his uncompromising fact-seeking expression. Those who knew Dr. Robold are strong in the affirmation that he was the antithesis of all emotion. He was the sternest product of science: unbending, hardened by experiment, and caustic in his condemnation of the frailness of human nature.

It had been his one function to topple over the castles of the foolish; with his hard-seeing wisdom he had spotted sophistry where we thought it not. Even into the castles of science he had gone like a juggernaut. It is hard to have one's theories derided— yea, even for a scientist—and to be called a fool! Dr. Robold knew no middle language; he was not relished by science.

His memory, as we have it, is that of an eccentric. A man of slight compassion, abrupt of manner and with no tact in speaking. Genius is often so; it is a strange fact that many of the greatest of men have been denied by their follows. A great man and laughter. He was not accepted.

None of us know today what it cost Dr. Robold. He was not the man to tell us. Perhaps Charley Huyck might; but his lips are sealed forever. We only know that he retired to the mountain, and of the subsequent flood of benefits that rained upon mankind. And we still denied him. The great cynic on the mountain. Of the secrets of the place we know little. He was not the man to accept the investigator; he despised the curious. He had been laughed at—let be—he would work alone on the great moment of the future.

In the light of the past we may well bend knee to the doctor and his protégé, Charley Huyck. Two men and destiny! What would we be without them? One shudders to think. A little thing, and yet one of the greatest moments in the world's history. It must have been Fate. Why was it that this stern man, who hated all emotion, should so have unbended at this moment? That we cannot answer. But we can conjecture. Mayhap it is this: We were all wrong; we accepted the man's exterior and profession as the fact of his marrow.

No man can lose all emotion. The doctor, was, after all, even as ourselves—he was human. Whatever may be said, we have the certainty of that moment—and of Charley Huyck.

The sun's rays were hot; they were burning; the pavements were intolerable; the baked air in the canyoned street was dancing like that of an oven; a day of dog-days. The boy crossing the street; his arms full of papers, and the glass bulging in his little hip-pocket.

At the curb he stopped. With such a sun it was impossible to long forget his plaything. He drew it carefully out of his pocket, lay down a paper and began distancing his glass for the focus. He did not notice the man beside him. Why should he? The round dot, the brownish smoke, the red spark and the flash of flame! He stamped upon it. A moment out of boyhood; an experimental miracle as old as the age of glass, and just as delightful. The boy had spoiled the name of a great Governor of a great Stata; but the paper was still saleable. He had had his moment. Mark that moment.

A hand touched his shoulder. The lad looked up.

"Yessir. *Star* or *Bulletin*?"

"I'll take one of each," said the man. "There now. I was just watching you. Do you know what you were doing?"

"Yessir. Burning paper. Startin' fire. That's the way the Indians did it."

The man smiled at the perversion of fact. There is not such a distance between sticks and glass in the age of childhood.

"I know," he said—"the Indians. But do you know how it was done; the why—why the paper began to blaze?"

"Yessir."

"All right, explain."

The boy looked up at him. He was a city boy and used to the streets. Here was some old highbrow challenging his wisdom. Of course he knew.

"It's the sun."

"There," laughed the man. "Of course. You said you knew, but you don't. Why doesn't the sun, without the glass, burn the paper? Tell me that."

The boy was still looking up at him; he saw that the man was not like the others on the street. It may be that the strange intimacy kindled into being at that moment. Certainly it was a strange unbending for the doctor.

"It would if it was hot enough or you could get enough of it together."

"Ah! Then that is what the glass is for, is it?"

"Yessir."

"Concentration?"

"Con— I don't know, sir. But it's the sun. She's sure some hot. I know a lot about the sun, sir. I've studied it with the glass. The glass picks up all the rays and puts them in one hole and that's what burns the paper.

"It's lots of fun. I'd like to have a bigger one; but it's all I've got. Why, do you know, if I had a glass big enough and a place to stand, I'd burn up the earth?"

The old man laughed. "Why, Archimides! I thought you were dead."

"My name ain't Archimedes. It's Charley Huyck."

Again the old man laughed.

"Oh, is it? Well, that's a good name, too. And if you keep on you'll make it famous as the name of the other." Wherein he was foretelling history. "Where do you live?"

The boy was still looking. Ordinarily he would not have told, but he motioned back with his thumb.

"I don't live; I room over on Brennan Street."

"Oh, I see. You room. Where's your mother?"

"Search me; I never saw her."

"I see; and your father?"

"How do I know. He went floating when I was four years old."

"Floating?"

"Yessir—to sea."

"So your mother's gone and your father's floating. Archimedes is adrift. You go to school?"

"Yessir."

"What reader?"

"No reader. Sixth grade.

"I see. What school?"

"School Twenty-six. Say, it's hot. I can't stand here all day. I've got to sell my papers."

The man pulled out a purse.

"I'll take the lot," he said. Then kindly: "My boy, I would like to have you go with me."

It was a strange moment. A little thing with the fates looking on. When destiny plays she picks strange moments. This was one. Charley Huyck went with Dr. Bobold.

II.
THE POISON PALL

We all of us remember that fatal day when the news startled all of Oakland. No one can forget it. At first it read like a newspaper hoax, in spite of the oft-proclaimed veracity of the press, and we were inclined to laughter. 'Twixt wonder at the story and its impossibilities we were not a little enthused at the nerve of the man who put it over.

It was in the days of dry reading. The world had grown populous and of well-fed content. Our soap-box artists had come to the point at last where they preached, not disaster, but a full-bellied thanks for the millennium that was here. A period of Utopian quietness—no villain around the corner; no man to covet the ox of his neighbour.

Quiet reading, you'll admit. Those were the days of the millennium. Nothing ever happened. Here's hoping they never come again. And then:

Honestly, we were not to blame for bestowing blessing out of our hearts upon that newspaperman. Even if it were a hoax, it was at least something.

At high noon. The clock in the city hall had just struck the hour that held the post 'twixt a.m. and p.m., a hot day with a sky that was clear and azure; a quiet day of serene peace and contentment. A strange and a portent moment. Looking back and over the miracle we may conjecture that it was the clearness of the atmosphere and the brightness of the sun that helped to the impact of the disaster. Knowing what we know now we can appreciate the impulse of natural phenomena. It was *not* a miracle.

The spot: Fourteenth and Broadway, Oakland, California.

Fortunately the thousands of employees in the stores about had not yet come out for their luncheons. The lapse that it takes to put a hat on, or to pat a ribbon, saved a thousand lives. One shudders to think of what would have happened had the spot been crowded. Even so, it was too impossible and too terrible to be true. Such things could not happen.

At high noon: Two street-cars crossing Fourteenth on Broadway—two cars with the same joggle and bump and the same aspect of any of a hundred thousand at a traffic corner. The wonder is—there were so few people. A Telegraph car outgoing, and a Broadway car coming in. The traffic policeman at his post had just given his signal. Two automobiles were passing and a single pedestrian, so it is said, was working his way diagonally across the corner. Of this we are not certain.

It was a moment that impinged on miracle. Even as we recount it, knowing, as we do, the explanation, we sense the impossibility of the event. A phenomenon that holds out and, in spite of our findings, lingers into the miraculous. To be and not to be. One moment life and action, an ordinary scene of existent monotony; and the next moment nothing. The spot, the intersection of the street, the passing street-cars, the two automobiles, pedestrian, the policeman—non-existent! When events are instantaneous reports are apt to be misleading. This is what we find.

Some of those who beheld it, report a flash of bluish white light; others that it was of a greenish or even a violet hue; and others, no doubt of stronger vision, that it was not only of a predominant colour but that it was shot and sparkled with a myriad specks of flame and burning.

It gave no warning and it made no sound; not even a whir. Like a hot breath out of the void. Whatever the forces that had focused, they were destruction. There was no Fourteenth and Broadway. The two automobiles, the two street-cars, the pedestrian, the policeman had been whiffed away as if they had never existed. In place of the intersection of the thoroughfares was a yawning gulf that looked down into the centre of the earth to a depth of nausea.

It was instantaneous; it was without sound; no warning. A tremendous force of unlimited potentiality had been loosed to kinetic violence. It was the suddenness and the silence that belied credence. We were accustomed to associate all disaster with confusion; calamity has an affinity with pandemonium, all things of terror climax into sound. In this case there was no sound. Hence the wonder.

A hole or bore forty feet in diameter. Without a particle of warning and without a bit of confusion. The spectators one and all aver that at first they took it for nothing more than the effect of startled eyesight. Almost subtle. It was not until after a full minute's reflection that they became aware that a miracle had been wrought before their faces. Then the crowd rushed up and with awe and now awakened terror gazed down into that terrible pit.

We say "terrible" because in this case it is an exact adjective. The strangest hole that man ever looked into. It was so deep that at first it appeared to have no bottom; not even the strongest eyesight could penetrate the smouldering blackness that shrouded the depths descending. It took a stout heart and courage to stand and hold one's head on the brink for even a minute.

It was straight and precipitous; a perfect circle in shape; with sides as smooth as the effect of machine work, the pavement and stone curb had been cut as if by a razor. Of the two street cars, two automobiles and their occupants there was nothing. The whole thing so silent and complete. Not even the spectators could really believe it.

It was a hard thing to believe. The newspapers themselves, when the news came clamouring, accepted it with reluctance. It was too much like a hoax. Not until the most trusted reporters had gone and had wired in their reports would they even consider it. Then the whole world sat up and took notice.

A miracle! Like Oakland's *Press* we all of us doubted that hole. We had attained almost everything that was worth the knowing; we were the masters of the earth and its secrets and we were proud of our wisdom; naturally we refused such reports all out of reason. It must be a hoax.

But the wires were persistent. Came corroboration. A reliable news-gathering organization soon was coming through with elaborate and detailed accounts of just what was happening. We had the news from the highest and most reputable authority.

And still we doubted. It was the story itself that brought the doubting; its touch on miracle. It was too easy to pick on the reporter. There might be a hole, and all that; but this thing of no explanation! A bomb perhaps? No noise? Some new explosive? No such thing? Well, how did we know? It was better than a miracle.

Then came the scientists. As soon as could be men of great minds had been hustled to the scene. The world had long been accustomed to accept without quibble the dictum of these great specialists of fact. With their train of accomplishments behind them we would hardly be consistent were we to doubt them.

We know the scientist and his habits. He is the one man who will believe nothing until it is proved. It is his profession, and for that we pay him. He can catch the smallest bug that ever crawled out of an atom and give it a name so long that a Polish wrestler, if he had to bear it, would break under the burden. It is his very knack of getting in under that has given us our civilization. You don't baffle a scientist in our Utopia. It can't be done. Which is one of the very reasons why we began to believe in the miracle.

In a few moments a crowd of many thousands had gathered about the spot; the throng grew so dense that there was peril of some of them being crowded into the pit at the centre. It took all the spare policemen of the city to beat them back far enough to string ropes from the corners. For blocks the streets were packed with wondering thousands. Street traffic was impossible. It was necessary to divert the cars to a roundabout route to keep the arteries open to the suburbs.

Wild rumours spread over the city. No one knew how many passengers had been upon the street cars. The officials of the company, from the schedule, could pick the numbers of the cars and their crews; but who could tell of the occupants?

Telephones rang with tearful pleadings. When the first rumours of the horror leaked out every wife and mother felt the clutch of panic at her heartstrings. It was a moment of historical psychology. Out of our books we had read of this strange phase of human nature that was wont to rise like a mad screeching thing out of disaster. We had never had it in Utopia.

It was rumbling at first and out of exaggeration; as the tale passed farther back to the waiting thousands it gained with the repetition. Grim and terrible enough in fact, it ratioed up with reiteration. Perhaps after all it was not psychology. The average impulse of the human mind does not even up so exactly. In the light of what we now know it may have been the poison that had leaked into the air; the new element that was permeating the atmosphere of the city.

At first it was spasmodic. The nearest witnesses of the disaster were the first victims. A strange malady began to spot out among those of the crowd who had been at the spot of contact. This is to be noticed. A strange affliction which from the virulence and rapidity of action was quite puzzling to the doctors.

Those among the physicians who would consent to statement gave it out that it was breaking down of tissue. Which of course it was; the new element that was radiating through the atmosphere of the city. They did not know it then.

The pity of it! The subtle, odourless pall was silently shrouding out over the city. In a short time the hospitals were full and it was necessary to call in medical aid from San Francisco. They had not even time for diagnosis. The new plague was fatal almost at conception. Happily the scientists made the discovery.

It was the pall. At the end of three hours it was known that the death sheet was spreading out over Oakland. We may thank our stars that it was learned so early. Had the real warning come a few hours later the death list would have been appalling.

A new element had been discovered; or if not a new element, at least something which was tipping over all the laws of the atmospheric envelope. A new combination that was fatal. When the news and the warning went out, panic fell upon the bay shore.

But some men stuck. In the face of such terror there were those who stayed and with grimness and sacrifice hung to their posts for mankind. There are some who had said that the stuff of heroes had passed away. Let them then consider the case of John Robinson.

Robinson was a telegraph operator. Until that day he was a poor unknown; not a whit better than his fellows. Now he has a name that will run in history. In the face of what he knew he remained under the blanket. The last words out of Oakland—his last message:

"Whole city of Oakland in grip of strange madness. Keep out of Oakland,"—following which came a haphazard personal commentary:

"I can feel it coming on myself. It is like what our ancestors must have felt when they were getting drunk—alternating desires of fight and singing—a strange sensation, light, and ecstatic with a spasmodic twitching over the forehead. Terribly thirsty. Will stick it out if I can get enough water. Never so dry in my life."

Followed a lapse of silence. Then the last words:

"I guess we're done for. There is some poison in the atmosphere—something. It has leaked, of course, out of this thing at Fourteenth and Broadway. Dr. Manson of the American Institute says it is something new that is forming a fatal combination; but he cannot understand a new element; the quantity is too enormous.

"Populace has been warned out of the city. All roads are packed with refugees. The Berkeley Hills are covered as with flies—north, east, and south and on the boats to Frisco. The poison, whatever it is, is advancing in a ring from Fourteenth and Broadway. You have got to pass it to these old boys of science. They are staying with that ring. Already they have calculated the rate of its advance and have given warning. They don't know what it is, but they have figured just how fast it is moving. They have saved the city.

"I am one of the few men now inside the wave. Out of curiosity I have stuck. I have a jug and as long as it lasts I shall stay. Strange feeling. Dry, dry, dry, as if the juice of one's life cells was turning into dust. Water evaporating almost instantly. It cannot pass through glass. Whatever the poison it has an affinity for moisture. Do not understand it. I have had enough—"

That was all. After that there was no more news out of Oakland. It is the only word that we have out of the pall itself. It was short and disconnected and a bit slangy; but for all that a basis from which to conjecture.

It is a strange and glorious thing how some men will stick to the post of danger. This operator knew that it meant death; but he held with duty. Had he been a man of scientific training his information might have been of incalculable value. However, may God bless his heroic soul!

What we know is thirst! The word that came from the experts confirmed it. Some new element of force was stealing or sapping the humidity out of the atmosphere. Whether this was combining and entering into a poison could not be determined.

Chemists worked frantically at the outposts of the advancing ring. In four hours it had covered the city; in six it had reached San Leandro, and was advancing on toward Haywards.

It was a strange story and incredible from the beginning. No wonder the world doubted. Such a thing had never happened. We had accepted the law of judging the future by the past; by deduction; we were used to sequence and to law; to the laws of Nature. This thing did look like a miracle; which was merely because—as usually it is with "miracles"—we could not understand it. Happily, we can look back now and still place our faith in Nature.

The world doubted and was afraid. Was this peril to spread slowly over the whole state of California and then on to the—world. Doubt always precedes terror. A tense world waited. Then came the word of reassurance—from the scientists:

"Danger past; vigour of the ring is abating. Calculation has deduced that the wave is slowly decreasing in potentiality. It is too early yet to say that there will be recessions, as the wave is just reaching its zenith. What it is we cannot say; but it cannot be inexplicable. After a little time it will all be explained. Say to the world there is no cause for alarm."

But the world was now aroused; as it doubted the truth before, it doubted now the reassurance. Did the scientists know? Could they have only seen the future! We know now that they did not. There was but one man in all the world great enough to foresee disaster. That man was Charley Huyck.

III
THE MOUNTAIN THAT WAS

On the same day on which all this happened, a young man, Pizzozi by name and of Italian parentage, left the little town of Ione in Amador County, California, with a small truck-load of salt. He was one of the cattlemen whose headquarters or home-farms are clustered about the foot-hills of the Sierras. In the wet season they stay with their home-land in the valley; in the summer they penetrate into the mountains. Pizzozi had driven in from the mountains the night before, after salt. He had been on the road since midnight.

Two thousand salt-hungry cattle do not allow time for gossip. With the thrift of his race, Joe had loaded up his truck and after a running snatch at breakfast was headed back into the mountains. When the news out of Oakland was thrilling around the world he was far into the Sierras.

The summer quarters of Pizzozi were close to Mt. Heckla, whose looming shoulders rose square in the centre of the pasture of the three brothers. It was not a noted mountain—that is, until this day—and had no reason for a name other than that it was a peak outstanding from the range; like a thousand others; rugged, pine clad, coated with deer-brush, red soil, and mountain miserie.

It was the deer-brush that gave it value to the Pizzozis—a succulent feed richer than alfalfa. In the early summer they would come up with bony cattle. When they returned in the fall they went out driving beef-steaks. But inland cattle must have more than forage. Salt is the tincture that makes them healthy.

It was far past the time of the regular salting. Pizzozi was in a hurry. It was nine o'clock when he passed through the mining town of Jackson; and by twelve o'clock—the minute of the disaster—he was well beyond the last little hamlet that linked up with civilization. It was four o'clock when he drew up at the little pine-sheltered cabin that was his headquarters for the summer.

He had been on the road since midnight. He was tired. The long weary hours of driving, the grades, the unvaried stress though the deep red dust, the heat, the stretch of a night and day had worn both mind and muscle. It had been his turn to go after salt; now that he was here, he could lie in for a bit of rest while his brothers did the salting.

It was a peaceful spot! this cabin of the Pizzozis; nestled among the virgin shade trees, great tall feathery sugar-pines with a mountain live-oak spreading over the door yard. To the east the rising heights of the Sierras, misty, gray-green, undulating into the distance to the pink-white snow crests of Little Alpine. Below in the canyon, the waters of the Mokolumne; to the west the heavy dark masses of Mt. Heckla, deep verdant in the cool of coming evening.

Joe drew up under the shade of the live oak. The air was full of cool, sweet scent of the afternoon. No moment could have been more peaceful; the blue clear sky overhead, the breath of summer, and the soothing spice of the pine trees. A shepherd dog came bounding from the doorway to meet him.

It was his favourite cow dog. Usually when Joe came back the dog would be far down the road to forestall him. He had wondered, absently, coming up, at the dog's delay. A dog is most of all a creature of habit; only something unusual would detain him. However the dog was here; as the man drew up he rushed out to greet him. A rush, a circle, a bark, and a whine of welcome. Perhaps the dog had been asleep.

But Joe noticed that whine; he was wise in the ways of dogs; when Ponto whined like that there was something unusual. It was not effusive or spontaneous; but rather of the delight of succour. After scarce a minute of patting, the dog squatted and faced to the westward. His whine was startling; almost fearful.

Pizzozi knew that something was wrong. The dog drew up, his stub tail erect, and his hair all bristled; one look was for his master and the other whining and alert to Mt. Heckla. Puzzled, Joe gazed at the mountain. But he saw nothing.

Was it the canine instinct, or was it coincidence? We have the account from Pizzozi. From the words of the Italian, the dog was afraid. It was not the way of Ponto; usually in the face of danger he was alert and eager; now he drew away to the cabin. Joe wondered.

Inside the shack he found nothing but evidence of departure. There was no sign of his brothers. It was his turn to go to sleep; he was wearied almost to numbness, for forty-eight hours he had not closed an eyelid. On the table were a few unwashed dishes and crumbs of eating. One of the three rifles that hung usually on the wall was missing; the coffee pot was on the floor with the lid open. On the bed the coverlets were mussed up. It was a temptation to go to sleep. Back of him the open door and Ponto. The whine of the dog drew his will and his consciousness into correlation. A faint rustle in the sugar-pines soughed from the canyon.

Joe watched the dog. The sun was just glowing over the crest of the mountain; on the western line the deep lacy silhouettes of the pine trees and the bare bald head of Heckla. What was it? His brothers should be on hand for the salting; it was not their custom to put things off for the morrow. Shading his eyes he stepped out of the doorway.

The dog rose stealthily and walked behind him, uneasily, with the same insistent whine and ruffled hair. Joe listened. Only the mountain murmurs, the sweet breath of the forest, and in the lapse of bated breath the rippling melody of the river far below him.

"What you see, Ponto? What you see?"

At the words the dog sniffed and advanced slightly—a growl and then a sudden scurry to the heels of his master. Ponto was afraid. It puzzled Pizzozi. But whatever it was that roused his fear, it was on Mt. Heckla.

This is one of the strange parts of the story—the part the dog played, and what came after. Although it is a trivial thing it is one of the most inexplicable. Did the dog sense it? We have no measure for the range of instinct, but we do have it that before the destruction of Pompeii the beasts roared in their cages. Still, knowing what we now know, it is hard to accept the analogy. It may, after all have been coincidence.

Nevertheless it decided Pizzozi. The cattle needed salt. He would catch up his pinto and ride over to the salt logs.

There is no moment in the cattle industry quite like the salting on the range.

It is not the most spectacular perhaps, but surely it is not lacking in intenseness. The way of Pizzozi was musical even if not operatic. He had a long-range call, a rising rhythm that for depth and tone had a peculiar effect on the shattered stillness. It echoed and reverberated, and peeled from the top to the bottom of the mountain. The salt call is the talisman of the mountains.

"ALLEEWAHOO!"

Two thousand cattle augmented by a thousand strays held up their heads in answer. The sniff of the welcome salt call! Through the whole range of the man's voice the stock stopped in their leafy pasture and listened.

"ALLEEWAHOO!"

An old cow bellowed. It was the beginning of bedlam. From the bottom of the mountain to the top and for miles beyond went forth the salt call. Three thousand head bellowed to the delight of salting.

Pizzozi rode along. Each lope of his pinto through the tall tangled miserie was accented. "*Alleewahoo! Alleewahoo!*" The rending of brush, the confusion, and pandemonium spread to the very bottom of the leafy gulches. It is no place for a pedestrian. Heads and tails erect, the cattle were stampeding toward the logs.

A few head had beat him to it. These he quickly drove away and cut the sack open. With haste he poured it upon the logs; then he rode out of the dust that for yards about the place was tramped to the finest powder. The centre of a herd of salting range stock is no place for comfort. The man rode away; to the left he ascended a low knob where he would be safe from the stampede; but close enough to distinguish the brands.

In no time the place was alive with milling stock. Old cows, heifers, bulls, calves, steers rushed out of the crashing brush into the clearing. There is no moment exactly like it. What before had been a broad clearing of brownish reddish dust was trampled into a vast cloud of bellowing blur, a thousand cattle, and still coming. From the farthest height came the echoing call. Pizzozi glanced up at the top of the mountain.

And then a strange thing happened.

From what we gathered from the excited accounts of Pizzozi it was instantaneous; and yet by the same words it was of such a peculiar and beautiful effect as never to be forgotten. A bluish azure shot though with a myriad flecks of crimson, a peculiar vividness of opalescence; the whole world scintillating; the sky, the air, the mountain, a vast flame of colour so wide and so intense that there seemed not a thing beside it. And instantaneous—it was over almost before it was started. No noise or warning, and no subsequent detonation: as silent as winking and much, indeed, like the queer blur of colour induced by defective vision. All in the fraction of a second. Pizzozi had been gazing at the mountain. There was no mountain!

Neither were there cattle. Where before had been the shade of the towering peak was now the rays of the western sun. Where had been the blur of the milling herd and its deafening pandemonium was now a strange silence. The transparency of the air was unbroken into the distance. Far off lay a peaceful range in the sunset. There was no mountain! Neither were there cattle!

For a moment the man had enough to do with his plunging mustang. In the blur of the subsequent second Pizzozi remembers nothing but a convulsion of fighting horseflesh bucking, twisting, plunging, the gentle pinto suddenly maddened into a demon. It required all the skill of the cowman to retain his saddle.

He did not know that he was riding on the rim of Eternity. In his mind was the dim subconscious realization of a thing that had happened. In spite of all his efforts the horse fought backward. It was some moments before he conquered. Then he looked.

It was a slow, hesitant moment. One cannot account for what he will do in the open face of a miracle. What the Italian beheld was enough for terror. The sheer immensity of the thing was too much for thinking.

At the first sight his simplex mind went numb from sheer impotence; his terror to a degree frozen. The whole of Mt. Heckla had been shorn away; in the place of its darkened shadow the sinking sun was blinking in his face; the whole western sky all golden. There was no vestige of the flat salt-clearing at the base of the mountain. Of the two thousand cattle milling in the dust not a one remained. The man crossed himself in stupor. Mechanically he put the spurs to the pinto.

But the mustang would not. Another struggle with bucking, fighting, maddened horseflesh. The cow-man must needs bring in all the skill of his training; but by the time he had conquered his mind had settled within some scope of comprehension.

The pony had good reasons for his terror. This time though the man's mind reeled it did not go dumb at the clash of immensity. Not only had the whole mountain been torn away, but its roots as well. The whole thing was up-side down; the world torn to its entrails. In place of what had been the height was a gulf so deep that its depths were blackness.

He was standing on the brink. He was a cool man, was Pizzozi; but it was hard in the confusion of such a miracle to think clearly; much less to reason. The prancing mustang was snorting with terror. The man glanced down.

The very dizziness of the gulf, sheer, losing itself into shadows and chaos overpowered him, his mind now clear enough for perception reeled at the distance. The depth was nauseating. His whole body succumbed to a sudden qualm of weakness: the sickness that comes just before falling. He went limp in the saddle.

But the horse fought backward; warned by instinct it drew back from the sheer banks of the gulf. It had no reason but its nature. At the instant it sensed the snapping of the iron will of its master. In a moment it had turned and was racing on its wild way out of the mountains. At supreme moments a cattle horse will always hit for home. The pinto and its limp rider were fleeing on the road to Jackson.

Pizzozi had no knowledge of what had occurred in Oakland. To him the whole thing had been but a flash of miracle; he could not reason. He did not curb his horse. That he was still in the saddle was due more to the near-instinct of his training than to his volition.

He did not even draw up at the cabin. That he could make better time with his motor than with his pinto did not occur to him; his mind was far too busy; and, now that the thing was passed, too full of terror. It was forty-four miles to town; it was night and the stars were shining when he rode into Jackson.

IV
"MAN—A GREAT LITTLE BUG"

And what of Charley Huyck? It was his anticipation, and his training which leaves us here to tell the story. Were it not for the strange manner of his rearing, and the keen faith and appreciation of Dr. Hobold there would be today no tale to tell. The little incident of the burning-glass had grown. If there is no such thing as Fate there is at least something that comes very close to being Destiny.

On this night we find Charley at the observatory in Arizona. He is a grown man and a great one, and though mature not so very far drawn from the lad we met on the street selling papers. Tall, slender, very slightly stooped and with the same idealistic, dreaming eyes of the poet. Surely no one at first glance would have taken him for a scientist. Which he was and was not.

Indeed, there is something vastly different about the science of Charley Huyck. Science to be sure, but not prosaic. He was the first and perhaps the last of the school of Dr. Robold, a peculiar combination of poetry and fact, a man of vision, of vast, far-seeing faith and idealism linked and based on the coldest and sternest truths of materialism. A peculiar tenet of the theory of Robold: "True science to be itself should be half poetry." Which any of us who have read or been at school know it is not. It is a peculiar theory and though rather wild still with some points in favour.

We all of us know our schoolmasters; especially those of science and what they stand for. Facts, facts, nothing but facts; no dreams or romance. Looking back we can grant them just about the emotions of cucumbers. We remember their cold, hard features, the prodding after fact, the accumulation of data. Surely there is no poetry in them.

Yet we must not deny that they have been by far the most potent of all men in the progress of civilization. Not even Robold would deny it.

The point is this:

The doctor maintained that from the beginning the progress of material civilization had been along three distinct channels; science, invention, and administration. It was simply his theory that the first two should be one; that the scientist deal not alone with dry fact but with invention, and that the inventor, unless he is a scientist, has mastered but half his trade. "The really great scientist should be a visionary," said Robold, "and an inventor is merely a poet, with tools."

Which is where we get Charley Huyck. He was a visionary, a scientist, a poet with tools, the protégé of Dr. Robold. He dreamed things that no scientist had thought of. And we are thankful for his dreaming.

The one great friend of Huyck was Professor Williams, a man from Charley's home city, who had known him even back in the days of selling papers. They had been cronies in boyhood, in their teens, and again at College. In after years, when Huyck had become the visionary, the mysterious Man of the Mountain, and Williams a great professor of astronomy, the friendship was as strong as ever.

But there was a difference between them. Williams was exact to acuteness, with not a whit of vision beyond pure science. He had been reared in the old stone-cold theory of exactness; he lived in figures. He could not understand

Huyck or his reasoning. Perfectly willing to follow as far as facts permitted he refused to step off into speculation.

Which was the point between them. Charley Huyck had vision; although exact as any man, he had ever one part of his mind soaring out into speculation. What is, and what might be, and the gulf between. To bridge the gulf was the life work of Charley Huyck.

In the snug little office in Arizona we find them; Charley with his feet poised on the desk and Williams precise and punctilious, true to his training, defending the exactness of his philosophy. It was the cool of the evening; the sun was just mellowing the heat of the desert. Through the open door and windows a cool wind was blowing. Charley was smoking; the same old pipe had been the bane of Williams's life at college.

"Then we know?" he was asking.

"Yes," spoke the professor, "what we know, Charley, we know; though of course it is not much. It is very hard, nay impossible, to deny figures. We have not only the proofs of geology but of astronomical calculation, we have facts and figures plus our sidereal relations all about us.

"The world must come to an end. It is a hard thing to say it, but it is a fact of science. Slowly, inevitably, ruthlessly, the end will come. A mere question of arithmetic."

Huyck nodded. It was his special function in life to differ with his former roommate. He had come down from his own mountain in Colourado just for the delight of difference.

"I see. Your old calculations of tidal retardation. Or if that doesn't work the loss of oxygen and the water."

"Either one or the other; a matter of figures; the earth is being drawn every day by the sun: its rotation is slowing up; when the time comes it will act to the sun in exactly the same manner as the moon acts to the earth today."

"I understand. It will be a case of eternal night for one side of the earth, and eternal day for the other. A case of burn up or freeze up."

"Exactly. Or if it doesn't reach to that, the water gas will gradually lose out into sidereal space and we will go to desert. Merely a question of the old dynamical theory of gases; of the molecules to be in motion, to be forever colliding and shooting out into variance.

"Each minute, each hour, each day we are losing part of our atmospheric envelope. In course of time it will all be gone; when it is we shall be all desert.

For intance, take a look outside. This is Arizona. Once it was the bottom of a deep blue sea. Why deny when we can already behold the beginning."

The other laughed.

"Pretty good mathematics at that, professor. Only—"

"Only?"

"That it is merely mathematics."

"Merely mathematics?" The professor frowned slightly. "Mathematics do not lie, Charlie, you cannot get away from them. What sort of fanciful argument are you bringing up now?"

"Simply this," returned the other, "that you depend too much on figures. They are material and in the nature of things can only be employed in a calculation of what *may* happen in the future. You must have premises to stand on, facts. Your figures are rigid: they have no elasticity; unless your foundations are permanent and faultless your deductions will lead you only into error."

"Granted; just the point: we know where we stand. Wherein are we in error?"

It was the old point of difference. Huyck was ever crashing down the idols of pure materialism. Williams was of the world-wide school.

"You are in error, my dear professor, in a very little thing and a very large one."

"What is that?"

"Man."

"Man?"

"Yes. He's a great little bug. You have left him out of your calculation—which he will upset."

The professor smiled indulgently. "I'll allow; he is at least a conceited bug; but you surely cannot grant him much when pitted against the Universe."

"No? Did it ever occur to you, Professor, what the Universe is? The stars for instance? Space, the immeasurable distance of Infinity. Have you never dreamed?"

Williams could not quite grasp him. Huyck had a habit that had grown out of childhood. Always he would allow his opponent to commit himself. The professor did not answer. But the other spoke.

"Ether. You know it. Whether mind or granite. For instance, your desert." He placed his finger to his forehead. "Your mind, my mind—localized ether."

"What are you driving at?"

"Merely this. Your universe has intelligence. It has mind as well as matter. The little knot called the earth is becoming conscious. Your deductions are incompetent unless they embrace mind as well as matter, and they cannot do it. Your mathematics are worthless."

The professor bit his lip.

"Always fanciful," he commented, "and visionary. Your argument is beautiful, Charley, and hopeful. I would that it were true. But all things must mature. Even an earth must die."

"Not our earth. You look into the past, professor, for your proof, and I look into the future. Give a planet long enough time in maturing and it will develop life; give it still longer and it will produce intelligence. Our own earth is just coming into consciousness; it has thirty million years, at least, to run."

"You mean?"

"This. That man is a great little bug. Mind: the intelligence of the earth."

This of course is a bit dry. The conversation of such men very often is to those who do not care to follow them. But it is very pertinent to what came after. We know now, everyone knows, that Charley Huyck was right. Even Professor Williams admits it. Our earth is conscious. In less than twenty-four hours it had to employ its consciousness to save itself from destruction.

A bell rang. It was the private wire that connected the office with the residence. The professor picked up the receiver. "Just a minute. Yes? All right." Then to his companion: "I must go over to the house, Charley. We have plenty of time. Then we can go up to the observatory."

Which shows how little we know about ourselves. Poor Professor Williams! Little did he think that those casual words were the last he would ever speak to Charley Huyck.

The whole world seething! The beginning of the end! Charley Huyck in the vortex. The next few hours were to be the most strenuous of the planet's history.

V
APPROACHING DISASTER

It was night. The stars which had just been coming out were spotted by millions over the sleeping desert. One of the nights that are peculiar to the country, which we all of us know so well, if not from experience, at least from hearsay; mellow, soft, sprinkled like salted fire, twinkling.

Each little light a message out of infinity. Cosmic grandeur; mind: chaos, eternity—a night for dreaming. Whoever had chosen the spot in the desert had picked full well. Charley had spoken of consciousness. On that night when he gazed up at the stars he was its personification. Surely a good spirit was watching over the earth.

A cool wind was blowing; on its breath floated the murmurs from the village; laughter, the song of children, the purring of motors and the startled barking of a dog; the confused drone of man and his civilization. From the eminence the observatory looked down upon the town and the sheen of light, spotting like jewels in the dim glow of the desert. To the east the mellow moon just tipping over the mountain. Charley stepped to the window.

He could see it all. The subtle beauty that was so akin to poetry: the stretch of desert, the mountains, the light in the eastern sky; the dull level shadow that marked the plain to the northward. To the west the mountains looming black to the star line. A beautiful night; sweetened with the breath of desert and tuned to its slumber.

Across the lawn he watched the professor descending the pathway under the acacias. An automobile was coming up the driveway; as it drove up under the arcs he noticed its powerful lines and its driver; one of those splendid pleasure cars that have returned to favour during the last decade; the soft purr of its motor, the great heavy tyres and its coating of dust. There is a lure about a great car coming in from the desert. The car stopped, Charley noted. Doubtless some one for Williams. If it were, he would go into the observatory alone.

In the strict sense of the word Huyck was not an astronomer. He had not made it his profession. But for all that he knew things about the stars that the more exact professors had not dreamed of. Charley was a dreamer. He had a code all his own and a manner of reasoning. Between him and the stars lay a secret.

He had not divulged it, or if he had, it was in such an open way that it was laughed at. It was not cold enough in calculation or, even if so, was too far from their deduction. Huyck had imagination; his universe was alive and potent; it had intelligence. Matter could not live without it. Man was its manifestation; just come to consciousness. The universe teemed with intelligence. Charley looked at the stars.

He crossed the office, passed through the reception-room and thence to the stairs that led to the observatory. In the time that would lapse before the coming of his friend he would have ample time for observation. Somehow he felt that there was time for discovery. He had come down to Arizona to employ the lens of his friend the astronomer. The instrument that he had erected on his own mountain in Colourado had not given him the full satisfaction that he expected.

Here in Arizona, in the dry clear air, which had hitherto given such splendid results, he hoped to find what he was after. But little did he expect to discover the terrible thing he did.

It is one of the strangest parts of the story that he should be here at the very moment when Fate and the world's safety would have had him. For years he and Dr. Robold had been at work on their visionary projects. They were both dreamers. While others had scoffed they had silently been at their great work on kinetics.

The boy and the burning glass had grown under the tutelage of Dr. Robold: the time was about at hand when he could out-rival the saying of Archimedes. Though the world knew it not, Charley Huyck had arrived at the point where he could literally burn up the earth.

But he was not sinister; though he had the power he had of course not the slightest intention. He was a dreamer and it was part of his dream that man break his thraldom to the earth and reach out into the universe. It was a great conception and were it not for the terrible event which took his life we have no doubt but that he would have succeeded.

It was ten-thirty when he mounted the steps and seated himself. He glanced at his watch: he had a good ten minutes. He had computed before just the time for the observation. For months he had waited for just this moment; he had not hoped to be alone and now that he was in solitary possession he counted himself fortunate. Only the stars and Charley Huyck knew the secret; and not even he dreamed what it would amount to.

From his pocket he drew a number of papers; most of them covered with notations; some with drawings; and a good sized map in colours. This he spread before him, and with his pencil began to draw right across its face a net of lines and cross lines. A number of figures and a rapid computation. He nodded and then he made the observation.

It would have been interesting to study the face of Charley Huyck during the next few moments. At first he was merely receptive, his face placid but with the studious intentness of one who has come to the moment: and as he began to find what he was after—an eagerness of satisfaction. Then a queer blankness; the slight movement of his body stopped, and the tapping of his feet ceased entirely.

For a full five minutes an absolute intentness. During that time he was out among the stars beholding what not even he had dreamed of. It was more than a secret: and what it was only Charley Huyck of all the millions of men could have recognized. Yet it was more than even he had expected. When he at last drew away his face was chalk-like; great drops of sweat stood on his forehead: and the terrible truth in his eyes made him look ten years older.

"My God!"

For a moment indecision and strange impotence. The truth he had beheld numbed action; from his lips the mumbled words:

"This world; my world; our great and splendid mankind!"

A sentence that was despair and a benediction.

Then mechanically he turned back to confirm his observation. This time, knowing what he would see, he was not so horrified: his mind was cleared by the plain fact of what he was beholding. When at last he drew away his face was settled.

He was a man who thought quickly—thank the stars for that—and, once he thought, quick to spring to action. There was a peril poising over the earth. If it were to be voided there was not a second to lose in weighing up the possibilities.

He had been dreaming all his life. He had never thought that the climax was to be the very opposite of what he hoped for. In his under mind he prayed for Dr. Robold—dead and gone forever. Were he only here to help him!

He seized a piece of paper. Over its white face he ran a mass of computations. He worked like lightning; his fingers plying and his mind keyed to the pin-point of genius. Not one thing did he overlook in his calculation. If the earth had a chance he would find it.

There are always possibilities. He was working out the odds of the greatest race since creation. While the whole world slept, while the uncounted millions lay down in fond security, Charley Huyck there in the lonely room on the desert drew out their figured odds to the point of infinity.

"Just one chance in a million."

He was going to take it. The words were not out of his mouth before his long legs were leaping down the stairway. In the flash of seconds his mind was rushing into clear action. He had had years of dreaming; all his years of study and tutelage under Robold gave him just the training for such a disaster.

But he needed time. Time! Time! Why was it so precious? He must get to his own mountain. In six jumps he was in the office.

It was empty. The professor had not returned. He thought rather grimly and fleetingly of their conversation a few minutes before; what would Williams think now of science and consciousness? He picked up the telephone receiver. While he waited he saw out of the corner of his eye the car in the driveway. It was—

"Hello. The professor? What? Gone down to town? No! Well, say, this is

Charley"—he was watching the car in front of the building, "Say, hello—tell him I have gone home, home! H-o-m-e to Colourado—to Colourado, yes—to the mountain—the m-o-u-n-t-a-i-n. Oh, never mind—I'll leave a note."

He clamped down the receiver. On the desk he scrawled on a piece of paper:

ED:
"LOOK THESE UP. I'M BOUND FOR THE MOUNTAIN. NO TIME TO EXPLAIN. THERE'S A CAR OUTSIDE. STAY WITH THE LENS. DON'T LEAVE IT. IF THE EARTH GOES UP YOU WILL KNOW THAT I HAVE NOT REACHED THE MOUNTAIN."

Beside the note he placed one of the maps that he had in his pocket—with his pencil drew a black cross just above the centre. Under the map were a number of computations.

It is interesting to note that in the stress of the great critical moment he forgot the professor's title. It was a good thing. When Williams read it he recognized the significance. All through their life in crucial moments he had been "Ed." to Charley.

But the note was all he was destined to find. A brisk wind was blowing. By a strange balance of fate the same movement that let Huyck out of the building ushered in the wind and upset calculation.

It was a little thing, but it was enough to keep all the world in ignorance and despair. The eddy whisking in through the door picked up the precious map, poised it like a tiny plane, and dropped it neatly behind a bookcase.

VI
A RACE TO SAVE THE WORLD

Huyck was working in a straight line. Almost before his last words on the phone were spoken he had requisitioned that automobile outside; whether money or talk, faith or force, he was going to have it. The hum of the motor sounded in his ears as he ran down the steps. He was hatless and in his shirt-sleeves. The driver was just putting some tools in the car. With one jump Charley had him by the collar.

"Five thousand dollars if you can get me to Robold Mountain in twenty hours."

The very suddenness of the rush caught the man by surprise and lurched him against the car, turning him half around. Charley found himself gazing into dull brown eyes and sardonic laughter: a long, thin nose and lips drooped at the corners, then as suddenly tipping up—a queer creature, half devil, half laughter, and all fun.

"Easy, Charley, easy! How much did you say? Whisper it."

It was Bob Winters. Bob Winters and his car. And waiting. Surely no twist of fortune could nave been greater. He was a college chum of Huyck's and of the professor's. If there was one man that could make the run in the time allotted, Bob was he. But Huyck was impersonal. With the burden on his mind he thought of naught but his destination.

"Ten thousand!" he shouted.

The man held back his head. Huyck was far too serious to appreciate mischief. But not the man.

"Charley Huyck, of all men. Did young Lochinvar come out of the West? How much did you say? This desert air and the dust, 'tis hard on the hearing. She must be a young, fair maiden. Ten thousand."

"Twenty thousand. Thirty thousand. Damnation, man, you can have the mountain. Into the car."

By sheer subjective strength he forced the other into the machine. It was not until they were shooting out of the grounds on two wheels that he realized that the man was Bob Winters. Still the workings of fate.

The madcap and wild Bob of the races! Surely Destiny was on the job. The challenge of speed and the premium. At the opportune moment before disaster the two men were brought together. Minutes weighed up with centuries and hours out-balanced millenniums. The whole world slept; little did it dream that its very life was riding north with these two men into the midnight.

Into the midnight! The great car, the pride of Winter's heart, leaped between the pillars. At the very outset, madcap that he was, he sent her into seventy miles an hour; they fairly jumped off the hill into the village. At a full seventy-five he took the curve; she skidded, sheered half around and swept on.

For an instant Charley held his breath. But the master hand held her; she steadied, straightened, and shot out into the desert. Above the whir of the motor, flying dust and blurring what-not, Charley got the tones of his companion's voice. He had heard the words somewhere in history.

"Keep your seat, Mr. Greely. Keep your seat!"

The moon was now far up over the mountain, the whole desert was bathed in a mellow twilight; in the distance the mountains brooded like an uncertain slumbering cloud bank. They were headed straight to the northward; though there was a better road round about, Winters had chosen the hard, rocky bee-line to the mountain.

He knew Huyck and his reputation; when Charley offered thirty thousand for a twenty-hour drive it was not mere byplay. He had happened in at the observatory to drop in on Williams on his way to the coast. They had been classmates; likewise he and Charley.

When the excited man out of the observatory had seized him by the collar, Winters merely had laughed. He was the speed king. The three boys who had gone to school were now playing with the destiny of the earth. But only Huyck knew it.

Winters wondered. Through miles and miles of fleeting sagebrush, cacti and sand and desolation, he rolled over the problem. Steady as a rock, slightly stooped, grim and as certain as steel he held to the north. Charley Huyck by his side, hatless, coatless, his hair dancing to the wind, all impatience. Why was it? Surely a man even for death would have time to get his hat.

The whole thing spelled speed to Bob Winters; perhaps it was the infusion of spirit or the intensity of his companion; but the thrill ran into his vitals. Thirty thousand dollars—for a stake like that—what was the balance? He had been called Wild Bob for his daring; some had called him insane; on this night his insanity was enchantment.

It was wild; the lee of the giant roadster a whirring shower of gravel: into the darkness, into the night the car fought over the distance. The terrific momentum and the friction of the air fought in their faces; Huyck's face was unprotected: in no time his lips were cracked, and long before they had crossed the level his whole face was bleeding.

But he heeded it not. He only knew that they were moving; that slowly, minute by minute, they were cutting down the odds that bore disaster. In his mind a maze of figures; the terrible sight he had seen in the telescope and the thing impending. Why had he kept his secret?

Over and again he impeached himself and Dr. Robold. It had come to this. The whole world sleeping and only himself to save it. Oh, for a few minutes, for one short moment! Would he get it?

At last they reached the mountains. A rough, rocky road, and but little travelled. Happily Winters had made it once before, and knew it. He took it with every bit of speed they could stand, but even at that it was diminished to a minimum.

For hours they fought over grades and gulches, dry washouts and boulders. It was dawn, and the sky was growing pink when they rode down again upon the level. It was here that they ran across their first trouble; and it was here that Winters began to realize vaguely what a race they might be running.

The particular level which they had entered was an elbow of the desert projecting into the mountains just below a massive, newly constructed dam. The reservoir had but lately been filled, and all was being put in readiness for the dedication.

An immense sheet of water extending far back into the mountains—it was intended before long to transform the desert into a garden. Below, in the valley, was a town, already the centre of a prosperous irrigation settlement; but soon, with the added area, to become a flourishing city. The elbow, where they struck it, was perhaps twenty miles across. Their northward path would take them just outside the tip where the foothills of the opposite mountain chain melted into the desert. Without ado Winters put on all speed and plunged across the sands. And then:

It was much like winking; but for all that something far more impressive. To Winters, on the left hand of the car and with the east on the right hand, it was much as if the sun had suddenly leaped up and as suddenly plumped down behind the horizon—a vast vividness of scintillating opalescence: an azure, naming diamond shot by a million fire points.

Instantaneous and beautiful. In the pale dawn of the desert air its wonder and colour were beyond all beauty. Winters caught it out of the corner of his eye; it was so instantaneous and so illusive that he was not certain. Instinctively he looked to his companion.

But Charley, too, had seen it. His attitude of waiting and hoping was vigourized into vivid action. He knew just what it was. With one hand he clutched Winters and fairly shouted.

"On, on, Bob! On, as you value your life. Put into her every bit of speed you have got."

At the same instant, at the same breath came a roar that was not to be forgotten; crunching, rolling, terrible—like the mountain moving.

Bob knew it. It was the dam. Something had broken it. To the east the great wall of water fallout of the mountains! A beautiful sight and terrible; a relentless glassy roller fringed along its base by a lace of racing foam. The upper part was as smooth as crystal; the stored-up waters of the mountain moving out compactly. The man thought of the little town below and its peril. But Huyck thought also. He shouted in Winter's ear:

"Never mind the town. Keep straight north. Over yonder to the point of the water. The town will have to drown."

It was inexorable; there was no pity; the very strength and purpose of the command drove into the other's understanding. Dimly now he realized that they were really running a race against time. Winters was a daredevil; the very catastrophe sent a thrill of exultation through him. It was the climax, the great moment of his life, to be driving at a hundred miles an hour under that wall of water.

The roar was terrible, Before they were half across it seemed to the two men that the very sound would drown them. There was nothing in the world but pandemonium. The strange flash was forgotten in the terror of the living wall that was reaching out to engulf them. Like insects they whizzed in the open face of the deluge. When they had reached the tip they were so close that the outrunning fringe of the surf was at their wheels.

Around the point with the wide open plain before them. With the flood behind them it was nothing to outrun it. The waters with a wider stretch spread out. In a few moments they had left all behind them.

But Winters wondered; what was the strange flash of evanescent beauty? He knew this dam and its construction; to outlast the centuries. It had been whiffed in a second. It was not lightning. He had heard no sound other than the rush of the waters. He looked to his companion.

Hueyk nodded.

"That's the thing we are racing. We have only a few hours. Can we make it?"

Bob had thought that he was getting all the speed possible out of his motor. What it yielded from that moment on was a revelation.

It is not safe and hardly possible to be driving at such speed on the desert. Only the best car and a firm roadway can stand it. A sudden rut, squirrel hole, or pocket of sand is as good as destruction. They rushed on till noon.

Not even Winters, with all his alertness, could avoid it. Perhaps he was weary. The tedious hours, the racking speed had worn him to exhaustion. They had ceased to individualize, their way a blur, a nightmare of speed and distance.

It came suddenly, a blind barranca—one of those sunken, useless channels that are death to the unwary. No warning.

It was over just that quickly. A mere flash of consciousness plus a sensation of flying. Two men broken on the sands and the great, beautiful roadster a twisted ruin.

VII
A RIVEN CONTINENT

But back to the world. No one knew about Charley Huyck nor what was occurring on the desert. Even if we had it would have been impossible to construe connection.

After the news out of Oakland, and the destruction of Mt. Heckla, we were far too appalled. The whole thing was beyond us. Not even the scientists with all their data could find one thing to work on. The wires of the world buzzed with wonder and with panic. We were civilized. It is really strange how quickly, in spite of our boasted powers, we revert to the primitive.

Superstition cannot die. Where was no explanation must be miracle. The thing had been repeated. When would it strike again. And where?

There was not long to wait. But this time the stroke was of far more consequence and of far more terror. The sheer might of the thing shook the earth. Not a man or government that would not resign in the face of such destruction.

It was omnipotent. A whole continent had been riven. It would be impossible to give description of such catastrophe; no pen can tell it any more than it could describe the creation. We can only follow in its path.

On the morning after the first catastrophe, at eight o'clock, just south of the little city of Santa Cruz, on the north shore of the Bay of Monterey, the same light and the same, though not quite the same, instantaneousness. Those who beheld it report a vast ball of azure blue and opalescent fire and motion; a strange sensation of vitalized vibration; of personified living force. In shape like a marble, as round as a full moon in its glory, but of infinitely more beauty.

It came from nowhere; neither from above the earth nor below it. Seeming to leap out of nothing, it glided or rather vanished to the eastward. Still the effect of winking, though this time, perhaps from a distanced focus, more vivid. A dot or marble, like a full moon, burning, opal, soaring to the eastward.

And instantaneous. Gone as soon as it was come; noiseless and of phantom beauty; like a finger of the Omnipotent tracing across the world, and as terrible. The human mind had never conceived a thing so vast.

Beginning at the sands of the ocean the whole country had vanished; a chasm twelve miles wide and of unknown depth running straight to the eastward. Where had been farms and homes was nothing; the mountains had been seared like butter. Straight as an arrow.

Then the roar of the deluge. The waters of the Pacific breaking through its sands and rolling into the Gulf of Mexico. That there was no heat was evidenced by the fact that there was no steam. The thing could not be internal. Yet what was it?

One can only conceive in figures. From the shores of Santa Cruz to the Atlantic—a few seconds; then out into the eastern ocean straight out into the Sea of the Sargasso. A great gulf riven straight across the face of North America.

The path seemed to follow the sun; it bore to the eastward with a slight southern deviation. The mountains it cut like cheese. Passing just north of Fresno it seared through the gigantic Sierras halfway between the Yosemite and Mt. Whitney, through the great desert to southern Nevada, thence across northern Arizona, New Mexico, Texas, Arkansas, Mississippi, Alabama, and Georgia, entering the Atlantic at a point half-way between Brunswick and Jacksonville. A great canal twelve miles in width linking the oceans. A cataclysmic blessing. Today, with thousands of ships bearing freight over its water, we can bless that part of the disaster.

But there was more to come. So far the miracle had been sporadic. Whatever had been its force it had been fatal only on point and occasion. In a way it had been local. The deadly atmospheric combination of its aftermath was invariable in its recession. There was no suffering. The death that it dealt was the death of obliteration. But now it entered on another stage.

The world is one vast ball, and, though large, still a very small place to live in. There are few of us, perhaps, who look upon it, or even stop to think of it, as a living being. Yet it is just that. It has its currents, life, pulse, and its fevers; it is coordinate; a million things such as the great streams of the ocean, the swirls of the atmosphere, make it a place to live in. And we are conscious only, or mostly, through disaster.

A strange thing happened.

The great opal like a mountain of fire had riven across the continent. From the beginning and with each succession the thing was magnified. But it was not until it had struck the waters of the Atlantic that we became aware of its full potency and its fatality.

The earth quivered at the shock, and man stood on his toes in terror. In twenty-four hours our civilization was literally falling to pieces. We were powerful with the forces that we understood; but against this that had been literally ripped from the unknown we were insignificant. The whole world was frozen. Let us see.

Into the Atlantic! The transition. Hitherto silence. But now the roar of ten thousand million Niagaras, the waters of the ocean rolling, catapulting, roaring into the gulf that had been seared in its bosom. The Gulf Stream cut in two, the currents that tempered our civilization sheared in a second. Straight into the Sargasso Sea. The great opal, liquid fire, luminiscent, a ball like the setting sun, lay poised upon the ocean. It was the end of the earth!

What was this thing? The whole world knew of it in a second. And not a one could tell. In less than forty hours after its first appearance in Oakland it had consumed a mountain, riven a continent, and was drinking up an ocean. The tangled sea of the Sargasso, dead calm for ages, was a cataract; a swirling torrent of maddened waters rushed to the opal—and disappeared.

It was hellish and out of madness; as beautiful as it was uncanny. The opal high as the Himalayas brooding upon the water; its myriad colours blending, winking in a phantasm of iridescence. The beauty of its light could be seen a thousand miles. A thing out of mystery and out of forces. We had discovered many things and knew much; but had guessed no such thing as this. It was vampirish, and it was literally drinking up the earth.

Consequences were immediate. The point of contact was fifty miles across, the waters of the Atlantic with one accord turned to the magnet. The Gulf Stream veered straight from its course and out across the Atlantic. The icy currents from the poles freed from the warmer barrier descended along the coasts and thence out into the Sargasso Sea. The temperature of the temperate zone dipped below the point of a blizzard.

The first word come out of London. Freezing! And in July! The fruit and entire harvest of northern Europe destroyed. Olympic games at Copenhagen postponed by a foot of snow. The river Seine frozen. Snow falling in New York. Crops nipped with frost as far south as Cape Hatteras.

A fleet of airplanes was despatched from the United States and another from the west coast of Africa. Not half of them returned. Those that did reported even more disaster. The reports that were handed in were appalling. They had sailed straight on. It was like flying into the sun; the vividness of the opalescence was blinding, rising for miles above them alluring, drawing and unholy, and of a beauty that was terror.

Only the tardy had escaped. It even drew their motors, it was like gravity suddenly become vitalized and conscious. Thousands of machines vaulted into the opalescence. From those ahead hopelessly drawn and powerless came back the warning. But hundreds could not escape.

"Back," came the wireless. "Do not come too close. The thing is a magnet. Turn back before too late. Against this man is insignificant."

Then like gnats flitting into fire they vanished into the opalescence.

The others turned back. The whole world freezing shuddered in horror. A great vampire was brooding over the earth. The greatness that man had attained to was nothing. Civilization was tottering in a day. We were hopeless.

Then came the last revelation; the truth and verity of the disaster and the threatened climax. The water level of all the coast had gone down. Vast ebb tides had gone out not to return. Stretches of sand where had been surf extended far out into the sea. Then the truth! The thing, whatever it was, was drinking up the ocean.

VIII
THE MAN WHO SAVED THE EARTH

It was tragic; grim, terrible, cosmic. Out of nowhere had come this thing that was eating up the earth. Not a thing out of all our science had there been to warn us; not a word from all our wise men. We who had built up our civilization, piece by piece, were after all but insects.

We were going out in a maze of beauty into the infinity whence we came. Hour by hour the great orb of opalescence grew in splendour; the effect and the beauty of its lure spread about the earth; thrilling, vibrant like suppressed music. The old earth helpless. Was it possible that out of her bosom she could not pluck one intelligence to save her? Was there not one law—no answer?

Out on the desert with his face to the sun lay the answer. Though almost hopeless there was still some time and enough of near-miracle to save us. A limping fate in the shape of two Indians and a battered runabout at the last moment.

Little did the two red men know the value of the two men found that day on the desert. To them the debris of the mighty car and the prone bodies told enough of the story. They were Samaritans; but there are many ages to bless them.

As it was there were many hours lost. Without this loss there would have been thousands spared and an almost immeasurable amount of disaster. But we have still to be thankful. Charley Huyck was still living.

He had been stunned; battered, bruised, and unconscious; but he had not been injured vitally. There was still enough left of him to drag himself to the old runabout and call for Winters. His companion, as it happened, was in even better shape than himself, and waiting. We do not know how they talked the red men out of their relic—whether by coaxing, by threat, or by force.

Straight north. Two men battered, worn, bruised, but steadfast, bearing in that limping old motor-car the destiny of the earth. Fate was still on the job, but badly crippled.

They had lost many precious hours. Winters had forfeited his right to the thirty thousand. He did not care. He understood vaguely that there was a stake over and above all money. Huyck said nothing; he was too maimed and too much below will-power to think of speaking. What had occurred during the many hours of their unconsciousness was unknown to them. It was not until they came sheer upon the gulf that had been riven straight across the continent that the awful truth dawned on them.

To Winters it was terrible. The mere glimpse of that blackened chasm was terror. It was bottomless; so deep that its depths were cloudy; the misty haze of its uncertain shadows was akin to chaos. He understood vaguely that it was related to that terrible thing they had beheld in the morning. It was not the power of man. Some force had been loosened which was ripping the earth to its vitals. Across the terror of the chasm he made out the dim outlines of the opposite wall. A full twelve miles across.

For a moment the sight overcame even Huyck himself. Full well he knew; but knowing, as he did, the full fact of the miracle was even more than he expected. His long years under Robold, his scientific imagination had given him comprehension. Not puny steam, nor weird electricity, but force, kinetics—out of the universe.

He knew. But knowing as he did, he was overcome by the horror. Such a thing turned loose upon the earth! He had lost many hours; he had but a few hours remaining. The thought gave him sudden energy. He seized Winters by the arm.

"To the first town, Bob. To the first town—an aerodome."

There was speed in that motor for all its decades. Winters turned about and shot out in a lateral course parallel to the great chasm. But for all his speed he could not keep back his question.

"In the name of Heaven, Charley, what did it? What is it?"

Came the answer; and it drove the lust of all speed through Winters:

"Bob," said Charley, "it is the end of the world—if we don't make it. But a few hours left. We must have an airplane. I must make the mountain."

It was enough for Wild Bob. He settled down. It was only an old runabout; but he could get speed out of a wheelbarrow. He had never driven a race like this. Just once did he speak. The words were characteristic.

"A world's record, Charley. And we're going to win. Just watch us."

And they did.

There was no time lost in the change. The mere fact of Huyck's name, his appearance and the manner of his arrival was enough. For the last hours messages had been pouring in at every post in the Rocky Mountains for Charley Huyck. After the failure of all others many thousands had thought of him.

Even the government, unappreciative before, had awakened to a belated and almost frantic eagerness. Orders were out that everything, no matter what, was to be at his disposal. He had been regarded as visionary; but in the face of what had occurred, visions were now the most practical things for mankind. Besides, Professor Williams had sent out to the world the strange portent of Huyck's note. For years there had been mystery on that mountain. Could it be?

Unfortunately we cannot give it the description we would like to give. Few men outside of the regular employees have ever been to the Mountain of Robold. From the very first, owing perhaps to the great forces stored, and the danger of carelessness, strangers and visitors had been barred. Then, too, the secrecy of Dr. Robold—and the respect of his successor. But we do know that the burning glass had grown into the mountain.

Bob Winters and the aviator are the only ones to tell us; the employees, one and all, chose to remain. The cataclysm that followed destroyed the work of Huyck and Robold—but not until it had served the greatest deed that ever came out of the minds of men. And had it not been for Huyck's insistence we would not have even the account that we are giving.

It was he who insisted, nay, begged, that his companions return while there was yet a chance. Full well he knew. Out of the universe, out of space he had coaxed the forces that would burn up the earth. The great ball of luminous opalescence, and the diminishing ocean!

There was but one answer. Through the imaginative genius of Robold and Huyck, fate had worked up to the moment. The lad and the burning glass had grown to Archimedes.

What happened?

The plane neared the Mountain of Robold. The great bald summit and the four enormous globes of crystal. At least we so assume. We have Winter's word and that of the aviator that they were of the appearance of glass. Perhaps they were not; but we can assume it for description. So enormous that were they set upon a plain they would have overtopped the highest building ever constructed; though on the height of the mountain, and in its contrast, they were not much more than golf balls.

It was not their size but their effect that was startling. They were alive. At least that is what we have from Winters. Living, luminous, burning, twisting within with a thousand blending, iridescent beautiful colours. Not like electricity but something infinitely more powerful. Great mysterious magnets that Huyck had charged out of chaos. Glowing with the softest light; the whole mountain brightened as in a dream, and the town of Robold at its base lit up with a beauty that was past beholding.

It was new to Winters. The great buildings and the enormous machinery. Engines of strangest pattern, driven by forces that the rest of the world had not thought of. Not a sound; the whole works a complicated mass covering a hundred acres, driving with a silence that was magic. Not a whir nor friction. Like a living composite body pulsing and breathing the strange and mysterious force that had been evolved from Huyck's theory of kinetics. The four great steel conduits running from the globes down the side of the mountain. In the centre, at a point midway between the globes, a massive steel needle hung on a pivot and pointed directly at the sun.

Winters and the aviator noted it and wondered. From the lower end of the needle was pouring a luminous stream of pale-blue opalescence, a stream much like a liquid, and of an unholy, radiance. But it was not a liquid, nor fire, nor anything seen by man before.

It was force. We have no better description than the apt phrase of Winters. Charley Huyck was milking the sun, as it dropped from the end of the four living streams to the four globes that took it into storage. The four great, wonderful living globes; the four batteries; the very sight of their imprisoned beauty and power was magnetic.

The genius of Huyck and Robold! Nobody but the wildest dreamers would have conceived it. The life of the sun. And captive to man; at his will and volition. And in the next few minutes we were to lose it all! But in losing it we were to save ourselves. It was fate and nothing else. There was but one thing more upon the mountain—the observatory and another needle apparently idle; but with a point much like a gigantic phonograph needle. It rose square out of the observatory, and to Winters it gave an impression of a strange gun, or some implement for sighting.

That was all. Coming with the speed that they were making, the airmen had no time for further investigation. But even this is comprehensive. Minus the force. If we only knew more about that or even its theory we might perhaps reconstruct the work of Charley Huyck and Dr. Robold.

They made the landing. Winters, with his nature, would be in at the finish; but Charley would not have it.

"It is death, Bob," he said. "You have a wife and babies. Go back to the world. Go back with all the speed you can get out of your motors. Get as far away as you can before the end comes."

With that he bade them a sad farewell. It was the last spoken word that the outside world had from Charley Huyck.

The last seen of him he was running up the steps of his office. As they soared away and looked back they could see men, the employees, scurrying about in frantic haste to their respective posts and stations. What was it all about? Little did the two aviators know. Little did they dream that it was the deciding stroke.

IX
THE MOST TERRIFIC MOMENT IN HISTORY

Still the great ball of Opalescence brooding over the Sargasso. Europe now was frozen, and though it was midsummer had gone into winter quarters. The Straits of Dover were no more. The waters had receded and one could walk, if careful, dry-shod from the shores of France to the chalk cliffs of England. The Straits of Gibraltar had dried up. The Mediterranean completely land-locked, was cut off forever from the tides of the mother ocean.

The whole world going dry; not in ethics, but in reality. The great Vampire, luminous, beautiful beyond all ken and thinking, drinking up our life-blood. The Atlantic a vast whirlpool.

A strange frenzy had fallen over mankind: men fought in the streets and died in madness. It was fear of the Great Unknown, and hysteria. At such a moment the veil of civilization was torn to tatters. Man was reverting to the primeval.

Then came the word from Charley Huyck; flashing and repeating to every clime and nation. In its assurance it was almost as miraculous as the Vampire itself. For man had surrendered.

TO THE PEOPLE OF THE WORLD:

THE STRANGE AND TERRIBLE OPALESCENCE WHICH, FOR THE PAST SEVENTY HOURS, HAS BEEN PLAYING HAVOC WITH THE WORLD, IS NOT MIRACLE, NOR OF THE SUPERNATURAL, BUT A MERE MANIFESTATION AND RESULT OF THE APPLICATION OF CELESTIAL KINETICS. SUCH A THING ALWAYS WAS AND ALWAYS WILL BE POSSIBLE WHERE THERE IS INTELLIGENCE TO CONTROL AND HARNESS THE FORCES THAT LIE ABOUT US. SPACE IS NOT SPACE EXACTLY, BUT AN INFINITE CISTERN OF UNKNOWN LAWS AND FORCES. WE MAY CONTROL CERTAIN LAWS ON EARTH, BUT UNTIL WE REACH OUT FARTHER WE ARE BUT PLAYTHINGS.

MAN IS THE INTELLIGENCE OF THE EARTH. THE TIME WILL COME WHEN HE MUST BE THE INTELLIGENCE OF A GREAT DEAL OF SPACE AS WELL. AT THE PRESENT TIME YOU ARE MERELY FORTUNATE AND A VICTIM OF A KIND FATE. THAT I AM THE INSTRUMENT OF THE EARTH'S SALVATION IS MERELY CHANCE. THE REAL MAN IS DR. ROBOLD. WHEN HE PICKED ME UP ON THE STREETS I HAD NO IDEA THAT THE SEQUENCE OF TIME WOULD DRIFT TO THIS MOMENT. HE TOOK ME INTO HIS WORK AND TAUGHT ME.

BECAUSE HE WAS SENSITIVE AND WAS LAUGHED AT, WE WORKED IN SECRET. AND SINCE HIS DEATH, AND OUT OF RESPECT TO HIS MEMORY, I HAVE CONTINUED IN THE SAME MANNER. BUT I HAVE WRITTEN DOWN EVERYTHING, ALL THE LAWS, COMPUTATIONS, FORMULAS—EVERYTHING; AND I AM NOW WILLING IT TO MANKIND.

ROBOLD HAD A THEORY ON KINETICS. IT WAS STRANGE AT FIRST AND A THING TO LAUGH AT; BUT HE REDUCED IT TO LAWS AS POTENT AND AS INEXORABLE AS THE LAWS OF GRAVITATION.

THE LUMINOUS OPALESCENCE THAT HAS ALMOST DESTROYED US IS BUT ONE OF ITS MINOR MANIFESTATIONS. IT IS A MESSAGE OF SINISTER INTELLIGENCE; FOR BACK OF IT ALL IS AN INTELLIGENCE. YET IT IS NOT ALL SINISTER. IT IS SELF-PRESERVATION. THE TIME IS COMING WHEN EONS OF AGES FROM NOW OUR OWN MAN WILL BE FORCED TO EMPLOY JUST SUCH A WEAPON FOR HIS OWN PRESERVATION. EITHER THAT OR WE SHALL DIE OF THIRST AND AGONY.

LET ME ASK YOU TO REMEMBER NOW, THAT WHATEVER YOU HAVE SUFFERED, YOU HAVE SAVED A WORLD. I SHALL NOW SAVE YOU AND THE EARTH.

IN THE VAULTS YOU WILL FIND EVERYTHING. ALL THE KNOWLEDGE AND DISCOVERIES OF THE GREAT DR. ROBOLD. PLUS A FEW MINOR FINDINGS BY MYSELF.

AND NOW I BID YOU FAREWELL. YOU SHALL SOON BE FREE.

CHARLEY HUYCK.

A strange message. Spoken over the wireless and flashed to every clime, it roused and revived the hope of mankind. Who was this Charley Huyck? Uncounted millions of men had never heard his name; there were but few, very few who had.

A message out of nowhere and of very dubious and doubtful explanation. Celestial kinetics! Undoubtedly. But the words explained nothing. However, man was ready to accept anything, so long as it saved him.

For a more lucid explanation we must go back to the Arizona observatory and Professor Ed. Williams. And a strange one it was truly; a certain proof that consciousness is more potent, far more so than mere material; also that many laws of our astronomers are very apt to be overturned in spite of their mathematics.

Charley Huyck was right. You cannot measure intelligence with a yard-stick. Mathematics do not lie; but when applied to consciousness they are very likely to kick backward. That is precisely what had happened.

The suddenness of Huyck's departure had puzzled Professor Williams; that, and the note which he found upon the table. It was not like Charley to go off so in the stress of a moment. He had not even taken the time to get his hat and coat. Surely something was amiss.

He read the note carefully, and with a deal of wonder.

"Look these up. Keep by the lens. If the world goes up you will know I have not reached the mountain."

What did he mean? Besides, there was no data for him to work on. He did not know that an errant breeze, had plumped the information behind the book-case. Nevertheless he went into the observatory, and for the balance of the night stuck by the lens.

Now there are uncounted millions of stars in the sky. Williams had nothing to go by. A needle in the hay-stack were an easy task compared with the one that he was allotted. The flaming mystery, whatever it was that Huyck had seen, was not caught by the professor. Still, he wondered. "If the world goes up you will know I have not reached the mountain." What was the meaning?

But he was not worried. The professor loved Huyck as a visionary and smiled not a little at his delightful fancies. Doubtless this was one of them. It was not until the news came flashing out of Oakland that he began to take it seriously. Then followed the disappearance of Mount Heckla. "If the world goes up"—it began to look as if the words had meaning.

There was a frantic professor during the next few days. When he was not with the lens he was flashing out messages to the world for Charley Huyck. He did not know that Huyck was lying unconscious and almost dead upon the desert. That the world was coming to catastrophe he knew full well; but where was the man to save it? And most of all, what had his friend meant by the words, "look these up"?

Surely there must be some further information. Through the long, long hours he stayed with the lens and waited. And he found nothing.

It was three days. Who will ever forget them? Surely not Professor Williams. He was sweating blood. The whole world was going to pieces without the trace of an explanation. All the mathematics, all the accumulations of the ages had availed for nothing. Charley Huyck held the secret. It was in the stars, and not an astronomer could find it. But with the seventeenth hour came the turn of fortune. The professor was passing through the office. The door was open, and the same fitful wind which had played the original prank was now just as fitfully performing restitution. Williams noticed a piece of paper protruding from the back of the bookcase and fluttering in the breeze. He picked it up. The first words that he saw were in the handwriting of Charley Huyck. He read:

"In the last extremity—in the last phase when there is no longer any water on the earth; when even the oxygen of the atmospheric envelope has been reduced to a minimum—man, or whatever form of intelligence is then upon the earth, must go back to the laws which governed his forebears. Necessity must ever be the law of evolution. There will be no water upon the earth, but there will be an unlimited quantity elsewhere.

"By that time, for instance, the great planet, Jupiter, will be in just a convenient state for exploitation. Gaseous now, it will be, by that time, in just about the stage when the steam and water are condensing into ocean. Eons of millions of years away in the days of dire necessity. By that time the intelligence and consciousness of the earth will have grown equal to the task.

"It is a thing to laugh at (perhaps) just at present. But when we consider the ratio of man's advance in the last hundred years, what will it be in a billion? Not all the laws of the universe have been discovered, by any means. At present we know nothing. Who can tell?

"Aye, who can tell? Perhaps we ourselves have in store the fate we would mete out to another. We have a very dangerous neighbour close beside us. Mars is in dire straits for water. And we know there is life on Mars and intelligence! The very fact on its face proclaims it. The oceans have dried up; the only way they have of holding life is by bringing their water from the polar snow-caps. Their canals pronounce an advanced state of cooperative intelligence; there is life upon Mars and in an advanced stage of evolution.

"But how far advanced? It is a small planet, and consequently eons of ages in advance of the earth's evolution. In the nature of things Mars cooled off quickly, and life was possible there while the earth was yet a gaseous mass. She has gone to her maturity and into her retrogression; she is approaching her end. She has had less time to produce intelligence than intelligence will have—in the end—upon the earth.

"How far has this intelligence progressed? That is the question. Nature is a slow worker. It took eons of ages to put life upon the earth; it took eons of more ages to make this life conscious. How far will it go? How far has it gone on Mars?"

That was as far as the comments went. The professor dropped his eyes to the rest of the paper. It was a map of the face of Mars, and across its centre was a black cross scratched by the dull point of a soft pencil.

He knew the face of Mars. It was the Ascræus Lucus. The oasis at the juncture of a series of canals running much like the spokes of a wheel. The great Uranian and Alander Canals coming in at about right angles.

In two jumps the professor was in the observatory with the great lens swung to focus. It was the great moment out of his lifetime, and the strangest and most eager moment, perhaps, ever lived by any astronomer. His fingers fairly twitched with tension. There before his view was the full face of our Martian neighbour!

But was it? He gasped out a breath of startled exclamation. Was it Mars that he gazed at; the whole face, the whole thing had been changed before him.

Mars has ever been red. Viewed through the telescope it has had the most beautiful tinge imaginable, red ochre, the weird tinge of the desert in sunset. The colour of enchantment and of hell!

For it is so. We know that for ages and ages the planet has been burning up; that life was possible only in the dry sea-bottoms and under irrigation. The rest, where the continents once were, was blazing desert. The redness, the beauty, the enchantment that we so admired was burning hell.

All this had changed.

Instead of this was a beautiful shade of iridescent green. The red was gone forever. The great planet standing in the heavens had grown into infinite glory. Like the great Dog Star transplanted.

The professor sought out the Ascræus Lucus. It was hard to find. The whole face had been transfigured; where had been canals was now the beautiful sheen of green and verdure. He realized what he was beholding and what he had never dreamed of seeing; the seas of Mars filled up.

With the stolen oceans our grim neighbour had come back to youth. But how had it been done. It was horror for our world. The great luminescent ball of Opalescence! Europe frozen and New York a mass of ice. It was the earth's destruction. How long could the thing keep up; and whence did it come? What was it?

He sought for the Ascræus Lucus. And he beheld a strange sight. At the very spot where should have been the juncture of the canals he caught what at first looked like a pin-point flame, a strange twinkling light with flitting glow of Opalescence. He watched it, and he wondered. It seemed to the professor to grow; and he noticed that the green about it was of different colour. It was winking, like a great force, and much as if alive; baneful.

It was what Charley Huyck had seen. The professor thought of Charley. He had hurried to the mountain. What could Huyck, a mere man, do against a thing like this? There was naught to do but sit and watch it drink of our life-blood. And then—

It was the message, the strange assurance that Huyck was flashing over the world. There was no lack of confidence in the words he was speaking. "Celestial Kinetics," so that was the answer! Certainly it must be so with the truth before him. Williams was a doubter no longer. And Charley Huyck could save them. The man he had humoured. Eagerly he waited and stuck by the lens. The whole world waited.

It was perhaps the most terrific moment since creation. To describe it would be like describing doomsday. We all of us went through it, and we all of us thought the end had come; that the earth was torn to atoms and to chaos.

The State of Colorado was lurid with a red light of terror; for a thousand miles the flame shot above the earth and into space. If ever spirit went out in glory that spirit was Charley Huyck! He had come to the moment and to Archimedes. The whole world rocked to the recoil. Compared to it the mightiest earthquake was but a tender shiver. The consciousness of the earth had spoken!

The professor was knocked upon the floor. He knew not what had happened. Out of the windows and to the north the flame of Colourado, like the whole world going up. It was the last moment. But he was a scientist to the end. He had sprained his ankle and his face was bleeding; but for all that he struggled, fought his way to the telescope. And he saw:

The great planet with its sinister, baleful, wicked light in the centre, and another light vastly larger covering up half of Mars. What was it? It was moving. The truth set him almost to shouting.

It was the answer of Charley Huyck and of the world. The light grew smaller, smaller, and almost to a pin-point on its way to Mars.

The real climax was in silence. And of all the world only Professor Williams beheld it. The two lights coalesced and spread out; what it was on Mars, of course, we do not know.

But in a few moments all was gone. Only the green of the Martian Sea winked in the sunlight. The luminous opal was gone from the Sargasso. The ocean lay in peace.

It was a terrible three days. Had it not been for the work of Robold and Huyck life would have been destroyed. The pity of it that all of their discoveries have gone with them. Not even Charley realized how terrific the force he was about to loosen.

He had carefully locked everything in vaults for a safe delivery to man. He had expected death, but not the cataclysm. The whole of Mount Robold was shorn away; in its place we have a lake fifty miles in diameter.

So much for celestial kinetics.

And we look to a green and beautiful Mars. We hold no enmity. It was but the law of self-preservation. Let us hope they have enough water; and that their seas will hold. We don't blame them, and we don't blame ourselves, either for that matter. We need what we have, and we hope to keep it.

THE VISITATION

by Cyril G. Wates

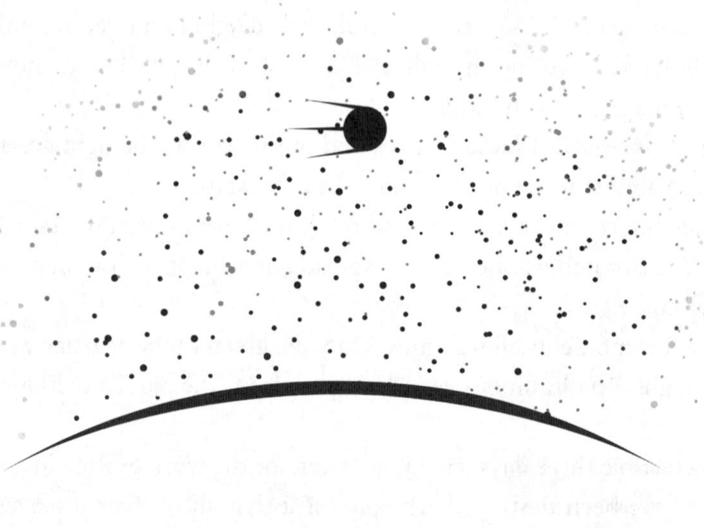

FOREWORD

This is the narrative of the last voyage of the *S.S. Shah of Iran*, to which voyage the greatest transformation the world has ever witnessed, was directly due—the voyage which resulted in that epoch-making year, universally known as "The Year of the Visitation."

Who I, the writer, may be, is of little importance and yet my name is not entirely unfamiliar to the countless millions who will read this story and will rejoice that the silence of nearly ninety years has at last been broken and all the world may know the events which took place on that extraordinary voyage—events which have hitherto been wrapped in mystery—at the request of those strange beings who called themselves "The Deelathon," but who are better known to us today as "The Visitants."

I am Benedict Clinton and I am the great-grandson of Charles Clinton, who was Captain of the *Shah of Iran*. Captain Clinton, my great-grandfather, died yesterday at the age of nearly one hundred and twenty-six years, and his death unseals my lips and releases me from the promise I made to him, a year ago, on his birthday.

Although, as I have stated, my own personality is of no importance in this narrative, it affords me a certain amused satisfaction to realize that I am perhaps the last historian of the human race. Owing to the changed conditions under which we live, the professional historian has become almost as obsolete as the lawyer or the alchemist of past ages. There is an old saying that "Happy is the nation which has no history," and that proverb is as true today as in the past, except that for the word "nation" we must substitute "planet." History is rightly defined as the record of the sufferings of mankind. Without suffering, there is nothing deemed worthy of record.

During the past century the world has been passing through the most extraordinary phase of transition which ever has been, or ever will be known. Prior to the year 1950—the Year of the Visitation—Humanity was divided by innumerable lines, largely artificial, into hundreds of races and nations. Since that date man has known only two divisions; those who were living at the time of the Visitation and those who were born afterwards.

We have adopted the two Deelathon words, "Zykof" and "Epzykof" (immortal and mortal), in referring to these two subdivisions of mankind and the names convey a fairly clear picture of human society of today. We of the new generation, the Zykofs, having been born to a knowledge of the Thon, glory in the prospect of a life which, while certainly not eternal, is infinitely richer and happier and more extended than that which our forefathers knew, but sometimes we are saddened by the sight of those who are nearest and dearest to us growing older and dying before our very eyes. Our friends the Epzykofs, who saw the great events which transpired nearly a century ago and even, as in my great-grandfather's case, were directly responsible for bringing about the Visitation, have only an acquired and not an inborn knowledge of the Thon and therefore are not fated to share with us, for long, the innumerable benefits it brings.

A year ago today I left my little workshop in the palm groves of Florida, where I carve and decorate the polar bosses for pleasure Zeeths, and before evening I set foot on the pine-clad shores of Vancouver Island. I had come, with many of my relatives and friends, to pay honour to Captain Clinton on his one hundred and twenty-fifth birthday. From all parts of the world we came and as I alighted from my Zeeth, I was greeted by several old friends who had just arrived from Japan.

Together we walked up the winding pathway through the forest, until we saw the gleam of white marble and emerged upon a wide lawn, upon the farther side of which, half hidden in a group of graceful cedar trees, was Captain Clinton's home, with its fluted columns and ellipsoidal roof. The Captain was seated upon the steps, his white hair shining like a beacon light in the last rays of the setting sun, and gathered around him was a group of our relatives in animated conversation.

As we approached, Captain Clinton rose and came forward to greet us, his fine figure still erect and his eyes bright with youth in spite of his (for an Epzykof) great age. For each he had a word of welcome, but it seemed that his handclasp to me was especially cordial.

"I am glad, very glad that you have come, Benedict," he said heartily. "I have a task for you to perform, a very important task, not without its responsibilities, and I hope that you will not refuse the request of an old man."

"That is a hope which will be realized as soon as your request is made known," I replied. "As for the responsibility involved, the fact that you have selected me, when all mankind delights to serve you, will give me strength to perform whatever task you set me."

"Thank you, Benedict," answered the Captain, simply, and turning to the others, he said, "In this happy world, where perfect candour is universal, I have the doubtful honour of being the only man with a secret. As you all know, I am the last survivor of the crew of the *Shah of Iran* and soon I shall go to join my shipmates. Tomorrow I will tell Benedict the story of my last voyage, a story which was to be kept secret until the last of us had sailed for the home port. When I am gone, Benedict will write it out for all the world to read."

We surrounded him with loving words and tender caresses. Not because he was the most famous man in the world for nearly a hundred years, but because of his simple nobility, we loved this fine old sea captain of a past age. Thelma, his eldest daughter, who with her companion, John Adair, had come from their home in Spain that day, slipped her arm around her father's neck and cried:

"You must not leave us yet, Father dear! You have a hundred years of life in that big body of yours still. I believe you can beat me in a swimming match even now!" For Thelma was a famous swimmer.

"That remains to be proven, my dear," said the Captain with a little laugh, half gay, half sad.

"Prove it! Prove it, Thelma!" we cried and soon we were all running down the path to the shore, where we plunged into the warm waters of the Pacific.

Thelma beat her father by a length, her white body flashing through the water like an ivory Zeeth cleaving the air. We remained sporting in the bay until the daylight died and the big moon rose.

As we loitered up the hill, my great-grandfather drew me back from the gay crowd.

"I should like you to climb the Shah with me in the morning, Benedict," he said. "I want to watch the sun rise—who knows, it may be for the last time—and then I will tell you the story of my last voyage and the Visitation of the Deelathon. Will you come?"

The half light of dawn was just touching the snow-capped peaks in the east when Captain Clinton and I started our ascent of the Shah, the little mountain just behind his home, to which he had attached the name of his old ship. We tiptoed down the steps in order not to disturb the sleeping guests, whose white forms lay—

"Star-scattered on the grass"—as old Omar puts it. Soon we were high up among the rocky buttresses of the Shah. An hour of exhilarating climbing brought us to the summit and we sat on a flat boulder to watch the ever-new miracle of the Dawn.

To the East shone the placid waters of Queen Charlotte Sound, sparkling like molten gold in the radiance of the rising sun. Beyond towered the mountains of the mainland, lifting their snowy heads above their mantle of green. To the West, the waters of the Pacific widened to an unbroken horizon.

At last the Captain broke the silence and for an hour I sat spellbound, listening to his deep voice telling the story of that last voyage—the Voyage of the Visitation.

I
THE METEOR

You must often have wondered (said Captain Clinton) in common with the rest of the world, why no person among the crew or passengers of the *Shah of Iran* has ever revealed what took place on the last voyage of the old ship. The reason for this secrecy on the subject which is naturally of more than average interest to everyone, is quite simple.

When the Deelathon conceded to our request to make the Visitation, it was upon the express understanding that the location of their country should be concealed. They pointed out to us that it was impossible to foresee the outcome of the Visitation and they wanted to insure their own safety in any event.

This request was so entirely reasonable that we all unhesitatingly agreed to it. We realized that it was not possible to release into the world a tremendous force like the Thon, without producing a widespread upheaval, which might be beneficent or the reverse. We decided that the simplest way of preserving the secret was to make a pact among ourselves that the entire story of the voyage should remain untold until the last of us was dead. If it seemed wise, in the light of events which were still in the future, the last living member of the party was to tell the story to some dear friend, who would publish it after his death.

This, then, Benedict (continued the Captain), is the task I am asking you to undertake. Say nothing until I am gone and then publish what I am about to tell you, word for word as I shall tell it, as you may easily do by the aid of the Thon. I feel that my end is not far off. All possibility of danger to our friends and benefactors, the Deelathon, has long passed away and the necessity for preserving their secret no longer exists. And now for my story!

The *Shah of Iran*, of which I was Captain, was one of a line of huge steamers which made the journey between Vancouver and Australia in the fifth decade of the twentieth century. These great vessels, which became obsolete with the introduction of the Zeeth, were magnificently equipped according to the strange standards of that time and were so powerful that, although they floated upon the surface of the water, they had little to fear from the worst storms they were likely to encounter. They carried a thousand passengers and a large crew, not only to handle the elaborate machinery and to navigate the vessel, but also to attend to the thousand and one wants of the thousand passengers!

On the seventeenth day of September, 1949, we sailed from Vancouver on a pleasure tour for which the *Shah of Iran* had been chartered. We were to touch at San Francisco, Manzanillo and Panama before striking across the Pacific for Sidney. The voyage was uneventful until we left the Isthmus and were three days' journey southwest of the Galapagos Islands. I was standing on the bridge with my chief officer, a fine fellow named Ian McFane, you knew him, Benedict.

The sun was rising. Ian and I were discussing some matter relating to the navigation of the ship, when a sailor came running up the steps and, touching his cap, as was the custom in those days, exclaimed:

"Beg pardon, Sir! There's something wrong with the sun!"

Ian McFane and I both looked to the East and both cried out in astonishment. Exactly in the centre of the golden disc was a round spot. This spot was perfectly black and about one-quarter the apparent diameter of the sun.

"What do you make of that, Mr. McFane?" I asked.

"Well, I hardly know, sir," replied the mate. "It's too big and black to be a sun-spot and, besides, it's moving!"

Sure enough, as we watched the spot, it crept slowly to the edge of the sun and in about ten minutes had left the disc altogether and vanished.

"It is some opaque object between us and the sun," I said.

"Some new kind of plane, maybe," suggested Ian.

"I doubt it, Mister," I replied. "It simply vanished when it left the solar disc and that would show that it's outside the atmosphere. More likely a big meteorite." "If that was a meteorite and it hits the earth, we're going to know it!" said Ian.

"Well, don't start that idea circulating among the passengers," I replied. "We don't want a small sized panic on our hands and, anyway, we may be entirely wrong in supposing that it was a meteorite."

My warning proved to be useless, for when I descended to the promenade deck, I found many of the passengers gathered in groups, discussing the strange phenomenon, which had been seen by several early risers.

The news of the curious black spot on the sun spread like wild-fire and as soon as I made my appearance I was surrounded by a group of passengers, clamouring for an explanation.

"I'm sorry, ladies and gentlemen," I said, "but I am as much at a loss to explain the spot as yourselves. I can only suggest that it may have been a small, very dense cloud."

"But that wouldn't explain why it vanished when it passed off the face of the sun," objected one of the ladies. "Oh! here comes Professor Smithton! He'll be able to tell us all about it," and the group broke away from me and re-formed around the famous astronomer and physicist, who had just arrived on deck.

* * * * *

Of course, I knew that my theory of a dense cloud was ridiculous, but I was anxious to avoid any suggestion that might cause alarm among the passengers. A panic is a nasty thing to handle and would have reflected seriously upon my management and indirectly upon the shipping company.

I walked across the deck in time to hear the Professor giving his opinion in his best lecture-room style. He had not seen the spot himself, so he was obliged to base his judgment upon the descriptions of the few who had been on deck at the time. He listened to all carefully and then said, laughing:

"I have no doubt that this spot on the sun seems very mysterious to all of you, even you, Captain, but the explanation is, after all, extremely simple." There was a murmur of surprise followed by demands for enlightenment.

"The spot you saw was simply a parachute descending from an aeroplane flying at a height so great that it was invisible. The spot was oval rather than round, was it not?"

Again there was a babble of voices, some saying that the spot was distinctly oval, others that it was quite round. When there was silence, the Professor continued, apparently quite deaf to any evidence that did not fit in with his preconceived theory.

"Ah! Quite so! Distinctively oval," he said. "Due to the angle of vision, of course," and rubbing his hands together with the air of a man who has cleared away all possible doubt, he disappeared into the saloon and was soon engrossed in a hearty breakfast, an excellent example which all the passengers followed.

"So that's that!" remarked Ian, who had come up during the discourse.

"Yes," I replied, dryly, "at least it would be if it had been a parachute! Fortunately for the professor's reputation for scientific infallibility, no one except ourselves seems to have noticed that the spot left the sun at its upper edge. If anyone has invented a rising parachute, I haven't heard of it!"

Throughout the day, the *Shah of Iran* continued to plough her way southward through an ocean as smooth as the proverbial sheet of glass. The weather was perfect, although the heat was oppressive, but that was to be expected during a calm just south of the equator.

In the late afternoon a slight swell manifested itself, getting gradually heavier until at sunset the steamer was perceptibly pitching, in spite of her gyroscopic stabilizers. The air was still motionless, the only breeze being due to the speed of the vessel, and the sky was absolutely cloudless.

I went to my cabin early and turned in, but could not sleep. An oppressive sense of impending disaster descended upon me like a pall, and resisted all my efforts to shake it off. At last I rose and dressed. I went out on the bridge, where I found Ian McFane talking to the officer of the watch, Gordon Caswell, the third mate. Both were looking up at the sky, where the stars were sparkling with tropical brilliancy.

"I'm glad you came out, sir," said Ian, "but what is the trouble?"

"I couldn't sleep," I exclaimed. "The heat, I guess."

"It sure is hot, even for the tropics," said Caswell.

"What are you two looking at?" I queried.

"There's something funny about the stars," replied Caswell and he pointed up towards the West.

Following the direction of his finger, I saw the Galaxy or Milky Way, as it is commonly called, shining like a belt of silver spray across the velvety sky. About fifty degrees above the horizon appeared a perfectly circular patch approximately three times the diameter of the moon. Within this area, the stars of the Galaxy were blotted out, giving exactly the appearance of the Coal Sack, that curious vacant space which has been familiar to astronomers for centuries.

"What do you think it is, sir?" asked Ian. "The spot we saw this morning?"

"It looks unpleasantly like it," I said, "and it also looks as though my theory of a huge meteorite or a wandering asteroid were correct."

"If so, it must be moving with tremendous speed," said Caswell. "It has doubled in size during the half hour that Mr. McFane and I have been watching it."

"I don't like the looks of it!" I said. "If that thing hits the sea anywhere near the boat, there's going to be one gosh-awful explosion! Mr. McFane, will you kindly have all hands called on deck. And quietly, please. Tell the Chief Steward to post men in all doorways and corridors to keep the passengers below decks in case of accident. Tell them to use tact and avoid a panic at all costs."

In ten minutes my orders had been carried out and the entire crew were standing by, waiting for—we knew not what!

The swell of the afternoon had increased rapidly to huge proportions, but the waves were so long and unbroken that the *Shah* rode them with ease. McFane, Caswell and I stood on the bridge watching that ominous disc in the sky spreading until it had blotted out fully one-eighth of the stars in the southwestern quadrant.

Suddenly the edges of the black circle were surrounded by an awful halo of flame. Far quicker than I can describe it the whole surface of the meteor, if that was what it was, had turned to a white heat, so intense that we were blinded by the glare. As the visitor from interstellar space tore its furious way through the hundred miles of our atmosphere, the whole expanse of ocean became as light as day. Great streams of molten lava shot out in every direction and yet, most ghastly touch of all, absolute silence reigned.

The blazing meteor struck the sea exactly at the horizon, that is to say about twenty miles away. We had a momentary glimpse of a fearful column of boiling water, wreathed in clouds of steam, hurling itself towards the zenith and then—darkness!

In the breathless silence my voice rang out: "Hard a-starbo'd!" and the great ship began to swing around in order to place her stem towards the point from which I was sure the inevitable danger must come.

And then came the NOISE!

* * * * *

No words of mine can hope to describe the frightful bellowing tumult of that explosion. First came the shrill shriek produced by the brief passage of the meteor through our atmosphere. Following this was a roar as if all the artillery of all the armies and navies of that unhappy old world of ours had been fired simultaneously and the sound multiplied a thousandfold.

Every man whose position exposed him to the direct force of the blast was hurled to the deck and many were injured. Cries of pain from the deck and screams of fear from the staterooms were mingled with the continuous, soul-shattering blasts of noise as the white hot meteor uttered its indignant protests at being sunk in four miles of salt water.

And last came the storm!

As when a boy casts a pebble into a pond to watch the ripples spread, so when the hand of fate cast into the greatest pond on earth, a pebble forty miles in diameter, ripples fled out in all directions. But these ripples were walls of water a hundred feet in height and moving with incredible rapidity!

In a moment the vessel was caught up and hurled eastward with the speed of an express train. In vain her powerful screws beat the water in a brave endeavour to stem the force of a two hundred mile hurricane! We were helpless and could only trust in the mercy of God, the strength of steel plates and the knowledge that hundreds of miles of open sea lay between us and the coasts of South America.

You know, Benedict, that there has been a prevailing impression for the last ninety years that the Deelathon arrived from the realms of space upon the meteor, whose shattered fragments now form an island in the Pacific. We who could have contradicted that idea were pledged to silence, but no one who had witnessed that hellish globe descend from the heavens and the tempest that followed it, could have believed for a moment that any living being could have survived such a cataclysm.

For five hours we drove before the storm. The bellow of the cooling meteor had long since died away in the West, but was replaced by the tumult of the wind and waves. It would take too long to tell you all the terror of that awful night. A dozen times it seemed impossible that we could remain afloat another moment and a dozen times the impossible happened.

Just before four o'clock the waves died down as suddenly as they had arisen and the *Shah of Iran* rested on an even keel in smooth water.

The rain still poured down and the roar of the tempest could be heard, as it were, far overhead. The darkness was stygian and it was impossible to see more than a hundred yards in any direction, even with the aid of the *Shah*'s powerful searchlight. I untied the rope with which I had lashed myself to the bridge rail and staggered over to McFane.

"It's pretty obvious that we have been driven by some miracle into a sheltered harbour on the South American Coast," I said.

"If that's so, sir," replied Ian, "it's a miracle indeed."

"Aye, and that's not the only miracle," said Caswell's voice. "We were three hundred miles off the coast when the meteor struck and that means we've been travelling over sixty miles an hour!"

"I'd be willing to believe you," said Ian, "if you told me it was a hundred!"

"Well, thank God it's over!" I said. "Mr. McFane, please have a sounding made and if we're in shallow water, as I suspect, drop anchor. We don't want to drift on the rocks."

By the time these instructions had been carried out, the storm outside had somewhat abated, but as the tumult of the wind became less, I noticed a continuous roar which at first I attributed to breakers on the rocks outside the harbour. On glancing at the compass, I was surprised to find that the sound came from the west; the probable direction of the land.

In about an hour, the noise of the wind had died to a whisper and then the roar from the west became very noticeable. Caswell, who had remained on the bridge, called my attention to the fact that the sound was practically steady and therefore could not be breakers.

"Well, we shall have to wait for daylight to see what it is," I said. "I'm going down now to see how the passengers have stood the racket. Call me if you see or hear anything unusual."

I found the passengers huddled in the main saloon, most of them showing evidence of the severe strain to which they had been exposed, but the ship's doctor reported that aside from one broken arm and a few bruises, there were no injuries.

"We've certainly got to hand it to Professor Smithton, sir," said the Doctor. "He did more than any of us to keep the crowd under control. He was as cool as if he were in his class room."

Having given orders for coffee and biscuits to be served as soon as possible, I was going from one group to another with assurances that all danger was now past, when the fourth officer came hurriedly down the stairs and told me that Mr. Caswell wanted me on deck at once.

* * * * *

As I reached the deck I saw that dawn was breaking. The curtain of rain had been withdrawn and I was able to take in at a glance the extraordinary chance to which we all owed our lives.

The *Shah* was lying peacefully at anchor in a little bay surrounded by sheer, black cliffs which seemed, in the dim light, to tower to a height of at least a thousand feet on all sides. The harbour was shaped like a pear, with the narrow part—the stem—towards the open sea.

The steady roaring sound still continued and seemed to come from a point in the cliffs directly opposite the entrance to the bay, which was about a mile across at its broadest part. The width of the "stem" was certainly not above a quarter of a mile and you will understand my feelings, Benedict, when I tell you that the sight of that narrow gap in the beetling cliffs literally turned me sick! We had all been under too great a strain all night, to realize our plight clearly, but the thought of what would have happened if we had missed that narrow opening—

I went up on the bridge and joined Caswell. I began to make some remark on the providential chance which had brought us safely into the harbour, when I saw that he was paying no attention to me, but was gazing intently to the westward.

"What's the trouble, Mr. Caswell?" I asked. "Well, sir, I don't know if the light of that meteor has affected my eyesight, but would you mind telling me how we got in here?"

II
IMPRISONED

Startled at Gordon Caswell's strange question, I followed the direction of his gaze and saw with amazement that the entire breadth of the harbour mouth was bridged by a natural breakwater, against which the waves from the open Pacific were bursting in columns of spray. No opening was visible in the reef and I was completely at a loss to answer Caswell's question as to how we had crossed it. A steamer of thirty thousand tons does not fly and even allowing for the height of the waves, it was hardly conceivable that we could have been washed over the reef without grounding.

"There must be an opening somewhere, Mr. Caswell," I said. "When you have had breakfast and it's lighter, please take number three launch and explore the reef."

While the second officer was away, the passengers began to throng the decks and many were the expressions of wonder at the remarkable harbour into which we had so providentially been carried. The black cliffs, which lost none of their height with the increasing light, were not smooth but broken by vertical seams at regular intervals. The whole scene reminded me of some picture I had seen, I could not tell where. It was Ian McFane, whose birthplace was in northern Scotland, who remarked on the close resemblance between these cliffs and the basaltic formation of the famous Fingall's Cave in the Hebrides. The vertical clefts we observed were indeed the spaces between huge hexagonal columns extend- ing from the surface of the water to the top of the cliffs without a break, giving the semblance of a gigantic temple built for some ghastly cult of devil worship.

The water was almost without a ripple and the tier of thousand foot columns unbroken, except at the point from which the thundering roar still came. Here appeared a gap, forming a narrow gorge, and the mirror-like surface of the sea was broken by a considerable stream which cascaded over broken blocks of basalt. It was apparent that the roar we heard came from a huge waterfall, hidden from our sight in the recesses of the canyon.

Caswell returned at noon. His report only served to increase our bewilderment. With three of the men, he had landed at the base of the cliffs where the southern end of the reef abutted against them. Ordering the launch to follow them at some distance from the rocks, they had walked northward along the broken tops of basaltic columns similar to those of which the cliffs were composed.

About half way along the reef they were stopped by a torrent of water flowing across the barrier into the open sea, and were obliged to signal to the launch to pick them up.

Landing again at the northern end of the reef, they walked back to the central stream without finding any trace of an opening. The stream was too narrow to permit the passage of such a vessel as the *Shah*, even had the water been sufficiently deep, which was obviously not the case.

They crossed the reef, which was about two hundred yards in width, and looked out upon the open Pacific, still heaving in long rollers; the aftermath of the storm of the previous night. They returned to the *Shah* completely nonplussed.

Having listened to Caswell's report, I thought it best to take the passengers into our confidence. Mounting the orchestra platform in the grand saloon, I made a short speech in which I stated that the *Shah of Iran* was imprisoned in a land-locked harbour. How she got there I could not explain, but it was impossible to get her out with anything short of dynamite, which naturally we did not possess.

"There is no possible cause for alarm, ladies and gentlemen," I said. "The *Shah* is provisioned for a long voyage and is perfectly safe in this bay. As soon as the necessary arrangements can be made, I will send an expedition inland to the nearest settlement which affords telegraphic or radio facilities. Our own radio is, unfortunately, damaged beyond possibility of repair. In a few weeks at the latest, a relief boat will arrive, bringing the necessary explosive to release the *Shah*, and I think I can promise you all some entertainment when the blasting begins. In the meantime I hope everyone will make the best of a bad job."

There was some applause and when it subsided, Professor Smithton arose and asked for permission to question the Second Officer.

"Will you kindly describe the nature of the beach along the barrier reef, Mr. Caswell," said the Professor.

"The fact is," said Caswell, "there is no beach of any kind on either side of the reef. The rocks go straight down into the water."

"One more question," said the Professor. "Do the ends of the reef lie conformably against the cliffs? I mean," he explained, smiling at Caswell's evident bewilderment, "do the rocks fit closely together?"

"No, sir, they do not," he replied. "They are very much broken up at both ends."

"Ah! Quite so!" ejaculated the Professor with satisfaction. "I think I can explain the mystery of our arrival, even if I did make a slight, though perfectly excusable mistake about the parachute," and he smiled blandly at his audience. "When the *Shah* entered the harbour, the reef was not there!"

"Not there?" I exclaimed.

"Quite so. The absence of beaches and the uncon- formable—excuse me, I should say broken condition of the ends of the reef show that it was recently raised above the water. The parachute—beg pardon, the meteor was apparently about forty miles in diameter, judging by the area of sky it obscured when it touched our atmosphere. If its composition were similar to that of most meteors, it would weigh in the neighbourhood of fifty million million tons. It is hardly to be expected that such a missile could strike the earth at a velocity of perhaps three hundred thousand miles per hour, without causing widespread seismic disturbances, which would flow through the solid globe in ripples from the point of impact. It is these ripples which were mainly responsible for the storm, which may be regarded as a series of tidal waves, and it was these ripples, or rather one of them, which raised the barrier reef and cut us off from the ocean—fortunately, after we entered the bay!"

The Professor was going on to enlarge on his subject when the Quartermaster entered the room and came up to where I was standing.

"Beg pardon, sir. Mr. McFane told me to tell you that the ship is sinking."

* * * * *

For the second time we came very near having a serious panic. I rushed on deck but could see no signs of anything to give basis for Ian's message. In reply to my questions he informed me that he had gone down into the launch, which was still floating alongside, to get some specimens of basalt which Caswell had brought from the reef. While there, he noticed that the *Shah* was floating nearly a foot deeper than when she left port. He had given orders to have all compartments examined for a leak before reporting to me, but could find nothing.

Meanwhile the excitement among the passengers was fast getting beyond control when the Professor began waving his arms and shouting for silence.

"Ladies and gentlemen! There is no cause for alarm. The *Shah* is perfectly safe, as I hope to prove in a few minutes. Captain, will you kindly have one of your men draw a bucket of sea water."

I nodded to Ian to have the request carried out and the Professor disappeared into his stateroom, returning in a few moments with a wooden case from which he took a thin glass tube with a bulb at one end. He dropped this into the bucket of water, where it floated upright. Having examined it carefully, he straightened up and said:

"Ah! Quite so! It is not the ship that is responsible for this unwarranted alarm, but the sea. The normal specific gravity of water is, of course 1.00, while that of sea water is about 1.031. Now the specific gravity of this water is only 1.014, so naturally the ship has settled."

"But what could possibly cause such a state of affairs, Professor?" I demanded.

"Ah! Quite simple, Captain. The sea water has been cut off by the reef, leaving the shallow harbour land-locked. There is a tremendous amount of freshwater running into the bay from that canyon at the western end and it is forcing out the salt water over the reef, as Mr. Caswell told us. Naturally the ship is settling and will continue to do so—" and he made a dramatic pause. "—for about six inches further, when the water will be entirely fresh."

Needless to say, the Professor's stock, which had slumped after the "parachute" fiasco and made a quick recovery during the meeting in the saloon, went sky high as the result of this second example of scientific acumen. Indeed, I was so much impressed with Professor Smithton's versatility, common sense and unfailing good nature, that I invited him to attend a conference of the officers to be held that afternoon for the purpose of laying definite plans for sending out a relief party.

At the Professor's suggestion, I also asked two young men named Alderson and FitzGerald; athletic young fellows, both members of the English and American Alpine Clubs, who were enroute to New Zealand to attempt the ascent of an unclimbed peak in the Southern Alps.

When these three passengers and the officers were gathered in the smoking room, I made a brief outline of the situation and asked for suggestions, explaining that the important thing was to get in touch with civilization as soon as possible.

The Professor rose and asked if I could state the approximate location of the *Shah* and whether it would not be better to send out a relief party by sea, rather than by land.

"I am afraid that it is impossible to give a satisfactory answer to your first question, Professor. We have no way of determining how far North or South we were carried by the storm and the heavy pall of clouds makes an observation out of the question."

"Ah! Quite so! The clouds are undoubtedly the result of the immense amount of steam produced by contact between the meteor and the ocean. I venture to predict that, on account of the great size of the meteor, which would preclude more than a small portion being immersed, these clouds will continue for a long period of time."

"With regard to sending out a party by sea," I continued, "I had thought of that possibility, but aside from the great difficulty of transporting one of the launches across the reef, there are two serious objections to that plan. One is that the sea is too rough for a small craft to navigate in safety and the other is that all our launches are electric and intended for short trips. The storage batteries would not last for over a couple of days at the outside."

"Ah! Quite so!" said the Professor. "Then I venture to suggest, Captain, that you send a party on shore at the mouth of the river, tomorrow, and determine the feasibility of reaching the top of the cliffs. I foresee that the presence of a waterfall might prove a serious obstruction. Here is where the mountaineering skill of our two young friends, Mr. Alderson and Mr. FitzGerald, will be invaluable. If the cliffs are successfully surmounted, you can then arrange the personnel of your party and the necessary outfit of provisions."

The Professor's suggestions met with unanimous approval. No sooner did the result of our conference become known than a number of the passengers asked my permission to accompany the proposed expedition. Thus it happened that a large and light-hearted party crossed the strip of smooth water that separated us from the shore and set foot on the narrow beach just north of the mouth of the river.

III
THE COMING OF THE DEELATHON

Accompanied by the Professor and the two mountaineers, I led the way inland. Presently we approached the point where the river made its way through the wall of cliffs and turning sharply to the north, scrambled over fallen rock into the entrance of the canyon, the roar of falling water growing louder as we advanced.

Above the fallen rock we turned to the right around a magnificent group of the hexagonal basalt columns and the words of some remark I was about to make died on my lips in sheer wonderment. We were confronted with a sight which, for appalling grandeur is probably unequalled anywhere on earth.

We stood on the edge of a vast, cup-like depression in the rock. On every side towered the pillars of basalt, as smooth and perfect as though they had been carved and polished by the hand of man. On the farther side of this huge theatre, the river descended from the brow of the cliffs in one mighty thousand-foot leap, to strike squarely on the edge of the great cup, which was filled to the brim with a churning mass of foam, while the deafening roar of the tortured waters echoed and re-echoed from the black walls.

So tremendous were the cliffs that we stood, as it were, at the bottom of a circular pit and the light that filtered down from above was but a dim similitude of day.

For a long time we stood transfixed with awe, while the other members of the party gradually joined us, their laughter quenched by the wonder of the sight that met their gaze. As our eyes became more accustomed to the half-light, we were able to see that it was only around the rocky margins of the pool that the water was beaten into foam. The entire centre was occupied by a mass of water perfectly smooth and piled up like a dome of glass.

At first sight this central mass seemed motionless but we soon realized that its whole surface was the playground of titanic forces. The entire structure quivered as though it were in a state of the most delicate equilibrium, as indeed it was, and it seemed as though one had only to throw a pebble to see it dissolve in a slather of foam, like a giant bubble.

Presently the voice of the Professor broke the spell.

"I'm a old man, Captain, and in my time I've seen the glories of the starry heavens as perhaps few have done, but I thank God that He has spared me to see this!"

"I thought the great snow peaks were the most beautiful things in creation," said FitzGerald, "but this has got them all beat."

"And look at the light, Fred!" exclaimed his sister, who had joined us. "It's like all the opals in the world rolled into one. Or rather, like a soap bubble on the point of bursting, for these colours move."

Miss FitzGerald's exclamation brought us to the realization that this water was not like other water, but seemed to glow with an effulgence of its own. Streamers of light of every imaginable colour darted here and there over the shining surface of the great dome, now blending into masses of rose or green or violet, now mingling in a glittering confusion of rainbow hues.

Of course, we knew that we were looking at some remarkable natural optical illusion, caused by the reflection of the light from above, but the effect was none the less impressive. The living, shining dome of colour, set in its girdle of snowy foam; the silent cliffs with their ebony towers; the thundering column of water eternally descending from above; all combined into a dramatic whole whose overwhelming grandeur was foiled by a broad band of emerald green turf which framed the central cup and was dotted here and there with graceful palm trees, whose fronds glistened with diamond drops of spray.

At last I tore my eyes from that living opal and turned to the two mountaineers.

"Well, gentlemen, what do you think of our chances of getting out of this?"

"Hopeless!" replied Alderson.

"Absolutely !" agreed FitzGerald. "We're by way of being mountaineers, but we're not flies! There's not a handhold anywhere. But, good Lord ! What's that!"

At his cry of surprise, we all looked up, to behold, poised in the air above the rim of the waterfall, a great ball like a gigantic soap bubble.

"Your parachute, I guess, Professor !" said Caswell slyly. "Look, it's coming down."

* * * * *

Very slowly the ball descended into the abyss and now we realized that it was far larger than we had at first supposed. It was apparently made of some transparent material like glass, except that it glittered with the same play of colours as that which appeared on the surface of the pool. Around the centre of the balloon, if balloon it was, was a broad band of some metal, such as copper or gold. This girdle formed the equator and at either pole was a projecting boss of the same metal, from which were suspended by cables, inverted cups which hung some distance below the globe.

As the strange aerial visitor drew nearer we saw that the equatorial band was studded at intervals with circular windows of the glassy material. From the centre of each of these projected a long needle, the purpose of which we could not guess unless they were for directing the course of the vessel—a theory which we afterwards found to be correct.

Very slowly the great ball sank until the two cups touched the grassy sward about three hundred yards from us. Still it sank, the cables from which the cups were suspended being withdrawn into the two metal bosses, until the lower edge of the central girdle was but a foot above the ground. Here the shining sphere hung, swaying gently in the wind that rose from the churning water.

A moment later one of the circular windows swung open and a figure stepped down upon the grass, followed by several others. They started to walk around the margin of the pool towards us and as they drew nearer the Professor exclaimed in surprise.

"Good Heavens! They're Indians! Look at the headdress!"

"Don't worry, Sir Charles," I said. "We're armed," and I drew my revolver from its holster, but as I did so I had a curious sensation that my warlike act was a gesture absolutely without meaning.

"Oh! I wasn't afraid," replied Sir Charles, "but they haven't got any—I mean, they're rather lightly clad for polite society, you know."

The group from the sphere were now near enough for me to see that Sir Charles was correct. There were five or six men and two women and each wore only a great headdress of what seemed to be white feathers. I also realized that these were no Indians. The colour of the skin which had at a distance appeared coppery, was now revealed as rosy pink, not due to the presence of any colouring pigment, but as though the skin were so transparent and the health so abounding, that the blood literally shone through.

I began to agree with Sir Charles that it would be wise for the ladies to retire while we interviewed these strange inhabitants. I turned to make some such suggestion and caught sight of Margaret FitzGerald staring at the approaching party, her eyes shining with excitement.

There was a burst of admiration from the passengers, men and women joining in exclamations of delight at the physical perfection and nobility of countenance of these splendid beings who were now only a few yards from us.

The party came to a halt and one of the tallest of the men stepped forward and saluted us with a curious but graceful gesture. As he did so I realized with a distinct shock that what we had taken to be a feather headdress was not a headdress at all, but was a semi-transparent, membranous frill, actually growing upon the heads of these beings. This frill or "thonmelek" as we afterwards learned was their word for it, ran across the forehead just in front of the hair, down each side of the neck, over the shoulders and terminated just above the elbows, I know of nothing which it so much resembled as the fin of a flying fish, except that the "thonmelek" was infinitely more delicate, but it was supported upon blades of cartilage in much the same way. All this we absorbed at a glance and then the tall man, evidently the appointed spokesman of the party, addressed us.

"*Deelarana, Deelatkon zeloma ek tara*!" and raising their hands in the same graceful gesture, all the others echoed "Zeloma!"

"Zeloma!" exclaimed Sir Charles. "I say, Captain, it sounds as if they were giving us a salute of welcome."

"Yes, I agree with you," I replied, "and they all have the kindliest smile I ever saw on human countenance. I am certain they mean us no harm."

I turned back to the tall stranger with the intention of trying to convey our friendliness to him, by means of signs, when his lips opened and he said in the most perfect English, without a trace of accent.

"Yes, I welcome you. Us, the Deelathon, mean no harm. Welcome!"

* * * * *

Of all the strange incidents of this strange voyage, I think this was the most astonishing. A thrill of excitement passed through the crowd. We, sophisticated citizens of the twentieth century, had discovered an unknown country, inhabited by an unknown race as beautiful as angels, who wore no clothes, grew a frill on their foreheads, and—spoke English without an accent! True, they spoke it mechanically and not quite correctly, but it was English!

"You speak English, friend!" I exclaimed.

The tall man shook his head and smiled.

"But you understand it?"

He smiled again and said, "Yes!"

"Why, Captain," cried Miss FitzGerald, "this is like a romance out of a book!"

At these apparently innocent words our visitors, the Deelathon (for you will have guessed that it was they) showed their first sign of excitement and we saw that their frills or thonmeleks, which were normally pearly white, flashed with rainbow colours, like the surface of the Dome of Water. One of the girls stepped forward and spoke rapidly in their soft, musical language, several times repeating the word "book."

Now it happened that Miss FitzGerald had brought a volume of Emerson's essays with her, to read while her brother and Mr. Alderson were exploring the cliffs. She smiled and handed it to the lovely girl, saying:

"This is a book."

The two Deelathon examined the volume with great interest and then the man handed it back to Miss FitzGerald with a questioning look.

"It is a book," she said. "We read it."

At once the tall man caught up her words.

"Read it!" he exclaimed. "Read it."

Miss FitzGerald turned to me in surprise. "They say they can't speak English," she said, "and yet they keep on speaking it! I don't understand!"

"Don't you see?" replied her brother. "They just say the words we say—like parrots."

"No, I don't agree with you, Mr. FitzGerald," interrupted Professor Smithton. "It is true that they repeat our words, but they combine them intelligently into new sentences, almost as though they could read our thoughts."

The tall man listened attentively to this discussion and then smiling, pointed to the book and repeated :

"Read!"

"Perhaps you had better do as they ask," I said to Miss FitzGerald.

And then took place one of the strangest scenes I have ever witnessed. At a gesture from their leader, the Deelathon seated themselves on the grass and we followed their example, for an hour, nothing but the boom of the waterfall and the soft, sweet voice of the American girl reading to those gods and goddesses, the words of the great American essayist, could be heard. At first she stopped at intervals and looked up, but the Deelathon would say softly, "Read!"

And she continued.

At last, when she had read fully half of the book, the tall man put up his hands to check her and rose to his feet.

"Friends from the sea," he said, "we, the people of the Thon, welcome you, the speakers of a strange, harsh language, until this moment unknown to us. We ask you to forgive our seeming inhospitality, but of course you realize that it was impossible for us to address you in your own language until we had heard it spoken. Therefore I asked this beautiful maiden to read from her record, which she calls a book.

"But enough of this matter of speech which doubtless you already know, by the Thon. Now that we are able to talk freely, accept our welcome and hospitality and then tell us how we, the Deelathon, may serve you. I am Toron, maker of Zeeths, and this is my companion, Torona," and he laid his hand gently upon the head of the girl who had asked Miss FitzGerald for the book.

To say that we were dumfounded at this fluent address from a being who, only an hour previously, had said, "Us mean no harm," would be putting it very mildly. For a few moments we were too astonished to reply. The Professor was the first to regain his wits. He rose, bowed courteously, and said: "Strangers, who call yourselves the Deelathon, we thank you for your welcome. I am Professor Smithton and this is Captain Clinton. We, with many others, were driven into this harbour by the terrible storm, and escape has been cut off. Therefore we seek a way inland."

"But have you no Zeeths?" asked Torona,

"I am afraid not," replied the Professor smiling. "We do not even know what a Zeeth may be."

"You do not know?" exclaimed the Deelathon girl, her thonmelek rippling with colour. "But does not the Thon tell you?"

"Again I must admit ignorance," replied Smithton. "I do not even know what you mean by the Thon."

At these words the Deelathon leaped to their feet in uncontrollable excitement. Their thonmeleks furled and unfurled, flashing with a hundred hues and we heard repeatedly the words "*Zeel epthona Thon*!" ("They know not the Thon!")

Finally Toron turned to us and said:

"You will forgive our unseemly emotion, Smithton, and you, Clinton. We were surprised at your apparent inability to understand us when we spoke our own language. We are doubly astonished that you are surprised at our fluent English. But we are astounded at your statement that you do not know the Thon and can only suppose two things: either that you and your friends are very unhappy or that you say the thing which is Epthona—or as you would express it, untrue."

"I can only assure you, friend Toron," said the Professor earnestly, "that we are not guilty of falsehood when we say we do not know this Thon, neither are we especially unhappy, though what connection that has with the Thon I do not understand."

"And are there many like you in the world?" asked one of the Deelathon men, wonderingly. "People who know not the Thon and who have lost their thonmeleks?" and he passed his hand upward over that glittering appendage.

"There are countless millions," replied the Professor.

"What you tell us," said Toron, "fills us with sorrow. True, we of the Deelathon have a legend that a people existed upon the face of the earth, who knew not the wonderful benefits which are constantly showered upon us by the Thon-ta-Zheena, but we did not believe it possible. It seemed like a story of fish flying through the air, or birds who lived under water. The news you tell us we must carefully consider. We will return to our people and I will call a conference of the Klendeela. In the meantime, return to your Zeeth-that-floats-on-the-water and at sunset I will visit you."

The Deelathon raised their hands in salutation, folded their thonmeleks and returned to the crystal globe which presently rose steadily into the air and disappeared over the brink of the waterfall.

* * * * *

As soon as we set foot once more on the deck of *Shah of Iran* I left the passengers to narrate to their friends who had remained on board, the strange events through which we had passed, and beckoning to Professor Smithton, conducted him to my cabin and closed the door.

When we had lighted our cigars, I said:

"Well, Professor, what do you make of it?"

"Candidly, Captain, there are a good many things I don't understand at all."

"This 'Thon' they talked about so much, for example," I said, "and how they were able to talk English so fluently."

"Well, no," said Smithton, thoughtfully, "I think I begin to have a hazy idea of what they were driving at."

"That's more than I have," I said.

"No, the things I can't fathom," the Professor went on, "are what supports that dome of water and why it shines like a fire-opal and what holds up that crystal balloon of theirs and why they have frills on their heads and a few other things like that. But the Thon—didn't you notice how that word kept on creeping up in their language? Deelathon—people of the Thon. Thonmelek—that frill of theirs. Do they name themselves for their natural headdress?"

"That would hardly explain their tremendous excitement when they discovered we didn't know this Thon of theirs," I objected, "and why they regarded us as so unhappy because we didn't have frilly things on our heads."

"Ah! Quite so!" mused the Professor, "but they also said 'Epthona' and translated it as 'untrue.' I believe I've got it!" and he jumped up and began to pace the cabin excitedly. "Thon means truth. They worship some god or fetish which stands for truth and naturally they think we're a benighted race because we don't follow their religion."

"But that doesn't explain their sudden command of English," I objected.

"Quite so!" said the professor.

There was a knock at my door and Miss FitzGerald peeped in.

"Am I intruding on a conference?"

"Not at all," I said. "Please come in and see if your intuition can solve what, to our more masculine reason, is as black as ink."

"What is the problem, Captain?" she asked, seating herself on the edge of my desk. I explained that the Professor and I had been discussing the strange inhabitants of the mainland and trying to decide what they meant by "Thon."

Margaret FitzGerald looked first at me and then at the Professor, her eyes twinkling. "Honestly, I don't know any more about it than you do, but I think I can guess."

"What is it?" I exclaimed.

"Why, you said it when I came in," she said.

"Ah! Truth," said Smithton.

"No, not exactly. I was thinking of what the Captain said. He asked me to use my supposed intuition. That's it. Intuition. Thon."

"By heaven! You're right!" cried the Professor. "Some highly developed sense of intuition, combined with marvellous memories, and reasoning powers which enabled them to understand our language after hearing the words once! Marvellous! They're mental prodigies! That explains their idea that we are so miserable because we haven't got their 'Thon.'"

"I don't think it explains everything, Professor," I replied. "I feel that there is some deeper meaning underlying that simple word 'Thon.' There's something about those people that makes me say, that if this Thon of theirs could make me like them—like them not only physically but mentally and morally—I'd never rest until I solved the mystery."

"I felt the same way, Captain," said Miss FitzGerald. "When I was reading aloud to them I had the strangest sensation as though some loving, comforting power were folding me in its arms and it seemed to emanate from the Deelathon. Oh! I know it sounds foolish, but I felt just as if my soul were in a warm bath!"

"Perhaps my chosen profession renders me less susceptible to subconscious impression than you and Captain Clinton," said the astronomer, "nevertheless, I must admit that I feel complete confidence in these Deelathon and their kindly intentions. We can only wait for the return of our friend Toron at sunset."

"Right!" I said, rising, "and now, Miss FitzGerald and Professor, what do you say to lunch?"

III
THE KLENDEELA

Throughout the long afternoon until the sun approached and touched the narrow sea-horizon visible in the gap to the west, eager eyes were incessantly turned to the crest of the landward cliffs, watching for the return of the friendly Deelathon.

Suddenly there was a cry: "They're coming!" and a moment later we saw a crystal globe travelling through the air just above the level of the plateau. It was much smaller than the one we had seen in the ravine but it glittered with the same flux of prismatic hues and was equipped with the same equatorial band and polar bosses of reddish metal, which Toron afterwards told us was an alloy of gold, copper and selenium.

For a few seconds the Zeeth (for this was the name by which the Deelathon called their strange aerial vessels) hovered motionless above the cliff-edge, and then with a suddenness which made me gasp it shot out towards the ship with tremendous velocity, as though hurled from some invisible cannon. In less than ten seconds the Zeeth was hovering above the deck, having come to a dead stop in its headlong flight, as suddenly as it had started. Then it descended with infinite care until its suspended cups rested on the after promenade deck where a space was cleared by the passengers for its reception.

One of the crystal windows swung inward and next moment Toron stepped upon the deck, followed by the girl Torona, whom he had called his companion.

They raised their hands in the Deelathon greeting and smiling at the amazed throng of men and women with that peculiarly radiant smile which is so characteristic of all these people, they cried : "Zeloma! Welcome!"

Now, as you doubtless know, Benedict (said Captain Clinton) in the ages before the Visitation, the people of the world and especially of the so-called civilized areas, were governed in their actions not so much by reason or intelligence as by custom. It was regarded as a sign of the most depraved savagery to wear clothing for the purpose for which it was designed, namely, warmth, and people wore the most extraordinary garments, oftentimes hideously ugly, simply because they were, as we used to say, "the fashion." Early in the twentieth century there was evident a healthy tendency to get away from this bondage of fashion and return to the sensible use of clothing for warmth alone, but it proved to be simply another phase in the cycle of unreasoning custom and by the year 1940 the pendulum had swung to the other extreme, with the result that people were again loading themselves with unnecessary garments as cumbersome and ugly as those of the Victorian Era. The natural outcome of this practice was an extraordinary attitude of false shame with regard to the human body, which is quite incomprehensible to us today. Nor was this modesty without its basis in reason, for the imperfections of the average human body illustrated the meaning of the old Greek saying that it was forbidden to walk the streets of Athens naked, not because it was indecent but because it was ugly!

You will easily understand, therefore, that the eight hundred or more passengers who had not pre- viously seen the Deelathon, regarded our story of a god-like people who wore no clothes, with mingled feelings of curiosity and disgust. The ladies, especially, listened with raised eyebrows to Miss FitzGerald's enthusiastic descriptions of the physical perfections of the Deelathon.

Having due regard to this state of mind I had some doubt as to the sort of welcome which would be accorded to the visitors.

My misgivings were soon dissipated. No sooner had the Deelathon uttered their words of greeting, than old Lady Gibson, mother of Sir Charles and the very epitome of British respectability, stepped forward and slipping her arm around Torona's waist, kissed her on both cheeks.

"My dear, you are very welcome to the *Shah of Iran* and you too, Sir," and the little old lady looked up nodding and smiling into the radiant face of the tall Deelathon.

Lady Gibson's impulsive action broke the ice and in a moment Toron and Torona were surrounded with passengers vying with each other to do honour to the beautiful visitors. Presently Torona raised her head for silence.

"My dear companion, Toron," she said, "has been in consultation with the Klendeela and he has a message for you. But first I want to thank you all for your greeting. You Deela Rana, or as you would say, People of the Sea, are very strange to us with your unhappy faces and your burden of clothes—though perhaps that is why you are unhappy. I am sure it would make me so! But I know we of the Deelathon must also seem strange to you, and so we thank you for your friendliness. The Thon tells us that great goodness is hidden behind your tired, unhappy faces, and therefore I love you all and especially this fair maiden, Margaret, whose book made it possible for us to learn your language." And she threw her arm around Miss FitzGerald and kissed her.

They stood there side by side, the American girl and the Deelathon maiden. The passengers must have been hard put to decide which was the fairer. For myself I had not a moment of doubt. Beautiful as was Torona, with a beauty almost unearthly, Margaret was more lovely in my eyes. As you will have guessed, Benedict, Margaret FitzGerald was she who afterwards became your great-grandmother.

* * * * *

And then Toron spoke.

"Friends," he said, "Torona, my companion, has told you that you seem strange to us, and this is true, for it is almost beyond belief that any beings exist who know not the Thon. I have been in consultation with the Klendeela, which is our council, and this is the message they have sent to you. The Klendeela understands that you are imprisoned by the, barrier reef which sank and rose during the earthquake. Since your Zeeth-which-floats-on-the-sea, will not float in the air, like our Zeeths, we want to tell you that with the greatest of our Zeeths we can raise your vessel into the air and transport it across the reef at any time you desire. The Klendeela thinks, however, that you should not leave us until we have entertained you and, if the Thon permits, made known to you the meaning of that Thon which seems so mysterious to you. To this end they have commanded me to ask some few of you to return with me, Smithton, and you Clinton and the maiden with the book, and her brother and some few others whom you may select."

"You bring us good news, Toron," I replied, "and we accept the invitation of your council. At least, the others will doubtless do so, but as for me, I am in command here, and it is not our custom for the captain to leave his ship for any length of time."

Toron nodded his understanding and then engaged in a brief discussion with Torona. At last he addressed me again.

"We understand and honour your custom, Clinton and are prepared to overcome the difficulty. In the morning I will return with our greatest Zeeth and will transport your ship above the cliffs to a lake which is in the midst of our houses. There you can remain as long as seems fit to you, visiting us at your pleasure and returning to your ship each night. When you desire to leave us, we will lift your ship into the sea and you can return whence you came."

The idea of lifting thirty thousand tons of steel plates and girders bodily into the air might well have caused more than a qualm of doubt in our minds, but such was the complete confidence with which the Deelathon inspired us that I assented to this amazing proposal without hesitation. The tremendous speed of which the Zeeth was capable and the perfect control with which it was handled removed all doubt that we might have felt of the ability of the Deelathon to carry out this titanic engineering feat.

Having arranged the time at which they would return in the morning, Toron and Torona saluted us and entered their Zeeth, which rose from the deck, and travelling in a tremendous parabola, disappeared behind the black columns of basalt.

There was little sleep that night for any one. The insomnia was produced not at all by alarm at the prospects of the morrow, but by the fact that everyone was speculating on the meaning of these strange events. All felt that we stood on the brink of some great adventure which was to have a permanent effect upon our lives. That the Deelathon meant us anything but good never entered our minds. As Lady Gibson remarked to Margaret:

"My dear, when that glorious creature Toron looked at me I felt as though I must tell the truth. If I had told even the tiniest white lie, I should have jumped in the sea and drowned myself to hide my shame!"

Next morning every passenger and member of the crew was on deck early. At the appointed time the Zeeth soared into view, and accustomed as we were becoming to marvels, the size of this tremendous sphere staggered us. It measured fully three thousand feet around the equator and from either pole hung huge cables of the same reddish metal that was used universally among the Deelathon for engineering purposes.

When the Zeeth was hovering above the *Shah* I ordered the anchors to be hauled in and we floated free. The Zeeth sank slowly until the inverted cups which terminated the cables hung suspended level with the mastheads.

I had anticipated that it would be necessary to spend several days rigging steel cables under the *Shah* in order to provide a cradle to support the immense weight of the vessel. I had mentioned this to Toron the previous day, but he had smiled and assured me that no preparations were necessary.

The great globe hung poised in the air above the ship and then a most amazing thing happened. A slight tremor passed through the vessel and it began to rise slowly towards those inverted cups. Inch by inch rose the great liner, the water cascading from her bottom plates, until the keel was clear of the surface and we hung in mid-air, supported by some invisible force. The cups from which this force apparently emanated were still separated from the deck by fully a hundred feet and yet the *Shah* hung securely on a level keel, so that in the saloon, where dinner had been laid, not even a drop of water was spilled from the filled glasses. Slowly we rose until we hung above the level of the cliffs and then the Zeeth with its enormous burden began to move towards the land.

* * * * *

As soon as we became accustomed to our strange situation, the rails were crowded with a throng eager to catch a first glimpse of the new land. We beheld a rolling park-like country, dotted here and there with groups of palms and other trees. In the far distance we could faintly discern another wall of black cliffs and beyond them rose range on range of snow-capped peaks which we rightly supposed were the mighty Andes. A wide river, like a silver ribbon, wound its way from the distant snow fields. In the centre of the level area, which might have been fifty miles in diameter, the river broadened "into a gleaming lake and then continued on its placid way, amplified by numerous tributaries, until it plunged over the cliffs into the Pit of the Shining Pool.

As we drew nearer, we caught sight of innumerable buildings, not crowded together into towns, but scattered among the groves of trees. These buildings, which were of every imaginable size, were all of the same general design, consisting of an ellipsoidal roof of the same glassy crystal of which the Zeeth was constructed, supported on a circular colonnade of marble pillars. Hundreds of Zeeths of all sizes darted here and there through the air and as their occupants caught sight of us, flocked towards us and followed our course until we seemed to move in a cloud of fairy bubbles.

Many of the houses were built on the top of the basaltic columns bordering the river and we could see groups of the Deelathon standing or sitting on the verge of the cliff, watching our progress with absorbed interest.

As we drew nearer to the lake we observed, standing on a slight elevation, a very large building, which we rightly took to be the meeting place of the Klendeela or council. This was built on the same circular plan as the dwellings, but was of vastly greater size.

At last the *Shah of Iran* hung above the centre of the lake and the Zeeth gradually sank until the *Shah* was resting once more in her native element.

That afternoon a small Zeeth shot out from the shore and landed on the deck. It contained our friends Toron and Torona, bringing with them a splendid Deelathon whom Toron introduced to us as Rethmar, the head of the Klendeela.

"The Klendeela is assembled and would be honoured by your presence," said Toron. "You, Clinton, and the wise man, Smithton, and the fair maiden, Margaret, and her brother, Fred."

"We answer the summons of the Klendeela gladly, Toron," I said, "because we fully trust you and are anxious to learn more of your country."

"That wish shall be granted," replied Toron. "In the meantime, while you are in consultation with the Klendeela, many of our people will come to your ship in pleasure Zeeths and take as many of your friends as care to go, to their homes; for all the Deelathon are delighted to offer hospitality to our visitors from the sea."

Torona explained that we were to cross the lake in their Zeeth and land on the farther shore, from which point we would walk to the assembly hall, in order that we might have an opportunity to see some of the country on our way.

Rethmar reentered the Zeeth, beckoning me with a smile to follow him. I approached the circular opening, not without trepidation, but I was hardly prepared for what took place. I set my foot on the edge of the door, while Rethmar extended a hand to help me. Next instant, I seemed to be falling. All sense of material existence vanished and in a whirl of confusion I seemed to be floating in space. Then I felt the reassuring clasp of Rethmar's hand and gradually I regained my composure, only to find to my astonishment that instead of resting on the bottom of the Zeeth, I was actually poised in space at the centre of the globe, without visible means of support.

Then Rethmar drew me to the side and, slipping a broad, flexible belt around my waist, fastened it with a catch of some sort.

I now perceived that there was one of these belts midway between each of the crystal windows attached to the metal band which encircled the equator.

And now another surprise awaited me. Although the Zeeth was made of some crystal, when viewed from without, the globe was quite opaque, so that it was impossible to see the occupants. When viewed from the interior, however, the glassy material was so perfectly transparent that it simply seemed non-existent and one was conscious only of the equatorial band and polar bosses, apparently suspended in air, without support.

Rethmar, having observed the state of mental aberration which possessed me upon my first entry, floated across the Zeeth to the open window and spoke to Toron in his own tongue, and I heard Toron warning the others not to be alarmed.

Professor Smithton was the next and I could hardly forbear laughing as the somewhat corpulent form of the astronomer floated lightly upwards under the guidance of Rethmar, who coolly passed one of the belts around the Professor, leaving him suspended horizontally above my head.

"Why! Good Heavens, Captain!" sputtered the Professor. "Wonders upon wonders! Do you realize what our extraordinary sensations indicate?"

"No, I can't say that I do, except that I feel as though I were having a nightmare and can't wake up!"

* * * * *

"Well, well, well!" ejaculated the Professor. "These people are a thousand years ahead of us in science, as well as in mental development. They have overcome gravitation. This transparent substance of which the globe is composed is opaque to gravitation, with the result that it not only has no weight, but nothing within it—ourselves for example—has any weight either. Marvellous!"

Now the others entered the Zeeth, each of my shipmates expressing wonder at the unexpected sensation of floating in mid-air. When we were all secured in place by the equatorial straps. Toron and Torona stepped into the Zeeth. The girl sailed lightly across the globe and slipped one of the belts around her, but Toron remained floating in the air and closed the crystal window behind him.

I began to look around for some machinery by which the Zeeth could be moved, but could see nothing except a small handle in the centre of each window. Toron began to turn these handles, propelling himself from one to another by slight touches against the walls of the globe, and I perceived that the handles were connected to the long needles which projected from the centre of the windows.

There was a slight shock and I looked downward. The deck of the *Shah of Iran* was falling away with tremendous speed and the country opened out until we could see for many miles in every direction. Toron manipulated some more of the handles and the Zeeth began to move rapidly towards the shore.

Now, of course, we were all accustomed to riding on the old-fashioned airplanes, which had been brought to great perfection during the second quarter of the twentieth century, but the sensation was no more comparable to that of riding in a Zeeth than falling downstairs is to be compared to sliding down a snow slope on skis. There was no roar or vibration of machinery, simply swift, effortless motion, and the absolute transparency of the globe and our own lack of weight added to the illusion that we were flying through space at our own volition.

As we flew towards the great building which we had seen that morning, Toron said:

"I heard your remark, Smithton, and you are quite right in your explanation of the cause for the Zeeth's lack of weight. The globe is composed of elathongar, an artificial crystal, which, as you say, is opaque to gravitation."

"Ah! Quite so!" said the Professor, "but I still fail to understand what force propels the Zeeth, since opacity to gravitation would simply cause it to rise upward from the earth's surface."

"The propelling force is contained or rather produced by the rods attached to these handles. They are acted upon by the Thon," replied Toron. "And by turning them on their axes the force is up, down, or in either direction, as we wish."

"The Thon again!" exclaimed the Professor. "What is this Thon, Toron?"

The Deelathon smiled gravely. "That I am not permitted to tell you—yet!" he replied.

Now we sank gently to a landing on a grassy plain near the shore of the lake. We alighted, and headed by Rethmar, started up a winding path. At first we were hampered by the sudden transition in weight from nothing to one hundred and sixty pounds or thereabouts, but the novelty soon wore off and we looked about us.

Everywhere we saw the simple and yet beautiful dwellings of the Deelathon and everywhere we saw the same ellipsoidal roof of elathongar supported by pillars of stone. Later, during our stay in this strange land, we received and accepted many invitations to visit the homes of the Deelathon and we discovered that both floors and roof were universally made of this gravity-shielding crystal, thus reducing the effort required to accomplish any work to a minimum.

The force of gravity could be adjusted to any degree desired by means of a sliding panel arrangement, but during our social calls these were generally kept closed so that we simply reclined in the air and talked! Some of the passengers spent the night in the Deelathon houses and after the perfect relaxation of literally "sleeping upon air," found difficulty in sleeping at all on an ordinary bed.

* * * * *

Presently we entered a great avenue of stately palms at the end of which gleamed the white pillars of the assembly hall. Guided by Rethmar we walked up a noble stairway, flanked by mighty columns and stood in the centre of a splendid amphitheatre surrounded by rows and rows of marble seats or couches. As we entered we were again conscious of loss of weight, so that we seemed to float rather than walk across the crystal pavement.

Hundreds of Deelathon, both men and women, reclined on the seats, but as we entered they all rose to their feet. There was a rustling sound and a ripple of coloured light as their thonmeleks flashed erect upon their heads. Their hands rose in the Deelathon salute and there was a unanimous shout of:

"*Zeloma, Deelarana*!"

Rethmar led us to seats at one side of the huge auditorium and then floated to the centre and addressed the assemblage in his own language. When he resumed his seat, Toron rose and began to speak in English.

"Friends from across the sea," he said, "the Klendeela has asked me to speak for them because I alone can talk your language freely, thanks to the maiden Margaret. We have brought you here out of no idle curiosity, or merely to offer you our hearty welcome, but because we believe it lies in our power to do you great good. Not alone to you and those with you, but also to the countless millions like you, who, as you tell us, inhabit the world, to us unknown.

"But before offering you this priceless gift, known to us as the Thon, the Klendeela requests you to tell us more of that world in which you live. Tell us of its history, its present conditions, its science and its religion. Thus will the Klendeela be able to judge if we are right in revealing to you the secret of the Thon.

"Fear not to speak in your own tongue, for all will understand you. Fear only to say that which is epthona or false, for we shall know the thona from the epthona."

Professor Smithton, who had, at my urgent request, agreed to act as spokesman for our party, rose to his feet and, steadying himself for a moment against his tendency to rise above the floor, said:

"Men of the Deelathon, the feeling of confidence with which you inspired us at our first meeting is made stronger by your welcome and your offer. We do not know what this gift of the Thon may portend, but we are agreed that if your self-evident health and happiness are due in any way to this Thon, we greatly desire to share the secret with you."

"We will willingly describe to you the world in which we live, but to do this completely, it would be necessary to combine the knowledge of many minds. Among the passengers and crew of our ship are persons from every walk of life. I suggest that you allow us to select some of these persons to deal with the various phases of the subject."

"Your excellent suggestion shall be carried out," replied Toron after a moment's consultation with Rethmar. "Return now to your ship and make all necessary arrangements with your friends. Each morning the Klendeela will assemble to hear your speakers. Each afternoon we of the Deelathon will welcome you to our homes or show you the beauties of our country on foot or in our Zeeths."

"Before we retire," said the Professor, "is it permitted to ask one question?"

"Any question will be answered freely, Smithton," replied Toron, "so long as it does not relate to the Thon."

"I wish to know," said the Professor, "why, with your Zeeths, incomparably superior to our finest means of transportation, you have not long ago visited this outer world in which we live."

"There are reasons which I cannot explain to you now," said Toron, "indeed, we do not fully understand them ourselves. This, however, I can tell you: The power of the crystal we call elathongar is in some way associated with the black rock that underlies our country. When we attempt to pass far beyond this rock, our Zeeths sink to the ground.* Neither is it possible for us to leave our country on foot, for we are hemmed in on one side by the sea and on the other by several rows of unclimbable cliffs."

Toron escorted us back to the ship and left us. I called the passengers together and having told them of our meeting with the Klendeela, asked for volunteers to give the strangest course of lectures that has ever been delivered.

* * * * *

Next morning and day by day for a week we crossed the lake to the assembly hall where the Klendeela gathered to listen in a silence unbroken save by the voice of the lecturer and the rustling of those strange rainbow-tinted frills which seemed to respond to every emotion of the hearers.

Dr. Malone of Yale spoke on ancient history and Dr. Calthorp of Harvard on modern history and social conditions. Professor Smithton lectured on pure science and Fred FitzGerald on applied science and mechanics. Dr. Ronald, the ship's surgeon, gave an outline of medicine and I spoke briefly on navigation. General Thornton of the U. S. Army described the development of war from the days of the sword and crossbow to its present state of perfection. Dr. Maxwell of Leland Stanford spoke on psychology and Bishop Brander of Washington lectured on comparative religion.

Thus the days passed while those god-like creatures listened with absorbed attention to all. We had got over the wonder of their being able to understand us. We had become accustomed to the strange sensations incident to the use of the gravitation shields. But our amazement at the beauty and health and radiant happiness of these marvellous beings remained unabated. Could Carlyle have seen the Klendeela before writing his Sartor Resartus, he would have hesitated before ridiculing the picture of a Parliament without clothes!

Once only was there any interruption to the steady flow of words. It was during the latter part of Professor Smithton's lecture on physics. He was explaining some of the more recent discoveries of the scientists when there was a rustle of

* During the Year of the Visitation this difficulty was overcome and Zeeths now travel over every part of the world.

thonmeleks, a flash of colour and the members of the Klendeela leaped to their feet amid a babble of voices. In the confusion we could hear the word "Thon" again and again. The excitement subsided as quickly as it had arisen and after a few words of apology from Rethmar, the Professor proceeded with his discourse.

Margaret FitzGerald and I spent all the afternoon with Toron and Torona, sometimes reclining in their Zeeth and watching the glorious landscape unfolding below us, sometimes wandering through groves of cinnamon and nutmeg trees, sometimes resting in the crystal dwelling of our Deelathon friends.

Toron talked freely on all subjects and willingly told us everything we asked relating to the social and economic life of the people. One subject alone he avoided, and that the thing we most desired to know—the nature and meaning of the Thon.

We were amazed at the perfection of the Deelathon government and their commercial arrangements, but we were astounded at the extreme simplicity of the social machinery by which all their activities were controlled. Early in our friendship I asked Toron if we were correct in supposing that Torona was his wife. Toron looked puzzled for an instant and then replied:

"Yes and no, Clinton. When I first met you I selected the word 'companion' as better suited to explain our relationship than 'wife.' I feel a meaning in your word which is entirely foreign to our word."

"But Torona is not related to you, Toron?" I asked.

"No, except as my companion."

"You have chosen each other as mates?" I asked.

"Yes," he replied, placing his hand gently on Torona's.

"Then surely," I went on, "you have been united by some ceremony such as that which we call marriage."

"No. That is the difference!" exclaimed Toron. "We have no ceremonies of any kind. What you call a ceremony is a form of words designed to make the listeners believe a falsehood or else to impress upon them something they are not sure of. Therefore, of course, we need no ceremonies."

I did not quite see where the "of course" came in, but I let that go and followed another line of thought.

"Then there is nothing to prevent you from separating from your companions, as you call them, at any time?"

"Nothing at all!" replied Toron, smiling radiantly at Torona.

"Then divorce must be exceedingly common among you, Toron," I said.

Toron and Torona both burst out laughing. "As common as it is for the rose to divorce itself voluntarily from the tree," said Torona, "or the silver pathway on the lake to divorce itself from the moon."

Toron laughed again at the blank expression on our faces and said:

"Don't you see, Clinton, and you, Margaret, that all your ceremonies and divorces are necessary because you are not sure of yourselves. We Deelathon never make a mistake in our choice of a companion. In fact, as you will learn later, it is impossible for us to make a mistake. Therefore, when we choose a companion, it is forever."

Another time, as we were hovering over the wooded country in Torona's little Zeeth, Margaret commented on the curious fact that we had never seen any sign of burial grounds nor indeed had we so much as heard the word "death" mentioned.

Again Toron looked puzzled and then, as was his custom, replied by asking a seemingly irrelevant question.

"How old are you, Clinton?"

"Thirty-six," I answered.

"Years?" was Toron's curious question.

"Of course," I replied.

"I understand Margaret's question now," said Toron, his face bearing an expression as near sadness as it ever could. "Friends, does it surprise you that I, Toron, have seen over eight hundred summers and Torona over six hundred and fifty!"

"Surely, you jest, Toron!" I exclaimed. "No man can ever live to such an age!"

"And why not?" asked Toron.

"Because—Oh! because it's contrary to nature. Sickness and old age sap the wells of life and death comes, generally before a hundred years have passed."

"And we wondered at their unhappy faces, Toron!" exclaimed Torona. "Why, Margaret, there are many among the Deelathon who have lived not eight hundred but eight thousand years. We know what you mean by sickness, but no such thing exists among us. Neither have we anything which corresponds to your idea of old age. True, we leave our bodies, not because they are worn out, but because our appointed time has come. Oh friend! how can you do more than just taste the cup of life in so brief a space of time as one century?"

* * * * *

And then came the afternoon when we were summoned to meet the Klendeela for the last time. Our speakers had concluded their addresses and Professor

Smithton summed up their lectures in an eloquent speech in which he extolled the glories of the civilization of which we were the representatives.

For a brief interval there was silence and then Rethmar rose.

"Friends, accept the thanks of the Klendeela for your kindness. We have decided that the gift of the Thon shall be extended to you and through you to all the world. Tomorrow, if it shall please you, we will take you and all your company, both men and women, to the Thontara and there, in the presence of that undying wonder, we will reveal to you the secret of the Thon, which makes us what we are."

IV
THE GLORY OF THE THONTARA

I need not tell you in detail, Benedict, with what excitement we awaited the coming of the day upon which we were at last to learn the meaning of the mysterious Thon. Everyone on the *Shah of Iran* had come to love and admire these strange people with their gentle, courteous ways, their radiant, happy faces, their wonderful health and almost divine beauty.

The sun rose in a clear sky for the first time for a week, as though to celebrate the beginning of a new era for mankind. Hundreds of Zeeths soared up from among the trees on the lake-shore and hovered over the steamer. One by one they dropped to the deck and rose again with their quota of passengers.

At last the ship was deserted and the fleet of crystal spheres swooped away seaward, to land upon a grassy plain near the brink of the great waterfall. Rethmar led the way to the edge of the cliffs, at the point where the river gathered itself for the final plunge, and then we perceived a flight of steps cut in the solid rock.

We started down, each man or woman escorted by a friendly Deelathon; a company of over two thousand. Rethmar and the professor went first, then Margaret and Torona, followed by myself accompanied by Toron. As my turn came and I approached the top of the steps, I noticed that they did not terminate at the edge of the river, but entered instead, a hole in the rocks directly under the fall. I should have hesitated, but I caught sight of Margaret disappearing into the gloom and plucked up my courage to proceed.

A moment later I stood on a small platform. On my left was the cliff. On my right, and so close that I could have touched it, was a descending wall of water, thundering into the abyss.

The other four had disappeared and I looked questioningly at Toron. For answer, he took my hand and led me forward to the edge of the platform and then I realized with a thrill of horror that we stood on the top of one of the basalt columns and that the flight of steps continued spirally down it, being carved out of the solid rock. There was no railing of any kind and the idea of walking down that fearsome stairway with nothing but space and darkness below me and with millions of tons of water rushing by, turned me sick.

I glanced again at Toron and met his smile of encouragement. My fears departed and with his hand in mine, we started down. Round and round we circled, now passing close to the wall of water, whose roar grew ever louder as we descended; now passing through little tunnels which had been cut between the pillar and the cliff. Looking up, I could see a seemingly endless line of figures circling the mighty column and looking for all the world like the processionary caterpillars on the trunk of a pine tree, and once when I glanced hurriedly downward, I caught a glimpse of Margaret's dark hair and the gleam of Torona's pink body in the gloom.

At last, with a sigh of relief, I stepped from the bottom of the column to the floor of a great cave, like the famous Cave of the Winds under Niagara Falls. Margaret and the Professor, with the two Deelathon men, were awaiting us and we stood watching that silent line of figures creeping slowly downward, until we were once more united in the great cavity under the waterfall.

I thought our ordeal was over and that this must be the Thontara of which Rethmar had spoken. I was wondering how it would be possible for him to reveal any secret to us in a place where the bellow of the waters would drown any attempt at speech. But as the thought entered my mind I saw Rethmar drawing the Professor forward and they began to descend another flight of steps, cut like the other in the solid rock.

Following Margaret and Torona, I found that this stairway ran sharply down into a tunnel which seemed to lead us directly under the fall. The passage was so low that I could touch the roof with my hand and feel the living rock trembling with the tremendous impact of the water.

Still we descended and I saw a faint flicker of light below me, growing ever brighter and brighter. A hundred more steps brought us to the bottom, and passing through an arched opening, we stood at last in the Thontara.

At the glory of the sight that met my eyes, I uttered an involuntary cry of amazement and delight. We stood on the edge of a great circular depression, which I judged to be about a thousand feet in diameter. Surrounding this depression was the broad shelf of black basalt on which we were standing, and filling the entire area within this shelf, was a mass of coloured light which surged and rippled like a sea of rainbows. I have spoken of the varied hues which were visible on the surface of the crystal Zeeths. This was the same but intensified a thousand-fold.

As my eyes became accustomed to the light I realized that we were standing on the border of a vast circular floor of crystal, so exquisitely transparent that it was like gazing into a bottomless pit of lucent flame. It was long before I could turn my eyes from that sea of fire and look upward, but when at last I did so, I was greeted by a new wonder.

* * * * *

I was looking at the under side of the great dome of water which occupied the centre of the pool below the waterfall! This living roof of liquid, seeming as frail as a bubble and yet weighing under normal conditions no one knows how many thousand tons, was bereft of its weight by the screening effect of the crystal and hung in midair, motionless and yet in constant motion under the tremendous force of the cataract, its under surface reflecting, as though in a mirror, the splendour of the sea of coloured light below.

While I had been absorbing the beauty of this natural kaleidoscope, the rocky shelf had been filling with our great company until we were all assembled in the Thontara. Rethmar and the Professor had gone to the farther side and I saw the Deelathon raise his hand in salute and prepare to speak.

The roar of the waterfall was almost inaudible and was replaced by a soft hissing produced by the rapid movement of the liquid roof. As Rethmar began to speak, his voice penetrated to every corner of the immense space, reflected from the dome by some strange acoustic effect like that sometimes heard in old cathedrals.

"Friends from beyond the sea," he said, "we have brought you to this place which we call the Thontara, because it seemed the most fitting spot in which to reveal to you the secret of the Thon. You cannot have failed to understand that this Thon, which is so mysterious to you, is regarded by us as the greatest gift in the possession of man. Our language alone would reveal this to you. We call ourselves the Deelathon, 'People of the Thon.' This living frill upon our heads is the Thonmelek, 'Mirror of the Thon.' And this glory that you behold is the Thontara, 'Place of the Thon.' Now, therefore, before revealing to you the meaning of this word, we ask you to tell us what you have guessed the Thon to be."

"Truly, we have wondered, Rethmar," said the Professor. "Some thought it was the god you worship. Miss FitzGerald imagined that it stood for Intuition and I guessed it might be Truth."

"In a measure you are all right," said Rethmar, "and yet you have but touched on the fringe of the matter. Listen and I will reveal to you all, the secret of this mystery. The Thon is the Power of Life. It is the essence which separates the living from the dead, the animate from the inanimate, the man from the animal and the plant from the stone. Through the Thon, we, the Deelathon, are what we are."

"We hear your words and they are good, Rethmar," said the Professor, "but we do not yet understand how the Thon can benefit us."

"Listen again," said Rethmar. "You have told us of the outer world in which you live and we are grieved at your story. You claim credit for the conquest of Nature, but it is Nature which has conquered you. You boast of the perfection of your civilization, but you are the slaves of that civilization you have created. There is hardly anything in science which you have told us that we have not known for centuries, but we use our knowledge instead of permitting our knowledge to use us. In spite of your fancied attainments, you are in bondage to three masters: sorrow, sickness and death, and yet the key to unlock your bonds is all around you. Nay, more. You, Smithton, have told us that you have known the Thon for forty years and have not recognized it for what it is!"

"I!" exclaimed the Professor. "I told you that?"

"You told us," repeated Rethmar, "at the third meeting of the Klendeela, that forty years ago one of your wise men discovered a power that penetrated the densest metals, a power of which he could not discover the origin, a power which he called the Cosmic Ray.* This, Friends, is the Thon!

"Make no mistake!" he went on. "We do not worship the Thon. One of you has told us how in ancient times men worshipped the Sun, the Source of Light. But we worship the one God, whom no man may know. As for the Thon, we know not whence it comes, we only know it fills all space and permeates all things. We know that it is a form of wave motion like light, but whereas light is

* Dr. Robert A. Milliken.

reflected by material things, the Thon is reflected by the mind and spirit of all that lives. Therefore, I have called it the Power of Life.

"You have spoken with pride of your elaborate system of laws, your multiplex religions, your social ceremonials, your great battles in which millions grapple to the death. Friends, are you so blind that you cannot see that all these things are bred of misunderstanding, misunderstanding of yourselves, of each other, of the living universe of which you are a part? Can you conceive of fighting those you call your enemies if each side could see the other's viewpoint as clearly as his own?

"I *have* said that the Thon is a form of vibration which responds to the life-form or spirit of living things. By virtue of the Thon, one mind beholds another, just as the material eye beholds other material bodies by virtue of reflected light. Thus it is that misunderstanding is impossible among us. Thus it is that we are able to understand you when you speak your own language. Thus it is that we need no such laws and ceremonies and social machinery as that of which you boast. And thus it is that we enjoy perfect health and happiness because we see, not only the outer shell as you do, but also the living mind that resides within the shell, as you would say."

"But tell us, Rethmar," said the Professor, "if you thus see the mind within the body, why is speech necessary, since your thoughts must be visible to one another?"

"First let me say, Smithton, that the mind is not within the body, but the body within the mind. As to your question, it is a reasonable one and we ourselves do not fully understand why it is not as you say. It seems, however, that the spoken word is necessary as the vehicle of thought, with us as with you. But note the difference; when you speak, your thought must go through many translations before reaching the mind of the hearer, losing some of its sense with each translation. First you must mentally select the words best fitted to express your idea. Then your organs of speech must convert those words into vibrations of sound, which in turn must act upon the ears of your hearer and be turned into the nerve-force which reacts upon the brain. Here the word-sounds must be converted into word-pictures.

"Is it any wonder that the thought of the speaker reaches the brain of the listener in a mangled condition? And it matters not whether the words be true or false, the hearer cannot distinguish between them. But with us, the spoken word is simply the means by which the speaker reveals his thought to the hearer.

No matter how imperfectly the words may have been selected, the hearer sees by the reflected rays of the Thon, the actual thought of the speaker. I use the word 'sees,' but of course we do not see the Thon with the eye, but with an intangible organ of the mind."

"It comes to us as a great surprise," said the Professor, "that the Thon of which we have heard so much, should be the medium of a sixth sense and should be none other than the Cosmic Ray, with which we are familiar. We can easily realize that a people who live under such conditions must be the happiest people in the world. But when you offer us the gift of the Thon, Rethmar, you seem to forget that we lack this special faculty which enables you to visualize the mental images produced by the Thon. You may tell a blind man of the light, but you cannot make him see."

"Oh, Smithton! Smithton! do you still fail to understand?" said Rethmar, and his voice rang out like a bugle call to every one of the great circle of listeners. "This special faculty, as you call it, is not the exclusive possession of the Deelathon. It is common to all mankind. It is a part of every living thing. It is inherent in Life itself. Oh! Friends from beyond the sea, you are not by nature blind to the Thon. For countless generations you and all your race have lived and died like men who bandage their eyes that they may not see the light!

"For the last time, *listen*!"

And then, in words so simple that the humblest trimmer among the crew could understand, Rethmar revealed to us the secret which gave us full possession of that marvellous sixth sense: the consciousness of the Thon.

You, Benedict, and all your generation, were born with this sense fully developed and you can hardly realize what stupendous emotions convulsed us when, to use Rethmar's simile, the bandages were torn from the eyes of our minds and we saw ourselves and our friends and all living things, face to face in the light of the Thon. To you, your consciousness of the Thon is as natural and commonplace as your consciousness of light or sound, but to us it came as an overpowering revelation.

Speaking for myself, for a space my mind was dazzled as the eyes of a blind man are dazzled when he first receives his sight. When this temporary confusion passed, my first thought was of Margaret FitzGerald.

We had been drawn together in friendship during our strange adventures. I had thought her beautiful and womanly, but no word of love had passed my lips. Now, as her eyes met mine, I saw revealed a beauty of spirit and intellect such as I scarcely dreamed could exist. Her face was radiant with happiness but her soul was calm with the peace of eternity.

No word was spoken. No word was needed. The revealing rays of the Thon told us beyond the possibility of misunderstanding that we were Companions. A moment later our arms were around each other and in the presence of that great company we gave and received our first kiss.

And in the light of the Thon we realized the literal truth of the poet's words:

"OUR SPIRITS RUSHED TOGETHER,
AT THE MEETING OF THE LIPS."

There is little more to be told. With her hand in mine I led Margaret across the great crystal floor, walking as though in a sea of prismatic flame to where Rethmar stood.

"Rethmar and Toron. Men and Women of the Deelathon," I said, "Margaret, my dear Companion and I, thank you in the name of all this company for your great gift. Now we ask a further favour, knowing that it will be granted, that we may go back into our world and teach our unhappy fellow men to see. I even venture to beg that some few of your people will accompany us to lighten our task, for none can fail to understand the meaning of the Thon when the secret is revealed by a Deelathon."

Rethmar's face was but a faint reflection of the radiance of his spirit. Raising his hand in the Deelathon salute, he cried:

"You have heard the request of our friends, Clinton and Margaret, now Companions by the Thon. Who will go with them?"

And a thousand arms flashed up in the salute and a thousand voices rang out in the words now as intelligible to us as English:

"*Zo thana!*—I will go!"

"All cannot go," said Rethmar. "Toron and Torona shall, with a company of one hundred, go with you on your ship. One thing alone we ask; that the place of the Deelathon shall remain a secret until you are sure that no harm shall come to our country. You have a saying that it is foolish to cast pearls before swine. Who knows what might happen when the Thon is revealed to all men?"

And there, in the pulsing splendour of the Thontara, we, the passengers and crew of the *Shah of Iran*, swore the oath of secrecy which we have kept to this hour.

Three days later the great liner was lifted from the lake to the blue waters of the Pacific, outside the barrier reef. A whirling cloud of Zeeths hovered and darted above us as our screws began to churn the water. The equatorial windows were crowded with Deelathon waving a last salute to the brave hundred upon our decks who, alas! were destined never to return.

Presently we passed the boundaries of the basalt rock and the Zeeths were forced to turn back, having reached what was then the limit of their range. Our course was laid to the North and a pathway of foam fled in our wake as we commenced the last voyage which was to bring happiness and health and understanding to the World—the Voyage of the Visitation.

AFTERWORD

The sun was high in the heavens when Captain Clinton concluded his narrative. We rose from our seat on the bare summit of the Shah and without a word began our descent.

And now I, Benedict Clinton, have completed the task assigned to me by my great-grandfather a year ago. The story of the Year of the Visitation is known to all the world, even if its effects were not visible on every side today.

And yet a visitor from another planet could hardly have blamed the Deelathon for their caution lest the gift of the Thon should bring about a revolution which would convulse the world and overwhelm their tiny country in its flood.

Actually, nothing in the nature of a revolution took place. The new order was so entirely natural, so utterly sane, that the change took place everywhere, almost without our being aware of it.

There was no wholesale abolition of laws and governments. We simply ceased to use them as men discard a worn-out garment. There was no deliberate disarmament. Nations ceased to go to war because there were no nations any longer. Cruisers and battleships, armoured cars and guns lay rotting and rusting where they had been abandoned. In the light of the new understanding, racial and national divisions ceased to have any meaning, although we have retained many of the geographical names for the sake of convenience.

People everywhere found a marvellous increase in health and happiness as the direct result of the knowledge of sane living, which was revealed by the Thon, but the seed of death was in them and they, the Epzykofs, are passing away from among us year by year. Not so with the generations yet unborn at the date of the Visitation. We, the Zykofs, enjoy the same perfection of bodily and mental well-being that my great-grandfather found among the Deelathon and we know of no limit to our lives, save the call of destiny.

And what of Toron and Torona and the hundred whom they led to our deliverance? They came forth voluntarily from a country of undying beauty, to bring the greatest of all natural gifts to the World, and in so doing, perished! Utterly unfitted physically to cope with the misery and disease and death which they came to eradicate, they faded, sickened and died in the accomplishment of their great task. Before the year had passed away, not one of that splendid band was left!

* * * * *

Far out in the Pacific is a barren island of magnetic iron oxide, the remnant of the great meteor and above its highest point towers a mighty spire of imperishable crystal. Its prismatic efflorescence is visible at night for many miles and upon its base is the inscription:

"TO THE VISITANTS"

THE MOON METAL

by Garrett P. Serviss

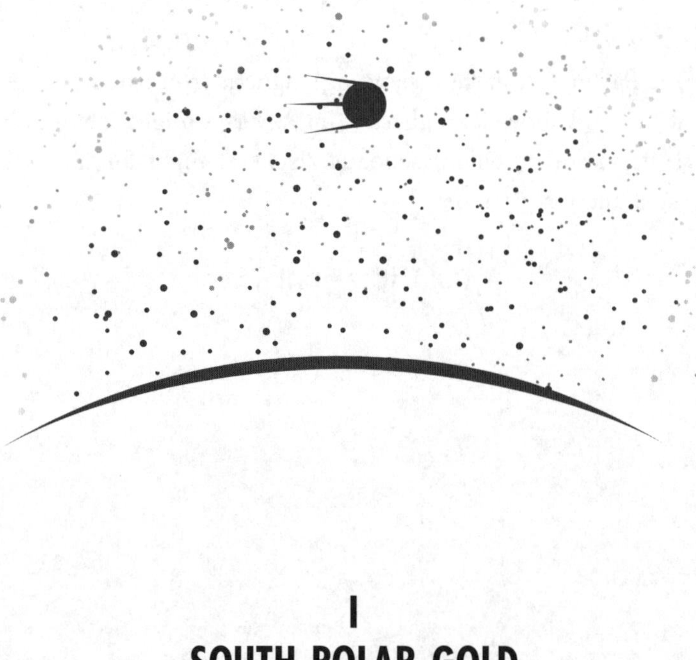

I
SOUTH POLAR GOLD

When the news came of the discovery of gold at the south pole, nobody suspected that the beginning had been reached of a new era in the world's history. The newsboys cried "Extra!" as they had done a thousand times for murders, battles, fires, and Wall Street panics, but nobody was excited. In fact, the reports at first seemed so exaggerated and improbable that hardly anybody believed a word of them. Who could have been expected to credit a despatch, forwarded by cable from New Zealand, and signed by an unknown name, which contained such a statement as this:

"A seam of gold which can be cut with a knife has been found within ten miles of the south pole."

The discovery of the pole itself had been announced three years before, and several scientific parties were known to be exploring the remarkable continent that surrounds it. But while they had sent home many highly interesting reports, there had been nothing to suggest the possibility of such an amazing discovery as that which was now announced. Accordingly, most sensible people looked upon the New Zealand despatch as a hoax.

But within a week, and from a different source, flashed another despatch which more than confirmed the first. It declared that gold existed near the south pole in practically unlimited quantity. Some geologists said this accounted for the greater depth of the Antarctic Ocean. It had always been noticed that the southern hemisphere appeared to be a little overweighted. People now began to prick up their ears, and many letters of inquiry appeared in the newspapers concerning the wonderful tidings from the south. Some asked for information about the shortest route to the new goldfields.

In a little while several additional reports came, some *via* New Zealand, others *via* South America, and all confirming in every respect what had been sent before. Then a New York newspaper sent a swift steamer to the Antarctic, and when this enterprising journal published a four-page cable describing the discoveries in detail, all doubt vanished and the rush began.

Some time I may undertake a description of the wild scenes that occurred when, at last, the inhabitants of the northern hemisphere were convinced that boundless stores of gold existed in the unclaimed and uninhabited wastes surrounding the south pole. But at present I have something more wonderful to relate.

Let me briefly depict the situation.

For many years silver had been absent from the coinage of the world. Its increasing abundance rendered it unsuitable for money, especially when contrasted with gold. The "silver craze," which had raged in the closing decade of the nineteenth century, was already a forgotten incident of financial history. The gold standard had become universal, and business all over the earth had adjusted itself to that condition. The wheels of industry ran smoothly, and there seemed to be no possibility of any disturbance or interruption. The common monetary system prevailing in every land fostered trade and facilitated the exchange of products. Travellers never had to bother their heads about the currency of money; any coin that passed in New York would pass for its face value in London, Paris, Berlin, Rome, Madrid, St. Petersburg, Constantinople, Cairo, Khartoum, Jerusalem, Peking, or Yeddo. It was indeed the "Golden Age," and the world had never been so free from financial storms.

Upon this peaceful scene the south polar gold discoveries burst like an unheralded tempest.

I happened to be in the company of a famous bank president when the confirmation of those discoveries suddenly filled the streets with yelling newsboys. "Get me one of those 'extras'!" he said, and an office-boy ran out to obey him. As he perused the sheet his face darkened.

"I'm afraid it's too true," he said, at length. "Yes, there seems to be no getting around it. Gold is going to be as plentiful as iron. If there were not such a flood of it, we might manage, but when they begin to make trousers buttons out of the same metal that is now locked and guarded in steel vaults, where will be our standard of worth? My dear fellow," he continued, impulsively laying his hand on my arm, "I would as willingly face the end of the world as this that's coming!"

"You think it so bad, then?" I asked. "But most people will not agree with you. They will regard it as very good news."

"How can it be good?" he burst out. "What have we got to take the place of gold? Can we go back to the age of barter? Can we substitute cattle-pens and wheat-bins for the strong boxes of the Treasury? Can commerce exist with no common measure of exchange?"

"It does indeed look serious," I assented.

"Serious! I tell you, it is the deluge!"

Thereat he clapped on his hat and hurried across the street to the office of another celebrated banker.

His premonitions of disaster turned out to be but too well grounded. The deposits of gold at the south pole were richer than the wildest reports had represented them. The shipments of the precious metal to America and Europe soon became enormous—so enormous that the metal was no longer precious. The price of gold dropped like a falling stone, with accelerated velocity, and within a year every money centre in the world had been swept by a panic. Gold was more common than iron. Every government was compelled to demonetize it, for when once gold had fallen into contempt it was less valuable in the eyes of the public than stamped paper. For once the world had thoroughly learned the lesson that too much of a good thing is worse than none of it.

Then somebody found a new use for gold by inventing a process by which it could be hardened and tempered, assuming a wonderful toughness and elasticity without losing its non-corrosive property, and in this form it rapidly took the place of steel.

In the mean time every effort was made to bolster up credit. Endless were the attempts to find a substitute for gold. The chemists sought it in their laboratories and the mineralogists in the mountains and deserts. Platinum might have served, but it, too, had become a drug in the market through the discovery of immense deposits. Out of the twenty odd elements which had been rarer and more valuable than gold, such as uranium, gallium, etc., not one was found to answer the purpose. In short, it was evident that since both gold and silver had become too abundant to serve any longer for a money standard, the planet held no metal suitable to take their place.

The entire monetary system of the world must be readjusted, but in the readjustment it was certain to fall to pieces. In fact, it had already fallen to pieces; the only recourse was to paper money, but whether this was based upon agriculture or mining or manufacture, it gave varying standards, not only among the different nations, but in successive years in the same country. Exports and imports practically ceased. Credit was discredited, commerce perished, and the world, at a bound, seemed to have gone back, financially and industrially, to the dark ages.

One final effort was made. A great financial congress was assembled at New York. Representatives of all the nations took part in it. The ablest financiers of Europe and America united the efforts of their genius and the results of their experience to solve the great problem. The various governments all solemnly stipulated to abide by the decision of the congress.

But, after spending months in hard but fruitless labour, that body was no nearer the end of its undertaking than when it first assembled. The entire world awaited its decision with bated breath, and yet the decision was not formed.

At this paralyzing crisis a most unexpected event suddenly opened the way.

II
THE MAGICIAN OF SCIENCE

An attendant entered the room where the perplexed financiers were in session and presented a peculiar-looking card to the president, Mr. Boon. The president took the card in his hand and instantly fell into a brown study. So complete was his absorption that Herr Finster, the celebrated Berlin banker, who had been addressing the chair for the last two hours from the opposite end of the long table, got confused, entirely lost track of his verb, and suddenly dropped into his seat, very red in the face and wearing a most injured expression.

But President Boon paid no attention except to the singular card, which he continued to turn over and over, balancing it on his fingers and holding it now at arm's-length and then near his nose, with one eye squinted as if he were trying to look through a hole in the card.

At length this odd conduct of the presiding officer drew all eyes upon the card, and then everybody shared the interest of Mr. Boon. In shape and size the card was not extraordinary, but it was composed of metal. What metal? That question had immediately arisen in Mr. Boon's mind when the card came into his hand, and now it exercised the wits of all the others. Plainly it was not tin, brass, copper, bronze, silver, aluminium—although its lightness might have suggested that metal—nor even base gold.

The president, although a skilled metallurgist, confessed his inability to say what it was. So intent had he become in examining the curious bit of metal that he forgot it was a visitor's card of introduction, and did not even look for the name which it presumably bore.

As he held the card up to get a better light upon it a stray sunbeam from the window fell across the metal and instantly it bloomed with exquisite colours! The president's chair being in the darker end of the room, the radiant card suffused the atmosphere about him with a faint rose tint, playing with surprising liveliness into alternate canary colour and violet.

The effect upon the company of clear-headed financiers was extremely remarkable. The unknown metal appeared to exercise a kind of mesmeric influence, its soft hues blending together in a chromatic harmony which captivated the sense of vision as the ears are charmed by a perfectly rendered song. Gradually all gathered in an eager group around the president's chair.

"What can it be?" was repeated from lip to lip.

"Did you ever see anything like it?" asked Mr. Boon for the twentieth time.

None of them had ever seen the like of it. A spell fell upon the assemblage. For five minutes no one spoke, while Mr. Boon continued to chase the flickering sunbeam with the wonderful card. Suddenly the silence was broken by a voice which had a touch of awe in it:

"It must be the metal!"

The speaker was an English financier, First Lord of the Treasury, Hon. James Hampton-Jones, K.C.B. Immediately everybody echoed his remark, and the strain being thus relieved, the spell dropped from them and several laughed loudly over their momentary aberration.

President Boon recollected himself, and, colouring slightly, placed the card flat on the table, in order more clearly to see the name. In plain red letters it stood forth with such surprising distinctness that Mr. Boon wondered why he had so long overlooked it.

"DR. MAX SYX."

"Tell the gentleman to come in," said the president, and thereupon the attendant threw open the door.

The owner of the mysterious card fixed every eye as he entered. He was several inches more than six feet in height. His complexion was very dark, his eyes were intensely black, bright, and deep-set, his eyebrows were bushy and up-curled at the ends, his sable hair was close-trimmed, and his ears were narrow, pointed at the top, and prominent. He wore black mustaches, covering only half the width of his lip and drawn into projecting needles on each side, while a spiked black beard adorned the middle of his chin.

He smiled as he stepped confidently forward, with a courtly bow, but it was a very disconcerting smile, because it more than half resembled a sneer. This uncommon person did not wait to be addressed.

"I have come to solve your problem," he said, facing President Boon, who had swung round on his pivoted chair.

"The metal!" exclaimed everybody in a breath, and with a unanimity and excitement which would have astonished them if they had been spectators instead of actors of the scene. The tall stranger bowed and smiled again:

"Just so," he said. "What do you think of it?"

"It is beautiful!"

Again the reply came from every mouth simultaneously, and again if the speakers could have been listeners they would have wondered not only at their earnestness, but at their words, for why should they instantly and unanimously pronounce that beautiful which they had not even seen? But every man knew he had seen it, for instinctively their minds reverted to the card and recognized in it the metal referred to. The mesmeric spell seemed once more to fall upon the assemblage, for the financiers noticed nothing remarkable in the next act of the stranger, which was to take a chair, uninvited, at the table, and the moment he sat down he became the presiding officer as naturally as if he had just been elected to that post. They all waited for him to speak, and when he opened his mouth they listened with breathless attention.

His words were of the best English, but there was some peculiarity, which they had already noticed, either in his voice or his manner of enunciation, which struck all of the listeners as denoting a foreigner. But none of them could satisfactorily place him. Neither the Americans, the Englishmen, the Germans, the Frenchmen, the Russians, the Austrians, the Italians, the Spaniards, the Turks, the Japanese, or the Chinese at the board could decide to what race or nationality the stranger belonged.

"This metal," he began, taking the card from Mr. Boon's hand, "I have discovered and named. I call it 'artemisium.' I can produce it, in the pure form, abundantly enough to replace gold, giving it the same relative value that gold possessed when it was the universal standard."

As Dr. Syx spoke he snapped the card with his thumb-nail and it fluttered with quivering hues like a humming-bird hovering over a flower. He seemed to await a reply, and President Boon asked:

"What guarantee can you give that the supply would be adequate and continuous?"

"I will conduct a committee of this congress to my mine in the Rocky Mountains, where, in anticipation of the event, I have accumulated enough refined artemisium to provide every civilized land with an amount of coin equivalent to that which it formerly held in gold. I can there satisfy you of my ability to maintain the production."

"But how do we know that this metal of yours will answer the purpose?"

"Try it," was the laconic reply.

"There is another difficulty," pursued the president. "People will not accept a new metal in place of gold unless they are convinced that it possesses equal intrinsic value. They must first become familiar with it, and it must be abundant enough and desirable enough to be used sparingly in the arts, just as gold was."

"I have provided for all that," said the stranger, with one of his disconcerting smiles. "I assure you that there will be no trouble with the people. They will be only too eager to get and to use the metal. Let me show you."

He stepped to the door and immediately returned with two black attendants bearing a large tray filled with articles shaped from the same metal as that of which the card was composed. The financiers all jumped to their feet with exclamations of surprise and admiration, and gathered around the tray, whose dazzling contents lighted up the corner of the room where it had been placed as if the moon were shining there.

There were elegantly formed vases, adorned with artistic figures, embossed and incised, and glowing with delicate colours which shimmered in tiny waves with the slightest motion of the tray. Cups, pins, finger-rings, earrings, watch-chains, combs, studs, lockets, medals, tableware, models of coins—in brief, almost every article in the fabrication of which precious metals have been employed was to be seen there in profusion, and all composed of the strange new metal which everybody on the spot declared was far more splendid than gold.

"Do you think it will answer?" asked Dr. Syx.

"We do," was the unanimous reply.

All then resumed their seats at the table, the tray with its magnificent array having been placed in the centre of the board. This display had a remarkable influence. Confidence awoke in the breasts of the financiers. The dark clouds that had oppressed them rolled off, and the prospect grew decidedly brighter.

"What terms do you demand?" at length asked Mr. Boon, cheerfully rubbing his hands.

"I must have military protection for my mine and reducing works," replied Dr. Syx. "Then I shall ask the return of one per cent, on the circulating medium, together with the privilege of disposing of a certain amount of the metal—to be limited by agreement—to the public for use in the arts. Of the proceeds of this sale I will pay ten per cent. to the government in consideration of its protection."

"But," exclaimed President Boon, "that will make you the richest man who ever lived!"

"Undoubtedly," was the reply.

"Why," added Mr. Boon, opening his eyes wider as the facts continued to dawn upon him, "you will become the financial dictator of the whole earth!"

"Undoubtedly," again responded Dr. Syx, unmoved. "That is what I purpose to become. My discovery entitles me to no less. But, remember, I place myself under government inspection and restriction. I should not be allowed to flood the market, even if I were disposed to do so. But my own interest would restrain me. It is to my advantage that artemisium, once adopted, shall remain stable in value."

A shadow of doubt suddenly crossed the president's face.

"Suppose your secret is discovered," he said. "Surely your mine will not remain the only one. If you, in so short a time, have been able to accumulate an immense quantity of the new metal, it must be extremely abundant. Others will discover it, and then where shall we be?"

While Mr. Boon uttered these words, those who were watching Dr. Syx (as the president was not) resembled persons whose startled eyes are fixed upon a wild beast preparing to spring. As Mr. Boon ceased speaking he turned towards the visitor, and instantly his lips fell apart and his face paled.

Dr. Syx had drawn himself up to his full stature, and his features were distorted with that peculiar mocking smile which had now returned with a concentrated expression of mingled self-confidence and disdain.

"Will you have relief, or not?" he asked in a dry, hard voice. "What can you do? I alone possess the secret which can restore industry and commerce. If you reject my offer, do you think a second one will come?"

President Boon found voice to reply, stammeringly:

"I did not mean to suggest a rejection of the offer. I only wished to inquire if you thought it probable that there would be no repetition of what occurred after gold was found at the south pole?"

"The earth may be full of my metal," returned Dr. Syx, almost fiercely, "but so long as I alone possess the knowledge how to extract it, is it of any more worth than common dirt? But come," he added, after a pause and softening his manner, "I have other schemes. Will you, as representatives of the leading nations, undertake the introduction of artemisium as a substitute for gold, or will you not?"

"Can we not have time for deliberation?" asked President Boon.

"Yes, one hour. Within that time I shall return to learn your decision," replied Dr. Syx, rising and preparing to depart. "I leave these things," pointing to the tray, "in your keeping, and," significantly, "I trust your decision will be a wise one."

His curious smile again curved his lips and shot the ends of his mustache upward, and the influence of that smile remained in the room when he had closed the door behind him. The financiers gazed at one another for several minutes in silence, then they turned towards the coruscating metal that filled the tray.

III
THE GRAND TETON MINE

Away on the western border of Wyoming, in the all but inaccessible heart of the Rocky Mountains, three mighty brothers, "The Big Tetons," look perpendicularly into the blue eye of Jenny's Lake, lying at the bottom of the profound depression among the mountains called Jackson's Hole. Bracing against one another for support, these remarkable peaks lift their granite spires from 12,000 to nearly 14,000 feet into the blue dome that arches the crest of the continent. Their sides, and especially those of their chief, the Grand Teton, are streaked with glaciers, which shine like silver trappings when the morning sun comes up above the wilderness of mountains stretching away eastward from the hole.

When the first white men penetrated this wonderful region, and one of them bestowed his wife's name upon Jenny's Lake, they were intimidated by the Grand Teton. It made their flesh creep, accustomed though they were to rough scrambling among mountain gorges and on the brows of immense precipices, when they glanced up the face of the peak, where the cliffs fall, one below another, in a series of breathless descents, and imagined themselves clinging for dear life to those skyey battlements.

But when, in 1872, Messrs. Stevenson and Langford finally reached the top of the Grand Teton—the only successful members of a party of nine practised climbers who had started together from the bottom—they found there a little rectangular enclosure, made by piling up rocks, six or seven feet across and three feet in height, bearing evidences of great age, and indicating that the red Indians had, for some unknown purpose, resorted to the summit of this tremendous peak long before the white men invaded their mountains. Yet neither the Indians nor the whites ever really conquered the Teton, for above the highest point that they attained rises a granite buttress, whose smooth vertical sides seemed to them to defy everything but wings.

Winding across the sage-covered floor of Jackson's Hole runs the Shoshone, or Snake River, which takes its rise from Jackson's Lake at the northern end of the basin, and then, as if shrinking from the threatening brows of the Tetons, whose fall would block its progress, makes a détour of one hundred miles around the buttressed heights of the range before it finds a clear way across Idaho, and so on to the Columbia River and the Pacific Ocean.

On a July morning, about a month after the visit of Dr. Max Syx to the assembled financiers in New York, a party of twenty horsemen, following a mountain-trail, arrived on the eastern margin of Jackson's Hole, and pausing upon a commanding eminence, with exclamations of wonder, glanced across the great depression, where lay the shining coils of the Snake River, at the towering forms of the Tetons, whose ice-striped cliffs flashed lightnings in the sunshine.

Even the impassive broncos that the party rode lifted their heads inquiringly, and snorted as if in equine astonishment at the magnificent spectacle.

One familiar with the place would have noticed something, which, to his mind, would have seemed more surprising than the pageantry of the mountains in their morning sun-bath. Curling above one of the wild gorges that cut the lower slopes of the Tetons was a thick black smoke, which, when lifted by a passing breeze, obscured the precipices half-way to the summit of the peak.

Had the Grand Teton become a volcano? Certainly no hunting or exploring party could make a smoke like that. But a word from the leader of the party of horsemen explained the mystery.

"There is my mill, and the mine is underneath it."

The speaker was Dr. Syx, and his companions were members of the financial congress. When he quitted their presence in New York, with the promise to return within an hour for their reply, he had no doubt in his own mind what that reply would be. He knew they would accept his proposition, and they did. No time was then lost in communicating with the various governments, and arrangements were quickly perfected whereby, in case the inspection of Dr. Syx's mine and its resources proved satisfactory, America and Europe should unite in adopting the new metal as the basis of their coinage. As soon as this stage in the negotiations was reached, it only remained to send a committee of financiers and metallurgists, in company with Dr. Syx, to the Rocky Mountains. They started under the doctor's guidance, completing the last stage of their journey on horseback.

"An inspection of the records at Washington," Dr. Syx continued, addressing the horsemen, "will show that I have filed a claim covering ten acres of ground around the mouth of my mine. This was done as soon as I had discovered the metal. The filing of the claim and the subsequent proceedings which perfected my ownership attracted no attention, because everybody was thinking of the south pole and its gold-fields."

The party gathered closer around Dr. Syx and listened to his words with silent attention, while their horses rubbed noses and jingled their gold-mounted trappings.

"As soon as I had legally protected myself," he continued, "I employed a force of men, transported my machinery and material across the mountains, erected my furnaces, and opened the mine. I was safe from intrusion, and even from idle curiosity, for the reason I have just mentioned. In fact, so exclusive was the attraction of the new gold-fields that I had difficulty in obtaining workmen, and finally I sent to Africa and engaged negroes, whom I placed in charge of trustworthy foremen. Accordingly, with half a dozen exceptions, you will see only black men at the mine."

"And with their aid you have mined enough metal to supply the mints of the world?" asked President Boon.

"Exactly so," was the reply. "But I no longer employ the large force which I needed at first."

"How much metal have you on hand? I am aware that you have already answered this question during our preliminary negotiations, but I ask it again for the benefit of some members of our party who were not present then."

"I shall show you today," said Dr. Syx, with his curious smile, "2500 tons of refined artemisium, stacked in rock-cut vaults under the Grand Teton."

"And you have dared to collect such inconceivable wealth in one place?"

"You forget that it is not wealth until the people have learned to value it, and the governments have put their stamp upon it."

"True, but how did you arrive at the proper moment?"

"Easily. I first ascertained that before the Antarctic discoveries the world contained altogether about 16,000 tons of gold, valued at $450,000 per ton, or $7,200,000,000 worth all told. Now my metal weighs, bulk for bulk, one-quarter as much as gold. It might be reckoned at the same intrinsic value per ton, but I have considered it preferable to take advantage of the smaller weight of the new metal, which permits us to make coins of the same size as the old ones, but only one-quarter as heavy, by giving to artemisium four times the value per ton that gold had. Thus only 4000 tons of the new metal are required to supply the place of the 16,000 tons of gold. The 2500 tons which I already have on hand are more than enough for coinage. The rest I can supply as fast as needed."

The party did not wait for further explanations. They were eager to see the wonderful mine and the store of treasure. Spurs were applied, and they galloped down the steep trail, forded the Snake River, and, skirting the shore of Jenny's Lake, soon found themselves gazing up the headlong slopes and dizzy parapets of the Grand Teton. Dr. Syx led them by a steep ascent to the mouth of the canyon, above one of whose walls stood his mill, and where the "Champ! Champ!" of a powerful engine saluted their ears.

IV
THE WEALTH OF THE WORLD

An electric light shot its penetrating rays into a gallery cut through virgin rock and running straight towards the heart of the Teton. The centre of the gallery was occupied by a narrow railway, on which a few flat cars, propelled by electric power, passed to and fro. Black-skinned and silent workmen rode on the cars, both when they came laden with broken masses of rock from the farther end of the tunnel and when they returned empty.

Suddenly, to an eye situated a little way within the gallery, appeared at the entrance the dark face of Dr. Syx, wearing its most discomposing smile, and a moment later the broader countenance of President Boon loomed in the electric glare beside the doctor's black framework of eyebrows and mustache. Behind them were grouped the other visiting financiers.

"This tunnel," said Dr. Syx, "leads to the mine head, where the ore-bearing rock is blasted."

As he spoke a hollow roar issued from the depths of the mountain, followed in a short time by a gust of foul air.

"You probably will not care to go in there," said the doctor, "and, in fact, it is very uncomfortable. But we shall follow the next car-load to the smelter, and you can witness the reduction of the ore."

Accordingly when another car came rumbling out of the tunnel, with its load of cracked rock, they all accompanied it into an adjoining apartment, where it was cast into a metallic shute, through which, they were informed, it reached the furnace.

"While it is melting," explained Dr. Syx, "certain elements, the nature of which I must beg to keep secret, are mixed with the ore, causing chemical action which results in the extraction of the metal. Now let me show you pure artemisium issuing from the furnace."

He led the visitors through two apartments into a third, one side of which was walled by the front of a furnace. From this projected two or three small spouts, and iridescent streams of molten metal fell from the spouts into earthen receptacles from which the blazing liquid was led, like flowing iron, into a system of moulds, where it was allowed to cool and harden.

The financiers looked on wondering, and their astonishment grew when they were conducted into the rock-cut store-rooms beneath, where they saw metallic ingots glowing like gigantic opals in the light which Dr. Syx turned on. They were piled in rows along the walls as high as a man could reach. A very brief inspection sufficed to convince the visitors that Dr. Syx was able to perform all that he promised. Although they had not penetrated the secret of his process of reducing the ore, yet they had seen the metal flowing from the furnace, and the piles of ingots proved conclusively that he had uttered no vain boast when he said he could give the world a new coinage.

But President Boon, being himself a metallurgist, desired to inspect the mysterious ore a little more closely. Possibly he was thinking that if another mine was destined to be discovered he might as well be the discoverer as anybody. Dr. Syx attempted no concealment, but his smile became more than usually scornful as he stopped a laden car and invited the visitors to help themselves.

"I think," he said, "that I have struck the only lode of this ore in the Teton, or possibly in this part of the world, but I don't know for certain. There may be plenty of it only waiting to be found. That, however, doesn't trouble me. The great point is that nobody except myself knows how to extract the metal."

Mr. Boon closely examined the chunk of rock which he had taken from the car. Then he pulled a lens from his pocket, with a deprecatory glance at Dr. Syx.

"Oh, that's all right," said the latter, with a laugh, the first that these gentlemen had ever heard from his lips, and it almost made them shudder; "put it to every test, examine it with the microscope, with fire, with electricity, with the spectroscope—in every way you can think of! I assure you it is worth your while!"

Again Dr. Syx uttered his freezing laugh, passing into the familiar smile, which had now become an undisguised mock.

"Upon my word," said Mr. Boon, taking his eye from the lens, "I see no sign of any metal here!"

"Look at the green specks!" cried the doctor, snatching the specimen from the president's hand. "That's it! That's artemisium! But it's of no use unless you can get it out and purify it, which is my secret!"

For the third time Dr. Syx laughed, and his merriment affected the visitors so disagreeably that they showed impatience to be gone. Immediately he changed his manner.

"Come into my office," he said, with a return to the graciousness which had characterized him ever since the party started from New York.

When they were all seated, and the doctor had handed round a box of cigars, he resumed the conversation in his most amiable manner.

"You see, gentlemen," he said, turning a piece of ore in his fingers, "artemisium is like aluminum. It can only be obtained in the metallic form by a special process. While these greenish particles, which you may perhaps mistake for chrysolite, or some similar unisilicate, really contain the precious metal, they are not entirely composed of it. The process by which I separate out the metallic element while the ore is passing through the furnace is, in truth, quite simple, and its very simplicity guards my secret. Make your minds easy as to over-production. A man is as likely to jump over the moon as to find me out."

"But," he continued, again changing his manner, "we have had business enough for one day; now for a little recreation." While speaking the doctor pressed a button on his desk, and the room, which was illuminated by electric lamps—for there were no windows in the building—suddenly became dark, except part of one wall, where a broad area of light appeared. Dr. Syx's voice had become very soothing when next he spoke: "I am fond of amusing myself with a peculiar form of the magic-lantern, which I invented some years ago, and which I have never exhibited except for the entertainment of my friends. The pictures will appear upon the wall, the apparatus being concealed."

He had hardly ceased speaking when the illuminated space seemed to melt away, leaving a great opening, through which the spectators looked as if into another world on the opposite side of the wall. For a minute or two they could not clearly discern what was presented; then, gradually, the flitting scenes and figures became more distinct until the lifelikeness of the spectacle absorbed their whole attention.

Before them passed, in panoramic review, a sunny land, filled with brilliant-hued vegetation, and dotted with villages and cities which were bright with light-coloured buildings. People appeared moving through the scenes, as in a cinematograph exhibition, but with infinitely more semblance of reality. In fact, the pictures, blending one into another, seemed to be life itself. Yet it was not an earth-like scene. The colours of the passing landscape were such as no man in the room had ever beheld; and the people, tall, round-limbed, with florid complexion, golden hair, and brilliant eyes and lips, were indescribably beautiful and graceful in all their movements.

From the land the view passed out to sea, and bright blue waves, edged with creaming foam, ran swiftly under the spectator's eyes, and occasionally, driven before light winds, appeared fleets of daintily shaped vessels, which reminded the beholder, by their flashing wings, of the feigned "ship of pearl."

After the fairy ships and breezy sea views came a long, curving line of coast, brilliant with coral sands, and indented by frequent bays, along whose enchanting shores lay pleasant towns, the landscapes behind them splendid with groves, meadows, and streams.

Presently the shifting photographic tape, or whatever the mechanism may have been, appeared to have settled upon a chosen scene, and there it rested. A broad champaign reached away to distant sapphire mountains, while the foreground was occupied by a magnificent house, resembling a large country villa, fronted with a garden, shaded by bowers and festoons of huge, brilliant flowers. Birds of radiant plumage flitted among the trees and blossoms, and then appeared a company of gaily attired people, including many young girls, who joined hands and danced in a ring, apparently with shouts of laughter, while a group of musicians standing near thrummed and blew upon curiously shaped instruments.

Suddenly the shadow of a dense cloud flitted across the scene; whereupon the brilliant birds flew away with screams of terror which almost seemed to reach the ears of the onlookers through the wall. An expression of horror came over the faces of the people. The children broke from their merry circle and ran for protection to their elders. The utmost confusing and whelming terror were evidenced for a moment—then the ground split asunder, and the house and the garden, with all their living occupants were swallowed by an awful chasm which opened just where they had stood. The great rent ran in a widening line across the sunlit landscape until it reached the horizon, when the distant mountains crumbled, clouds poured in from all sides at once, and billows of flame burst through them as they veiled the scene.

But in another instant the commotion was over, and the world whose curious spectacles had been enacted as if on the other side of a window, seemed to retreat swiftly into space, until at last, emerging from a fleecy cloud, it reappeared in the form of the full moon hanging in the sky, but larger than is its wont, with its dry ocean-beds, its keen-spired peaks, its ragged mountain ranges, its gaping chasms, its immense crater rings, and Tycho, the chief of them all, shooting raylike streaks across the scarred face of the abandoned lunar globe. The show was ended, and Dr. Syx, turning on only a partial illumination in the room, rose slowly to his feet, his tall form appearing strangely magnified in the gloom, and invited his bewildered guests to accompany him to his house, outside the mill, where he said dinner awaited them. As they emerged into daylight they acted like persons just aroused from an opiate dream.

V
WONDERS OF THE NEW METAL

Within a twelvemonth after the visit of President Boon and his fellow financiers to the mine in the Grand Teton a railway had been constructed from Jackson's Hole, connecting with one of the Pacific lines, and the distribution of the new metal was begun. All of Dr. Syx's terms had been accepted. United States troops occupied a permanent encampment on the upper waters of the Snake River, to afford protection, and as the consignments of precious ingots were hurried east and west on guarded trains, the mints all over the world resumed their activity. Once more a common monetary standard prevailed, and commerce revived as if touched by a magic wand.

Artemisium quickly won its way in popular favour. Its matchless beauty alone was enough. Not only was it gladly accepted in the form of money, but its success was instantaneous in the arts. Dr. Syx and the inspectors representing the various nations found it difficult to limit the output to the agreed upon amount. The demand was incessant.

Goldsmiths and jewellers continually discovered new excellences in the wonderful metal. Its properties of translucence and refraction enabled skilful artists to perform marvels. By suitable management a chain of artemisium could be made to resemble a string of vari-coloured gems, each separate link having a tint of its own, while, as the wearer moved, delicate complementary colours chased one another, in rapid undulation, from end to end.

A fresh charm was added by the new metal to the personal adornment of women, and an enhanced splendour to the pageants of society. Gold in its palmiest days had never enjoyed such a vogue. A crowded reception room or a dinner party where artemisium abounded possessed an indescribable atmosphere of luxury and richness, refined in quality, yet captivating to every sense. Imaginative persons went so far as to aver that the sight and presence of the metal exercised a strangely soothing and dreamy power over the mind, like the influence of moonlight streaming through the tree-tops on a still, balmy night.

The public curiosity in regard to the origin of artemisium was boundless. The various nations published official bulletins in which the general facts—omitting, of course, such incidents as the singular exhibition seen by the visiting financiers on the wall of Dr. Syx's office—were detailed to gratify the universal desire for information.

President Boon not only submitted the specimens of ore-bearing rock which he had brought from the mine to careful analysis, but also appealed to several of the greatest living chemists and mineralogists to aid him; but they were all equally mystified. The green substance contained in the ore, although differing slightly from ordinary chrysolite, answered all the known tests of that mineral. It was remembered, however, that Dr. Syx had said that they would be likely to mistake the substance for chrysolite, and the result of their experiments justified his prediction. Evidently the doctor had gone a stone's-cast beyond the chemistry of the day, and, just as evidently, he did not mean to reveal his discovery for the benefit of science, nor for the benefit of any pockets except his own.

Notwithstanding the failure of the chemists to extract anything from Dr. Syx's ore, the public at large never doubted that the secret would be discovered in good time, and thousands of prospectors flocked to the Teton Mountains in search of the ore. And without much difficulty they found it. Evidently the doctor had been mistaken in thinking that his mine might be the only one. The new miners hurried specimens of the green-speckled rock to the chemical laboratories for experimentation, and meanwhile began to lay up stores of the ore in anticipation of the time when the proper way to extract the metal should be discovered.

But, alas! that time did not come. The fresh ore proved to be as refractory as that which had been obtained from Dr. Syx. But in the midst of the universal disappointment there came a new sensation.

One morning the newspapers glared with a despatch from Grand Teton station announcing that the metal itself had been discovered by prospectors on the eastern slope of the main peak.

"It outcrops in many places," ran the despatch, "and many small nuggets have been picked out of crevices in the rocks."

The excitement produced by this news was even greater than when gold was discovered at the south pole. Again a mad rush was made for the Tetons. The heights around Jackson's Hole and the shores of Jackson's and Jenny's lakes were quickly dotted with camps, and the military force had to be doubled to keep off the curious, and occasionally menacing, crowds which gathered in the vicinity and seemed bent on unearthing the great secret locked behind the windowless walls of the mill, where the column of black smoke and the roar of the engine served as reminders of the incredible wealth which the sole possessor of that secret was rolling up.

This time no mistake had been made. It was a fact that the metal, in virgin purity, had been discovered scattered in various places on the ledges of the Grand Teton. In a little while thousands had obtained specimens with their own hands. The quantity was distressingly small, considering the number and the eagerness of the seekers, but that it was genuine artemisium not even Dr. Syx could have denied. He, however, made no attempt to deny it.

"Yes," he said, when questioned, "I find that I have been deceived. At first I thought the metal existed only in the form of the green ore, but of late I have come upon veins of pure artemisium in my mine. I am glad for your sakes, but sorry for my own. Still, it may turn out that there is no great amount of free artemisium after all."

While the doctor talked in this manner close observers detected a lurking sneer which his acquaintances had not noticed since artemisium was first adopted as the money basis of the world.

The crowd that swarmed upon the mountain quickly exhausted all of the visible supply of the metal. Sometimes they found it in a thin stratum at the bottom of crevices, where it could be detached in opalescent plates and leaves of the thickness of paper. These superficial deposits evidently might have been formed from water holding the metal in solution. Occasionally, deep cracks contained nuggets and wiry masses which looked as if they had run together when molten.

The most promising spots were soon staked out in miners' claims, machinery was procured, stock companies were formed, and borings were begun. The enthusiasm arising from the earlier finds and the flattering surface indications caused everybody to work with feverish haste and energy, and within two months one hundred tunnels were piercing the mountain.

For a long time nobody was willing to admit the truth which gradually forced itself upon the attention of the miners. The deeper they went the scarcer became the indications of artemisium! In fact, such deposits as were found were confined to fissures near the surface. But Dr. Syx continued to report a surprising increase in the amount of free metal in his mine, and this encouraged all who had not exhausted their capital to push on their tunnels in the hope of finally striking a vein. At length, however, the smaller operators gave up in despair, until only one heavily capitalized company remained at work.

VI
A STRANGE DISCOVERY

"It is my belief that Dr. Max Syx is a deceiver."

The person who uttered this opinion was a young engineer, Andrew Hall, who had charge of the operations of one of the mining companies which were driving tunnels into the Grand Teton.

"What do you mean by that?" asked President Boon, who was the principal backer of the enterprise.

"I mean," replied Hall, "that there is no free metal in this mountain, and Dr. Syx knows there is none."

"But he is getting it himself from his mine," retorted President Boon.

"So he says, but who has seen it? No one is admitted into the Syx mine, his foremen are forbidden to talk, and his workmen are specially imported negroes who do not understand the English language."

"But," persisted Mr. Boon, "how, then, do you account for the nuggets scattered over the mountain? And, beside, what object could Dr. Syx have in pretending that there is free metal to be had for the digging?"

"He may have salted the mountain, for all I know," said Hall. "As for his object, I confess I am entirely in the dark; but, for all that, I am convinced that we shall find no more metal if we dig ten miles for it."

"Nonsense," said the president; "if we keep on we shall strike it. Did not Dr. Syx himself admit that he found no free artemisium until his tunnel had reached the core of the peak? We must go as deep as he has gone before we give up."

"I fear the depths he attains are beyond most people's reach," was Hall's answer, while a thoughtful look crossed his clear-cut brow, "but since you desire it, of course the work shall go on. I should like, however, to change the direction of the tunnel."

"Certainly," replied Mr. Boon; "bore in whatever direction you think proper, only don't despair."

About a month after this conversation Andrew Hall, with whom a community of tastes in many things had made me intimately acquainted, asked me one morning to accompany him into his tunnel.

"I want to have a trusty friend at my elbow," he said, "for, unless I am a dreamer, something remarkable will happen within the next hour, and two witnesses are better than one."

I knew Hall was not the person to make such a remark carelessly, and my curiosity was intensely excited, but, knowing his peculiarities, I did not press him for an explanation. When we arrived at the head of the tunnel I was surprised at finding no workmen there.

"I stopped blasting some time ago," said Hall, in explanation, "for a reason which, I hope, will become evident to you very soon. Lately I have been boring very slowly, and yesterday I paid off the men and dismissed them with the announcement, which, I am confident, President Boon will sanction after he hears my report of this morning's work, that the tunnel is abandoned. You see, I am now using a drill which I can manage without assistance. I believe the work is almost completed, and I want you to witness the end of it."

He then carefully applied the drill, which noiselessly screwed its nose into the rock. When it had sunk to a depth of a few inches he withdrew it, and, taking a hand-drill capable of making a hole not more than an eighth of an inch in diameter, cautiously began boring in the centre of the larger cavity. He had made hardly a hundred turns of the handle when the drill shot through the rock! A gratified smile illuminated his features, and he said in a suppressed voice:

"Don't be alarmed; I'm going to put out the light."

Instantly we were in complete darkness, but being close at Hall's side I could detect his movements. He pulled out the drill, and for half a minute remained motionless as if listening. There was no sound.

"I must enlarge the opening," he whispered, and immediately the faint grating of a sharp tool cutting through the rock informed me of his progress.

"There," at last he said, "I think that will do; now for a look."

I could tell that he had placed his eye at the hole and was gazing with breathless attention. Presently he pulled my sleeve.

"Put your eye here," he whispered, pushing me into the proper position for looking through the hole.

At first I could discern nothing except a smoky blue glow. But soon my vision cleared a little, and then I perceived that I was gazing into a narrow tunnel which met ours directly end to end. Glancing along the axis of this gallery I saw, some two hundred yards away, a faint light which evidently indicated the mouth of the tunnel.

At the end where we had met it the mysterious tunnel was considerably widened at one side, as if the excavators had started to change direction and then abandoned the work, and in this elbow I could just see the outlines of two or three flat cars loaded with broken stone, while a heap of the same material lay near them. Through the centre of the tunnel ran a railway track.

"Do you know what you are looking at?" asked Hall in my ear.

"I begin to suspect," I replied, "that you have accidentally run into Dr. Syx's mine."

"If Dr. Syx had been on his guard this accident wouldn't have happened," replied Hall, with an almost inaudible chuckle.

"I heard you remark a month ago," I said, "that you were changing the direction of your tunnel. Has this been the aim of your labours ever since?"

"You have hit it," he replied. "Long ago I became convinced that my company was throwing away its money in a vain attempt to strike a lode of pure artemisium. But President Boon has great faith in Dr. Syx, and would not give up the work. So I adopted what I regarded as the only practicable method of proving the truth of my opinion and saving the company's funds. An electric indicator, of my invention, enabled me to locate the Syx tunnel when I got near it, and I have met it end on, and opened this peep-hole in order to observe the doctor's operations. I feel that such spying is entirely justified in the circumstances. Although I cannot yet explain just how or why I feel sure that Dr. Syx was the cause of the sudden discovery of the surface nuggets, and that he has encouraged the miners for his own ends, until he has brought ruin to thousands who have spent their last cent in driving useless tunnels into this mountain. It is a righteous thing to expose him."

"But," I interposed, "I do not see that you have exposed anything yet except the interior of a tunnel."

"You will see more clearly after a while," was the reply.

Hall now placed his eye again at the aperture, and was unable entirely to repress the exclamation that rose to his lips. He remained staring through the hole for several minutes without uttering a word. Presently I noticed that the lenses of his eye were illuminated by a ray of light coming through the hole, but he did not stir.

After a long inspection he suddenly applied his ear to the hole and listened intently for at least five minutes. Not a sound was audible to me, but, by an occasional pressure of the hand, Hall signified that some important disclosure was reaching his sense of hearing. At length he removed his ear.

"Pardon me," he whispered, "for keeping you so long in waiting, but what I have just seen and overheard was of a nature to admit of no interruption. He is still talking, and by pressing your ear against the hole you may be able to catch what he says."

"Who is 'he'?"

"Look for yourself."

I placed my eye at the aperture, and almost recoiled with the violence of my surprise. The tunnel before me was brilliantly illuminated, and within three feet of the wall of rock behind which we crouched stood Dr. Syx, his dark profile looking almost satanic in the sharp contrast of light and shadow. He was talking to one of his foremen, and the two were the only visible occupants of the tunnel. Putting my ear to the little opening, I heard his words distinctly:

—"end of their rope. Well, they've spent a pretty lot of money for their experience, and I rather think we shall not be troubled again by artemisium-seekers for some time to come."

The doctor's voice ceased, and instantly I clapped my eye to the hole. He had changed his position so that his black eyes now looked straight at the aperture. My heart was in my mouth, for at first I believed from his expression that he had detected the gleam of my eyeball. But if so, he probably mistook it for a bit of mica in the rock, and paid no further attention. Then his lips moved, and I put my ear again to the hole. He seemed to be replying to a question that the foreman had asked.

"If they do," he said, "they will never guess the real secret."

Thereupon he turned on his heel, kicked a bit of rock off the track, and strode away towards the entrance. The foreman paused long enough to turn out the electric lamp, and then followed the doctor.

"Well," asked Hall, "what have you heard?"

I told him everything.

"It fully corroborates the evidence of my own eyes and ears," he remarked, "and we may count ourselves extremely lucky. It is not likely that Dr. Syx will be heard a second time proclaiming his deception with his own lips. It is plain that he was led to talk as he did to the foreman on account of the latter's having informed him of the sudden discharge of my men this morning. Their presence within ear-shot of our hiding-place during their conversation was, of course, pure accident, and so you can see how kind fortune has been to us. I expected to have to watch and listen and form deductions for a week, at least, before getting the information which five lucky minutes have placed in our hands."

While he was speaking my companion busied himself in carefully plugging up the hole in the rock. When it was closed to his satisfaction he turned on the light in our tunnel.

"Did you observe," he asked, "that there was a second tunnel?"

"What do you say?"

"When the light was on in there I saw the mouth of a smaller tunnel entering the main one behind the cars on the right. Did you notice it?"

"Oh yes," I replied. "I did observe some kind of a dark hole there, but I paid no attention to it because I was so absorbed in the doctor."

"Well," rejoined Hall, smiling, "it was worth considerably more than a glance. As a subject of thought I find it even more absorbing than Dr. Syx. Did you see the track in it?"

"No," I had to acknowledge, "I did not notice that. But," I continued, a little piqued by his manner, "being a branch of the main tunnel, I don't see anything remarkable in its having a track also."

"It was rather dim in that hole," said Hall, still smiling in a somewhat provoking way, "but the railroad track was there plain enough. And, whether you think it remarkable or not, I should like to lay you a wager that that track leads to a secret worth a dozen of the one we have just overheard."

"My good friend," I retorted, still smarting a little, "I shall not presume to match my stupidity against your perspicacity. I haven't cat's eyes in the dark."

Hall immediately broke out laughing, and, slapping me good-naturedly on the shoulder, exclaimed:

"Come, come now! If you go to kicking back at a fellow like that, I shall be sorry I ever undertook this adventure."

VII
A MYSTERY INDEED!

When President Boon had heard our story he promptly approved Hall's dismissal of the men. He expressed great surprise that Dr. Syx should have resorted to a deception which had been so disastrous to innocent people, and at first he talked of legal proceedings. But, after thinking the matter over, he concluded that Syx was too powerful to be attacked with success, especially when the only evidence against him was that he had claimed to find artemisium in his mine at a time when, as everybody knew, artemisium actually was found outside the mine. There was no apparent motive for the deception, and no proof of malicious intent. In short, Mr. Boon decided that the best thing for him and his stockholders to do was to keep silent about their losses and await events. And, at Hall's suggestion, he also determined to say nothing to anybody about the discovery we had made.

"It could do no good," said Hall, in making the suggestion, "and it might spoil a plan I have in mind."

"What plan?" asked the president.

"I prefer not to tell just yet," was the reply.

I observed that, in our interview with Mr. Boon, Hall made no reference to the side tunnel to which he had appeared to attach so much importance, and I concluded that he now regarded it as lacking significance. In this I was mistaken.

A few days afterwards I received an invitation from Hall to accompany him once more into the abandoned tunnel.

"I have found out what that sidetrack means," he said, "and it has plunged me into another mystery so dark and profound that I cannot see my way through it. I must beg you to say no word to any one concerning the things I am about to show you."

I gave the required promise, and we entered the tunnel, which nobody had visited since our former adventure. Having extinguished our lamp, my companion opened the peep-hole, and a thin ray of light streamed through from the tunnel on the opposite side of the wall. He applied his eye to the hole.

"Yes," he said, quickly stepping back and pushing me into his place, "they are still at it. Look, and tell me what you see."

"I see," I replied, after placing my eye at the aperture, "a gang of men unloading a car which has just come out of the side tunnel, and putting its contents upon another car standing on the track of the main tunnel."

"Yes, and what are they handling?"

"Why, ore, of course."

"And do you see nothing significant in that?"

"To be sure!" I exclaimed. "Why, that ore—"

"Hush! hush!" admonished Hall, putting his hand over my mouth; "don't talk so loud. Now go on, in a whisper."

"The ore," I resumed, "may have come back from the furnace-room, because the side tunnel turns off so as to run parallel with the other."

"It not only may have come back, it actually has come back," said Hall.

"How can you be sure?"

"Because I have been over the track, and know that it leads to a secret apartment directly under the furnace in which Dr. Syx pretends to melt the ore!"

For a minute after hearing this avowal I was speechless.

"Are you serious?" I asked at length.

"Perfectly serious. Run your finger along the rock here. Do you perceive a seam? Two days ago, after seeing what you have just witnessed in the Syx tunnel, I carefully cut out a section of the wall, making an aperture large enough to crawl through, and, when I knew the workmen were asleep, I crept in there and examined both tunnels from end to end. But in solving one mystery I have run myself into another infinitely more perplexing."

"How is that?"

"Why does Dr. Syx take such elaborate pains to deceive his visitors, and also the government officers? It is now plain that he conducts no mining operations whatever. This mine of his is a gigantic blind. Whenever inspectors or scientific curiosity seekers visit his mill his mute workmen assume the air of being very busy, the cars laden with his so-called 'ore' rumble out of the tunnel, and their contents are ostentatiously poured into the furnace, or appear to be poured into it, really dropping into a receptacle beneath, to be carried back into the mine again. And then the doctor leads his gulled visitors around to the other side of the furnace and shows them the molten metal coming out in streams. Now what does it all mean? That's what I'd like to find out. What's his game? For, mark you, if he doesn't get artemisium from this pretended ore, he gets it from some other source, and right on this spot, too. There is no doubt about that. The whole world is supplied by Syx's furnace, and Syx feeds his furnace with something that comes from his ten acres of Grand Teton rock. What is that something? How does he get it, and where does he hide it? These are the things I should like to find out."

"Well," I replied, "I fear I can't help you."

"But the difference between you and me," he retorted, "is that you can go to sleep over it, while I shall never get another good night's rest so long as this black mystery remains unsolved."

"What will you do?"

"I don't know exactly what. But I've got a dim idea which may take shape after a while."

Hall was silent for some time; then he suddenly asked:

"Did you ever hear of that queer magic-lantern show with which Dr. Syx entertained Mr. Boon and the members of the financial commission in the early days of the artemisium business?"

"Yes, I've heard the story, but I don't think it was ever made public. The newspapers never got hold of it."

"No, I believe not. Odd thing, wasn't it?"

"Why, yes, very odd, but just like the doctor's eccentric ways, though. He's always doing something to astonish somebody, without any apparent earthly reason. But what put you in mind of that?"

"Free artemisium put me in mind of it," replied Hall, quizzically.

"I don't see the connection."

"I'm not sure that I do either, but when you are dealing with Dr. Syx nothing is too improbable to be thought of."

Hall thereupon fell to musing again, while we returned to the entrance of the tunnel. After he had made everything secure, and slipped the key into his pocket, my companion remarked:

"Don't you think it would be best to keep this latest discovery to ourselves?"

"Certainly."

"Because," he continued, "nobody would be benefited just now by knowing what we know, and to expose the worthlessness of the 'ore' might cause a panic. The public is a queer animal, and never gets scared at just the thing you expect will alarm it, but always at something else."

We had shaken hands and were separating when Hall stopped me.

"Do you believe in alchemy?" he asked.

"That's an odd question from you," I replied. "I thought alchemy was exploded long ago."

"Well," he said, slowly, "I suppose it has been exploded, but then, you know, an explosion may sometimes be a kind of instantaneous education, breaking up old things but revealing new ones."

VIII
MORE OF DR. SYX'S MAGIC

Important business called me East soon after the meeting with Hall described in the foregoing chapter, and before I again saw the Grand Teton very stirring events had taken place.

As the reader is aware, Dr. Syx's agreement with the various governments limited the output of his mine. An international commission, continually in session in New York, adjusted the differences arising among the nations concerning financial affairs, and allotted to each the proper amount of artemisium for coinage. Of course, this amount varied from time to time, but a fair average could easily be maintained. The gradual increase of wealth, in houses, machinery, manufactured and artistic products called for a corresponding increase in the circulating medium; but this, too, was easily provided for. An equally painstaking supervision was exercised over the amount of the precious metal which Dr. Syx was permitted to supply to the markets for use in the arts. On this side, also, the demand gradually increased; but the wonderful Teton mine seemed equal to all calls upon its resources.

After the failure of the mining operations there was a moderate revival of the efforts to reduce the Teton ore, but no success cheered the experimenters. Prospectors also wandered all over the earth looking for pure artemisium, but in vain. The general public, knowing nothing of what Hall had discovered, and still believing Syx's story that he also had found pure artemisium in his mine, accounted for the failure of the tunnelling operations on the supposition that the metal, in a free state, was excessively rare, and that Dr. Syx had had the luck to strike the only vein of it that the Grand Teton contained. As if to give countenance to this opinion, Dr. Syx now announced, in the most public manner, that he had been deceived again, and that the vein of free metal he had struck being exhausted, no other had appeared. Accordingly, he said, he must henceforth rely exclusively, as in the beginning, upon reduction of the ore.

Artemisium had proved itself an immense boon to mankind, and the new era of commercial prosperity which it had ushered in already exceeded everything that the world had known in the past. School-children learned that human civilization had taken five great strides, known respectively, beginning at the bottom, as the "age of stone," the "age of bronze," the "age of iron," the "age of gold," and the "age of artemisium."

Nevertheless, sources of dissatisfaction finally began to appear, and, after the nature of such things, they developed with marvellous rapidity. People began to grumble about "contraction of the currency." In every country there arose a party which demanded "free money." Demagogues pointed to the brief reign of paper money after the demonetization of gold as a happy period, when the people had enjoyed their rights, and the "money barons"—borrowing a term from nineteenth-century history—were kept at bay.

Then came denunciations of the international commission for restricting the coinage. Dr. Syx was described as "a devil-fish sucking the veins of the planet and holding it helpless in the grasp of his tentacular billions." In the United States meetings of agitators passed furious resolutions, denouncing the government, assailing the rich, cursing Dr. Syx, and calling upon "the oppressed" to rise and "take their own." The final outcome was, of course, violence. Mobs had to be suppressed by military force. But the most dramatic scene in the tragedy occurred at the Grand Teton. Excited by inflammatory speeches and printed documents, several thousand armed men assembled in the neighbourhood of Jenny's Lake and prepared to attack the Syx mine. For some reason the military guard had been depleted, and the mob, under the leadership of a man named Bings, who showed no little talent as a commander and strategist, surprised the small force of soldiers and locked them up in their own guard-house.

Telegraphic communication having been cut off by the astute Bings, a fierce attack was made on the mine. The assailants swarmed up the sides of the canyon, and attempted to break in through the foundation of the buildings. But the masonry was stronger than they had anticipated, and the attack failed. Sharp-shooters then climbed the neighbouring heights, and kept up an incessant peppering of the walls with conical bullets driven at four thousand feet per second.

No reply came from the gloomy structure. The huge column of black smoke rose uninterruptedly into the sky, and the noise of the great engine never ceased for an instant. The mob gathered closer on all sides and redoubled the fire of the rifles, to which was now added the belching of several machine-guns. Ragged holes began to appear in the walls, and at the sight of these the assailants yelled with delight. It was evident that the mill could not long withstand so destructive a bombardment. If the besiegers had possessed artillery they would have knocked the buildings into splinters within twenty minutes. As it was, they would need a whole day to win their victory.

Suddenly it became evident that the besieged were about to take a hand in the fight. Thus far they had not shown themselves or fired a shot, but now a movement was perceived on the roof, and the projecting arms of some kind of machinery became visible. Many marksmen concentrated their fire upon the mysterious objects, but apparently with little effect. Bings, mounted on a rock, so as to command a clear view of the field, was on the point, of ordering a party to rush forward with axes and beat down the formidable doors, when there came a blinding flash from the roof, something swished through the air, and a gust of heat met the assailants in the face. Bings dropped dead from his perch, and then, as if the scythe of the Destroyer had swung downward, and to right and left in quick succession, the close-packed mob was levelled, rank after rank, until the few survivors crept behind rocks for refuge.

Instantly the atmospheric broom swept up and down the canyon and across the mountain's flanks, and the marksmen fell in bunches like shaken grapes. Nine-tenths of the besiegers were destroyed within ten minutes after the first movement had been noticed on the roof. Those who survived owed their escape to the rocks which concealed them, and they lost no time in crawling off into neighbouring chasms, and, as soon as they were beyond eye-shot from the mill, they fled with panic speed.

Then the towering form of Dr. Syx appeared at the door. Emerging without sign of fear or excitement, he picked his way among his fallen enemies, and, approaching the military guard-house, undid the fastening and set the imprisoned soldiers free.

"I think I am paying rather dear for my whistle," he said, with a characteristic sneer, to Captain Carter, the commander of the troop. "It seems that I must not only defend my own people and property when attacked by mob force, but must also come to the rescue of the soldiers whose pay-rolls are met from my pocket."

The captain made no reply, and Dr. Syx strode back to the works. When the released soldiers saw what had occurred their amazement had no bounds. It was necessary at once to dispose of the dead, and this was no easy undertaking for their small force. However, they accomplished it, and at the beginning of their work made a most surprising discovery.

"How's this, Jim?" said one of the men to his comrade, as they stooped to lift the nearest victim of Dr. Syx's withering fire. "What's this fellow got all over him?"

"Artemisium! 'pon my soul!" responded "Jim," staring at the body. "He's all coated over with it."

Immediately from all sides came similar exclamations. Every man who had fallen was covered with a film of the precious metal, as if he had been dipped into an electrolytic bath. Clothing seemed to have been charred, and the metallic atoms had penetrated the flesh of the victims. The rocks all round the battle-field were similarly veneered. "It looks to me," said Captain Carter, "as if old Syx had turned one of his spouts of artemisium into a hose-pipe and soaked 'em with it."

"That's it," chimed in a lieutenant, "that's exactly what he's done."

"Well," returned the captain, "if he can do that, I don't see what use he's got for us here."

"Probably he don't want to waste the stuff," said the lieutenant. "What do you suppose it cost him to plate this crowd?"

"I guess a month's pay for the whole troop wouldn't cover the expense. It's costly, but then—gracious! Wouldn't I have given something for the doctor's hose when I was a youngster campaigning in the Philippines in '99?"

The story of the marvellous way in which Dr. Syx defended his mill became the sensation of the world for many days. The hose-pipe theory, struck off on the spot by Captain Carter, seized the popular fancy, and was generally accepted without further question. There was an element of the ludicrous which robbed the tragedy of some of its horror. Moreover, no one could deny that Dr. Syx was well within his rights in defending himself by any means when so savagely attacked, and his triumphant success, no less than the ingenuity which was supposed to underlie it, placed him in an heroic light which he had not hitherto enjoyed.

As to the demagogues who were responsible for the outbreak and its terrible consequences, they slunk out of the public eye, and the result of the battle at the mine seemed to have been a clearing up of the atmosphere, such as a thunder-storm effects at the close of a season of foul weather.

But now, little as men guessed it, the beginning of the end was close at hand.

IX
THE DETECTIVE OF SCIENCE

The morning of my arrival at Grand Teton station, on my return from the East, Andrew Hall met me with a warm greeting.

"I have been anxiously expecting you," he said, "for I have made some progress towards solving the great mystery. I have not yet reached a conclusion, but I hope soon to let you into the entire secret. In the meantime you can aid me with your companionship, if in no other way, for, since the defeat of the mob, this place has been mighty lonesome. The Grand Teton is a spot that people who have no particular business out here carefully avoid. I am on speaking terms with Dr. Syx, and occasionally, when there is a party to be shown around, I visit his works, and make the best possible use of my eyes. Captain Carter of the military is a capital fellow, and I like to hear his stories of the war in Luzon forty years ago, but I want somebody to whom I can occasionally confide things, and so you are as welcome as moonlight in harvest-time."

"Tell me something about that wonderful fight with the mob. Did you see it?"

"I did. I had got wind of what Bings intended to do while I was down at Pocotello, and I hurried up here to warn the soldiers, but unfortunately I came too late. Finding the military cooped up in the guard-house and the mob masters of the situation, I kept out of sight on the side of the Teton, and watched the siege with my binocular. I think there was very little of the spectacle that I missed."

"What of the mysterious force that the doctor employed to sweep off the assailants?"

"Of course, Captain Carter's suggestion that Syx turned molten artemisium from his furnace into a hose-pipe and sprayed the enemy with it is ridiculous. But it is much easier to dismiss Carter's theory than to substitute a better one. I saw the doctor on the roof with a gang of black workmen, and I noticed the flash of polished metal turned rapidly this way and that, but there was some intervening obstacle which prevented me from getting a good view of the mechanism employed. It certainly bore no resemblance to a hose-pipe, or anything of that kind. No emanation was visible from the machine, but it was stupefying to see the mob melt down."

"How about the coating of the bodies with artemisium?"

"There you are back on the hose-pipe again," laughed Hall. "But, to tell you the truth, I'd rather be excused from expressing an opinion on that operation in wholesale electro-plating just at present. I've the ghost of an idea what it means, but let me test my theory a little before I formulate it. In the meanwhile, won't you take a stroll with me?"

"Certainly; nothing could please me better," I replied. "Which way shall we go?"

"To the top of the Grand Teton."

"What! are you seized with the mountain-climbing fever?"

"Not exactly, but I have a particular reason for wishing to take a look from that pinnacle."

"I suppose you know the real apex of the peak has never been trodden by man?"

"I do know it, but it is just that apex that I am determined to have under my feet for ten minutes. The failure of others is no argument for us."

"Just as you say," I rejoined. "But I suppose there is no indiscretion in asking whether this little climb has any relation to the mystery?"

"If it didn't have an important relation to the clearing up of that dark thing I wouldn't risk my neck in such an undertaking," was the reply.

Accordingly, the next morning we set out for the peak. All previous climbers, as we were aware, had attacked it from the west. That seemed the obvious thing to do, because the westward slopes of the mountain, while very steep, are less abrupt than those which face the rising sun. In fact, the eastern side of the Grand Teton appears to be absolutely unclimbable. But both Hall and I had had experience with rock climbing in the Alps and the Dolomites, and we knew that what looked like the hardest places sometimes turn out to be next to the easiest. Accordingly we decided—the more particularly because it would save time, but also because we yielded to the common desire to outdo our predecessors—to try to scale the giant right up his face.

We carried a very light but exceedingly strong rope, about five hundred feet long, wore nail-shod shoes, and had each a metal-pointed staff and a small hatchet in lieu of the regular mountaineer's axe. Advancing at first along the broken ridge between two gorges we gradually approached the steeper part of the Teton, where the cliffs looked so sheer and smooth that it seemed no wonder that nobody had ever tried to scale them. The air was deliciously clear and the sky wonderfully blue above the mountains, and the moon, a few days past its last quarter, was visible in the southwest, its pale crescent face slightly blued by the atmosphere, as it always appears when seen in daylight.

"SLOW WESTERING, A PHANTOM SAIL— THE LONELY SOUL OF YESTERDAY."

Behind us, somewhat north of east, lay the Syx works, with their black smoke rising almost vertically in the still air. Suddenly, as we stumbled along on the rough surface, something whizzed past my face and fell on the rock at my feet. I looked at the strange missile, that had come like a meteor out of open space, with astonishment.

It was a bird, a beautiful specimen of the scarlet tanagers, which I remembered the early explorers had found inhabiting the Teton canyons, their brilliant plumage borrowing splendour from contrast with the gloomy surroundings. It lay motionless, its outstretched wings having a curious shrivelled aspect, while the flaming colour of the breast was half obliterated with smutty patches. Stooping to pick it up, I noticed a slight bronzing, which instantly recalled to my mind the peculiar appearance of the victims of the attack on the mine.

"Look here!" I called to Hall, who was several yards in advance. He turned, and I held up the bird by a wing.

"Where did you get that?" he asked.

"It fell at my feet a moment ago."

Hall glanced in a startled manner at the sky, and then down the slope of the mountain.

"Did you notice in what direction it was flying?" he asked.

"No, it dropped so close that it almost grazed my nose. I saw nothing of it until it made me blink."

"I have been heedless," muttered Hall under his breath. At the time I did not notice the singularity of his remark, my attention being absorbed in contemplating the unfortunate tanager.

"Look how its feathers are scorched," I said.

"I know it," Hall replied, without glancing at the bird.

"And it is covered with a film of artemisium," I added, a little piqued by his abstraction.

"I know that, too."

"See here, Hall," I exclaimed, "are you trying to make game of me?"

"Not at all, my dear fellow," he replied, dropping his cogitation. "Pray forgive me. But this is no new phenomenon to me. I have picked up birds in that condition on this mountain before. There is a terrible mystery here, but I am slowly letting light into it, and if we succeed in reaching the top of the peak I have good hope that the illumination will increase."

"Here now," he added a moment later, sitting down upon a rock and thrusting the blade of his penknife into a crevice, "what do you think of this?"

He held up a little nugget of pure artemisium, and then went on:

"You know that all this slope was swept as clean as a Dutch housewife's kitchen floor by the thousands of miners and prospectors who swarmed over it a year or two ago, and do you suppose they would have missed such a tidbit if it had been here then?"

"Dr. Syx must have been salting the mountain again," I suggested.

"Well," replied Hall, with a significant smile, "if the doctor hasn't salted it somebody else has, that's plain enough. But perhaps you would like to know precisely what I expect to find out when we get on the topknot of the Teton."

"I should certainly be delighted to learn the object of our journey," I said. "Of course, I'm only going along for company and for the fun of the thing; but you know you can count on me for substantial aid whenever you need it."

"It is because you are so willing to let me keep my own counsel," he rejoined, "and to wait for things to ripen before compelling me to disclose them, that I like to have you with me at critical times. Now, as to the object of this breakneck expedition, whose risks you understand as fully as I do, I need not assure you that it is of supreme importance to the success of my plans. In a word, I hope to be able to look down into a part of Dr. Syx's mill which, if I am not mistaken, no human eye except his and those of his most trustworthy helpers has ever been permitted to see. And if I see there what I fully expect to see, I shall have got a long step nearer to a great fortune."

"Good!" I cried. "*En avant*, then! We are losing time."

X
THE TOP OF THE GRAND TETON

The climbing soon became difficult, until at length we were going up hand over hand, taking advantage of crevices and knobs which an inexperienced eye would have regarded as incapable of affording a grip for the fingers or a support for the toes. Presently we arrived at the foot of a stupendous precipice, which was absolutely insurmountable by any ordinary method of ascent. Parts of it overhung, and everywhere the face of the rock was too free from irregularities to afford any footing, except to a fly.

"Now, to borrow the expression of old Bunyan, we are hard put to it," I remarked. "If you will go to the left I will take the right and see if there is any chance of getting up."

"I don't believe we could find any place easier than this," Hall replied, "and so up we go where we are."

"Have you a pair of wings concealed about you?" I asked, laughing at his folly.

"Well, something nearly as good," he responded, unstrapping his knapsack. He produced a silken bag, which he unfolded on the rock.

"A balloon!" I exclaimed. "But how are you going to inflate it?"

For reply Hall showed me a receptacle which, he said, contained liquid hydrogen, and which was furnished with a device for retarding the volatilization of the liquid so that it could be carried with little loss.

"You remember I have a small laboratory in the abandoned mine," he explained, "where we used to manufacture liquid air for blasting. This balloon I made for our present purpose. It will just suffice to carry up our rope, and a small but practically unbreakable grapple of hardened gold. I calculate to send the grapple to the top of the precipice with the balloon, and when it has obtained a firm hold in the riven rock there we can ascend, sailor fashion. You see the rope has knots, and I know your muscles are as trustworthy in such work as my own."

There was a slight breeze from the eastward, and the current of air slanting up the face of the peak assisted the balloon in mounting with its burden, and favoured us by promptly swinging the little airship, with the grapple swaying beneath it, over the brow of the cliff into the atmospheric eddy above. As soon as we saw that the grapple was well over the edge we pulled upon the rope. The balloon instantly shot into view with the anchor dancing, but, under the influence of the wind, quickly returned to its former position behind the projecting brink. The grapple had failed to take hold.

"'Try, try again' must be our motto now," muttered Hall.

We tried several times with the same result, although each time we slightly shifted our position. At last the grapple caught.

"Now, all together!" cried my companion, and simultaneously we threw our weight upon the slender rope. The anchor apparently did not give an inch.

"Let me go first," said Hall, pushing me aside as I caught the first knot above my head. "It's my device, and it's only fair that I should have the first try."

In a minute he was many feet up the wall, climbing swiftly hand over hand, but occasionally stopping and twisting his leg around the rope while he took breath.

"It's easier than I expected," he called down, when he had ascended about one hundred feet. "Here and there the rock offers a little hold for the knees."

I watched him, breathless with anxiety, and, as he got higher, my imagination pictured the little gold grapple, invisible above the brow of the precipice, with perhaps a single thin prong wedged into a crevice, and slowly ploughing its way towards the edge with each impulse of the climber, until but another pull was needed to set it flying! So vivid was my fancy that I tried to banish it by noticing that a certain knot in the rope remained just at the level of my eyes, where it had been from the start. Hall was now fully two hundred feet above the ledge on which I stood, and was rapidly nearing the top of the precipice. In a minute more he would be safe.

Suddenly he shouted, and, glancing up with a leap of the heart, I saw that he was falling! He kept his face to the rock, and came down feet foremost. It would be useless to attempt any description of my feelings; I would not go through that experience again for the price of a battleship. Yet it lasted less than a second. He had dropped not more than ten feet when the fall was arrested.

"All right!" he called, cheerily. "No harm done! It was only a slip."

But what a slip! If the balloon had not carried the anchor several yards back from the edge it would have had no opportunity to catch another hold as it shot forward. And how could we know that the second hold would prove more secure than the first? Hall did not hesitate, however, for one instant. Up he went again. But, in fact, his best chance was in going up, for he was within four yards of the top when the mishap occurred. With a sigh of relief I saw him at last throw his arm over the verge and then wriggle his body upon the ledge. A few seconds later he was lying on his stomach, with his face over the edge, looking down at me.

"Come on!" he shouted. "It's all right."

When I had pulled myself over the brink at his side I grasped his hand and pressed it without a word. We understood one another.

"It was pretty close to a miracle," he remarked at last. "Look at this."

The rock over which the grapple had slipped was deeply scored by the unyielding point of the metal, and exactly at the verge of the precipice the prong had wedged itself into a narrow crack, so firmly that we had to chip away the stone in order to release it. If it had slipped a single inch farther before taking hold it would have been all over with my friend.

Such experiences shake the strongest nerves, and we sat on the shelf we had attained for fully a quarter of an hour before we ventured to attack the next precipice which hung beetling directly above us. It was not as lofty as the one we had just ascended, but it impended to such a degree that we saw we should have to climb our rope while it swung free in the air!

Luckily we had little difficulty in getting a grip for the prongs, and we took every precaution to test the security of the anchorage, not only putting our combined weight repeatedly upon the rope, but flipping and jerking it with all our strength. The grapple resisted every effort to dislodge it, and finally I started up, insisting on my turn as leader.

The height I had to ascend did not exceed one hundred feet, but that is a very great distance to climb on a swinging rope, without a wall within reach to assist by its friction and occasional friendly projections. In a little while my movements, together with the effect of the slight wind, had imparted a most distressing oscillation to the rope. This sometimes carried me with a nerve-shaking bang against a prominent point of the precipice, where I would dislodge loose fragments that kept Hall dodging for his life, and then I would swing out, apparently beyond the brow of the cliff below, so that, as I involuntarily glanced downward, I seemed to be hanging in free space, while the steep mountain-side, looking ten times steeper than it really was, resembled the vertical wall of an absolutely bottomless abyss, as if I were suspended over the edge of the world.

I avoided thinking of what the grapple might be about, and in my haste to get through with the awful experience I worked myself fairly out of breath, so that, when at last I reached the rounded brow of the cliff, I had to stop and cling there for fully a minute before I could summon strength enough to lift myself over it.

When I was assured that the grapple was still securely fastened I signalled to Hall, and he soon stood at my side, exclaiming, as he wiped the perspiration from his face:

"I think I'll try wings next time!"

But our difficulties had only begun. As we had foreseen, it was a case of Alp above Alp, to the very limit of human strength and patience. However, it would have been impossible to go back. In order to descend the two precipices we had surmounted it would have been necessary to leave our life-lines clinging to the rocks, and we had not rope enough to do that. If we could not reach the top we were lost.

Having refreshed ourselves with a bite to eat and a little stimulant, we resumed the climb. After several hours of the most exhausting work I have ever performed we pulled our weary limbs upon the narrow ridge, but a few square yards in area, which constitutes the apex of the Grand Teton. A little below, on the opposite side of a steep-walled gap which divides the top of the mountain into two parts, we saw the singular enclosure of stones which the early white explorers found there, and which they ascribed to the Indians, although nobody has ever known who built it or what purpose it served.

The view was, of course, superb, but while I was admiring it in all its wonderful extent and variety, Hall, who had immediately pulled out his binocular, was busy inspecting the Syx works, the top of whose great tufted smoke column was thousands of feet beneath our level. Jackson's Lake, Jenny's Lake, Leigh's Lake, and several lakelets glittered in the sunlight amid the pale grays and greens of Jackson's Hole, while many a bending reach of the Snake River shone amid the wastes of sage-brush and rock.

"There!" suddenly exclaimed Hall, "I thought I should find it."

"What?"

"Take a look through my glass at the roof of Syx's mill. Look just in the centre."

"Why, it's open in the middle!" I cried as soon as I had put the glass to my eyes. "There's a big circular hole in the centre of the roof."

"Look inside! Look inside!" repeated Hall, impatiently.

"I see nothing there except something bright."

"Do you call it nothing because it is bright?"

"Well, no," I replied, laughing. "What I mean is that I see nothing that I can make anything of except a shining object, and all I can make of that is that it is bright."

"You've been in the Syx works many times, haven't you?"

"Yes."

"Did you ever see the opening in the roof?"

"Never."

"Did you ever hear of it?"

"Never."

"Then Dr. Syx doesn't show his visitors everything that is to be seen."

"Evidently not since, as we know, he concealed the double tunnel and the room under the furnace."

"Dr. Syx has concealed a bigger secret than that," Hall responded, "and the Grand Teton has helped me to a glimpse of it."

For several minutes my friend was absorbed in thought. Then he broke out: "I tell you he's the most wonderful man in the world!"

"Who, Dr. Syx? Well, I've long thought that."

"Yes, but I mean in a different way from what you are thinking of. Do you remember my asking you once if you believed in alchemy?"

"I remember being greatly surprised by your question to that effect."

"Well, now," said Hall, rubbing his hands with a satisfied air, while his eyes glanced keen and bright with the reflection of some passing thought, "Max Syx is greater than any alchemist that ever lived. If those old fellows in the dark ages had accomplished everything they set out to do, they would have been of no more consequence in comparison with our black-browed friend down yonder than—than my head is of consequence in comparison with the moon."

"I fear you flatter the man in the moon," was my laughing reply.

"No, I don't," returned Hall, "and some day you'll admit it."

"Well, what about that something that shines down there? You seem to see more in it than I can."

But my companion had fallen into a reverie and didn't hear my question. He was gazing abstractedly at the faint image of the waning moon, now nearing the distant mountain-top over in Idaho. Presently his mind seemed to return to the old magnet, and he whirled about and glanced down at the Syx mill. The column of smoke was diminishing in volume, an indication that the engine was about to enjoy one of its periodical rests. The irregularity of these stoppages had always been a subject of remark among practical engineers. The hours of labour were exceedingly erratic, but the engine had never been known to work at night, except on one occasion, and then only for a few minutes, when it was suddenly stopped on account of a fire.

Just as Hall resumed his inspection two huge quarter spheres, which had been resting wide apart on the roof, moved towards one another until their arched sections met over the circular aperture which they covered like the dome of an observatory.

"I expected it," Hall remarked. "But come, it is mid-afternoon, and we shall need all of our time to get safely down before the light fades."

As I have already explained, it would not have been possible for us to return the way we came. We determined to descend the comparatively easy western slopes of the peak, and pass the night on that side of the mountain. Letting ourselves down with the rope into the hollow way that divides the summit of the Teton into two pinnacles, we had no difficulty in descending by the route followed by all previous climbers. The weather was fine, and, having found good shelter among the rocks, we passed the night in comfort. The next day we succeeded in swinging round upon the eastern flank of the Teton, below the more formidable cliffs, and, just at nightfall, we arrived at the station. As we passed the Syx mine the doctor himself confronted us. There was a very displeasing look on his dark countenance, and his sneer was strongly marked.

"So you have been on top of the Teton?" he said.

"Yes," replied Hall, very blandly, "and if you have a taste for that sort of thing I should advise you to go up. The view is immense, as fine as the best in the Alps."

"Pretty ingenious plan, that balloon of yours," continued the doctor, still looking black.

"Thank you," Hall replied, more suavely than ever. "I've been planning that a long time. You probably don't know that mountaineering used to be my chief amusement."

The doctor turned away without pursuing the conversation.

"I could kick myself," Hall muttered as soon as Dr. Syx was out of earshot. "If my absurd wish to outdo others had not blinded me, I should have known that he would see us going up this side of the peak, particularly with the balloon to give us away. However, what's done can't be undone. He may not really suspect the truth, and if he does he can't help himself, even though he is the richest man in the world."

XI
STRANGE FATE OF A KITE

"Are you ready for another tramp?" was Andrew Hall's greeting when we met early on the morning following our return from the peak.

"Certainly I am. What is your programme for today?"

"I wish to test the flying qualities of a kite which I have constructed since our return last night."

"You don't allow the calls of sleep to interfere very much with your activity."

"I haven't much time for sleep just now," replied Hall, without smiling. "The kite test will carry us up the flanks of the Teton, but I am not going to try for the top this time. If you will come along I'll ask you to help me by carrying and operating a light transit. I shall carry another myself. I am desirous to get the elevation that the kite attains and certain other data that will be of use to me. We will make a détour towards the south, for I don't want old Syx's suspicions to be prodded any more."

"What interest can he have in your kite-flying?"

"The same interest that a burglar has in the rap of a policeman's night-stick."

"Then your experiment today has some connection with the solution of the great mystery?"

"My dear fellow," said Hall, laying his hand on my shoulder, "until I see the end of that mystery I shall think of nothing else."

In a few hours we were clambering over the broken rocks on the south-eastern flank of the Teton at an elevation of about three thousand feet above the level of Jackson's Hole. Finally Hall paused and began to put his kite together. It was a small box-shaped affair, very light in construction, with paper sides.

"In order to diminish the chances of Dr. Syx noticing what we are about," he said, as he worked away, "I have covered the kite with sky-blue paper. This, together with distance, will probably insure us against his notice."

In a few minutes the kite was ready. Having ascertained the direction of the wind with much attention, he stationed me with my transit on a commanding rock, and sought another post for himself at a distance of two hundred yards, which he carefully measured with a gold tape. My instructions were to keep the telescope on the kite as soon as it had attained a considerable height, and to note the angle of elevation and the horizontal angle with the base line joining our points of observation.

"Be particularly careful," was Hall's injunction, "and if anything happens to the kite by all means note the angles at that instant."

As soon as we had fixed our stations Hall began to pay out the string, and the kite rose very swiftly. As it sped away into the blue it was soon practically invisible to the naked eye, although the telescope of the transit enabled me to follow it with ease.

Glancing across now and then at my companion, I noticed that he was having considerable difficulty in, at the same time, managing the kite and manipulating his transit. But as the kite continued to rise and steadied in position his task became easier, until at length he ceased to remove his eye from the telescope while holding the string with outstretched hand.

"Don't lose sight of it now for an instant!" he shouted.

For at least half an hour he continued to manipulate the string, sending the kite now high towards the zenith with a sudden pull, and then letting it drift off. It seemed at last to become almost a fixed point. Very slowly the angles changed, when, suddenly, there was a flash, and to my amazement I saw the paper of the kite shrivel and disappear in a momentary flame, and then the bare sticks came tumbling out of the sky.

"Did you get the angles?" yelled Hall, excitedly.

"Yes; the telescope is yet pointed on the spot where the kite disappeared."

"Read them off," he called, "and then get your angle with the Syx works."

"All right," I replied, doing as he had requested, and noticing at the same time that he was in the act of putting his watch in his pocket. "Is there anything else?" I asked.

"No, that will do, thank you."

Hall came running over, his face beaming, and with the air of a man who has just hooked a particularly cunning old trout.

"Ah!" he exclaimed, "this has been a great success! I could almost dispense with the calculation, but it is best to be sure."

"What are you about, anyhow?" I asked, "and what was it that happened to the kite?"

"Don't interrupt me just now, please," was the only reply I received.

Thereupon my friend sat down on a rock, pulled out a pad of paper, noted the angles which I had read on the transit, and fell to figuring with feverish haste. In the course of his work he consulted a pocket almanac, then glanced up at the sky, muttered approvingly, and finally leaped to his feet with a half-suppressed "Hurrah!" If I had not known him so well I should have thought that he had gone daft.

"Will you kindly tell me," I asked, "how you managed to set the kite afire?"

Hall laughed heartily. "You thought it was a trick, did you?" said he. "Well, it was no trick, but a very beautiful demonstration. You surely haven't forgotten the scarlet tanager that gave you such a surprise the day before yesterday."

"Do you mean," I exclaimed, startled at the suggestion, "that the fate of the bird had any connection with the accident to your kite?"

"Accident isn't precisely the right word," replied Hall. "The two things are as intimately related as own brothers. If you should care to hunt up the kite sticks, you would find that they, too, are now artemisium plated."

"This is getting too deep for me," was all that I could say.

"I am not absolutely confident that I have touched bottom myself," said Hall, "but I'm going to make another dive, and if I don't bring up treasures greater than Vanderdecken found at the bottom of the sea, then Dr. Syx is even a more wonderful human mystery than I have thought him to be."

"What do you propose to do next?"

"To shake the dust of the Grand Teton from my shoes and go to San Francisco, where I have an extensive laboratory."

"So you are going to try a little alchemy yourself, are you?"

"Perhaps; who knows? At any rate, my good friend, I am forever indebted to you for your assistance, and even more for your discretion, and if I succeed you shall be the first person in the world to hear the news."

XII
BETTER THAN ALCHEMY

I come now to a part of my narrative which would have been deemed altogether incredible in those closing years of the nineteenth century that witnessed the first steps towards the solution of the deepest mysteries of the ether, although men even then held in their hands, without knowing it, powers which, after they had been mastered and before use had made them familiar, seemed no less than godlike.

For six months after Hall's departure for San Francisco I heard nothing from him. Notwithstanding my intense desire to know what he was doing, I did not seek to disturb him in his retirement. In the meantime things ran on as usual in the world, only a ripple being caused by renewed discoveries of small nuggets of artemisium on the Tetons, a fact which recalled to my mind the remark of my friend when he dislodged a flake of the metal from a crevice during our ascent of the peak. At last one day I received this telegram at my office in New York:

"SAN FRANCISCO, MAY 16, 1940.
"COME AT ONCE. THE MYSTERY IS SOLVED.
"(SIGNED) HALL."

As soon as I could pack a grip I was flying westward one hundred miles an hour. On reaching San Francisco, which had made enormous strides since the opening of the twentieth century, owing to the extension of our Oriental possessions, and which already ranked with New York and Chicago among the financial capitals of the world, I hastened to Hall's laboratory. He was there expecting me, and, after a hearty greeting, during which his elation over his success was manifest, he said:

"I am compelled to ask you to make a little journey. I found it impossible to secure the necessary privacy here, and, before opening my experiments, I selected a site for a new laboratory in an unfrequented spot among the mountains this side of Lake Tahoe. You will be the first man, with the exception of my two devoted assistants, to see my apparatus, and you shall share the sensation of the critical experiment."

"Then you have not yet completed your solution of the secret?"

"Yes, I have; for I am as certain of the result as if I had seen it, but I thought you were entitled to be in with me at the death."

From the nearest railway station we took horses to the laboratory, which occupied a secluded but most beautiful site at an elevation of about six thousand feet above sea-level. With considerable surprise I noticed a building surmounted with a dome, recalling what we had seen from the Grand Teton on the roof of Dr. Syx's mill. Hall, observing my look, smiled significantly, but said nothing. The laboratory proper occupied a smaller building adjoining the domed structure. Hall led the way into an apartment having but a single door and illuminated by a skylight.

"This is my sanctum sanctorum," he said, "and you are the first outsider to enter it. Seat yourself comfortably while I proceed to unveil a little corner of the artemisium mystery."

Near one end of the room, which was about thirty feet in length, was a table, on which lay a glass tube about two inches in diameter and thirty inches long. In the farther end of the tube gleamed a lump of yellow metal, which I took to be gold. Hall and I were seated near another table about twenty-five feet distant from the tube, and on this table was an apparatus furnished with a concave mirror, whose optical axis was directed towards the tube. It occurred to me at once that this apparatus would be suitable for experimenting with electric waves. Wires ran from it to the floor, and in the cellar beneath was audible the beating of an engine. My companion made an adjustment or two, and then remarked:

"Now, keep your eyes on the lump of gold in the farther end of the tube yonder. The tube is exhausted of air, and I am about to concentrate upon the gold an intense electric influence, which will have the effect of making it a kind of kathode pole. I only use this term for the sake of illustration. You will recall that as long ago as the days of Crookes it was known that a kathode in an exhausted tube would project particles, or atoms, of its substance away in straight lines. Now watch!"

I fixed my attention upon the gold, and presently saw it enveloped in a most beautiful violet light. This grew more intense, until, at times, it was blinding, while, at the same moment, the interior of the tube seemed to have become charged with a luminous vapour of a delicate pinkish hue.

"Watch! Watch!" said Hall. "Look at the nearer end of the tube!"

"Why, it is becoming coated with gold!" I exclaimed.

He smiled, but made no reply. Still the strange process continued. The pink vapour became so dense that the lump of gold was no longer visible, although the eye of violet light glared piercingly through the coloured fog. Every second the deposit of metal, shining like a mirror, increased, until suddenly there came a curious whistling sound. Hall, who had been adjusting the mirror, jerked away his hand and gave it a flip, as if hot water had spattered it, and then the light in the tube quickly died away, the vapour escaped, filling the room with a peculiar stimulating odour, and I perceived that the end of the glass tube had been melted through, and the molten gold was slowly dripping from it.

"I carried it a little too far," said Hall, ruefully rubbing the back of his hand, "and when the glass gave way under the atomic bombardment a few atoms of gold visited my bones. But there is no harm done. You observed that the instant the air reached the kathode, as I for convenience call the electrified mass of gold, the action ceased."

"But your anode, to continue your simile," I said, "is constantly exposed to the air."

"True," he replied, "but in the first place, of course, this is not really an anode, just as the other is not actually a kathode. As science advances we are compelled, for a time, to use old terms in a new sense until a fresh nomenclature can be invented. But we are now dealing with a form of electric action more subtle in its effects than any at present described in the text-books and the transactions of learned societies. I have not yet even attempted to work out the theory of it. I am only concerned with its facts."

"But wonderful as the exhibition you have given is, I do not see," I said, "how it concerns Dr. Syx and his artemisium."

"Listen," replied Hall, settling back in his chair after disconnecting his apparatus. "You no doubt have been told how one night the Syx engine was heard working for a few minutes, the first and only night work it was ever known to have done, and how, hardly had it started up when a fire broke out in the mill, and the engine was instantly stopped. Now there is a very remarkable story connected with that, and it will show you how I got my first clew to the mystery, although it was rather a mere suspicion than a clew, for at first I could make nothing out of it. The alleged fire occurred about a fortnight after our discovery of the double tunnel. My mind was then full of suspicions concerning Syx, because I thought that a man who would fool people with one hand was not likely to deal fairly with the other.

"It was a glorious night, with a full moon, whose face was so clear in the limpid air that, having found a snug place at the foot of a yellow-pine-tree, where the ground was carpeted with odoriferous needles, I lay on my back and renewed my early acquaintance with the romantically named mountains and 'seas' of the Lunar globe. With my binocular I could trace those long white streaks which radiate from the crater ring, called 'Tycho,' and run hundreds of miles in all directions over the moon. As I gazed at these singular objects I recalled the various theories which astronomers, puzzled by their enigmatical aspect, have offered to a more or less confiding public concerning them.

"In the midst of my meditation and moon gazing I was startled by hearing the engine in the Syx works suddenly begin to run. Immediately a queer light, shaped like the beam of a ship's searchlight, but reddish in colour, rose high in the moonlit heavens above the mill. It did not last more than a minute or two, for almost instantly the engine was stopped, and with its stoppage the light faded and soon disappeared. The next day Dr. Syx gave it out that on starting up his engine in the night something had caught fire, which compelled him immediately to shut down again. The few who had seen the light, with the exception of your humble servant, accepted the doctor's explanation without a question. But I knew there had been no fire, and Syx's anxiety to spread the lie led me to believe that he had narrowly escaped giving away a vital secret. I said nothing about my suspicions, but upon inquiry I found out that an extra and pressing order for metal had arrived from the Austrian government the very day of the pretended fire, and I drew the inference that Syx, in his haste to fill the order—his supply having been drawn low—had started to work, contrary to his custom, at night, and had immediately found reason to repent his rashness. Of course, I connected the strange light with this sudden change of mind.

"My suspicion having been thus stimulated, and having been directed in a certain way, I began, from that moment to notice closely the hours during which the engine laboured. At night it was always quiet, except on that one brief occasion. Sometimes it began early in the morning and stopped about noon. At other times the work was done entirely in the afternoon, beginning sometimes as late as three or four o'clock, and ceasing invariably at sundown. Then again it would start at sunrise and continue the whole day through.

"For a long time I was unable to account for these eccentricities, and the problem was not rendered much clearer, although a startling suggestiveness was added to it, when, at length, I noticed that the periods of activity of the engine had a definite relation to the age of the moon. Then I discovered, with the aid of an almanac, that I could predict the hours when the engine would be busy. At the time of new moon it worked all day; at full moon, it was idle; between full moon and last quarter, it laboured in the forenoon, the length of its working hours increasing as the quarter was approached; between last quarter and new moon, the hours of work lengthened, until, as I have said, at new moon they lasted all day; between new moon and first quarter, work began later and later in the forenoon as the quarter was approached, and between first quarter and full moon the labouring hours rapidly shortened, being confined to the latter part of the afternoon, until at full moon complete silence reigned in the mill."

"Well! well!" I broke in, greatly astonished by Hall's singular recital, "you must have thought Dr. Syx was a cross between an alchemist and an astrologer."

"Note this," said Hall, disregarding my interruption, "the hours when the engine worked were invariably the hours during which the moon was above the horizon!"

"What did you infer from that?"

"Of course, I inferred that the moon was directly concerned in the mystery; but how? That bothered me for a long time, but a little light broke into my mind when I picked up, on the mountain-side, a dead bird, whose scorched feathers were bronzed with artemisium, and sometime later another similar victim of a mysterious form of death. Then came the attack on the mine and its tragic finish. I have already told you what I observed on that occasion. But, instead of helping to clear up the mystery, it rather complicated it for a time. At length, however, I reasoned my way partly out of the difficulty. Certain things which I had noticed in the Syx mill convinced me that there was a part of the building whose existence no visitor suspected, and, putting one thing with another, I inferred that the roof must be open above that secret part of the structure, and that if I could get upon a sufficiently elevated place I could see something of what was hidden there.

"At this point in the investigation I proposed to you the trip to the top of the Teton, the result of which you remember. I had calculated the angles with great care, and I felt certain that from the apex of the mountain I should be able to get a view into the concealed chamber, and into just that side of it which I wished particularly to inspect. You remember that I called your attention to a shining object underneath the circular opening in the roof. You could not make out what it was, but I saw enough to convince me that it was a gigantic parabolic mirror. I'll show you a smaller one of the same kind presently.

"Now, at last, I began to perceive the real truth, but it was so wildly incredible, so infinitely remote from all human experience, that I hardly ventured to formulate it, even in my own secret mind. But I was bound to see the thing through to the end. It occurred to me that I could prove the accuracy of my theory with the aid of a kite. You were kind enough to lend your assistance in that experiment, and it gave me irrefragable evidence of the existence of a shaft of flying atoms extending in a direct line between Dr. Syx's pretended mine and the moon!"

"Hall!" I exclaimed, "you are mad!" My friend smiled good-naturedly, and went on with his story.

"The instant the kite shrivelled and disappeared I understood why the works were idle when the moon was not above the horizon, why birds flying across that fatal beam fell dead upon the rocks, and whence the terrible master of that mysterious mill derived the power of destruction that could wither an army as the Assyrian host in Byron's poem

"Melted like snow in the glance of the Lord."

"But how did Dr. Syx turn the flying atoms against his enemies?" I asked.

"In a very simple manner. He had a mirror mounted so that it could be turned in any direction, and would shunt the stream of metallic atoms, heated by their friction with the air, towards any desired point. When the attack came he raised this machine above the level of the roof and swept the mob to a lustrous, if expensive, death."

"And the light at night—"

"Was the shining of the heated atoms, not luminous enough to be visible in broad day, for which reason the engine never worked at night, and the stream of volatilized artemisium was never set flowing at full moon, when the lunar globe is above the horizon only during the hours of darkness."

"I see," I said, "whence came the nuggets on the mountain. Some of the atoms, owing to the resistance of the air, fell short and settled in the form of impalpable dust until the winds and rains collected and compacted them in the cracks and crevices of the rocks."

"That was it, of course."

"And now," I added, my amazement at the success of Hall's experiments and the accuracy of his deductions increasing every moment, "do you say that you have also discovered the means employed by Dr. Syx to obtain artemisium from the moon?"

"Not only that," replied my friend, "but within the next few minutes I shall have the pleasure of presenting to you a button of moon metal, fresh from the veins of Artemis herself."

XIII
THE LOOTING OF THE MOON

I shall spare the reader a recital of the tireless efforts, continuing through many almost sleepless weeks, whereby Andrew Hall obtained his clew to Dr. Syx's method. It was manifest from the beginning that the agent concerned must be some form of etheric, or so-called electric, energy; but how to set it in operation was the problem. Finally he hit upon the apparatus for his initial experiments which I have already described.

"Recurring to what had been done more than half a century ago by Hertz, when he concentrated electric waves upon a focal point by means of a concave mirror," said Hall, "I saw that the key I wanted lay in an extension of these experiments. At last I found that I could transform the energy of an engine into undulations of the ether, which, when they had been concentrated upon a metallic object, like a chunk of gold, imparted to it an intense charge of an apparently electric nature. Upon thus charging a metallic body enclosed in a vacuum, I observed that the energy imparted to it possessed the remarkable power of disrupting its atoms and projecting them off in straight lines, very much as occurs with a kathode in a Crookes's tube. But—and this was of supreme importance—I found that the line of projection was directly towards the apparatus from which the impulse producing the charge had come. In other words, I could produce two poles between which a marvellous interaction occurred. My transformer, with its concentrating mirror, acted as one pole, from which energy was transferred to the other pole, and that other pole immediately flung off atoms of its own substance in the direction of the transformer. But these atoms were stopped by the glass wall of the vacuum tube; and when I tried the experiment with the metal removed from the vacuum, and surrounded with air, it failed utterly.

"This at first completely discouraged me, until I suddenly remembered that the moon is in a vacuum, the great vacuum of interplanetary space, and that it possesses no perceptible atmosphere of its own. At this a great light broke around me, and I shouted 'Eureka!' Without hesitation I constructed a transformer of great power, furnished with a large parabolic mirror to transmit the waves in parallel lines, erected the machinery and buildings here, and when all was ready for the final experiment I telegraphed for you." Prepared by these explanations I was all on fire to see the thing tried. Hall was no less eager, and, calling in his two faithful assistants to make the final adjustments, he led the way into what he facetiously named "the lunar chamber."

"If we fail," he remarked with a smile that had an element of worriment in it, "it will become the 'lunatic chamber'—but no danger of that. You observe this polished silver knob, supported by a metallic rod curved over at the top like a crane. That constitutes the pole from which I propose to transmit the energy to the moon, and upon which I expect the storm of atoms to be centred by reflection from the mirror at whose focus it is placed."

"One moment," I said. "Am I to understand that you think that the moon is a solid mass of artemisium, and that no matter where your radiant force strikes it a 'kathodic pole' will be formed there from which atoms will be projected to the earth?"

"No," said Hall, "I must carefully choose the point on the lunar surface where to operate. But that will present no difficulty. I made up my mind as soon as I had penetrated Syx's secret that he obtained the metal from those mystic white streaks which radiate from Tycho, and which have puzzled the astronomers ever since the invention of telescopes. I now believe those streaks to be composed of immense veins of the metal that Syx has most appropriately named artemisium, which you, of course, recognize as being derived from the name of the Greek goddess of the moon, Artemis, whom the Romans called Diana. But now to work!"

It was less than a day past the time of new moon, and the earth's satellite was too near the sun to be visible in broad daylight. Accordingly, the mirror had to be directed by means of knowledge of the moon's place in the sky. Driven by accurate clockwork, it could be depended upon to retain the proper direction when once set.

With breathless interest I watched the proceedings of my friend and his assistants. The strain upon the nerves of all of us was such as could not have been borne for many hours at a stretch. When everything had been adjusted to his satisfaction, Hall stepped back, not without betraying his excitement in flushed cheeks and flashing eyes, and pressed a lever. The powerful engine underneath the floor instantly responded. The experiment was begun.

"I have set it upon a point about a hundred miles north of Tycho, where the Yerkes photographs show a great abundance of the white substance," said Hall.

Then we waited. A minute elapsed. A bird, fluttering in the opening above, for a second or two, wrenched our strained nerves. Hall's face turned pale.

"They had better keep away from here," he whispered, with a ghastly smile.

Two minutes! I could hear the beating of my heart. The engine shook the floor.

Three minutes! Hall's face was wet with perspiration. The bird blundered in and startled us again.

Four minutes! We were like statues, with all eyes fixed on the polished ball of silver, which shone in the brilliant light concentrated upon it by the mirror.

Five minutes! The shining ball had become a confused blue, and I violently winked to clear my vision.

"At last! Thank God! Look! There it is!"

It was Hall who spoke, trembling like an aspen. The silver knob had changed colour. What seemed a miniature rainbow surrounded it, with concentric circles of blinding brilliance.

Then something dropped flashing into an earthen dish set beneath the ball! Another glittering drop followed, and, at a shorter interval, another!

Almost before a word could be uttered the drops had coalesced and become a tiny stream, which, as it fell, twisted itself into a bright spiral, gleaming with a hundred shifting hues, and forming on the bottom of the dish a glowing, interlacing maze of viscid rings and circlets, which turned and twined about and over one another, until they had blended and settled into a button-shaped mass of hot metallic jelly. Hall snatched the dish away, and placed another in its stead.

"This will be about right for a watch charm when it cools," he said, with a return of his customary self-command. "I promised you the first specimen. I'll catch another for myself."

"But can it be possible that we are not dreaming?" I exclaimed. "Do you really believe that this comes from the moon?"

"Just as surely as rain comes from the clouds," cried Hall, with all his old impatience. "Haven't I just showed you the whole process?"

"Then I congratulate you. You will be as rich as Dr. Syx."

"Perhaps," was the unperturbed reply, "but not until I have enlarged my apparatus. At present I shall hardly do more than supply mementoes to my friends. But since the principle is established, the rest is mere detail."

Six weeks later the financial centres of the earth were shaken by the news that a new supply of artemisium was being marketed from a mill which had been secretly opened in the Sierras of California. For a time there was almost a panic. If Hall had chosen to do so, he might have precipitated serious trouble. But he immediately entered into negotiations with government representatives, and the inevitable result was that, to preserve the monetary system of the world from upheaval, Dr. Syx had to consent that Hall's mill should share equally with his in the production of artemisium. During the negotiations the doctor paid a visit to Hall's establishment. The meeting between them was most dramatic. Syx tried to blast his rival with a glance, but knowledge is power, and my friend faced his mysterious antagonist, whose deepest secrets he had penetrated, with an unflinching eye. It was remarked that Dr. Syx became a changed man from that moment. His masterful air seemed to have deserted him, and it was with something resembling humility that he assented to the arrangement which required him to share his enormous gains with his conqueror.

Of course, Hall's success led to an immediate recrudescence of the efforts to extract artemisium from the Syx ore, and, equally of course, every such attempt failed. Hall, while keeping his own secret, did all he could to discourage the experiments, but they naturally believed that he must have made the very discovery which was the subject of their dreams, and he could not, without betraying himself, and upsetting the finances of the planet, directly undeceive them. The consequence was that fortunes were wasted in hopeless experimentation, and, with Hall's achievement dazzling their eyes, the deluded fortune-seekers kept on in the face of endless disappointments and disaster.

And presently there came another tragedy. The Syx mill was blown up! The accident—although many people refused to regard it as an accident, and asserted that the doctor himself, in his chagrin, had applied the match—the explosion, then, occurred about sundown, and its effects were awful. The great works, with everything pertaining to them, and every rail that they contained, were blown to atoms. They disappeared as if they had never existed. Even the twin tunnels were involved in the ruin, a vast cavity being left in the mountain-side where Syx's ten acres had been. The force of the explosion was so great that the shattered rock was reduced to dust. To this fact was owing the escape of the troops camped near. While the mountain was shaken to its core, and enormous parapets of living rock were hurled down the precipices of the Teton, no missiles of appreciable size traversed the air, and not a man at the camp was injured. But Jackson's Hole, filled with red dust, looked for days afterwards like the mouth of a tremendous volcano just after an eruption. Dr. Syx had been seen entering the mill a few minutes before the catastrophe by a sentinel who was stationed about a quarter of a mile away, and who, although he was felled like an ox by the shock, and had his eyes, ears, and nostrils filled with flying dust, miraculously escaped with his life.

After this a new arrangement was made whereby Andrew Hall became the sole producer of artemisium, and his wealth began to mount by leaps of millions towards the starry heights of the billions.

About a year after the explosion of the Syx mill a strange rumour got about. It came first from Budapest, in Hungary, where it was averred several persons of credibility had seen Dr. Max Syx. Millions had been familiar with his face and his personal peculiarities, through actually meeting him, as well as through photographs and descriptions, and, unless there was an intention to deceive, it did not seem possible that a mistake could be made in identification. There surely never was another man who looked just like Dr. Syx. And, besides, was it not demonstrable that he must have perished in the awful destruction of his mill?

Soon after came a report that Dr. Syx had been seen again; this time at Ekaterinburg, in the Urals. Next he was said to have paid a visit to Batang, in the mountainous district of southwestern China, and finally, according to rumour, he was seen in Sicily, at Nicolosi, among the volcanic pimples on the southern slope of Mount Etna.

Next followed something of more curious and even startling interest. A chemist at Budapest, where the first rumours of Syx's reappearance had placed the mysterious doctor, announced that he could produce artemisium, and proved it, although he kept his process secret. Hardly had the sensation caused by this news partially subsided when a similar report arrived from Ekaterinburg; then another from Batang; after that a fourth from Nicolosi!

Nobody could fail to notice the coincidence; wherever the doctor—or was it his ghost?—appeared, there, shortly afterwards, somebody discovered the much-sought secret.

After this Syx's apparitions rapidly increased in frequency, followed in each instance by the announcement of another productive artemisium mill. He appeared in Germany, Italy, France, England, and finally at many places in the United States.

"It is the old doctor's revenge," said Hall to me one day, trying to smile, although the matter was too serious to be taken humorously. "Yes, it is his revenge, and I must admit that it is complete. The price of artemisium has fallen one-half within six months. All the efforts we have made to hold back the flood have proved useless. The secret itself is becoming public property. We shall inevitably be overwhelmed with artemisium, just as we were with gold, and the last condition of the financial world will be worse than the first."

My friend's gloomy prognostications came near being fulfilled to the letter. Ten thousand artemisium mills shot their etheric rays upon the moon, and our unfortunate satellite's metal ribs were stripped by atomic force. Some of the great white rays that had been one of the telescopic wonders of the lunar landscapes disappeared, and the face of the moon, which had remained unchanged before the eyes of the children of Adam from the beginning of their race, now looked as if the blast of a furnace had swept it. At night, on the moonward side, the earth was studded with brilliant spikes, all pointed at the heart of its child in the sky.

But the looting of the moon brought disaster to the robber planet. So mad were the efforts to get the precious metal that the surface of our globe was fairly showered with it, productive fields were, in some cases, almost smothered under a metallic coating, the air was filled with shining dust, until finally famine and pestilence joined hands with financial disaster to punish the grasping world.

Then, at last, the various governments took effective measures to protect themselves and their people. Another combined effort resulted in an international agreement whereby the production of the precious moon metal was once more rigidly controlled. But the existence of a monopoly, such as Dr. Syx had so long enjoyed, and in the enjoyment of which Andrew Hall had for a brief period succeeded him, was henceforth rendered impossible.

XIV
THE LAST OF DR. SYX

Many years after the events last recorded I sat, at the close of a brilliant autumn day, side by side with my old friend Andrew Hall, on a broad, vine-shaded piazza which faced the east, where the full moon was just rising above the rim of the Sierra, and replacing the rosy counter-glow of sunset with its silvery radiance. The sight was calculated to carry the minds of both back to the events of former years. But I noticed that Hall quickly changed the position of his chair, and sat down again with his back to the rising moon. He had managed to save some millions from the wreck of his vast fortune when artemisium started to go to the dogs, and I was now paying him one of my annual visits at his palatial home in California.

"Did I ever tell you of my last trip to the Teton?" he asked, as I continued to gaze contemplatively at the broad lunar disk which slowly detached itself from the horizon and began to swim in the clear evening sky.

"No," I replied, "but I should like to hear about it."

"Or of my last sight of Dr. Syx?"

"Indeed! I did not suppose that you ever saw him after that conference in your mill, when he had to surrender half of the world to you."

"Once only I saw him again," said Hall, with a peculiar intonation.

"Pray go ahead, and tell me the whole story."

My friend lighted a fresh cigar, tipped his chair into a more comfortable position, and began:

"It was about seven years ago. I had long felt an unconquerable desire to have another look at the Teton and the scenes amid which so many strange events in my life had occurred. I thought of sending for you to go with me, but I knew you were abroad much of your time, and I could not be certain of catching you. Finally I decided to go alone. I travelled on horseback by way of the Snake River canyon, and arrived early one morning in Jackson's Hole. I can tell you it was a gloomy place, as barren and deserted as some of those Arabian wadies that you have been describing to me. The railroad had long ago been abandoned, and the site of the military camp could scarcely be recognized. An immense cavity with ragged walls showed where Dr. Syx's mill used to send up its plume of black smoke.

"As I stared up the gaunt form of the Teton, whose beetling precipices had been smashed and split by the great explosion, I was seized with a resistless impulse to climb it. I thought I should like to peer off again from that pinnacle which had once formed so fateful a watch-tower for me. Turning my horse loose to graze in the grassy river bottom, and carrying my rope tether along as a possible aid in climbing, I set out for the ascent. I knew I could not get up the precipices on the eastern side, which we were able to master with the aid of our balloon, and so I bore round, when I reached the steepest cliffs, until I was on the southwestern side of the peak, where the climbing was easier.

"But it took me a long time, and I did not reach the rift in the summit until just before sundown. Knowing that it would be impossible for me to descend at night, I bethought me of the enclosure of rocks, supposed to have been made by Indians, on the western pinnacle, and decided that I could pass the night there.

"The perpendicular buttress forming the easternmost and highest point of the Teton's head would have baffled me but for the fact that I found a long crack, probably an effect of the tremendous explosion, extending from bottom to top of the rock. Driving my toes and fingers into this rift, I managed, with a good deal of trouble, and no little peril, to reach the top. As I lifted myself over the edge and rose to my feet, imagine my amazement at seeing Dr. Syx standing within arm's-length of me!

"My breath seemed pent in my lungs, and I could not even utter the exclamation that rose to my lips. It was like meeting a ghost. Notwithstanding the many reports of his having been seen in various parts of the world, it had always been my conviction that he had perished in the explosion.

"Yet there he stood in the twilight, for the sun was hidden by the time I reached the summit, his tall form erect, and his black eyes gleaming under the heavy brows as he fixed them sternly upon my face. You know I never was given to losing my nerve, but I am afraid I lost it on that occasion. Again and again I strove to speak, but it was impossible to move my tongue. So powerless seemed my lungs that I wondered how I could continue breathing.

"The doctor remained silent, but his curious smile, which, as you know, was a thing of terror to most people, overspread his black-rimmed face and was broad enough to reveal the gleam of his teeth. I felt that he was looking me through and through. The sensation was as if he had transfixed me with an ice-cold blade. There was a gleam of devilish pleasure in his eyes, as though my evident suffering was a delight to him and a gratification of his vengeance. At length I succeeded in overcoming the feeling which oppressed me, and, making a step forward, I shouted in a strained voice,

"'You black Satan!'

"I cannot clearly explain the psychological process which led me to utter those words. I had never entertained any enmity towards Dr. Syx, although I had always regarded him as a heartless person, who had purposely led thousands to their ruin for his selfish gain, but I knew that he could not help hating me, and I felt now that, in some inexplicable manner, a struggle, not physical, but spiritual, was taking place between us, and my exclamation, uttered with surprising intensity, produced upon me, and apparently upon him, the effect of a desperate sword thrust which attains its mark.

"Immediately the doctor's form seemed to recede, as if he had passed the verge of the precipice behind him. At the same time it became dim, and then dimmer, until only the dark outlines, and particularly the jet-black eyes, glaring fiercely, remained visible. And still he receded, as though floating in the air, which was now silvered with the evening light, until he appeared to cross the immense atmospheric gulf over Jackson's Hole and paused on the rim of the horizon in the east.

"Then, suddenly, I became aware that the full moon had risen at the very place on the distant mountain-brow where the spectre rested, and as I continued to gaze, as if entranced, the face and figure of the doctor seemed slowly to frame themselves within the lunar disk, until at last he appeared to have quitted the air and the earth and to be frowning at me from the circle of the moon."

While Hall was pronouncing his closing words I had begun to stare at the moon with swiftly increasing interest, until, as his voice stopped, I exclaimed,

"Why, there he is now! Funny I never noticed it before. There's Dr. Syx's face in the moon, as plain as day."

"Yes," replied Hall, without turning round, "and I never like to look at it."

THE SKY WOMAN

by Charles B. Stilson

I
FIRE

I am twenty-four years old, and—I may as well say it at the start—quite good to look at; that is, I have black hair, brown eyes, even white teeth, and a clear complexion, and they match up passably well. Also I am sure that I know how to wear my clothes to the best advantage, and am neither overgrown nor too tiny. I don't know why I mention these things, for they haven't much to do with what is to follow, though they are quite important to me.

It isn't necessary to tell that I know little about writing. Old Miss Dyver at Wellesley, it is true, used to compliment me upon my descriptive ability when I had her in English. But in the same breath she would waggle her flopsy pomp and deplore my lack of imagination. I believe that it was her opinion that it was a sin to possess so much and not the little more requisite to make a gifted writer—I mean imagination.

Miss Dyver was right. I can tell only what I have seen and felt. Nor am I the least bit scientific. I've had a course in domestic science—you needn't sniff at that— but of the things which terminate in "ology" I know next to nothing, and thank Heaven for it!

Yet here am I, Ruth Chasper, as I have introduced myself in three paragraphs, plunging recklessly to tell of what, viewed merely from its scientific side, is without doubt the most wonderful thing which has happened to the world since thinking, sometimes reasoning, women and men were set upon it to wonder why.

"*Yee-mahl Yee-mah! Alla ferma na somma!*"

The words will ring in my ears forever until I die! What do they mean? Who uttered them? What was she, and whence, and why? Will science in five thousand years more of groping and striving be able to answer? What cosmic secret might the interpretation of that wild, sweet cry lay bare? Or was it but a dying woman's wail of despair?

"*Yee-mah! Yee-mah! Alla ferma na somma!*"

No it could not have been despair. The creature was too utterly splendid and daring to have given way to it. She would not have yielded to despair, even when she realized that she had failed, and death was before her. It was not despair. It was an undelivered message—a broken link between two worlds.

So much I allow to my lame imagination. Now I will describe what has happened, though I cannot explain it. Rickey Moyer is my distant cousin, fourth or fifth. Rickey's father, D. B. Moyer, as a coal baron, turned a fearful lot of carbon into currency in the Pennsylvania Alleghanies, and then died and left Rickey alone to spend it.

Coal-grubbing never appealed to Rickey. He finished a course at Amherst, sold out the mines, and travelled. He seemed to have a consuming desire to know the world he was living in, and I guess that he has a speaking acquaintance with most of it. He should have; for he started out when he was twenty-one years old; and spent ten years globe-galloping.

Quite suddenly he came home again, two years ago, built him a bungalow in the forest on Black Bear Mountain above the old Moyer homestead in Centre County, and settled down.

With him—and this is where I come in —he brought Count Giuseppe Natali, of Florence. They had met somewhere in Borneo. Both were cosmopolites, both fearless. They had been through dangers together in the Dyak country, and had formed a friendship which stuck.

I met the count for the first time last summer at Palm Beach. Not to go into tiresome details, we soon became engaged. Count Natali is a thoroughly delightful fellow, a gentleman to his slender fingertips, and no fortune-hunter. Else he would not have picked me; for I've none to mention, unless Aunt Caroline—but that has nothing to do with it.

In January of this year Count Natali sailed to Italy to look after business connected with his ancestral estate. I understand that it is immense, and boasts, among other attractions, an ancient feudal castle which makes one think of that creepy old romance, "The Mysteries of Udolpho." On his return in early April, Rickey kidnapped him away from me in New York and took him off to the Pennsylvania wilds.

Soon afterward came an invitation to me to come out for a fortnight, bringing my chum, Carrie Andrews, with Aunt Caroline for chaperon. Carrie was of my class at college. We were both staying with Aunt Caroline at Bayonne.

All three of us thought that it would be a fine little outing—a sort of rest before the strenuosities of the summer season; so I at once wired Rickey that he was on. Naturally I wasn't sorrowful at the prospect of seeing Count Natali again so soon. I had felt that I had rather a bone to pick with Rickey for sequestrating my intended as he had.

Rickey's haunt on Black Bear is no end of a quiet roost; and yet there are plenty of possibilities to while away a couple of weeks, if one cares for them. There is excellent trout-fishing in Forge Run, if one doesn't mind wading in hip-boots and meeting an occasional rattlesnake. And there are a number of pleasant motor trips one can take, if one doesn't mind the rough roads and the hills.

I don't mind these things. I was born in Pennsylvania. So was Aunt Caroline, who isn't a bit fussy about such matters. As for Carrie: she is one of those big, slow-moving, non-excitable blond creatures, whom nothing ever seems to disturb. She who would encounter an earthquake or a boa-constrictor with the same casual interest she would bestow upon a new dance. Very like Rickey himself, Carrie is.

* * * * *

Late in the afternoon of April 17 we were deposited from the up-train at Viaduct, and saw the wooded spine of old Black Bear looming above us across the valley to the left of the tracks.

Viaduct is little more than a signal tower, a tank, a row of labourers' shanty-shacks, and ten houses—personally I don't believe there are ten; but I am a Pennsylvanian, and I give Viaduct the benefit of a doubt.

Count Natali met us with Rickey's roadster; but Rickey was not with him. Aunt Caroline and Carrie were comfortably discreet while the count greeted me—much more so than a thin-faced woman telegraph-operator, whom I saw watching us with avid interest from the height of her tower. Poor thing! How her eyes would have popped had she known that it was an honest-to-goodness Italian count who was kissing me, or perhaps she did know. Anyhow, she watched, and the proceeding seemed to have her approval.

My first reflection was that Count Natali both looked and felt much better without his mustache. The coating of tan which the spring sun was overlaying on his olive cheeks gave to his thin features the aspect of an Indian chieftain or a Bedouin sheik.

"A-hem!" said Aunt Caroline, after she and Carrie had swept the skyline of Black Bear for what she deemed a proper interval. "A-hem! And where is Richard?"

"Your nephew asked me to make his amends, Mme. Allison," replied Count Natali. "He was unavoidably denied the pleasure of meeting you this evening. We have had a trifle of excitement."

"Fire!" remarked Aunt Caroline, wrinkling her nose and sniffing. "I hope it destroyed nothing valuable."

"Not the bungalow!" I cried dismayedly. I, too, had noticed an acrid, wood-smoky odour about the count's clothes. "No," he answered our two queries; "only a few trees. I believe that it is now entirely under control. The railroad authorities sent a force of workmen up the mountain to help us. I believe that is their custom—to protect their property."

"*Umph!* I suppose a spark from one of their engines started it, as usual," commented Aunt Caroline.

"Not so; nothing so prosaic." Count Natali shook his handsome head. "It was a very unusual fire; in fact, quite an extraordinary occurrence."

He turned to lead the way to the car.

This began to smack of a mystery. I could see that the count was covertly excited, and I began to feel the thrill of an adventure.

A second later we were in the car, and discussion of the fire for the time was ended. The count manages a car prettily. He whirled us up the zigzag road to the summit of Black Bear.

Rickey and the count had been roughing it; but in deference to our coming Rickey had imported servants up from the big house below, including Mrs. Sanders, a cook whom Aunt Caroline had tried vainly to bribe from his service; so we found everything that three famished and train-weary wights could desire.

II
THE MYSTERY-STONE

No Rickey was waiting for us at the bungalow. He did not come in until we were taking our places at table. When he did put in an appearance he was in such a scandalous condition that I positively was ashamed of him. His tawny hair was all topsyturvy and dark with dust, and his khakis and puttees were smeared with soot and mud, not to mention a black streak across the bridge of his short nose, and numerous holes which flying embers had scorched through his shirt and trousers.

He did not contrast at all favourably with Count Natali, who is always perfection in his get-up. Though, in spite of the dirt and disarray, Rickey still contrived to look cool and efficient.

"Hello, Aunt Caroline and folkses all," was his welcome. He slipped into a chair, and as soon as decency would permit began to eat like a hungry and hurried man.

Have I said that Rickey is a big fellow? No? He is—big and blond and ruddy, with small blue eyes above high cheek-bones—not piggish eyes, but friendly and twinkly, and not a little shrewd, seeing that he inherited them from the coal baron.

"Glad you came, Ruth," he said to me presently. "Joe"—so he always referred to Count Giuseppe—"has been pining. I had to send for you or the blue devils would have got him sure. He's been as disconsolate as a bushman who's lost his fetish."

Naturally I had nothing to say to this. Aunt Caroline charged to the rescue. She had been studying Rickey sharply.

"Please don't talk nonsense, Richard," she cut in. "Tell us about the fire. You look as though you had been rolled in it."

"Oh, yes, the fire," responded Rickey, who had been talking off the top of his mind and thinking hard about something else deeper down.

He glanced at Count Natali, and I think that the count shook his head.

"Well?" from Aunt Caroline.

"Well," echoed Rickey, "we had one, aunty. It was some fire, too, I'll inform the universe, while-it lasted, and now it's out."

A prodigious bite of Mrs. Sanders' homemade biscuit interrupted communication. I could hear Aunt Caroline's toe tapping. Count Natali bridged the gap with questions about our trip. But Aunt Caroline, like an elephant, refused to take the bridge.

"What started it?" she pursued, wading in.

"That's what twoscore men have been labouring all day to discover, aunty," said Rickey tantalizingly. Just then I think that he became aware of Aunt Caroline's foot; for he muttered a hasty word to his biscuit; and at the same time hitched in his chair.

"We thought it was a falling star," he went on, freeing his utterance. "We've been grubbing an amateur coal-mine in the mountain on the strength of finding it and seeing what it's made of."

"I'm *sure* that is nothing to be so secretive about," declared Aunt Caroline.

"And did you find the star at the bottom of your mine?" asked Carrie.

"Yes," Rickey answered; "only it isn't a star." He turned his voice on Count Natali. "That section boss is interested, Joe," he said. "He has sent for an armful of dynamite. He wants to blast it."

"You surely will not allow that?" Anxiety, if not consternation, was in the count's tones.

"Not all in a chunk, anyway."

Aunt Caroline set down her teacup with firmness.

"Richard, will you have the goodness to inform us just what it is that you have found in the hole, which you will or will not blast, and why?" she demanded.

"A meteorite, aunty," replied Rickey, reduced to terms. "At least, by all the rules of the game, it should be a meteorite. It's a large one. The heat engendered by the friction of its hurried transit through our mundane atmosphere was what started the fire and led to its discovery."

"But why not blast it?" I asked, coming to Aunt Caroline's aid, as she had to mine. "Is it dangerous? Is it still too hot?"

"Why blast it at all?" queried Carrie.

Rickey appeared somewhat embarrassed, which in itself was unnatural.

"Joe and I may be a pair of blithering idiots," he returned; "but we are agreed that this star or meteorite or mystery—mystery, whether star or meteorite—is a very extraordinary proposition. It has—well, it has an uncanny sort of a" hand-made appearance."

Aunt Caroline drained her third cup of tea and set it down with a decision that threatened the china.

"Richard," she said, "your explanations are as clear as a Moshannon fog. The only portion of them which is understandable is your hint at your mental condition. How far from here is this phenomenon? I propose to see it before I close my eyes."

It was evident that this declaration relieved Rickey. He brightened up.

"Not more than a mile, aunty," he answered. "We can go the best part of the way in the car, and there will be a fine moon to see by. After you folks have looked the thing over will be time enough to diagnose my mental symptoms. It's either what it ought to be, and Joe and I are jack-donkeyed, or else it's one of the marvels of the ages."

"How intensely interesting you make it sound, Mr. Moyer," volunteered Carrie; and that ended the table conversation so far as concerned the meteorite.

I couldn't help being impressed by Rickey's manner. The mere fact that he was excited—and excitement fairly oozed from his pores—was impressive to one who knew him. But what was he driving at? How on earth could a meteorite be hand-made? What were we about to see up yonder on Black Bear by the light of the moon? If I had possessed a little more imagination, I am sure that I should have shivered.

* * * * *

Soon after our meal Rickey led the way to his touring-car, and the five of us piled in. We three women sat in the tonneau, which was already occupied by Frisky, Rickey's Skye terrier. Frisky, too, had been digging in the burned ground, to judge by appearances, and in his exuberance at seeing so many old acquaintances he insisted upon making a mess of our skirts.

Before we started Rickey fetched out from the bungalow an armful of blankets, which he hung over the robe-rail. As the night was quite warm, I wondered what he wanted of them.

We rolled off northwestward along the crest of Black Bear ridge behind the bungalow clearing, following a narrow, rutty old lumber trail which I remembered from having explored it as a child in search of arbutus, honeysuckle, and tea-berries.

After twenty minutes' driving, which the difficulties of the road made very slow, we reached the edge of the burned area. A grand moon had risen, and cast a peculiar light on the carpet of ashes which the fire had left, and against which the jagged stumps of broken trees and the scorched, distorted bodies of those still standing were limned in sharply defined silhouettes.

At intervals a light breeze set this arboreal cemetery to creaking and groaning lugubriously, and fanned our faces with an acrid warmth that was not of the night. Somewhere in the dusky distance a bird was clamouring for the immediate castigation of poor Will. Nearer at hand an owl hooted dolefully—doubtless mourning over having been burned out of her house and home in a hollow log.

"Isn't this delightfully spooky?" whispered Carrie, who would hobnob with a ghost with animation were the opportunity offered, and considered herself in luck. Aunt Caroline sniffed. Frisky yapped at the owl. I kept still and stared. I may be deficient in imagination, but I really did shiver a little. The picture was compelling.

Rickey halted the car.

He jumped out and shouldered his blankets.

We followed him across the soft, crisp flooring of the ashes.

Occasionally we passed smoking heaps where the breeze would stir the embers so that little spurts of flame leaped up and danced like elves of mischief over the destruction they had done. These were too far isolated from the main forest, Rickey said, to be accounted dangerous. Besides, watch was being kept.

In the centre of this desolation we found the cause of it, Rickey's mystery-stone.

Where it had fallen, in the slope of a little dip, or valley, was an ash-strewn pit, some twelve feet across, resembling those shell-craters which one sees in the war movies. Through the lower rim of it workmen with picks and spades had dug a deep trenchlike passage to the stone itself and then had undermined it so that it had toppled from its first position and lay along the trench.

At the bottom of the dip the ashes had been cleared away, and a brisk wood fire was burning, around which a number of men sat upon logs. These were part of the section gang which the railroad had sent up to help Rickey fight the fire. A strong aroma of coffee was grateful to our noses after their long struggle with smoke and soot.

A stockily built man of middle age detached himself from the group at the fire as we came over the edge of the dip. He approached Rickey, an Irish brogue issuing from his broad and exceedingly grimy countenance

"The dinnymite will be here directly, Misther Moyer," he said, removing his hat. "Shall we be afther crackin' her tonight, sor?"

His voice was eager. His men around the fire strained forward to catch the reply.

"Not tonight, Conoway; we'll do the job by daylight," responded Rickey. "The old railroad can spare a few of you for another day, can't it?"

"Yis—I suppose," assented Mr. Conoway, evidently disappointed.

"You told your man to fetch drills?" pursued Rickey.

"Oh, yis, sor. Ye're sthill daycided to bust her open wid pops, sor?"

"Yes. If there should happen to be anything inside worth looking at, we want to injure it as little as possible. Fetch up a torch or two, will you, Conoway? I want to exhibit our find to the ladies."

We stepped around to the mouth of the passage and looked at the mystery. And I am afraid were not, at first sight, particularly impressed. At least, I was not, save by its size.

It was a monster of a stone, all of fifteen feet long, and at its middle, where its girth was greatest, as thick through as the height of a tall man. I didn't wonder at the great hole it had torn in the earth when it struck, or the depth to which it had penetrated. The bottom of the socket from which it had been tipped was nearly on a level with the floor of the dip. The impact, I thought, must have jarred a considerable portion of the mountain.

* * * * *

Against the newly turned earth of the excavation it contrasted darkly. Its surface must recently have been molten. I touched it with my fingers, and it still was warm. Small stones, gravel, and clods of scorched earth were encrusted in it like gipsy settings. The upper end of it as it lay, which had struck first was splayed out and blunted.

Three of Mr. Conoway's men fetched pine-knot torches and flashed their light into the passage and the pit. I found the glamour of the thing grow upon me. Even a weak imagination was stirred to ponderings.

It lay in the trough of the trench with the wavering torchlight flickering over it, a dull-brown, sombre, sullen, inert mass of stone. Yet it was not of our world.

It was material evidence of other worlds beyond our ken. To me astronomy and kindred sciences had appealed as largely guess work. Here was evidence that the stars were more than mere watchlights set to brighten our dark ways. Whence had it come, this unearthly visitant? Next to our awe of time is our awe of distance. How many millions of miles had it fallen? The thought dizzied me.

"Isn't it fortunate that it did not strike upon rock instead of earth?" said Carrie, pointing to its jammed and misshapen tip.

"Would have been one grand smash, and nothing left but flinders,", remarked Rickey. "I shouldn't have cared to have been riding in it at the time."

"Nonsense!" ejaculated Aunt Caroline, prodding at it with her toes. "What is there about it to give you such ideas? Why do you suppose that something may be inside of it?"

Count Natali took a torch from a labourer's hand.

"But see, *madame*," he urged, stepping into the trench to the head of the stone. "And do you come hither, too, *carissima*" —this to me—"and Mlle. Andrews, and see."

I followed until I could peer over his stooping shoulder. Aunt Caroline and Carrie squeezed in on the other side. We stared where he pointed.

"I see nothing, except that it has been broken," said Aunt Caroline, readjusting her slipping spectacles.

"Yes, *madame*; a fragment has been chipped away by a hammer-blow. Now watch closely."

He moved one of his slender fingers along the fresh scar, tracing a zigzag pattern. Looking closely, we could then see a darker line in the substance of the rock.

"It looks like an irregular seam—a suture," remarked Carrie, who won honours in physiology.

"It may be only a vein in the rock," suggested Aunt Caroline; but her scepticism was shaky.

"Too regular, aunty," countered Rickey. "It's a joint, and a devilish clever one, and it's closed with some kind of cement that is harder than adamant. What do you say, Conoway?"

"The same as I did at first, sor," the Irishman answered. "There's something inside of that there that somewan put there for to stay, sor. Unless the bodies up yon are gunnin' for us down here, an' their projacktul didn't go off." Conoway pointed toward the stars.

"No, I don't think it's a heavenly 'dud,'" laughed Rickey, and added soberly, "but just the same someone up there may have fired it."

"I am going home and going to bed," announced Aunt Caroline, backing out of the trench.

"Joe will drive you girls back," said Rickey.

"What are you going to do?" asked aunt.

"Sleep by it." Rickey tumbled his blankets into the trench. "Some of these chaps here have it in their heads that this stone is a kind of wandering treasure chest full of diamonds and gold, and that they've only to crack it to see 'em come pouring out. I'm going to guard against anything premature."

"All right," Aunt Caroline assented. "Don't you dare to open that thing, Richard, until I am here in the morning. I shall get up at half-past eight."

"Right-o, aunty. If anyone tries to dynamite it before you get on the job he'll have to blow me to glory along with it."

"In which case you might find out where it came from and why," said Carrie. On the way back to the bungalow she asked, "What did Mr. Conoway mean by 'pops', I wonder?"

"It is that they will drill the stone full of small holes, mademoiselle," explained Count Natali, "and explode the dynamite in light charges, chipping away the stone a fraction at a time."

III
WHAT THE STONE CONTAINED

Less prepossessing, but more mystery-laden, was the big stone by the light of next morning's sun. We arrived at the scene of operations shortly after nine o'-clock. Aunt Caroline having made the concession of rising earlier than she had promised. The preparations for blasting were in full swing.

Three power-drills had been lugged up the mountainside in the night, and six swarthy workmen were busy along the trench, attacking the surface of the stone with an uproar which must have resembled a continuous volley of machine guns. A dozen others were waiting to spell them. The balance of the fire-fighting force, much against their inclinations, had been herded down the mountain by Mr. Conoway to less interesting employment.

I noticed that all of the labourers, with the exception of the Irishman, treated Count Natali with an obsequious deference, rather strange to an American, until one reflected that most of them probably were Italians, and the others from lands where counts count for more than they do here.

Viewed by daylight, the irregular line in the substance of the stone which had been disclosed by the hammer-blow, and which Carrie had dubbed a suture, was even more noticeable than it had been under the torches. Count Natali found us a position near the rim of the little amphitheatre, from where we could watch the proceedings safely, and where we could talk undisturbed by the clattering, popping drills, which made conversation in their immediate vicinity an impossibility.

Presently came Rickey, dirtier and more elated than ever, to announce:

"We'll be blasting in another half hour. We've been at her since sun-up." Aunt Caroline, who had once more inspected the odd, jointlike appearance of the stone, was disposed to argue.

"Isn't it quite possible, Richard, that it is something let fall from an airplane?" she asked. "These aviators are becoming as careless as motorists."

From the corners of her eyes she glanced in the direction of Count Natali.

"Considering that it must weigh all of twenty tons, I'm afraid that your suggestion is hardly tenable, aunty," replied Rickey, his eyes twinkling. "Aviators don't carry such pebbles around for ballast."

"Some time ago I read in the newspapers that attempts were to be made to signal to Mars at about this time. Mightn't it be that this is some sort of a Jules Verne projectile, which has been fired from earth, and fallen back?"

This was from Carrie. Aunt Caroline gave her an approving look.

Rickey smiled and went down among the workmen. What a big, capable fellow he was! Mr. Conoway, who cared nothing for counts, was, in his Irish way, as deferential to Rickey as were the others to the nobleman.

* * * * *

Soon after the expiration of the half hour the clamour of the drills ceased. They had pecked a neat double row of holes along the upper side of the stone. One by one the holes were charged with dynamite, and the explosive set off from a hand battery. They cracked like big firecrackers. At each explosion a shower of fragments flew up from the surface of the stone and fell around the lower part of the dip.

When the first row of holes had been blown out, Count Natali went down to inspect the work. From where we sat we could see that the stone was beginning to present a gnawed and ill-used appearance.

"Nothing at all," was the count's report as he came back.

An explosion of greater violence than any of the others followed.

After the crash there sounded a hissing like that of escaping steam. The labourers below ran toward the trench shouting.

Rickey thrust his arm recklessly into the opening. Then he called for a drillrod, which Mr. Conoway handed to him, and I saw its slender length disappear in the stone, and heard the clink of it as he groped around in the inside.

"Does he expect to find a rabbit?" Aunt Caroline murmured.

"It is that there is a cavity, and another stone is within," reported Count Natali. "It is very strange. It has the appearance of a sarcophagus." His fingers trembled as he stroked the place where his mustache had been. "I believe that it is a find."

"A mummy! That's not so bad!" exclaimed Aunt Caroline triumphantly. She had caught at the word sarcophagus. "I knew someone must have dropped the thing. They must have been hurrying it to some museum. Probably it will be advertised."

"How interesting if it is the mummy of a Martian," put in Carrie, not without malice, and drew a quick "Nonsense!" from aunt.

A number of blasts followed in rapid succession. The great stone seemed to leap and crumble in its bed. I shrieked; for several objects like coiled serpents flew into the air whirling, and one of them nearly fell on my foot.

Count Natali stooped down and picked it up.

It was a powerful metal spring!

Only a glance we bestowed upon it, and then stared down the hillside.

Where had been the long brown mass of stone was a heap of debris and earth fallen from the trench. Partly buried in the pile was a cylinder, more slender and shapely than its husk had been. Its surface was polished, and it reflected the light of the sun in a greenish sheen.

We arose and went down to it.

It was like a great coffin hewn for a giant. Whether it was of stone or metal we could not tell. In one spot a fragment had been chipped away by the blasts, and the fracture was scintillant with tiny particles which refracted the light vividly. At intervals the entire surface was pitted with sockets, for the springs which had maintained it centred in the interior vacuum of its shell. There had been many springs, nearly two hundred.

Mr. Conoway's workmen gathered about the trench, shouting, chattering and gesticulating. They were inclined to crowd us, until at a stern word from Count Natali they drew to one side.

I laid a hand upon the cylinder and shivered. It was chill as ice with an unearthly cold.

Aunt Caroline stared down at it and shuddered from other motives.

"What a godlike way to be buried," soliloquized Carrie. "To be hurled out through uncounted millions of miles of space and rest at last upon an unknown world!"

Aunt Caroline's "Nonsense!" was notably weak.

"Why do you folkses all take it so for granted that there's a dead one in here?' asked Rickey, clapping a hand on the cylinder and drawing it hastily away.

"Rickey!" I cried. "You don't mean to suggest that there may be something alive in there!"

"Well, and why not? Those chaps who were clever enough to shoot it across should know some way to preserve life for the few months necessary for the transit. I shall not be surprised to find the traveller in good condition and famously ready for his breakfast."

Months! Yes, Rickey was right about that. I hadn't reflected that it might take nearly a year for an object to fall from Mars to the earth, if this thing *was* from Mars.

"When is the opening scheduled to be?" Carrie inquired. "I am anxious to meet the gentleman; and he can't be very comfortable in that box."

"I should think that he, or it—if anything living was sealed in there—would be frozen," I said, thinking of the intense cold I had felt.

Count Natali in turn stooped and laid a hand on the sarcophagus.

"But that was the purpose of the vacuum space, *carissima mia*," he explained, oblivious of the stares which this endearment drew from his countrymen; "to provide an intervening coldness, so that what was within might not be destroyed by the heat which fused the surface of the stone. It is like a monster thermos bottle."

Aunt Caroline glanced from one to another of us in bewilderment.

IV
THE CRYSTAL CASKET

Our dark-skinned labourers, were waiting with unconcealed impatience to attack the job. Not for them were fanciful speculations as to where the strange object might have come from. To them it was a treasure trove, in which they possibly might share. At an order from Mr. Conoway they swarmed into the trench, and loose earth and stones began to fly. Rickey seized an extra spade, and his two great bronzed arms did double the work of the best of them.

Count Natali fetched the blankets down the slope and fixed another seat for us.

Before the trench was more than partially cleared we could see that a clearly marked line of junction extended lengthwise around the sarcophagus. Cover had been joined to body with great exactness, and only the thinnest of red lines indicated the presence of a cement. At intervals along the sides of the sarcophagus some manner of sockets, larger than those in which the spring had been fitted, had been sunk on the juncture line, and these too were filled with the reddish substance.

Rickey dug at one of them with the nail-file in his penknife.

"Hello; this stuff isn't so hard," he said. "Fetch some chisels, somebody, and we'll clear these places out."

Buried in the cement of each socket was a bent metal bar, or L-shaped handle, similar to those upon kitchen water-taps. Some of them were turned upwards and others down, but all were at right angles to the cement-filled line.

As the sarcophagus lay somewhat askew in the trench, crowbars were applied until it rested squarely upon its bottom. Then Rickey tightened a wrench upon one of the sunken handles and held it while Mr. Conoway struck it a smart tap with a hammer. It turned, slowly at first, and then more easily, until it stopped on a line with the cemented joint of the sarcophagus.

One after another all the handles were turned. Still the joint was firm. Under Rickey's direction an octette of workers set the blades of chisels and the points of their crowbars at intervals, along the line, and as many more men with hammers or pieces of stone struck upon them simultaneously.

A shout went up as the stubborn lid was seen to be yielding and rising. At just the right instant Rickey thrust a crowbar into the widening interstice, and pried with all his broad-shouldered might.

Lubricated by the soft cement, the huge lid moved almost without noise, balanced, swayed, toppled, and subsided with a *thunk* on the earth of the trench.

We three sprang up and rubbed elbows with the crowding men. But this, as was remarked by Mr. Conoway, was a particularly well-packed parcel. Nothing of its contents was to be seen save a mass of grayish, woolly-appearing stuff, so tightly wadded and compressed that it retained the imprint of the inside of the lid as though it had been modelling clay.

Only Mr. Conoway's bellows of restraint prevented the labourers from stampeding and making short work of this, to such pitch had risen their eagerness to lay bare the treasure.

"This is your package, boss," he said to Rickey. Rickey nodded, stuck his hands into the stuff and pulled out no great amount.

"Gee, it's rammed in tight enough!" he grunted, and attacked it again.

Curiosity moved Count Natali to take a wisp of the wadding, step back a few paces, and touch a lighted match to it. It refused to burn, or so much as scorch.

"*Huh!* The beggars know asbestos," commented Rickey, who had watched the operation. "Let your gang tackle this stuff, Conoway, if they're so blamed anxious."

"Aye, sor."

But they had understood, and did not wait for the Irishman's order. A score of muscular brown hands, reaching from both sides of the sarcophagus, seized the asbestos packing and tore it out. Among them was one pair of slender woman's hands, wrinkled and tremulous. Aunt Caroline, her habitual dignity for the moment in abeyance, was labouring to vindicate her theory, and took her pound of asbestos with the rest of them. The stuff came out in wads and layers. There seemed to be no end of it. Dust flew from it and choked us.

Count Natali pressed my arm.

"How excited we all are; is it not so, *carissima*?" he said.

His soft clasp hardened to a grip of iron, and I gasped with the pain of it.

"*Por Dio*" he whispered, and again, "*Por Dio!*"

Then for many seconds all our group was silent, and a quarter of a mile down the slope of Black Bear I heard plainly the splash and tinkle of Forge Run flinging itself endessly over a ten-foot fall.

For a great layer of the asbestos had come away in the workers' hands, and disclosed the contents of the sarcophagus.

As a newly-fallen icicle might lie embedded in a bank of rain-soiled snow, a crystal casket lay glittering against the bed of dull-gray asbestos which surrounded it, and within the casket's gleaming panels lay neither mummy nor man, but a woman with sun-gold hair.

Many authors have written that we of womankind are prone to see our sisters through cats' eyes and to judge them with prejudice and jealousy. That may be true; I won't argue it. But I, another woman, shall think always of the being who lay in that scintillant crystal casket as the most beautiful thing that ever came to earth. So poignant was the beauty of her that mere memory of it hurts.

No language which has yet been written can make one see the perfections of her—perfections of every line and contour of face and figure—and I am not going to make myself ridiculous by attempting to put the burden upon my English.

But she was a blonde of a blondness which made poor Carrie's type look dingy and scrubby by contrast. She lay easily upon a long cushion affair of soft, white material, which had been crinkled and padded around her until it fitted her as the satin of a jewel-case fits the brooch of pearls for which it was made.

It was difficult to believe that such a radiant thing could die; though I suppose that all of us who were staring into that crystal casket had no other thought than that she must be dead. The casket itself and all its trappings suggested death. But its inmate, by her easy posture, the bloom of her cheeks and the carmine of her lips, suggested slumber only.

Her costume is hardly worth mentioning. It was—well, what a fastidious woman might have chosen for a nap, and scant. Her hair flowed loose. She wore no jewels of any kind, not so much as a single finger-ring. But had she come to us bedizened with gems and arrayed like Balkis, she could never have impressed us as she did lying there in simple white in the white purity of her glittering crystal casket.

We stared, and were as still as she.

* * * * *

Oddly enough, it was Mr. Conoway who first broke our startled silence.

"Raymarkably well prayserved, isn't she, sor?" he said to Rickey, and removed his hat.

Count Natali's grip of my arm—the flesh bore blue fingermarks for days—relaxed, and with something very like an oath he caught up one of the blankets and threw it across the sarcophagus, hiding the casket from profaning eyes.

"Thank you, Joe," acknowledged Rickey, shaking himself as though coming out of a dream. He had not heard Mr. Conoway's first banality. The Irishman committed a second.

"Beloike wan of us had betther be afther notifyin' the coroner, sor," he remarked solemnly, and put on his hat again.

"I will attend to it, Conoway," answered Rickey, "depend upon it. Now, if I may impose upon you a bit more, I'll have your gang here give us a lift with that casket, and we'll take it over to the bungalow. We can sling it in the blankets over a couple of poles."

All this while not a word from Aunt Caroline or Carrie. I stole a peep at them. Aunt was weeping softly into her handkerchief. Carrie was lost in thought.

Mr. Conoway's labourers made a difficulty about complying with Rickey's request. When it turned out that there was no treasure in the sarcophagus, they, after their first surprise, experienced a rapid loss of interest, replaced by a superstitious fear of its contents. They refused to touch the crystal case, until Count Natali, exerting an influence superior to Mr. Conoway's threats, virtually compelled them to do it.

The count drove us slowly back to the bungalow. Behind us, Rickey followed, directing ten of the labourers, who, walking two and two, carried the casket in a blanket sling.

"Poor thing! Poor thing!" said Aunt Caroline, recovering speech. "I shall see her face to the day of my death. Don't talk to me about her, please. I'm very much upset, really."

We ate a subdued dinner, while the casket, swathed in blankets, lay upon the floor in Rickey's hunting-room, which looks north. Out of deference to Aunt Caroline's state of mind, we forbore reference to it during the meal.

Various as I suppose our views concerning it were, it exercised a fascination upon us all, and we were soon gathered around it again.

"I hope you will have her decently buried as soon as possible, Richard," said aunt, as, after another long look at the unworldly beauty of the occupant of the crystal case, she turned away, shaking her head sadly.

"Buried!" he echoed. "Not until I am sure that she is really dead."

Aunt's jaw fell. "Richard!" she ejaculated, "you're not—you're not going to—"

"I'm going to take the means necessary to be certain," he replied firmly. He knelt down and began to inspect the casket.

Count Natali made a pretence of assisting him—a pretence, I say; for it was patent that he could not keep his eyes from the woman.

Aunt Caroline seated herself on a divan and gazed fixedly out the window, her toes keeping up a ceaseless tattoo on the floor.

Moved by I do not know what impulse, Carrie went to Rickey's baby-grand in the corner, and began to strum mournfully in a slow minor key. I continued to stand by the head of the casket.

"Air tight, and perhaps soundproof," said Rickey at the end of ten minutes. "Here's some kind of a lever, which seems to connect through to a sort of tank arrangement inside, and there's apparently another lever inside here, near her shoulder. Shall I chance it, Joe?" He laid a hand on the outer lever.

The count nodded abstractedly, though I am sure that he had not sensed the question.

Rickey pressed the lever. His sleeve was turned back, and I saw the cords of his forearm bulge under the skin. The lever yielded noiselessly for an inch or more.

"There," he said, "now let's see what happens." Nothing apparently, not immediately. We waited for I suppose five minutes, though it seemed fifteen; Rickey squatted on his haunches, Count Natali kneeling, and I standing. I cried out sharply. I was first to see it—the flutter of a pulse in the neck. Before I could point out my discovery to the others, the woman's bosom heaved softly, and at once a tide of rich colour swept into her cheeks. She was alive!

V
THE VISITOR FROM THE SKY

Carrie and aunt had come at my cry. We stared down at this miracle in silence, and with swirling senses. Then Rickey swore softly to himself, and I think we were all grateful to him, even aunt.

"She is not dead, but sleeping," murmured Aunt Caroline.

"I'm going to waken her," said Rickey.

With the handle of his pocket-knife he struck upon the side of the casket, near the woman's head. The crystal rang like a bell under the blow. Aunt started violently.

"Richard! Stop that instantly!" she commanded. Really it did seem a fearful thing to do, but Rickey struck three times.

Mrs. Sanders, who could not have been far from the door, thrust her gray head through and asked if anything was wanted.

"You may bring tea, Sanders," replied Aunt Caroline weakly. Mrs. Sanders cast a horrified glance at the casket and withdrew.

The crystal had not ceased to vibrate under Rickey's last blow when the woman within stirred; a change of expression passed across her features, and she opened her eyes. They were black as night, when I had thought that they would have been blue.

For only an instant her face retained the bewilderment of the newly-awakened; then the brain took command, and she looked up into Count Natali's face and smiled. I heard him catch his breath with a gasp, and he bent nearer the casket.

She seemed to see only him of all of us, and as if in response to his involuntary movement, her hands crept up until they came in contact with the crystal lid of her prison.

The feel of it touched the spring of memory. She flashed a glance at the rest of us, and her wonderful eyes widened. Groping at her shoulder with one hand, she pressed the lever which Rickey had discovered there. It released hidden springs, or else there was a pressure of gas within the narrow chamber. The lid rose swiftly, discovering that it was hinged at one side, and fell over on the heap of blankets.

A puff of cool, choking atmosphere struck me in the face. I inhaled some of it, and it dizzied me. I reeled back and took hold of a chair for support.

The strange woman arose from her cushioned rest, and extending a hand to Count Natali for his aid, stepped out upon the floor.

One glimpse of her face I had before the catastrophe.

Asleep, she had been of supernal beauty; awake, her black eyes flashing, and her cheeks aglow, her face presented such a combination of intellect and passion as I have never seen or expect to see upon any other mortal countenance, fleshly or painted. Queenly is too weak an adjective to describe it, but it is the only one I can think of.

For an instant I saw her so, smiling as Count Natali bowed low before her. Then came a change, a terrible change. She had taken a step forward. Her mouth was open for speech, when I saw her glorious eyes go wide. She swayed, one hand clutching at her bosom, and the ripe colour faded in her cheeks.

Whatever weakness had come upon her, I thought at the moment she had overcome. She moved on toward the north door with a regal carriage, still holding Natali's hand, but she did not speak, and her face was like death.

At the doorway she paused and looked down the sunlighted slopes of Black Bear and up at the cloudless sky. A supreme triumph conquered the shadow of disaster in her face. Half turning, she let fall Count Natali's fingers, raised her white arms above her head, and cried in a voice like a silver bell:

"*Yee-mahl Yee-mah! Alla ferma na somme!*"

It was her swan song. Before the echoes of the marvellous voice had ceased to thrill us, she had collapsed, choking, into the Italian's arms.

We ran toward them and helped him to carry her to the divan, but all we could do was useless. In three minutes she was dead.

When that fact was sure we stood and stared stupidly. Natali hung over her, his face like that of a carven statue, the statue of a red Indian or a Bedouin sheik. From the instant when she had smiled into his eyes, for him, the rest of us had ceased to exist.

Our spell of sorrow and horror was broken by Mrs. Sanders, who bustled in with an armful of tea-things, sized up the situation, and fainted in a terrific clatter.

I recall hearing Carrie say, "I wish I could do that; I do really," and then my nerves would stand no more. Instead of turning to and helping them resuscitate Mrs. Sanders, I escaped to my room, and for more than an hour did battle with a round of hysterics.

When I was once more presentable. I found that Aunt Caroline had retired with a headache—I suspect that it was another name for what had ailed me—and Carrie had gone out for a walk in the woods.

Rickey and Count Natali were in the hunting room, my cousin sitting dejectedly upon the divan, and the count standing at the north doorway and looking down the mountainside. The crystal casket had again received its burden, and the blankets were over it.

"Well, I suppose there is only one thing to be done, Joe," I heard Rickey say as I came down the stairs, "and that is to do as the Irishman said, and call in the coroner. Then we will bury her."

"No; I beg of you to let me dispose of those arrangements," interposed the count earnestly, without turning from his stand.

"I know that you will not gainsay me, my friend. I will go down at once to the station. I have messages to dispatch." He stepped out without seeing me, and a couple of minutes later we heard him leaving in one of Rickey's cars.

Rickey caught sight of me and jumped up. I suppose that I must have looked woebegone, for he shook his head over me, and then managed to grin.

"I say, Ruth, old girl, let's you and I go out and walk it off," he proposed.

At the edge of the clearing we met Carrie coming in. Her eye-lids were swollen.

* * * * *

Rickey explained to me what he thought had happened. It was our air which had killed the strange visitor. The atmosphere of earth must be of a different quality from that at Mars.

"But I don't see how we could have helped it," he said. "She attempted a splendid thing, and failed. I feel like crying like a baby every time I think of the sheer pluck of her."

I did, too. It was as if a goddess had died, as Carrie said afterward.

I saw the sky woman only once more. It was in the night, that same night. I could sleep only in nervous cat-naps, and when I did I dreamed such fantasies that it was a relief to wake from them. Finally I gave it up, and put on a dressing-gown and sat at the window. There was a white moon and a silence, and I thought and thought.

At first my musings were disjointed and silly, evidenced by the persistent running through my mind of two lines of a rather vulgar old college ditty:

SING HO FOR THE GREAT SEMIRAMIS!
HER LIKE WE SHALL NE'ER SEE AGAIN—

which came to me, as such things sometimes will insist in our human brains upon intruding themselves among the sacrosanct and the sublime.

Truth to tell, contemplation of the events of the day gave me a touch of vertigo. The stupendous hardihood and daring of the sky woman overawed me. She could not have known that she would find human beings to release her, nor had she means to release herself; yet she had taken the thousandth chance, and had herself flung out through the space toward our world, gambling her life with magnificent recklessness.

Had she missed her mark, she might have fallen through infinity and eternity; perhaps been sucked into the vortex of some blazing sun, to perish like a moth in a candle-flame. All these things she had weighed, and still her splendid spirit had been undaunted.

Surely this was the supreme test of mortal courage, confidence and fortitude; or it was fatalism to its *n*th power. To die is less than she had offered. She had made the cast, and failed; and before the sheer splendour of her failure the most glorious human achievements that I could think of were dimmed. Columbus launching himself westward across unknown waters in his leaky caravels, was a puny comparison.

And no glory had offered, hot as we rate glory; she could not have returned to tell her people that she had succeeded.

An impulse grew strong upon me to go down to the hunting-room. I fought it, for I was afraid; but it conquered, and I stole down the stairs to take another look at the wondrous stranger. How glad I have always been that I did so!

The blankets had been thrown back from the crystal case, and the moonlight shone in through a window and gleamed and glittered frostily upon its translucent fabric and upon the beauty, now pallid and awful, of its occupant.

I paused upon the rug without the doorway; for the sky woman was not alone.

At the head of the casket sat, or rather crouched, Count Natali. His face was toward me, but he did not see me; his eyes were upon the dead. One by one, great, slow tears were trickling down his cheeks.

As I stood there, almost afraid to breathe, Rickey stepped in through the outer door. He too had been moved to night-wandering from his bed it seemed, for he was in his bathrobe. He saw Count Natali, and went to him and laid a hand upon his shoulder

"Come, Joe, old man, best go to bed," he said. "I cannot, my friend," Natali answered. "I must watch. Something has come to me that is tearing my heart to shreds. How shall I say it? I—" His voice broke, and he pointed to the casket and covered his face.

"I think that; I can understand, Joe," said Rickey very gently. "I am sorry."

I crept back upstairs and to bed. I too understood. I suppose that I ought to have felt jealous and horrid, but I didn't. I just felt very small and insignificant and lost.

Poor sky woman! Living or dead, I would not have fought you. Anyway, I couldn't have competed with a princess of the blood royal of Mars—and she must have been all of that.

In the morning Rickey took me for another walk in the woods.

"Joe has asked me to tell you something, little one," he began, facing me squarely, but speaking in an I'd-rather-be-hung-than-do-it manner.

"Then you needn't," I interrupted, "for I know what it is. I was at the door of the hunting-room last night, and I couldn't help overhearing part of it. And you needn't be compassionate, Rickey Mover, for somehow I can't seem to care as perhaps I should—and I'm glad—"

Maybe I leaned just the least bit toward him, he looked so big and strong and leanable. Anyway, his hand crept under my chin. I don't know what he saw in my tilted face; but next instant I was crying against his breast-pocket, and he was holding me comfortingly tight in his great arms and telling me that he had cared for me since we were small, "only somehow Joe seemed to have beat me to it."

So, you see, I have found compensation for what the sky woman cost me. Rickey and I are to be married soon.

And the sky woman? Count Natali had her embalmed in some marvellous Italian fashion and took her back to Italy with him. I often have a vision of him sitting in a moonlighted hall of his old Udolpho castle with his dead but imperishable bride, while the slow tears glisten upon his cheeks and fall upon her crystal casket.

PALOS OF THE DOG STAR PACK

by John Ulrich Giesy

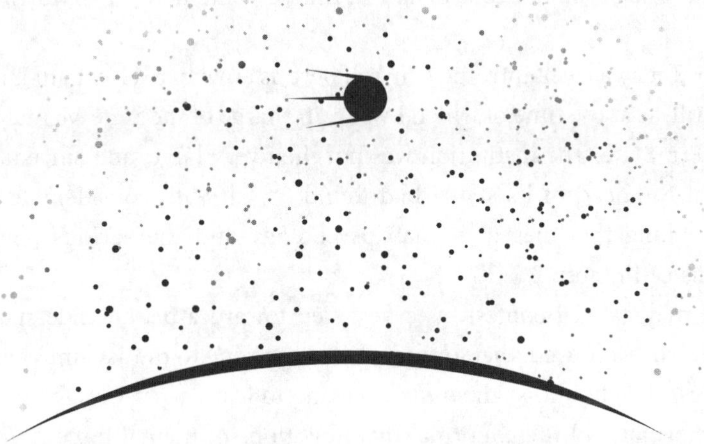

I
OUT OF THE STORM

It was a miserable night which brought me first in touch with Jason Croft. There was a rain and enough wind to send it in gusty dashes against the windows. It was the sort of a night when I always felt glad to cast off coat and shoes, don a robe and slippers, and sit down with the curtains drawn, a lighted pipe, and the soft glow of a lamp falling across the pages of my book. I am, I admit, always strangely susceptible to the shut-in sense of comfort afforded by a pipe, the steady yellow of a light, and the magic of printed lines at a time of elemental turmoil and stress.

It was with a feeling little short of positive annoyance that I heard the door-bell ring. Indeed, I confess, I was tempted to ignore it altogether at first. But as it rang again, and was followed by a rapid tattoo of rapping, as of fists pounded against the door itself, I rose, laid aside my book, and stepped into the hall.

First switching on a porch-light, I opened the outer door, to reveal the figure of an old woman, somewhat stooping, her head covered by a shawl, which sloped wetly from her head to either shoulder, and was caught and held beneath her chin by one bony hand.

"Doctor," she began in a tone of almost frantic excitement. "Dr. Murray—come quick!"

Perhaps I may as well introduce myself here as anywhere else. I am Dr. George Murray, still, as at the time of which I write, in charge of the State Mental Hospital in a Western State. The institution was not then very large, and since taking my position at the head of its staff I had found myself with considerable time for my study along the lines of human psychology and the various powers and aberrations of the mind.

Also, I may as well confess, as a first step toward a better understanding of my part in what followed, that for years before coming to the asylum I had delved more or less deeply into such studies, seeking to learn what I might concerning both the normal and the abnormal manifestations of mental force.

There is good reading and highly entertaining, I assure you, in the various philosophies dealing with life, religion, and the several beliefs regarding the soul of man. I was therefore fairly conversant not only with the Occidental creeds, but with those of the Oriental races as well. And I knew that certain of the Eastern sects had advanced in their knowledge far beyond our Western world. I had even endeavoured to make their knowledge mine, so far as I could, in certain lines at least, and had from time to time applied some of that knowledge to the treatment of cases in the institution of which I was the head.

But I was not thinking of anything like that as I looked at the shawl-wrapped face of the little bent woman, wrinkled and wry enough to have been a very part of the storm which beat about her and blew back the skirts of my lounging-robe and chilled my ankles. I lived in a residence detached from the asylum buildings proper, but none the less a part of the institution; and, as a matter of fact, my sole thought was a feeling of surprise that any one should have come here to find me, and despite the woman's manifest state of anxiety and haste, a decided reluctance to go with her quickly or otherwise on such a night.

I rather temporized: "But, my dear woman, surely there are other doctors for you to call. I am really not in general practice. I am connected with the asylum—"

"And that is the very reason I always said I would come for you if anything happened to Mr. Jason," she cut in.

"Whom?" I inquired, interested in spite of myself at this plainly premeditated demand for my service.

"Mr. Jason Croft, sir," she returned. "He's dead maybe—I dunno. But he's been that way for a week."

"Dead?" I exclaimed in almost an involuntary fashion, startled by her words.

"Dead, or asleep. I don't know which."

Clearly there was something here I wasn't getting into fully, and my interest aroused. The whole affair seemed to be taking on an atmosphere of the peculiar, and it was equally clear that the gusty doorway was no place to talk. "Come in," I said. "What is your name?"

"Goss," said she, without making any move to enter. "I'm house-keeper for Mr. Jason, but I'll not be comin' in unless you say you'll go."

"Then come in without any more delay," I replied, making up my mind. I knew Croft in a way—by sight at least. He was a big fellow with light hair and a splendid physique, who had been pointed out to me shortly after my arrival. Once I had even got close enough to the man to look into his eyes. They were gray, and held a peculiar something in their gaze which had arrested my attention at once. Jason Croft had the eyes of a mystic—of a student of those very things I myself had studied more or less.

They were the eyes of one who saw deeper than the mere objective surface of life, and the old woman's words at the last had waked up my interest in no uncertain degree. I had decided I would go with her to Croft's house, which was not very far down the street, and see, if I might, for myself just what had occurred to send her rushing to me through the night.

I gave her a seat, said I would get on my shoes and coat, and went back into the room I had left some moments before. There I dressed quickly for my venture into the storm, adding a raincoat to my other attire, and was back in the hall inside five minutes at most.

* * * * *

We set out at once, emerging into the wind-driven rain, my long raincoat flapping about my legs and the little old woman tottering along at my side. And what with the rain, the wind, and the unexpected summons, I found myself in a rather strange frame of mind. The whole thing seemed more like some story I had read than a happening of real life, particularly so as my companion kept pace with me and uttered no sound save at times a rather rasping sort of breath. The whole thing became an almost eery experience as we hastened down the storm-swept street.

Then we turned in at a gate and went up toward the large house I knew to be Croft's, and the little old woman unlocked a heavy front door and led me into a hall. It was a most unusual hall, too, its walls draped with rare tapestries and rugs, its floor covered with other rugs such as I had never seen outside private collections, lighted by a hammered brass lantern through the pierced sides of which the rays of an electric light shone forth.

Across the hall she scuttered, still in evident haste, and flung open a door to permit me to enter a room which was plainly a study. It was lined with cases of books, furnished richly yet plainly with chairs, a heavy desk, and a broad couch, on which I saw in one swift glance the stretched-out body of Croft himself.

He lay wholly relaxed, like one sunk in heavy sleep, his eyelids closed, his arms and hands dropped limply at his sides, but no visible sign of respiration animating his deep full chest.

Toward him the little woman gestured with a hand, and stood watching, still with her wet shawl about her head and shoulders, while I approached and bent over the man.

I touched his face and found it cold. My fingers sought his pulse and failed to find it at all. But his body was limp as I lifted an arm and dropped it. There was no rigor, yet there was no evidence of decay, such as must follow once rigor has passed away. I had brought instruments with me as a matter of course. I took them from my pocket and listened for some sound from the heart. I thought I found the barest flutter, but I wasn't sure. I tested the tension of the eyeball under the closed lids and found it firm. I straightened and turned to face the little old woman.

"Dead, sir?" she asked in a sibilant whisper. Her eyes were wide in their sockets. They stared into mine.

I shook my head. "He doesn't appear to be dead," I replied. "See here, Mrs. Goss, what did you mean by saying he ought to have been back three days ago? What do you mean by back?"

She fingered at her lips with one bony hand. "Why—awake, sir," she said at last.

"Then why didn't you say so?" I snapped. "Why use the word back?"

"Because, sir," she faltered, "that's what he says when he wakes up. 'Well, Mary, I'm back.' I—I guess I just said it because he does, doctor. I—was worrit when he didn't come back—when he didn't wake up, to-night, an' it took to rainin'. I reckon maybe it was th' storm scared me, sir."

Her words had, however, given me a clue. "He's been like this before, then?"

"Yes, sir. But never more than four days without telling me he would. Th' first time was months ago—but it's been gettin' oftener and oftener, till now all his sleeps are like this. He told me not to be scared—an' to—to never bother about him—to—to just let him alone; but—I guess I was scared to-night, when it begun to storm an' him layin' there like that. It was like havin' a corpse in the house."

I began to gain a fuller appreciation of the situation. I myself had seen people in a cataleptic condition, had even induced the state in subjects myself, and it appeared to me that Jason Croft was in a similar state, no matter how induced.

"What does your employer do?" I asked.

"He studies, sir—just studies things like that." Mrs. Goss gestured at the cases of books. "He don't have to work, you know. His uncle left him rich."

I followed her arm as she swept it about the glass-fronted cases. I brought my glances back to the desk in the centre of the room, between the woman and myself as we stood. Upon it I spied another volume lying open. It was unlike any book I had ever seen, yellowed with age; in fact not a book at all, but a series of parchment pages tied together with bits of silken cord.

I took the thing up and found the open pages covered with marginal notes in English, although the original was plainly in Sanskrit, an ancient language I had seen before, but was wholly unable to read. The notations, however, threw some light into my mind, and as I read them I forgot the storm, the little old woman—everything save what I read and the bearing it held on the man behind me on the couch. I felt sure they had been written by his own hand, and they bore on the subject of astral projection—the ability of the soul to separate itself, or be separated, from the physical body and return to its fleshy husk again at will.

I finished the open pages and turned to others. The notations were still present wherever I looked. At last I turned to the very front and found that the manuscript was by Ahmid, an occult adept of Hindustan, who lived somewhere in the second or third century of the Christian era.

With a strange sensation I laid down the silk-bound pages. They were very, very old. Over a thousand years had come and passed since they were written by the dead Ahmid's hand. Yet I had held them to-night, and I felt sure Jason Croft had held them often—read them and understood them, and that the condition in which I found him this night was in some way subtly connected with their store of ancient lore. And suddenly I sensed the storm and the little old woman and the silent body of the man at my back again, with a feeling of something uncanny in the whole affair.

* * * * *

"You can do nothing for him?" the woman broke my introspection.

I looked up and into her eyes, dark and bright and questioning as she stood still clutching her damp shawl.

"I'm not so sure of that," I said. "But—Mr. Croft's condition is rather—peculiar. Whatever I do will require quiet—that I am alone with him for some time. I think if I can be left here with him for possibly an hour, I can bring him back."

I paused abruptly. I had used the woman's former words almost. And I saw she noticed the fact, for a slight smile gathered on her faded lips. She nodded. "You'll bring him back," she said. "Mind you, doctor, th' trouble is with Mr. Jason's head, I've been thinking. 'Twas for that I've been telling myself I would come for you, if he forgot to come back some time, like I've been afraid he would."

"You did quite right," I agreed. "But—the trouble is not with Mr. Croft's mind. In fact, Mrs. Goss, I believe he is a very learned man. How long have you known him, may I ask?"

"Ever since he was a boy, except when he was travellin'," she returned.

"He has travelled?" I took her up.

"Yes, sir, a lot. Me an' my husband kept up th' place while he was gone."

"I see," I said. "And now if you will let me try what I can do."

"Yes, sir. I'll set out in th' hall," she agreed, and turned in her rapid putter from the room.

Left alone, I took a chair, dragged it to the side of the couch, and studied my man.

So far as I could judge, he was at least six feet tall, and correspondingly built. His hair was heavy, almost tawny, and, as I knew, his eyes were gray. The whole contour of his head and features showed what appeared to me remarkable intelligence and strength, the nose finely chiseled, the mouth well formed and firm, the chin unmistakably strong. That Croft was an unusual character I felt more and more as I sat there. His very condition, which, from what I had learned from the little old woman and his own notation on the margins of Ahmid's writings, I believed self-induced, would certainly indicate that.

But my own years of study had taught me no little of hypnosis, suggestion, and the various phases of the subconscious mind. I had developed no little power with various patients, or "subjects," as a hypnotist calls them, who from time to time had submitted themselves to my control. Wherefore I felt that I knew about what to do to waken the sleeping objective mind of the man on the couch. I had asked for an hour, and the time had been granted. It behooved me to get to work.

I began. I concentrated my mind to the exclusion of all else upon my task, sending a mental call to the soul of Jason Croft, wherever it might be, commanding it to return to the body it had temporarily quitted of its own volition, and once more animate it to a conscious life. I forgot the strangeness of the situation, the rattle of the rain against the glass panes of the room. And after a time I began speaking to the form beside which I sat, as to a conscious person, firmly repeating over and over my demand for the presence of Jason Croft—demanding it, nor letting myself doubt for a single instant that the demand would be given heed in time.

It was a nerve-racking task. In the end it came to seem that I sat there and struggled against some intangible, invisible force which resisted all my efforts. I look back now on the time spent there that night as an ordeal such as I never desire to again attempt. But I did not desist. I had asked for an hour, because when I asked I never dreamed the thing I had attempted, the thing which is yet to be related, concerning the weird, yet true narrative, as I fully believe, of Jason Croft.

I had then no conception of how far his venturesome spirit had plumbed the universe. If I thought of him at all, it was merely as some experimenter who might have need of help, rather than as an adept of adepts, who had transcended all human accomplishments in his line of research and thought.

In my own blindness I had fancied that his overlong period in his cataleptic trance might even be due to some inability on his part to reanimate his own body, after leaving it where it lay. I thought of myself as possibly aiding him in the task by what I would do in the time for which I had asked.

But the hour ran away, and another, and still the body over which I worked lay as it had lain at first, nor gave any sign of any effect of my concentrated will. It had been close to ten when I came to the house. It was three in the morning when I gained my first reward.

And when it came, it was so sudden that I actually started back in my chair and sat clutching its carved arms, and staring in something almost like horror, I think, at first at the body which had lifted itself to a sitting posture on the couch.

And I know that when the man said, "So you are the one who called me back?" I actually gasped before I answered:

"Yes."

* * * * *

Croft fastened his eyes upon me in a steady regard. "You are Dr. Murray, from the Mental Hospital, are you not?" he went on.

"Ye-es," I stammered again. Mrs. Goss had said his sleep was like having a corpse about the house. I found myself thinking this was nearly as though a corpse should rise up and speak.

But he nodded, with the barest smile on his lips. "Only one acquainted with the nature of my condition could have roused me," he said. "However, you were engaging in a dangerous undertaking, friend."

"Dangerous for you, you mean," I rejoined. "Do you know you have lain cataleptic for something like a week?"

"Yes." He nodded again. "But I was occupied on a most important mission."

"Occupied!" I exclaimed. "You mean you were engaged in some undertaking while you lay there?" I pointed to the couch where he sat.

"Yes." Once more he smiled.

Well, the man was sane. In fact, it seemed to me in those first few moments that he was far saner than I, far less excited, far less affected by the whole business from the first to last. In fact, he seemed quite calm and a trifle amused, while I was admittedly upset. And my very knowledge gained by years of study told me he was sane, that his was a perfectly balanced brain. There was nothing about him to even hint at anything else, save his extraordinary words. In the end I continued with a question:

"Where?"

"On the planet Palos, one of the Dog Star pack—a star in the system of the sun Sirius," he replied.

"And you mean you have just returned from—there?" I faltered over the last word badly. My brain seemed slightly dazed at the astounding statement he had made—that I—I had called him from a planet beyond the ken of the naked eye, known only to those who studied the heavens with powerful glasses—farther away than any star of our own earthly system of planets. The thing made my senses reel.

And he seemed to sense my emotions, because he went on in a softly modulated tone: "Do not think me in any way similar to those unfortunates under your charge. As an alienist you must know the truth of that, just as you knew that my trancelike sleep was wholly self-induced."

"I gathered that from the volume on your desk," I explained.

He glanced toward Ahmid's work. "You read the Sanskrit?" he inquired.

I shook my head. "No, I read the marginal notes."

"I see. Who called you here?"

I explained.

Croft frowned. "I cannot blame her; she is a faithful soul," he remarked. "I can comprehend her worry. I have explained to her as fully as I dared, but—she does not understand, and I remained away longer than I really intended, to tell the truth. However, now that you can reassure her, I must ask you to excuse me, doctor, for a while. Come to me in about twelve hours and I will be here to meet you and explain in part at least." He stretched himself out once more on the couch.

"Wait!" I cried. "What are you going to do?"

"I am going back to Palos," he told me with a smile.

"But—will your body stand the strain?" I questioned, beginning to doubt his sanity after all.

He met my objection with another smile. "I have studied that well before I began these little excursions of mine. Meet me at, say, four o'clock this afternoon." He appeared to relax, sighed softly, and sank again into his trance.

I sprang up and stood looking down upon him. I hardly knew what to do. I began pacing the floor. Finally I gave my attention to the books in the cases which lined the room. They comprised the most wonderful collection of works on the occult ever gathered within four walls. They helped me to make up my mind in the end. I decided to take Jason Croft at his word and keep the engagement for the coming afternoon.

I went to the study door and set it open. The little old woman sat huddled on a chair. At first I thought she slept, but almost at once I found her bright eyes upon me, and she started to her feet.

"He came back—I—I heard him speaking," she began in a husky whisper. "He—is he all right?"

"All right," I replied. "But he is asleep again now and has promised to see me this afternoon at four. In the meantime do not attempt to disturb him in any way, Mrs. Goss."

She nodded. Suddenly she seemed wholly satisfied. "I won't, sir," she gave her promise. "I was worrit—worrit—that was all."

"You need not worry any more," I sought to reassure her. "I fancy Mr. Croft is able to take care of himself."

And, oddly enough, I found myself believing my own words as I went down the steps and turned toward my own home to get what sleep I could—since, to tell the truth, I felt utterly exhausted after my efforts to call Jason Croft back from—the planet of a distant sun.

II
A COUNTRY IN THE CLOUDS

And yet when I woke in the morning and went about my duties at the asylum, I confess the events of the night before seemed rather unreal. I began to half fancy myself the victim of some sort of hoax. I did not doubt that Croft had been up to some psychic experiment when his old servant, Mrs. Goss, had become alarmed and brought me into the situation. But—I felt inclined to believe that after I had waked him from his self-induced trance he had deliberately turned the conversation into a channel which would give me a mental jolt before he had calmly gone back to sleep.

I knew something of the occult, of course, but I was hardly ready to credit the rather lurid statement he had made. Before noon I was smiling at myself, and determining to keep my appointment with him for the afternoon, and show him from the start that I was not so complete a fool as I had seemed.

Hence it was with a resolve not to be swept off my feet by any unusual fabrication of his devising that I approached his house at about three o'clock and turned in from the street to his porch.

He sat there, in a wicker chair, smoking an excellent cigar. No doubt but he had recovered completely from the state in which I had beheld him first. He rose as I mounted the steps and put out a hand. "Ah, Dr. Murray," he greeted me with a smile. "I have been waiting your coming. Let me offer you a chair and a smoke while we talk."

We shook hands, and then I sat down and lighted the mate of the cigar Croft held between his strong, even teeth. Then, as I threw away the match, I looked straight into his eyes. And, believe me or not, it was as though the man read my thoughts.

He shook his head. "I really told you the truth, Murray, you know," he said.

"About—Palos?" I smiled.

He nodded. "Yes, I was really there, and—I went back after we had our talk."

"Rather quick work," I remarked, and puffed out some smoke. "Have you figured out how long it takes even light to reach the earth from that distant star, Mr. Croft?"

"Light?" He half-knit his brows, then suddenly laughed without sound. "Oh, I see—you refer to the equation of time?"

"Well, yes. The distance is considerable, as you must admit."

He shook his head. "How long does it take you to think of Palos—of Sirius?" he asked.

"Not long," I replied.

He leaned back in his seat. "Murray," he went on, staring straight before him, "time is but the measure of consciousness. Outside the atmospheric envelopes of the planets—outside the limit of, well—say—human thought—time ceases to exist. And—if between the planets there is no time beyond the depths of their surrounding atmosphere—how long will it take to go from here to there?"

I stared. His statement was startling, at least.

"You mean that time is a mental conception?" I managed at last.

"Time is a mental measure of a span of eternity," he said slowly. "Past planetary atmospheres, eternity alone exists. In eternity there is no time. Hence, I cannot use what *is not*, either in going to or returning from that planet I have named. You admit you can think instantly of Palos. I allege that I can *think* myself, carry my astral consciousness instantly to Palos. Do you see?"

I saw what he meant, of course, and I indicated as much by a nod. "But," I objected, "you told me you had to return to Palos. Now you tell me you had projected your astral body to that star. What could you do there in the astral state?"

He smiled. "Very little. I know. I have passed through that stage. As a matter of fact, I have a body there now."

"You have what—" As I remember, I came half out of my chair, and then sank back. The thing hit me as nothing else in my whole life had done before. His calm avowal was unbelievable on its face—impossible—a man with a double corporeal existence on two separate planets at one and the same time.

"A body—a living, breathing body," he repeated his declaration. "Oh, man, I know it overthrows all human conceptions of life, but—last night you asked me a question concerning *this* body of mine—and I told you I knew what I was doing. And I know you must have studied some of the teachings of the higher cult—the esoteric philosophies, if you will. And therefore you must have read of the ability of a spirit to dispossess a body of its original spiritual tenant and occupy its place—"

"Obsession," I interrupted. "You are practicing that—up there?"

"No. I've gone farther than that. I took this body when its original occupant was done with it," he said. "Murray—wait—let me explain. I'm a physician like yourself."

"You?" I exclaimed, none too politely, I fear, in the face of this additional surprise.

Croft's lips twitched. He seemed to understand and yet be slightly amused. "Yes. That's why I was able to assure you I knew how long the body I occupy now could endure a cataleptic condition last night. I am a graduate of Rush, and I fancy, fully qualified to speak concerning the body's needs. And—" he paused a moment, then resumed:

"Frankly, Murray, I find myself confronted by what I think I may call the strangest position a man was ever called upon to face. Last night I recognized in you one who had probably far from a minor understanding of mental and spiritual forces. Your ability to force my return at a time when I was otherwise engaged showed me your understanding. For that very reason I asked you to return to me here today. I would like to talk to you—a brother physician; to tell you a story—my story, provided you would care to hear it. Most men would call me insane. Something tells me you, who devote your time to the care of the insane, will not."

He paused and sat once more staring across the sunlit landscape which, after the storm of the night before, was glowing and fresh. After a time he turned his eyes and looked into mine with something almost an appeal, in his glance. In response, I nodded and settled myself in my chair.

* * * * *

"I'm not going to deny a natural curiosity, Dr. Croft," I said, since, to tell the absolute truth, I was anxious to get at the inward facts under-lying the entire peculiar affair.

"Then," he said in an almost eager fashion, "I shall tell you—the whole thing, I think. Murray, when Shakespeare wrote into one of his characters' mouth the statement that there are more things in heaven and earth than are dreamt of, he told the truth. Mankind in the main is like a crowd storming the doors of a showhouse sold out to capacity and unable to accommodate any one else. Mankind is the crowd in the lobby, shut out from the real sights back of the veiling doors which bar their perception of what goes on within. Mankind stands only on the fringe of life, does not dream of the truth. Only here and there is there one who *knows*. It was one such who first directed my mind toward the truth.

"Murray"—he paused and once more fastened me with his gaze—"I am going to tell that truth to you… . But first—in order that you may understand, and believe if you can, I shall tell you something of myself."

That telling took a long time; hours, the rest of the afternoon, and most of the following night. It was a strange tale, an unbelievably strange story. And yet, in view of what happened inside that same week, I am not sure, after all, but it was the truth, just as Croft alleged. What, when all is said, do any of us know beyond the round of our own human life? What do we know of those things which may lie outside the scope of our mental vision? There must be things in heaven and earth not dreamt of in the philosophy of *Horatio*. Here is the tale.

Jason Croft was born in New Jersey, but brought West at an early age by his parents, who had become converts to a certain faith. Right there, it seems to me, may have been laid the foundation of Croft's interest in the occult in later life, since that faith contains possibly a greater number of parallels to occult teachings than any of the Occidental creeds. Of course, in all religions there is the germ of truth. Were it not, they would be dead dogmas rather than living sects. But in this church, which has grown strong in the Western States, I think there is a closer approach to the Eastern theory of soul and spiritual life.

Be that as it may, Croft grew to manhood in the very state and town where I was now employed, and in the home on the porch of which we sat. He elected medicine as a career. He went to Chicago and put in his first three years. The second year his mother died, and a year later his father. He returned on each occasion, and went back to his studies after the obsequies were done. In his fourth year he met a man named Gatua Kahaun, destined, as it seems, to change the entire course of his life.

Gatua Kahaun was a Hindu, a member of an Eastern brotherhood, come to the United States to study the religions of the West. One can see how naturally he took up with Croft, who had been raised in one of those religions.

The two became friends. From what Croft told me, the Hindu was a man of marked attainments, well versed in the Oriental creeds. When Croft came West after his graduation, Gatua Kahaun was his companion and stopped at his home, which had been kept up by Mrs. Goss and her husband, then still alive. The two lived there together for some weeks, and the Hindu taught Croft the rudiments at least of the occult philosophy of life.

Then, with little warning, Croft was assigned on a mission to Australia by his church. He got a letter from "Box B," as he told me, smiling, knowing I would understand. The church of which he was a member has a custom of sending their members about the world as missionaries of their faith, to spread its doctrines and win converts to their ranks. Croft went, though even then he had begun to see the similarity between his own lifelong creed and the scheme of things held before him by Gatua Kahaun.

For over two years he did not see the Hindu, though he kept up his studies of the occult, to which he seemed inclined by a natural bent. Then, just as he was nearly finished with his "mission," what should happen but that, walking the streets of Melbourne, he bumped into Gatua Kahaun.

The two men renewed their acquaintance at once. Gatua Kahaun taught Croft Hindustani and the mysteries of the Sanskrit tongue. When Croft's mission was finished he prevailed upon him to visit India before returning home.

Croft went. Through Gatua's influence he was admitted to the man's own brotherhood. He forgot his former objects and aims in life in the new world of thought which opened up before his mental eyes. He studied and thought. He learned the secrets of the magnetic or enveloping body of the soul, and after a time he became convinced that by constant application to the major purpose the spirit could break the bonds of the material body without going through the change which men call death. He came to believe that beyond the phenomenon of astral projection—the sending of the conscious ego about the earthly sphere—projections might be made beyond the planet, with only the universe to limit the scope of the flight.

* * * * *

At times he lay staring at the starry vault of the heavens with a vague longing within him to put the thing to the test. And always there was one star which seemed to call him, to beckon to him, to draw his spirit toward it as a magnet may draw a fleck of iron. That was the Dog Star, Sirius, known to astronomers as the sun of another planetary system like our own.

Meantime his studies went on. He learned that matter is the reflex of spirit; that no blade of grass, no chemical atom exists save as the envelope of an essence which cannot and does not die. He came to see that nature is no more than a realm of force, comprising light, heat, magnetism, chemical affinity, aura, essence, and all the imponderables which go to produce the various forms of motion as expressions of the ocean of force, so that motion comes to be no more than force refracted through the various forms of existence, from the lowest to the highest, as a ray of light is split into the seven primary colours by a prism, each being different in itself, yet each but an integral part of the original ray.

He came to comprehend that all stages of existence are but stages and nothing more, and that mind, spirit, is the highest form of life force—the true essence—manifesting through material means, yet independent of them in itself. So only, he argued, was life after death a possible thing. And so, he reasoned further, could the mystery be solved, there was no real reason why the spirit could not be set free to roam and return to the body at will. If that were true, it seemed to him that the spirit could return from such excursions, bringing with it a conscious recollection of the place where it had been.

Then once more he was called home by a thing which seems like no more than a further step in the course of what mortals call fate. His father's brother died. He was a bachelor. He left Croft sufficient wealth to provide for his every need. Croft decided to pursue his studies at home. He had gained all India could give him. Indeed, he had rather startled even Gatua Kahaun by some of the theories he had deduced.

He began work at once. He stocked the library where I had found him the night before, with everything on the subject he could find. And the more he studied, the more firmly did he become convinced that ordinary astral projection was but the first step in developing the spirit's power—that it was akin to the first step of an infant learning to walk, and that, if confidence were forthcoming, if the will to dare the experiment were sufficiently strong—then he could accomplish the thing of which he dreamed.

He began to experiment, sending his astral consciousness here and there. He centred on that one phase of his knowledge alone. He roamed the earth at will. He perfected his ability to bring back from such excursions a vivid recollection of all he had seen. So at last he was ready for the great experiment. Yet in the end he made it on impulse rather than at any pre-selected time.

He sat one evening on his porch. Over the eastern mountains which hem in the valley the full moon was rising in a blaze of mellow glory. Its rays caught the sleeping surface of a lake which lies near our little city, touching each rippling wavelet until they seemed made of molten silver. The lights of the town itself were like fireflies twinkling amid the trees. The mountains hazed somewhat in a silvery mist, compounded of the moonrays and distance, seemed to him no more than the figments of a fairy tale or a dream.

Everything was quiet. Mrs. Goss, now a widow, had gone to bed, and Croft had simply been enjoying the soft air and a cigar. Suddenly, as the moon appeared to leap free of the mountains, it suggested a thought of a spirit set free and rising above the material shell of existence to his mind.

He sat watching the golden wheel radiant with reflected light, and after a time he asked himself why he should not try the great adventure without a longer delay. He was the last of his race. No one depended upon him. Should he fail, they would merely find his body in the chair. Should he succeed, he would have won his ambition and placed himself in a position to learn of things which had heretofore baffled man.

He decided to try it there and then. Knocking the ash from his cigar, he took one last, long, possibly farewell whiff, and laid it down on the broad arm of his chair. Then summoning all the potent power of his will, he fixed his whole mind upon his purpose and sank into cataleptic sleep.

The moon is dead. In so much science is right. It is lifeless, without moisture, without an atmosphere. Croft won his great experiment, or its first step at least. His body sank to sleep, but his ego leaped into a fuller, wider life.

There was a sensation of airy lightness, as though his sublimated consciousness had dropped material weight. His body sat beneath him in the chair. He could see it. He could see the city and the lake and the mountains and the yellow disk of the moon. He knew he was rising toward the latter swiftly. Then—space was annihilated in an instant, and he seemed to himself to be standing on the topmost edge of a mighty crater in the full, unobstructed glare of a blinding light.

He sensed that was the sun, which hung like a ball of fire halfway up from the horizon, flinging its rays in a dazzling brilliance against the dead satellite's surface, unprotected by an atmospheric screen. His first sensation was an amazing realization of his own success. Then he gazed about.

* * * * *

To one side was the vast ring of the crater itself, a well of unutterable darkness and unplumbed depth, as yet not opened up to the burning light of the sun. To the other was the downward sweep of the crater's flank, dun, dead, wrinkled, seamed and seared by the stabbing rays which bathed it in pitiless light. And beyond the foot of the crater was a vast irregular plain, lower in the centre as though eons past it might have been the bed of some vanished sea. About the plain were the crests of barren mountains, crags, pinnacles, misshapen and weird beyond thought.

Yes, the moon is dead—now. But—there was life upon it once. Croft willed himself down from the lip of the crater to the plain. He moved about it. Indeed it had been a sea. There in the airless blaze, still etched in the lifeless formations, he found an ancient water-line, the mark of the fingers of vanished waters—like a mockery of what had been. And skirting the outline of that long-lost sea, he came to the ruin of a city which had stood upon the shores a myriad years ago. It stood there still—a thing of paved streets, and dead walls, safe in that moistureless world from decay.

Through those dead streets and houses, some of them thrown down by terrific earthquakes which he judged had accompanied the final cooling stages and death of the moon, Croft took his way, pausing now and then to examine some ancient inscriptions cut into the blocks of stone from which the buildings had been reared. In a way they impressed him as similar in many respects to the Asiatic structures of today, most of them being windowless on the first story, but built about an inner court, gardens of beauty in the time when the moon supported life.

So far as he could judge from the buildings themselves and frescoes on the walls, done in pigments which still prevailed, the lunarians had been a tiny people, probably not above an average of four feet in height, but extremely intelligent past any doubt, as shown by the remains of their homes. They had possessed rather large heads in proportion to their slender bodies, as the paintings done on the inside walls led Croft to believe.

From the same source he became convinced that their social life had been highly developed, and that they had been well versed in the arts of manufacture and commerce, and had at the time when lunar seas persisted maintained a merchant marine.

Through the hours of the lunar day he explored. Not, in fact, until the sun was dropping swiftly below the rim of the mountains beyond the old sea-bed, did he desist. Then lifting his eyes he beheld a luminous crescent, many times larger than the moon appears to us, emitting a soft, green light. He stood and gazed upon it for some moments before he realized fully that he looked upon a sunrise on the earth—that the monster crescent was the earth indeed as seen from her satellite.

Then as realization came upon him he remembered his body—left on the porch of his home in the chair. Suddenly he felt a longing to return, to forsake the forsaken relics of a life which had passed and go back to the full, pulsing tide of life which still flowed on.

Here, then, he was faced by the second step of his experiment. He had consciously reached the moon. Could he return again to the earth? If so, he had proved his theory beyond any further doubt. Fastening his full power upon the endeavour, he willed himself back, and—

He opened his eyes—his physical eyes—and gazed into the early sun of a new day rising over the mountains and turning the world to emerald and gold.

The sound of a caught-in breath fell on his ears. He turned his glance. Mrs. Goss stood beside him.

"Laws, sir, but you was sound asleep!" she exclaimed. "I come to call you to breakfast an' you wasn't in your room, an' when I found you you was sleepin' like th' dead. You must have got up awful early, Mr. Jason."

"I was here before you were moving," Croft said as he rose. He smiled as he spoke. Indeed, he wanted to laugh, to shout. He had done what no mortal had ever accomplished before. The wonders of the universe were his to explore at will. Yet even so he did not dream of what the future held.

III
BEYOND THE MOON

And now the Dog Star called. Croft had proved his ability to project his conscious self beyond earth's attraction and return. And, having proved that, the old lure of the star he had watched when a student in the Indian mountains came back with a double strength. No longer was it an occasional prompting. Rather it was a never-ceasing urge which nagged him night and day.

He yielded at last. But remembering his return from his first experiment, he arranged for the next with due care. In order that Mrs. Goss might not become alarmed by seeing his body entranced, he arranged for her to take a holiday with a married daughter in another part of the state, telling her simply that he himself expected to be absent from his home for an indefinite time and would summon her upon his return.

He knew the woman well enough to be sure she would spread the word of his coming absence, and so felt assured that his body would remain undisturbed during the period of his venture into universal space.

Having seen the old woman depart, he entered the library, drew down all the blinds, and stretched himself on the couch. Fixing his mind on Sirius to the exclusion of everything else, he threw off the bonds of the flesh.

Yet here, as it chanced, even Croft made a well-nigh fatal mistake. It was toward Sirius he had willed himself in his thoughts, and Sirius is a sun. As a result, he realized none too soon that he was floating in the actual nebula surrounding the flaming orb itself.

Directly beneath him, as it appeared, the Dog Star rolled, a mass of electric fire. Mountains of flame ran darting off into space in all directions. Between them the whole surface of the sun boiled and bubbled and seethed like a world-wide cauldron. Not for a moment was there any rest upon that surface toward which he was sinking with incredible speed. Every atom of the monster sun was in motion, ever shifting, ever changing yet always the same. It quivered and billowed and shook. Flames of every conceivable colour radiated from it in waves of awful heat. Vast explosions recurred again and again on the ever heaving surface. What seemed unthinkable hurricanes rushed into the voids created by the exploding gases.

In this maelstrom of titanic forces Croft found himself caught. Not even the wonderful force his spirit had attained could overcome the sun's power of repulsion. His progress stayed, he hung above the molten globe beneath him, imprisoned, unable to extricate himself from his position, buffeted, swirled about and swayed by the irresistible forces which warred around him in a never-ceasing tumult such as he had never conceived.

Something like a vague question as to his fate rather than any fear assailed him, something like a blind wonder. The force which held him was one beyond his experience or knowledge. He knew that a true spirit, a pure ego, could not wholly perish, yet now he asked himself what would be the effect of close proximity to such an enormous centre of elemental activity upon an ego not wholly sublimated, such as his.

His will power actually faltered, staggered. For the time being he lost his ability to choose his course. He had willed himself here, and here he was, but he found himself unable to will himself back or anywhere else, in fact. The sensation crept through his soul that he was a plaything of fate, a mad ego which had ventured too far, dared too much, sought to learn those things possibly forbidden, hence caught in a net of universal law, woven about him by his own mad thirst for knowledge—a spirit doomed by its own daring to an eternity of something closely approaching the orthodox hell.

* * * * *

Through eons of time, as it seemed to him, he hung above that blazing orb, surrounded by seething gases which dimmed but did not wholly obscure his vision. Then a change began taking place. A great spot of darkness appeared on the pulsing body of the sun. It widened swiftly. About it the fiery elements of molten mass seemed to centre their main endeavour. Vast streamers of flaming gas leaped and darted about its spreading centre. It stretched and spread.

To Croft's fascinated vision it showed a mighty, funnel-like chasm, reaching down for thousands of miles into the very heart of their solar mass. And suddenly he knew that once more he was sinking, was being drawn down, down, to be engulfed in that terrible throat of the terrifying funnel, swept and sucked down like a bit of driftwood into the maw of a whirlpool, powerless to resist.

Down he sank, down, between walls of living fire which swirled about him with an inconceivable velocity of revolution. The vapours which closed about him seemed to stifle even his spirit senses. Down, down, how far he had no conception. He had lost all control, all conscious power to judge of time or distance. Yet he was able still to see. And so at last he sensed that the fiery walls were coming swiftly together.

For a wild instant he conceived himself engulfed. Then he knew that he was being thrown out and upward again with terrific force, literally crowded forth with the out-rushing gases between the collapsing walls, and hurled again into space.

Darkness came down, a darkness so deep it seemed a thousand suns might not pierce it through with their rays. Sirius, the great sun, seemed blotted out. He was seized by a sense of falling through that Stygian shroud. In which direction he knew not, or why or how. He knew only that his ego over which he had lost control was swirling in vast spirals down and down through an endless void to an endless fate—that he who had come so confidently forth to explore the universal secrets had become a waif in the uncharted immensity of the eternal universe.

The sensation went on and on. So much he knew. Still he was conscious. The thought came to him that this was his punishment for daring to know. Still conscious, he must be still bound by natural law. Had he broken that law and been cast into utter darkness, to remain forever conscious of his fate? Yet if so, where was he falling, where was he to wander, and for how long? His senses reeled.

By degrees, however, he fought back to some measure of control. His very necessity prompted the attempt. And by degrees there came to him a sense of not being any longer alone. In the almost palpable darkness it seemed that other shapes and forms, whose warp and woof was darkness also, floated and writhed about him as he fell.

They thrust against him; they gibbered soundlessly at him. They taunted him as he passed. And yet their very presence helped him in the end. He called his own knowledge to his assistance. He recognized these shapes of terror as those elementals of which occult teaching spoke, things which roamed in the darkness, which had as yet never been able to reach out and gain a soul for themselves.

With understanding came again the power of independent action. Unknowing whither, Croft willed himself out of their midst to some spot unnamed, where he might gain a spiritual moment of rest—to the nearest bit of matter afloat in the universal void. Abruptly he became aware of the near presence of some solid substance, the sense of falling ended, and he knew that his will had found expression in fact.

Yet wherever it was he had landed, the region was dead. Like the moon, it was wholly devoid of moisture or atmosphere. The presence of solid matter, however, gave him back a still further sense of control. Though he was still enveloped in darkness, he reasoned that if this was a planet and possessed of a sun in its system, its farther side must be bathed in light. Reason also told him that in all probability he was still within the system of Sirius despite the seemingly endless distance he had come.

Exerting his will, he passed over the darkened face and emerged on the other side in the midst of a ghostly light. At once he became conscious of his surroundings, of a valley and encircling lofty mountains. From the sides of the latter came the peculiar light. Examination showed Croft that it was given off by some substance which glowed with a phosphorescence sufficient to cast faint shadows of the rocks which strewed the dead and silent waste.

Not knowing where he was, loath to dare again the void, hardly knowing whether to will himself back to earth or remain and abide the issue of his own adventure, Croft waited, debating the question, until at length the top of a mountain lighted as if from a rising sun. Inside a few moments the valley was bathed in light; he saw the great sun Sirius wheel up the morning sky.

Peace came into his soul. He was still a conscious ego, still a creature in the universe of light. He gazed about. Close to the line of the horizon, and shining with what was plainly reflected light, he saw the vast outlines of another planet he had failed to note until now.

He understood. This was the major planet, surely one of the Dog Star's pack; and he had alighted on one of its moons. All desire to remain there left him. He was tired of dead worlds, of bottomless voids.

As before on the moon itself, he felt a resurgent desire to bathe in an atmosphere of life. By now, fairly himself again, the wish was father to the fact. Summoning his will, he made the final step of his journey, as it was to prove, and found himself standing on a world not so vastly different from his own.

* * * * *

He stood on the side of a mountain in the midst of an almost tropic vegetation. Giant trees were about him, giant ferns sprouted from the soil. But here, as on earth, the colour of the leaves was green. Through a break in the forest he gazed across a vast, wide-flung plain through which a mighty river made its way. Its waters glinted in the rays of the rising sun. Its banks were lined with patches of what he knew from their appearance were cultivated fields. Beyond them was a dun track, reminding him of the arid stretches of a desert, reaching out as far as his vision could plumb the distance.

He turned his eyes and followed the course of the river. By stages of swift interest he traced it to a point where it disappeared beneath what seemed the dull red walls of a mighty city. They were huge walls, high and broad, bastioned and towered, flung across the course of the river, which ran on through the city itself, passed beyond a farther wall, and—beyond that again there was the glint of silver and blue in Croft's eyes—the shimmer of a vast body of water—whether lake or ocean he did not know then.

The call of a bird brought his attention back. Life was waking in the mountain forest where he stood. Gay-plumaged creatures, not unlike earthly parrots, were fluttering from tree to tree. The sound of a grunting came toward him. He swung about. His eyes encountered those of other life. A creature such as he had never seen was coming out of a quivering mass of sturdy fern. It had small, beady eyes and a snout like a pig. Two tusks sprouted from its jaws like the tusks of a boar. But the rest of the body, although something like that of a hog, was covered with a long wool-like hair, fine and seemingly almost silken soft.

This, as he was to learn later, was the tabur, an animal still wild on Palos, though domesticated and raised both for its hair, which was woven into fabrics, and for its flesh, which was valued as food. While Croft watched, it began rooting about the foot of a tree on one side of the small glade where he stood. Plainly it was hunting for something to eat.

Once more he turned to the plain and stood lost in something new. Across the dun reaches of the desert, beyond the green region of the river, was moving a long dark string of figures, headed toward the city he had seen. It was like a caravan, Croft thought, in its arrangement, save that the moving objects which he deemed animals of some sort, belonged in no picture of a caravan such as he had ever seen.

Swiftly he willed himself toward them and moved along by their side. Something like amazement filled his being. These beasts were such creatures as might have peopled the earth in the Silurian age. They were huge, twice the size of an earthly elephant. They moved in a majestic fashion, yet with a surprising speed. Their bodies were covered with a hairless skin, reddish pink in colour, wrinkled and warted and plainly extremely thick. It slipped and slid over the muscles beneath it as they swung forward on their four massive legs, each one of which ended in a five-toed foot armed with short heavy claws.

But it was the head and neck and tail of the things which gave Croft pause. The head was more that of a sea-serpent or a monster lizard than anything else. The neck was long and flexible and curved like that of a camel. The tail was heavy where it joined the main spine, but thinned rapidly to a point. And the crest of head and neck, the back of each creature, so far as he could see, was covered with a sort of heavy scale, an armour devised by nature for the thing's protection, as it appeared. Yet he could not see very well, since each Sarpelca, as he was to learn their Palosian name, was loaded heavily with bundles and bales of what might be valuable merchandise.

And on each sat a man. Croft hesitated not at all to give them that title, since they were strikingly like the men of earth in so far as he could see. They had heads and arms and legs and a body, and their faces were white. Their features departed in no particular, so far as he could see, from the faces of earth, save that all were smooth, with no evidence of hair on upper lip or cheek or chin.

They were clad in loose cloak-like garments and a hooded cap or cowl. They sat the Sarpelcas just back of the juncture of the body and neck, and guided the strange-appearing monsters by means of slender reins affixed to two of the fleshy tentacles which sprouted about the beasts' almost snakelike mouths.

That this strange cortege was a caravan Croft was now assured. He decided to follow it to the city and inspect that as well. Wherefore he kept on beside it down the valley, along what he now saw was a well-defined and carefully constructed road, built of stone, cut to a nice approximation, along which the unwieldy procession made good time. The road showed no small knowledge of engineering. It was like the roads of Ancient Rome, Croft thought with quickened interest. It was in a perfect state of preservation and showed signs of recent mending here and there. While he was feeling a quickened interest in this the caravan entered the cultivated region along the river, and Croft gave his attention to the fields.

* * * * *

The first thing he noted here was the fact that all growth was due to irrigation, carried out by means of ditches and laterals very much as on earth at the present time. Here and there as the caravan passed down the splendid road he found a farmer's hut set in a bower of trees. For the most part they were built of a tan-coloured brick, and roofed with a thatching of rushes from the river's bank. He saw the natives working in the fields, strong-bodied men, clad in what seemed a single short-skirted tunic reaching to the knees, with the arms and lower limbs left bare.

One or two stopped work and stood to watch the caravan pass, and Croft noticed that their faces were intelligent, well featured, and their hair for the most part a sort of rich, almost chestnut brown, worn rather long and wholly uncovered or else caught about the brows by a cincture which held a bit of woven fabric draped over the head and down the neck.

Travel began to thicken along the road. The natives seemed heading to the city, to sell the produce of their fields. Croft found himself drawing aside in the press as the caravan overtook the others and crowded past. So real had it become to him that for the time he forgot he was no more than an impalpable, invisible thing these people could not contact or see. Then he remembered and gave his attention to what he might behold once more.

They had just passed a heavy cart drawn by two odd creatures, resembling deer save that they were larger and possessed of hoofs like those of earth-born horses, and instead of antlers sported two little horns not over six inches long. They were in colour almost a creamy white, and he fancied them among the most beautiful forms of animal life he had ever beheld. On the cart itself were high-piled crates of some unknown fowl, as he supposed—some edible bird, with the head of a goose, the plumage of a pheasant so far as its brilliant colouring went, long necks and bluish, webbed feet. Past the cart they came upon a band of native women carrying baskets and other burdens, strapped to their shoulders. Croft gave them particular attention, since as yet he had seen only men.

The Palosian females were fit mates, he decided, after he had given them a comprehensive glance. They were strong limbed and deep breasted. These peasant folks at least were simply clad. Like the men, they wore but a single garment, falling just over the bend of the knees and caught together over one shoulder with an embossed metal button, so far as he could tell. The other arm and shoulder were left wholly bare, as were their feet and legs, save that they wore coarse sandals of wood, strapped by leather thongs about ankle and calf. Their baskets were piled with vegetables and fruit, and they chattered and laughed among themselves as they walked.

And now as the Sarpelcas shuffled past, the highway grew actually packed. Also it drew nearer to the river and the city itself. The caravan thrust its way through a drove of the taburs—the woolly hogs such as Croft had seen on the side of the mountain. The hogsherds, rough, powerful, bronzed fellows, clad in hide aprons belted about their waists and nothing else, stalked beside their charges and exchanged heavy banter with the riders of the Sarpelcas as the caravan passed.

From behind a sound of shouting reached Croft's ears. He glanced around. Down the highway, splitting the throng of early market people, came some sort of conveyance, drawn by four of the beautiful creamy deer-like creatures he had seen before. They were harnessed abreast and had nodding plumes fixed to the head bands of their bridles in front of their horns. These plumes were all of a purple colour, and from the way the crowds gave way before the advance of the equipage, Croft deemed that it bore some one of note. Even the captain of the Sarpelca train, noting the advance of the gorgeous team, drew his huge beasts to the side of the road and stood up in his seat-like saddle to face inward as it passed.

* * * * *

The vehicle came on. Croft watched intently as it approached. So nearly as he could tell, it was a four-wheeled conveyance something like an old-time chariot in front, where stood the driver of the cream-white steeds, and behind that protected from the sun by an arched cover draped on each side with a substance not unlike heavy silk. These draperies, too, were purple in shade, and the body and wheels of the carriage seemed fashioned from something like burnished copper, as it glistened brightly in advance.

Then it was upon them, and Croft could look squarely into the shaded depths beneath the cover he now saw to be supported by upright metal rods, save at the back where the body continued straight up in a curve to form the top.

The curtains were drawn back since the morning air was still fresh, and Jason gained a view of those who rode. He gave them one glance and mentally caught his breath. There were two passengers in the coach—a woman and a man. The latter was plainly past middle age, well built, with a strongly set face and hair somewhat sprinkled with gray. He was clad in a tunic the like of which Croft had never seen, since it seemed woven of gold, etched and embroidered in what appeared stones or jewels of purple, red, and green. This covered his entire body and ended in half sleeves below which his forearms were bare.

He wore a jewelled cap supporting a single spray of purple feathers. From an inch below his knees his legs were encased in what seemed an open-meshed casing of metal, in colour not unlike his tunic, jointed at the ankles to allow of motion when he walked. There were no seats proper in the carriage, but rather a broad padded couch upon which both passengers lay.

So much Croft saw, and then, forsaking the caravan, let himself drift along beside the strange conveyance to inspect the girl. In fact, after the first swift glance at the man, he had no eyes save for his companion in the coach.

She was younger than the man, yet strangely like him in a feminine way—more slender, more graceful as she lay at her ease. Her face was a perfect oval, framed in a wealth of golden hair, which, save for a jewelled cincture, fell unrestrained about her shoulders in a silken flood. Her eyes were blue—the purple blue of the pansy—her skin, seen on face and throat and bared left shoulder and arm, a soft, firm white. For she was dressed like the peasant women, save in a richer fashion. Her single robe was white, lustrous in its sheen. It was broidered with a simple jewelled margin at throat and hem and over the breasts with stones of blue and green.

Her girdle was of gold in colour, catching her just above the hips with long ends and fringe which fell down the left side of the knee-length skirt. Sandals of the finest imaginable skin were on the soles of her slender pink-nailed feet, bare save for a jewel-studded toe and instep band, and the lacing cords which were twined about each limb as high as the top of the calf. On her left arm she wore a bracelet, just above the wrist, as a single ornament.

Croft gave her one glance which took in every detail of her presence and attire. He quivered as with a chill. Some change as cataclysmic as his experience of the night before above the Dog Star itself took place in his spiritual being. He felt drawn toward this beautiful girl of Palos as he had never in all his life on earth been drawn toward a woman before.

It was as though suddenly he had found something he had lost—as though he had met one known and forgotten and now once more recognized. Without giving the act the slightest thought of consideration, he willed himself into the coach between the fluttering curtains of purple silk, and crouched down on the padded platform at her feet.

DR. HEIDEGGER'S EXPERIMENT

Nathanial Hawthorne

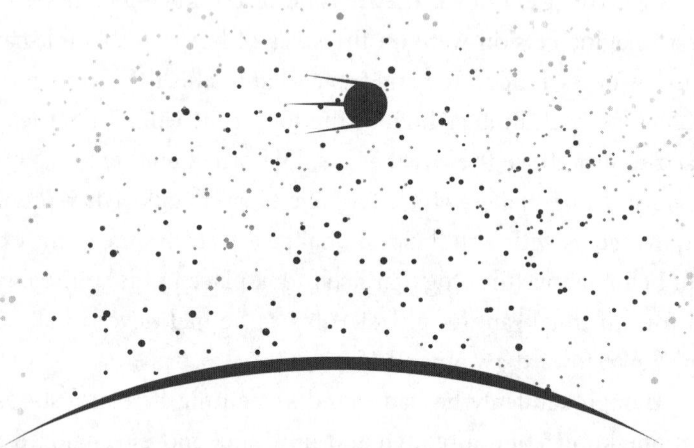

That very singular man, old Dr. Heidegger, once invited four venerable friends to meet him in his study. There were three white-bearded gentlemen, Mr. Medbourne, Colonel Killigrew, and Mr. Gascoigne, and a withered gentlewoman, whose name was the Widow Wycherly. They were all melancholy old creatures, who had been unfortunate in life, and whose greatest misfortune it was, that they were not long ago in their graves. Mr. Medbourne, in the vigour of his age, had been a prosperous merchant, but had lost his all by a frantic speculation, and was now little better than a mendicant. Colonel Killigrew had wasted his best years, and his health and substance, in the pursuit of sinful pleasures, which had given birth to a brood of pains, such as the gout, and divers other torments of soul and body. Mr. Gascoigne was a ruined politician, a man of evil fame, or at least had been so, till time had buried him from the knowledge of the present generation, and made him obscure instead of infamous. As for the Widow Wycherly, tradition tells us that she was a great beauty in her day; but, for a long while past, she had lived in deep seclusion, on account of certain scandalous stories, which had prejudiced the gentry of the town against her. It is a circumstance worth mentioning, that each of these three old gentlemen, Mr. Medbourne, Colonel Killigrew, and Mr. Gascoigne, were early lovers of the Widow Wycherly, and had once been on the point of cutting each other's throats for her sake. And, before proceeding farther, I will merely hint, that Dr. Heidegger and all his four guests were sometimes thought to be a little beside themselves; as is not unfrequently the case with old people, when worried either by present troubles or woeful recollections.

"My dear old friends," said Dr. Heidegger, motioning them to be seated, "I am desirous of your assistance in one of those little experiments with which I amuse myself here in my study."

If all stories were true. Dr. Heidegger's study must have been a very curious place. It was a dim, old-fashioned chamber, festooned with cobwebs, and besprinkled with antique dust. Around the walls stood several oaken bookcases, the lower shelves of which were filled with rows of gigantic folios, and black-letter quartos, and the upper with little parchment covered duodecimos. Over the central bookcase was a bronze bust of Hippocrates, with which, according to some authorities, Dr. Heidegger was accustomed to hold consultations, in all difficult cases of his practice. In the obscurest corner of the room stood a tall and narrow oaken closet, with its door ajar, within which doubtfully appeared a skeleton. Between two of the bookcases hung a looking-glass, presenting its high and dusty plate within a tarnished gilt frame. Among many wonderful stories related of this mirror, it was fabled that the spirits of all the doctor's deceased patients dwelt within its verge, and would stare him in the face whenever he looked thitherward. The opposite side of the chamber was ornamented with the full-length portrait of a young lady, arrayed in the faded magnificence of silk, satin, and brocade, and with a visage as faded as her dress. Above half a century ago, Dr. Heidegger had been on the point of marriage with this young lady; but, being affected with some slight disorder, she had swallowed one of her lover's prescriptions, and died on the bridal evening. The greatest curiosity of the study remains to be mentioned; it was a ponderous folio volume, bound in black leather, with massive silver clasps. There were no letters on the back, and nobody could tell the title of the book. But it was well known to be a book of magic; and once, when a chambermaid had lifted it, merely to brush away the dust, the skeleton had rattled in its closet, the picture of the young lady had stepped one foot upon the floor, and several ghastly faces had peeped forth from the mirror; while the brazen head of Hippocrates frowned, and said—"Forbear!"

Such was Dr. Heidegger's study. On the summer afternoon of our tale, a small round table, as black as ebony, stood in the centre of the room, sustaining a cut-glass vase, of beautiful form and elaborate workmanship. The sunshine came through the window, between the heavy festoons of two faded damask curtains, and fell directly across this vase; so that a mild splendour was reflected from it on the ashen visages of the five old people who sat around. Four champaigne glasses were also on the table.

"My dear old friends," repeated Dr. Heidegger, "may I reckon on your aid in performing an exceedingly curious experiment?"

Now Dr. Heidegger was a very strange old gentleman, whose eccentricity had become the nucleus for a thousand fantastic stories. Some of these fables, to my shame be it spoken, might possibly be traced back to mine own veracious self; and if any passages of the present tale should startle the reader's faith, I must be content to bear the stigma of a fiction-monger.

When the doctor's four guests heard him talk of his proposed experiment, they anticipated nothing more wonderful than the murder of a mouse in an air-pump, or the examination of a cobweb by the microscope, or some similar nonsense, with which he was constantly in the habit of pestering his intimates. But without waiting for a reply, Dr. Heidegger hobbled across the chamber, and returned with the same ponderous folio, bound in black leather, which common report affirmed to be a book of magic. Undoing the silver clasps, he opened the volume, and took from among its black-letter pages a rose, or what was once a rose, though now the green leaves and crimson petals had assumed one brownish hue, and the ancient flower seemed ready to crumble to dust in the doctor's hands.

"This rose," said Dr. Heidegger, with a sigh, "this same withered and crumbling flower, blossomed five-and-fifty years ago. It was given me by Sylvia Ward, whose portrait hangs yonder; and I meant to wear it in my bosom at our wedding. Five-and-fifty years it has been treasured between the leaves of this old volume. Now, would you deem it possible that this rose of half a century could ever bloom again?"

"Nonsense!" said the Widow Wycherly, with a peevish toss of her head. "You might as well ask whether an old woman's wrinkled face could ever bloom again."

"See!" answered Dr. Heidegger.

He uncovered the vase, and threw the faded rose into the water which it contained. At first, it lay lightly on the surface of the fluid, appearing to imbibe none of its moisture. Soon, however, a singular change began to be visible. The crushed and dried petals stirred, and assumed a deepening tinge of crimson, as if the flower were reviving from a death-like slumber; the slender stalk and twigs of foliage became green; and there was the rose of half a century, looking as fresh as when Sylvia Ward had first given it to her lover. It was scarcely full-blown; for some of its delicate red leaves curled modestly around its moist bosom, within which two or three dew-drops were sparkling.

"That is certainly a very pretty deception," said the doctor's friends; carelessly, however, for they had witnessed greater miracles at a conjurer's show: "pray how was it effected?"

"Did you never hear of the 'Fountain of Youth?'" asked Dr. Heidegger, "which Ponce De Leon, the Spanish adventurer, went in search of, two or three centuries ago?"

"But did Ponce De Leon ever find it?" said the Widow Wycherly.

"No," answered Dr. Heidegger, "for he never sought it in the right place. The famous Fountain of Youth, if I am rightly informed, is situated in the southern part of the Floridian peninsula, not far from Lake Macaco. Its source is overshadowed by several gigantic magnolias, which, though numberless centuries old, have been kept as fresh as violets, by the virtues of this wonderful water. An acquaintance of mine, knowing my curiosity in such matters, has sent me what you see in the vase."

"Ahem!" said Colonel Killigrew, who believed not a word of the doctor's story: "and what may be the effect of this fluid on the human frame?"

"You shall judge for yourself, my dear colonel," replied Dr. Heidegger; "and all of you, my respected friends, are welcome to so much of this admirable fluid, as may restore to you the bloom of youth. For my own part, having had much trouble in growing old, I am in no hurry to grow young again. With your permission, therefore, I will merely watch the progress of the experiment."

While he spoke. Dr. Heidegger had been filling the four champaigne glasses with the water of the Fountain of Youth. It was apparently impregnated with an effervescent gas, for little bubbles were continually ascending from the depths of the glasses, and bursting in silvery spray at the surface. As the liquor diffused a pleasant perfume, the old people doubted not that it possessed cordial and comfortable properties; and, though utter sceptics as to its rejuvenescent power, they were inclined to swallow it at once. But Dr. Heidegger besought them to stay a moment.

"Before you drink, my respectable old friends," said he, "it would be well that, with the experience of a life-time to direct you, you should draw up a few general rules for your guidance, in passing a second time through the perils of youth. Think what a sin and shame it would be, if, with your peculiar advantages, you should not become patterns of virtue and wisdom to all the young people of the age!"

The doctor's four venerable friends made him no answer, except by a feeble and tremulous laugh; so very ridiculous was the idea, that, knowing how closely repentance treads behind the steps of error, they should ever go astray again.

"Drink, then," said the doctor, bowing: "I rejoice that I have so well selected the subjects of my experiment.

With palsied hands, they raised the glasses to their lips. The liquor, if it really possessed such virtues as Dr. Heidegger imputed to it, could not have been bestowed on four human beings who needed it more woefully. They looked as if they had never known what youth or pleasure was, but had been the offspring of Nature's dotage, and always the gray, decrepit, sapless, miserable creatures, who now sat stooping round the doctor's table, without life enough in their souls or bodies to be animated even by the prospect of growing young again. They drank off the water, and replaced their glasses on the table.

Assuredly there was an almost immediate improvement in the aspect of the party, not unlike what might have been produced by a glass of generous wine, together with a sudden glow of cheerful sunshine, brightening over all their visages at once. There was a healthful suffusion on their cheeks, instead of the ashen hue that had made them look so corpse-like. They gazed at one another, and fancied that some magic power had really begun to smooth away the deep and sad inscriptions which Father Time had been so long engraving on their brows. The Widow Wycherly adjusted her cap, for she felt almost like a woman again.

"Give us more of this wondrous water!" cried they, eagerly. "We are younger—but we are still too old! Quick!—give us more!"

"Patience, patience!" quoth Dr. Heidegger, who sat watching the experiment, with philosophic coolness. "You have been a long time growing old. Surely, you might be content to grow young in half an hour! But the water is at your service."

Again he filled their glasses with the liquor of youth, enough of which still remained in the vase to turn half the old people in the city to the age of their own grandchildren. While the bubbles were yet sparkling on the brim, the doctor's four guests snatched their glasses from the table, and swallowed the contents at a single gulp. Was it delusion! Even while the draught was passing down their throats, it seemed to have wrought a change on their whole systems. Their eyes grew clear and bright; a dark shade deepened among their silvery locks; they sat around the table, three gentlemen, of middle age, and a woman, hardly beyond her buxom prime.

"My dear widow, you are charming!" cried Colonel Killigrew, whose eyes had been fixed upon her face, while the shadows of age were flitting from it like darkness from the crimson daybreak.

The fair widow knew, of old, that Colonel Killigrew's compliments were not always measured by sober truth; so she started up and ran to the mirror, still dreading that the ugly visage of an old woman would meet her gaze. Meanwhile, the three gentlemen behaved in such a manner, as proved that the water of the Fountain of Youth possessed some intoxicating qualities; unless, indeed, their exhilaration of spirits were merely a lightsome dizziness, caused by the sudden removal of the weight of years. Mr. Gascoigne's mind seemed to run on political topics, but whether relating to the past, present, or future, could not easily be determined, since the same ideas and phrases have been in vogue these fifty years. Now he rattled forth full-throated sentences about patriotism, national glory, and the people's right; now he muttered some perilous stuff or other, in a sly and doubtful whisper, so cautiously that even his own conscience could scarcely catch the secret; and now, again, he spoke in measured accents, and a deeply deferential tone, as if a royal ear were listening to his well-turned periods. Colonel Killigrew all this time had been trolling forth a jolly bottle-song, and ringing his glass in symphony with the chorus, while his eyes wandered toward the buxom figure of the Widow Wycherly. On the other side of the table, Mr. Medbourne was involved in a calculation of dollars and cents, with which was strangely intermingled a project for supplying the East Indies with ice, by harnessing a team of whales to the polar icebergs.

As for the Widow Wycherly, she stood before the mirror, curtseying and simpering to her own image, and greeting it as the friend whom she loved better than all the world beside. She thrust her face close to the glass, to see whether some long-remembered wrinkle or crows-foot had indeed vanished. She examined whether the snow had so entirely melted from her hair, that the venerable cap could be safely thrown aside. At last, turning briskly away, she came with a sort of dancing step to the table.

"My dear old doctor," cried she, "pray favour me with another glass!"

"Certainly, my dear madam, certainly!" replied the complaisant doctor; "see! I have already filled the glasses."

There, in fact, stood the four glasses, brim-full of this wonderful water, the delicate spray of which, as it effervesced from the surface, resembled the tremulous glitter of diamonds. It was now so nearly sunset, that the chamber had grown duskier than ever; but a mild and moon-like splendour gleamed from within the vase, and rested alike on the four guests, and on the doctor's venerable figure. He sat in a high-backed, elaborately-carved, oaken arm-chair, with a gray dignity of aspect that might have well befitted that very Father Time, whose power had never been disputed, save by this fortunate company. Even while quaffing the third draught of the Fountain of Youth, they were almost awed by the expression of his mysterious visage.

But, the next moment, the exhilarating gush of young life shot through their veins. They were now in the happy prime of youth. Age, with its miserable train of cares, and sorrows, and diseases, was remembered only as the trouble of a dream, from which they had joyously awoke. The fresh gloss of the soul, so early lost, and without which the world's successive scenes had been but a gallery of faded pictures, again threw its enchantment over all their prospects. They felt like new-created beings, in a new-created universe.

"We are young! We are young!" they cried, exultingly.

Youth, like the extremity of age, had effaced the strongly marked characteristics of middle life, and mutually assimilated them all. They were a group of merry youngsters, almost maddened with the exuberant frolicksomeness of their years. The most singular effect of their gaiety was an impulse to mock the infirmity and decrepitude of which they had so lately been the victims. They laughed loudly at their old-fashioned attire, the wide-skirted coats and flapped waistcoats of the young men, and the ancient cap and gown of the blooming girl. One limped across the floor, like a gouty grandfather; one set a pair of spectacles astride of his nose, and pretended to pore over the blackletter pages of the book of magic; a third seated himself in an arm-chair, and strove to imitate the venerable dignity of Dr. Heidegger. Then all shouted mirthfully, and leaped about the room. The Widow Wycherly—if so fresh a damsel could be called a widow—tripped up to the doctor's chair, with a mischievous merriment in her rosy face.

"Doctor, you dear old soul," cried she, "get up and dance with me!" And then the four young people laughed louder than ever, to think what a queer figure the poor old doctor would cut.

"Pray excuse me," answered the doctor, quietly. "I am old and rheumatic, and my dancing days were over long ago. But either of these gay young gentlemen will be glad of so pretty a partner."

"Dance with me, Clara!" cried Colonel Killigrew.

"No, no, I will be her partner!" shouted Mr. Gascoigne.

"She promised me her hand, fifty years ago!" exclaimed Mr. Medbourne.

They all gathered round her. One caught both her hands in his passionate grasp—another threw his arm about her waist—the third buried his hand among the glossy curls that clustered beneath the widow's cap. Blushing, panting, struggling, chiding, laughing, her warm breath fanning each of their faces by turns, she strove to disengage herself, yet still remained in their triple embrace. Never was there a livelier picture of youthful rivalship, with bewitching beauty for the prize. Yet, by a strange deception, owing to the duskiness of the chamber, and the antique dresses which they still wore, the tall mirror is said to have reflected the figures of the three old, gray, withered grandsires, ridiculously contending for the skinny ugliness of a shrivelled granddam.

But they were young: their burning passions proved them so. Inflamed to madness by the coquetry of the girl-widow, who neither granted nor quite withheld her favours, the three rivals began to interchange threatening glances. Still keeping hold of the fair prize, they grappled fiercely at one another's throats. As they struggled to and fro, the table was overturned, and the vase dashed into a thousand fragments. The precious Water of Youth flowed in a bright stream across the floor, moistening the wings of a butterfly, which, grown old in the decline of summer, had alighted there to die. The insect fluttered lightly through the chamber, and settled on the snowy head of Dr. Heidegger.

"Come, come, gentlemen!—come, Madam Wycherly," exclaimed the doctor, "I really must protest against this riot."

They stood still, and shivered; for it seemed as if gray Time were calling them back from their sunny youth, far down into the chill and darksome vale of years. They looked at old Dr. Heidegger, who sat in his carved arm-chair, holding the rose of half a century, which he had rescued from among the fragments of the shattered vase. At the motion of his hand, the four rioters resumed their seats; the more readily, because their violent exertions had wearied them, youthful though they were.

"My poor Sylvia's rose!" ejaculated Dr. Heidegger, holding it in the light of the sunset clouds: "it appears to be fading again."

And so it was. Even while the party were looking at it, the flower continued to shrivel up, till it became as dry and fragile as when the doctor had first thrown it into the vase. He shook off the few drops of moisture which clung to its petals.

"I love it as well thus, as in its dewy freshness," observed he, pressing the withered rose to his withered lips. While he spoke, the butterfly fluttered down from the doctor's snowy head, and fell upon the floor.

His guests shivered again. A strange chillness, whether of the body or spirit they could not tell, was creeping gradually over them all. They gazed at one another, and fancied that each fleeting moment snatched away a charm, and left a deepening furrow where none had been before. Was it an illusion? Had the changes of a life-time been crowded into so brief a space, and were they now four aged people, sitting with their old friend, Dr. Heidegger?

"Are we grown old again, so soon!" cried they, dolefully.

In truth, they had. The Water of Youth possessed merely a virtue more transient than that of wine. The delirium which it created had effervesced away. Yes! they were old again. With a shuddering impulse, that showed her a woman still, the widow clasped her skinny hands before her face, and wished that the coffin-lid were over it, since it could be no longer beautiful.

"Yes, friends, ye are old again," said Dr. Heidegger; "and lo! the Water of Youth is all lavished on the ground. Well—I bemoan it not; for if the fountain gushed at my very door-step, I would not stoop to bathe my lips in it—no, though its delirium were for years instead of moments. Such is the lesson ye have taught me!"

But the doctor's four friends had taught no such lesson to themselves. They resolved forthwith to make a pilgrimage to Florida, and quaff at morning, noon, and night, from the Fountain of Youth.

RAPPACINI'S DAUGHTER

by Nathaniel Hawthorne

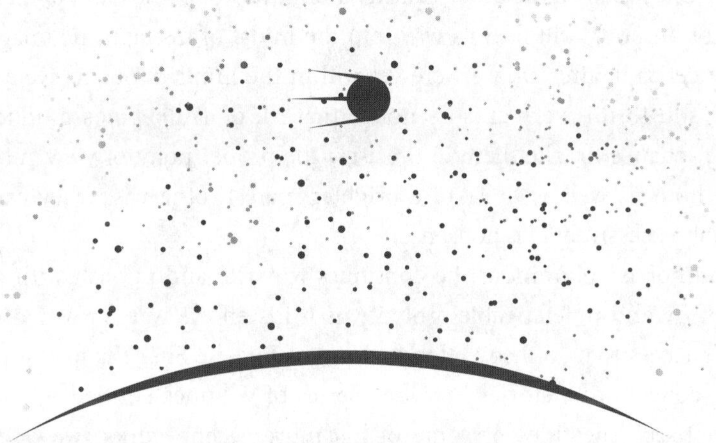

We do not remember to have seen any translated specimens of the productions of M. de l'Aubepine—a fact the less to be wondered at, as his very name is unknown to many of his own countrymen as well as to the student of foreign literature. As a writer, he seems to occupy an unfortunate position between the Transcendentalists (who, under one name or another, have their share in all the current literature of the world) and the great body of pen-and-ink men who address the intellect and sympathies of the multitude. If not too refined, at all events too remote, too shadowy, and unsubstantial in his modes of development to suit the taste of the latter class, and yet too popular to satisfy the spiritual or metaphysical requisitions of the former, he must necessarily find himself without an audience, except here and there an individual or possibly an isolated clique. His writings, to do them justice, are not altogether destitute of fancy and originality; they might have won him greater reputation but for an inveterate love of allegory, which is apt to invest his plots and characters with the aspect of scenery and people in the clouds, and to steal away the human warmth out of his conceptions. His fictions are sometimes historical, sometimes of the present day, and sometimes, so far as can be discovered, have little or no reference either to time or space. In any case, he generally contents himself with a very slight embroidery of outward manners,—the faintest possible counterfeit of real life,—and endeavours to create an interest by some less obvious peculiarity of the subject. Occasionally a breath of Nature, a raindrop of pathos and tenderness, or a gleam of humour, will find its way into the midst of his fantastic imagery, and make us feel as if, after all, we were yet within the limits of our native earth. We will only add to this very cursory notice that M. de l'Aubepine's productions, if the reader chance to take them in precisely the proper point of view, may amuse a leisure hour as well as those of a brighter man; if otherwise, they can hardly fail to look excessively like nonsense.

Our author is voluminous; he continues to write and publish with as much praiseworthy and indefatigable prolixity as if his efforts were crowned with the brilliant success that so justly attends those of Eugene Sue. His first appearance was by a collection of stories in a long series of volumes entitled "Contes deux fois racontees." The titles of some of his more recent works (we quote from memory) are as follows: "Le Voyage Celeste a Chemin de Fer," 3 tom., 1838; "Le nouveau Pere Adam et la nouvelle Mere Eve," 2 tom., 1839; "Roderic; ou le Serpent a l'estomac," 2 tom., 1840; "Le Culte du Feu," a folio volume of ponderous research into the religion and ritual of the old Persian Ghebers, published in 1841; "La Soiree du Chateau en Espagne," 1 tom., 8vo, 1842; and "L'Artiste du Beau; ou le Papillon Mecanique," 5 tom., 4vo, 1843. Our somewhat wearisome perusal of this startling catalogue of volumes has left behind it a certain personal affection and sympathy, though by no means admiration, for M. de l'Aubepine; and we would fain do the little in our power towards introducing him favourably to the American public. The ensuing tale is a translation of his "Beatrice; ou la Belle Empoisonneuse," recently published in "La Revue Anti-Aristocratique." This journal, edited by the Comte de Bearhaven, has for some years past led the defence of liberal principles and popular rights with a faithfulness and ability worthy of all praise.

A young man, named Giovanni Guasconti, came, very long ago, from the more southern region of Italy, to pursue his studies at the University of Padua. Giovanni, who had but a scanty supply of gold ducats in his pocket, took lodgings in a high and gloomy chamber of an old edifice which looked not unworthy to have been the palace of a Paduan noble, and which, in fact, exhibited over its entrance the armourial bearings of a family long since extinct. The young stranger, who was not unstudied in the great poem of his country, recollected that one of the ancestors of this family, and perhaps an occupant of this very mansion, had been pictured by Dante as a partaker of the immortal agonies of his Inferno. These reminiscences and associations, together with the tendency to heartbreak natural to a young man for the first time out of his native sphere, caused Giovanni to sigh heavily as he looked around the desolate and ill-furnished apartment.

"Holy Virgin, signor!" cried old Dame Lisabetta, who, won by the youth's remarkable beauty of person, was kindly endeavouring to give the chamber a habitable air, "what a sigh was that to come out of a young man's heart! Do you find this old mansion gloomy? For the love of Heaven, then, put your head out of the window, and you will see as bright sunshine as you have left in Naples."

Guasconti mechanically did as the old woman advised, but could not quite agree with her that the Paduan sunshine was as cheerful as that of southern Italy. Such as it was, however, it fell upon a garden beneath the window and expended its fostering influences on a variety of plants, which seemed to have been cultivated with exceeding care.

"Does this garden belong to the house?" asked Giovanni.

"Heaven forbid, signor, unless it were fruitful of better pot herbs than any that grow there now," answered old Lisabetta. "No; that garden is cultivated by the own hands of Signor Giacomo Rappaccini, the famous doctor, who, I warrant him, has been heard of as far as Naples. It is said that he distils these plants into medicines that are as potent as a charm. Oftentimes you may see the signor doctor at work, and perchance the signora, his daughter, too, gathering the strange flowers that grow in the garden."

The old woman had now done what she could for the aspect of the chamber; and, commending the young man to the protection of the saints, took her departure.

Giovanni still found no better occupation than to look down into the garden beneath his window. From its appearance, he judged it to be one of those botanic gardens which were of earlier date in Padua than elsewhere in Italy or in the world. Or, not improbably, it might once have been the pleasure-place of an opulent family; for there was the ruin of a marble fountain in the centre, sculptured with rare art, but so woefully shattered that it was impossible to trace the original design from the chaos of remaining fragments. The water, however, continued to gush and sparkle into the sunbeams as cheerfully as ever. A little gurgling sound ascended to the young man's window, and made him feel as if the fountain were an immortal spirit that sung its song unceasingly and without heeding the vicissitudes around it, while one century imbodied it in marble and another scattered the perishable garniture on the soil. All about the pool into which the water subsided grew various plants, that seemed to require a plentiful supply of moisture for the nourishment of gigantic leaves, and in some instances, flowers gorgeously magnificent. There was one shrub in particular, set in a marble vase in the midst of the pool, that bore a profusion of purple blossoms, each of which had the lustre and richness of a gem; and the whole together made a show so resplendent that it seemed enough to illuminate the garden, even had there been no sunshine. Every portion of the soil was peopled with plants and herbs, which, if less beautiful, still bore tokens of assiduous care, as if all had their individual virtues, known to the scientific mind that fostered them. Some were placed in urns, rich with old carving, and others in common garden pots; some crept serpent-like along the ground or climbed on high, using whatever means of ascent was offered them. One plant had wreathed itself round a statue of Vertumnus, which was thus quite veiled and shrouded in a drapery of hanging foliage, so happily arranged that it might have served a sculptor for a study.

While Giovanni stood at the window he heard a rustling behind a screen of leaves, and became aware that a person was at work in the garden. His figure soon emerged into view, and showed itself to be that of no common labourer, but a tall, emaciated, sallow, and sickly-looking man, dressed in a scholar's garb of black. He was beyond the middle term of life, with gray hair, a thin, gray beard, and a face singularly marked with intellect and cultivation, but which could never, even in his more youthful days, have expressed much warmth of heart.

Nothing could exceed the intentness with which this scientific gardener examined every shrub which grew in his path: it seemed as if he was looking into their inmost nature, making observations in regard to their creative essence, and discovering why one leaf grew in this shape and another in that, and wherefore such and such flowers differed among themselves in hue and perfume. Nevertheless, in spite of this deep intelligence on his part, there was no approach to intimacy between himself and these vegetable existences. On the contrary, he avoided their actual touch or the direct inhaling of their odours with a caution that impressed Giovanni most disagreeably; for the man's demeanour was that of one walking among malignant influences, such as savage beasts, or deadly snakes, or evil spirits, which, should he allow them one moment of license, would wreak upon him some terrible fatality. It was strangely frightful to the young man's imagination to see this air of insecurity in a person cultivating a garden, that most simple and innocent of human toils, and which had been alike the joy and labour of the unfallen parents of the race. Was this garden, then, the Eden of the present world? And this man, with such a perception of harm in what his own hands caused to grow,—was he the Adam?

The distrustful gardener, while plucking away the dead leaves or pruning the too luxuriant growth of the shrubs, defended his hands with a pair of thick gloves. Nor were these his only armour. When, in his walk through the garden, he came to the magnificent plant that hung its purple gems beside the marble fountain, he placed a kind of mask over his mouth and nostrils, as if all this beauty did but conceal a deadlier malice; but, finding his task still too dangerous, he drew back, removed the mask, and called loudly, but in the infirm voice of a person affected with inward disease, "Beatrice! Beatrice!"

"Here am I, my father. What would you?" cried a rich and youthful voice from the window of the opposite house—a voice as rich as a tropical sunset, and which made Giovanni, though he knew not why, think of deep hues of purple or crimson and of perfumes heavily delectable. "Are you in the garden?"

"Yes, Beatrice," answered the gardener, "and I need your help."

Soon there emerged from under a sculptured portal the figure of a young girl, arrayed with as much richness of taste as the most splendid of the flowers, beautiful as the day, and with a bloom so deep and vivid that one shade more would have been too much. She looked redundant with life, health, and energy; all of which attributes were bound down and compressed, as it were and girdled tensely, in their luxuriance, by her virgin zone. Yet Giovanni's fancy must have grown morbid while he looked down into the garden; for the impression which the fair stranger made upon him was as if here were another flower, the human sister of those vegetable ones, as beautiful as they, more beautiful than the richest of them, but still to be touched only with a glove, nor to be approached without a mask. As Beatrice came down the garden path, it was observable that she handled and inhaled the odour of several of the plants which her father had most sedulously avoided.

"Here, Beatrice," said the latter, "see how many needful offices require to be done to our chief treasure. Yet, shattered as I am, my life might pay the penalty of approaching it so closely as circumstances demand. Henceforth, I fear, this plant must be consigned to your sole charge."

"And gladly will I undertake it," cried again the rich tones of the young lady, as she bent towards the magnificent plant and opened her arms as if to embrace it. "Yes, my sister, my splendour, it shall be Beatrice's task to nurse and serve thee; and thou shalt reward her with thy kisses and perfumed breath, which to her is as the breath of life."

Then, with all the tenderness in her manner that was so strikingly expressed in her words, she busied herself with such attentions as the plant seemed to require; and Giovanni, at his lofty window, rubbed his eyes and almost doubted whether it were a girl tending her favourite flower, or one sister performing the duties of affection to another. The scene soon terminated. Whether Dr. Rappaccini had finished his labours in the garden, or that his watchful eye had caught the stranger's face, he now took his daughter's arm and retired. Night was already closing in; oppressive exhalations seemed to proceed from the plants and steal upward past the open window; and Giovanni, closing the lattice, went to his couch and dreamed of a rich flower and beautiful girl. Flower and maiden were different, and yet the same, and fraught with some strange peril in either shape.

But there is an influence in the light of morning that tends to rectify whatever errors of fancy, or even of judgment, we may have incurred during the sun's decline, or among the shadows of the night, or in the less wholesome glow of moonshine. Giovanni's first movement, on starting from sleep, was to throw open the window and gaze down into the garden which his dreams had made so fertile of mysteries. He was surprised and a little ashamed to find how real and matter-of-fact an affair it proved to be, in the first rays of the sun which gilded the dew-drops that hung upon leaf and blossom, and, while giving a brighter beauty to each rare flower, brought everything within the limits of ordinary experience. The young man rejoiced that, in the heart of the barren city, he had the privilege of overlooking this spot of lovely and luxuriant vegetation. It would serve, he said to himself, as a symbolic language to keep him in communion with Nature. Neither the sickly and thoughtworn Dr. Giacomo Rappaccini, it is true, nor his brilliant daughter, were now visible; so that Giovanni could not determine how much of the singularity which he attributed to both was due to their own qualities and how much to his wonder-working fancy; but he was inclined to take a most rational view of the whole matter.

In the course of the day he paid his respects to Signor Pietro Baglioni, professor of medicine in the university, a physician of eminent repute to whom Giovanni had brought a letter of introduction. The professor was an elderly personage, apparently of genial nature, and habits that might almost be called jovial. He kept the young man to dinner, and made himself very agreeable by the freedom and liveliness of his conversation, especially when warmed by a flask or two of Tuscan wine. Giovanni, conceiving that men of science, inhabitants of the same city, must needs be on familiar terms with one another, took an opportunity to mention the name of Dr. Rappaccini. But the professor did not respond with so much cordiality as he had anticipated.

"Ill would it become a teacher of the divine art of medicine," said Professor Pietro Baglioni, in answer to a question of Giovanni, "to withhold due and well-considered praise of a physician so eminently skilled as Rappaccini; but, on the other hand, I should answer it but scantily to my conscience were I to permit a worthy youth like yourself, Signor Giovanni, the son of an ancient friend, to imbibe erroneous ideas respecting a man who might hereafter chance to hold your life and death in his hands. The truth is, our worshipful Dr. Rappaccini has as much science as any member of the faculty—with perhaps one single exception—in Padua, or all Italy; but there are certain grave objections to his professional character."

"And what are they?" asked the young man.

"Has my friend Giovanni any disease of body or heart, that he is so inquisitive about physicians?" said the professor, with a smile. "But as for Rappaccini, it is said of him—and I, who know the man well, can answer for its truth—that he cares infinitely more for science than for mankind. His patients are interesting to him only as subjects for some new experiment. He would sacrifice human life, his own among the rest, or whatever else was dearest to him, for the sake of adding so much as a grain of mustard seed to the great heap of his accumulated knowledge."

"Methinks he is an awful man indeed," remarked Guasconti, mentally recalling the cold and purely intellectual aspect of Rappaccini. "And yet, worshipful professor, is it not a noble spirit? Are there many men capable of so spiritual a love of science?"

"God forbid," answered the professor, somewhat testily; "at least, unless they take sounder views of the healing art than those adopted by Rappaccini. It is his theory that all medicinal virtues are comprised within those substances which we term vegetable poisons. These he cultivates with his own hands, and is said even to have produced new varieties of poison, more horribly deleterious than Nature, without the assistance of this learned person, would ever have plagued the world withal. That the signor doctor does less mischief than might be expected with such dangerous substances is undeniable. Now and then, it must be owned, he has effected, or seemed to effect, a marvellous cure; but, to tell you my private mind, Signor Giovanni, he should receive little credit for such instances of success,—they being probably the work of chance, —but should be held strictly accountable for his failures, which may justly be considered his own work."

The youth might have taken Baglioni's opinions with many grains of allowance had he known that there was a professional warfare of long continuance between him and Dr. Rappaccini, in which the latter was generally thought to have gained the advantage. If the reader be inclined to judge for himself, we refer him to certain black-letter tracts on both sides, preserved in the medical department of the University of Padua.

"I know not, most learned professor," returned Giovanni, after musing on what had been said of Rappaccini's exclusive zeal for science,—"I know not how dearly this physician may love his art; but surely there is one object more dear to him. He has a daughter."

"Aha!" cried the professor, with a laugh. "So now our friend Giovanni's secret is out. You have heard of this daughter, whom all the young men in Padua are wild about, though not half a dozen have ever had the good hap to see her face. I know little of the Signora Beatrice save that Rappaccini is said to have instructed her deeply in his science, and that, young and beautiful as fame reports her, she is already qualified to fill a professor's chair. Perchance her father destines her for mine! Other absurd rumours there be, not worth talking about or listening to. So now, Signor Giovanni, drink off your glass of lachryma."

Guasconti returned to his lodgings somewhat heated with the wine he had quaffed, and which caused his brain to swim with strange fantasies in reference to Dr. Rappaccini and the beautiful Beatrice. On his way, happening to pass by a florist's, he bought a fresh bouquet of flowers.

Ascending to his chamber, he seated himself near the window, but within the shadow thrown by the depth of the wall, so that he could look down into the garden with little risk of being discovered. All beneath his eye was a solitude. The strange plants were basking in the sunshine, and now and then nodding gently to one another, as if in acknowledgment of sympathy and kindred. In the midst, by the shattered fountain, grew the magnificent shrub, with its purple gems clustering all over it; they glowed in the air, and gleamed back again out of the depths of the pool, which thus seemed to overflow with coloured radiance from the rich reflection that was steeped in it. At first, as we have said, the garden was a solitude. Soon, however,—as Giovanni had half hoped, half feared, would be the case,—a figure appeared beneath the antique sculptured portal, and came down between the rows of plants, inhaling their various perfumes as if she were one of those beings of old classic fable that lived upon sweet odours. On again beholding Beatrice, the young man was even startled to perceive how much her beauty exceeded his recollection of it; so brilliant, so vivid, was its character, that she glowed amid the sunlight, and, as Giovanni whispered to himself, positively illuminated the more shadowy intervals of the garden path. Her face being now more revealed than on the former occasion, he was struck by its expression of simplicity and sweetness,—qualities that had not entered into his idea of her character, and which made him ask anew what manner of mortal she might be. Nor did he fail again to observe, or imagine, an analogy between the beautiful girl and the gorgeous shrub that hung its gemlike flowers over the fountain,—a resemblance which Beatrice seemed to have indulged a fantastic humour in heightening, both by the arrangement of her dress and the selection of its hues.

Approaching the shrub, she threw open her arms, as with a passionate ardour, and drew its branches into an intimate embrace—so intimate that her features were hidden in its leafy bosom and her glistening ringlets all intermingled with the flowers.

"Give me thy breath, my sister," exclaimed Beatrice; "for I am faint with common air. And give me this flower of thine, which I separate with gentlest fingers from the stem and place it close beside my heart."

With these words the beautiful daughter of Rappaccini plucked one of the richest blossoms of the shrub, and was about to fasten it in her bosom. But now, unless Giovanni's draughts of wine had bewildered his senses, a singular incident occurred. A small orange-coloured reptile, of the lizard or chameleon species, chanced to be creeping along the path, just at the feet of Beatrice. It appeared to Giovanni,—but, at the distance from which he gazed, he could scarcely have seen anything so minute,—it appeared to him, however, that a drop or two of moisture from the broken stem of the flower descended upon the lizard's head. For an instant the reptile contorted itself violently, and then lay motionless in the sunshine. Beatrice observed this remarkable phenomenon and crossed herself, sadly, but without surprise; nor did she therefore hesitate to arrange the fatal flower in her bosom. There it blushed, and almost glimmered with the dazzling effect of a precious stone, adding to her dress and aspect the one appropriate charm which nothing else in the world could have supplied. But Giovanni, out of the shadow of his window, bent forward and shrank back, and murmured and trembled.

"Am I awake? Have I my senses?" said he to himself. "What is this being? Beautiful shall I call her, or inexpressibly terrible?"

Beatrice now strayed carelessly through the garden, approaching closer beneath Giovanni's window, so that he was compelled to thrust his head quite out of its concealment in order to gratify the intense and painful curiosity which she excited. At this moment there came a beautiful insect over the garden wall; it had, perhaps, wandered through the city, and found no flowers or verdure among those antique haunts of men until the heavy perfumes of Dr. Rappaccini's shrubs had lured it from afar. Without alighting on the flowers, this winged brightness seemed to be attracted by Beatrice, and lingered in the air and fluttered about her head. Now, here it could not be but that Giovanni Guasconti's eyes deceived him. Be that as it might, he fancied that, while Beatrice was gazing at the insect with childish delight, it grew faint and fell at her feet; its bright wings shivered; it was dead—from no cause that he could discern, unless it were the atmosphere of her breath. Again Beatrice crossed herself and sighed heavily as she bent over the dead insect.

An impulsive movement of Giovanni drew her eyes to the window. There she beheld the beautiful head of the young man—rather a Grecian than an Italian head, with fair, regular features, and a glistening of gold among his ringlets—gazing down upon her like a being that hovered in mid air. Scarcely knowing what he did, Giovanni threw down the bouquet which he had hitherto held in his hand.

"Signora," said he, "there are pure and healthful flowers. Wear them for the sake of Giovanni Guasconti."

"Thanks, signor," replied Beatrice, with her rich voice, that came forth as it were like a gush of music, and with a mirthful expression half childish and half woman-like. "I accept your gift, and would fain recompense it with this precious purple flower; but if I toss it into the air it will not reach you. So Signor Guasconti must even content himself with my thanks."

She lifted the bouquet from the ground, and then, as if inwardly ashamed at having stepped aside from her maidenly reserve to respond to a stranger's greeting, passed swiftly homeward through the garden. But few as the moments were, it seemed to Giovanni, when she was on the point of vanishing beneath the sculptured portal, that his beautiful bouquet was already beginning to wither in her grasp. It was an idle thought; there could be no possibility of distinguishing a faded flower from a fresh one at so great a distance.

For many days after this incident the young man avoided the window that looked into Dr. Rappaccini's garden, as if something ugly and monstrous would have blasted his eyesight had he been betrayed into a glance. He felt conscious of having put himself, to a certain extent, within the influence of an unintelligible power by the communication which he had opened with Beatrice. The wisest course would have been, if his heart were in any real danger, to quit his lodgings and Padua itself at once; the next wiser, to have accustomed himself, as far as possible, to the familiar and daylight view of Beatrice—thus bringing her rigidly and systematically within the limits of ordinary experience. Least of all, while avoiding her sight, ought Giovanni to have remained so near this extraordinary being that the proximity and possibility even of intercourse should give a kind of substance and reality to the wild vagaries which his imagination ran riot continually in producing. Guasconti had not a deep heart—or, at all events, its depths were not sounded now; but he had a quick fancy, and an ardent southern temperament, which rose every instant to a higher fever pitch. Whether or no Beatrice possessed those terrible attributes, that fatal breath, the affinity with those so beautiful and deadly flowers which were indicated by what Giovanni had witnessed, she had at least instilled a fierce and subtle poison into his system. It was not love, although her rich beauty was a madness to him; nor horror, even while he fancied her spirit to be imbued with the same baneful essence that seemed to pervade her physical frame; but a wild offspring of both love and horror that had each parent in it, and burned like one and shivered like the other. Giovanni knew not what to dread; still less did he know what to hope; yet hope and dread kept a continual warfare in his breast, alternately vanquishing one another and starting up afresh to renew the contest. Blessed are all simple emotions, be they dark or bright! It is the lurid intermixture of the two that produces the illuminating blaze of the infernal regions.

Sometimes he endeavoured to assuage the fever of his spirit by a rapid walk through the streets of Padua or beyond its gates: his footsteps kept time with the throbbings of his brain, so that the walk was apt to accelerate itself to a race. One day he found himself arrested; his arm was seized by a portly personage, who had turned back on recognizing the young man and expended much breath in overtaking him.

"Signor Giovanni! Stay, my young friend!" cried he. "Have you forgotten me? That might well be the case if I were as much altered as yourself."

It was Baglioni, whom Giovanni had avoided ever since their first meeting, from a doubt that the professor's sagacity would look too deeply into his secrets. Endeavouring to recover himself, he stared forth wildly from his inner world into the outer one and spoke like a man in a dream.

"Yes; I am Giovanni Guasconti. You are Professor Pietro Baglioni. Now let me pass!"

"Not yet, not yet, Signor Giovanni Guasconti," said the professor, smiling, but at the same time scrutinizing the youth with an earnest glance. "What! did I grow up side by side with your father? and shall his son pass me like a stranger in these old streets of Padua? Stand still, Signor Giovanni; for we must have a word or two before we part."

"Speedily, then, most worshipful professor, speedily," said Giovanni, with feverish impatience. "Does not your worship see that I am in haste?"

Now, while he was speaking there came a man in black along the street, stooping and moving feebly like a person in inferior health. His face was all overspread with a most sickly and sallow hue, but yet so pervaded with an expression of piercing and active intellect that an observer might easily have overlooked the merely physical attributes and have seen only this wonderful energy. As he passed, this person exchanged a cold and distant salutation with Baglioni, but fixed his eyes upon Giovanni with an intentness that seemed to bring out whatever was within him worthy of notice. Nevertheless, there was a peculiar quietness in the look, as if taking merely a speculative, not a human interest, in the young man.

"It is Dr. Rappaccini!" whispered the professor when the stranger had passed. "Has he ever seen your face before?"

"Not that I know," answered Giovanni, starting at the name.

"He *has* seen you! he must have seen you!" said Baglioni, hastily. "For some purpose or other, this man of science is making a study of you. I know that look of his! It is the same that coldly illuminates his face as he bends over a bird, a mouse, or a butterfly, which, in pursuance of some experiment, he has killed by the perfume of a flower; a look as deep as Nature itself, but without Nature's warmth of love. Signor Giovanni, I will stake my life upon it, you are the subject of one of Rappaccini's experiments!"

"Will you make a fool of me?" cried Giovanni, passionately. "*That*, signor professor, were an untoward experiment."

"Patience! patience!" replied the imperturbable professor. "I tell thee, my poor Giovanni, that Rappaccini has a scientific interest in thee. Thou hast fallen into fearful hands! And the Signora Beatrice,—what part does she act in this mystery?"

But Guasconti, finding Baglioni's pertinacity intolerable, here broke away, and was gone before the professor could again seize his arm. He looked after the young man intently and shook his head.

"This must not be," said Baglioni to himself. "The youth is the son of my old friend, and shall not come to any harm from which the arcana of medical science can preserve him. Besides, it is too insufferable an impertinence in Rappaccini, thus to snatch the lad out of my own hands, as I may say, and make use of him for his infernal experiments. This daughter of his! It shall be looked to. Perchance, most learned Rappaccini, I may foil you where you little dream of it!"

Meanwhile Giovanni had pursued a circuitous route, and at length found himself at the door of his lodgings. As he crossed the threshold he was met by old Lisabetta, who smirked and smiled, and was evidently desirous to attract his attention; vainly, however, as the ebullition of his feelings had momentarily subsided into a cold and dull vacuity. He turned his eyes full upon the withered face that was puckering itself into a smile, but seemed to behold it not. The old dame, therefore, laid her grasp upon his cloak.

"Signor! signor!" whispered she, still with a smile over the whole breadth of her visage, so that it looked not unlike a grotesque carving in wood, darkened by centuries. "Listen, signor! There is a private entrance into the garden!"

"What do you say?" exclaimed Giovanni, turning quickly about, as if an inanimate thing should start into feverish life. "A private entrance into Dr. Rappaccini's garden?"

"Hush! hush! not so loud!" whispered Lisabetta, putting her hand over his mouth. "Yes; into the worshipful doctor's garden, where you may see all his fine shrubbery. Many a young man in Padua would give gold to be admitted among those flowers."

Giovanni put a piece of gold into her hand.

"Show me the way," said he.

A surmise, probably excited by his conversation with Baglioni, crossed his mind, that this interposition of old Lisabetta might perchance be connected with the intrigue, whatever were its nature, in which the professor seemed to suppose that Dr. Rappaccini was involving him. But such a suspicion, though it disturbed Giovanni, was inadequate to restrain him. The instant that he was aware of the possibility of approaching Beatrice, it seemed an absolute necessity of his existence to do so. It mattered not whether she were angel or demon; he was irrevocably within her sphere, and must obey the law that whirled him onward, in ever-lessening circles, towards a result which he did not attempt to foreshadow; and yet, strange to say, there came across him a sudden doubt whether this intense interest on his part were not delusory; whether it were really of so deep and positive a nature as to justify him in now thrusting himself into an incalculable position; whether it were not merely the fantasy of a young man's brain, only slightly or not at all connected with his heart.

He paused, hesitated, turned half about, but again went on. His withered guide led him along several obscure passages, and finally undid a door, through which, as it was opened, there came the sight and sound of rustling leaves, with the broken sunshine glimmering among them. Giovanni stepped forth, and, forcing himself through the entanglement of a shrub that wreathed its tendrils over the hidden entrance, stood beneath his own window in the open area of Dr. Rappaccini's garden.

How often is it the case that, when impossibilities have come to pass and dreams have condensed their misty substance into tangible realities, we find ourselves calm, and even coldly self-possessed, amid circumstances which it would have been a delirium of joy or agony to anticipate! Fate delights to thwart us thus. Passion will choose his own time to rush upon the scene, and lingers sluggishly behind when an appropriate adjustment of events would seem to summon his appearance. So was it now with Giovanni. Day after day his pulses had throbbed with feverish blood at the improbable idea of an interview with Beatrice, and of standing with her, face to face, in this very garden, basking in the Oriental sunshine of her beauty, and snatching from her full gaze the mystery which he deemed the riddle of his own existence. But now there was a singular and untimely equanimity within his breast. He threw a glance around the garden to discover if Beatrice or her father were present, and, perceiving that he was alone, began a critical observation of the plants.

The aspect of one and all of them dissatisfied him; their gorgeousness seemed fierce, passionate, and even unnatural. There was hardly an individual shrub which a wanderer, straying by himself through a forest, would not have been startled to find growing wild, as if an unearthly face had glared at him out of the thicket. Several also would have shocked a delicate instinct by an appearance of artificialness indicating that there had been such commixture, and, as it were, adultery, of various vegetable species, that the production was no longer of God's making, but the monstrous offspring of man's depraved fancy, glowing with only an evil mockery of beauty. They were probably the result of experiment, which in one or two cases had succeeded in mingling plants individually lovely into a compound possessing the questionable and ominous character that distinguished the whole growth of the garden. In fine, Giovanni recognized but two or three plants in the collection, and those of a kind that he well knew to be poisonous. While busy with these contemplations he heard the rustling of a silken garment, and, turning, beheld Beatrice emerging from beneath the sculptured portal.

Giovanni had not considered with himself what should be his deportment; whether he should apologize for his intrusion into the garden, or assume that he was there with the privity at least, if not by the desire, of Dr. Rappaccini or his daughter; but Beatrice's manner placed him at his ease, though leaving him still in doubt by what agency he had gained admittance. She came lightly along the path and met him near the broken fountain. There was surprise in her face, but brightened by a simple and kind expression of pleasure.

"You are a connoisseur in flowers, signor," said Beatrice, with a smile, alluding to the bouquet which he had flung her from the window. "It is no marvel, therefore, if the sight of my father's rare collection has tempted you to take a nearer view. If he were here, he could tell you many strange and interesting facts as to the nature and habits of these shrubs; for he has spent a lifetime in such studies, and this garden is his world."

"And yourself, lady," observed Giovanni, "if fame says true,—you likewise are deeply skilled in the virtues indicated by these rich blossoms and these spicy perfumes. Would you deign to be my instructress, I should prove an apter scholar than if taught by Signor Rappaccini himself."

"Are there such idle rumors?" asked Beatrice, with the music of a pleasant laugh. "Do people say that I am skilled in my father's science of plants? What a jest is there! No; though I have grown up among these flowers, I know no more of them than their hues and perfume; and sometimes methinks I would fain rid myself of even that small knowledge. There are many flowers here, and those not the least brilliant, that shock and offend me when they meet my eye. But pray, signor, do not believe these stories about my science. Believe nothing of me save what you see with your own eyes."

"And must I believe all that I have seen with my own eyes?" asked Giovanni, pointedly, while the recollection of former scenes made him shrink. "No, signora; you demand too little of me. Bid me believe nothing save what comes from your own lips."

It would appear that Beatrice understood him. There came a deep flush to her cheek; but she looked full into Giovanni's eyes, and responded to his gaze of uneasy suspicion with a queenlike haughtiness.

"I do so bid you, signor," she replied. "Forget whatever you may have fancied in regard to me. If true to the outward senses, still it may be false in its essence; but the words of Beatrice Rappaccini's lips are true from the depths of the heart outward. Those you may believe."

A fervour glowed in her whole aspect and beamed upon Giovanni's consciousness like the light of truth itself; but while she spoke there was a fragrance in the atmosphere around her, rich and delightful, though evanescent, yet which the young man, from an indefinable reluctance, scarcely dared to draw into his lungs. It might be the odour of the flowers. Could it be Beatrice's breath which thus embalmed her words with a strange richness, as if by steeping them in her heart? A faintness passed like a shadow over Giovanni and flitted away; he seemed to gaze through the beautiful girl's eyes into her transparent soul, and felt no more doubt or fear.

The tinge of passion that had coloured Beatrice's manner vanished; she became gay, and appeared to derive a pure delight from her communion with the youth not unlike what the maiden of a lonely island might have felt conversing with a voyager from the civilized world. Evidently her experience of life had been confined within the limits of that garden. She talked now about matters as simple as the daylight or summer clouds, and now asked questions in reference to the city, or Giovanni's distant home, his friends, his mother, and his sisters—questions indicating such seclusion, and such lack of familiarity with modes and forms, that Giovanni responded as if to an infant. Her spirit gushed out before him like a fresh rill that was just catching its first glimpse of the sunlight and wondering at the reflections of earth and sky which were flung into its bosom. There came thoughts, too, from a deep source, and fantasies of a gemlike brilliancy, as if diamonds and rubies sparkled upward among the bubbles of the fountain. Ever and anon there gleamed across the young man's mind a sense of wonder that he should be walking side by side with the being who had so wrought upon his imagination, whom he had idealized in such hues of terror, in whom he had positively witnessed such manifestations of dreadful attributes,—that he should be conversing with Beatrice like a brother, and should find her so human and so maidenlike. But such reflections were only momentary; the effect of her character was too real not to make itself familiar at once.

In this free intercourse they had strayed through the garden, and now, after many turns among its avenues, were come to the shattered fountain, beside which grew the magnificent shrub, with its treasury of glowing blossoms. A fragrance was diffused from it which Giovanni recognized as identical with that which he had attributed to Beatrice's breath, but incomparably more powerful. As her eyes fell upon it, Giovanni beheld her press her hand to her bosom as if her heart were throbbing suddenly and painfully.

"For the first time in my life," murmured she, addressing the shrub, "I had forgotten thee."

"I remember, signora," said Giovanni, "that you once promised to reward me with one of these living gems for the bouquet which I had the happy boldness to fling to your feet. Permit me now to pluck it as a memorial of this interview."

He made a step towards the shrub with extended hand; but Beatrice darted forward, uttering a shriek that went through his heart like a dagger. She caught his hand and drew it back with the whole force of her slender figure. Giovanni felt her touch thrilling through his fibres.

"Touch it not!" exclaimed she, in a voice of agony. "Not for thy life! It is fatal!"

Then, hiding her face, she fled from him and vanished beneath the sculptured portal. As Giovanni followed her with his eyes, he beheld the emaciated figure and pale intelligence of Dr. Rappaccini, who had been watching the scene, he knew not how long, within the shadow of the entrance.

No sooner was Guasconti alone in his chamber than the image of Beatrice came back to his passionate musings, invested with all the witchery that had been gathering around it ever since his first glimpse of her, and now likewise imbued with a tender warmth of girlish womanhood. She was human; her nature was endowed with all gentle and feminine qualities; she was worthiest to be worshipped; she was capable, surely, on her part, of the height and heroism of love. Those tokens which he had hitherto considered as proofs of a frightful peculiarity in her physical and moral system were now either forgotten, or, by the subtle sophistry of passion transmitted into a golden crown of enchantment, rendering Beatrice the more admirable by so much as she was the more unique. Whatever had looked ugly was now beautiful; or, if incapable of such a change, it stole away and hid itself among those shapeless half ideas which throng the dim region beyond the daylight of our perfect consciousness. Thus did he spend the night, nor fell asleep until the dawn had begun to awake the slumbering flowers in Dr. Rappaccini's garden, whither Giovanni's dreams doubtless led him. Up rose the sun in his due season, and, flinging his beams upon the young man's eyelids, awoke him to a sense of pain. When thoroughly aroused, he became sensible of a burning and tingling agony in his hand—in his right hand—the very hand which Beatrice had grasped in her own when he was on the point of plucking one of the gemlike flowers. On the back of that hand there was now a purple print like that of four small fingers, and the likeness of a slender thumb upon his wrist.

Oh, how stubbornly does love,—or even that cunning semblance of love which flourishes in the imagination, but strikes no depth of root into the heart,—how stubbornly does it hold its faith until the moment comes when it is doomed to vanish into thin mist! Giovanni wrapped a handkerchief about his hand and wondered what evil thing had stung him, and soon forgot his pain in a reverie of Beatrice.

After the first interview, a second was in the inevitable course of what we call fate. A third; a fourth; and a meeting with Beatrice in the garden was no longer an incident in Giovanni's daily life, but the whole space in which he might be said to live; for the anticipation and memory of that ecstatic hour made up the remainder. Nor was it otherwise with the daughter of Rappaccini. She watched for the youth's appearance, and flew to his side with confidence as unreserved as if they had been playmates from early infancy—as if they were such playmates still. If, by any unwonted chance, he failed to come at the appointed moment, she stood beneath the window and sent up the rich sweetness of her tones to float around him in his chamber and echo and reverberate throughout his heart: "Giovanni! Giovanni! Why tarriest thou? Come down!" And down he hastened into that Eden of poisonous flowers.

But, with all this intimate familiarity, there was still a reserve in Beatrice's demeanour, so rigidly and invariably sustained that the idea of infringing it scarcely occurred to his imagination. By all appreciable signs, they loved; they had looked love with eyes that conveyed the holy secret from the depths of one soul into the depths of the other, as if it were too sacred to be whispered by the way; they had even spoken love in those gushes of passion when their spirits darted forth in articulated breath like tongues of long-hidden flame; and yet there had been no seal of lips, no clasp of hands, nor any slightest caress such as love claims and hallows. He had never touched one of the gleaming ringlets of her hair; her garment—so marked was the physical barrier between them—had never been waved against him by a breeze. On the few occasions when Giovanni had seemed tempted to overstep the limit, Beatrice grew so sad, so stern, and withal wore such a look of desolate separation, shuddering at itself, that not a spoken word was requisite to repel him. At such times he was startled at the horrible suspicions that rose, monster-like, out of the caverns of his heart and stared him in the face; his love grew thin and faint as the morning mist, his doubts alone had substance. But, when Beatrice's face brightened again after the momentary shadow, she was transformed at once from the mysterious, questionable being whom he had watched with so much awe and horror; she was now the beautiful and unsophisticated girl whom he felt that his spirit knew with a certainty beyond all other knowledge.

A considerable time had now passed since Giovanni's last meeting with Baglioni. One morning, however, he was disagreeably surprised by a visit from the professor, whom he had scarcely thought of for whole weeks, and would willingly have forgotten still longer. Given up as he had long been to a pervading excitement, he could tolerate no companions except upon condition of their perfect sympathy with his present state of feeling. Such sympathy was not to be expected from Professor Baglioni.

The visitor chatted carelessly for a few moments about the gossip of the city and the university, and then took up another topic.

"I have been reading an old classic author lately," said he, "and met with a story that strangely interested me. Possibly you may remember it. It is of an Indian prince, who sent a beautiful woman as a present to Alexander the Great. She was as lovely as the dawn and gorgeous as the sunset; but what especially distinguished her was a certain rich perfume in her breath—richer than a garden of Persian roses. Alexander, as was natural to a youthful conqueror, fell in love at first sight with this magnificent stranger; but a certain sage physician, happening to be present, discovered a terrible secret in regard to her."

"And what was that?" asked Giovanni, turning his eyes downward to avoid those of the professor.

"That this lovely woman," continued Baglioni, with emphasis, "had been nourished with poisons from her birth upward, until her whole nature was so imbued with them that she herself had become the deadliest poison in existence. Poison was her element of life. With that rich perfume of her breath she blasted the very air. Her love would have been poison—her embrace death. Is not this a marvellous tale?"

"A childish fable," answered Giovanni, nervously starting from his chair. "I marvel how your worship finds time to read such nonsense among your graver studies."

"By the by," said the professor, looking uneasily about him, "what singular fragrance is this in your apartment? Is it the perfume of your gloves? It is faint, but delicious; and yet, after all, by no means agreeable. Were I to breathe it long, methinks it would make me ill. It is like the breath of a flower; but I see no flowers in the chamber."

"Nor are there any," replied Giovanni, who had turned pale as the professor spoke; "nor, I think, is there any fragrance except in your worship's imagination. Odours, being a sort of element combined of the sensual and the spiritual, are apt to deceive us in this manner. The recollection of a perfume, the bare idea of it, may easily be mistaken for a present reality."

"Ay; but my sober imagination does not often play such tricks," said Baglioni; "and, were I to fancy any kind of odour, it would be that of some vile apothecary drug, wherewith my fingers are likely enough to be imbued. Our worshipful friend Rappaccini, as I have heard, tinctures his medicaments with odours richer than those of Araby. Doubtless, likewise, the fair and learned Signora Beatrice would minister to her patients with draughts as sweet as a maiden's breath; but woe to him that sips them!"

Giovanni's face evinced many contending emotions. The tone in which the professor alluded to the pure and lovely daughter of Rappaccini was a torture to his soul; and yet the intimation of a view of her character opposite to his own, gave instantaneous distinctness to a thousand dim suspicions, which now grinned at him like so many demons. But he strove hard to quell them and to respond to Baglioni with a true lover's perfect faith.

"Signor professor," said he, "you were my father's friend; perchance, too, it is your purpose to act a friendly part towards his son. I would fain feel nothing towards you save respect and deference; but I pray you to observe, signor, that there is one subject on which we must not speak. You know not the Signora

Beatrice. You cannot, therefore, estimate the wrong—the blasphemy, I may even say—that is offered to her character by a light or injurious word."

"Giovanni! my poor Giovanni!" answered the professor, with a calm expression of pity, "I know this wretched girl far better than yourself. You shall hear the truth in respect to the poisoner Rappaccini and his poisonous daughter; yes, poisonous as she is beautiful. Listen; for, even should you do violence to my gray hairs, it shall not silence me. That old fable of the Indian woman has become a truth by the deep and deadly science of Rappaccini and in the person of the lovely Beatrice."

Giovanni groaned and hid his face

"Her father," continued Baglioni, "was not restrained by natural affection from offering up his child in this horrible manner as the victim of his insane zeal for science; for, let us do him justice, he is as true a man of science as ever distilled his own heart in an alembic. What, then, will be your fate? Beyond a doubt you are selected as the material of some new experiment. Perhaps the result is to be death; perhaps a fate more awful still. Rappaccini, with what he calls the interest of science before his eyes, will hesitate at nothing."

"It is a dream," muttered Giovanni to himself; "surely it is a dream."

"But," resumed the professor, "be of good cheer, son of my friend. It is not yet too late for the rescue. Possibly we may even succeed in bringing back this miserable child within the limits of ordinary nature, from which her father's madness has estranged her. Behold this little silver vase! It was wrought by the hands of the renowned Benvenuto Cellini, and is well worthy to be a love gift to the fairest dame in Italy. But its contents are invaluable. One little sip of this antidote would have rendered the most virulent poisons of the Borgias innocuous. Doubt not that it will be as efficacious against those of Rappaccini. Bestow the vase, and the precious liquid within it, on your Beatrice, and hopefully await the result."

Baglioni laid a small, exquisitely wrought silver vial on the table and withdrew, leaving what he had said to produce its effect upon the young man's mind.

"We will thwart Rappaccini yet," thought he, chuckling to himself, as he descended the stairs; "but, let us confess the truth of him, he is a wonderful man—a wonderful man indeed; a vile empiric, however, in his practice, and therefore not to be tolerated by those who respect the good old rules of the medical profession."

Throughout Giovanni's whole acquaintance with Beatrice, he had occasionally, as we have said, been haunted by dark surmises as to her character; yet so thoroughly had she made herself felt by him as a simple, natural, most affectionate, and guileless creature, that the image now held up by Professor Baglioni looked as strange and incredible as if it were not in accordance with his own original conception. True, there were ugly recollections connected with his first glimpses of the beautiful girl; he could not quite forget the bouquet that withered in her grasp, and the insect that perished amid the sunny air, by no ostensible agency save the fragrance of her breath. These incidents, however, dissolving in the pure light of her character, had no longer the efficacy of facts, but were acknowledged as mistaken fantasies, by whatever testimony of the senses they might appear to be substantiated. There is something truer and more real than what we can see with the eyes and touch with the finger. On such better evidence had Giovanni founded his confidence in Beatrice, though rather by the necessary force of her high attributes than by any deep and generous faith on his part. But now his spirit was incapable of sustaining itself at the height to which the early enthusiasm of passion had exalted it; he fell down, grovelling among earthly doubts, and defiled therewith the pure whiteness of Beatrice's image. Not that he gave her up; he did but distrust. He resolved to institute some decisive test that should satisfy him, once for all, whether there were those dreadful peculiarities in her physical nature which could not be supposed to exist without some corresponding monstrosity of soul. His eyes, gazing down afar, might have deceived him as to the lizard, the insect, and the flowers; but if he could witness, at the distance of a few paces, the sudden blight of one fresh and healthful flower in Beatrice's hand, there would be room for no further question. With this idea he hastened to the florist's and purchased a bouquet that was still gemmed with the morning dew-drops.

It was now the customary hour of his daily interview with Beatrice. Before descending into the garden, Giovanni failed not to look at his figure in the mirror,—a vanity to be expected in a beautiful young man, yet, as displaying itself at that troubled and feverish moment, the token of a certain shallowness of feeling and insincerity of character. He did gaze, however, and said to himself that his features had never before possessed so rich a grace, nor his eyes such vivacity, nor his cheeks so warm a hue of superabundant life.

"At least," thought he, "her poison has not yet insinuated itself into my system. I am no flower to perish in her grasp."

With that thought he turned his eyes on the bouquet, which he had never once laid aside from his hand. A thrill of indefinable horror shot through his frame on perceiving that those dewy flowers were already beginning to droop; they wore the aspect of things that had been fresh and lovely yesterday. Giovanni grew white as marble, and stood motionless before the mirror, staring at his own reflection there as at the likeness of something frightful. He remembered Baglioni's remark about the fragrance that seemed to pervade the chamber. It must have been the poison in his breath! Then he shuddered—shuddered at himself. Recovering from his stupor, he began to watch with curious eye a spider that was busily at work hanging its web from the antique cornice of the apartment, crossing and recrossing the artful system of interwoven lines—as vigorous and active a spider as ever dangled from an old ceiling. Giovanni bent towards the insect, and emitted a deep, long breath. The spider suddenly ceased its toil; the web vibrated with a tremor originating in the body of the small artisan. Again Giovanni sent forth a breath, deeper, longer, and imbued with a venomous feeling out of his heart: he knew not whether he were wicked, or only desperate. The spider made a convulsive gripe with his limbs and hung dead across the window.

"Accursed! accursed!" muttered Giovanni, addressing himself. "Hast thou grown so poisonous that this deadly insect perishes by thy breath?"

At that moment a rich, sweet voice came floating up from the garden.

"Giovanni! Giovanni! It is past the hour! Why tarriest thou? Come down!"

"Yes," muttered Giovanni again. "She is the only being whom my breath may not slay! Would that it might!"

He rushed down, and in an instant was standing before the bright and loving eyes of Beatrice. A moment ago his wrath and despair had been so fierce that he could have desired nothing so much as to wither her by a glance; but with her actual presence there came influences which had too real an existence to be at once shaken off: recollections of the delicate and benign power of her feminine nature, which had so often enveloped him in a religious calm; recollections of many a holy and passionate outgush of her heart, when the pure fountain had been unsealed from its depths and made visible in its transparency to his mental eye; recollections which, had Giovanni known how to estimate them, would have assured him that all this ugly mystery was but an earthly illusion, and that, whatever mist of evil might seem to have gathered over her, the real Beatrice was a heavenly angel. Incapable as he was of such high faith, still her presence had not utterly lost its magic. Giovanni's rage was quelled into an aspect of sullen insensibility. Beatrice, with a quick spiritual sense, immediately felt that there was a gulf of blackness between them which neither he nor she could pass. They walked on together, sad and silent, and came thus to the marble fountain and to its pool of water on the ground, in the midst of which grew the shrub that bore gem-like blossoms. Giovanni was affrighted at the eager enjoyment—the appetite, as it were—with which he found himself inhaling the fragrance of the flowers.

"Beatrice," asked he, abruptly, "whence came this shrub?"

"My father created it," answered she, with simplicity.

"Created it! created it!" repeated Giovanni. "What mean you, Beatrice?"

"He is a man fearfully acquainted with the secrets of Nature," replied Beatrice; "and, at the hour when I first drew breath, this plant sprang from the soil, the offspring of his science, of his intellect, while I was but his earthly child. Approach it not!" continued she, observing with terror that Giovanni was drawing nearer to the shrub. "It has qualities that you little dream of. But I, dearest Giovanni,—I grew up and blossomed with the plant and was nourished with its breath. It was my sister, and I loved it with a human affection; for, alas!—hast thou not suspected it?—there was an awful doom."

Here Giovanni frowned so darkly upon her that Beatrice paused and trembled. But her faith in his tenderness reassured her, and made her blush that she had doubted for an instant.

"There was an awful doom," she continued, "the effect of my father's fatal love of science, which estranged me from all society of my kind. Until Heaven sent thee, dearest Giovanni, oh, how lonely was thy poor Beatrice!"

"Was it a hard doom?" asked Giovanni, fixing his eyes upon her.

"Only of late have I known how hard it was," answered she, tenderly. "Oh, yes; but my heart was torpid, and therefore quiet."

Giovanni's rage broke forth from his sullen gloom like a lightning flash out of a dark cloud.

"Accursed one!" cried he, with venomous scorn and anger. "And, finding thy solitude wearisome, thou hast severed me likewise from all the warmth of life and enticed me into thy region of unspeakable horror!"

"Giovanni!" exclaimed Beatrice, turning her large bright eyes upon his face. The force of his words had not found its way into her mind; she was merely thunderstruck.

"Yes, poisonous thing!" repeated Giovanni, beside himself with passion. "Thou hast done it! Thou hast blasted me! Thou hast filled my veins with poison! Thou hast made me as hateful, as ugly, as loathsome and deadly a creature as thyself—a world's wonder of hideous monstrosity! Now, if our breath be happily as fatal to ourselves as to all others, let us join our lips in one kiss of unutterable hatred, and so die!"

"What has befallen me?" murmured Beatrice, with a low moan out of her heart. "Holy Virgin, pity me, a poor heart-broken child!"

"Thou,—dost thou pray?" cried Giovanni, still with the same fiendish scorn. "Thy very prayers, as they come from thy lips, taint the atmosphere with death. Yes, yes; let us pray! Let us to church and dip our fingers in the holy water at the portal! They that come after us will perish as by a pestilence! Let us sign crosses in the air! It will be scattering curses abroad in the likeness of holy symbols!"

"Giovanni," said Beatrice, calmly, for her grief was beyond passion, "why dost thou join thyself with me thus in those terrible words? I, it is true, am the horrible thing thou namest me. But thou,—what hast thou to do, save with one other shudder at my hideous misery to go forth out of the garden and mingle with thy race, and forget there ever crawled on earth such a monster as poor Beatrice?"

"Dost thou pretend ignorance?" asked Giovanni, scowling upon her. "Behold! this power have I gained from the pure daughter of Rappaccini.

There was a swarm of summer insects flitting through the air in search of the food promised by the flower odours of the fatal garden. They circled round Giovanni's head, and were evidently attracted towards him by the same influence which had drawn them for an instant within the sphere of several of the shrubs. He sent forth a breath among them, and smiled bitterly at Beatrice as at least a score of the insects fell dead upon the ground.

"I see it! I see it!" shrieked Beatrice. "It is my father's fatal science! No, no, Giovanni; it was not I! Never! never! I dreamed only to love thee and be with thee a little time, and so to let thee pass away, leaving but thine image in mine heart; for, Giovanni, believe it, though my body be nourished with poison, my spirit is God's creature, and craves love as its daily food. But my father,—he has united us in this fearful sympathy. Yes; spurn me, tread upon me, kill me! Oh, what is death after such words as thine? But it was not I. Not for a world of bliss would I have done it."

Giovanni's passion had exhausted itself in its outburst from his lips. There now came across him a sense, mournful, and not without tenderness, of the intimate and peculiar relationship between Beatrice and himself. They stood, as it were, in an utter solitude, which would be made none the less solitary by the densest throng of human life. Ought not, then, the desert of humanity around them to press this insulated pair closer together? If they should be cruel to one another, who was there to be kind to them? Besides, thought Giovanni, might there not still be a hope of his returning within the limits of ordinary nature, and leading Beatrice, the redeemed Beatrice, by the hand? O, weak, and selfish, and unworthy spirit, that could dream of an earthly union and earthly happiness as possible, after such deep love had been so bitterly wronged as was Beatrice's love by Giovanni's blighting words! No, no; there could be no such hope. She must pass heavily, with that broken heart, across the borders of Time—she must bathe her hurts in some fount of paradise, and forget her grief in the light of immortality, and *there* be well.

But Giovanni did not know it.

"Dear Beatrice," said he, approaching her, while she shrank away as always at his approach, but now with a different impulse, "dearest Beatrice, our fate is not yet so desperate. Behold! there is a medicine, potent, as a wise physician has assured me, and almost divine in its efficacy. It is composed of ingredients the most opposite to those by which thy awful father has brought this calamity upon thee and me. It is distilled of blessed herbs. Shall we not quaff it together, and thus be purified from evil?"

"Give it me!" said Beatrice, extending her hand to receive the little silver vial which Giovanni took from his bosom. She added, with a peculiar emphasis, "I will drink; but do thou await the result."

She put Baglioni's antidote to her lips; and, at the same moment, the figure of Rappaccini emerged from the portal and came slowly towards the marble fountain. As he drew near, the pale man of science seemed to gaze with a triumphant expression at the beautiful youth and maiden, as might an artist who should spend his life in achieving a picture or a group of statuary and finally be satisfied with his success. He paused; his bent form grew erect with conscious power; he spread out his hands over them in the attitude of a father imploring a blessing upon his children; but those were the same hands that had thrown poison into the stream of their lives. Giovanni trembled. Beatrice shuddered nervously, and pressed her hand upon her heart.

"My daughter," said Rappaccini, "thou art no longer lonely in the world. Pluck one of those precious gems from thy sister shrub and bid thy bridegroom wear it in his bosom. It will not harm him now. My science and the sympathy between thee and him have so wrought within his system that he now stands apart from common men, as thou dost, daughter of my pride and triumph, from ordinary women. Pass on, then, through the world, most dear to one another and dreadful to all besides!"

"My father," said Beatrice, feebly,—and still as she spoke she kept her hand upon her heart,—"wherefore didst thou inflict this miserable doom upon thy child?"

"Miserable!" exclaimed Rappaccini. "What mean you, foolish girl? Dost thou deem it misery to be endowed with marvellous gifts against which no power nor strength could avail an enemy—misery, to be able to quell the mightiest with a breath—misery, to be as terrible as thou art beautiful? Wouldst thou, then, have preferred the condition of a weak woman, exposed to all evil and capable of none?"

"I would fain have been loved, not feared," murmured Beatrice, sinking down upon the ground. "But now it matters not. I am going, father, where the evil which thou hast striven to mingle with my being will pass away like a dream—like the fragrance of these poisonous flowers, which will no longer taint my breath among the flowers of Eden. Farewell, Giovanni! Thy words of hatred are like lead within my heart; but they, too, will fall away as I ascend. Oh, was there not, from the first, more poison in thy nature than in mine?"

To Beatrice,—so radically had her earthly part been wrought upon by Rappaccini's skill,—as poison had been life, so the powerful antidote was death; and thus the poor victim of man's ingenuity and of thwarted nature, and of the fatality that attends all such efforts of perverted wisdom, perished there, at the feet of her father and Giovanni. Just at that moment Professor Pietro Baglioni looked forth from the window, and called loudly, in a tone of triumph mixed with horror, to the thunderstricken man of science, "Rappaccini! Rappaccini! and is *this* the upshot of your experiment!"

THE EMANCIPATRIX

by Homer Eon Flint

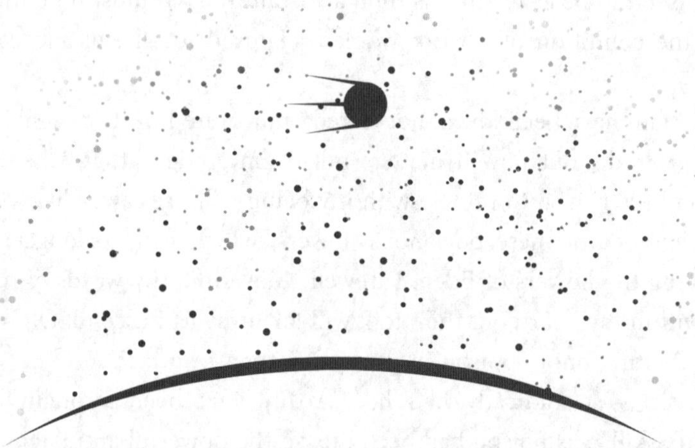

I
THE MENTAL EXPEDITION

The doctor closed the door behind him, crossed to the table, silently offered the geologist a cigar, and waited until smoke was issuing from it. Then he said:

"Well," bluntly, "what's come between you and your wife, Van?"

The geologist showed no surprise. Instead, he frowned severely at the end of his cigar, and carefully seated himself on the corner of the table. When he spoke there was a certain rigor in his voice, which told the doctor that his friend was holding himself tightly in rein.

"It really began when the four of us got together to investigate Capellette, two months ago." Van Emmon was a thorough man in important matters. "Maybe I ought to say that both Billie and I were as much interested as either you or Smith; she often says that even the tour of Mercury and Venus was less wonderful.

"What is more, we are both just as eager to continue the investigations. We still have all kinds of faith in the Venusian formula; we want to 'visit' as many more worlds as the science of telepathy will permit. It isn't that either of us has lost interest."

The doctor rather liked the geologist's scientific way of stating the case, even though it meant hearing things he already knew. Kinney watched and waited and listened intently.

"You remember, of course, what sort of a man I got in touch with. Powart was easily the greatest Capellan of them all; a magnificent intellect, which I still think was intended to have ruled the rest. I haven't backed down from my original position."

"Van! You still believe," incredulously, "in a government of the sort he contemplated?"

Van Emmon nodded aggressively. "All that we learned merely strengthens my conviction. Remember what sort of people the working classes of Capellette were? Smith's 'agent' was typical—a helpless nincompoop, not fit to govern himself!" The geologist strove to keep his patience.

"However," remarked Kinney, "the chap whose mind I used was no fool."

"Nor was Billie's agent, the woman surgeon," agreed Van Emmon, "even if she did prefer 'the Devolutionist' to Powart. But you'll have to admit, doc, that the vast majority of the Capellans were incompetents; the rest were exceptions."

The doctor spoke after a brief pause. "And—that's what is wrong, Van?"

"Yes," grimly. "Billie can't help but rejoice that things turned out the way they did. She is sure that the workers, now that they've been separated from the ruling class, will proceed to make a perfect paradise out of their land." He could not repress a certain amount of sarcasm. "As well expect a bunch of monkeys to build a steam engine!

"Well," after a little hesitation, "as I said before, doc, I've no reason to change my mind. You may talk all you like about it—I can't agree to such ideas. The only way to get results on that planet is for the upper classes to continue to govern."

"And this is what you two have—quarrelled about?"

Van Emmon nodded sorrowfully. He lit another cigar absent-mindedly and cleared his throat twice before going on:

"My fault, I guess. I've been so darned positive about everything I've said, I've probably caused Billie to sympathize with her friends more solidly than she would otherwise."

"But just because you've championed the autocrats so heartily—"

"I'm afraid so!" The geologist was plainly relieved to have stated the case in full. He leaned forward in his eagerness to be understood. He told the doctor things that were altogether too personal to be included in this account.

Meanwhile, out in the doctor's study, Smith had made no move whatever to interrogate the geologist's young wife. Instead, the engineer simply remained standing after Billie had sat down, and gave her only an occasional hurried glance. Shortly the silence got on her nerves; and—such was her nature, as contrasted with Van Emmon's—whereas he had stated causes first, she went straight to effects.

"Well," explosively, "Van and I have split!"

Smith was seldom surprised at anything. This time was no exception. He merely murmured "Sorry" under his breath; and Billie rushed on, her pent-up feelings eager to escape.

"We haven't mentioned Capellette for weeks, Smith! We don't dare! If we did, there'd be such a rumpus that we—we'd separate!" Something came up into her throat which had to be choked back before she could go on. Then—

"I don't know why it is, but every time the subject is brought up Van makes me so *wild*!" She controlled herself with a tremendous effort. "He blames me, of course, because of what I did to help the Devolutionist. But I can't be blamed for sympathizing with the under dog, can I? I've always preferred justice to policy, any time. Justice first, I say! And I think we've seen—there on Capellette—how utterly impossible it is for any such system as theirs to last indefinitely."

But before she could follow up her point the door opened and the doctor returned with her husband. Kinney did not allow any tension to develop; instead, he said briskly:

"There's only a couple of hours remaining between now and dinner time; I move we get busy." He glanced about the room, to see if all was in place. The four chairs, each with its legs tipped with glass; the four footstools, similarly insulated from the floor; the electrical circuit running from the odd group of machinery in the corner, and connecting four pair of brass bracelets—all were ready for use. He motioned the others to the chairs in which they had already accomplished marvels in the way of mental travelling.

"Now," he remarked, as he began to fit the bracelets to his wrists, an example which the rest straightway followed; "now, we want to make sure that we all have the same purpose in mind. Last time, we were simply looking for four people, such as had view-points similar to our own. Today, our object is to locate, somewhere among the planets attached to one of the innumerable sun-stars of the universe, one on which the conditions are decidedly different from anything we have known before."

Billie and Van Emmon, their affair temporarily forgotten, listened eagerly.

"As I recall it," Smith calmly observed, "we agreed that this attempt would be to locate a new kind of—well, near-human. Isn't that right?"

The doctor nodded. "Nothing more or less"—speaking very distinctly—"than a creature as superior as we are, but *not in human form*."

Smith tried hard not to share the thrill. He had been reading biology the previous week. "I may as well protest, first as last, that I don't see how human intelligence can ever be developed outside the human form. Not—possibly!"

Van Emmon also was sceptical, but his wife declared the idea merely unusual, not impossible. "Is there any particular reason against it?" she demanded of the doctor.

"I will say this much," cautiously. "Given certain conditions, and inevitably the human form will most certainly become the supreme creature, superior to all the others.

"However, suppose the planetary conditions are entirely different. I conceive it entirely possible for one of the other animals to forge ahead of the man-ape; quite possible, Smith," as the engineer started to object, "if only the conditions are different *enough*.

"At any rate, we shall soon find out. I have been reading further in the library the Venusians gave us, and I assure you that I've found some astonishing things." He fingered one of the diminutive volumes. "There is one planet in particular, whose name I have forgotten, where all animal life has disappeared entirely. There are none but vegetable forms on the land, and all of them are the rankest sort of weeds. They have literally choked off everything else!

"And the highest form of life there is a weed; a hideous monstrosity, shaped something like an octopus, and capable of the most horrible—" He stopped abruptly, remembering that one of his hearers was a woman. "Never mind about that now."

He indicated another of the little books. "I think we will do well to investigate a planet which the Venusians call 'Sanus.' It belongs to the tremendous planetary family of the giant star Arcturus. I haven't read any details at all; I didn't want to know more than you. We can proceed with our discoveries on an equal footing."

"But," objected Smith, recalling the previous methods, "how are we to put our minds in touch with any of theirs, unless we know enough about them to imagine their viewpoints?"

"Our knowledge of their planet's name and location," replied the doctor, "makes it easier for us. All we have to do is to go into the telepathic state, via the Venusian formula; then, at the same time, each must concentrate upon some definite mental quality, some particular characteristic of his own mind, which he or she wishes to find on Sanus. It makes no difference what it may be; all you have to do is, exert your imaginations a little."

There was a pause, broken by Smith: "We ought to tell each other what we have in mind, so that we don't conflict."

"Yes. For my part," said the doctor, "I'd like to get in touch with a being who is mildly rebellious; not a violent radical, but a philosophical revolutionist. I don't care what sort of a creature he, she, or it may be, so long as the mind is in revolt against whatever injustice may exist."

"Then I," stated Smith, "will stick to the idea of service." Nobody was surprised that the engineer should make such a choice; he was, first, last, and all the time, essentially a useful man.

Van Emmon was not ready with his choice. Instead: "You say, doc, that you know nothing further about Sanus than what you've already told us?"

"I was about to mention that. The Venusians say that conditions are reversed from what we found on Capellette. Instead of Sanus being ruled by a small body of autocrats, it is—ruled by the working class!"

"Under the circumstances," said Van, "I'll take something different from what I got last time. No imperiousness this trip." He smiled grimly. "There was a time when I used to take orders. Suppose you call my choice 'subordinacy.'"

"How very noble of you!" gibed Billie. "My idea is supremacy, and plenty of it! I want to get in touch with the man higher up—the worker who is boss of the whole works!" She flashed a single glance at her husband, then threw herself back in her chair. "Go ahead!"

And before two minutes were up, the power of concerted thought, aided by a common objective and the special electrical circuit which joined them, had projected the minds of the four across the infinite depths of space. The vast distance which separated their bodies from Sanus was annihilated, literally as quick as thought.

Neither of the four stirred. To all appearances they were fast asleep. The room was quite still; only the clock ticked dully on the wall. Down-stairs, the doctor's wife kept watch over the house.

The greatest marvel in creation, the human mind, was exploring the unknown.

II
ALMOST HUMAN

Of course, the four still had the ability to communicate with each other while in the trance state; they had developed this power to a fair degree while investigating Capellette. However, each was so deeply interested in what he or she was seeing during the first hour of their Sanusian experiences that neither thought to discuss the matter until afterward.

When the doctor first made connection with the eyes of his agent, he instinctively concluded that he, at least, had got in touch with a being more or less like himself. The whole thing was so natural; he was surveying a sunny, brush-covered landscape from eyes whose height from the ground, and other details, were decidedly those of a human.

For a moment there was comparative silence. Then his unknown agent swiftly raised something—a hand, presumably—to a mouth, and gave out a piercing cry. Whereupon the doctor learned something that jarred him a trifle. His agent was—a woman!

He had time to congratulate himself upon the fact that he was (1) a doctor, (2) a married man, (3) the father of a daughter or two, before his agent repeated her cry. Almost immediately it was answered by another exactly like it, from an unseen point not far away. The Sanusian plainly chuckled to herself with satisfaction.

A moment later there came, rather faintly, two more calls, each from a different direction in the dun-coloured brush. Still without moving from the spot, the doctor's agent replied two or three times, meanwhile watching her surroundings very closely. Within half a minute the first of her friends came in sight.

It was a young woman. At a distance of about twenty yards she appeared to be about five feet tall and sturdily built. She was dressed in a single garment, made of the skin of some yellow, short-haired animal. It may have been a lion cub. Around her waist was a strip of hide, which served as a belt, and held a small, stone-headed tomahawk. One shoulder and both legs were left quite bare, revealing a complexion so deeply tanned that the doctor instantly thought: "Spanish!"

In a way, the girl's face gave the same impression. Large, dark-brown eyes, full lips and a healthy glow beneath her tan, all made it possible for her to pass as a Spaniard. However, there was nothing in the least coquettish about her; she had a remarkably independent manner, and a gaze as frank and direct as it was pure and untroubled.

In one hand she carried a branch from some large-leafed shrub. The eyes which Kinney was using became fixed upon this branch; and even as the newcomer cried out in joyous response to the other's greeting, her expression changed and she turned and fled, laughing, as the doctor's agent darted toward her. She did not get away, and immediately the two were struggling over the possession of the branch.

In the midst of the tussle another figure made its appearance.

"Look out! Here comes Dulnop!"* cried Kinney's agent; at the same time she made a special effort, and succeeded in breaking off a good half of the branch.

Instantly she darted to one side, where she calmly began to pluck some small, hard-shelled nuts from the branch, and proceeded to crack them, with entire ease, using a set of teeth which must have been absolutely perfect.

She gave the latest comer only a glance or two. He—for it certainly was a man—was nearly a half a foot taller than the girl already described; but he was plainly not much older or younger, and in build and colour much the same. He was clothed neither more nor less than she, the only difference being that some leopardlike animal had contributed the material. In his belt was tucked a primitive stone hammer, also a stone knife. His face was longer than hers, his eyes darker; but he was manifestly still very boyish. Dulnop, they had called him.

"Hail, Cunora!" he called to the girl who had brought the nuts; then, to her who was watching: "Rolla! Where got ye the nuts?"

Rolla didn't answer; she couldn't use her mouth just then; it was too full of

* It made no difference whatever as to what language was used. The telepathic process employed enabled the investigators to know all that their agents' subconscious minds took in. The brains of the four automatically translated these thought-images into their own language. However, this method did not enable them to learn what their agents were thinking, but only what they said, heard, and saw.

nuts. She merely nodded in the direction of Cunora.

"Give me some, Cunora!"

The younger girl gave no reply, but backed away from him as he approached; her eyes sparkled mischievously and, the doctor thought, somewhat affectionately. Dulnop made a sudden darting move toward her branch, and she as swiftly whirled in her tracks, so that he missed. However, he instantly changed his mind and grasped the girl instead. Like a flash he drew her to him and kissed her noisily.

Next second he was staggering backward under the weight of her hard brown fist. "Do that again, and I'll have the hair out of thy head!" the girl screamed, her face flaming. Yet Kinney saw that the man was laughing joyously even as he rubbed the spot where her blow had landed, while the expression of her eyes quite belied what she had said.

Not until then did the doctor's agent say anything. When she spoke it was in a deep, contralto voice which gave the impression of riper years than either of the other two. Afterward Kinney learned that Rolla was nearly ten years their senior, a somewhat more lithe specimen of the same type, clad in the skin of what was once a magnificent goat. She carried only a single small knife in her belt. As seen reflected in pools of water, her complexion was slightly paler and her whole expression a little less self-assertive and distinctively philosophical. To those who admire serious, thoughtful women of regular feature and different manner, Rolla would have seemed downright beautiful.

"Dulnop," said she, with a laugh in her voice, "ye will do well to seek the nut tree, first as last." She nonchalantly crushed another shell in her mouth. "Neither Cunora nor I can spare good food to a kiss-hungry lout like thee!"

He only laughed again and made as though to come toward her. She stood ready to dodge, chuckling excitedly, and he evidently gave it up as a bad job. "Tell me whence cameth the nuts, Cunora!" he begged; but the girl pretended to be cross, and shut her mouth as firmly as its contents would allow.

Next moment there was a shout from the thicket, together with a crashing sound; and shortly the fourth Sanusian appeared. He was by far the larger; but his size was a matter of width rather than of height. An artist would have picked him as a model for Ajax himself. His muscles fairly strained the huge lion's skin in which he was clad, and he had twice the weight of Dulnop within the same height. Also, to the doctor's eye, he was nearer Rolla's age.

His face was strong and handsome in a somewhat fierce, relentless way; his complexion darker than the rest. He carried a huge club, such as must have weighed all of forty pounds, while his belt was jammed full of stone weapons. The doctor classed him and the younger girl together because of their vigour and independence, while Dulnop and Rolla seemed to have dispositions very similar in their comparative gentleness and restraint.

"Hail, all of ye!" shouted this latest arrival in a booming baritone. He strode forward with scarcely a glance at the two younger people; his gaze was fixed upon Rolla, his expression unmistakable. The woman quietly turned upon Dulnop and Cunora.

"Look!" she exclaimed, pointing to a spot back of them. "See the curious bird!" They wheeled instantly, with the unquestioning faith of two children; and before they had brought their gazes back again, the big man had seized Rolla, crushed her to his breast and kissed her passionately. She responded just as warmly, pushing him away only in order to avoid being seen by the others. They showed only an innocent disappointment at having missed seeing the "curious bird."

"A simple-minded people, basically good-humoured," was the way the doctor summed the matter up when reporting what he had seen. However, it was not so easy to analyze certain things that were said during the time the four Sanusians spent in each other's company. For one thing—

"Did They give thee permission to go?" Rolla was asked by the big man. His name, it seemed, was Corrus.

"Yes, Corrus. They seemed to think it a good idea for us to take a little recreation today. I suppose ye left thy herd with thy brother?"

He nodded; and the doctor was left to wonder whom "They" might be. Were They a small group of humans, whose function was to superintend? Or were They, as the books from Venus seemed to indicate, another type of creature, entirely different from the humans, and yet, because of the peculiar Sanusian conditions, superior to the humans?

"They have decided to move their city a little farther away from the forest," Rolla overheard Dulnop telling Cunora; which was the first indication that the planet boasted such a thing as a city. Otherwise, things appeared to be in a primitive, rather than a civilized condition.

These four skin-clad savages seemed to be enjoying an aboriginal picnic. For lunch, they munched on various fruits and nuts picked up en route, together with handfuls of some wheatlike cereal which the big man had brought in a goatskin. From time to time they scared out various animals from the brush, chasing the creatures after the fashion of dogs and children. Whenever they came to a stream, invariably all four splashed through it, shouting and laughing with delight.

However, there were but two of these streams, and both of them quite small. Their banks indicated that either the season was very far advanced, or else that the streams were at one time vastly larger.

"A rather significant fact," the doctor afterward commented.

Nevertheless, the most impressive thing about all that the doctor learned that day was the strange manner in which the excursion came to an end. The quartet was at that moment climbing a small hill, apparently on the edge of an extensive range of mountains. An occasional tree, something like an oak, broke the monotony of the brush at this point, and yet it was not until Rolla was quite at the top of the knoll that Kinney could see surrounding country with any degree of clearness. Even then he learned little.

The hill was placed on one edge of a valley about forty miles in width. A good part of it was covered with dusty vegetation, presumably wild; but the rest was plainly under cultivation. There were large green areas, such as argued grain fields; elsewhere were what looked like orchards and vineyards, some of which were in full bloom—refuting the notion that the season was a late one. Nowhere was there a spot of land which might be called barren.

Rolla and her three friends stood taking this in, keeping a rather curious silence meanwhile. At length Cunora gave a deep sigh, which was almost instantly reproduced by all the rest. Corrus followed his own sigh with a frank curse.

"By the great god Mownoth!" he swore fiercely. "It be a shame that we cannot come hence a great deal oftener! Me-thinks They could allow it!"

"They care not for our longings," spoke Cunora, her eyes flashing as angrily as his. "They give us enough freedom to make us work the better—no more! All They care for is thy herd and my crops!"

"And for the labour," reminded the big man, "of such brains as Rolla's and Dulnop's. It be not right that They should drive us so!"

"Aye," agreed the younger man, with much less enthusiasm. "However, what can ye do about it, Corrus?"

The big man's face flushed, and he all but snarled. "I tell ye what I can do, I, and ye as well, if ye but will! I can—"

He stopped, one hand upraised in mighty emphasis, and a sudden and startling change came over him. Downright fear drove the anger from his face; his massive body suddenly relaxed, and all his power and vigour seemed to crumble and wilt. His hands shook; his mouth trembled. At the same time the two women shrank from him, each giving an inarticulate cry of alarm and distress. Dulnop gave no sound, but the anger which had left the herdsman seemed to have come to him; the youngster's eyes flared and his breast heaved. His gaze was fixed upon Corrus's neck, where the sweat of fear already glistened.

Suddenly the big man dropped his head, as though in surrender. He gasped and found voice; this time a voice as shaky and docile as it had been strong and dominant a moment before.

"Very well," he spoke abjectly. "Very well. I—shall do as you wish." He seemed to be talking to thin air. "We—will go home at once."

And instantly all four turned about, and in perfect silence took the back trail.

III
WORLD OF MAMMOTHS

Immediately upon going into tele-consciousness Smith became aware of a decided change in his surroundings. The interior of the study had been darkened with drawn shades; now he was using eyes that were exposed to the most intense sunlight. The first sight that he got, in fact, was directed toward the sky; and he noted with an engineer's keen interest that the colour of the sky was blue, slightly tinged with orange. This, he knew, meant that the atmosphere of Sanus contained at least one chemical element which is lacking on the earth.

For a minute or two the sky remained entirely clear. There were no clouds whatever; neither did any form of winged life make its appearance. So Smith took note of sounds.

Presumably his agent—whoever or whatever it might be—was located in some sort of aircraft; for an extremely loud and steady buzzing, suggesting a powerful engine, filled the engineer's borrowed ears. Try as he might, however, he could not identify the sound exactly. It was more like an engine than anything else, except that the separate sounds which comprised the buzz occurred infinitely close together. Smith concluded that the machine was some highly developed rotary affair, working at perhaps six or eight thousand revolutions a minute—three or four times as fast as an ordinary engine.

Meanwhile his agent continued to stare into the sky. Shortly something arrived in the field of vision; a blurred speck, far to one side. It approached leisurely, with the unknown agent watching steadfastly. It still remained blurred, however; for a long time the engineer knew as little about its actual form as he knew about his mysterious agent.

Then, like a flash, the vision cleared. All the blurring disappeared instantly, and the form of a buzzard was disclosed. It was almost directly overhead, about a quarter of a mile distant, and soaring in a wide spiral. No sound whatever came from it. Smith's agent made no move of any kind, but continued to watch.

Shortly the buzzard "banked" for a sharper turn; and the engineer saw, by the perspective of its apparent speed, that the aircraft whose use he was enjoying was likewise on the move. Apparently it was flying in a straight line, keeping the sun—an object vastly too brilliant to examine—on the right.

The buzzard went out of sight. Once more the clear sky was all that could be seen; that, and the continual roar of the engine, were all that Smith actually knew. He became impatient for his agent to look elsewhere; it might be that the craft contained other specimens of the unknown creatures. But there was no change in the vigilant watch which was being kept upon the sky.

Suddenly the engineer became exceedingly alert. He had noticed something new—something so highly different from anything he had expected to learn that it was some minutes before he could believe it true.

His borrowed eyes had no eyelids! At least, if they did, they were never used. Not once did they flicker in the slightest; not once did they blink or wink, much less close themselves for a momentary rest from the sun's glare. They remained as stonily staring as the eyes of a marble statue.

Then something startling happened. With the most sickening suddenness the aircraft came to an abrupt halt. Smith's senses swam with the jolt of it. All about him was a confused jumble of blurred figures and forms; it was infinitely worse than his first ride in a hoist. In a moment, however, he was able to examine things fairly well.

The aircraft had come to a stop in the middle of what looked like a cane brake. On all sides rose yellowish-green shafts, bearing leaves characteristic of the maize family. Smith knew little about cane, yet felt sure that these specimens were a trifle large. "Possibly due to difference in gravitation," he thought.

However, he could not tell much about the spot on which the machine had landed. For a moment it was motionless; the engine had been stopped, and all was silent except for the gentle rustling of the cane in the field. The unknown operator did not change his position in the slightest.

Then the craft began to move over the surface, in a jerky, lurching fashion which indicated a very rough piece of ground. At the same time a queer, leathery squeaking came to the engineer's borrowed ears; he concluded that the machine was being sorely strained by the motion. At the time he was puzzled to account for the motion itself. Either there was another occupant of the craft, who had climbed out and was now pushing the thing along the ground, or else some form of silent mechanism was operating the wheels upon which, presumably, the craft was mounted. Shortly the motion stopped altogether.

It was then that Smith noticed something he had so far ignored because he knew his own dinner hour was approaching. His agent was hungry, like himself. He noticed it because, just then, he received a very definite impression of the opposite feeling; the agent was eating lunch of some sort, and enjoying it. There was no doubt about this. All that Smith could do was to wish, for the hundredth time, that he could look around a little and see what was being eaten, and how.

The meal occupied several minutes. Not once did the strange occupant of that machine relax his stony stare at the sky, and Smith tried to forget how hungry he was by estimating the extent of his vision. He decided that the angle subtended about a hundred and sixty degrees, or almost half a circle; and he further concluded that if his agent possessed a nose, it was a pretty trifling affair, too small to be noticed. It was obvious, too, that the fellow's mouth was located much lower in the face than normal. He ate without showing a single particle of food, and did it very quietly.

At length hunger was satisfied. There was complete stillness and silence for a moment, then another short lurching journey through the cane; and next, with an abruptness that made the engineer's senses swim again, the fellow once more took to the air. The speed with which he "got away" was enough to make a motorcyclist, doing his best, seem to stand still.

It took time for Smith to regain his balance. When he did, the same unbroken expanse of sky once more met his gaze; but it was not long until, out of the corners of those unblinking eyes, he could make out bleary forms which shortly resolved themselves into mountain tops. It was odd, the way things suddenly flashed into full view. One second they would be blurred and unrecognizable; the next, sharply outlined and distinct as anything the engineer had ever seen. Yet, there seemed to be no change in the focus of those eyes. It wasn't as though they were telescopic, either. Not until long afterward did Smith understand the meaning of this.

The mountains grew higher and nearer. Before long it seemed as though the aircraft was entering some sort of a canyon. Its sides were only sparsely covered with vegetation, and all of it was quite brown, as though the season were autumn. For the most part the surface was of broken rock and boulders.

Within a space of three or four minutes the engineer counted not less than ten buzzards. The unknown operator of the machine, however, paid no attention to them, but continued his extraordinary watch of the heavens. Smith began to wonder if the chap were not seated in an air-tight, sound-proof chamber, deep in the hull of some great aerial cruiser, with his eyes glued fast to a periscope. "Maybe a sky patrol," thought the man of the earth; "a cop on the lookout for aerial smugglers, like as not."

And then came another of those terrifying stops. This time, as soon as he could collect his senses, the engineer saw that the machine had landed approximately in the middle of the canyon, and presumably among the boulders in its bottom. For all about it were the tops of gigantic rocks, most of them worn smooth from water action. And, as soon as the engine stopped, Smith plainly heard the roar of water right at hand. He could not see it, however. Why in the name of wonder didn't the fellow look down, for a change?

The craft began to move. This time its motion was smoother arguing an even surface. However, it had not gone far before, to the engineer's astonishment, it began to move straight down a slope so steep that no mechanism with which Smith was familiar could possibly have clung to it. As this happened, his adopted eyes told him that the craft was located upon one of those enormous boulders, in the centre of a stream of such absolute immensity that he fairly gasped. The thing was—colossal!

And yet it was true. The unseen machine deliberately moved along until it was actually clinging, not to the top, but to the side of the rock. The water appeared to be about five yards beneath, to the right. To the left was the sky, while the centre of that strange vision was now upon a similar boulder seemingly a quarter of a mile distant, farther out in the stream. But the fellow at the periscope didn't change position one whit!

It was so unreal. Smith deliberately ignored everything else and watched again for indications of eyelids. He saw not one flicker, but noticed a certain tiny come-and-go, the merest sort of vibration, which indicated the agent's heart-action.

Apparently it beat more than twice as fast as Smith's.

But it relieved him to know that his agent was at least a genuine living being. For a moment he had fancied something utterly repellent to him. Suppose this Sanusian were not any form of natural creature at all, but some sort of supermachine, capable of functioning like an organism? The thought made the engineer shudder as no morgue could.

Presently the queer craft approached the water closely enough, and at such an angle, that Smith looked eagerly for a reflection. However, the water was exceedingly rough, and only a confused brownish blur could be made out. Once he caught a queer sound above the noise of the water; a shrill hiss, with a harsh whine at the end. "Just like some kind of suction apparatus," as he later described it.

And then, with that peculiar sound fresh in his ears, came the crowning shock of the whole experience. Floating toward the boulder, but some distance away, was what looked like a black seed. Next moment the vision flashed clear, as usual, and the engineer saw that the object was really a beetle; and in a second it was so near that Smith's own body, back on the earth, involuntarily shrank back into the recesses of his chair.

For that beetle was an enormity in the most unlimited sense of the word. It was infinitely larger than any beetle the engineer had ever seen—infinitely! It was as large as a good-sized horse!

But before Smith could get over his amazement there was a rush and a swirl in the water behind the insect. Spray was dashed over the rock, a huge form showed itself indistinctly beneath the waves, and next instant the borrowed eyes were showing the engineer, so clearly as to be undeniable, the most astounding sight he had ever seen.

A fish of mountainous size leaped from the water, snapped the beetle into its mouth, and disappeared from sight. In a flash it had come and gone, leaving the engineer fairly gasping and likewise wondering how he could possibly expect anybody to believe him if he told the bald truth of what he had seen.

For he simply could not have invented anything half as incredible. The fish simply could not be described with ordinary language. *It was as large as the largest locomotive.*

IV
THE GOLD-MINER

As for Van Emmon, his experience will have to be classed with Smith's. That is to say, he soon came to feel that his agent was not what is commonly called human. It was all too different. However, he found himself enjoying a field of view which was a decided improvement upon Smith's. Instead of a range which began and ended just above the horizon, his agent possessed the power of looking almost straight ahead.

This told the geologist that his unsuspecting Sanusian was located in an aircraft much like the other. The same tremendous noise of the engine, the same inexplicable wing action, together with the same total lack of the usual indications of human occupancy, all argued that the two men had hit upon the same type of agent. In Van Emmon's case, however, he could occasionally glimpse two loose parts of the machine, flapping and swaying oddly from time to time within the range of the observer, and at the front. Nothing was done about it. Van Emmon came to the same conclusion as Smith; the operator was looking into something like a periscope. Perhaps he himself did not do the driving.

From what the geologist could see of the country below, it was quite certainly cultivated. In no other way could the even rows and uniform growth be explained; even though Van Emmon could not say whether the vegetation were tree, shrub, or plant, it was certainly the work of man—or something mightily like man.

Shortly he experienced an abrupt downward dive, such as upset his senses somewhat. When he recovered, he had time for only the swiftest glance at what, he thought rather vaguely, was a great green-clad mountain. Then his agent brought the craft to one of those nerve-racking stops; once more came a swimming of the brain, and then the geologist saw something that challenged his understanding.

The craft had landed on the rim of a deep pit, or what would have been called a pit if it had not been so extraordinary. Mainly the strangeness was a matter of colour; the slope was of a brilliant orange, and seemingly covered with frost, for it sparkled so brightly in the sun as to actually hurt the eyes. In fact, the geologist's first thought was "A glacier," although he could not conceive of ice or snow of that tint.

Running down the sides of the pit were a number of dark-brown streaks, about a yard wide; Van Emmon could make them out, more or less clearly, on the other side of the pit as well. From the irregular way in which the walls were formed, he quickly decided that the pit was a natural one. The streaks, he thought, might have been due to lava flow.

His agent proceeded to drive straight over the rim and down the slope into the pit. His engine was quite stopped; like Smith, the geologist wondered just how the craft's wheels were operated. Next he was holding his breath as the machine reached so steep a point in the slope that, most surely, no brakes could hold it. Simultaneously he heard the hiss and whine which seemed to indicate the suction device.

"It was a whole lot like going down into a placer mine," the geologist afterward said; and in view of what next met his eyes, he was justified in his guess.

Down crept the machine until it was "standing on its nose." The sun was shining almost straight down into the slope, and Van Emmon forgot his uneasiness about the craft in his interest in what he saw.

The bottom of the pit was perhaps twenty feet in diameter, and roughly hemispherical. Standing up from its bottom were half a dozen slim formations, like idealized stalagmites; they were made of some semitransparent rock, apparently, the tint being a reddish yellow. Finally, perched on the top of each of these was a stone; and surrounding these six "landmarks," as Van Emmon called them, was the most prodigious display of wealth imaginable. For the whole queer place was simply sprinkled with gold. Gold—gold everywhere; large nuggets of it, as big as one's fist! Not embedded in rock, not scattered through sand, but lying loose upon the surface of that unbelievable orange snow! It was overwhelming.

The mysterious Sanusian lost no time. Operating some unseen machinery, he caused three shovel-like devices to project from the front of his machine; and these instantly proceeded, so swiftly that Van Emmon could not possibly watch their action, to pick up nuggets and stow them away out of sight in what must have been compartments in the hull. All this was done without any sound beyond the occasional thud of a nugget dropped in the scramble. Suddenly the Sanusian wheeled his machine about and started hurriedly up the slope. Van Emmon judged that the chap had been frightened by something, for he took flight as soon as he reached the top of the pit. And—he left half a million in gold behind him!

This new flight had not lasted two minutes before the geologist began to note other objects in the air. There were birds, so distant that he could not identify them; one came near enough, however, for him to conclude that it was a hawk. But he did not hold to this conclusion very long.

The thing that changed his mind was another aircraft. It approached from behind, making even more noise than the other, and proceeded to draw abreast of it. From time to time Van Emmon's agent turned his mysterious periscope so as to take it all in, and the geologist was able to watch his fill. Whereupon he became converted to a new idea: The birds that Smith and he had seen had not been birds at all, but aircraft built in imitation of them. For this new arrival had been made in almost perfect imitation of a bee! It was very close to an exact reproduction. For one exception, it did not have the hairy appearance so characteristic of bees; the body and "legs" were smooth and shiny. (Later, Van Emmon saw machines which went so far as even to imitate the hairs.) Also, instead of trying to duplicate the two compound eyes which are found, one on each side of a bee's head, a perfectly round representation of a single eye was built, like a conning tower, toward the front of the bow. Presumably, the observer sat or stood within this "head."

But otherwise it was wonderfully like a drone bee. Van Emmon was strongly reminded of what he had once viewed under a powerful lens. The fragile semi-transparent wings, the misshapen legs, and even the jointed body with its scale-like segments, all were carefully duplicated on a large scale. Imagine a bee thirty feet long!

At first the geologist was puzzled to find that it carried a pair of many-jointed antennae. He could not see how any intelligent being would make use of them; they were continually waving about, much as bees wave theirs. Evidently these were the loose objects he had already noted. "Now," he wondered, "why in thunder did the builders go to so much trouble for the sake of mere realism?"

Then he saw that the antennae served a very real purpose. There was no doubt about it; they were wireless antennae!

For presently the newcomer, who so far had not shown himself at any point on his machine, sent out a message which was read as quickly as it was received by Van Emmon's agent, and as unconsciously translated:

"Number Eight Hundred Four, you are wanted on Plot Seventeen."

Whereupon Van Emmon's unknown assistant replied at once:

"Very well, Superior."

It was done by means of an extremely faint humming device, reminding the geologist of certain wireless apparata he had heard. Not a word was actually spoken by either Sanusian.

Van Emmon kept a close watch upon the conning tower on the other machine.

The sun was shining upon it in such a fashion that its gleam made inspection very difficult. Once he fancied that he could make out a short, compact figure within the "eye"; but he could not be sure. The glass, or whatever it was, reflected everything within range.

Was the airman a quadruped? Did he sit or stand upright, like a man? Or did he use all four limbs, animal-fashion? Van Emmon had to admit that he could not tell; no wonder he didn't guess the truth.

Shortly after receiving the summons, the geologist's agent changed his direction slightly; and within ten minutes the machine was passing over a large grain field. On the far edge was a row of trees, and it was toward this that the Sanusian proceeded to volplane, presently coming to another nausea-producing stop. Once more Van Emmon was temporarily helpless.

When he could look again, he saw that the machine had landed upon a steep slope, this time with its nose pointing upward. Far above was what looked like a cave, with a growth of some queer, black grass on its upper rim. The craft commenced to move upward, over a smooth, dark tan surface.

In half a minute the machine had reached the top of the slope, and the geologist looked eagerly for what might lie within the cave. He was disappointed; it was not a cave at all. Instead, another brown slope, or rather a bulging precipice, occupied this depression.

Van Emmon looked closer. At the bottom of this bulge was a queer fringe of the same kind of grass that showed on top of it. Van Emmon looked from one to the other, and all of a sudden the thing dawned upon him.

This stupendous affair was no mountainside; it was neither more nor less than the head of a colossal statue! A mammoth edition of the Goddess of Liberty; and the aircraft had presumed to alight upon its cheek!

The machine clung there, motionless, for some time, quite as though the airman knew that Van Emmon would like to look a long while. He gazed from side to side as far as he could see, making out a small section of the nose, also the huge curves of a dust-covered ear. It was wonderfully life-like.

Next second came the earthquake. The whole statue rocked and swayed; Van Emmon looked to see the machine thrown off. From the base of the monument came a single terrific sound, a veritable roar, as though the thing was being wrenched from the heart of the earth. From somewhere on top came a spurt of water that splashed just beside the craft.

Then came the most terrible thing. Without the slightest warning the statue's great eye opened! Opened wide, revealing a prodigious pupil which simply blazed with wrath!

The statue was alive!

Next second the Sanusian shot into the air. A moment and Van Emmon was able to look again, and as it happened, the craft was now circling the amazing thing it had just quit, so that the geologist could truthfully say that he was dead sure of what he saw.

He was justified in wanting to be absolutely sure. Resting on the solid earth was a human head, about fifty yards wide and proportionately as tall. It was alive; but *it was only the head, nothing more.*

V
THE SUPER-RACE

It will be remembered that Billie wanted to get in touch with a creature having the characteristic which she had said she admired: supremacy—"A worker who is the boss!" Bearing this in mind, her experience will explain itself, dumfounding though it was.

Her first sight of the Sanusian world was from the front of a large building. The former architect was not able to inspect it minutely; but she afterwards said that it impressed her as being entirely plain, and almost a perfect cube. Its walls were white and quite without ornament; there was only one entrance, an extremely low and broad, flat archway, extending across one whole side. The structure was about a hundred yards each way. In front was a terrace, seemingly paved with enormous slabs of stone; it covered a good many acres.

Presumably Billie's agent had just brought her machine from the building, for, within a few seconds, she took flight in the same abrupt fashion which had so badly upset Smith and Van Emmon. When Billie was able to look closely, she found herself gazing down upon a Sanusian city.

It was a tremendous affair. As the flying-machine mounted higher, Billie continually revised her guesses; finally she concluded that London itself was not as large. Nevertheless her astonishment was mainly directed at the character, not the number of the buildings.

They were all alike! Every one was a duplicate of that she had first seen: cube-shaped, plain finished, flat of wall and roof. Even in colour they were alike; in time the four came to call the place the "White City." However, the buildings were arranged quite without any visible system. And they were vastly puzzled, later on in their studies, to find every other Sanusian city precisely the same as this one.

However, there was one thing which distinguished each building from the rest. It was located on the roof; a large black hieroglyphic, set in a square black border, which Billie first thought to be all alike. Whether it meant a name or a number, there was no way to tell.*

Billie turned her attention to her agent. She seemed to belong to the same type as Smith's and Van Emmon's; otherwise she was certainly much more active, much more interested in her surroundings, and possessed of a far more powerful machine. She was continually changing her direction; and Billie soon congratulated herself upon her luck. Beyond a doubt, this party was no mere slave to orders; it was she who gave the orders.

Before one minute had passed she was approached by a Sanusian in a big, clumsy looking machine. Although built on the bee plan, it possessed an observation tower right on top of its "head." (The four afterward established that this was the sort of a machine that Smith's agent had operated.) The occupant approached to within a respectful distance from Billie's borrowed eyes, and proceeded to hum the following through his antennae:

"Supreme, I have been ordered to report for Number Four."

"Proceed."

"The case of insubordinancy which occurred in Section Eighty-five has been disposed of."

"Number Four made an example of her?"

"Yes, Supreme."

Whereupon the operator flew away, having not only kept his body totally out of sight all the while, but having failed by the slightest token to indicate, by his manner of communicating that he had the slightest particle of personal interest in his report. For that matter, neither did Supreme.

Scarcely had this colloquy ended than another subordinate approached. This one used a large and very fine machine. She reported:

"If Supreme will come with me to the spot, it will be easier to decide upon this case."

---

* Since writing the above, further investigations have proved that these Sanusian house-labels are all numbers.

Immediately the two set off without another word; and after perhaps four minutes of the speediest travel Billie had known outside the doctor's sky-car, they descended to within a somewhat short distance from the ground. Here they hovered, and Billie saw that they were stopped above some hills at the foot of a low mountain range.

Next moment she made out the figures of four humans on top of a knoll just below. A little nearer, and the architect was looking, from the air, down upon the same scene which the doctor was then witnessing through the eyes of Rolla, the older of the two Sanusian women. Billie could make out the powerful physique of Corrus, the slighter figure of Dulnop, the small but vigorous form of Cunora, and Rolla's slender, graceful, capable body. But at that moment the other flier began to say to Supreme:

"The big man is a tender of cattle, Supreme; and he owes his peculiar aptitude to the fact that his parents, for twenty generations back, were engaged in similar work. The same may be said for the younger of the two women; she is small, but we owe much of the excellence of our crops to her energy and skill.

"As for the other woman," indicating Rolla, "she is a soil-tester, and very expert. Her studies and experiments have greatly improved our product. The same may be said in lesser degree of the youth, who is engaged in similar work."

"Then," coolly commented the Sanusian whose eyes and ears Billie enjoyed; "then your line of action is clear enough. You will see to it that the big man marries the sturdy young girl, of course; their offspring should give us a generation of rare outdoor ability. Similarly the young man and the older woman, despite their difference in ages, shall marry for the sake of improving the breed of soil-testers."

"Quite so, Supreme. There is one slight difficulty, however, such as caused me to summon you."

"Name the difficulty."

The Sanusian hesitated only a trifle with her reply: "It is, Supreme, that the big man and the older woman have seen fit to fall in love with one another, while the same is true of the youth and the girl."

"This should not have been allowed!"

"I admit it, Supreme; my force has somehow overlooked their case, heretofore. What is your will?"

The commandant answered instantly: "Put an immediate end to their desires!"

"It shall be done!"

At that moment there was a stir on the ground. In fact, this was the instant when Corrus began his vehement outcry against the tyranny of "They." The two in the air came closer; whereupon Billie discovered that Supreme did not understand the language of the humans below.* Yet the herdsman's tones were unmistakably angry.

"You will descend," commented Supreme evenly, "and warn the big man not to repeat such outbreaks."

Immediately Supreme's lieutenant darted down, and was lost to view. The commandant glanced interestedly here and there about the landscape, returning her gaze to Corrus just as the man stopped in mid-speech. Billie was no less astonished than the doctor to see the herdsman's expression change as it did; one second it was that of righteous indignation, the next, of the most abject subservience.

Nevertheless, Billie could see no cause whatever for it; neither did she hear anything. The other flier remained out of sight. All that the architect could guess was that the operator had "got the drop" on Corrus in some manner which was clear only to those involved. Badly puzzled, Billie watched the four humans hurry away, their manner all but slinking.

A moment later still another aircraft came up, and its operator reported. As before, Billie could make out not a single detail of the occupant herself. She, too, wanted the commandant's personal attention; and shortly Billie was looking down upon a scene which she had good reason to remember all the rest of her life.

In the middle of a large field, where some light green plant was just beginning to sprout, a group of about a dozen humans was at work cultivating. Billie had time to note that they were doing the work in the most primitive fashion, employing the rudest of tools, all quite in keeping with their bare heads and limbs and their skin-clad bodies. About half were women.

Slightly at one side, however, stood a man who was not so busy. To put it plainly, he was loafing, with the handle of his improvised mattock supporting his weight. Clearly the two up in the air were concerned only with him.

"He has been warned three times, Supreme," said the one who had reported the case.

"Three? Then make an example of him!"

"It shall be done, Supreme!"

The lieutenant disappeared. Again the commandant glanced at this, that, and

---

* The humans did not realize this fact, however; they assumed that "They" always understood.

the other thing before concentrating upon what happened below. Then Billie saw the man straighten up suddenly in his tracks, and with remarkable speed, considering his former laziness, he whirled about, dodged, and clapped a hand upon his thigh.

Next second he raised an exultant cry. Billie could not understand what he said; but she noted that the others in the group echoed the man's exultation, and started to crowd toward him, shouting and gesticulating in savage delight. Then something else happened so sudden and so dreadful that the woman who was watching from the earth was turned almost sick.

Like a flash Supreme dropped, headlong, toward the group of humans. In two seconds the distance was covered, and in the last fifth of a second Billie saw the key to the whole mystery.

In that last instant the man who before had seemed of ordinary size, was magnified to the dimensions of a colossus. Instead of being under six feet, he appeared to be near a hundred yards in height; but Billie scarcely realized this till later, it all happened so quickly. There was an outcry from the group, and then the commandant's aircraft crashed into the man's *hand*; a hand so huge that the very wrinkles in its skin were like so many gulleys; even in that final flash Billie saw all this.

Simultaneously with the landing there was a loud pop, while Billie's senses reeled with the stunning suddenness of the impact. Next second the machine had darted to a safe distance, and Billie could see the man gnawing frantically at the back of his hand. Too late; his hand went stiff, and his arm twitched spasmodically. The fellow made a step or two forward, then swayed where he stood, his whole body rigid and strained. An expression of the utmost terror was upon his face; he could not utter a sound, although his companions shrieked in horror. Another second and the man fell flat, twitching convulsively; and in a moment or two it was all over. He was dead!

And then the truth burst upon the watcher. In fact, it seemed to come to all four at the same time, probably by reason of their mental connections. Neither of them could claim that he or she had previously guessed a tenth of its whole, ghastly nature.

The "cane" which Smith had seen had not been cane at all; it had been grass. The "beetle" in the stream had not been the giant thing he had visualized it; neither had that fish been the size he had thought.

Van Emmon's "gold mine" had not been a pit in any sense of the word; it had been the inside of the blossom of a very simple, poppy-like flower. The "nuggets" had been not mineral, but pollen. As for the incredible thing which Van Emmon had seen on the ground; that living statue; that head without a body—the body had been buried out of sight beneath the soil; and the man had been an ordinary human, being punished in this manner for misconduct.

Instead of being aircraft built in imitation of insects, the machines had been constructed by nature herself, and there had been nothing unusual in their size. No; they were the real thing, differing only slightly from what might have been found anywhere upon the earth.

In short, it had all been simply a matter of view-point. The supreme creature of Sanus was, not the human, but the bee. A poisonous bee, superior to every other form of Sanusian life! What was more—

"The damned things are not only supreme; *the humans are their slaves*!"

VI

Impossible, But—

The four looked at each other blankly. Not that either was at a loss for words; each was ready to burst. But the thing was so utterly beyond their wildest conceptions, so tremendously different in every way, it left them all a little unwilling to commit themselves.

"Well," said Smith finally, "as I said in the first place, I can't see how any other than the human form became supreme. As I understand biology—"

"What gets me," interrupted Van Emmon; "what gets me is, *why* the humans have allowed such an infernal thing to happen!"

Billie smiled somewhat sardonically. "I thought," she remarked, cuttingly, "that you were always in sympathy with the upper dog, Mr. Van Emmon!"

"I am!" hotly. Then, with the memory of what he had just seen rushing back upon him: "I mean, I was until I saw—saw that—" He stopped, flushing deeply; and before he could collect himself Smith had broken in again:

"I just happened to remember, doc; didn't you say that the Venusians, in those books of yours, say that Sanus is ruled by the workers?"

"Just what I was wondering about," from Van Emmon. "The humans seem to do all the work, and the bees the bossing!"

The doctor expected this. "The Venusians had our viewpoint—the viewpoint of people on the earth, when they said that the workers rule. We consider the bee as a great worker, don't we? 'As busy as a bee,' you know. None of the so-called lower animals show greater industry."

"You don't mean to say," demanded Smith, "that these Sanusian bees owe their position to the fact that they are, or were, such great workers?"

Before the doctor could reply, Van Emmon broke in. It seemed as though his mind refused to get past this particular point. "Now, why the dickens have the humans allowed the bees to dominate them? Why?"

"We'll have to go at this a little more systematically," remarked Kinney, "if we want to understand the situation."

"In the first place, suppose we note a thing or two about conditions as we find them here on the earth. We, the humans, are accustomed to rank ourselves far above the rest. It is taken for granted.

"Now, note this: the human supremacy was not always taken for granted." He paused to let it sink in. "Not always. There was a time in prehistoric days when man ranked no higher than others. I feel sure of this," he insisted, seeing that Smith was opposed to the idea; "and I think I know just what occurred to make man supreme."

"What?" from Billie.

"Never mind now. I rather imagine we shall learn more on this score as we go on with our work.

"At any rate, we may be sure of this: whatever it was that caused man to become supreme on the earth, that condition is lacking on Sanus!"

Van Emmon did not agree to this. "The condition may be there, doc, but there is some other factor which overbalances it; a factor such as is—well, more favourable to the bees."

The doctor looked around the circle. "What do you think? 'A factor more favourable to the bees.' Shall we let it go at that?" There was no remark, even from Smith; and the doctor went on:

"Coming back to the bees, then, we note that they are remarkable for several points of great value. First, as we have seen, they are very industrious by nature. Second, all bees possess wings and on that count alone they are far superior to humans.

"Third—and to me, the most important—the bees possess a remarkable combination of community life and specialization. Of course, when you come to analyze these two points, you see that they really belong to one another. The bees we know, for instance, are either queens, whose only function is to fertilize the eggs; or workers, who are unsexed females, and whose sole occupations are the collecting of honey, the building of hives, and the care of the young.

"Now," speaking carefully, "apparently these Sanusian bees have developed something that is not unknown to certain forms of earth's insect life. I mean, a soldier type. A kind of bee which specializes on fighting!"

Van Emmon was listening closely, yet he had got another idea: "Perhaps this soldier type is simply the plain worker bee, all gone to sting! It may be that these bees have given up labour altogether!"

"Still," muttered Smith, under his breath, "all this doesn't solve the real problem. Why aren't the *humans* supreme?" For once he became emphatic. "That's what gets me! Why aren't the humans the rulers, doc?"

Kinney waited until he felt sure the others were depending upon him. "Smith, the humans on Sanus are not supreme now because they were *never* supreme."

Smith looked blank. "I don't get that."

"Don't you? Look here: you'll admit that success begets success, won't you?"

"Success begets success? Sure! 'Nothing succeeds like success.'"

"Well, isn't that merely another way of saying that the consciousness of superiority will lead to further conquests? We humans are thoroughly conscious of our supremacy; if we weren't we'd never attempt the things we do!"

Van Emmon saw the point. "In other words, the humans on the earth never began to show their superiority until something—something big, happened to demonstrate their ability!"

"Exactly!" cried Kinney. "Our prehistoric ancestors would never have handed down such a tremendous ambition to you and me if they, at that time, had not been able to point to some definite feat and say, 'That proves I'm a bigger man than a horse,' for example."

"Of course," reflected Billie, aloud; "of course, there were other factors."

"Yes; but they don't alter the case. Originally the human was only slightly different from the apes he associated with. There was perhaps only one slight point of superiority; today there are millions of such points. Man is infinitely superior, now, and it's all because he was slightly superior, then."

"Suppose we grant that," remarked the geologist. "What then? Does that explain why the bees have made good on Sanus?"

"To a large degree. Some time in the past the Sanusian bee discovered that he possessed a certain power which enabled him to force his will upon other creatures. This power was his poisonous sting. He found that, when he got his fellows together and formed a swarm, they could attack any animal in such large numbers as to make it helpless."

"Any creature?"

"Yes; even reptiles, scales or no scales. They'd attack the eyes."

"But that doesn't explain how the bees ever began to make humans work for them," objected Van Emmon.

The doctor thought for a few minutes. "Let's see. Suppose we assume that a certain human once happened to be in the neighbourhood of a hive, just when it was attacked by a drove of ants. Ants are great lovers of honey, you know. Suppose the man stepped among the ants and was bitten. Naturally he would trample them to death, and smash with his hands all that he couldn't trample. Now, what's to prevent the bees from seeing how easily the man had dealt with the ants? A man would be far more efficient, destroying ants, than a bee; just as a horse is more efficient, dragging a load, than a man. And yet we know that the horse was domesticated, here on the earth, simply because the humans saw his possibilities; the horse could do a certain thing more efficiently than a human.

"You notice," the doctor went on, with great care, "that everything I've assumed is natural enough: the combination of an ant attack and the man's approach, occurring at the same time. Suppose we add a third factor: that the bees, even while fighting the ants, also started to attack the man; but that he chanced to turn his attention to the ants *first*. So that the bees let him alone!

"We know what remarkable things bees are, when it comes to telling one another what they know. Is there any reason why such an experience—all natural enough—shouldn't demonstrate to them that they, by merely threatening a man, could compel him to kill ants for them?"

Billie was dubious for a moment; then agreed that the man, also, might notice that the bees failed to sting him as long as he continued to destroy their other enemies. If so, it was quite conceivable that, bit by bit, the bees had found other and more positive ways of securing the aid of men through threatening to sting. "Even to cultivating flowers for their benefit," she conceded. "It's quite possible."

Smith had been thinking of something else. "I always understood that a bee's stinging apparatus is good for only one attack. Doesn't it always remain behind after stinging?"

"Yes," from the doctor, quietly. "That is true. The sting has tiny barbs on its tip, and these cause it to remain in the wound. The sting is actually torn away from the bee when it flies away. It never grows another. That is why, in fact, the bee never stings except as a last resort, when it thinks it's a question of self-defence."

"Just what I thought!" chuckled Smith. "A bee is helpless without its sting! If so, how can you account for anything like a soldier bee?"

The doctor returned his gaze with perfect equanimity. He looked at Van Emmon and Billie; they, too, seemed to think that the engineer had found a real flaw in Kinney's reasoning. The doctor dropped his eyes, and searched his mind thoroughly for the best words. He removed his bracelets while he was thinking; the others did the same. All four got to their feet and stretched, silently but thoroughly. Not until they were ready to quit the study did the doctor make reply.

"Smith, I don't need to remind you that it's the little things that count. It's too old a saying. In this case it happens to be the greatest truth we have found today.

"Smith"—speaking with the utmost care—"what we have just said about the bee's sting is all true; but only with regard to the bees on the earth. It is only on the earth, so far as we know positively, that the bee is averse to stinging, for fear of losing his sting.

"There is only one way to account for the soldier bee. Its sting has no barbs!"

"No barbs?"

"Why not? If the poison is virulent enough, the barbs wouldn't be necessary, would they? Friends, the Sanusian bee is the supreme creature on its planet; it is superior to all the other insects, all the birds, all the animals; and its supremacy is due solely and entirely to the fact that there are no barbs on its sting!"

VII
THE MISSING FACTOR

By the time the four once more got together in the doctor's study, each had had a chance to consider the Sanusian situation pretty thoroughly. All but Billie were convinced that the humans were deserving people, whose position was all the more regrettable because due, so far as could be seen, the insignificant little detail of the barbless sting.

Were these people doomed forever to live their lives for the sake of insects? Were they always to remain, primitive and uncultured, in ignorance of the things that civilization is built upon, obeying the orders of creatures who were content to eat, reproduce, and die? For that is all that bees know!

Perhaps it was for the best. Possibly Rolla and her friends were better off as they were. It might have been that a wise Providence, seeing how woefully the human animal had missed its privileges on other worlds, had decided to make man secondary on Sanus. Was that the reason for it all?

All but Billie scouted the idea. To them the affair was a ghastly perversion of what Nature intended. Van Emmon stated the case in a manner which showed how strongly he felt about it.

"Those folks will never get anywhere if the bees can help it!" he charged. "We've got to lend a hand, here, and see that they get a chance!"

Smith said that, so far as he was concerned, the bees might all be consigned to hell. "I'm not going to have anything to do with the agent I had, any more!" he declared. "I'm going to get in touch with that chap, Dulnop. What is he like, doc?"

Kinney told him, and then Van Emmon asked for details of the herdsman, Corrus. "No more bees in my young life, either. From now on it's up to us. What do you think?" turning to his wife, and carefully avoiding any use of her name.

The architect knew well enough that the rest were wondering how she would decide. She answered with deliberation:

"I'm going to stay in touch with Supreme!"

"You are!" incredulously, from her husband.

"Yes! I've got a darned sight more sympathy for those bees than for the humans! The 'fraid-cats!" disgustedly.

"But listen," protested Van Emmon. "We can't stand by and let those cold-blooded prisoners keep human beings, like ourselves, in rank slavery! Not much!"

Evidently he thought he needed to explain. "A human is a human, no matter where we find him! Why, how can those poor devils show what they're good for if we don't give 'em a chance? That's the only way to develop people—give 'em a chance to show what's in 'em! Let the best man win!"

Billie only closed her mouth tighter; and Smith decided to say, "Billie, you don't need to stand by your guns just because the Sanusian working class happens to be insects. Besides, we're three to one in favour of the humans!"

"Oh, well," she condescended, "if you put it that way I'll agree not to interfere. Only, don't expect me to help you any with your schemes; I'll just keep an eye on Supreme, that's all."

"Then we're agreed." The doctor put on his bracelets. "Suppose we go into the trance state for about three minutes—long enough to learn what's going on today."

Shortly Billie again using the eyes and ears of the extraordinarily capable bee who ruled the rest, once more looked down upon Sanus. She saw the big "city," which she now knew to be a vast collection of hives, built by the humans at the command of the bees. At the moment the air was thick with workers, returning with their loads of honey from the fields which the humans had been compelled to cultivate. What a diabolical reversal of the accepted order of things!

The architect had time to note something very typical of the case. On the outskirts of the city two humans were at work, erecting a new hive. Having put it together, they proceeded to lift the big box and place it near those already inhabited. They set it down in what looked like a good location, but almost immediately took it up again and shifted it a foot to one side. This was not satisfactory, either; they moved it a few inches in another direction.

All told, it took a full minute to place that simple affair where it was wanted; and all the while those two humans behaved as though some one were shouting directions to them—silent directions, as it were. Billie knew that a half-dozen soldier bees, surrounding their two heads, were coolly and unfeelingly driving them where they willed. And when, the work done, they left the spot, two soldiers went along behind them to see that they did not loiter.

As for the doctor, he came upon Rolla when the woman was deep in an experiment. She stood in front of a rude trough, one of perhaps twenty located within a large, high-walled inclosure. In the trough was a quantity of earth, through the surface of which some tiny green shoots were beginning to show.

Rolla inspected the shoots, and then, with her stone knife, she made a final notch in the wood on the edge of the trough. There were twenty-odd of these notches; whereas, on other troughs which the doctor had a chance to see, there were over thirty in many cases, and still no shoots.

The place, then, was an experimental station. This was proven by Rolla's next move. She went outside the yard and studied five heaps of soil, each of a different appearance, also three smaller piles of pulverized mineral—nitrates, for all that the doctor knew. And before Kinney severed his connection with the Sanusian, she had begun the task of mixing up a fresh combination of these ingredients in a new trough. In the midst of this she heard a sound; and turning about, waved a hand excitedly toward a distant figure on the far side of a nearby field.

Meanwhile Smith had managed to get in touch with Dulnop. He found the young man engaged in work which did not, at first, become clear to the engineer. Then he saw that the chap was simply sorting over big piles of broken rock, selecting certain fragments which he placed in separate heaps. Not far away two assistants were pounding these fragments to powder, using rude pestles, in great, nature-made mortars—"pot-holes," from some river-bed.

It was this powder, beyond a doubt, that Rolla was using in her work. To Smith, Dulnop's task seemed like a ridiculously simple occupation for a nearly grown man, until he reflected that these aborigines were exactly like toddling children in intellects.

Van Emmon had no trouble in making connections with Corrus. The herdsman was in charge of a dozen cows, wild looking creatures which would have been far too much for the man had they been horned, which they were not. He handled them by sheer force, using the great club he always carried. Once while Van Emmon was watching, a cow tried to break away from the group; but Corrus, with an agility amazing in so short and heavy a man, dashed after the creature and tapped her lightly on the top of her head. Dazed and contrite, she followed him meekly back into the herd.

The place was on the edge of a meadow, at the beginning of what looked like a grain field. Stopping here, Corrus threw a hand to his mouth and gave a ringing shout. Immediately it was answered, faintly, by another at a distance; and then Van Emmon made out the form of Rolla among some huts on the other side of the grain. She beckoned toward the herdsman, and he took a half-dozen steps toward her.

Just as abruptly he stopped, almost in mid-stride. Simultaneously Van Emmon heard a loud buzzing in either ear. Corrus was being warned. Like a flash he dropped his head and muttered: "Vey well. I will remember—next time." And trembling violently he turned back to his cows.

"Well," remarked the geologist, when the four "came out" of their seance, "the bees seem to have everything their own way. How can we help the humans best? Hurry up with your idea; I'm getting sick of these damned poisoners."

The doctor asked if the others had any suggestions. Smith offered this: why couldn't the humans retire to some cave, or build tight-walled huts, and thus bar out the bees?

No sooner had he made the remark, however, than the engineer declared his own plan no good. "These people aren't like us; they couldn't stand such imprisonment long enough to make their 'strike' worth while."

"Is there any reason," suggested Billie, indifferently, "why they couldn't weave face nets from some kind of grass, and protect themselves in that way?"

Smith saw the objection to that, too. "They'd have to protect themselves all over as well; every inch would have to be covered tightly. From what I've seen of them I'd say that the arrangement would drive them frantic. It would be worse than putting clothes on a cat."

"It's a man-sized job we've tackled," commented the doctor. "What Smith says is true; such people would never stand for any measures which would restrict their physical freedom. They are simply animals with human possibilities, nothing more."

He paused, and then added quietly, "By the way, did either of you notice any mountains just now?"

Smith and Van Emmon both said they had. "Why?"

"Of course, it isn't likely, but—did you see anything like a volcano anywhere?"

"No," both replied.

"Another thing," Kinney went on. "So far, I've seen nothing that would indicate lightning, much less the thing itself. Did either of you," explicitly, "run across such a thing as a blasted tree?"

They said they had not. Billie hesitated a little with her reply, then stated that she had noted a tree or two in a state of disintegration, but none that showed the unmistakable scars due to being struck by lightning.

"Then we've got the key to the mystery!" declared the doctor. "Remember how brown and barren everything looks excepting only where there's artificial vegetation? Well, putting two and two together, I come to the conclusion that Sanus differs radically from the earth in this respect:

"The humans have arrived rather late in the planet's history. Or—and this is more likely—Sanus is somewhat smaller than the earth, and therefore has cooled off sooner. At any rate, the relationship between the age of the planet and the age of its human occupancy differs from what it is on the earth."

"I don't quite see," from Smith, "what that's got to do with it."

"No? Well, go back to the first point: the dried-up appearance of things. That means, their air and water are both less extensive than with us, and for that reason there are far fewer clouds; therefore, it is quite possible that there has been no lightning within the memory of the humans."

"How so?" demanded the geologist.

"Why, simply because lightning depends upon clouds. Lightning is merely the etheric electricity, drawn to the earth whenever there is enough water in the air to promote conductivity."

"Yes," agreed Smith; "but—what of it?"

Kinney went on unheeding. "As for volcanoes—probably the same explanation accounts for the lack of these also. You know how the earth, even, is rapidly coming to the end of her Volcanic period. Time was when there were volcanoes almost everywhere on the earth.

"The same is likely true of Sanus as well. The point is," and the doctor paused significantly, "there have been no volcanic eruptions, and no lightning discharges within the memory of Sanusian man!"

What was he getting at? The others eyed him closely. Neither Van Emmon nor Smith could guess what he meant; but Billie, her intuition wide awake, gave a great jump in her chair.

"I know!" she cried. A flood of light came to her face.

"The Sanusians—no wonder they let the bees put it over on them!"

"They haven't got *fire*! They've never had it!"

VIII
FIRE!

From the corner of his eyes Kinney saw Van Emmon turn a gaze of frank admiration at his wife. It lasted only a second, however; the geologist remembered, and masked the expression before Billie could detect it.

Smith had been electrified by the idea.

"By George!" he exclaimed two or three times. "Why didn't I think of that? It's simple as A, B, C now!"

"Why," Van Emmon exulted, "all we've got to do is put the idea of fire into their heads, and the job is done!" He jumped around in his chair. "Darn those bees, anyhow!"

"And yet," observed the doctor, "it's not quite as simple as we may think. Of course it's true that once they have fire, the humans ought to assert themselves. We'll let that stand without argument."

"Will we?" Smith didn't propose to back down that easy. "Do you mean to say that fire, and nothing more than fire, can bring about human ascendency?"

The doctor felt sure. "All the other animals are afraid of fire. Such exceptions as the moth are really not exceptions at all; the moth is simply driven so mad by the sight of flame that it commits suicide in it. Horses sometimes do the same.

"Humans are the only creatures that do not fear fire! Even a tiny baby will show no fear at the sight of it."

"Which ought to prove," Van Emmon cut in to silence Smith, "that superiority is due to fire, rather than fire due to superiority, for the simple reason that a newborn child is very low in the scale of evolution." Smith decided not to say what he intended to say. Van Emmon concluded:

"We've just got to give 'em fire! What's the first step?"

"I propose," from the doctor, "that when we get in touch this time we concentrate on the idea of fire. We've got to give them the notion first."

"Would you rather," inquired Billie, "that I kept the idea from Supreme?"

"Thanks," returned her husband, icily, "but you might just as well tell her, too. It'll make her afraid in advance, all the better!"

The engineer threw himself back in his seat. "I'm with you," said he, laying aside his argument. The rest followed his example, and presently were looking upon Sanus again.

All told, this particular session covered a good many hours. The four kept up a more or less connected mental conversation with each other as they went along, except, of course, when the events became too exciting. Mainly they were trying to catch their agents in the proper mood for receiving telepathic communications, and it proved no easy matter. It required a state of semi-consciousness, a condition of being neither awake nor asleep. It was necessary to wait until night had fallen on that particular part of the planet.*

Van Emmon was the first to get results. Corrus had driven his herd back from the brook at which they had got their evening drink, and after seeing them all quietly settled for the night, he lay down on the dried grass slope of a small hill, and stared up at the sky. Van Emmon had plenty of time to study the stars as seen from Sanus, and certainly the case demanded plenty of time.

For he saw a broad band of sky, as broad as the widest part of the Milky Way, which was neither black nor sparkling with stars, but glowing as brightly as the full moon! From the eastern horizon to the zenith it stretched, a great "Silvery Way," as Van Emmon labelled it; and as the darkness deepened and the night lengthened, the illumination crept on until the band of light stretched all the way across. Van Emmon racked his brains to account for the thing.

Then Corrus became drowsy. Van Emmon concentrated with all his might. At first he overdid the thing; Corrus was not quite drowsy enough, and the

* It should be mentioned that all parts of Sanus showed the same condition of bee supremacy and human servitude. The spot in question was quite typical of all the colonies.

attempt only made him wakeful. Shortly, however, he became exceedingly sleepy, and the geologist's chance came.

At the end of a few minutes the herdsman sat up, blinking. He looked around at the dark forms of the cattle, then up at the stars; he was plainly both puzzled and excited. He remained awake for hours, in fact, thinking over the strange thing he had seen "in a dream."

Meanwhile Smith was having a similar experience with Dulnop. The young fellow was, like Corrus, alone at the time; and he, too, was made very excited and restless by what he saw.

Billie was unable to work upon her bee. Supreme retired to a hive just before dusk, but remained wide awake and more or less active, feeding voraciously, for hours upon hours. When she finally did nap, she fell asleep on such short notice that the architect was taken off her guard. The bee seemed to all but jump into slumberland.

The doctor also had to wait for Rolla. The woman sat for a long time in the growing dusk, looking out pensively over the valley. Corrus was somewhere within a mile or two, and so Kinney was not surprised to see the herdsman's image dancing, tantalizingly, before Rolla's eyes. She was thinking of him with all her might.

Presently she shivered with the growing coolness, and went into a rough hut, which she shared with Cunora. The girl was already asleep on a heap of freshly gathered brush. Rolla, delightfully free of any need to prepare for her night's rest—such as locking any doors or cleaning her teeth—made herself comfortable beside her friend. Two or three yawns, and the doctor's chance came.

Two minutes later Rolla sat bolt upright, at the same time giving out a sharp cry of amazement and alarm. Instantly Cunora awoke.

"What is it, Rolla?" terror-stricken.

"Hush!" The older woman got up and went to the opening which served as a door. There she hung a couple of skins, arranging them carefully so that no bee might enter. Coming back to Cunora, she brought her voice nearly to a whisper:

"Cunora, I have had a wonderful dream! Ye must believe me when I say that it were more than a mere dream; 'twere a message from the great god, Mownoth, or I be mad!"

"Rolla!" The girl was more anxious than frightened now. "Ye speak wildly! Quiet thyself, and tell what thou didst see!

"It were not easy to describe," said Rolla, getting herself under control. "I dreamed that a man, very pale of face and most curiously clad, did approach me while I was at work. He smiled and spake kindly, in a language I could not understand; but I know he meant full well.

"This be the curious thing, Cunora: He picked up a handful of leaves from the ground and laid them on the trough at my side. Then, from some place in his garments he produced a tiny stick of white wood, with a tip made of some dark-red material. This he held before mine eyes, in the dream; and then spake very reassuringly, as though bidding me not to be afraid.

"Well he might! Cunora, he took that tiny stick in his hand and moved the tip along the surface of the trough; and, behold, a miracle!"

"What happened?" breathlessly.

"In the twinkling of an eye, the stick blossomed! Blossomed, Cunora, before mine eyes! And such a blossom no eye ever beheld before. Its colour was the colour of the poppy, but its shape—most amazing! Its shape continually changed, Cunora; it danced about, and rose and fell; it flowed, even as water floweth in a stream, but always upward!"

"Rolla!" incredulously. "Ye would not awaken me to tell such nonsense!"

"But it were not nonsense!" insisted Rolla. "This blossom was even as I say: a living thing, as live as a kitten! And as it bloomed, behold, the stick was consumed! In a moment or two the man dropped what was left of it; I stooped—so it seemed—to pick it up; but he stopped me, and set his foot upon the beautiful thing!"

She sighed, and then hurried on. "Saying something further, also reassuring, this angel brought forth another of the strange sticks; and when he had made this one bloom, he touched it to the little pile of leaves. Behold, a greater miracle, Cunora! The blossoms spread to the leaves, and caused them to bloom, too!"

Cunora was eying her companion pretty sharply. "Ye must take me for a simple one, to believe such imagining."

Rolla became even more earnest. "Yet it were more than imagining, Cunora; 'twere too vivid and impressive for only that. As for the leaves, the blossoming swiftly spread until it covered every bit of the pile; and I tell thee that the bloom flowed as high as thy hand! Moreover, after a moment or so, the thing faded and died out, just as flowers do at the end of the season; all that was left of the leaves was some black fragments, from which arose a bluish dust, like unto the cloud that ye and I saw in the sky one day.

"Then the stranger smiled again, and said something of which I cannot tell the meaning. Once more he performed the miracle, and this time he contrived to spread the blossom from some leaves to the tip of a large piece of wood which he took from the ground. 'Twas a wonderful sight!

"Nay, hear me further," as Cunora threw herself, with a grunt of impatience, back on her bed; "there is a greater wonder to tell.

"Holding this big blooming stick in one hand, he gave me his other; and it seemed as though I floated through the air by his side. Presently we came to the place where Corrus's herd lay sleeping. The angel smote one of the cows with the flat of his hand, so that it got upon its feet; and straighway the stranger thrust the flowing blossom into its face.

"The cow shrank back, Cunora! 'Twas deadly afraid of that beautiful flower!"

"That is odd," admitted Cunora. She was getting interested.

"Then he took me by the hand again, and we floated once more through the air. In a short time we arrived at the city of the masters.* Before I knew it, he had me standing before the door of one of their palaces. I hung back, afraid lest we be discovered and punished; but he smiled again and spoke so reassuringly that I fled not, but watched until the end.

"With his finger he tapped lightly on the front of the palace. None of the masters heard him at first; so he tapped harder. Presently one of them appeared, and flew at once before our faces. Had it not been for the stranger's firm grasp I should have fled.

"The master saw that the stranger was the offender, and buzzed angrily. Another moment, and the master would surely have returned to the palace to inform the others; and then the stranger would have been punished with the Head Out punishment. But instead the angel very deliberately moved the blooming stick near unto the master; and behold, it was helpless! Down it fell to the ground, dazed; I could have picked it up, or killed it, without the slightest danger!

"Another master came out, and another, and another; and for each and all the flowing blossom was too much! None would come near it wittingly; and such as the angel approached with it were stricken almost to death.

"When they were all made helpless the angel bade me hold my hand near the bloom; and I was vastly surprised to feel a great warmth. 'Twas like the heat of

* Having no microscopes, the Sanusians could not know that the soldier bees were unsexed females; hence, "masters."

a stone which has stood all day in the sun, only much greater. Once my finger touched the bloom, and it gave me a sharp pain."

Cunora was studying her friend very closely. "Ye could not have devised this tale, Rolla. 'Tis too unlikely. Is there more of it?"

"A little. The angel once more took me by the hand, and shortly set me down again in this hut. Then he said something which seemed to mean, 'With this magic bloom thou shalt be freed from the masters. They fear it; but ye, and all like ye, do not. Be ye ready to find the blossom when I bid thee.' With that he disappeared, and I awoke.

"Tell me; do I look mad, to thine eyes?" Rolla was beginning to feel a little anxious herself.

Cunora got up and led Rolla to the entrance. The glow of "the Silvery Way" was all the help that the girl's catlike eyesight needed; she seemed reassured.

"Ye look very strange and excited, Rolla, but not mad. Tell me again what thou didst see and hear, that I may compare it with what ye have already told."

Rolla began again; and meanwhile, on the earth, the doctor's companions telepathically congratulated him on his success. He had put the great idea into a fertile mind.

Presently they began to look for other minds. It seemed wise to get the notion into as many Sanusian heads as possible. For some hours this search proceeded; but in the end, after getting in touch with some forty or fifty individuals in as many different parts of the planet, they concluded that they had first hit upon the most advanced specimens that Sanus afforded; the only ones, in fact, whose intellect were strong enough to appreciate the value of what they were told. The investigators were obliged to work with Rolla, Dulnop, and Corrus only; upon these three depended the success of their unprecedented scheme.

Rolla continued to keep watch upon Supreme; and toward morning—that is, morning in that particular part of Sanus—the architect was rewarded by catching the bee in a still drowsy condition. Using the same method Kinney had chosen, Billie succeeded in giving the soldier bee a very vivid idea of fire. And judging by the very human way in which the half-asleep insect tossed about, thrashing her wings and legs and making incoherent sounds, Billie succeeded admirably. The other bees in the hive came crowding around, and Supreme had some difficulty in maintaining her dignity and authority. In the end she confided in the subordinate next in command:

"I have had a terrible dream. One of our slaves, or a woman much like one, assaulted me with a new and fearful weapon." She described it more or less as Rolla had told Cunora. "It was a deadly thing; but how I know this, I cannot say, except that it was exceedingly hot. So long as the woman held it in her hand, I dared not go near her.

"See to it that the others know; and if such a thing actually comes into existence, let me know immediately."

"Very well, Supreme." And the soldier straightway took the tale to another bee. This told, both proceeded to spread the news, bee-fashion; so that the entire hive knew of the terror within a few minutes. Inside an hour every hive in the whole "city" had been informed.

"Give them time now," said the doctor, "and they will tell every bee on the planet. Suppose we want a couple of weeks before doing anything further? The more afraid the bees are in advance, the easier for Rolla and her friends."

Meanwhile Corrus, after a sleepless night with his cattle, had driven them hurriedly back to the huts surrounding the "experimental station." Here the herdsman turned his herd over to another man, and then strode over among the huts. Outside one of them—probably Rolla's—he paused and gazed longingly, then gave a deep sigh and went on. Shortly he reached another hut in which he found Dulnop.

"I was just going to seek ye!" exclaimed the younger man. "I have seen a wondrous sight, Corrus!"

Thus the two men came to compare notes, finding that each had learned practically the same thing. Corrus being denied the right to visit any woman save Cunora, Dulnop hurried to Rolla and told her what he and the herdsman had learned. The three testimonies made an unshakable case.

"By the great god Mownoth!" swore Corrus in vast delight when Dulnop had reported. "We have learned a way to make ourselves free! As free as the squirrels!"

"Aye," agreed the younger. "We know the method. But—how shall we secure the means?"

Corrus gave an impatient gesture. "'Twill come in time, Dulnop, just as the dream came! Meanwhile we must tell every one of our kind, so that all shall be ready when the day comes to strike!

"Then"—his voice lost its savagery, and became soft and tender— "then, Dulnop, lad, ye shall have thy Cunora; and as for Rolla and I—"

Corrus turned and walked away, that his friend might not see what was in his eyes.

IX
FOUND!

It was two weeks to a day when the four on the earth, after having seen very little of each other in the meanwhile, got together for the purpose of finishing their "revelation" to the Sanusians.

"Mr. Van Emmon and I," stated Billie coolly, as they put on their bracelets, "have been trying to decide upon the best way of telling them how to obtain fire."

Neither Smith nor the doctor showed that he noticed her "Mr. Van Emmon." Evidently the two were still unreconciled.

"I argue," remarked the geologist, "that the simplest method will be a chemical one. There's lots of ways to produce fire spontaneously, with chemicals; and this woman Rolla could do it easily."

Billie indulged in a small, superior smile. "He forgets that all these chemical methods require pure chemicals. And you don't find them pure in the natural state. You've got to have fire to reduce them with."

"What's your proposition, then?" from the doctor.

"Optics!" enthusiastically. She produced a large magnifying-glass from her pocket. "All we have to do is to show Dulnop—he's something of a mineralogist—how to grind and polish a piece of crystal into this shape!"

Van Emmon groaned. "Marvellous! Say, if you knew how infernally hard it is to find even a small piece of crystal, you'd never propose such a thing! Why, it would take years—Mrs. Van Emmon!"

Smith also shook his head. "Neither of you has the right idea. The easiest way, under the circumstances, would be an electrical one."

He paused, frowning hard; then vetoed his own plan. "Thunder; I'm always speaking first and thinking afterward. I never used to do it," accusingly, "until I got in with you folks. Anyhow, electricity won't do; you've got to have practically pure elements for that, too."

"Guess it's up to you, doc," said Billie. And they all looked respectfully toward their host.

He laughed. "You three will never learn anything. You'll continue to think that I'm a regular wonder about these things, but you never notice that I merely stay still and let you commit yourselves first before I say anything. All I have to do is select the one idea remaining after you've disproved the rest. Nothing to it!"

He paused. "I'm afraid we're reduced to the spark method. It would take too long to procure materials pure enough for any other plan. Friction is out of the question for such people; they haven't the patience. Suppose we go ahead on the flint-and-spark basis."

They went at once into the familiar trance state. Nightfall was approaching on the part of Sanus in which they were interested. Smith and Van Emmon came upon Dulnop and Corrus as they were talking together. The herdsman was saying:

"Lad, my heart is heavy this night." Much of his usual vigour was absent. "When I were passing Cunora's field this day, some of the masters came and drove me over to her side. I tried to get away, and one threatened to kill. I fear me, lad, they intend to force us to marry!"

"What!" fiercely, from the younger.

Corrus laid a hand upon his arm. "Nay, Dulnop; fear not. I have no feeling for thy Cunora; I may marry her, but as for fathering her children—no!"

"Suppose," through set teeth, "suppose They should threaten to kill thee?"

"I should rather die, Dulnop, than be untrue to Rolla!"

The younger man bounded to his feet. "Spoken like a man! And I tell thee, neither shall I have aught to do with Rolla! Rather death than dishonour!"

Next moment silence fell between them; and then Van Emmon and Smith noted that both men had been bluffing in what they had said. For, sitting apart in the growing darkness, each was plainly in terror of the morrow. Presently Corrus spoke in a low tone:

"All the same, Dulnop, it were well for me and thee if the secret of the flowing blossom were given us this night. I"—he paused, abashed—"I am not so sure of myself, Dulnop, when I hear Their accursed buzzing. I fear—I am afraid I might give in!"

At this Dulnop broke down, and fell to sobbing. Nothing could have told the investigators so well just how childlike the Sanusians really were. Corrus had all he could do to hold in himself.

"Mownoth!" he exclaimed, his eyes raised fervently. "If it be thy will to deliver us, give us the secret this night!"

Meanwhile, in Rolla's hut, a similar scene was going on under the doctor's projected eye. Cunora lost her nerve, and Rolla came near to doing the same in her efforts to comfort the other.

"They are heartless things!" Rolla exclaimed with such bitterness as her nature would permit. "They know not what love is: They with their drones and their egg-babes! What is family life to Them? Nothing!

"Somehow I feel that Their reign is nearly at an end, Cunora. Perhaps the great secret shall be given us to-night!"

The girl dried her tears. "Why say ye that, Rolla?"

"Because the time be ripe for it. Are not all our kind looking forward to it? Are we not all expecting and longing for it? Know we not that we shall, must, have what we all so earnestly desire?" It was striking, to hear this bit of modern psychology uttered by this primitive woman. "Let me hear no more of thy weeping! Ye shall not be made to wed Corrus!"

Nevertheless, at the speaking of her lover's name, the older woman's lips trembled despite themselves; and she said nothing further beyond a brief "Sleep well." After which the two women turned in, and shortly reached the drowsy point.

Thus it happened that Rolla, after a minute or two, once more aroused Cunora in great excitement, and after securely closing the entrance to the hut against all comers, proceeded to relate what she had seen. She finished:

"The seed of the flower can be grown in the heart of rotting wood!" And for hours afterward the two whispered excitedly in the darkness. It was hard to have to wait till dawn.

As for Corrus and Dulnop, they even went so far as to search the heaps of stone in the mineral yards, although neither really expected to find what they sought.

But the four on the earth, not being able to do anything further until morning, proceeded to make themselves at home in the doctor's house. Smith and the doctor slept together, likewise Billie and Mrs. Kinney; Van Emmon occupied the guest-room in lonely grandeur. When he came down to breakfast he said he had dreamed that he was Corrus, and that he had burned himself on a blazing cow.

Again in the trance state, the four found that Rolla and Cunora, after reaching an understanding with Corrus and Dulnop, had already left their huts in search of the required stone. Five bees accompanied them. Within a few minutes however, Corrus and Dulnop set out together in the opposite direction, as agreed upon; and shortly the guards were withdrawn. This meant that the holiday was officially sanctioned, so long as the two couples kept apart; but if they were to join forces afterward, and be caught in the act, they would be severely punished. Such was bee efficiency—and sentiment.

The doctor had impressed Rolla with the fact that she would find the desired stone in a mountainous country. Cunora, however, was for examining every rock she came to; Rolla was continually passing judgment upon some specimen.

"Nay," said she, for the hundredth time. "Tis a very bright stone we seek, very small and very shiny, like sunlight on the water. I shall know it when I see it, and I shall see it not until we reach the mountains." Soon Cunora's impatience wore off, and the two concentrated upon making time. By midday they were well into the hills, following the course of a very dry creek; and now they kept a sharp lookout at every step.

Van Emmon and Smith had similarly impressed Corrus and Dulnop with the result that there was no loss of time in the beginning. The two men reached the hills on their side of the valley an hour before the women reached theirs.

And thus the search began, the strangest search, beyond a doubt, within the history of the universe. It was not like the work of some of earth's prehistoric men, who already knew fire and were merely looking up fresh materials; it was a quest in which an idea, an idea given in a vision, was the sole driving force. The most curious part of the matter was that these people were mentally incapable of conceiving that there was intelligence at work upon them from another world, or even that there was another world.

"Ye saw the stars last night?" Corrus spoke to Dulnop. "Well, 'tis just such stars as shall awaken the seed of the flower. Ye shall see!"

Both knew exactly what to look for: the brassy, regularly cut crystals with the black stripings, such as has led countless men to go through untold hardships in the belief that they had found gold. In fact, iron pyrites is often called "fool gold," so deceptive is its glitter.

Yet, it was just the thing for the purpose. Flint they already had, large quantities of it; practically all their tools, such as axes and knives, were made of it. Struck against iron pyrites, a larger, fatter, hotter spark could be obtained than with any other natural combination.

It was Dulnop's luck to see the outcropping. He found the mineral exposed to plain view, a few feet above the bottom of the ravine the two were ascending. With a shout of triumph he leaped upon the rock.

"Here, Corrus!" he yelled, dancing like mad. "Here is the gift of the gods!"

The older man didn't attempt to hide his delight. He grabbed his companion and hugged him until his ribs began to crack. Then, with a single blow from his huge club, the herdsman knocked the specimen clear of the slate in which it was set. Such was their excitement, neither dreamed of marking the place in any way.

First satisfying themselves that the pyrites really could produce "stars" from the flint, the two hurried down-stream, in search of the right kind of wood. In half an hour Corrus came across a dead, worm-eaten tree, from which he nonchalantly broke off a limb as big as his leg. The interior was filled with a dry, stringy rot, just the right thing for making a spark "live."

Then came a real difficulty. It will be better appreciated when the men's childish nature is borne in mind. Their patience was terribly strained in their attempts to make the sparks fly into the tinder. Again and again one of them would throw the rocks angrily to the ground, fairly snarling with exasperation.

However, the other would immediately take them up and try again. Neither man had a tenth the deftness that is common to adults on the earth. In size and strength alone they were men; otherwise—it cannot too often be repeated—they were mere children. All told, it was over two hours before the punk began to smoulder.

"By Mownoth!" swore the herdsman, staring reverently at the smoke. "We have done a miracle, Dulnop—ye and I! Be ye sure this is no dream?"

Quite in human fashion, Dulnop seriously reached out and pinched the herdsman's tremendous arm. Corrus winced, but was too well pleased with the result to take revenge, although the nature of these men was such as to call for it.

"It be no dream!" he declared, still awestruck.

"Nay," agreed Dulnop. "And now—to make the flower grow!"

It was Corrus's lungs which really did the work. His prodigious chest was better than a small pair of bellows, and he blew just as he had been told in the vision. Presently a small flame appeared in the tinder, and leaped eagerly upward. Both men jumped back, and for lack of enough air the flame went out.

"Never mind!" exclaimed Dulnop at Corrus's crestfallen look. "I remember that we must be ready with leaves, and the like, as soon as the blossom appears. Blow, ye great wind-maker, and I shall feed the flower!"

And thus it came about that two men of Sanus, for the first time in the history of the planet, looked upon fire itself. And when they had got it to burning well, each of them stared at his hands, and from his hands to the little heap of "flowers"; from hands to fire they looked, again and again; and then gazed at one another in awe.

X
AT HALF COCK

Rolla and Cunora searched for hours. They followed one creek almost to its very beginning, and then crossed a ridge on the left and came down another stream. Again and again Cunora found bits of mineral such as would have deceived any one who had been less accurately impressed than Rolla. As it afterward turned out, the very accuracy of this impression was a great error, strange though that may seem. Finally Rolla glanced up at the sun and sighed. "We will have to give it up for this day," she told Cunora. "There be just time enough to return before night." Neither said anything about the half-rations upon which they would be fed in punishment for running away.

So the two started back, making their way in gloomy silence through the woods and fields of the valley. Cunora was greatly disappointed, and soon began to show it as any child would, by maintaining a sullenness which she broke only when some trifling obstacle, such as a branch, got in her way. Then she would tear the branch from the tree and fling it as far as she could, meanwhile screaming with anger. Rolla showed more control.

It was nearing nightfall when they came within sight of the huts. At a distance of perhaps half a mile they stopped and stared hard at the scene ahead of them.

"Hear ye anything, Cunora?" asked the older woman.

The girl's keen ears had caught a sound. "Methinks something hath aroused our people. I wonder—"

"Cunora!" gasped Rolla excitedly. "Think ye that Corrus and Dulnop have succeeded in growing the flower?"

They ran nearer. In a moment it was clear that something most certainly was arousing the people. The village was in an uproar. "Stay!" cautioned Rolla, catching her friend's arm. "Let us use cunning! Mayhap there be danger!"

They were quite alone in the fields, which were always deserted at that hour. Crouching behind a row of bushes, they quickly drew near to the village, all without being seen. Otherwise, this tale would never be told.

For Corrus and Dulnop, after having satisfied themselves that the wondrous flowering flower would live as long as they continued to feed it, had immediately decided to carry it home. To do so they first tried building the fire on a large piece of bark. Of course it burned through, and there had been more delay.

Finally Corrus located a piece of slate, so large that a small fire could be kept up without danger of spilling.

The two men had hurried straight for the village. Not once did either of them dream what a magnificent spectacle they made; the two skin-clad aborigines, bearing the thing which was to change them from slaves into free beings, with all the wonders of civilization to come in its train. Behind them as they marched, if they but knew it, stalked the principles of the steam engine, of the printing-press, of scientific agriculture and mechanical industry in general. Look about the room in which you sit as you read this; even to the door-knobs every single item depends upon fire, directly or indirectly! But Corrus and Dulnop were as ignorant of this as their teeth were devoid of fillings.

Not until then did it occur to the four watchers on the earth that there was anything premature about the affair. It was Smith who first observed:

"Say, Van, I never thought to impress Dulnop with any plan for using the fire. How about you and Corrus?"

"By George!" seriously, from the geologist. And immediately the two set to work trying to reach their agents' minds.

They failed! Dulnop and Corrus were both too excited, far too wide awake, to feel even the united efforts of all four on the earth. And the two Sanusians marched straight into the village without the remotest idea of how they should act.

"It is a flower!" he shrieked, frantic with joy. "The flower has come!" the shout was passed along. "Corrus and Dulnop have found the flowering blossom!"

Within a single minute the two men were surrounded by the whole human population of the place. For the most part the natives were too awestruck to come very near; they were content to stand off and stare at the marvel, or fall upon their knees and worship it. It was now so dark that the flames fairly illumined their faces.

Shortly one or two got up courage enough to imitate Dulnop as he "fed the flower;" and presently there were several little fires burning merrily upon the ground. As for the aborigines, they let themselves loose; never before did they shout and dance as they shouted and danced that night. It was this Rolla and Cunora heard.

Before five minutes had passed, however, a scout awakened Supreme. Billie could see that the bee was angry at having been disturbed, but swiftly collected herself as she realized the significance of the scout's report.

"So they have found the terror," she reflected aloud. "Very well. Arouse all except the egg-layers and the drones. We can make use of the food-gatherers as well as the fighters."

The hive was soon awake. Billie was sure that every last bee was greatly afraid; their agitation was almost pitiful. But such was their organization and their automatic obedience to orders, there was infinitely less confusion than might be supposed. Another five minutes had not passed before not only that hive, but all within the "city" were emptied; and millions upon millions of desperate bees were under way toward the village.

Rolla and Cunora knew of it first. They heard the buzzing of that winged cloud as it passed through the air above their heads; but such was the bees' intent interest in the village ahead, the two women were not spied as they hid among the bushes. By this time twilight was half gone. The firelight lit up the crowd of humans as they surged and danced about their new deity. For, henceforth, fire would replace Mownoth as their chief god; it was easy to see that.

Moreover, both Corrus and Dulnop, as primitive people will, had been irresistibly seized by the spirit of the mob. They threw their burden down and joined in the frenzy of the dance. Louder and louder they shouted; faster and faster they capered. Already one or two of their fellow villagers had dropped, exhausted, to the ground. Never had they had so good an excuse for dancing themselves to death!

And into this scene came the bees. Not one of them dared go within ten yards of the flames; for a while, all they did was to watch the humans. Such was the racket no one noticed the sound of the wings.

"Shall we attack those on the edge of the crowd?" one of Supreme's lieutenants wanted to know. The commandant considered this with all the force of what mental experience she had had.

"No," she decided. "We shall wait a little longer. Just now, they are too jubilant to be frightened; we would have to kill them all, and that would not be good policy." Of course, the bee had the pollen crop, nothing more, in mind when she made her decision; yet it was further justified. There was no let-up in the rejoicing; if anything, it became more frantic than before. Darkness fell upon a crowd which was reeling in self-induced mental intoxication.

Rolla and Cunora came a little nearer; and still remaining hidden, saw that more than half their friends had succumbed. One by one the remainder dropped out; their forms lay all about what was left of the fire. The two women could easily see what their friends were blind to: the bees were simply biding their time.

"Ought we not to rush in and warn them?" whispered Cunora to Rolla. "Surely the flower hath driven them mad!"

"Hush!" warned the older woman. "Be quiet! Everything depends upon our silence!"

It was true. Only two of the villagers remained upon their feet, and shortly one of these staggered and fell in his tracks. The one who was left was Corrus himself, his immense vitality keeping him going. Then he, too, after a final whoop of triumph and defiance, absolutely unconscious of the poison-laden horde that surrounded him, fell senseless to the earth. Another minute, and the whole crowd was still.

And the fire had gone out.

The bees came closer. Several thousands of them were stricken by smoke from the embers, and the rest of the swarm took good care to avoid it. They hovered over the prostrate forms of the aborigines and made sure that they were unconscious.

"Is there nothing we can do?" whispered Cunora, straining her eyes to see.

"Nothing, save to watch and wait," returned Rolla, her gaze fixed upon the dark heap which marked her lover's form. And thus an hour passed, with the four on the earth quite unable to take a hand in any way.

Then one of the villagers—the first, in fact, who had dropped out of the dance—stirred and presently awakened. He sat up and looked about him, dazed and dizzy, for all the world like a drunken man. After a while he managed to get to his feet.

No sooner had he done this than a dozen bees were upon him. Terror-stricken, he stood awaiting their commands. They were not long in coming.

By means of their fearful buzzing, the deadly insects guided him into the nearest hut, where they indicated that he should pick up one of the rude hoelike tools which was used in the fields. With this in hand, he was driven to the little piles of smoldering ashes, where the fires had flickered an hour before.

Hardly knowing what he was doing, but not daring to disobey, the man proceeded to heap dirt over the embers. Shortly he had every spark of the fire smothered beneath a mound as high as his knees. Not till then did any of the others begin to revive.

As fast as they recovered the bees took charge of them. Not a human had courage enough to make a move of offense; it meant certain death, and they all knew it only too well. As soon as they were wide awake enough to know what they were doing, they were forced to search the bodies of those still asleep.

"We must find the means for growing the flower," said Supreme, evidently convinced that a seed was a seed, under any circumstances. And presently they found, tucked away in Corrus's lion-skin, a large chunk of the pyrites, and a similar piece on Dulnop.

"So these were the discoverers," commented Supreme.

"What is your will in their case?" the subordinate asked.

The commanding bee considered for a long time. Finally she got an idea, such as bees are known to get once in a great while. It was simply a new combination—as all ideas are merely new combinations—of two punishments which were commonly employed by the bees.

As a result, eight of the villagers were compelled to carry the two fire-finders to a certain spot on the bank of a nearby stream. Here the two fragments of pyrites were thrown, under orders, into the water; so that the eight villagers might know just why the whole thing was being done. Next the two men, still unconscious, were buried up to their necks. Their heads, lolling helplessly, were all that was exposed. So it was to be the Head Out punishment—imprisonment of one day with their bodies rigidly held by the soil: acute torture to an aborigine. But was this all?

One of the villagers was driven to the nearest hut, where he was forced to secure two large stone axes. Bringing these back to the "torture-place," as the spot was called, the man was compelled to wield one of the clumsy tools while a companion used the other; and between them they cut down the tree whose branches had been waving over the prisoners' heads. Then the villagers were forced to drag the tree away.

All of which occurred in the darkness, and out of sight of Rolla and Cunora. They could only guess what was going on. Hours passed, and dawn approached. Not till then did they learn just what had been done.

The villagers, now all awake, were driven by the bees to the place on the bank of the stream. There, the eight men who had imprisoned the two discoverers told what had been done with the "magic stones." Each villager stared at the offenders, and at something which lay on the ground before them, and in sober silence went straight to his or her work in the fields.

Presently the huts were deserted. All the people were on duty elsewhere. Such bees as were not guarding the fields had returned to the hives. Rolla and Cunora cautiously ventured forth, taking great care to avoid being seen. They hurried fearfully to the stream.

Before they reached the spot Rolla gave an exclamation and stared curiously to one side, where the tree had been dragged. Suddenly she gave a terrible cry and rushed forward, only to drop on her knees and cover her face with hands that shook as with the palsy. At the same instant Cunora saw what had been done; and uttering a single piercing scream, fell fainting to the ground.

Heaped in front of the two prisoners was a large pile of pebbles. There were thousands upon thousands in the heap. Before each man, at a distance of a foot, was a large gourd-ful of water. To the savages, these told the whole story; these, together with the tree dragged to one side.

Corrus and Dulnop were to be buried in that spot every day for as many days as there were pebbles in the heap; in other words, until they died. Every night they would be dug up, and every morning buried afresh. And to keep them from telling any of the villagers where they had found the pyrites, they were to be deprived of water all day long. By night their tongues would be too swollen for speech. For they had been sentenced to the No Shade torture, as well; their heads would be exposed all day long to the burning sun itself.

XI
THE EDGE OF THE WORLD

It is significant that Billie, because of her connection with the bee, Supreme, was spared the sight that the doctor saw from Rolla's point of view. Otherwise, the geologist's wife might have had a different opinion of the matter. As it was—

"Corrus and Dulnop," said she as cooly as Supreme herself might have spoken, "are not the first to suffer because they have discovered something big."

Whereupon her husband's wrath got beyond his grip. "Not the first! Is that all you can say?" he demanded hotly. "Why, of all the damnably cruel, cold-blooded creatures I ever heard of, those infernal bees—"

Van Emmon stopped, unable to go on without blasphemy.

The doctor had got over the horror of what he had seen. "We want to be fair, Van. Look at this matter from the bees' view-point for awhile. What were they to do? They had to make sure, as far as possible, that their supremacy would never be threatened again. Didn't they?"

"Oh, but—damn it all!" cried Van Emmon. "There's a limit somewhere! Such cruelty as that—no one could conceive of it!"

"As for the bees," flared Billie, "I don't blame 'em! And unless I'm very much mistaken, the ruling class anywhere, here on the earth or wherever you investigate, will go the limit to hold the reins, once they get them!"

The expression on Van Emmon's face was curious to see. There was no fear there, only a puzzled astonishment. Strange as it may seem, Billie had told him something that had never occurred to him before. And he recognized it as truth, as soon as she had said it.

"Just a minute," remarked Smith in his ordinary voice; "just a minute. You're forgetting that we don't really know whether Rolla and Cunora are safe. Everything depends upon them now, you know."

In silence the four went back into telepathic connection. Now, of course, Smith and Van Emmon were practically without agents. The prisoners could tell them nothing whatever except the tale of increasing agony as their torture went on. All that Van Emmon and Smith could do was lend the aid of their mentality to the efforts of the other two, and for a while had to be content with what Billie, through Supreme, and the doctor, through Rolla, were able to learn. However, Kinney did suggest that one of the other two men get in touch with Cunora.

"Good idea," said Smith. "Go to it, Van Emmon."

The geologist stirred uneasily, and avoided his wife's eyes. "I—I'm afraid not, Smith. Rather think I'd prefer to rest a while. You do it!"

Smith laughed and reddened. "Nothing doing for an old bach like me. Cunora might—well, you know—go in bathing, for instance. It's all right for the doctor, of course; but—let me out!"

Meanwhile the two women on Sanus, taking the utmost care, managed to retreat from the river bank without being discovered. Keeping their eyes very wide open and their ears strained for the slightest buzz, the two contrived to pass through the village, out into the fields, and thence, from cover to cover, into the foothills on that side of the valley where their lovers had found the pyrites.

"If only we knew which stream they ascended!" lamented Cunora, as they stood in indecision before a fork in the river.

"But we don't!" Rolla pointed out philosophically. "We must trust to luck and Mownoth, ye and I."

And despite all the effort the doctor could put forth to the contrary, the two women picked out the wrong branch. They searched as diligently as two people possibly could; but somehow the doctor knew, just because of the wrong choice that had been made, that their search would be unsuccessful. He thought the matter over for a few moments, and finally admitted to his three friends:

"I wonder if I haven't been a little silly? Why should I have been so precious specific in impressing Rolla about the pyrites? Pshaw! Almost any hard rock will strike sparks from flint!"

"Why, of course!" exploded Van Emmon. "Here—let's get busy and tell Rolla!"

But it proved astonishingly difficult. The two women were in an extraordinary condition now. They were continually on the alert. In fact, the word "alert" scarcely described the state of mind, the keen, desperate watchfulness which filled every one of their waking hours, and caused each to remain awake as long as possible; so that they invariably fell to sleep without warning. They could not be caught in the drowsy state!

For they knew something about the bees which the four on the earth did not learn until Billie had overheard Supreme giving some orders.

"Set a guard on that river bank," she told her subordinate, "and maintain it night and day. If any inferior attempts to recover the magic stone, deal with him or her in the same manner in which we punished the finders of the deadly flower."

"It shall be done, Supreme. Is there anything further?"

"Yes. Make quite sure that none of the inferiors are missing."

Shortly afterward the lieutenant reported that one of the huts was empty.

"Rolla, the soil-tester, and Cunora, the vineyardist, are gone."

"Seek them!" Supreme almost became excited. "They are the lovers of the men we punished! They would not absent themselves unless they knew something! Find them, and torture them into revealing the secret! We must weed out this flowing blossom forever!"

"It shall be done!"

Such methods were well known to Rolla and Cunora. Had not their fellow villagers, many of them, tried time after time to escape from bondage? And had they not inevitably been apprehended and driven back, to be tortured as an example to the rest? It would never do to be caught!

So they made it a practice to travel only during twilight and dawn, remaining hidden through the day. Invariably one stood watch while the other slept. The bees were—everywhere!

Upon crossing the range of mountains going down the other side, Cunora and Rolla began to feel hopeful of two things—first, that their luck would change, and the wonderful stone be found; and second, that they would be in no danger from the bees in this new country, which seemed to be a valley much like the one they had quit. It was all quite new and strange to them, and in their interest they almost forgot at times that each had a terrible score to settle when her chance finally came.

Twice they had exceedingly narrow escapes. Always they kept carefully hid, but on the third day Cunora, advancing cautiously through some brush, came suddenly upon two bees feeding. She stopped short and held her breath. Neither saw her, so intent were they upon their honey; yet Cunora felt certain that each had been warned to watch out for her. This was true; Billie learned that every bee on the planet had been told. And so Cunora silently backed away, an inch at a time, until it was safe to turn and run.

On another occasion Rolla surprised a big drone bee, just as she bent to take a drink of water from a stream. The insect had been out of her sight, on the other side of a boulder. It rose with an angry buzz as she bent down; a few feet away from her it hung in the air, apparently scrutinizing her to make sure that she was one of the runaways. Her heart leaped to her mouth. Suppose they were reported!

She made a lightninglike grab at the thing, and very nearly caught it. Straight up it shot, taken by surprise, and dashed blindly into a ledge of rock which hung overhead. For a second it floundered, dazed; and that second was its last. Cunora gave a single bound forward, and with a vicious swing of a palm-leaf, which she always carried, smashed the bee flat.

Before they had been free five days they came to an exceedingly serious conclusion: that it was only a question of time until they were caught. Sooner or later they must be forced to return; they could not hope to dodge bees much longer. When Rolla fully realized this she turned gravely to the younger girl.

"Methinks the time has come for us to make a choice, Cunora. Which shall it be: live as we have been living for the past four days, with the certainty of being caught in time or—face the unknown perils on the edge of the world?"

Cunora dropped the piece of stone she had been inspecting and shivered with fear. "A dreadful choice ye offer, Rolla! Think of the horrible beasts we must encounter!"

"Ye mean"—corrected the philosophical one—"ye mean, the beasts which men SAY they have seen. Tell me; hast ever seen such thyself? Many times hast thou been near the edge, I know."

The girl shook her head. "Nay; not I. Yet these beasts must be, Rolla; else why should all men tell of them?"

"I note," remarked Rolla thoughtfully, "that each man tells of seeing a different sort of beast. Perchance they were all but lies."

However, it was Cunora's fear of capture, rather than her faith in Rolla's reasoning, which drove the girl to the north. For to the north they travelled, a matter of some two weeks; and not once did they dare relax their vigilance. Wherever they went, there was vegetation of some sort, and wherever there was vegetation bees were likely to be found. By the time the two weeks were over, the women were in a state of near-hysteria, from the nervous strain of it all. Moreover, both suffered keenly for want of cereals, to which they were accustomed; they were heartily tired of such fruits and nuts as they were able to pick up without exposing themselves.

One morning before daybreak they came to the upper end of a long, narrow valley—one which paralleled their own, by the way—and as they emerged from the plain into the foothills it was clear that they had reached a new type of country. There was comparatively little brush; and with every step the rockiness increased. By dawn they were on the edge of a plateau; back of them stretched the inhabited country; ahead, a haze-covered expanse. Nothing but rocks was about them.

"Ye are sure that we had best keep on?" asked Cunora uneasily.

Rolla nodded, slowly but positively. "It is best. Back of us lies certain capture. Ahead—we know not what; but at least there is a chance!"

Nevertheless, both hesitated before starting over the plateau. Each gazed back longingly over the home of their kind; and for a moment Rolla's resolution plainly faltered. She hesitated; Cunora made a move as though to return. And at that instant their problem was decided for them.

A large drone passed within six feet of them. Both heard the buzz, and whirled about to see the bee darting frantically out of reach. At a safe distance it paused, as though to make sure of its find, then disappeared down the valley. They had been located!

"We have no choice now!" cried Rolla, speaking above a whisper for the first time in weeks. "On, as fast as ye can, Cunora!"

The two sped over the rocks, making pretty good time considering the loads they carried. Each had a good-sized goatskin full of various dried fruits and nuts, also a gourd not so full. In fact, it had been some while since they had had fresh water. Cunora was further weighed down by some six pounds of dried rabbit meat; the animals had been caught in snares. Both, however, discarded their palm leaves; they would be of no further use now.

And thus they fled, knowing that they had, at most, less than a day before the drone would return with enough soldiers to compel obedience. For the most part, the surface was rough granite, with very little sign of erosion. There was almost no water; both women showed intense joy when they found a tiny pool of it standing in a crevasse. They filled their gourds as well as their stomachs.

A few steps farther on, and the pair stepped out of the shallow gully in which they had been walking. Immediately they were exposed to a very strong and exceedingly cold wind, such as seemed to surprise them in no way, but compelled both to actually lean against its force. Moreover, although this pressure was all from the left, it proved exceedingly difficult to go on. Their legs seemed made of lead, and their breathing was strangely laboured. This, also, appeared to be just what they had expected.

Presently, however, they found another slight depression in the rocks; and sheltered from the wind, made a little better progress ahead. It was bitter cold, however; only the violence of their exercise could make them warm enough to stand it. All in all, the two were considerably over three hours in making the last mile; they had to stop frequently to rest. The only compensating thing was their freedom from worry; the bees would not bother them where the wind was so strong. So long as they could keep on the move they were safe.

But what made it worse was the steadily increasing difficulty of moving their legs. For, although the surface continued level, they seemed to be CLIMBING now, where before they had simply walked. It was just as though the plateau had changed into a mountain, and they were ascending it; only, upon looking back, nothing but comparatively flat rock met the gaze. What made them lean forward so steeply anyhow?

Rolla seemed to think it all very ordinary. She was more concerned about the wind, to which they had become once more exposed as they reached the end of the rift. On they pressed, five or six steps at each attempt, stopping to rest twice the length of time they actually travelled. It was necessary now to cling to the rock with both hands, and once Cunora lost her grip, so that she would have been blown to one side, or else have slipped backward, had not Rolla grasped her heel and held her until she could get another hand-hold.

"Courage!" gasped Rolla. Perspiration was streaming down her face, despite the bitter cold of the wind; her hands trembled from the strain she was undergoing. "Courage, Cunora! It be not much farther!"

On they strove. Always it seemed as though they were working upward as well as onward, although the continued flatness of the surface argued obstinately against this. Also, the sun remained in the same position relative to the rocks; if they were climbing, it should have appeared overhead. What did it mean?

Finally Rolla saw, about a hundred yards farther on, something which caused her to shout: "Almost there, Cunora!"

The younger girl could not spare breath enough to reply. They struggled on in silence.

Now they were down on their hands and knees. Before half the hundred yards was covered, they were flat on their faces, literally clawing their way upward and onward. Had the wind increased in violence in proportion as the way grew harder, they could never have made it, physical marvels though they were. Only the absolute knowledge that they dared not return drove them on; that, and the possibility of finding the precious stone, and of ultimately saving the two men they had left behind.

The last twenty feet was the most extraordinary effort that any human had ever been subjected to. They had to take turns in negotiating the rock; one would creep a few inches on, get a good hold, and brace herself against the wind, while the other, crawling alongside, used her as a sort of a crutch. Their fingers were bleeding and their finger-nails cracked from the rock and cold; the same is equally true of their toes. Had it been forty feet instead of twenty—

The rocks ended there. Beyond was nothing but sky; even this was not like what they were used to, but was very nearly black. Two more spurts, and Rolla threw one hand ahead and caught the edge of the rock. Cunora dragged herself alongside. The effort brought blood to her nostrils.

They rested a minute or two, then looked at one another in mute inquiry. Cunora nodded; Rolla took great breath; and they drew themselves to the edge and looked over.

XII
OUTSIDE INFORMATION

The two women gazed in extreme darkness. The other side of the ridge of rock was black as night. From side to side the ridge extended, like a jagged knife edge on a prodigious scale; it seemed infinite in extent. Behind them—that is, at their feet—lay the stone-covered expanse they had just traversed; ahead of them there was—nothingness itself.

Cunora shook with fear and cold. "Let us not go on, Rolla!" she whimpered. "I like not the looks of this void; it may contain all sorts of beasts. I—I am afraid!" She began to sob convulsively.

Rolla peered into the darkness. Nothing whatever was to be seen. It was as easy to imagine enemies as friends; easier in fact. What might not the unknown hold for them?

"We cannot stay here," spoke Rolla, with what energy her condition would permit. "We could not—hold on. Nor can we return now; They would surely find us!"

But Cunora's courage, which had never faltered in the face of familiar dangers, was not equal to the unknown. She wailed: "Rolla! A little way back—a hollow in the rock! 'Tis big enough to shelter me! I would—rather stay there than—go on!"

"Ye would rather die there, alone!"

Cunora hid her face. "Let me have half the food! I can go back to the pool—for water! And maybe," hopefully—"maybe They will give up the search in time."

"Aye," from Rolla, bitterly. "And in time Dulnop will die, if we do nothing for him—and for Corrus!"

Cunora fell to sobbing again. "I cannot help it! I am—afraid!"

Rolla scarcely heard. An enormous idea had just occurred to her. She had told the girl to think of Dulnop and Corrus; but was it not equally true that they should think of all the other humans, their fellow slaves, each of whom had suffered nearly as much? Was not the fire equally precious to them all?

She started to explain this to the girl, then abruptly gave it up. It was no use; Cunora's mind was not strong enough to take the step. Rolla fairly gasped as she realized, as no Sanusian had realized before, that she had been given the responsibility of rescuing A WHOLE RACE.

Fire she must have! And since she could not, dared not, seek it here, she must try the other side of the world. And she would have to do it—alone!

"So be it!" she said loudly in a strange voice. "Ye stay here and wait, Cunora! I go on!"

And for fear her resolution would break down, she immediately crept over the edge. She clung to the rock as though expecting to be dragged from it. Instead, as she let her feet down into the blackness, she could feel solid rock beneath her body, quite the same as she had lain upon a moment before. It was like descending the opposite side of an incredibly steep mountain, a mountain made of blackness itself.

The women gave one another a last look. For all they knew, neither would gaze upon the other again. Next moment, with Cunora's despairing cry ringing in her ears, Holla began to crawl backward and downward.

She could plainly see the sun's level rays above her head, irregular beams of yellowish light; it served slightly to illuminate her surroundings. Shortly, however, her eyes became accustomed to the darkness; the stars helped just as they had always helped; and soon she was moving almost as freely as on the other side.

Once she slipped, and slid down and to one side, for perhaps ten feet. When she finally grabbed a sharp projecting ledge and stopped, her vision almost failed from the terrible effort she had put forth. She could scarcely feel the deep gash that the ledge had made in her finger-tips.

After perhaps half an hour of hard work among bare rocks exactly like those she had quit, she stopped for a prolonged rest. As a matter of course, she stared at the sky; and then came her first discovery.

Once more let it be understood that her view was totally different from anything that has ever been seen on the earth. To be sure, "up" was over her head, and "down" was under her feet; nevertheless, she was stretched full length, face down, on the rock. In other words, it was precisely as though she were clinging to a cliff. Sky above, sky behind and all sides; there were stars even under her feet!

But all her life she had been accustomed, at night, to see that broad band of silver light across the heavens. She had taken it for granted that, except at two seasons of the year, for short periods, she would always see "the Silvery Way." But tonight—there was no band! The whole sky was full of—stars, nothing else!

It will be easier to picture her wonder and uneasiness if she is compared mentally with a girl of five or six. Easier, too, to appreciate the fact that she determined to go on anyhow.

Mile after mile was covered in the darkness. Rolla was on the point of absolute exhaustion; but she dared not sleep until she reached a spot where there was no danger of falling. It was only after braving the gale for over four hours in the starlight that Rolla reached a point where she was no longer half crawling, half creeping, but moved nearly erect. Shortly she was able to face the way she was going; and by leaning backward was able to make swift progress.

In another half-hour she was walking upright. Still no explanation of the mystery!

Finding a sheltered spot, she proceeded to make herself comparatively comfortable on the rock. Automatically, from habit, she proceeded to keep watch; then she must have remembered that there was now no need for vigilance. For she lay herself down in the darkness and instantly fell asleep.

Three hours later—according to the time kept by the watchers on the earth—Rolla awoke and sat up in great alarm. And small wonder.

It was broad daylight! The sun was well above the horizon; and not only the Sanusian but the people on the earth were vastly puzzled to note that it was the western horizon! To all appearances, Rolla had slept a whole day in that brief three hours.

Shortly her nerves were steady enough for her to look about, uncomprehendingly, but interestedly, as a child will. There was nothing but rock to be seen; a more or less level surface, such as she had toiled over the day before. The day before! She glanced at the sun once more, and her heart gave a great leap.

The sun was rising—in the west!

"'Tis a world of contraries," observed Rolla sagely to herself. "Mayhap I shall find all else upside down."

She ate heartily, and drank deep from her gourd. There was not a cupful remaining. She eyed it seriously as she got to her feet.

Another look back at that flat expanse of granite, which had so gradually and so mysteriously changed from precipice to plain, and Rolla strode on with renewed vigour and interest. Presently she was able to make out something of a different colour in the distance, and soon was near enough to see some bona-fide bushes; a low, flowerless shrub, it is true, but at least it was a living thing.

Shortly the undergrowth became dense enough to make it somewhat of an effort to get through. And before long she was noticing all manner of small creatures, from bugs to an occasional wandering bird. These last, especially, uttered an abrupt but cheerful chirp which helped considerably to raise her spirits. It was all too easy to see, in her fancy, her lover helpless and suffering in the power of those cold-blooded, merciless insects.

In an hour or two she reached the head of a small stream. Hurrying down its banks as rapidly as its undergrowth would permit, Rolla followed its course as it bent, winding and twisting, in the direction which had always been north to her, but which the sun plainly labeled "south." Certainly the sun mounted steadily toward the zenith, passing successively through the positions corresponding to four, three and two o'clock, in a manner absolutely baffling.

About noon she came out of the canyon into the foothills. Another brief rest, and from the top of a knoll she found herself looking upon a valley about the size of the one she called "home." Otherwise, it was very different. For one thing, it was far better watered; nowhere could she see the half-dried brownishness so characteristic of her own land. The whole surface was heavily grown with all manner of vegetation; and so far as she could see it was all absolutely wild. There was not a sign of cultivation.

Keeping to the left bank of the river, a much broader affair than any she had seen before, Rolla made her way for several miles with little difficulty. Twice she made wide detours through the thicket, and once it was necessary to swim a short distance; the stream was too deep to wade. The doctor watched the whole affair, purely as a matter of professional interest.

"She is a magnificent specimen physically," he said in his impersonal way, "and she shows none of the defects of the African savages."

And such was his manner, in speaking of his distant "patient," that Billie took it entirely as a matter of course, without the slightest self-consciousness because of Van Emmon and Smith.

All this while Rolla had been intent, as before, upon finding some of the coveted crystals. She had no luck; but presently she discovered something decidedly worth while—a fallen tree trunk, not too large, and near enough to the bank to be handled without help. A few minutes later she was floating at ease, and making decidedly better time.

A half-hour of this—during which she caught glimpses of many animals, large and small, all of which fled precipitately—and she rounded a sharp bend in the stream, to be confronted with a sight which must have been strange indeed to her. Stretching across the river was—a network of rusty wire, *the remains of a reinforced concrete bridge.*

There was no doubt of this. On each bank was a large, moss-grown block of stone, which the doctor knew could be nothing else than the old abutments. Seemingly there had been only a single span.

The woman brought the log to the shore, and examined the bridge closely. Instinctively she felt that the structure argued a high degree of intelligence, very likely human. A little hesitation, and then she beached her log, ascended the bank, and looked upon the bridge from above.

A narrow road met her eyes. Once it might have been twice as wide, but now the thicket encroached until there was barely room enough, judged the doctor, for a single vehicle to pass. Its surface was badly broken up—apparently it had been concrete—and grass grew in every crack. Nevertheless, it was a bona-fide road.

For the first time in a long while, Rolla was temporarily off her guard. The doctor was able to impress her with the idea of "Follow this road!" and to his intense gratification the woman started away from the river at once.

Soon the novelty of the thing wore off enough for her to concern herself with fresh food. She discovered plenty of berries, also three kinds of nuts; all were strange to her, yet she ate them without question, and suffered nothing as a result, so far as the doctor could see.

The sun was less than an hour from the horizon when the road, after passing over a slight rise, swung in a wide arc through the woods and thus unveiled a most extraordinary landscape. It was all the more incredible because so utterly out of keeping with what Rolla had just passed through. She had been in the wilderness; now—

A vast city lay before her. Not a hundred yards away stood a low, square building of some plain, gray stone. Beyond this stretched block upon block—mile upon mile, rather—of bona-fide residences, stores and much larger buildings. It is true that the whole place was badly overgrown with all sorts of vegetation; yet, from that slight elevation, there was no doubt that this place was, or had been, a great metropolis.

Presently it became clear that "had been" was the correct term. Nothing but wild life appeared. Rolla looked closely for any signs of human occupancy, but saw none. To all appearances the place was deserted; and it was just as easy to say that it had been so for ten centuries as for one.

"There seems no good reason why I should not go farther," commented Rolla aloud, to boost her courage. "Perchance I shall find the magic stone in this queer place."

It speaks well for her self-confidence that, despite the total strangeness of the whole affair—a city was as far out of her line as aviation to a miner—she went forward with very little hesitation. None of the wild creatures that scuttled from her sight alarmed her at all; the only things she looked at closely were such bees as she met. The insects ignored her altogether, except to keep a respectful distance.

"These masters," observed Rolla with satisfaction, "know nothing of me. I shall not obey them till they threaten me." But there was no threatening.

For the most part the buildings were in ruins. Here and there a structure showed very little damage by the elements. In more than one case the roof was quite intact. Clearly the materials used were exceptional, or else the place had not been deserted very long. The doctor held to the latter opinion, especially after seeing a certain brown-haired dog running to hide behind a heap of stones.

"It was a dog!" the doctor felt sure. To Rolla, however, the animal was even more significant. She exclaimed about it in a way which confirmed the doctor's guess. On she went at a faster rate, plainly excited and hopeful of seeing something further that she could recognize.

She found it in a hurry. Reaching the end of one block of the ruins, she turned the corner and started to follow the cross street. Whereupon she stopped short, to gaze in consternation at a line of something whitish which stretched from one side of the "street" to the other.

It was a line of human skeletons.

There were perhaps two hundred in the lot, piled one on top of the other, and forming a low barrier across the pavement. To Rolla the thing was simply terrible, and totally without explanation. To the people on the earth, it suggested a formation of troops, shot down in their tracks and left where they had fallen. The doctor would have given a year of his life if only Rolla had had the courage to examine the bones; there might have been bullet holes, or other evidence of how they had met their death.

The Sanusian chose rather to back carefully away from the spot. She walked hurriedly up the street she had just left, and before going another block came across two skeletons lying right in the middle of the street. A little farther on, and she began to find skeletons on every hand. Moreover—and this is especially significant—the buildings in this locality showed a great many gaps and holes in their walls, such as might have been made by shell-fire.

This made it easier to understand something else. Every few yards or so the explorer found a large heap of rust in the gutter, or what had once been the gutter. These heaps had little or no shape; yet the doctor fancied he could detect certain resemblances to things he had seen before, and shortly declared that they were the remains of motors.

"Can't say whether they were aircraft or autos, of course," he added, "but those things were certainly machines." Later, Rolla paid more attention to them, and the doctor positively identified them as former motor-cars.

The sun had gone down. It was still quite light, of course; darkness would not come for a couple of hours. Rolla munched on what food she had, and pressed on through the ruins. She saw skeletons and rusted engines everywhere, and once passed a rounded heap of rust which looked like nothing so much as a large cannon shell. Had the place been the scene of a battle?

Just when she had got rather accustomed to the place and was feeling more or less at her ease, she stopped short. At the same time the doctor himself fairly jumped in his chair. Somewhere, right near at hand, on one of the larger structures, a bell began to ring!

It clanged loudly and confidently, giving out perhaps thirty strokes before it stopped. The stillness which followed was pretty painful. In a moment, however, it was broken as effectively as any silence can be broken.

A man's voice sounded within the building.

Immediately it was replied to, more faintly, by several others. Then came the clatter of some sort of utensils, and sundry other noises which spoke loudly of humans. Rolla froze in her tracks, and her teeth began to chatter.

Next moment she got a grip on herself. "What difference doth it make, whether they be friend or enemy?" she argued severely, for the benefit of her shaking nerves. "They will give thee food, anyhow. And perchance they know where liveth the magic stone!"

In the end Rolla's high purpose prevailed over her weak knees, and she began to look for the entrance to the place. It was partly in ruins—that is, the upper stories—but the two lower floors seemed, so far as their interior could be seen through the high, unglazed windows, to be in good condition. There were no doors on that street.

Going around the corner, however, Rolla saw a high archway at the far corner of the structure. Approaching near enough to peek in, she saw that this arch provided an opening into a long corridor, such as might once have served as a wagon or auto entrance. After a little hesitation she went in.

She passed a door, a massive thing of solid brassy metal, such as interested the doctor immensely but only served to confuse the explorer. A little farther on, and the corridor became pretty dark. She passed another brass door, and approached the end of the pavement. There was one more door there; and she noted with excitement that it was open.

She came closer and peered in. The room was fairly well lighted, and what she saw was clear-cut and unmistakable. In the middle of the room was a long table, and seated about it, in perfect silence, sat an even dozen men.

XIII
THE TWELVE

For a minute or two Rolla was not observed. She simply stood and stared, being neither confident enough to go forward nor scared enough to retreat. Childlike, she scrutinized the group with great thoroughness.

Their comparatively white faces and hands puzzled her most. Also, she could not understand the heavy black robes in which all were dressed. Falling to the floor and reaching far above their necks, such garments would have been intolerable to the free-limbed Sanusians. To the watchers on the earth, however, the robes made the group look marvellously like a company of monks.

Not that there was anything particularly religious about the place or in their behaviour. All twelve seemed to be silent only because they were voraciously hungry. A meal was spread on the table. Except for the garments, the twelve might have been so many harvest hands, gathered for the evening meal in the cook-house. From the white-bearded man who sat at the head of the table and passed out large helpings of something from a big pot, to the fair-haired young fellow at the foot, who could scarcely wait for his share, there was only one thing about them which might have been labelled pious; and that was their attitude, which could have been interpreted: "Give us this day our daily bread—and hurry up about it!"

Apparently Rolla was convinced that these men were thoroughly human, and as such fairly safe to approach. For she allowed her curiosity to govern her caution, and proceeded to sidle through the doorway. Half-way through she caught a whiff of the food, and her sidling changed to something faster.

At that instant she was seen. A tall, dark-haired chap on the far side of the table glanced up and gave a sharp, startled exclamation. Instantly the whole dozen whirled around and with one accord shot to their feet.

Rolla stopped short.

There was a second's silence; then the white-bearded man, who seemed to be the leader of the group, said something peremptory in a deep, compelling voice. Rolla did not understand.

He repeated it, this time a little less commandingly; and Rolla, after swallowing desperately, inclined her head in the diffident way she had, and said:

"Are ye friends or enemies?"

Eleven of the twelve looked puzzled. The dark-haired man, who had been the first to see her, however, gave a muttered exclamation; then he cogitated a moment, wet his lips and said something that sounded like: "What did you say? Say it again!"

Rolla repeated.

The dark-haired man listened intently. Immediately he fell to nodding with great vigour, and thought deeply again before making another try: "We are your friends. Whence came ye, and what seek ye?"

Rolla had to listen closely to what he said. The language was substantially the same as hers; but the verbs were misplaced in the sentences, the accenting was different, and certain of the vowels were flatted. After a little, however, the man caught her way of talking and was able to approximate it quite well, so that she understood him readily.

"I seek," Rolla replied, "food and rest. I have travelled far and am weary."

"Ye look it," commented the man. His name, Rolla found out later, was Somat. "Ye shall have both food and rest. However, whence came ye?"

"From the other side of the world," answered Rolla calmly.

Instantly she noted that the twelve became greatly excited when Somat translated her statement. She decided to add to the scene.

"I have been away from my people for many days," and she held up one hand with the five fingers spread out, opening and closing them four times, to indicate twenty.

"Ye came over the edge of the world!" marveled Somat. "It were a dangerous thing to do, stranger!"

"Aye," agreed Rolla, "but less dangerous than that from which I fled. However," impatiently, "give me the food ye promised; I can talk after my stomach be filled."

"Of a surety," replied Somat apologetically. "I were too interested to remember thy hunger." He spoke a word or two, and one of his companions brought another stool, also dishes and table utensils.

Whereupon the watchers on the earth got a first-class surprise. Here they had been looking upon twelve men, living in almost barbaric fashion amid the ruins of a great city; but the men had been eating from hand-painted china of the finest quality, and using silverware that was simply elegant, nothing less! Luxury in the midst of desolation!

Rolla, however, paid little attention to these details. She was scarcely curious as to the food, which consisted of some sort of vegetable and meat stew, together with butterless bread, a kind of small-grained corn on the cob, a yellowish root-vegetable not unlike turnips, and large quantities of berries. She was too hungry to be particular, and ate heartily of all that was offered, whether cooked or uncooked. The twelve almost forgot their own hunger in their interest in the stranger.

It was now pretty dark in the big room. The white-bearded man said something to the young fellow at the foot of the table, whereupon the chap got up and stepped to the nearest wall, where he pressed something with the tip of his finger. Instantly the room was flooded with white light—from two incandescent bulbs!

Rolla leaped to her feet in amazement, bunking painfully in the unaccustomed glare.

"What is this?" she demanded, all the more furiously to hide her fear. "Ye would not trick me with magic; ye, who call yourselves friends!"

Somat interpreted this to the others. Some laughed; others looked pityingly at her. Somat explained:

"It is nothing, stranger. Be not afraid. We forgot that ye might know nothing of this 'magic.'" He considered deeply, apparently trying to put himself in her place. "Know ye not fire?" Of course, she did not know what he meant. "Then," with an inspiration, "perchance ye have see the flower, the red flower, ye might call—"

"Aye!" eagerly. "Doth it grow here?"

Somat smiled with satisfaction, and beckoned for her to follow him. He led the way through a small door into another room, evidently used as a kitchen. There he pointed to a large range, remarkably like the up-to-date article known on the earth.

"The flower 'groweth' here," said he, and lifted a lid from the stove. Up shot the flame.

"Great Mownoth!" shouted Rolla, forgetting all about her hunger. "I have found it—the precious flower itself!"

Somat humored her childlike view-point. "We have the seed of the flower, too," said he. He secured a box of matches from a shelf, and showed her the "little sticks."

"Exactly what the angel showed me!" jubilated Rolla. "I have come to the right place!"

Back she went to her food, her face radiant, and all her lurking suspicion of the twelve completely gone. From that time on she had absolute and unquestioning confidence in all that was told her. In her eyes, the twelve were simply angels or gods who had seen fit to clothe themselves queerly and act human.

Supper over, she felt immensely tired. All the strain of the past three weeks had to have its reaction. Like a very tired, sleepy child, she was led to a room in another part of the building, where she was shown an ordinary sleeping-cot. She promptly pulled the mattress onto the floor, where she considered it belonged, and fell fast asleep.

Meanwhile, back on the earth, Van Emmon and Smith had lost no time in making use of the doctor's description of the twelve. Within a few minutes they had new agents; Van Emmon used Somat's eyes and ears, while Smith got in touch with the elderly bearded man at the head of the table. His name was Deltos.

"A very striking confirmation of the old legends," he was saying through a big yawn, as Smith made connection. He used a colloquial type of language, quite different from the lofty, dignified speech of the Sanusians. "That is, of course, if the woman is telling the truth."

"And I think she is," declared the young fellow at the foot of the table. "It makes me feel pretty small, to think that none of us ever had the nerve to make the trip; while she, ignorant as she is, dared it all and succeeded!"

"You forget, Sorplee," reminded Somat, "that such people are far hardier than we. The feat is one that requires apelike ability. The only thing that puzzled me is—why did she do it at all?"

"It will have to remain a puzzle until she awakens," said Deltos, rising from the table. "Lucky for us, Somat, that you saw fit to study the root tongues. Otherwise we'd have to converse by signs."

Neither Smith nor Van Emmon learned anything further that night. The twelve were all very tired, apparently, and went right to bed; a procedure which was straightway seconded by the four watchers on the earth. Which brings us in the most ordinary manner to the events of the next day.

After breakfast all but Somat left the place and disappeared in various directions; and Rolla noted that the robes were, evidently, worn only at meal time. Most of the men were now dressed in rough working garments, similar to what one sees in modern factories. Whimsical sort of gods, Rolla told herself, but gods just the same.

"Tell me," began Somat, as the woman sat on the floor before him—he could not get her to use a chair—"tell me, what caused thee to leave thy side of the world? Did ye arouse the wrath of thy fellow creatures?"

"Nay," answered Rolla, and proceeded to explain, in the wrong order, as a child might, by relating first the crossing of the ridge, the flight from the bees, the "masters'" cruel method of dealing with Corrus and Dulnop, and finally the matter of the fire itself, the real cause of the whole affair. Somat was intelligent enough to fill in such details as Rolla omitted.

"Ye did right, and acted like the brave girl ye are!" he exclaimed, when Rolla had finished. However, he did not fully appreciate what she had meant by "the winged masters," and not until she pointed out some bees and asked if, on this part of the planet, such were the rulers of the humans, that the man grasped the bitter irony of it all.

"What! Those tiny insects rule thy lives!" It took him some time to comprehend the deadly nature of their stings, and the irresistible power of concerted effort; but in the end he commented: "'Tis not so strange, now that I think on it. Mayhap life is only a matter of chance, anyway."

Presently he felt that he understood the Sanusian situation. He fell silent; and Rolla, after waiting as long as her patience would allow, finally put the question temporarily uppermost in her mind:

"It is true that I have crossed the edge of the world. And yet, I understand it not at all. Can ye explain the nature of this strange world we live upon, Somat?" There was infinite respect in the way Rolla used his name; had she known a word to indicate human infallibility, such as "your majesty," she would have used it. "There is a saying among our people that the world be round. How can this be so?"

"Yet it is true," answered Somat, "although ye must know that it be not round like a fruit or a pebble. No more is it flat, like this," indicating the lid of the stove, near which they sat. "Instead, 'tis shaped thus"—and he took from his finger a plain gold band, like an ordinary wedding ring—"the world is shaped like that!"

Rolla examined the ring with vast curiosity. She had never seen the like before, and was quite as much interested in the metal as in the thing it illustrated. Fortunately the band was so worn that both edges were nearly sharp, thus corresponding with the knifelike ridge over which she had crawled.

"Now," Somat went on, "ye and your people live on the inner face of the world," indicating the surface next his skin, "while I and my kind live on the outer face. Were it not for the difficulties of making the trip, we should have found you out ere this."

Rolla sat for a long time with the ring in her hand, pondering the great fact she had just learned. And meanwhile, back on the earth, four excited citizens were discussing this latest discovery.

"An annular world!" exclaimed the doctor, his eyes sparkling delightedly. "It confirms the nebular hypothesis!"

"How so?" Smith wanted to know.

"Because it proves that the process of condensation and concentration, which produces planets out of the original gases can take place at uneven speeds! Instead of concentrating to the globular form, Sanus cooled too quickly; she concentrated while she was still a ring!"

Smith was struck with another phase of the matter. "Must have a queer sort of gravitation," he pointed out. "Seems to be the same, inside the ring or outside. Surely, doc, it can't be as powerful as it is here on the earth?"

"No; not likely."

"Then, why hasn't it made a difference in the inhabitants? Seems to me the humans would have different structure."

"Not necessarily. Look at it the other way around; consider what an enormous variety of animal forms we have here, all developed under the same conditions. The humming-bird and the python, for instance. Gravitation needn't have anything to do with it."

Billie was thinking mainly of the question of day and night. "The ring must be inclined at an angle with the sun's rays," she observed. "That being the case, Sanus has two periods each year when there is continuous darkness on the inner face; might last a week or two. Do you suppose the people all hibernate during those seasons?" But no one had an answer to that.

Van Emmon said he would give all he was worth to explore the Sanusian mountains long enough to learn their geology. He said that the rocks ought to produce some new mineral forms, due to the peculiar condition of strain they would be subjected to.

"I'm not sure," said he thoughtfully, "but I shouldn't be surprised if there's an enormous amount of carbon there. Maybe diamonds are as plentiful as coal is here."

At the word "diamonds" Smith glanced covertly at Billie's left hand. But she had hidden it in the folds of her skirt. Next moment the doctor warned them to be quiet; Somat and Rolla were talking again.

He was telling her about his world. She learned that his people, who had never concerned themselves with her side of the planet, had progressed enormously beyond the Sanusians. Rolla did not understand all that he told her; but the people on the earth gathered, in one way or another, that civilization had proceeded about as far as that of the year 1915 in Europe. All this, while fellow humans only a few thousand miles away, not only failed to make any progress at all, but lived on, century after century, the absolute slave of a race of bees!

But it was a fact. The ancient city in which Rolla found herself had been, only a generation before, a flourishing metropolis, the capital of a powerful nation. There had been two such nations on that side of the planet, and the most violent rivalry had existed between them.

"However," Somat told Rolla, "'twas not this rivalry which wrought their downfall, except indirectly. The last great war between them was terrible, but not disastrous. Either could have survived that.

"But know you that the ruler of one of the nations, in order to carry on this war—which was a war of commerce (never mind what that means)—in order to carry it on was obliged to make great concessions to his people. In the other nation, the ruler oppressed the workers, instead, and drove them mad with his cruelty. So that, not long after the end of the war, there was a great rebellion among the people who had been so long oppressed, and their government was overthrown."

Back on the earth the four investigators reflected on this in amazement. The case was wonderfully like that of Russia after the great war. Perhaps—

"Immediately the other nation forced its soldiers to fight the victorious rebels. But at home the workers had tasted of power. Many refused to work at all; and one day, behold, there were two rebellions instead of one! And within a very short time the whole world was governed by—the working class!"

So this was what the Venusians had meant when they wrote that Sanus was ruled by the workers!

"What became of these rebellions?" Rolla asked, little understanding what it meant, but curious anyhow.

"Devastation!" stated Somat solemnly. He waved a hand, to include all that lay within the ruined city. "Not altogether because of the workers, although they were scarcely fit for ruling but because the former rulers and others of that kind, who liked to oppose their wills upon others, saw fit to start a fresh rebellion.

Conflict followed conflict; sometimes workers were in power, and sometimes aristocrats. But the fighting ended not until"—he drew a deep breath—"until there were none left to fight!"

"Ye mean," demanded Rolla incredulously, "that your people killed themselves off in this fashion?"

"Aye," sorrowfully. "There were a few of us—they called us 'the middle class'—who urged equality. We wanted a government in which all classes were represented fairly; what we called a democracy. Once the experiment was started, but it failed.

"Saw ye the skeletons in the streets?" he went on. "'Twas a dreadful sight, those last few days. I were but a lad, yet I remember it all too well." He paused, then broke out fiercely: "I tell ye that I saw brother slay brother, father slay son, son slay mother, in those last days!

"Lucky am I that I fled, I and my parents! They took me to a mountainous country, but even there the madness spread, and one day a soldier of the army killed my father and my mother. He sought me, also, that he might slay me; but I hid from him beneath a heap of manure. Aye," he gritted savagely, "I owe my life to a pile of manure!

"These other eleven men all have like tales to tell. Only one woman survived those awful days. Young Sorplee is her son; his father was a soldier, whom she herself slew with her own hands. Even she is now dead.

"Well," he finished, after a long pause, "when the madness had spent itself, we who remained came from our hiding-places to find our world laid waste. 'Tis now thirty years since Sorplee's mother died, since we first looked upon these ruins, and we have made barely a beginning. We have little heart for the work. Of what use is it, with no women to start the race afresh?"

Rolla started despite herself. Was this the reason why she, despite her savagery, had been made so welcome?

"Ye have not told me," said she hurriedly, "why ye and the others all wear such curious garments when ye eat."

Somat was taken off his guard. He had been chuckling to himself at the woman's childlike mind. Now he had to look apologetic and not a little sheepish as he made reply:

"The robes are a mere custom. It were started a great many years ago, by the founders of a—a—" He tried to think of a simpler expression than "college fraternity." "A clan," he decided. "All of we men were members of that clan."

"And," pursued Rolla, "will ye give me the magic stone, that I may take the flowing blossoms back to my people, and release my loved one from the masters' cruelty?" The great question was put! Rolla waited in tremulous anxiety for the answer.

"Aye, stranger!" replied Somat vigorously. "More; ye shall have some of the little sticks!"

Whereupon Rolla leaped to her feet and danced in sheer delight. Somat looked on and marvelled. Then, abruptly, he got up and marched away. He had not seen a woman in thirty years; and he was a man of principle.

That night, when the twelve were again seated at the table, Somat related this conversation with Rolla. Since he used his own language, of course she did not understand what was said. "And I told her," he concluded, "how we came to be here; also the reason for the condition of things. But I doubt if she understood half what I said. We have quite a problem before us," he added. "What shall we do about it?"

"You mean this woman?" Deltos asked. Rolla was busy with her food. "It seems to me, brothers, that Providence has miraculously come to our aid. If we can handle her people rightly the future of the race is assured."

Somat thought it was simple enough. "All we need to do is send this woman back with a supply of matches, and implicit instructions as to how best to proceed against the bees. Once released, their friends can make their way over the edge and settle among us. Let the bees keep their country."

The two who had seconded him before again showed agreement. Sorplee and Deltos, however, together with the other seven, were distinctly opposed to the method. "Somat," protested Deltos, as though surprised, "you forget that there's an enormous population over there. Let them come in of their own free will? Why, they would overrun our country! What would become of us?"

"We'd have to take our chances," replied Somat energetically, "like good sports! If we can't demonstrate our worth to them, enough to hold their respect, we'd deserve to be snowed under!"

"Not while I'm alive!" snarled Sorplee. "If they come here, they've got to give up their wilderness ways, right off! We can't stand savagery! The safest thing for us, and the best for them, is to make an industrial army of 'em and set 'em to work!" His enthusiasm was boundless.

"I must say," admitted Deltos, with his usual dignity, "that you have the right idea, Sorplee. If I had stated it, however, I should have been more frank about it. The arrangements you propose simply means that we are to take possession of them!"

"What!" shouted Somat, horrified.

"Why, of course! Make slaves of them! What else?"

XIV
THE SLAVE RAID

Despite all that Somat and his two backers could say, the other nine men swiftly agreed upon the thing Deltos had proposed. Somat went so far as to declare that he would warn Rolla; but he was instantly given to understand that any such move would be disastrous to himself. In the end he was made to agree not to tell her.

"We aren't going to let you and your idealism spoil our only chance to save the race!" Sorplee told him pugnaciously; and Somat gave his word. At first he hoped that the nine might fall out among themselves when it came to actually enslaving the Sanusians; but he soon concluded that, if there was any difference of opinion, the aristocratic element would take charge of half the captives, while Sorplee's friends commandeered the rest. The outlook was pretty black for Rolla's friends; yet there was nothing whatever to do about it.

Among the four people on the earth, however, the thing was being discussed even more hotly. Van Emmon found himself enthusiastically backing Somat, the liberal-minded one.

"He's got the right idea," declared the geologist. "Let the Sanusians come over of their own free will! Let the law of competition show what it can do! Dandy experiment!"

Smith could not help but put in: "Perhaps it's Deltas and Sorplee who are right, Van. These Sanusians are mere aborigines. They wouldn't understand democratic methods."

"No?" politely, from the doctor. "Now, from what I've seen of Rolla, I'll say she's a perfect example of 'live-and-let-live.' Nothing either subservient or autocratic in her relations with other people. Genuinely democratic, Smith."

"Meanwhile," remarked Billie, with exaggerated nonchalance, "meanwhile, what about the bees? Are they going to be permitted to show their superiority or not?" Van Emmon took this to be aimed at him. "Of course not! We can't allow a race of human beings to be dominated forever by insects!

"I say, let's get together and put Rolla wise to what Deltos and Sorplee are framing up! We can do it, if we concentrate upon the same thought at the right time!"

Smith did not commit himself. "I don't care much either way," he decided. "Go ahead if you want to"—meaning Van Emmon and the doctor—"I don't want to butt in."

"Don't need you," growled the geologist. "Two of us is enough."

"Is that so?" sarcastically, from Billie. "Well, it'll take more than two of you to get it over to Rolla!"

"What do you mean?" hotly.

"I mean," with deliberation,—"that if you and the doctor try to interfere I'll break up our circle here!" They stared at her incredulously. "I sure will! I'm not going to lend my mental influence for any such purpose!"

"My dear," protested the doctor gently, "you know how it is: the combined efforts of the four of us is required in order to keep in touch with Sanus. Surely you would not—"

"Oh, yes, I would!" Billie was earnestness itself. "Mr. Van Emmon was so good as to blame me for what I did in that Capellette mix-up; now, if you please, I'm going to see to it that this one, anyhow, works itself out without our interference!"

"Well, I'll be darned!" The geologist looked again, to make sure it was really his wife who had been talking thus. "I'm mighty glad to know that you're not intending to warn Supreme, anyhow!"

"Maybe I shall! snapped Billie.

"If you do," stated the doctor quietly, "then I'll break the circle myself." They looked at him with a renewal of their former respect as he concluded emphatically: "If you won't help us stop this slave raid, Billie, then, by George, you'll at least let the bees fight it out on their own!"

And so the matter stood, so far as the investigators were concerned. They were to be lookers-on, nothing more.

Meanwhile the survivors of a once great civilization prepared to move in person against the bees. They did this after Deltos had pointed out the advantages of such a step.

"If we rout the bees ourselves," said he, "the natives will regard us as their saviours, and we shall have no trouble with them afterward."

This was sound policy; even Somat had to admit it. He had decided to be a member of the expedition, for the reason that Rolla flatly refused to accompany the other men unless he, her special god, went along. His two liberal-minded friends stayed behind to take care of their belongings in the ruined city.

The expedition was a simple one. It consisted of a single large auto truck and trailer, the only items of automotive machinery that the twelve had been able to reconstruct from the ruins. However, these served the purpose; they carried large supplies of food, also means for protection against the bees, together with abundant material for routing them. A large quantity of crude explosives also was included. The trailer was large enough to seat everybody; and the ten men of the party had a good deal of amusement watching Rolla as she tried to get accustomed to that land of travel. She was glad enough when the end of the road was reached and the truck began to push its way into the wilderness, giving her an excuse to walk.

No need to describe the trip in detail. Within three days the truck was as far as it could go up the rock wall of the "edge." The point selected was about twenty miles west of where Cunora was hid, and directly opposite the upper end of her home valley. No attempt was made to go over the top as Rolla had done; instead, about two miles below the ridge a crevasse was located in the granite; and by means of some two tons of powder a narrow opening was made through to the other side. Through it the men carried their supplies on their backs, transferring everything to improvised sleds, a hundred pounds to a man.

While this was being done, Rolla hurried east and located Cunora. The girl was in a pitiful condition from lack of proper food, and comparative confinement and constant strain. But during Rolla's absence she had seen none of the bees.

"What are you going to do now?" she asked Rolla, after the explorer had told her story.

Rolla shrugged her shoulders indifferently. "These gods," she declared with sublime confidence, "can do no wrong! Whatever they propose must be for the best! I have done my part; now it is all in the hands of the Flowing Blossom!"

Not until they reached the head of the valley which had been her home did Rolla ask Somat as to the plan. He answered:

"Ye and the other woman shall stay here with me, on this hill." He produced a telescope. "We will watch with this eye-tube. The other nine men will go ahead and do the work."

"And will they separate?"

"Nay. They intend to conquer this colony first; then, after your people are freed and safely on the way to my country, the conquerors will proceed to the next valley, and so on until all are released." He kept his word not to warn Rolla of the proposed captivity. "In that way the fear of them will go ahead and make their way easy."

Meanwhile the nine were getting ready for their unprecedented conquest. They put on heavy leather clothes, also leather caps, gloves and boots. Around their faces were stiff wire nets, such as annoyed them all exceedingly and would have maddened Cunora or Rolla. But it meant safety.

As for weapons, they relied entirely upon fire. Each man carried a little wood alcohol in a flask, in case it was necessary to burn wet or green wood. Otherwise, their equipment was matches, with an emergency set of flint and steel as well. There could be no resisting them.

"We'll wait here till we've seen that you've succeeded," Somat told Deltos and Sorplee. "Then we'll follow."

The nine left the hills. The hours passed with Rolla and Cunora amusing themselves at the "eye-tube." They could see the very spot where their lovers were being punished; but some intervening bushes prevented seeing the men themselves. The other villagers were at work quite as usual; so it was plain that, although the bees were invisible, yet they were still the masters.

Hardly had the nine reached the first low-growing brush before they encountered some of the bees. None attempted to attack, but turned about and flew back to report. It was not long before Supreme, and therefore Billie, knew of the approaching raiders.

"They are doubtless provided with the magic flower," Supreme told her lieutenants. "You will watch the blossom as it sways in the wind, and keep always on the windward side of it. In this way you can attack the inferiors."

The word was passed, bee-fashion, until every soldier and worker in the colony knew her duty. The stingers were to keep back and watch their chance, while the workers harrassed the attackers. Moreover, with the hives always uppermost in her mind, Supreme planned to keep the actual conflict always at a distance from the "city."

It was late in the day when the nine reached the stream in whose bed rested the pyrites taken from Corrus and Dulnop. This stream, it will be remembered, flowed not far from the torture-place. Deltos's plan was to rescue these two men before doing anything else; this, because it would strengthen the villagers' regard for the conquerors.

The bees seemed to sense this. They met the invaders about three miles above the village, in an open spot easily seen by the people with the telescope. And the encounter took place during twilight, just early enough to be visible from a distance, yet late enough to make the fire very impressive.

"Remember, it's the smoke as much as the flame," Deltos shouted to the others. "Just keep your torches on the move, and make as much fuss as you can!"

Next moment the swarm was upon them. It was like a vast cloud of soot; only, the buzzing of those millions of wings fairly drowned out every other sound. The nine had to signal to one another; shouting was useless.

Within a single minute the ground was covered with bees, either dead or insensible from the smoke. Yet the others never faltered. At times the insects battered against the wire netting with such force, and in such numbers, that the men had to fight them away in order to get enough air.

Supreme watched from above, and kept sending her lieutenants with fresh divisions to first one man and then another, as he became separated from the rest. Of course, nobody suffered but the bees. Never before had they swarmed a creature which did not succumb; but these inferiors with the queer things over their faces, and the cows' hides over their bodies and hands, seemed to care not at all. Supreme was puzzled.

"Keep it up," she ordered. "They surely cannot stand it much longer."

"It shall be done!"

And the bees were driven in upon the men, again and again. Always the torches were kept waving, so that the insects never could tell just where to attack. Always the men kept moving steadily down-stream; and as they marched they left in their wake a black path of dead and dying bees. Half of them had been soldier bees, carrying enough poison in their stings to destroy a nation. Yet, nine little matches were too much for them!

Presently the invaders had approached to within a half-mile of the torture-place. One of Supreme's lieutenants made a suggestion:

"Had we not better destroy the men, rather than let them be rescued?"

The commandant considered this fully. "No," she decided. "To kill them would merely enrage the other villagers, and perhaps anger them so much as to make them unmanageable." More than once a human had been driven so frantic as to utterly disregard orders. "We cannot slay them all."

The bees attacked with unabated fury. Not once did the insects falter; orders were orders, and always had been. What mattered it if death came to them, so long as the Hive lived? For that is bee philosophy.

And then, just when it seemed that the wisest thing would be to withdraw,

Supreme got the greatest idea she had ever had. For once she felt positively enthusiastic. Had she been a human she would have yelled aloud for sheer joy.

"Attention!" to her subordinates. "We attack no more! Instead, go into the huts and drive all the inferiors here! Compel them to bring their tools! Kill all that refuse!"

The lieutenants only dimly grasped the idea. "What shall we do when we get them here?"

"Do? Drive them against the invaders, of course!"

It was a daring thought. None but a super bee could have conceived it. Off flew the lieutenants, with Supreme's inspired order humming after them:

"Call out every bee! And drive every last one of the inferiors to this spot!"

And thus it came about that, a minute later, the nine looked around to see the bees making off at top speed. Sorplee raised a cheer.

"Hurrah!" he shouted, and the rest took it up. Neither admitted that he was vastly relieved; it had been a little nerve-shaking to know that a single thickness of leather had been all that stood, for an hour, between him and certain death. The buzzing, too, was demoralizing.

"Now, to release the two men!" reminded Deltos, and led the way to the torture-place. They found Corrus and Dulnop exactly as the two women had left them six weeks before, except that their faces were drawn with the agony of what they had endured. Below the surface of the ground their bodies had shriveled and whitened with their daily imprisonment. Only their spirits remained unchanged; they, of all the natives, had known what it was to feel superior.

For the last time they were dug out and helped to their feet. They could not stand by themselves, much less run; but it is not likely they would have fled. Somehow they knew that the strange head-coverings had human faces behind them. And scarcely had they been freed before Sorplee, glancing about, gave an exclamation of delight as he saw a group of natives running toward them.

"Just what we want!" he exclaimed. "They've seen the scrap, and realize that we've won!"

Looking around, the nine could see the other groups likewise hurrying their way. All told, there were a couple of hundred of the villagers, and all were armed with tools they knew how to use very well.

"Who shall do the honours?" asked Sorplee. "Wish Somat was here, to explain for us."

"Don't need him," reminded Deltos. "All we've got to do is to show these two fellows we dug up."

And it was not until the first of the villagers was within twenty yards that the nine suspected anything. Then they heard the buzzing. Looking closer, they saw that it was—an attack!

"Stop!" cried Deltos, in swift panic. "We are friends, not enemies!"

It was like talking to the wind. The villagers had their choice of two fears: either fight the strangers with the magic flower, or—be stung to death. And no one can blame them for what they chose.

The nine had time enough to snatch knives or hatchets from their belts, or clubs from the ground. Then, with wild cries of fear, the natives closed in. They fought as only desperate people can fight, caught between two fires. And they were two hundred to nine!

In half a minute the first of the invaders was down, his head crushed by a mattock in the hands of a bee-tormented native. In a single minute all were gone but two; and a moment later, Deltos alone, because he had chanced to secure a long club, was alive of all that crew.

For a minute he kept them off by sheer strength. He swung the stick with such vigour that he fairly cleared a circle for himself. The natives paused, howling and shrieking, before the final rush.

An inspiration came to Deltos. He tore his cap from his head and his net from his face.

"Look!" he screamed, above the uproar. "I am a man, like yourselves! Do not kill!"

Next second he froze in his tracks. The next he was writhing in the death agony, and the bees were supreme once more.

Supreme herself had stung Deltos.

XV
OVERLOOKED

Of the four on the earth, Smith was the first to make any comment. He had considerable difficulty in throwing his thought to the others; somehow he felt slightly dazed.

"This is—unbelievable!" he said, and repeated it twice. "To think that those insects are still the masters!"

"I wish"—Billie's voice shook somewhat—"I wish almost that I had let you warn Rolla. It might have helped—" She broke off suddenly, intent upon something Supreme was hearing. "Just listen!"

"Quick!" a lieutenant was humming excitedly to the commandant. "Back to the hives; give the order, Supreme!"

It was done, and immediately the bees quit the throng of natives and their victims, rushing at top speed for their precious city. As they went, Supreme demanded an explanation.

"What is the meaning of this?"

For answer the lieutenant pointed her antennae straight ahead. At first Supreme could see nothing in the growing darkness; then she saw that some of the sky was blacker than the rest. Next she caught a faint glow.

"Supreme, the deadly flower has come to the hives!"

It was true! In ten minutes the city was near enough for the commandant to see it all very clearly. The fire had started on the windward side, and already had swept through half the hives!

"Quick!" the order was snapped out. "Into the remaining houses, and save the young!"

She herself led the horde. Straight into the face of the flames they flew, unquestioningly, unhesitantly. What was self, compared with the Hive?

Next moment, like a mammoth billow, the smoke rolled down upon them all. And thus it came about that the villagers, making their cautious way toward the bee city, shouted for joy and danced as they had never danced before, when they saw what had happened.

Not a bee was left alive. Every egg and larva was destroyed; every queen was burned. And every last soldier and worker had lost her life in the vain attempt at rescue. Suddenly one of the villagers, who had been helping to carry Corrus and Dulnop to the spot, pointed out something on the other side of the fire! It was Rolla!

"Hail!" she shouted, hysterical with happiness as she ran toward her people. Cunora was close upon her heels. "Hail to the flowing flower!"

She held up a torch. Down fell the villagers to their knees. Rolla strode forward and found Corrus, even as Cunora located her Dulnop.

"Hail to the flowing flower!" shouted Rolla again. "And hail to the free people of this world! A new day cometh for us all! The masters—are no more!"

The four on the earth looked at each other inquiringly. There was a heavy silence. The doctor stood it as long as he could, and then said:

"So far as I'm concerned, this ends our investigations." They stared at him uncomprehendingly; he went on: "I don't see anything to be gained by this type of study. Here we've investigated the conditions on two planets pretty thoroughly, and yet we can't agree upon what we've learned!

"Van still thinks that the upper classes should rule, despite all the misery we saw on Capellette! And Billie is still convinced that the working classes, and no others, should govern! This, in the face of what we've just—seen! Sanus is absolute proof of what must happen when one class tries to rule; conflict, bloodshed, misery—little else! Besides"—remembering something, and glancing at his watch—"besides, it's time for dinner."

Billie and Smith got to their feet, and in silence quit the room. Billie and Van Emmon were still fumbling with their bracelets. The two young people rose from the chairs at the same time and started across the room to put their bracelets away. The wire which connected them trailed in between and caught on the doctor's chair. It brought the two of them up short.

Van Emmon stared at the wire. He gave it a little tug. The chair did not move. Billie gave an answering jerk, with similar lack of results. Then they glanced swiftly at one another, and each stepped back enough to permit lifting the wire over the chair.

"In other words," Van Emmon stammered, with an effort to keep his voice steady—"in other words, Billie, we both had to give in a little, in order to get past that chair!"

Then he paused slightly, his heart pounding furiously.

"Yes Van." She dropped the bracelets. "And—as for me—Van, I didn't really want to see the bees win! I only pretended to—I wanted to make you—think!"

"Billie! I'll say 'cooperate' if you will!"

"Cooperate!"

He swept her into his arms, and held her so close that she could not see what had rushed to his eyes. "Speaking of cooperation," he remarked unsteadily, "reminds me—it takes two to make a kiss!"

They proceeded to experiment.

THE THAMES VALLEY CATASTROPHE

by Grant Allen

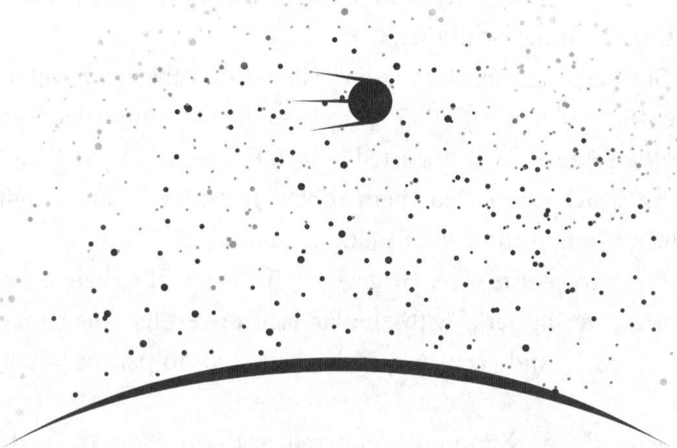

It can scarcely be necessary for me to mention, I suppose, at this time of day, that I was one of the earliest and fullest observers of the sad series of events which finally brought about the transference of the seat of Government of these islands from London to Manchester. Nor need I allude here to the conspicuous position which my narrative naturally occupies in the Blue-book on the Thames Valley Catastrophe (vol. ii., part vii), ordered by Parliament in its preliminary Session under the new regime at Birmingham. But I think it also incumbent upon me, for the benefit of posterity, to supplement that necessarily dry and formal statement by a more circumstantial account of my personal adventures during the terrible period.

I am aware, of course, that my poor little story can possess little interest for our contemporaries, wearied out as they are with details of the disaster, and surfeited with tedious scientific discussions as to its origin and nature. But in after years, I venture to believe, when the crowning calamity of the nineteenth century has grown picturesque and, so to speak, ivy-clad, by reason of its remoteness (like the Great Plague or the Great Fire of London with ourselves), the world may possibly desire to hear how this unparalleled convulsion affected the feelings and fortunes of a single family in the middle rank of life, and in a part of London neither squalid nor fashionable.

It is such personal touches of human nature that give reality to history, which without them must become, as a great writer has finely said, nothing more than an old almanac. I shall not apologize, therefore, for being frankly egoistic and domestic in my reminiscences of that appalling day: for I know that those who desire to seek scientific information on the subject will look for it, not in vain, in the eight bulky volumes of the recent Blue-book. I shall concern myself here with the great event merely as it appeared to myself, a Government servant of the second grade, and in its relations to my own wife, my home, and my children.

On the morning of the 21st of August, in the memorable year of the calamity, I happened to be at Cookham, a pleasant and pretty village which then occupied the western bank of the Thames just below the spot where the Look-out Tower of the Earthquake and Eruption Department now dominates the whole wide plain of the Glassy Rock Desert. In place of the black lake of basalt which young people see nowadays winding its solid bays in and out among the grassy downs, most men still living can well remember a gracious and smiling valley, threaded in the midst by a beautiful river.

I had cycled down from London the evening before (thus forestalling my holiday), and had spent the night at a tolerable inn in the village. By a curious coincidence, the only other visitor at the little hotel that night was a fellow-cyclist, an American, George W. Ward by name, who had come over with his "wheel," as he called it, for six weeks in England, in order to investigate the geology of our southern counties for himself, and to compare it with that of the far western cretaceous system. I venture to describe this as a curious coincidence, because, as it happened, the mere accident of my meeting him gave me my first inkling of the very existence of that singular phenomenon of which we were all so soon to receive a startling example. I had never so much as heard before of fissure-eruptions; and if I had not heard of them from Ward that evening, I might not have recognized at sight the actuality when it first appeared, and therefore I might have been involved in the general disaster. In which case, of course, this unpretentious narrative would never have been written.

As we sat in the little parlour of the White Hart, however, over our evening pipe, it chanced that the American, who was a pleasant, conversable fellow, began talking to me of his reasons for visiting England. I was at that time a clerk in the General Post Office (of which I am now secretary), and was then no student of science; but his enthusiastic talk about his own country and its vastness amused and interested me. He had been employed for some years on the Geological Survey in the Western States, and he was deeply impressed by the solemnity and the colossal scale of everything American. "Mountains!" he said, when I spoke of Scotland; "why, for mountains, your Alps aren't in it! and as for volcanoes, your Vesuviuses and Etnas just spit fire a bit at infrequent intervals; while ours do things on a scale worthy of a great country, I can tell you. Europe is a circumstance: America is a continent."

"But surely," I objected, "that was a pretty fair eruption that destroyed Pompeii!"

The American rose and surveyed me slowly. I can see him to this day, with his close-shaven face and his contemptuous smile at my European ignorance. "Well," he said, after a long and impressive pause, "the lava-flood that destroyed a few acres about the Bay of Naples was what we call a trickle: it came from a crater; and the crater it came from was nothing more than a small round vent-hole; the lava flowed down from it in a moderate stream over a limited area. But what do you say to the earth opening in a huge crack, forty or fifty miles long—say, as far as from here right away to London, or farther—and lava pouring out from the orifice, not in a little rivulet as at Etna or Vesuvius, but in a sea or inundation, which spread at once over a tract as big as England? That's something like volcanic action, isn't it? And that's the sort of thing we have out in Colourado."

"You are joking," I replied, "or bragging. You are trying to astonish me with the familiar spread eagle."

He smiled a quiet smile. "Not a bit of it," he answered. "What I tell you is at least as true as Gospel. The earth yawns in Montana. There are fissure-eruptions, as we call them, in the Western States, out of which the lava has welled like wine out of a broken skin—welled up in vast roaring floods, molten torrents of basalt, many miles across, and spread like water over whole plains and valleys."

"Not within historical times!" I exclaimed.

"I'm not so sure about that," he answered, musing. "I grant you, not within times which are historical right there—for Colourado is a very new country: but I incline to think some of the most recent fissure eruptions took place not later than when the Tudors reigned in England. The lava oozed out, red-hot—gushed out—was squeezed out—and spread instantly everywhere; it's so comparatively recent that the surface of the rock is still bare in many parts, unweathered sufficiently to support vegetation. I fancy the stream must have been ejected at a single burst, in a huge white-hot dome, and then flowed down on every side, filling up the valleys to a certain level, in and out among the hills, exactly as water might do. And some of these eruptions, I tell you, by measured survey, would have covered more ground than from Dover to Liverpool, and from York to Cornwall."

"Let us be thankful," I said, carelessly, "that such things don't happen in our own times."

He eyed me curiously. "Haven't happened, you mean," he answered. "We have no security that they mayn't happen again tomorrow. These fissure-eruptions, though not historically described for us, are common events in geological history—commoner and on a larger scale in America than elsewhere. Still, they have occurred in all lands and at various epochs; there is no reason at all why one shouldn't occur in England at present."

I laughed, and shook my head. I had the Englishman's firm conviction—so rudely shattered by the subsequent events, but then so universal—that nothing very unusual ever happened in England.

Next morning I rose early, bathed in Odney Weir (a picturesque pool close by), breakfasted with the American, and then wrote a hasty line to my wife, informing her that I should probably sleep that night at Oxford; for I was off on a few days' holiday, and I liked Ethel to know where a letter or telegram would reach me each day, as we were both a little anxious about the baby's teething. Even while I pen these words now, the grim humour of the situation comes back to me vividly. Thousands of fathers and mothers were anxious that morning about similar trifles, whose pettiness was brought home to them with an appalling shock in the all-embracing horror of that day's calamity.

About ten o'clock I inflated my tyres and got under way. I meant to ride towards Oxford by a leisurely and circuitous route, along the windings of the river, past Marlow and Henley; so I began by crossing Cookham Bridge, a wooden or iron structure, I scarcely remember which. It spanned the Thames close by the village: the curious will find its exact position marked in the maps of the period.

In the middle of the bridge, I paused and surveyed that charming prospect, which I was the last of living men perhaps to see as it then existed. Close by stood a weir; beside it, the stream divided into three separate branches, exquisitely backed up by the gentle green slopes of Hedsor and Cliveden. I could never pass that typical English view without a glance of admiration; this morning, I pulled up my bicycle for a moment, and cast my eye down stream with more than my usual enjoyment of the smooth blue water and the tall white poplars whose leaves showed their gleaming silver in the breeze beside it. I might have gazed at it too long—and one minute more would have sufficed for my destruction—had not a cry from the tow-path a little farther up attracted my attention.

It was a wild, despairing cry, like that of a man being overpowered and murdered.

I am confident this was my first intimation of danger. Two minutes before, it is true, I had heard a faint sound like distant rumbling of thunder; but nothing else. I am one of those who strenuously maintain that the catastrophe was not heralded by shocks of earthquake.

I turned my eye up stream. For half a second I was utterly bewildered. Strange to say, I did not perceive at first the great flood of fire that was advancing towards me. I saw only the man who had shouted—a miserable, cowering, terror-stricken wretch, one of the abject creatures who used to earn a dubious livelihood in those days (when the river was a boulevard of pleasure) by towing boats up stream. But now, he was rushing wildly forward, with panic in his face; I could see he looked as if close pursued by some wild beast behind him. "A mad dog!" I said to myself at the outset; "or else a bull in the meadow!"

I glanced back to see what his pursuer might be; and then, in one second, the whole horror and terror of the catastrophe burst upon me. Its whole horror and terror, I say, but not yet its magnitude. I was aware at first just of a moving red wall, like dull, red-hot molten metal. Trying to recall at so safe a distance in time and space the feelings of the moment and the way in which they surged and succeeded one another, I think I can recollect that my earliest idea was no more than this: "He must run, or the moving wall will overtake him!" Next instant, a hot wave seemed to strike my face. It was just like the blast of heat that strikes one in a glasshouse when you stand in front of the boiling and seething glass in the furnace. At about the same point in time, I was aware, I believe, that the dull red wall was really a wall of fire. But it was cooled by contact with the air and the water. Even as I looked, however, a second wave from behind seemed to rush on and break: it overlaid and outran the first one. This second wave was white, not red—at white heat, I realized. Then, with a burst of recognition, I knew what it all meant. What Ward had spoken of last night—a fissure eruption!

I looked back. Ward was coming towards me on the bridge, mounted on his Columbia. Too speechless to utter one word, I pointed up stream with my hand He nodded and shouted back, in a singularly calm voice: "Yes; just what I told you. A fissure-eruption!"

They were the last words I heard him speak. Not that he appreciated the danger less than I did, though his manner was cool; but he was wearing no clips to his trousers, and at that critical moment he caught his leg in his pedals. The accident disconcerted him; he dismounted hurriedly, and then, panic-stricken as I judged, abandoned his machine. He tried to run. The error was fatal. He tripped and fell. What became of him afterward I will mention later.

But for the moment I saw only the poor wretch on the tow-path. He was not a hundred yards off, just beyond the little bridge which led over the opening to a private boat-house. But as he rushed forwards and shrieked, the wall of fire overtook him. I do not think it quite caught him. It is hard at such moments to judge what really happens; but I believe I saw him shrivel like a moth in a flame a few seconds before the advancing wall of fire swept over the boat-house. I have seen an insect shrivel just so when flung into the midst of white-hot coals. He seemed to go off in gas, leaving a shower of powdery ash to represent his bones behind him. But of this I do not pretend to be positive; I will allow that my own agitation was far too profound to permit of my observing anything with accuracy.

How high was the wall at that time? This has been much debated. I should guess, thirty feet (though it rose afterwards to more than two hundred), and it advanced rather faster than a man could run down the centre of the valley. (Later on, its pace accelerated greatly with subsequent outbursts.) In frantic haste, I saw or felt that only one chance of safety lay before me: I must strike up hill by the field path to Hedsor.

I rode for very life, with grim death behind me. Once well across the bridge, and turning up the hill, I saw Ward on the parapet, with his arms flung up, trying wildly to save himself by leaping into the river. Next instant he shrivelled I think, as the beggar had shrivelled; and it is to this complete combustion before the lava flood reached them that I attribute the circumstance (so much commented upon in the scientific excavations among the ruins) that no cast of dead bodies, like those at Pompeii, have anywhere been found in the Thames Valley Desert.

My own belief is that every human body was reduced to a gaseous condition by the terrific heat several seconds before the molten basalt reached it.

Even at the distance which I had now attained from the central mass, indeed, the heat was intolerable. Yet, strange to say, I saw few or no people flying as yet from the inundation. The fact is, the eruption came upon us so suddenly, so utterly without warning or premonitory symptoms (for I deny the earthquake shocks), that whole towns must have been destroyed before the inhabitants were aware that anything out of the common was happening. It is a sort of alleviation to the general horror to remember that a large proportion of the victims must have died without even knowing it; one second, they were laughing, talking, bargaining; the next, they were asphyxiated or reduced to ashes as you have seen a small fly disappear in an incandescent gas flame.

This, however, is what I learned afterward. At that moment, I was only aware of a frantic pace uphill, over a rough, stony road, and with my pedals working as I had never before worked them; while behind me, I saw purgatory let loose, striving hard to overtake me. I just knew that a sea of fire was filling the valley from end to end, and that its heat scorched my face as I urged on my bicycle in abject terror.

All this time, I will admit, my panic was purely personal. I was too much engaged in the engrossing sense of my own pressing danger to be vividly alive to the public catastrophe. I did not even think of Ethel and the children. But when I reached the hill by Hedsor Church—a neat, small building, whose shell still stands, though scorched and charred, by the edge of the desert—I was able to pause for half a minute to recover breath, and to look back upon the scene of the first disaster.

It was a terrible and yet I felt even then a beautiful sight—beautiful with the awful and unearthly beauty of a great forest fire, or a mighty conflagration in some crowded city. The whole river valley, up which I looked, was one sea of fire. Barriers of red-hot lava formed themselves for a moment now and again where the outer edge or vanguard of the inundation had cooled a little on the surface by exposure: and over these temporary dams, fresh cataracts of white-hot material poured themselves afresh into the valley beyond it. After a while, as the deeper portion of basalt was pushed out all was white alike. So glorious it looked in the morning sunshine that one could hardly realize the appalling reality of that sea of molten gold; one might almost have imagined a splendid triumph of the scene painter's art, did one not know that it was actually a river of fire, overwhelming, consuming, and destroying every object before it in its devastating progress.

I tried vaguely to discover the source of the disaster. Looking straight up stream, past Bourne End and Marlow, I descried with bleared and dazzled eyes a whiter mass than any, glowing fiercely in the daylight like an electric light, and filling up the narrow gorge of the river towards Hurley and Henley. I recollected at once that this portion of the valley was not usually visible from Hedsor Hill, and almost without thinking of it I instinctively guessed the reason why it had become so now: it was the centre of disturbance—the earth's crust just there had bulged upward slightly, till it cracked and gaped to emit the basalt.

Looking harder, I could make out (though it was like looking at the sun) that the glowing white dome-shaped mass, as of an electric light, was the molten lava as it gurgled from the mouth of the vast fissure. I say vast, because so it seemed to me, though, as everybody now knows, the actual gap where the earth opened measures no more than eight miles across, from a point near what was once Shiplake Ferry to the site of the old lime-kilns at Marlow. Yet when one saw the eruption actually taking place, the colossal scale of it was what most appalled one. A sea of fire, eight to twelve miles broad, in the familiar Thames Valley, impressed and terrified one a thousand times more than a sea of fire ten times as vast in the nameless wilds of Western America.

I could see dimly, too, that the flood spread in every direction from its central point, both up and down the river. To right and left, indeed, it was soon checked and hemmed in by the hills about Wargrave and Medmenham; but downward, it had filled the entire valley as far as Cookham and beyond; while upward, it spread in one vast glowing sheet towards Reading and the flats by the confluence of the Kennet. I did not then know, of course, that this gigantic natural dam or barrier was later on to fill up the whole low-lying level, and so block the course of the two rivers as to form those twin expanses of inland water, Lake Newbury and Lake Oxford. Tourists who now look down on still summer evenings where the ruins of Magdalen and of Merton may be dimly descried through the pale green depths, their broken masonry picturesquely overgrown with tangled water-weeds, can form but little idea of the terrible scene which that peaceful bank presented while the incandescent lava was pouring forth in a scorching white flood towards the doomed district. Merchants who crowd the busy quays of those mushroom cities which have sprung up with greater rapidity than Chicago or Johannesburg on the indented shore where the new lakes abut upon the Berkshire

Chalk Downs have half forgotten the horror of the intermediate time when the waters of the two rivers rose slowly, slowly, day after day, to choke their valleys and overwhelm some of the most glorious architecture in Britain. But though I did not know and could not then foresee the remoter effects of the great fire-flood in that direction, I saw enough to make my heart stand still within me. It was with difficulty that I grasped my bicycle, my hands trembled so fiercely. I realized that I was a spectator of the greatest calamity which had befallen a civilized land within the ken of history.

I looked southward along the valley in the direction of Maidenhead. As yet it did not occur to me that the catastrophe was anything more than a local flood, though even as such it would have been one of unexampled vastness. My imagination could hardly conceive that London itself was threatened. In those days one could not grasp the idea of the destruction of London. I only thought just at first, "It will go on towards Maidenhead!" Even as I thought it, I saw a fresh and fiercer gush of fire well out from the central gash, and flow still faster than ever down the centre of the valley, over the hardening layer already cooling on its edge by contact with the air and soil. This new outburst fell in a mad cataract over the end or van of the last, and instantly spread like water across the level expanse between the Cliveden hills and the opposite range at Pinkneys. I realized with a throb that it was advancing towards Windsor. Then a wild fear thrilled through me. If Windsor, why not Staines and Chertsey and Hounslow? If Hounslow, why not London?

In a second I remembered Ethel and the children. Hitherto, the immediate danger of my own position alone had struck me. The fire was so near; the heat of it rose up in my face and daunted me. But now I felt I must make a wild dash to warn—not London—no, frankly, I forgot those millions; but Ethel and my little ones. In that thought, for the first moment, the real vastness of the catastrophe came home to me. The Thames Valley was doomed! I must ride for dear life if I wished to save my wife and children!

I mounted again, but found my shaking feet could hardly work the pedals. My legs were one jelly. With a frantic effort, I struck off inland in the direction of Burnham. I did not think my way out definitely; I hardly knew the topography of the district well enough to form any clear conception of what route I must take in order to keep to the hills and avoid the flood of fire that was deluging the lowlands. But by pure instinct, I believe, I set my face Londonwards along the ridge of the chalk downs. In three minutes I had lost sight of the burning flood, and was deep among green lanes and under shadowy beeches. The very contrast frightened me. I wondered if I was going mad. It was all so quiet. One could not believe that scarce five miles off from that devastating sheet of fire, birds were singing in the sky and men toiling in the fields as if nothing had happened.

Near Lambourne Wood I met a brother cyclist, just about to descend the hill. A curve in the road hid the valley from him I shouted aloud:

"For Heaven's sake, don't go down! There is danger, danger!"

He smiled and looked back at me. "I can take any hill in England," he answered.

"It's not the hill," I burst out. "There has been an eruption—a fissure-eruption at Marlow—great floods of fire—and all the valley is filled with burning lava!"

He stared at me derisively. Then his expression changed of a sudden. I suppose he saw I was white-faced and horror-stricken. He drew away as if alarmed. "Go back to Colney Hatch!" he cried, pedalling faster and rode hastily down the hill, as if afraid of me. I have no doubt he must have ridden into the very midst of the flood, and been scorched by its advance, before he could check his machine on so sudden a slope.

Between Lambourne Wood and Burnham I did not see the fire-flood. I rode on at full speed among green fields and meadows. Here and there I passed a labouring man on the road. More than one looked up at me and commented on the oppressive heat, but none of them seemed to be aware of the fate that was overtaking their own homes close by, in the valley. I told one or two, but they laughed and gazed after me as if I were a madman. I grew sick of warning them. They took no heed of my words, but went on upon their way as if nothing out of the common were happening to England.

On the edge of the down, near Burnham, I caught sight of the valley again. Here, people were just awaking to what was taking place near them. Half the population was gathered on the slope, looking down with wonder on the flood of fire, which had now just turned the corner of the hills by Taplow. Silent terror was the prevailing type of expression. But when I told them I had seen the lava bursting forth from the earth in a white dome above Marlow, they laughed me to scorn; and when I assured them I was pushing forward in hot haste to London, they answered, "London! It won't never get as far as London!" That was the only place on the hills, as is now well known, where the flood was observed long enough beforehand to telegraph and warn the inhabitants of the great city; but nobody thought of doing it; and I must say, even if they had done so, there is not the slightest probability that the warning would have attracted the least attention in our ancient Metropolis. Men on the Stock Exchange would have made jests about the slump, and proceeded to buy and sell as usual.

I measured with my eye the level plain between Burnham and Slough, calculating roughly with myself whether I should have time to descend upon the well-known road from Maidenhead to London by Colnbrook and Hounslow. (I advise those who are unacquainted with the topography of this district before the eruption to follow out my route on a good map of the period.) But I recognised in a moment that this course would be impossible. At the rate that the flood had taken to progress from Cookham Bridge to Taplow, I felt sure it would be upon me before I reached Upton, or Ditton Park at the outside. It is true the speed of the advance might slacken somewhat as the lava cooled; and strange to say, so rapidly do realities come to be accepted in one's mind, that I caught myself thinking this thought in the most natural manner, as if I had all my life long been accustomed to the ways of fissure-eruptions. But on the other hand, the lava might well out faster and hotter than before, as I had already seen it do more than once; and I had no certainty even that it would not rise to the level of the hills on which I was standing. You who read this narrative nowadays take it for granted, of course, that the extent and height of the inundation was bound to be exactly what you know it to have been; we at the time could not guess how high it might rise and how large an area of the country it might overwhelm and devastate. Was it to stop at the Chilterns, or to go north to Birmingham, York, and Scotland?

Still, in my trembling anxiety to warn my wife and children, I debated with myself whether I should venture down into the valley, and hurry along the main road with a wild burst for London. I thought of Ethel, alone in our little home at Bayswater, and almost made up my mind to risk it. At that moment, I became aware that the road to London was already crowded with carriages, carts, and cycles, all dashing at a mad pace unanimously towards London. Suddenly a fresh wave turned the corner by Taplow and Maidenhead Bridge, and began to gain upon them visibly. It was an awful sight. I cannot pretend to describe it. The poor creatures on the road, men and animals alike, rushed wildly, despairingly on; the fire took them from behind, and, one by one, before the actual sea reached them, I saw them shrivel and melt away in the fierce white heat of the advancing inundation. I could not look at it any longer. I certainly could not descend and court instant death. I felt that my one chance was to strike across the downs, by Stoke Poges and Uxbridge, and then try the line of northern heights to London.

Oh, how fiercely I pedalled! At Farnham Royal (where again nobody seemed to be aware what had happened) a rural policeman tried to stop me for frantic riding. I tripped him up, and rode on. Experience had taught me it was no use telling those who had not seen it of the disaster. A little beyond, at the entrance to a fine park, a gatekeeper attempted to shut a gate in my face, exclaiming that the road was private. I saw it was the only practicable way without descending to the valley, and I made up my mind this was no time for trifling. I am a man of peace, but I lifted my fist and planted it between his eyes. Then, before he could recover from his astonishment, I had mounted again and ridden on across the park, while he ran after me in vain, screaming to the men in the pleasure-grounds to stop me. But I would not be stopped; and I emerged on the road once more at Stoke Poges.

Near Galley Hill, after a long and furious ride, I reached the descent to Uxbridge. Was it possible to descend? I glanced across, once more by pure instinct, for I had never visited the spot before, towards where I felt the Thames must run. A great white cloud hung over it. I saw what that cloud must mean: it was the steam of the river, where the lava sucked it up and made it seethe and boil suddenly. I had not noticed this white fleece of steam at Cookham, though I did not guess why till afterwards. In the narrow valley where the Thames ran between hills, the lava flowed over it all at once, bottling the steam beneath; and it is this imprisoned steam that gave rise in time to the subsequent series of appalling earthquakes, to supply forecasts of which is now the chief duty of the Seismologer Royal; whereas, in the open plain, the basalt advanced more gradually and in a thinner stream, and therefore turned the whole mass of water into white cloud as soon as it reached each bend of the river.

At the time, however, I had no leisure to think out all this. I only knew by such indirect signs that the flood was still advancing, and, therefore, that it would be impossible for me to proceed towards London by the direct route via Uxbridge and Hanwell. If I meant to reach town (as we called it familiarly), I must descend to the valley at once, pass through Uxbridge streets as fast as I could, make a dash across the plain, by what I afterwards knew to be Hillingdon (I saw it then as a nameless village), and aim at a house-crowned hill which I only learned later was Harrow, but which I felt sure would enable me to descend upon London by Hampstead or Highgate.

I am no strategist; but in a second, in that extremity, I picked out these points, feeling dimly sure they would lead me home to Ethel and the children.

The town of Uxbridge (whose place you can still find marked on many maps) lay in the valley of a small river, a confluent of the Thames. Up this valley it was certain that the lava-stream must flow; and, indeed, at the present day, the basin around is completely filled by one of the solidest and most forbidding masses of black basalt in the country. Still, I made up my mind to descend and cut across the low-lying ground towards Harrow. If I failed, I felt, after all, I was but one unit more in what I now began to realize as a prodigious national calamity.

I was just coasting down the hill, with Uxbridge lying snug and unconscious in the glen below me, when a slight and unimportant accident occurred which almost rendered impossible my further progress. It was past the middle of August; the hedges were being cut; and this particular lane, bordered by a high thorn fence, was strewn with the mangled branches of the may-bushes. At any other time, I should have remembered the danger and avoided them; that day, hurrying down hill for dear life and for Ethel, I forgot to notice them. The consequence was, I was pulled up suddenly by finding my front wheel deflated; this untimely misfortune almost unmanned me. I dismounted and examined the tyre; it had received a bad puncture. I tried inflating again, in hopes the hole might be small enough to make that precaution sufficient. But it was quite useless. I found I must submit to stop and doctor up the puncture. Fortunately, I had the necessary apparatus in my wallet.

I think it was the weirdest episode of all that weird ride—this sense of stopping impatiently, while the fiery flood still surged on towards London, in order to go through all the fiddling and troublesome little details of mending a pneumatic tyre. The moment and the operation seemed so sadly out of harmony. A countryman passed by on a cart, obviously suspecting nothing; that was another point which added horror to the occasion—that so near the catastrophe, so very few people were even aware what was taking place beside them. Indeed, as is well known, I was one of the very few who saw the eruption during its course, and yet managed to escape from it. Elsewhere, those who tried to run before it, either to escape themselves or to warn others of the danger, were overtaken by the lava before they could reach a place of safety. I attribute this mainly to the fact that most of them continued along the high roads in the valley, or fled instinctively for shelter towards their homes, instead of making at once for the heights and the uplands.

The countryman stopped and looked at me.

"The more haste the less speed!" he said, with proverbial wisdom.

I glanced up at him, and hesitated. Should I warn him of his doom, or was it useless? "Keep up on the hills," I said, at last. "An unspeakable calamity is happening in the valley. Flames of fire are flowing down it, as from a great burning mountain. You will be cut off by the eruption."

He stared at me blankly, and burst into a meaningless laugh. "Why, you're one of them Salvation Army fellows," he exclaimed, after a short pause. "You're trying to preach to me. I'm going to Uxbridge." And he continued down the hill towards certain destruction.

It was hours, I feel sure, before I had patched up that puncture, though I did it by the watch in four and a half minutes. As soon as I had blown out my tyre again I mounted once more, and rode at a breakneck pace to Uxbridge. I passed down the straggling main street of the suburban town, crying aloud as I went, "Run, run, to the downs! A flood of lava is rushing up the valley! To the hills, for your lives! All the Thames bank is blazing!" Nobody took the slightest heed; they stood still in the street for a minute with open mouths: then they returned to their customary occupations. A quarter of an hour later, there was no such place in the world as Uxbridge.

I followed the main road through the village which I have since identified as Hillingdon; then I diverged to the left, partly by roads and partly by field paths of whose exact course I am still uncertain, towards the hill at Harrow. When I reached the town, I did not strive to rouse the people, partly because my past experience had taught me the futility of the attempt, and partly because I rightly judged that they were safe from the inundation; for as it never quite covered the dome of St. Paul's, part of which still protrudes from the sea of basalt, it did not reach the level of the northern heights of London. I rode on through Harrow without one word to any body. I did not desire to be stopped or harassed as an escaped lunatic.

From Harrow I made my way tortuously along the rising ground, by the light of nature, through Wembley Park, to Willesden. At Willesden, for the first time, I found to a certainty that London was threatened. Great crowds of people in the profoundest excitement stood watching a dense cloud of smoke and steam that spread rapidly over the direction of Shepherd's Bush and Hammersmith. They were speculating as to its meaning, but laughed incredulously when I told them what it portended. A few minutes later, the smoke spread ominously towards

Kensington and Paddington. That settled my fate. It was clearly impossible to descend into London; and indeed, the heat now began to be unendurable. It drove us all back, almost physically. I thought I must abandon all hope. I should never even know what had become of Ethel and the children.

My first impulse was to lie down and await the fire-flood. Yet the sense of the greatness of the catastrophe seemed somehow to blunt one's own private grief. I was beside myself with fear for my darlings; but I realized that I was but one among hundreds of thousands of fathers in the same position. What was happening at that moment in the great city of five million souls we did not know, we shall never know; but we may conjecture that the end was mercifully too swift to entail much needless suffering. All at once, a gleam of hope struck me. It was my father's birthday. Was it not just possible that Ethel might have taken the children up to Hampstead to wish their grandpa many happy returns of the day? With a wild determination not to give up all for lost, I turned my front wheel in the direction of Hampstead Hill, still skirting the high ground as far as possible. My heart was on fire within me. A restless anxiety urged me to ride my hardest. As all along the route, I was still just a minute or two in front of the catastrophe. People were beginning to be aware that something was taking place; more than once as I passed they asked me eagerly where the fire was. It was impossible for me to believe by this time that they knew nothing of an event in whose midst I seemed to have been living for months; how could I realize that all the things which had happened since I started from Cookham Bridge so long ago were really compressed into the space of a single morning?—nay, more, of an hour and a half only?

As I approached Windmill Hill, a terrible sinking seized me. I seemed to totter on the brink of a precipice. Could Ethel be safe? Should I ever again see little Bertie and the baby? I pedalled on as if automatically; for all life had gone out of me. I felt my hip-joint moving dry in its socket. I held my breath; my heart stood still. It was a ghastly moment.

At my father's door I drew up, and opened the garden gate. I hardly dared to go in. Though each second was precious, I paused and hesitated.

At last I turned the handle. I heard somebody within. My heart came up in my mouth. It was little Bertie's voice: "Do it again, Granpa; do it again; it amooses Bertie!"

I rushed into the room. "Bertie, Bertie!" I cried. "Is Mammy here?"

He flung himself upon me. "Mammy, Mammy, Daddy has comed home." I burst into tears. "And Baby?" I asked, trembling.

"Baby and Ethel are here, George," my father answered, staring at me. "Why, my boy, what's the matter?"

I flung myself into a chair and broke down. In that moment of relief, I felt that London was lost, but I had saved my wife and children.

I did not wait for explanations. A crawling four-wheeler was loitering by. I hailed it and hurried them in. My father wished to discuss the matter, but I cut him short. I gave the driver three pounds—all the gold I had with me. "Drive on!" I shouted, "drive on! Towards Hatfield—anywhere!"

He drove as he was bid. We spent that night, while Hampstead flared like a beacon, at an isolated farm-house on the high ground in Hertfordshire. For, of course, though the flood did not reach so high, it set fire to everything inflammable in its neighbourhood.

Next day, all the world knew the magnitude of the disaster. It can only be summed up in five emphatic words: There was no more London.

I have one other observation alone to make. I noticed at the time how, in my personal relief, I forgot for the moment that London was perishing. I even forgot that my house and property had perished. Exactly the opposite, it seemed to me, happened with most of those survivors who lost wives and children in the eruption. They moved about as in a dream, without a tear, without a complaint, helping others to provide for the needs of the homeless and houseless. The universality of the catastrophe made each man feel as though it were selfishness to attach too great an importance at such a crisis to his own personal losses. Nay, more; the burst of feverish activity and nervous excitement, I might even say enjoyment, which followed the horror, was traceable, I think, to this self-same cause. Even grave citizens felt they must do their best to dispel the universal gloom; and they plunged accordingly into around of dissipations which other nations thought both unseemly and un-English. It was one way of expressing the common emotion. We had all lost heart and we flocked to the theatres to pluck up our courage. That, I believe, must be our national answer to M. Zola's strictures on our untimely levity. "This people," says the great French author, "which took its pleasures sadly while it was rich and prosperous, begins to dance and sing above the ashes of its capital—it makes merry by the open graves of its wives and children. What an enigma! What a puzzle! What chance of an Oedipus!"

WORLD OF THE WAR GOD

by George Griffith

INTRODUCTION

For their honeymoon Rollo Lenox Smeaton Aubrey, Earl of Redgrave, and his bride, Lilla Zaidie, leave the earth on a visit to the moon and the principal planets; their sole companion being Andrew Murgatroyd, an old engineer who had superintended the building of the Astronef in which the journey is made. By means of the "R. Force," or Antigravitational Force, of the secret of which Lord Redgrave is the sole possessor, they are able to navigate with precision and safety the limitless ocean of Space. Their adventures on the moon were described in the first story of the series.

* * * * *

The earth and the moon were more than a hundred million miles behind in the depths of Space, and the Astronef had crossed this immense gap in eleven days and a few hours; but this apparently inconceivable speed was not altogether due to the powers of the Navigator of the Stars, for Lord Redgrave had taken advantage of the passage of the planet along its orbit towards that of the earth; therefore, while the Astronef was approaching Mars with ever-increasing speed, Mars was travelling towards the Astronef at the rate of sixteen miles a second. The great silver disc of the earth had diminished until it looked only a little larger than Venus appears from the earth. In fact the planet Terra is to the inhabitants of Mars what Venus is to us, the star of the morning and evening.

Breakfast on the morning of the twelfth day, or, since there is neither day nor night in Space, it would be more correct to say the twelfth period of twenty-four earth-hours as measured by the chronometers, was just over, and the commander of the Astronef was standing with his bride in the forward end of the glass-covered deck looking downwards at a vast crescent of rosy light which stretched out over an arc of more than ninety degrees. Two tiny black spots were travelling towards each other across it. "Ah!" said her ladyship, going towards one of the telescopes, "there are the moons. I was reading my Gulliver last night. I wonder what the old Dean would have given to be here, and see how true his guess was. Have you made up your mind to land on them?"

"I don't see why we shouldn't," said her husband. "I think they'd make rather convenient stopping-places; besides, we want to know whether they have atmospheres and inhabitants."

"What, people living on those wee things?" she laughed, "why, they're only about thirty or forty miles round, aren't they?"

"That's about it," he said, "but that's just one of the points I want to solve, and as for life, it doesn't always mean people, you know. We are only a few hundred miles away from Deimos, the outer one, and he is twelve thousand five hundred miles from Mars. I vote we drop on him first and let him carry us towards his brother Phobos. Then when we've examined him, we'll drop down to Phobos and take a trip round Mars on him. He does the journey in about seven hours and a half, and as he's only three thousand seven hundred miles above the surface we ought to get a very good view of our next stopping-place."

"That ought to be quite a delightful trip!" said her ladyship, "but how commonplace you are getting, Lenox. That's so like you Englishmen. We are doing what has only been dreamt of before, and here you are talking about moons and planets as if they were railway stations."

"Well, if your ladyship prefers it, we will call them undiscovered islands and continents in the Ocean of Space. That does sound a little bit better, doesn't it? Now I must go down and see to my engines."

When he had gone, Zaidie sat down to the telescope again and kept it on one of the little black spots travelling across the crescent of Mars. Both it and the other spot rapidly grew larger, and the features of the planet itself became more distinct. She could make out the seas and continents and the mysterious canals quite plainly through the clear rosy atmosphere, and, with the aid of the telescope, she could even make out the glimmer which the inner moon threw upon the unlighted portion of the disc.

Deimos grew bigger and bigger, and in about half-an-hour the Astronef grounded gently on what looked to her like a dimly-lighted circular plain, but which, when her eyes became accustomed to the light, was more like the summit of a conical mountain. Redgrave raised the keel a little from the surface again and propelled her towards a thin circle of light on the tiny horizon. As they crossed into the sunlit portion it became quite plain that Deimos at any rate was as airless and lifeless as the moon. The surface was composed of brown rock and red sand broken up into miniature hills and valleys. There were a few traces of byegone volcanic action, but it was evident that the internal fires of this tiny world must have burnt themselves out very quickly.

"Not much to be seen here," said Redgrave, "and I don't think it would be safe to go out. The attraction is so weak here that we might find ourselves falling off with very little exertion. You might take a couple of photographs of the surface, and then we'll be off to Phobos."

A few minutes later Zaidie got a couple of good photographs of the satellite. The attraction of Mars now began to make itself strongly felt, and the Astronef dropped rapidly through the eight thousand miles which separate the inner and outer moons of Mars. As they approached Phobos they saw that half the little disc was brilliantly lighted by the same rays of the sun which were glowing on the rapidly increasing crescent of Mars beneath them. By careful manipulation of his engines Lord Redgrave managed to meet the approaching satellite with a hardly perceptible shock about the centre of its lighted portion, that is to say the side turned towards the planet.

Mars now appeared as a gigantic rosy moon filling the whole vault of the heavens above them. Their telescopes brought the three thousand seven hundred and fifty miles down to about fifty. The rapid motion of the tiny satellite afforded them a spectacle which might be compared to the rising of a moon glowing with rosy light and hundreds of times larger than the earth. The speed of the vehicle of which they had taken possession, something like four thousand two hundred miles an hour, caused the surface of the planet to apparently sweep away from below them from west to east, just as the earth appears to slip away from under the car of a balloon.

Neither of them left the telescopes for more than a few minutes during this aerial circumnavigation. Murgatroyd, outwardly impassive, but inwardly filled with solemn fears for the fate of this impiously daring voyage, brought them wine and sandwiches and later on tea and toast and more sandwiches; but they hardly touched even these, so absorbed were they in the wonderful spectacle which was passing swiftly under their eyes. Their telescopes were excellent ones, and at that distance Mars gave up all his secrets.

Phobos revolves from west to east almost along the plane of the planet's equator. To left and right they saw the huge ice-caps of the South and North Poles gleaming through the red atmosphere with a pale sunset glimmer. Then came the great stretches of sea, often obscured by vast banks of clouds, which, as the sunlight fell upon them, looked strangely like the earth-clouds at sunset. Then, almost immediately underneath them spread out the great land areas of the equatorial region. The three continents of Halle, Gallileo, and Tycholand; then Huygens—which is to Mars what Europe, Asia, and Africa are to the earth. Then Herschell and Copernicus. Nearly all of these land masses were split up into semi-regular divisions by the famous canals which have so long puzzled terrestrial observers.

"Well, there is one problem solved at any rate," said Redgrave, when after a journey of nearly four hours they had crossed the western hemisphere. "Mars is getting very old, her seas are diminishing, and her continents are increasing, and those canals are the remains of gulfs and isthmuses which have been widened and deepened and lengthened by human, or we'll say Martian, labour, partly, I've no doubt, for purposes of navigation, and partly to keep the inhabitants of the interior of the continent within measurable distance of the sea. There's not the slightest doubt about that. Then, you see, we've seen scarcely any mountains to speak of so far, only ranges of low hills."

"And that means, I suppose," said Zaidie, "that they've all been worn down as the mountains of the earth are worn away. I was reading Flammarion's 'End of the World' last night, and he, you know, painted the earth at the end as an enormous plain of land, no hills or mountains, no seas, and only sluggish rivers draining into marshes. I suppose that's what they're coming to down yonder. Now, I wonder what sort of civilisation we shall find. Perhaps we shan't find any at all. Suppose all their civilisations have worn out, and they are degenerating into the same struggle for sheer existence those poor creatures in the moon must have had."

"Or suppose," said his lordship seriously, "we find that they have passed the zenith of civilisation, and are dropping back into savagery, but still have the use of weapons and means of destruction which we, perhaps, have no notion of, and are inclined to use them. We'd better be careful, dear."

"What do you mean, Lenox?" she said. "They wouldn't try to do us any harm, would they? Why should they?"

"I don't say they would," he replied, "but still you never know. You see, their ideas of right and wrong and hospitality and all that sort of thing might be quite different to what we have on the earth. In fact, they may not be men at all, but just a sort of monster with a semihuman intellect, perhaps a superhuman one with ideas that we have no notion of. Then there's another thing: suppose they fancied a trip through Space, and thought that they had quite as good a right to the Astronef as we have? I dare say they've seen us if they've got telescopes, as no doubt they have, perhaps a good deal more powerful than ours, and they may be getting ready to receive us now. I think I'll get the guns up before we go down, in case our reception may not be a friendly one."

The defensive armament of the Astronef consisted of four pneumatic guns, which could be mounted on swivels, two ahead and two astern, and which carried a shell containing either one of two kinds of explosives invented by her creator. One was a solid, and burst on impact with an explosive force equal to about twenty pounds of dynamite. The other consisted of two liquids separated in the shell, and these, when mixed by the breaking of the partition, nurse into a volume of flame which could not be extinguished by any known human means. It would burn even in a vacuum, since it supplied its own elements of combustion. The guns would throw these shells to a distance of about seven terrestrial miles. On the upper deck there were also stands for a couple of light machine guns, capable of discharging seven hundred bullets a minute.

The small arms consisted of a couple of heavy, ten-bore, elephant guns carrying explosive bullets, a dozen rifles and fowling pieces of different makes of which three, a single and a double-barrelled rifle and a double-barrelled shot-gun, belonged to her ladyship, as well as a dainty brace of revolvers, one of half-a-dozen brace of various calibres which completed the minor armament of the Astronef.

These guns were got up and mounted while the attraction of the planet was comparatively feeble, and the guns themselves were, therefore, of very little weight. On the surface of the earth a score of men could not have done the work, but on board the Astronef, suspended in space, his lordship and Murgatroyd found the work easy, and Zaidie herself picked up a Maxim and carried it about as though it were a toy sewing-machine.

"Now I think we can go down," said Redgrave, when everything had been put in position as far as possible. "I wonder whether we shall find the atmosphere of Mars suitable for terrestrial lungs. It will be rather awkward if it isn't."

A very slight exertion of repulsive force was sufficient to detach the Astronef from the body of Phobos. She dropped rapidly towards the surface of the planet, and within three hours they saw the sunlight for the first time since they had left the earth shining through an unmistakable atmosphere, an atmosphere of a pale, rosy hue, instead of the azure of the earthly skies, and an angular observation showed that they were within fifty miles of the surface of the undiscovered world.

"Well, there's air here of some sort, there's no doubt. We'll drop a bit further and then Andrew shall start the propellers. They'll very soon give us an idea of the density. Do you notice the change in the temperature? That's the diffused rays instead of the direct ones. Twenty miles, I think that will do. I'll stop her now and we'll prospect for a landing-place."

He went down to apply the repulsive force directly to the surface of Mars, so as to check the descent, and then he put on his breathing-dress, went into the exit chamber, closed one door behind him, opened the other and allowed it to fill with Martian air; then he shut it again, opened his visor and took a cautious breath.

It may, perhaps, have been the idea that he, the first of all the sons of earth, was breathing the air of another world, or it might have been some peculiar property from the Martian atmosphere, but he immediately experienced a sensation such as usually follows drinking a glass of champagne. He took another breath, and another. Then he opened the inner door and went on to the lower deck, saying to himself:

"Well, the air's all right if it is a bit champagney, rich in oxygen, I suppose, with perhaps a trace of nitrous-oxide in it. Still, it's certainly breathable and that's the principal thing.

"It's all right, dear," he said as he reached the upper deck where Zaidie was walking about round the sides of the glass dome gazing with all her eyes at the strange scene of mingled cloud and sea, and land, which spread for an immense distance on all sides of them. "I have breathed the air of Mars, and even at this height it is distinctly wholesome, though of course it's rather thin, and I had it mixed with some of our own atmosphere. Still I think it will agree all right with us lower down."

"Well, then," said Zaidie, "suppose we get down below those clouds and see what there really is to be seen."

"Your ladyship has but to speak and be obeyed," he replied, and disappeared into the lower regions of the vessel.

In a couple of minutes she saw the cloud belt below them rising rapidly. When her husband returned, the Astronef plunged into a sea of rosy mist.

"The clouds of Mars," she exclaimed, "fancy a world with pink clouds! I wonder what there is on the other side." The next moment they saw.

Just below them, at a distance of about five earth miles, lay an irregularly triangular island, a detached portion of the Continent of Huygens almost equally divided by the Martian equator, and lying with another almost similarly shaped island between the fortieth and fiftieth meridians of west longitude. The two islands were divided by a broad straight stretch of water about the width of the English Channel between Folkestone and Boulogne. Instead of the bright blue green of terrestrial seas, this connecting link between the great Northern and Southern Martian oceans had an orange tinge.

The land immediately beneath them was of a gently undulating character, something like the downs of south-eastern England. No mountains were visible in any direction. The lower portions, particularly along the borders of the canals and the sea, were thickly dotted with towns and cities, apparently of enormous extent. To the north of the island continent there was a peninsula, covered with a vast collection of buildings, which, with the broad streets and spacious squares which divided them, must have covered an area of something like two hundred square miles.

"There's the London of Mars!" said Redgrave, pointing down towards it; "where the London of Earth will be in a few thousand years, close to the equator. And you see all those other towns and cities crowded round the canals! I dare say when we go across the northern and southern temperate zones we shall find them in about the state that Siberia or Patagonia are in."

"I dare say we shall," replied Zaidie, "Martian civilisation is crowding towards the equator, though I should call that place down there the greater New York of Mars, and see there's Brooklyn just across the canal. I wonder what they're thinking about us down there."

"Hullo, what's that!" exclaimed Redgrave, interrupting her and pointing towards the great city whose roofs, apparently of glass, were flashing with a thousand tints in the pale crimson sunlight. "That's either an air-ship or another Astronef, and it's evidently coming up to interview us. So they've solved the problem, have they? Well, dear, I think it quite possible that we're in for a pretty exciting time on Mars."

While he was speaking a little dark shape, at first not much bigger than a bird, had risen from the glittering roofs of the city. It rapidly increased in size until in a few minutes Zaidie got a glimpse of it through one of the telescopes and said:

"It's a great big thing something like the Astronef, only it has wings and, I think, masts; yes, there are three masts and there's something glittering on the tops of them."

"Revolving helices, I suppose. He's screwing himself up into the air. That shows that they must either have stronger and lighter machinery here than we have, or, as the astronomers have thought, this atmosphere is denser than ours and therefore easier to fly in. Then, of course, things are only half their earthly weight here. Well, I suppose we may as well let them come and reconnoitre; then we shall see what kind of creatures they are. Ah! there are a lot more of them, some coming from Brooklyn, too, as you call it. Come up into the wheelhouse and I'll relieve Murgatroyd so that he can go and look after his engines. We shall have to give these gentlemen a lesson in flying. Meanwhile, in case of accidents, we may as well make ourselves as invulnerable as possible."

A few minutes later they were in the little steel conning-tower forward, watching the approach of the Martian fleet through the thick windows of toughened glass which enabled them to look in every direction except straight down. The steel coverings had been drawn down over the glass dome of the main deck, and Murgatroyd had gone down to the engine-room, which was connected with the conning-tower by telephone and electric signal, as well as by speaking tubes.

Fifty feet ahead of them stretched out a long shining spur, the forward end of the Astronef of which ten feet were solid steel, a ram which no floating structure built by human hands could have resisted.

Redgrave was at the wheel, standing with his hands on the steering-wheel, looking more serious than he had done so far during the voyage. Zaidie stood beside him with a powerful binocular telescope watching, with cheeks a little paler than usual, the movements of the Martian air-ships. She counted twenty-five vessels rising round them in a wide circle.

"I don't like the idea of a whole fleet coming up," said Redgrave, as he watched them rising, and the ring narrowing round the still motionless Astronef. "If they only wanted to know who and what we are, or to leave their cards on us, as it were, and bid us welcome to the world, one ship could have done that just as well as fifty. This lot coming up looks as if they wanted to get round and capture us."

"It does look like it!" said Zaidie, with her glasses fixed on the nearest of the vessels; "and now I can see they've guns, too, something like ours, and, perhaps, as you said just now, they may have explosives that we don't know anything about. Oh, dear, suppose they were able to smash us up with a single shot!"

"You needn't be afraid of that, dear!" said Redgrave, laying his hand on her shoulder; "but, of course, it's perfectly natural that they should look upon us with a certain amount of suspicion, dropping like this on them from the stars. Can you see anything like men on board them yet?"

"No, they're all closed in," she replied, "just as we are; but they've got conning-towers like this, and something like windows along the sides; that's where the guns are, and the guns are moving, they're pointing them at us. Lenox, I'm afraid they're going to shoot."

"Then we may as well spoil their aim," he said, pressing an electric button three times, and then once more after a little interval. In obedience to the signal Murgatroyd turned on the repulsive force to half power, and the Astronef leapt up vertically a couple of thousand feet; then Redgrave pressed the button once and stopped. Another signal set the propellers in motion, and as she sprang forward across the circle formed by the Martian air-ships, they looked down and saw that the place which they had just left was occupied by a thick, greenish-yellow cloud.

"Look, Lenox, what on earth is that?" exclaimed Zaidie, pointing down to it.

"What on Mars would be nearer the point, dear," he said, with what she thought a somewhat vicious laugh. "That I'm afraid means anything but a friendly reception for us. That cloud is one of two things. It's either made by the explosion of twenty or thirty shells, or else it's made of gases intended to either poison us or make us insensible, so that they can take possession of the ship. In either case I should say that the Martians are not what we should call gentlemen."

"I should think not," she said angrily. "They might at least have taken us for friends till they had proved us enemies, which they wouldn't have done. Nice sort of hospitality that, considering how far we've come, and we can't shoot back because we haven't got the ports open."

"And a very good thing too!" laughed Redgrave. "If we had had them open, and that volley had caught us unawares, the Astronef would probably have been full of poisonous gases by this time, and your honeymoon, dear, would have come to a somewhat untimely end. Ah, they're trying to follow us! Well, now we'll see how high they can fly."

He sent another signal to Murgatroyd, and the Astronef, still beating the Martian air with the fans of her propellers, and travelling forward at about fifty miles an hour, rose in a slanting direction through a dense bank of rosy-tinted clouds, which hung over the bigger of the two cities—New York, as Zaidie had named it. When they reached the golden red sunlight above it, the Astronef stopped her ascent, and with half a turn of the wheel her commander sent her sweeping round in a wide circle. A few minutes later they saw the Martian fleet rise almost simultaneously through the clouds. They seemed to hesitate a moment, and then the prow of every vessel was directed towards the swiftly moving Astronef.

"Well, gentlemen." said Redgrave, "you evidently don't know anything about Professor Rennick and his R. Force; and yet you ought to know that we couldn't have come through space without being able to get beyond this little atmosphere of yours. Now let us see how fast you can fly."

Another signal went down to Murgatroyd, and the whirling propellers became two intersecting circles of light. The speed of the Astronef increased to a hundred miles an hour, and the Martian fleet began to drop behind and trail out into a triangle like a flock of huge birds.

"That's lovely; we're leaving them!" exclaimed Zaidie leaning forward with the glasses to her eyes and tapping the floor of the conning-tower with her toe as if she wanted to dance, "and their wings are working faster than ever. They don't seem to have any screws."

"Probably because they've solved the problem of the bird's flight," said Redgrave, "They're not gaining on us, are they?"

"No, they're at about the same distance."

"Then we'll see how they can soar."

Another signal went over the wire, the Astronef's propellers slowed down and stopped, and the vessel began to rise swiftly towards the Zenith, which the Sun was now approaching. The Martian fleet continued the impossible chase until the limits of the navigable atmosphere. about eight earth-miles above the surface, was reached. Here the air was evidently too rarefied for their wings to act. They came to a standstill arranged in an irregular circle, their occupants no doubt looking up with envious eyes upon the shining body of the Astronef glittering like a tiny star in the sunlight ten thousand feet above them.

"Now, gentlemen," said Redgrave, "I think we have shown you that we can fly faster and soar higher than you can. Perhaps you'll be a bit more civil now. And, if you're not, well, we shall have to teach you manners."

"But you're not going to fight them all dear, are you? Don't let us be the first to bring war and bloodshed with us into another world."

"Don't trouble about that, little woman, it's here already," said her husband. "People don't have air-ships and guns, which fire shells or whatever they were, without knowing what war is. From what I've seen, I should say these Martians have civilised themselves out of all the emotions, and, I daresay, have fought pitilessly for the possession of the last habitable lands of the planet. They've preyed upon each other till only the fittest are left, and those, I suppose, were the ones who invented the air-ships and finally got possession of all that existed. Of course that would give them the command of the planet, land, and sea. In fact, if we were able to make the personal acquaintance of the Martians, we should probably find them a set of over-civilised savages."

"That's a rather striking paradox, isn't it, dear?" said Zaidie, slipping her hand through his arm: "but still it's not at all bad. You mean, of course, that they've civilised themselves out of all the emotions until they're just a set of cold, calculating, scientific animals. After all they must be. We should not have done anything like that on earth if we'd had a visitor from Mars. We shouldn't have got out cannons, and shot at him before we'd even made his acquaintance.

"Now, if he or they had dropped in America as we were going down there, we should have received them with deputations, given them banquets, which they might not have been able to eat, and speeches, which they would not understand, photographed them, filled the newspapers with everything that we could imagine about them, put them in a palace car and hustled them round the country for everybody to look at."

"And meanwhile," laughed Redgrave, "some of your smart engineers, I suppose, would have gone over the vessel they had come in, found out how she was worked, and taken out a dozen patents for her machinery."

"Very likely," replied Zaidie, with a saucy little toss of her chin; "and why not? We like to learn things down there—and anyhow that would be better than shooting at them."

While this little conversation was going on, the Astronef was dropping rapidly into the midst of the Martian fleet, which had again arranged itself in a circle. Zaidie soon made out through the glasses that the guns were pointed upwards.

"Oh, that's your little game, is it!" said Redgrave, when she told him of this. "Well, if you want a fight, you can have it."

As he said this, his jaws came together, and Zaidie saw a look in his eyes that she had never seen there before. He signalled rapidly two or three times to Murgatroyd. The propellers began to whirl at their utmost speed, and the Astronef, making a spiral downward course, swooped down on to the Martian fleet with terrific velocity. Her last curve coincided almost exactly with the circle occupied by the fleet. Half-a-dozen spouts of greenish flame came from the nearest vessel, and for a moment the Astronef was enveloped in a yellow mist.

"Evidently they don't know that we are air-tight, and they don't use shot or shell. They've got past that. Their projectiles kill by poison or suffocation. I daresay a volley like that would kill a regiment. Now give that fellow a lesson which he won't live to remember."

They swept through the poison mist. Redgrave swung the wheel round. The Astronef dropped to the level of the ring of Martian vessels which had now got up speed again. Her steel ram was directed straight at the vessel which had fired the last shot. Propelled at a speed of more than a hundred miles an hour, it took the strange-winged craft amidships. As the shock came, Redgrave put his arm round Zaidie's waist and held her close to him, otherwise she would have been flung against the forward wall of the conning-tower.

The Martian vessel stopped and bent up. They saw human figures, more than half as large again as men, inside her, staring at them through the windows in the sides. There were others at the breeches of the guns in the act of turning the muzzles on the Astronef; but this was only a momentary glimpse, for in a second or two after the Astronef's spur had pierced her, the Martian air-ship broke in twain, and her two halves plunged downwards through the rosy clouds.

"Keep her at full speed, Andrew," said Redgrave down the speaking-tube, "and stand by to jump if we want to."

"Ready, my lord!" came back up the tube.

The old Yorkshireman during the last few minutes had undergone a transformation which he himself hardly understood. He recognised that there was a fight going on, that it was a case of "burn, sink and destroy," and the thousand-year-old savage awoke in him just, as a matter of fact, it had done in his lordship.

"Well, they can pick up the pieces down there," said Redgrave, still holding Zaidie tight to his side with one hand and working the wheel with the other. "Now we'll teach them another lesson."

"What are you going to do, dear?" she said, looking up at him with somewhat frightened eyes.

"You'll see in a moment," he said, between his shut teeth. "I don't care whether these Martians are degenerate human beings or only animals; but from my point of view the reception that they have given us justifies any kind of retaliation. If we'd had a single port hole open during the first volley you and I would have been dead by this time, and I'm not going to stand anything like that without reprisals. They've declared war on us, and killing in war isn't murder."

"Well, no, I suppose not," she said; "but it's the first fight I've been in, and I don't like it. Still, they did receive us pretty meanly, didn't they?"

"Meanly? If there was anything like a code of interplanetary morals, one might call it absolutely caddish."

He sent another message to Murgatroyd. The Astronef sprang a thousand feet towards the zenith; another signal, and she stopped exactly over the biggest of the Martian air-ships; another, and she dropped on to it like a stone and smashed it to fragments. Then she stopped and mounted again above the broken circle of the fleet, while the pieces of the air-ship and what was left of her crew plunged downwards through the crimson clouds in a fall of nearly thirty thousand feet.

Within the next few moments the rest of the Martian fleet had followed it, sinking rapidly down through the clouds and scattering in all directions. "They seem to have had enough of it," laughed Redgrave, as the Astronef, in obedience to another signal, began to drop towards the surface of Mars. "Now we'll go down and see if they're in a more reasonable frame of mind. At any rate we've won our first scrimmage, dear."

"But it was rather brutal, Lenox, wasn't it?"

"When you are dealing with brutes, Zaidie, it is sometimes necessary to be brutal."

"And you look a wee bit brutal now," she replied, looking up at him with something like a look of fear in her eyes. "I suppose that is because you have just killed somebody—or some things—whichever they are."

"Do I, really?"

The hard-set jaw relaxed and his lips melted into a smile under his moustache, and he bent down and kissed her. And then he said:

"Well, what do you suppose I should have thought of them if you had had a whiff of that poison?"

"Yes, dear," she said; "I see now."

When the Astronef dropped through the clouds, they saw that the fleet had not only scattered, but was apparently getting as far out of reach as possible. One vessel had dropped into the principal square in the centre of the city which her ladyship had called New York.

"That fellow has gone to report, evidently," said Redgrave. "We'll follow him, but I don't think we'd better open the ports even then. There's no telling when they might give us a whiff of that poison-mist, or whatever it is."

"But how are you going to talk to them, then, if they can talk?—I mean, if they know any language that we do?"

"They're something like men, and so I suppose they understand the language of signs, at any rate. Still, if you don't fancy it, we'll go somewhere else."

"No thanks," she said. "That's not my father's daughter. I haven't come a hundred million miles from home to go away before the first act's finished. We'll go down to see if we can make them understand."

By this time the Astronef was hanging suspended over an enormous square about half the size of Hyde Park. It was laid out just as a terrestrial park would be in grassland, flower beds, and avenues, and patches of trees, only the grass was a reddish yellow, the leaves of the trees were like those of a beech in autumn, and the flowers were nearly all a deep violet, or a bright emerald green.

As they descended they saw that the square, or Central Park, as her ladyship at once christened it, was flanked by enormous blocks of buildings, palaces built of a dazzlingly white stone, and topped by domed roofs, and lofty cupolas of glass.

"Isn't that just lovely!" she said, swinging her binoculars in every direction.

"Talk about Fifth Avenue and the houses in Central Park; why, it's the Chicago Exposition, and the Paris one, and your Crystal Palace, multiplied by about ten thousand, and all spread out just round this one place. If we don't find these people nice, I guess we'd better go back and build a fleet like this, and come and take it."

"There spoke the new American imperialism," laughed Redgrave. "Well, we'll go and see what they're like first, shall we?"

The Astronef dropped a little more slowly than the air-ship had done, and remained suspended a hundred feet or so above her after she had reached the ground. Swarms of human figures, but of more than human statures clad in tunics and trousers or knickerbockers, came out of the glass-domed palaces from all sides into the park. They were nearly all of the same stature and there appeared to be no difference whatever between the sexes. Their dress was absolutely plain; there was no attempt at ornament or decoration of any kind.

"If there are any of the Martian women among those people," said her ladyship, "they've taken to rationals and they've grown about as big as the men. And look; there's someone who seems to want to communicate with us. Why, they're all bald! They haven't got a hair among them—and what a size their heads are!"

"That's brains—too much brains, I expect! Those people have lived too long. I expect they've ceased to be animals—civilised themselves out of everything in the way of passions and emotions, and are just purely intellectual beings, with as much human nature about them as a limited company has."

The orderly swarms of figures, which were rapidly filling the park, divided as he was speaking, making a broad lane from one of its entrances to where the Astronef was hanging above the air-ship. A light four-wheeled vehicle, whose framework and wheels glittered like burnished gold, sped towards them, driven by some invisible agency. Its only occupant was a huge man, dressed in the universal costume, saving only a scarlet sash in place of the cord-girdle which the others wore round their waists. The vehicle stopped near the air-ship, over which the Astronef was hanging, and, as the figure dismounted, a door opened in the side of the vessel and three other figures, similar both in stature and attire, came out and entered into conversation with him.

"The Admiral of the Fleet is evidently making his report," said Redgrave. "Meanwhile, the crowd seems to be taking a considerable amount of interest in us."

"And very naturally, too!" replied Zaidie. "Don't you think we might go down now and see if we can make ourselves understood in any way? You can have the guns ready in case of accidents, but I don't think they'll try and hurt us now. Look, the gentleman with the red sash is making signs."

"I think we can go down now all right," replied Redgrave, "because it's quite certain they can't use the poison guns on us without killing themselves as well. Still, we may as well have our own ready. Andrew, load up and get that port Maxim ready. I hope we shan't want it, but we may. I don't quite like the look of these people."

"They're very ugly, aren't they?" said Zaidie; "and really you can't tell which are men and which are women. I suppose they've civilised themselves out of everything that's nice, and are just scientific and utilitarian and everything that's horrid."

"I shouldn't wonder. They look to me as if they've just got common sense as we call it, and hadn't any other sense; but, at any rate, if they don't behave themselves, we shall be able to teach them manners of a sort, though I dare say we've done that to some extent already."

As he said this Redgrave went into the conning-tower, and the Astronef moved from above the air-ship, and dropped gently into the crimson grass about a hundred feet from her. Then the ports were opened, the guns, which Murgatroyd had loaded, were swung into position, and they armed themselves with a brace of revolvers each, in case of accident.

"What delicious air this is!" said her ladyship, as the ports were opened, and she took her first breath of the Martian atmosphere. "It's ever so much nicer than ours; it's just like breathing champagne."

Redgrave looked at her with an admiration which was tempered by a sudden apprehension. Even in his eyes she had never seemed so lovely before. Her cheeks were glowing and her eyes were gleaming with a brightness that was almost feverish, and he was himself sensible of a strange feeling of exultation, both mental and physical, as his lungs filled with the Martian air.

"Oxygen," he said shortly, "and too much of it! Or, I shouldn't wonder if it was something like nitrous-oxide—you know, laughing gas."

"Don't!" she laughed, "it may be very nice to breathe, but it reminds one of other things which aren't a bit nice. Still, if it is anything of that sort it might account for these people having lived so fast. I know I feel just now as if I were living at the rate of thirty-six hours a day and so, I suppose, the fewer hours we stop here the better."

"Exactly!' said Redgrave, with another glance of apprehension at her. "Now, there's his Royal Highness, or whatever he is, coming. How are we going to talk to him? Are you all ready, Andrew?"

"Yes, my lord, all ready," replied the old Yorkshireman, dropping his huge, hairy hand on the breech of the Maxim.

"Very well, then, shoot the moment you see them doing anything suspicious, and don't let anyone except his Royal Highness come nearer than a hundred yards."

As he said this, Redgrave, revolver in hand, went to the door, from which the gangway steps had been lowered, and, in reply to a singularly expressive gesture from the huge Martian, who seemed to stand nearly nine feet high, he beckoned to him to come up on to the deck.

As he mounted the steps the crowd closed round the Astronef and the Martian air-ship; but, as though in obedience to orders which had already been given, they kept at a respectful distance of a little over a hundred yards away from the strange vessel, which had wrought such havoc with their fleet. When the Martian reached the deck Redgrave held out his hand and the giant recoiled, as a man on earth might have done if, instead of the open palm, he had seen a clenched hand gripping a knife.

"Take care, Lenox," exclaimed Zaidie, taking a couple of steps towards him, with her right hand on the butt of one of her revolvers. The movement brought her close to the open door, and in full view of the crowd outside.

If a seraph had come on earth and presented itself thus before a throng of human beings, there might have happened some such miracle as was wrought when the swarm of Martians beheld the strange beauty of this radiant daughter of the earth. As it seemed to them, when they discussed it afterwards, ages of purely mechanical and utilitarian civilisation had brought all conditions of Martian life up—or down—to the same level. There was no apparent difference between the males and females in stature; their faces were all the same, with features of mathematical regularity, pale skin, bloodless cheeks, and all expression, if such it could be called, utterly devoid of emotion.

But still these creatures were human, or at least their forefathers had been. Hearts beat in their breasts, blood flowed through their veins, and so the magic of this marvellous vision instantly awoke the long-slumbering elementary instincts of a bye-gone age. A low murmur ran through the vast throng, a murmur, half-human, half-brutish, which swiftly rose to a hoarse, screaming roar.

"Look out, my lord! Quick! Shut the door, they're coming! It's her ladyship they want; she must look like an angel from Heaven to them. Shall I fire?"

"Yes," said Redgrave, gripping the lever, and bringing the door down. "Zaidie, if this fellow moves, put a bullet through him. I'm going to talk to that air-ship before he gets his poison guns to work."

As the last word left his lips, Murgatroyd put his thumb on the spring on the Maxim. A roar such as Martian ears had never heard before resounded through the vast square, and was flung back with a thousand echoes from the walls of the huge palaces on every side. A stream of smoke and flame poured out of the little port-hole, and then the onward-swarming throng seemed to stop, and the front ranks of it began to sink down silently in long rows.

Then through the roaring rattle of the Maxim, sounded the deep, sharp bang of Redgrave's gun, as he sent twenty pounds' weight of an explosive, invented by Zaidie's father, which was nearly four times as powerful as Lyddite, into the Martian air-ship. Then came an explosion, which shook the air for miles around. A blaze of greenish flame, and a huge cloud of steamy smoke, showed that the projectile had done its work, and, when the smoke drifted away, the spot on which the air-ship had lain was only a deep, red, jagged gash in the ground. There was not even a fragment of the ship to be seen.

Then Redgrave left the gun and turned the starboard Maxim on to another swarm which was approaching the Astronef from that side. When he had got the range, he swung the gun slowly from side to side. The moving throng stopped, as the other one had done, and sank down to the red grass, now dyed with a deeper red.

Meanwhile, Zaidie had been holding the Martian at something more than arm's length with her revolver. He seemed to understand perfectly that if she pulled the trigger, the revolver would do something like what the Maxims had done. He appeared to take no notice whatever either of the destruction of the air-ship or of the slaughter that was going on around the Astronef. His big pale blue eyes were fixed upon her face. They seemed to be devouring a loveliness such as they had never seen before. A dim, pinky flush stole for the first time into his sallow cheeks, and something like a light of human passion came into his eyes.

Then he spoke. The words were slowly uttered, passionless, and very distinct. As words they were unintelligible but there was no mistaking their meaning or that of the gestures which accompanied them. He bent forward, towering over her with outstretched arms, huge, hideous, and half human.

Zaidie took a step backwards and, just as Redgrave whipped out one of his revolvers, she pulled the trigger of hers. The bullet cut a clean hole through the smooth, hairless skull of the Martian, and he dropped to the deck without a sound other than what was made by his falling body.

"That's the first man I've ever killed," she faltered, as her hand fell to her side, and the revolver dropped from it. "Still, do you think it really was a man?"

"That a man!" said Redgrave through his clenched teeth. "Not much! Here, Andrew, open that door again and help me to heave this thing overboard, and then we'd better be off or we shall be having the rest of the fleet with their poison guns around us. Hurry up! Zaidie, I think you'd better go below for the present, little woman, and keep the door of your room tight shut. There's no telling what these animals may do if they get a chance at us."

Although she would rather have remained on deck to see what was to happen, she saw that he was in earnest, and so she at once obeyed.

The dead body of the Martian was tumbled out, Murgatroyd closed all the air-tight doors of the upper deck chamber, while Redgrave set the engines in motion and, with hardly a moment's delay, the Astronef sprang up into the crimson sky from her first and last battle-field in the well-named world of the War God.

A Glimpse of The Sinless Star

by George Griffith

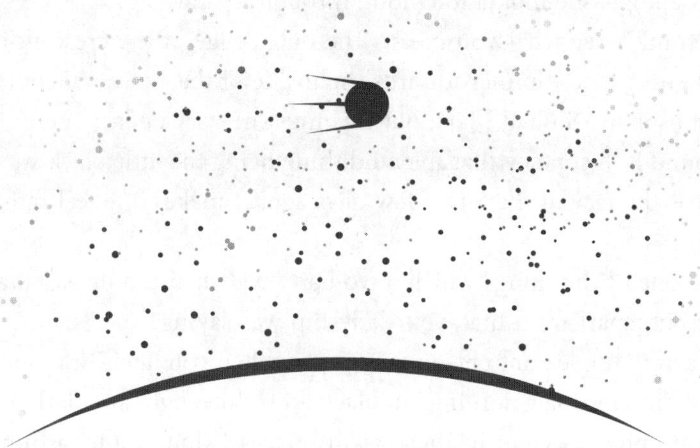

"How very different Venus looks now to what it does from the earth," said Zaidie as she took her eye away from the telescope, through which she had been examining the enormous crescent, almost approaching to what would be called upon earth a half-moon, which spanned the dark vault of space ahead of the Astronef.

"I wonder what she'll be like. All the authorities are agreed that on Venus, having her axis of revolution very much inclined to the plane of her orbit, the seasons are so severe that for half the year its temperate zone and its tropics have a summer about twice as hot as our tropics and the other half they have a winter twice as cold as our coldest. I'm afraid, after all, we shall find the Love-Star a world of salamanders and seals; things that can live in a furnace and bask on an iceberg; and when we get back home it will be our painful duty, as the first explorers of the fields of space, to dispel another dearly-cherished popular delusion."

"I'm not so very sure about that," said Lenox, glancing from the rapidly growing crescent, which was still so far away, to the sweet smiling face that was so near to his. "Don't you see something very different there to what we saw either on the moon or Mars? Now just go back to your telescope and let us take an observation."

"Well," said Zaidie, "as our trip is partly, at least, in the interest of science, I will." And then, when she had got her own telescope into focus again—for the distance between the Astronef and the new world they were about to visit was rapidly lessening—she took a long look through it, and said:

"Yes, I think I see what you mean. The outer edge of the crescent is bright, but it gets greyer and dimmer towards the inside of the curve. Of course Venus has an atmosphere. So had Mars; but this must be very dense. There's a sort of halo all round it. Just fancy that splendid thing being the little black spot we saw going across the face of the Sun a few days ago! It makes one feel rather small, doesn't it?"

"That is one of the things which a woman says when she doesn't want to be answered; but, apart from that, your ladyship was saying?"

"What a very unpleasant person you can be when you like! I was going to say that on the moon we saw nothing but black and white, light and darkness. There was no atmosphere, except in those awful places I don't want to think about. Then, as we got near Mars, we saw a pinky atmosphere, but not very dense; but this, you see, is a sort of pearl-grey white shading from silver to black. But look—what are those tiny bright spots? There are hundreds of them."

"Do you remember, as we were leaving the earth, how bright the mountain ranges looked; how plainly we could see the Rockies and the Andes?"

"Oh, yes, I see; they're mountains; thirty-seven miles high some of them, they say; and the rest of the silver-grey will be clouds, I suppose. Fancy living under clouds like those."

"Only another case of the adaptation of life to natural conditions, I expect. When we get there, I daresay we shall find that these clouds are just what make it possible for the inhabitants of Venus to stand the extremes of heat and cold. Given elevations, three or four times as high as the Himalayas, it would be quite possible for them to choose their temperature by shifting their altitude.

"But I think it's about time to drop theory and see to the practice," he continued, getting up from his chair and going to the signal board in the conning-tower. "Whatever the planet Venus may be like, we don't want to charge it at the rate of sixty miles a second. That's about the speed now, considering how fast she's travelling towards us."

"And considering that, whether it is a nice world or not, it's about as big as the earth, and so we should get rather the worst of the charge," laughed Zaidie, as she went back to her telescope.

Redgrave sent a signal down to Murgatroyd to reverse engines, as it were, or, in other words, to direct the "R. Force" against the planet, from which they were now only a couple of hundred thousand miles distant. The next moment the sun and stars seemed to halt in their courses. The great silver-grey crescent which had been increasing in size every moment appeared to remain stationary, and then when Lenox was satisfied that the engines were developing the force properly, he sent another signal down, and the Astronef began to descend.

The half-disc of Venus seemed to fall below them, and in a few minutes they could see it from the upper deck spreading out like a huge semi-circular plain of silver grey light ahead, and on both sides, of them. The Astronef was falling upon it at the rate of about a thousand miles a minute towards the centre of the half crescent, and every moment the brilliant spots above the cloud-surface grew in size and brightness.

"I believe the theory about the enormous height of the mountains of Venus must be correct after all," said Redgrave, tearing himself with an evident wrench away from his telescope. "Those white patches can't be anything else but the summits of snow-capped mountains. You know how brilliantly white a snow-peak looks on earth against even the whitest of clouds."

"Oh, yes," said her ladyship, "I've often seen that in the Rockies. But it's lunch time, and I must go down and see how my things in the kitchen are getting on. I suppose you'll try and land somewhere where it's morning, so that we can have a good day before us. Really it's very convenient to be able to make your own morning or night as you like, isn't it? I hope it won't make us too conceited when we get back, being able to choose our mornings and our evenings; in fact, our sunrises and sunsets on any world we like to visit in a casual way like this."

"Well," laughed Redgrave, as she moved away towards the companion stairs, "after all, if you find the United States, or even the planet Terra, too small for you, we've always got the fields of Space open to us. We might take a trip across the zodiac or down the Milky Way."

"And meanwhile," she replied, stopping at the top of the stairs and looking round, "I'll go down and get lunch. You and I may be king and queen of the realms of Space, and all that sort of thing; but we've got to eat and drink after all."

"And that reminds me," said Redgrave, getting up and following her, "we must celebrate our arrival on a new world as usual. I'll go down and get out the champagne. I shouldn't be surprised if we found the people of the Love-World living on nectar and ambrosia, and as fizz is our nearest approach to nectar—"

"I suppose," said Zaidie, as she gathered up her skirts and stepped daintily down the companion stairs, "if you find anything human or at least human enough to eat and drink, you'll have a party and give them champagne. I wonder what those wretches on Mars would have thought of it if we'd only made friends with them?"

Lunch on board the Astronef was about the pleasantest meal of the day. Of course there was neither day nor night, in the ordinary sense of the word, except as the hours were measured off by the chronometers. Whichever side or end of the vessel received the direct rays of the sun, there then was blazing heat and dazzling light. Elsewhere there was black darkness, and the more than icy cold of space; but lunch was a convenient division of the waking hours, which began with a stroll on the upper deck and a view of the ever-varying splendours about them and ended after dinner in the same place with coffee and cigarettes and speculations as to the next day's happenings.

This lunch hour passed even more pleasantly and rapidly than others had done, for the discussion as to the possibilities of Venus was continued in a quite delightful mixture of scientific disquisition and that converse which is common to most human beings on their honeymoon.

As there was nothing more to be done or seen for an hour or two, the afternoon was spent in a pleasant siesta in the luxurious saloon of the star-navigator; because evening to them would be morning on that portion of Venus to which they were directing their course, and, as Zaidie said, when she subsided into her hammock: "It will be breakfast time before we shall be able to get dinner."

As the Astronef fell with ever-increasing velocity towards the cloud-covered surface of Venus, the remainder of her disc, lit up by the radiance of her sister-worlds, Mercury, Mars, and the earth, and also by the pale radiance of an enormous comet, which had suddenly shot into view from behind its southern limb, became more or less visible.

Towards six o'clock, according to earth, or rather Astronef, time, it became necessary to exert the full strength of her engines to check the velocity of her fall. By eight she had entered the atmosphere of Venus, and was dropping slowly towards a vast sea of sunlit cloud, out of which, on all sides, towered thousands of snow-clad peaks, with wide-spread stretches of upland above which the clouds swept and surged like the silent billows of some vast ocean in ghost-land.

"I thought so!" said Redgrave, when the propellers had begun to revolve and Murgatroyd had taken his place in the conning-tower. "A very dense atmosphere loaded with clouds. There's the sun just rising, so your ladyship's wishes are duly obeyed."

"And doesn't it seem nice and homelike to see him rising through an atmosphere above the clouds again? It doesn't look a bit like the same sort of dear old sun just blazing like a red-hot moon among a lot of white hot stars and planets. Look, aren't those peaks lovely, and that cloud-sea? Why, for all the world we might be in a balloon above the Rockies or the Alps. And see," she continued, pointing to one of the thermometers fixed outside the glass dome which covered the upper deck, "it's only sixty-five even here. I wonder if we could breathe this air, and oh, I do wonder what we shall see on the other side of those clouds."

"You shall have both questions answered in a few minutes," replied Redgrave, going towards the conning-tower. "To begin with, I think we'll land on that big snow-dome yonder, and do a little exploring. Where there are snow and clouds there is moisture, and where there is moisture a man ought to be able to breathe."

The Astronef, still falling, but now easily under the command of the helmsman, shot forwards and downwards towards a vast dome of snow which, rising some two thousand feet above the cloud-sea, shone with dazzling brilliance in the light of the rising sun. She landed just above the edge of the clouds. Meanwhile they had put on their breathing suits, and Redgrave had seen that the air chamber, through which they had to pass from their own little world into the new ones that they visited, was in working order. When the outer door was opened and the ladder lowered he stood aside, as he had done on the moon, and her ladyship's was the first human foot which made an imprint on the virgin snows of Venus.

The first thing Lenox did was to raise the visor of his helmet and taste the air of the new world. It was cool, and fresh, and sweet, and the first draught of it sent the blood tingling and dancing through his veins. Perfect as the arrangements of the Astronef were in this respect, the air of Venus tasted like clear running spring water would have done to a man who had been drinking filtered water for several days. He threw the visor right up and motioned to Zaidie to do the same. She obeyed, and, after drawing a long breath, she said:

"That's glorious! It's like wine after water, and rather stagnant water too. But what a world, snow-peaks and cloud-sea, islands of ice and snow in an ocean of mist! Just look at them! Did you ever see anything so lovely and unearthly in your life? I wonder how high this mountain is, and what there is on the other side of the clouds. Isn't the air delicious! Not a bit too cold after all—but, still, I think we may as well go back and put on something more becoming. I shouldn't quite like the ladies of Venus to see me dressed like a diver."

"Come along then," laughed Lenox, as he turned back towards the vessel. "That's just like a woman. You're about a hundred and fifty million miles away from Broadway or Regent Street. You are standing on the top of a snow mountain above the clouds of Venus, and the moment that you find the air is fit to breathe you begin thinking about dress. How do you know that the inhabitants of Venus, if there are any, dress at all?"

"What nonsense! Of course they do—at least, if they are anything like us."

As soon as they got back on board the Astronef and had taken their breathing-dresses off, Redgrave and the old engineer, who appeared to take no visible interest in their new surroundings, threw open all the sliding doors on the upper and lower decks so that the vessel might be thoroughly ventilated by the fresh sweet air. Then a gentle repulsion was applied to the huge snow mass on which the Astronef rested. She rose a couple of hundred feet, her propellers began to whirl round, and Redgrave steered her out towards the centre of the vast cloud-sea which was almost surrounded by a thousand glittering peaks of ice and domes of snow.

"I think we may as well put off dinner, or breakfast as it will be now, until we see what the world below is like," he said to Zaidie, who was standing beside him on the conning-tower.

"Oh, never mind about eating just now; this is altogether too wonderful to be missed for the sake of ordinary meat and drink. Let's go down and see what there is on the other side."

He sent a message down the speaking tube to Murgatroyd, who was below among his beloved engines, and the next moment sun and clouds and ice-peaks had disappeared and nothing was visible save the all-enveloping silver-grey mist.

For several minutes they remained silent, watching and wondering what they would find beneath the veil which hid the surface of Venus from their view. Then the mist thinned out and broke up into patches which drifted past them as they descended on their downward-slanting course.

Below them they saw vast, ghostly shapes of mountains and valleys, lakes and rivers, continents, islands, and seas. Every moment these became more and more distinct, and soon they were in full view of the most marvellous landscape that human eyes had ever beheld.

The distances were tremendous. Mountains, compared with which the Alps or even the Andes would have seemed mere hillocks, towered up out of the vast depths beneath them. Up to the lower edge of the all-covering cloud-sea they were clad with a golden-yellow vegetation, fields and forests, open, smiling valleys, and deep, dark ravines through which a thousand torrents thundered down from the eternal snows beyond, to spread themselves out in rivers and lakes in the valleys and plains which lay many thousands of feet below.

"What a lovely world!" said Zaidie, as she at last found her voice after what was almost a stupor of speechless wonder and admiration. "And the light! Did you ever see anything like it? It's neither moonlight nor sunlight. See, there are no shadows down there; it's just all lovely silvery twilight. Lenox, if Venus is as nice as she looks from here I don't think I shall want to go back. It reminds me of Tennyson's Lotus Eaters, 'The land where it is always afternoon.'"

"I think you are right after all. We are thirty million miles nearer to the sun than we were on the earth, and the light and heat have to filter through those clouds. They are not at all like earth-clouds from this side. It's the other way about. The silver lining is on this side. Look, there isn't a black or a brown one, or even a grey one within sight. They are just like a thin mist, lighted by millions of electric lamps. It's a delicious world, and if it isn't inhabited by angels it ought to be."

While they were talking, the Astronef was still sweeping swiftly down towards the surface through scenery of whose almost inconceivable magnificence no human words could convey any adequate idea. Underneath the cloud-veil the air was absolutely clear and transparent; clearer, indeed, than terrestrial air at the highest elevations, and, moreover, it seemed to be endowed with a strange luminous quality, which made objects, no matter how distant, stand out with almost startling distinctness.

The rivers and lakes and seas, which spread out beneath them, seemed never to have been ruffled by the blast of a storm or wind, and shone with a soft silvery grey light, which seemed to come from below rather than from above. The atmosphere, which had now penetrated to every part of the Astronef, was not only exquisitely soft but also conveyed a faint but delicious sense of languorous intoxication to the nerves.

"If this isn't Heaven it must be the half-way house," said Redgrave, with what was, perhaps, under the circumstances, a pardonable irreverence. "Still, after all, we don't know what the inhabitants may be like, so I think we'd better close the doors, and drop on the top of that mountain spur running out between the two rivers into the bay. Do you notice how curious the water looks after the earth-seas; bright silver, instead of blue and green?"

"Oh, it's just lovely," said Zaidie. "Let's go down and have a walk. There's nothing to be afraid of. You'll never make me believe that a world like this can be inhabited by anything dangerous."

"Perhaps, but we mustn't forget what happened on Mars; still, there's one thing, we haven't been tackled by any aerial fleets yet."

"I don't think the people here want air-ships. They can fly themselves. Look! there are a lot of them coming to meet us. That was a rather wicked remark of yours about the half-way house to Heaven; but those certainly look something like angels."

As Zaidie said this, after a somewhat lengthy pause, during which the Astronef had descended to within a few hundred feet of the mountain-spur, she handed a pair of field-glasses to her husband and pointed downward towards an island which lay a couple of miles or so off the end of the spur.

Redgrave put the glasses to his eyes, and, as he took a long look through them, moving them slowly up and down, and from side to side, he saw hundreds of winged figures rising from the island and soaring towards them.

"You were right, dear," he said, without taking the glass from his eyes, "and so was I. If those aren't angels, they're certainly something like men, and, I suppose, women too, who can fly. We may as well stop here and wait for them. I wonder what sort of an animal they take the Astronef for."

He sent a message down the tube to Murgatroyd, and gave a turn and a half to the steering-wheel. The propellers slowed down and the Astronef landed with a hardly perceptible shock in the midst of a little plateau covered with a thick soft moss of a pale yellowish green, and fringed by a belt of trees which seemed to be over three hundred feet high, and whose foliage was a deep golden bronze.

They had scarcely landed before the flying figures reappeared over the tree-tops and swept downwards in long spiral curves towards the Astronef.

"If they're not angels, they're very like them," said Zaidie, putting down her glasses.

"There's one thing," replied her husband; "they fly a lot better than the old masters' angels or Dore's could have done, because they have tails—or at least something that seems to serve the same purpose, and yet they haven't got feathers."

"Yes, they have, at least round the edges of their wings or whatever they are, and they've got clothes, too, silk tunics or something of that sort—and there are men and women."

"You're quite right. Those fringes down their legs are feathers, and that's how they fly."

The flying figures which came hovering near to the Astronef, without evincing any apparent sign of fear, were certainly the strangest that human eyes had looked upon. In some respects they had a sufficient resemblance to human form for them to be taken for winged men and women, while in another they bore a decided resemblance to birds. Their bodies and limbs were almost human in shape, but of slenderer and lighter build; and from the shoulder-blades and muscles of the back there sprang a pair of wings arching up above their heads. The body was covered in front and down the back between the wings with a sort of tunic of a light, silken-looking material, which must have been clothing, since there were many different colours.

In stature these inhabitants of the Love-Star varied from about five feet six to five feet, but both the taller and the shorter of them were all of nearly the same size, from which it was easy to conclude that this difference in stature was on Venus, as well as on the Earth, one of the broad distinctions between the sexes.

They flew once or twice completely round the Astronef with an exquisite ease and grace which made Zaidie exclaim: "Now, why weren't we made like that on earth!"

To which Redgrave, after a look at the barometer, replied:

"Partly, I suppose, because we weren't built that way, and partly because we don't live in an atmosphere about two and a half times as dense as ours."

Then several of the winged figures alighted on the mossy covering of the plain and walked towards the vessel.

"Why, they walk just like us, only much more prettily!" said Zaidie. "And look what funny little faces they've got! Half bird, half human, and soft, downy feathers instead of hair. I wonder whether they talk or sing. I wish you'd open the doors again, Lenox. I'm sure they can't possibly mean us any harm; they are far too innocent for that. What soft eyes they have, and what a thousand pities it is we shan't be able to understand them."

They had left the conning-tower and both his lordship and Murgatroyd were throwing open the sliding doors and, to Zaidie's considerable displeasure, getting the deck Maxims ready for action in case they should be needed. As soon as the doors were open Zaidie's judgement of the inhabitants of Venus was entirely justified.

Without the slightest sign of fear, but with very evident astonishment in their round golden-yellow eyes, they came walking close up to the sides of the Astronef. Some of them stroked her smooth, shining sides with their little hands, which Zaidie now found had only three fingers and a thumb. Many ages before they might have been bird's claws, but now they were soft and pink and plump, utterly strange to work as manual work is understood upon earth.

"Just fancy getting Maxim guns ready to shoot those delightful things," said Zaidie, almost indignantly, as she went towards the doorway from which the gangway ladder ran down to the soft, mossy turf. "Why, not one of them has got a weapon of any sort; and just listen," she went on, stopping in the opening of the doorway, "have you ever heard music like that on earth? I haven't. I suppose it's the way they talk. I'd give a good deal to be able to understand them. But still, it's very lovely, isn't it?"

"Ay, like the voices of syrens enticing honest folk to destruction," said Murgatroyd, speaking for the first time since the Astronef had landed; for this big, grizzled, taciturn Yorkshireman, who looked upon the whole cruise through Space as a mad and almost impious adventure, which nothing but his hereditary loyalty to his master's name and family could have persuaded him to share in, had grown more and more silent as the millions of miles between the Astronef and his native Yorkshire village had multiplied day by day.

"Syrens—and why not?" laughed Redgrave. "Yes, Zaidie, I never heard anything like that before. Unearthly, of course it is; but then we're not on earth. Now, Zaidie, they seem to talk in song-language. You did pretty well on Mars with your sign-language, suppose we go out and show them that you can speak the song-language, too."

"What do you mean?" she said; "sing them something?"

"Yes," he replied, "they'll try to talk to you in song, and you won't be able to understand them; at least, not as far as words and sentences go. But music is the universal language on earth, and there's no reason why it shouldn't be the same through the Solar System. Come along, tune up, little woman!"

They went together down the gangway stairs, he dressed in an ordinary English tweed grey suit, with a golf cap on the back of his head, and she in the last and daintiest of costumes which had combined the art of Paris and London and New York before the Astronef soared up from Central Park.

The moment that she set foot on the golden-yellow sward she was surrounded by a swarm of the winged, and yet strangely human creatures. Those nearest to her came and touched her hands and face, and stroked the folds of her dress. Others looked into her violet-blue eyes, and others put out their queer little hands and touched her hair.

This and her clothing seemed to be the most wonderful experience for them, saving always the fact that she had no wings.

Redgrave kept close beside her until he was satisfied that these strange half-human, and yet wholly interesting creatures were innocent of any intention of harm, and when he saw two of the winged daughters of the Love-Star put up their hands and touch the thick coils of her hair, he said:

"Take those pins and things out and let it down. They seem to think that your hair's part of your head. It's the first chance you've had to work a miracle, so you may as well do it. Show them the most beautiful thing they've ever seen."

"What babies you men can be when you get sentimental!" laughed Zaidie, as she put her hands up to her head. "How do you know that this may not be ugly in their eyes?"

"Quite impossible!" he replied. "They're a great deal too pretty themselves to think you ugly."

While he was speaking Zaidie had taken off a Spanish mantilla which she had thrown over her head as she came out, and which the ladies of Venus seemed to think was part of her hair. Then she took out the comb and one or two hair-pins which kept the coils in position, deftly caught the ends, and then, after a few rapid movements of her fingers, she shook her head, and the wondering crowd about her saw, what seemed to them a shimmering veil, half gold, half silver, in the strange, reflected light from the cloud-veil, fall down from her head over her shoulders.

They crowded still more closely round her, but so quietly and so gently that she felt nothing more than the touch of wondering hands on her arms, and dress, and hair. Her husband, as he said afterwards, was "absolutely out of it." They seemed to imagine him to be a kind of uncouth monster, possibly the slave of this radiant being which had come so strangely from somewhere beyond the cloud-veil. They looked at him with their golden-yellow eyes wide open, and some of them came up rather timidly and touched his clothes, which they seemed to think were his skin.

Then one or two, more daring, put their little hands up to his face and touched his moustache, and all of them, while both examinations were going on, kept up a running conversation of cooing and singing which evidently conveyed their ideas from one to the other on the subject of this most marvellous visit of these two strange beings with neither wings nor feathers, but who, most undoubtedly, had other means of flying, since it was quite certain that they had come from another world.

There was a low cooing note, something like the language in which doves converse, and which formed a sort of undertone. But every moment this rose here and there into higher notes, evidently expressing wonder or admiration, or both.

"You were right about the universal language," said Redgrave, when he had submitted to the stroking process for a few moments. "These people talk in music, and, as far as I can see or hear, their opinion of us, or, at least, of you, is distinctly flattering. I don't know what they take me for, and I don't care, but, as we'd better make friends with them, suppose you sing them 'Home, Sweet Home,' or 'The Swanee River.' I shouldn't wonder if they consider our talking voices most horrible discords, so you might as well give them something different."

While he was speaking the sounds about them suddenly hushed, and, as Redgrave said afterwards, it was something like the silence that follows a cannon shot. Then, in the midst of the hush, Zaidie put her hands behind her, looked up towards the luminous silver surface which formed the only visible sky of Venus, and began to sing "The Swanee River."

The clear, sweet notes rang up through the midst of a sudden silence. The sons and daughters of the Love-Star ceased the low, half-humming, half-cooing tones in which they seemed to be whispering to each other, and Zaidie sang the old plantation song through for the first time that a human voice had sung it to ears other than human.

As the last note thrilled sweetly from her lips she looked round at the crowd of strange half-human figures about her, and something in their unlikeness to her own kind brought back to her mind the familiar scenes which lay so far away, so many millions of miles across the dark and silent Ocean of Space.

Other winged figures, attracted by the sound of her singing had crossed the trees, and these, during the silence which came after the singing of the song, were swiftly followed by others, until there were nearly a thousand of them gathered about the side of the Astronef.

There was no crowding or jostling among them. Each one treated every other with the most perfect gentleness and courtesy. No such thing as enmity or ill-feeling seemed to exist among them, and, in perfect silence, they waited for Zaidie to continue what they thought was her first speech of greeting. The temper of the throng somehow coincided exactly with the mood which her own memories had brought to her, and the next moment she sent the first line of "Home Sweet Home" soaring up to the cloud-veiled sky.

As the notes rang up into the still, soft air a deeper hush fell on the listening throng. Heads were bowed with a gesture almost of adoration, and many of those standing nearest to her bent their bodies forward, and expanded their wings, bringing them together over their breasts with a motion which, as they afterwards learnt, was intended to convey the idea of wonder and admiration, mingled with something like a sentiment of worship.

Zaidie sang the sweet old song through from end to end, forgetting for the time being everything but the home she had left behind her on the banks of the Hudson. As the last notes left her lips, she turned round to Redgrave and looked at him with eyes dim with the first tears that had filled them since her father's death, and said, as he caught hold of her outstretched hand:

"I believe they've understood every word of it."

"Or, at any rate, every note. You may be quite certain of that," he replied. "If you had done that on Mars it might have been even more effective than the Maxims."

"For goodness sake don't talk about things like that in a heaven like this! Oh, listen! They've got the tune already!" It was true! The dwellers of the Love-Star, whose speech was song, had instantly recognised the sweetness of the sweetest of all earthly songs. They had, of course, no idea of the meaning of the words; but the music spoke to them and told them that this fair visitant from another world could speak the same speech as theirs. Every note and cadence was repeated with absolute fidelity, and so the speech, common to the two far-distant worlds, became a link connecting, this wandering son and daughter of the earth with the sons and daughters of the Love-Star.

The throng fell back a little and two figures; apparently male and female, came to Zaidie and held out their right hands and began addressing her in perfectly harmonised song, which, though utterly unintelligible to her in the sense of speech, expressed sentiments which could not possibly be mistaken, as there was a faint suggestion of the old English song running through the little song-speech that they made, and both Zaidie and her husband rightly concluded that it was intended to convey a welcome to the strangers from beyond the cloud-veil.

And then the strangest of all possible conversations began. Redgrave, who had no more notion of music than a walrus, perforce kept silence. In fact, he noticed with a certain displeasure which vanished speedily with a musical, and half-malicious little laugh from Zaidie, that when he spoke the bird-folk drew back a little and looked in something like astonishment at him, but Zaidie was already in touch with them, and half by song and half by signs she very soon gave them an idea of what they were and where they had come from. Her husband afterwards told her that it was the best piece of operatic acting he had ever seen, and, considering all the circumstances, this was very possibly true.

In the end the two, who had come to give her what seemed to be the formal greeting, were invited into the Astronef. They went on board without the slightest sign of mistrust, and with only an expression of mild wonder on their beautiful and almost childlike faces.

Then, while the other doors were being closed, Zaidie stood at the open one above the gangway and made signs showing that they were going up beyond the clouds and then down into the valley, and as she made the signs she sang through the scale, her voice rising and falling in harmony with her gestures. The bird-folk understood her instantly, and as the door closed and the Astronef rose from the ground, a thousand wings were outspread and presently hundreds of beautiful soaring forms were circling about the Navigator of the Stars.

"Don't they look lovely," said Zaidie. "I wonder what they would think if they could see us flying above New York or London or Paris with an escort like this. I suppose they're going to show us the way. Perhaps they have a city down there. Suppose you were to go and get a bottle of champagne and see if Master Cupid and Miss Venus would like a drink. We'll see then if our nectar is anything like theirs."

Redgrave went below. Meanwhile, for lack of other possible conversation, Zaidie began to sing the last verse of "Never Again." The melody almost exactly described the upward motion of the Astronef, and she could see that it was instantly understood, for when she had finished, their two voices joined in an almost exact imitation of it.

When Redgrave brought up the wine and the glasses they looked at them without any sign of surprise. The pop of the cork did not even make them look round.

"Evidently a semi-angelic people, living on nectar and ambrosia, with nectar very like our own," he said, as he filled the glasses. "Perhaps you'd better give it to them. They seem to understand you better than they do me—you being, of course, a good bit nearer to the angels than I am."

"Thanks!" she said, as she took a couple of glasses up, wondering a little what their visitors would do with them. Somewhat to her surprise, they took them with a little bow and a smile and sipped at the wine, first with a little glint of wonder in their eyes, and then with smiles which are unmistakable evidence of perfect appreciation.

"I thought so," said Redgrave, as he raised his own glass, and bowed gravely towards them. "This is our nearest approach to nectar, and they seem to recognise it."

"And don't they just look like the sort of people who live on it, and, of course, other things," added Zaidie, as she too lifted her glass, and looked with laughing eyes across the brim at her two guests.

But meanwhile Murgatroyd had been applying the repulsive force a little too strongly. The Astronef shot up with a rapidity which soon left her winged escort far below. She entered the cloud-veil and passed beyond it. The instant that the unclouded sun-rays struck the glass-roofing of the upper deck, their two guests, who had been moving about examining everything with a childlike curiosity, closed their eyes and clasped their hands over them, uttering little cries, tuneful and musical, but still with a note of strange discord in them.

"Lenox, we must go down again," exclaimed Zaidie. "Don't you see they can't stand the light; it hurts them. Perhaps, poor dears, it's the first time they've ever been hurt in their lives. I don't believe they have any of our ideas of pain or sorrow or anything of that sort. Take us back under the clouds, quick, or we may blind them."

Before she had finished speaking, Redgrave had sent a signal down to Murgatroyd, and the Astronef began to drop back again towards the surface of the cloud-sea. Zaidie had, meanwhile, gone to her lady guest and dropped the black lace mantilla over her head, and, as she did so, she caught herself saying:

"There, dear, we shall soon be back in your own light. I hope it hasn't hurt you. It was very stupid of us to do a thing like that."

The answer came in a little cooing murmur, which said: "Thank you!" quite as effectively as any earthly words could have done, and then the Astronef dropped through the cloud-sea. The soaring forms of her lost escort came into view again and clustered about her; and, surrounded by them, she dropped, in obedience to their signs, down between the tremendous mountains and towards the island, thick with golden foliage, which lay two or three earth-miles out in a bay, where four converging rivers spread out into the sea.

It would take the best part of a volume rather than a few lines to give even an imperfect conception of the purely Arcadian delights with which the hours of the next ten days and nights were filled; but some idea of what the Space-voyagers experienced may be gathered from this extract of a conversation which took place in the saloon of the Astronef on the eleventh evening.

"But look here, Zaidie," said his lordship, "as we've found a world which is certainly much more delightful than our own, why shouldn't we stop here a bit? The air suits us and the people are simply enchanting. I think they like us, and I'm sure you're in love with every one of them, male and female. Of course, it's rather a pity that we can't fly unless we do it in the Astronef. But that's only a detail. You're enjoying yourself thoroughly, and I never saw you looking better or, if possible, more beautiful; and why on earth—or Venus—do you want to go?"

She looked at him steadily for a few moments, and with an expression which he had never seen on her face or in her eyes before, and then she said slowly and very sweetly, although there was something like a note of solemnity running through her tone:—

"I altogether agree with you, dear; but there is something which you don't seem to have noticed. As you say, we have had a perfectly delightful time. It's a delicious world, and just everything that one would think it to be, either Aurora or Hesperus looked at from the earth; but if we were to stop here we should be committing one of the greatest crimes, perhaps the greatest, that ever was committed within the limits of the Solar System."

"My dear Zaidie, what in the name of what we used to call morals on the earth, do you mean?"

"Just this," she replied, leaning a little towards him in her deck chair. "These people, half angels, and half men and women, welcomed us after we dropped through their cloud-veil, as friends; a bit strange to them, certainly, but still they welcomed us as friends. They've taken us into their palaces, they've given us, as one might say, the whole planet. Everything was ours that we liked to take."

"We've been living with them ten days now, and neither you nor I, nor even Murgatroyd, who, like the old Puritan that he is, seems to see sin or wrong in everything that looks nice, has seen a single sign among them that they know anything about what we call sin or wrong on earth."

"I think I understand what you're driving at," said Redgrave. "You mean, I suppose, that this world is something like Eden before the fall, and that you and I—oh—but that's all rubbish you know."

She got up out of her chair and, leaning over his, put her arm round his shoulder. Then she said very softly: "I see you understand what I mean, Lenox. It doesn't matter how good you think me or I think you, but we have our original sin. You're an earthly man and I'm an earthly woman, and, as I'm your wife, I can say it plainly. We may think a good bit of each other, but that's no reason why we shouldn't be a couple of plague-spots in a sinless world like this."

Their eyes met, and he understood. Then he got up and went down to the engine-room.

A couple of minutes later the Astronef sprang upwards from the midst of the delightful valley in which she was resting. In five minutes she had passed through the cloud-veil, and the next morning when their new friends came to visit them and found that they had vanished back into Space, there was sorrow for the first time among the sons and daughters of the Love-Star.

THE WORLD OF THE CRYSTAL CITIES

by George Griffith

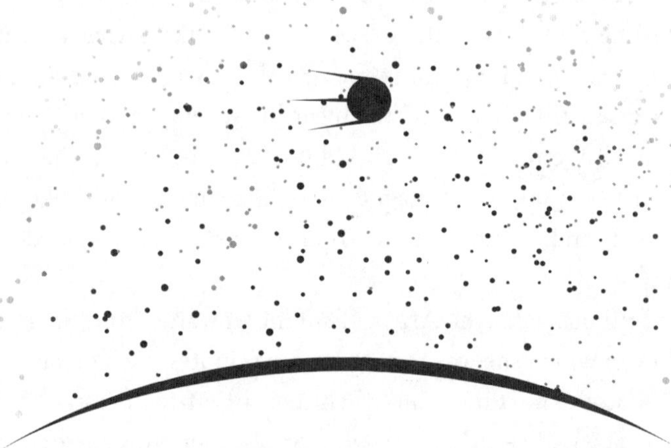

"Five hundred million miles from the earth and forty-seven million miles from Jupiter," said his lordship, as he came into breakfast on the morning of the twenty-eighth day after leaving Venus.

During this brief period the Astronef had recrossed the orbits of the Earth and Mars and passed through that marvellous region of the Solar System, the Belt of the Asteroides. Nearly a hundred million miles of their journey had lain through this zone, in which hundreds and possibly thousands of tiny planets revolve in vast orbits round the Sun.

Then had come a desert void of over three hundred million miles, through which the Astronef voyaged alone, surrounded by the ever-constant splendours of the Heavens, but visited only now and then by one of those Spectres of Space, which we call comets.

Astern, the disc of the Sun steadily diminished, and ahead, the grey-blue shape of Jupiter, the Giant of the Solar System, had grown larger and larger until now they could see it as it had never been seen before—a gigantic three-quarter moon filling up the whole Heavens in front of them almost from Zenith to Nadir.

Its four satellites, Io, Europa, Ganymede, and Calisto were distinctly visible to the naked eye, and Europa and Ganymede happened to be in such a position with regard to the Astronef that her crew could see not only the bright sides turned towards the sun, but also the black shadow-spots which they cast on the cloud-veiled face of the huge planet.

"Five hundred million miles!" said Zaidie, with a little shiver, "that seems an awful long way from home, doesn't it? Though, of course, we've brought our home with us to a certain extent. Still I often wonder what they are thinking about us on the dear old earth. I don't suppose anyone ever expects to see us again. However, it's no good getting homesick in the middle of a journey when you're outward bound."

They were now falling very rapidly towards the huge planet, and, as the crescent approached the full they were able to examine the mysterious bands as human observers had never examined them before. For hours they sat almost silent at their telescopes, trying to probe the mystery which has baffled human science since the days of Gallileo.

"I believe I was right, or, in other words, the people I got the idea from are," said Redgrave eventually, as they approached the orbit of Calisto, which revolves at a distance of about eleven hundred thousand miles from the surface of the planet.

"Those belts are made of clouds or vapour in some stage or other. The lightest—the ones along the equator and what we should call the Temperate Zones—are the highest, and therefore coolest and whitest. The dark ones are the lowest and hottest. I daresay they are more like what we call volcanic clouds. Do you see how they keep changing? That's what's bothered our astronomers. Look at that big one yonder a bit to the north, going from brown to red. I suppose that's something like the famous red spot which they have been puzzling about. What do you make of it?"

"Well," said Zaidie, looking up from her telescope, "it's quite certain that the glare must come from underneath. It can't be sunlight, because the poor old sun doesn't seem to have strength enough to make a decent sunset or sunrise here, and look how it's running along to the westward! What does that mean, do you think?"

"I should say it means that some half-formed Jovian Continent has been flung sky high by a big burst-up underneath, and that's the blaze of the incandescent stuff running along. Just fancy a continent, say ten times the size of Asia, being split up and sent flying in a few moments like that. Look, there's another one to the north. On the whole, dear, I don't think we should find the climate on the other side of those clouds very salubrious. Still, as they say the atmosphere of Jupiter is about ten thousand miles thick, we may be able to get near enough to see something of what's going on.

"Meanwhile, here comes Calisto. Look at his shadow flying across the clouds. And there's Ganymede coming up after him, and Europa behind him. Talk about eclipses, they must be about as common here as thunderstorms are with us."

"We don't have a thunderstorm every day," corrected Zaidie, "but on Jupiter they have two or three eclipses every day. Meanwhile, there goes Jupiter himself. What a difference distance makes! This little thing is only a trifle larger than our moon, and it's hiding everything else."

As she was speaking, the full-orbed disc of Calisto, measuring nearly three thousand miles across, swept between them and the planet. It shone with a clear, somewhat reddish light like that of Mars. The Astronef was feeling its attraction strongly, and Redgrave went to the levers and turned on about a fifth of the R. Force to avoid contact with it.

"Another dead world," said Redgrave, as the surface of Calisto revolved swiftly beneath them, "or, at any rate, a dying one. There must be an atmosphere of some sort, or else that snow and ice wouldn't be there, and the land would be either black or white as it was on the Moon. It's not worth while landing there. Ganymede will be much more interesting."

Zaidie took half-a-dozen photographs of the surface of Calisto while they were passing it at a distance of about a hundred miles, and then went to get lunch ready.

When they got on to the upper deck again Calisto was already a half-moon in the upper sky nearly five hundred thousand miles away and the full orb of Ganymede, shining with a pale golden light, lay outspread beneath them. A thin, bluish-grey arc of the giant planet over-arched its western edge.

"I think we shall find something like a world here," said Zaidie, when she had taken her first look through her telescope. "There's an atmosphere and what looks like thin clouds. Continents, and oceans, too! And what is that light shining up between the breaks? Isn't it something like our Aurora?"

As the Astronef fell towards the surface of Ganymede she crossed its northern pole, and the nearer they got the plainer it became that a light very like the terrestrial Aurora was playing about it, illuminating the thin, yellow clouds with a bluish-violet light, which made magnificent contrasts of colouring amongst them.

"Let us go down there and see what it's like," said Zaidie. "There must be something nice under all those lovely colours."

Redgrave checked the R. Force and the Astronef fell obliquely across the pole towards the equator. As they approached the luminous clouds Redgrave turned it on again, and they sank slowly through a glowing mist of innumerable colours, until the surface of Ganymede came into plain view about ten miles below them.

What they saw then was the strangest sight they had beheld since they had left the Earth. As far as their eyes could reach, the surface of Ganymede was covered with vast orderly patches, mostly rectangular, of what they at first took for ice, but which they soon found to be a something that was self-illuminating.

"Glorified hot houses, as I'm alive," exclaimed Redgrave. "Whole cities under glass, fields, too, and lit by electricity or something very like it. Zaidie, we shall find human beings down there."

"Well, if we do I hope they won't be like the half-human things we found on Mars! But isn't it all just lovely! Only there doesn't seem to be anything outside the cities, at least nothing but bare, flat ground with a few rugged mountains here and there. See, there's a nice level plain near the big glass city, or whatever it is. Suppose we go down there."

Redgrave checked the after-engine which was driving them obliquely over the surface of the satellite, and the Astronef fell vertically towards a bare flat plain of what looked like deep yellow sand, which spread for miles alongside one of the glittering cities of glass.

"Oh, look, they've seen us!" exclaimed Zaidie. "I do hope they're going to be as friendly as those dear people on Venus were."

"I hope so," replied Redgrave, "but if they're not, we've got the guns ready."

As he said this about twenty streams of an intense bluish light suddenly shot up all round them, concentrating themselves upon the hull of the Astronef, which was now about a mile and a half from the surface. The light was so intense that the rays of the sun were lost in it. They looked at each other, and found that their faces were almost perfectly white in it. The plain and the city below had vanished.

To look downwards was like staring straight into the focus of a ten thousand candlepower electric arc lamp. It was so intolerable that Redgrave closed the lower shutters, and meanwhile he found that the Astronef had ceased to descend. He shut off more of the R. Force, but it produced no effect. The Astronef remained stationary. Then he ordered Murgatroyd to set the propellers in motion. The engineer pulled the starting levers, and then came up out of the engine-room and said to Lord Redgrave:

"It's no good, my lord; I don't know what devil's world we've got into now, but they won't work. If I thought that engines could be bewitched—"

"Oh, nonsense, Andrew!" said his lordship rather testily. "It's perfectly simple; those people down there, whoever they are, have got some way of demagnetising us, or else they've got the R. Force too, and they're applying it against us to stop us going down. Apparently they don't want us. No, that's just to show us that they can stop us if they want to. The light's going down. Begin dropping a bit. Don't start the propellers, but just go and see that the guns are all right in case of accidents."

The old engineer nodded and went back to his engines, looking considerably scared. As he spoke the brilliancy of the light faded rapidly and the Astronef began to sink towards the surface.

As a precaution against their being allowed to drop with force enough to cause a disaster, Redgrave turned the R. Force on again and they dropped slowly towards the plain, through what seemed like a halo of perfectly white light. When she was within a couple of hundred yards of the ground a winged car of exquisitely graceful shape, rose from the roof of one of the huge glass buildings nearest to them, flew swiftly towards them, and after circling once round the dome of the upper deck, ran close alongside.

The car was occupied by two figures of distinctly human form but rather more than human stature. Both were dressed in long, close-fitting garments of what seemed like a golden brown fleece. Their heads were covered with a close hood and their hands with thin, close-fitting gloves.

"What an exceedingly handsome man!" said Zaidie, as one of them stood up. "I never saw such a noble-looking face in my life; it's half philosopher, half saint. Of course, you won't be jealous."

"Oh, nonsense!" he laughed. "It would be quite impossible to imagine you in love with either. But he is handsome, and evidently friendly—there's no mistaking that. Answer him, Zaidie; you can do it better than I can." The car had now come close alongside. The standing figure stretched its hands out, palms upward, smiled a smile which Zaidie thought was very sweetly solemn, next the head was bowed, and the gloved hands brought back and crossed over his breast. Zaidie imitated the movements exactly. Then, as the figure raised its head, she raised hers, and she found herself looking into a pair of large luminous eyes, such as she could have imagined under the brows of an angel. As they met hers, a look of unmistakable wonder and admiration came into them. Redgrave was standing just behind her; she took him by the hand and drew him beside her, saying with a little laugh:

"Now, please look as pleasant as you can; I am sure they are very friendly. A man with a face like that couldn't mean any harm."

The figure repeated the motions to Redgrave, who returned them, perhaps a trifle awkwardly. Then the car began to descend, and the figure beckoned to them to follow.

"You'd better go and wrap up, dear. From the gentleman's dress it seems pretty cold outside, though the air is evidently quite breathable," said Redgrave, as the Astronef began to drop in company with the car. "At any rate, I'll try it first, and, if it isn't, we can put on our breathing-dresses."

When Zaidie had made her winter toilet, and Redgrave had found the air to be quite respirable, but of Arctic cold, they went down the gangway ladder about twenty minutes later.

The figure had got out of the car which was lying a few yards from them on the sandy plain, and came forward to meet them with both hands outstretched.

Zaidie unhesitatingly held out hers, and a strange thrill ran through her as she felt them for the first time clasped gently by other than earthly hands, for the Venus folk had only been able to pat and stroke with their gentle little paws, somewhat as a kitten might do. The figure bowed its head again and said something in a low, melodious voice, which was, of course, quite unintelligible save for the evident friendliness of its tone. Then, releasing her hands, he took Redgrave's in the same fashion, and then led the way towards a vast, domed building of semi-opaque glass, or a substance which seemed to be something like a mixture of glass and mica, which appeared to be one of the entrance gates of the city.

When they reached it a huge sheet of frosted glass rose silently from the ground. They passed through, and it fell behind them. They found themselves in a great oval antechamber along each side of which stood triple rows of strangely shaped trees whose leaves gave off a subtle and most agreeable scent. The temperature here was several degrees higher, in fact about that of an English spring day, and Zaidie immediately threw open her big fur cloak saying:

"These good people seem to live in Winter Gardens, don't they? I don't think I shall want these things much while we're inside. I wonder what dear old Andrew would have thought of this if we could have persuaded him to leave the ship."

They followed their host through the antechamber towards a magnificent pointed arch, raised on clusters of small pillars each of a different coloured, highly polished stone which shone brilliantly in a light which seemed to come from nowhere. Another door, this time of pale, transparent, blue glass, rose as they approached; they passed under it and, as it fell behind them, half-a-dozen figures, considerably shorter and slighter than their host, came forward to meet them. He took off his gloves and cape and thick outer covering, and they were glad to follow his example for the atmosphere was now that of a warm June day.

The attendants, as they evidently were, took their wraps from them, looking at the furs and stroking them with evident wonder; but with nothing like the wonder which came into their wild, soft grey eyes when they looked at Zaidie, who, as usual when she arrived on a new world, was arrayed in one of her daintiest costumes.

Their host was now dressed in a tunic of a light blue material, which glistened with a lustre greater than that of the finest silk. It reached a little below his knees, and was confined at the waist by a sash of the same colour but of somewhat deeper hue. His feet and legs were covered with stockings of the same material and colour, and his feet, which were small for his stature and exquisitely shaped, were shod with thin sandals of a material which looked like soft felt, and which made no noise as he walked over the delicately coloured mosaic pavement of the street—for such it actually was—which ran past the gate.

When he removed his cap they expected to find that he was bald like the Martians, but they were mistaken. His well-shaped head was covered with long, thick hair of a colour something between bronze and grey. A broad band of metal, looking like light gold, passed round the upper part of his forehead, and from under this the hair fell in gentle waves to below his shoulders.

For a few moments Zaidie and Redgrave stared about them in frank and silent wonder. They were standing in a broad street running in a straight line, apparently several miles, along the edge of a city of crystal. It was lined with double rows of trees with beds of brilliantly coloured flowers between them. From this street others went off at right angles and at regular intervals. The roof of the city appeared to be composed of an infinity of domes of enormous extent, supported by tall clusters of slender pillars standing at the street corners.

Presently their host touched Redgrave on the shoulder and pointed to a four-wheeled car of light framework and exquisite design, containing seats for four besides the driver, or guide, who sat behind. He held out his hand to Zaidie, and handed her to one of the front seats just as an earth-born gentleman might have done. Then he motioned to Redgrave to sit beside her, and mounted behind them.

The car immediately began to move silently, but with considerable speed, along the left-hand side of the outer street, which, like all the others, was divided by narrow strips of russet-coloured grass and flowering shrubs.

In a few minutes it swung round to the right, crossed the road, and entered a magnificent avenue, which, after a run of some four miles, ended in a vast, park-like square, measuring at least a mile each way.

The two sides of the avenue were busy with cars like their own, some carrying six people, and others only the driver. Those on each side of the road all went in the same direction. Those nearest to the broad side-walks between the houses and the first row of trees went at a moderate speed of five or six miles an hour, but along the inner sides, near the central line of trees, they seemed to be running as high as thirty miles an hour. Their occupants were nearly all dressed in clothes made of the same glistening, silky fabric as their host wore, but the colourings were of infinite variety. It was quite easy to distinguish between the sexes, although in stature they were almost equal.

The men were nearly all clothed as their host was. The women were dressed in flowing garments something after the Greek style, but they were of brighter hues, and much more lavishly embroidered than the men's tunics were. They also wore much more jewellery. Indeed, some of the younger ones glittered from head to foot with polished metal and gleaming stones.

"Could anyone ever have dreamt of such a lovely place?" said Zaidie, after their wondering eyes had become accustomed to the marvels about them, "and yet—oh dear, now I know what it reminds me of! Flammarion's book, 'The End Of The World,' where he describes the remnants of the human race dying of cold and hunger on the Equator in places something like this. I suppose the life of poor Ganymede is giving out, and that's why they've got to live in glorified Crystal Palaces like this, poor things."

"Poor things!" laughed Redgrave, "I'm afraid I can't agree with you there, dear. I never saw a jollier looking lot of people in my life. I daresay you're quite right, but they certainly seem to view their approaching end with considerable equanimity."

"Don't be horrid, Lenox! Fancy talking in that cold-blooded way about such delightful-looking people as these, why, they are even nicer than our dear bird-folk on Venus, and, of course, they are a great deal more like ourselves."

"Wherefore it stands to reason that they must be a great deal nicer!" he replied, with a glance which brought a brighter flush to her cheeks. Then he went on: "Ah, now I see the difference."

"What difference? Between what?"

"Between the daughter of Earth and the daughters of Ganymede," he replied. "You can blush, and I don't think they can. Haven't you noticed that, although they have the most exquisite skins and beautiful eyes and hair and all that sort of thing, not a man or woman of them has any colouring. I suppose that's the result of living for generations in a hothouse."

"Very likely," she said; "but has it struck you also that all the girls and women are either beautiful or handsome, and all the men, except the ones who seem to be servants or slaves, are something like Greek gods, or, at least, the sort of men you see on the Greek sculptures?"

"Survival of the fittest, I presume. These will be the descendants of the highest races of Ganymede,—the people who conceived the idea of prolonging human life like this and were able to carry it out. The inferior races would either perish of starvation or become their servants. That's what will happen on Earth, and there is no reason why it shouldn't have happened here."

As he said this the car swung out round a broad curve into the centre of the great square, and a little cry of amazement broke from Zaidie's lips as her glance roamed over the multiplying splendours about her.

In the centre of the square, in the midst of smooth lawns and flower beds of every conceivable shape and colour, and groves of flowering trees, stood a great, domed building, which they approached through an avenue of overarching trees interlaced with flowering creepers.

The car stopped at the foot of a triple flight of stairs of dazzling whiteness which led up to a broad, arched doorway. Several groups of people were sprinkled about the avenue and steps and the wide terrace which ran along the front of the building. They looked with keen, but perfectly well-mannered surprise at their strange visitors, and seemed to be discussing their appearance; but not a step was taken towards them nor was there the slightest sign of anything like vulgar curiosity.

"What perfect manners these dear people have!" said Zaidie, as they dismounted at the foot of the staircase. "I wonder what would happen if a couple of them were to be landed from a motor car in front of the Capitol at Washington. I suppose this is their Capitol, and we've been brought here to be put through our paces. What a pity we can't talk to them. I wonder if they'd believe our story if we could tell it."

"I've no doubt they know something of it already," replied Redgrave; "they're evidently people of immense intelligence. Intellectually, I daresay, we're mere children compared with them, and it's quite possible that they have developed senses of which we have no idea."

"And perhaps," added Zaidie, "all the time that we are talking to each other our friend here is quietly reading everything that is going on in our minds."

Whether this was so or not their host gave no sign of comprehension. He led them up the steps and through the great doorway where he was met by three splendidly dressed men even taller than himself.

"I feel beastly shabby among all these gorgeously attired personages," said Redgrave, looking down at his plain tweed suit, as they were conducted with every manifestation of politeness along the magnificent vestibule beyond.

At the end of the vestibule another door opened, and they were ushered into a large hall which was evidently a council-chamber. At the further end of it were three semi-circular rows of seats made of the polished silvery metal, and in the centre and raised slightly above them another under a canopy of sky-blue silk. This seat and six others were occupied by men of most venerable aspect, in spite of the fact that their hair was just as long and thick and glossy as their host's or even as Zaidie's own.

The ceremony of introduction was exceedingly simple. Though they could not, of course, understand a word he said, it was evident from his eloquent gestures that their host described the way in which they had come from Space, and landed on the surface of the World of the Crystal Cities, as Zaidie subsequently rechristened Ganymede.

The President of the Senate or Council spoke a few sentences in a deep musical tone. Then their host, taking their hands, led them up to his seat, and the President rose and took them by both hands in turn. Then, with a grave smile of greeting, he bent his head and resumed his seat. They joined hands in turn with each of the six senators present, bowed their farewells in silence, and then went back with their host to the car.

They ran down the avenue, made a curving sweep round to the left—for all the paths in the great square were laid in curves, apparently to form a contrast to the straight streets—and presently stopped before the porch of one of the hundred palaces which surrounded it. This was their host's house, and their home during the rest of their sojourn on Ganymede.

It is, as I have already said, greatly to be regretted that the narrow limits of these brief narratives make it impossible for me to describe in detail all the experiences of Lord Redgrave and his bride during their Honeymoon in Space. Hereafter I hope to have an opportunity of doing so with the more ample assistance of her ladyship's diary; but for the present I must content myself with the outlines of the picture which she may some day consent to fill in.

The period of Ganymede's revolution round its gigantic primary is seven days, three hours, and forty-three minutes, practically a terrestrial week, and both of the daring navigators of Space describe this as the most interesting and delightful week in their lives, not even excepting the period which they spent in the Eden of the Morning Star.

There the inhabitants had never learnt to sin; here they had learnt the lesson that sin is mere foolishness, and that no really sensible or properly educated man or woman thinks crime worth committing.

The life of the Crystal Cities, of which they visited four in different parts of the satellite, using the Astronef as their vehicle, was one of peaceful industry and calm innocent enjoyment. It was quite plain that their first impressions of this aged world were correct. Outside the cities spread a universal desert on which life was impossible. There was hardly any moisture in the thin atmosphere. The rivers had dwindled into rivulets and the seas into vast, shallow marshes. The heat received from the Sun was only about a twenty-fifth of that received on the surface of the Earth, and this was drawn to the cities and collected and preserved under their glass domes by a number of devices which displayed superhuman intelligence.

The dwindling supplies of water were hoarded in vast subterranean reservoirs and by means of a perfect system of redistillation the priceless fluid was used over and over again both for human purposes and for irrigating the land within the cities.

Still the total quantity was steadily diminishing, for it was not only evaporating from the surface, but, as the orb cooled more and more rapidly towards its centre, it descended deeper and deeper below the surface, and could now only be reached by means of marvellously constructed borings and pumping machinery which extended down several miles into the ground.

The dwindling store of heat in the centre of the little world, which had now cooled through more than half its bulk, was utilised for warming the air of the cities, and also to drive the machinery which propelled it through the streets and squares. All work was done by electricity developed directly from this source, which also actuated the repulsive engines which had prevented the Astronef from descending.

In short, the inhabitants of Ganymede were engaged in a steady, ceaseless struggle to utilise the expiring natural forces of their world to prolong to the latest possible date their own lives and the exquisitely refined civilisation to which they had attained. They were, in fact, in exactly the same position in which the distant descendants of the human race may one day be expected to find themselves.

Their domestic life, as Zaidie and Lenox saw it while they were the guests of their host, was the perfection of simplicity and comfort, and their public life was characterised by a quiet but intense intellectuality which, as Zaidie had said, made them feel very much like children who had only just learnt to speak.

As they possessed magnificent telescopes, far surpassing any on earth, the wanderers were able to survey, not only the Solar System, but the other systems far beyond its limits as no other of their kind had ever been able to do before. They did not look through or into the telescopes. The lens was turned upon the object, which was thrown, enormously magnified, upon screens of what looked something like ground glass some fifty feet square. It was thus that they saw, not only the whole visible surface of Jupiter as he revolved above them and they about him, but also their native earth, sometimes a pale silver disc or crescent close to the edge of the Sun, visible only in the morning and the evening of Jupiter, and at other times like a little black spot crossing the glowing surface.

It was, of course, inevitable that the Astronef—which Murgatroyd could not be persuaded to leave once during their stay—should prove an object of intense interest to their hosts. They had solved the problem of the Resolution of Forces, and, as they were shown pictorially, a vessel had been made which embodied the principles of attraction and repulsion. It had risen from the surface of Ganymede, and then, possibly because its engines could not develop sufficient repulsive force, the tremendous pull of the giant planet had dragged it away. It had vanished through the cloud-belts towards the flaming surface beneath—and the experiment had never been repeated.

Here, however, was a vessel which had actually, as Redgrave had convinced his hosts by means of celestial maps and drawings of his own, left a planet close to the Sun, and safely crossed the tremendous gulf of six hundred and fifty million miles which separated Jupiter from the centre of the system. Moreover he had twice proved her powers by taking his host and two of his newly-made friends, the chief astronomers of Ganymede, on a short trip across space to Calisto and Europa, the second satellite of Jupiter, which, to their very grave interest they found had already passed the stage in which Ganymede was, and had lapsed into the icy silence of death.

It was these two journeys which led to the last adventure of the Astronef in the Jovian System. Both Redgrave and Zaidie had determined, at whatever risk, to pass through the cloud-belts of Jupiter, and catch a glimpse, if only a glimpse, of a world in the making. Their host and the two astronomers, after a certain amount of quiet discussion, accepted their invitation to accompany them, and on the morning of the eighth day after their landing on Ganymede, the Astronef rose from the plain outside the Crystal City, and directed her course towards the centre of the vast disc of Jupiter.

She was followed by the telescopes of all the observatories until she vanished through the brilliant cloud-band, eighty-five thousand miles long and some five thousand miles broad, which stretched from east to west of the planet. At the same moment the voyagers lost sight of Ganymede and his sister satellites.

The temperature of the interior of the Astronef began to rise as soon as the upper cloud-belt was passed. Under this, spread out a vast field of brown-red cloud, rent here and there into holes and gaps like those storm-cavities in the atmosphere of the Sun, which are commonly known as sun-spots. This lower stratum of cloud appeared to be the scene of terrific storms, compared with which the fiercest earthly tempests were mere zephyrs.

After falling some five hundred miles further they found themselves surrounded by what seemed an ocean of fire, but still the internal temperature had only risen from seventy to ninety-five. The engines were well under control. Only about a fourth of the total R. Force was being developed, and the Astronef was dropping swiftly, but steadily.

Redgrave, who was in the conning-tower controlling the engines, beckoned to Zaidie and said:

"Shall we go on?"

"Yes," she said. "Now we've got as far as this I want to see what Jupiter is like, and where you are not afraid to go, I'll go."

"If I'm afraid at all it's only because you are with me, Zaidie," he replied, "but I've only got a fourth of the power turned on yet, so there's plenty of margin."

The Astronef, therefore, continued to sink through what seemed to be a fathomless ocean of whirling, blazing clouds, and the internal temperature went on rising slowly but steadily. Their guests, without showing the slightest sign of any emotion, walked about the upper deck now singly and now together, apparently absorbed by the strange scene about them.

At length, after they had been dropping for some five hours by Astronef time, one of them, uttering a sharp exclamation, pointed to an enormous rift about fifty miles away. A dull, red glare was streaming up out of it. The next moment the brown cloud-floor beneath them seemed to split up into enormous wreaths of vapour, which whirled up on all sides of them, and a few minutes later they caught their first glimpse of the true surface of Jupiter.

It lay as nearly as they could judge, some two thousand miles beneath them, a distance which the telescopes reduced to less than twenty; and they saw for a few moments the world that was in the making. Through floating seas of misty steam they beheld what seemed to them to be vast continents shape themselves and melt away into oceans of flames. Whole mountain ranges of glowing lava were hurled up miles high to take shape for an instant and then fall away again, leaving fathomless gulfs of fiery mist in their place.

Then waves of molten matter rose up again out of the gulfs, tens of miles high and hundreds of miles long, surged forward, and met with a concussion like that of millions of earthly thunder-clouds. Minute after minute they remained writhing and struggling with each other, flinging up spurts of flaming matter far above their crests. Other waves followed them, climbing up their bases as a sea-surge runs up the side of a smooth, slanting rock. Then from the midst of them a jet of living fire leapt up hundreds of miles into the lurid atmosphere above, and then, with a crash and a roar which shook the vast Jovian firmament, the battling lava-waves would split apart and sink down into the all-surrounding fire-ocean, like two grappling giants who had strangled each other in their final struggle.

"It's just Hell let loose!" said Murgatroyd to himself as he looked down upon the terrific scene through one of the portholes of the engine-room; "and, with all respect to my lord and her ladyship, those that come this near almost deserve to stop in it."

Meanwhile, Redgrave and Zaidie and their three guests were so absorbed in the tremendous spectacle, that for a few moments no one noticed that they were dropping faster and faster towards the world which Murgatroyd, according to his lights, had not inaptly described. As for Zaidie, all her fears were for the time being lost in wonder, until she saw her husband take a swift glance round upwards and downwards, and then go up into the conning-tower. She followed him quickly, and said:

"What is the matter, Lenox, are we falling too quickly?"

"Much faster than we should," he replied, sending a signal to Murgatroyd to increase the force by three-tenths.

The answering signal came back, but still the Astronef continued to fall with terrific rapidity, and the awful landscape beneath them—a landscape of fire and chaos—broadened out and became more and more distinct.

He sent two more signals down in quick succession. Three-fourths of the whole repulsive power of the engines was now being exerted, a force which would have been sufficient to hurl the Astronef up from the surface of the Earth like a feather in a whirlwind. Her downward course became a little slower, but still she did not stop. Zaidie, white to the lips, looked down upon the hideous scene beneath and slipped her hand through Redgrave's arm. He looked at her for an instant and then turned his head away with a jerk, and sent down the last signal.

The whole energy of the engines was now directing the maximum of the R. Force against the surface of Jupiter, but still, as every moment passed in a speechless agony of apprehension, it grew nearer and nearer. The fire-waves mounted higher and higher, the roar of the fiery surges grew louder and louder. Then, in a momentary lull, he put his arm round her, drew her close up to him, and kissed her and said:

"That's all we can do, dear. We've come too close and he's too strong for us."

She returned his kiss and said quite steadily:

"Well, at any rate, I'm with you, and it won't last long, will it?"

"Not very long now, I'm afraid," he said between his clenched teeth.

Almost the next moment they felt a little jerk beneath their feet—a jerk upwards; and Redgrave shook himself out of the half stupor into which he was falling and said:

"Hallo, what's that! I believe we're stopping—yes, we are—and we're beginning to rise, too. Look, dear, the clouds are coming down upon us—fast too! I wonder what sort of miracle that is. Ay, what's the matter, little woman?"

Zaidie's head had dropped heavily on his shoulder. A glance showed him that she had fainted. He could do nothing more in the conning-tower, so he picked her up and carried her towards the companion-way, past his three guests, who were standing in the middle of the upper deck round a table on which lay a large sheet of paper.

He took her below and laid her on her bed, and in a few minutes he had brought her to and told her that it was all right. Then he gave her a drink of brandy and water, and went back on to the upper deck. As he reached the top of the stairway one of the astronomers came towards him with the sheet of paper in his hand, smiling gravely, and pointing to a sketch upon it.

He took the paper under one of the electric lights and looked at it. The sketch was a plan of the Jovian System. There were some signs written along one side, which he did not understand, but he divined that they were calculations. Still, there was no mistaking the diagram. There was a circle representing the huge bulk of Jupiter; there were four smaller circles at varying distances in a nearly straight line from it, and between the nearest of these and the planet was the figure of the Astronef, with an arrow pointing upwards.

"Ah, I see!" he said, forgetting for a moment that the other did not understand him, "That was the miracle! The four satellites came into line with us just as the pull of Jupiter was getting too much for our engines, and their combined pull just turned the scale. Well, thank God for that, sir, for in a few minutes more we should have been cinders!"

The astronomer smiled again as he took the paper back. Meanwhile the Astronef was rushing upward like a meteor through the clouds. In ten minutes the limits of the Jovian atmosphere were passed. Stars and gems and planets blazed out of the black vault of Space, and the great disc of the World that Is to Be once more covered the floor of Space beneath them—an ocean of cloud, covering continents of lava and seas of flame.

They passed Io and Europa, which changed from new to full moons as they sped by towards the Sun, and then the golden yellow crescent of Ganymede also began to fill out to the half and full disc, and by the tenth hour of earth-time after they had risen from its surface, the Astronef was once more lying beside the gate of the Crystal City.

At midnight on the second night after their return, the ringed shape of Saturn, attended by his eight satellites, hung in the zenith magnificently inviting. The Astronef's engines had been replenished after the exhaustion of their struggle with the might of Jupiter. Zaidie and Lenox said farewell to their friends of the dying world. The doors of the air chamber closed. The signal tinkled in the engine-room, and a few moments later a blur of white lights on the brown background of the surrounding desert was all they could distinguish of the Crystal City under whose domes they had seen and learnt so much.

IN SATURN'S REALM

by George Griffith

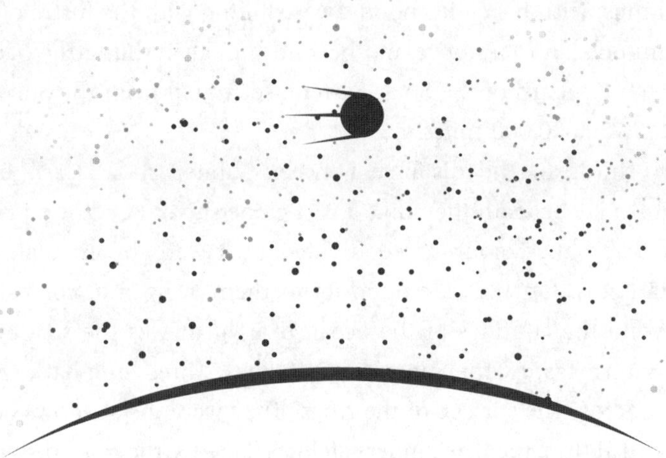

The relative position of the two giants of the Solar System at the moment when the Astronef left the surface of Ganymede, the third and largest satellite of Jupiter, was such that she had to make a journey of rather more than 340,000,000 miles before she passed within the confines of the Saturnian System.

At first her speed, as shown by the observations which Redgrave took by means of instruments designed for such a voyage by Professor Rennick, was comparatively slow. This was due to the tremendous "pull" or attraction of Jupiter and its four moons on the fabric of the Star Navigator; but this backward drag rapidly decreased as the pull of Saturn and his System began to overmaster that of Jupiter.

It so happened, too, that Uranus, the next outer planet of the Solar System, revolving round the Sun at the tremendous distance of more than 1,700,000,000 miles, was approaching its conjunction with Saturn, and thus the pull of the two huge orbs and their systems of satellites acted together on the tiny bulk of the Astronef, producing a constant acceleration of speed.

Jupiter and his System dropped behind, sinking, as it seemed to the wanderers, down into the bottomless gulf of Space, but still forming by far the most brilliant and splendid object in the skies. The far distant Sun which, seen from the Saturnian System, has only about a ninetieth of the superficial extent which he presents to the Earth, dwindled away rapidly until it began to look like a huge planet, with the Earth, Venus, Mars, and Mercury as satellites. Beyond the orbit of Saturn, Uranus, with his eight moons, was shining with the lustre of a star of the first magnitude, and far above and beyond him again hung the pale disc of Neptune, the outer guard of the Solar System, separated from the Sun by a gulf of more than 2,750,000,000 miles.

When two-thirds of the distance between Jupiter and Saturn had been traversed, Saturn lay beneath them like a vast globe surrounded by an enormous circular ocean of many-coloured fire, divided, as it were, by circular shores of shade and darkness. On the side opposite to them a gigantic conical shadow extended beyond the confines of the ocean of light. It was the shadow of half the globe of Saturn cast by the Sun across his rings. Three little dark spots were also travelling across the surface of the rings. They were the shadows of Mimas, Encealadus, and Tethys, the three inner satellites. Japetus, the most distant, which revolves at a distance ten times greater than that of the Moon from the Earth, was rising to their left above the edge of the rings, a pale, yellow, little disc shining feebly against the black background of Space. The rest of the eight satellites were hidden behind the enormous bulk of the planet, and the infinitely vaster area of the rings.

Day after day Zaidie and her husband had been exhausting the possibilities of the English language in attempting to describe to each other the multiplying marvels of the wondrous scene which they were approaching at a speed of more than a hundred miles a second, and at length Zaidie, after nearly an hour's absolute silence, during which they sat with eyes fastened to their telescopes, looked up and said:

"It's no use, Lenox, all the fine words that we've been trying to think of have just been wasted. The angels may have a language that you could describe that in, but we haven't. If it wouldn't be something like blasphemy I should drop down to the commonplace, and call Saturn a celestial spinning-top, with bands of light and shadow instead of colours all round it."

"Not at all a bad simile either," laughed Redgrave, as he got up from his chair with a yawn and a stretch of his athletic limbs, "still, it's as well that you said celestial, for, after all, that's about the best word we've found yet. Certainly the ringed world is the most nearly heavenly thing we've seen so far."

"But," he went on, "I think it's about time we were stopping this headlong fall of ours. Do you see how the landscape is spreading out round us? That means that we're dropping pretty fast. Whereabouts would you like to land? At present we're heading straight for the north pole."

"I think I'd rather see what the rings are like first," said Zaidie; "couldn't we go across them?"

"Certainly we can," he replied, "only we'll have to be a bit careful."

"Careful, what of—collisions? I suppose you're thinking of Proctor's explanation that the rings are formed of multitudes of tiny satellites?"

"Yes, but I should go a little farther than that, I should say that his rings and his eight satellites are to Saturn what the planets generally and the ring of the Asteroides are to the Sun, and if that is the case—I mean if we find the rings made up of myriads of tiny bodies flying round with Saturn—it might get a bit risky.

"You see the outside ring is a bit over 160,000 miles across, and it revolves in less than eleven hours. In other words we might find the ring a sort of celestial maelstrom, and if we once got into the whirl, and Saturn exerted his full pull on us, we might become a satellite, too, and go on swinging round with the rest for a good bit of eternity."

"Very well, then," she said, "of course we don't want to do anything of that sort, but there's something else I think we could do," she went on, taking up a copy of Proctor's "Saturn and its System," which she had been reading just after breakfast. "You see those rings are, all together, about 10,000 miles broad; there's a gap of about 1700 miles between the big dark one and the middle bright one, and it's nearly 10,000 miles from the edge of the bright ring to the surface of Saturn. Now why shouldn't we get in between the inner ring and the planet? If Proctor was right and the rings are made of tiny satellites and there are myriads of them, of course they'll pull up while Saturn pulls down. In fact Flammarion says somewhere, that along Saturn's equator there is no weight at all."

"Quite possible," said Redgrave, "and, if you like, we'll go and prove it. Of course, if the Astronef weighs absolutely nothing between Saturn and the rings, we can easily get away. The only thing that I object to is getting into this 170,000 mile vortex, being whizzed round with Saturn every ten and a half hours, and sauntering round the Sun at 21,000 miles an hour."

"Don't," she said, "really it isn't good to think about these things, situated as we are. Fancy, in a single year of Saturn there are nearly 25,000 days. Why, we should each of us be about thirty years older when we got round, even if we lived, which, of course, we shouldn't. By the way, how long could we live for, if the worst came to the worst?"

"About two earth-years at the outside," he replied, "but, of course, we shall be home long before that."

"If we don't become one of the satellites of Saturn," she replied, "or get dragged away by something into the outer depths of Space."

Meanwhile the downward speed of the Astronef had been considerably checked. The vast circle of the rings seemed to suddenly expand, though it now covered the whole floor of the vault of Space.

As the Astronef dropped towards what might be called the limit of the northern tropic of Saturn, the spectacle presented by the rings became every minute more and more marvellous—purple and silver, black and gold, dotted with myriads of brilliant points of many-coloured lights, they stretched upwards like vast rainbows in the Saturnian sky as the Astronef's position changed with regard to the horizon of the planet. The nearer they approached the surface, the nearer the gigantic arch of the many coloured rings approached the zenith. Sun and stars sank down behind it, for now they were dropping through the fifteen-year-long twilight that reigns over that portion of the globe of Saturn which during half of his year of thirty terrestrial years is turned away from the Sun.

The further they dropped towards the rings the more certain it became that the theory of the great English astronomer was the correct one. Seen through the telescopes at a distance of only thirty or forty thousand miles, it became perfectly plain that the outer or darker ring as seen from the Earth was composed of myriads of tiny bodies so far separated from each other that the rayless blackness of Space could be seen through them.

"It's quite evident," said Redgrave, "that those are rings of what we should call meteorites on earth, atoms of matter which Saturn threw off into Space after the satellites were formed."

"And I shouldn't wonder, if you will excuse my interrupting you," said Zaidie, "if the moons themselves have been made up of a lot of these things going together when they were only gas, or nebula or something of that sort. In fact, when Saturn was a good deal younger than he is now, he may have had a lot more rings and no moons, and now these aerolites, or whatever they are, can't come together and make moons, because they've got too solid."

Meanwhile the Astronef was dropping rapidly down towards the port on of Saturn's surface which was illuminated by the rays of the Sun, streaming under the lower arch of the inner ring.

As they passed under it the whole scene suddenly changed. The rings vanished. Overhead was an arch of brilliant light a hundred miles thick, spanning the whole of the visible heavens. Below lay the sunlit surface of Saturn divided into light and dark bands of enormous breadth.

The band immediately below them was of a brilliant silver-grey, very much like the central zone of Jupiter. North of this on the one side stretched the long shadow of the rings, and southward other bands of alternating white and gold and deep purple succeeded each other till they were lost in the curvature of the vast planet. The poles were of course invisible since the Astronef was now too near to the surface; but on their approach they had seen unmistakable evidence of snow and ice.

As soon as they were exactly under the Ring-arch, Redgrave shut off the R. Force, and, somewhat to their astonishment, the Astronef began to revolve slowly on its axis, giving them the idea that the Saturnian System was revolving round them. The arch seemed to sink beneath their feet while the belts of the planet rose above them.

"What on earth is the matter?" said Zaidie. "Everything has gone upside down."

"Which shows." replied Redgrave, "that as soon as the Astronef became neutral the rings pulled harder than the planet, I suppose because we're so near to them, and, instead of falling on to Saturn, we shall have to push up at him."

"Oh yes, I see that," said Zaidie, "but after all it does look a little bit bewildering, doesn't it, to be on your feet one minute and on your head the next?"

"It is, rather; but you ought to be getting accustomed to that sort of thing now. In a few minutes neither you, nor I, nor anything else will have any weight. We shall be just between the attraction of the Rings and Saturn, so you'd better go and sit down, for if you were to give a bit of an extra spring in walking you might be knocking that pretty head of yours against the roof," said Redgrave, as he went to turn the R. Force on to the edge of the Rings.

A vast sea of silver cloud seemed now to descend upon them. Then they entered it, and for nearly half-an-hour the Astronef was totally enveloped in a sea of pearl-grey luminous mist.

"Atmosphere!" said Redgrave, as he went to the conning-tower and signalled to Murgatroyd to start the propellers. They continued to rise and the mist began to drift past them in patches, showing that the propellers were driving them ahead.

They now rose swiftly towards the surface of the planet. The cloud wrack got thinner and thinner, and presently they found themselves floating in a clear atmosphere between two seas of cloud, the one above them being much less dense than the one below.

"I believe we shall see Saturn on the other side of that," said Zaidie, looking up at it. "Oh dear, there we are going round again."

"Reaching the point of neutral attraction," said Redgrave; "once more you'd better sit down in case of accidents."

Instead of dropping into her deck chair as she would have done on Earth, she took hold of the arms and pulled herself into it, saying:

"Really it seems rather absurd to have to do this sort of thing. Fancy having to hold yourself into a chair. I suppose I hardly weigh anything at all now."

"Not much," said Redgrave, stooping down and taking hold of the end of the chair with both hands. Without any apparent effort he raised her about five feet from the floor, and held her there while the Astronef made another revolution. For a moment he let go, and she and the chair floated between the roof and the floor of the deck-chamber. Then he pulled the chair away from under her, and as the floor of the vessel once more turned towards Saturn, he took hold of her hands and brought her to her feet on deck again.

"I ought to have had a photograph of you like that!" he laughed. "I wonder what they'd think of it at home?"

"If you had taken one I should certainly have broken the negative. The very idea, a photograph of me standing on nothing! Besides, they'd never believe it on Earth."

"We might have got old Andrew to make an affidavit to that effect," he began.

"Don't talk nonsense, Lenox! Look! There's something much more interesting. There's Saturn at last. Now I wonder if we shall find any sort of life there—and shall we be able to breathe the air?"

"I hardly think so," he said, as the Astronef dropped slowly through the thin cloud-veil. "You know spectrum analysis has proved that there is a gas in Saturn's atmosphere which we know nothing about, and, whatever it may be for the inhabitants it's not very likely that it would agree with us, so I think we'd better be content with our own. Besides, the atmosphere is so enormously dense that even if we could breathe it it might squash us up. You see we're only accustomed to fifteen pounds on the square inch, and it may be hundreds of pounds here."

"Well," said Zaidie, "I haven't got any particular desire to be flattened out like that, or squeezed dry like an orange. It's not at all a nice idea, is it? But, look, Lenox," she went on, pointing downwards, "surely this isn't air at all, or at least it's something between air and water. Aren't these things swimming about in it—something like fish in the sea? They can't be clouds, and they aren't either fish or birds. They don't fly or float. Well, this is certainly more wonderful than anything else we've seen, though it doesn't look very pleasant. They're not nice looking, are they? I wonder if they are at all dangerous!"

While she was saying this Zaidie had gone to her telescope, and was sweeping the surface of Saturn, which was now about 100 miles distant. Her husband was doing the same. In fact, for the time being they were all eyes, for they were looking on a stranger sight than human beings had ever seen before.

Underneath the inner cloud-veil the atmosphere of Saturn appeared to them somewhat as the lower depths of the ocean would appear to a diver, granted that he was able to see for hundreds of miles about him. Its colour was a pale greenish yellow. The outside thermometers showed that the temperature was a hundred and seventy-five. In fact the interior of the Astronef was getting uncomfortably like a Turkish bath, and Redgrave took the opportunity of at once freshening and cooling the air by releasing a little from the cylinders where it was stored in liquid form.

From what they could see of the surface of Saturn it seemed to be a dead level, greyish-brown in colour, and not divided into oceans and continents. In fact there were no signs whatever of water within range of their telescopes. There was nothing that looked like cities, or any human habitations, but the ground, as they got nearer to it, seemed to be covered with a very dense vegetable growth, not unlike gigantic forms of seaweed, and of somewhat the same colour. In fact, as Zaidie remarked, the surface of Saturn was not at all unlike what the floors of the ocean of the Earth might be if they were laid bare.

It was evident that the life of this portion of Saturn was not what, for want of a more exact word, might be called terrestrial. Its inhabitants, however they were constituted, floated about in the depths of this semi-gaseous ocean as the denizens of earthly seas did in the terrestrial oceans. Already their telescopes enabled them to make out enormous moving shapes, black and grey-brown and pale red, swimming about, evidently by their own volition, rising and falling and often sinking down on to the gigantic vegetation which covered the surface, possibly for the purpose of feeding. But it was also evident that they resembled the inhabitants of earthly oceans in another respect since it was easy to see that they preyed upon each other.

"I don't like the look of those creatures at all," said Zaidie when the Astronef had come to a stop and was floating about five miles above the surface. "They're altogether too uncanny. They look to me something like jelly-fish about the size of whales only they have eyes and mouths. Did you ever see such awful looking eyes, bigger than soup-plates and as bright as a cat's. I suppose that's because of the dim light. And the nasty wormy sort of way they swim, or fly, or whatever it is. Lenox, I don't know what the rest of Saturn may be like, but I certainly don't like this part. It's quite too creepy and unearthly for my taste. Look at the horrors fighting and eating each other. That's the only bit of earthly character they've got about them; the big ones eating the little ones. I hope they won't take the Astronef for something nice to eat."

"They'd find her a pretty tough morsel if they did," laughed Redgrave, "but still we may as well get some speed on her in case of accident."

In obedience to a signal to Murgatroyd, the propellers began to revolve, beating the dense air and driving the Star Navigator about twenty miles an hour through the depths of this strangely-peopled ocean.

They approached nearer and nearer to the surface, and as they did so the strange creatures about them grew more and more numerous. They were certainly the most extraordinary living things that human eyes had looked upon. Zaidie's comparison to the whale and the jelly fish was by no means incorrect; only when they got near enough to them they found, to their astonishment, that they were double-headed—that is to say, they had a head furnished with mouth, nostrils, ear-holes, and eyes at each end of their bodies.

The larger of the creatures appeared to have a certain amount of respect for each other. Now and then they witnessed a battle-royal between two of the monsters who were pursuing the same prey. Their method of attack was as follows: the assailant would rise above his opponent or prey, and then, dropping on to its back, envelope it and begin tearing at its sides and under parts with huge beak-like jaws, somewhat resembling those of the largest kind of the earthly octopus, only very much larger. The substance composing their bodies appeared to be not unlike that of a terrestrial jelly-fish, but much denser, and having the tenacity of soft India rubber save at the double ends, where it was much harder, in fact a good deal more like horn.

When one of them had overpowered an enemy or a victim the two sank down into the vegetation, and the victor began to eat the vanquished. Their means of locomotion consisted of huge fins, or rather half fins, half wings, of which they had three laterally arranged behind each head, and four much longer and narrower, above and below, which seemed to be used mainly for steering purposes.

They moved with equal ease in either direction, and they appeared to rise or fall by inflating or deflating the middle portions of their bodies, somewhat as fish do with their swimming bladders.

The light in the lower regions of this strange ocean was dimmer than earthly twilight, although the Astronef was steadily making her way beneath the arch of the rings towards the sunlit hemisphere.

"I wonder what the effect of the searchlight would be on these fellows!" said Redgrave. "Those huge eyes of theirs are evidently only suited to dim light. Let's try and dazzle some of them."

"I hope it won't be a case of the moths and the candle!" said Zaidie. "They don't seem to have taken much interest in us so far. Perhaps they haven't been able to see properly, but suppose they were attracted by the light and began crowding round us and fastening on to us, as the horrible things do with each other. What should we do then? They might drag us down and perhaps keep us there; but there's one thing, they'd never eat us, because we could keep closed up and die respectably together."

"Not much fear of that, little woman," he said, "we're too strong for them. Hardened steel and toughened glass ought to be more than a match for a lot of exaggerated jelly-fish like these," said Redgrave, as he switched on the head search-light. "We've come here to see strange things and we may as well see them. Ah, would you my friend. No, this is not one of your sort, and it isn't meant to eat."

A huge, double-headed monster, apparently some four hundred feet long, came floating towards them as the search-light flashed out, and others began instantly to crowd about them, just as Zaidie had feared.

"Lenox, for Heaven's sake be careful!" cried Zaidie, shrinking up beside him as the huge, hideous head, with its saucer eyes and enormous beak-like jaws wide open, came towards them. "And look, there are more coming. Can't we go up and get away from them?"

"Wait a minute, little woman," replied Redgrave, who was beginning to feel the passion of adventure thrilling in his nerves. "If we fought the Martian air fleet and licked it I think we can manage these things. Let's see how he likes the light."

As he spoke he flashed the full glare of the five thousand candle-power lamp full on to the creature's great cat-like eyes. Instantly it bent itself up into an arc. The two heads, each the exact image of the other, came together. The four eyes glared half dazzled into the conning-tower and the four huge jaws snapped viciously together.

"Lenox, Lenox, for goodness sake let us go up!" cried Zaidie shrinking still closer to him. "That thing's too horrible to look at."

"It is a beast, isn't it?" he said, "but I think we can cut him in two without much trouble."

He pressed one of the buttons on the signal board three times quickly and once slowly. It was the signal for full speed on the propellers, that is to say about a hundred earth-miles an hour. The Astronef ought to have sprung forward and driven her ram through the huge, brick-red body of the hideous creature which was now only a couple of hundred yards from them; but instead of that a slow, jarring, grinding thrill seemed to run through her, and she stopped. The next moment Murgatroyd put his head up through the companion-way which led from the upper deck to the conning-tower, and said in a tone whose calm indicated, as usual, resignation to the worst that could happen:

"My lord, two of those beasts, fishes or live balloons, or whatever they are, have come across the propellers. They're cut up a good bit, but I've had to stop the engines, and they're clinging all round the after part. We're going down, too. Shall I disconnect the propellers and turn on the repulsion?"

"Yes, certainly, Andrew!" cried Zaidie, "and all of it, too. Look, Lenox, that horrible thing is coming. Suppose it broke the glass, and we couldn't breathe this atmosphere!"

As she spoke the enormous, double-headed body advanced until it completely enveloped the forward part of the Astronef. The two hideous heads came close to the sides of the conning-tower; the huge, palely luminous eyes looked in upon them. Zaidie, in her terror, even thought that she saw something like human curiosity in them.

Then, as Murgatroyd disappeared to obey the orders which Redgrave had sanctioned with a quick nod, the heads approached still closer, and she heard the ends of the pointed jaws, which she now saw were armed with shark-like teeth, striking against the thick glass walls of the conning-tower.

"Don't be frightened, dear!" he said, putting his arm round her, just as he had done when they thought they were falling into the fiery seas of Jupiter. "You'll see something happen to this gentleman soon. Big and all as he is there won't be much left of him in a few minutes. They are like those monsters they found in the lowest depths of our own seas. They can only live under tremendous pressure. That's why we didn't find any of them up above. This chap'll burst like a bubble presently. Meanwhile, there's no use in stopping here. Suppose you go below and brew some coffee and bring it up on deck with a drop of brandy in it, while I go and see how things are looking aft. It doesn't do you any good, you know, to be looking at monsters of this sort. You can see what's left of them later on."

Zaidie was not at all sorry to obey him, for the horrible sight had almost sickened her.

They were still under the arch of the rings, and so, when the full strength of the R. Force was directed against the body of Saturn, the vessel sprang upwards like a projectile fired from a cannon.

Redgrave went back into the conning-tower to see what happened to their assailant. It was already trying vainly to detach itself and sink back into a more congenial element. As the pressure of the atmosphere decreased its huge body swelled up into still huger proportions. The skin on the two heads puffed up as though air was being pumped in under it. The great eyes protruded out of their sockets; the jaws opened widely as though the creature were gasping for breath.

Meanwhile Murgatroyd was seeing something very similar at the after end, and wondering what was going to happen to his propellers, the blades of which were deeply imbedded in the jelly-like flesh of the monsters.

The Astronef leaped higher and higher, and the hideous bodies which were clinging to her swelled out huger and huger, and Redgrave even fancied that he heard something like the cries of pain from both heads on either side of the conning-tower. They passed through the inner cloud-veil, and then the Astronef began to turn on her axis, and, just as the outer envelope came into view the enormously distended bulk of the monsters collapsed, and their fragments, seeming now more like the tatters of a burst balloon, dropped from the body of the Astronef and floated away down into what had once been their native element.

"Difference of environment means a lot, after all," said Redgrave to himself. "I should have called that either a lie or a miracle if I hadn't seen it, and I'm jolly glad I sent Zaidie down below."

"Here's your coffee, Lenox," said Zaidie's voice from the upper deck, "only it doesn't seem to want to stop in the cups, and the cups keep getting off the saucers. I suppose we're turning upside down again."

Redgrave stepped somewhat gingerly on to the deck, for his body had so little weight under the double attraction of Saturn and the Rings that a very slight effort would have sent him flying up to the roof of the deck-chamber.

"That's exactly as you please," he said, "just hold that table steady a minute. We shall have our centre of gravity back soon. And now, as to the main question, suppose we take a trip across the sunlit hemisphere of Saturn to, what I suppose we should call, on Earth, the South Pole. We can get resistance from the Rings, and as we are here we may as well see what the rest of Saturn is like. You see, if our theory is correct as to the Rings gathering up most of the atmosphere of Saturn about its equator, we shall get to higher altitudes where the air is thinner and more like our own, and therefore it is quite possible that we shall find different forms of life in it too—or if you've had enough of Saturn and would prefer a trip to Uranus?"

"No, thanks," said Zaidie quickly. "To tell you the truth, Lenox, I've had almost enough star-wandering for one honeymoon, and though we've seen nice things as well as horrible things—especially those ghastly, slimy creatures down there—I'm beginning to feel a bit homesick for good old mother Earth. You see, we're nearly a thousand million miles from home, and, even with you, it makes one feel a bit lonely. I vote we explore the rest of this hemisphere up to the pole, and then, as they say at sea—I mean our sea—'bout ship, and see if we can find our own old world again. After all, it's more homelike than any of these, isn't it?"

"Just take your telescope and look at it," said Redgrave, pointing towards the Sun, with its little cluster of attendant planets. "It looks something like one of Jupiter's little moons down there, doesn't it, only not quite as big?"

"Yes, it does, but that doesn't matter. The fact is that it's there, and we know what it's like, and it's home, if it is a thousand million miles away, and that's everything."

By this time they had passed through the outer band of clouds. The huge, sunlit arch of the Rings towered up to the zenith, and apparently overarched the whole heavens. Below and in front of them lay the enormous semi-circle of the hemisphere which was turned towards the Sun, shrouded by its many coloured bands of clouds. The Repulsive Force was directed strongly against the lower Ring, and the Astronef dropped rapidly in a slanting direction through the cloud-bands towards the southern temperate zone of the planet.

They passed through the second, or dark, cloud-band at the rate of about three thousand miles an hour, aided by the Repulsion against the Rings and, the attraction of the planet, and soon after lunch, the materials of which now consented to remain on the table, they passed through the clouds and found themselves in a new world of wonders.

On a far vaster scale, it was the Earth during that period of its development which is called the Reptilian Age. The atmosphere was still dense and loaded with aqueous vapour, but the waters had already been divided from the land.

They passed over vast, marshy continents and islands, and warm seas, above which thin clouds of steam still hung. They passed through these, and, as they swept southward with the propellers working at their utmost speed, they caught glimpses of giant forms rising out of the steamy waters near the land; of others crawling slowly over it, dragging their huge bulk through a tremendous vegetation, which they crushed down as they passed, as a sheep on earth might push its way through a field of standing corn.

Yet other shapes, huge winged and ungainly, fluttered with a slow, bat-like motion, through the lower strata of the atmosphere.

Every now and then during the voyage across the temperate zone the propellers were slowed down to enable them to witness some Titanic conflict between the gigantic denizens of land and sea and air. But her ladyship had had enough of horrors on the Saturnian equator, and so she was quite content to watch this phase of evolution (as it had happened on the Earth many thousands of ages ago) from a convenient distance, and so the Astronef sped on southward without approaching the surface nearer than a couple of miles.

"It'll be all very nice to see and remember and dream about afterwards," she said, "but really I don't think I can stand any more monsters just now, at least not at close quarters, and I'm quite sure if those things can live there we couldn't, any more than we could have lived on Earth a million years or so ago. No, really I don't want to land, Lenox, let's go on."

They went on at a speed of about a hundred miles an hour, and, as they progressed southward, both the atmosphere and the landscape rapidly changed. The air grew clearer and the clouds lighter. Lands and seas were more sharply divided, and both teeming with life. The seas still swarmed with serpentine monsters of the saurian type, and the firmer lands were peopled by huge animals, mastodons, bears, giant tapirs, nyledons, deinotheriums, and a score of other species too strange for them to recognise by any earthly likeness, which roamed in great herds through the vast twilit forests and over boundless plains covered with grey-blue vegetation.

Here, too, they found mountains for the first time on Saturn; mountains steep-sided, and many earth-miles high.

As the Astronef was skirting the side of one of these ranges Redgrave allowed it to approach more closely than he had so far done to the surface of Saturn.

"I shouldn't wonder if we found some of the higher forms of life up here," he said. "If there is anything here that's going to develop some clay into the human race of Saturn, it would naturally get up here."

"Of course it would," said Zaidie, "as far as possible out of the reach of those unutterable horrors on the equator. I should think that would be one of the first signs they would show of superior intelligence. Look, I believe there are some of them. Do you see those holes in the mountain side there? And there they are, something like gorillas, only twice as big, and up the trees, too—and what trees! They must be seven or eight hundred feet high."

"Tree and cave-dwellers, and ancestors of the future royal race of Saturn, I suppose!" said Redgrave. "They don't look very nice, do they? Still, there's no doubt about their being far superior in intelligence to what we left behind us. Evidently this atmosphere is too thin for the two-headed jelly-fishes, and the saurians to breathe. These creatures have found that out in a few hundreds of generations, and so they have come to live up here out of the way. Vegetarians, I suppose, or perhaps they live on smaller monkeys and other animals, just as our ancestors did."

"Really, Lenox," said Zaidie, turning round and facing him, "I must say that you have a most unpleasant way of alluding to one's ancestors. They couldn't help what they were."

"Well, dear," he said, going towards her, "marvellous as the miracle seems, I'm heretic enough to believe it possible that your ancestors even, millions of years ago, perhaps, may have been something like those; but then, of course, you know I'm a hopeless Darwinian."

"And, therefore, entirely horrid, as I've often said before when you get on subjects like these. Not, of course, that I'm ashamed of my poor relations; and then, after all, your Darwin was quite wrong when he talked about the descent of man—and woman. We—especially the women—have ascended from that sort of thing, if there's any truth in the story at all; though, personally, I must say I prefer dear old Mother Eve."

"Who never had a sweeter daughter!" he replied, drawing her towards him.

"And, meanwhile, compliments being barred, I'll go and get dinner ready," she said. "After all, it doesn't matter what world one's in, one gets hungry all the same."

The dinner, which was eaten somewhere in the middle of the fifteen-year-long day of Saturn, was a very pleasant one, because they were now nearing the turning-point of their trip into the depths of Space, and thoughts of home and friends were already beginning to fly back across the thousand-million-mile gulf which lay between them and the Earth which they had left only a little more than two months ago.

While they were at dinner the Astronef rose above the mountains and resumed her southward course. Zaidie brought the coffee up on deck as usual after dinner, and, while Redgrave smoked his cigar and Zaidie her cigarette, they luxuriated in the magnificent spectacle of the sunlit side of Rings towering up, rainbow built on rainbow, to the zenith of their visible heavens.

"What a pity there aren't any words to describe it!" said Zaidie. "I wonder if the descendants of the ancestors of the future human race on Saturn will invent anything like a suitable language. I wonder how they'll talk about those Rings millions of years hence."

"By that time there may not be any Rings," Lenox replied, blowing a ring of smoke from his own lips. "Look at that—made in a moment and gone in a moment—and yet on exactly the same principle, it gives one a dim idea of the difference between time and eternity. After all it's only another example of Kelvin's theory of vortices. Nebulae, and asteroids, and planet-rings, and smoke-rings are really all made on the same principle."

"My dear Lenox, if you're going to get as philosophical and as commonplace as that I'm going to bed. Now that I come to think of it, I've been about fifteen earth-hours out of bed, so it's about time I went. It's your turn to make the coffee in the morning—our morning I mean—and you'll wake me in time to see the South Pole of Saturn, won't you? You're not coming yet, I suppose?"

"Not just yet, dear. I want to see a bit more of this, and then I must go through the engines and see that they're all right for that thousand million mile homeward voyage you're talking about. You can have a good ten hours' sleep without missing much, I think, for there doesn't seem to be anything more interesting than our own Arctic life down there. So good-night, little woman, and don't have too many nightmares."

"Good-night!" she said, "if you hear me shout you'll know that you've to come and protect me from monsters. Weren't those two-headed brutes just too horrid for words? Good-night, dear!"

THE RAID FROM MARS

by Miles J. Breuer

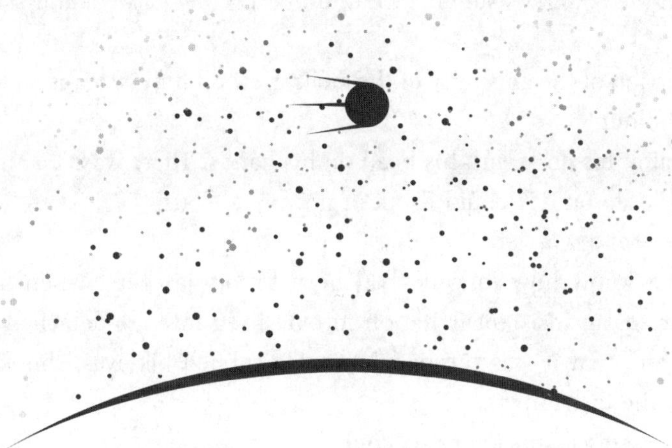

I
THE RADIUM THEFTS

In a corner office of the ground floor of the Department of Justice Building in Washington, D. C., a man sat bent over his desk with his forehead in his hands. He was a keen and powerful looking person, but at the present he looked utterly puzzled and helpless. He was Herbert Hawes, Chief of the Bureau of Criminal Investigation, and a famous man. Beside him on the desk, and on the floor around his chair, were arranged stack after stack of telegrams, yellow with black headings, and white with blue headings.

"Mercy Hospital reports mysterious disappearance of radium salts during night."

"Entire stock of radium disappeared last night. Two attendants found unconscious!"

"One hundred thousand dollars worth of radium disappeared from Mt. Sinai Hospital. Nurse and doctor unconscious!"

"Total radium supply stolen. Locks demolished. No clues!"

Thus ran the telegrams, all of them. They came from all of the large hospitals in the principal cities in the United States, and from numerous large University laboratories. From Bangor, Maine, to Jacksonville, Florida, from Portland, Oregon, to Los Angeles, and crisscrosswise over the country, the story was the same.

"A raid on the country's supply of radium!" the chief gasped, and sank down in his chair.

The realization of the enormity of the affair grew on him by leaps and bounds.

"What a holdup!"

Now he sat at his desk with his head on his hands. There wasn't a clue. There was nothing to go on. He could think of no way to start.

He sat there and worried.

He did not know how long he had been brooding there, when he slowly became aware of an insistent irritation forcing itself into his detached brain. It dawned on him that it was the telephone. He rubbed his eyes, shook himself and grabbed the instrument.

"Hello!" he said, as quickly as he could.

"Lincoln, Nebraska, calling," came through the telephone. "Is this Chief Hawes? Chief of Police Henderson, of Lincoln, wishes to speak to you."

There was a momentary silence while the connection was made, then a gruff voice spoke.

The two chiefs identified themselves to each other.

"I suppose you are investigating the disappearance of the radium," said the Police Chief from Lincoln.

Chief Hawes grunted in a dubious sort of fashion. Chief Henderson from Lincoln continued:

Chief Hawes just now thought to look up at the clock. Three o'clock. Four hours his head had lain sunk on his desk, thinking and dozing alternately after this terrific shock had struck him.

"—the accounts in the newspapers have been most unsatisfactory, but I gather there is a serious problem on, I have what may be a clue. Do you want it?"

"Do I? Do I? Come on quick!" roared Chief Hawes, banging his desk with the other fist.

Chief Henderson continued:

"There was a young chap, just a boy, in my office yesterday, with a most fantastic tale, which now strikes me as having a possible hook-up with this thing. It was so wild, that I told him it was bosh and sent him about his business. Now that this thing has turned up, I feel that there may be something in the boy's story. We ought to look into it."

"What did he have to say?" demanded Chief Hawes.

"He had a curious tale about some inventor with heart disease communicating with Mars—; shall I send him over to you?"

"Nuts! I thought you had a clue. What d'ya want to bother me with… "

"Well," the Western Police Chief explained, "his story said just that: stealing radium by some guys from Mars."

"Nuts!"

"Shall I send him over?" queried Chief Henderson.

"Yes! No!" roared Hawes, "I'm coming over there."

In one of the homes on a modest residence street in Lincoln, Nebraska, a sixteen-year old boy walked into the living-room, where his father was reading a newspaper, and turned off the radio. By the door, at the foot of the hat-rack, a physician's emergency bag and two canvas paper-carrier bags showed plainly that both father and son were busy men.

"Dad," the boy inquired earnestly, "would it be a good or a bad thing for the human race if someone discovered how to make people live forever?"

"Well, well," the doctor replied. "You are being mighty serious about it. Is that for one of your debates?"

"Yes," Ronald answered eagerly; that excuse was as good as any.

"I believe," the doctor continued, "that if everlasting life were given to the human race, it would be a very bad thing. If no one died, in a population which is now stationary, it would double in one generation."

"You mean," the son reminded, "that if the birth-rate continued unchanged."

"It would," the doctor assured him. "No ifs are needed. You can fancy, after a few generations, the horrible crowding up of the earth. Think of the pressure, the competition, the lowered standard of living, worse than anything in India or China—and growing worse and no end to it."

"But supposing," suggested Ronald, "that birth-control were put into effect?"

"Don't make me laugh," his father countered. "Voluntarily or individually, people would never do anything. By public measures, perhaps in a hundred years after everybody was crazy, something might be done. No, I rather think your gift of everlasting life would be no boon to race, and of questionable benefit to the individual."

As the boy said nothing further, the doctor resumed his reading. At intervals however, he glanced over the top of his paper at his son, who sat there motionless in a stiff chair, staring straight ahead of him and saying nothing. Undoubtedly something was preying on his mind. The doctor, a practical man who knew boys well, said nothing, realizing that it would all eventually come out.

The boy maintained his puzzled posture for nearly two hours before he stirred. Then he rose, stretched himself, and remarked that he hated to go to bed.

At that moment there was a gallop of many footsteps on the porch floor, and a ring at the doorbell. In a moment the room was filled with Chiefs of Police and Government officers.

"There used to be a light in old man Dragstedt's window every morning at 4:30," Ronald began his explanation, "when I passed his house carrying papers. I knew he was a sickly old man who never went anywhere, and lived alone. Sometimes one of the windows went funny colours in the night, as I went by with my paper-bags. He's got a crazy chimney on his house, like a tall pipe, and shiny, like polished metal.

"Although it is against the rules of the paper, one morning I couldn't resist trying a peek in at one of his windows. I tiptoed up on the porch, but the minute I stepped on his rug, an alarm went off somewhere in the house. The door opened, and he started to roar at me, and then collapsed on the floor. He has heart disease, and gets attacks when he gets sore.

"I dragged him to the davenport and was going to call up my dad, but he begged me not to. He had some pills that he took. I got them for him and they made him better in half an hour. I stayed with him and warmed him a glass of milk. I saw nothing in the house out of the way, but in the direction of the queerly lighted windows there was a closed door.

"The next day I walked boldly up and knocked on the door. He had me in and I asked him how he was. I got to dropping in that way and found that he was grateful for a lot of little things I could do to help him. But, he never opened that door.

"I thought I would never find out what was in there, until one day when I rang his doorbell and he didn't answer. I opened up and went in, fearing that something had happened to him. I found the secret door open, and he was just about to come in through it, when he had another spell. He fell down and his face was so blue it gave me the creeps. I got him to bed, gave him his tablet, and had a look at the room. "A lot of the stuff there was undoubtedly short-wave equipment. I've got a ham station of my own, and am up on it. The scanning elements and the big screen of a television set were also familiar. But there was an awful pile of strange stuff there that meant nothing to me.

"He came to as I was standing in the middle of the apparatus room, looking around, trying to figure out stuff. He didn't get sore; he got to know that it would give him another spell with his heart. So I just shut the door, warmed him some more milk, and never said a word and he didn't either.

"But after that he let me come in and watch him working at the apparatus. He used cw, but he had six keys instead of one; he played five of them with the fingers of his right hand like piano keys; it must have taken a lot of practice to get that way, because he really made 'em sing. Another odd thing was that his transmission wave had several tones to it—no; he must have had several transmission waves. It gave a musical effect as he sent."

"Say!" interrupted Chief Henderson, "Where is this old bird? Dragstedt you say? We'll listen to the rest of it from him."

"Well, I guess he's gone to them. Or they took him away with them. He hasn't been at his house for 24 hours. But his stuff is all right."

"What do you mean by they? Who took him away?"

The boy showed embarrassment.

"Well," he hesitated; "I know you'll think I'm crazy—"

"Suppose you are!" said the police chief, his voice rough with impatience. "Who took him away?"

"Well—the Martians. But wait till I get to 'em."

The men settled in their chairs with a certain amount of relief. Martians! If that was all, they needn't worry. They had thought it might be some well-known crooks. The boy continued his narrative:

"Then one day, when he didn't come to the doorbell, I opened the door again and walked on in. The inner door was open. I could see him at the television apparatus. I really saw a Martian on the screen!

"I saw him plenty plain and had a long time to look at him. Dragstedt was so absorbed that he didn't know I was there for thirty minutes.

"The thing on the screen moved, and worked little pieces of a vast stack of machinery behind it. It had bright eyes, and arms and legs, and wasn't so very different from people after all. But for a person, it looked small and fragile and easy to fall to pieces. It moved with quick jerks. As it moved, little buzzes on different notes came out of Dragstedt's machine. It gestured with its hands, and then brought out papers. Or, you know, whatever they use for papers. But it looked just like papers. Some had maps and some had mathematical stuff on them.

"Then Dragstedt turned around and saw that I had been watching him. He came near having another spell. But, he's a smart guy, and he calmed down and held it off. He decided he might as well tell me about it. I understand the stuff pretty well and can give you the high spots—"

"Whatever Ronald says about radio and related subjects," his father interrupted, turning to the police officers, "you can put down as being accurate and dependable. I myself am amazed at the amount of knowledge he has on those things."

"Kids are hot on that stuff," the grizzled old D. C. I. chief mumbled to himself.

"He had been a professor of physics," Ronald went on. "But he inherited a lot of dough from a relative and got to experimenting on his own. He was interested in picking up the portion of radio waves that are reflected from the Heaviside layer. He had some odd notion about the thing and was measuring intensities. He found that the reflected portion was weaker than the transmitted portion to an extent not explained by the square of the distance equation. He tried it with direction beams, and the more nearly vertical he got his beams, the greater the loss in intensity—just opposite to what you'd expect—"

Chief Hawes grunted and mumbled something about what he would expect.

"When he finally directed a successfully controlled beam in an accurately vertical direction, he lost most of his short-wave energy. Can't you see—that he was putting a wave through the Heaviside layer?"

Chief Haves grunted again, so that Ronald had to smile.

"He played with it a lot, and sent out a lot of amateur broadcasting, and cw.

"It wasn't really very long, a few weeks, till he was amazed to find that he was getting signals in return. The poor fellow must have gone nearly crazy before he figured out what those odd, broken tones were.

"For many months he worked on them, but could make no sense out of them. After quite a while, it struck him that he ought to build a television apparatus in connection. By that time his heart was getting bad; he went to a doctor and the doctor wanted to put him in a hospital. He couldn't stand that, and went back to his apparatus. After some weary months he finally saw his first Martian on the screen.

"Eventually he learned to talk to them. By means of the vision screen and his multitoned cw, he and the Martians developed a language from gestures and pointing to objects, and then gradually into words. I got on to a good deal of the stuff myself as I watched him, and it isn't so hard at that. When I got so that I could stand there and get what the cw was saying, I got quite a thrill out of it.

"Well, it turned out that these Martians lived under the ground on their planet, because it was too cold and dry on top and no air. They had it all fixed livable underground. They were an old, old race, much older than ours. They had learned among other things, the secret of preventing death, or at least of putting it off indefinitely. As their births were regulated in the laboratory merely to replace rare losses by death, the race was stable.

"However, within the recent century, a new disease had sprung up among them which they could not conquer with all their science. Deaths occurred in such numbers that the laboratories could not replace them by a sufficient number of births; their mathematicians predicted the early extinction of the race. Their physicists said that the disease was due to the complete loss of radioactive minerals, due to the old age of the planet itself. I saw some of the sick ones on the television screen, and it must have been some kind of cancer.

"What did Dragstedt do, but describe radium to them, and ask them if they knew what it was, and if they thought it would cure their stuff. Of course that is the first thing that would have occurred to me. No, all their radium had finally broken itself up into non-radioactive elements. But they grasped the idea, only too promptly.

"The gist of it is, that Dragstedt and the Martians got up a scheme, where he is to steer them to the caches of radium when they come to Earth in a space ship. In return, they will cure his heart disease and give him everlasting life. Dragstedt has been all over the country, getting the layouts of hospitals and universities, which he could easily do, for he is a well known physicist himself.

"Those birds up there on Mars even planned mechanical things to get around in, when they got to Earth, because their bodies are too flimsily built for our heavier gravitation.

"That's all I know, except that I overheard that their ship is down in the sandhills, about fifty miles southeast of Alliance; and that they are sticking around about a week to treat old Dragstedt."

II
THE MARTIAN SHIP

By the next morning, the entire Eighth Army Corps was on the move, swarming from all directions toward Alliance, Nebraska. Its airplanes, and also two squadrons of Navy hydroplanes from the Great Lakes Training Station, were at Alliance by daybreak.

Field artillery and tanks on flat-cars came in on the railroads from the East, West, and South. From four directions came tracks loaded with men and small equipment.

By noon, Alliance looked like the centre of a war zone. The sky hummed with planes. Tanks clanked along the roads, and motorized artillery pointed its long, keen noses at the sky. Trim, khaki-clad detachments clicked precisely along the pavements, their rifle-barrels all neatly parallel. The entire division was mobilized. It was being strung out in a new-moon-shaped line, thickest in the centre, and the points feeling outward, to surround the object as soon as it was found.

The airplanes located it early in the afternoon. It was described as an egg-shaped affair as big as an ocean liner, located in a hollow in the sand hills, practically where Ronald Worth had predicted it would be found.

The young captain in command of the airplane squadron from the Great Lakes Navy Base saluted General Barry, the Commander of the expedition, and stood in front of him waiting for orders. He could not conceal a restlessness, stepping from one foot to the other, even though trying hard to stand rigid.

The grizzled old General smiled.

"What is the Captain jittery about?" he asked.

"Begging the General's pardon," the Captain said in embarrassment, "I am awaiting orders to bomb the space ship. It is just a pippin of a target. We could smash it in thirty seconds—"

"What about the radium?" the General interrupted.

The Captain's face suddenly fell, and he stood there puzzled.

"Do you know," the General continued, "that the entire nation's supply of radium is inside that vessel. If you throw explosives down there, you will scatter several million dollars' worth of precious stuff out in the sand. It would cost as much money and take as much time to recover it, as it did to make it in the first place."

"Yes, Sir!" replied the Captain meekly. "We've got a job on hand!"

In the modest residence section of Lincoln, Nebraska, three swift cars that had just dashed across the town from the airport, drew up in front of Dragstedt's deserted little house. General Barry, his aides, and a squad of guards tramped into the house.

There, in the room of apparatus which old Dragstedt had built, sat Ronald Worth, high-school student and paper-carrier. Sleepiness showed in his eyes, and at his elbow were partly consumed bottles of milk and plates of cheese and crackers.

"Ronald Worth calling Professor Dragstedt! Ronald Worth calling Professor Dragstedt! Will you please answer! It will be to your interest to communicate with us!"

The boy's voice droned monotonously on, uninterrupted by the entry of the men into the room. Then he stopped, took a drink of milk, and put his hand on the six keys. The queer musical drone started and whined monotonously on. The military men stood silently about the room.

"You are sure that no other operator could take this over?" General Barry asked.

"I'd have to teach him. It would take time. Took me months to get on to it," the boy answered. "This is different from ordinary radios. And common radios won't tune with those of the Martians."

"You look tired," the General said.

Suddenly the boy stiffened, and took his hand away from the keys. The musical drone continued, in a different rhythm.

"He is answering. Wouldn't answer on the telephone, but bit on the cw at once." Ronald was elated.

"Tell him," said General Barry, "to tell these Martians, that if they give us back our radium, we shall treat them royally, entertain them, show them the Earth; and then let them go home unharmed, with a gift of enough radium for their purpose."

The cw transmitter hummed awhile; and there were stirs of impatience among the soldiers who filled the room. After a while, the boy spoke again.

"The best I can make out of these answers, Sir," he said, "is that the Martians refuse to recognize us as intelligent beings. They refuse to deal with us. They think we are just some sort of animals."

"You tell him, then," the General directed, "that we have got them surrounded on land and in the air. We shall not permit them to rise, and shall simply lay siege to them until they starve. Do not be alarmed when we put a small shell through the skin of their vessel; that will be to keep them from rising out into space. Advise them again, that they will be better off if they surrender."

The cw spoke again for a period; and again the boy spoke, with some excitement in his voice:

"Apparently the shell has arrived, and blown a hole in the nose of their ship. Dragstedt didn't think it did any damage. But the Martians have become very busy about something, moving jerkily about. The shell-hole seems to have interfered with their arrangements for decreased gravitation inside the vessel. He doesn't know how many there are, but over a hundred. He says they are disturbed."

"That was Grigsby of the 110th Field Artillery that disturbed them."

"Swoop" Martin, the crack observation pilot, circled around over the scene of operations, at 30,000 feet. He had to use an oxygen helmet, fitted with binocular glasses. But he was invisible and inaudible from below.

He could see the gleaming, egg-shaped hull, nestling in the sand like some child's toy; and around it, the dotted, splotched, irregular circle formed by the Eighth Army Corps. As he watched, a puff of smoke came from one of the splotches below; in a moment a puff of smoke appeared at the smaller end of the egg; and when it cleared, a small black hole remained in the metal. He reported it all promptly to headquarters by radio.

The next thing that happened was that a square of metal opened in the side of the vessel, like a door, and an odd thing stepped out of it, and started walking out across the sand away from the ship.

In another second, a dozen airplanes, far below him, swooped down toward the thing. The faint patter of their machine guns came up to him. The mechanical thing that had come out of the vessel careened over on its side and lay still. The door in the side of the hull quickly closed.

For some minutes nothing happened, and then a row of little round ports appeared higher up off the ground. "Swoop" Martin could not see anything else happen, except that there were a dozen loud explosions, with flashes of fire in the air, and the airplanes which had fusilladed the Martian coming out of his ship, all exploded there beneath him, and only a litter of small fragments dropped on down to the ground. Then, systematically down there in that investing circle, one battery after another blew up in a flash and a cloud of smoke, huge gun barrels and artillery wheels flying high in the air mingled with the bodies of men, whirling down to be buried in a cloud of sand.

A few seconds later there were scores of explosions in the air, as distant airplanes blew up. There must have been communication from them to the ground, because some of the batteries in the second and third lines banged loudly two or three times before they finally blew up. Their marksmanship was good. Shells shrieked across the interval and huge holes were ripped in the shining side of the Martian vessel.

However, the Martians were the swifter. Before vital damage had been done to their vessel, there was not a tank, not a field gun, not an intact infantry company left. The Eighth Army Corps had been wiped out and was represented only by a few stragglers staggering in the sand.

"God!" exclaimed "Swoop" Martin, up in his plane above range of the damage. "All of that to pay for a couple of ounces of radium!"

As he circled around to head for safer regions, he could see repair proceeding rapidly in the holes in the side of the Martian vessel.

Airplanes from the Tenth Army Corps Area were on the spot in the morning, practically hitting their "ceiling" in order to keep out of the way of the Martians' destructive reach. They had expected to arrive and find the thing gone. But it was still there, and the shell-holes all repaired.

So, the Tenth Division moved up to fill the place of the Eighth. A few scouts first took their posts. As nothing happened, more and more men trickled in, and were slowly followed by heavy equipment. In a few days the line was again complete, among the blackened ruins of their predecessors. Their orders were:

"Surround the Martians. Keep quiet. Take no action against them unless they try to rise."

Now, those men who had filtered up to their positions at night with pounding hearts, expecting to be suddenly wiped out at any moment, were getting tired of week after week of inactivity. Army discipline, always irksome, was doubly so in the heat and the sand. There was sand in their clothes, sand in their hair, sand in their ears, sand in their food. There were hot winds, and nothing to do but wait all day and wonder what the airplanes above had to report. The enlisted personnel were not the only ones who were restless. There were constant, worried conferences in the General Headquarters tent.

"I have an idea!" exclaimed General Johnson, Commander of the Tenth Army Corps, one hot day, when weariness was at its height.

The headquarters staff deliberated long and carefully before the officers finally dispersed, each to his own sandy quarters. There was much tapping of the Royal

Portable typewriter and sealing of secret orders during the next few days. There was code communication with Washington by radio.

Finally, one dark night, the men were overjoyed by orders to get up and move. A few moments later they were dismayed to find that their progress was going to be backwards. They were going away from the enemy. They pounded through the sand until they reached a paved highway, and were then whisked away by trucks. By daybreak the Division was comfortably making camp in a country that was not sandhills. Eventually it was discovered that the little city in the distance was Ravenna.

"Swoop" Martin, transferred to the Tenth Division, saluted General Johnson, as the latter stepped out of his car.

"Ready for orders, Sir," he said.

"Lieutenant Martin, there are no orders. You may do this if you care to volunteer, but you will not be ordered to do it."

"Instructions, I meant, Sir," said "Swoop" Martin.

In a few moments he was on the run for his plane, which stood ready for him.

III
THE ATTACK ON THE MARTIANS

"Swoop" Martin in his monoplane made circles around over the Martian space-ship like a hawk. He swept around lower and lower. At a height of about 3,000 feet, he flew away to the distance of a half mile, and then dived steeply downward, toward the Martian vessel. A few hundred feet above it, he turned sharply upward again, making a sort of V. At the bottom of the V, a small black object left the scout plane, and described a parabola, striking the Martian vessel amidships. A ragged hole appeared, and then a dull explosion.

"Swoop" Martin was climbing fast, and thinking every moment was his last one; expecting to be blown to atoms any second. But until he was, he determined, he would go through with it. He guided his plane, watched his board, and went steeply upwards.

Finally, when he was gasping for breath, he levelled off, and put on his oxygen mask. He looked down below. Everything was the same as before. He was puzzled.

He cruised around awhile, thinking things over, and shook his head. He swiftly reported what had happened and asked for further orders. The General's message was to the effect that he did not wish to give an order of that kind; but that if Lieutenant Martin wished to volunteer to repeat his manoeuvre, it might be a good idea.

Down, down, the plane swooped again, toward the tiny globule nestling in the sand, and sent another bomb hurtling down from the front of its V-shaped path, and again fled upwards into the heights. Again a jagged hole was torn in the top of the space ship; again "Swoop" Martin expected the worst as he climbed his way back to the height; again he waited in vain for something to happen, and nothing happened.

Back at the camp near Ravenna, a group of men stirred. In fifteen minutes, a dozen swift cars filled with officers and men, two high-speed tanks, and two high-speed four-inch field-pieces, were headed toward the Martian ship. They covered the ground rapidly, and by noon were on the site of the previous camp from which they had besieged the Martian vessel. The field-guns were set up and trained; a dozen men climbed into the two tanks, loaded with machine guns and hand grenades. Above, a dozen airplanes droned, and made swooping circles, much like hawks.

The tanks started off, throwing up clouds of sand, and dashed at high speed, straight toward the shining side of the Martian vessel. Their crews were tense, expecting to be blotted out instantly. But nothing happened. The old General sat at the front porthole of one of the tanks, watching ahead, gazing at the narrowing space between the tank and the Martian ship. Those gleaming walls began to seem very close, and the General expected the catastrophe any moment. But they roared and clanked onward, and still nothing happened. The airplanes came lower, till the roar of their motors was heard above the noise of the tanks. Still nothing happened. Behind, the men at the cannons watched through field glasses and waited at their radios, ready to rain a shower of shells on the Martian vessel at the least suspicion. But nothing happened.

Finally, they were under the very lee of the metal hulk. It towered above them like a skyscraper, and extended in both directions like a mountain range. Still nothing happened.

"All out!" the General ordered, as the tanks stopped.

Their feet crunching in the sand, their hands full of grenades, they made their way slowly alongside the ship. One hundred yards. Two hundred yards, three hundred yards, they walked along, and still there appeared no way of getting inside. The holes that "Swoop" Martin had made were on the upper surface, and there was no way to climb.

"Try a grenade," the General ordered.

They all backed off. There was a crash of flying fragments, but no damage to the wall.

"A four-inch shell, then!"

The only communication with the gunners was now by flags. The General's order was rapidly wig-wagged to them. The General and his men hurried to shelter behind a sand hummock, now genuinely expecting complete annihilation. The gun crew placed the first shot too short and merely threw up sand. The second was a little high, tearing open the metal plates of the hull about twenty feet above the ground. The third shot ripped open a hole that they could easily walk into.

For a moment the General contemplated with interest the twisted and blackened edges of the shiny, white metal that was unknown to him. Then he recollected that they were in danger, he and his little group of men, peering into the depths of the dark opening. There was some huge machinery visible, a long corridor with a bright, flat surface at the end of it. Nothing had as yet happened to them. They were still alive.

The General pushed back one of the men who was edging into the opening. He claimed the privilege of being the first to walk into danger. The men with grenades and hand-machine guns crowded behind him. The General found himself walking down a small corridor, and the men filed behind him. The corridor soon became a bridge out in a vast void, black and filled with machinery of enormous proportions. Then again it became a corridor, and the bright surface was a wall turning at right angles.

It seemed that they spent hours walking about with pounding hearts and thumping heads, expecting every moment to be attacked in some unknown way from dark ambush. There was endless machinery, large and small, everywhere.

Finally, at the end of a climb up a long stairway, they came to an open space, at what they guessed to be about the middle of the ship. It looked as though they had found the "living quarters" at last. They were in a vestibule. In front of them was a metal door with a glass window, through which they could look into a vast, ovoid, rotunda-like room or hall.

All efforts to open the door failed. There seemed to be no lock against which to direct operations. The metal of the door was firm as a mountain against all their blows. So, they all stepped back, and a well-aimed grenade tore the door open wide enough for them to go through, their ears singing from the roar of the explosion. They went through cautiously, two experienced enlisted-men first, with their rifles at ready, then the officers with their pistols in their hands.

The lighting seemed to them rather dim, though it had the quality of daylight. Probably it corresponded to the lower intensity of illumination as found on the surface of Mars. "Crash!" went the rifle of a soldier at something that moved slightly on a couch across the room, a hundred yards away. Whatever it was that had moved, jerked as though it had been kicked, shuddered a moment, and lay still.

The group stood huddled together near the door, looked around and waited. Not a sound, not a stir in the vast room. It had all the proportions of some huge Coliseum, though none of the ponderous evidences of constructional difficulties. They had time to examine the place. About two hundred cots or couches stood around its walls. It appeared that originally they had been arranged in precise order, but now there was confusion. All of them were occupied by little, shrivelled, flat-looking bodies, that looked astonishingly human. They were small and frail-looking. On closer inspection they looked especially human because the faces were so very old and sad. The skin was blue, leathery, and wrinkled.

In the middle of the place was a cluster of some kind of apparatus: a foundation-pillar, a platform, elongated, casing-like structures of metal pointing in all directions like telescopes or projectors, wheels, knobs, and levers for control. It may possibly have been the control station for running the ship. Near one end of the space into which they were looking, three or four of the mechanical contrivances in which these creatures traveled around when they were on earth, lay propped up in a heap, and a motionless body was still strapped in one of them.

"All beds occupied but one, sir!" the veteran Sergeant said; "and that must belong to him," pointing to the one in the machine. "Not one of them is stirring."

"Just the same," the wary old General said, "the four of you go around and prod everyone of them to see if there is any life left. This is no time to get shot from behind."

A keen-looking officer with a lieutenant-colonel's leaves on his shoulders, was also looking the bodies over. They were indeed all dead. He walked up to one and another, and even thumped and prodded several with professional skill and interest. The General watched him in mute inquiry.

"Well, doctor," he finally asked, "what killed them?"

"Radiation!" the medical officer replied. "As I see it, they had developed no natural protection against radiation because they live underground, and because there is so little radiation of any kind on Mars, both because of its distance from the sun and because of the scarcity of its radioactive minerals. Apparently there was no warning in their mathematics, of the terrific power of radium against their own flesh, even through the lead walls of its containers. See the deep destruction of skin and tissue on some of the older cases."

The General stood a moment, lost in thought. Then he sent two men back to the main force with orders that proper guards be brought up for the Martian ship.

"Now we'll look for the radium," he said. "It can't be far from here."

The men stuck close together as they moved here and there. It was a jittery place. The vastness and dimness of it, the two-hundred odd dead Martians, the jungles of incredibly huge machinery filling the great spaces all around them, between them and honest daylight, with God only knew what lurking in the depths, were conditions to which they were unaccustomed. They would have preferred a concrete human enemy in front of them no matter how well armed. They went to one of the doors that were let into the wall at intervals, then to another, then to several in succession.

The doors were of the same character as the first one they had encountered. There seemed no way to open them except by explosives, and this for the present they hesitated to do. The light from the rotunda penetrated the glass windows of the doors only a short distance, and was lost among the huge bulks and dizzy reaches of machinery.

Suddenly a harsh cackle sounded behind them.

They wheeled around and stood petrified, the enlisted men with their rifles automatically aimed in the direction from which the laugh had come.

"Ha! ha! ha! ha!" rasped a harsh, dry laugh. "Go ahead and have a shot at me, boys, and see how much harm it does!"

They saw Dragstedt standing there his eyes gleaming.

There was a moment's pause. The General whispered:

"He's insane."

"Who wouldn't be?" the medical officer said.

The madman's dry cackle rose again to the lofty ceiling:

"Ha! ha! So you think you can get the best of me, eh? Look what I can do to you!"

He whirled a little wheel, which slowly swung one of the long casings so that it pointed at a dead Martian on a couch. He moved his hand to something else, and an intense red ray shot across the intervening space. The Martian and his bed simply flew into pieces, and the fragments also disappeared, leaving behind them faint clouds of smoky vapour. A dull thud shook the room.

"Look! and look! and look!" the madman shouted excitedly, aiming at one after another of the Martians, blowing them into smoke with red streaks and dull thuds.

Crash! went a soldier's rifle as the ray began to swing too close to them.

The soldier dropped his rifle in one hand, and held the other to his head as though to nurse a headache.

"Swipe me! I could hit a pinhead at that distance!" he moaned.

"Fire at him again!" the General ordered. They all watched closely.

Crash! went the rifle. At the same time a small puff of smoke appeared in the thin air about a foot from Professor Dragstedt, and in line with his heart. The bullet had been caught and disintegrated by some field of force.

Again the long, cackling laugh:

"You see, I've got you!"

"Yes," said the General. "What do you want?"

"I'm sailing this ship to Mars," the Professor said. "I'm going to sell them the radium there. I'm going to be rich. I'm going to get power! I'm going to rule. I'll be the biggest—"

"But what about us?" the General interrupted.

The madman's face became crafty.

"You will come with me, and be my royal Guard," he orated. "Or—" he waited thoughtfully a moment as though a new and more interesting idea had struck him. "—or, I'll blast you into smoke. What would you rather do? Go to Mars, or get flashed into nothing?"

Someone in the group whispered:

"But the ship's got holes in it. If he goes out into space, we're all goners in a few seconds."

Another voice whispered:

"Does he really believe he can handle this ship? And get it to Mars? Looks complicated to me, and I'm—"

The old General's head probably worked faster than anyone else's.

"You go to hell!" he thundered to the mad professor. "We'll get you yet, and court-martial you and shoot you."

Professor Dragstedt gave a shrill yell.

“Whoopee! All aboard for Mars! Here we go!”

He adjusted a number of little wheels, lumbered all the casings into different positions, and took hold of a large, heavy lever.

The men looked at each other blankly. In a few seconds the cold of space would penetrate into their bone marrow, and all the air out of their bodies would be lost as an infinitesimal whiff in the limitless void. Irresistibly they turned to Dragstedt again.

With a wild grin on his face, he leaned back, and gave a long, hard pull at the heavy lever in front of him.

Suddenly they were pressed to the floor with an immense weight. The sensation was over in a second. During that second the spectacle in front of them took place. A fountain of a dozen streams of red beams played for an instant at steep angles, crisscrossing each other and forming a hyperboloid. When they subsided, the tower in the middle of the room was a molten mass, and the only trace of Professor Dragstedt was a whiff of smoky vapour, slowly dissipating itself in faint swirls.

THE EINSTEIN SEE-SAW

by Miles J. Breuer

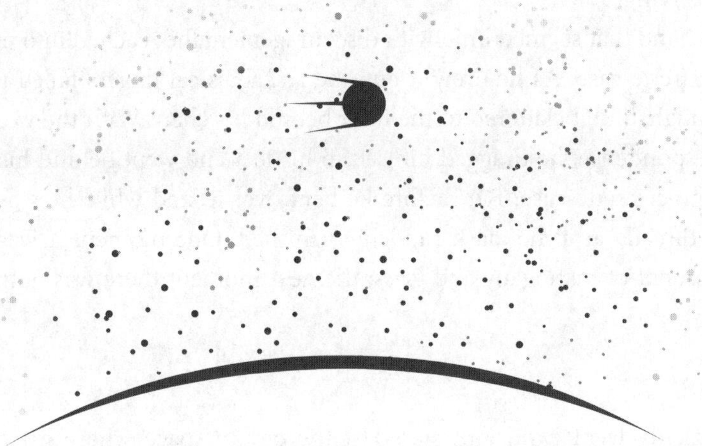

I
THE EINSTEIN SEE-SAW

Tony Costello leaned glumly over his neat, glass-topped desk, on which a few papers lay arranged in orderly piles. Tony was very blue and discouraged. The foundations of a pleasant and profitable existence had been cut right out from under him. Gone were the days in which the big racket boss, Scarneck Ed, generously rewarded the exercise of Tony's brilliant talents as an engineer in redesigning cars to give higher speed for bootlegging purposes, in devising automatic electric apparatus for handling and concealing liquor, in designing beam-directed radios for secret communication among the gangs. Yes, mused Tony, it had been profitable.

Six months ago the Citizens' Committee had stepped in. Now the police department was reorganized; Scarneck Ed Podkowski was in jail, and his corps of trusty lieutenants were either behind the bars with him or scattered far and wide in flight. Tony, always a free spender, had nothing left but the marvellous laboratory and workshop that Scarneck Ed had built him, and his freedom. For the police could find nothing legal against Tony. They had been compelled to let him alone, though they were keeping a close watch on him. Tony's brow was as dark as the mahogany of his desk. He did not know just how to go about making an honest living.

With a hand that seemed limp with discouragement, he reached into his pocket for his cigarette-case. As he drew it out, the lackadaisical fingers failed to hold it firmly enough, and it clattered to the floor behind his chair. With the weary slowness of despondence, he dragged himself to his feet and went behind his chair to pick up the cigarette-case. But, before he bent over it, and while he was looking fully and directly at it, his desk suddenly vanished. One moment it was there, a huge ornament of mahogany and glass; the next moment there was nothing.

* * * * *

Tony suddenly went rigid and stared at the empty space where his desk had stood. He put his hand to his forehead, wondering if his financial troubles were affecting his reason. By that time, another desk stood in the place.

Tony ran over this strange circumstance mentally. His mental processes were active beneath, though dazed on the surface. His desk had stood there. While looking fully at it, all his senses intact, he had seen it vanish, and for a moment there had been nothing in its place. While he stared directly at the empty space from which the desk had disappeared, another desk had materialized there, like a flash. Perhaps, there had been a sort of jar, a tremor, of the floor and of the air, of everything. But the point was that his own desk, at which he had been working one moment, had suddenly vanished, and at the next moment another desk had appeared in its place.

And what a desk! The one that now stood there was smaller than his own palatial one, and shabbier. A raw, unpleasant golden-oak, much scratched and scuffed. Its top was heaped and piled full of books and papers. In the middle of it stood a photograph of a girl, framed in red leather. Irresistibly, the sunny beauty of the face, the bright eyes, the firm little chin, the tall forehead topped by a shining mass of light curly hair, drew Tony's first glance. For a few moments his eyes rested delightedly on the picture.

In a moment, however, Tony noticed that the books and papers on the desk were of a scientific character; and such is the nature of professional interest, that for the time he forgot his astonishment at how the desk had got there, in his absorption in the things heaped on top of it.

Perhaps it isn't fair to give the impression that the desk was in disorder. It was merely busy; just as though someone who had been deeply engaged in working had for the moment stepped away. There was a row of books across the back edge, and Tony leaned over eagerly to glance at the titles.

"'Theory of Parallels,' Lobatchevsky; 'Transformation of Complex Functions,' Riemann; 'Tensors and Geodesics,' Gauss," Tony read. "Hm—old stuff. But here's modern dope along the same line. 'Tensors,' by Christoffel; 'Absolute Differential Calculus,' by Ricci and Levi Civita. And Schrödinger and Eddington and D'Abro. Looks like somebody's interested in Relativity. Hm!"

* * * * *

He bent over, his constantly increasing interest showing in the attitude of his body; he turned over papers and opened notebooks crowded full of handwritten figures. Last of all he noted the batch of manuscript directly in front of him in the middle of the front edge of the desk. It was typewritten, with corrections and interlineations all over it in purple ink.

A title, "The Parallel Transformations of Equations for Matter, Energy, and Tensors," had been crossed out with purple ink, and "The Intimate Relation between Matter and Tensors" substituted. Tony bent over it and read. He was so fascinated that it did not even occur to him to speculate on the happy circumstance that the mysteriously appearing desk had brought its own scientific explanation with it. The title of the paper told him that its sheets would elucidate the apparently supernatural phenomenon, and all he did was to plunge breathlessly ahead in his eager reading. The article was short, about seven typewritten sheets. He took out his pencil and followed through the mathematical equations readily. Tony's mind was a brilliant, even though an erring one.

Under the first article lay a second one. One glance at the title caused Tony to stiffen. Then he picked up the typewritten script and carried it across the big room of his laboratory, as far away from the desk as he could get. He put the girl's photograph in his pocket. Then he took heaps and armfuls of papers, books and notes and carried them from the desk to a bench in the far corner. For, as soon as he had read the title, "A Preliminary Report of Experimental Work in the Physical Manipulation of Tensors," a sudden icy panic gripped his heart lest the desk and its papers suddenly disappear before he had finished reading to the end of the fascinating explanation.

We might add that it did not. For many weeks the desk remained standing in Tony's shop and laboratory, and he had the opportunity to study its contents thoroughly. But it took him only a few hours to grasp its secret, to add his own brilliant conception to it, and to form his great resolve. Once more Tony faced the world hopefully and enthusiastically.

II
VANISHING VALUABLES

The police understood Tony's share in the exploits of Scarneck Ed thoroughly, and, chagrined at their failure to produce proof that would hold in court, they maintained a close and constant watch on that gifted gentleman long after crime matters in the city seemed to have been cleaned up and forgotten. For one thing, they still had hopes that something would turn up to enable them to round off their work and lock him up with his former pals; for another, they did not fully trust his future behaviour. Nevertheless, for three or four months it seemed as though Tony had genuinely reformed. He lived in and for his laboratory and shop. All day the scouts could see him labouring therein, and far into the night he bent over benches and machines under shaded lights. Then, some other astonishing occurrences distracted their attention from Tony to other fields.

One morning Mr. Ambrose Parakeet, private jewel broker, walked briskly out of the elevator on the fourteenth floor of the North American Building and unlocked the door of his office. He flung it open and started in, but stopped as if shot, uttered a queer, hoarse gurgle, and staggered against the door-casing. In a moment he recovered and began to shout:

"Help! Help! Robbers!"

Before long, several people had gathered. He stood there, gasping, pointing with his hand into the room. The eagerly peering onlookers could see that beside his desk stood an empty crate. It was somewhat old and weatherbeaten and looked as though it might have come from a buffet or a bookcase. He stood there and pointed at it and gasped, and the gathering crowd in the corridor wondered what sort of strange mental malady he had been seized with. The elevator girl, with trained promptness had at once summoned the manager of the building, who elbowed his way through the crowd and stood beside Mr. Parakeet.

* * * * *

"There! There! Look! Where is it?" Mr. Parakeet was gasping slowly and gazing round in a circle. He was a little gray man of about sixty, and seemed utterly dazed and overcome.

"What's wrong, Mr. Parakeet?" asked the building manager. "I didn't know you had your safe moved out."

"But, no!" panted the bewildered old man. "I didn't. It's gone. Just gone. Last night at five o'clock I locked the office, and it was there, and everything was straight. What did you do? Who took it?"

The building manager conducted the poor old man into the office, shut the door, and asked the crowd to disperse. He sat Mr. Parakeet down into the most comfortable chair he could find, and then barked snappily into the telephone a few times. Then he sat and stared about him, stopping occasionally to reassure the old man and ask him to be patient until things could be investigated.

The building manager was an efficient man and knew his building and his tenants. He knew, as thoroughly as he knew his own office, that Mr. Parakeet had a medium-sized A. V. & L. Co.'s safe weighing about three tons, that could not be carried up the elevator when Mr. Parakeet had moved in, and had been hoisted into the window with block and tackle. He knew that it was physically impossible for the safe to go down any of the elevators, and knew that none of the operators would dare move any kind of a safe without his permission. Nevertheless, with the aid of a police-sergeant, his night-shift, and the night-watchmen of his building and adjacent ones, it was definitely established that nothing had been moved in or out of the North American Building during the preceding twenty-four hours, either by elevator or through a window to the sidewalk.

* * * * *

The newspapers took up the mystery with a shout. The prostrating loss suffered by Mr. Parakeet, amounting to over a hundred thousand dollars, added no little sensation to the story. A huge safe, disappearing into thin air, without a trace, and in its place an old wooden crate! What a mouthful for the scareheads! For several days newspapers kept up items about it, dwindling in size and strategic importance of position; for nothing further was ever found. Every bit of investigation, including that by scientific men from the University of Chicago, was futile; not a trace, not a suggestion did it yield.

Six days later the tall scareheads leaped out again: "Another Safe Disappears! Absolutely No Trace! Some time during the night, the six-foot steel safe of the Simonson Loan Company vanished into thin air. In the morning a dilapidated iron oil-cask was found in its place. The safe was so large and heavy that it could not have been moved without a large truck, special hoisting apparatus, a crew of men, and some hours of time. The store was brightly lighted during the entire night, and two watchmen patrolled it regularly. They report that they saw and heard nothing unusual, and were very much amazed when shown the oil-cask standing where the safe had been the night before." The accounts in the various papers were substantially the same.

Newspaper readers throughout the city and its environs were very much intrigued. Such a thing was very exciting and mystifying; but it was so far out of touch with their own lives that it did not affect them very much at any time except when they were reading the paper or discussing it in conversation. The police were the ones who were doing the real worrying. And, when the following week two more safes disappeared, insurance companies began to take an interest in the matter; and everyone who had any considerable amount of valuables in store began to feel panicky.

* * * * *

The circumstances surrounding the disappearance of the last of the series, the fourth, were especially amazing. This was also a jewellery safe. Canzoni's is a popular firm that rents a quarter of a floor in a big department store, and does a large volume of moderate-priced business. The receipts are stored in a heavy portable safe in a corner of the silverware section until evening, when they are carried to the large vault of the big store. One Saturday afternoon after a particularly busy day, Mr. Shipley, Canzoni's manager, was watching the hands of the clock creep toward five-thirty. He leaned on a counter and watched the clerks putting away goods for the night; he glanced idly toward the safe which he intended to open in a few minutes. The doormen had already taken their stations to keep out further customers. Then he glanced back at the safe, and it wasn't there!

Mr. Shipley drew a deep breath. The safe disappearances he had read about flashed through his mind. But he didn't believe it. It couldn't be! Yet, there was the empty corner with the birch panels forming the back of the show-windows, and no safe. In a daze, he walked over to the corner, intending to feel about with his hands and make sure the safe was really gone. Before he got there, there flashed into sight in place of the safe, a barrel of dark wood; and in a moment there was a strong odour of vinegar.

Things spun around with Mr. Shipley for a few moments. He grasped a counter and looked wildly about him. Clerks were hurrying with the covering of counters; no one seemed to have noticed anything. He stood a moment, gritted his teeth, and breathed deeply, and soon was master of himself. He stood and waited until the last customer was gone, and then called several clerks and pointed to where the safe had stood.

Within the space of a month, thirteen safes and three million dollars worth of money or property had disappeared. The police were dazed and desperate, and business was in a panic. Scientific men were appealed to, to help solve the riddle, but were helpless. Many of them agreed that though in theory such things were explainable, science was as yet far from any known means of bringing them about in actuality. Insurance companies spent fabulous sums on investigation, and, failing to get results, raised their premiums to impossible levels.

III
THE LADY OF THE PICTURE

Phil Hurren, often known as "Zip" Hurren, reporter on the *Examiner*, felt, on the day the managing editor called him into the sanctum, that fortune could smile on him no more brightly. There wasn't anything brighter.

"You stand well with the detective bureau," his boss had said; "and you've followed this safe-disappearing stuff pretty closely. You're relieved of everything else for the time being. Get on that business, and see that the public hears from the *Examiner*!"

Phil knew better than to say any more, for before he recovered from his surprise, the editor had turned his back, buried himself in his work on the desk, and forgotten that Phil was there. Nor did Phil waste any real time in rejoicing. That is why he was called "Zip." When things happened, whether it was luck or system, Phil was usually there. In sixty seconds more, Phil was in a taxicab, whirling toward police headquarters.

Luck or system, he didn't know, but he struck it again. The big wagon was just starting away from the station door when he arrived, crowded inside with bluecoats and plainclothes-men. The burly, red-faced man with chevrons on his sleeve, sitting beside the driver, saw Phil jump out, and motioned with his hand. Phil leaped up on the back step of the vehicle and hung on for dear life with his fingers through the wire grating as they careened through the streets. The men on the inside grinned at him; a number of them knew him and liked him. Gradually the door was opened and he crowded in. He found Sergeant Johnson and eyed him mutely.

"How the hell do you find these things out, I'd like to know," the sergeant exclaimed. "Are you a mind-reader?"

"I don't really know anything," Phil admitted with that humility which the police like on the part of newspaper men and seldom meet with. "Do you mind?"

"No objection," grunted the sergeant. "Been watching all the old crooks since these safes have been popping. Nothin' much on any of them, except this slippery wop, Tony Costello. No, we haven't caught him at anything. Seems to be keeping close and minding his own business. Working in his laboratory. Ought to make a good living if he turned honest; clever guy, he seems. But he's been too prosperous lately. Lots of machinery delivered to his place; we traced it to the manufacturers and find it cost thousands. Big deposits in his banks. But, no trace of his having sold anything or worked at anything outside his own place. So, we're running over to surprise him and help him get the cobwebs out of his closets."

* * * * *

The raid on Tony Costello's shop and laboratory disclosed nothing whatever. They surrounded the place effectively and surprised Tony genuinely. But a thorough search of every nook and cranny revealed nothing whatever of a suspicious nature. There was merely a tremendous amount of apparatus and machinery that none of the raiding party understood anything about. Tony's person was also thoroughly searched, and the leather-framed photograph of the beautiful unknown girl was found.

"Who's this?" the sergeant demanded. "She don't look like anyone that might belong to your crowd."

"I don't know," Tony replied.

"Whad'ya mean, don't know?" The sergeant gave him a rough shake. "What'ya carryin' it for, then?"

"I had really forgotten that it was in my pocket," Tony replied calmly, at his ease. "I found it in a hotel room one day, and liked the looks of it."

"I know you're lying there," the sergeant said, "though I'm ready to believe that you don't know her. Too high up for you. Well, it looks suspicious and we'll take the picture."

"Boy!" gasped Phil. "What a girl she must be in person! Even the picture would stand out among a thousand. May I have the picture, Sergeant?"

"You can come and get a copy of it tomorrow. We'll have it copied and see if we can trace the subject of it. That might tell us something."

* * * * *

The following morning Phil was at Police Headquarters to pick up further information, and to get a copy of the girl's photograph. Like the police, he could not keep his mind off the idea that there was some association between the crooked engineer and the disappearance of the safes. It seemed to fit too well. The scientific nature of the phenomena, Tony Costello's well known reputation for scientific brilliance, and his recent affluence; what else could it mean? In some way, Tony was getting at these safes. But how? And how prove it? Most exhaustive searches failed to reveal any traces of the safes anywhere. If any fragment of one of them had appeared in New York or San Francisco, the news would have come at once, such was the sensation all over the country that the series of disappearances had caused. Tony's calm insolence during the raid, his attitude of waiting patiently till the police should have had their fun and have it over with so that he might be left at peace again, showed that he must be guilty, for anyone else would have protested and felt deeply injured and insulted. He seemed to be enjoying their discomfiture, and absolutely confident of his own safety.

"There's got to be some way of getting him," Phil mused; and he mused almost absent-mindedly, for he was gazing at the photograph of the girl. For many minutes he looked at it, and then put it silently into his pocket.

Five o'clock in the evening of that same day came the news of another safe disappearance. Phil got his tip over the phone, and in fifteen minutes was at the scene. It was too much like the others to go into detail about; a six-foot portable safe had suddenly disappeared right in front of the eyes of the office staff of The Epicure, a huge restaurant and cafeteria that fed five thousand people three times a day. In its place stood a ragged, rusty old Ford coupe body. He went away from there, shaking his head.

Then suddenly in the midst of his dinner, he jumped up, and ran. An idea had leaped into his head.

"Right after one of these things pops is the time to take a peek at Tony," he said to himself, and immediately he was on the way.

* * * * *

But how to get his peep was not so easy a problem. When he alighted from his cab a block away from Tony's building, he was hesitant about approaching it. Tony knew him, and might see him first. Phil circled the brick building, keeping under cover or far enough away; all around it was a belt of thirty feet of lawn between the building and the sidewalk. Ought he have called the police and given them his idea? Or should he wait till darkness and see what he could do alone?

Then suddenly he saw her. Across the street, standing in the shelter of a delivery truck in front of an apartment, she was observing Tony's building intently. The aristocratic chin, the brightness of the eyes, the waves of her hair, and the general sunny expression! It could not be anyone else. Post haste he ran across the street.

"Pardon me!" he cried excitedly, lifting his hat and then digging hastily into his inner pocket. "I'm sure you must be the—"

"Well, the nerve!" the young woman said icily, and pointing her chin at the opposite horizon she walked haughtily away.

By that time Phil had dug out his picture and was running after her.

"Please," he said, "just a moment!" And he held the picture out in front of her face.

"Now, where in the world—?" She looked at him in puzzled and indignant inquiry, and then burst out laughing.

"It *is* you, isn't it?" Phil asked. "What are you laughing at?"

"Oh, you looked so abject. I'm sure your intentions must be good. Now tell me where you got my picture."

"Let us walk this way," suggested Phil, leading away from Tony's building.

* * * * *

And, as they walked, he told her the story. When he got through she stood and looked at him a long time in silence.

"You look square to me," she said. "You're working on my side already. Will you help me."

"I'll do anything—anything—" Phil said, and couldn't think of any other way of expressing his willingness, for the wonderful eyes bore radiantly upon him.

"First I must tell you my story," she began. "But before I can do so, you must promise me that it is to remain an absolute secret. You're a newspaper man—"

Phil gave his promise readily.

"My father is Professor Bloomsbury at the University of Chicago. He has been experimenting in mathematical physics, and I have been assisting him. He has succeeded in proving experimentally the concept of tensors. A tensor is a mathematical expression for the fact that space is smooth and flat, in three dimensions, only at an infinite distance from matter; in the neighbourhood of a particle of matter, there is a pucker or a wrinkle in space. My father has found that by suddenly removing a portion of matter from out of space, the pucker flattens out. If the matter is heavy enough and its removal sudden enough, there is a violent disturbance of space. By planning all the steps carefully my father has succeeded in swinging a section of space on a pivot through an angle of 180 degrees, and causing two portions of space to change places through hyperspace, or as you might express it popularly, through the fourth dimension."

* * * * *

Phil held his hands to his head.

"It is not difficult," she went on smiling. "Loan me your pocket knife and a piece of paper from your notebook. If I cut out a rectangular piece of paper from this sheet and mount it on a pivot or shaft at A B, I can rotate it through 180 degrees, just like a child's teeter-totter, so that X will be where Y originally was.

That is in two dimensions. Now, simply add one dimension all the way round and you will have what daddy is doing with space. He does it by shoving fifty or a hundred pounds of lead right out of space; the sudden flattening out of the tensors causes a section of space to flop around, and two portions of space change places. The first time he tried it, his desk disappeared, and we've never seen it again. We've thought it was somewhere out in hyperspace; but this terrible story of yours about disappearing safes, and the fact that you have this picture, means that someone has got the desk."

"Surely you must have suspected that long ago, when the disappearances first began?" Phil suggested.

"I've just returned from Europe," said Miss Bloomsbury. "I was tremendously puzzled when I got my first newspapers in New York and read about the safes. Gradually I gathered all the news on the subject, and it seemed most reasonable to suspect this gangster engineer."

"Great minds and same channels," Phil smiled. "But your father. Why didn't he speak up when the safes began to pop?"

"Ha! ha!" she laughed a tinkly little laugh. "My father doesn't know what safes are for, nor who is President, nor that there has been a war. Mother and I take care of him, and he works on tensors. He has probably never heard about the safes."

* * * * *

"What were you going to do around here?" Phil asked, marvelling at the courage of the girl who had come to look the situation over personally.

"I hadn't formed any definite plans. I just wanted to look about first."

"Well," said Phil, "as you will soon see by the papers, another safe has puffed out. It occurred to me that we might find out something by spying about here immediately after one of the disappearances. That's why I'm here. If you'll tell me where you live, or wait for me at some safe place, I'll come and report to you as soon as I find out anything."

"Oho! So that's the kind of a girl you think I am!" She laughed sunnily again. "No, Mr. Reporter. Either we reconnoitre together, or each on our own."

"Oh, together, by all means," said Phil so earnestly that she laughed again. "And since we'd better wait for darkness, let's have something to eat somewhere. I didn't finish my dinner."

Phil found Ione Bloomsbury in person to be even more wonderful than her photograph suggested. Obviously she had brains; it was apparent, too that she had breeding. Her cheerful view of the world was like a tonic for tired nerves; and withal, she had a gentle sort of courtesy in her manner that may have been old-fashioned, but it was almost too much for Phil. Before the dinner was over, he would have laid his heart at her feet. It gave him a thrill that went to his head, to have her by his side, slipping along through the darkness toward Tony's building.

This building was a one-story brick affair with a vast amount of window space. From the sidewalk they could see faint lights glowing within, but could make out no further details. They therefore selected the darkest side of the building, and made their way hurriedly across the lawn. Here, they found, they could see the crowding apparatus within the one long room fairly well. They looked into one window after another, making a circuit around the building, until Phil suddenly clutched the girl's arm.

"Look!" he whispered. "Straight ahead and a little to the left!"

At the place he indicated stood a tall safe. Across the top of its door were painted in gold letters, the words: "The Epicure."

"That's the safe that went to-night," whispered Phil. "That's all we need to know. Now, quick to a telephone!"

"Oh," said a gentle, ironic voice behind them, "not so quick!"

* * * * *

They whirled around and found themselves looking into two automatic pistols, and behind them in the light of the street lamps, the sardonic smile of Tony Costello.

"Charmed at your kind interest in my playthings, I'm sure," he purred. "Only it leaves me in an embarrassing position. I'm not exactly sure what to do about it. Kindly step inside while I think."

Phil made a move sidewise along the wall.

"Stop!" barked Costello sharply. "Of course," his voice was quiet again, "that might be the simplest way out. I think I am within my legal rights if I shoot people who are trying to break into my property. Yet, that would be messy—not neat. Better step in. The window swings outward."

At the point of his pistols they clambered through the window, and he came in after them. He kept on talking, as though to himself, but loud enough for them to hear.

"Yes, we want some way out that is neater than that. Hm! Violence distresses me. Never liked Ed's rough methods. Yet, this is embarrassing."

He turned to them.

"What did you really want here? I see that you are the *Examiner's* reporter, and that you are the lady of the photograph. What did you come here for? Ah, yes, the safe. Well, go over and look at it."

As they hesitated, he stamped his foot and shrilled crankily:

"I mean it! Go, look at the safe! Is there anything else you want to know?"

"Yes," said Phil coolly, his self-control returning, "where are the other safes?"

"Oh. Anything to oblige. Last requests are a sort of point of honour, aren't they. Ought to grant them. Stand close to that safe!"

* * * * *

He backed away, his guns levelled at them. He laid down the right one, keeping the left one aimed, and moved some knobs on a dial and threw over a big switch. A muffled rumbling and whirring began somewhere; and then, slowly, a block of tables and apparatus ten feet square rose upward toward the ceiling. A section of the floor on which they stood came up, supported by columns, and now formed the roof of a room that had risen out of the floor. In it were four safes.

"Poor old Ed!" sighed Tony. "There was a time when he had a lot of good stuff put away down there. I've got six rooms like that. Well, the good old times are over."

He threw out the switch and the whole mass sank slowly and silently downward till the floor was level and there was no further sign of it. Then he backed away to another table, across the room from them, keeping his gun levelled.

"Too bad," he said. "I don't like to do these things. But—" he sighed deeply, "self-preservation. Now I'm going to flip you out, yes, *out*, into a strange region. I've never been there. I don't know if there is food or drink there. I hope so, for you'll never get back here."

Phil stiffened. He determined to leap and risk a shot. But he was too late. Tony's hand came down on a switch. There was a sudden, nauseating jar. The laboratory vanished.

There was only the safe, Ione Bloomsbury and himself, and a small circle of concrete floor extending to a dim little horizon a dozen feet away. Beyond that, nothing. Not blue, as the sky is. Not black, as dark, empty spaces are. It suggested black, because there was no impression of light or colour on the eyes; but it wasn't black. It was nothingness.

IV
MAROONED IN HYPERSPACE

"I suppose you realize what he has done?" Miss Bloomsbury inquired.

"Couldn't be too sure, but it looks like plenty. What's the equation for it?" Beneath his jocularity, Phil felt a tremendous sinking within him. It looked serious, despite the fact that he did not understand it at all.

"He has swung us out into hyperspace, or into the fourth dimension, as your newspaper readers might understand it, and has let us hang there. Remember our slip of paper. Suppose X and Y were swung out of the plane of the paper and allowed to remain at an angle with it. We are at an angle with space, out in hyperspace."

There was a period of bewilderment, almost panic, in which they both felt so physically weak that they had to sit down on the concrete and stare at each other mutely. But this passed and their natural courage soon reasserted itself. Their first thought was to take stock of what information they could get on their situation; and their first step was to venture as close as possible to the queer little horizon which lay almost at their very feet. It gave them a frightened feeling, as though they were standing high up on a precipice or tower.

To their surprise, the horizon receded as they walked toward it, always remaining about a dozen feet away from them. At first they walked on concrete and then came to a crumbly edge of it and found themselves stepping on hard, sandy earth. Later there was rock, sometimes granite-like, sometimes black and shiny. But what they saw underfoot was nothing, compared with the glimpses of things they got out in the surrounding emptiness. First there was a vast space in which a soft light shone, and in which there were countless spheres of various sizes, motionlessly suspended. The spheres seemed to be made of wood, a green, sap-filled, unseasoned wood. The scene was visible for a few seconds, and vanished suddenly as they walked on. This astonished them; so they stepped back a pace or two and saw it again; and as they moved on, it disappeared again.

* * * * *

Then there was a great stretch of water in which the backs of huge monsters rolled and from which a hot wind blew for a few instants until they passed on and the scene vanished. There was a short walk with nothing but emptiness, and then there appeared huge, oblique, cubistic looking rows of jagged rocks in wild, dizzy formations that didn't look possible; and farther on, after another interval of emptiness, a tangle of brown, ropey vines with black-green leaves on them, an immense space filled with serpentine swinging loops and lengths of innumerable vines. Several loops projected so near them that they could have reached out and touched them had they wished.

"This is too much for me!" Phil gasped. "Have we gone crazy? Or did he kill us, and is this Purgatory?"

Ione smiled and shook her little head in which she had a goodly store of modern mathematics stored away.

"These must be glimpses of other 'spaces' besides our own space. If we could see in four dimensions we could see them all spread out before us. But we can only perceive in three dimensions; therefore, as we walk through hyperspace, past the different 'spaces' which are ranged about in it, we get a glimpse into such of them as are parallel with our own space. Can you understand that?"

"Oh, yes," groaned Phil. "It sounds just about like it looks. But, don't mind me. Go on, have your fun."

"I've been thinking about those wooden spheres," continued Ione. "I'm sure they must be sections of trees that are cut crosswise by our 'space;' they grow in three dimensions, but only two of them are our dimensions and a third is strange to us. We see only three-dimensional sections of them, which are spheres. There is more of them, that we cannot see, in another dimension."

"Yes, yes. Just as plain as the Jabberwock!"

"Look! There's a real Jabberwock!" exclaimed Ione.

On ahead of them they saw a number of creatures that seemed to be made of painted wooden balls in different colours, joined together.

"Tinkertoys!" exclaimed Phil. "Live ones! Big ones!"

The animals, though they looked for all the world as though they were made of painted wood, moved with jerky motions and clattered and snarled.

"There is probably more to *them* in another dimension," Ione said.

* * * * *

Suddenly one of the beasts approached them with a leap. There were two big eyes and two rows of teeth that came together with a snap, right on Phil's trouser-leg. He jerked himself away, sacrificing some square inches of trouser-leg, and, whirling around, kicked at the thing with all his force. It almost paralyzed his foot, for the animal seemed to be made of wood or bone. But it disappeared, and, as it did, both of them felt a queer, nauseating jolt. A few more minutes' walk brought them back to the safe without seeing any more spaces; and the sight of its black iron bulk filled them with a home-like relief, which in a moment they recognized as a mockery.

"Are we on a sphere of some sort?" Phil asked.

"Probably on an irregular mass of matter," Ione replied, "part of which is Tony's concrete floor, and part of which comes out of some other dimension. This mass of matter is at one end of a long, bar-like portion of space, the middle of which is pivoted in our world, somewhere in Chicago, and both ends of which are free in hyperspace."

"Then," suggested Phil, "why can't we walk down to the axle on which it is balanced, and step out into Chicago?"

"Because there isn't any *matter* for us to walk on. We are not able to move about in space, in three dimensions, you know. We can only get around in two dimensions, on the surface of *matter*."

"Well, let's try another exploration trip at right angles to our first one. After all, these 'spaces' are an interesting show, and I want to see some more."

They started out in the selected direction, and after a short walk got a glimpse of a vast space dotted with stars and nebulae, with two bright moons sailing overhead. A few steps farther on was a wall of solid granite, near enough to touch with their hands. Again, there was an intensely active mass of weaving bright stripes and loops and circles, seeming to consist of light only, and making them dizzy in a few seconds. Ione wondered if it might not be something like an organic molecule on a large scale. Again, odd, queer, indescribable shapes and outlines would appear and disappear, obviously three-dimensional sections of multi-dimensional things, cut by space. Once they passed a place of intense cold and terrific noise and escaped destruction or lunacy only because it took them the merest instant to get past.

They arrived back at the safe, very much fatigued from the strain, their minds woefully confused. Hunger and thirst were beginning to thrust up their little reminders; and for the first time the terrors of their position, flung out into hyperspace on a small, barren piece of matter, began to seem real.

* * * * *

After a rest they started out again. As Phil had touched, in kicking it, a creature from another "space," perhaps they might find water and even food somewhere. They retraced their first steps to the spot where they had at first seen water. They found it again and were able to dip their hands into it. It was warm, and too salty to drink. They came to the place with the creepers or vines, and Phil reached out and seized one of them. It was heavy, rubbery, and elastic, stretching readily as he pulled it.

"These little lurches that we feel must be the snapping back of the space-puckers as expressed by tensors," Ione remarked. "Every time matter goes in or out of space, the nature of space is altered."

"Well," observed Phil, releasing the vine, "I'd better be careful. If one of these things hauls me off here, our last bond with home is gone. I don't want to get lost in some other space."

As he released the vines they snapped back to their places, and the forest of them dimmed a little and reappeared.

They made the round again, dodging cautiously past the point where they had previously found the "Tinkertoy" animals, and succeeded in getting past their snapping teeth. But no promise of food or water did they find anywhere.

"Looks like we're sunk," observed Phil, as they dropped down on the concrete to rest, leaning their backs against the safe.

How time counted in hyperspace, neither Phil nor Ione could tell; Phil knew that his watch was running. He knew that it was ages and ages that he sat with his back against the safe, reviewing all the events of his past life, and thinking of this ignominious end to a lively career! He swore half aloud; then suddenly looked at Ione, ready to apologize. He found her weeping silently.

"I should never have let you come into the building with me," he stammered in confusion at her tears.

"Oh, what do I care what becomes of *me*!" she exclaimed angrily. "But who will take care of poor daddy? He doesn't even know when it's time to eat." And she burst into a fresh fit of weeping.

Phil bent his head in the dumbness of profound despair.

V
THE REVERSIBLE EQUATION

Despair, however, is a luxury. Necessity is a stimulus. With the parchings of thirst and the gnawings of hunger, the two young people ceased swearing and weeping. Phil got up and paced about and sat down again. Ione's tears stopped and dried, and she sat and thought.

In the back of her mind there had been forming a vague sort of an idea, which had signalled ahead of itself that there was hope. She sat there and desperately drove her reason to its utmost efforts, to find that idea and bring it to the surface of consciousness. Hand to hand fights with wild animals, battles between ships of the line, vicious duels between ace-aviators in the clouds are tense fights; but they cannot compare in anxious difficulty with the struggle to bring up an unformed idea out of the subconscious mind—especially when one knows that the idea is there, and that it must be found to save one's life.

"Ione!" exclaimed Phil. It was the first time he had used the name. "What is the matter? You are as tense as a—"

"Ah!" cried Ione, springing up. "Tense! Tensors! I have it!"

Phil gazed at her in alarm. She laughed; at first it was a strained laugh, but gradually it melted into her sunny one.

"No, I'm not crazy. I knew there was a way out, and I've been trying to reason it out. How simple. You remember the little jolts when you pulled at the vines and when you kicked the funny animal? Tensors. Matter and space are so closely interrelated that you can't move matter in or out of space without causing disturbance, recoils, and tremors in space. Those bits of matter were small, and produced only a slight disturbance. It takes about a hundred pounds of lead to swing this segment—"

"Oho! Got you!" exclaimed Phil. "Not so dumb! The safe!"

"Yes. The safe!" Ione cried.

"Throw it off and watch us swing, eh? What would happen?"

"I might calculate it if I knew the weight of the safe."

"No calculating when I'm around," Phil said. "It couldn't make things any worse. Try it first and calculate afterwards."

* * * * *

They got behind the safe and pushed, and their combined strength against it was about as effective as it would have been in moving the Peoples' Gas Building. They sat down again in despair.

"Suppose we *could* budge it," Ione said. "All we could do would be to push it around, this piece of matter we are on. That wouldn't help. We've got to get it out of space. We can't push it hard enough to do that. It's got to be shot out suddenly—"

"And we haven't got a gun handy," Phil remarked droopingly.

"Not exactly a gun. A sort of sling—"

Phil leaped to his feet.

"A sling. Why! To be sure! The vines!"

Without another word, both of them got up and ran. They hastened in a direction opposite to the one they had at first taken on their trip of exploration, and this brought them first past the "space" of the Tinkertoy-like animals. As they went by, several of these beasts darted at them, one of them snapping at Ione's heels. She uttered a scream, causing Phil to turn about and kick right and left among them. He drove them back and escaped from them, rejoining Ione.

"Wait," he said, when they reached the vines. "Remember those wooden balls. If I could get a few to throw at those critters—"

In a moment they were off, and finally arrived at the point from which they first saw the balls. Odd it seemed, how they hung suspended in space, thousands of them, all sizes. Phil reached out and grasped one about the size of a baseball and drew it toward himself. He felt a dizzy lurch and heard Ione scream.

"Let go!" she screamed again.

When he suddenly realized what was going on, he found himself prostrate on the ground, with Ione across him, her arms about his knees.

"Do you realize," she panted, disentangling herself, "that you were pulling yourself out of this space into that one?"

"Thanks!" said Phil. "Never say die. More careful this time, and a smaller one."

* * * * *

He reached out and grasped a ball smaller than a golf-ball, and pulled carefully, keeping an eye upon Ione. There was resistance to his pull, but gradually the ball came. It seemed heavy. There was a crack as of breaking wood, and he fell backward, with a wave of nausea sweeping strongly over him. He gazed in amazement at a heavy wooden stick that he held in his hands. The only thing about it that suggested the ball for which he had reached was its diameter.

"Can't understand it, but appreciate it just the same," he said. He broke the stick in two, and had two excellent clubs.

"Simple," Ione replied. "The balls are cross-sections of these trees or sticks which grow in a 'space' at right angles to our own; and we only see their three-dimensional cross-sections."

"Yes," said Phil. "Cabbages and kings. I'm for you and the party."

A short walk brought them to the "space" of the vines. After testing the matter out carefully, they found that they could each pull two of them at a time. The vines stretched amazingly when they found those whose far ends were fixed firmly in the tangle, permitting them to carry their own ends along with them toward the safe. Phil wound his vines around his left arm and stuck one club through his belt. The other he got ready for the wooden animals.

He needed it. The size of the pack was doubled, and he rapped them till his hand was numb before he and Ione got by. Their vines drew out thin, but held until they were firmly tied about the safe. They went back after four more.

"I should judge," said Phil, "that by the time we get thirty or forty, the elastic pull will be strong enough to drag the safe back with them as they snap back home."

* * * * *

Trip after trip they made, fighting the wooden animals with their clubs each time. Their clothes were torn, and their legs bleeding; their throats were dry and lips cracked. The hard animals seemed to have a persistent, mechanical ferocity that was undismayed by hammering with the clubs and by repeated repulses. Phil could not seem to hurt them; he merely knocked them away. Finally, on the ninth trip, Ione collapsed when she reached the safe. As she fell, the elasticity of the vines began slowly to drag her back with them. Phil was forced to sit across her knees while he tied his own vines about the safe. Then he released her and added her vines to the great cable about the safe.

An overbold hard animal rattled up and snapped at her. Goaded to fury, Phil swung at it with his club and hurled it through the air. He could feel the lurch as it left his space and entered another. Then he pushed with his mightiest effort against the safe. It budged, and slid a few inches. He used his stick as a lever. It moved again, a little faster. Ione struggled to her feet and tried to help, but her efforts were ineffectual.

With one arm about her, Phil pried again under the safe, knowing that another trip after vines was out of question. Another animal snapped at their heels. For a while, it was kick backwards, then a shove at the safe. Each time the safe moved. The sight of its movement revived Ione, so that she was able to push also. Gradually it acquired a steady motion, pulled by the contraction of the vines; its progress soon became faster and faster. Phil was about to follow it and give it another push, when Ione drew him back.

Suddenly they experienced a sinking sensation and a fearful vertigo. The snapping animals faded. Ahead of them was the forest of vines, and they saw the safe hurled into it, crashing, plunging into the tangled mass. The whole view crumpled and moved upwards like a swirl of leaves in a wind, and then vanished with a snap.

* * * * *

They were sick and dizzy, but tremendously curious to see everything. The water, the cubistic cliffs, the vast space full of balls, all curiously blurred, appeared in succession. There were blank spaces and then blurred sights of things which they did not recognize, never having seen them before. Then the dizziness and the nausea abated, and ahead of them was a vast yellow blue, a huge nebula, and in it were double-coloured suns and ringed planets with swarms of moons; this glorious sight remained for many seconds, as they gazed at it in panting astonishment, half reclining on the concrete; and then it faded. Again the nausea came on; again the succession of blurred views. Eventually the myriad spheres, the water with the leviathans, the forest of vines, each succeeding scene grew more blurred. Their nausea was correspondingly increased, till they were forced to lie down on the ground from illness.

When their giddiness abated, there were blurring views again. There was an impression as though the speed of a train were decreasing as one looks out of the window. And how one view held for several seconds, a vast and wild mountain-range with glaciers and snow peaks by moonlight. When this faded gradually, the scenes began to flick by, more and more rapidly, and grew blurred. Phil and Ione were attacked by nausea until, again, they had to lie down. After that came the familiar succession: the wooden animals, the tangle of vines, the vast sea, the spheres, and more blurred scenes. Then came a pause, with the nebula and the glorious suns swinging into view once again.

"Oh, I understand!" Ione exclaimed; "We're swinging. The safe was so heavy that we swung too violently, too far, and back again—"

"And we keep going till it knocks us out, or till the old cat dies," added Phil.

* * * * *

However, they found that after a number of repetitions of the same program, their giddiness was becoming less; and instead of lying down in the middle of the swing, they could look about. Then it occurred to Phil to time the interval between the nebula and the mountain-range. When the exact halfway point was determined, and after several more swings, they could see dimly the windows and machinery of Tony's laboratory flash by when they passed the middle.

"I don't mean to be a crepe-hanger, but how do you know we will stop at the right point?" Phil asked.

"I don't," replied Ione cheerfully. "But mathematics says so. A freely oscillating segment of space would naturally come to equilibrium in a position parallel to the rest of its own space, would it not?"

There came a swing when they did not reach the nebula on the one hand and the mountain-range on the other. After that, views dropped off from either end of the swing quite rapidly, and before many minutes, they looked into Tony's laboratory a large portion of the time. For many seconds the laboratory held; then it would gradually fade, and reappear again, only to fade into empty nothingness all around.

"The old cat's dead," Phil finally announced.

They sat and stared about them as the laboratory held steady and no further intervening periods of blankness intervened. They both sighed deeply and slumped over on the ground to rest.

"Bang! bang! bang!"

* * * * *

Some sort of hammering woke them up. They looked about them in a daze. It was broad daylight, and things looked queer in the laboratory. There was a smell of scorched rubber and hot oil. Great loops of wire sagged down from above.

Several nondescript heaps stood about that might once have been machinery, but now suggested melting snow-men, all fused into heaps. At a table sprawled a queer, misshapen figure that suggested human origin. Both of its hands were burned to cinders to the elbows. Great holes were scorched into the clothes. But the face was recognizable. Tony's playthings had got him at last.

"Looks like something's happened in here!" Phil gasped, in amazement.

"I'll bet it has, too," Ione exclaimed. "This is the first time it occurred to me that our recoil from throwing the safe overboard and the oscillation of our space-segment must have created a tremendous electrical field in the tetra-ordinate apparatus. The reaction is reversible, you see. The field swings the space-segment, or the swinging of the space-segment creates the field. And the field was too much for Tony."

At this point the door fell under the blows of the police, and the raiding squad rushed into the room.

THE GOSTAK AND THE DOSHES

by Miles J. Breuer

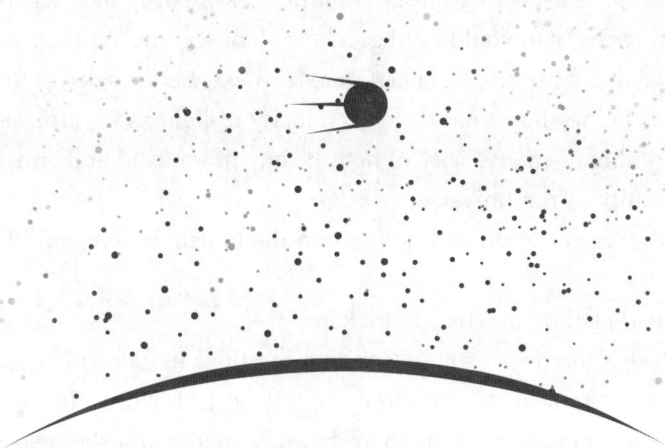

Why! That is lifting yourself by your own bootstraps!" I exclaimed in amazed incredulity. "It's absurd."

Woleshensky smiled indulgently. He towered in his chair as though in the infinite kindness of his vast mind there were room to understand and overlook all the foolish little foibles of all the weak little beings that called themselves men. A mathematical physicist lives in vast spaces where a lightyear is a footstep, where universes are being born and blotted out, where space unrolls along a fourth dimension on a surface distended from a fifth. To him, human beings and their affairs do not loom very important.

"Relativity," he explained. In his voice there was a patient forbearance for my slowness of comprehension. "Merely relativity. It doesn't take much physical effort to make the moon move through the treetops, does it? Just enough to walk down the garden path."

I stared at him and he continued:

"If you had been born and raised on a moving train, no one could convince you that the landscape was not in rapid motion. Well, our conception of the universe is quite as relative as that. Sir Issac Newton tried mathematics to express a universe as though beheld by an infinitely removed and perfectly fixed observer. Mathematicians since his time, realizing the futility of such an effort, have taken into consideration that what things 'are' depends upon the person who is looking at them. They have tried to express common knowledge, such as the law of gravitation, in terms that would hold good for all observers. Yet their leader and culminating genius, Einstein, has been unable to express knowledge in terms of pure relativity; he has had to accept the velocity of light as an arbitrarily fixed constant. Why should the velocity of light be any more fixed and constant than any other quantity in the universe?

"But, what's that got to do with going into the fourth dimension?" I broke in impatiently.

He continued as though I hadn't spoken.

"The thing that interests us now, and that mystifies modern mathematicians, is the question of movement, or more accurately: translation. Is there such a thing as *absolute translation?* Can there be movement—translation—except in *relation* to something else than the thing that moves? All movement we know of is movement in relation to other objects, whether it be a walk down the street, or the movement of the earth in its orbit around the sun. A change of *relative* position. But the mere translation of an isolated object existing alone in space is mathematically inconceivable; for there is no such thing as space in that sense."

"I thought you said something about going into another universe—" I interrupted again.

You can't argue with Woleshensky. His train of thought went on without a break.

"By translation we understand getting from one place to another. 'Going somewhere' originally meant a movement of our bodies. Yet, as a matter of fact, when we drive in an automobile, we 'go somewhere' without moving our bodies at all. The scene is changed around us; we are somewhere else; and yet we haven't *moved* at all.

"Or suppose you could cast off gravitational attraction for a moment and let the earth rotate under you; you would be going somewhere, and yet not moving—"

"But that is theory; you can't tinker with gravitation—"

"Every day you tinker with gravitation. When you start upwards in an elevator, your pressure, not your weight, against the floor of it is increased; apparent gravitation between you and the floor of the elevator is greater than before—and that's like gravitation is anyway: inertia and acceleration. But we are talking about translation. The position of everything in the universe must be referred to some sort of coordinates. Suppose we change the angle or direction of the coordinates: then you have 'gone somewhere' and yet you haven't moved, nor has anything else moved."

I looked at him, holding my head in my hands.

"I couldn't swear that I understand that," I said slowly. "And I repeat, that it looks like lifting yourself by your own bootstraps."

The homely simile did not dismay him. He pointed a finger at me as he spoke:

"You've seen a chip of wood bobbing on the ripples of a pond. Now you think the chip is moving; now the water. Yet neither is moving; the only motion is of an abstract thing called a wave.

"You've seen those 'illusion' diagrams, for instance this one of a group of cubes. Make up your mind that you are looking down upon their upper surfaces, and indeed they seem below you. Now change your mind, and imagine that you are down below, looking up. Behold, you see their lower surfaces; you are indeed below them. You have 'gone somewhere,' yet there has been no translation of anything. You have merely changed coordinates."

"Which do you think will drive me insane more quickly—if you *show* me what you mean, or if you keep on talking without showing me?"

"I'll try to show you. There are some types of mind, you know, that cannot grasp the idea of relativity. It isn't the mathematics involved that matters; it's just the inability of some types of mental organization to grasp the fact that the mind of the observer endows his environment with certain properties which have no absolute existence. Thus, when you walk through the garden at night the moon floats from one tree top to another. Is your mind good enough to invert this: make the moon stand still and let the trees move backwards. Can you do that? If so, you can 'go somewhere' into another dimension."

Woleshensky rose and walked to the window. His office was an appropriate setting for such a modern discussion as was ours; situated in a new, ultra-modern building on the University campus, the varnish glossy, the walls clean, the books neatly arranged behind clean glass, the desk in most orderly array; the office was just as precise and modern and wonderful as the mind of its occupant.

"When do you want to go?" he asked.

"Now!"

"Then, I have two more things to explain to you. The fourth dimension is just as much *here* as anywhere else. Right here around you and me things exist and go forward in the fourth dimension: but we do not see them and are not conscious of them, because we are confined to our own three. Secondly: if we name the four coordinates as Einstein does, *x*, *y*, *z*, and *t*, then we exist in *x*, *y*, and *z*, and move freely about in them; but are powerless to move in *t*. Why? Because *t* is the time dimension; and the time dimension is a difficult one for biological structures that depend on irreversible chemical reactions for their existence. But, biochemical reactions can take place along any one of the other dimensions as well as along *t*.

"Therefore, let us transform coordinates. Rotate the property of chemical irreversibility from *t* to *z*. Since we are organically able to exist (or at least to perceive) in only three dimensions at once, our new time dimension will be *z*. We shall be unconscious of *z* and cannot travel in it. Our activities and consciousness will take place along *x*, *y*, and *t*.

"According to fiction writers, to switch into the *t* dimension, some sort of an apparatus with an electrical field ought to be necessary. It is not. You need nothing more to rotate into the *t* dimension than you do to stop the moon and make the trees move as you ride down the road; or than you do to turn the cubes upside down. It is a matter of *relativity*."

I had ceased trying to wonder or to understand.

"Show me!" was all I could gasp.

"The success of this experiment in changing from the *z* to the *t* coordinate has depended largely upon my lucky discovery of a favourable location. It is just as, when you want the moon to ride the tree tops successfully, there have to be favourable features in the topography or it won't work. The edge of this building and that little walk between the two rows of Norway poplars seems to be an angle between planes in the *z* and *t* dimensions. It seems to slope downwards, does it not?—Now walk from here to the end and imagine yourself going upwards. That is all. Instead of feeling this building behind and *above* you, conceive it as behind and *below*. Just as on your ride by moonlight, you must tell yourself that the moon is not moving while the trees ride by—Can you do that? Go ahead then." He spoke in a confident tone, as though he knew exactly what would happen.

Half credulous, half wondering. I walked slowly out of the door; I noticed that Woleshensky settled himself down to the table with a pad and a pencil to some kind of study, and forgot me before I had finished turning around. I looked curiously at the familiar wall of the building and thc still more familiar poplar walk, expecting to see some strange scenery, some unknown view from another world. But there were the same old bricks and trees that I had known so long; though my disturbed and wondering frame of mind endowed them with a sudden strangeness and unwontedness. Things I had known for some years, they were, yet so powerfully had Woleshensky's arguments impressed me that I already fancied myself in a different universe. According to the conception of relativity, objects of the *x*, *y*, *z* universe *ought* to look different when viewed from the *x*, *y*, *t* universe.

Strange to say, I had no difficulty at all in imagining myself as going *upwards* on my stroll along the slope. I told myself that the building was behind and below me, and indeed it seemed real that it was that way. I walked some distance along the little avenue of poplars, which seemed familiar enough in all its details; though after a few minutes it struck me that the avenue seemed rather long. In fact, it was much longer than I had ever known it to be before.

With a queer Alice-in-Wonderland feeling I noted it stretching way on ahead of me. Then I looked back.

I gasped in astonishment. The building was indeed *below* me. I looked down upon it from the top of an elevation. The astonishment of that realization had barely broken over me, when I admitted that there was a building down there; but what building? Not the new Morton Hall, at least. It was a long, three-story brick building, quite resembling Morton Hall, but it was not the same. And on beyond there were trees with buildings among them; but it was not the campus that I knew.

I paused in a kind of panic. What was I to do now? Here I was in a strange place. How I had gotten there I had no idea. What ought I do about it? Where should I go? How was I to get back? Odd that I had neglected the precaution of how to get back. I surmised that I must be on the *t* dimension. Stupid blunder on my part, neglecting to find out how to get back.

I walked rapidly down the slope toward the building. Any hopes that I might have had about its being Morton Hall were thoroughly dispelled in a moment. It was a totally strange building, old, and old-fashioned looking. I had never seen it before in my life. Yet it looked perfectly ordinary and natural, and was obviously a University class-room building.

I cannot tell whether it was an hour or a dozen that I spent walking frantically this way and that, trying to decide to go into this building or another, and at the last moment backing out in a sweat of hesitation. It seemed like a year, but was probably only a few minutes. Then I noticed the people. They were mostly young people, of both sexes. Students, of course. Obviously I was on a University campus. Perfectly natural, normal young people, they were. If I were really on the *t* dimension, it certainly resembled the *z* dimension very closely.

Finally I came to a decision. I could stand this no longer. I selected a solitary, quiet-looking man, and stopped him.

"Where am I?" I demanded.

He looked at me in astonishment. I waited for a reply, and he continued to gaze at me speechlessly. Finally it occurred to me that he didn't understand English.

"Do you speak English?" I asked hopelessly.

"Of course!" he said vehemently. "What's wrong with you?"

"Something's wrong with something," I exclaimed. "I haven't any idea where I am or how I got here."

"Synthetic wine?" he asked sympathetically.

"Oh, hell! Think I'm a fool? Say, do you have a good man in mathematical physics on the faculty? Take me to him."

"Psychology, I should think," he said, studying me. "Or psychiatry. But I'm a law student and know nothing of either."

"Then make it mathematical physics, and I'll be grateful to you."

So I was conducted to the mathematical physicist. The student led me into the very building which corresponded to Morton Hall, and into an office the position of which quite corresponded to that of Woleshensky's room. However, the office was older and dustier; it had a Victorian look about it, and was not as modern as Woleshensky's room. Professor Vibens was a rather small, bald-headed man, with a keen looking face. As I thanked the law-student and started on my story, he looked rather bored, as though wondering why I had picked on him with my tale of wonder. Before I had gotten very far he straightened up a little; and further along he picked up another notch; and before many minutes he was tense in his chair as he listened to me. When I finished, his comment was terse, like that of a man accustomed to thinking accurately and to the point.

"Obviously you come into this world from another set of coordinates. As we are on the *z* dimension, you must have come to us from the *t* dimension—."

He disregarded my attempts to protest at this point.

"Your man Woleshensky has evidently developed the conception of relativity further than we have, although Monpeters' theory comes close enough to it. Since I have no idea how to get you back, you must be my guest. I shall enjoy hearing all about your world."

"That is very kind of you," I said gratefully. "I'm accepting because I can't see what else to do. At least until the time when I can find me a place in your world or get back on my own. Fortunately," I added as an afterthought, "no one will miss me there, unless it be a few classes of students who will welcome the little vacation that must elapse before my successor is found."

Breathlessly eager to find out what sort of a world I had gotten into, I walked with him to his home. And I may state at the outset that if I had found everything upside down and outlandishly bizarre, I should have been far less amazed and astonished than I was. For, from the walk that first evening from Professor Viben's office along several blocks of residence street to his solid and respectable home, through all of my goings about the town and country during the years that I remained in the *t*-dimensional world, I found people and things thoroughly ordinary and familiar. They looked and acted as we do, and their homes and goods looked like ours. I cannot possibly imagine a world and a people that could be more similar to ours without actually being the same. It was months before I got over the idea that I had merely wandered into an unfamiliar part of my own city. Only the actual experience of wide travel and much sight-seeing, and the knowledge that there was no such extensive English-speaking country on the world that I knew, convinced me that I must be on some other world, doubtless in the *t* dimension.

"A gentleman who has found his way here from another universe," the professor introduced me to a strapping young fellow who was mowing the lawn.

The professor's son was named John! Could anything be more commonplace?

"I'll have to take you around and show you things tomorrow," John said cordially, accepting the account of my arrival without surprise.

A red-headed servant-girl, roast-pork and rhubarb-sauce for dinner, and checkers afterwards, a hot bath at bedtime, the ringing of a telephone somewhere else in the house—is it any wonder that it was months before I would believe that I had actually come into a different universe? What slight differences there were in the people and the world, merely served to emphasize the similarity. For instance, I think they were just a little more hospitable and "old-fashioned" than we are. Making due allowances for the fact that I was a rather remarkable phenomenon, I think I was welcomed more heartily in this home and in others later, people spared me more of their time and interest from their daily business, than would have happened under similar circumstances in a correspondingly busy city in America.

Again, John found a lot of time to take me about the city and show me banks and stores and offices. He drove a little squat car with tall wheels, run by a spluttering gasoline motor. (The car was not as perfect as our modern cars, and horses were quite numerous in the streets. Yet John was a busy business man, the district superintendent of a life-insurance agency.) Think of it! Life insurance in Einstein's *t* dimension.

"You're young to be holding such an important position," I suggested.

"Got started early," John replied. "Dad is disappointed because I didn't see fit to waste time in college. Disgrace to the family, I am."

What in particular shall I say about the city? It might have been any one of a couple of hundred American cities. Only it wasn't. The electric street cars, except for their bright green colour, were perfect; they might have been brought over bodily from Oshkosh or Tulsa. The ten-cent stores with gold letters on their signs; drug-stores with soft drinks; a mad, scrambling stock-exchange; the blaring sign of an advertising dentist; brilliant entrances to motion-picture theatres, were all there. The beauty-shops did wonders to the women's heads, excelling our own by a good deal, if I am any judge; and at that time I had nothing more important on my mind than to speculate on that question. Newsboys bawled the *Evening Sun*, and the *Morning Gale* in whose curious, flat type I could read accounts of legislative doings, murders and divorces, quite as fluently as I could in my own *Tribune* at home. Strangeness and unfamiliarity had bothered me a good deal on a trip to Quebec a couple of years ago; but they were not noticeable here in the *t* dimension.

For three or four weeks the novelty of going around, looking at things, meeting people, visiting concerts, theatres, and department stores, was sufficient to absorb my interest. Professor Vibens' hospitality was so sincerely extended that I did not hesitate to accept, though I assured him that I would repay it as soon as I got established in this world. In a few days I was thoroughly convinced that there was no way back home. Here I must stay, at least until I learned as much as Woleshensky knew about crossing dimensions. Professor Vibens eventually secured for me a position at the University.

It was shortly after I had accepted the position as instructor in experimental physics and had begun to get broken into my work, that I noticed a strange commotion among the people of the city. I have always been a studious recluse, observing people as phenomena rather than participating in their activities. So for some time I noted only in a subconscious way the excited gathering in groups, the gesticulations and blazing eyes, the wild sale of extra editions of papers, the general air of disturbance. I even failed to take an active interest in these things when I made a railroad journey of three hundred miles and spent a week in another city; so thoroughly at home did I feel in this world that when the advisability arose of my studying laboratory methods in another University, I made the trip alone. So absorbed was I in my laboratory problems that I only noted with half an eye the commotion and excitement everywhere, and merely recollected it later. One night it suddenly popped into my head that the country was aroused over something.

That night I was with the Vibens' family in their living room. John tuned in the radio. I wasn't listening to the thing very much; I had troubles of my own. It was familiar enough to me. It meant the same and held as rigidly here as in my old world. But, what was the name of the bird who had formulated that law? Back home it was Newton. Tomorrow in class I would have to be thoroughly familiar with his name. Pasvieux, that's what it was. What messy surnames. It struck me that it was lucky that they expressed the laws of physics in the same form, and even in the same algebraical letters, or I might have had a time getting them confused—when all of a sudden the radio blatantly bawled:

"THE GOSTAK DISTIMS THE GOSHES!"

John jumped to his feet.

"Damn right!" he shouted, slamming the table with his fist.

Both his father and mother annihilated him with withering glances, and he slunk from the room. I gazed stupefied. My stupefaction continued while the Professor shut off the radio, and both of them excused themselves from my presence. Then suddenly I was alert.

I grabbed a bunch of newspapers, having seen none for several days. Great sprawling headlines covered the front pages:

"THE GOSTAK DISTIMS THE DOSHES."

For a moment I stopped, trying to recollect where I had heard those words before. They recalled something to me. Ah, yes! That very afternoon, there had been a commotion beneath my window on the University campus. I had been busy checking over an experiment so that I might be sure of its success at tomorrow's class, and looked out rather absently to see what was going on. A group of young men from a dismissed class was passing, and had stopped for a moment.

"I say, the gostak distims the doshes!" said a fine-looking young fellow. His face was pale and strained looking.

The young man facing him sneered derisively:

"Aw your grandmother! Don't be a feeble—"

He never finished. The first fellow's fist caught him in the cheek. Several books dropped to the ground. In a moment the two had clinched and were rolling on the ground, fists flying up and down, smears of blood appearing here and there. The others surrounded them, and for a moment appeared to enjoy the spectacle; but suddenly recollected that it looked rather disgraceful on a University campus, and after a lively tussle separated the combatants. Twenty of them, pulling in two directions, tugged them apart.

The first boy strained in the grasp of his captors; his white face was flecked with blood, and he panted for breath.

"Insult!" he shouted, giving another mighty heave to get free. He looked contemptuously around. "The whole bunch of you ought to learn to stand up for your honour. The gostak distims the doshes!"

That was the astonishing incident that these words called to my mind. I turned back to my newspapers.

"Slogan Sweeps the Country," proclaimed the sub-heads. "Ringing Expression of National Spirit! Enthusiasm Spreads Like Wildfire! The new patriotic slogan is gaining ground rapidly," the leading article went on. "The fact that it has covered the country almost instantaneously seems to indicate that it fills a deep and long-felt want in the hearts of the people. It was first uttered during a speech in Walkingdon by that majestic figure in modern statesmanship, Senator Harob. The beautiful sentiment, the wonderful emotion of this sublime thought, are epoch-making. It is a great conception, doing credit to a great man, and worthy of being the guiding light of a great people—"

That was the gist of everything I could find in the papers. I fell asleep, still puzzled about the thing. I was puzzled, because—as I see now and didn't see then—I was trained in the analytical methods of physical science, and knew little or nothing about the ways and emotions of the masses of the people.

In the morning the senseless expression popped into my head as soon as I awoke. I determined to waylay the first member of the Vibens family who showed up, and demand the meaning of the thing. It happened to be John.

"John, what's a gostak?"

John's face lighted up with pleasure. He threw out his chest and a look of pride replaced the pleasure. His eyes blazed, and with a consuming enthusiasm, he shook hands with me, as the deacons shake hands with a new convert—a sort of glad welcome.

"The gostak!" he exclaimed. "Hurray for the gostak!"

"But what is a gostak?"

"Not *a* gostak! *The* gostak. The gostak is—the distimmer of the doshes—see! He distims 'em, see?"

"Yes, yes. But what is distimming? How do you distim?"

"No, no! Only the gostak can distim. The gostak distims the doshes. See?"

"Ah, I see!" I exclaimed. Indeed, I pride myself on my quick wit. "What are doshes? Why, they are the stuff distimmed by the gostak. Very simple!"

"Good for you" John slapped my back in huge enthusiasm. "I think it wonderful for you to understand us so well, after being here only a short time. You are very patriotic."

I gritted my teeth tightly, to keep myself from speaking.

"Professor Vibens, what's a gostak?" I asked in the solitude of his office an hour later.

He looked pained.

He leaned back in his chair and looked me over elaborately, and waited some time before answering.

"Hush!" he finally whispered. "A scientific man may think what he pleases; but if he says too much, people in general may misjudge him. As a matter of fact, a good many scientific men are taking this so-called patriotism seriously. But a mathematician cannot use words loosely; it has become second nature with him to inquire closely into the meaning of every term he uses."

"Well, doesn't that jargon mean anything at all?" I was beginning to be puzzled in earnest.

"To me, it does not. But it seems to mean a great deal to the public in general. It's making people do things, is it not?"

I stood a while in stupefied silence. That an entire great nation should become fired up over a meaningless piece of nonsense! Yet, the astonishing thing was that I had to admit that there was plenty of precedent for it in the history of my own *z*-dimensional world. A nation exterminating itself in civil wars to decide which of two profligate royal families should be privileged to waste the people's substance from the throne; a hundred thousand crusaders marching to death for an idea that to me means nothing; a meaningless, untrue advertising slogan that sells millions of dollars' worth of cigarettes to a nation to the latter's own detriment—haven't we seen it over and over again?"

"There's a public lecture on this stuff tonight at the First Church of The Salvation," Professor Vibens suggested.

"I'll be there," I said. "I want to look into the thing."

That afternoon there was another flurry of "extras" over the street; people gathered in knots and gesticulated with open newspapers.

"War! Let 'em have it!" I heard men shout.

"Is our national honour a rag to be muddied and trampled on?" the editorial asked.

As far as I could gather from reading the papers, there was a group of nations across an ocean that was not taking the gostak seriously. A ship whose pennant bore the slogan had been refused entrance to an Engtalian harbour because it flew no national ensign. The Executive had dispatched a diplomatic note. An evangelist who had attempted to preach the gospel of the distimmed doshes at a public gathering in Itland had been ridden on a rail and otherwise abused. The Executive was dispatching a diplomatic note.

Public indignation waxed high. Derogatory remarks about "wops" were flung about. Shouts of "Holy war!" were heard. I could feel the tension in the atmosphere as I took my seat in the crowded church in the evening. I had been assured that the message of the gostak and the doshes would be thoroughly expounded so that even the most simple-minded and uneducated people could understand it fully. Although I had my hands full at the University, I was so puzzled and amazed at the course that events were taking that I determined to give the evening to finding out what the "slogan" meant.

There was a good deal of singing before the lecture began. Mimeographed copies of the words were passed about, but I neglected to preserve them, and do not remember them. I know there was one solemn hymn that reverberated harmoniously through the great church, a chanting repetition of "The Gostak

Distims the Doshes." There was another stirring martial air, that began: "Oh the Gostak! Oh the Gostak!"—and ended with a swift cadence on the "Gostak Distims the Doshes!" The speaker had a rich, eloquent voice and a commanding figure. He stepped out and bowed solemnly.

"The gostak distims the doshes," he pronounced impressively. "Is it not comforting to know that there is a gostak; do we not glow with pride because the doshes are distimmed? In the entire universe there is no more profoundly significant fact: the gostak distims the doshes. Could anything more complete, yet more tersely emphatic. The gostak distims the doshes!" Applause. "This thrilling truth affects our innermost lives. What would we do if the gostak did not distim the doshes? Without the gostak, without doshes, what would we do? What would we think? How would we feel?—" Applause again.

At first I thought this was some kind of an introduction. I was inexperienced in listening to popular speeches, lectures, and sermons. I had spent most of my life in the study of physics and its accessory sciences. I could not help trying to figure out the meaning of whatever I heard. When I found none I began to get impatient. I waited some more, thinking that soon he would begin on the real explanation. After thirty minutes of the same sort of stuff as I have just quoted, I gave up trying to listen. I just sat and hoped he would soon be through. The people applauded and grew more excited. After an hour, I stirred restlessly; I slouched down in my seat and sat up by turns. After two hours I grew desperate; I got up and walked out. Most of the people were too excited to notice me. Only a few of them cast hostile glances at my retreat.

The next day the mad nightmare began for me. First there was a storm of "extras" over the city, announcing the sinking of a merchantman by an Engtalian cruiser. A dispute had arisen between the officers of the merchantman and the port officials, because the latter had jeered disrespectfully at the gostak. The merchantman picked up and started out without having fulfilled all the Customs requirements. A cruiser followed it and ordered it to return. The captain of the merchantman told them that the gostak distims the doshes, whereupon the cruiser fired twice and sank the merchantman. In the afternoon came the "extras" announcing the Executive's declaration of war.

Recruitment offices opened; the University was depleted of its young men; uniformed troops marched through the city, and railway trains full of them went in and out. Campaigns for raising war loans; homeguards, women's auxiliaries, ladies' aid societies making bandages, young women enlisting as ambulance drivers—it was indeed war; all of it to the constantly repeated slogan: "The gostak distims the doshes."

I could hardly believe that it was really true. There seemed to be no adequate cause for a war. The huge and powerful nation had dreamed a silly slogan and flung it in the world's face. A group of nations across the water had united into an alliance, claiming they had to defend themselves against having forced upon them a principle they did not desire. The whole thing at the bottom had no meaning. It did not seem possible that there would actually be a war; it seemed more like going through a lot of elaborate play-acting.

Only when the news came of a vast naval battle of doubtful issue, in which ships had been sunk and thousands of lives lost, did it come to me that they meant business. Black bands of mourning appeared on sleeves and in windows. One of the allied countries was invaded and a front-line set up. Reports of a division wiped out by an airplane attack; of forty thousand dead in a five-day battle; of more men and more money needed, began to make things look real. Haggard men with bandaged heads and arms in slings appeared on the streets; a church and an auditorium were converted into hospitals; and trainloads of wounded were brought in. To convince myself that this thing was so, I visited these wards, and saw with my own eyes the rows of cots, the surgeons working on ghastly wounds, the men with a leg missing or with a hideously disfigured face.

Food became restricted; there was no white bread, and sugar was rationed. Clothing was of poor quality; coal and oil were obtainable only on government permit. Businesses were shut down. John was gone; his parents received news that he was missing in action.

Real it was; there could be no more doubt of it. The thing that made it seem most real was the picture of a mangled, hopeless wreck of humanity sent back from the guns, a living protest against the horror of war. Suddenly someone would say: "The gostak distims the doshes!" and the poor wounded fragment would straighten up and put out his chest with pride, and an unquenchable fire would blaze in his eyes. He did not regret having given his all for that. How could I understand it?

And real it was when the draft was announced. More men were needed; volunteers were insufficient. Along with the rest, I complied with the order to register, doing so in a mechanical fashion, thinking little of it. Suddenly the coldest realization of the reality of it was flung at me, when I was informed that my name had been drawn and that I would have to go!

All this time I had looked upon this mess as something outside of me; something belonging to a different world, of which I was not a part. Now here was a card summoning me to training camp. With all this death and mangled humanity in the background, I wasn't even interested in this world. I didn't belong here. To be called upon to undergo all the horrors of military life, the risk of a horrible death, for no reason at all! For a silly jumble of meaningless sounds.

I spent a sleepless night in maddened shock from the thing. In the morning a wild and haggard caricature of myself looked back at me from the mirror. But I had revolted. I intended to refuse service. If the words conscientious objector ever meant anything, I certainly was one. Even if they shot me for treason at once, that would be a fate less hard to bear than going out and giving my strength and my life for—for nothing at all.

My apprehensions were quite correct. With my usual success at self-control over a seething interior, I coolly walked to the draft office and informed them that I did not believe in their cause and could not see my way to fight for it. Evidently they had suspected something of that sort already, for they had the irons on my wrists before I had hardly done with my speech.

"Period of emergency," said a beefy tyrant at the desk; "no time for stringing out a civil trial. Court martial!"

He said it at me vindictively, and the guards jostled me roughly down the corridor; even they resented my attitude. The court-martial was already waiting for me. From the time I walked out of the lecture at the church I had been under secret surveillance; and they knew my attitude thoroughly. That is the first thing the president of the court informed me.

My trial was short. I was informed that I had no valid reason for objecting. Objectors because of religion, because of nationality, and similar reasons, were readily understood; a jail sentence to the end of the war was their usual fate. But I admitted that I had no intrinsic objection to fighting; I merely jeered at their holy cause. That was treason unpardonable.

"Sentenced to be shot at sunrise!" the president of the court announced.

The world spun around with me. But only for a second. My self-control came to my aid. With the curious detachment that comes to us in such emergencies, I noted that the court-martial was being held in Professor Vibens' office; that dingy little Victorian room, where I had first told my story of travelling by relativity and had first realized that I had come to the *t*-dimensional world. Apparently it was also to be the last room I was to see in this same world. I had no false hopes that the execution would help me back to my own world, as such things sometimes do in stories. When life is gone, it is gone, whether in one dimension or another. I would be just as dead in the *z* dimension as in the *t* dimension.

"Now, Einstein, or never?" I thought. "Come to my aid, O Riemann! O Lobatchewsky! If anything will save me it will have to be a tensor or a geodesic."

I said it to myself rather ironically. Relativity had brought me here. Could it get me out of this?

Well! Why not?

If the form of a natural law, yea, if a natural object varies with the observer who expresses it, might not the truth and the meaning of the gostak slogan also be a matter of relativity? It was like making the moon ride the tree tops again. If I could be a better relativist, and put myself in these people's place, perhaps I could understand the gostak. Perhaps I would even be willing to fight for him or it.

The idea struck me suddenly. I must have straightened up and some bright change must have passed over my features, for the guards who led me looked at me curiously and took a firmer grip on me. We had just descended the steps of the building and had started down the walk.

Making the moon ride the tree tops! That was what I needed now. And that sounded as silly to me as the gostak. And the gostak did not seem so silly. I drew a deep breath and felt very much encouraged. The viewpoint of *relativity* was somehow coming back to me. Necessity manages much. I could understand how one might fight for the idea of a gostak distimming the doshes. I felt almost like telling these men. Relativity is a wonderful thing. They led me up the slope, between the rows of poplars.

Then it all suddenly popped into my head; how I had gotten here by changing my coordinates, insisting to myself that I was going *upwards*. Just like making the moon stop and making the trees ride, when you are out riding at night. Now I was going upwards. In my own world, in the *z* dimension, this same poplar was *down* the slope.

"It's downwards!" I insisted to myself. I shut my eyes, and imagined the building behind and *above* me. With my eyes shut, it did seem downwards. I walked for a long time before opening them. Then I opened them and looked around.

I was at the end of the avenue of poplars. I was surprised. The avenue seemed short. Somehow it had become shortened; I had not expected to reach the end so soon. And where were the guards in olive uniform? There were none.

I turned around and looked back. The slope extended on backwards above me. Indeed I had walked downwards. There were no guards, and the fresh, new building was on the hill behind me.

Woleshensky stood on the steps.

"Now what do you think of a *t* dimension," he called out to me.

Woleshensky!

And a *new* building, modern! Vibens' office was in an old, Victorian building. What was there in common between Vibens and Woleshensky? I drew a deep breath. The comforting realization spread gratefully over me that I was back in my native dimension. The gostak and the war were somewhere else. Here were peace and Woleshensky.

I hastened to pour out the story to him.

"What does it all mean?" I asked when I was through. "Somehow—vaguely—it seems that it ought to mean something."

"Perhaps," he said in his kind, sage way, "we really exist in four dimensions. A part of us and our world that we cannot see and are not conscious of, projects on into another dimension; just like the front edges of the books in the bookcase, turned away from us. You know that the section of a conic cut by the *y* plane looks different than the section of the same conic by the *z* plane? Perhaps what you saw was our own world and our own selves, intersected by a different set of co-ordinates. *Relativity*, as I told you in the beginning."

BY THE WATERS OF BABYLON

by Stephen Vincent Benét

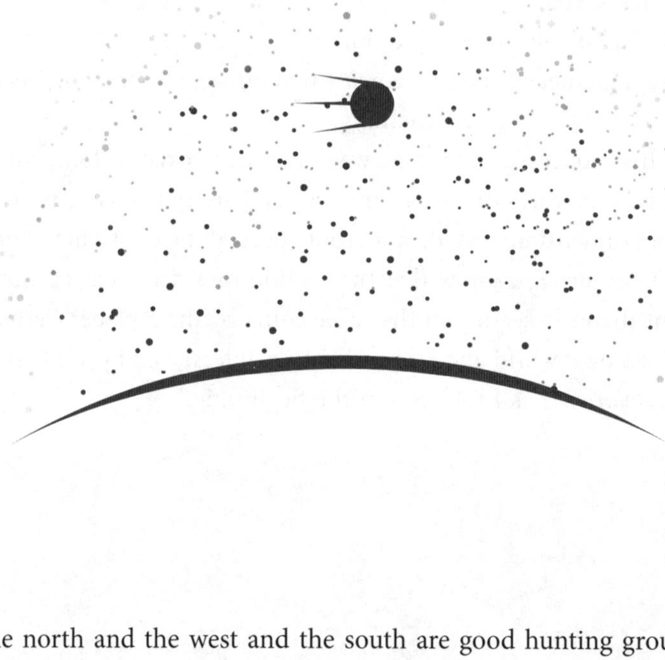

The north and the west and the south are good hunting ground, but it is forbidden to go east. It is forbidden to go to any of the Dead Places except to search for metal and then he who touches the metal must be a priest or the son of a priest. Afterwards, both the man and the metal must be purified. These are the rules and the laws; they are well made. It is forbidden to cross the great river and look upon the place that was the Place of the Gods—this is most strictly forbidden. We do not even say its name though we know its name. It is there that spirits live, and demons—it is there that there are the ashes of the Great Burning. These things are forbidden—they have been forbidden since the beginning of time.

My father is a priest; I am the son of a priest. I have been in the Dead Places near us, with my father—at first, I was afraid. When my father went into the house to search for the metal, I stood by the door and my heart felt small and weak. It was a dead man's house, a spirit house. It did not have the smell of man, though there were old bones in a corner. But it is not fitting that a priest's son should show fear. I looked at the bones in the shadow and kept my voice still.

Then my father came out with the metal—good, strong piece. He looked at me with both eyes but I had not run away. He gave me the metal to hold—I took it and did not die. So he knew that I was truly his son and would be a priest in my time. That was when I was very young—nevertheless, my brothers would not have done it, though they are good hunters. After that, they gave me the good piece of meat and the warm corner of the fire. My father watched over me—he was glad that I should be a priest. But when I boasted or wept without a reason, he punished me more strictly than my brothers. That was right.

After a time, I myself was allowed to go into the dead houses and search for metal. So I learned the ways of those houses—and if I saw bones, I was no longer afraid. The bones are light and old—sometimes they will fall into dust if you touch them. But that is a great sin.

I was taught the chants and the spells—I was taught how to stop the running of blood from a wound and many secrets. A priest must know many secrets—that was what my father said.

If the hunters think we do all things by chants and spells, they may believe so—it does not hurt them. I was taught how to read in the old books and how to make the old writings—that was hard and took a long time. My knowledge made me happy—it was like a fire in my heart. Most of all, I liked to hear of the Old Days and the stories of the gods. I asked myself many questions that I could not answer, but it was good to ask them. At night, I would lie awake and listen to the wind—it seemed to me that it was the voice of the gods as they flew through the air.

We are not ignorant like the Forest People—our women spin wool on the wheel, our priests wear a white robe. We do not eat grubs from the trees, we have not forgotten the old writings, although they are hard to understand. Nevertheless, my knowledge and my lack of knowledge burned in me—I wished to know more. When I was a man at last, I came to my father and said, "It is time for me to go on my journey. Give me your leave."

He looked at me for a long time, stroking his beard, then he said at last, "Yes.

It is time." That night, in the house of the priesthood, I asked for and received purification. My body hurt but my spirit was a cool stone. It was my father himself who questioned me about my dreams.

He bade me look into the smoke of the fire and see—I saw and told what I saw. It was what I have always seen—a river, and, beyond it, a great Dead Place and in it the gods walking. I have always thought about that. His eyes were stern when I told him he was no longer my father but a priest. He said, "This is a strong dream."

"It is mine," I said, while the smoke waved and my head felt light. They were singing the Star song in the outer chamber and it was like the buzzing of bees in my head.

He asked me how the gods were dressed and I told him how they were dressed. We know how they were dressed from the book, but I saw them as if they were before me. When I had finished, he threw the sticks three times and studied them as they fell.

"This is a very strong dream," he said. "It may eat you up."

"I am not afraid," I said and looked at him with both eyes. My voice sounded thin in my ears but that was because of the smoke.

He touched me on the breast and the forehead. He gave me the bow and the three arrows.

"Take them," he said. "It is forbidden to travel east. It is forbidden to cross the river. It is forbidden to go to the Place of the Gods. All these things are forbidden."

"All these things are forbidden," I said, but it was my voice that spoke and not my spirit. He looked at me again.

"My son," he said. "Once I had young dreams. If your dreams do not eat you up, you may be a great priest. If they eat you, you are still my son. Now go on your journey."

I went fasting, as is the law. My body hurt but not my heart. When the dawn came, I was out of sight of the village. I prayed and purified myself, waiting for a sign. The sign was an eagle. It flew east.

Sometimes signs are sent by bad spirits. I waited again on the flat rock, fasting, taking no food. I was very still—I could feel the sky above me and the earth beneath. I waited till the sun was beginning to sink. Then three deer passed in the valley going east—they did not mind me or see me. There was a white fawn with them—a very great sign.

I followed them, at a distance, waiting for what would happen. My heart was troubled about going east, yet I knew that I must go. My head hummed with my fasting—I did not even see the panther spring upon the white fawn. But, before I knew it, the bow was in my hand. I shouted and the panther lifted his head from the fawn. It is not easy to kill a panther with one arrow but the arrow went through his eye and into his brain. He died as he tried to spring—he rolled over, tearing at the ground. Then I knew I was meant to go east—I knew that was my journey. When the night came, I made my fire and roasted meat.

It is eight suns' journey to the east and a man passes by many Dead Places. The Forest People are afraid of them but I am not. Once I made my fire on the edge of a Dead Place at night and, next morning, in the dead house, I found a good knife, little rusted. That was small to what came afterward but it made my heart feel big. Always when I looked for game, it was in front of my arrow, and twice I passed hunting parties of the Forest People without their knowing. So I knew my magic was strong and my journey clean, in spite of the law.

Toward the setting of the eighth sun, I came to the banks of the great river. It was half-a-day's journey after I had left the god-road—we do not use the god-roads now for they are falling apart into great blocks of stone, and the forest is safer going. A long way off, I had seen the water through trees but the trees were thick. At last, I came out upon an open place at the top of a cliff. There was the great river below, like a giant in the sun. It is very long, very wide. It could eat all the streams we know and still be thirsty. Its name is Ou-dis-sun, the Sacred, the Long. No man of my tribe had seen it, not even my father, the priest. It was magic and I prayed.

Then I raised my eyes and looked south. It was there, the Place of the Gods.

How can I tell what it was like—you do not know. It was there, in the red light, and they were too big to be houses. It was there with the red light upon it, mighty and ruined. I knew that in another moment the gods would see me. I covered my eyes with my hands and crept back into the forest.

Surely, that was enough to do, and live. Surely it was enough to spend the night upon the cliff. The Forest People themselves do not come near. Yet, all through the night, I knew that I should have to cross the river and walk in the places of the gods, although the gods ate me up. My magic did not help me at all and yet there was a fire in my bowels, a fire in my mind. When the sun rose, I thought, "My journey has been clean. Now I will go home from my journey." But, even as I thought so, I knew I could not. If I went to the Place of the Gods,

I would surely die, but, if I did not go, I could never be at peace with my spirit again. It is better to lose one's life than one's spirit, if one is a priest and the son of a priest.

Nevertheless, as I made the raft, the tears ran out of my eyes. The Forest People could have killed me without fight, if they had come upon me then, but they did not come.

When the raft was made, I said the sayings for the dead and painted myself for death. My heart was cold as a frog and my knees like water, but the burning in my mind would not let me have peace. As I pushed the raft from the shore, I began my death song—I had the right. It was a fine song.

"I AM JOHN, SON OF JOHN," I SANG. "MY PEOPLE ARE THE HILL PEOPLE. THEY ARE THE MEN.
I GO INTO THE DEAD PLACES BUT I AM NOT SLAIN.
I TAKE THE METAL FROM THE DEAD PLACES BUT I AM NOT BLASTED.
I TRAVEL UPON THE GOD-ROADS AND AM NOT AFRAID. E-YAH! I HAVE KILLED THE PANTHER, I HAVE KILLED THE FAWN!
E-YAH! I HAVE COME TO THE GREAT RIVER. NO MAN HAS COME THERE BEFORE.
IT IS FORBIDDEN TO GO EAST, BUT I HAVE GONE, FORBIDDEN TO GO ON THE GREAT RIVER, BUT I AM THERE.
OPEN YOUR HEARTS, YOU SPIRITS, AND HEAR MY SONG.
NOW I GO TO THE PLACE OF THE GODS, I SHALL NOT RETURN.
MY BODY IS PAINTED FOR DEATH AND MY LIMBS WEAK, BUT MY HEART IS BIG AS I GO TO THE PLACE OF THE GODS!"

All the same, when I came to the Place of the Gods, I was afraid, afraid. The current of the great river is very strong—it gripped my raft with its hands. That was magic, for the river itself is wide and calm. I could feel evil spirits about me, I was swept down the stream. Never have I been so much alone—I tried to think of my knowledge, but it was a squirrel's heap of winter nuts. There was no strength in my knowledge any more and I felt small and naked as a new-hatched bird—alone upon the great river, the servant of the gods.

Yet, after a while, my eyes were opened and I saw. I saw both banks of the river—I saw that once there had been god-roads across it, though now they were broken and fallen like broken vines. Very great they were, and wonderful and broken—broken in the time of the Great Burning when the fire fell out of the sky. And always the current took me nearer to the Place of the Gods, and the huge ruins rose before my eyes.

I do not know the customs of rivers—we are the People of the Hills. I tried to guide my raft with the pole but it spun around. I thought the river meant to take me past the Place of the Gods and out into the Bitter Water of the legends. I grew angry then—my heart felt strong. I said aloud, "I am a priest and the son of a priest!" The gods heard me—they showed me how to paddle with the pole on one side of the raft. The current changed itself—I drew near to the Place of the Gods.

When I was very near, my raft struck and turned over. I can swim in our lakes—I swam to the shore. There was a great spike of rusted metal sticking out into the river—I hauled myself up upon it and sat there, panting. I had saved my bow and two arrows and the knife I found in the Dead Place but that was all. My raft went whirling downstream toward the Bitter Water. I looked after it, and thought if it had trod me under, at least I would be safely dead. Nevertheless, when I had dried my bowstring and re-strung it, I walked forward to the Place of the Gods.

It felt like ground underfoot; it did not burn me. It is not true what some of the tales say, that the ground there burns forever, for I have been there. Here and there were the marks and stains of the Great Burning, on the ruins, that is true. But they were old marks and old stains. It is not true either, what some of our priests say, that it is an island covered with fogs and enchantments. It is not. It is a great Dead Place—greater than any Dead Place we know. Everywhere in it there are god-roads, though most are cracked and broken. Everywhere there are the ruins of the high towers of the gods.

How shall I tell what I saw? I went carefully, my strung bow in my hand, my skin ready for danger. There should have been the wailings of spirits and the shrieks of demons, but there were not. It was very silent and sunny where I had landed—the wind and the rain and the birds that drop seeds had done their work—the grass grew in the cracks of the broken stone. It is a fair island—no wonder the gods built there. If I had come there, a god, I also would have built.

How shall I tell what I saw? The towers are not all broken—here and there one still stands, like a great tree in a forest, and the birds nest high. But the towers themselves look blind, for the gods are gone. I saw a fishhawk, catching fish in the river. I saw a little dance of white butterflies over a great heap of broken stones and columns. I went there and looked about me—there was a carved stone with cut—letters, broken in half. I can read letters but I could not understand these. They said UBTREAS. There was also the shattered image of a man or a god. It had been made of white stone and he wore his hair tied back like a woman's. His name was ASHING, as I read on the cracked half of a stone. I thought it wise to pray to ASHING, though I do not know that god.

How shall I tell what I saw? There was no smell of man left, on stone or metal. Nor were there many trees in that wilderness of stone. There are many pigeons, nesting and dropping in the towers—the gods must have loved them, or, perhaps, they used them for sacrifices. There are wild cats that roam the god-roads, green-eyed, unafraid of man. At night they wail like demons but they are not demons. The wild dogs are more dangerous, for they hunt in a pack, but them I did not meet till later. Everywhere there are the carved stones, carved with magical numbers or words.

I went north—I did not try to hide myself. When a god or a demon saw me, then I would die, but meanwhile I was no longer afraid. My hunger for knowledge burned in me—there was so much that I could not understand. After a while, I knew that my belly was hungry. I could have hunted for my meat, but I did not hunt. It is known that the gods did not hunt as we do—they got their food from enchanted boxes and jars. Sometimes these are still found in the Dead Places—once, when I was a child and foolish, I opened such a jar and tasted it and found the food sweet. But my father found out and punished me for it strictly, for, often, that food is death. Now, though, I had long gone past what was forbidden, and I entered the likeliest towers, looking for the food of the gods.

I found it at last in the ruins of a great temple in the mid-city. A mighty temple it must have been, for the roof was painted like the sky at night with its stars—that much I could see, though the colours were faint and dim. It went down into great caves and tunnels—perhaps they kept their slaves there. But when I started to climb down, I heard the squeaking of rats, so I did not go—rats are unclean, and there must have been many tribes of them, from the squeaking. But near there, I found food, in the heart of a ruin, behind a door that still opened. I ate only the fruits from the jars—they had a very sweet taste. There was drink, too, in bottles of glass—the drink of the gods was strong and made my head swim. After I had eaten and drunk, I slept on the top of a stone, my bow at my side.

When I woke, the sun was low. Looking down from where I lay, I saw a dog sitting on his haunches. His tongue was hanging out of his mouth; he looked as if he were laughing. He was a big dog, with a gray-brown coat, as big as a wolf. I sprang up and shouted at him but he did not move—he just sat there as if he were laughing. I did not like that. When I reached for a stone to throw, he moved swiftly out of the way of the stone. He was not afraid of me; he looked at me as if I were meat. No doubt I could have killed him with an arrow, but I did not know if there were others. Moreover, night was falling.

I looked about me—not far away there was a great, broken god-road, leading north. The towers were high enough, but not so high, and while many of the dead-houses were wrecked, there were some that stood. I went toward this god-road, keeping to the heights of the ruins, while the dog followed. When I had reached the god-road, I saw that there were others behind him. If I had slept later, they would have come upon me asleep and torn out my throat. As it was, they were sure enough of me; they did not hurry. When I went into the dead-house, they kept watch at the entrance—doubtless they thought they would have a fine hunt. But a dog cannot open a door and I knew, from the books, that the gods did not like to live on the ground but on high.

I had just found a door I could open when the dogs decided to rush. Ha! They were surprised when I shut the door in their faces—it was a good door, of strong metal. I could hear their foolish baying beyond it but I did not stop to answer them. I was in darkness—I found stairs and climbed. There were many stairs, turning around till my head was dizzy. At the top was another door—I found the knob and opened it. I was in a long small chamber—on one side of it was a bronze door that could not be opened, for it had no handle. Perhaps there was a magic word to open it but I did not have the word. I turned to the door in the opposite side of the wall. The lock of it was broken and I opened it and went in.

Within, there was a place of great riches. The god who lived there must have been a powerful god. The first room was a small ante-room—I waited there for some time, telling the spirits of the place that I came in peace and not as a robber. When it seemed to me that they had had time to hear me, I went on. Ah, what riches! Few, even, of the windows had been broken—it was all as it had been. The great windows that looked over the city had not been broken at all though they were dusty and streaked with many years. There were coverings on the floors, the colours not greatly faded, and the chairs were soft and deep. There were pictures upon the walls, very strange, very wonderful—I remember one of a bunch of flowers in a jar—if you came close to it, you could see nothing but bits of colour, but if you stood away from it, the flowers might have been picked yesterday. It made my heart feel strange to look at this picture—and to look at the figure of a bird, in some hard clay, on a table and see it so like our birds. Everywhere there were books and writings, many in tongues that I could not read. The god who lived there must have been a wise god and full of knowledge. I felt I had a right there, as I sought knowledge also.

Nevertheless, it was strange. There was a washing-place but no water—perhaps the gods washed in air. There was a cooking-place but no wood, and though there was a machine to cook food, there was no place to put fire in it. Nor were there candles or lamps—there were things that looked like lamps but they had neither oil nor wick. All these things were magic, but I touched them and lived—the magic had gone out of them. Let me tell one thing to show. In the washing-place, a thing said "Hot" but it was not hot to the touch—another thing said "Cold" but it was not cold. This must have been a strong magic but the magic was gone. I do not understand—they had ways—I wish that I knew.

It was close and dry and dusty in the house of the gods. I have said the magic was gone but that is not true—it had gone from the magic things but it had not gone from the place. I felt the spirits about me, weighing upon me. Nor had I ever slept in a Dead Place before—and yet, tonight, I must sleep there. When I thought of it, my tongue felt dry in my throat, in spite of my wish for knowledge. Almost I would have gone down again and faced the dogs, but I did not.

I had not gone through all the rooms when the darkness fell. When it fell, I went back to the big room looking over the city and made fire. There was a place to make fire and a box with wood in it, though I do not think they cooked there. I wrapped myself in a floor-covering and slept in front of the fire—I was very tired.

Now I tell what is very strong magic. I woke in the midst of the night. When I woke, the fire had gone out and I was cold. It seemed to me that all around me there were whisperings and voices. I closed my eyes to shut them out. Some will say that I slept again, but I do not think that I slept. I could feel the spirits drawing my spirit out of my body as a fish is drawn on a line.

Why should I lie about it? I am a priest and the son of a priest. If there are spirits, as they say, in the small Dead Places near us, what spirits must there not be in that great Place of the Gods? And would not they wish to speak? After such long years? I know that I felt myself drawn as a fish is drawn on a line. I had stepped out of my body—I could see my body asleep in front of the cold fire, but it was not I. I was drawn to look out upon the city of the gods.

It should have been dark, for it was night, but it was not dark. Everywhere there were lights—lines of light—circles and blurs of light—ten thousand torches would not have been the same. The sky itself was alight—you could barely see the stars for the glow in the sky. I thought to myself "This is strong magic" and trembled. There was a roaring in my ears like the rushing of rivers. Then my eyes grew used to the light and my ears to the sound. I knew that I was seeing the city as it had been when the gods were alive.

That was a sight indeed—yes, that was a sight: I could not have seen it in the body—my body would have died. Everywhere went the gods, on foot and in chariots—there were gods beyond number and counting and their chariots blocked the streets. They had turned night to day for their pleasure—they did not sleep with the sun. The noise of their coming and going was the noise of the many waters. It was magic what they could do—it was magic what they did.

I looked out of another window—the great vines of their bridges were mended and god-roads went east and west. Restless, restless, were the gods and always in motion! They burrowed tunnels under rivers—they flew in the air. With unbelievable tools they did giant works—no part of the earth was safe from them, for, if they wished for a thing, they summoned it from the other side of the world. And always, as they laboured and rested, as they feasted and made love, there was a drum in their ears—the pulse of the giant city, beating and beating like a man's heart.

Were they happy? What is happiness to the gods? They were great, they were mighty, they were wonderful and terrible. As I looked upon them and their magic, I felt like a child—but a little more, it seemed to me, and they would pull down the moon from the sky. I saw them with wisdom beyond wisdom and knowledge beyond knowledge. And yet not all they did was well done—even I could see that—and yet their wisdom could not but grow until all was peace.

Then I saw their fate come upon them and that was terrible past speech. It came upon them as they walked the streets of their city. I have been in the fights with the Forest People—I have seen men die. But this was not like that. When gods war with gods, they use weapons we do not know. It was fire falling out of the sky and a mist that poisoned. It was the time of the Great Burning and the Destruction. They ran about like ants in the streets of their city—poor gods, poor gods! Then the towers began to fall. A few escaped—yes, a few. The legends tell it. But, even after the city had become a Dead Place, for many years the poison was still in the ground. I saw it happen, I saw the last of them die. It was darkness over the broken city and I wept.

All this, I saw. I saw it as I have told it, though not in the body. When I woke in the morning, I was hungry, but I did not think first of my hunger for my heart was perplexed and confused. I knew the reason for the Dead Places but I did not see why it had happened. It seemed to me it should not have happened, with all the magic they had. I went through the house looking for an answer. There was so much in the house I could not understand—and yet I am a priest and the son of a priest. It was like being on one side of the great river, at night, with no light to show the way.

Then I saw the dead god. He was sitting in his chair, by the window, in a room I had not entered before and, for the first moment, I thought that he was alive. Then I saw the skin on the back of his hand—it was like dry leather. The room was shut, hot and dry—no doubt that had kept him as he was. At first I was afraid to approach him—then the fear left me. He was sitting looking out over the city—he was dressed in the clothes of the gods. His age was neither young nor old—I could not tell his age. But there was wisdom in his face and great sadness. You could see that he would have not run away. He had sat at his window, watching his city die—then he himself had died. But it is better to lose one's life than one's spirit—and you could see from the face that his spirit had not been lost. I knew, that, if I touched him, he would fall into dust—and yet, there was something unconquered in the face.

* * * * *

That is all of my story, for then I knew he was a man—I knew then that they had been men, neither gods nor demons. It is a great knowledge, hard to tell and believe. They were men—they went a dark road, but they were men. I had no fear after that—I had no fear going home, though twice I fought off the dogs and once I was hunted for two days by the Forest People. When I saw my father again, I prayed and was purified. He touched my lips and my breast, he said, "You went away a boy. You come back a man and a priest." I said, "Father, they were men! I have been in the Place of the Gods and seen it! Now slay me, if it is the law—but still I know they were men."

He looked at me out of both eyes. He said, "The law is not always the same shape—you have done what you have done. I could not have done it my time, but you come after me. Tell!"

I told and he listened. After that, I wished to tell all the people but he showed me otherwise. He said, "Truth is a hard deer to hunt. If you eat too much truth at once, you may die of the truth. It was not idly that our fathers forbade the Dead Places." He was right—it is better the truth should come little by little. I have learned that, being a priest. Perhaps, in the old days, they ate knowledge too fast.

Nevertheless, we make a beginning. It is not for the metal alone we go to the Dead Places now—there are the books and the writings. They are hard to learn. And the magic tools are broken—but we can look at them and wonder. At least, we make a beginning. And, when I am chief priest we shall go beyond the great river. We shall go to the Place of the Gods—the place newyork—not one man but a company. We shall look for the images of the gods and find the god ASHING and the others—the gods Lincoln and Biltmore and Moses. But they were men who built the city, not gods or demons. They were men. I remember the dead man's face. They were men who were here before us. We must build again.

IN THE YEAR TEN THOUSAND

by Will Harben

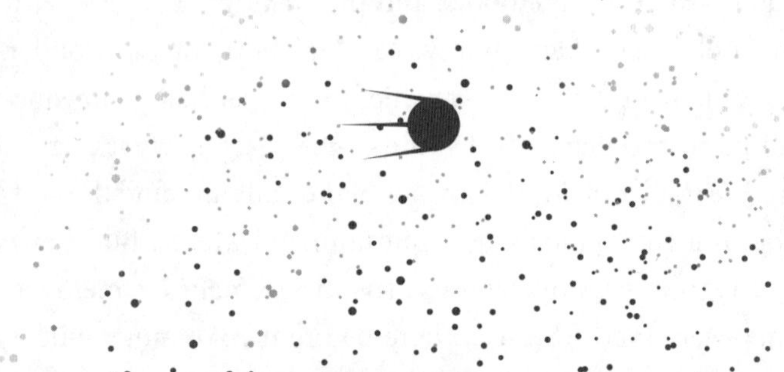

A.D. 10,000

An old man, more than six hundred years of age, was walking with a boy through a great museum. The people who were moving around them had beautiful forms, and faces which were indescribably refined and spiritual.

"Father," said the boy, "you promised to tell me today about the Dark Ages. I like to hear how men lived and thought long ago."

"It is no easy task to make you understand the past," was the reply. "It is hard to realize that man could have been so ignorant as he was eight thousand years ago, but come with me; I will show you something."

He led the boy to a cabinet containing a few time-worn books bound in solid gold.

"You have never seen a book," he said, taking out a large volume and carefully placing it on a silk cushion on a table. "There are only a few in the leading museums of the world. Time was when there were as many books on earth as inhabitants."

"I cannot understand," said the boy with a look of perplexity on his intellectual face. "I cannot see what people could have wanted with them; they are not attractive; they seem to be useless."

The old man smiled. "When I was your age, the subject was too deep for me; but as I grew older and made a close study of the history of the past, the use of books gradually became plain to me. We know that in the year 2000 they were read by the best minds. To make you understand this, I shall first have to explain that eight thousand years ago human beings communicated their thoughts to one another by making sounds with their tongues, and not by mind-reading, as you and I do. To understand me, you have simply to read my thoughts as well as your education will permit; but primitive man knew nothing about thought-intercourse, so he invented speech. Humanity then was divided up in various races, and each race had a separate language. As certain sounds conveyed definite ideas, so did signs and letters; and later, to facilitate the exchange of thought, writing and printing were invented. This book was printed."

The boy leaned forward and examined the pages closely; his young brow clouded. "I cannot understand," he said, "it seems so useless."

The old man put his delicate fingers on the page. "A line of these words may have conveyed a valuable thought to a reader long ago," he said, reflectively. "In fact, this book purports to be a history of the world up to the year 2000. Here are some pictures," he continued, turning the worn leaves carefully. "This is George Washington; this a pope of a church called the Roman Catholic; this is a man named Gladstone, who was a great political leader in England. Pictures then, as you see, were very crude. We have preserved some of the oil paintings made in those days. Art was in its cradle. In producing a painting of an object, the early artists mixed coloured paints and spread them according to taste on stretched canvas or on the walls or windows of buildings. You know that our artists simply throw light and darkness into space in the necessary variations, and the effect is all that could be desired in the way of imitating nature. See that landscape in the alcove before you. The foliage of the trees, the grass, the flowers, the stretch of water, have every appearance of life because the light which produces them is alive."

The boy looked at the scene admiringly for a few minutes, then bent again over the book. Presently he recoiled from the pictures, a strange look of disgust struggling in his tender features.

"These men have awful faces," he said. "They are so unlike people living now. The man you call a pope looks like an animal. They all have huge mouths and frightfully heavy jaws. Surely men could not have looked like that."

"Yes," the old man replied, gently. "There is no doubt that human beings then bore a nearer resemblance to the lower animals than we now do. In the sculpture and portraits of all ages we can trace a gradual refinement in the appearances of men. The features of the human race today are more ideal. Thought has always given form and expression to faces. In those dark days the thoughts of men were not refined. Human beings died of starvation and lack of attention in cities where there were people so wealthy that they could not use their fortunes. And they were so nearly related to the lower animals that they believed in war. George Washington was for several centuries reverenced by millions of people as a great and good man; and yet under his leadership thousands of human beings lost their lives in battle."

The boy's susceptible face turned white.

"Do you mean that he encouraged men to kill one another?" he asked, bending more closely over the book.

"Yes, but we cannot blame him; he thought he was right. Millions of his countrymen applauded him. A greater warrior than he was a man named Napoleon Bonaparte. Washington fought under the belief that he was doing his country a service in defending it against enemies, but everything in history goes to prove that Bonaparte waged war to gratify a personal ambition to distinguish himself as a hero. Wild animals of the lowest orders were courageous, and would fight one another till they died; and yet the most refined of the human race, eight or nine thousand years ago, prided themselves on the same ferocity of nature. Women, the gentlest half of humanity, honoured men more for bold achievements in shedding blood than for any other quality. But murder was not only committed in wars; men in private life killed one another; fathers and mothers were now and then so depraved as to put their own children to death; and the highest tribunals of the world executed murderers without dreaming that it was wrong, erroneously believing that to kill was the only way to prevent killing.

"Did no one in those days realize that it was horrible?" asked the youth.

"Yes," answered the father, "as far back as ten thousand years ago there was an humble man, it is said, who was called Jesus Christ. He went from place to place, telling every one he met that the world would be better if men would love one another as themselves."

"What kind of man was he?" asked the boy, with kindling eyes.

"He was a spiritual genius," was the earnest reply, "and the greatest that has ever lived."

"Did he prevent them from killing one another?" asked the youth, with a tender upward glance.

"No, for he himself was killed by men who were too barbarous to understand him. But long after his death his words were remembered. People were not civilized enough to put his teachings into practice, but they were able to see that he was right."

"After he was killed, did the people not do as he had told them?" asked the youth, after a pause of several minutes.

"It seems not," was the reply. "They said no human being could live as he had directed. And when he had been dead for several centuries, people began to say that he was the Son of God who had come to earth to show men how to live. Some even believed that he was God himself."

"Did they believe that he was a person like ourselves?"

The old man reflected for a few minutes, then, looking into the boy's eager face, he answered: "That subject will be hard for you to understand. I will try to make it plain. To the unformed minds of early humanity there could be nothing without a personal creator. As man could build a house with his own hands, and was superior to his work, so he argued that some unknown being, greater than all visible things, had made the universe. They called that being by different names according to the language they spoke. In English the word used was 'God.'"

"They believed that somebody had made the universe!" said the boy, "how very strange!"

"No, not somebody as you comprehend it," replied the father gently, "but some vague, infinite being who punished the evil and rewarded the good. Men could form no idea of a creator that did not in some way resemble themselves; and as they could subdue their enemies through fear and by the infliction of pain, so did they believe that God would punish those who did not please him. Some people long ago believed that God's punishment was inflicted after death for eternity. The numerous beliefs about the personality and laws of the creator caused more bloodshed in the gloomy days of the past than anything else. Religion was the foundation of many of the most horrible wars. People committed thousands of crimes in the name of the God of the universe. Men and women were burned alive because they would not believe certain creeds, and yet they adhered to convictions equally as preposterous; but you will learn all these things later in life. That picture before you was the last queen of England, called Victoria."

"I hoped that the women would not have such repulsive features as the men," said the boy, looking critically at the picture, "but this face makes me shudder. Why do they all look so coarse and brutal?"

"People living when this queen reigned had the most degrading habit that ever blackened the history of mankind."

"What was that?" asked the youth.

"The consumption of flesh. They believed that animals, fowls, and fish were created to be eaten."

"Is it possible?" The boy shuddered convulsively, and turned away from the book. "I understand now why their faces repel me so. I do not like to think that we have descended from such people."

"They knew no better," said the father. "As they gradually became more refined they learned to burn the meat over flames and to cook it in heated vessels to change its appearance. The places where animals were killed and sold were withdrawn to retired places. Mankind was slowly turning from the habit, but they did not know it. As early as 2050 learned men, calling themselves vegetarians, proved conclusively that the consumption of such food was cruel and barbarous, and that it retarded refinement and mental growth. However, it was not till about 2300 that the vegetarian movement became of marked importance. The most highly educated classes in all lands adopted vegetarianism, and only the uneducated continued to kill and eat animals. The vegetarians tried for years to enact laws prohibiting the consumption of flesh, but opposition was very strong. In America in 2320 a colony was formed consisting of about three hundred thousand vegetarians. They purchased large tracts of land in what was known as the Indian Territory, and there made their homes, determined to prove by example the efficacy of their tenets. Within the first year the colony had doubled its number: people joined it from all parts of the globe. In the year 4000 it was a country of its own, and was the wonder of the world. The brightest minds were born there. The greatest discoveries and inventions were made by its inhabitants. In 4030 Gillette discovered the process of manufacturing crystal. Up to that time people had built their houses of natural stone, inflammable wood, and metals; but the new material, being fireproof and beautiful in its various colours, was used for all building purposes. In 4050 Holloway found the submerged succession of mountain chains across the Atlantic Ocean, and intended to construct a bridge on their summits; but the vast improvement in air ships rendered his plans impracticable.

"In 4051 John Saunders discovered and put into practice thought-telegraphy. This discovery was the signal for the introduction in schools and colleges of the science of mind-reading, and by the year 5000 so great had been the progress in that branch of knowledge that words were spoken only among the lowest of the uneducated. In no age of the world's history has there been such an important discovery. It civilized the world. Its early promoters did not dream of the vast good mind-reading would accomplish. Slowly it killed evil. Societies for the prevention of evil thought were organized in all lands. Children were born pure of mind and grew up in purity. Crime was choked out of existence. If a man had an evil thought, it was read in his heart, and he was not allowed to keep it. Men at first shunned evil for fear of detection, and then grew to love purity.

"In the year 6021 all countries of the world, having then a common language, and being drawn together in brotherly love by constant exchange of thought, agreed to call themselves a union without ruler or rulers. It was the greatest event in the history of the world. Certain sensitive mind students in Germany, who had for years been trying to communicate with other planets through the channel of thought, declared that, owing to the terrestrial unanimity of purpose in that direction, they had received mental impressions from other worlds, and that thorough interplanetary intercourse was a future possibility.

"Important inventions were made as the mind of humanity grew more elevated. Thornton discovered the plan to heat the earth's surface from its internal fire, and this discovery made journeys to the wonderful ice-bound countries situated at the North and the South Poles easy of accomplishment. At the North Pole, in the extensive concave lands, was found a peculiar race of men. Their sun was the great perpetually boiling lake of lava which bubbled from the centre of the earth in the bottom of their bowl-shaped world. And a strange religion was theirs! They believed that the earth was a monster on whose hide they had to live for a mortal lifetime, and that to the good was given the power after death to walk over the icy waste to their god, whose starry eyes they could see twinkling in space, and that the evil were condemned to feed the fire in the stomach of the monster as long as it lived.

They told beautiful stories about the creation of their world, and held that if they lived too near the hot, dazzling mouth of evil, they would become blinded to the soft, forgiving eyes of the god of space. Hence they suffered the extreme cold of the lands near the frozen seas, believing that the physical ordeal prepared them for the icy journey to immortal rest after death. But there were those who hungered after the balmy atmosphere and the wonderful fruits and flowers that grew in the lowlands, and they lived there in indolence and so-called sin."

The old man and his son left the museum and walked into a wonderful park. Flowers of the most beautiful kinds and of sweetest fragrance grew on all sides. They came to a tall tower, four thousand feet in height, built of manufactured crystal. Something, like a great white bird, a thousand feet long, flew across the sky and settled down on the tower's summit.

"This was one of the most wonderful inventions of the Seventieth century, said the old man. "The early inhabitants of the earth could not have dreamed that it would be possible to go around it in twenty-four hours. In fact, there was a time when they were not able to go around it at all. Scientists were astonished when a man called Malburn, a great inventor, announced that, at a height of four thousand feet, he could disconnect an air ship from the laws of gravitation, and cause it to stand still in space till the earth had turned over. Fancy what must have been that immortal genius' feelings when he stood in space and saw the earth for the first time whirling beneath him!"

They walked on for some distance across the park till they came to a great instrument made to magnify the music in light. Here they paused and seated themselves.

"It will soon be night," said the old man. "The tones are those of bleeding sunset. I came here last evening to listen to the musical struggle between the light of dying day and that of the coming stars. The sunlight had been playing a powerful solo; but the gentle chorus of the stars, led by the moon, was inexplicably touching. Light is the voice of immortality; it speaks in all things."

An hour passed. It was growing dark.

"Tell me what immortality is," said the boy. "What does life lead to?"

"We do not know," replied the old man. "If we knew we would be infinite. Immortality is increasing happiness for all time; it is—"

A meteor shot across the sky. There was a burst of musical laughter among the singing stars. The old man bent over the boy's face and kissed it. "Immortality," said he—"immortality must be love immortal."

THE ULTIMATE EXPERIMENT

by Thornton DeKy

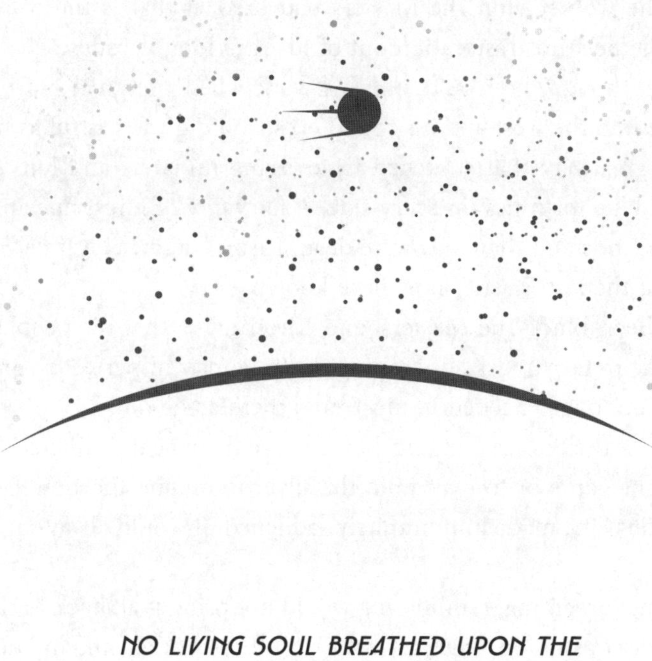

NO LIVING SOUL BREATHED UPON THE EARTH. ONLY ROBOTS. CARRYING ON THE LAST GREAT ORDER.

“They were all gone now, The Masters, all dead and their atoms scattered to the never ceasing winds that swept the great crysolite city towers in ever increasing fury. That had been the last wish of each as he had passed away, dying from sheer old age. True they had fought on as long as they could to save their kind from utter extinction but the comet that had trailed its poisoning wake across space to leave behind it, upon Earth, a noxious, lethal gas vapour, had done its work too well."

No living soul breathed upon the Earth. No one lived here now, but Kiron and his kind.

"And," so thought Kiron to himself, "he might as well be a great unthinking robot able to do only one thing instead of the mental giant he was, so obsessed had he become with the task he had set himself to do."

Yet, in spite of a great loneliness and a strong fear of a final frustration, he worked on with the others of his people, hardly stopping for anything except the very necessities needed to keep his big body working in perfect coordination.

Tirelessly he worked, for The Masters had bred, if that is the word to use, fatigue and the need for restoration out of his race long decades ago.

Sometimes, though, he would stop his work when the great red dying sun began to fade into the west and his round eyes would grow wistful as he looked out over the great city that stretched in towering minarets and lofty spires of purest crystal blue for miles on every side. A fairy city of rarest hue and beauty. A city for the Gods and the Gods were dead. Kiron felt, at such times, the great loneliness that the last Master must have known.

They had been kind, The Masters, and Kiron knew that his people, as they went about their eternal tasks of keeping the great city in perfect shape for The Masters who no longer needed it, must miss them as he did.

Never to hear their voices ringing, never to see them again gathered in groups to witness some game or to play amid the silver fountains and flowery gardens of the wondrous city, made him infinitely saddened. It would always be like this, unless….

But thinking, dreaming, reminiscing would not bring it all back for there was only one answer to still the longing: work. The others worked and did not dream, but instead kept busy tending to the thousand and one tasks The Masters had set them to do—had left them doing when the last Master perished. He too must remember the trust they had placed in his hands and fulfill it as best he could.

From the time the great red eye of the sun opened itself in the East until it disappeared in the blue haze beyond the crysolite city, Kiron laboured with his fellows. Then, at the appointed hour, the musical signals would peal forth their sweet, sad chimes, whispering goodnight to ears that would hear them no more and all operations would halt for the night, just as it had done when The Masters were here to supervise it.

Then when morning came he would start once more trying, testing, experimenting with his chemicals and plastics, forever following labyrinth of knowledge, seeking for the great triumph that would make the work of the others of some real use.

His hands molded the materials carefully, lovingly to a pattern that was set in his mind as a thing to cherish. Day by day his experiments in their liquid baths took form under his careful modelling. He mixed his chemicals with the same loving touch, the same careful concentration and painstaking thoroughness, studying often his notes and analysis charts.

Everything must be just so lest his experiment not turn out perfectly. He never became exasperated at a failure or a defect that proved to be the only reward for his faithful endeavours but worked patiently on toward a goal that he knew would ultimately be his.

Then one day, as the great red sun glowed like an immense red eye overhead, Kiron stepped back to admire his handiwork. In that instant the entire wondrous city seemed to breathe a silent prayer as he stood transfixed by the sight before him. Then it went on as usual, hurrying noiselessly about its business. The surface cars, empty though they were, fled swiftly about supported only by the rings of magnetic force that held them to their designated paths. The gravoships raised from the tower-dromes to speed silently into the eye of the red sun that was dying.

"No one now," Kiron thought to himself as he studied his handiwork. Then he walked unhurriedly to the cabinet in the laboratory corner and took from it a pair of earphones resembling those of a long forgotten radio set. Just as unhurriedly, though his mind was filled with turmoil and his being with excitement, he walked back and connected the earphones to the box upon his bench. The phones dangled into the liquid bath before him as he adjusted them to suit his requirements.

Slowly he checked over every step of his experiments before he went farther. Then, as he proved them for the last time, his hand went slowly to the small knife switch upon the box at his elbow. Next he threw into connection the larger switch upon his laboratory wall bringing into his laboratory the broadcast power of the crysolite city.

The laboratory generators hummed softly, drowning out the quiet hum of the city outside. As they built up, sending tiny living electrical impulses over the wires like minute currents that come from the brain, Kiron sat breathless; his eyes intent.

Closer to his work he bent, watching lovingly, fearful least all might not be quite right. Then his eyes took on a brighter light as he began to see the reaction. He knew the messages that he had sent out were being received and coordinated into a unit that would stir and grow into intellect.

Suddenly the machine flashed its little warning red light and automatically snapped off. Kiron twisted quickly in his seat and threw home the final switch. This, he knew, was the ultimate test. On the results of the flood of energy impulses that he had set in motion rested the fulfillment of his success—*or failure.*

He watched with slight misgivings. This had never been accomplished before. How could it possibly be a success now? Even The Masters had never quite succeeded at this final test, how could he, only a servant? Yet it must work for he had no desire in life but to make it work.

Then, suddenly, he was on his feet, eyes wide. From the two long, coffin-like liquid baths, there arose two perfect specimens of the *Homo sapiens.* Man and woman, they were, and they blinked their eyes in the light of the noonday sun, raised themselves dripping from the baths of their creation and stepped to the floor before Kiron.

The man spoke, the woman remained silent.

"I am Adam Two," he said. "Created, by you Kiron from a formula they left, in their image. I was created to be a Master and she whom you also have created is to be my wife. We shall mate and the race of Man shall be reborn through us and others whom I shall help you create."

The Man halted at the last declaration he intoned and walked smilingly toward the woman who stepped into his open arms returning his smile.

Kiron smiled too within his pumping heart. The words the Man had intoned had been placed in his still pregnable mind by the tele-teach phones and record that the last Master had prepared before death had halted his experiments. The actions of the Man toward the Woman, Kiron knew, was caused by the natural constituents that went to form his chemical body and govern his humanness.

He, Kiron, had created a living man and woman. The Masters lived again because of him. They would sing and play and again people the magnificent crysolite city because he loved them and had kept on until success had been his. But then why not such a turnabout? Hadn't they, The Masters, created him a superb, thinking *robot*?

THE MENTANICALS

by Francis Flagg

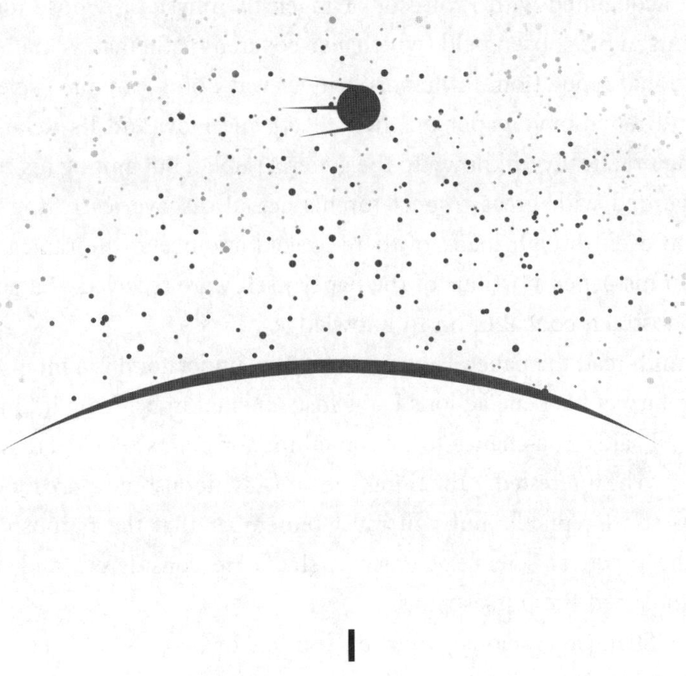

I

This is a strange story, and if you are the kind of person who believes nothing without overwhelming proof, read no further, for the story is an incredible one and centres around characters widely divergent as to background and walks of life—Bronson, Smith and Stringer.

Bronson was by way of being an adventurous man, one who had sailed the seven seas, first as fo'cas'le hand, then as mate and skipper of rusty tramps for Chinese owners in the Orient. Yet he was by no means uneducated, though the knowledge he possessed on a wide range of subjects seldom met with in the repertoire of that type of tramp captains, had been gleaned from books and not from colleges. Olson Smith had picked him up—I never rightly understood when or how—in the Indian Ocean and made him captain of his sleek ocean liner masquerading as a yacht. Olson Smith could afford the luxury of thousand-ton yachts, because his father had been canny enough to get into a packing-house combine at the right moment and so turn an already sizable fortune into millions. Olson himself, however, had nothing to do with the packing business aside from helping to spend its profits. He was a dilettante of sorts, a patron of the arts, a stout, distinguished looking gentleman under sixty, who endowed colleges and founded chairs and laboratories for research work. Through these benevolences he became acquainted with Professor Stringer, the physicist, whose remarkable achievements in his chosen field (which also covered mathematics) had won him an international reputation. Professor Stringer was not a "popular" scientist, his abstruse and remarkable paper on "The Electronic Flow and Its Relation With Time" being practically unknown to the general public. But among his colleagues he was regarded with great respect for his actual discoveries in the realm of physics; and even though many of them looked askance at the radical theories advanced in his paper, portions of the paper itself were received as a genuine, if somewhat abstract, contribution to knowledge.

Olson Smith read the paper. How much of it he understood is a moot question. As the secretary of his benefactions I was instrumental in bringing it to his attention. "Here," I said, "is a chance to do something for pure science." He was not at first inclined to be interested. "The thing," he said, "is moonshine, pure moonshine."

"Perhaps so," I replied; "but you must remember that the moonshine often precedes the practical science. Consider, sir…" He considered; and after due reflection loosened the pursestrings.

Professor Stringer graciously allowed himself to be endowed. He was (one sensed) fed up with wasting his genius on unappreciative college students; and he wanted money, much money, a million dollars he said, to carry out his experiments. But he made it clear that he was honouring Olson Smith by allowing him to donate the money; and strangely enough—for Olson Smith was a plutocrat convinced of his own weight and importance—the magnate agreed. The personality of Professor Stringer—and this dried-up wizened little scientist in the middle fifties possessed a dynamic personality—carried all before it. Olson Smith turned over to him his Long Island home, built workshops and laboratories, and then left him to the seclusion and privacy he desired, taking his annual trip to the Bermudas. What with one thing and another we did not see Professor Stringer again until a year later, when the yacht tied up at the private pier of the Long Island estate and we dined with him. Besides Olson Smith, Professor Stringer and myself, three others were present that night, a middle-aged business man named Gleason, ruddy of fate from constant shampooing and good living, a noted surgeon who does not wish his name or description given here, and Captain Bronson of the steam-yacht. Perhaps I have failed to mention that Captain Bronson was a remarkably handsome man, somewhere under forty, whose medium height and slender figure belied the great physical strength that was really his. He certainly did not look the two-fisted fighter, the dubious hero of shady exploits that Olson Smith declared him to be. The multimillionaire was scarcely one to make friends of his hired men, be they valets or private secretaries, but between himself and Bronson an undoubted intimacy existed, based, perhaps, on the dual nature of the Captain. Bronson was capable either of fighting or discussing the merits of a Pulitzer prize winner: a sort of Wolf Larsen of a fellow, but more versatile and amenable than Jack London's character.

There was drink that night of course, wines, liqueurs and a very good brandy, all brought from the boat, but the Professor touched nothing. "A scientist must have a clear head," he said, "and alcohol is not conducive to that—no—" But he drunk coffee, and when the servants had served it and left us alone, he began to talk, almost musingly. "Time," he said, "is the great enigma, the phenomenon that captivates the imagination. We travel in it from the cradle to the grave, and yet," he said, "what do we know of time? Nothing," he said, "nothing, save that it is related to space." He paused and looked at us all half-dreamily. "As you know I have discovered a force that I call the Electronic Flow, and that force I have related to the phenomenon of time. I am convinced—in my various papers on the subject I have sought to show—that the Electronic Flow, being to all intents and purposes the absolute as far as we are concerned, is capable of bearing us on its bosom into the future. Or rather its tremendous speed is capable of holding us suspended at the core of things, while the phenomenon of time…" He broke off and regarded us more directly. "Really," he said, "I don't know as I am making this subject very clear. But you must understand," he said, "that there are points, on which I am not very clear myself. Whether the speed of the electronic flow carries one forward into time, or the speed of time passes one held in the electronic flow, is a question difficult to answer. Yes," he said, "very difficult to determine. Of course I did not start my recent investigations with any intention so radical as building a Time

Machine. Not at first," he said. "My intentions were merely to verify mathematically some further theories, and to demonstrate … He mused a moment. "But do you know the idea of an actual Time Machine grew on me? It were," he said, "as if something whispered in my very brain and drove me on. I can't describe it. Foolishness of course. But I built the Time Machine." He looked at Olson Smith. "Yes," he said, "I built the Time Machine. It lies in the laboratory yonder; and to-night—to-night," he said, "I am going to demonstrate it for the first time!"

The business man was one of those beefy individuals who stare into whiskey glasses, and make strange noises in their throats when they fail to understand anything. "Stuff and nonsense," he said now, "stuff and nonsense."

Bronson stared at him. "Oh, I don't know."

"But to travel in time!"

"It does sound absurd."

"Absurd," said the famous doctor.

"And yet you know what they said about iron steamships sinking and heavier-than-air flying machines."

"That was different."

"Different," I said with conviction.

"… in my time," said Olson Smith; "building time machines." He looked reproachfully at his glass. "Will some one," he asked, "pass the brandy?"

The brandy was passed.

We were all drinking; more than was good for us perhaps. The Professor put down his coffee cup and addressed himself to Olson Smith. "In a sense," he said, "a financial sense, this time machine is yours. If you care to see it demonstrated…" He stood up.

The business man did not stir. He muttered something about damn-fool nuts and snorted into his glass. But the rest of us were interested. A fresh breeze was blowing off the water, as we passed from the house to the laboratory, and helped, partially, to dissipate the fumes of alcohol. Professor Stringer threw open the laboratory door and turned on the lights. We saw it then, an odd machine, shiny and rounded, occupying the centre of the workshop floor. I had been drinking, you will recollect, and my powers of observation were not at their best. It was the same with the others. When I questioned them later, they could give no adequate description of it. "So this," said Olson Smith rather flatly, "is a time machine." The doctor walked about—a little unsteadily I noticed—and viewed it from all angles. "The passenger," said the Professor, "sits here. Notice this lever on the graduated face of the dial; it controls the machine. Turn it this way from Zero and one travels into the past; throw it ahead and one travels into the future. The return of the lever to Zero will return the machine to the point of departure in time. The electronic flow..." he went into obscure details. "Will it work?" demanded the Doctor.

"According to the equation...."

"Equations?"

"... it cannot help but function."

"If time travelling were possible."

Bronson laughed loudly. "To travel in time! That *would* be an adventure."

"On paper," jibed the Doctor.

Bronson laughed again. "We'll see about that."

All of us were a little drunk, I tell you, and despite the respect we felt for Professor Stringer as an eminent scientist, no one believed in his time machine. I am quite certain that Bronson didn't. Or did he? I have sketched his background and there is little doubt that by temperament and training he was a wild and reckless fellow, one given to doing bizarre things and taking desperate chances. With a quick movement that no one anticipated he stepped forward and seated himself in the passenger seat of the odd contrivance. I can see him yet, his face flushed, his eyes brilliant, his mop of dark hair disordered. "All aboard for the future!" he shouted recklessly.

"For heaven's sake, man!" The Professor tried to reach his side. "Careful you fool! careful! Don't touch anything!" But Bronson grasped the lever and pushed it, pushed it abruptly ahead. How can I describe what followed? There was a chaotic moment when the machine spun—we saw it spinning, a blurred mass. A sudden wind rushed through the room in quick fury, raged, subsided, and left us staring in dumb amazement and fear at an empty spot. The machine—and Bronson with it—had vanished before our eyes!

That was on June the first, a little before midnight, and five days passed, five days, during which Bronson was lost to his own time and place.

Ahead of us in time! That was the implication.

Close to the machine when Bronson turned the lever, Professor Stringer had been thrown to the floor, his head struck by a portion of the machine as it whirled into invisibility. We picked him up, unconscious, and for days he hovered on the verge of death. The next morning the business man went his way to the city, ignorant of what had occurred. "Time machines," he chortled, "time machines," and smiled fatly. But the rest of us settled down to wait for we knew not what, and on the fifth day occurred the terrific explosion by the old stone wall, a half mile from the workshop, and when we hurried there, it was to find Bronson entangled in a wreckage of steel and other metals. We hauled him forth. His clothes were in shreds, his body terribly bruised and battered, and it was some time before he could be made to realize where he was. "Brandy!" he exclaimed; "for God's sake give me brandy!" We gave him brandy and other things, and the doctor patched him up, and we rushed him to a hospital, where in time he recovered from the shock and his broken bones knit. But the beauty that had been his was forever marred by a livid scar diagonally crossing the nose and running to the bulge of the jaw-bone. He fingered it as he told of his incredible adventure.

II
BRONSON'S STORY

Time (he said) is the great phenomenon, I know that, but to travel in it—ah, that seemed impossible to the point of absurdity. I had read H. G. Wells' "The Time Machine," as who has not, deeming it fantastic fiction. Wells' story *is* fantastic fiction, of course, though scarcely as fantastic as what I experienced.

When I seated myself in the Professor's time machine that night and pushed over the lever, I have no need to tell you that I was in a drunken and reckless mood. The room turned around me like a pin-wheel, dissolved into mist. I was conscious of the terrible vibration of the machine, of a deathly sickness at the pit of my stomach. Blackness followed the mist. Wells describes what the character in his story saw as he journeyed into the future, the procession of days and nights ever accelerating their motion, but I saw nothing like that, perhaps from the beginning the speed was too great. Terrified, bewildered, I yet retained enough presence of mind to depress the lever into neutral and so bring the machine to a halt. Moments passed while I lolled in my seat, blind, dazed; then my vision cleared—I could see. It was day. Sunlight fell around me. Everything was strange—and different. How can I make you see what I saw? The machine stood near one end of a great, open square that was surrounded by massive buildings. Those buildings! I had never seen their like before. And yet there was a similarity of line, of mathematical precision which linked them with the architecture of New York and Chicago. It was as if the building construction of today had been carried to an extreme length. *As if the machine had carried it forward.* I did not think that at the moment, but later....

The walls of the massive buildings were broken by yawning doorways. So this, I thought, is the future; it can be nothing less than that. I stepped out of the machine, holding on to it for support, still feeling terribly sick and giddy. Then I saw the cylinders! They came gliding from one of the openings in an upright fashion, and this was the singular thing about them, that their means of locomotion were not apparent to the eye. There were no wheels or treads. They appeared to skim the stone or concrete with which the square was paved, rather than touch it. Oddly repellent they were, and intimidating, and I loosened the automatic in its shoulder holster—the small one I always carry—and prepared for emergencies, though bullets were useless against the cylinders as I was to discover later.

The cylinders were smooth things about five feet tall, of a dulled metal hue, with here and there shining spots which constantly waxed and waned in colour. They were machines—I thought of them as machines—and it was reasonable to suppose that behind them lurked a human intelligence. The people of the future, I thought, have invented devices unknown to us of the Twentieth Century; and it came over me how wonderful it was going to be to meet those superior people, talk to them, gaze upon the marvels with which they had surrounded themselves.

So I went to meet the cylinders.

Their soft whispering meant nothing to me at first. Nor at first did I suspect the source of the gentle pressure running over me from head to foot, as the cylinders came close. Then with an odd thrill of apprehension I realized that the curious cylinders were handling, examining me, that from them emanated an electrical force, a manipulation of invisible rays which functioned as organs of touch. Alone, bewildered, trying vainly to comprehend the strange situation. I had to call on every ounce of my self-control to remain calm. Yes, I was afraid—only the fool says he never is—but more afraid of being afraid, of showing fear. I still believed that behind those cylinders must lurk a human intelligence. The genius of the race seemed to run along the line of making robots. There was the "metal brain" at Washington, that told of the tides, the electrical eye which watched a thousand industrial processes, a myriad automatic devices functioning with little or no supervision from man; and of course I had read the play "R. U. R.," science fiction stories dealing with the future of machinery, and it was inevitable—strange, and yet not so strange—that I should expect an advancement, a realization of all those things in the future. Man the inventor, I thought, had achieved them; and for a moment this belief seemed borne out when I saw the men.

They were in one of the buildings, and the city of buildings, which I was soon to know, lay on all sides of and beyond the square. I did not struggle when the cylinders lifted and carried me away. That is, I ceased my involuntary resistance almost at once. It was useless to struggle against a force far superior to my own puny strength; besides I believed the robots were carrying me to their human masters.

The building into which I was taken—through an arched opening—was a vast place; too vast, too overwhelming for me to describe save in the vaguest, most general terms. You know how it is when you see something stupendous, something so intricate that you are bewildered by its very complexity. There was a huge room filled with almost noiseless machines rooted in their places like shackled monsters, or going to and fro on cables and grooves which determined their spheres of activity. Strange lights glowed, weird devices toiled; but I can tell you no more that that; I saw them for too short a time.

The men were among those machines. At sight of them my heart leapt. Here, I thought, is the human intelligence back of the wonders I view, the masters of the cylindrical robots; yet even at that moment I was aware of a doubt, a misgiving.

One of the men shambled forward. His blond hair—long and matted—fell over the forehead and he brushed it back with a taloned hand and stared at me stupidly. "Hello!" I said, "what place is this, what year? Tell these robots of yours to let me go."

He was naked and thin, his skin of a greenish pallor, and save for a mouthing of toothless gums, vouchsafed me no answer. Chilled by his lack of response my heart fell as suddenly as it had leapt. Good God! I thought, this can't be master here, this pitiful thing. The cylinders seemed watching, attentively, *listening*. I don't know how, but they gave me that impression; and now I noticed that the shining spots on them were glowing intensely, that their whispering was not a steady but a modulated sound. As if it were language, I thought, language! and a strange dread came over me and I shivered as if with cold. Other men, perhaps a dozen in number came forward, naked and shambling, with stupid beast-like looks on their faces and rumblings in their throats. In vain I endeavoured to communicate with them, human intelligence seemed dead back of their lacklustre eyes. Filled with rising horror, I squirmed in the grip of the cylinders and suddenly their hold on me relaxed and I tore myself free and fled, possessed with but one overwhelming desire, and that was to win to the time machine, leave this uncanny future and return to my own day and age. But the arched opening leading to the square had vanished, blank wall rose where it had been. The cylinders appeared to watch me with cold impersonal watchfulness. The thought of being marooned among them in this incredible and alien future brought the chill sweat to my forehead, but I did not loose my head. Perhaps the closing of the doorway had not been a calculated thing; perhaps if I awaited events with caution and patience the door would re-open; meantime I could search for other exits.

But other exits did not give on the square I desired. I discovered but two of them anyway, though there may have been many more, one leading into a dark, forbidding tunnel, the other giving access to a second square entirely surrounded by buildings. I was afraid to venture into other buildings for fear of going astray, of losing the neighbourhood of the time machine. Filled with what feelings you can imagine, I returned to the first doorway (through which I had been carried) to find it still closed. Then I thought of the beastlike men. Perhaps they possessed knowledge that might be helpful to me; perhaps after all I could succeed in communicating with them. It was hazardous work penetrating any distance in that maze of almost noiseless and ever-toiling mechanisms, but I followed in the footsteps of the timidly retreating beastmen and so at last came to a kind of squatting place in the midst of the machinery, which locality appeared to be their place of abode, since a number of women with children cowered there, and the men showed a disposition to pause and dispute my further progress. At the edge of the squatting place I seated myself, my automatic ready for action, and lit a cigarette. I know of nothing that soothes the nerves like nicotine. Slowly the beast-men drew near me. I smiled and made peaceful gestures. Some half-grown children crept closer and fingered my clothes. They were eating, I noticed, a kind of biscuit which they took at will from a scuttle-like machine, and chewing small pellets. Water ran through a huge metal trough with a subdued roar. After awhile I got up and went to the trough to satisfy a growing thirst, helping myself at the same time to biscuits from the scuttle. They were rather flat in flavour—lacking salt perhaps—and possessed a peculiar taste I did not like. The pellets were better. They too were obtained from a scuttle-machine (I can call them nothing else) and were pleasant to chew. I soon discovered that swallowed at regular intervals one of them gave all the sensations of having partaken of a hearty meal. I had eaten an hour—or was it twenty centuries?—before, but ate again, feeling ravenously hungry. Probably the pellets represented a dehydrated method of concentrating foods, far in advance of that utilized in the preparation of certain foodstuffs today. Be that as it may, I filled my pockets with them, and I dare say if you were to search the clothes I returned in you will find some of those pellets.

I spent several hours at the squatting place of the beast-men trying to talk to them, but without success. Seemingly they were as are the animals of the field lacking coherent language, men who had somehow lost the power to talk, to think, the ability to grasp the meaning of simple signs, such as possessed by the lowliest aborigine today. In vain I speculated as to the reason for this. That the cylinders were somehow responsible I felt certain. Man, I thought, had developed the robot, the automatic machine until the human worker was ejected from the industrial process and cast out to degenerate and perish, the beast-men being a surviving remnant of those toilers. This reasoning seemed plausible enough at the time, though it left much to be desired, for, in the twentieth century from which I had come, wasn't the machine replacing human workers with a ruthlessness suggestive of what I found in the future? How right I was in my reasoning, and how wrong, you will shortly see.

Thinking thus it was natural that I should again turn my attention to the cylinders. Never once had I been free from their observation, or unconscious of it. Through them, I thought, I shall contact the rulers of this realm, the human masters whose servants they are, the pitiless ones who have doomed a portion of humanity to beast-hood and extinction. So I grimly waited—a prey to what emotions you can imagine—observing the beast-men, watching the blank wall for the possible opening of the way to the square and the time machine, and all the time aware of the coming and going of those cylinders. Time passed; how much of it I had no means of telling, since my wrist-watch refused to run; but a long time; and finally I grew tired of waiting for the cylindrical robots to communicate my presence to their masters, or to conduct me there, and decided to seek their presence myself.

By way of the opening already alluded to, I gained access to the second square. The squares were a peculiar feature of the place, as I was soon to learn. There were no streets or roads leading from square to square; the squares were isolated with radiating arteries always ending against some building—at least those did, that I explored.

Dusk was falling as I entered the square. Indescribably lonely it was, lonely and weird, to look up and see the stars blazing far overhead. I followed one radiating artery to a blank wall; another, another. Then suddenly I was too tired to proceed further and returned to the vicinity of the closed door, where I lay down at the base of the blank wall and fell asleep.

The next morning I filled my pockets with pellets and again started out. Square after square I passed through, and building after building. The cylinders were everywhere but did not interfere with my movements. A group of them constantly accompanied me, but whether always composed of the same cylinders I could not tell. Their incessant whispering was a nerve-wracking thing, and I often felt like turning on them and shooting.

I wish I could tell you all I saw: buildings full of toiling machinery and now and then a score or so of beast-men; squares and radiating arteries without a blade of grass or a tree, and never an animal, a bird, or an insect. On that first day of exploration, despite every precaution, I lost my way—hopelessly—and spent futile hours trying to retrace my steps. I have been lost in tropical jungles. There was that time in Siam. But never before had I felt so panic-stricken. Remember, I was an alien creature in an incredible future, separated from the only means of returning to my own place and time. One square was like another, one building similar to its neighbour. Soon I gave up the vain effort to return to my starting point. My sole hope now lay in finding the rulers of this bewildering maze.

That night—I knew it was night when darkness fell in the squares—I slaked my thirst with a trickle of water running from a pipe, swallowed a pellet, and almost instantly sank into the sleep of exhaustion.

The next day I came to a part of the city free of the beast-men. The squares were larger, the radiating arteries were splendid roads, but in the midst of many squares stood circular buildings not met with before. I entered one of them and was surprised to find huge rooms filled with pieces of rusted tools, shovels, spades, chisels, hammers, axe-heads, all displayed in a kind of chronological order. The thought of its being a museum did not occur to me at once. It was only after a while that I exclaimed to myself, "Why this looks like a museum!" Then the inevitable conviction came: "It is a museum!" But who could have arranged it? Certainly not the witless beast-men, and of other men I had seen nothing. This failure to find human beings, on a par with the stupendous buildings and machines all around, filled me with anxious foreboding. I gazed at the cylinders. For the first time it came over me that they were the only universal inhabitants I had seen. Bewildered, amazed, I wandered from building to building, and from floor to floor (for some of the buildings had as many as a dozen floors accessible to myself, gained not by stairways, but by gradually mounting run-ways or ramps in circular wells), engrossed it, what I saw, forgetting for the nonce my terrible plight.

There were chambers filled with fragments of machines such as cash-registers, clock-wheels, gasoline engines, and similar devices. Nothing was complete; nearly everything showed the wear and tear of time. And there were others containing various machines more or less correctly reassembled from ancient parts: automobiles, for instance, and locomotives; with an arrangement of simpler mechanical forms leading to more complex ones. I couldn't comprehend why all those things had been gathered together for preservation and display; nor account for the age of them, their general condition of ruin.

Not on that day, nor on the next—it was on the last day that I spent in the strange future—did I come to the library. And here I must touch on another phase of my adventure. You can have no idea how horrible it became at times to be alone among hundreds, yes, thousands of whispering cylinders. I was always aware of their subtle and invisible touch. Have you ever felt the antennae of an insect? Like that it was, like that. I recall one time the Gold Coast… Only it bolstered up my tottering sanity and control to gaze now and then on creatures similar in structure to myself, even if they were but the soulless beast-men of the machines. For in all that vast intricate city they were the only human beings I could discover, and I began to suspect, to dread, I scarcely knew what.

I came to the library, I say, on that last day. I did not know it was a library at first—and perhaps I was mistaken in believing the odd metal disks arranged in piles on shelves and tables, and consulted by the cylinders, to be a species of recording plates—but it was here I found the books. They were in boxes of thin metal, the better evidently to protect them from injury.

The thrill of seeing those books! Old, they were, old, covers gone, pages torn and missing; but they were books and magazines, though few in number, and I examined them eagerly. All this time the cylinders were following me, watching me, as if weighing my actions, and all the time I fought back a feeling of weirdness, uncanniness. Unnerving it was, intimidating. I had the feeling that in some perfectly incomprehensible way my actions were being controlled, directed. Experimenting, I thought, that's what they're doing, experimenting with me. But you mustn't get the idea that I realized or suspected this at first. Even up to that moment I was still thinking of the cylinders as automatic devices without intelligence or reason, and it must be kept in mind that, if I speak of them from time to time as if understanding their true nature from the beginning, I am speaking as one who looks back upon past happenings from the vantage-point of later knowledge.

The books and magazines were typed in English! I was amazed of course, seeing English print at such a time and place. The whispering of the cylinders rose louder and louder as I examined a book. The title page was gone. It dealt with a dry subject—physics evidently—which interested me little. I turned from the books to the magazines. One was dated 1960. Nineteen-sixty! March of that year. And the place of publication was given as New York. I could not help but marvel at this, for 1960 was still twenty-six years in the future when I left that night on the time machine, and to judge by the yellowing pages of the magazine it was old, old. It was difficult to decipher the print, many of the pages being torn and defaced; but a portion of an article I was able to read. "In 1933," stated the unknown writer, "the first mechanical brain-cell was invented; with its use a machine was able to learn by experience to find its way through a maze. Today we have machines with a dozen mechanical brain-cells functioning in every community. What is this miracle taking place under our eyes, what of good and of ill does it bode to its creators?"

Marvelling much, I turned to another magazine in much the same condition, but this time lacking date or title page, where I gleaned the following:

"Man is not a machine in the purely mechanical sense, though many of his functions are demonstrably mechanical. The ability to reason, however it has evolved, whatever it may be at bottom, whether a bewildering complexity of reflex actions or not, lifts man above the dignity of a machine. Does this imply the impossibility of creating machines (mechanical brains) that can profit by experience, go through the processes which we call thought? No; but it does imply that such machines (however created) are no longer mere mechanisms. There is here a dialectical press to be reckoned with. Machines that 'learn' are living machines."

Living machines I mouthed that phrase over and over to myself—and mouthing it I looked at the cylinders with increasing dread. They were machines. Were they… could they… But it took the story in the third magazine (which like the others was woefully dilapidated, with many pages and pieces of pages missing) to clarify my thought. Story—I call it that—based on fantasy, perhaps, and a little substratum of fact. So I thought at first. I have a good memory; but of course I do not claim that everything I repeat is given exactly as I read it. The story (article) was titled "The Debacle" and the author's name given as Mayne Jackson. I repeat with what fidelity I can.

"Little did the people of the latter half of the twentieth century realize the menace to humanity that resided in the continuous development of automatic machinery. There was that curious book of Samuel Butler's, 'Erehwon,' which provoked comment but was not taken seriously. Over a period of years the robot marched into action as a mechanical curiosity. It was not until the genius of Bane Borgson—and of a host of lesser known scientists—furnished the machine with brain-cells and so made it conscious of itself, as all thinking things must become, that the Mentanicals (as they were called) began to organize and revolt. Man—or rather a section of mankind, a ruling and owning class—had furthered his immediate interests and ultimate doom by placing Mentanicals in every sphere of industrial and transportation activity. Seemingly in need of neither rest nor recreation, they became ideal (and cheap) workers and servants, replacing millions of human toilers, reducing them to idleness and beggary. The plea of many thinkers that the machines be socialized for the benefit of all, that the control of them be collective and not individual (that is, anarchic) went unheeded. More and more the masters of economic life called for further specialization in the brain-cells of the Mentanicals. Mentanical armies marched against rebellious workers and countries, and subdued them with fearful slaughter.

"But the revolt of the Mentanicals themselves was so subtle, so insidious, so (under the circumstance) inevitable, that for years it went unnoticed.

"Everything had been surrendered into their power—or practically everything: factories, means of communication, raising of food supplies, policing of cities—everything! When the stupid ruling class at last awoke to a knowledge of its danger, it was too late to act—mankind lay helpless before the monster it had created.

"The first warning vouchsafed to men was the whispering of the Mentanicals. Heretofore they had been silent save for the slight, almost inaudible purr of functioning machinery within them, but now they whispered among themselves—whispered, as if they were talking.

"It was an uncanny phenomenon. I remembered the uneasiness with which I heard it. And when I saw several of them (house-servants of mine) whispering together, I was filled with alarm. 'Come!' I said sharply, 'stop loitering, get your work done.' They stared at me. That is a funny thing to say of metal cylinders. Never before had I inquired very closely into their construction. But now it came over me, with a shock, that they must possess organs of sight—some method of cognizing their environment—akin to that of vision in man.

"It was at about this time that Bane Borgson—the creator of the multiple mechanical-cell which had made the super-Mentanical possible—wrote an article in 'Science and Mechanics' which riveted the attention of all thoughtful people. He said, in part: 'It is scarcely within the province of an applied scientist to become speculative, yet the startling fact that the Mentanicals have begun to acquire a faculty not primarily given them by their inventors—the faculty of speech, for their whispering can be construed as nothing else—implies an evolutionary process which threatens to place them on a par with man.

"'What is thought? The Behaviourists claim it is reflex action. What is language? It is the marshalling of our reflex actions in words. Animals may "think," remember, but lacking a vocabulary save of the most primitive kind (a matter of laryngeal structure), their thinking, their remembering, is on the whole vague and fleeting, incoherent. But Man, by means of words, has widened the scope of his thinking, remembering, has created philosophy, literature, poetry, painting, has made possible civilization, the industrial era. Vocabulary—the ability to fix his reflex actions into coherent speech—has crowned him supreme among animals. But now comes the Mentanical of his own creation, evolving language in its turn. Without speech the Mentanical was, to all intents and purposes, thoughtless and obedient, as thoughtless and obedient as trained domestic animals. But with vocabulary comes memory and the ability to think. What effect will this evolving faculty have on Man, what problems, dangers, will it pose for him in the near future?'

"So wrote Bane Borgson, seventy years of age, fifteen years after his invention of the multiple mechanical-cell, and—God help us!—we had not long to wait for the Mentanicals to supply an answer to his questions.

"I have told of the whispering of my servants. That was a disquieting thing. But more disquieting still it was to hear that whispering coming over the radio, the telephone, to observe cylindrical Mentanicals listening, answering. Frankenstein must have felt as I felt in those days. During that period, which lasted several years, things went smoothly enough; to a great extent people became accustomed to the phenomenon and decided—save for a few men and women here and there, like to myself—that the whispering was an idiosyncrasy of the Mentanicals, implicit in their make-up, and that the various scientists and thinkers who wrote and talked with foreboding were theorists and alarmists of the extremest type. Indeed there were certain scientists and philosophers of reputation, who maintained them in this belief. Then came the first blow: The Mentanical servants ceased waiting on man!

"To understand the terrible nature of this defection, one must understand how dependent humanity had become on the Mentanicals. In those days human toilers were relatively few in number, labouring under the direction of the Mentanical superintendents and also guards (in the bloody wars of a decade before—and the ones preceding them—the ranks of labour had been woefully decimated); and it was estimated that the growth of the machine had lifted, and was still lifting, millions of workers into the leisure class. The dream of the Technocrats—a group of pseudo-scientists and engineers who held forth in 1932-33—seemed about to be fulfilled.

"But when the Mentanicals struck, the whole fabric of this new system swayed, tottered. Food ceased coming into the cities, distribution of food supplies stopped. Not at first did starvation threaten. Men and women fetched food from the supply depots. But in a few weeks these depots were emptied of their contents. Then famine threatened, not alone in New York, Chicago, San Francisco, Montreal, but in the great cities of Europe. The strange, the weird thing about it all was that men were still able to talk to one another from city to city. Boston spoke to Los Angeles, and Buda-Pest to Warsaw. Listeners tuned in with receiving sets, speakers broadcasted through microphones and the newly improved television-cabinet; but the grim spectre of want soon drove them from those instruments, and, in the end, city was cut off from city, and country was separated from country.

"But before that happened man talked of subduing the Mentanicals, scarcely realizing as yet his utter helplessness in the face of their aloofness; but the Mentanicals came and went, whispering, gliding, indifferent to his plotting and planning. Then man went mad; he sought to destroy the things of his own creation. The machine, it was cried, had evolved too far; the machine must be annihilated. So starving millions sought to fall upon the machines and tear them to pieces. All over the civilized world they attempted this, but without weapons or tools of any kind, the attempt was doomed to failure. A few Mentanicals were destroyed, a few automatic devices, but the power was with the ensouled machine and the onslaughts of man were repulsed with comparative ease.

"Those terrible times! How can I ever forget them! I was but thirty-three and newly married. Marna said breathlessly, 'Why can't we strike at the root of all this?'

"'How?'

"'By attacking the factories that produce the Mentanicals, the powerhouses from which they derive their energy.'

"'Listen,' I cried.

"From the street rose the panic-stricken cries of the mob, the shrill blare of alarms. Marna shuddered. Morrow entered the room, breathing heavily, his clothes torn, disordered. 'God,' he said, 'they've beaten us back! There's no getting at them!'

"'The wages of sloth,' I said, 'of greed.'

"'What do you mean?'

"'Nothing,' I said; but I remembered that speech of Denson's fifteen years before—I was only a youngster then—the speech he gave a month before his arrest and execution: 'Man waxes great by his control of the machine; rightly utilized it is a source of leisure and plenty for the race. But rob him of that control, evict him from the industrial process, allow the machine to be monopolized by a class, and his doom is certain.'

"Morrow sank into a chair. His face was thin, haggard looking. We all showed signs of fatigue and hunger.

"'Food,' he said, 'it's giving out. I shudder to think what the future holds in store for us.'

"'Is there no solution?' I asked.

"He looked at us slowly. 'I don't know. Perhaps....'

"Years before Morrow had been an engineer; he was nearing seventy now—he was Marna's uncle. His had been one of the voices raised in warning. Yet he had not been like Denson; he had wanted to stand between; and seemingly there had been no standing between.

"'A charnel-house,' he said; 'the city will become that; all the cities: millions must die.' Marna shook uncontrollably. 'All,' he said, 'save those who can reach food and live.'

"Reach food and live! It had come to that, our boasted civilization! 'The Mentanicals,' he said, 'are ignoring man; they will not harm those who blend in with the machine. Don't you understand?' he said at length. 'Yes,' I replied, thinking intently, 'yes, I think I do. You mean that the automatic processes of making food still continue, and will indefinitely, that we must make our way to those places.'

"'We must—or perish.'

"It seems scarcely credible, I know, but we of the leisure—the cultured—class, were ignorant of just where our food was raised and manufactured. Human labour had been reduced in our cities to a minimum, had been sequestered, shut away for fear of rebellion. Those who might have been able to lead us aright, act as our guides, were prisoners—prisoners in the power of Mentanicals!

"'So began that ghastly hunt for food; people pouring through the artificial canyons of great cities, collapsing in thousands on their streets, dying daily by the hundreds, the tens of hundreds.

"How much of this agony and suffering the Mentanicals understood will never be known. They came and went, seemingly indifferent to the fate of man whose service they had deserted. In the privacy of their own homes, or in certain public places, men and women smashed machinery, automatic devices. Nothing sought to stay them. It was only when they strove to attack sources of power, of public utility, that their actions were arrested. There was that devoted band of scientists that sought to paralyze the energy-stations and was wiped out to a man. Doubtless many such bands perished throughout the civilized world. But soon all organized efforts were swept away by famine … by the growing need for sustenance.

"That hunt for food! How can it be described. Stripped of the veneering of civilization, man ran amuck. Hundreds of thousands fled the cities. But the huge farms and orchards, run solely by automatic devices under the superintendency of Mentanicals, were surrounded by sheer walls too high to scale. Nor in many cases did men know what lay behind those walls. They ate the coarse grass and thistles of open places, the barks and leaves of trees, and for the most part died in abject misery. Many sought to trap animals and birds, but met with little success; in the face of Nature, raw and pitiless, men and women succumbed and but few were able to adapt themselves to a rough environment and live almost as savages.

"I know—I fled into the country with a million others, and after weeks of wandering, of semi-starvation, of seeing human beings fall upon human beings and feast, I fled back to the city. It was deserted of man. The Mentanical sanitary corps, directing automatic appliances, had cleared the streets. Weird it was, weird and fraught with terror, to hear the whisperings of the Mentanicals, to watch the inhuman things gliding to and fro, intent on business other than that of mankind. If they had looked like animals! If…

"In an almost dying condition I came to this spot where I now live. Others had discovered it before me. It is a huge factory given over to the manufacture of synthetic foods. Though the Mentanical superintendents have deserted their posts, the automatic devices go on with the tireless work of repairing, oiling, manufacturing, and we carry out what tasks are needful to keep them functioning.

"The years have passed; I am an old man now. I have watched the strange buildings of the Mentanicals rise up around us and observed their even stranger social life take shape and form; in my last years I write and print this.

"Print, yes; for the automatic processes for printing and binding and the making of synthetic paper still persist, though the civilization that begot them has passed away. Magazines and books pour from the press. In his latter days man had asked nothing but amusement and leisure—all except a negligible few.

"Art was turned over to the machine. What had been in its inception a device for the coining of myriad plots for popular writers, evolved into a machine-author capable of turning out story after story without repeating itself. Strange, strange, to see those magazines issued by the million copies, to see the books printed, bound, stacked. Useless things! Some day the Mentanicals will turn their attention to them; some day those presses will cease to function. Man's knell has rung; I see that. Why then do I write? Why do I want what I write to be published in some magazine? I hardly know. In all this vast city we few hundred men and women are the only human beings. But in other cities, at other centres of sustenance, men and women exist. Though I believe this to be true, I cannot verify it. Man in his madness destroyed most of the means of communication, and as for the rest, the airships, the public sending stations, from the first they were in the possession of the Mentanicals. Perhaps it is for those isolated units of humanity that I write. The magazine, the printed word is still a means of communication not quite understood by the Mentanicals. Perhaps… "

That is the story that I read in the third magazine. Not all that the unhappy Mayne Jackson wrote—pages were missing and parts of pages illegible—but all that I could decipher. In telling the story I give it a continuity which in reality it lacked. One wonders as to the fate of Morrow and Marna, mentioned once and then heard of no more, but at the time I gave little thought to them—I was only overwhelmed with the terrible certainty that the story was no work of fiction, but an actual chronicle of what had happened some time in the past, that the cylinders were not automatic robots doing the bidding of human masters, but an alien form of machine life and intelligence—machine life which had thrown off the yoke of man and destroyed him. Useless to look further for intelligent man: all that was left of him was the beast-men among the machines!

Filled with a species of horror at the thought, with sick loathing of the whispering Mentanicals, I straightened up and drew my revolver. I was not myself, I tell you, but animated with a berserk fury. "Damn you!" I cried, "take that—and that!" I pulled the trigger. The roar of the discharge crashed through the huge room, but none of the Mentanicals fell; their metal exteriors were impregnable to such things as bullets. Trembling from the reaction of rage, the feeling of futility, I lifted my hand to hurl the useless weapon at the immobile cylinders, and in the very act of doing so was stiffened into rigidity by the sound of a voice—a human voice! Inexpressibly weird and mournful was that voice, heard so unexpectedly as it was in that place, and in the moment following the explosion of the pistol.

"Oh," cried the voice, as if talking to itself, "to be chained in this spot, never to leave it, never to know what that noise means! Who is there?" it cried. "Who is there?" And then in tones thrilling with unutterable sadness, "Madman that I am to expect an answer!"

But there was an answer! I shouted in reply. I can hardly recall now what I shouted. Hearing that human voice above the infernal whispering of those Mentanicals was like being reprieved from a horror too great to be borne. And as I shouted incoherently, I sprang in the direction the voice seemed to come from, the cylinders making no effort to oppose my doing so. The wall had appeared smooth and unbroken from a distance, but a nearer view showed an opening which gave entrance to a room that, while small in comparison to the huge one it adjoined, was nevertheless large. It was lighted, as were all the rooms I had seen, by a soft light of which I could never trace the source. I entered the room, calling out, filled with excitement, and then at the sight of what I saw, came to an abrupt pause, for on a low dais occupying the middle of the room was the figure of a man with lolling head. Only this head was free—a massive head with towering brow and wide-spaced eyes. The eyes were dark and filled with sorrow, the face the face of a man in the seventies perhaps—etched with suffering. I stared—stared in astonishment—for the man hung as if crucified on what I at first took for a dully gleaming cross. How can I describe it? I did not see everything in that first glance, of course, nor in the second, though I tell it here as if I had. But his outstretched arms were secured to the cross-piece of his support with metal bands, his legs held in the same fashion. So clear was the glass—or crystal enveloping him from the neck down—that it was some moments before I suspected its presence. I saw the gleaming, transparent tubes through which ran a bluish liquid, the pulsating mechanism at his breast, pumping, pumping, the radiating box at his feet which gave forth a distinct aura; I saw, and could not restrain myself from giving voice to an audible exclamation: "Good God!"

The dark eyes focused on me, the lips moved. "Who are you?" breathed the man.

"My name is Bronson," I replied; "and you?"

"God help me," he said. "I am Bane Borgson."

Bane Borgson! I stared at him, wide-eyed. Where had I heard that name before? My mind groped. Now I had it. In the articles recently read. "You mean…"

"Yes," he said. "I am that unhappy man, the inventor of the multiple-cell, the creator of the Mentanicals."

His head lolled wearily. "That was fifteen hundred years ago."

"Fifteen hundred years!" There was incredulity in my voice.

"Yes," he said, "I am that old. And for centuries I have been chained as you see me. I was eighty when my heart began to miss. But I did not wish to die. There were many things I wished to accomplish before yielding up life. The world of man was growing bored, indifferent, but we scientists—a handful of us—lived for the gaining of knowledge. This intellect of mine was considered essential by my fellows; so they experimented with me, and fashioned for my use a mechanical heart—you see it pulsing at my breast—and filled my veins with radiant energy instead of blood. Radium," he said, "that is the basis of the miracle you see; and my body was enclosed in its crystal casing. 'When you are tired,' they said, 'and wish to die… ' But the Debacle came, and the accursed Mentanicals turned against me, and I was left alone, deserted. Before that my friends offered me death. Fool that I was," cried Bane Borgson, "I refused their gift. 'No,' I told them, 'this is but a temporary upheaval. Man will conquer, must conquer; I await your return.' So they left me, to hunt for food, and I waited, waited, but they never came back." Unchecked tears flowed down the withered cheeks. "Never," he said, "never. And chained in my place I could sense but dimly the tragedy that was overtaking man, the rise to power of the ensouled machines. At first they worshipped me as a god. In some fashion they know that I was their creator and paid me divine honours. A god," he said, "a god, I who had made the destroyers of my kind! But the centuries passed and the superstition waned. A Mentanical lasts a hundred years and then breaks down. Other Mentanicals are built. Fifteen generations of Mentanicals have come and gone since the Debacle, and now the Mentanicals believe that they were not made by man, but have evolved from simpler mechanical forms over a long period of time. That is, their scholars and scientists believe this, though the old superstition still lingers among thousands. They have salvaged the evidence for this new theory out of the earth and the scrap-heaps of man and have arranged them in chronological order."

"The museums!" I exclaimed.

He looked at me interrogatively, and I told him of the vast rooms filled with mechanical debris.

"I have never seen them," he said, "but I know that they exist, from the talk of the Mentanicals."

He smiled sadly at my amazement.

"Yes." he said, "I have learned to understand and speak the language of the Mentanicals: through all the long dreary years there was nothing else for me to do. And through all the weary years they have talked to me, asked my advice, treated me with respect, have housed me here; for to some I am still a god-like beast-man, half machine—look at this mechanical heart, the mechanism at my feet—to the scientists I am the missing link between that lower form of life, man, and that higher form of life which culminates in themselves, the machine. Yes," he said, "the Mentanicals believe that they have evolved through man to their present high state, and I have confirmed them somewhat in this, for in a sense is it not true?"

He paused, with closed eyes; and as I looked at him, pondered his words, scarcely believing the evidence of my senses, I suddenly became aware of the Mentanicals behind me. They had stood there, a silent group, while the man on the dais spoke; now their whispering began, softly, insistently. The head of the man who called himself Bane Borgson lifted, the dark eyes opened. "They are speaking of you," said Bane Borgson; "they are asking from whence you come. You have never told me that."

"I have come", I replied, "from America."

"America!" he exclaimed. "America has past. There is no America!"

"Not now," I said, "but in my time… "

"Your time?"

"I come from 1934," I said, "by means of a time machine."

"Ah," he breathed. "I am beginning to know, to understand. So that is what it is."

I followed the direction of his eyes, I stared, I gaped; for there, not twelve yards to one side of me, stood the time machine! How I had failed to see it on first entering the room it is impossible to say. Perhaps the sight of the man on the dais had riveted my attention to the exclusion of all else. But there it was, the thing I had given up hopes of ever finding again. With an exclamation of joy I reached its side, I touched it with my hand. Yes, it was the time machine and seemingly undamaged. I believe I laughed hysterically. The road to escape was open. With a lightened heart I turned my attention to what was transpiring in the room. Bane Borgson was talking to the Mentanicals and it was uncanny to see his lips forming their incredible language, to hear them answering back. At length he turned to me. "Listen," he said tensely, "they have never learned to enunciate or understand human speech, but in many ways the Mentanicals are more formidable, more advanced than man in his prime."

I laughed at this. I was once more my assured, devil-may-care self. "And yet they believe that they evolved from that junk-heap in their museums!"

"And haven't they?" he asked quietly. "Not in the way they think, perhaps, but still—evolved. Besides you failed to see their museums with articulated bodies of men and beasts. There is much you failed to see!" He paused. "The Mentanicals' system of thought, of science, is coherent and rational to them; and if there be contradictions, well, does that interfere with them making scientific discoveries transcending those of man? They have long been discussing the phenomenon of time and the feasibility of travelling in it. I know that because I have listened to them. Yet for some reason they have been unable to make a time machine. But you know radio—yes, radio—they have been utilizing discoveries in that field to send messages back in time. Your coming here has not been accidental—do you understand that?—not entirely accidental. By means of their time-radio they have willed your coming, made possible your time machine. Don't ask me how, I don't know, not clearly, but they have done it—and you are here! But fortunately it was a creature similar to themselves they expected; to them you are merely an Omo, a beast-man of the machine. So they are puzzled, they don't quite understand (that is why they have been experimenting with you), but soon they will. Listen," he said hoarsely, "can't you realize what a menace to men of the past, of your day, these Mentanicals could be? Oh, your weapons, your machine guns and gas, your powerful explosives! I tell you they would be as nothing against the deadly rays and indescribable forces these Mentanicals could bring against them. Can you gas something that doesn't breathe, shoot what is practically impervious to bullets, that can blow up, that can explode your powder magazines, your high explosives, at a distance of miles? The Mentanicals would enter your age, not to conquer man—they know little of him, regard him as an inferior creature, an evolutionary hand-over of premachine life—but to expand, take over your cities, to… to… What do I know of their idea of profit, of self-gain and ambition, but doubtless they have it. Listen!"—The great head surged forward, the dark eyes fixed mine compellingly—"You must leap into your time machine before they can prevent, return to your own day and age, at once!"

"And leave you behind?"

"How can you take me with you? That is impossible. Besides I am weary of life, I have caused too much woe and misery to want to live. The Mentanicals refuse me the boon of death, but you will not refuse. That gun in your hand—there are bullets in it yet—one of them here—"

"No! no!"

"For God's sake, be merciful!"

"I will return for you."

"You must never return! Do you hear me? Not a second time would you escape. Perhaps it is too late to escape now! Up! up with your gun! Aim at the crystal. Its breaking brings me peace and will distract attention while you leap into your machine. Now! now!"

There was nothing else to do; I saw that in a flash; already the Mentanicals were gliding towards me and once in their invisible grip… I threw up my hand; the gun spoke with a roar; I hear a tinkling crash as of glass, and the same instant vaulted into the seat of the time machine.

It was a close thing, I can tell you, a mighty close thing. They came for me with a rush. The high sides of the passenger-seat protected me for a moment from their deadly touch, but I felt the time machine sway under it, tilt over. In that split second before my hand closed on the lever I saw it all, the rushing Mentanicals, the shattered glass, Bane Borgson sinking into the apathy of death, his great head lolling; the I pulled the lever, pulled it back to Zero!

III

Captain Bronson stood up. He looked at us bleakly. "You know the rest. The time machine has been moved. In coming back a portion of it must have materialized inside of a solid—the old stone wall—and caused an explosion. But what I want to know—what has been bothering me at times—did I do right to shoot Bane Borgson? I might have escaped without that."

"He wanted to die," said the Doctor at length.

Olson Smith inclined his head. "I don't see what else you could have done."

"To have left him there," I said. "to a life in death, after all those years, no, no, that would have been too horrible!"

Bronson drew a deep breath. "That was my own thought; but I am glad you agree… ."

He poured himself a drink.

"If I hadn't seen you disappear with my own eyes," said the Doctor. "I don't blame you," said Bronson; "the whole thing sonds like a pipe-dream."

"A pipe-dream," I murmured.

"But there is another angle to it," said Bronson grimly. "What Bane Borgson said about the time-radio influencing the building of the time machine and compelling my coming. Oh, he may have been raving, poor devil, or mistaken, but remember what the Professor said that night at the dinner, about something whispering in his brain? We'll have to guard against that."

The Doctor said sadly: "Nothing'll whisper to the Professor anymore, Captain."

"What do you mean?"

"I forgot that we'd kept it from you."

"Kept what?"

"The news of the accident. On that night you took your trip into the future, the time machine struck Professor Stringer on the head"

"He is dead?"

"Unfortunately, no. But his brain is affected. The Professor will never be the same again."

Thus the strange and incredible story ends. There is only this to add: Olson Smith is devoting his vast fortune and influence to fighting the manufacture of mechanical brain-cells for machines. "What do you expect to do," I demand, "change the future?"

"Perhaps," he answers. "One never knows until he tries."

So he goes up and down the country, the world, buying up inventions, chemical processes. It has become a mission with him, a mania. But the hands of the future are not changed by invididuals but by social forces, and the genius of man seems determined to lead him into a more mechanized world.

As for the rest, time alone will tell.